PRAISE FOR ELENA FERRANTE'S NEAPOLITAN QUARTET

MW00852085

FROM THE UNITED STATES

"Ferrante's writing is so unencumbered, so natural, and yet so lovely, brazen, and flush. The constancy of detail and the pacing that zips and skips then slows to a real-time crawl have an almost psychic effect, bringing you deeply into synchronicity with the discomforts and urgency of the characters' emotions. Ferrante is unlike other writers—not because she's innovative, but rather because she's unselfconscious and brutally, diligently honest."　　　　　—Minna Proctor, *Bookforum*

"Everyone should read anything with Ferrante's name on it."
　　　　　　　　　　　　　　　　　　—*The Boston Globe*

"In these bold, gorgeous, relentless novels, Ferrante traces the deep connections between the political and the domestic. This is a new version of the way we live now—one we need, one told brilliantly, by a woman."
　　　—Roxana Robinson, *The New York Times Book Review*

"An intoxicatingly furious portrait of enmeshed friends Lila and Elena, bright and passionate girls from a raucous neighborhood in world-class Naples. Ferrante writes with such aggression and unnerving psychological insight about the messy complexity of female friendship that the real world can drop away when you're reading her."
　　　　　　　　　　　　　　　　　—*Entertainment Weekly*

"Ferrante can do a woman's interior dialogue like no one else, with a ferocity that is shockingly honest, unnervingly blunt."
—*Booklist*

"Elena Ferrante's gutsy and compulsively readable new novel, the first of a quartet, is a terrific entry point for Americans unfamiliar with the famously reclusive writer, whose go-for-broke tales of women's shadow selves—those ambivalent mothers and seething divorcées too complex or unseemly for polite society (and most literary fiction, for that matter)—shimmer with Balzacian human detail and subtle psychological suspense . . . The Neapolitan novels offer one of the more nuanced portraits of feminine friendship in recent memory—from the make-up and break-up quarrels of young girls to the way in which we carefully define ourselves against each other as teens—Ferrante wisely balances her memoir-like emotional authenticity with a wry sociological understanding of a society on the verge of dramatic change."   —Megan O'Grady, *Vogue*

"Elena Ferrante will blow you away."   —Alice Sebold

"An engrossing, wildly original contemporary epic about the demonic power of human (and particularly female) creativity checked by the forces of history and society."
—*The Los Angeles Review of Books*

"*My Brilliant Friend* is a sweeping family-centered epic that encompasses issues of loyalty, love, and a transforming Europe. This gorgeous novel should bring a host of new readers to one of Italy's most acclaimed authors."
—*The Barnes and Noble Review*

"[Ferrante's Neapolitan Novels] don't merely offer a teeming vision of working-class Naples, with its cobblers and professors, communists and mobbed-up businessmen, womanizing poets and downtrodden wives; they present one of modern fiction's richest portraits of a friendship."

—John Powers, "Fresh Air", NPR

"Ferrante tackles girlhood and friendship with amazing force."

—Gwyneth Paltrow

"Ferrante draws an indelible picture of the city's mean streets and the poverty, violence and sameness of lives lived in the same place forever . . . She is a fierce writer."   —*Shelf Awareness*

"Ferrante transforms the love, separation and reunion of two poor urban girls into the general tragedy of their city."

—*The New York Times*

"Elena Ferrante: the best angry woman writer ever!"

—John Waters

"Beautifully translated by Ann Goldstein . . . Ferrante writes with a ferocious, intimate urgency that is a celebration of anger. Ferrante is terribly good with anger, a very specific sort of wrath harbored by women, who are so often not allowed to give voice to it. We are angry, a lot of the time, at the position we're in—whether it's as wife, daughter, mother, friend—and I can think of no other woman writing who is so swift and gorgeous in this rage, so bracingly fearless in mining fury."

—Susanna Sonnenberg, *The San Francisco Chronicle*

"The through-line in all of Ferrante's investigations, for me, is nothing less than one long, mind-and-heart-shredding howl for the history of women (not only Neapolitan women), and its implicit *j'accuse* . . . Ferrante's effect, critics agree, is inarguable. 'Intensely, violently personal' and 'brutal directness, familial torment' is how James Wood ventures to categorize her—descriptions that seem mild after you've encountered the work."   —Joan Frank, *The San Francisco Chronicle*

"Lila, mercurial, unsparing, and, at the end of this first episode in a planned trilogy from Ferrante, seemingly capable of starting a full-scale neighborhood war, is a memorable character."
            —*Publishers Weekly*

"Ferrante's own writing has no limits, is willing to take every thought forward to its most radical conclusion and backward to its most radical birthing."   —*The New Yorker*

FROM THE UNITED KINGDOM

"Nothing quite like it has ever been published."—*The Guardian*

"*The Story of a New Name*, like its predecessor, is fiction of the very highest order."   —*Independent on Sunday*

"*My Brilliant Friend*, translated by Ann Goldstein, is stunning: an intense, forensic exploration of the friendship between Lila and the story's narrator, Elena. Ferrante's evocation of the working-class district of Naples where Elena and Lila first meet as two wiry eight-year-olds is cinematic in the density of its detail."   —*The Times Literary Supplement*

"This is a story about friendship as a mass of roiling currents—love, envy, pity, spite, dependency and Schadenfreude coiling around one another, tricky to untangle."   —*Intelligent Life*

"Elena Ferrante may be the best contemporary novelist you

have never heard of. The Italian author has written six lavishly praised novels. But she writes under a pseudonym and will not offer herself for public consumption. Her characters likewise defy convention . . . Her prose is crystal, and her storytelling both visceral and compelling." —*The Economist*

FROM ITALY

"*Those Who Leave and Those Who Stay* evokes the vital flux of a heartbeat, of blood flowing through our veins."—*La Repubblica*

"We don't know who she is, but it doesn't matter. Ferrante's books are enthralling self-contained monoliths that do not seek friendship but demand silent, fervid admiration from her passionate readers . . . The thing most real in these novels is the intense, almost osmotic relationship that unites Elena and Lila, the two girls from a neighborhood in Naples who are the peerless protagonists of the Neapolitan novels."—*Famiglia Cristiana*

"Today it is near impossible to find writers capable of bringing smells, tastes, feelings, and contradictory passions to their pages. Elena Ferrante, alone, seems able to do it. There is no writer better suited to composing the great Italian novel of her generation, her country, and her time." —*Il Manifesto*

"Regardless of who is behind the name Elena Ferrante, the mysterious pseudonym used by the author of the Neapolitan novels, two things are certain: she is a woman and she knows how to describe Naples like nobody else. She does so with a style that recalls an enchanted spider web with its expressive power and the wizardry with which it creates an entire world." —*Huffington Post* (Italy)

"A marvel that is without limits and beyond genre."
—*Il Salvagente*

"Elena Ferrante is proving that literature can cure our present ills; it can cure the spirit by operating as an antidote to the nervous attempts we make to see ourselves reflected in the present-day of a country that is increasingly repellent."
—*Il Mattino*

"*My Brilliant Friend* flows from the soul like an eruption from Mount Vesuvius."
—*La Repubblica*

FROM AUSTRALIA

"No one has a voice quite like Ferrante's. Her gritty, ruthlessly frank novels roar off the page with a barbed fury, like an attack that is also a defense . . . Ferrante's fictions are fierce, unsentimental glimpses at the way a woman is constantly under threat, her identity submerged in marriage, eclipsed by motherhood, mythologised by desire. Imagine if Jane Austen got angry and you'll have some idea of how explosive these works are."
—John Freeman, *The Australian*

"One of the most astounding—and mysterious—contemporary Italian novelists available in translation, Elena Ferrante unfolds the tumultuous inner lives of women in her thrillingly menacing stories of lost love, negligent mothers and unfulfilled desires."
—*The Age*

"Ferrante bewitches with her tiny, intricately drawn world . . . *My Brilliant Friend* journeys fearlessly into some of that murkier psychological territory where questions of individual identity are inextricable from circumstance and the ever-changing identities of others."   —*The Melbourne Review*

"The Neapolitan novels move far from contrivance, logic or respectability to ask uncomfortable questions about how we live, how we love, how we singe an existence in a deeply flawed world that expects pretty acquiescence from its women. In all their beauty, their ugliness, their devotion and deceit, these girls enchant and repulse, like life, like our very selves."
                                        —*The Sydney Morning Herald*

From Spain

"Elena Ferrante's female characters are genuine works of art . . . It is clear that her novel is the child of Italian neorealism and an abiding fascination with scene."   —*El País*

THE STORY
OF THE LOST CHILD

Elena Ferrante

THE STORY
OF THE LOST CHILD

Book Four, The Neapolitan Quartet
Maturity, Old Age

*Translated from the Italian
by Ann Goldstein*

Europa
editions

Europa Editions
1 Penn Plaza Suite 6282
New York, N.Y. 10019
www.europaeditions.com
info@europaeditions.com

Copyright © 2015 by Edizioni E/O
First Publication 2015 by Europa Editions
Twenty-fifth printing, 2021

Translation by Ann Goldstein
Original title: *Storia della bambina perduta*
Translation copyright © 2015 by Europa Editions

Library of Congress Cataloguing in Publication Data is available
ISBN 978-1-60945-286-5

Ferrante, Elena
The Story of the Lost Child

Book design by Emanuele Ragnisco
www.mekkanografici.com

Cover photo © Cultura/Hybrid Images/Getty
Prepress by Grafica Punto Print – Rome

Printed in Italy

THE STORY
OF THE LOST CHILD

INDEX OF CHARACTERS

The Cerullo family (the shoemaker's family):

Fernando Cerullo, shoemaker, Lila's father.

Nunzia Cerullo, Lila's mother.

Raffaella Cerullo, called Lina, or Lila. She was born in August, 1944, and is sixty-six when she disappears from Naples without a trace. At the age of sixteen, she marries Stefano Carracci, but during a vacation on Ischia she falls in love with Nino Sarratore, for whom she leaves her husband. After the disastrous end of her relationship with Nino, the birth of her son Gennaro (also called Rino), and the discovery that Stefano is expecting a child with Ada Cappuccio, Lila leaves him definitively. She moves with Enzo Scanno to San Giovanni a Teduccio, but several years later she returns to the neighborhood with Enzo and Gennaro.

Rino Cerullo, Lila's older brother. He is married to Stefano's sister, Pinuccia Carracci, with whom he has two sons.

Other children.

The Greco family (the porter's family):

Elena Greco, called Lenuccia or Lenù. Born in August, 1944, she is the author of the long story that we are reading. After elementary school, Elena continues to study, with increasing success, obtaining a degree from the Scuola Normale, in Pisa, where she meets Pietro Airota. She marries him, and they move to Florence. They have two children, Adele, called Dede, and Elsa, but Elena, disappointed by marriage, begins an affair with Nino Sarratore, with whom she

has been in love since childhood, and eventually leaves
Pietro and the children.

Peppe, *Gianni*, and *Elisa*, Elena's younger siblings. Despite
Elena's disapproval, Elisa goes to live with Marcello Solara.

The father, a porter at the city hall.

The mother, a housewife.

The Carracci family (Don Achille's family):

Don Achille Carracci, dealer in the black market, loan shark.
He was murdered.

Maria Carracci, wife of Don Achille, mother of Stefano,
Pinuccia, and Alfonso. The daughter of Stefano and Ada
Cappuccio bears her name.

Stefano Carracci, son of Don Achille, shopkeeper and Lila's
first husband. Dissatisfied by his stormy marriage to Lila,
he initiates a relationship with Ada Cappuccio, and they
start living together. He is the father of Gennaro, with Lila,
and of Maria, with Ada.

Pinuccia, daughter of Don Achille. She is married to Lila's
brother, Rino, and has two sons with him.

Alfonso, son of Don Achille. He resigns himself to marrying
Marisa Sarratore after a long engagement.

The Peluso family (the carpenter's family):

Alfredo Peluso, carpenter and Communist, dies in prison.

Giuseppina Peluso, devoted wife of Alfredo, commits suicide
after his death.

Pasquale Peluso, older son of Alfredo and Giuseppina, construction worker, militant Communist.

Carmela Peluso, called *Carmen*. Pasquale's sister, she was the
girlfriend of Enzo Scanno for a long time. She subsequently
marries Roberto, the owner of the gas pump on the *stradone,*
with whom she has two children.

Other children.

THE STORY OF THE LOST CHILD · 17

The Cappuccio family (the mad widow's family):

Melina, a widow, a relative of Nunzia Cerullo. She nearly lost her mind after her relationship with Donato Sarratore ended.

Melina's *husband*, who died in mysterious circumstances.

Ada Cappuccio, Melina's daughter. For a long time the girlfriend of Pasquale Peluso, she becomes the lover of Stefano Carracci, and goes to live with him. From their relationship a girl, Maria, is born.

Antonio Cappuccio, her brother, a mechanic. He was Elena's boyfriend.

Other children.

The Sarratore family (the railway-worker poet's family):

Donato Sarratore, a great womanizer, who was the lover of Melina Cappuccio. Elena, too, at a very young age, gives herself to him on the beach in Ischia, driven by the suffering that the relationship between Nino and Lila has caused her.

Lidia Sarratore, wife of Donato.

Nino Sarratore, the oldest of the five children of Donato and Lidia, has a long secret affair with Lila. Married to Eleonora, with whom he has Albertino and Lidia, he begins an affair with Elena, who is also married and has children.

Marisa Sarratore, sister of Nino. Married to Alfonso Carracci. She becomes the lover of Michele Solara, with whom she has two children.

Pino, Clelia, and *Ciro Sarratore*, younger children of Donato and Lidia.

The Scanno family (the fruit-and-vegetable seller's family):

Nicola Scanno, fruit-and-vegetable seller, dies of pneumonia.

Assunta Scanno, wife of Nicola, dies of cancer.

Enzo Scanno, son of Nicola and Assunta, also a fruit-and-vegetable seller. He was for a long time the boyfriend of Carmen

Peluso. He takes on responsibility for Lila and her son, Gennaro, when she leaves Stefano Carracci, and takes them to live in San Giovanni a Teduccio.
Other children.

The Solara family (the family of the owner of the Solara bar-pastry shop):
Silvio Solara, owner of the bar-pastry shop.
Manuela Solara, wife of Silvio, moneylender. As an old woman, she is killed in the doorway of her house.
Marcello and Michele Solara, sons of Silvio and Manuela. Rejected by Lila, *Marcello*, after many years, goes to live with Elisa, Elena's younger sister. *Michele*, married to Gigliola, the daughter of the pastry maker, takes Marisa Sarratore as his lover, and has two more children with her. Yet he continues to be obsessed with Lila.

The Spagnuolo family (the baker's family):
Signor Spagnuolo, pastry maker at the Solaras' bar-pastry shop.
Rosa Spagnuolo, wife of the pastry maker.
Gigliola Spagnuolo, daughter of the pastry maker, wife of Michele Solara and mother of two of his children.
Other children.

The Airota family:
Guido Airota, professor of Greek literature.
Adele Airota, his wife.
Mariarosa Airota, their daughter, professor of art history in Milan.
Pietro Airota, a very young university professor, Elena's husband and the father of Dede and Elsa.

The teachers:
Ferraro, teacher and librarian.

Maestra Oliviero, teacher.
Professor Gerace, high-school teacher.
Professor Galiani, high-school teacher.

Other characters:
Gino, son of the pharmacist; Elena's first boyfriend.
Nella Incardo, the cousin of Maestra Oliviero.
Armando, doctor, son of Professor Galiani. Married to Isabella, with whom he has a son named Marco.
Nadia, student, daughter of Professor Galiani, was Nino's girlfriend. During a period of militant political activity, she becomes attached to Pasquale Peluso.
Bruno Soccavo, friend of Nino Sarratore and the heir to a sausage factory. He is killed in his factory.
Franco Mari, Elena's boyfriend during her first years at the university, has devoted himself to political activism. He loses an eye in a Fascist attack.
Silvia, a university student and political activist. She has a son, Mirko, from a brief relationship with Nino Sarratore.

MATURITY
THE STORY OF THE LOST CHILD

1.

From October 1976 until 1979, when I returned to Naples to live, I avoided resuming a steady relationship with Lila. But it wasn't easy. She almost immediately tried to reenter my life by force, and I ignored her, tolerated her, endured her. Even if she acted as if there were nothing she wanted more than to be close to me at a difficult moment, I couldn't forget the contempt with which she had treated me.

Today I think that if it had been only the insult that wounded me—You're an idiot, she had shouted on the telephone when I told her about Nino, and she had never, *ever* spoken to me like that before—I would have soon calmed down. In reality, what mattered more than that offense was the mention of Dede and Elsa. Think of the harm you're doing to your daughters, she had warned me, and at the moment I had paid no attention. But over time those words acquired greater weight, and I returned to them often. Lila had never displayed the slightest interest in Dede and Elsa; almost certainly she didn't even remember their names. If, on the phone, I mentioned some intelligent remark they had made, she cut me off, changed the subject. And when she met them for the first time, at the house of Marcello Solara, she had confined herself to an absentminded glance and a few pat phrases—she hadn't paid the least attention to how nicely they were dressed, how neatly their hair was combed, how well both were able to express themselves, although they were still small. And yet *I* had given birth to them, *I* had brought them up, they were part of me, who had been her friend forever: she should have taken this into account—I won't say out of affection but at least out of politeness—for my maternal pride. Yet she hadn't even attempted a little good-natured sarcasm; she had displayed indifference and nothing more. Only now—out of jealousy, surely, because I had taken Nino—did she remember the girls, and wanted to emphasize that I was a terrible mother, that although I was happy, I was causing them unhappiness. The minute I thought about it I became anxious. Had Lila worried about Gennaro when she left Stefano, when she abandoned the child to the neighbor because of her work in the factory, when she sent him to me as if to get him out of the way? Ah, I had my faults, but I was certainly more a mother than she was.

2.

Such thoughts became a habit in those years. It was as if Lila, who, after all, had uttered only that one malicious remark about Dede and Elsa, had become the defense lawyer for their needs as daughters, and, every time I neglected them to devote myself to myself, I felt obliged to prove to her that she was wrong. But it was a voice invented by ill feeling; what she really thought of my behavior as a mother I don't know. Only she can say if, in fact, she has managed to insert herself into this extremely long chain of words to modify my text, to purposely supply the missing links, to unhook others without letting it show, to say of me more than I want, more than I'm able to say. I wish for this intrusion, I've hoped for it ever since I began to write our story, but I have to get to the end in order to check all the pages. If I tried now, I would certainly get stuck. I've been writing for too long, and I'm tired; it's more and more dif-ficult to keep the thread of the story taut within the chaos of the years, of events large and small, of moods. So either I tend to pass over my own affairs to recapture Lila and all the complications she brings with her or, worse, I let myself be carried away by the events of my life, only because it's easier to write them. But I have to avoid this choice. I mustn't take the first path, on which, if I set myself aside, I would end up finding ever fewer traces of Lila—since the very nature of our relationship dictates that I can reach her only by passing through myself. But I shouldn't take the second, either. That, in fact, I speak of my experience in increasingly greater detail is just what she would certainly favor. Come on—she would say—tell us what turn your life took, who cares about mine, admit that it doesn't even interest you. And she would conclude: I'm a scribble on a scribble, completely unsuitable for one of your books; forget it, Lenù, one doesn't tell the story of an erasure.

What to do, then? Admit yet again that she's right? Accept that to be adult is to disappear, is to learn to hide to the point of vanishing? Admit that, as the years pass, the less I know of Lila?

This morning I keep weariness at bay and sit down again at the desk. Now that I'm close to the most painful part of our story, I want to seek on the page a balance between her and me that in life I couldn't find even between myself and me.

3.

Of the days in Montpellier I remember everything except the city; it's as if I'd never been there. Outside the hotel, outside the vast assembly hall where the academic conference that Nino was attending took place, today I see only a windy autumn and a blue sky resting on white clouds. And yet in my memory that place-name, Montpellier, has for many reasons remained a symbol of escape. I had been out of Italy once, in Paris, with Franco, and I had felt exhilarated by my own audacity. But then it seemed to me that my world was and would forever remain the neighborhood, Naples, while the rest was like a brief outing in whose special climate I could imagine myself as I would never in fact be. Montpellier, on the other hand, although it was far less exciting than Paris, gave me the impression that my boundaries had burst and I was expanding. The pure and simple fact of being in that place constituted in my eyes the proof that the neighborhood, Naples, Pisa, Florence, Milan, Italy itself were only tiny fragments of the world and that I would do well not to be satisfied with those fragments any longer. In Montpellier I felt the limitations of my outlook, of the language in which I expressed myself and in which I had written. In Montpellier it seemed to me evident how restrictive, at thirty-two, being a wife and mother might be. And in all those days charged with love I felt, for the first time, freed from the chains I had accumulated over the years—those of my origins, those I had acquired through academic success, those derived from the choices I had made in life, especially marriage. There I also understood the reasons for the pleasure I had felt, in the past, on seeing my first book translated into other languages and, at the same time, the reasons for my disappointment at finding few readers outside Italy. It was marvelous to cross borders, to let oneself go within other cultures, discover the provisional nature of what I had taken for absolute. The fact that Lila had never been out of Naples, that she was afraid even of San Giovanni a Teduccio—if in the past I had judged it an arguable choice that she was nevertheless able, as usual, to turn into an advantage—now seemed to me simply a sign of mental limitation. I reacted the way you do to someone who insults you by using the same formulations that offended you. *You were wrong about me? No, my dear, it's I, I who was wrong about you: you will spend the rest of your life looking out at the trucks passing on the* stradone.

The days flew by. The organizers of the conference had reserved for Nino a single room in the hotel, and since I had decided so late to go with him, there was no way to change it to a double. So we had separate rooms, but every night I took a shower, got ready for bed, and then, with trepidation, went to his room. We slept together, clinging to each other, as if we feared that a hostile force would separate us in sleep. In the morning we had breakfast in bed, a luxury that I had seen only in movies; we laughed, we were happy. During the day I went with him to the assembly hall and, although the speakers read their endless pages in a bored tone, being with him was exciting; I sat next to him but without disturbing him. Nino followed the talks attentively, took notes, and every so often whispered in my ear ironic comments and words of love. At lunch and dinner we mixed with academics from all over the world, foreign names, foreign languages. Of course, the participants with bigger reputations were at a table of their own; we sat in a large group of younger scholars. But I was struck by Nino's mobility, both during the events and at the restaurants. How different he was from the student of long ago, even from the youth who had defended me in the bookstore in Milan almost ten years earlier. He had abandoned polemical tones, he tactfully crossed academic barriers, established relations with a serious yet engaging demeanor. Now in English (excellent), now in French (good), he conversed brilliantly, displaying his old devotion to figures and efficiency. I was filled with pride at how well liked he was. In a few hours he had charmed everyone, and was invited here and there.

There was a single moment when he changed abruptly. The evening before he was to speak at the conference, he became aloof and rude; he seemed overwhelmed by anxiety. He began to disparage the text he had prepared, he kept repeating that writing for him wasn't as easy as it was for me, he became angry because he hadn't had time to work well. I felt guilty—

was it our complicated affair that had distracted him?—and tried to help, hugging him, kissing him, urging him to read me the pages. He did read them, with the air of a frightened schoolboy, which touched me. To me the speech seemed as dull as the ones I had heard in the assembly hall, but I praised it and he calmed down. The next morning he performed with practiced warmth and was applauded. That evening one of the big-name academics, an American, invited him to sit with him. I was left alone, but I wasn't sorry. When Nino was there, I didn't talk to anyone, while in his absence I was forced to manage with my halting French, and I became friendly with a couple from Paris. I liked them because I quickly discovered that they were in a situation not very different from ours. Both considered the institution of the family suffocating, both had painfully left spouses and children, both seemed happy. He, Augustin, was around fifty, with a ruddy face, lively blue eyes, a bushy pale-blond mustache. She, Colombe, was a little over thirty, like me; she had very short black hair, eyes and lips drawn sharply on a tiny face, a charming elegance. I talked mainly to Colombe, who had a child of seven.

"In a few months," I said, "my older daughter will turn seven, but she's going into second grade this year—she's very bright."

"My son is extremely clever and imaginative."

"How did he take the separation?"

"Fine."

"He didn't get even a little upset?"

"Children aren't rigid, the way we are: they're flexible."

She dwelled on the flexibility she ascribed to childhood; it seemed to reassure her. She added: in our world it's fairly common for parents to separate, and children know it's possible. But just as I was saying that I didn't know other separated women, apart from one friend, her tone changed abruptly and she began to complain about the child: he's smart but slow, she exclaimed, at school they say he's unruly. I was struck by the change; she expressed herself without tenderness, almost bitterly, as if her son were behaving like that to spite her, and this made me anxious. Her companion must have noticed, and he interrupted, boasting about *his* two boys, fourteen and eighteen, and joking about how attractive they were to women, both old and young. When Nino returned, the two men—especially Augustin—began to criticize the speakers. Colombe joined in almost immediately, with a slightly artificial gaiety. The maliciousness soon created a bond. Augustin talked and drank a lot all evening, his companion laughed whenever Nino managed to say a word. They invited us to drive to Paris with them, in their car.

The conversation about children, and that invitation that we didn't say yes or no to, brought me back to reality. Until that moment Dede and Elsa, and also Pietro, had been on my mind constantly, but as if suspended in a parallel universe, motionless around the kitchen table in Florence, or in front of the television, or in their beds. Suddenly my world and theirs were back in communication. I realized that the days in Montpellier were about to end, that inevitably Nino and I would return to our homes, that we would have to face our respective marital crises, I in Florence, he in Naples. And the children's bodies rejoined mine, I felt the contact violently. I had no news of them for five days, and as I became aware of that I felt an intense nausea, an unbearable longing for them. I was afraid not of the future in general, which now seemed inescapably occupied by Nino, but of the hours that were about to come, of tomorrow, of the day after. I couldn't resist and although it was almost midnight—what's the difference, I said to myself, Pietro is always awake—I tried to telephone.

It was fairly laborious, but finally the call went through. Hello, I said. Hello, I repeated. I knew that Pietro was at the other end of the line, I called him by name: Pietro, it's Elena, how are the girls. The connection was cut off. I waited a few minutes, then I asked the operator to call again. I was determined to continue all night, but this time Pietro answered.

"What do you want?"

"Tell me about the children."

"They're sleeping."

"I know, but how are they?"

"What is it to you."

"They're my children."

"You left them, they don't want to be your children anymore."

"They told you?"

"They told my mother."

"You had Adele come?"

"Yes."

"Tell them I'll be home in a few days."

"No, don't come back. Neither I, nor the children, nor my mother wants to see you again."

4.

I had a cry, then I calmed down and went to Nino. I wanted to tell him about that phone call, I wanted him to console me. But as I was about to knock on his door I heard him talking to someone. I hesitated. He was on the phone. I couldn't understand what he was saying, or even what language he was speaking, but right away I thought that he was talking to his wife. So did this happen every evening? When I went to my room to get ready for the night and he was alone, he telephoned Eleonora? Were they looking for a way to separate without fighting? Or were they reconciling and, once the interlude of Montpellier was over, she would take him back?

I decided to knock. Nino broke off, silence, then he began

talking again but lowered his voice. I became nervous, I knocked again, nothing happened. I had to knock a third time, hard, before he came to the door. I immediately confronted him, I accused him of hiding me from his wife, I cried that I had telephoned Pietro, that my husband didn't want to let me see my children, that I was calling into question my entire life, while he was cooing on the telephone with Eleonora. It was a terrible night of quarreling; we struggled to make up. Nino tried everything to soothe me: he laughed nervously, he got angry at Pietro for the way he had treated me, he kissed me, I pushed him away, he said I was crazy. But no matter how I pressed him he never admitted that he was talking to his wife, in fact he swore on his son that since the day he left Naples he hadn't talked to her.

"Then who were you calling?"

"A colleague here in the hotel."

"At midnight?"

"At midnight."

"Liar."

"It's the truth."

I refused for a long time to make love, I couldn't, I was afraid that he no longer loved me. Then I yielded, in order not to have to believe that it was all already over.

The next morning, for the first time in almost five days of living together, I woke in a bad mood. We had to leave, the conference was nearly over. But I didn't want Montpellier to be merely an interlude; I was afraid to go home, afraid that Nino would go home, afraid of losing my children forever. When Augustin and Colombe again suggested that we drive to Paris with them, and even offered to put us up, I turned to Nino, hoping that he, too, wanted nothing more than the chance to extend this time, put off the return. But he shook his head sadly, he said: Impossible, we have to go back to Italy, and he talked about flights, tickets, trains, money. I was fragile, I felt disappointment and rancor. I was right, I thought, he lied to me, the break with his wife isn't conclusive. He had talked to her every night, he had pledged to return home after the conference, he couldn't delay even a couple of days. And me?

I remembered the publisher in Nanterre and my short, scholarly story about the male invention of woman. Until that moment I hadn't talked about myself to anyone, even Nino. I had been the smiling but nearly mute woman who slept with the brilliant professor from Naples, the woman always pasted to him, attentive to his needs, to his thoughts. But now I said with false cheer: It's Nino who has to return, I have an engagement in Nanterre; a work of mine is about to come out—or maybe it's already out—a half essay, half story; I just might leave with you, and stop in at the publisher's. The two looked at me as if only at that moment had I actually begun to exist, and they went on to ask me about my work. I told them, and it turned out that Colombe knew well the woman who was the head of the small but—as I discovered at that moment—prestigious publishing house. I let myself go, I talked with too much vivacity and maybe I exaggerated a little about my literary career. I did it not for the two French people but, rather, for Nino. I wanted to remind him that I had a rewarding life of my own, that if I had been capable of leaving my children and Pietro, then I could also do without him, and not in a week, not in ten days: immediately.

He listened, then he said seriously to Colombe and Augustin: All right, if it's not a bother for you we'll take advantage of the ride. But when we were alone he made me a speech anxious in tone and passionate in content, whose sense was that I should trust him, that although our situation was complicated we would surely untangle it, that to do so, however, we had to go home, we couldn't flee from Montpellier to Paris and then to who knows what other city, we had to confront our spouses and begin our life together. Suddenly I felt that he was not only reasonable but sincere. I was confused, I embraced him, I murmured agreement. And yet we left for Paris; I wanted just a few more days.

5.

It was a long trip. There was a strong wind, and sometimes rain. The landscape had a rust-caked pallor, but at times the sky broke and everything became brilliant, starting with the rain. I clung to Nino and, now and then, fell asleep on his shoulder; I began again to feel, with pleasure, that I was far beyond my margins. I liked the foreign language that echoed in the car, I was pleased that I was heading in the direction of a book that I had written in Italian and that, thanks to Mariarosa, was being published first in another language. What an extraordinary fact—how many amazing things were happening to me. That little volume was like a rock that I had hurled along an unpredictable trajectory and at a speed that had no comparison with that of the rocks that as girls Lila and I had thrown at the gangs of boys.

But the journey wasn't always pleasant; sometimes I became sad. And I quickly formed the impression that Nino was talking to Colombe in a tone that he didn't use with Augustin, not to mention that too often he touched her shoulder with his fingertips. My bad mood gradually worsened, as I saw the two of them were getting very friendly. When we arrived in Paris they were the best of friends, chatting away; she laughed often, smoothing her hair with a careless gesture.

Augustin lived in a nice apartment on Canal Saint-Martin; Colombe had recently moved in. Even after they showed us our room, they wouldn't let us to go bed. It seemed to me that they were afraid to be alone, they wouldn't stop talking. I was tired and nervous; I was the one who had wanted to go to

Paris, and now it seemed absurd to be in that house, among strangers, far from my daughters, with Nino paying scant attention to me. Once in the room I asked him:

"Do you like Colombe?"

"She's nice."

"I asked if you like her."

"Do you want to quarrel?"

"No."

"Then think about it: how can I like Colombe if I love you?"

It scared me when his tone became even slightly harsh; I was afraid I would have to acknowledge that something between us wasn't working. He is simply nice to anyone who has been nice to us, I said to myself, and fell asleep. But I slept badly. At one point I had the impression that I was alone in the bed; I tried to wake up, but was drawn back into sleep. I emerged again sometime later. Nino now was standing in the dark, or so it seemed to me. Sleep, he said. I fell asleep again.

The next day our hosts took us to Nanterre. The whole way Nino continued to joke with Colombe, to talk to her in an allusive way. I tried not to pay attention. How could I think of living with him if I had to spend my time watching him? When we reached our destination and he became genial and charming with Mariarosa's friend, the owner of the publishing house, and her partner—one around forty, the other sixty—I drew a sigh of relief. It's innocent, I concluded, he's like that with all women. And finally I felt better.

The two women greeted me warmly, full of praise, and asked about Mariarosa. I knew that my volume had only just arrived in the bookstores, but already a couple of reviews had appeared. The older woman showed them to me; she seemed amazed herself at how positive they were, and, turning to Colombe, to Augustin, to Nino, she kept repeating it. I read the articles, two lines here, four there. They were written by women—I had never heard of them, but Colombe and the two women had—and they praised the book enthusiastically. I should have been pleased; the day before, I had been compelled to sing my own praises, and now I no longer needed to. Yet I found that I couldn't feel excited. It was as if, since I loved Nino and he loved me, that love made everything good that happened to me and would happen to me nothing but a pleasant secondary effect. I showed my satisfaction graciously and gave a feeble assent to my publishers' plans for promotion. You'll have to return soon, the older woman exclaimed, or at least we hope so. The younger added: Mariarosa told us about your marital crisis; we hope you'll come out of it without too much suffering.

In this way I discovered that the news of the break between me and Pietro had reached not only Adele but Milan and even France. Better that way, I thought; it will be easier to make the separation permanent. I said to myself: I'll take what's mine, and I mustn't live in fear of losing Nino, I mustn't worry about Dede and Elsa. I'm fortunate, he will always love me, my daughters are my daughters, everything will work out.

6.

We returned to Rome. We promised each other everything as we said goodbye, we did nothing but promise. Then Nino left for Naples and I for Florence.

I returned home almost on tiptoe, convinced that one of the most difficult trials of my life awaited me. Instead the children greeted me with apprehensive joy, and began tagging after me through the house—not only Elsa but Dede, too—as if they were afraid that if they lost sight of me I would disappear again. Adele was polite and didn't mention even once the situation that had brought her to my house; Pietro, very pale, confined himself to handing me a piece of paper with a list of phone calls for me (Lila's name appeared at least four times), muttered that he had to go to work, and two hours later had disappeared, without even saying goodbye to his mother or the children.

It took a few days for Adele to manifest her opinion plainly: she wanted me to return to myself and to my husband. But it took several weeks to convince her that I really didn't want either of those things. In that time she never raised her voice, never lost her temper, didn't even comment sarcastically about my frequent long phone calls to Nino. She was more interested in the phone calls from the two women in Nanterre, who were keeping me informed of the progress of the book and of a calendar of engagements that would lead to a tour in France. She wasn't surprised at the positive reviews in the French papers; she was sure that the book would soon get the same attention in Italy, she said that in our papers she would have been able to obtain better. Above all she insistently praised my intelligence, my education, my courage, and on no account did she defend her son, who, besides, was never around.

I assumed that Pietro did not really have work obligations outside of Florence. Rather, I was immediately convinced, with rage and even a hint of contempt, that he had entrusted the resolution of our crisis to his mother and was holed up somewhere to work on his interminable book. Once, I couldn't contain myself and I said to Adele:

"It was really difficult to live with your son."

"There's no man it's not difficult to live with."

"With him, believe me, it's been especially difficult."

"You think it will go better with Nino?"

"Yes."

"I've asked around, the talk about him in Milan is very nasty."

"I don't need the talk of Milan. I've loved him for twenty

THE STORY OF THE LOST CHILD · 37

years and you can spare me the gossip. I know more about him than anyone else."

"How you like saying you love him."

"Why shouldn't I like it?"

"You're right, why? I was wrong: it's pointless to open the eyes of someone in love."

From then on we stopped talking about Nino. And when I left the girls with her to rush to Naples she didn't bat an eye. She didn't bat an eye even when I told her that, when I returned from Naples, I would have to go to France and would be there for a week. She asked only, with a slightly ironic inflection: "Will you be here for Christmas? Will you be with the children?"

The question almost offended me, I answered:

"Of course."

I filled my suitcase mainly with elegant underwear and stylish dresses. At the announcement of my new departure Dede and Elsa, who never asked about their father, even though they hadn't seen him for a long time, were extremely upset. Dede went so far as to yell words that were surely not hers: go, get out, you're mean and hateful. I glanced at Adele, hoping that she would try to get her to play, and distract her, but she did nothing. When they saw me go to the door they began to cry. Elsa started it, shrieking, I want to come with you. Dede resisted, she tried to show me all her indifference, maybe even her scorn, but finally she gave in and became even more desperate than her sister. I had to tear myself away from them, they held on to my dress, they wanted me to leave the suitcase. Their cries pursued me to the street.

The trip to Naples seemed very long. Nearing the city I looked out the window. As the train slowed down, sliding into the urban space, I was seized by an anxious exhaustion. I noticed the ugliness of the periphery, with the small gray apartment buildings beyond the tracks; the pylons, the lights of the signals, the stone parapets. When the train entered the station it seemed to me that the Naples I felt bound to, the Naples I was returning to, was now summed up only in Nino. I knew that he was in worse trouble than I was. Eleonora had thrown him out of the house; for him, too, everything had become provisional. For several weeks he had been staying at the house of a university colleague who lived near the Duomo. Where would he take me, what would we do? And, above all, what decisions would we make, since we hadn't the least idea of a concrete solution to our situation? The only thing clear to me was that I was burning with desire, I couldn't wait to see him. I got out of the train terrified that something had kept him from coming to meet me. But he was there: tall as he was, he stood out in the stream of travelers.

This reassured me, and I was even more reassured to find that he had taken a room in a small hotel in Mergellina, thus showing that he had no intention of hiding me in his friend's house. We were mad with love, the time flew. In the evening we walked along the sea clinging to each other; he put an arm around my shoulders, and every so often leaned over to kiss me. I tried in every way possible to persuade him to go to France with me. He was tempted, then retreated, taking refuge behind his work at the university. He never spoke of Eleonora or Albertino, as if the mere mention of them could ruin the joy of our being together. I instead told him about the girls' desperation, I said we had to find a solution as quickly as possible. I felt he was nervous; I was sensitive to the slightest tension, I was afraid that at any moment he might say: I can't do it, I'm going home. But I was wide of the mark. When we went to dinner he revealed what the problem was. He said, becoming suddenly serious, that there was some vexing news.

"Let's hear it," I whispered.

"This morning Lina called me."

"Ah."

"She wants to see us."

7.

The evening was spoiled. Nino said it was my mother-in-law who had told Lila that I was in Naples. He spoke with great embarrassment, choosing his words carefully, emphasizing points like: she didn't have my address; she asked my sister for the phone number of my colleague; she telephoned a little before I was about to leave for the station; I didn't tell you right away because I was afraid you would get angry and our day would be ruined. He concluded, desolate:

"You know what she's like, I've never been able to say no to her. We have an appointment with her tomorrow at eleven, she'll be at the entrance to the metro at Piazza Amedeo."

I couldn't control myself:

"How long have you been back in touch? Have you seen each other?"

"What are you talking about? Absolutely not."

"I don't believe you."

"Elena, I swear I haven't talked to or seen Lila since 1963."

"You know the child wasn't yours?"

"She told me this morning."

"So you talked for a long time, and about intimate things."

"She was the one who brought up the child."

"And you—in all this time you were never curious to know more about it?"

"It's my problem, I don't see the need to discuss it."

"Your problems are also mine now. We have a lot to talk about, time is short, and I didn't leave my children to waste it with Lina. How could it possibly have occurred to you to make this date?"

"I thought it would please you. But there's the telephone: call your friend and tell her that we have a lot to do, you can't see her."

There, suddenly he lost patience, I was silent. Yes, I knew what Lila was like. Ever since I returned to Florence she had been calling often, but I had other things to think about and not only did I always hang up, I had also asked Adele—if she happened to answer—to say that I wasn't home. Lila, however, hadn't given up. It was therefore likely that she had found out from Adele about my presence in Naples, likely that she had taken for granted that I would not go to the neighborhood, likely that, to see me, she had found a way of getting in touch with Nino. What was the harm? And above all what did I expect? I had always known that he had loved Lila and that Lila had loved him. So? It had happened long ago, and to be jealous was inappropriate. I slowly caressed his hand, I murmured: All right, tomorrow we'll go to Piazza Amedeo.

We ate, and he talked for a long time about our future. Nino made me promise that I would ask for a separation as soon as I returned from France. Meanwhile he assured me that he had already been in touch with a lawyer friend of his and that even if it was all complicated, and certainly Eleonora and her relatives would make things hard for him, he had decided to go ahead. You know, he said, here in Naples these things are more difficult: when it comes to a backward mentality and bad manners my wife's relatives are no different from mine and yours, even if they have money and are high-ranking professionals. And, as if to explain himself better, he began to speak well of my in-laws. Unfortunately, he exclaimed, I'm not dealing, as you are, with respectable people, like the Airotas, people he described as having grand cultural traditions, admirable civility.

I listened, but now Lila was there between us, at our table, and I couldn't push her away. While Nino talked, I remembered the trouble she had got herself in just to be with him, heedless of what Stefano could do to her, or her brother, or Michele Solara. And the mention of our parents for a fraction of a second brought me back to Ischia, to the evening on the beach of the Maronti—Lila with Nino in Forio, I on the damp sand with Donato—and I felt horror. This, I thought, is a secret that I will never be able to tell him. How many words remain unsayable even between a couple in love, and how the risk is increased that others might say them, destroying it. His father and I, he and Lila. I tore away revulsion, I mentioned Pietro, what he was suffering. Nino flared up, it was his turn to be jealous, I tried to reassure him. He demanded clean breaks and full stops, I demanded them, too: they seemed to us indispensable to the start of a new life. We discussed when, where. Work chained Nino inescapably to Naples, the children chained me to Florence.

"Come and live here," he said suddenly. "Move as soon as you can."

"Impossible, Pietro has to be able to see the children."

"Take turns: you'll take them to him, the next time he'll come here."

"He won't agree."

"He'll agree."

The evening went on like that. The more we examined the question, the more complicated it seemed; the more we imagined a life together—every day, every night—the more we desired it and the difficulties vanished. Meanwhile in the empty restaurant the waiters whispered to each other, yawned. Nino paid, and we went back along the sea walk, which was still lively. For a moment, as I looked at the dark water and smelled its odor, it seemed that the neighborhood was much farther away than when I had gone to Pisa, to Florence. Even Naples, suddenly, seemed very far from Naples. And Lila from Lila, I felt that beside me I had not her but my own anxieties.

Only Nino and I were close, very close. I whispered in his ear:
Let's go to bed.

8.

The next day I got up early and shut myself in the bathroom.
I took a long shower, I dried my hair carefully, worrying that the
hotel hair dryer, which blew violently, would give it the wrong
wave. A little before ten I woke Nino, who, still dazed by sleep,
was full of compliments for my dress. He tried to pull me down
beside him, I drew back. Although I made an effort to pretend
there was nothing wrong, I had trouble forgiving him. He had
transformed our new day of love into Lila's day, and now the time
was completely indelibly marked by that looming encounter.

I dragged him to breakfast, he followed submissively. He
didn't laugh, he didn't tease me, he said, touching my hair with
his fingertips: You look very nice. Evidently he perceived that
I was anxious. And I was, I was afraid that Lila would arrive
looking her best. I was made as I was made; she was elegant by
nature. And, besides, she had new money, if she wanted she
could take care of herself as she had done as a girl with
Stefano's money. I didn't want Nino to be dazzled by her again.

We left around ten-thirty, in a cold wind. We walked, unhurried, toward Piazza Amedeo. I was shivering, even though I was
wearing a heavy coat and he had an arm around my shoulders.
We never mentioned Lila. Nino talked in a somewhat artificial
way about how Naples had improved now that there was a
Communist mayor, and he began pressing me again to join him
as soon as possible with the children. He held me close as we
walked, and I hoped he would keep holding me until we
reached the subway station. I wanted Lila to be at the metro
entrance, to see us from a distance, to find us handsome, to be
forced to think: a perfect couple. But, a few meters from the

meeting place, he released his arm, lighted a cigarette. I took his hand instinctively, squeezed it hard, and we entered the piazza like that.

I didn't see Lila right away and for a moment I hoped she hadn't come. Then I heard her call me—she called me in her usual imperative way, as though it could never even occur to her that I wouldn't hear her, wouldn't turn, wouldn't obey her voice. She was in the doorway of the café opposite the metro tunnel, her hands stuck in the pockets of an ugly brown coat, thinner than usual, slightly bent, her shining black hair traversed by trails of silver and tied in a ponytail. She seemed to me the usual Lila, the adult Lila, a Lila marked by the factory experience: she had done nothing to dress up. She hugged me tight, in an intense embrace that I returned without energy, then she kissed me on the cheeks with two sharp smacks, and a contented laugh. She held out her hand to Nino absently.

We sat inside the café; she did almost all the talking and addressed me as if we were alone. She immediately confronted my hostility, which evidently she read in my face, and said affectionately, smiling: All right, I was wrong, I offended you, but now, enough, how is it that you've become so touchy, you know that I like everything about you, let's make up.

I avoided her, with tepid half-smiles, I didn't say yes or no. She was sitting opposite Nino, but she never looked or spoke to him. She was there for me; once, she took my hand but I quietly withdrew it. She wanted us to be reconciled, she intended to reinstate herself in my life again, even if she didn't agree with the direction I was taking it. I realized this from the way she added question to question without paying attention to the answers. She was so eager to reoccupy every corner that she had scarcely touched on one subject when she immediately went on to another.

"With Pietro?"

"Badly."

"And your daughters?"

"They're well."

"You'll get divorced?"

"Yes."

"And you two will live together?"

"Yes."

"Where, what city?"

"I don't know."

"Come back here to live."

"It's complicated."

"I'll find you an apartment."

"If it's necessary I'll let you know."

"Are you writing?"

"I've published a book."

"Another?"

"Yes."

"No one's said anything about it."

"For now it's only come out in France."

"In French?"

"Yes."

"A novel?"

"A story, but it has a thesis."

"What's it about?"

I was vague, I cut her off. I preferred to ask about Enzo, about Gennaro, about the neighborhood, about her work. At the mention of her son she took on a look of amusement, and declared that I would see him soon; he was still at school now, but he was coming with Enzo and there would also be a nice surprise. About the neighborhood, on the other hand, she assumed an attitude of indifference. Alluding to the terrible death of Manuela Solara and the turmoil it had unleashed, she said: It's nothing, people are murdered here the way they are everywhere in Italy. Then, surprisingly, she mentioned my mother, praising her energy and her resourcefulness, even though she was well aware of our turbulent relationship. And, just as surprisingly, she seemed affectionate toward her own parents; she said that she was putting money aside to buy the apartment where they had always lived, to give them some peace of mind. It's a pleasure for me—she explained, as if she had to apologize for that generosity—I was born there, I'm attached to it, and if Enzo and I work hard we can afford it. She worked as much as twelve hours a day now, not only for Michele Solara but also for other clients. I'm studying—she said—a new machine, the System 32, much better than the one I showed you when you came to Acerra: it's a white case that incorporates a tiny six-inch monitor, a keyboard, and a printer. She talked on and on about more advanced systems that were coming. She was very well informed, as usual she got excited about the new things, even though she'd be sick of them in a few days. The new machine had a beauty of its own, according to her. Too bad, she said, that apart from the machine, everything was shit.

At that point Nino broke in, and did exactly the opposite of what until that moment I had done: he began to give her detailed information. He spoke with excitement about my book, he said that it was coming out soon in Italy, too; he cited the success of the French reviews, he pointed out that I had a lot of problems with my husband and my daughters, he talked about his break with his wife, he repeated that the only solution was to live in Naples, he even encouraged her to find us a house, he asked some knowledgeable questions about her and Enzo's work.

I listened somewhat apprehensively. His manner as he spoke was distant, to show me, first, that he really hadn't seen Lila before; and, second, that she no longer had any influence over him. And not for an instant did he use the seductive tones that he had used with Colombe and which habitually came to him with women. He didn't invent sentimental locutions, he never looked her straight in the eye, he didn't touch her: his voice became a little warmer only when he praised me.

This didn't prevent me from remembering the beach at Citara, and how he and Lila had made use of the most varied subjects to reach an understanding and cut me out. But it seemed to me that now the opposite was happening. Even when they asked each other questions and answered them, they ignored each other and addressed me, as if I were their only interlocutor.

They went on talking for a good half hour without agreeing about anything. I was surprised especially by the way they insisted on their differences about Naples. My political knowledge was by now feeble: the care of the children, the study in preparation for my little book, the writing of it, and, above all, the upheaval of my personal life had kept me even from reading the newspaper. The two of them, on the other hand, knew everything about everything. Nino listed names of Neapolitan Communists and socialists he knew well, and trusted. He praised an administration that, finally, was honest, led by a mayor whom he called respectable, likable, a stranger to the usual old corruption. He concluded: now at last there are good reasons to live and work here, this is a great opportunity, we have to be part of it. But Lila made sarcastic comments about everything he said. Naples, she said, is disgusting, exactly as it was before, and if you're not teaching the monarchists, fascists, and Christian Democrats a good lesson for all the filthy things they've done, if you just forget about it, as the left is doing, soon the shopkeepers—she laughed a little harshly after saying the word—will take back the city, along with the city bureaucracy, the lawyers, the accountants, the banks, and the Camorrists. I was quickly forced to realize that even at the center of that discussion they had put me. They both wanted me to return to Naples, but each was openly intent on detaching me from the influence of the other and was urging me to move to the city that each was imagining: Nino's was at peace and heading toward good government; Lila's was taking revenge on all the predators, it didn't give a damn about Communists and socialists, it was starting over from zero.

I studied them the whole time. It struck me that, the more complex the themes that emerged in the conversation, the more Lila tended to unfold her secret Italian, which I knew she was capable of but which on that occasion astonished me, because every sentence demonstrated that she was more cultured than she wished to appear. As for Nino, who was usually brilliant, self-confident, he chose his words warily, and at times seemed intimidated. They're both uneasy, I thought. In the past they exposed themselves to each other openly and now they're ashamed of having done so. What is happening at this moment? Are they deceiving me? Are they really fighting over me or are they only trying to keep their old attraction under control? I purposely gave signs of impatience. Lila noticed, she got up and disappeared as if to go to the bathroom. I didn't say a word, I was afraid of seeming aggressive toward Nino, and he, too, was silent. When Lila returned, she exclaimed cheerfully:

"Come on, it's time, let's go see Gennaro."

"We can't," I said, "we have an engagement."

"My son is really fond of you, he'll be disappointed."

"Say hello from me, tell him I love him, too."

"I have an appointment in Piazza dei Martiri: it's just ten minutes, we'll say hello to Alfonso and then you'll go."

I stared at her, she suddenly narrowed her eyes as if to hide them. Was that her plan, then? She wanted to take Nino to the Solaras' old shoe store, take him back to the place where, for almost a year, they had been secret lovers?

I answered with a half smile: No, I'm sorry, we really have to run. And I glanced at Nino, who immediately gestured to the waiter, to pay. Lila said: I've already done it, and while he protested she turned to me again, insisting in a cajoling tone:

"Gennaro isn't coming by himself, Enzo's bringing him. And someone else is coming with them, someone who's dying to see you, it would really be terrible if you left without seeing him."

The person was Antonio Cappuccio, my teenage boyfriend, whom the Solaras, after the murder of their mother, had swiftly recalled from Germany.

9.

Lila told me that Antonio had come by himself for Manuela's funeral, so thin that he was almost unrecognizable. Within a few days he had rented a place near Melina, who lived with Stefano and Ada, and had sent for his German wife and three children. It was true, then, that he was married, it was true that he had children. Separate segments of life came together in my head. Antonio was an important part of the world I came from, Lila's words about him diminished the weight of the morning: I felt lighter. I whispered to Nino: Just a few minutes, all right? He shrugged his shoulders and we set off toward Piazza dei Martiri.

All the way, as we went along Via dei Mille and Via Filangieri, Lila monopolized me, and while Nino followed us, hands in pockets, head lowered, certainly in a bad mood, she talked to me with her usual assurance. She said that at the first opportunity I should meet Antonio's family. She vividly described his wife and children. She was beautiful, fairer than I was, and the three children were also fair, not one had taken after their father, who was as dark as a Saracen: when the five of them walked along the *stradone*, the wife and children, so pale, with those shining heads, seemed like prisoners of war he was leading around the neighborhood. She laughed, then she listed those who, besides Antonio, were waiting to greet me: Carmen—who, however, had to work, she would stay a few minutes and rush off with Enzo—Alfonso, of course, who still managed the Solaras' shop, Marisa with the children. Give them just a few minutes, she said, and you'll make them happy: they love you.

While she talked, I thought that all those people I was about to see again would spread through the neighborhood the news of the end of my marriage, that my parents, too, would find out, that my mother would learn I had become the lover of the son of Sarratore. But I noticed that it didn't bother me, in fact it pleased me that my friends would see me with Nino, that they would say behind my back: She's a person who does as she likes, she's left her husband and children, she's gone with someone else. I realized, to my surprise, that I *wanted* to be officially associated with Nino, I wanted to be seen with him, I wanted to erase the Elena-Pietro couple and replace it with the Nino-Elena couple. And I felt suddenly calm, almost well disposed toward the net in which Lila wished to trap me.

The words followed one another without pause; at one point, assuming an old habit, she took me by the arm. That gesture left me indifferent. She wants to prove that we're still the same, I said to myself, but it's time to acknowledge that we've used each other up, that arm of hers is like a wooden limb or the phantom remains of the thrilling contact of long ago. I remembered, by contrast, the moment when, years before, I had wished that she would get sick and die. Then—I thought—in spite of everything our relationship was alive, intense, therefore painful. Now there was a new fact. All the passion I was capable of—even what had harbored that terrible wish—was concentrated on the man I had always loved. Lila thought that she still had her old power, that she could drag me with her where she wanted. But in the end what had she orchestrated: the revisiting of bitter loves and adolescent passions? What a few moments earlier had seemed to me malicious suddenly appeared as harmless as a museum. Something else was important for me, whether she liked it or not. Nino and I were important, Nino and I, and even to cause scandal in the small world of the neighborhood seemed a pleasing recognition of us as a couple. I no longer felt Lila, there was no life in her arm, it was only fabric against fabric.

We arrived in Piazza dei Martiri. I turned to Nino to warn him that his sister and her children were also at the shop. He muttered in irritation. The sign appeared—SOLARA—we entered, and even though all eyes were on Nino, I was greeted as if I were alone. Only Marisa spoke to her brother, and neither seemed pleased by the encounter. She immediately reproached him because she never heard from him or saw him, exclaiming: Mamma is ill, Papa is unbearable, and you don't give a damn. He didn't answer, he kissed his nephews absentmindedly, and only because Marisa continued to attack him he said: I've got my own troubles, Marì, leave me alone. While I was pulled affectionately this way and that, I continued to keep my eye on him, not jealously now—I was worried only about his uneasiness. I didn't know if he remembered Antonio, if he recognized him, I alone knew about the beating my former boyfriend had given him. I saw that they exchanged a very reserved greeting—a movement of the head, a slight smile—no different from what right afterward occurred between Enzo and him, Alfonso and him, Carmen and him. For Nino they were all strangers, Lila's and my world, he had had almost nothing to do with it. Afterward, he wandered through the shop smoking, and no one, not even his sister, said a word to him. He was there, he was present, it was he I had left my husband for. Even Lila—especially Lila—had finally to acknowledge the fact. Now that everyone had studied him carefully, I wanted to drag him out of there as quickly as possible and take him away with me.

10.

For the half hour that I was in that place there was a chaotic collision of past and present: the shoes Lila designed, her wedding photograph, the evening of the inauguration and the miscarriage, she who for her own purposes had transformed the shop into a salon and a love nest; and the present-day plot, all of us over thirty, with our very different stories, the open rumors, the secret ones.

I affected composure, I assumed a happy tone. I exchanged kisses, hugs, and a few words with Gennaro, who was now an overweight boy of twelve with a dark strip of fuzz on his upper lip, so similar in features to the adolescent Stefano that Lila, in conceiving him, seemed to have taken away herself entirely. I felt obliged to be equally affectionate with Marisa's children and with Marisa herself, who, pleased with my attention, began to make allusive remarks, the remarks of someone who knew the turn my life was taking. She said: Now that you'll be in Naples more often, please, come see us; we know you two are busy, you're scholarly people and we aren't, but you'll find a little time.

She sat next to her husband and restrained her children, who were eager to run outside. In vain I sought in her face traces of a blood tie with Nino, but she had nothing of her brother or even of her mother. Now that she was heavier she resembled, rather, Donato; she had also inherited his artificial patter, with which she was trying to give me the impression that she had a lovely family and a good life. And Alfonso, to support her, nodded yes, and smiled at me silently, displaying gleaming white teeth. How disorienting his looks were. He was stylishly dressed, and his long black hair, tied in a ponytail, showed off the grace of his features, but there was something in his gestures, in his face, that I couldn't understand, something unexpected that made me uneasy. He was the only one there, except for Nino and me, who had had an education, and—it seemed to me—rather than fading over time it had more profoundly penetrated his slender body, the fine contours of his face. How handsome he was, how polite. Marisa had wanted him at all costs, even though he fled, and now look at them, she who as she aged was taking on masculine features, he who fought virility by becoming more feminine, and those two children of theirs, who were said to be the children of Michele Solara. Yes, Alfonso whispered, joining his wife's invitation, if you would come to dinner sometime at our house you would make us very happy. And Marisa: When will you write a new book, Lenù? We're waiting; but you have to keep up. You seemed dirty, but you weren't dirty enough—have you seen the pornographic stuff they write today?

Although no one there showed any liking for Nino, there was no hint of criticism for my change of feeling, not even a glance, or a half smile. On the contrary, as I did my rounds, hugging and talking, they tried to impress on me their affection and their respect. Enzo put into his embrace the force of his seriousness, and although he merely smiled, without a word, it seemed to me that he was saying: I love you whatever you decide to do. Carmen, instead, drew me almost immediately into a corner—she was very nervous, and kept looking at the clock—and spoke in a rush about her brother, as one speaks to a good authority who knows everything and can do everything, and no false step can dim that aura. She made no mention of her children, her husband, her personal life or mine. I realized that she had taken upon herself the weight of Pasquale's reputation as a terrorist, but only in order to recast it. In our few minutes of conversation she did not confine herself to saying that her brother was unjustly persecuted: she wanted to restore courage and goodness to him. Her eyes were burning with the determination to be always and no matter what on his side. She said that she had to know where to find me, she wanted my telephone number and my address. You are an important person, Lenù—she whispered—you know people who, if Pasquale isn't murdered, can help him. Then she indicated Antonio, who was standing apart, a few steps from Enzo. Come here—she said softly—you tell her, too. And Antonio came over, head down, and spoke timid phrases whose meaning was: I know Pasquale trusts you, he came to your house before making the choice he made, so if you see him again, warn him. He has to disappear, he'd better not be seen in Italy; because, as I told Carmen, too, the problem isn't the carabinieri, the problem is the Solaras. They're convinced that he murdered Signora Manuela, and if they find him—now, tomorrow, years from now—I can't help him. While he was making that speech, in a grave tone, Carmen kept interrupting to ask me: Do you understand, Lenù? She watched me with an anxious gaze. Finally she hugged me, kissed me, whispered: You and Lina are my sisters, and she went off with Enzo, they had things to do.

So I remained alone with Antonio. I seemed to have before me two people present in the same body and yet very distinct. He was the boy who long ago had held me tight at the ponds, who had idolized me, and whose intense odor had remained in my memory like a desire that is never truly satisfied. And he was the man of now, without an ounce of fat, all big bones and taut skin that went from his hard blank face to his feet, in enormous shoes. I said, embarrassed, that I didn't know anyone who could help Pasquale, that Carmen overestimated me. But I realized right away that if Pasquale's sister had an exaggerated idea of my prestige, his was even more exaggerated. Antonio said that I was modest as usual, that he had read my book, in German no less, that I was known all over the world. Although he had lived for a long time abroad, and had certainly seen and done terrible things for the Solaras, he had remained someone from the neighborhood and continued to imagine—or maybe he was pretending, who knows, to please me—that I had power, the power of respectable people, because I had a degree, because I spoke in Italian, I wrote books. I said, laughing: you're the only person in Germany who bought that book. And I asked about his wife, his children. He answered in monosyllables, but meanwhile he drew me outside, into the square. There he said kindly:

"Now you have to admit that I was right."

"In what."

"You wanted him, and you lied to me."

"I was a girl."

"No, you were grown up. And you were more intelligent than me. You don't know the harm you did letting me believe I was crazy."

"Stop it."

He was silent, I retreated toward the shop. He followed me, and held me back on the threshold. For a few seconds he stared at Nino, who had sat down in a corner. He murmured:

"If he hurts you, too, tell me."

I laughed: "Of course."

"Don't laugh, I talked to Lina. She knows him well, she says you shouldn't trust him. We respect you, he doesn't."

Lila. Here she was using Antonio, making him her messenger of possible misfortunes. Where had she gone? I saw that she was off in a corner, playing with Marisa's children, but in fact she was observing each one of us, with her eyes narrowed. And in her usual way she was ruling over everyone: Carmen, Alfonso, Marisa, Enzo, Antonio, her son and the children of others, perhaps even the owners of the shop. I told myself again that she would no longer exercise any authority over me, that that long phase was over. I said goodbye, she hugged me tight, as if she wanted to pull me into herself. As I said goodbye to them all, one by one, I was again struck by Alfonso, but this time I understood what had disturbed me. The little that had marked him as the son of Don Achille and Maria, as the brother of Stefano and Pinuccia, had disappeared from his face. Now, mysteriously, with that long hair in a ponytail, he resembled Lila.

11.

I returned to Florence, I talked to Pietro about our separation. We quarreled violently while Adele tried to protect the children and perhaps herself, shutting herself up with them in her room. At a certain point we realized not that we were overdoing it but that the presence of our daughters did not allow us to overdo it as we felt the need to do. So we went out, continuing to fight in the street. When Pietro walked off, I don't know where—I was furious, I didn't want to see or hear him anymore—I went home. The children were sleeping. I found Adele sitting in the kitchen reading.

I said: "You see how he treats me?"

"And you?"

"I?"

"Yes, you: do you see how you treat him, how you've treated him?"

I turned away and shut myself in the bedroom, slamming the door. The contempt she had put into those words surprised me, wounded me. It was the first time she had turned against me so explicitly.

I left the next day for France, full of guilt because of the children's crying and the books I had to study on the trip. But as I concentrated on the reading, the pages became more and more mixed up with Nino, Pietro, my daughters, the defense of Pasquale made by his sister, Antonio's words, Alfonso's mutation. I arrived in Paris after an exhausting train trip, more confused than ever. Yet at the station, when I recognized the younger of the two women publishers on the platform, I became cheerful, I found again the pleasure of extending myself that I had had with Nino in Montpellier. This time there were no hotels and monumental lecture halls; everything was more modest. The two women took me around to big cities and small towns, every day a journey, every evening a debate in a bookstore or even in a private apartment. As for meals and sleep, there was home cooking, a cot, or, occasionally, a couch.

I was very tired, and paid less and less attention to my appearance; I lost weight. And yet my editors and the audiences I encountered night after night liked me. Moving here and there, discussing with this and that person in a language that wasn't mine but that I rapidly learned to manage, I gradually rediscovered an aptitude that I had displayed years before, with my previous book: I had a natural ability to transform small private events into public reflection. Every night I improvised successfully, starting from my own experience. I talked about the world I came from, about the poverty and squalor, male and also female rages, about Carmen and her bond with her brother, her justifications for violent actions that she would surely never commit. I talked about how, since I was a girl, I had observed in my mother and other women the most humiliating aspects of family life, of motherhood, of subjection to males. I talked about how, for love of a man, one could be driven to be guilty of every possible infamy toward other women, toward children. I talked about my difficult relationship with the feminist groups in Florence and Milan, and, as I did, an experience that I had underestimated suddenly became important: I discovered in public what I had learned by watching that painful effort of excavation. I talked about how, to assert myself, I had always sought to be male in intelligence— I started off every evening saying I felt that I had been invented by men, colonized by their imagination—and I told how I had recently seen a male childhood friend of mine make every effort possible to subvert himself, extracting from himself a female.

I drew often on that half hour spent in the Solaras' shop, but I only realized it later, maybe because Lila never came to my mind. I don't know why I didn't at any point allude to our friendship. Probably it seemed to me that, although she had dragged me into the swelling sea of her desires and those of our childhood friends, she didn't have the capacity to decipher what she had put before my eyes. Did she see, for example, what in a flash I had seen in Alfonso? Did she reflect on it? I ruled that out. She was mired in the *lota*, the filth, of the neighborhood, she was satisfied with it. I, on the other hand, in those French days, felt that I was at the center of chaos and yet had tools with which to distinguish its laws. That conviction, reinforced by the small success of my book, helped me to be somewhat less anxious about the future, as if, truly, everything that I was capable of adding up with words written and spoken were destined to add up in reality as well. Look, I said to myself, the couple collapses, the family collapses, every cultural cage collapses, every possible social-democratic accommodation collapses, and meanwhile everything tries violently to assume another form that up to now would have been unthinkable: Nino and me, the sum of my children and his, the hegemony of the working class, socialism and Communism, and above all the unforeseen subject, the woman, I. Night after night, I went around recognizing myself in an idea that suggested general disintegration and, at the same time, new composition.

Meanwhile, always somewhat breathlessly, I telephoned Adele and talked to the children, who answered in monosyllables, or asked, over and over, like a refrain: When are you coming home? Around Christmas, I tried to take leave of my publishers, but by now they had taken my fate to heart, and didn't want to let me go. They had read my first book, they wanted to republish it, and to this purpose they dragged me to the offices of the French publishing house that had printed it years earlier, unsuccessfully. I timidly got involved in discussions and negotiations, sustained by the two women, who, unlike me, were very combative, and knew how to cajole and threaten. Finally, in part thanks to the mediation of the Milan publisher, they came to an agreement: my text would be reissued the following year under the imprint of my new publishers.

I told Nino on the phone, and he seemed very excited. But then, sentence by sentence, his displeasure emerged.

"Maybe you don't need me anymore," he said.

"What are you talking about? I can't wait to hold you."

"You're so involved in your own affairs that there's not even a tiny spot left for me."

"You're wrong. It's thanks to you that I wrote this book, that I seem to have everything clear in my mind."

"Then let's see each other in Naples, or even in Rome, now, before Christmas."

But by this point a meeting was impossible, the editorial matters had taken up my time, I had to get back to the children. Yet I couldn't resist, and we decided to meet in Rome at least for a few hours. I traveled in a sleeping car, and arrived in the capital exhausted on the morning of December 23rd. I spent pointless hours in the station: Nino wasn't there. I was worried, I was desolate. I was about to take a train for Florence when he appeared, sweating despite the cold. He had had endless difficulties, and had come by car, by train he would never have made it. We ate something quickly, we found a hotel in Via Nazionale, close to the station, and shut ourselves in the room. I wanted to go in the afternoon, but I didn't have the strength to leave him, and I delayed my departure until the next day. We woke up happy to have slept together: ah, it was wonderful to stretch out a foot and discover, after the unconsciousness of sleep, that he was there in the bed, beside me. It was Christmas Eve, and we went out to get each other presents. My departure was postponed hour by hour and so was his. Not until the late afternoon did I drag myself with my suitcase to his car, I couldn't leave him. Finally he started the engine, drove off, disappeared in the traffic. Laboriously I trudged from Piazza della Repubblica to the station, but I had delayed too long, and I missed the train by a few minutes. I was desperate: I would arrive in Florence in the middle of the night. And yet it had happened that way. I resigned myself to telephoning home. Pietro answered.

"Where are you?"

"In Rome, the train is stuck here in the station and I don't know when it's leaving."

"Ah, these trains. Shall I tell the girls that you won't be here for Christmas Eve dinner?"

"Yes, I probably won't arrive in time."

He burst into laughter, he hung up.

I traveled in a totally empty, frigid train. Not even the conductor came by. I felt as if I had lost everything and was heading toward nothingness, prisoner of a bleakness that accentuated my guilt. I arrived in Florence in the middle of the night, and couldn't find a taxi. I carried my suitcase through the cold, on the deserted streets; even the Christmas bells had long since vanished into the night. I used my keys to enter. The apartment was dark and there was an anguished silence. I went through the rooms, no trace of the children, or of Adele. Tired, terrified, but also exasperated, I looked for at least a note that would tell me where they had gone. Nothing.

The house was in perfect order.

12.

I had ugly thoughts. Maybe Dede or Elsa or both had got sick and Pietro and his mother had taken them to the hospital.

Or my husband had ended up in the hospital, because he had done some mad thing, and Adele and the children were with him.

I wandered through the house consumed by anxiety, I didn't know what to do. At some point I thought that, whatever had happened, it was likely that my mother-in-law had told Mariarosa, and although it was three in the morning I decided to call her. My sister-in-law answered eventually; I had a hard time waking her. But finally I found out from her that Adele had decided to take the children to Genoa—they had left two days earlier—to allow me and Pietro to confront our situation freely, and Dede and Elsa to enjoy Christmas vacation in peace.

On the one hand, the news calmed me, on the other it made me furious. Pietro had lied to me: when I telephoned he already knew there would be no Christmas Eve dinner, that the children weren't expecting me, that they had left with their grandmother. And Adele? How dare she take away my daughters! I vented on the telephone while Mariarosa listened to me in silence. I asked: Am I wrong about everything, do I deserve what is happening to me? She took a serious tone, but she was encouraging. She said that I had the right to have my life and the duty to continue to study and write. Then she offered to let me stay with her, along with the children, any time I found myself in trouble.

Her words soothed me, yet I couldn't sleep. I turned things over and over in my breast: anguish, rage, desire for Nino, unhappiness because he would spend the holiday with his family, with Albertino, and I was reduced to a woman alone, without affection, in an empty house. At nine in the morning I heard the door open, it was Pietro. I confronted him immediately, I yelled at him: Why did you hand over the children to your mother without my permission? He was disheveled, unshaven, he stank of wine, but he didn't seem drunk. He let me scream without reacting, he merely repeated over and over, in a depressed tone: I have work to do, I can't take care of them, and you have your lover, you don't have time for them.

I forced him to sit down, in the kitchen. I tried to calm myself, I said:

"We have to come to an agreement."

"Explain yourself, what type of agreement."

"The children will live with me, and you'll see them on the weekend."

"On the weekend where?"

"At my house."

"And where is your house?"

"I don't know, I'll decide later: here, in Milan, in Naples."

That word was enough: Naples. As soon as he heard it he jumped to his feet, opened his eyes wide, opened his mouth as if to bite me, raised his fist with such a ferocious expression that I was terrified. It was an endless moment. The faucet was dripping, the refrigerator humming, someone laughed in the courtyard. Pietro was large, he had big white knuckles. He had already hit me once, I knew that he would hit me now so violently that he would kill me, and I raised my arms abruptly to protect myself. But suddenly he changed his mind, turned, and once, twice, three times punched the metal closet where I kept the brooms. He would have continued if I hadn't clung to his arm crying: Stop it, enough, you'll hurt yourself.

The result of that rage was that what I had feared on my return really happened: we ended up in the hospital. His arm was put in a cast, and on the way home he seemed almost cheerful. I remembered that it was Christmas and I made something to eat. We sat down at the table, and he said, point-blank:

"Yesterday I called your mother."

I jumped.

"How did that occur to you?"

"Well, someone had to tell her. I told her what you did to me."

"It was my job to talk to her."

"Why? To lie to her the way you lied to me?"

I became agitated again, but I tried to contain myself; I was afraid that he would start breaking his bones again to avoid breaking mine. Instead I saw that he smiled calmly, looking at his arm in the cast.

"So I can't drive," he muttered.

"Where do you have to go?"

"To the station."

I discovered that my mother had set out by train on Christmas Day—the day she normally assumed domestic centrality, the highest of her responsibilities—and was about to arrive.

13.

I was tempted to flee. I thought of going to Naples—escaping to my mother's city just as she was arriving in mine—and seeking some tranquility with Nino. But I didn't move. Although I felt that I was changed, I had remained the disciplined person who had never avoided anything. And besides, I said to myself, what can she do to me? I'm a woman, not a child. At most she'll bring something good to eat, like that Christmas ten years ago, when I was sick and she came to see me in the dormitory at the Normale.

I went with Pietro to get my mother at the station; I drove. She got off the train proudly, she had new clothes, a new purse, new shoes, even a little powder on her cheeks. You look well, I said, you're very stylish. She hissed: No thanks to you, and didn't say another word to me. To make up for it she was very affectionate toward Pietro. She asked about his cast, and since he was vague—he said he had bumped into a door—she began to mumble in hesitant Italian: Bumped, I know who made you bump it. I imagine, bumped.

Once we got home she ended her feigned composure. She made me a long speech, limping back and forth in the living room. She praised my husband in an exaggerated fashion, she ordered me to ask his forgiveness immediately. When I didn't, she began to beg him herself to forgive me and swore on Peppe, Gianni, and Elisa that she would not go home if the two of us did not make peace. At first, with all her hyperbole, she seemed to be making fun of both me and my husband. The list she made of Pietro's virtues appeared infinite, and—I have to admit—she didn't stint on mine, either. She emphasized endlessly that, when it came to intelligence and scholarship, we were made for each other. She urged us to think of Dede's good—Dede was her favorite granddaughter, she forgot to mention Elsa—the child understood everything and it wasn't right to make her suffer.

My husband, while she spoke, appeared to agree, even though he wore the incredulous expression he assumed in the face of any spectacle of excess. She hugged him, kissed him, thanked him for his generosity, before which—she shouted at me—I should go down on my knees. She kept pushing us with rude claps toward each other, so that we would hug and kiss each other. I drew back, I was aloof. The whole time I thought: I can't bear her, I can't bear that at a moment like this, in front of Pietro, I *also* have to account for the fact that I am the daughter of this woman. And meanwhile I tried to calm myself by saying: It's her usual scene, soon she'll get tired and go to bed. But when she grabbed me for the hundredth time, insisting I admit that I had made a serious mistake, I couldn't take it anymore, her hands offended me and I pulled away. I said something like: Enough, Ma, it's pointless, I can't stay with Pietro anymore, I love someone else.

It was a mistake. I knew her, she was just waiting for a small provocation. Her litany broke off, things changed in a flash. She slapped me violently, shouting nonstop: Shut up, you whore, shut up, shut up. And she tried to grab me by the hair, she cried that she couldn't stand it any longer, that it wasn't possible that I, *I*, should want to ruin my life, running after Sarratore's son, who was worse, much worse, than that man of shit who was his father. Once, she cried, I thought it was your friend Lina leading you on this evil course, but I was wrong, you, *you*, are the shameless one; without you, she's become a fine person. Damn me that I didn't break your legs when you were a child. You have a husband of gold who makes you a lady in this beautiful city, who loves you, who has given you two daughters, and you repay him like this, bitch? Come here, I gave birth to you and I'll kill you.

She was on me, I felt as if she really wanted to kill me. In those moments I felt all the truth of the disappointment that I was causing her, all the truth of the maternal love that despaired of subjecting me to what she considered my good—that is, what she had never had and what I instead had and what until the day before had made her the most fortunate mother in the neighborhood—and was ready to turn into hatred and destroy me to punish me for my waste of God's gifts. So I pushed her away, I pushed her shouting louder than she was. I pushed her involuntarily, instinctively, with such force that I made her lose her balance and she fell to the floor.

Pietro was frightened. I saw it in his face, in his eyes: my world colliding with his. Certainly in all his life he had never witnessed a scene like that, words so aggressive, reactions so frenzied. My mother had overturned a chair, she had fallen heavily. Now she had trouble getting up, because of her bad leg, she was waving one arm in an effort to grab the edge of the table and pull herself up. But she didn't stop, she went on screaming threats and insults at me. She didn't stop even when Pietro, shocked, helped her up with his good arm. Her voice choked, angry and at the same time truly grieved, eyes staring, she gasped: You're not my child anymore, he's my child, him, not even your father wants you anymore, not even your siblings; Sarratore's son is bound to stick you with the clap and syphilis, what did I do wrong to come to a day like this, oh God, oh God, God, I want to die this minute, I want to die now. She was so overwhelmed by her suffering that—incredibly—she burst into tears.

I ran away and locked myself in the bedroom. I didn't know what to do; never would I have expected that a separation would involve such torture. I was frightened, I was devastated. From what obscure depth, what presumption, had come the determination to push back my mother with her own physical violence? I became calmer only when, after a while, Pietro knocked and said softly, with an unexpected gentleness: Don't open the door, I'm not asking you to let me in; I just want to say that I didn't want this, it's too much, not even you deserve it.

14.

I hoped that my mother would soften, that in the morning, with one of her abrupt swerves, she would find a way of affirming that she loved me and in spite of everything was proud of me. But she didn't. I heard her talking to Pietro all night. She flattered him, she repeated bitterly that I had always been her cross, she said, sighing, that one had to have patience with me. The next day, to avoid quarreling again, I wandered through the house or tried to read, without ever joining their councils. I was very unhappy. I was ashamed of the shove I had given her, I was ashamed of her and of myself, I wanted to apologize, embrace her, but I was afraid that she would misunderstand and be convinced that I had given in. If she had gone so far as to assert that I was the black soul of Lila, and not Lila mine, I must have been a truly intolerable disappointment to her. I said to myself, to excuse her: her unit of measure is the neighborhood; there everything, in her eyes, is arranged for the best; she feels related to the Solaras thanks to Elisa; her sons finally work for Marcello, whom she proudly calls her son-in-law; in those new clothes she wears the sign of the prosperity that has rained down on her; it's natural therefore that Lila, working for Michele Solara, in a stable home with Enzo, so rich she wants to bequeath her parents the small apartment they live in, appears to her much more successful than me. But arguments like that served only to further mark the distance between her and me; we no longer had any point of contact.

She departed without our having spoken a word to each other. Pietro and I took her to the station in the car, but she acted as if I were not driving. She confined herself to wishing Pietro all the best and urging him, until a moment before the train left, to keep her informed about his broken arm and about the children.

As soon as she left I realized with some surprise that her irruption had had an unhoped-for effect. My husband, as we were returning home, went beyond the few phrases of solidarity whispered outside my door the night before. That intemperate encounter with my mother must have revealed to him about me, about how I had grown up, more than what I had told him and he had imagined. He felt sorry for me, I think. He returned abruptly to himself, our relations became polite, a few days later we went to a lawyer, who talked for a moment about this and that, then asked:

"You're sure you don't want to live together anymore?"

"How can one live with a person who no longer loves you?" Pietro answered.

"You, Signora, you no longer want your husband?"

"It's my business," I said. "All you have to do is settle the practical details of the separation."

When we were back on the street Pietro laughed: "You're just like your mother."

"It's not true."

"You're right, it's not true: you're like your mother if she had had an education and had started writing novels."

"What do you mean?"

"I mean you're worse."

I was angry but not very. I was glad that within the limits of the possible he had come to his senses. I drew a sigh of relief and began to focus on what to do. In the course of long phone calls to Nino, I told him everything that had happened since the moment we parted, and we discussed my moving to Naples; out of prudence I didn't tell him that Pietro and I had begun to sleep under the same roof, even if in separate rooms, naturally. Most important, I talked to my daughters often and I told Adele, with explicit hostility, that I would come to get them.

"Don't worry," my mother-in-law tried to reassure me, "you can leave them as long as you need to."

"Dede has school."

"We can send her here, nearby, I would take care of everything."

"No, I need them with me."

"Think about it. A woman separated, with two children and your ambitions, has to take account of reality and decide what she can give up and what she can't."

Everything, in that last sentence, bothered me.

15.

I wanted to leave immediately for Genoa, but I got a phone call from France. The older of my two publishers asked me to put into writing, for an important journal, the arguments she had heard me make in public. So right away I found myself in a situation in which I had to choose between going to get my daughters and starting work. I put off my departure, I worked day and night with the anxiety of doing well. I was still trying to give my text an acceptable form when Nino announced to me that, before returning to the university, he had some free days and was eager to see me. I couldn't resist; we drove to Argentario. I was dazed by love. We spent marvelous days devoted to the winter sea and, as had never happened with either Franco or, even less, Pietro, to the pleasure of eating and drinking, conversation, sex. Every morning at dawn I dragged myself out of bed and began writing.

One evening, in bed, Nino gave me some pages he had written, saying that he would value my opinion. It was a complicated essay, on Italsider in Bagnoli. I read it lying close beside him, while now and then he murmured, self-critical: I write badly, correct it if you want, you're better, you were better in high school. I praised his work highly, and suggested some corrections. But he wasn't satisfied, he urged me to intervene further. Then, finally, as if to convince me of the need for my corrections, he said that he had a terrible thing to reveal to me. Half embarrassed, half ironic, he described this secret: "the most shameful thing I've done in my life." And he said that it had to do with the article I had written in high school about my fight with the religion teacher, the one that he had commissioned for a student magazine.

"What did you do?" I asked, laughing.

"I'll tell you, but remember I was just a boy."

I felt that he was seriously ashamed and I became slightly worried. He said that when he read my article he couldn't believe that someone could write in such a pleasing and intelligent way. I was content with that compliment, I kissed him, I remembered how I had labored over those pages with Lila, and meanwhile I described to him in a self-ironic way the disappointment, the pain I had felt when the magazine hadn't had space to publish it.

"I told you that?" Nino asked, uneasily.

"Maybe, I don't remember now."

He had an expression of dismay.

"The truth is that there was plenty of space."

"Then why didn't they publish it?"

"Out of envy."

I burst out laughing.

"The editors were envious of me?"

"No, it was *I* who felt envy. I read your pages and threw them in the wastebasket. I couldn't bear that you were so good."

For a few moments I said nothing. How important that article had been to me, how much I had suffered. I couldn't believe it: was it possible that Professor Galiani's favorite had been so envious of the lines of a middle-school student that he threw them away? I felt that Nino was waiting for my reaction, but I didn't know how to place such a petty act within the radiant aura I had given him as a girl. The seconds passed and I tried, disoriented, to keep it close to me, so that it could not reinforce the bad reputation that, according to Adele, Nino had in Milan, or the invitation not to trust him that had come to me from Lila and Antonio. Then I shook myself, the positive side of that confession leaped to my eyes, and I embraced him. There was, in essence, no need for him to tell me that episode, it was a bad deed that was very distant in time. And yet he had just told me, and that need of his to be sincere, greater than any personal gain, even at the risk of putting himself in a terrible light, moved me. Suddenly, starting from that moment, I felt that I could always believe him.

We loved each other that night with more passion than usual. Upon waking I realized that, in confessing his sin, Nino had confessed that in his eyes I had always been a girl out of the ordinary, even when he was Nadia Galiani's boyfriend, even when he had become Lila's lover. Ah, how exciting it was to feel that I was not only loved but esteemed. He entrusted his text to me, I helped him give it a more brilliant form. In those days in Argentario I had the impression that I had now definitively expanded my capacity to feel, to understand, to express myself, something that—I thought with pride—was confirmed by the modest welcome that the book I had written goaded by him, to please him, had received outside Italy. I had everything, at that moment. Only Dede and Elsa were left in the margins.

16.

I said nothing to my mother-in-law about Nino. I told her instead about the French journal and portrayed myself as being fully absorbed by what I was writing. Meanwhile, if reluctantly, I thanked her for taking care of her grandchildren.

Although I didn't trust her, I understood at that point that Adele had raised a real problem. What could I do to keep my life and my children together? Certainly I intended to go and live with Nino soon, somewhere, and in that case we would help each other. But meanwhile? It wouldn't be easy to balance the need to see each other, Dede, Elsa, the writing, the public engagements, the pressures that Pietro, although he had become more reasonable, would nevertheless subject me to. Not to mention the problem of money. Very little remained of my own, and I still didn't know how much the new book would earn. It was out of the question that at the moment I could pay rent, telephone, daily life for my daughters and me. And then where would our daily life take shape? Any moment now, I would go and get the children, but to take them where? To Florence, to the apartment where they were born and in which, finding a gentle father, a courteous mother, they would be convinced that everything had miraculously gone back to normal? Did I want to delude them, knowing that as soon as Nino burst in I would disappoint them even more? Should I tell Pietro to leave, even though I was the one who had broken with him? Or was it up to me to leave the apartment?

I went to Genoa with a thousand questions and no decision.

My in-laws received me with polite coldness, Elsa with uncertain enthusiasm, Dede with hostility. I didn't know the house in Genoa well, only an impression of light remained in my mind. In reality there were entire rooms full of books, old furniture, crystal chandeliers, floors covered with precious carpets, heavy curtains. Only the living room was bright: it had a big window that framed a section of light and sea, displaying it like a prized object. My daughters—I realized—moved through the entire apartment with more freedom than in their own house: they touched everything, they took what they wanted with never a reproach, and they spoke to the maid in the courteous but commanding tones they had learned from their grandmother. In the first hours after I arrived they showed me their room, they wanted me to get excited about the many expensive toys that they would never have received from me and their father, they told me about the many wonderful things they had done and seen. I slowly realized that Dede had become very attached to her grandfather, while Elsa, although she had hugged and kissed me as much as she could, turned to Adele for anything she needed or, when she was tired, climbed up on her lap and looked at me from there with a melancholy gaze, her thumb in her mouth. Had the children learned to do without me in so short a time? Or, rather, were they exhausted by what they had seen and heard in the past months and now, apprehensive of the swarm of disasters I conjured up, were afraid to take me back? I don't know. Certainly I didn't dare to say immediately: Pack your things and let's go. I stayed a few days, I began to care for them again. And my in-laws never interfered; rather, at the first recourse to their authority against mine, especially by Dede, they withdrew, avoiding any conflict.

Guido in particular was very careful to speak about other

things; at first he didn't even allude to the break between me
and his son. After dinner, when Dede and Elsa went to bed and
he, politely, stayed with me for a while before shutting himself
in his study to work late into the night (evidently Pietro did little more than apply his father's model), he was embarrassed.
He usually took refuge in political talk: the deepening crisis of
capitalism, the cure-all of austerity, the broadening area of mar-
ginalization, the earthquake in Friuli as the symbol of a precarious Italy, the great difficulties of the left, old parties and factions. But he did it without displaying any interest in my
opinions, and I, in turn, made no effort to have any. If he actually decided to encourage me to say something, he fell back on
my book, whose Italian edition I saw for the first time in that
house: it was a slender volume, not very conspicuous, which
arrived along with the many books and magazines that piled up
continuously on the tables, waiting to be perused. One evening
he asked some questions, and I—knowing that he hadn't read
it and wouldn't—summarized for him the arguments, read him
a few lines. In general he listened seriously, attentive. In one
case only did he offer some learned criticisms on a passage of
Sophocles that I had cited inappropriately, and he assumed
professorial tones that shamed me. He was a man who
emanated authority, even though authority is a patina and at
times it doesn't take much to crack it, if only for a few minutes,
and glimpse a less edifying person. At a mention of feminism
Guido's composure suddenly shattered, an unexpected malice
appeared in his eyes, and he began to hum sarcastically, red in
the face—he who in general had an anemic complexion—a
couple of slogans he had heard: *Sex, sex behind the wall, who
has orgasms of us all? No one*; and also: *We're not machines for
reproduction but women fighting for liberation*. He sang in a low
voice and laughed, all excited. When he realized that he had
unpleasantly surprised me, he grabbed his glasses, cleaned
them carefully, withdrew to his study.

On those few evenings Adele was almost always silent, but I soon realized that both she and her husband were looking for a way to draw me out into the open. Since I wouldn't bite, my father-in-law finally confronted the problem in his own way. When Dede and Elsa said good night, he asked his grand-daughters in a sort of good-humored ritual:

"What is the name of these two lovely young ladies?"

"Dede."

"Elsa."

"And then? Grandfather wants to hear the whole name."

"Dede Airota."

"Elsa Airota."

"Airota like who?"

"Like Papa."

"And also?"

"Like Grandpa."

"And what's Mamma's name?"

"Elena Greco."

"And is your name Greco or Airota?"

"Airota."

"Bravo. Good night, dear ones, sweet dreams."

Then, as soon as the children left the room, accompanied by Adele, he said as if following a thread that started from the answers of the two children: I've learned that the break with Pietro is due to Nino Sarratore. I jumped, I nodded yes. He smiled, he began to praise Nino, but not with the absolute support of years earlier. He said that he was very intelligent, someone who knew what was what, but—he said, emphasizing the adversative conjunction—he is *fickle*, and he repeated the word as if to make sure that he had chosen the right one. Then he emphasized: I didn't like Sarratore's most recent writings. And in a suddenly contemptuous tone he relegated him to the heap of those who considered it more urgent to make the gears of neocapitalism function rather than to continue to demand transformations in social relations and in production. He used that language, but giving every word the substance of an insult.

I couldn't bear it. I struggled to convince him that he was wrong. Adele returned just as I was citing the essays of Nino's that seemed to me most radical, and Guido listened to me, emitting the dull sound he usually resorted to when he was suspended between agreement and disagreement. I suddenly stopped, rather agitated. For a few minutes my father-in-law seemed to soften his judgment (*After all, it's difficult for all of us to orient ourselves in the chaos of the Italian crisis, and I can understand that young men like him find themselves in trouble, especially when they have a desire to act*), then he rose to go to his study. But before he disappeared he had a second thought. He paused in the doorway and uttered harshly: *But there is doing and doing, Sarratore is intelligence without traditions, he would rather be liked by those in charge than fight for an idea, he'll become a very useful technocrat.* And he broke off, but still he hesitated, as if he had something much crueler on the tip of his tongue. He confined himself instead to muttering good night and went into his study.

I felt Adele's gaze on me. I ought to retreat, I thought, I have to make up an excuse, say I'm tired. But I hoped that Adele would find a conciliating phrase that might soothe me, and so I asked:

"What does it mean that Nino is intelligence without traditions?"

She looked at me ironically.

"That he's no one. And for a person who is no one to become someone is more important than anything else. The result is that this Signor Sarratore is an unreliable person."

"I, too, am an intelligence without traditions."

She smiled.

"Yes, you are, too, and in fact you are unreliable."

Silence. Adele had spoken serenely, as if the words had no

emotional charge but were limited to recording the facts. Still, I felt offended.

"What do you mean?"

"That I trusted a son to you and you didn't treat him honestly. If you wanted someone else, why did you marry him?"

"I didn't know I wanted someone else."

"You're lying."

I hesitated, I admitted: "I'm lying, yes, but why do you force me to give you a linear explanation; linear explanations are almost always lies. You also spoke badly of Pietro, in fact you supported me against him. Were you lying?"

"No. I was really on your side, but within a pact that you should have respected."

"What pact?"

"Remaining with your husband and children. You were an Airota, your daughters were Airotas. I didn't want you to feel unsatisfied and unhappy, I tried to help you be a good mother and a good wife. But if the pact is broken everything changes. From me and from my husband you'll have nothing anymore, in fact I'll take away everything I've given you."

I took a deep breath, I tried to keep my voice calm, just as she continued to do.

"Adele," I said, "I am Elena Greco and my daughters are my daughters. I don't give a damn about you Airotas."

She nodded, pale, and her expression was now severe.

"It's obvious that you are Elena Greco, it's now far too obvious. But the children are my son's daughters and we will not allow you to ruin them."

17.

That was the first clash with my in-laws. Others followed, though they never reached such explicit contempt. Later my in-laws confined themselves to demonstrating in every possible way that, if I insisted on being concerned with myself above all, I had to entrust Dede and Elsa to them.

I resisted, naturally: there was not a day that I didn't get angry and decide to take my children away with me immediately, to Florence, to Milan, to Naples—anywhere, just so as not to leave them in that house a moment longer. But soon I would give in, put off my departure; something always happened that bore witness against me. Nino, for example, telephoned and, unable to refuse, I rushed to meet him wherever he wanted. And then in Italy, too, the new book had begun to make a small wave, and, although it was ignored by the reviewers of the big papers, it was nevertheless finding an audience. So often I added encounters with readers to the meetings with my lover, which extended the time that I was away from the children.

I separated from them unwillingly. I felt their accusing gaze on me, and I suffered. And yet already in the train, as I studied, as I prepared for some public discussion, as I imagined my meeting with Nino, an impudent joy began to bubble up inside me. I soon discovered that I was getting used to being happy and unhappy at the same time, as if that were the new, inevitable law of my life. When I returned to Genoa I felt guilty—Dede and Elsa were now comfortable, they had school, friends, everything they wanted, independently of me—but as soon as I left the guilt became a tedious obstacle; it weakened. I realized this, naturally, and the alternation made me wretched. It was humiliating to have to admit that a little fame, and love for Nino, could obscure Dede and Elsa. And yet it was so. The echo of Lila's phrase, *Think of the harm you're doing to your daughters,* became in that period a sort of permanent epigraph that introduced unhappiness. I traveled, I was often in a new bed, often I couldn't sleep. My mother's curses returned to mind, and were mixed up with Lila's words.

She and my friend, although they had always been, for me, the opposite of one another, in those nights often came together. Both were hostile, estranged from my new life: on the one hand this seemed the proof that I had finally become an autonomous person; on the other it made me feel alone, at the mercy of my troubles.

I tried to repair relations with my sister-in-law. As usual she showed herself to be very willing, and organized an event in honor of my book at a bookstore in Milan. Most of those who came were women, and I was now much criticized, now much praised by opposing groups. At first I was frightened, but Mariarosa interceded with authority and I discovered in myself an unsuspected capacity to summarize disagreement and agreement, choosing in the meantime a role as mediator. I was good at saying in a convincing way: *That isn't exactly what I meant.* In the end I was celebrated by everyone, especially by her.

Afterward I had dinner and stayed at her house. I found Franco there, I found Silvia with her son Mirko. The whole time, all I did was observe the child—I calculated that he must be eight—and register the physical resemblances to Nino, and even resemblances in personality. I had never told him that I knew about that child and had decided that I never would, but all evening I talked to him, cuddled him, played with him, held him on my lap. In what disorder we lived, how many fragments of ourselves were scattered, as if to live were to explode into splinters. In Milan, there was this child, in Genoa my daughters, in Naples Albertino. I couldn't restrain myself, I began talking about that dispersion with Silvia, with Mariarosa, with Franco, assuming the attitude of a disillusioned thinker. In reality I expected that my former boyfriend would, as usual, take over the conversation and arrange everything according to a skillful dialectic that settled the present and anticipated the future, reassuring us. But he was the true surprise of the evening. He spoke of the imminent end of a period that had been *objectively*—he used the adverb sarcastically—revolutionary but that now, he said, was declining, was sweeping away all the categories that had served as a compass.

"I don't think so," I objected, but only to provoke him. "In Italy things are very lively and combative."

"You don't think so because you're pleased with yourself."

"Not at all, I'm depressed."

"The depressed don't write books. People who are happy write, people who travel, are in love, and talk and talk with the conviction that, one way or another, their words always go to the right place."

"Isn't that how it is?"

"No, words rarely go to the right place, and if they do, it's only for a very brief time. Otherwise they're useful for speaking nonsense, as now. Or for pretending that everything is under control."

"Pretending? You who have always kept everything under control, you were pretending?"

"Why not? It's unavoidable to pretend a little. We who wanted to enact the revolution were the ones who, even in the midst of chaos, were always inventing an order and pretending to know exactly how things were going."

"You're accusing yourself?"

"Yes. Good grammar, good syntax. An explanation ready for everything. And such great skill in logic: this derives from that and leads necessarily to that. The game is over."

"It doesn't work anymore?"

"Oh, it works very well. It's so comfortable never to be confused by anything. No infected bedsores, no wound without its stitches, no dark room that frightens you. Only that at a certain point the trick no longer functions."

"Meaning what?"

"Blah blah blah, Lena, blah blah blah. The meaning is leaving the words."

And he didn't stop there. He mocked what he had just said, making fun of himself and of me. Then he said: What a lot of nonsense I'm talking, and he spent the rest of the evening listening to the three of us.

It struck me that if in Silvia the terrible marks of violence had completely disappeared, in him the beating suffered several years earlier had gradually exposed another body and another spirit. He got up often to go to the bathroom; he limped, though not conspicuously; the purple socket, in which the false eye was clumsily set, seemed more combative than the other eye, which, although it was alive, seemed opaque with depression. Above all, both the pleasantly energetic Franco of long ago and the shadowy Franco of convalescence had disappeared. He seemed gently melancholy, capable of an affectionate cynicism. While Silvia said that I should take my daughters back, and Mariarosa said that, as long as I hadn't found a stable arrangement, Dede and Elsa were fine with their grandparents, Franco exaggerated his praise of my capacities, ironically defined as male, and insisted that I should continue to refine them without getting lost in female obligations.

When I went to my room I had trouble falling asleep. What was bad for my children, what was their good? And bad for me, and my good, what did those consist of, and did they correspond to or diverge from what was bad and good for the children? That night Nino faded into the background, Lila reemerged. Lila alone, without the support of my mother. I felt the need to argue with her, shout at her: Don't just criticize me, take responsibility, tell me what to do. Finally I slept. The next day I returned to Genoa and said point-blank to Dede and Elsa, in the presence of my in-laws:

"Girls, I have a lot of work at the moment. In a few days I have to leave again and then again and again. Do you want to come with me or stay with your grandparents?"

Even today as I write that question I'm ashamed.

First Dede and then, right afterward, Elsa answered:
"With Grandma and Grandpa. But come back whenever
you can and bring us presents."

18.

It took me more than two years, filled with joys, torments,
nasty surprises, and agonizing mediations, to put some order
into my life. Meanwhile, although I was privately suffering,
publicly I continued to be successful. The scant hundred pages
I had written to make a good impression on Nino were translated into German and English. My book of ten years earlier
reappeared in both France and Italy, and I began writing again
for newspapers and journals. My name and my physical person
gradually reacquired their modest fame, the days became
crowded, as they had been in the past, I gained the interest, and
at times the respect, of people who at the time were well known
on the public stage. But what helped my self-confidence was
some gossip from the director of the Milan publishing house,
who had liked me from the start. One evening when I was
having dinner with him to talk about my publishing future,
but also—I have to say—to propose a collection of Nino's
essays, he revealed that, the preceding Christmas, Adele had
pressured him to block the publication of my book.

He said, jokingly, "The Airotas are used to plotting the rise
of an undersecretary at breakfast and deposing a minister at
dinner, but with your book they didn't succeed. The volume
was ready and we sent it to the printer."

According to him, my mother-in-law was also behind the
meager number of reviews in the Italian press. As a result, if
the book had nevertheless made a name for itself, certainly the
credit should go not to kind second thoughts from Dottoressa
Airota but to the force of my writing. Thus I learned that this

time I owed nothing to Adele, although she continued to tell me I did whenever I went to Genoa. That gave me confidence, made me proud, I was finally convinced that the period of my dependence was over.

Lila didn't notice at all. She, from the depths of the neighborhood, from that area that now seemed to me infinitesimal, continued to consider me an appendage of hers. From Pietro she got the telephone number in Genoa, and she began to use it without worrying about annoying my in-laws. When she managed to reach me she pretended not to notice my terseness and talked for both of us, without pause. She talked about Enzo, about work, about her son, who was doing well in school, about Carmen, about Antonio. When I wasn't there, she persisted in telephoning, with neurotic perseverance, enabling Adele—who wrote in a notebook the calls that came for me, putting down, I don't know, such and such month, such and such day, Sarratore (three calls), Cerullo (nine calls)—to complain about the nuisance I caused. I tried to convince Lila that if they said I wasn't there it was pointless to insist, that the house in Genoa wasn't my house, and that she was embarrassing me. Useless. She went so far as to call Nino. It's hard to say how things really went: he was embarrassed, he made light of it, he was afraid of saying something that would irritate me. Early on he told me that Lila had telephoned Eleonora's house repeatedly, angering her, then I gathered that she had tried to get him on the phone at Via Duomo directly, finally that he himself had hastened to track her down to prevent her from constantly telephoning his wife. Whatever had happened, the fact was that Lila had forced him to meet her. Not alone, however: Nino was immediately eager to explain that she had come with Carmen, since it was Carmen—mainly Carmen—who urgently needed to get in touch with me.

I listened to the account of the meeting without emotion. First, Lila had wanted to know in detail how I behaved in public when I talked about my books: what dress I wore, how I did my hair and my makeup, if I was shy, if I was entertaining, if I read, if I improvised. Otherwise she was silent, she had left the field to Carmen. So it turned out that all that eagerness to talk to me had to do with Pasquale. Through her own channels, Carmen had found out that Nadia Galiani had fled to safety abroad, and so she wanted to ask a favor again, that I get in touch with my high-school teacher to ask her if Pasquale, too, was safe. Carmen had exclaimed a couple of times: I don't want the children of the rich people to get out and not the ones like my brother. Then she had urged him to let me know—as if she herself considered her worry about Pasquale to be an indictable crime that could involve me, too—that if I wanted to help her I shouldn't use the telephone either to get in touch with the professor or to get in touch with her. Nino concluded: Both Carmen and Lina are imprudent, better to let it go, they can get you in trouble.

I thought that, a few months earlier, an encounter between Nino and Lila, even in the presence of Carmen, would have alarmed me. Now I was discovering instead that it left me indifferent. Evidently I was now so sure of Nino's love that, although I couldn't rule out that she wanted to take him away from me, it seemed impossible that she could succeed. I caressed his cheek, I said, amused, Don't *you* get into trouble, please: How is it that you never have a free moment and now you found the time for this?

19.

I noted for the first time, during that period, the rigidity of the perimeter that Lila had established for herself. She was less and less interested in what happened outside the neighborhood. If she became excited by something whose dimensions were not merely local, it was because it concerned people she had known since childhood. Even her work, as far as I knew, interested her only within a very narrow radius. Enzo occasionally had to spend time in Milan, or Turin. Not Lila, she had never moved, and I only began to notice that closing off of herself seriously when my own taste for travel intensified.

I took every possible opportunity to travel outside of Italy, at the time, especially if it was possible to do so with Nino. For example, when the small German publisher who had brought out my little book organized a promotional tour in West Germany and Austria, Nino canceled all his engagements and acted as my cheerful and obedient driver. We travelled all over for some two weeks, gliding from one landscape to the next as if beside paintings with dazzling colors. Every mountain or lake or city or monument entered our life as a couple only to become part of the pleasure of being there, at that moment, and it always seemed like a refined contribution to our happiness. Even when rude reality intervened and frightened us because it corresponded to the darkest words that I uttered night after night in front of radical audiences, we recounted the fear to each other afterward as if it had been a pleasant adventure.

One night when we were driving back to the hotel, the police stopped us. The German language, in the dark, in the mouths of men in uniform, guns in hand, sounded, both to my ear and to Nino's, sinister. The police pulled us out of the car, and separated us; I ended up, yelling, in one car, Nino in another. We were reunited in a small room, left to ourselves, then brutally questioned: documents, reason for our stay, job. On one wall there was a long row of photos: grim faces, mostly bearded, some women with short hair. I surprised myself by looking anxiously for the faces of Pasquale and Nadia; I didn't find them. We were released at dawn, returned to the place where we had been forced to leave our car. No one apologized:

we had an Italian license plate, we were Italians, the check was obligatory.

I was surprised by my instinct to seek in Germany, among the mug shots of criminals all over the world, that of the very person who was then close to Lila's heart. Pasquale Peluso, that night, seemed to me a sort of rocket launched from the narrow space in which Lila had enclosed herself to remind me, in my much broader space, of her presence in the whirlwind of planetary events. For a few seconds Carmen's brother became the point of contact between her diminishing world and my expanding world.

On the evenings when I talked about my book in foreign cities I knew nothing about, there was a host of questions on the harshness of the political climate, and I got by with generic phrases that in essence rotated around the word "repress." As a fiction writer, I felt obliged to be imaginative. No space is spared, I said. A steamroller is moving from land to land, from West to East, to put the whole planet in order: the workers to work, the unemployed to waste away, the starving to perish, the intellectuals to speak nonsense, blacks to be black, women to be women. But at times I felt the need to say something truer, genuine, my own, and I told the story of Pasquale in all its tragic stages, from childhood to the choice of a clandestine life. I didn't know how to make more concrete speeches, the vocabulary was what I had appropriated ten years earlier, and I felt that the words had meaning only when I connected them to certain facts of the neighborhood, for it was only old, worn-out material, of certain effect. What's more, if at the time of my first book I had sooner or later ended by appealing to revolution, as that seemed to be the general feeling, now I avoided the word: Nino had begun to find it naïve; from him I was learning the complexity of politics and I was more cautious. I resorted, rather, to the formula *to rebel is just*, and immediately afterward added that it was necessary to broaden the consensus, that the state would last longer than we had imagined, that it was urgent to learn to govern. I wasn't always satisfied with myself on those evenings. In some cases it seemed to me that I lowered my tone only to make Nino happy, as he sat listening to me in smoky rooms, among beautiful foreigners who were my age or younger. Often I couldn't resist and I overdid it, indulging the old obscure impulse that in the past had pushed me to argue with Pietro. It happened mainly when I had an audience of women who had read my book and expected cutting remarks. We must be careful not to become policemen of ourselves, I said then, the struggle is to the last drop of blood and will end only when we win. Nino teased me afterward, he said that I always had to exaggerate, and we laughed together.

Some nights I curled up next to him and tried to explain myself to myself. I confessed that I liked subversive words, words that denounced the compromises of the parties and the violence of the state. Politics—I said—politics the way you think about it, *as it certainly is*, bores me, I leave it to you, I'm not made for that sort of engagement. But then I had second thoughts and added that I didn't feel cut out, either, for the other sort of engagement that I had forced myself into in the past, dragging the children along with me. The threatening shouts of the demonstrators frightened me, as did the aggressive fringes, the armed gangs, the dead on the streets, the revolutionary hatred of everything. I have to speak in public, I confessed, and I don't know what I am, I don't know to what point I seriously believe what I say.

Now, with Nino, I seemed able to put into words the most secret feelings, even things I didn't say to myself, even the incongruities, the acts of cowardice. He was so sure of himself, solid, he had detailed opinions about everything. I felt as if I had pasted onto the chaotic rebellion of childhood neat cards bearing phrases suited to making a good impression. At a conference in Bologna—we were part of a determined exodus headed to the city of freedom—we ran into constant police checks, and were stopped at least five times. Weapons leveled against us, out of the car, documents, there against the wall. I was frightened, at the time, even more than in Germany: it was my land, it was my language, I became anxious, I wanted to be silent, to obey, and instead I began to shout, I slipped into dialect without realizing it, I unloaded insults at the police for pushing me rudely. Fear and rage were mixed up, and often I couldn't control either one. Nino instead remained calm, he joked with the policemen, humored them, calmed me. For him only the two of us counted. Remember that we're here, now, together, he said, the rest is background and will change.

20.

We were always moving, in those years. We wanted to be present, observe, study, understand, argue, bear witness, and most of all love each other. The wailing police sirens, the checkpoints, the crack of helicopter blades, the murdered—all were paving stones on which we marked the time of our relationship, the weeks, the months, the first year, and then a year and a half, starting from the night when, in the house in Florence, I had gone to Nino in his room. It was then that—we said to each other—our true life had begun. And what we called *true life* was that impression of miraculous splendor that never abandoned us even when everyday horrors took the stage.

We were in Rome in the days following the kidnapping of Aldo Moro. I had joined Nino, who was to discuss a book by a Neapolitan colleague on southern politics and geography. Very little was said about the volume, while there was a lot of argument about Moro, the head of the Christian Democrats. Part of the audience rose up, scaring me, when Nino said it was

Moro himself who threw mud at the state, who embodied its worst aspects, who created the conditions for the birth of the Red Brigades, and thus obscured uncomfortable truths about his corrupt party, and indeed identified it with the state to avoid every accusation and every punishment. Even when he concluded that defending the institutions meant not hiding their misdeeds but making them transparent, without omissions, efficient, capable of justice in every nerve center, the people didn't calm down, and insults flew. I saw Nino turn pale, and I dragged him away as soon as possible. We took refuge in us as if in shining armor.

The times had that rhythm. Things went badly for me, too, one evening, in Ferrara. Moro's body had been found a little more than a month earlier and I let slip a description of his kidnappers as murderers. It was always difficult with words, my audience required that I calibrate them according to the current usage of the radical left, and I was very careful. But often I would get excited and then I made pronouncements with no filter. "Murderers" did not sit well with that audience—*the fascists are the murderers*—and I was attacked, criticized, jeered. I was silent. How I suffered in situations where approval suddenly vanished: I lost confidence, I felt dragged down to my origins, I felt politically incapable, I felt I was a woman who would have been better off not opening her mouth, and for a while I avoided every occasion of public confrontation. *If one murders someone, is one not a murderer?* The evening ended unpleasantly, Nino nearly came to blows with someone at the back of the room. But even in that situation only the return to the two of us counted. That's how it was: if we were together, there was no critic who could truly touch us; in fact we became arrogant, nothing else made sense except our opinions. We hurried to dinner, to good food, wine, sex. We wanted only to hold each other, cling to each other.

21.

The first cold shower arrived at the end of 1978, from Lila, naturally. It was the end of a series of unpleasant events that began in mid-October, when Pietro, returning from the university, was openly attacked by a couple of kids—reds, blackshirts, who knew anymore—armed with clubs. I hurried to the hospital, convinced that I would find him more depressed than ever. Instead, in spite of his bandaged head and a black eye, he was cheerful. He greeted me with a conciliatory tone, then he forgot about me and talked the whole time with some of his students, among whom a very pretty girl was conspicuous. When most of them left, she sat next to him, on the edge of the bed, and took one of his hands. She wore a white turtleneck sweater and a blue miniskirt, and her brown hair hung down her back. I was polite, I asked her about her studies. She said she had two more exams before getting her degree, but she was already working on her thesis, on Catullus. She's very good, Pietro praised her. Her name was Doriana and the whole time we were in the ward she only let go of his hand to rearrange the pillows.

That night, in the house in Florence, my mother-in-law appeared with Dede and Elsa. I talked to her about the girl, she smiled with satisfaction, she knew about her son's relationship. She said: You left him, what did you expect. The next day we all went together to the hospital. Dede and Elsa were immediately charmed by Doriana, by her necklaces and bracelets. They paid little attention to either their father or me, they went out to the courtyard to play with her and their grandmother. A new phase has begun, I said to myself, and I cautiously tested the ground with Pietro. Even before the beating his visits to his daughters had decreased, and now I understood why. I asked him about the girl. He talked about her as he knew how to do, with devotion. I asked: Will she come to live with you? He said that it was too soon, he didn't know, but yes, maybe so. We have to discuss the children, I said. He agreed.

As soon as possible, I took up this new situation with Adele. She must have thought that I wanted to complain but I explained that I wasn't unhappy about it, my problem was the children.

"What do you mean?" she asked, alarmed.

"Until now I've left them with you out of necessity and because I thought that Pietro needed to resettle himself, but now that he has a life of his own things have changed. I, too, have the right to some stability."

"And so?"

"I'll take a house in Naples and move there with my daughters."

We had a violent quarrel. She was very attached to the girls and didn't trust leaving them to me. She accused me of being too self-absorbed to take care of them properly. She insinuated that setting up house with a stranger—she meant Nino—when you have two female children was a very serious imprudence. Finally she swore that she would never allow her grandchildren to grow up in a disorderly city like Naples.

We shouted insults. She brought up my mother—her son must have told her about the terrible scene in Florence.

"When you have to go away who will you leave them with, her?"

"I'll leave them with whoever I like."

"I don't want Dede and Elsa to have any contact with people who are out of control."

I answered:

"In all these years I believed that you were the mother figure I'd always felt the need for. I was wrong, my mother is better than you."

22.

I subsequently brought up the subject again with Pietro, and it became evident that, despite his protests, he would agree to whatever arrangement allowed him to be with Doriana as much as possible. At that point I went to Naples to talk to Nino; I didn't want to reduce such a delicate moment to a phone call. I stayed in the apartment on Via Duomo, as I had often done now. I knew that he was still living there, it was his home, and although I always had a sense of temporariness and the dirty sheets annoyed me, I was glad to see him and I went there willingly. When I told him that I was ready to move, with my daughters, he had a real explosion of joy. We celebrated, he promised to find us an apartment as soon as possible, he wanted to take on all the inevitable annoyances.

I was relieved. After so much running around and traveling and pain and pleasure, it was time to settle down. Now I had some money, I would get some from Pietro for the children's maintenance, and I was about to sign a favorable contract for a new book. I felt that I was finally an adult, with a growing reputation, in a state in which returning to Naples could be an exciting risk and fruitful for my work. But mainly I wished to live with Nino. How lovely it was to walk with him, meet his friends, talk, come home late. I wanted to find a light-filled house, with a view of the sea. My daughters mustn't feel the lack of the comforts of Genoa.

I avoided calling Lila and telling her my decision. I assumed that she would inevitably get mixed up in my affairs and I didn't want her to. Instead I called Carmen, with whom in the past year I had established a good relationship. To please her I had met Nadia's brother, Armando, who—I had discovered—was now, besides a doctor, a prominent member of the Proletarian Democracy party. He had treated me with great respect. He had praised my last book, insisting that I come and talk about it somewhere in the city, had brought me to a popular radio station he had founded; there, in the most wretched disorder, he had interviewed me. But as for what he ironically called my recurrent curiosity about his sister, he had been evasive. He said that Nadia was well, that she had gone on a long trip with their mother, and nothing else. About Pasquale he knew nothing nor was he interested in knowing: people like him—he had said emphatically—had been the ruin of an extraordinary political period.

To Carmen, obviously, I had given a toned-down report of that meeting, but she was unhappy just the same. A decorous unhappiness, which in the end had led me to see her occasionally when I went to Naples. I felt in her an anguish that I understood. Pasquale was *our* Pasquale. We both loved him, whatever he had done or was doing. Of him I now had a drifting, fragmentary memory: the time we had been together at the neighborhood library, the time of the fight in Piazza dei Martiri, the time he had come in the car to take me to Lila, the time he had showed up at my house in Florence with Nadia. Carmen on the other hand I felt as more consistent. Her suffering as a child—I had a clear memory of her father's arrest—was welded to her suffering for her brother, to the tenacity with which she tried to watch over his fate. If she had once been only the childhood friend who had ended up behind the counter in the Carraccis' new grocery store thanks to Lila, now she was a person I saw willingly and was fond of.

We met in a coffee shop on Via Duomo. The place was dark, and we sat near the street door. I told her in detail about my plans, I knew she would talk to Lila and I thought: That's as it should be. Carmen, wearing dark colors, with her dark complexion, listened attentively and without interrupting. I felt frivolous in my elegant outfit, talking about Nino and my desire to live in a nice house. At a certain point she looked at the clock, announced:

"Lina's coming."

That made me nervous; I had a date with her, not with Lila. I looked in turn at the clock, and said, "I have to go."

"Wait, five minutes and she'll be here."

She began to speak of her with affection and gratitude. Lila took care of her friends. Lila took care of everyone: her parents, her brother, even Stefano. Lila had helped Antonio find an apartment and had become very friendly with the German woman he had married. Lila intended to set up her own computer business. Lila was sincere, she was rich, she was generous, if you were in trouble she reached into her purse. Lila was ready to help Pasquale in any way. Ah, she said, Lenù, how lucky you two are to have always been so close, how I envied you. And I seemed to hear in her voice, to recognize in a movement of her hand, the tones, the gestures of our friend. I thought again of Alfonso, I remembered my impression that he, a male, resembled Lila even in his features. Was the neighborhood settling in her, finding its direction?

"I'm going," I said.

"Wait a minute, Lila has something important to tell you."

"You tell me."

"No, it's up to her."

I waited, with growing reluctance. Finally Lila arrived. This time she had paid much more attention to her looks than when I'd seen her in Piazza Amedeo, and I had to acknowledge that, if she wanted, she could still be very beautiful. She exclaimed:

"So you've decided to return to Naples."

"Yes."

"And you tell Carmen but not me?"

"I would have told you."

"Do your parents know?"

"No."

"And Elisa?"

"Not her, either."

"Your mother's not well."

"What's wrong?"

"She has a cough, but she won't go to the doctor."

I became restless, I turned to look at the clock.

"Carmen says you have something important to tell me."

"It's not a nice thing."

"Go ahead."

"I asked Antonio to follow Nino."

I jumped.

"Follow in what sense?"

"See what he does."

"Why?"

"I did it for your own good."

"I'll worry about my own good."

Lila glanced at Carmen as if to get her support, then she turned back to me.

"If you act like that I'll shut up: I don't want you to feel offended again."

"I'm not offended, go on."

She looked me straight in the eye and revealed, in curt phrases, in Italian, that Nino had never left his wife, that he continued to live with her and his son, that as a reward he had been named, just recently, the director of an important research institute financed by the bank that his father-in-law headed. She concluded gravely:

"Did you know?"

I shook my head.

"No."

"If you don't believe me let's go see him and I'll repeat everything to his face, word for word, just as I told you now."

I waved a hand to let her know there was no need.

"I believe you," I whispered, but to avoid her eyes I looked out the door, at the street.

Meanwhile from very far away came Carmen's voice saying:

If you're going to Nino I want to come, too; the three of us will settle things properly. I felt her lightly touching my arm to get my attention. As small girls we had read photo-romances in the garden next to the church and had felt the same urge to help the heroine when she was in trouble. Now, surely, she had the same feeling of solidarity of those days, but with the gravity of today, and it was a genuine feeling, brought on by a wrong that was not fictional but real. Lila on the other hand had always scorned such reading and there was no doubt that at that moment she was sitting across from me with other motives. I imagined that she felt satisfied, as Antonio, too, must have been when he discovered Nino's falseness. I saw that she and Carmen exchanged a look, a sort of mute consultation, as if to make a decision. It was a long moment. No, I read on Carmen's lips, and that breath was accompanied by an imperceptible shaking of her head.

No to what?

Lila stared at me again, her mouth half open. As usual she was taking on the job of sticking a pin in my heart not to stop it but to make it beat harder. Her eyes were narrowed, her broad forehead wrinkled. She waited for my reaction. She wanted me to scream, weep, hand myself over to her. I said softly:

"I really have to go now."

23.

I cut Lila out of everything that followed.

I was hurt, not because she had revealed that for more than two years Nino had been telling me lies about the state of his marriage but because she had succeeded in proving to me what in fact she had said from the start: that my choice was mistaken, that I was stupid.

A few hours later I met Nino, but I acted as if nothing were wrong, I limited myself only to avoiding his embraces. I was swallowed up by bitterness. I spent the whole night with my eyes wide open, the desire to cling to that long male body was ruined. The next day he wanted to take me to see an apartment on Via Tasso, and I agreed when he said: If you like it, don't worry about the rent, I'll take care of it, I'm about to get a position that will resolve all our financial problems. But that night I couldn't take it anymore and I exploded. We were in the apartment on Via Duomo, and his friend as usual wasn't there. I said to him:

"Tomorrow I'd like to see Eleonora."

He looked at me in bewilderment.

"Why?"

"I have to talk to her. I want to know what she knows about us, when you left home, when you stopped sleeping together. I want to know if you asked for a legal separation. I want her to tell me if her father and mother know that your marriage is over."

He remained calm.

"Ask me: if something isn't clear I'll explain it to you."

"No, I trust only her, you're a liar."

At that point I started yelling, I switched to dialect. He gave in immediately, he admitted everything, I had no doubt that Lila had told me the truth. I hit him in the chest with my fists and as I did I felt as if there were a me unglued from me who wished to hurt him even more, who wanted to beat him, spit in his face as I had seen people do as a child in the neighborhood quarrels, call him a shit, scratch him, tear out his eyes. I was surprised, frightened. *Am I always this furious other I? I, here in Naples, in this filthy house, I, who if I could would kill this man, plunge a knife into his heart with all my strength? Should I restrain this shadow—my mother, all our female ancestors—or should I let her go?* I shouted, I hit him. And at first he warded off the blows, pretending to be amused, then suddenly he darkened, sat down heavily, stopped defending himself.

I slowed down, my heart was about to burst. He murmured:

"Sit down."

"No."

"At least give me a chance to explain."

I collapsed onto a chair, as far away as possible, and let him speak. You know—he began in a choked voice—that before Montpellier I had told Eleonora everything and that the break was irreparable. But when he returned, he said, things had become complicated. His wife had gone crazy, even Albertino's life seemed in danger. Thus, to be able to continue he had had to tell her that we were no longer seeing each other. For a while the lie had held up. But since the explanations he gave Eleonora for all his absences were increasingly implausible, the scenes had begun again. Once his wife had grabbed a knife and tried to stab herself in the stomach. Another time she had gone out on the balcony and wanted to jump. Yet another time she had left home, taking the child; she had disappeared for an entire day and he was dying with fear. But when he finally tracked her down at the house of a beloved aunt, he realized that Eleonora had changed. She was no longer angry, there was just a hint of contempt. One morning—Nino said, breathlessly—she asked if I had left you. I said yes. And she said: All right, I believe you. She said it just like that and from then on she began to pretend to believe me, *pretend*. Now we live in this fiction and things are working well. In fact, as you see, I'm here with you, I sleep with you, if I want I'll go away with you. And she knows everything, but she behaves as if she knew nothing.

Here he took a breath, cleared his throat, tried to understand if I was listening or harboring only rage. I continued to say nothing, I looked in another direction. He must have thought that I was yielding and he continued to explain with greater determination. He talked and talked, he was good at it, he put everything into it. He was winning, self-mocking, suffering, desperate. But when he tried to approach, I pushed him away, shouting. Then he couldn't bear it and burst into tears. He gesticulated, he leaned toward me, he murmured between tears: I don't want you to pardon me, I want only to be understood. I interrupted him, angrier than ever, I cried: You lied to her and you lied to me, and you didn't do it for love of either of us, you did it for yourself, because you don't have the courage of your choices, because you're a coward. Then I moved on to repugnant words in dialect, and he let himself be insulted, he muttered just some phrases of regret. I felt as if I were suffocating, I gasped, I was silent, and that allowed him to return to the charge. He tried again to demonstrate that lying to me had been the only way to avoid a tragedy. When it seemed to him that he had succeeded, when he whispered to me that now, thanks to Eleonora's acquiescence, we could try to live together without trouble, I said calmly that it was over between us. I left, I returned to Genoa.

24.

The atmosphere in my in-laws' house became increasingly tense. Nino telephoned constantly, I either hung up on him or quarreled too loudly. A couple of times Lila called, she wanted to know how it was going. I said to her: Well, very well, just the way you wanted it to go, and hung up. I became intractable, I yelled at Dede and Elsa for no reason. But mainly I began to fight with Adele. One morning I threw in her face what she had done to hinder the publication of my book. She didn't deny it, in fact she said: It's a pamphlet, it doesn't have the dignity of a book. I replied: If I write pamphlets, you in your whole life haven't been capable of writing even that, and it's not clear where all this authority of yours comes from. She was offended, she hissed: You don't know anything about me. Oh no, I knew things that she couldn't imagine. That time I managed to keep my mouth shut, but a few days later I had a violent quarrel with Nino; I yelled on the phone in dialect, and when my mother-in-law reproached me in a contemptuous tone I reacted by saying:

"Leave me alone, worry about yourself."

"What do you mean?"

"You know."

"I don't know anything."

"Pietro told me that you've had lovers."

"I?"

"Yes, you, don't be so taken aback. I assumed my responsibilities in front of everyone, even Dede and Elsa, and I'm paying for the consequences of my actions. You, who give yourself so many airs, you're just a hypocritical little bourgeois who hides her dirt under the carpet."

Adele turned pale, she was speechless. Rigid, her face tense, she got up and closed the door of the living room. Then she said to me in a low voice, almost a whisper, that I was an evil woman, that I couldn't understand what it meant to truly love and to give up one's beloved, that behind a pleasing and docile façade I concealed an extremely vulgar craving to grab everything, which neither studying nor books could ever tame. Then she concluded: Tomorrow get out, you and your children; I'm sorry only that if the girls had grown up here they might have tried not to be like you.

I didn't answer, I knew I had gone too far. I was tempted to apologize but I didn't. The next morning Adele ordered the maid to help me pack. I'll do it myself, I exclaimed, and without even saying goodbye to Guido, who was in his study pretending nothing was happening, I found myself at the station loaded with suitcases, the two children watching me, trying to understand what my intentions were.

I remember the exhaustion, the echo of the station hall, the waiting room. Dede reproached me for shoving: Don't push me, don't always shout, I'm not deaf. Elsa asked: Are we going to Papa? They were cheerful because there was no school, but I felt that they didn't trust me and they asked cautiously, ready to be silent if I got angry: What are we doing, when are we going back to Grandma and Grandpa's, where are we going to eat, where will we sleep tonight.

At first, desperate as I was, I thought of going to Naples and showing up with the children, without warning, at Nino and Eleonora's house. I said to myself: Yes, that's what I should do, my daughters and I are in this situation because of him, and he has to pay. I wanted my disorder to crash into him and overwhelm him, as it was overwhelming me. He had deceived me. He had held on to his family and, like a toy, me, too. I had chosen definitively, he hadn't. I had left Pietro, he had kept Eleonora. I was in the right, then. I had the right to invade his life and say to him: Well, my dear, we are here; if you're worried about your wife because she does crazy things, now I'm doing crazy things, let's see how you manage it.

But while I was preparing for a long, excruciating journey to Naples I changed my mind in a flash—an announcement on the loudspeaker was enough—and left for Milan. In this new situation I needed money more than ever. I said to myself that first of all I should go to a publisher and beg for work. Only on the train did I realize the reason for that abrupt change of plan. In spite of everything, love writhed fiercely inside me and the mere idea of doing harm to Nino was repugnant to me. Although I now wrote about women's autonomy and discussed it everywhere, I didn't know how to live without his body, his voice, his intelligence. It was terrible to confess it, but I still wanted him, I loved him more than my own daughters. At the idea of hurting him and of no longer seeing him I withered painfully, the free and educated woman lost her petals, separated from the woman-mother, and the woman-mother was disconnected from the woman-lover, and the woman-lover from the furious whore, and we all seemed on the point of flying off in different directions. As I traveled toward Milan, I discovered that, with Lila set aside, I didn't know how to give myself substance except by modeling myself on Nino. *I* was incapable of being a model for myself. Without him I no longer had a nucleus from which to expand outside the neighborhood and through the world, I was a pile of debris.

I arrived worn out and frightened at Mariarosa's house.

25.

How long did I stay there? Several months, and at times it was a difficult cohabitation. My sister-in-law already knew about the fight with Adele and she said with her usual frankness: You know I love you, but you were wrong to treat my mother like that.

"She behaved very badly."

"Now. But she helped you before."

"She did it only so that her son wouldn't look bad."

"You're unfair."

"No, I'm direct."

She looked at me with an irritation that was unusual in her. Then, as if she were stating a rule whose violation she could not tolerate, she said:

"I want to be direct, too. My mother is my mother. Say what you like about my father and my brother, but leave her alone."

Otherwise she was polite. She welcomed us to her house in her casual way, assigned us a big room with three cots, gave us towels, and then left us to ourselves, as she did with all the guests who appeared and disappeared in the apartment. I was struck, as usual, by her vivacious gaze; her entire organism seemed to hang from her eyes like a worn dressing gown. I scarcely noticed that she had an unusual pallor and had lost weight. I was absorbed in myself, in my suffering, and soon I paid her no attention at all.

I tried to put some order into the room, which was dusty, dirty, crowded with things. I made my bed and the girls' beds. I made a list of everything they and I needed. But that organizational effort didn't last long. My head was in the clouds, I didn't know what decisions to make, and for the first days I was constantly on the telephone. I missed Nino so much that I immediately called him. He got Mariarosa's number and from then on he called me continuously, even if every conversation ended in a fight. At first I was overjoyed to hear his voice, and at times I was close to giving in. I said to myself: I hid from him the fact that Pietro returned home and we were sleeping under the same roof. Then I grew angry with myself, I realized that it wasn't the same thing: I had never slept with Pietro, he slept with Eleonora; I had started the process of separation, he had consolidated his marriage bond. So we started quarreling again, I told him, shouting, never to call again. But the telephone rang regularly morning and evening. He said that he couldn't do without me, he begged me to come to Naples. One day he announced that he had rented the apartment on Via Tasso and that everything was ready to welcome me and my daughters. He said, he declared, he promised, he appeared ready for everything, but he could never make up his mind to say the most important words: *It's really over now with Eleonora.* So there was always a moment when, paying no attention to the children or to the people coming and going around the house, I screamed at him to stop tormenting me and hung up angrier than ever.

26.

I lived those days despising myself, I couldn't tear Nino out of my mind. I finished my work lethargically, I departed out of duty, I returned out of duty, I despaired, I was collapsing. And I felt that the facts were proving Lila right: I was forgetting my daughters, I was leaving them with no care, with no school.

Dede and Elsa were enchanted by the new arrangement. They scarcely knew their aunt, but they adored the sense of absolute freedom that she radiated. The house in Sant'Ambrogio continued to be a port in a storm; Mariarosa welcomed everyone with the tone of a sister or perhaps a nun without prejudices, and she didn't care about dirt, mental problems, crime, drugs. The girls had no duties; they wandered through the rooms until late at night, curious. They listened to speeches and jargons of every type, they were entertained when people made music, when they sang and danced. Their aunt went out in the morning to the university and returned in the late afternoon. She was never anxious, she made them laugh, she chased them around the apartment, played hide-and-seek or blind-man's buff. If she stayed home, she undertook great cleaning efforts, involving me, them, stray guests. But more than our bodies she looked after our minds. She had organized evening courses, and invited her colleagues from the university. Sometimes she herself gave lectures that were witty and packed with information, and she kept her nieces beside her, addressing them, involving them. The apartment at those times was crowded with her friends, men and women, who came just to listen to her.

One evening, during one of those lessons, there was a knock on the door and Dede ran to open it; she liked to greet people. Returning to the living room, she said excitedly: It's the police. In the small assembly there was an angry, almost threatening murmur. Mariarosa rose calmly and went to speak to the police. There were two, they said that the neighbors had complained, or something like that. She was cordial, insisted that they come in, almost forced them to sit with us in the living room, and returned to her lecture. Dede had never seen a policeman up close, and started talking to the younger one, resting her elbow on his knee. I remember her opening remark, by which she intended to explain that Mariarosa was a good person:

"In fact," she said, "my aunt is a professor."

"In fact," the cop said faintly, with an uncertain smile.

"Yes."

"How well you speak."

"Thank you. In fact, her name is Mariarosa Airota and she teaches art history."

The boy whispered something to his older companion. They remained prisoners for ten minutes or so and then they left. Dede led them to the door.

Later I, too, was assigned one of these educational projects, and for my evening more people showed up than usual. My daughters sat on cushions in the first row, in the big living room, and they listened obediently. Starting then, I think, Dede began to observe me with curiosity. She had great respect for her father, her grandfather, and now Mariarosa. She knew nothing about me and didn't want to know anything. I was her mother, I forbade everything, she couldn't stand me. She must have been amazed that I was listened to with an attention that she on principle would never have given me. And maybe she also liked the composure with which I responded to criticisms; that evening they came surprisingly from Mariarosa. My sister-in-law was the only one among the women present who did not agree with even a word of what I was saying—she who, long ago, had encouraged me to study, to write, to publish. Without asking my permission, she told the story of the fight I had had with my mother in Florence, demonstrating that she knew about it in detail. "Resorting to many learned citations," she theorized that a woman without love for her origins is lost.

27.

When I had to travel I left the children to my sister-in-law, but I soon realized that it was really Franco who took care of them. Generally he stayed in his room, he didn't join in the lectures, he paid no attention to the constant coming and going. But he was fond of my daughters. When necessary he cooked for them, he invented games, in his way he instructed them. Dede learned from him to challenge the silly fable—so she described it, telling me about it—of Menenius Agrippa, which she had been taught in the new school I had decided to enroll her in. She laughed and said: *The patrician Menenius Agrippa, Mamma, bewildered the common people with his talk, but he couldn't prove that one man's limbs are nourished when another man's stomach is filled. Ha ha ha.* From him she also learned, on a big map of the world, the geography of inordinate prosperity and intolerable poverty. She couldn't stop repeating: It's the greatest injustice.

One evening when Mariarosa wasn't there, my boyfriend from the days of Pisa said, in a serious tone of regret, alluding to the children, who followed him around the house with drawn-out cries: Imagine, they could have been ours. I corrected him: They'd be a few years older by now. He nodded yes. I observed him for a few seconds while he stared at his shoes. I compared him in my mind to the rich, educated student of fifteen years earlier: it was him and yet it was not him. He no longer read, he didn't write, within the past year he had reduced to the minimum his participation in assemblies, debates, demonstrations. He talked about politics—his only true interest—without his former conviction and passion; rather, he accentuated the tendency to mock his own grim prophecies of disaster. In hyperbolic tones he listed the catastrophes that in his view were approaching: one, the decline of the revolutionary subject par excellence, the working class; two, the definitive dispersion of the political patrimony of socialists and Communists, who were already perverted by their daily quarrel over which was playing the role of capital's crutch; three, the end of every hypothesis of change, what was there was there and we would have to adapt to it. I asked skeptically: You really think it's going to end like that? Of course— he laughed—but you know that I'm a skilled debater, and if you want I'll prove to you, by means of thesis, antithesis, and synthesis, the exact opposite: Communism is inevitable, the dictatorship of the proletariat is the highest form of democracy, the Soviet Union and China and North Korea and Thailand are much better than the United States, shedding blood in rivulets or rivers in certain cases is a crime and in certain others is just. Would you prefer that I do that?

Only twice did I see him as he had been as a youth. One morning Pietro appeared, without Doriana, assuming the attitude of someone who was making an inspection to check on what conditions his daughters were living in, what school I had put them in, if they were happy. It was a moment of great tension. The children perhaps told him too much, and with a childish taste for fantastic exaggeration, about the way they were living. So he began to quarrel ponderously first with his sister and then with me, he said to us both that we were irresponsible. I lost my temper, and shouted at him: You're right, take them away, you take care of them, you and Doriana. And at that point Franco came out of his room, intervened, rolled out his old skill with words, which in the past had enabled him to control raucous meetings. He and Pietro ended up having a learned discussion on the couple, the family, the care of children, and even Plato, forgetting about Mariarosa and me. My husband left, his face flushed, his eyes clear, nervous and yet pleased to have found someone with whom he could have an intelligent and civilized conversation.

Stormier—and terrible for me—was the day when Nino appeared without warning. He was tired from the long drive, unkempt in appearance, very tense. At first I thought he had come to decide, on his own authority, the fate of me and the children. Enough, I hoped he would say, I've cleared up my situation and we're going to live in Naples. I felt disposed to give in without any more nonsense, I was exhausted by the provisional nature of things. But it didn't turn out like that. We closed ourselves in a room, and he, amid endless hesitations, twisting his hands, his hair, his face, repeated, against all my expectations, that it was impossible for him to separate from his wife. He was agitated, he tried to embrace me, he struggled to explain that only by staying with Eleonora would it be possible for him not to give up me and our life together. At another moment I would have pitied him; it was evident that his suffering was sincere. But, at the time, I didn't care in the least how much he was suffering, I looked at him in astonishment.

"What are you saying to me?"

"That I can't leave Eleonora, but I can't live without you."

"So if I understand you: you are proposing, as if it were a reasonable solution, that I abandon the role of lover and accept that of parallel wife."

"What do you mean, it's not like that."

I attacked him, *Of course it's like that*, and I pointed to the door: I was tired of his tricks, his inspired ideas, his every wretched word. Then, in a voice that strained to come out of his throat, and yet with the air of someone who is uttering definitively the irrefutable reasons for his own behavior, he confessed to me a thing that—he cried—*he didn't want others to tell me*, and so he had come to tell me in person: Eleonora was seven months pregnant.

28.

Now that much of my life is behind me I know that my reaction to that news was overblown, and as I write I realize that I'm smiling to myself. I know many men and many women who can recount experiences that aren't very different: love and sex are unreasonable and brutal. But at the time I couldn't bear it. That fact—*Eleonora is seven months pregnant*—seemed to me the most intolerable wrong that Nino could do to me. I remembered Lila, the moment of uncertainty when she and Carmen had looked at each other, as if they had had something else to tell me. Had Antonio discovered the pregnancy, too? Did they know? And why had Lila relinquished her chance to tell me? Had she claimed the right to measure out my suffering in doses? Something broke in my chest and in my stomach. While Nino was suffocating with anxiety and struggling to justify himself, saying that the pregnancy, if on the one hand it had served to calm his wife, on the other had made it even more difficult to leave her, I was doubled over with suffering, arms locked, my whole body was ill, I couldn't speak, or cry out. Only Franco was in the apartment. No crazy women, desolate women, singers, sick people. Mariarosa had taken the children out to give Nino and me time to confront each other. I opened the door of the room and called my old boyfriend from Pisa in a weak voice. He came right away and I pointed to Nino. I said in a sort of rattle: throw him out.

He didn't throw him out, but he signaled him to be silent. He avoided asking what had happened, he grabbed my wrists, he held me steady, he let me retake possession of myself. Then he led me to the kitchen, made me sit down. Nino followed us.

I was gasping for breath, making choking sounds of despair. Throw him out, I repeated, when Nino tried to come near me. Franco kept him away, said calmly: Leave her alone, leave the room. Nino obeyed and I told Franco everything in the most confused way. He listened without interrupting, until he realized that I had no more energy. Only at that point did he say, in his refined way, that it was a good rule not to expect the ideal but to enjoy what is possible. I got mad at him, too: The usual male talk, I shouted, who gives a damn about the possible, you're talking nonsense. He wasn't offended, he wanted me to examine the situation for what it was. All right, he said, this man has lied to you for two and a half years, he told you he had left his wife, he said he didn't have relations with her, and now you discover that seven months ago he made her pregnant. You're right, it's horrible, Nino is an abject being. But once it was known—he pointed out—he could have disappeared, forgotten about you. Why, then, did he drive from Naples to Milan, why did he travel all night, why did he humiliate himself, accusing himself, why did he beg you not to leave him? All that should signify something. It signifies, I cried, that he is a liar, that he is a superficial person, that he is incapable of making a choice. And he kept nodding yes, he agreed. But then he asked: What if he loved you, seriously, and yet knew that he could love you only in this way?

I didn't have time to say that that was exactly Nino's argument. The house door opened and Mariarosa appeared. The girls recognized Nino with charming bashfulness and at the idea of getting his attention immediately forgot that that name had for days, for months, sounded in their father's mouth like a curse. He devoted himself to them, Mariarosa and Franco took care of me. How difficult everything was. Dede and Elsa were now talking in loud voices, laughing, and my two hosts turned to me with serious arguments. They wanted to help me reason, but with underlying feelings that not even they could keep under control. Franco revealed a surprising tendency to give space to affectionate mediation instead of to clean breaks, as he used to do. My sister-in-law at first was full of understanding for me, then she also tried to understand Nino's motives and, especially, Eleonora's plight, in the end wounding me, maybe without wishing to, maybe intentionally. Don't get angry, she said, try to reflect: what does a woman of your understanding feel at the idea that her happiness becomes the ruin of someone else?

It went on like that. Franco urged me to take what I could within the limits imposed by the situation, Mariarosa portrayed Eleonora abandoned with a small child and another on the way, and advised me: establish a relationship with her, look at one another. The nonsense of someone who doesn't know, I thought, with no energy now, of someone who can't understand. Lila would come out of it as she always does, Lila would advise me: You've already made a big enough mistake, spit in their faces and get out, it was the ending she'd always wished for. But I was frightened, I felt even more confused by what Franco and Mariarosa were saying, I was no longer listening to them. I observed Nino instead. How handsome he was as he regained my daughters' trust. Here, he was coming back into the room with them, pretending nothing had happened, praising them as he addressed Mariarosa—See, aunt, what exceptional young ladies?—and the charm came naturally to him, the light touch of his fingers on her bare knee. I dragged him out of the house, insisted on a long walk through Sant'Ambrogio.

It was hot, I remember. We drifted alongside a red brick stain, the air was full of fuzz flying off the plane trees. I told him that I had to get used to doing without him, but that for now I couldn't, I needed time. He answered that he, instead, would never be able to live without me. I replied that he had never been able to separate himself from anything or anyone. He repeated that it wasn't true, that circumstances were to blame, that to have me he was compelled to hold on to everything. I understood that to force him to go beyond that position was in vain, he could see before him only an abyss and he was frightened by it. I walked him to his car, I sent him away. A moment before he left he asked: What do you think you'll do. I didn't answer, even I didn't know.

29.

What happened a few weeks later made my decision for me. Mariarosa had gone, she had an engagement in Bordeaux. Before she left she took me aside and delivered a confused speech about Franco, on the need for me to stay close to him during her absence. She described him as very depressed, and I suddenly understood what until that moment I had only intuited in fits and starts and then missed through distraction: with Franco she was playing the good Samaritan as she did with everyone; she loved him seriously, she had become for him mother-sister-lover, and her expression of suffering, her withered body were due to permanent anxiety about him, the certainty that he had become too fragile and might break at any moment.

She was away for eight days. With some effort—I had other things on my mind—I was cordial to Franco. I stayed up late talking with him every evening, and I was glad that instead of talking about politics he preferred to recall, to himself more than to me, how well we had got on together: our walks through Pisa in the spring, the terrible smell of the street along the Arno, the times he had confided to me things he'd never said to anyone about his childhood, his parents, his grandparents. Above all I was pleased that he let me talk about my anxieties, about the new contract I had signed with the publishing house, about the need therefore to write a new book, about a possible return to Naples, about Nino. He never attempted generalizations or superfluous words. He was, rather, sharp, almost vulgar. If he is more important to you than yourself— he said one evening, seeming almost dazed—you should take him as he is: wife, children, that permanent tendency to sleep with other women, the vulgar things he is and will be capable of. Lena, Lenuccia, he murmured, affectionately, shaking his head. And then he laughed, got up from the chair, said obscurely that in his view love ended only when it was possible to return to oneself without fear or disgust, and left the room with shuffling steps, as if he wanted to reassure himself of the materiality of the floor. I don't know why Pasquale came to mind, that night, a person very far from him in social background, culture, political choices. And yet, for an instant, I imagined that if my friend from the neighborhood had managed to reemerge alive from the darkness that had swallowed him he would have the same way of walking.

For an entire day Franco didn't come out of his room. That night I had an engagement for work, I knocked, I asked him if he could give Dede and Elsa dinner. He promised to do it. I got home late, and, contrary to his usual habit, he had left the kitchen in great disorder. I cleared the table, I washed the dishes. I didn't sleep much, at six I was already awake. On the way to the bathroom I passed his room and was attracted by a sheet of notebook paper attached to the door with a thumbtack. On it was written: *Lena, don't let the children in.* I thought that Dede and Elsa had been bothering him, or that the evening before they had made him angry, and I went to make breakfast with the intention of scolding them. Then I thought again. Franco had a good relationship with my daughters, I ruled out that he was angry with them for some reason. Around eight I knocked discreetly. No answer. I knocked harder, I opened the door cautiously, the room was dark. I called him, silence, I turned on the light.

There was blood on the pillow and on the sheet, a large blackish stain that extended to his feet. Death is so repellent. Here I will say only that when I saw that body deprived of life, that body which I knew intimately, which had been happy and active, which had read so many books and had been exposed to so many experiences, I felt both repulsion and pity. Franco had been a living material saturated with political culture, with generous purposes and hopes, with good manners. Now he offered a horrible spectacle of himself. He had rid himself so fiercely of memory, language, the capacity to find meaning that it seemed obvious the hatred he had for himself, for his own skin, for his moods, for his thoughts and words, for the brutal corner of the world that had enveloped him.

In the days that followed I thought of Pasquale and Carmen's mother, Giuseppina. She, too, had stopped being able to tolerate herself and the segment of life that remained to her. But Giuseppina came from the time that preceded me, Franco instead was of my time, and that violent removal from it didn't just make an impression, it was devastating. I thought for a long time about his note, the only one he left. It was addressed to me and in substance was saying: Don't let the children in, I don't want them to see me; but you can enter, you *must* see me. I still think about that double imperative, one explicit, one implicit. After the funeral, which was attended by a crowd of militants with weakly clenched fists (Franco was still at the time well known and highly respected), I tried to re-establish a bond with Mariarosa. I wanted to be close to her, I wanted to talk about him, but she wouldn't let me. Her untidy appearance got worse, her features took on a morbid distrust that diminished even the vivacity of her eyes. The house slowly emptied. Any sisterly feeling toward me vanished, and she became increasingly hostile. Either she stayed at the university all the time or, if she was at home, she shut herself in her room and didn't want to be disturbed. She got angry if the girls made noise playing, she got even angrier if I scolded them for their noisy games. I packed the bags, I left for Naples with Dede and Elsa.

30.

Nino had been sincere, he had actually rented the apartment on Via Tasso. I went to live there right away, even though it was infested with ants and the furniture came down to a double bed without a headboard, cots for the children, a table, some chairs. I didn't talk about love, I didn't mention the future.

I told him that my decision had to do mostly with Franco, and I limited myself to bringing him good news and bad. The good was that my publisher had agreed to bring out his collection of essays, provided he made a new draft that was a little less dry; the bad was that I didn't want him to touch me. He greeted the first piece of news joyfully, he was desperate about the second. But then, as it turned out, we spent every evening sitting together, rewriting his essays, and with that closeness I couldn't keep my rage alive. Eleonora was still pregnant when we began to love each other again. And when she gave birth to a girl, who was named Lidia, Nino and I had returned to being lovers, a couple with our habits, a nice house, two children, an intense life, both private and public.

"Don't think," I said from the start, "that I'm at your command: I'm not capable of leaving you now, but sooner or later it will happen."

"It won't happen, you won't have any reason to."

"I have plenty of reasons."

"Everything will change soon."

"We'll see."

But it was a stage set, I passed off as very reasonable what was in fact unreasonable and humiliating. I'm taking—I said, adapting Franco's words—what is indispensable to me now, and as soon as I've consumed his face, his words, every desire, I'll send him away. When I waited for him in vain for days I told myself it was better that way, I was busy, he was with me too much. And when I felt the sting of jealousy I tried to calm myself by whispering: *I am the woman he loves*. And if I thought of his children I said to myself: He spends more time with Dede and Elsa than with Albertino and Lidia. Naturally it was all true and all false. Yes, the force of Nino's attraction would wear out. Yes, I had a lot of things to do. Yes, Nino loved me, he loved Dede and Elsa. But there were also others, yes, whom I pretended to ignore. Yes, I was more attracted to him than ever. Yes, I was ready to neglect everything and everyone if he needed me. Yes, his ties to Eleonora, Albertino, and the newborn Lidia were at least as strong as his ties to me and my daughters. I lowered dark curtains over those yeses, and if in fact here or there a tear in the fabric made evident the true state of things I quickly resorted to big words about the world to come: everything is changing, we are inventing new forms of living together, and other nonsense of the sort that I myself uttered in public or wrote every time it happened.

But the difficulties hammered at me every day, cracks were continually opening up. The city hadn't improved at all, its malaise wore me out immediately. Via Tasso turned out to be inconvenient. Nino got me a used car, a white Renault 4 that I immediately became attached to, but then I was always stuck in traffic, and I soon gave it up. I struggled to meet the endless demands of daily life much more than I ever had in Florence, Genoa, Milan. From the first day of school Dede hated her teacher and her classmates. Elsa, now in first grade, always came home depressed, her eyes red, and refused to tell me what had happened to her. I began to scold them both. I said they didn't know how to deal with adversity, they didn't know how to assert themselves, they didn't know how to adapt, and they had to learn. As a result the two sisters joined forces against me: they began to speak of their grandmother Adele and aunt Mariarosa as if they were divinities who had organized a happy world made just for them, they mourned them in an increasingly explicit way. When, in an attempt to win them back, I drew them to me, cuddled them, they hugged me unwillingly, and sometimes pushed me away. And my work? It became more and more evident that, especially in that successful period, I would have done better to stay in Milan and find a job at a publisher's. Or even settle in Rome, since I had met people on my promotional tours who had offered to help me. What were my daughters and I doing in Naples? Were we there just to make Nino happy? Was I lying to myself when I portrayed myself as free and autonomous? And was I lying to my audience when I played the part of someone who, with her two small books, had sought to help every woman confess what she couldn't say to herself? Were they mere formulas that it was convenient for me to believe in while in fact I was no different from my more traditional contemporaries? In spite of all the talk was I letting myself be *invented* by a man to the point where his needs were imposed on mine and those of my daughters?

I learned to avoid myself. It was enough for Nino to knock on the door and the bitterness vanished. I said to myself: Life *now* is this and can't be other. Meanwhile I tried to give myself some discipline, I didn't resign myself, I tried to be assertive, sometimes I even managed to feel happy. The house shone with light. From my balcony I saw Naples stretching to the edges of the yellow-blue reflection of the sea. I had taken my daughters away from the temporariness of Genoa and Milan, and the air, the colors, the sounds of the dialect in the streets, the cultured people Nino brought to see me even late into the night gave me confidence, made me cheerful. I took the girls to see Pietro in Florence and was pleased when he came to see them in Naples. Over Nino's protests I let him stay in my house. I made him a bed in the girls' room; their affection for him was a performance, as if they wanted to keep him with them through a display of how much they loved him. We tried to have a casual relationship, I inquired about Doriana, I asked about his book, which was always about to be published when further details emerged that had to be examined. When the children held tight to their father, ignoring me, I took a little break. I went down through the Arco Mirelli and walked along Via Caracciolo, beside the sea. Or I went up to Via Aniello Falcone and came to the Floridiana. I chose a bench, I read.

31.

From Via Tasso the old neighborhood was a dim, distant rockpile, indistinguishable urban debris at the foot of Vesuvius. I wanted it to stay that way: I was another person now, I would make sure that it did not recapture me. But in that case, too, the purpose I tended to attribute to myself was fragile. A mere three or four days after the first harried arrangement of the apartment I gave in. I dressed the children carefully, dressed up myself, and said: Now let's go see Grandmother Immacolata and Grandfather Vittorio and the uncles.

We left early in the morning and at Piazza Amedeo took the metro; the children were excited by the violent wind produced by the train's arrival, which ruffled their hair, pasted their dresses to their bodies, took away their breath. I hadn't seen or talked to my mother since the scene in Florence. I was afraid she would refuse to see me and maybe for that reason I didn't telephone to announce my visit. But I have to be honest, there was another, more obscure reason. I was reluctant to say to myself: I am here for this or that other reason, I want to go here or I want to go there. The neighborhood for me, even more than my family, was Lila: to plan that visit would also mean asking myself how I wanted to arrange things with her. And I still didn't have definite answers, and so leaving it to chance was better. In any case, since it was possible that I would run into her, I had devoted the greatest attention to the children's appearance and to my own. If it happened, I wanted her to realize that I was a lady of refinement and that my daughters weren't suffering, weren't falling apart, were doing very well.

It turned out to be an emotionally charged day. I went through the tunnel, I avoided the gas pump where Carmen worked with her husband, Roberto, and crossed the courtyard. My heart pounding, I climbed the crumbling stairs of the old building where I was born. Dede and Elsa were very excited, as if they were heading into some unknown adventure; I arrayed them in front of me and rang the bell. I heard the limping gait of my mother, she opened the door, she widened her eyes as if we were ghosts. I, too, in spite of myself, showed astonishment. The person I expected to see had come unglued from the one who was in fact before me. My mother was very changed. For a fraction of a second she seemed to be a cousin of hers whom I had seen a few times as a child, and who resembled her, although she was six or seven years older. She was much thinner, the bones of her face, her nose, her ears seemed enormous.

I tried to hug her, she drew back. My father wasn't there, nor were Peppe and Gianni. To find out anything about them was impossible, for a good hour she barely spoke a word to me. With the children she was affectionate. She praised them mightily and then, enveloping them in large aprons, she began making sugar candies with them. For me it was very awkward; the whole time she acted as if I weren't there. When I tried to say to the children that they were eating too many candies, Dede quickly turned to her grandmother:

"Can we have some more?"

"Eat as many as you want," my mother said, without looking at me.

The same scene was repeated when she told her grandchildren that they could go play in the courtyard. In Florence, in Genoa, in Milan I had never let them go out alone. I said:

"No, girls, you can't, stay here."

"Grandma, can we go?" my daughters asked, almost in unison.

"I told you yes."

We remained alone. I said to her anxiously, as if I were still a child: "I moved. I've taken an apartment on Via Tasso."

"Good."

"Three days ago."

"Good."

"I've written another book."

"What do I care?"

I was silent. With an expression of disgust, she cut a lemon in two and squeezed the juice into a glass.

"Why are you having a lemonade?" I asked.

"Because seeing you turns my stomach."

She added water to the lemon, put in some bicarbonate of soda, drank the foamy effervescence in one gulp.

"Are you not well?"

"I'm very well."

"It's not true. Have you been to the doctor?"

"Imagine if I'll throw away money on doctors and medicine."

"Elisa knows you don't feel well?"

"Elisa is pregnant."

"Why didn't you or she tell me anything?"

She didn't answer. She placed the glass on the sink with a long, tired sigh, wiped her lips with the back of her hand. I said:

"I'll take you to the doctor. What else do you feel?"

"Everything that you brought on. Because of you a vein in my stomach ruptured."

"What do you mean?"

"Yes, you've killed this body."

"I love you very much, Mamma."

"Not me. You've come to stay in Naples with the children?"

"Yes."

"And your husband's not coming?"

"No."

"Then don't ever show up in this house again."

"Ma, today it's not like it used to be. You can be a respectable person even if you leave your husband, even if you go with someone else. Why do you get so angry with me when you don't say anything about Elisa, who's pregnant and not married?"

"Because you're not Elisa. Did Elisa study the way you did? From Elisa did I expect what I expected from you?"

"I'm doing things you should be happy about. Greco is becoming an important name. I even have a little reputation abroad."

"Don't boast to me, you're nobody. What you think you are means nothing to normal people. I'm respected here not because I had you but because I had Elisa. She didn't study, she didn't even graduate from middle school, but she's a lady. And you who have a university degree—where did you end up? I'm just sorry for the two children, so pretty and they speak so well. Didn't you think of them? With that father they were growing up like children on television, and you, what do you do, you bring them to Naples?"

"I'm the one who brought them up, Ma, not their father. And wherever I take them they'll still grow up like that."

"You are presumptuous. *Madonna*, how many mistakes I made with you. I thought Lina was the presumptuous one, but it's you. Your friend bought a house for her parents, did you do that? Your friend orders everyone around, even Michele Solara, and who do you order around, that piece of shit son of Sarratore?"

At that point she began to sing Lila's praises: Ah, how pretty Lina is, how generous, now she's got her own business, no less, she and Enzo—they've known how to get ahead. I understood that the greatest sin she charged to me was forcing her to admit, with no way out, that I was worth less than Lila. When she said she wanted to cook something for Dede and Elsa, deliberately excluding me, I realized that it would pain her to invite me to lunch and, taking the children, I went away bitterly.

32.

Once on the *stradone* I hesitated: wait at the gate for my father's return, wander the streets in search of my brothers, see if my sister was home? I found a telephone booth, I called Elisa, I dragged the girls to her big apartment, from which you could see Vesuvius. My sister showed no signs yet of pregnancy, and yet I found her very changed. The simple fact of being pregnant must have made her expand suddenly, but distorting her. She was as if coarsened in her body, in her words, in her voice. She had an ashy complexion and was so poisoned by animosity that she welcomed us reluctantly. Not for a moment did I find any trace of the affection nor the slightly childish admiration she had always had for me. And when I mentioned our mother's health she took an aggressive tone that I wouldn't have thought her capable of, at least with me. She exclaimed:

"Lenù, the doctor said she's fine, it's her soul that suffers. Mamma is very healthy, she has her health, there's nothing to treat except sorrow. If you hadn't disappointed her the way you have she wouldn't be in this state."

"What sort of nonsense is that?"

She became even more rancorous.

"Nonsense? I'll just tell you this: my health is worse than Mamma's. And anyway, now that you're in Naples and you know more about doctors, you take care of her, don't leave it all on my shoulders. Enough for you to give her a bit of attention and she'll be healthy again."

I tried to control myself, I didn't want to quarrel. Why was she talking to me like that? Had I, too, changed for the worse, like her? Were our good times as sisters over? Or was Elisa, the youngest of the family, the outward sign that the life of the neighborhood was even more ruinous than in the past? I told the children, who sat obediently, in silence, but disappointed that their aunt paid them not the slightest attention, that they could finish the candies from their grandmother. Then I asked my sister:

"How are things with Marcello?"

"Very good, how should they be? If it weren't for all the worries he's had since his mother died, we'd really be happy."

"What worries?"

"Worries, Lenù, worries. Go think about your books, life is something else."

"Peppe and Gianni?"

"They work."

"I never see them."

"Your fault that you never come around."

"I'll come more often now."

"Good for you. Then try to talk to your friend Lina, too."

"What's happening?"

"Nothing. But among Marcello's many worries she's one."

"What do you mean?"

"Ask Lina, and if she answers, tell her that she'd better stay where she belongs."

I recognized the threatening reticence of the Solaras and I

realized that we would never regain our old intimacy. I told her that Lila and I had grown apart, but I had just heard from our mother that she had stopped working for Michele and had set up on her own. Elisa muttered:

"Set up on her own with our money."

"Explain."

"What is there to explain, Lenù? She twists Michele around her finger. But not my Marcello."

33.

Elisa didn't invite us to lunch, either. Only when she led us to the door did she seem to become aware that she had been rude, and she said to Elsa: Come with your aunt. They disappeared for a few minutes, making Dede suffer; she clutched my hand in order not to feel neglected. When they reappeared Elsa had a serious expression but a cheerful gaze. My sister, who seemed worn out by being on her feet, closed the door as soon as we started down the stairs.

Once we were in the street the child showed us her aunt's secret gift: twenty thousand lire. Elisa had given her money the way, when we were small, certain relatives did who were scarcely better off than we were. But at that time the money was only in appearance a gift for us children: we were bound to hand it over to my mother, who spent it on necessities. Elisa, too, evidently, had wanted to give the money to me rather than to Elsa, but for another purpose. With that twenty thousand lire—the equivalent of three books in quality bindings—she meant to prove to me that Marcello loved her and she led a life of luxury.

I calmed the children, who were squabbling. Elsa had to be subjected to persistent questioning in order to admit that, according to their aunt's wishes, the money should be divided, ten thousand to her and ten thousand to Dede. They were still wrangling and tugging at each other when I heard someone calling me. It was Carmen, bundled up in a blue gas-station attendant's smock. Distracted, I hadn't taken a detour around the gas pump. Now she was making signs of greeting, her hair curly and black, her face broad.

It was hard to resist. Carmen closed the pump, wanted to take us to her house for lunch. Her husband, whom I had never met, arrived. He had gone to get the children at school: two boys, one the same age as Elsa, the other a year younger. He turned out to be a gentle, very cordial man. He set the table, getting the children to help him, he cleared, he washed the dishes. Until that moment I had never seen a couple of my generation get along so well, so obviously content to live together. Finally I felt welcomed, and I saw that my daughters, too, were at ease: they ate heartily, with maternal tones they devoted themselves to the two boys. In other words I felt reassured, I had a couple of hours of tranquility. Then Roberto hurried out to reopen the pump, and Carmen and I were alone.

She was discreet, she didn't ask about Nino, if I had moved to Naples to live with him, even though she seemed to know everything. Instead she talked about her husband, a hard worker, and attached to the family. Lenù, she said, amid so much suffering he and the children are the only consolation. She recalled the past: the terrible story of her father, the sacrifices of her mother and her mother's death, the period when she worked in Stefano Carracci's grocery store, and then when Ada replaced Lila and had tortured her. We even laughed a little about the time when she was Enzo's girlfriend: What nonsense, she said. She didn't mention Pasquale even once; I had to ask. But she stared at the floor, shook her head, jumped up as if to push away something she wouldn't or couldn't tell me.

"I'm going to call Lina," she said. "If she knows we saw each other and I didn't tell her she'll never speak to me again."

"Forget it, she'll be working."

"Come on, she's the boss now and she does as she likes."

I tried to keep her talking, and asked her cautiously about the relations between Lila and the Solaras. But she was embarrassed, she answered that she didn't know much about it and went to call. I heard her announcing excitedly that my daughters and I were in her house. When she returned she said:

"She's very pleased, she'll be right over."

From that moment I began to get nervous. And yet I felt well disposed, it was comfortable in that modest, respectable house, the four children playing in the other room. The bell rang, Carmen went to the door, there was Lila's voice.

34.

I didn't notice Gennaro at first, nor did I see Enzo. They became visible only after a long series of seconds in which I heard only Lila and felt an unexpected sense of guilt. Maybe it seemed wrong that it was she, yet again, who was eager to see me, while I insisted on keeping her outside of my life. Or maybe it seemed to me rude that she continued to be interested in me, while I, by my silence, by my absence, intended to signal to her that she no longer interested me. I don't know. Certainly as she hugged me I thought: if she doesn't attack me with spiteful talk about Nino, if she pretends not to know about his new child, if she is nice to my daughters, I'll be polite, then we'll see.

So we sat down. We hadn't seen each other since the meeting in the bar on Via Duomo. It was Lila who spoke first. She pushed Gennaro forward—a large adolescent, his face marked by acne—and immediately began to complain about his scholastic performance. She said, but in an affectionate tone: he did well in elementary school, he did well in middle school, but this year they're failing him, he can't manage Latin and

Greek. I gave the boy a pat, I consoled him: you just have to practice, Gennà, come to me, I'll tutor you. And impulsively I decided to take the initiative, confronting what for me was the burning issue, I said: I moved to Naples a few days ago, things with Nino are resolved within the limits of the possible, everything's fine. Then, calmly, I called my daughters, and when they looked in I exclaimed, Here are the children, how do you find them, see how they've grown. There was confusion. Dede recognized Gennaro and happily pulled him after her with a seductive look, she nine and he nearly fifteen; Elsa in turn tugged at him, in order not to be outdone by her sister. I looked at them with motherly pride and was glad that Lila meanwhile said: You've done well to return to Naples, one should do what one feels like doing, the girls look really well, how pretty they are.

At that point I felt relieved. Enzo, making conversation, asked me about work. I boasted a little about the success of the last book, but I immediately understood that though people in the neighborhood had heard of my first book at the time and some had even read it, not even Enzo and Carmen, or Lila, knew about the second. So I circled around it in a self-mocking tone and then I asked about their activities, I said, laughing: I know you've gone from being workers to bosses. Lila made a face as if to disparage this, and turned to Enzo, who tried to explain in simple terms. He said that computers in recent years had evolved, he said that IBM had put machines on the market that were completely different from the earlier ones. As usual he got lost in technical details that bored me. He cited products, the System 34, the 5120, and explained that there were no longer either perforated cards or punch-card machines and checkers but a different programming language, BASIC, while the machines kept getting smaller, with less power for calculation and storage but much less costly. In the end I understood only that that new technology had been crucial for them; they had begun to study up and had decided that they could go out on their own. So they had started their own business, Basic Sight—*in English, because otherwise they don't take you seriously*—and of that business, with headquarters in the rooms of their house (*hardly bosses*), he, Enzo, was the majority partner and administrator, but the soul, the true soul—Enzo pointed to her with a gesture of pride—was Lila. Look at the logo, he said, she designed it.

I examined the logo, a swirl around a vertical line. I stared at it with sudden emotion, as a further manifestation of her ungovernable mind—I wondered how many I had missed. I felt a sudden longing for the good moments of our past. Lila learned, set aside, learned. She couldn't stop, she never retreated: the 34, the 5120, BASIC, Basic Sight, the logo. Lovely, I said, and I felt then the way I hadn't felt with my mother and my sister. They all seemed happy to have me among them again, and drew me generously into their lives. Enzo, as if to demonstrate that his ideas hadn't changed in spite of prosperity, began to relate in his dry manner what he saw when he went around to the factories: people were working in terrible conditions for practically nothing, and sometimes he was ashamed at having to transform the filth of exploitation into the tidiness of programming. Lila, for her part, said that to obtain that tidiness the bosses had been forced to show her all their dirt close up, and she spoke sarcastically about the duplicity, the tricks, the scams that were behind the façade of orderly accounts. Carmen was not to be outdone, she talked about gas, she exclaimed: Here, too, there's shit everywhere. And only at that point she mentioned her brother, citing all the right reasons that had led him to do wrong things. She recalled the neighborhood of our childhood and adolescence. She told the story—she had never told it before—of when she and Pasquale were children and their father listed point by point what the fascists, led by Don Achille, had done to him: the time he had been beaten up right at the entrance to the tunnel; the time they'd made him kiss the photograph of Mussolini but he had spit on it, and if they hadn't murdered him, if he hadn't disappeared like so many comrades—*there is no history of those whom the fascists killed and then "disappeared"*—it was only because he had the carpentry shop and was well known in the neighborhood, and if they had removed him from the face of the earth everyone would have noticed.

So the time passed. At a certain point there was such a strong feeling of friendship that they decided to give me real proof of it. Carmen consulted Enzo and Lila with a look, then she said warily: We can trust Lenuccia. When she saw that they agreed she said that they had recently seen Pasquale. He had appeared one night at Carmen's house, and she had called Lila, and Lila had hurried over with Enzo. Pasquale was well. He was clean, not a hair out of place, very well dressed, he looked like a surgeon. But they had found him sad. His ideas had remained the same, but he was incredibly sad. He had said that he would never surrender, that they would have to kill him. Before leaving he had looked in at his nephews as they slept: he didn't even know their names. Carmen here began to cry, but silently, so that her children wouldn't come in. We said, she first of all, she more than me, more than Lila (Lila was laconic, Enzo confined himself to nodding), that we didn't like Pasquale's choices, that we felt horror at the bloody disorder of Italy and the world, but that he knew the same essential things that we knew, and even if he had committed whatever terrible acts—among those you read about in the papers—and even if we were comfortable with our lives in information technology, Latin and Greek, books, gas, we would never reject him. None of those who loved him would do so.

The day ended there. There was only one last question, which I asked Lila and Enzo, because I was feeling at ease and had in mind what Elisa had said to me a little earlier. I asked:

And the Solaras? Enzo immediately stared at the floor. Lila shrugged, she said: The usual pieces of shit. Then she said sarcastically that Michele had gone mad: after his mother's death he had left Gigliola, he had thrown his wife and children out of the house on Posillipo and if they showed up there he beat them. The Solaras—she said, with a hint of gratification—are finished: imagine, Marcello goes around saying it's my fault that his brother is behaving like that. And here she narrowed her eyes, with an expression of satisfaction, as if what Marcello said were a compliment. Then she concluded: A lot of things have changed, Lenù, since you left; you should stay with us now; give me your phone number, we ought see each other as much as we can; and then I want to send you Gennaro, you have to see if you can help him.

She took a pen and got ready to write. I dictated the first two numbers right away, then I got confused, I had learned the number only a few days earlier and I couldn't remember it. When, however, it did come to mind precisely, I hesitated again, I was afraid she would come back and settle in my life; I dictated two more numbers, and got the other numbers wrong on purpose.

It was a good thing. Just as I was about to leave with the girls Lila asked me in front of everyone, including Dede and Elsa:

"Will you have a child with Nino?"

35.

Of course not, I responded, and laughed in embarrassment. But on the street I had to explain, to Elsa especially—Dede was grimly silent—that I would not have other children, they were my children and that was that. And for two days I had a headache, I couldn't sleep. A few deliberately placed words and Lila had disrupted an encounter that had seemed to me pleasant. I said to myself: There's nothing to be done, she's incurable, she always knows how to complicate my existence. And I wasn't alluding only to the anxieties she had unleashed in Dede and Elsa. Lila had struck with precision a point in myself that I kept carefully hidden and which had to do with the urge for motherhood I'd noticed for the first time a dozen years ago, when I had held little Mirko, in Mariarosa's house. It had been a completely irrational impulse, a sort of command of love, which at the time had overwhelmed me. I had intuited even then that it was not a simple wish to have a child, I wanted a particular child, a child like Mirko, a child of Nino's. And in fact that yearning had not been alleviated by Pietro and the conception of Dede and Elsa. Rather, it had reemerged recently, when I saw Silvia's child and, especially, when Nino had told me that Eleonora was pregnant. Now, with increasing frequency, it rummaged around in me, and Lila, with her usual acute gaze, *had seen* it. It's her favorite game—I said to myself—she does it with Enzo, with Carmen, with Antonio, with Alfonso. She must have behaved the same way with Michele Solara, with Gigliola. She pretends to be a kind and affectionate person, but then she gives you a slight nudge, she moves you a tiny bit, and she ruins you. She wants to go back to acting like that with me, and with Nino, too. She had managed to bring out into the open a secret tremor that in general I tried to ignore, as one ignores the twitching of an eyelid.

For days, in the house on Via Tasso, alone and in company, I was constantly agitated by the question: *Will you have a child with Nino?* But now it wasn't Lila's question, I asked it of myself.

36.

After that, I returned often to the neighborhood, especially when Pietro came to stay with the girls. I walked to Piazza

Amedeo, I took the metro. Sometimes I stopped on the railroad bridge and looked down on the *stradone*, sometimes I just went through the tunnel and walked to the church. But more often I went to fight with my mother, insisting that she go to a doctor, and I involved my father, Peppe, Gianni in that battle. She was a stubborn woman, she got angry at her husband and sons as soon as they alluded to her health problems. With me, it was always the same, she cried: Shut up, you're the one who's killing me, and she threw me out, or locked herself in the bathroom.

Lila instead had what it takes, and everyone knew it; Michele, for example, had realized it long ago. So Elisa's aversion toward her was due not only to some disagreement with Marcello but to the fact that Lila had yet again broken off from the Solaras and, after using them, had done well. Basic Sight was earning her a growing reputation for innovation and for profit. It was no longer a matter of the brilliant person who since she was a child had had the capacity to take the disorder from your head and heart to give it back to you well organized or, if she couldn't stand you, to confuse your ideas and leave you depressed. Now she also embodied the possibility of learning a new job, a job that no one knew anything about but was lucrative. The business was going so well—people said—that Enzo was looking for a space for a proper office and not the makeshift one that he had installed between the kitchen and the bedroom. But who was Enzo, clever though he might be? Only a subordinate of Lila. It was she who moved things, who made and unmade. So, to exaggerate just slightly, the situation in the neighborhood seemed in a short time to have become the following: you learned either to be like Marcello and Michele or to be like Lila.

Of course, it might be that it was my obsession, but in that phase, at least, I seemed increasingly to see her in all the people who had been or were close to her. Once, for example, I ran into Stefano Carracci, much heavier, his complexion yellowish, shabbily dressed. There was absolutely nothing left of the young shopkeeper Lila had married, least of all his money. And yet from the little conversation we had it seemed to me that he used many of his wife's phrases. And Ada, too, who at that point had great respect for Lila and said nice things about her, because of the money she gave Stefano, seemed to imitate her gestures, maybe even her way of laughing.

Relatives and friends crowded around her in search of a job, making an effort to appear suitable. Ada herself was hired out of the blue at Basic Sight, she was to begin by answering the telephone, then maybe she would learn other things. Rino, too—who one bad day had quarreled with Marcello and left the supermarket—inserted himself into his sister's activity without even asking permission, boasting that he could learn in no time all there was to learn. But the most unexpected news for me—Nino told me one night, he had heard it from Marisa—was that even Alfonso had ended up at Basic Sight. Michele Solara, who continued to act in a crazy way, had closed the shop in Piazza dei Martiri for no reason and Alfonso was left without a job. As a result now he, too—and successfully—was being retrained, thanks to Lila.

I could have found out more, and maybe I would have liked to, all I had to do was call her, stop by. But I never did. Once only I met her on the street and stopped reluctantly. She must have been offended that I had told her the wrong phone number, that I had offered to give lessons to her son and instead had disappeared, that she had done everything to reconcile with me and I had withdrawn. She said she was in a hurry, she asked in dialect:

"Are you still living on Via Tasso?"

"Yes."

"It's out of the way."

"It has a view of the sea."

"What's the sea, from up there? A bit of color. Better if

you're closer, that way you notice that there's filth, mud, piss, polluted water. But you who read and write books like to tell lies, not the truth."

I cut her short, I said:

"For now I'm there."

She cut me even shorter:

"One can always change. How many times do we say one thing and then do another? Take a place here."

I shook my head, I said goodbye. Was that what she wanted? To bring me back to the neighborhood?

37.

Then in my already complicated life two completely unexpected things happened at the same time. Nino's research institute was invited to New York for some important job and a tiny publishing house in Boston published my book. Those two events turned into a possible trip to the United States.

After endless hesitations, endless discussions, some quarrels, we decided to take that vacation. But I would have to leave Dede and Elsa for two weeks. Even under normal conditions I had a hard time making arrangements: I wrote for some journals, I did translations, I took part in debates in places large and small, I compiled notes for a new book, and to arrange for the children with all that hectic activity was always extremely difficult. In general I turned to Mirella, a student of Nino's, who was very reliable and didn't ask much, but if she wasn't available I left them with Antonella, a neighbor of around fifty, the competent mother of grown children. This time I tried to get Pietro to take them, but he said it was impossible just then to have them for so long. I examined the situation (I had no relationship with Adele, Mariarosa had left and

no one knew where she was, my mother was weakened by her
elusive illness, Elisa was increasingly hostile), and there didn't
seem to be an acceptable solution. It was Pietro who finally
said to me: Ask Lina, she left her son with you for months,
she's in your debt. I had a hard time making up my mind. The
more superficial part of me imagined that, although she had
showed that in spite of her work obligations she was available,
she would treat my daughters like fussy, demanding little dolls,
she would torment them, or leave them to Gennaro; while a
more hidden part, which perhaps upset me more than the first,
considered her the only person I knew who would devote herself entirely to making them comfortable. It was the urgency of
finding a solution that drove me to call her. To my tentative
and evasive request she responded without hesitation, as usual
surprising me:

"Your daughters are more than my daughters, bring them
to me whenever you like and go do your things as long as you
want."

Even though I had told her that I was going with Nino, she
never mentioned him, not even when, with all kinds of cau-
tions, I brought her the children. And so in May of 1980, consumed by misgivings and yet excited, I left for the United
States. It was an extraordinary experience. I felt again that I had
no limits, I was capable of flying over oceans, expanding over
the entire world: an exhilarating delirium. Naturally the two
weeks were very exhausting and very expensive. The women
who had published my book had no money and even though
they were generous I still spent a lot. As for Nino, he had trouble getting reimbursed even for his airplane ticket. Yet we were
happy. I, at least, have never been so happy as in those days.

When we got back I was sure I was pregnant. Already
before leaving for America I had had some suspicions, but I
hadn't said anything to Nino and for the entire vacation I had
savored the possibility in secret, with a heedless pleasure. But

when I went to get my daughters I had no more doubts and, feeling so literally full of life, I was tempted to confide in Lila. As usual, however, I gave up on the idea, I thought: She'll say something unpleasant, she'll remind me that I claimed I didn't want another child. I was radiant and Lila, as if my happiness had infected her, greeted me with an air that was no less content, she exclaimed: How beautiful you look. I gave her the gifts I had brought for her, for Enzo, and for Gennaro. I told her in detail about the cities I had seen, the encounters I'd had. From the plane, I said, I saw a piece of the Atlantic Ocean through a hole in the clouds. The people are very friendly, they're not reserved the way they are in Germany, or arrogant, as in France. Even if you speak English badly they listen to you with attention and make an effort to understand. In the restaurants everybody shouts, more than in Naples. If you compare the skyscraper on Corso Novara with the ones in Boston or New York, you realize it's not a skyscraper. The streets are numbered, they don't have the names of people everyone's forgotten by now. I never mentioned Nino, I didn't say anything about him and his work, I acted as if I had gone by myself. She listened attentively, she asked questions I wasn't able to answer, and then she praised my daughters sincerely, she said she had got on very well with them. I was pleased, and again I was on the point of telling her that I was expecting a child. But Lila didn't give me time, she whispered seriously: Lucky you're back, Lenù, I've just had some good news and it makes me happy to tell you first of all. She, too, was pregnant.

38.

Lila had dedicated herself to the children body and soul. And it could not have been easy to wake them in time in the morning, get them washed and dressed, give them a solid but

quick breakfast, take them to school in the Via Tasso neighborhood amid the morning chaos of the city, pick them up
punctually in that same turmoil, bring them back to the neighborhood, feed them, supervise their homework, and keep up
with her job, her domestic tasks. But, when I questioned Dede
and Elsa closely, it became clear that she had managed very
well. And now for them I was a more inadequate mother than
ever. I didn't know how to make pasta with tomato sauce the
way Aunt Lina did, I didn't know how to dry their hair and
comb it with the skill and gentleness she had, I didn't know
how to perform any task that Aunt Lina didn't approach with
a superior sensitivity, except maybe singing certain songs that
they loved and that she had admitted she didn't know. To this
it should be added that, especially in Dede's eyes, that marvelous woman whom I didn't visit often enough (*Mamma, why
don't we go see Aunt Lina, why don't you let us sleep at her
house more, don't you have to go away anymore?*) had a specific
quality that made her unequalled: she was the mother of
Gennaro, whom my older daughter usually called Rino, and
who seemed to her the most wonderful person of the male sex
in the world.

At the moment I was hurt. My relations with the children
were not wonderful and their idealization of Lila made things
worse. Once, at yet another criticism of me, I lost my patience,
I yelled: O.K., go to the market of mothers and buy another
one. That market was a game of ours that generally served to
alleviate conflicts and reconcile us. I would say: Sell me at the
market of mothers if I'm no good for you; and they would
answer, no, Mamma, we don't want to sell you, we like you the
way you are. On that occasion, however, maybe because of my
harsh tone, Dede answered: Yes, let's go right now, we can sell
you and buy Aunt Lina.

That was the atmosphere for a while. And certainly it wasn't
the best one for telling the children that I had lied to them. My

emotional state was complicated: shameless, shy, happy, anxious, innocent, guilty. And I didn't know where to begin, the conversation was difficult: children, I thought I didn't want another child, but I did, and in fact I'm pregnant, you'll have a little brother or maybe another sister, but the father isn't your father, the father is Nino, who already has a wife and two children, and I don't know how he'll take it. I thought about it, thought about it again, and put it off.

Then out of the blue came a conversation that surprised me. Dede, in front of Elsa, who listened in some alarm, said in the tone she took when she wanted to explain a problem full of perils:

"You know that Aunt Lina sleeps with Enzo, but they're not married?"

"Who told you?"

"Rino. Enzo isn't his father."

"Rino told you that, too?"

"Yes. So I asked Aunt Lina and she explained to me."

"What did she explain?"

She was tense. She observed me to see if she was making me angry.

"Shall I tell you?"

"Yes."

"Aunt Lina has a husband just as you do, and that husband is Rino's father, his name is Stefano Carracci. Then she has Enzo, Enzo Scanno, who sleeps with her. And the exact same thing happens with you: you have Papa, whose name is Airota, but you sleep with Nino, whose name is Sarratore."

I smiled to reassure her.

"How did you ever learn all those surnames?"

"Aunt Lina talked to us about it, she said that they're stupid. Rino came out of her stomach, he lives with her, but he's called Carracci like his father. We came out of your stomach, we live much more with you than with Papa, but we're called Airota."

"So?"

"Mamma, if someone talks about Aunt Lina's stomach he doesn't say this is Stefano Carracci's stomach, he says this is Lina Cerullo's stomach. The same goes for you: your stomach is Elena Greco's stomach, not Pietro Airota's."

"And what does that mean?"

"That it would be more correct for Rino to be called Rino Cerullo and us Dede and Elsa Greco."

"Is that your idea?"

"No, Aunt Lina's."

"What do you think?"

"I think the same thing."

"Yes?"

"Yes, absolutely."

But Elsa, since the atmosphere seemed favorable, tugged at me and intervened:

"It's not true, Mamma. She said that when she gets married she'll be called Dede Carracci."

Dede exclaimed furiously: "Shut up, you're a liar."

I turned to Elsa:

"Why Dede Carracci?"

"Because she wants to marry Rino."

I asked Dede:

"You like Rino?"

"Yes," she said in an argumentative tone, "and even if we don't get married I'll sleep with him just the same."

"With Rino?"

"Yes. Like Aunt Lina with Enzo. And also like you with Nino."

"Can she do that, Mamma?" Elsa asked, dubiously.

I didn't answer, I was evasive. But that exchange improved my mood and initiated a new phase. It didn't take much, in fact, to recognize that with this and other conversations about real and pretend fathers, about old and new last names, Lila

had managed to make the living situation into which I had cast
Dede and Elsa not only acceptable in their eyes but even interesting. In fact almost miraculously my daughters stopped talking about how they missed Adele and Mariarosa; they stopped
saying, when they returned from Florence, that they wanted to
go and stay forever with their father and Doriana; they stopped
making trouble for Mirella, the babysitter, as if she were their
worst enemy; they stopped rejecting Naples, the school, the
teachers, their classmates, and, above all, the fact that Nino
slept in my bed. In short, they seemed more serene. And I
noted those changes with relief. However vexing it might be
that Lila had entered the lives of my daughters, binding them
to her, the last thing I could accuse her of was not having given
them the utmost affection, the utmost care, assistance in reducing their anxieties. That was the Lila I loved. She could emerge
unexpectedly from within her very meanness, surprising me.
Suddenly every offense faded—*she's malicious, she always has
been, but she's also much more, you have to put up with her*—
and I acknowledged that she was helping me do less harm to
my daughters.

One morning I woke up and thought of her without hostility for the first time in a long while. I remembered when she
got married, her first pregnancy: she was sixteen, only seven or
eight years older than Dede. My daughter would soon be the
age of the ghosts of our girlhood. I found it inconceivable that
in a relatively small amount of time, my daughter could wear a
wedding dress, as Lila had, end up brutalized in a man's bed,
lock herself into the role of Signora Carracci; I found it equally
inconceivable that, as had happened to me, she could lie under
the heavy body of a grown man, at night, on the Maronti,
smeared with dark sand, damp air, and bodily fluids, just for
revenge. I remembered the thousands of odious things we had
gone through and I let the solidarity regain force. What a waste
it would be, I said to myself, to ruin our story by leaving too

much space for ill feelings: ill feelings are inevitable, but the essential thing is to keep them in check. I grew close to Lila again with the excuse that the children liked seeing her. Our pregnancies did the rest.

39.

But we were two very different pregnant women. My body reacted with eager acceptance, hers with reluctance. And yet from the beginning Lila emphasized that she had *wanted* that pregnancy, she said, laughing: I planned it. Yet there was something in her body that, as usual, put up resistance. Thus while I immediately felt as if a sort of rose-colored light flickered inside me, she became greenish, the whites of her eyes turned yellow, she detested certain smells, she threw up continuously. What should I do, she said, I'm happy, but that thing in my belly isn't, it's mad at me. Enzo denied it, he said: Come on, he's happier than anyone. And according to Lila, who made fun of him, he meant: I put it in there, trust me, I saw that it's good and you mustn't worry.

When I ran into Enzo I felt more liking for him than usual, more admiration. It was as if to his old pride a new one had been added, which was manifested in a vastly increased desire to work and, at the same time, in a vigilance at home, in the office, on the street, all aimed at defending his companion from physical and metaphysical dangers and anticipating her every desire. He took on the task of giving Stefano the news; he didn't blink, he half grimaced and withdrew, maybe because by now the old grocery made almost nothing and the subsidies he got from his ex-wife were essential, maybe because every connection between him and Lila must have seemed to him a very old story, what did it matter to him if she was pregnant, he had other problems, other desires.

But, mainly, Enzo took on the job of telling Gennaro. Lila in fact had reasons to feel embarrassment with her son that were no different from mine—but certainly more justified— for feeling embarrassed with Dede and Elsa. Gennaro wasn't a child and childish tones and words couldn't be used with him. He was a boy in the full crisis of puberty who couldn't find an equilibrium. Failed twice in a row in high school, he had become hypersensitive, unable to hold back tears, or emerge from his humiliation. He spent days wandering the streets or in his father's grocery, sitting in a corner, picking at the pimples on his broad face and studying Stefano in every gesture and expression, without saying a word.

He'll take it really badly, Lila worried, but meanwhile she was afraid that someone else would tell him, Stefano for exam- ple. So one evening Enzo took him aside and told him about the pregnancy. Gennaro was impassive, Enzo urged him: Go hug your mother, let her know that you love her. The boy obeyed. But a few days later Elsa asked me in secret:

"Mamma, what's a tramp?"

"A beggar."

"You're sure?"

"Yes."

"Rino told Dede that Aunt Lina is a tramp."

Problems, in other words. I didn't talk to Lila about it, that seemed pointless. And then I had my own difficulties: I couldn't bring myself to tell Pietro, I couldn't tell the children, mainly I couldn't tell Nino. I was sure that when Pietro found out I was pregnant he would be resentful, even though he now had Doriana, and would turn to his parents, would induce his mother to make trouble for me in every way possible. I was sure that Dede and Elsa would become hostile again. But my real worry was Nino. I hoped that the birth of the child would bind him definitively to me. I hoped that Eleonora, once she found out about that new fatherhood, would leave him. But it was a feeble hope, usually fear predominated. Nino had told me clearly: he preferred that double life—even though it caused all sorts of problems, anxieties, tensions—to the trauma of an absolute break with his wife. I was afraid he would ask me to have an abortion. So every day I was on the point of telling him and every day I said to myself: No, better tomorrow.

Instead everything began to sort itself out. One night I telephoned Pietro and told him: I'm pregnant. There was a long silence, he cleared his throat, he said softly that he expected it. He asked:

"Have you told the children?"

"No."

"Do you want me to tell them?"

"No."

"Be careful."

"All right."

That was it. He began to call more often. His tone was affectionate, he was worried about how the girls would react, he offered every time to talk to them about it. But in the end it was neither of us. It was Lila, who, although she had refused to tell her own son, convinced Dede and Elsa that it would be a wonderful thing to occupy themselves, when the time came, with the funny live doll that I had made with Nino and not with their father. They took it well. Since Aunt Lina had called it a doll, they began to use the same word. They were interested in my stomach, and every morning when they woke up they asked, Mamma, how's the doll?

Between telling Pietro and telling the girls, I finally confronted Nino. It went like this. One afternoon when I felt especially anxious I went to see Lila to complain, and asked her:

"What if he wants me to have an abortion?"

"Well," she said, "then everything becomes perfectly clear."

"What's clear?"

"That his wife and children come first, then you."

Direct, brutal. Lila hid many things from me, but not her aversion to my union. I wasn't sorry, in fact I knew that it did me good to speak explicitly. In the end she had said what I didn't dare say to myself, that Nino's reaction would provide proof of the solidity of our bond. I muttered something like: It's possible, we'll see. When, soon afterward, Carmen arrived with her children, and Lila drew her, too, into the conversation, the afternoon became like afternoons of our adolescence. We confided in each other, we plotted, we planned. Carmen got mad, she said that if Nino was opposed she was ready to go and speak to him in person. And she added: I don't understand how it's possible, Lenù, that a person at your level can let someone walk all over you. I tried to justify myself and to justify my companion. I said that his in-laws had helped and were helping him, that everything Nino and I could afford was possible only because, thanks to his wife's family, he had a good income. I admitted that, with what I got from my books and from Pietro, the girls and I would have a hard time scraping by in a respectable way. And I added: Don't get the wrong idea, though, Nino is very affectionate, he sleeps at my house at least four times a week, he has always avoided humiliating me in any way, when he can he takes care of Dede and Elsa as if they were his. But as soon as I stopped speaking Lila almost ordered me:

"Then tell him tonight."

I obeyed. I went home and when he arrived we had dinner, I put the children to bed, and finally I told him that I was pregnant. There was a very long moment, then he hugged me, kissed me, he was very happy. I whispered with relief: I've known for a while, but I was afraid you would be angry. He reproached me, and said something that amazed me: We have to go with Dede and Elsa to my parents and give them this good news, too—my mother will be pleased. He wanted in that way to sanction our union, he wanted to make his new

paternity official. I gave a halfhearted sign of agreement, then
I said:

"But you'll tell Eleonora?"

"It's none of her business."

"You're still her husband."

"It's pure form."

"You'll have to give your name to our child."

"I'll do it."

I became agitated.

"No, Nino, you won't do it, you'll pretend it's nothing, as
you've done up to now."

"Aren't you happy with me?"

"I'm very happy."

"Do I neglect you?"

"No. But *I* left my husband, *I* came to live in Naples, *I*
changed my life from top to bottom. *You* instead still have
yours, and it's intact."

"My life is you, your children, this child who's about to
arrive. The rest is a necessary background."

"Necessary to whom? To you? Certainly not to me."

He hugged me tight, he whispered:

"Have faith."

The next day I called Lila and said to her: Everything's fine,
Nino was really happy.

40.

Complicated weeks followed; I often thought that if my
body hadn't reacted with such delighted naturalness to pregnancy, if I had been in Lila's state of continuous physical suffering, I wouldn't have held up. My publisher, after much
resistance, finally brought out Nino's collection of essays,
and I—continuing to imitate Adele, in spite of our terrible

relationship—took on the job of persuading both the few prominent people I knew to cover it in the newspapers, and the many, very many, he knew, but out of pride refused to telephone. Around at the same time, Pietro's book also was published, and he brought a copy to me himself when he came to Naples to see his daughters. He waited anxiously while I read the dedication (embarrassing: *to Elena, who taught me to love with suffering*), we were both excited, he invited me to a celebration in his honor in Florence. I had to go, if only to bring the children. But then I was forced to face not only the open hostility of my in-laws but also, before and after, Nino's agitation: he was jealous of every contact with Pietro, angry about the dedication, surly because I had said that my ex-husband's book was really good and was talked about with great respect within the academic world and outside it, unhappy because his volume was going completely unnoticed.

How exhausting our relationship was, and how many hazards were concealed in every gesture, in every sentence that I uttered, that he uttered. He didn't even want to hear Pietro's name, he darkened if I recalled Franco, he became jealous if I laughed too much with some friend of his, yet he found it completely normal to divide himself between me and his wife. A couple of times I ran into him on Via Filangieri with Eleonora and the two children: the first time they pretended not to see me, and kept going; the second I stopped in front of them with a warm smile, I said a few words referring to my pregnancy, even though it wasn't visible, I went off in a rage, with my heart pounding in my throat. When, later, he reproached me for what he called a needlessly provocative attitude, we quarreled (*I didn't tell her that you're the father: all I said was I'm pregnant*), I threw him out of the house, I welcomed him back.

At those moments I saw myself suddenly for what I was: a slave, willing to always do what he wanted, careful not to exaggerate in order not to get him in trouble, not to displease him.

I wasted my time cooking for him, washing the dirty clothes he left in the house, listening to all his troubles at the university and in the many responsibilities that he was accumulating, thanks to the aura of good feeling that surrounded him and the small powers of his father-in-law; I always welcomed him joyfully, I wanted him to be happier with me than in the other house, I wanted him to relax, to confide, I felt sorry that he was continuously overwhelmed by obligations; I even wondered if Eleonora might love him more than I did, since she accepted every insult just to feel that he was still hers. But sometimes I couldn't stand it anymore and I yelled at him, despite the risk that the girls might hear: Who am I for you, tell me why I'm in this city, why I wait for you every night, why I tolerate this situation.

He became frightened and begged me to calm down. It was probably to show me that I—I alone—was his wife, and Eleonora had no importance in his life, that he really wanted to take me to lunch one Sunday at his parents', in their house on Via Nazionale. I didn't know how to say no. The day passed slowly and the mood was one of affection. Lidia, Nino's mother, was an old woman, worn down by weariness; her eyes seemed terrified not by the external world but by a threat she felt from within. As for Pino, Clelia, and Ciro, whom I had known as children, they were adults, who studied, who worked, Clelia had recently gotten married. Soon Marisa and Alfonso arrived with their children, and the lunch began. There were innumerable courses, and it lasted from two in the afternoon until six at night, in an atmosphere of forced gaiety, but also of sincere feeling. Lidia, especially, treated me as if I were her real daughter-in-law, she wanted to keep me beside her, she complimented my daughters, and congratulated me for the child I carried in my womb.

Naturally the only source of tension was Donato. Seeing him after twenty years made an impression on me. He wore a dark blue smoking jacket, and on his feet brown slippers. He was as if shrunken and broadened, he kept waving his stubby hands, with their dark age spots and a blackish arc of dirt under the nails. His face seemed to have spread over the bones, his gaze was opaque. He covered his bald crown with his sparse hair, dyed a vaguely reddish color, and when he smiled the spaces where the teeth were missing showed. At first he tried to assume his former attitude of a man of the world, and he kept staring at my bosom, and made allusive remarks. Then he began to complain: Nothing is in its place, the Ten Commandments have been abolished, women, who can restrain them, it's all a whorehouse. But his children shut him up, ignored him, and he was silent. After lunch he drew Alfonso into a corner—so refined, so delicate, as good-looking in my eyes as Lila and more—to indulge his craving to be the center of attention. Every so often I looked, incredulous, at that old man, I thought: it's not possible that I, I as a girl, at the Maronti was with that foul man, it can't really have happened. Oh, my God, look at him: bald, slovenly, his obscene glances, next to my so deliberately feminine classmate, a young woman in male clothes. And I in the same room with him, so very different from the me of Ischia. What time is *now*, what time was *then*.

At a certain point Donato called me over, he said politely, Lenù. And Alfonso, too, insisted with a gesture, a look, that I join them. I went to their corner uneasily. Donato began to praise me loudly, as if he were speaking to a vast audience: This woman is a great scholar, a writer who has no equal anywhere in the world; I'm proud to have known her as a girl; at Ischia, when she came to vacation at our house she was a child, she discovered literature through her interest in my poor verses, she read my book before going to sleep:—isn't it true, Lenù?

He looked at me uncertainly, suddenly a supplicant. His eyes pleaded with me to confirm the role of his words in my literary vocation. And I said yes, it's true, as a girl I couldn't believe that I knew personally someone who had written a book of poetry and whose thoughts were printed in the newspaper. I thanked him for the review that a dozen years earlier he had given my first book, I said it had been very useful. And Donato turned red with joy, he took off, he began to celebrate himself and at the same time to complain that the envy of mediocrities had kept him from becoming known as he deserved. Nino had to intervene, and roughly. He brought me over to his mother again.

On the street he reproached me, saying: You know what my father's like, there's no need to encourage him. I nodded, and meanwhile I looked at him out of the corner of my eye. Would Nino lose his hair? Would he get fat? Would he utter rancorous words against those who had been more fortunate? He was so good-looking now, I didn't even want to think about it. He was saying of his father: he can't resign himself, the older he gets the worse he is.

41.

During that same period my sister, after endless anxieties and protests, gave birth. She had a boy whom she named Silvio, after Marcello's father. Since our mother was still not well I tried to help Elisa. She was white with exhaustion and terrified by the newborn. Seeing her son all smeared with blood and liquids had given her the impression of a small body in its death throes and she was disgusted. But Silvio was all too alive, he wailed desperately with clenched fists. And she didn't know how to hold him, how to bathe him, how to take care of the wound from the umbilical cord, how to cut his nails. Even the fact that he was a male repulsed her. I tried to instruct her, but it didn't last long. Marcello, always rather clumsy, treated me immediately with an apprehension beneath which I perceived annoyance, as if my presence in the house complicated his day. And Elisa, too, instead of being grateful, appeared annoyed by everything I said, by my very generosity. Every day I said to myself: that's it, I have so many things to do, tomorrow I won't go. But I kept going, until events decided for me.

Terrible events. One morning when I was at my sister's house—it was very hot and the neighborhood was dozing in the burning-hot dust; several days earlier the station in Bologna had been blown up—a phone call came from Peppe: our mother had fainted in the bath. I hurried to her, she was in a cold sweat, trembling, she had an unbearable pain in her stomach. Finally I managed to make her see a doctor. Tests of various sorts followed and in a short time a serious illness was diagnosed, an evasive term that I learned to use immediately. The neighborhood resorted to it whenever the problem was cancer and the doctors did the same. They translated their diagnosis into a similar formula, maybe just a little more refined: the illness, rather than serious, was *inexorable*.

My father at that news immediately fell apart, he couldn't tolerate the situation, and became depressed. My brothers, their expressions vaguely dazed, their complexions pasty, hovered for a while with an air of wanting to help, and then, absorbed day and night by their mysterious jobs, disappeared, leaving money, which was needed for doctors and medicines. As for my sister, she stayed in her house, frightened, untidy, in her nightgown, ready to stick a nipple in Silvio's mouth if he merely hinted at a wail. Thus, in the fourth month of my pregnancy, the full weight of my mother's illness fell on me.

I wasn't sorry, I wanted my mother to understand, even if she had always tormented me, that I loved her. I became very active: I involved both Nino and Pietro, asking them to direct me to the best doctors; I took her to the various luminaries; I stayed with her in the hospital when she had an urgent operation, when she was discharged. I took care of everything once I brought her home.

The heat was unbearable, and I was constantly worried. While my stomach began to swell happily and in it grew a heart different from the one in my breast, I daily observed, with sorrow, my mother's decline. I was moved by her clinging to me in order not to get lost, the way I, a small child, had clung to her hand. The frailer and more frightened she became, the prouder I was of keeping her alive.

At first she was as ill-tempered as usual. Whatever I said, she always objected with rude refusals, there was nothing she didn't claim to be able to do without me. The doctor? She wanted to see him alone. The hospital? She wanted to go alone. The treatments? She wanted to take care of them alone. I don't need anything, she grumbled, get out, you only bother me. Yet she got angry if I was just a minute late (*Since you had other things to do it was pointless to tell me you were coming*); she insulted me if I wasn't ready to bring her immediately what she asked for and she would set off with her limping gait to show me that I was worse than Sleeping Beauty, that she was much more energetic than I (*There, there, who are you thinking about, your head's not there, Lenù, if I wait for you I'll get cold*); she criticized me fiercely for being polite to doctors and nurses, hissing, *If you don't spit in their faces, those pieces of shit don't give a damn about you, they only help if they're scared of you.* But meanwhile inside her something was changing. Often she was frightened by her own agitation. She moved as if she feared that the floor might open beneath her feet. Once when I surprised her in front of the mirror—she looked at herself often, with a curiosity she had never had—she asked me, in embarrassment, do you remember when I was young? Then, as if there were a connection, she insisted—returning to her old violence—that I swear I wouldn't take her to the hospital again, that I wouldn't let her die alone in a ward. Her eyes filled with tears.

What worried me most was that she became emotional

easily: she had never been that way. She was moved if I mentioned Dede, if she suspected that my father had no clean
socks, if she spoke of Elisa struggling with her baby, if she
looked at my growing stomach, if she remembered the countryside that had once extended all around the houses of the
neighborhood. With the illness there came, in other words, a
weakness she hadn't had before, and that weakness lessened
her anxiety, transformed it into a capricious suffering that frequently brought tears to her eyes. One afternoon she burst out
crying because she had thought of Maestra Oliviero, although
she had always detested her. You remember, she said, how she
insisted that you take the test for admission to middle school?
And the tears poured down without restraint. Ma, I said, calm
down, what's there to cry about? It shocked me seeing her so
desperate for nothing, I wasn't used to it. She, too, shook her
head, incredulous, she laughed and cried, she laughed to let
me know that she didn't know what there was to cry about.

42.

It was this frailty that slowly opened the way to an intimacy
we had never shared. At first she was ashamed of being ill. If
my father or my brothers or Elisa and Silvio were present at a
moment of weakness she hid in the bathroom, and when they
urged her tactfully (*Ma, how do you feel, open the door*) she
wouldn't open it, she answered inevitably: I'm fine, what do
you want, why don't you leave me in peace in the bathroom, at
least. With me, on the other hand, out of the blue, she let go,
she decided to show me her sufferings unashamedly.

It began one morning, at her house, when she told me why
she was lame. She did it spontaneously, with no preamble. The
angel of death, she said proudly, touched me when I was a
child, with the exact same illness as now, but I screwed him,

even though I was just a girl. And you'll see, I'll screw him again, because I know how to suffer—I learned at the age of ten, I haven't stopped since—and if you know how to suffer the angel respects you, after a while he goes away. As she spoke she pulled up her dress and showed me the injured leg like the relic of an old battle. She smacked it, observing me with a fixed half-smile on her lips and terrified eyes.

From then on her periods of bitter silence diminished and those of uninhibited confidences increased. Sometimes she said embarrassing things. She revealed that she had never been with any man but my father. She revealed with coarse obscenities that my father was perfunctory, she couldn't remember if sleeping with him had ever truly given her pleasure. She revealed that she had always loved him and that she still did, but as a brother. She revealed that the only good thing in her life was the moment I came out of her belly, I, her first child. She revealed that the worst sin she had committed—a sin for which she would go to Hell—was that she had never felt attached to her other children, she had considered them a punishment, and still did so. She revealed finally, without circumlocutions, that her only true child was me. When she said this—I remember that we were at the hospital for an examination—her distress was such that she wept even more than usual. She whispered: I worried only about you, always, the others for me were stepchildren; so I deserve the disappointment you've given me, what a blow, Lenù, what a blow, you shouldn't have left Pietro, you shouldn't have gone with Sarratore's son, he's worse than the father, an honest man who is married, who has two children, doesn't take someone else's wife.

I defended Nino. I tried to reassure her, I told her that there was divorce now, that we would both get divorced and then would marry. She listened without interrupting me. She had almost completely used up the energy with which she once rebelled, and insisted on being right, and now she confined herself to shaking her head. She was skin and bones, pale, if she contradicted me she did it with the slow voice of despair.

"When? Where? Must I watch you become worse than me?"

"No, Ma, don't worry, I'll move forward."

"I don't believe it anymore, Lenù, you've come to a halt."

"You'll see, I'll make you happy, we'll all make you happy, my siblings and I."

"I abandoned your brothers and sister and I'm ashamed."

"It's not true. Elisa has everything she wants, and Peppe and Gianni work, have money, what more do you want?"

"I want to fix things. I gave all three of them to Marcello and I was wrong."

Like that, in a low voice. She was inconsolable, she sketched a picture that surprised me. Marcello is more criminal than Michele, she said, he pulled my children into the mud, he seems the better of the two but it's not true. He had changed Elisa, who now felt more Solara than Greco and was on his side in everything. She talked for hours, whispering, as if we were waiting our turn not in the ugly, crowded waiting room of one of the best hospitals in the city but in some place where Marcello lurked nearby. I tried to make light of it, to calm her, illness and old age were making her exaggerate. You worry too much, I said. She answered: I worry because I know and you don't, ask Lina if you don't believe me.

It was here, on the wave of those melancholy words describing how the neighborhood had changed for the worse (*We were better off when Don Achille Carracci was in charge*), that she began to talk about Lila with an even more marked approval than before. Lila was the only one capable of putting things in order in the neighborhood. Lila was capable of harnessing the good and, even more, the bad. Lila knew everything, even the most terrible acts, but she never condemned you, she understood that anyone can make a mistake, herself first of all, and so she helped you. Lila appeared to her as a kind of holy warrior who spread avenging light over the *stradone*, the gardens, amid the old buildings and the new.

As I listened it seemed to me that now I counted, in her eyes, only because of my relationship with the neighborhood's new authority. She described the friendship between me and Lila as a useful friendship, which I ought to cultivate forever, and I immediately understood why.

"Do me a favor," she said, "talk to her and to Enzo, see if they can take your brothers off the street, see if they can hire them."

I smiled at her, I smoothed a lock of gray hair. She claimed she had never taken care of her other children, meanwhile, bent over, hands trembling, nails white as she clutched my arm, she worried about them most of all. She wanted to take them away from the Solaras and give them to Lila. It was her way of remedying a tactical mistake in the war between the desire to do harm and the desire to do good in which she had been engaged forever. Lila, I observed, seemed to her the incarnation of the desire to do good.

"Mamma," I said, "I'll do everything you want, but Peppe and Gianni, even if Lina would take them—and I don't think she would, they'd need to study there—would never go to work for her, they earn more with the Solaras."

She nodded bleakly, but insisted:

"Try anyhow. You've been away and you're not well informed, but here everyone knows how Lina put down Michele. And now that she's pregnant, you'll see, she'll become stronger. The day she makes up her mind to, she'll crush both of the Solaras."

43.

The months of pregnancy passed quickly for me, in spite of my worries, and very slowly for Lila. We couldn't avoid noting that the feelings of expecting were very different for each of us. I said things like I'm *already* at the fourth month, she said things like I'm *only* at the fourth month. Of course, Lila's complexion soon improved, her features softened. But our bodies, although undergoing the same process of reproducing life, continued to experience the phases in different ways, mine with active collaboration, hers with dull resignation. And even the people we dealt with were surprised at how time hurried along for me and dragged for her.

I remember that one Sunday we were walking along Toledo with the children and we ran into Gigliola. That encounter was important; it was disturbing to me and proved that Lila really had had something to do with Michele Solara's crazy behavior. Gigliola was wearing heavy makeup but she was shabbily dressed, her hair was uncombed, she flaunted her uncontainable breasts and hips, her broad buttocks. She seemed happy to see us, she wouldn't let us go. She made a fuss over Dede and Elsa, she dragged us to Gambrinus, she ordered all sorts of things, both salty and sweet, and ate greedily. She soon forgot about my children, and they her: when she began to tell us in detail, in a very loud voice, about all the wrongs Michele had done to her, they got bored and, curious, went off to explore the restaurant.

Gigliola couldn't accept the way she had been treated. He's a beast, she said. He went so far as to shout at her: Don't just threaten to do it, kill yourself for real, jump off the balcony, die. Or he thought he could fix everything with no concern for her feelings, sticking in her bosom and in her pocket hundreds of thousands of lire. She was furious, she was desperate. She recounted—turning to me, because I had been away for a long time and wasn't up to date—that her husband had thrown her out of the house on Posillipo, kicking and hitting her, that he had sent her to live, with the children in the old neighborhood, in two dark rooms. But the moment she began to wish on Michele all the most atrocious diseases she could think of and a terrible death, she switched listeners, and addressed herself exclusively to Lila. I was amazed, she spoke to her as if she could help her make the curses effective, she considered her an ally. You did well, she said excitedly, to make him pay dearly for your work and then quit. In fact, even better if you screwed him out of some money. Lucky you, you know how to treat him, you have to keep making him bleed. She screamed: What he can't bear is that you don't care, he can't accept that the less you see him the better off you are, well done, well done, make him go nuts for good, make him die cursed.

At that point she drew a sigh of false relief. She remembered our two pregnant bellies, she wanted to touch them. She placed her broad hand almost on my pubic bone, she asked what month I was in. As soon as I said the fourth she exclaimed: No way you're already in the fourth. Of Lila, on the other hand, she said, suddenly unfriendly: There are women who never give birth, they want to keep the child inside forever, you're one of those. It was pointless to remind her that we were in the same month, that we would both give birth in January of the following year. She shook her head, she said to Lila: Just think, I was sure you'd already had it. And she added, with an incoherent note of pain: The more Michele sees you with that belly, the more he suffers; so make it last a long time, you can manage, stick it in front of him, let him drop dead. Then she announced that she had very urgent things to do, but meanwhile she repeated two or three times that we ought to see each other more often (*Let's reestablish the group from when we were girls, ah, how nice it was, we should have said fuck off to all those shits and thought only of ourselves*). She didn't even wave goodbye to the children, who were now play-ing outside, and she went off after making some obscene remarks to the waiter, laughing.

"She's an idiot," Lila said, sulkily. "What's wrong with my stomach?"

"Nothing."

"And me?"

"Nothing, don't worry."

44.

It was true, nothing was wrong with Lila: nothing new. She remained the same restless creature with an irresistible force of attraction, and that force made her special. Every one of her affairs, for better or for worse (how she was reacting to the pregnancy, what she had done to Michele and how she had subdued him, how she was asserting herself in the neighbor-hood), continued to seem to us more intense than ours, and it was for that reason that time for her seemed to move slowly. I saw her frequently, above all because my mother's illness brought me to the neighborhood. But with a new sense of bal-ance. Maybe because of my public persona, maybe because of all my private troubles, I felt more mature than Lila by now, and I was increasingly convinced that I could welcome her back into my life, acknowledging her fascination without suf-fering from it.

In those months I rushed frantically here and there, but the days flew by; paradoxically I felt light even when I crossed the city to take my mother to a doctor's appointment in the hospi-tal. If I didn't know what to do with the children I turned to Carmen, or sometimes even Alfonso, who had telephoned me often to tell me I could count on him. But naturally the person in whom I had the most confidence, the one whom Dede and

Elsa went to most willingly, was Lila, although she was always
burdened by work and exhausted by pregnancy. The differences between my belly and hers were increasing. I had a
large, wide stomach, which seemed to expand sideways rather
than forward; she had a small stomach, squeezed between narrow hips, sticking out like a ball that was about to tumble out
of her lap.

As soon as I told Nino about my condition, he took me to
a gynecologist who was the wife of a colleague, and since I
liked the doctor—very skilled, very available, very different in
manner and perhaps also in competence from the gruff doctors in Florence—I had told Lila about her enthusiastically and
urged her to come with me at least once, to try. Now we went
together for our examinations, and had arranged to see her at
the same time: when it was my turn, she stood quietly in a corner, and when it was her turn, I held her hand, because doctors still made her nervous. But the best part was in the waiting room. In those moments I forgot about my mother's
suffering and we became girls again. We liked sitting next to
each other, I fair, she dark, I calm, she anxious, I likable, she
malicious, the two of us opposite and united, and separate
from the other pregnant women, whom we observed ironically.

It was a rare hour of joy. Once, thinking of the tiny creatures who were defining themselves in our bodies, I remembered when—sitting next to each other in the courtyard, as we
were now in the waiting room—we played at being mothers
with our dolls. Mine was called Tina, hers Nu. She had
thrown Tina into the shadows of the cellar and I, out of spite,
had done the same with Nu. Do you remember, I asked. She
seemed bewildered, she had the faint smile of someone struggling to recapture a memory. Then, when I whispered to her,
with a laugh, how fearful we were, how bold, climbing up to
the door of the terrible Don Achille Carracci, the father of her
future husband, and accusing him of the theft of our dolls, she

began to find it funny, we laughed like idiots, disturbing the inhabited stomachs of the other patients, who were more sedate.

We stopped only when the nurse called us, Cerullo and Greco: we had both given the surnames we had had as girls. She was a large good-humored woman, who never failed to say to Lila, touching her stomach, There's a boy in here; and to me, Here's a girl. Then she showed us in and I whispered to Lila: I already have two girls, if you really have a boy will you give it to me: and she replied, Yes, let's do an exchange, no problem.

The doctor always found us in good health, the tests were excellent, everything was going smoothly. Or rather—since she focused her attention on our weight, and Lila remained as usual very thin while I tended to get fat—at every examination she judged that Lila was healthier than me. And although we both had many worries, on those occasions we were almost always happy to have found again, at the age of thirty-six, a pathway to affection: though distant in every way we were still close.

But when I went back up to Via Tasso and she hurried to the neighborhood, the gap that we put between us made other gaps conspicuous. This new solidarity was undoubtedly real. We liked being together, it lightened our lives. But there was one unequivocal fact: I told her almost everything about myself, she said almost nothing about herself. While I couldn't not tell her about my mother, or an article that I was writing, or problems with Dede and Elsa, or even about my situation as a lover-wife (it was enough not to specify the lover-wife of whom, not to utter the name of Nino too often; otherwise I could confide freely), when she talked about herself, her parents, her siblings, Rino, the anxieties Gennaro caused her, our friends and acquaintances, Enzo, Michele and Marcello Solara, the entire neighborhood, she was vague, she didn't seem to trust me completely. Evidently I remained the one who had gone away, and who, even though I had returned, now had

another view, lived in upper-class Naples, could not be fully
welcomed back.

45.

That I had a sort of double identity was true. Up on Via
Tasso Nino brought me his educated friends, who treated me
with respect, loved my second book in particular, wanted me to
look at what they were working on. We talked late into the
night with an attitude of worldliness. We wondered if there was
still a proletariat or not, we alluded to the socialist left and, with
bitterness, to the Communists (*They're more cops than the cops
and the priests*), we argued about the governability of an increasingly depleted country, some boldly used drugs, we were sarcastic about a new illness that everyone thought was an exaggeration of Pope John Paul II's to block the free expression of
sexuality in all its possible versions.

But I wasn't confined to Via Tasso; I moved around, I didn't
want to be a prisoner of Naples. I often went to Florence with
the children. Pietro, who had long since broken politically with
his father, was now—unlike Nino, who was growing closer to
the socialists—openly Communist. I stayed a few hours, listening to him in silence. He sang the praises of the competent honesty of his party, he cited the problems of the university, he
informed me of the success his book was having among academics, especially the English and Americans. Then I set off
again. I left the girls with him and Doriana and went to Milan,
to the publisher, in particular to oppose the campaign of deni-
gration in which Adele was persisting. My mother-in-law—the
director himself had reported, one evening when he took me to
dinner—did not miss any opportunity to say bad things about
me and was labeling me with the reputation of a fickle and unreliable person. As a result I tried to be engaging with everyone I

happened to meet at the publisher's. I made sophisticated conversation, I was agreeable to every request from the publicity
department, I claimed to the editor that my new book was at a
good point, even though I hadn't even started it. Then I set off
again, stopped to get the children, and slipped into Naples,
readjusting to the chaotic traffic, to the endless transactions to
obtain each thing that was mine by right, to exhausting and
quarrelsome lines, to the struggle to assert myself, to the permanent anxiety of going with my mother to doctors, hospitals, labs
for tests. The result was that on Via Tasso and throughout Italy
I felt like a woman with a small reputation, whereas in Naples,
especially in the neighborhood, I lost my refinement, no one
knew anything about my second book, if injustices enraged me
I moved into dialect and the coarsest insults.

The only bond between high and low seemed to me blood.
There was more and more killing, in the Veneto, in Lombardy,
in Emilia, in Lazio, in Campania. I glanced at the newspaper in
the morning and sometimes the neighborhood seemed more
tranquil than the rest of Italy. It wasn't true, of course, the violence was the same. Men fought with each other, women were
beaten, people were murdered for obscure reasons. Sometimes, even among the people I loved, the tension rose and
tones became threatening. But I was treated with respect.
Toward me there was the benevolence that is shown to a guest
who is welcomed but mustn't stick her nose into matters she's
not familiar with. And in fact I felt like an external observer,
with inadequate information. I constantly had the impression
that Carmen or Enzo or others knew much more than I did,
that Lila told them secrets that she didn't reveal to me.

One afternoon I was with the children in the office of Basic
Sight—three little rooms from whose windows you could see
the entrance to our elementary school—and, knowing I was
there, Carmen also stopped by. I alluded to Pasquale out of
sympathy, out of affection, even though I imagined him now as

a fighter on the run, ever more deeply involved in infamous crimes. I wanted to know if there was news, but it seemed to me that both Carmen and Lila stiffened, as if I had said something reckless. They didn't avoid it, on the contrary, we talked for a long time about him, or rather we let Carmen go on about her anxieties. But I had the impression that for some reason they had decided that they couldn't say more to me.

Two or three times I also ran into Antonio. Once he was with Lila, another, I think, with Lila, Carmen, and Enzo. It struck me how the friendship among them had solidified again, and it seemed surprising that he, a henchman of the Solaras, behaved as if he had changed masters, he seemed to be working for Lila and Enzo. Of course, we had all known each other since we were children, but I felt it wasn't a question of old habits. The four of them, on seeing me, behaved as if they had met by chance, and it wasn't true, I perceived a sort of secret pact that they didn't intend to extend to me. Did it have to do with Pasquale? With the operations of the business? With the Solaras? I don't know. Antonio said only, on one of those occasions, but absentmindedly: you're very pretty with that belly. Or at least that's the only remark of his that I remember.

Was it distrust? I don't think so. At times I thought that, because of my *respectable* identity, I had lost, especially in Lila's eyes, the capacity to understand and so she wanted to protect me from moves that I might in my ignorance misunderstand.

46.

Yet something wasn't right. It was a sensation of indeterminacy, which I felt even when everything appeared explicit and it seemed only one of Lila's old childish diversions: to orchestrate situations in which she let you perceive that under the facts there was something else.

One morning—again at Basic Sight—I exchanged a few words with Rino, whom I hadn't seen for many years. He seemed unrecognizable. He was thin, his eyes were dull, he greeted me with exaggerated affection, he even touched me as if I were made of rubber. He talked a lot of nonsense about computers, about the great business affairs he managed. Then suddenly he changed, he was seized by a kind of asthma attack, and for no evident reason he began, in a low voice, to rail against his sister. I said: Calm down, and wanted to get him a glass of water, but he stopped me in front of Lila's closed door and disappeared as if he were afraid that she would reprimand him.

I knocked and went in. I asked her warily if her brother was sick. She had an expression of irritation, she said: You know what he's like. I nodded yes, I thought of Elisa, I said that with siblings things aren't always straightforward. Meanwhile I thought of Peppe and Gianni, I said my mother was worried about them, she wanted to get them away from Marcello Solara and had asked me to see if she had any way of giving them a job. But those phrases—*get them away from Marcello Solara, give them a job*—made her narrow her eyes, she looked at me as if she wanted to know how far my knowledge when it came to meaning of the words I had uttered. Since she must have decided that I didn't know their real meaning, she said bitterly: I can't take them here, Lenù; Rino's already enough, not to mention the risks that Gennaro runs. At first I didn't know how to answer. *Gennaro, my brothers, hers, Marcello Solara.* I returned to the subject, but she retreated, she talked about other things.

That evasiveness happened later in the case of Alfonso, too. He now worked for Lila and Enzo, but not like Rino, who hung around there without a job. Alfonso had become very good, they sent him to the companies they consulted for to collect data. The bond between him and Lila, however, immediately seemed to me much stronger than anything to do with work. It wasn't the attraction-repulsion that Alfonso had confessed to me in the past but something more. There was on his part a need—I don't know how to put it—not to lose sight of her. It was a singular relationship, based on a secret flow that, moving from her, remodeled him. I was soon convinced that the closing of the shop in Piazza dei Martiri and the firing of Alfonso had to do with that flow. But if I tried to ask questions—what happened with Michele, how did you manage to get rid of him, why did he fire Alfonso—Lila gave a little laugh, she said: what can I say, Michele doesn't know what he wants, he closes, he opens, he creates, he destroys, and then he gets mad at everyone.

The laugh wasn't of mockery, of contentment, or of satisfaction. The laugh served to prevent me from insisting. One afternoon we went shopping on Via dei Mille and since that area had for years been Alfonso's domain, he offered to go with us, he had a friend with a shop that would suit us. People knew by now of his homosexuality. He continued formally to live with Marisa, but Carmen had confirmed to me that his children were Michele's, and she had whispered: Marisa is now Stefano's lover—yes, Stefano, Alfonso's brother, Lila's ex-husband, that was the new gossip. But—she added with explicit understanding—Alfonso doesn't give a damn, he and his wife lead separate lives and they get on. So I wasn't surprised that the shopkeeper friend—as Alfonso himself introduced him, smiling—was a homosexual. What surprised me instead was the game that Lila led him into.

We were trying on maternity clothes. We came out of the dressing rooms, looked at ourselves in the mirror, and Alfonso and his friend admired, recommended, recommended against, in a generally pleasant atmosphere. Then for no reason Lila began to get restless, scowling. She didn't like anything, she touched her pointy stomach, she was tired, she made remarks to Alfonso like: What are you saying, don't give me bad advice, would you wear a color like this?

I perceived in what was happening around me the usual

164 - ELENA FERRANTE

oscillation between the visible and the hidden. At a certain point Lila grabbed a beautiful dark dress and, as if the mirror in the shop were broken, said to her former brother-in-law: show me how it looks on *me*. She said those incongruous words as if they expressed a normal request, so that Alfonso didn't wait to be asked again, he grabbed the dress and shut himself up in the dressing room for a long time.

I continued to try on clothes. Lila looked at me absentmindedly, the owner of the shop complimented every item I put on, and I waited in bewilderment for Alfonso to reappear. When he did I was speechless. My old desk mate, with his hair down, in the elegant dress, was a copy of Lila. His tendency to resemble her, which I had long noted, came abruptly into focus, and maybe at that moment he was even handsomer, more beautiful than she, a male-female of the type I had talked about in my book, ready, male and female, to set off on the road leading to the black Madonna of Montevergine.

He asked Lila with some anxiety: Do you like it, this way? And the shop owner applauded enthusiastically, he said conspiratorially: I know exactly who'd like you, you're beautiful. Allusions. Facts that I didn't know and they did. Lila had a malicious smile, she muttered: I want to give it to you. Nothing more. Alfonso accepted it happily but nothing else was said, as if Lila had commanded him and his friend, silently, that it was enough, I had seen and heard enough.

47.

That deliberate oscillation of hers between the obvious and the opaque struck me in a particularly painful way once—the only time—when things went badly at one of our appointments with the gynecologist. It was November and yet the city gave off heat as if summer had never ended. Lila felt sick on the way, and we sat in a café for a few minutes, then went, slightly alarmed, to the doctor. Lila explained to her in self-mocking tones that the now large thing she had inside was kicking her, pushing her, stifling her, disturbing her, weakening her. The gynecologist listened, amused, calmed her, said: You'll have a son like you, very lively, very imaginative. All good, then, very good. But before leaving I insisted with the doctor:

"You're sure everything's all right?"

"Very sure."

"What's the matter with me?" Lila protested.

"Nothing that has to do with your pregnancy."

"What does it have to do with?"

"With your head."

"What do you know about my head?"

"Your friend Nino was full of praise for it."

Nino? Friend? Silence.

When we left I had to struggle to persuade Lila not to change doctors. Before going off she said, in her fiercest tones: your lover is certainly not my friend, but in my view he's not your friend, either.

Here I was, then, driven forcefully into the heart of my problems: the unreliability of Nino. In the past Lila had showed me that she knew things about him I didn't know. Was she now suggesting that there were still other facts known to her and not to me? It was pointless to ask her to explain; she left, cutting short any conversation.

48.

Afterward I quarreled with Nino for his lack of tact, for the confidences that, although he denied it indignantly, he must surely have made to the wife of his colleague, for everything I kept inside me and that this time, too, in the end I stifled.

I didn't say to him: Lila considers you a traitorous liar. It was pointless, he would have started laughing. But the suspicion remained that that mention of his unreliability alluded to something concrete. It was a slow, reluctant suspicion, I myself had no intention of transforming it into some intolerable certainty. And yet it persisted. So one Sunday in November, I went first to my mother, then, around six, to Lila's house. My daughters were in Florence with their father, Nino was celebrating his father-in-law's birthday with his family (that was how I put it now: *your* family). I knew that Lila was alone; Enzo had had to go and see some relatives of his in Avellino and had taken Gennaro.

The creature in my womb was nervous, I blamed the heavy air. Lila, too, complained that the baby was moving too much, she said it was forever creating a choppy sea in her belly. To calm him she wanted to take a walk, but I had brought pastries; I made the coffee myself, I wanted to have a private conversation, in the intimacy of that bare house with windows onto the *stradone*.

I pretended I was in the mood for idle talk. I mentioned matters that interested me less—*Why does Marcello say you're the ruin of his brother, what did you do to Michele*—and in a tone partly of fun, as if they were just something to laugh about. I counted on slowly getting to the question that I really cared about: What do you know about Nino that I don't know.

Lila answered unwillingly. She sat down, she got up, she said her stomach felt as if she had swallowed liters of carbonated drinks, she complained about the smell of the cannoli, which she usually liked but which now seemed to her bad. Marcello—you know what he's like, she said, he's never forgotten what I did to him as a girl, and since he's a coward he doesn't say things to your face, he acts like a good person, harmless, but he spreads gossip. Then she took the tone she always had in that phase, affectionate and at the same time slightly teasing: But you're a lady, forget my troubles, tell me how your mother is. As usual she wanted me to talk about myself, but I didn't yield. Moving from my mother, from her worries about Elisa and my brothers, I led her back to the Solaras. She grumbled, she said sarcastically that men place such an enormous importance on fucking, she laughed: not Marcello—although even he doesn't joke—but Michele, who went crazy, he's been obsessed with me for a long time, and even runs after the shadow of my shadow. She repeated that expression allusively—*shadow of my shadow*—she said that was why Marcello was angry and threatened her, he couldn't bear the fact that she had put a leash on his brother and led him in directions that in his view were humiliating. She laughed again, she muttered: Marcello thinks he can scare me, but look, the only person who really knew how to scare people was his mother and you know how she ended up.

As she talked she kept touching her forehead, she complained of the heat, of the slight headache she'd had since the morning. I understood that she wanted to reassure me but also, in a contradictory manner, show me a little of what was there where she lived and worked every day, behind the façade of the houses, on the streets of the new neighborhood and the old one. Thus on the one hand she repeatedly denied the danger, on the other drew me a picture of spreading crime, extortion, assault, theft, usury, revenge followed by revenge. The secret red book that Manuela maintained and that after her death had passed to Michele was now controlled by Marcello, who was also taking away from his brother—out of distrust— the management of the legal and illegal trafficking, the political friendships. She said suddenly: Marcello has been bringing drugs to the neighborhood for several years, and I want to see where it's going to end up. A remark like that. She was very pale, fanning herself with the edge of her skirt.

Of all her allusions, only the one to drugs struck me, particularly because of her tone of disgust and disapproval. Drugs for me at that time meant Mariarosa's house, or, on certain evenings, the apartment on Via Tasso. I had never used drugs, apart from smoking once or twice, out of curiosity, but I wasn't outraged if others did, in the circles I had frequented and did frequent no one was outraged. So, to keep the conversation going, I stated an opinion, drawing on the days in Milan, and on Mariarosa, for whom taking drugs was one of many channels for individual well-being, a way of freeing oneself from taboos, a cultivated form of release. But Lila shook her head in opposition: What release, Lenù, the son of Signora Palmieri died two weeks ago, they found him in the gardens. And I perceived the irritation she felt at that word, *release*, at my way of saying it, assigning it a positive value. I stiffened, I ventured: He must have had some heart trouble. She answered, He had heroin trouble, and she quickly added: That's enough, I'm fed up, I don't want to spend Sunday talking about the revolting activities of the Solaras.

Yet she had done so, and more than usual. A long moment slipped by. Out of restlessness, out of weariness, out of choice—I don't know—Lila had slightly widened the net of her conversation, and I realized that even if she hadn't said much she had filled my head with new images. I had long known that Michele wanted her—wanted her in that abstractly obsessive way that was harmful to him—and it was clear that she had taken advantage of it by bringing him to his knees. But now she had evoked the *shadow of her shadow*, and with that expression had thrust before my eyes Alfonso, the Alfonso who posed as a reflection of her in a maternity dress in the store on Via dei Mille, and I had seen Michele, a dazzled Michele, lifting his dress, holding him tight. As for Marcello, in a flash drugs stopped being what they had seemed to me, a liberating game for wealthy people, and moved into the sticky theater of the gardens beside the church, they had become a viper, a poison that spread through the blood of my brothers, of Rino, perhaps of Gennaro, and murdered, and brought money into the red book once kept by Manuela Solara and now—having passed from Michele to Marcello—by my sister, in her house. I felt all the fascination of the way Lila governed the imagination of others or set it free, at will, with just a few words: that speaking, stopping, letting images and emotions go without adding anything else. I'm wrong, I said to myself in confusion, to write as I've done until now, recording everything I know. I should write the way she speaks, leave abysses, construct bridges and not finish them, force the reader to establish the flow: Marcello Solara who takes off quickly with my sister Elisa, with Silvio, with Peppe, with Gianni, with Rino, with Gennaro, with Michele enthralled by the shadow of the shadow of Lila; suggest that they all slip inside the veins of Signora Palmieri's son, a boy I don't even know and who now causes me pain, veins far away from those of the people Nino brings to Via Tasso, from Mariarosa's, from those of a friend of hers—I now remembered—who was sick, and had to detox, and my sister-in-law, too, wherever she is, I haven't heard from her for a long time, some people are always saved and some perish.

I tried to expel images of voluptuous penetrations between men, of needles in veins, of desire and death. I tried to resume the conversation but something wasn't right, I felt the heat of that late afternoon in my throat, I remember that my legs felt heavy and my neck was sweaty. I looked at the clock on the kitchen wall, it was just after seven-thirty. I discovered I no longer felt like talking about Nino, like asking Lila, sitting opposite me in a low yellowish light, what do you know about him that I don't know. She knew a lot, too much, she could make me imagine whatever she wanted and I would never be able to erase the images from my mind. They had slept together, they had studied together, she had helped him write his articles, as I had done with the essays. For a moment jealousy and envy returned. They hurt me and I repressed them.

Or probably what actually repressed them was a kind of thunder under the building, under the *stradone*, as if one of the trucks that were constantly passing had swerved in our direction, was descending rapidly underground with the engine at top speed, and running into our foundations, crashing and shattering everything.

49.

My breath was cut short, and for a fraction of a second I couldn't understand what was happening. The coffee cup trembled on the saucer, the leg of the table bumped my knee. I jumped up, and realized that Lila, too, was alarmed, she was trying to get up. The chair was tilting backward, she tried to grasp it, but slowly, bent over, one hand reaching in front of her, in my direction, the other extended toward the chair back, her eyes narrowing, the way they did when she concentrated before reacting. Meanwhile thunder rumbled beneath the building, a stormy underground wind lifted waves of a secret sea against the floor. I looked at the ceiling; the light was swaying, along with the pink glass cover.

Earthquake, I cried. The earth was moving, an invisible tempest exploding under my feet, shaking the room with the howl of a forest subdued by gusts of wind. The walls creaked, they appeared distended, they came unstuck and were pasted together again at the corners. A cloud of dust rained down from the ceiling, adding to the cloud that came out of the walls. I rushed toward the door, shouting again: earthquake. But the movement was mere intention, I couldn't take a step. My feet were like lead, everything was heavy, my head, my chest, above all my stomach. And yet the ground on which I wanted to step was receding: for a fraction of a second it was there and then immediately it subsided.

I remembered Lila, I sought her with my gaze. The chair had finally fallen over, the ceiling light was swaying, the furniture—especially an old sideboard with its knickknacks, glasses, silverware, chinoiserie—vibrated along with the windowpanes, like weeds growing in the eaves, stirred by the breeze. Lila was standing in the middle of the room, leaning forward, head down, eyes narrowed, brow furrowed, her hands holding her stomach as if she were afraid that it would slip away from her and get lost in the cloud of plaster dust. The seconds slid by, but nothing appeared to want to return to order; I called to her. She didn't respond, she seemed solid, the only one of all the shapes impervious to jolts, tremors. She seemed to have erased every feeling: her ears didn't hear, her throat didn't inhale air, her mouth was locked, her eyelids canceled her gaze. She was a motionless organism, rigid, alive only in the hands that, fingers spread, gripped her stomach.

Lila, I called. I moved to grab her, drag her away, it was the most urgent thing to do. The lower part of me, the part I thought was exhausted but, instead, here it was reviving, suggested to me: maybe you should be like her, stand still, bend over to protect your infant, don't run away, think calmly. I struggled to make up my mind, to reach her was difficult, and yet it was just a step. Finally I seized her by the arm, I shook her, and she opened her eyes, which seemed white. The noise was unbearable, the whole city was making noise, Vesuvius, the streets, the sea, the old houses of the Tribunali and the Quartieri, the new ones of Posillipo. She wriggled free, she cried: Don't touch me. It was an angry shout, and shocked me even more than the long seconds of the earthquake. I realized that I was mistaken: Lila, always in control of everything, at that moment wasn't in control of anything. She was immobilized by horror, fearful that if I merely touched her she would break.

50.

I dragged her outside, tugging her violently, pushing, entreating. I was afraid the tremor that had paralyzed us would be followed immediately by another, more terrible, final, and that everything would collapse on top of us. I admonished her, I begged her, I reminded her that we had to rescue the creatures we carried in our wombs. So we flung ourselves into the wake of terrified cries, a growing clamor joined to frenzied movements—it seemed that the heart of the neighborhood, of the city, was about to burst. As soon as we reached the courtyard, Lila threw up; I fought the nausea that gripped my stomach.

The earthquake—the earthquake of November 23, 1980, with its infinite destruction—entered into our bones. It expelled the habit of stability and solidity, the confidence that every second would be identical to the next, the familiarity of sounds and gestures, the certainty of recognizing them. A sort of suspicion of every form of reassurance took over, a tendency to believe in every prediction of bad luck, an obsessive attention to signs of the brittleness of the world, and it was hard to take control again. Minutes and minutes and minutes that wouldn't end.

Outside was worse than inside, everything was moving and shouting, we were assaulted by rumors that multiplied the terror. Red flashes could be seen in the direction of the railroad. Vesuvius had reawakened. The sea was beating against Mergellina, the city hall, Chiatamone. The cemetery of the Pianto had sunk, along with the dead, Poggioreale had collapsed entirely. The prisoners were either under the ruins or had escaped and now were murdering people just for the hell of it. The tunnel that led to the Marina had collapsed, burying half the fleeing neighborhood. Fantasies fed on one another, and Lila, I saw, believed everything, she trembled as she clung to my arm. The city is dangerous, she whispered, we have to go, the houses are cracking, everything is falling on us, the sewers are spurting into the air, look how the rats are escaping. Since people were running to their cars and the streets were becoming congested, she began to pull me, she whispered, they're all going to the countryside, it's safer there. She wanted to run to her car, she wanted to get to an open space where only the sky, which seemed weightless, could fall on our heads. I couldn't calm her.

We reached the car, but Lila didn't have the keys. We had fled without taking anything, we had pulled the door shut behind us and, even if we had found the courage, we couldn't go back to the house. I seized one of the door handles with all my strength and pulled it, shook it, but Lila shrieked, she put her hands over her ears as if my action produced intolerable sounds and vibrations. Looking around, I saw a big rock that had fallen out of a wall, and used it to break a window. I'll get it fixed later, I said, now let's stay here, it will pass. We settled ourselves in the car, but nothing passed, we felt a continuous trembling of the earth. Beyond the dusty windshield, we watched the people of the neighborhood, who had gathered in small groups to talk. But when at last things seemed quiet someone ran by shouting, which caused a general stampede, and people slammed into our car with heart-stopping violence.

51.

I was afraid, yes, I was terrified. But to my great amazement I wasn't as frightened as Lila. In those seconds of the earthquake she had suddenly stripped off the woman she had been until a moment before—the one who was able to precisely calibrate thoughts, words, gestures, tactics, strategies—as if in that situation she considered her a useless suit of armor. Now she was someone else. She was the person I had glimpsed the time

Melina walked along the *stradone* eating soap; or the one of the night of New Year's Eve in 1958, when the fireworks war broke out between the Carraccis and the Solaras; or the one who had sent for me in San Giovanni a Teduccio, when she worked in Bruno Soccavo's factory and, thinking something was wrong with her heart, wanted to leave me Gennaro because she was sure she would die. But now that other person seemed to have emerged directly from the churning guts of the earth; she bore almost no resemblance to the friend who a few minutes before I had envied for her ability to choose words deliberately; there was no resemblance even in the features, disfigured by anguish.

I could never have undergone such an abrupt metamorphosis, my self-discipline was stable, the world existed around me, in a natural way, even in the most terrible moments. I knew that Dede and Elsa were with their father in Florence, and Florence was an elsewhere out of danger, which in itself calmed me. I hoped that the worst had passed, that no house in the neighborhood had collapsed, that Nino, my mother, my father, Elisa, my brothers were surely, like us, frightened, but surely, like us, alive. She, on the other hand, no, she couldn't think in that way. She writhed, she trembled, she caressed her stomach, she no longer seemed to believe in solid connections. For her Gennaro and Enzo had lost every connection with each other and with us, they were destroyed. She emitted a sort of death rattle, eyes wide, she clutched herself, held tight. And she repeated obsessively adjectives and nouns that were completely incongruous with the situation we were in, she uttered sentences without sense and yet she uttered them with conviction, tugging on me.

For a long time it was useless for me to point out people we knew, to open the window, wave my arms, call out to anchor her to names, to voices that would have their own stories of that terrible experience and so draw her into an orderly conversation. I pointed out Carmen with her husband and children, and others, hurrying, on foot, toward the station. I pointed out Antonio with his wife and children, I was astonished at how handsome they all were, like characters in a film, as they calmly got into a green van, which then left. I pointed out to her the Carracci family and their relations, husbands, wives, fathers, mothers, people living together, lovers—that is to say Stefano, Ada, Melina, Maria, Pinuccia, Rino, Alfonso, Marisa, and all their children—who appeared and disappeared in the throng, shouting continuously for fear of losing each other. I pointed out Marcello Solara's fancy car that was trying, with a roar, to get free of the jam of vehicles; he had my sister Elisa with her child next to him, and in the back seat the pale shadows of my mother and father. I shouted names with the window open, I tried to involve Lila, too. But she wouldn't move. In fact, I realized that the people—especially those we knew well—frightened her even more, especially if they were agitated, if they were shouting, if they were running. She squeezed my hand hard and closed her eyes when, against all the rules, Marcello's car went up on the sidewalk honking and made its way amid the people who were standing there talking, or were hauling things along. She exclaimed: Oh Madonna, an expression I had never heard her use. What's wrong, I asked. Gasping for breath, she cried out that the car's boundaries were dissolving, the boundaries of Marcello, too, at the wheel were dissolving, the thing and the person were gushing out of themselves, mixing liquid metal and flesh.

She used that term: *dissolving boundaries*. It was on that occasion that she resorted to it for the first time; she struggled to elucidate the meaning, she wanted me to understand what the dissolution of boundaries meant and how much it frightened her. She was still holding my hand tight, breathing hard. She said that the outlines of things and people were delicate, that they broke like cotton thread. She whispered that for her it had always been that way, an object lost its edges and poured into another, into a solution of heterogeneous materials, a merging and mixing. She exclaimed that she had always had to struggle to believe that life had firm boundaries, for she had known since she was a child that it was not like that—*it was absolutely not like that*—and so she couldn't trust in their resistance to being banged and bumped. Contrary to what she had been doing, she began to utter a profusion of overexcited sentences, sometimes kneading in the vocabulary of the dialect, sometimes drawing on the vast reading she had done as a girl. She muttered that she mustn't ever be distracted: if she became distracted real things, which, with their violent, painful contortions, terrified her, would gain the upper hand over the unreal ones, which, with their physical and moral solidity, pacified her; she would be plunged into a sticky, jumbled reality and would never again be able to give sensations clear outlines. A tactile emotion would melt into a visual one, a visual one would melt into an olfactory one, ah, what is the real world, Lenù, nothing, nothing, nothing about which one can say conclusively: it's like that. And so if she didn't stay alert, if she didn't pay attention to the boundaries, the waters would break through, a flood would rise, carrying everything off in clots of menstrual blood, in cancerous polyps, in bits of yellowish fiber.

52.

She spoke for a long time. It was the first and last time she tried to explain to me the feeling of the world she moved in. Up to now, she said—and here I summarize in my own words, of the present—I thought it was a matter of bad moments that came and then passed, like a childhood illness. Do you remember New Year's Eve of 1958, when the Solaras shot at us? The shots were the least frightening part. First, even before they started shooting, I was afraid that the colors of the fireworks were sharp—the green and the purple especially were razor-like—that they could butcher us, that the trails of the rockets were scraping my brother Rino like files, like rasps, and broke his flesh, caused another, disgusting brother to drip out of him, whom I had to put back inside right away—inside his usual form—or he would turn against me and hurt me. All my life I've done nothing, Lenù, but hold back moments like those. Marcello scared me and I protected myself with Stefano. Stefano scared me and I protected myself with Michele. Michele scared me and I protected myself with Nino. Nino scared me and I protected myself with Enzo. But what does that mean, protect, it's only a word. I could make you, now, a detailed list of all the coverings, large and small, that I constructed to keep myself hidden, and yet they were of no use to me. Do you remember how the night sky of Ischia horrified me? You all said how beautiful it is, but I couldn't. I smelled an odor of rotten eggs, eggs with a greenish-yellow yolk inside the white and inside the shell, a hard-boiled egg cracked open. I had in my mouth poisoned egg stars, their light had a white, gummy consistency, it stuck to your teeth, along with the gelatinous black of the sky, I crushed it with disgust, I tasted a crackling of grit. Am I clear? Am I making myself clear? And yet on Ischia I was happy, full of love. But it was no use, my head always finds a chink to peer through, beyond—above, beneath, on the side—where the fear is. In Bruno's factory, for example, the bones of the animals cracked in your fingers if you merely touched them, and a rancid marrow spilled out. I was so afraid that I thought I was sick. But was I sick? Did I really have a murmur in my heart? No. The only problem has always been the disquiet of my mind. I can't stop it, I always have to do, redo, cover, uncover, reinforce, and then suddenly undo, break. Take Alfonso, he's always made me nervous, ever since he was a boy, I've felt that the cotton thread that held him together was about to break. And Michele? Michele thought he was who knows what, and yet all I had to do was find his boundary line and pull, oh, oh, oh, I broke it, I broke his cotton thread and tangled it with Alfonso's, male material inside male material, the fabric that I weave by day is unraveled by night, the head finds a way. But it's not much use, the terror remains, it's always in the crack between one normal thing and the other. It's there waiting, I've always suspected it, and since yesterday evening I've known for certain: nothing lasts, Lenù, even here in my belly, you think the creature will endure but it won't. You remember when I married Stefano and I wanted the neighborhood to start again from the beginning, to be only beautiful things, the ugliness of before was not supposed to be there anymore. How long did it last? Good feelings are fragile, with me love doesn't last. Love for a man doesn't last, not even love for a child, it soon gets a hole in it. You look in the hole and you see the nebula of good intentions mixed up with the nebula of bad. Gennaro makes me feel guilty, this thing here in my belly is a responsibility that cuts me, scratches me. Loving courses together with hating, and I can't, I can't manage to solidify myself around any goodwill. Maestra Oliviero was right, I'm bad. I don't even know how to keep friendship alive. You're kind, Lenù, you've always had a lot of patience. But tonight I finally understood it: there is always a solvent that acts slowly, with a gentle heat, and undoes everything, even when there's no earthquake. So please, if I insult you, if I say ugly things to you, stop up your ears, I don't want to do it and yet I do. Please, please, don't leave me, or I'll fall in.

53.

Yes—I kept saying—all right, but now rest. I held her tight beside me, and finally she fell asleep. I stayed awake watching her, as she had once begged me to do. Every so often I felt new small aftershocks, someone in a car shouted with terror. Now the *stradone* was empty. The infant moved in my belly like rolling waters, I touched Lila's stomach, hers was moving, too. Everything was moving: the sea of fire under the crust of the earth, and the furnaces of the stars, and the planets, and the universes, and the light within the darkness and the silence in the cold. But, even now as I pondered the wave of Lila's distraught words, I felt that in me fear could not put down roots, and even the lava, the fiery stream of melting matter that I imagined inside the earthly globe, and the fear it provoked in me, settled in my mind in orderly sentences, in harmonious images, became a pavement of black stones like the streets of Naples, a pavement where I was always and no matter what the center. I gave myself weight, in other words, I knew how to do that, whatever happened. Everything that struck me—my studies, books, Franco, Pietro, the children, Nino, the earthquake— would pass, and I, whatever *I* among those I was accumulating, *I* would remain firm, I was the needle of the compass that stays fixed while the lead traces circles around it. Lila on the other hand—it seemed clear to me now, and it made me proud, it calmed me, touched me—struggled to feel stable. She couldn't, she didn't believe it. However much she had always dominated all of us and had imposed and was still imposing a way of being, on pain of her resentment and her fury, she perceived herself as a liquid and all her efforts were, in the end, directed only at containing herself. When, in spite of her defensive manipulation of persons and things, the liquid prevailed, Lila lost Lila, chaos seemed the only truth, and she—so active, so courageous—erased herself and, terrified, became nothing.

54.

The neighborhood emptied, the *stradone* became quiet, the air turned cold. In the buildings, transformed into dark rocks, there was not a single lamp lighted, no colorful glow of a television. I, too, fell asleep. I awoke with a start, it was still dark. Lila had left the car, the window on her side was half open. I opened mine, I looked around. The stopped cars were all inhabited, people coughed, groaned in their sleep. I didn't see Lila, I grew concerned, I went toward the tunnel. I found her not far from Carmen's gas pump. She was moving amid fragments of cornices and other debris, she looked up toward the windows of her house. Seeing me she had an expression of embarrassment. I wasn't well, she said, I'm sorry, I filled your head with nonsense, luckily we were together. There was the hint of an uneasy smile on her face, she said one of the many almost incomprehensible phrases of that night—*"Luckily" is a breath of perfume that comes out when you press the pump*—and she shivered. She still wasn't well, I persuaded her to return to the car. In a few minutes she fell asleep again.

As soon as it was day I woke her. She was calm, she wanted to apologize. She said softly, making light of it: You know I'm like that, every so often there's something that grabs me here in my chest. I said: It's nothing, there are periods of exhaustion, you're looking after too many things, and anyway it's been terrible for everyone, it wouldn't end. She shook her head: I know how I'm made.

We organized ourselves, we found a way of returning to her house. We made a great number of phone calls, but either they didn't go through or the phone rang in vain. Lila's parents didn't answer, the relatives in Avellino, who could have given us news of Enzo and Gennaro, didn't answer, no one answered at Nino's number, his friends didn't answer. I talked to Pietro, he had just found out about the earthquake. I asked him to keep the girls for a few days, long enough to be sure the danger had passed. But as the hours slid by, the dimensions of the disaster grew. We hadn't been frightened for nothing. Lila murmured as if to justify herself: You see, the earth was about to split in two.

We were dazed by emotions and by weariness, but still we walked through the neighborhood and through a sorrowing city, now silent, now streaked by the nagging sounds of sirens. We kept talking to alleviate anxiety: where was Nino, where was Enzo, where was Gennaro, how was my mother, where had Marcello Solara taken her, where were Lila's parents. I realized that she needed to return to the moments of the earthquake, and not so much to recount again its traumatic effects as to feel them as a new heart around which to restructure sensibility. I encouraged her every time, and it seemed to me that the more she regained control of herself the more evident became the destruction and death of entire towns of the South. Soon she began to speak of the terror without being ashamed and I was reassured. But something indefinable nevertheless remained: her more cautious steps, a hint of apprehension in her voice. The memory of the earthquake endured, Naples contained it. Only the heat was departing, like a foggy breath that rose from the body of the city and its slow, strident life.

We reached the house of Nino and Eleonora. I knocked for a long time, I called, no answer. Lila stood a hundred meters away, staring at me, her belly stretched, pointed, a sulky expression on her face. I talked to a man who came out of the entrance with two suitcases, he said that the whole building was deserted. I stayed another moment, unable to make up my mind to leave. I observed Lila's figure. I remembered what she had said and implied shortly before the earthquake, I had the impression that a legion of demons was pursuing her. She used Enzo, she used Pasquale, she used Antonio. She remodeled Alfonso. She subdued Michele Solara, leading him into a mad love for her, for him. And Michele was thrashing about to free himself, he fired Alfonso, he closed the shop in Piazza dei Martiri, but in vain. Lila humiliated him, continued to humiliate him, subjugating him. How much did she know now of the two brothers' business. She had set eyes on their affairs when she collected data for the computer, she even knew about the drug money. That's why Marcello hated her, that's why my sister Elisa hated her. Lila knew everything. She knew everything out of pure, simple fear of all that was living or dead. Who knows how many ugly facts she knew about Nino. She seemed to say to me from a distance: Forget him, we both know that he's safely with his family and doesn't give a damn about you.

55.

It turned out to be essentially true. Enzo and Gennaro returned to the neighborhood in the evening, worn-out, overwhelmed, looking like survivors of an atrocious war, with a single preoccupation: How was Lila. Nino, on the other hand, reappeared many days later, as if he'd come back from a vacation. I couldn't understand anything, he said, I took my children and fled.

His children. What a responsible father. And the one I carried in my belly?

He said in his confident voice that he had taken refuge with the children, Eleonora, his in-laws in a family villa in Minturno. I sulked. I kept him away for days, I didn't want to see him, I was worried about my parents. I heard from Marcello himself, who had returned alone to the neighborhood, that he had brought them to a safe place, with Elisa and Silvio, to a property he had in Gaeta. Another savior of *his* family.

Meanwhile I returned to Via Tasso, alone. It was very cold now, the apartment was freezing. I checked the walls one by one, there didn't seem to be any cracks. But at night I was afraid to fall asleep, I feared that the earthquake would return, and I was glad that Pietro and Doriana had agreed to keep the children for a while.

Then Christmas came; I couldn't help it, I made peace with

Nino. I went to Florence to get Dede and Elsa. Life began again but like a convalescence whose end I couldn't see. Now, every time I saw Lila, I felt on her part a mood of uncertainty, especially when she took an aggressive tone. She looked at me as if to say: You know what is behind my every word.

But did I really know? I crossed barricaded streets and passed by countless uninhabitable buildings, shored up by strong wooden beams. I often ended up in the havoc caused by the basest complicit inefficiency. And I thought of Lila, of how she immediately returned to work, to manipulate, motivate, deride, attack. I thought of the terror that in a few seconds had annihilated her, I saw the trace of that terror in her now habitual gesture of holding her hands around her stomach with the fingers spread. And I wondered apprehensively: who is she now, what can she become, how can she react? I said to her once, to underline that a bad moment had passed:

"The world has returned to its place."

She replied teasingly:

"What place?"

56.

In the last month of pregnancy everything became a struggle. Nino was hardly ever around: he had to work, and that exasperated me. When he did appear, he was rude. I thought: I'm ugly, he doesn't want me anymore. And it was true, by now I couldn't look at myself in the mirror without disgust. I had puffy cheeks and an enormous nose. My bosom and stomach seemed to have consumed the rest of my body, I saw myself without a neck, with short legs and fat ankles. I had become like my mother, but not the one of now, who was a thin, frightened old woman; rather, I resembled the venomous figure I had always feared, who now existed only in my memory.

That persecuting mother was unleashed. She began to act through me, venting because of the difficulties, the anxieties, the pain the dying mother was causing me with her frailties, the gaze of a person who is about to drown. I became intractable, every complication seemed like a plot, I often started shouting. I had the impression, in my moments of greatest unhappiness, that the chaos of Naples had settled even in my body, that I was losing the capacity to be nice, to be likable. Pietro called to talk to the children and I was brusque. The publisher called me, or some daily paper, and I protested, I said: I'm in my ninth month, I'm stressed, leave me alone.

With my daughters, too, I got worse. Not so much with Dede, since she resembled her father, and I was by now accustomed to her mixture of intelligence, affection, and harassing logic. It was Elsa who began to upset me. The meek little girl was becoming a being with blurry features, whose teacher did nothing but complain about her, calling her sly and violent, while I myself, in the house or on the street, constantly scolded her for picking fights, taking others' things and breaking them when she had to give them back. A fine trio of women we are, I said to myself, it's obvious that Nino is avoiding us, that he prefers Eleonora, Albertino, and Lidia. When I couldn't sleep at night because of the creature stirring in my womb, as if it were made of mobile air bubbles, I hoped against every prediction that the new baby would be a male, that he would resemble Nino, that he would please him, and that Nino would love him more than his other children.

But although I forced myself to return to the image I preferred of myself—I had always wanted to be an even-tempered person who wisely curbed petty or even violent feelings—in those final days I was unable to find an equilibrium. I blamed the earthquake, which at the time didn't seem to have disturbed me a great deal but perhaps remained deep inside, right in my belly. If I drove through the tunnel of Capodimonte I was gripped by panic, I was afraid that a new shock would make it collapse. If I took the Corso Malta viaduct, which vibrated anyway, I accelerated to escape the shock that might shatter it at any moment. In that phase I even stopped battling the ants, which often and willingly appeared in the bathroom: I preferred to let them live and every so often observe them; Alfonso claimed that they could anticipate disaster.

But it wasn't only the aftermath of the earthquake that upset me; Lila's fantastical hints also entered into it. I now looked on the streets for syringes like the ones I had absent-mindedly noticed in the days of Milan. And if I saw some in the gardens in the neighborhood a querulous mist rose around me, I wanted to go and confront Marcello and my brothers, even if it wasn't clear to me what arguments I would use. Thus I ended up doing and saying hateful things. To my mother, who harassed me, asking if I had talked to Lila about Peppe and Gianni, I responded rudely one day: Ma, Lina can't take them, she already has a brother who's a drug addict, and she's afraid for Gennaro, you can't all burden her with the problems you can't fix. She looked at me in horror, she had never alluded to drugs, I had said a word that shouldn't be said. But if in earlier times she would have started shouting in defense of my brothers and against my lack of sensitivity, now she shut herself in a dark corner of the kitchen and didn't breathe a word, so that I had to say, repentant: Don't worry, come on, we'll find a solution.

What solution? I made things even more complicated. I tracked down Peppe in the gardens—who knows where Gianni was—and made an angry speech about how terrible it was to earn money from the vices of others. I said: Go find any job but not this, you'll ruin yourself and make our mother die of worry. The whole time he was cleaning the nails of his right hand with the nail of his left thumb, and he listened to me uneasily, eyes lowered. He was three years younger than me and felt like the little brother in front of the big sister who was an important person. But that didn't keep him from saying to me, at the end, with a sneer: Without my money Mamma would already be dead. He went away with a faint wave of farewell.

That answer got me even more upset. I let a day or two go by and went to see Elisa, hoping to find Marcello, too. It was very cold, the streets of the new neighborhood were as damaged and dirty as those of the old. Marcello wasn't there; the house was untidy; and I found my sister's slovenliness annoying: she hadn't washed or dressed, all she did was take care of her son. I almost scolded her: Tell your husband—and I stressed that word *husband* even though they weren't married—that he's ruining our brothers; if he has to sell drugs, let him do it himself. I expressed myself like that, in Italian, and she turned pale, she said: Lenù, leave my house immediately, who do you think you're talking to, all those fancy people you know? Get out, you're presumptuous, you always were. As soon as I tried to reply she shouted: Don't ever come here again acting like the professor about my Marcello: he's a good person, we owe everything to him; if I want to I can buy you, that whore Lina, and all the shits you admire so much.

57.

I got more and more involved in the neighborhood that, because of Lila, I had glimpsed, and realized only later that I was getting mixed up in activities that were difficult to sort out, and was violating among other things a rule I had made when I returned to Naples: not to be sucked back into the place where I was born. One afternoon when I had left the children with Mirella, I went to see my mother, and then, I don't know whether to soothe my agitation or to give vent to it, I went to Lila's office. Ada opened the door, cheerfully. Lila was closed in her room and arguing with a client, Enzo had gone with Rino to visit some business or other, and she felt it her duty to keep me company. She entertained me with talk about her daughter, Maria, on how big she was, how good she was in school. But then the telephone rang, she hurried to answer, calling to Alfonso: Lenuccia's here, come. With a certain embarrassment, my former schoolmate, more feminine than ever in his ways, in his hair, in the colors of his clothes, led me into a small bare space. There to my surprise I found Michele Solara.

I hadn't seen him for a long time, and an unease took possession of all three of us. Michele seemed very changed. He had gone gray, and his face was lined, although his body was still young and athletic. But the oddest thing was that he appeared to be embarrassed by my presence, and behaved in a completely uncharacteristic way. First of all he stood up when I entered. Then he was polite but said very little, his usual teasing patter had disappeared. He kept looking at Alfonso as if he were seeking help, then immediately looked away, as if merely looking at him could be compromising. And Alfonso was just as uncomfortable. He kept smoothing his long hair, he smacked his lips in search of something to say, and the conversation soon languished. The moments seemed fragile to me. I became nervous, but I didn't know why. Maybe it annoyed me that they were hiding—*from me*, no less, as if I couldn't understand; *from me,* who had frequented and did frequent circles more progressive than that little neighborhood room, who had written a book praised even abroad on how brittle sexual identities were. On the tip of my tongue was the wish to exclaim: If I've understood correctly, you are lovers. I didn't do it only out of fear of having mistaken Lila's hints. But certainly I couldn't bear the silence and I talked a lot, pushing the conversation in that direction.

I said to Michele:

"Gigliola told me you're separated."

"Yes."

"I'm also separated."

"I know, and I also know you you're with."

"You never liked Nino."

"No, but people have to do what they feel like, otherwise they get sick."

"Are you still in Posillipo?"

Alfonso interrupted enthusiastically:

"Yes, and the view is fabulous."

Michele looked at him with irritation, he said:

"I'm happy there."

I answered:

"People are never happy alone."

"Better alone than in bad company," he answered.

Alfonso must have perceived that I was looking for a chance to say something unpleasant to Michele and he tried to focus my attention on himself.

He exclaimed:

"And I am about to separate from Marisa." And he related in great detail certain quarrels with his wife on money matters. He never mentioned love, sex, or even her infidelities. Instead he continued to insist on the money, he spoke obscurely of Stefano and alluded only to the fact that Marisa had pushed out Ada (*Women take men away from other women without any scruples, in fact with great satisfaction*). His wife, in his words, seemed no more than an acquaintance whose doings could be talked about with irony. Think what a waltz, he said, laughing—Ada took Stefano from Lila and now Marisa is taking him away from her, hahaha.

I sat listening and slowly rediscovered—but as if I were dragging it up from a deep well—the old solidarity of the time when we sat at the same desk. Yet only then did I understand that even if I had never been aware that he was different, I was fond of him precisely because he wasn't like the other boys, precisely because of that peculiar alienation from the male behaviors of the neighborhood. And now, as he spoke, I discovered that that bond endured. Michele, on the other hand, annoyed me more than ever. He muttered some vulgarities about Marisa, he was impatient with Alfonso's conversation, at a certain point he interrupted in the middle of a sentence almost angrily (Will you let me have a word with Lenuccia?) and asked about my mother, he knew she was ill. Alfonso became suddenly silent, blushing. I started talking about my mother, purposely emphasizing how worried she was about my brothers. I said:

"She's not happy that Peppe and Gianni work for your brother."

"What's the problem with Marcello?"

"I don't know, you tell me. I heard that you don't get along anymore."

He looked at me almost in embarrassment.

"You heard wrong. And anyway, if your mother doesn't like Marcello's money, she can send them to work under someone else."

I was on the point of reproaching him for that *under*: my brothers *under* Marcello, *under* him, *under* someone else: *my* brothers, whom I hadn't helped with school and now, because of me, they were *under*. Under? No human being should be under, much less under the Solaras. I felt even more dissatisfied and had a desire to quarrel. But Lila came out.

"Ah, what a crowd," she said, and turned to Michele: "You need to talk to me?"

"Yes."

"Will it take long?"

"Yes."

"Then first I'll talk to Lenuccia."

He nodded timidly. I got up, and, looking at Michele but touching Alfonso on the arm as if to push him toward Michele, said:

"One of these nights you two must invite me to Posillipo, I'm always alone. I can do the cooking."

Michele opened his mouth but no sound came out, Alfonso intervened anxiously:

"There's no need, I'm a good cook. If Michele invites us, I'll do everything."

Lila led me away.

She stayed in her room with me for a long time, we talked about this and that. She, too, was near the end of her term, but the pregnancy no longer seemed to weigh on her. She said, smiling, as she placed her hand in a cup shape under her stomach: Finally I've gotten used to it, I feel good, I'd almost keep the child inside forever. With a vanity that she had rarely displayed, she turned sideways to be admired. She was tall, and her slender figure had beautiful curves: the small bosom, the stomach, the back and the ankles. Enzo, she said, laughing, with a trace of vulgarity, likes me pregnant even more, how annoying that it'll end. I thought: the earthquake seemed so terrible to her that each moment now is uncertain, and she would like everything to stand still, even her pregnancy. Every so often I looked at the clock, but she wasn't worried that Michele was waiting; rather, she seemed to be wasting time with me on purpose.

"He's not here for work," she said when I reminded her that he was waiting, "he's pretending, he's looking for excuses."

"For what?"

"Excuses. But you stay out of it: either mind your own business, or these are matters you have to take seriously. Even that remark about dinner at Posillipo, maybe it would have been better if you hadn't said it."

I was embarrassed. I murmured that it was a time of constant tensions, I told her about the fight with Elisa and Peppe, I told her I intended to confront Marcello. She shook her head, she repeated:

"Those, too, are things you can't interfere in and then go back up to Via Tasso."

"I don't want my mother to die worrying about her sons."

"Comfort her."
"How."
She smiled.
"With lies. Lies are better than tranquilizers."

58.

But in those low-spirited days I couldn't lie even for a good cause. Only because Elisa reported to our mother that I had insulted her and as a result she wanted nothing more to do with me; only because Peppe and Gianni shouted at her that she must never dare send me to make speeches like a cop, I finally decided to tell her a lie. I told her that I had talked to Lila and Lila had promised to take care of Peppe and Gianni. But she perceived that I wasn't really convinced and she said grimly: Yes, well done, go home, go, you have children. I was angry at myself, and on the following days she was even more agitated, she grumbled that she wanted to die soon. But once when I took her to the hospital she seemed more confident.

"She telephoned me," she said in her hoarse, sorrowful voice.
"Who?"
"Lina."
I was speechless with surprise.
"What did she tell you?"
"That I can stop worrying, she'll take care of Peppe and Gianni."
"In what sense?"
"I don't know, but if she promised it means she'll find a solution."
"That's certainly true."
"I trust her, she knows what's right."
"Yes."
"Have you seen how pretty she looks?"

"Yes."

"She told me if she has a girl she'll call her Nunzia, like her mother."

"She'll have a boy."

"But if it's a girl she'll call her Nunzia," she repeated, and as she spoke she looked not at me but at the other suffering faces in the waiting room. I said:

"I am certainly going to have a girl, just look at this belly."

"So?"

I forced myself to promise her:

"Then I'll give her your name, don't worry."

"Sarratore's son will want to name her for his mother."

59.

I denied that Nino had a say in it, at that stage the mere mention of him made me angry. He had vanished, he always had something to do. But on the day I made that promise to my mother, in the evening, as I was having dinner with the children, he unexpectedly appeared. He was cheerful, he pretended not to notice that I was bitter. He ate with us, he put Dede and Elsa to bed with jokes and stories, he waited for them to fall asleep. His casual superficiality made my mood worse. He had dropped in now, but he would leave again and who could say for how long. What was he afraid of, that my labor would start while he was in the house, while he was sleeping with me? That he would have to take me to the clinic? That he would then have to say to Eleonora: I have to stay with Elena because she is bringing my child into the world?

The girls were asleep, he came back to the living room. He caressed me, he knelt in front of me, he kissed my stomach. It was a flash, Mirko came to mind: how old would he be now, maybe twelve.

"What do you hear about your son?" I asked without pre-amble.

He didn't understand, naturally, he thought I was talking about the child I had in my belly, and he smiled, disoriented. Then I explained, with pleasure breaking the promise I had long ago made to myself:

"I mean Silvia's child, Mirko. I've seen him, he's identical to you. But you? Did you acknowledge him? Have you ever had anything to do with him?"

He frowned, he got up.

"Sometimes I don't know what to do with you," he mur-mured.

"Do what? Explain."

"You're an intelligent woman, but every so often you become another person."

"What do you mean? Unreasonable? Stupid?"

He gave a small laugh and made a gesture as if to brush off an annoying insect.

"You pay too much attention to Lina."

"What does Lina have to do with it?"

"She ruins your head, your feelings, everything."

Those words made me lose my temper completely. I said to him:

"Tonight I want to sleep alone."

He didn't resist. With the expression of someone who in order to live peacefully gives in to a serious injustice he softly closed the door behind him.

Two hours later, as I was wandering around the house, with no desire to sleep, I felt small contractions, as if I had men-strual cramps. I called Pietro, I knew that he still spent the nights studying. I said: I'm about to give birth, come and get Dede and Elsa tomorrow. I had barely hung up when I felt a warm liquid drip down my legs. I grabbed a bag that I had long since packed with what I needed, then I kept my finger on the neighbors' doorbell until they answered. I had already made an arrangement with Antonella, and though she was half asleep she wasn't surprised. I said:

"The time has come, I'm leaving you the girls."

Suddenly my rage and all my anxieties disappeared.

60.

It was January 22, 1981, the day my third child was delivered. Of the first two experiences I didn't have a particularly painful memory, but this one was absolutely the easiest, so much so that I considered it a happy liberation. The gynecologist praised my self-control, she was happy that I hadn't caused her any problems. If only they were all like you, she said: You're made for bringing children into the world. She whispered: Nino is waiting outside, I've let him know.

The news pleased me, but I was even happier to discover that my resentments were gone. Delivering the child relieved me of the bitterness of the past month and I was glad, I felt capable again of a good nature that could take things less seriously. I welcomed the new arrival lovingly, she was a girl of seven pounds, purple, bald. I said to Nino, when I let him come in, after neatening myself to hide the evidence of the exertion: now we're four females, I'll understand if you leave me. I made no allusion to the quarrel we had had. He embraced me, kissed me, swore he couldn't do without me. He gave me a gold necklace with a pendant. I thought it was beautiful.

As soon as I felt better I called the neighbor. I learned that Pietro, diligent as usual, had arrived. I talked to him, he wanted to come to the clinic with the children. I had him put them on the phone, but they were distracted by the pleasure of being with their father, and answered in monosyllables. I told my ex-husband I would prefer that he take them to Florence for a few days. He was very affectionate, I would have liked to thank him for his care, tell him that I loved him. But I felt Nino's inquiring gaze and I gave up on the idea.

Right afterward I called my parents. My father was cold, maybe out of timidity, maybe because my life seemed to him a disaster, maybe because he shared my brothers' resentment at my recent tendency to stick my nose in their business, when I had never let them meddle in mine. My mother wanted to see the child immediately, and I struggled to calm her down. Afterward I called Lila, she commented, amused: Things always go smoothly for you, for me nothing's moving yet. Maybe because she was busy with work she was brusque, she didn't mention a visit to the clinic. Everything normal, I thought, good-humoredly, and fell asleep.

When I woke I took it for granted that Nino had disappeared, but he was there. He talked for a long time with his friend the gynecologist, he asked about acknowledgment of paternity, he showed no anxiety about Eleonora's possible reaction. When I said I wanted to give the baby my mother's name he was pleased. And as soon as I recovered we went to a city clerk to officially register the child I had just delivered as Immacolata Sarratore.

Nino didn't appear uncomfortable on that occasion, either. I was the confused one, I said that I was married to Giovanni Sarratore, I corrected myself, I said *separated* from Pietro Airota, I came out with a disorderly pile of names, surnames, imprecise information. But the moment seemed lovely to me and I went back to believing that, to put my life in order, I needed only a little patience.

In those early days Nino neglected his endless duties and demonstrated in every possible way how important I was to him. He darkened only when he discovered that I didn't want to baptize the child.

"Children are baptized," he said.

196 · ELENA FERRANTE

"Are Albertino and Lidia baptized?"

"Of course."

Thus I learned that, in spite of the anti-religiousness that he often flaunted, baptism seemed necessary to him. There were moments of embarrassment. I had thought, ever since we were in high school, that he wasn't a believer, and he, on the other hand, said to me that, precisely because of the argument with the religion teacher in middle school, he was sure that I was a believer.

"Anyway," he said, bewildered, "believer or not, children are baptized."

"What sort of reasoning is that."

"It's not reasoning, it's feeling."

I assumed a playful tone.

"Let me be consistent," I said. "I didn't baptize Dede and Elsa, I won't baptize Immacolata. They'll decide themselves when they grow up."

He thought about it for a moment and burst out laughing: "Well, yes, who cares, it was an excuse for a celebration."

"Let's do it anyway."

I promised that I would organize something for all his friends. In those first hours of our daughter's life I observed him in every gesture, in the expressions of disappointment and those of approval. I felt happy and yet disoriented. Was it him? Was he the man I had always loved? Or a stranger I was forcing to assume a clear and definite character?

61.

None of my relatives, none of my friends from the neighborhood came to the clinic. Maybe—I thought, once I got home—I should have a little party for them, too. I had kept my origins so far from myself that, although I spent quite a bit of time in the neighborhood, I had never invited a single person who had to do with my childhood and adolescence to the apartment on Via Tasso. I regretted it, I felt that sharp separation as a residue of more fragile periods of my life, almost a sign of immaturity. I still had that thought in mind when the telephone rang. It was Lila.

"We're about to arrive."

"Who."

"Your mother and I."

It was a cold afternoon, Vesuvius had a dusting of snow on top, that visit seemed ill-timed.

"In this cold? Going out will make her ill."

"I told her but she won't listen."

"In a few days I'll have a party, I'll invite everyone, tell her she'll see the baby then."

"You tell her."

I gave up the discussion, but every idea of celebration left me, I felt that visit as an intrusion. I had only been home for a short time. With feeding, bathing, some sutures that bothered me, I was tired. And at that moment Nino was in the house. I didn't want my mother to be unhappy, and it made me uneasy that he and Lila should meet at a moment when I wasn't yet in shape. I tried to get rid of Nino, but he didn't seem to understand, in fact he seemed happy that my mother was coming, and stayed.

I went into the bathroom to fix myself up. When they knocked I rushed to open the door. I hadn't seen my mother for ten days. The contrast was violent between Lila, still carrying two lives, beautiful and energetic, and my mother, gripping her arm like a life preserver in a storm, more bent over than ever, at the end of her strength, close to sinking. I had her lean on me, I led her to a chair at the window. She murmured: how beautiful the bay is. And she stared past the balcony, maybe so as not to look at Nino. But he came over to her and in his winning way began to point out to her the foggy outlines between sea and sky: That's Ischia, there is Capri, come, you can see better here, lean on me. He never spoke to Lila, he didn't even greet her. I talked to her.

"You've recovered quickly," she said.

"I'm a little tired but I'm well."

"You insist on staying up here, it's hard to get here."

"But it's beautiful."

"Well."

"Come, let's go get the baby."

I took her into Immacolata's room.

"You already have your looks back," she praised me. "Your hair is so nice. And that necklace?"

"Nino gave it to me."

I picked the baby up from the cradle. Lila sniffed her, put her nose in her neck, said she smelled her scent as soon as she came into the house.

"What scent?"

"Of talcum powder, milk, disinfectant, newness."

"You like it?"

"Yes."

"I expected her to weigh more. Evidently only I was fat."

"Who knows what mine is like."

She spoke of him always in the masculine now.

"He'll be wonderful."

She nodded yes, but as if she hadn't heard, she was looking at the baby carefully. She ran a finger over her forehead, one ear. She repeated the pact we had jokingly made:

"If necessary we'll make an exchange."

I laughed, I brought the baby to my mother, who was leaning on Nino's arm, near the window. She was staring up at him with pleasure, she was smiling, it was as if she had forgotten herself and imagined that she was young.

"Here's Immacolata," I said.

She looked at Nino. He exclaimed quickly:

"It's a beautiful name."

My mother murmured:

"It's not true. But you can call her Imma, which is more modern."

She left Nino's arm, she gestured to me to give her her granddaughter. I did, but fearful that she didn't have the strength to hold her.

"*Madonna*, how beautiful you are," she whispered, and turned to Lila: "Do you like her?"

Lila was distracted, she was staring at my mother's feet.

"Yes," she said without taking her eyes off them. "But sit down."

I also looked where she was looking. Blood was dripping from under my mother's black dress.

62.

I snatched the infant with an instinctive jerk. My mother realized what was happening and I saw in her face disgust and shame. Nino grabbed her a moment before she fainted. Mamma, mamma, I called while he struck her lightly on one cheek with his fingertips. I was alarmed, she didn't regain consciousness, and meanwhile the baby began to wail. She'll die, I thought, terrified, she held out until the moment she saw Immacolata and then she let go. I kept repeating *Mamma* in a louder and louder voice.

"Call an ambulance," Lila said.

I went to the telephone, I stopped, confused, I wanted to give the baby to Nino. But he avoided me, he turned to Lila instead, he said that it would be quicker to take her to the hospital in the car. I felt my heart in my throat, the baby was crying, my mother regained consciousness and began to moan.

She whispered, weeping, that she didn't want to set foot in the hospital, she reminded me, pulling on my skirt, that she had been admitted once and didn't want to die in that abandonment. Trembling, she said: I want to see the baby grow up.

Nino at that point assumed the firm tone he had had even as a student when he had to confront difficult situations. Let's go, he said and picked up my mother in his arms. Since she protested weakly he reassured her, he told her that he would take care of arranging everything. Lila looked at me perplexed, I thought: the professor who attends to my mother at the hospital is a friend of Eleonora's family, Nino at this moment is indispensable, lucky he's here. Lila said, leave me the baby, you go. I agreed, I was about to hand her Immacolata but with a hesitant gesture, I was connected to her as if she were still inside me. And, anyway, I couldn't separate myself now, I had to feed her, bathe her. But to my mother, too, I felt bound as never before, I was shaking, what was that blood, what did it mean.

"Come on," Nino said impatiently to Lila, "hurry up."

"Yes," I said, "go and let me know."

Only when the door closed did I feel the wound of that situation: Lila and Nino together were taking my mother away, they were taking care of her when it should have been me.

I felt weak and confused. I sat on the couch, giving my breast to Immacolata to soothe her. I couldn't take my eyes off the blood on the floor as I imagined the car speeding over the frozen streets of the city, the handkerchief outside the window signaling an emergency, the finger on the horn, my mother dying in the back seat. The car was Lila's, was she driving or had he gotten behind the wheel? I have to stay calm, I said to myself.

I placed the baby in the cradle, and decided to call Elisa. I minimized what had happened, I was silent about Nino, I mentioned Lila. My sister immediately lost her temper, burst out crying, insulted me. She shouted that I had sent our mother who knows where with a stranger, that I should have called an ambulance, that I thought only of my own affairs and convenience, that if our mother died I was responsible. Then I heard her calling Marcello repeatedly in a commanding tone unfamiliar to me, petulant yet anguished cries. I said to her: What does "who knows where" mean, Lina took her to the hospital, why must you speak like that. She slammed down the telephone.

But Elisa was right. I had lost my head. I really should have called an ambulance. Or torn the baby away and given her to Lila. I was subject to Nino's authority, to that craving of men to make a good impression by appearing determined, saviors. I waited by the telephone for them to call me.

An hour passed, an hour and a half, finally the phone rang. Lila said calmly:

"They admitted her. Nino knows the doctors, they told him it's all under control. Be calm."

"Is she alone?"

"Yes, they won't let anyone in."

"She doesn't want to die alone."

"She won't die."

"She's frightened, Lila, do something, she's not what she used to be."

"That's how the hospital works."

"Did she ask about me?"

"She said you should bring her the baby."

"What are you doing now?"

"Nino is still with the doctors, I'm going."

"Go, yes, thank you, don't get tired."

"He'll phone as soon as he can."

"O.K."

"And stay calm, otherwise your milk won't come."

That allusion to the milk helped me. I sat next to Immacolata's cradle as if her nearness could preserve my swollen breasts. What was the body of a woman: I had nourished my daughter in the womb, now that she was out she was nourished by my breast. I thought, there was a moment when I, too, had been in my mother's womb, had sucked at her breast. A breast as big as mine, or maybe even bigger. Until shortly before my mother got sick my father had often alluded obscenely to that bosom. I had never seen her without a bra, in any stage of her life. She had always concealed herself, she didn't trust her body because of the leg. Yet at the first glass of wine she would counter my father's obscenities with words just as coarse in which she boasted of her attractions, an exhibition of shamelessness that was pure show. The telephone rang again and I hurried to answer. It was Lila again, now she had a curt tone.

"There's trouble here, Lenù."

"Is she worse?"

"No, the doctors are confident. But Marcello showed up and he's acting crazy."

"Marcello? What does Marcello have to do with it?"

"I don't know."

"Let me talk to him."

"Wait, he's arguing with Nino."

I recognized in the background Marcello's thick voice, loaded with dialect, and Nino's, in good Italian, but strident, which happened when he lost his temper.

"Tell Nino to forget it, in fact send him away."

Lila didn't answer, I heard her join a discussion that I was ignorant of and then suddenly shout in dialect: What the fuck are you saying, Marcè, go fuck yourself, get out. Then she shouted at me: Talk to this shit, please, you two come to an agreement, I don't want to get involved. Distant voices. After a few seconds Marcello came to the phone. He said, trying to assume a polite tone, that Elisa had insisted that we not leave our mother in the hospital and that he had come to get her and take her to a nice clinic in Capodimonte. He asked as if he seriously sought my permission:

"Am I right? Tell me if I'm right."

"Calm down."

"I'm calm, Lenù. But you gave birth in a clinic, Elisa gave birth in a clinic: why should your mother die here?"

I said uneasily:

"The doctors who are taking care of her work there."

He became aggressive as he had never been toward me:

"The doctors are where the money is. Who's in charge here, you, Lina, or that shit?"

"It's not a question of being in charge."

"Yes, it is. Either tell your friends that I can take her to Capodimonte or I'll break someone's face and take her all the same."

"Give me Lina," I said.

I had trouble standing up, my temples were pounding. I said: Ask Nino if my mother can be moved, make him talk to the doctors, then call me back. I hung up wringing my hands, I didn't know what to do.

A few minutes went by and the phone rang again. It was Nino.

"Lenù, control that beast, otherwise I'll call the police."

"Did you ask the doctors if my mother can be moved?"

"No, she can't be moved."

"Nino, did you ask or not? She doesn't want to stay in the hospital."

"Private clinics are even more disgusting."

"I know, but calm down."

"I'm perfectly calm."

"All right, but come home now."

"And here?"

"Lina will take care of it."

"I can't leave Lina with that guy."

I raised my voice:

"Lina can take care of herself. I can't stand up, the baby's crying, I have to bathe her. I told you, come home right now."

I hung up.

63.

Those were difficult hours. Nino arrived distraught, he was speaking in dialect, he was extremely nervous, he repeated: Now let's see who wins. I realized that my mother's admission to the hospital had become for him a question of principle. He was afraid that Solara really would take her to some unsuitable place, one of those which operate just to make money. In the hospital, he exclaimed, returning to Italian, your mother has high-level specialists available, professors who, in spite of the advanced stage of the illness, have so far kept her alive in a dignified way.

I shared his fears, and he took the matter to heart. Although it was dinnertime he telephoned important people, names well known in Naples at the time, I don't know if to complain or to gain support in a possible battle against Marcello's aggression. But I could hear that as soon as he uttered the name Solara the conversation became complicated, and he was silent, listening. He calmed down only around ten. I was in despair, but I tried not to let him see it, so that he wouldn't decide to go back to the hospital. My agitation spread to Immacolata. She wailed, I nursed her, she was quiet, she wailed again.

I didn't close my eyes. The telephone rang again at six in the morning, I rushed to answer hoping that neither the baby nor Nino would wake up. It was Lila, she had spent the night in the hospital. She gave me the report in a tired voice. Marcello had apparently given in, and had left without even saying goodbye to her. She had sneaked through stairways and corridors, had found the ward where they had brought my mother. It was a room of agony, there were five other suffering women, they groaned and cried, all abandoned to their suffering. She had found my mother, who, motionless, eyes staring, was whispering at the ceiling, *Madonna*, let me die soon, her whole body shaking with the effort of enduring the pain. Lila had squatted beside her, had calmed her. Now she had had to get out because it was day and the nurses were beginning to show up. She was pleased at how she had violated all the rules; she always enjoyed disobedience. But in that circumstance it seemed to me that she was pretending, in order not to make me feel the weight of the effort she had undertaken for me. She was close to giving birth, I imagined her exhausted, tortured by her own needs. I was worried about her at least as much as about my mother.

"How do you feel?"

"Fine."

"Sure?"

"Very sure."

"Go and sleep."

"Not until Marcello arrives with your sister."

"You're sure they'll be back?"

"As if they would give up making a scene."

While I was on the phone Nino appeared, sleepy. He listened for a while, then said:

"Let me speak to her."

I didn't hand him the phone, I muttered: She already hung up. He complained, he said he had mobilized a series of people to ensure that my mother would have the best care possible and he wanted to know if there had been any result of his interest. For now, no, I answered. We made a plan for him to take me to the hospital with the baby, even though there was a strong, cold wind. He would stay in the car with Immacolata and I would go to my mother between feedings. He said all right, and his helpfulness softened me toward him, then annoyed me, because he had taken care of everything except the practicality of noting the visiting hours. I called to find out, we carefully bundled up the baby, and went. Lila hadn't been heard from; I was sure we would find her in the hospital. But when we arrived we found that not only was she not there but neither was my mother. She had been discharged.

64.

I learned later from my sister what had happened. She told me as if she were saying: You give yourself a lot of airs, but without us you are no one. At exactly nine Marcello had arrived at the hospital with some head physician—he had taken the trouble himself to pick him up at home in the car. Our mother had been immediately transferred by ambulance to the Capodimonte clinic. There, Elisa said, she's like a queen, we relatives can stay as much as we want, there's a bed for Papa, who will keep her company at night. And she specified, contemptuously: Don't worry, we'll pay for it. What followed was explicitly threatening. Maybe your friend the professor, she said, doesn't understand who he's dealing with, you'd better explain it to him. And tell that shit Lina that she may be very intelligent, but Marcello has changed, Marcello isn't her little boyfriend from long ago, and he's not like Michele, whom she twists around her little finger: Marcello said that if she raises her voice again with me, if she insults me the way she did in front of everyone in the hospital, he'll kill her.

I didn't report anything to Lila and I didn't even want to know in what terms she had quarreled with my sister. But in the days that followed I became more affectionate, I telephoned often to let her know that I was grateful, that I loved her and couldn't wait until she, too, gave birth.

"Everything all right?" I asked.

"Yes."

"Nothing moving?"

"Of course not. Do you want help today?"

"No, tomorrow if you can."

The days were intense, with a complicated adding up of old restraints and new. My whole body was still in symbiosis with Imma's tiny organism, I couldn't separate from her. But I also missed Dede and Elsa, so I telephoned Pietro and he finally brought them back. Elsa immediately pretended to love her new little sister dearly, but she didn't hold out for long, in a few hours she began to make faces of disgust at her, she said: You made her really ugly. Dede, on the other hand, wanted to prove that she could be a much more capable mamma than I was and was in constant danger of dropping her or drowning her in the bath.

I needed a lot of help, at least in those early days, and I have to say that Pietro offered it. He, who as a husband had barely exerted himself to make things easier, now that we were officially separated didn't want to leave me alone with three children, one of whom was a newborn, and offered to stay for a few days. But I had to send him away, and not because I didn't want his help but because during the few hours he was in Via Tasso Nino harassed me, he kept calling to find out if Pietro had gone and if he could come *to his house* without being forced to meet him. Naturally when my ex-husband left Nino was overwhelmed by his job and his political engagements, so I was on my own: in order to shop, take the children to school, pick them up, read a book or write a few lines, I had to leave Imma with the neighbor.

But that was the least of it. Much more complicated was arranging to go and see my mother in the clinic. I didn't trust Mirella, two children and a newborn seemed too much for her. So I decided to take Imma with me. I bundled her up, called a taxi, and was driven to Capodimonte, taking advantage of the time when Dede and Elsa were in school.

My mother had recovered. Of course, she was frail, and if she didn't see us children every day she feared catastrophe and began to cry. Also, she was permanently in bed, while before, even if laboriously, she had moved, gone out. But it seemed indisputable that the luxuries of the clinic were beneficial to her. To be treated like a great lady became a game that distracted her from the illness and that, with the help of some drug, diminished the pain, making her at times euphoric. She liked the large luminous room, she found the mattress comfortable, she was proud of having her own bathroom, and in the room, no less. A real bathroom—she pointed out—not a toilet, and she wanted to get up and show it to me. Not to mention that there was the new granddaughter. When I went with Imma to see her she held the baby next to her, talked to her in baby talk, grew excited, claiming—which was very unlikely—that Imma had smiled at her.

But in general her interest in the infant didn't last long. She began to speak of her own childhood, of adolescence. She went back to when she was five, then she slid to twelve, then fourteen, and she related to me from within those ages things that had happened to her and her companions of that time. One morning she said to me in dialect: As a child I knew about death, I've always known about it, but I never thought it would happen to me, and even now I can't believe it. Another time, following her own thoughts, she began to laugh, and whispered: You're right not to baptize the baby, it's nonsense; now that I'm dying I know that I'll turn into little bits and pieces. But mostly it was in those slow hours that I truly felt I was her favorite child. When she embraced me before I left, it was as if she meant to slip inside me and stay there, as once I had been inside her. That contact with her body, which had irritated me when she was healthy, I now liked.

65.

It was odd how the clinic soon became a place of meeting for the old and the young of the neighborhood.

My father slept there with my mother, and when I saw him in the morning his beard was unshaven, his eyes were frightened. We barely greeted each other, but that didn't seem unusual. I had never had much contact with him: at times affectionate, often distracted, occasionally in support of me against my mother. But it had almost always been superficial. My mother had given him a role and taken it away according to convenience, and especially when it came to me—making and unmaking my life was to be only for her—she had pushed him into the background. Now that the energy of his wife had almost completely vanished, he didn't know how to talk to me nor I to him. I said hi, he said hi, then he added: while you keep her company, I'll go smoke a cigarette. Sometimes I wondered how he had managed to survive, a man so ordinary, in the fierce world he had moved in, in Naples, in his job, in the neighborhood, even at home.

When Elisa arrived with her baby I saw that there was a greater intimacy between her and our father. Elisa treated him with affectionate authority. Often she stayed all day and sometimes all night, sending him home to sleep in his own bed. As soon as she arrived, my sister had to criticize everything, the dust, the windows, the food. She did it to make herself respected, she wanted it to be clear that she was in charge. And Peppe and Gianni matched her. When they felt my mother was suffering and my father desperate, both would get upset, press the bell, call the nurse. If the nurse delayed, my brothers reprimanded her harshly and then, contradicting themselves, gave her lavish tips. Gianni especially, before leaving, would stick some money in her pocket, saying: Stay right outside the door and hop up as soon as Mamma calls you, have your coffee when you're off duty, is that clear? Then, to let it be understood that our mother was a person of consequence, he would mention three or four times the name of the Solaras. Signora Greco—he would say—is the Solaras' business.

The Solaras' business. Those words enraged me, I was ashamed. But meanwhile I thought, either this or the hospital, and I said to myself: but *afterward* (what I meant by *afterward* I didn't admit even to myself) I'll have to clear up a lot of things with my siblings and with Marcello. For now it gave me pleasure to arrive in the room and find my mother with her friends from the neighborhood, all her contemporaries, to whom she boasted weakly, saying things like, My children wanted it like this, or, pointing to me: Elena is a famous writer, she has a house on Via Tasso from which the sea is visible, look what a beautiful baby, she's called Immacolata, like me. When her friends left, murmuring, Sleep, I went in to check on her, then returned with Imma to the corridor, where the air seemed fresher. I left the door of the room open so I could monitor my mother's heavy breathing; after the fatigue of those visits, she often fell asleep and groaned in her sleep.

Occasionally the days were simpler. Carmen, for example, sometimes came to get me in her car. And Alfonso did the same. Naturally it was a sign of affection for me. They spoke respectfully to my mother, at most they gave her some satisfaction by praising her granddaughter and the comfort of the room. The rest of the time they spent either talking in the corridor with me or waiting outside, in the car, to be in time to take me to pick up the girls at school. The mornings with them were always intense and created a curious effect: they brought together the neighborhood of my mother, now near its end, and the one being constructed under Lila's influence.

I told Carmen what our friend had done for my mother. She said with satisfaction: You know no one can stop Lina, and she spoke of her as if she attributed to her magical powers. But I learned more from a quarter of an hour spent with Alfonso in the spotless corridor of the clinic, while the doctor was with my mother. He, too, usually, was inflamed with gratitude toward Lila, but what struck me was that for the first time he talked explicitly about himself. He said: Lina taught me a job with a great future. He exclaimed: Without her what would I have been, nothing, a piece of living flesh, without fulfillment. He compared Lila with his wife's behavior: I left Marisa free to betray me as much as she wanted, I gave my name to her children, but just the same she's angry at me, she tormented me and torments me, she has spit in my face countless times, she says I cheated her. He defended himself: How did I cheat, Lenù, you're an intellectual and you can understand me, the one who was cheated was me, cheated by myself, and if Lina hadn't helped me I would have died cheated. His eyes were shining. The most beautiful thing she did for me was to impose clarity on me, teach me to say: If I touch the bare foot of this woman I feel nothing, while I die of desire if I touch the foot of that man, there, and caress his hands, cut his nails with scissors, squeeze his blackheads, be with him on a dance floor and say to him, If you know how to waltz lead me, let me feel how well you lead. He recalled faraway events: Do you remember when you and Lina came to my house to ask my father to give you back the dolls and he called me, he asked, teasing, Alfò, did you take them—because I was the shame of the family, I played with my sister's dolls and I tried on Mamma's necklaces? He explained to me, but as if I already knew everything and was useful only in enabling him to express his true nature. Even as a child, he said, I knew I wasn't what the others thought but not what I thought, either. I said to myself: I'm another thing, a thing that is hidden in the veins, it has no name and waits. But I didn't know what that thing was and especially I didn't know how it could be me, until Lila forced me—I don't know how to say it—to take a little of her. You

212 · ELENA FERRANTE

know what she's like, she said: start here and see what happens; so we were mixed up—it was a lot of fun—and now I'm not what I was and I'm not Lila, either, but another person who is slowly defining himself.

He was happy to share these confidences and I was happy, too, that he made them. A new intimacy arose between us, different from when we used to walk home from school. And with Carmen, too, I had the impression that our relationship was becoming more trusting. Then I realized that both, if in different ways, were asking something more of me. It happened twice, both times connected to Marcello's presence in the clinic.

My sister Elisa and her baby were usually driven to the clinic by an old man named Domenico. Domenico left them there and drove our father back to the neighborhood. But sometimes it was Marcello himself who brought Elisa and Silvio. One morning when he appeared in person Carmen was there with me. I was sure there would be tensions between them, but they exchanged a greeting that wasn't warm but not confrontational, either, and she hovered around him like an animal ready to approach at the first hint of favor. Once we were alone she confided to me nervously, in a low voice, that even if the Solaras hated her she was trying to be friendly and she did it for love of Pasquale. But—she exclaimed—I can't do it, Lenù, I hate them, I want to strangle them, it's only out of necessity. Then she asked: How would you act in my place?

Something similar happened with Alfonso. One morning when he took me to see my mother, Marcello appeared and Alfonso panicked just at the sight of him. And yet Solara behaved just as he usually did: he greeted me with awkward politeness, and gave Alfonso a nod, pretending not to see the hand that he had mechanically extended. To avoid friction I pushed my friend into the hall with the excuse that I had to nurse Imma. Once outside the room Alfonso muttered: If they murder me, remember it was Marcello. I said: Don't exaggerate.

But he was tense, he began sarcastically to make a list of the people in the neighborhood who would gladly kill him, people I didn't know and people I knew. On the list he put his brother Stefano (he laughed; *he fucks my wife only to demonstrate that we're not all fags in the family*) and also Rino (he laughed; *ever since he realized I'm able to look like his sister, he would do to me what he can't do to her*). But at the top he always left Marcello, according to him it was Marcello who hated him most. He said it with satisfaction and yet anguish: he thinks Michele went mad because of me. And he added, sneering: Lila encouraged me to be like her, she likes the effort I make, she likes to see how I distort her, she's pleased with the effect that this distortion has on Michele, and I'm pleased, too. Then he stopped, he asked me: What do you think?

I listened, nursing the baby. He and Carmen were not satisfied that I lived in Naples, that every so often we met: they wanted me to be fully reintegrated into the neighborhood, they asked me to stand beside Lila as a guardian deity, they urged that we act as divinities at times in agreement, at times in competition, but in any case attentive to their problems. That request for greater involvement in their affairs, which in her way Lila, too, often made and which in general seemed an inappropriate pressure, in that situation moved me, I felt that it reinforced the tired voice of my mother when she proudly pointed me out to her friends of the neighborhood as an important part of herself. I hugged Imma to my breast and adjusted the blanket to protect her from the drafts.

66.

Only Nino and Lila never came to the clinic. Nino was explicit: I have no desire to meet that Camorrist, I'm sorry for your mother, give her my best, but I can't go with you. Sometimes

I convinced myself that it was a way of justifying his disappearances, but more often he seemed truly hurt, because he had gone
to a lot of trouble for my mother and then I and my whole family had ended up going along with the Solaras. I explained to him
that it was a difficult system. I said: It doesn't have to do with
Marcello, we only agreed to what made our mother happy. But
he grumbled: that's why Naples will never change.

As for Lila, she said nothing about the move to the clinic.
She continued to help me out even though she was about to
give birth herself at any moment. I felt guilty. I said: Don't worry
about me, you should look after yourself. But no—she answered
pointing to her stomach with an expression between sarcasm
and alarm—he's late, I don't want to and he doesn't want to.
And as soon as I needed something she hurried over. Naturally,
she never offered to drive me to Capodimonte, as Carmen and
Alfonso did. But if the children had a fever and I couldn't send
them to school—as happened several times in Immacolata's
first three weeks of life, which were cold and rainy—she was
available, she left the job to Enzo and Alfonso, she came up to
Via Tasso to take all three of them.

I was glad; the time Dede and Elsa spent with Lila was
always valuable. She was able to bring the two sisters closer to
the third, making Dede take responsibility, keeping Elsa under
control, soothing Imma without sticking the pacifier in her
mouth, as Mirella did. The only problem was Nino. I was
afraid I would discover that—though he was always busy when
I was alone—he had miraculously managed to find time to
help Lila when she was with the girls. And so in a hidden corner of myself I was never really serene. Lila arrived, I gave her
endless advice, I wrote down the number of the clinic, I alerted
my neighbor just in case, I hurried to Capodimonte. I stayed
with my mother no longer than an hour and then I slipped
away to get home in time for nursing, for cooking. But sometimes, on the way home, I'd have a flash of entering the house

and finding Nino and Lila together, talking about everything under the sun, as they used to do in Ischia. I also tended, naturally, to more intolerable fantasies, but I repressed them, horrified. The most persistent fear was a different one, and, while I drove, it appeared to me the most well founded. I imagined that her labor would begin while Nino was there, so that he would have to take her to the emergency room, leaving Dede to play, terrified, the part of the sensible woman, Elsa to rummage in Lila's bag and steal something, Imma to wail in her cradle, tormented by hunger and diaper rash.

Something like that did happen, but Nino had no part in it. I returned home one morning, punctual, within the half hour, and discovered that Lila wasn't there; her labor had begun. An intolerable anguish seized me. More than anything she feared the shaking and bending of matter, she hated illness in any form, she detested the hollowness of words when they were emptied of any possible meaning. So I prayed that she would hold up.

67.

I know about the birth from two sources, her and the gynecologist. Here I'll put down the stories in succession and summarize the situation in my own words. It was raining. I had given birth three weeks earlier. My mother had been in the clinic for a couple of weeks and, if I didn't appear, she wept like an anxious child. Dede had a slight fever, Elsa refused to go to school, insisting that she wanted to take care of her sister. Carmen wasn't available, nor was Alfonso. I called Lila, I set out the usual conditions: If you don't feel well, if you have to work, forget it, I'll find another solution. She replied in her teasing way that she felt very well and that when you're the boss you give the orders and take all the time off you want. She loved the two girls, but she especially liked taking care of Imma with them; it was a game that made all four of them happy. I'm leaving right away, she said. I figured that she would arrive in an hour at most, but she was late. I waited a while, but since I knew that she would keep her promise, I said to the neighbor: It's a matter of minutes, and left the children with her to go to my mother.

But Lila was late because of a sort of presentiment in her body. Although she wasn't having contractions she didn't feel well and, finally, as a precaution, had Enzo take her to my house. Even before she went in she felt the first pains. She immediately called Carmen, ordering her to come and give the neighbor a hand, then Enzo took her to the clinic where our gynecologist worked. The contractions suddenly became violent but not decisive: the labor lasted sixteen hours.

Lila's account was almost funny. It's not true, she said, that you suffer only with the first child and afterward it's easier—you always suffer. And she brought out arguments as fierce as they were humorous. It seemed to her pointless to safeguard the child in your womb and at the same time long to get rid of it. It's ridiculous, she said, that this exquisite nine months of hospitality is accompanied by the desire to throw out the guest as violently as possible. She shook her head indignantly at the inconsistency of the mechanism. It's crazy, she exclaimed, resorting to Italian, it's your own body that's angry with you, and in fact rebels against you until it becomes its own worst enemy, until it achieves the most terrible pain possible. For hours she had felt in her belly sharp cold flames, an unbearable flow of pain that hit her brutally in the pit of her stomach and then returned, penetrating her kidneys. Come on, she said sarcastically, you're a liar, where is the great experience. And she swore—this time seriously—that she would never get pregnant again.

But according to the gynecologist, whom Nino invited to dinner one night with her husband, the delivery had been normal, any other woman would have given birth without all that talk. What complicated it was only Lila's teeming head. The doctor had been very irritated. You're doing the opposite of what you should, she had reprimanded her, you hold on when instead you should push: go on, go, push. According to her—she now felt an open aversion toward her patient, and there in my house, at dinner, she didn't hide it but, rather, displayed it in a conspiratorial way, especially to Nino—Lila had done her best not to bring her infant into the world. She held onto it with all her strength and meanwhile gasped: Cut my stomach open, you get it out, I can't do it. When the gynecologist continued to encourage her, Lila shouted vulgar insults at her. She was soaked in sweat, the gynecologist told us, her eyes were bloodshot below her broad forehead, and she was screaming: You talk, you give orders, you come here and do it, you piece of shit, you push the baby out if you can, it's killing me.

I was annoyed and I said to the doctor: You shouldn't tell us these things. She became even more irritated, she exclaimed: I'm telling you because we're among friends. But then, stung, she assumed the tone of the doctor and said with an affected seriousness that if we loved Lila we should (she meant Nino and me, obviously) help her concentrate on something that truly gave her satisfaction, otherwise, with her dancing brain (she used precisely that expression), she would get herself and those around her in trouble. Finally, she repeated that in the delivery room she had seen a struggle against nature, a terrible clash between a mother and her child. It was, she said, a truly unpleasant experience.

The infant was a girl, a girl and not a boy as everyone had predicted. When I was able to go to the clinic, Lila, although she was exhausted, showed me her daughter proudly. She asked:

"How much did Imma weigh?"

"Seven pounds."

"Nunzia weighs almost nine pounds: my belly was small but she is large."

She really had named her for her mother. And in order not to upset Fernando, her father, who was even more irascible in old age than he'd been as a young man, and Enzo's relatives, she had her baptized in the neighborhood church and held a big party in the Basic Sight offices.

68.

The babies immediately became an excuse to spend more time together. Lila and I talked on the phone, met to take them for a walk, spoke endlessly, no longer about ourselves but about them. Or at least so it seemed to us. In reality a new richness and complexity in our relationship began to manifest itself through a mutual attention to our daughters. We compared them in every detail as if to assure ourselves that the health or illness of the one was the precise mirror of the health or illness of the other and as a result we could readily intervene to reinforce the first and cut off the second. We told each other everything that seemed good and useful for healthy development, engaging in a sort of virtuous competition of who could find the best food, the softest diaper, the most effective cream for a rash. There was no pretty garment acquired for Nunzia—but now she was called Tina, the diminutive of Nunziatina—that Lila did not also get for Imma, and I, within the limits of my finances, did the same. This onesie was cute on Tina, so I got one for Imma, too—she'd say—or these shoes were cute on Tina and I got some for Imma, too.

"You know," I said one day, smiling, "that you've given her the name of my doll?"

"What doll?"

"Tina, you don't remember?"

She touched her forehead as if she had a headache, and said:

"It's true, but I didn't do it on purpose."

"She was a beautiful doll—I was attached to her."

"My daughter is more beautiful."

Meanwhile the weeks passed; already the scents of spring were flaring. One morning my mother got worse, and there was a moment of panic. Since the doctors at the clinic didn't seem qualified even to my siblings, the idea of taking her back to the hospital was mentioned. I asked Nino to find out if, through the doctors who were connected to his in-laws and had taken care of my mother before, it would be possible to avoid the wards and get a private room. But Nino said that he was opposed to using connections or appeals, that in a public institution treatment should be the same for everyone, and he muttered ill-humoredly: in this country we have to stop thinking that even for a bed in the hospital you have to be a member of a lodge or rely on the Camorra. He was angry with Marcello, naturally, not with me, but I felt humiliated anyway. On the other hand I'm sure that in the end he would have helped if my mother, although suffering atrociously, hadn't made it clear in every way possible that she preferred to die amid comforts rather than return, even for a few hours, to a hospital ward. So one morning Marcello, surprising us yet again, brought to the clinic one of the specialists who had treated our mother. The specialist, who had been curt when he was working in the hospital, was extremely cordial and returned often, greeted deferentially by the doctors in the private clinic. Things improved.

But soon the clinical picture worsened again. At that point my mother gathered all her strength and did two contradictory but in her eyes equally important things. Lila just then had found a way of getting jobs for Peppe and Gianni with a client of hers in Baiano, but they had disregarded the offer, so she— heaping blessings on my friend for her generosity—summoned her two sons and became, at least for a moment, what she had been in the past. Her eyes were furious, she threatened to pursue them from the kingdom of the dead if they didn't accept the offer: she made them weep, she reduced them to lambs, she didn't let go until she was sure she had subdued them. Then she took up an initiative that ran in the opposite direction. She summoned Marcello, from whom she had just wrested Peppe and Gianni, and made him swear solemnly that he would marry her younger daughter before she closed her eyes forever. Marcello reassured her, he told her that he and Elisa had put off getting married only because they were waiting for her to recover, and now that her recovery was imminent he would immediately take care of the paperwork. Now my mother brightened. She made no distinction between the power she attributed to Lila and that which she attributed to Marcello. She had pressured both and was happy to have gained benefits for her children from the most important people in the neighborhood; that is, in her view, in the world.

For a few days she lingered in a state of peaceful joy. I brought Dede, whom she loved dearly, and I let her hold Imma. She was even affectionate toward Elsa, whom she had never liked much. I observed her: she was a gray, wrinkled old woman, even though she wasn't a hundred but sixty. I then first felt the impact of time, the force that was pushing me toward forty, the velocity with which life was consumed, the concreteness of the exposure to death: *If it's happening to her,* I thought, *there's no escape, it will happen to me as well.*

One morning, when Imma was just over two months old, my mother said weakly: Lenù, I'm truly content now, it's only you I'm worried about, but you are you and you've always been able to arrange things as you liked, so I have confidence. Then she went to sleep and fell into a coma. She held out for a few more days; she didn't want to die. I remember that I was in her room with Imma; by now the death rattle was continuous, it had become one of the ordinary sounds of the clinic. My father, who couldn't bear to hear it anymore, had stayed home that night, weeping. Elisa had taken Silvio out to the courtyard to get some air, my brothers were smoking in a room nearby. I stared for a long time at that insubstantial bulge under the sheet. My mother was diminished almost to nothing, and yet she had been truly burdensome, weighing on me, making me feel like a worm under a rock, protected and crushed. I wished that wheeze would stop, right away, now, and, to my surprise, it did. Suddenly the room was silent. I waited, I couldn't find the strength to get up and go to her. Then Imma clicked her tongue and the silence was broken. I left the chair, went over to the bed. The two of us—I and the infant, greedily seeking my nipple in her sleep, to feel that she was still part of me— were, in that place of illness, the only living and healthy part of my mother that remained.

That day, I don't know why, I had put on the bracelet she had given me more than twenty years before. I hadn't worn it for a long time; I usually wore the finer jewelry that Adele had recommended. From then on I wore it often.

69.

I struggled to accept my mother's death. Even though I didn't shed a tear, the pain lasted for a long time and perhaps has never really gone away. I had considered her an insensitive and vulgar woman, I had feared her and fled. Right after her funeral I felt the way you feel when it suddenly starts raining hard, and you look around and find no place to take shelter. For weeks I saw and heard her everywhere, night and day. She was a vapor that in my imagination continued to burn without a wick. I missed the different way of being together we had discovered during her illness, I prolonged it by retrieving positive memories of when I was a child and she was young. My sense of guilt wanted to compel her to endure. In a drawer I put a hairpin of hers, a handkerchief, a pair of scissors, but they all seemed inadequate objects, even the bracelet was worthless. My pregnancy had brought back the pain in my hip and Imma's birth hadn't relieved it, but maybe that was why I decided not to go to the doctor. I nurtured that pain like a bequest preserved in my body.

The words she had said to me at the end (*You're you, I have confidence*) also stayed with me for a long time. She died convinced that because of how I was made, because of the resources I had accumulated, I would not be overwhelmed by anything. That idea worked inside me and in the end helped me. I decided to prove to her that she had been right. I began again in a disciplined way to take care of myself. I returned to using every bit of empty time for reading and writing. I lost what little interest I'd had in petty politics—I couldn't get excited at the intrigues of the five governing parties and their quarrels with the Communists, as Nino now was actively doing—but I continued to follow closely the corrupt and violent drift of the country. I collected feminist readings and, still fortified by the small success of my last book, proposed articles to the new journals directed at women. But, I have to admit, a great part of my energy was focused on convincing my publisher that I was moving along with the new novel.

A few years earlier half of a substantial advance had been paid, but in the meantime I had done very little, I was stumbling along, still looking for a story. The editor in chief, who was responsible for that generous sum, had never pressured me, he inquired discreetly, and if I was elusive, because to admit the truth seemed to me shameful, he let me be elusive. Then a small unpleasant event occurred. A semi-sarcastic article appeared in the *Corriere della Sera* that, after praising a first novel that had had a modest success, alluded to the failed promise of the new

Italian literature, and included my name. A few days later the editor passed through Naples—he was to take part in a prestigious conference—and asked if we could meet.

His serious tone immediately worried me. In almost fifteen years he had never insisted on his authority, he had sided with me against Adele, he had always treated me kindly. With forced warmth I invited him to dinner on Via Tasso, which cost me anxiety and hard work, but I did it partly because Nino wanted to propose a new collection of essays.

The editor was polite but not affectionate. He expressed his condolences for my mother, he praised Imma, he gave Dede and Elsa some colorful books, he waited patiently for me to maneuver between dinner and daughters, leaving Nino to talk to him about his possible book. When we got to dessert he brought up the true reason for the meeting: he wanted to know if he could plan to bring out my novel the following fall. I turned red.

"Fall of 1982?"

"Fall of 1982."

"Maybe, but I'll know better in a little while."

"You have to know now."

"I'm still nowhere near the end."

"You could let me read something."

"I don't feel ready."

Silence. He took a sip of wine, then said in a serious tone:

"Up to now you've been very lucky, Elena. The last book went particularly well, you're respected, you've gained a good number of readers. But readers have to be cultivated. If you lose them, you lose the chance to publish other books."

I was displeased. I understood that Adele, by force of repetition, had gotten through even to that very civilized and polite man. I imagined the words of Pietro's mother, her choice of terms—*She's an untrustworthy southerner who behind a charming appearance weaves crafty tissues of lies*—and I hated myself because I was proving to that man that those words

were true. At dessert, the editor, in a few curt phrases, liqui-
dated Nino's proposal, saying that it was a difficult moment for
essays. The awkwardness increased, no one knew what to say,
I talked about Imma until finally the guest looked at his watch
and said that he had to go. At that point I couldn't take it and
I said:

"All right, I'll deliver the book in time for it to come out in
the fall."

70.

My promise soothed the editor. He stayed another hour, he
chatted about this and that, he made an effort to be more well
disposed to Nino. He embraced me as he left, whispering, I'm
sure you're writing a wonderful story.

As soon as I closed the door I exclaimed: Adele is still plotting against me, I'm in trouble. But Nino didn't agree. Even
the slim possibility that his book would be published had
cheered him. Besides, he had been in Palermo recently for the
Socialist Party Congress, where he had seen both Guido and
Adele, and the professor had indicated that he admired some
of his recent work. So he said, conciliatory:

"Don't exaggerate the intrigues of the Airotas. All you had
to do was promise you'd get to work and you saw how things
changed?"

We quarreled. I had just promised a book, yes, but how,
when would I be able to write it with the necessary concentration and continuity? Did he realize what my life had been, and
still was? I listed randomly the illness and death of my mother,
the care of Dede and Elsa, the household tasks, the pregnancy,
the birth of Imma, his lack of interest in her, the rushing from
this conference to that congress, more and more often without
me, and the disgust, yes, the disgust at having to share him with

Eleonora. *I*, I shouted at him, *I* am now nearly divorced from
Pietro, and you wouldn't even separate. Could I work among so
many tensions, by myself, without any help from him?

The fight was pointless, Nino reacted as he always did. He
looked depressed, he whispered: You don't understand, you
can't understand, you're unfair, and he swore fiercely that he
loved me and couldn't do without Imma, the children, me.
Finally he offered to pay for a housekeeper.

He had encouraged me on other occasions to find someone
who could take care of the house, the shopping, the cooking,
the children, but, in order not to seem excessively demanding,
I had always responded that I didn't want to be a bigger economic burden than necessary. Generally I tended to give more
importance not to what would be helpful to me but to what he
would appreciate. And then I didn't want to admit that the
same problems I had already experienced with Pietro were
surfacing in our relationship. But this time, surprising him, I
said immediately: Yes, all right, find this woman as soon as
possible. And it seemed to me that I was speaking in the voice
of my mother, not in the feeble voice of recent times but in strident tones. Who gave a damn about the shopping, I had to
take care of my future. And my future was to write a novel in
the next few months. And that novel had to be very good. And
nothing, not even Nino, would prevent me from doing my
work well.

71.

I examined the situation. The two previous books, which
for years had produced a little money, partly thanks to translations, had stopped selling. The advance I had received for my
new book and hadn't yet earned was nearly gone. The articles
I wrote, working late into the night, either brought in little or

were not paid at all. I lived, in other words, on the money that Pietro contributed punctually every month and that Nino supplemented by taking on the rent for the house, the bills, and, I have to admit, often giving me money for clothes for myself and the children. But as long as I had had to confront all the upheavals and inconveniences and sufferings that followed my return to Naples, it had seemed fair. Now instead—after that evening—I decided that it was urgent to become as autonomous as possible. I had to write and publish regularly, I had to reinforce my profile as an author, I had to earn money. And the reason was not any literary vocation, the reason had to do with the future: Did I really think that Nino would take care of me and my daughters forever?

It was then that a part of me—only a part—began to emerge that consciously, without particular suffering, admitted that it couldn't really count on him. It wasn't just the old fear that he would leave me; rather it seemed to me an abrupt contraction of perspective. I stopped looking into the distance, I began to think that in the immediate future I couldn't expect from Nino more than what he was giving me, and that I had to decide if it was enough.

I continued to love him, of course. I liked his long slender body, his methodical intelligence. And I had a great admiration for his work. His old ability to assemble facts and interpret them was a skill that was much in demand. Recently he had published a highly regarded work—maybe that was the one Guido had liked so much—on the economic crisis and on the karstic movement of capital that was being shifted from sources to be investigated toward construction, finance, private television. Yet something about him had begun to bother me. For example, I was wounded by his delight in finding favor with my former father-in-law. Nor did I like the way he had begun again to differentiate Pietro—*a petty professor with no imagination, highly praised only because of his surname and his obtuse activity in the Communist Party*—from his father, the *real* Professor Airota, whom he praised unrestrainedly as the author of fundamental volumes on Hellenism and as an outstanding and combative figure of the socialist left. His renewed liking for Adele further wounded me; he was constantly calling her a great lady, extraordinary at public relations. He seemed to me, in other words, sensitive to the approval of those who had authority and ready to catch out, or even, at times, humiliate, out of envy, those who did not yet have enough of it and those who did not have it at all but could have it. Something that marred the image that I had always had of him and that he generally had of himself.

It wasn't only that. The political and cultural climate was changing, other readings were emerging. We had all stopped making extreme speeches, and I was surprised to find myself agreeing with positions that years earlier I had opposed in Pietro, out of a wish to contradict him, out of the need to quarrel. But Nino went too far, he now found ridiculous not only every subversive statement but also every ethical declaration, every display of purity. He said, making fun of me:

"There are too many sensitive souls around."

"Meaning?"

"People who are outraged, as if they didn't know that either the parties do their job or you get armed gangs and Masonic lodges."

"What do you mean?"

"I mean that a party can't be anything other than a distributor of favors in exchange for support, ideals are part of the furniture."

"Well, then I'm a sensitive soul."

"I know that."

I began to find his craving to be politically surprising unpleasant. When he organized dinners at my house he embarrassed his own guests by defending from the left positions of the right. The fascists—he maintained—aren't always wrong and we should learn to talk to each other. Or: You can't simply condemn, you have to get your hands dirty if you want to change things. Or even: Justice should as soon as possible be subordinated to the rights of those who have the task of governing, otherwise the judges become loose cannons, dangerous for the preservation of the democratic system. Or again: Wages have to be frozen, the mechanism of the wage index scale is ruinous for Italy. If someone disagreed with him he became contemptuous, he sneered, he let it be understood that it wasn't worth the trouble to argue with people wearing blinders, whose heads were full of old slogans.

I retreated into an uneasy silence, in order not to take sides against him. He loved the shifting sands of the present, the future for him was decided there. He knew about everything that happened in the parties and in parliament, about the internal movements of capital and of the organization of labor. I, on the other hand, persisted in reading only what had to do with the dark conspiracies, the kidnappings and bloody last-ditch efforts of the armed red gangs, the debate on the decline of the centrality of workers, the identification of new opposition subjects. As a result I felt more comfortable with the language of the other diners than with his. One evening he quarreled with a friend who taught in the school of architecture. He became inflamed by passion, disheveled, handsome.

"You can't distinguish between a step forward, a step back, and standing still."

"What's a step forward?" the friend asked.

"A prime minister who isn't the same old Christian Democrat."

"And standing still?"

"A demonstration by steelworkers."

"And a step back?"

"Asking who's cleaner, the socialists or the Communists."

"You're turning cynical."

"You, on the other hand, have always been a shit."

No, Nino no longer persuaded me the way he used to. He expressed himself, I don't know how to say it, in a provocative and yet opaque way, as if precisely he, who extolled the long view, were able to follow only the daily moves and counter-moves of a system that to me, to his own friends, seemed rotten to the core. Enough, he would insist, let's end the childish aversion to power: one has to be on the inside in the places where things are born and die: the parties, the banks, television. And I listened, but when he turned to me I lowered my gaze. I no longer concealed from myself that his conversation partly bored me, and partly seemed to point to a brittleness that dragged him down.

One time he was lecturing Dede, who had to do some sort of crazy research for her teacher, and to soften his pragmatism I said:

"The people, Dede, always have the possibility of turning everything upside down."

Good-humoredly he replied, "Mamma likes to make up stories, which is a great job. But she doesn't know much about how the world we live in functions, and so whenever there's something she doesn't like she resorts to a magic word: let's turn everything upside down. You tell your teacher that we have to make the world that exists function."

"How?" I asked.

"With laws."

"But if you say that the judges should be controlled."

Displeased with me, he shook his head, just as Pietro used to do.

"Go and write your book," he said, "otherwise you'll complain it's our fault that you can't work."

He started a lesson with Dede on the division of powers, which I listened to in silence and agreed with from A to Z.

72.

When Nino was home he staged a comic ritual with Dede and Elsa. They dragged me into the little room where I had my desk, ordered me peremptorily to get to work, and shut the door behind them, scolding me in chorus if I dared to open it.

In general, if he had time, he was very available to the children: to Dede, whom he judged very intelligent but too rigid, and to Elsa, whose feigned acquiescence, behind which lurked malice and cunning, amused him. But what I hoped would happen never did: he didn't become attached to little Imma. He played with her, of course, and sometimes he really seemed to enjoy himself. For example, with Dede and Elsa he would bark at her, to get her to say the word "dog." I heard them howling through the house as I sought in vain to make some notes, and if Imma by pure chance emitted from the depths of her throat an indistinct sound that resembled d, Nino shrieked in unison with the children: she said it, hooray, d. But nothing more. In fact he used the infant as a doll to entertain Dede and Elsa. The increasingly rare times when he spent a Sunday with us and the weather was fine, he went with them and Imma to the Floridiana, encouraging them to push their sister's stroller along the paths of the park. When they returned they were all pleased. But a few words were enough for me to guess that Nino had abandoned Dede and Elsa to play mamma to Imma, while he went off to converse with the real mothers of the Vomero who were taking their children out for air and sun.

Over time I had become used to his penchant for seductive behavior, I considered it a sort of tic. I was used above all to the way women immediately liked him. But at a certain point something was spoiled there, too. I began to notice that he had an impressive number of women friends, and that they all seemed to brighten in his vicinity. I knew that light well, I wasn't surprised. Being close to him gave you the impression of being visible, especially to yourself, and you were content. It was natural, therefore, that all those girls, and older women, too, were fond of him, and if I didn't exclude sexual desire I also didn't consider it essential. I stood confused on the edge of the remark made long ago by Lila, *In my opinion he's not your friend, either*, and tried as infrequently as possible to transmute it into the question: *Are these women his lovers?* So it wasn't the hypothesis that he was betraying me that disturbed me but something else. I was convinced that Nino encouraged in those people a sort of maternal impulse to do, within the limits of the possible, what could be useful to him.

Shortly after Imma's birth, things began to go better for him. When he appeared he told me proudly of his successes, and I was quickly forced to register that, just as in the past his career had had a boost thanks to his wife's family, so, too, behind every new responsibility he got was the mediation of a woman. One had obtained for him a biweekly column in *Il Mattino*. One had recommended him for the keynote speech at an important conference in Ferrara. One had put him on the managing editorial board of a Turinese journal. Another— originally from Philadelphia and married to a NATO officer stationed in Naples—had recently added his name as a consultant for an American foundation. The list of favors was continuously lengthening. Besides, hadn't I myself helped him publish a book with an important publishing house? And, if I thought about it, hadn't Professor Galiani been the source of his reputation as a high-school student?

I began to study him while he was engaged in that work of seduction. He often invited young and not so young women to dinner at my house, alone or with their husbands or companions. I observed with some anxiety that he knew how to give them space: he ignored the male guests almost completely, making the women the center of his attention, and at times focusing on one in particular. Many evenings I witnessed conversations that, although they took place in the presence of other people, he was able to conduct as if he were alone, in private, with the only woman who at that moment appeared to interest him. He said nothing allusive, or compromising, he merely asked questions.

"And then what happened?"

"I left home. I left Lecce at eighteen and Naples wasn't an easy city."

"Where did you live?"

"In a run-down apartment in the Tribunali, with two other girls. There wasn't even a quiet corner where I could study."

"And men?"

"Certainly not."

"There must have been someone."

"There was one, and, just my luck, he's here, I'm married to him."

Although the woman had brought up her husband as if to include him in the conversation, Nino ignored him and continued to talk to her in his warm voice. He had a curiosity about the world of women that was genuine. But—this I knew very well by now—he didn't in the least resemble the men who in those years made a show of giving up at least a few of their privileges. I thought not only of professors, architects, artists who came to our house and displayed a sort of feminization of behaviors, feelings, opinions; but also of Carmen's husband, Roberto, who was really helpful, and Enzo, who with no hesitation would have sacrificed all his time to Lila's needs. Nino was sincerely interested in how women found themselves. There was no dinner at which he did not repeat that to think *along with* them was now the only way to a true thought. But he held tight to his spaces and his numerous activities, he put first of all, always and only, himself, he didn't give up an instant of his time.

On one occasion I tried, with affectionate irony, to show him up as a liar in front of everyone:

"Don't believe him. At first he helped me clear, he washed the dishes: today he doesn't even pick his socks up off the floor."

"That's not true," he protested.

"Yes, it is. He wants to liberate the women of others but not his."

"Well, your liberation shouldn't necessarily signify the loss of my freedom."

In remarks like this, too, uttered playfully, I soon recognized, uneasily, echoes of my conflicts with Pietro. Why had I gotten so angry at my ex-husband while with Nino I let it go? I thought: maybe every relationship with men can only reproduce the same contradictions and, in certain environments, even the same smug responses. But then I said to myself: I mustn't exaggerate, there's a difference, with Nino it's certainly going better.

But was it really? I was less and less sure. I remembered how, when he was our guest in Florence, he had supported me against Pietro, I thought again with pleasure of how he had encouraged me to write. But now? Now that it was crucial for me to seriously get to work, he seemed unable to instill in me the same confidence as before. Things had changed over the years. Nino always had his own urgent needs, and even if he wanted to he couldn't devote himself to me. To mollify me he had hurried to get, through his mother, a certain Silvana, a massive woman of around fifty, with three children, always cheerful, very lively, and good with the three girls. Generously he had glossed over what he paid her, and after a week had asked: Everything in order, it's working? But it was evident that he felt that the expense authorized him not to be concerned with me. Of course he was attentive, he regularly asked: Are you writing? But that was it. The central place that my effort to write had had at the start of our relationship had vanished. And it wasn't only that. I myself, with a certain embarrassment, no longer recognized him as the authority he had once been. I discovered, in other words, that the part of me that confessed I could not really depend on Nino also no longer saw around his every word the flaming halo I had seemed to perceive since childhood. I gave him a still shapeless paragraph to read and he exclaimed: Perfect. I summarized a plot and characters that I was sketching out and he said: Great, very intelligent. But he didn't convince me, I didn't believe him, he expressed enthusiastic opinions about the work of too many women. His recurring phrase after an evening with other couples was almost always: What a boring man, she is certainly better than he is. His women friends, inasmuch as they were his friends, were always judged extraordinary. And his judgment of women in general was, as a rule, tolerant. Nino could justify even the sadistic obtuseness of the employees of the post office, the ignorant narrow-mindedness of Dede and Elsa's teachers. In other words I no longer felt unique, I was a form that was valid for all women. But if for him I wasn't unique, what help could his opinion give me, how could I draw energy from it to do well?

Exasperated, one evening, by the praise he had heaped on a biologist friend in my presence, I asked him:

"Is it possible that a stupid woman doesn't exist?"

"I didn't say that: I said that as a rule you are better than us."

"I'm better than you?"

"Absolutely, yes, and I've known it for a very long time."

"All right, I believe you, but at least once in your life, have you met a bitch?"

"Yes."

"Tell me her name."

I knew what he would say, and yet I insisted, hoping he would say Eleonora. I waited, he became serious:

"I can't."

"Tell me."

"If I tell you you'll get mad."

"I won't get mad."
"Lina."

73.

If in the past I had believed somewhat in his recurring hostility toward Lila, now I found it less and less convincing, partly
because it was joined not infrequently to moments when, as had
happened a few nights earlier, he demonstrated a completely
different feeling. He was trying to finish an essay on work and
the automation of Fiat, but I saw that he was in trouble (*What
precisely is a microprocessor, what's a chip, how does this stuff
function in practice*). I had said to him: talk to Enzo Scanno, he's
smart. He had asked absentmindedly: Who is Enzo Scanno?
Lina's companion, I answered. He said with a half smile: Then
I prefer to talk to Lina, she certainly knows more. And, as if the
memory had returned, he added, with a trace of resentment:
Wasn't Scanno the idiot son of the fruit seller?

That tone struck me. Enzo was the founder of a small, innovative business—a miracle, considering that the office was in
the heart of the old neighborhood. Precisely because he was a
scholar, Nino should have displayed interest and admiration
toward him. Instead, he had returned him, thanks to that
imperfect—*was*—to the time of elementary school, when he
helped his mother in the shop or went around with his father
and the cart and didn't have time to study and didn't shine. He
had, with irritation, taken every virtue away from Enzo, and
given them all to Lila. That was how I realized that if I had
forced him to delve into himself, it would have emerged that
the highest example of female intelligence—maybe his own
worship of female intelligence, even certain lectures claiming
that the waste of women's intellectual resources was the greatest waste of all—had to do with Lila, and that if our season of

love was already darkening, the season of Ischia would always remain radiant for him. The man for whom I left Pietro, I thought, is what he is because his encounter with Lila reshaped him that way.

74.

This idea occurred to me one frigid fall morning when I was taking Dede and Elsa to school. I was driving distractedly, and the idea took root. I distinguished the love for the neighborhood boy, the high-school student—a feeling of *mine* that had as its object a fantasy of *mine*, conceived *before* Ischia— from the passion that had overwhelmed me for the young man in the bookstore in Milan, the person who had appeared in my house in Florence. I had always maintained a connection between those two emotional blocks, and that morning instead it seemed to me that there was no connection, that the continuity was a trick of logic. In the middle, I thought, there had been a rupture—his love for Lila—that should have cancelled Nino forever from my life, but which I had refused to reckon with. To whom, then, was I bound, and whom did I still love today?

Usually Silvana drove the children to school, and, while Nino was still asleep, I took care of Imma. That day, however, I had arranged things so that I could stay out all morning; I wanted to see if I could find in the Biblioteca Nazionale an old volume by Roberto Bracco, entitled *In the World of Women*. Meanwhile, I advanced slowly through the morning traffic with that thought in mind. I was driving, I was answering the children's questions, I was returning to a Nino made of two parts, one that belonged to me, the other alien. When, with countless warnings and bits of advice, I left Dede and Elsa at their respective schools, the thought had become an image and, as happened often in that period, had been transformed into the nucleus of a possible story. It could be, I said to myself as I descended toward the sea, a novel in which a woman marries the man she's been in love with since childhood, but on their wedding night she realizes that while a part of his body belongs to her, the other part is physically inhabited by a childhood friend of hers. Then in a flash everything was swept away by a sort of domestic alarm bell: I had forgotten to buy diapers for Imma.

Daily life frequently erupted, like a slap, making irrelevant if not ridiculous every meandering little fantasy. I pulled up, angry at myself. I was so burdened that, although I scrupulously wrote down on a notepad the things I needed to buy, I ended up forgetting the list itself. I fumed, I could never organize myself as I should. Nino had an important appointment for work, maybe he had already left, and anyway it was useless to count on him. I couldn't send Silvana to the pharmacy because she would have had to leave the baby alone in the house. As a result there were no diapers, Imma couldn't be changed and would have a rash for days. I went back to Via Tasso. I hurried to the pharmacy, I bought the diapers, I arrived home out of breath. I was sure I would hear Imma screaming from the landing but I opened the door with the key and entered a silent apartment.

I glimpsed the baby in the living room, sitting in her playpen, without a diaper, playing with a doll. I slipped past so that she wouldn't see me, or she would start howling to be picked up, and I wanted to hand over the package to Silvana and try again to get to the library. A faint noise came from the big bathroom (we had a small bathroom that Nino generally used, and a large one for the girls and me), I thought that Silvana must be straightening it. I went there, the door was half open, I pushed it. First I saw, in the luminous space of the long mirror, Silvana's head bent forward, and I was struck by the stripe of the center part, the two black bands of her hair

238 · ELENA FERRANTE

threaded with white. Then I became aware of Nino's closed
eyes, his open mouth. Suddenly, in a flash, the reflected image
and the real bodies came together. Nino was in his undershirt
and otherwise naked, his long thin legs parted, his feet bare.
Silvana, curved forward, with both hands resting on the sink,
had her big underpants at her knees and the dark smock
pulled up around her waist. He, while he stroked her sex holding her heavy stomach with his arm, was gripping an enormous
breast that stuck out of the smock and the bra, and meanwhile
was thrusting his flat stomach against her large white buttocks.

I pulled the door hard toward myself just as Nino opened
his eyes and Silvana suddenly raised her head, throwing me a
frightened gaze. I rushed to get Imma from the playpen and
while Nino shouted, Elena, wait, I was already out of the
house, I didn't even call the elevator, I ran down the stairs with
the baby in my arms.

75.

I took refuge in the car, I started the engine, and with Imma
on my knees I left. The baby seemed happy, she wanted to honk
the horn, as Elsa had taught her, she spoke her incomprehensible little words alternating with shrieks of joy at my presence. I
drove without a goal, I wanted only to get as far away from the
house as possible. Finally I found myself at Sant'Elmo. I
parked, turned off the engine, and discovered that I had no
tears, I wasn't suffering, I was only frozen with horror.

I couldn't believe it. Was it possible that that Nino whom I
had discovered as he was thrusting his taut sex inside the sex
of a mature woman—a woman who cleaned my house, did my
shopping, cooked, took care of my children; a woman marked
by the struggle to survive, large, worn-out, the absolute opposite of the cultivated, elegant women he brought to dinner—

was the boy of my adolescence? For the whole time I was driving blindly, perhaps scarcely feeling the weight of the half-naked Imma, who was pounding the horn in vain and happily calling me, I couldn't give him a stable identity. I felt as if, entering the house, I had suddenly found out in the open, in my bathroom, an alien creature who usually stayed hidden inside the skin of the father of my third daughter. The stranger had the features of Nino, but wasn't him. Was it the other, the one born after Ischia? But which one? The one who had impregnated Silvia? The lover of Mariarosa? The husband of Eleonora, unfaithful and yet closely bound to her? The married man who had said to me, a married woman, that he loved me, wanted me at all costs?

Along the entire route that led me to the Vomero, I had tried to cling to the Nino of the neighborhood and of high school, the Nino of tenderness and love, to get myself out of the revulsion. Only when I stopped at Sant'Elmo did the bathroom return to mind, and the moment when he had opened his eyes and seen me in the mirror, standing on the threshold. Then everything seemed clearer. There was no split between that man who came after Lila and the boy with whom—before Lila—I had been in love since childhood. Nino was only one, and the expression he had on his face while he was inside Silvana was the proof. It was the expression of his father, Donato, not when he deflowered me on the Maronti but when he touched me between the legs, under the sheet, in Nella's kitchen.

Nothing alien, then, but much that was ugly. Nino was what he wouldn't have wanted to be and yet always had been. When he rhythmically hammered against Silvana's buttocks and was also kindly taking care to give her pleasure, he wasn't lying, just as he wasn't lying when he wronged me and was sorry, apologized, begged me to forgive him, swore that he loved me. *He is like that*, I said to myself. But that didn't console me. I felt, rather, that the horror, instead of fading, found

a more solid refuge in that statement. Then a warm liquid
spread down to my knees. I shook myself: Imma was naked,
she had peed on me.

76.

Going home seemed unthinkable, even though it was cold
and Imma risked getting sick. I wrapped her in my coat as if
we were playing, I bought a new package of diapers, I put one
on after cleaning her with a baby wipe. Now I had to decide
what to do. Dede and Elsa would get out of school soon, irritable and hungry; Imma was already hungry. I, my jeans wet,
without a coat, nerves tense, was shivering with cold. I looked
for a telephone, I called Lila, I asked:

"Can I come to lunch at your house with the children?"

"Of course."

"Enzo won't be annoyed?"

"You know he'll be pleased."

I heard Tina's happy little voice, Lila said to her: Quiet.
Then she asked me with a wariness that she normally didn't
have:

"Is something wrong?"

"Yes."

"What happened?"

"What you predicted."

"Did you fight with Nino?"

"I'll tell you later, I have to go now."

I arrived early at school. Imma had by now lost any interest
in me, the steering wheel, the horn, and was howling. I forced
her yet again to stay wrapped in the jacket and we went to find
some cookies. I thought I was acting calmly—inside I felt
tranquil: not fury but disgust still prevailed, a revulsion not
different from what I would have felt if I had seen two lizards

coupling—but I realized that the passersby were looking at me with curiosity, with alarm, as I hurried along the street in my wet pants, talking aloud to the baby, who, squeezed tight in the coat, was wriggling and wailing.

At the first cookie Imma quieted down, but her calm freed my anxiety. Nino must have put off his appointment, he was probably looking for me, I was in danger of finding him at school. Since Elsa came out before Dede, who was in her second year of middle school, I went and stood in a corner from which I could watch the entrance of the elementary school without being seen. My teeth were chattering with cold, Imma was smearing my coat with saliva-soaked cookie crumbs. I surveyed the area, nervously, but Nino didn't appear. And he didn't appear at the entrance of the middle school, from which Dede soon emerged in a flood of pushing and shoving, shouts, and insults in dialect.

The children paid little attention to me; they were very interested in the novelty of my coming to get them with Imma.

"Why are you holding her in the coat?" Dede asked.

"Because she's cold."

"Did you see she's ruining it?"

"It doesn't matter."

"Once when I got you dirty you slapped me," Elsa complained.

"It's not true."

"It's very true."

Dede investigated:

"Why is it that she has only a shirt and diaper on?"

"She's fine like that."

"Did something happen?"

"No. Now we're going to have lunch at Aunt Lina's."

They greeted the news with their usual enthusiasm, then they settled in the car, and while the baby talked to her sisters in her obscure language, happy to be the center of their attention, they began to fight over who got to hold her. I insisted that they hold her together, without pulling her this way and that: She's not made of rubber, I cried. Elsa wasn't pleased with that solution and swore at Dede in dialect. I tried to slap her, I said, staring at her in the rearview mirror: What did you say, repeat it, what did you say? She didn't cry, she abandoned Imma to Dede, muttering that taking care of her sister bored her. Then, when the baby reached out her hands to play, she pushed her away roughly. She shouted, assaulting my nerves: Imma, that's enough, you're bothering me, you're getting me dirty. And to me: Mamma, make her stop. I couldn't bear it anymore, I let out a scream that frightened all three of them. We crossed the city in a state of tension broken only by the whispering of Dede and Elsa, who were trying to understand if, again, something irreparable was about to happen in their lives.

I couldn't even tolerate that consultation. I couldn't bear anything anymore: their childhood, my role as mother, Imma's babbling. And then the presence of my daughters in the car clashed with the images of coitus that were constantly before me, with the odor of sex that was still in my nostrils, with the rage that was beginning to advance, along with the most vulgar dialect. Nino had fucked the servant and then gone to his appointment, not giving a shit about me or even about his daughter. Ah, what a piece of shit, all I did was make mistakes. Was he like his father? No, too simple. Nino was very intelligent, Nino was extraordinarily cultured. His propensity for fucking did not come from a crude, naïve display of virility based on half-fascistic, half-southern clichés. What he had done to me, what he was doing to me, was filtered by a very refined knowledge. He dealt in complex concepts, he knew that this way he would offend me to the point of destroying me. But he had done it just the same. He had thought: I can't give up my pleasure just because that shit can be a pain in the ass. Like that, just like that. And surely he judged as philistine—

that adjective was still very widespread in our world—my possible reaction. Philistine, philistine. I even knew the line he would resort to in sophisticated justification: What's the harm, the flesh is weak and I've read all the books. Exactly those words, nasty son of a bitch. Rage had opened up a pathway in the horror. I shouted at Imma—*even at Imma*—to be quiet. When I reached Lila's house I hated Nino as until that moment I had never hated anyone.

77.

Lila had made lunch. She knew that Dede and Elsa adored orecchiette with tomato sauce and she announced this, creating a rowdy scene of enthusiasm. That wasn't all. She took Imma from my arms and cared for her and Tina as if suddenly her daughter had doubled. She changed them both, washed them, dressed them identically, cuddled them with an extraordinary display of maternal care. Then, since the two little girls had recognized each other at once and were playing, she put them down on an old carpet, to crawl around, babble. How different they were. Bitterly I compared the daughter of Nino and me to the daughter of Lila and Enzo. Tina seemed prettier, healthier than Imma: she was the sweet fruit of a solid relationship.

Meanwhile Enzo came home from work, cordially laconic as usual. At the table neither he nor Lila asked me why I wasn't eating. Only Dede intervened, as if to take me away from her own bad thoughts and those of the others. She said: my Mamma always eats just a little because she doesn't want to get fat, and I'm doing that, too. I exclaimed, threatening: You have to clean your plate down to the last bite. And Enzo, perhaps to protect my daughters from me, started a comical contest to see who could eat the most and finish first. He patiently answered Dede's many questions about Rino—my daughter had hoped to see him at least for lunch—and explained that he had started a job in a workshop and was out all day. Then, at the end of the meal, in great secrecy, he took the two sisters into Gennaro's room to show them all the treasures there. After a few minutes there was a burst of furious music, and they didn't come back.

I was alone with Lila, and I told her every detail, in a tone between sarcasm and suffering. She listened without interrupting. I realized, the more I put into words what had happened, the more ridiculous the scene of sex between that fat woman and skinny Nino seemed. He woke up—at a certain point the words emerged in dialect—he found Silvana in the bathroom, and even before peeing he pulled up her skirt and stuck it in. Then I burst out laughing in a vulgar fashion and Lila looked at me uneasily. She used such tones, she didn't expect them from me. You have to calm down, she said, and since Imma was crying we went into the other room.

My daughter, fair-haired, red in the face, was shedding large tears, her mouth open, and as soon as she saw me she raised her arms to be picked up. Tina, dark, pale, stared at her, disconcerted, and when her mother appeared she didn't move, she called to her as if she wanted her to help her understand, saying "Mamma" clearly. Lila picked up both babies, settled one on each arm, kissed mine, drying her tears with her lips, spoke to her, soothed her.

I was amazed. I thought: Tina says "Mamma" clearly, all the syllables, Imma doesn't do that yet and is almost a month older. I felt at a loss and sad. 1981 was about to end. I would get rid of Silvana. I didn't know what to write, the months would fly by, I wouldn't deliver my book, I would lose ground as well as my reputation as a writer. I would remain without a future, dependent on financial support from Pietro, alone with three daughters, without Nino. Nino lost, Nino over. The part of me that continued to love him appeared again, not as in Florence but, rather, as the child in elementary school had loved him, seeing him coming out of school. In confusion I searched for an excuse to forgive him in spite of the humiliation, I couldn't bear to drive him out of my life. Where was he? Was it possible that he hadn't even tried to look for me? I put together Enzo, who had immediately taken care of the two children, and Lila, who had freed me of every task and had listened, leaving me all the space I wanted. I finally understood that they had known everything before I arrived in the neighborhood. I asked:

"Did Nino call?"

"Yes."

"What did he say?"

"That it was foolish, that I should stay with you, that I should help you understand, that today people live like this. Talk."

"And you?"

"I slammed the telephone down on him."

"But he'll call again?"

"Of course he'll call again."

I felt discouraged.

"Lila, I don't know how to live without him. It all lasted such a short time. I broke up my marriage, I came to live here with the children, I had another child. Why?"

"Because you made a mistake."

I didn't like the remark, it sounded like the echo of an old offense. She was reminding me that I had made a mistake even though she had tried to get me out of the mistake. She was saying that I had *wanted* to make a mistake, and as a result *she* had been mistaken, I wasn't intelligent, I was a stupid woman. I said:

"I have to talk to him, I have to confront him."

"All right, but leave me the children."

"You can't do it, there are four."

"There are five, there's also Gennaro. And he's the most difficult of all."

"You see? I'll take them."

"Don't even mention it."

I admitted that I needed her help, I said:

"I'll leave them until tomorrow, I need time to resolve the situation."

"Resolve it how?"

"I don't know."

"You want to continue with Nino?"

I could hear her opposition and I almost shouted:

"What can I do?"

"The only thing possible: leave him."

For her it was the right solution, she had always wanted it to end like that, she had never concealed it from me. I said:

"I'll think about it."

"No, you won't think about it. You've already decided to pretend it was nothing and go on."

I avoided answering but she pressed me, she said that I shouldn't throw myself away, that I had another destiny, that if I went on like that I would lose myself. I noticed that she was becoming harsh, I felt that to restrain me she was on the point of telling me what for a long time I had wanted to know and what for a long time she had been silent about. I was afraid, but had I not myself, on various occasions, tried to urge her to be clear? And now, had I not come to her *also* so that finally she would tell me everything?

"If you have something to tell me," I said, "speak."

And she made up her mind, she looked at me, I looked down. She said that Nino had often sought her out. She said that he had asked her to come back to him, both before he had become involved with me and after. She said that when they took my mother to the hospital he had been particularly insistent. She said that while the doctors were examining my mother and they were waiting for the results in the waiting room he had sworn to her that he was with me only to feel closer to her.

"Look at me," she whispered. "I know I'm mean to tell you

these things, but he is much worse than I am. He has the worst
kind of meanness, that of superficiality."

78.

I returned to Via Tasso determined to cut off every relation
with Nino. I found the house empty and in perfect order, I sat
beside the French door that led to the balcony. Life in that
apartment was over, in a couple of years the reasons for my
very presence in Naples had been consumed.

I waited with growing anxiety for him to appear. Several
hours passed, I fell asleep, I woke with a start, when it was
dark. The telephone was ringing.

I hurried to answer, sure that it was Nino, but it was Antonio.
He was calling from a café nearby, he asked if I could meet
him. I said: Come up. I heard his hesitation, then he agreed. I
had no doubt that Lila had sent him, and he admitted it himself right away.

"She doesn't want you to do something foolish," he said,
making an effort to speak in Italian.

"You can stop me?"

"Yes."

"How?"

He sat down in the living room, after refusing the coffee I
wanted to make for him, and deliberately, in the tone of someone who is used to giving detailed reports, listed all Nino's
lovers: names, surnames, professions, relatives. Some I didn't
know, they were relationships from long ago. Others he had
brought to dinner at my house and I remembered them, affectionate with me and the children. Mirella, who had taken care
of Dede, Elsa, and also Imma, had been with him for three
years. And his relationship with the gynecologist who had
delivered my daughter, and Lila's too, was even longer. Antonio

enumerated a sizable number of females—he used that word—
with whom, at various times, Nino had applied the same
scheme: an intense period of meetings, then occasional encounters, in no case a definitive break. He's faithful, Antonio said,
sarcastically, he never really cuts off relations: now he goes to
that one, now he goes to that other.

"Does Lina know?"

"Yes."

"Since when?"

"Recently."

"Why didn't you tell me right away?"

"I wanted to tell you right away."

"And Lina?"

"She said to wait."

"And you obeyed her. You two let me cook and set the table
for people he had betrayed me with the day before or would
betray me with the day after. I ate with people whose foot or
knee or something else he touched under the table. I entrusted
my children to a girl he jumped on as soon as I looked away."

Antonio shrugged, he looked at his hands, clasped them,
and left them between his knees.

"If they tell me to do a thing I do it," he said in dialect.

But then he got confused. I almost always do it, he said, and
tried to explain: sometimes I obey money, sometimes respect,
in some cases myself. As for infidelities, he said, if you don't
find out about them at the right moment they're of no use:
when you're in love you forgive everything. For infidelities to
have their real impact some lovelessness has to develop first.
And he went on like that, piling up painful remarks about the
blindness of people in love. As if by way of example, he told
me again about how, years before, he had spied on Nino and
Lila for the Solaras. In that case, he said proudly, I didn't do
what they ordered. He hadn't felt like handing Lila over to
Michele and had called Enzo so that he could get her out of

trouble. He spoke again of the beating he had given Nino. I did it, he muttered, most of all because you loved him and not me, and then because if that piece of shit went back to Lina, she would have stayed faithful to him and would be ruined forever. You see, he concluded, in that case, too, there was little to be gained by talking, Lina wouldn't have listened to me, love not only doesn't have eyes, it doesn't have ears, either.

I asked him, stunned:

"In all these years you never told Lina that Nino was going back to her that night?"

"No."

"You should have."

"Why? When my head says, it's better to act in this way, I do it, and I don't think about it anymore. If you go back to it you only make trouble."

How wise he had become. That was when I learned that the story of Nino and Lila would have lasted a little longer if Antonio hadn't cut it off with a beating. But I immediately discarded the hypothesis that they would have loved each other all their lives, and perhaps both he and she would have become utterly different people: to me it seemed not only unlikely but unbearable. Instead I sighed with impatience. Antonio had decided for his own reasons to save Lila and now Lila had sent him to save me. I looked at him, I said with explicit sarcasm something about his role as a protector of women. He should have showed up in Florence, I thought, when I was hanging in the balance, when I didn't know what to do, and made the decision for me with his gnarled hands, as years before he had decided for Lila. I asked him teasingly:

"What orders do you have now?"

"Before sending me here, Lina forbade me to break the face of that shit. But I did it once and I'd like to do it again."

"You're unreliable."

"Yes and no."

"Meaning?"

"It's a complicated situation, Lenù, stay out of it. You just tell me that the son of Sarratore should repent the day he was born and I'll make him repent."

I couldn't contain myself, I burst out laughing at the mannered seriousness with which he expressed himself. It was the tone he had learned in the neighborhood as a boy, the formal tone of the upright male: he who in reality had been timid and fearful. What an effort it must have been, but now it was *his* tone, he wouldn't have known how to have any other. The only difference, in relation to the past, was that in that situation he was making an effort to speak in Italian and the difficult language was coming to him with a foreign accent.

He darkened because of my laughter, he looked at the black panes of the window, he said: Don't laugh. I saw that his forehead was shiny in spite of the cold, he was sweating from the shame of having seemed ridiculous to me. He said: I know I don't express myself well, I know German better than Italian. I became aware of his odor, the way it had smelled at the time of the ponds. I'm laughing, I apologized, at the situation, at you, who've wanted to kill Nino forever, and at me, who if he showed up now would say to you: Yes, kill him. I'm laughing out of despair, because I've never been so offended, because I feel humiliated in a way that I don't know if you can imagine, because at this moment I'm so ill that I think I'm fainting.

In fact I felt weak, and dead inside. So I was suddenly grateful to Lila for having had the sensitivity to send me Antonio, he was the only person whose affection at that moment I didn't doubt. Besides, his lean body, his big bones, his thick eyebrows, his coarse features had remained familiar to me, they didn't repel me, I wasn't afraid of them. At the ponds, I said, it was cold and we didn't feel it: I'm trembling, can I sit next to you?

He looked at me uncertainly, but I didn't wait for his assent. I got up, I sat on his knees. He didn't move, he extended only

his arms, for fear of touching me, and let them fall to the sides
of the chair. I leaned against him, resting my face between his
neck and his shoulder, it seemed to me that for a few seconds
I fell asleep.

"Lenù."

"Yes?"

"Do you not feel well?"

"Hold me, I have to warm up."

"No."

"Why?"

"I'm not sure you want me."

"I want you now, this time only: it's something you owe me
and I you."

"I don't owe you anything. I love you and you, instead, have
always loved only him."

"Yes, but I never desired anyone the way I desired you, not
even him."

I talked for a long time, I told him the truth, the truth of
that moment and the truth of the faraway time of the ponds.
He was the discovery of excitement, he was the pit of the stomach that grew warm, that opened up, that turned liquid, releas-
ing a burning indolence. Franco, Pietro, Nino had stumbled
on that expectation but had never managed to satisfy it,
because it was an expectation without a definite object, it was
the hope of pleasure, the hardest to fulfill. The taste of
Antonio's mouth, the perfume of his desire, his hands, the large
sex taut between his thighs constituted a *before* that couldn't be
matched. The *after* had never been truly equal to our afternoons hidden by the skeleton of the canning factory, although
they consisted of love without penetration and often without
orgasm.

I spoke in an Italian that was complex. I did it more to
explain to myself what I was doing than to clarify to him, and
this must have seemed to him an act of trust, he seemed content.

He held me, he kissed me on one shoulder, then on the neck, finally on the mouth. I don't think I've had any other sexual relation like that, which abruptly joined the ponds of more than twenty years earlier and the room on Via Tasso, the chair, the floor, the bed, suddenly sweeping away everything that was between us, that divided us, what was me, what was him. Antonio was delicate, he was brutal, and I was the same, no less than him. He demanded things and I demanded things with a fury, an anxiety, a need for violation that I didn't think I harbored. At the end he was annihilated by wonder and I was, too.

"What happened?" I asked, stunned, as if the memory of that absolute intimacy had already vanished.

"I don't know," he said, "but luckily it happened."

I smiled.

"You're like everybody else, you've betrayed your wife."

I wanted to joke, but he took me seriously, he said in dialect:

"I haven't betrayed anyone. My wife—*before now*—doesn't exist yet."

An obscure formulation but I understood. He was trying to tell me that he agreed with me, seeking to communicate, in turn, a sense of time outside the present chronology. He wanted to say that we had lived *now* a small fragment of a day that belonged to twenty years earlier. I kissed him, I whispered: Thank you, and I told him I was grateful because he had chosen to ignore the brutal reasons for all that sex—mine and his—and to see in it only the need to close our accounts.

Then the telephone rang, I went to answer, it might be Lila who needed me for the children. But it was Nino.

"Luckily you're home," he said breathlessly. "I'm coming right away."

"No."

"When?"

"Tomorrow."

"Let me explain, it's essential, it's urgent."

"No."

"Why?"

I told him and hung up.

79.

It was hard to separate from Nino; it took months. I don't think I've ever suffered so much for a man; it tortured me both to keep him away and to take him back. He wouldn't admit that he had made romantic and sexual offers to Lila. He insulted her, he mocked her, he accused her of wanting to destroy our relationship. But he was lying. At first he always lied, he even tried to convince me that what I had seen in the bathroom was a mistake due to weariness and jealousy. Then he began to give in. He confessed to some relationships but backdated them, as for others, indisputably recent, he said they had been meaningless, he swore that with those women it was friendship, not love. We quarreled all through Christmas, all winter. Sometimes I silenced him, worn out by his skill at accusing himself, defending himself, and *expecting* forgiveness, sometimes I yielded in the face of his despair, which seemed real—he often arrived drunk—sometimes I threw him out because, out of honesty, pride, maybe even dignity, he never promised that he would stop seeing those he called his friends, nor would he assure me that he would not lengthen the list.

On that theme he often undertook long, very cultured monologues in which he tried to convince me that it wasn't his fault but that of nature, of astral matter, of spongy bodies and their excessive liquids, of the immoderate heat of his loins—in short, of his exorbitant virility. No matter how much I add up all the books I've read, he murmured, in a tone that was sincere, pained, and yet vain to the point of ridiculousness, no matter how much I add up the languages I've learned, the mathematics, the sciences, the literature, and most of all my love for you—yes, the love and the need I have for you, the terror of not being able to have you anymore—believe me, I beg you, believe me, there's nothing to be done, I can't I can't I can't, the occasional desire, the most foolish, the most obtuse, prevails.

Sometimes he moved me, more often he irritated me, in general I responded with sarcasm. And he was silent, he nervously ruffled his hair, then he started again. But when I said to him coldly one morning that perhaps all that need for women was the symptom of a labile heterosexuality that in order to endure needed constant confirmation, he was offended, he harassed me for days, he wanted to know if I had been better with Antonio than with him. Since I was now tired of all that distraught talk, I shouted yes. And since in that phase of excruciating quarrels some of his friends had tried to get into my bed, and I, out of boredom, out of spite, had sometimes consented, I mentioned names of people he was fond of, and to wound him I said they had been better than him.

He disappeared. He had said that he couldn't do without Dede and Elsa, he had said that he loved Imma more than his other children, he had said that he would take care of the three children even if I hadn't wanted to go back to him. In reality not only did he forget about us immediately but he stopped paying the rent in Via Tasso, along with the bills for the electricity, the gas, the telephone.

I looked in vain for a cheaper apartment in the area: often, apartments that were uglier and smaller commanded even higher rents. Then Lila said to me that there were three rooms and a kitchen available just above her. The rent was almost nothing, from the windows you could see both the *stradone* and the courtyard. She said it in her way, in the tone of someone who signals: I'm only giving you the information, do as you like.

I was depressed, I was frightened. Elisa had recently yelled at me during a quarrel: Papa is alone, go live with him, I'm tired of having to take care of him myself. And naturally I had refused, in my situation I couldn't take care of my father, too. I was already the slave of my daughters. Imma was constantly sick, as soon as Dede got over the flu Elsa had it, she wouldn't do her homework unless I sat with her, Dede got mad and said: Then you have to help me, too. I was exhausted, a nervous wreck. And then, in the great chaos I had fallen into, I didn't have even that bit of active life that until then I had guaranteed myself. I turned down invitations and articles and trips, I didn't dare answer the telephone for fear it was the publisher asking for the book. I had ended up in a vortex that was pulling me down, and a hypothetical return to the neighborhood would be the proof that I had touched bottom. To immerse myself again, and my daughters, in that mentality, let myself be absorbed by Lila, by Carmen, by Alfonso, by everyone, just as in fact they wanted. No, no, I swore to myself that I would go and live in Tribunali, in Duchesca, in Lavinaio, in Forcella, amid the scaffolding that marked the earthquake damage, rather than return to the neighborhood. In that atmosphere the editor called.

"How far along are you?"

It was an instant, a flame kindled in my head illuminating it like day. I knew what I had to say and what I had to do.

"I finished just yesterday."

"Seriously? Send it today."

"Tomorrow morning I'll go to the post office."

"Thank you. As soon as the book arrives, I'll read it and let you know."

"Take your time."

I hung up. I went to a big box I kept in the bedroom closet, I pulled out the typescript that years before neither Adele nor Lila had liked, I didn't even attempt to reread it. The next morning I took the children to school and went with Imma to send the package. I knew that it was a risky move, but it seemed to me the only one possible to save my reputation. I had promised to deliver a novel and here it was. Was it an unsuccessful novel, irrefutably bad? Well, it wouldn't be published. But I had worked hard, I hadn't deceived anyone, I would soon do better.

The line at the post office was exhausting, I had to protest continually against people who didn't respect it. In that situation my disaster became obvious to me. *Why am I here, why am I wasting time like this. The girls and Naples have eaten me alive. I don't study, I don't write, I've lost all discipline.* I had gained a life very far from what might have been expected for me, and look how I had ended up. I felt exasperated, guilty toward myself and especially toward my mother. Furthermore, Imma had been making me anxious: when I compared her with Tina I was sure she was suffering from some developmental problem. Lila's daughter, although she was three weeks younger, was very lively, seemed more than a year old, whereas Imma seemed unresponsive and had a vacant look. I observed her obsessively, I harassed her with tests that I invented on the spot. I thought: it would be terrible if Nino not only had ruined my life but had given me a daughter with problems. And yet people stopped me on the street because she was so plump, so fair. Here, even at the post office, the women in line complimented her, how chubby she was. But she didn't even smile. A man offered her a candy and Imma stretched out her hand reluctantly, took it, dropped it. Ah, I was constantly anxious, every day a new worry was added to the others. When I came out of the post office and the package had been sent and there was no way to stop it, I jumped, I remembered my mother-in-law. Good Lord, what had I done. Was it possible that I hadn't considered that the publisher would give the manuscript to Adele? It was she, after all, who had wanted the publication of both my first book and the second, they owed it to her if only out of courtesy. And she would say: Greco is cheating you, this isn't a new text, I read it years ago and it's terrible. I broke out in a cold sweat, I felt weak. To plug one leak I had created another. I was no longer able to keep under control, even within the limits of the possible, the chain of my actions.

80.

Just then, to complicate things, Nino showed up again. He had never given me back the keys, even though I had insisted on having them, and so he reappeared without calling, without knocking. I told him to go, the house was mine, he wasn't paying the rent and wasn't giving me a cent for Imma. He swore that, annihilated by grief at our separation, he had forgotten. He seemed sincere; he had a feverish look, and was very thin. He promised with an involuntarily comic solemnity to start paying the next month, he spoke in a sorrowful voice of his love for Imma. Then, apparently in a good-humored way, he began to ask again about my encounter with Antonio, about how it had gone, first in general and then sexually. From Antonio he moved on to his friends. He tried to make me admit that I had yielded ("yield" seemed to him the right verb) to this one or that one not out of genuine attraction but only out of spite. I was alarmed when he began to caress my shoulder, my knee, my cheek. I soon saw—in his eyes and in his words—that what made him desperate was not that he had lost my love but that I had been with those other men, and that sooner or later I would be with others and would prefer them to him. He had showed up, that morning, only to reenter my bed. He demanded that I vilify those recent lovers by showing him that my only desire was to be penetrated again by him. He wanted, in other words, to reassert his primacy, then surely he would again disappear. I managed to get the keys back and I threw him out. I realized then, and to my surprise, that I no longer felt anything for him. The long time that I had loved him dissolved conclusively that morning.

The next day I began to ask about what I had to do to get a job, even as a substitute, in the middle schools. I quickly realized that it wouldn't be simple, and that in any case I would have to wait for the new school year. Since I took for granted the break with the publisher, which was followed in my imagination by the devastating collapse of my identity as a writer, I was frightened. From birth, the children had been used to a comfortable life, I myself—ever since my marriage to Pietro—couldn't imagine being without books, magazines, newspapers, records, movies, theater. I had to think immediately of some provisional job, and I put advertisements in the local shops offering private lessons.

Then one morning in June the editor called. He had received the manuscript, he had read it.

"Already?" I said with feigned indifference.

"Yes. And it's a book that I would never have expected from you, but that you, surprisingly, wrote."

"You're saying it's bad?"

"It is, from the first line to the last, pure pleasure of narration."

My heart was going crazy in my chest.

"Is it good or not?"

"It's extraordinary."

81.

I was proud. In a few seconds I not only regained faith in myself, I relaxed, I began to speak of my work with a childish enthusiasm, I laughed too much, I questioned the editor

closely to get a more articulated approval. I quickly understood that he had read my pages as a sort of autobiography, an
arrangement in novel form of my experience of the poorest
and most violent Naples. He said he had feared the negative
effects of a return to my city, but now he had to admit that that
return had helped me. I didn't say that the book had been written several years earlier in Florence. It's a harsh novel, he
emphasized, I would say masculine, but paradoxically also delicate, in other words a big step forward. Then he discussed
organizational questions. He wanted to move the publication
to the spring of 1983 to devote himself to careful editing and
to prepare the launch. He concluded, with some sarcasm:

"I talked about it with your ex-mother-in-law. She said that
she had read an old version and hadn't liked it; but evidently
either her taste has aged or your personal problems kept her
from giving a dispassionate evaluation."

I quickly admitted that long ago I had let Adele read a first
draft. He said: It's clear that the air of Naples has given free
rein to your talent. When he hung up I felt hugely relieved. I
changed, I became particularly affectionate toward my daughters. The publisher paid the rest of the advance and my economic situation improved. Suddenly I began to look at the city
and especially at the neighborhood as an important part of my
life; not only should I not dismiss it but it was essential to the
success of my work. It was a sudden leap, going from distrust
to a joyful sense of myself. What I had felt as a precipice not
only acquired literary nobility but seemed to me a determined
choice of a cultural and political arena. The editor himself had
sanctioned it authoritatively, saying: For you, returning to the
point of departure has been a step forward. Of course, I hadn't
said that the book was written in Florence, that the return to
Naples had had no influence on the text. But the narrative
material, the human depth of the characters came from the
neighborhood, and surely the turning point was there. Adele

hadn't had the sensitivity to understand, so she had lost. All the Airotas had lost. Nino had lost, too, as in essence he had considered me one of the women on his list, without distinguishing me from the others. And—what for me was even more significant—Lila had lost. She hadn't liked my book, she had been severe, it was one of the few times in her life she had cried, when she had had to wound me with her negative judgment. But I didn't want it from her, rather I was pleased that she was wrong. From childhood I had given her too much importance, and now I felt as if unburdened. Finally it was clear that what I was wasn't her, and vice versa. Her authority was no longer necessary to me, I had my own. I felt strong, no longer a victim of my origins but capable of dominating them, of giving them a shape, of taking revenge on them for myself, for Lila, for whomever. What before was dragging me down was now the material for climbing higher. One morning in July of 1982 I called her and said:

"All right, I'll take the apartment above you, I'm coming back to the neighborhood."

82.

I moved in midsummer, Antonio took care of the logistics. He assembled some brawny men who emptied the apartment on Via Tasso and arranged everything in the apartment in the neighborhood. The new house was dark and repainting the rooms didn't help brighten it. But, contrary to what I had thought since I returned to Naples, this didn't bother me; in fact the dusty light that had always struggled to penetrate the windows had the effect on me of an evocative childhood memory. Dede and Elsa, on the other hand, protested at length. They had grown up in Florence, Genoa, in the bright light of Via Tasso, and they immediately hated the floors of uneven tiles, the small dark bathroom, the din of the *stradone*. They resigned themselves only because now they could enjoy some not insignificant advantages: see Aunt Lina every day, get up later because the school was nearby, go there by themselves, spend time on the street and in the courtyard.

I was immediately seized by a yearning to regain possession of the neighborhood. I enrolled Elsa in the elementary school where I had gone and Dede in my middle school. I resumed contact with anyone, old or young, who remembered me. I celebrated my decision with Carmen and her family, with Alfonso, with Ada, with Pinuccia. Naturally I had misgivings, and Pietro, who was very unhappy with the decision, made them worse. He said on the telephone:

"On the basis of what criteria do you want to bring up our daughters in a place that you fled?"

"I won't bring them up here."

"But you've taken a house and enrolled them in school without considering that they deserve something else."

"I have a book to finish and I can only do it well here."

"I could have taken them."

"You would also take Imma? All three are my daughters and I don't want the third to be separated from the other two."

He calmed down. He was happy that I had left Nino and he soon forgave the move. Keep at your work, he said, I have confidence in you, you know what you're doing. I hoped it was true. I watched the trucks that passed noisily along the *stradone*, raising dust. I walked in the gardens that were full of syringes. I went into the neglected, empty church. I felt sad in front of the parish cinema, which had closed, in front of the party offices, which were like abandoned dens. I listened to the shouting of men, women, children in the apartments, especially at night. The feuds between families, the hostilities between neighbors, the ease with which things came to blows, the wars between gangs of boys. When I went to the pharmacy

I remembered Gino; I felt revulsion at the sight of the place where he had been killed, and went cautiously around it. I spoke compassionately to his parents, who were still behind the old dark-wood counter, more bent over, white-haired in their white smocks, and as kind as ever. As a child I endured all this, I thought, let's see if now I can control it.

"How is it that you decided to do it?" Lila asked some time after the move. Maybe she wanted an affectionate answer, or maybe a sort of recognition of the validity of her choices, words like: You were right to stay, going out into the world was of no use, now I understand. Instead I answered:

"It's an experiment."

"Experiment in what?"

We were in her office. Tina was near her, Imma was wandering on her own. I said:

"An experiment in recomposition. You've managed to have your whole life here, but not me: I feel I'm in pieces scattered all over."

She had an expression of disapproval.

"Forget these experiments, Lenù, otherwise you'll be disappointed and leave again. I'm also in pieces. Between my father's shoe repair shop and this office it's only a few meters, but it's as if they were at the North Pole and the South Pole."

I said, pretending to be amused:

"Don't discourage me. In my job I have to paste one fact to another with words, and in the end everything has to seem coherent even if it's not."

"But if the coherence isn't there, why pretend?"

"To create order. Remember the novel I gave you to read and you didn't like? There I tried to set what I know about Naples within what I later learned in Pisa, Florence, Milan. Now I've given it to the publisher and he thought it was good. It's being published."

She narrowed her eyes. She said softly:

"I told you that I don't understand anything."

I felt I had wounded her. It was as if I had thrown it in her face: if you can't connect your story of the shoes with the story of the computers, that doesn't mean that it can't be done, it means only that you don't have the tools to do it. I said hastily: You'll see, no one will buy the book and you'll be right. Then I listed somewhat randomly all the defects that I myself attributed to my text, and what I wanted to keep or change before it was published. But she escaped, it was as if she wanted to regain altitude, she started talking about computers and she did it as if to point out: You have your things, I mine. She said to the children: Do you want to see a new machine that Enzo bought?

She led us into a small room. She explained to Dede and Elsa: This machine is called a personal computer, it costs a lot of money but it can do wonderful things, look how it works. She sat on a stool and first she settled Tina on her knees, then she began patiently to explain every element, speaking to Dede, to Elsa, to the baby, never to me.

I looked at Tina the whole time. She talked to her mother, asked, pointing: What's this, and if her mother didn't pay attention she tugged on the edge of her shirt, grabbed her chin, insisted: Mamma, what's this. Lila explained it to her as if she were an adult. Imma wandered around the room, pulling a little wagon, and sometimes she sat down on the floor, disoriented. Come, Imma, I said, over and over, listen to what Aunt Lina is saying. But she continued to play with the wagon.

My daughter did not have the qualities of Lila's daughter. A few days earlier the anxiety that she was in some way retarded had dissipated. I had taken her to a very good pediatrician, the child showed no retardation of any sort. I was reassured. And yet comparing Imma to Tina continued to make me uneasy. How lively Tina was: to see her, to hear her talk put you in a good mood. And to see mother and daughter together was touching. As long as Lila talked about the computer—we were starting then to use that word—I observed them both with admiration. At that moment I felt happy, satisfied with myself, and so I also felt, very clearly, that I loved my friend for how she was, for her virtues and her flaws, for everything, even for that being she had brought into the world. The child was full of curiosity, she learned everything in an instant, she had a large vocabulary and a surprising manual dexterity. I said to myself: She has little of Enzo, she's like Lila, look how she widens her eyes, narrows them, look at the ears that have no lobe. I still didn't dare to admit that Tina attracted me more than my daughter, but when that demonstration of skill ended, I was very excited about the computer, and full of praise for the little girl, even though I knew that Imma might suffer from it (*How clever you are, how pretty, how well you speak, how many things you learn*), I complimented Lila, mainly to diminish the unease I had caused her by announcing the publication of my book, and, finally, I drew an optimistic portrait of the future that awaited my three daughters and hers. They'll study, I said, they'll travel all over the world, goodness knows what they'll be. But Lila, after smothering Tina with kisses—*yes, she's sooo clever*—replied bitterly: Gennaro was clever, too, he spoke well, he read, he was very good in school, and look at him now.

83.

One night when Lila was speaking disparagingly of Gennaro, Dede gathered her courage and defended him. She became red-faced, she said: He's extremely intelligent. Lila looked at her with interest, smiled, replied: You're very nice, I'm his mamma and what you say gives me great pleasure.

From then on Dede felt authorized to defend Gennaro on every occasion, even when Lila was very angry at him. Gennaro was now a large boy of eighteen, with a handsome face, like his father's as a youth, but he was stockier and had a surly nature. He didn't even notice Dede, who was twelve, he had other things on his mind. But she never stopped thinking of him as the most astonishing human creature who had ever appeared on the face of the earth and whenever she could she sang his praises. Sometimes Lila was in a bad mood and didn't respond. But on other occasions she laughed, she exclaimed: Certainly not, he's a delinquent. You three sisters, on the other hand, you're clever, you'll be better than your mother. And Dede, although pleased with the compliment (when she could consider herself better than me she was happy), immediately began to belittle herself in order to elevate Gennaro.

She adored him. She would often sit at the window to watch for his return from the shop, shouting at him as soon as he appeared: Hi, Rino. If he answered hi (usually he didn't) she hurried to the landing to wait for him to come up the stairs and then tried to start a serious conversation, like: You're tired, what did you do to your hand, aren't you hot in those overalls, things of that sort. Even a few words from him excited her. If she happened to get more attention than usual, in order to prolong it she grabbed Imma and said: I'm taking her down to Aunt Lina, so she can play with Tina. I didn't have time to give her permission before she was out of the house.

Never had so little space separated Lila and me, not even when we were children. My floor was her ceiling. Two flights of stairs down brought me to her house, two up brought her to mine. In the morning, in the evening, I heard their voices: the indistinct sounds of conversations, Tina's trills that Lila responded to as if she, too, were trilling, the thick tonality of Enzo, who, silent as he was, spoke a lot to his daughter, and often sang to her. I supposed that the signs of my presence also reached Lila. When she was at work, when my older daughters were at school, when only Imma and Tina—who often stayed

with me, sometimes even to sleep—were at home, I noticed the
emptiness below, I listened for the footsteps of Lila and Enzo
returning.

Things soon took a turn for the better. Dede and Elsa frequently looked after Imma; they carried her down to the courtyard with them or to Lila's. If I had to go out Lila took care of
all three. It was years since I had had so much time available. I
read, I revised my book, I was at ease without Nino and free of
the anxiety of losing him. Also my relationship with Pietro
improved. He came to Naples more often to see the girls, he
got used to the small, dreary apartment and to their Neapolitan
accents, Elsa's especially, and he often stayed overnight. At
those times, he was polite to Enzo, and talked a lot to Lila.
Even though in the past Pietro had had definitely negative
opinions of her, it seemed clear that he was happy to spend
time in her company. As for Lila, as soon as he left she began
to talk about him with an enthusiasm she rarely showed for
anyone. How many books must he have studied, she said seriously, fifty thousand, a hundred thousand? I think she saw in
my ex-husband the incarnation of her childhood fantasies
about people who read and write for knowledge, not as a
profession.

"You're very smart," she said to me one evening, "but he
has a way of speaking that I truly like: he puts the writing into
his voice, but he doesn't speak like a printed book."

"I do?" I asked, as a joke.

"A little."

"Even now?"

"Yes."

"If I hadn't learned to speak like that I would never have
had any respect, outside of here."

"He's like you, but more natural. When Gennaro was little,
I thought—even though I didn't know Pietro yet—I thought
I'd want him to become just like that."

She often talked about her son. She said she should have given him more, but she hadn't had time, or consistency, or ability. She accused herself of having taught him the little she could and of having then lost confidence and stopped. One night she went from her first child to the second without interruption. She was afraid that Tina, too, as she grew up would be a waste. I praised Tina, sincerely, and she said in a serious tone:

"Now that you're here you have to help her become like your daughters. It's important to Enzo, too, he told me to ask you."

"All right."

"You help me, I'll help you. School isn't enough, you remember Maestra Oliviero, with me it wasn't enough."

"They were different times."

"I don't know. I gave Gennaro what was possible, but it went badly."

"It's the fault of the neighborhood."

She looked at me gravely, she said:

"I don't have much faith in it, but since you've decided to stay here with us, let's change the neighborhood."

84.

In a few months we became very close. We got in the habit of going out together to do the shopping, and on Sundays, rather than strolling amid the stalls on the *stradone*, we insisted on going to the center of town with Enzo so that our daughters could have the sun and the sea air. We walked along Via Caracciolo or in the Villa Comunale. He carried Tina on his shoulders, he pampered her, maybe too much. But he never forgot my daughters, he bought balloons, sweets, he played with them. Lila and I stayed behind them on purpose. We talked about everything, but not the way we had as adolescents: those times would never return. She asked questions about things she had heard on television and I answered volubly. I talked about the postmodern, the problems of publishing, the latest news of feminism, whatever came into my mind, and Lila listened attentively, her expression just slightly ironic, interrupting only to ask for further explanations, never to say what she thought. I liked talking to her. I liked her look of admiration, I liked it when she said: How many things you know, how many things you think, even when I felt she was teasing. If I pressed for her opinion she retreated, saying: No, don't make me say something stupid, you talk. Often she asked me about famous people, to find out if I knew them, and when I said no she was disappointed. She was also disappointed—I should say—when I reduced to ordinary dimensions well-known people I'd had dealings with.

"So," she concluded one morning, "those people aren't what they seem."

"Not at all. Often they're good at their work. But otherwise they're greedy, they like hurting you, they're allied with the strong and they persecute the weak, they form gangs to fight other gangs, they treat women like dogs on a leash, they'll utter obscenities and put their hands on you exactly the way they do on the buses here."

"You're exaggerating?"

"No, to produce ideas you don't have to be a saint. And anyway there are very few true intellectuals. The mass of the educated spend their lives commenting lazily on the ideas of others. They engage their best energies in sadistic practices against every possible rival."

"Then why are you with them?"

I answered: I'm not with them, I'm here. I wanted her to feel that I was part of an upper-class world and yet different. She herself pushed me in that direction. She was amused if I was sarcastic about my colleagues. Sometimes I had the impression that she insisted so that I would confirm that I really was one of those who told people how things stood and what they should think. The decision to live in the neighborhood made sense to her only if I continued to count myself among those who wrote books, contributed to magazines and newspapers, appeared sometimes on television. She wanted me as her friend, her neighbor, provided I had that aura. And I supported her. Her approval gave me confidence. I was beside her in the Villa Comunale, with our daughters, and yet I was definitively different, I had a wide-ranging life. It flattered me to feel that, compared to her, I was a woman of great experience and I felt that she, too, was pleased with what I was. I told her about France, Germany, and Austria, about the United States, the debates I had taken part in, here and there, the men there had been recently, after Nino. She was attentive to every word with a half smile, never saying what she thought. Not even the story of my occasional relationships set off in her a need to confide.

"Are you happy with Enzo?" I asked one morning.

"Enough."

"And you've never been interested in someone else?"

"No."

"Do you really love him?"

"Enough."

There was no way of getting anything else out of her, it was I who talked about sex and often in an explicit way. My ramblings, her silences. Yet, whatever the subject, during those walks, something was released from her very body that enthralled me, stimulating my brain as it always had, helping me reflect.

Maybe that was why I sought her out. She continued to emit an energy that gave comfort, that reinforced a purpose, that spontaneously suggested solutions. It was a force that struck not only me. Sometimes she invited me to dinner with the children, more often I invited her, with Enzo and, naturally, Tina. Gennaro, no, there was nothing to be done, he often stayed out and came home late at night. Enzo—I soon realized—was wor-ried about him, whereas Lila said: He's grown-up, let him do as he likes. But I felt she spoke that way to reduce her partner's anxiety. And the tone was identical to that of our conversations. Enzo nodded, something passed from her to him like an invig-orating tonic.

It was no different on the streets of the neighborhood. Going shopping with her never ceased to amaze me: she had become an authority. She was constantly stopped, people drew her aside with a respectful familiarity, they whispered something to her, and she listened, without reacting. Did they treat her like that because of the success she had had with her new business? Because she gave off the sense of someone who could do any-thing? Or because, now that she was nearly forty, the energy she had always had imbued her with the aura of a magician who cast spells and instilled fear? I don't know. Of course it struck me that people paid more attention to her than to me. I was a well-known writer and the publishing house was making sure that, in view of my new book, I was often mentioned in the newspapers: the *Repubblica* had come out with a fairly large photograph of me to illustrate a short article on forthcoming books, which at a certain point said: *Highly anticipated is the new novel by Elena Greco, a story set in an unknown Naples, with bloodred colors*, et cetera. And yet next to her, in the place where we were born, I was only a decoration, that is, I bore witness to Lila's merits. Those who had known us from birth attributed to her, to the force of her attraction, the fact that the neighborhood could have on its streets an esteemed person like me.

85.

I think there were many who wondered why I, who in the newspapers seemed rich and famous, had come to live in a wretched apartment, situated in an increasingly run-down area. Maybe the first not to understand were my daughters. Dede came home from school one day disgusted:

"An old man peed in our doorway."

Another day Elsa arrived terrified:

"Today someone was knifed in the gardens."

At such times I was afraid. The part of me that had long ago left the neighborhood was indignant, was worried about the children, and said, Enough. At home, Dede and Elsa spoke a good Italian, but occasionally I heard them from the window or coming up the stairs, and I realized that Elsa especially used a very aggressive, sometimes obscene dialect. I reprimanded her, she pretended to be sorry. But I knew that it took a lot of self-discipline to resist the lure of bad behavior and so many other temptations. Was it possible that while I was devoting myself to making literature they were getting lost? I calmed myself by repeating the temporal limit of this stay: after the publication of my book I would definitively leave Naples. I said it to myself and said it again: I needed only to reach a final draft of the novel.

The book was undoubtedly benefiting from everything that came from the neighborhood. But the work proceeded so well mainly because I was attentive to Lila, who had remained completely within that environment. Her voice, her gaze, her gestures, her meanness and her generosity, her dialect were all intimately connected to our place of birth. Even Basic Sight, in spite of the exotic name (people called her office *basissìt*), didn't seem some sort of meteorite that had fallen from outer space but rather the unexpected product of poverty, violence, and blight. Thus, drawing on her to give truth to my story seemed indispensable. Afterward I would leave for good, I intended to move to Milan.

I had only to sit in her office for a while to understand the background against which she moved. I looked at her brother, who was now openly consumed by drugs. I looked at Ada, who was crueler every day, the sworn enemy of Marisa, who had taken Stefano away from her. I looked at Alfonso—in whose face, in whose habits, the feminine and the masculine continually broke boundaries with effects that one day repelled me, the next moved me, and always alarmed me—who often had a black eye or a split lip because of the beatings he got, who knows where, who knows when. I looked at Carmen, who, in the blue jacket of a gas-pump attendant, drew Lila aside and interrogated her like an oracle. I looked at Antonio, who hovered around her with unfinished sentences or stood in a serene silence when he brought to the office, as if on a courtesy visit, his beautiful German wife, the children. Meanwhile I picked up endless rumors. Stefano Carracci is about to close the grocery, he doesn't have a lira, he needs money. It was Pasquale Peluso who kidnapped so-and-so, and if it wasn't him he certainly has something to do with it. That other so-and-so set fire to the shirt factory in Afragola by himself to fuck the insurance company. Watch out for Dede, they're giving children drugged candy. There's a faggot hanging around the elementary school who lures children away. The Solaras are opening a night club in the new neighborhood, women and drugs, the music will be so loud that no one will sleep again. Big trucks pass by on the *stradone* at night, transporting stuff that can destroy us faster than the atomic bomb. Gennaro has started hanging out with a bad crowd, and, if he continues like that, I won't even let him go to work. The person they found murdered in the tunnel looked like a woman but was a man: there was so much blood in the body that it flowed all the way down to the gas pump.

I observed, I listened, from the vantage point of what Lila and I as children had imagined becoming and what I had actually become: the author of a big book that I was polishing—or at times rewriting—and that would soon be published. In the first draft—I said to myself—I put too much dialect. And I erased it, rewrote. Then it seemed that I had put in too little and I added ·

some. I was in the neighborhood and yet safe in that role, within that setting. The ambitious work justified my presence there and, as long as I was occupied with it, gave meaning to the poor light in the rooms, the rough voices of the street, the risks that the children ran, the traffic on the *stradone* that raised dust when the weather was good and water and mud when it rained, Lila and Enzo's swarm of clients, small provincial entrepreneurs, big luxury cars, clothes of a vulgar wealth, heavy bodies that moved sometimes aggressively, sometimes with servile manners.

Once when I was waiting for Lila at Basic Sight with Imma and Tina, everything seemed to become clearer: Lila was doing new work but totally immersed in our old world. I heard her shouting at a client in an extremely crude way about a question of money. I was shaken, where had the woman who graciously emanated authority suddenly gone? Enzo hurried in, and the man—a small man around sixty, with an enormous belly—went away cursing. Afterward I said to Lila:

"Who are you really?"

"In what sense?"

"If you don't want to talk about it, forget it."

"No, let's talk, but explain what you mean."

"I mean: in an environment like this, with the people you have to deal with, how do you behave?"

"I'm careful, like everyone."

"That's all?"

"Well, I'm careful and I move things around in order to make them go the way I say. Haven't we always behaved that way?"

"Yes, but now we have responsibilities, toward ourselves and our children. Didn't you say we have to change the neighborhood?"

"And to change it what do you think needs to be done?"

"Resort to the law."

I was startled myself by what I was saying. I made a speech in which I was, to my surprise, even more legalistic than my

274 · ELENA FERRANTE

ex-husband and, in many ways, more than Nino. Lila said teasingly:

"The law is fine when you're dealing with people who pay attention if you merely say the word 'law'. But you know how it is here."

"And so?"

"So if people have no fear of the law, you have to instill the fear yourself. We did a lot of work for that shit you saw before, in fact a huge amount, but he won't pay, he says he has no money. I threatened him, I told him: I'll sue you. And he answered: Sue me, who gives a damn."

"But you'll sue him."

She laughed: "I'll never see my money that way. Some time ago, an accountant stole millions from us. We fired him and filed charges. But the law didn't lift a finger."

"So?"

"I was fed up with waiting and I asked Antonio. The money was returned immediately. And this money, too, will return, without a trial, without lawyers, and without judges."

86.

So Antonio did that sort of work for Lila. Not for money but out of friendship, or personal respect. Or, I don't know, maybe she asked Michele if she could borrow him, since Antonio worked for Michele, and Michele, who agreed to everything Lila asked, let her.

But did Michele really satisfy her every request? If it had certainly been true before I moved to the neighborhood, now it wasn't clear if things really were like that. First I noticed some odd signs: Lila no longer uttered Michele's name with condescension but, rather, with irritation or obvious concern; mainly, though, he hardly ever appeared at Basic Sight.

It was at the wedding celebration of Marcello and Elisa, which was ostentatious and lavish, that I became aware something had changed. During the entire reception Marcello stayed close to his brother; he often whispered to him, they laughed together, he put an arm around his shoulders. As for Michele, he seemed revived. He had returned to making long, pompous speeches, as he used to, while the children and Gigliola, now extraordinarily fat, sat obediently beside him, as if they had decided to forget the way he had treated them. It struck me how the vulgarity, which was still very provincial at the time of Lila's wedding, had been as if modernized. It had become a metropolitan vulgarity, and Lila herself was appropriate to it, in her habits, in her language, in her clothes. Nothing clashed, in other words, except for me and my daughters, who with our sobriety were completely out of place in that triumph of excessive colors, excessive laughter, excessive luxuries.

Perhaps that was why Michele's burst of rage was especially alarming. He was making a speech in honor of the newlyweds, but meanwhile little Tina was claiming something that Imma had taken away from her, and was screaming in the middle of the room. He was talking, Tina was crying. Suddenly Michele broke off and, with the eyes of a madman, shouted: Fuck, Lina, will you shut that piece of shit kid up? Like that, exactly in those words. Lila stared at him for a long second. She didn't speak, she didn't move. Very slowly, she placed one hand on the hand of Enzo, who was sitting next to her. I quickly got up from my table and took the two little girls outside.

The episode roused the bride, that is to say, my sister Elisa. At the end of the speech, when the sound of applause reached me, she came out, in her extravagant white dress. She said cheerfully: My brother-in-law has returned to himself. Then she added: But he shouldn't treat babies like that. She picked up Imma and Tina, and, laughing and joking returned to the hall with the two children. I followed her, confused.

For a while I thought that she, too, had returned to herself. Elisa in fact did change greatly, after her marriage, as if what had ruined her had been the absence, until that moment, of the marriage bond. She became a calm mother, a tranquil yet firm wife, her hostility toward me ended. Now when I went to her house with my daughters and, often, Tina, she welcomed me politely and was affectionate with the children. Even Marcello—when I ran into him—was courteous. He called me the sister-in-law who writes novels (*How is the sister-in-law who writes novels?*), said a cordial word or two, and disappeared. The house was always tidy, and Elisa and Silvio welcomed us dressed as if for a party. But my sister as a little girl— I soon realized—had vanished forever. The marriage had inaugurated a completely fake Signora Solara, never an intimate word, only a good-humored tone and a smile, all copied from her husband. I made an effort to be loving, with her and especially with my nephew. But I didn't find Silvio appealing, he was too much like Marcello, and Elisa must have realized it. One afternoon she turned bitter again for a few minutes. She said: You love Lina's child more than mine. I swore it wasn't true, I hugged the child, kissed him. But she shook her head, whispered: Besides, you went to live near Lina and not near me or Papa. She continued, in other words, to be angry with me and now also with our brothers. I think she accused them of behaving like ingrates. They lived and worked in Baiano and they weren't even in touch with Marcello, who had been so generous with them. Family ties, said Elisa, you think they're strong, but no. She talked as if she were stating a universal principle, then she added: To keep from breaking those ties, you need, as my husband has shown, goodwill. Michele had turned into an idiot, but Marcello restored his mind to him: Did you notice what a great speech he made at my wedding?

87.

Michele's return to his senses was marked not only by a return to his flowery speech but also by the absence among the guests of a person who during that period of crisis had been very close to him: Alfonso. Not to be invited was for my former schoolmate a source of great suffering. For days he did nothing but complain, asking aloud how he had wronged the Solaras. I worked for them for so many years, he said, and they didn't invite me. Then something happened that caused a sensation. One evening he came to dinner at my house with Lila and Enzo, very depressed. But Alfonso, who had never dressed as a woman in my presence except the day he tried on the maternity dress in the shop on Via Chiaia, arrived in women's clothes, leaving Dede and Elsa speechless. He was troublesome all evening; he drank a lot. He asked Lila obsessively: Am I getting fat, am I getting ugly, do I not look like you anymore? And Enzo: Who's prettier, her or me? At a certain point he complained that he had a blocked intestine, that he had a terrible pain in what—addressing the girls—he called his ass. And he began to insist that I look and see what was wrong. Look at my ass, he said, laughing in an obscene way, and Dede stared at him in bewilderment, Elsa tried to stifle a laugh. Enzo and Lila had to take him away in a hurry.

But Alfonso didn't calm down. The next day, without makeup, in male clothes, eyes red with crying, he left Basic Sight saying that he was going to have a coffee at the Bar Solara. At the entrance he met Michele, and they said something to each other. Michele, after a few minutes, began to punch and kick him, then he grabbed the pole that was used to lower the shutter and beat him methodically, for a long time. Alfonso returned to the office badly battered, but he couldn't stop repeating: It's my fault, I don't how to control myself. Control in what way we couldn't understand. Certainly, he got even worse, and Lila seemed worried. For days she tried in vain to soothe Enzo, who couldn't bear the violence of the strong against the weak, and wanted to go to Michele to see if he could beat him, Enzo, the way he had beaten Alfonso. From my apartment I heard Lila saying: Stop it, you're frightening Tina.

88.

January arrived, and my book was now enriched by echoes of many small details of the neighborhood. A great anguish came over me. When I was at the last stage of proofs I timidly asked Lila if she had the patience to reread it (*It's very changed*) but she answered decisively no. I didn't read the last one you published, she said, those are things in which I have no expertise. I felt alone, at the mercy of my own pages, and I was even tempted to call Nino to ask if he would do me a favor and read it. Then I realized that, although he knew my address and phone number, he had never appeared, in all those months he had ignored both me and his daughter. So I gave up. The text moved beyond the final provisional stage and disappeared. Separating from it frightened me, I would see it again only in its definitive guise, and every word would be irremediable.

The publicity office telephoned. Gina said: at *Panorama* they've read the proofs and are very interested, they'll send a photographer. Suddenly I missed the elegant apartment on Via Tasso. I thought: I don't want to be photographed again at the entrance of the tunnel, or in this dreary apartment, or even in the gardens, amid the syringes of the addicts; I'm not the girl of fifteen years ago, this is my third book, I want to be treated properly. But Gina insisted, the book had to be promoted. I told her: Give the photographer my phone number—I wanted at least to be notified ahead of time, attend to my appearance, put off the meeting if I didn't feel in good shape.

In those days I tried to keep the house in order, but no one called. I concluded that there were already enough photographs of me around and that *Panorama* had decided not to do the article. But one morning, when Dede and Elsa were at school and I was sitting on the floor, in jeans and a worn-out sweater, my hair uncombed, playing with Imma and Tina, the doorbell rang. The two little girls were building a castle with blocks that were scattered around, and I was helping them. In the past few months it had seemed to me that the distance between my daughter and Lila's had been bridged: they collaborated on the construction with precise gestures, and if Tina appeared more imaginative and often asked me surprising questions in a pure Italian, always clearly pronounced, Imma was more decisive, maybe more disciplined, and her only disadvantage was a constricted language that we often needed her friend to decipher. Since I delayed going to the door as I finished answering some question or other of Tina's, there was a commanding ring. I opened the door and found myself facing a beautiful woman of around thirty, with blond curls, a long blue raincoat. She was the photographer.

She turned out to be a very gregarious Milanese, expensively dressed. I lost your number, she said, but just as well—the less you expect to be photographed the better the photos. She looked around. What a job to get here, what a wretched place, but it's exactly what's needed: are these your babies? Tina smiled at her, Imma didn't, but it was obvious that they both considered her a kind of fairy. I introduced them: Imma is my daughter and Tina the daughter of a friend. But even as I was speaking, the photographer began to wander around, snapping photos constantly with different cameras and all her equipment. I have to pull myself together, I tried to say. Not at all, you're fine like that.

She pushed me into every part of the house: the kitchen, the children's room, my bedroom, even in front of the bathroom mirror.

"Do you have your book?"

"No, it's not out yet."

"A copy of the last one you wrote?"

"Yes."

"Take it and sit here, pretend to be reading."

I obeyed in a daze. Tina grabbed a book, too, and assumed the same pose, saying to Imma: Take a picture of me. This excited the photographer, she said: Sit on the floor with the children. She took a lot of pictures, Tina and Imma were happy. She exclaimed: Now let's do one alone with your daughter. I tried to pull Imma to me, but she said: No, the other one, she has a fantastic face. She pushed Tina toward me, she took an infinite number of pictures, Imma became upset. Me, too, she said. I opened my arms, I called to her: Yes, come to Mamma.

The morning flew by. The woman in the blue raincoat dragged us out of the house, but was somewhat tense. She asked a couple of times: They won't steal my equipment? Then she got carried away, she wanted to photograph every squalid corner of the neighborhood. She placed me on a broken-down bench, against a flaking wall, next to the old urinal. I said to Imma and Tina: Stay here, don't move, because the cars are going by, I'm warning you. They held each other by the hand, one fair and one dark, the same height, and waited.

Lila returned from work at dinnertime, and came up to get her daughter. Tina didn't wait for her to come in before she told her all about it.

"A beautiful lady came."

"More beautiful than me?"

"Yes."

"Even more beautiful than Aunt Lenuccia?"

"No."

"So Aunt Lenuccia is the prettiest of all?"

"No, me."

"You? What nonsense you talk."

"It's true, Mamma."

"And what did this lady do?"

"Took photos."

"Of whom?"

"Of me."

"Only you?"

"Yes."

"Liar. Imma, come here, tell me what you did."

89.

I waited for *Panorama* to come out. I was pleased now, the publicity office was doing a good job, I felt proud of being the subject of an entire photographic feature. But a week passed, and the feature didn't appear. Two weeks passed, nothing. It was the end of March, the book was in the bookstores, and still nothing. I was absorbed in other things, an interview on the radio, one in *Il Mattino*. At a certain point I had to go to Milan for the launch of the book. I did it in the same bookstore as fifteen years earlier, introduced by the same professor. Adele didn't come, nor did Mariarosa, but the audience was bigger than in the past. The professor talked about the book without much warmth but positively, and some members of the audience—it was mostly women—spoke up enthusiastically about the complex humanity of the protagonist. A rite that I knew well by now. I left the next morning and returned to Naples, exhausted.

I remember that I was heading home, dragging my suitcase, when a car pulled up along the *stradone*. At the wheel was Michele, next to him sat Marcello. I remembered when the two Solaras had tried to pull me into their car—they had done it with Ada, too—and Lila had defended me. I had on my wrist, as I had then, my mother's bracelet, and, though objects are impassive by nature, I drew back with a start to protect it. But Marcello stared straight ahead without greeting me, he didn't even say in his usual good-humored tone: Here's the sister-in-law who writes novels. Michele spoke, he was furious:

"Lenù, what the fuck did you write in that book? Despicable things about the place you were born? Despicable things about my family? Despicable things about the people who watched you grow up and who admire you and love you? Despicable things about this beautiful city of ours?"

He turned around and took from the backseat a copy of *Panorama*, fresh from the printer, and held it out through the window.

"You like talking shit?"

I looked. The weekly was open to the page about me. There was a big color photo that showed Tina and me sitting on the floor at my apartment. The caption struck me immediately: *Elena Greco with her daughter Tina*. At first I thought that the problem was the caption and I didn't understand why Michele was so angry. I said bewildered:

"They made a mistake."

But he shouted out a sentence, even more incomprehensible:

"They aren't the ones who made a mistake, it was *you two*."

At that point Marcello interrupted, he said with irritation:

"Forget it, Michè, Lina manipulates her and she doesn't even realize it."

He took off, tires screeching, and left me on the sidewalk with the magazine in my hand.

90.

I stood stock-still, my suitcase beside me. I read the article, four pages with pictures of the ugliest places in the neighborhood: the only one with me was the one with Tina, a beautiful picture in which the bleak background of the apartment gave our two figures a particular refinement. The writer wasn't reviewing my book and didn't speak of it as a novel, but used it to give an account of what he called "the dominion of the Solara brothers," a borderland territory, perhaps tied to the new organized Camorra, perhaps not. Of Marcello it said little, alluding mainly to Michele, to whom it attributed initiative, unscrupulousness, a tendency to jump from one political cart to the next, according to the logic of business. What business? *Panorama* made a list, mixing the legal and the illegal: the bar-pastry shop, hides, shoe factories, mini-markets, night clubs, loan sharking, cigarette smuggling, receiving stolen goods, drugs, infiltration of the post-earthquake construction sites.

I broke into a cold sweat.

What had I done, how could I have been so imprudent.

In Florence I had invented a plot, drawing on facts of my childhood and adolescence with the boldness that came from distance. Naples, seen from there, was almost a place of imagination, a city like the ones in films, which although the streets and buildings are real serve only as a background for crime stories or romances. Then, since I had moved and saw Lila every day, a mania for reality had gripped me, and although I hadn't named it I had told the story of the neighborhood. But I must have overdone it, and the relationship between truth and fiction must have gone awry: now every street, every building had become recognizable, and maybe even the people, even the violent acts. The photographs were proof of what my pages really contained, they identified the area conclusively, and the neighborhood ceased to be, as it had always been for me while I was writing, an invention. The author of the article told the history of the neighborhood, even mentioning the murders of Don Achille Carracci and Manuela Solara. He went on at length about the latter, hypothesizing that it had been either the visible point of a conflict between

Camorra families or an execution at the hands of the "dangerous terrorist Pasquale Peluso, born and raised in the area, former bricklayer, former secretary of the local section of the Communist Party." But I hadn't written anything about Pasquale, I hadn't written anything about Don Achille or Manuela. The Carraccis, the Solaras had been for me only outlines, voices that had been able to enrich, with the cadence of dialect, gestures, at times violent tonalities, a completely imagined scheme. I didn't want to stick my nose in their real business, what did "the dominion of the Solara brothers" have to do with it.

I had written a novel.

91.

I went to Lila's house in a state of great agitation, the children were with her. You're back already, said Elsa, who felt freer when I wasn't there. And Dede greeted me distractedly, murmuring with feigned restraint: Just a minute, Mamma, I'll finish my homework and then hug you. The only enthusiastic one was Imma, who pressed her lips to my cheek and kissed me for a long time, refusing to let go. Tina wanted to do the same. But I had other things on my mind, and paid them almost no attention. I immediately showed Lila *Panorama*. I told her about the Solaras, suppressing my anxiety. I said: They're angry. Lina read the article calmly and made a single comment: Nice photos. I exclaimed:

"I'll send a letter, I'll protest. Let them do a report on Naples, let them do it on, I don't know, the kidnapping of Cirillo, on Camorra deaths, on what they want, but they shouldn't use my book gratuitously."

"And why?"

"Because it's literature, I didn't narrate real events."

"I recall that you did."

I looked at her uncertainly.

"What do you mean?"

"You didn't use the names, but a lot of things were recognizable."

"Why didn't you tell me?"

"I told you I didn't like the book. Things are told or not told: you remained in the middle."

"It was a novel."

"Partly a novel, partly not."

I didn't answer, my anxiety increased. Now I didn't know if I was more unhappy about the Solaras' reaction or because she, serenely, had just repeated her negative judgment of years earlier. I looked at Dede and Elsa, who had taken possession of the magazine, but almost without seeing them. Elsa exclaimed:

"Tina, come see, you're in the newspaper."

Tina approached and looked at herself, eyes wide with wonder and a pleased smile on her face. Imma asked Elsa:

"Where am I?"

"You're not there because Tina is pretty and you're ugly," her sister answered.

Imma then turned to Dede to find out if it was true. And Dede, after reading the *Panorama* caption aloud twice, tried to convince her that since her name was Sarratore and not Airota, she wasn't truly my daughter. I couldn't take it anymore, I was tired, upset, I cried: That's enough, let's go home. They all three objected, supported by Tina and by Lila, who insisted that we stay for dinner.

I stayed. Lila tried to soothe me, she even tried to make me forget that she had again been critical of my book. She started off in dialect and then began to speak in the Italian she brought out on important occasions, which never failed to surprise me. She cited the experience of the earthquake, for more

286 · ELENA FERRANTE

than two years she had done nothing except complain of how the city had deteriorated. She said that since then she had been careful never to forget that we are very crowded beings, full of physics, astrophysics, biology, religion, soul, bourgeoisie, proletariat, capital, work, profit, politics, many harmonious phrases, many unharmonious, the chaos inside and the chaos outside. So calm down, she said laughing, what do you expect the Solaras to be. Your novel is done: you wrote it, you rewrote it, being here was evidently useful to you, to make it truer, but now it's out and you can't take it back. The Solaras are angry? So what. Michele threatens you? Who gives a damn. There could be another earthquake at any moment, even stronger. Or the whole universe could collapse. And then what is Michele Solara? Nothing. And Marcello is nothing. The two of them are merely flesh that spouts out threats and demands for money. She sighed. She said in a low voice: The Solaras will always be dangerous beasts, Lenù, there's nothing to be done; I thought I had tamed one but his brother made him ferocious again. Did you see how many blows Michele gave Alfonso? They're blows he wanted to give me but he hasn't got the courage. And that rage at your book, at the article in *Panorama*, at the photos, is all rage against me. So don't give a shit, the way I don't give a shit. You put them in the newspaper and the Solaras can't tolerate it, it's bad for business and for scams. To us, on the other hand, it's a pleasure, no? What do we have to worry about?

I listened. When she talked like that, with those high-flown pronouncements, the suspicion returned that she had continued to consume books, the way she had as a girl, but that for incomprehensible reasons she kept it hidden from me. In her house not a single volume was to be seen, apart from the hypertechnical pamphlets that had to do with the work. She wanted to present herself as an uneducated person, and yet suddenly here she was talking about biology, psychology, about how complicated human beings are. Why did she act like that with me? I didn't know, but I needed support and I trusted her just the same. In other words, Lila managed to soothe me. I reread the article and I liked it. I examined the photographs: the neighborhood was ugly but Tina and I were pretty. We began to cook, and the preparations helped me reflect. I decided that the article, the photos, would be useful for the book and that the text of Florence, filled out in Naples, in the apartment above hers, really was improved. Yes, I said, let's screw the Solaras. And I relaxed, I was nice to the children again.

Before dinner, after who knows what councils, Imma came over to me, Tina trailing behind. In her language made up of words that were pronounced clearly and words that were barely comprehensible she said:

"Mamma, Tina wants to know if your daughter is me or her."

"And do you want to know?" I asked her.

Her eyes were shining: "Yes."

Lila said:

"We are mammas of you both and we love you both."

When Enzo returned from work he was excited about the photograph of his daughter. The next day he bought two copies of *Panorama* and stuck up in his office both the whole image and the image of his daughter alone. Naturally he cut off the mistaken caption.

92.

Today, as I write, I'm embarrassed at the way fortune continued to favor me. The book immediately aroused interest. Some were thrilled by the pleasure of reading it. Some praised the skill with which the protagonist was developed. Some talked about a brutal realism, some extolled my baroque imagination, some admired a female narrative that was gentle and embracing. In other words there were many positive judgments, but often in sharp contrast to one another, as if the reviewers hadn't read the book that was in the bookstores but, rather, each had evoked a fantasy book fabricated from his own biases. On one thing, after the article in *Panorama*, they all agreed: the novel was absolutely different from the usual kind of writing about Naples.

When my copies arrived from the publisher, I was so happy that I decided to give one to Lila. I hadn't given her my previous books, and I took it for granted that, at least for the moment, she wouldn't even look at it. But I felt close to her, she was the only person I could truly rely on, and I wanted to show her my gratitude. She didn't react well. Obviously that day she had a lot to do, and was involved in her usual aggressive way in the neighborhood conflicts over the forthcoming elections on June 26th. Or maybe something had annoyed her, I don't know. The fact is that I gave her the book and she didn't even look at it, she said I shouldn't waste my copies.

I was disappointed. Enzo saved me from embarrassment. Give it to me, he said, I've never had a passion for reading, but I'll save it for Tina, so when she grows up she'll read it. And he wanted me to write a dedication to the child. I remember that I wrote with some uneasiness: For Tina, who will do better than all of us. Then I read the dedication aloud and Lila exclaimed: It doesn't take much to do better than me, I hope she'll do much more. Pointless words, with no motivation: I had written *better than all of us* and she had reduced it to *better than me*. Both Enzo and I dropped it. He put the book on a shelf among the computer manuals and we talked about the invitations I was receiving, the trips I would have to make.

93.

In general those moments of hostility were open, but sometimes they also persisted behind an appearance of availability and affection. Lila, for example, still seemed happy to take care of my daughters, and yet, with a mere inflection of her voice, she could make me feel indebted, as if she were saying: What you are, what you become, depends on what I, sacrificing, allow you to be, to become. If I perceived that tone I darkened and suggested getting a babysitter. But both she and Enzo were almost offended, it shouldn't even be mentioned. One morning when I needed her help she alluded in irritation to problems that were putting her under pressure and I said coldly that I could find other solutions. She became aggressive: Did I tell you I can't? If you need me, I'll arrange it: have your daughters ever complained, have I neglected them? So I convinced myself that she wanted only a sort of declaration of indispensability and I admitted with sincere gratitude that my public life would have been impossible if she had been less supportive. Then I gave in to my commitments without any more qualms.

Thanks to the competence of the publicity office, I appeared in a different newspaper every day, and a couple of times even on television. I was excited and extremely tense, I liked the increasing attention but I was afraid of saying the wrong thing. At the moments of greatest anxiety I didn't know whom to ask and I resorted to Lila for advice:

"If they ask me about the Solaras?"

"Say what you think."

"And if the Solaras get angry?"

"At the moment you're more dangerous for them than they are for you."

"I'm worried, Michele seems crazier and crazier."

"Books are written so their authors can be heard, not so that they remain silent."

In reality I always tried to be cautious. It was the middle of a heated electoral campaign, and I was careful, in interviews, not to get mixed up in politics, not to mention the Solaras, who—it was known—were involved in funneling votes for the five governing parties. Instead I talked a lot about the conditions of life in the neighborhood, of the further deterioration after the earthquake, of poverty and illegal trafficking, of institutional complicity. And then—depending on the questions and the whim of the moment—I talked about myself, about my education, about the effort I had had to make in order to study, about misogyny at the Normale, about my mother, about my daughters, about feminist thought. It was a complicated moment in the literary market; writers of my age, hesitating between the avant-garde and traditional storytelling, struggled to define and establish themselves. But I had an advantage. My first book had come out at the end of the sixties, with my second I had demonstrated a solid education and a broad range of interests, and I was one of the few who had a small publication history and even a following. So the telephone began to ring more and more often. But rarely, it should be said, did the journalists want opinions or comments on literary questions; they asked me mainly for sociological reflections and statements about the current state of Naples. I engaged in this willingly. And soon I began to contribute to *Il Mattino* on an array of subjects, and I accepted a column in *We Women*, I presented the book wherever I was invited, adapting it to the requirements of the audience I found. I couldn't believe what was happening to me. The preceding books had done well but not with the same momentum. A couple of well-known writers whom I had never had a chance to meet telephoned me. A famous director wanted to meet me, he wanted to make my novel into a film. Every day I learned that the book had been requested for reading by this or that foreign publisher. I was more and more content.

But I got particular satisfaction from two unexpected phone calls. The first was from Adele. She spoke to me very cordially, she asked about her grandchildren, she said that she knew all about them from Pietro, that she had seen pictures of them and they were beautiful. I listened to her, I confined myself to a few polite remarks. About the book she said: I read it again, well done, you improved it a lot. And as she said good-bye she made me promise that if I came to present the book in Genoa I should let her know, I should bring the children, leave them with her for a while. I promised, but I ruled out that I would keep my promise.

A few days later Nino called. He said that my novel was fantastic (*a quality of writing unimaginable in Italy*), he asked to see the three children. I invited him to lunch. He devoted himself to Dede, Elsa, and Imma, and then naturally he spoke a great deal about himself. He spent very little time in Naples now, he was always in Rome, he worked a lot with my former father-in-law, he had important responsibilities. He repeated: Things are going well, Italy is finally setting out on the road to modernity. Then suddenly he exclaimed, fixing his eyes on mine: Let's get back together. I burst out laughing: When you want to see Imma, call; but the two of us have nothing more to say to each other. It seems to me that I conceived the child with a ghost, certainly you weren't in the bed. He went away sulkily and didn't show up again. He forgot about us—Dede, Elsa, Imma, and me—for a long period. He probably forgot about us as soon as I closed the door behind him.

94.

At that point, what more did I want? My name, the name of a nobody, was definitely becoming the name of a somebody. That was why Adele Airota had telephoned me as if to

apologize, that was why Nino Sarratore had tried to be forgiven and to return to my bed, that was why I was invited
everywhere. Of course, it was difficult to separate from the
children and stop, if just for a few days, being their mother. But
even that tug became habitual. The need to make a good
impression in public soon replaced the sense of guilt. My head
became crowded with countless things, Naples and the neighborhood lost substance. Other landscapes imposed themselves, I went to beautiful cities I had never seen before, I
thought I would like to go and live in them. I met men who
attracted me, who made me feel important, who made me
happy. A range of alluring possibilities opened up before me in
the space of a few hours. And the chains of motherhood weakened, sometimes I forgot to call Lila, to say goodnight to the
girls. Only when I noticed that I would have been capable of
living without them did I return to myself, did I feel remorse.

Then there was an especially bad moment. I left for a long
promotional tour in the south. I was to stay away for a week,
but Imma didn't feel well, she looked depressed, she had a
bad cold. It was my fault, I couldn't be angry with Lila: she
was very attentive, but she had endless things to do and
couldn't keep an eye on the children if they got sweaty when
they ran around, and the drafts. Before I left I asked the publicity office to get me the telephone numbers of the hotels
where I was to stay and I left them with Lila for any eventuality. If there are problems, I insisted, telephone me and I'll be
right home.

I departed. At first I thought only of Imma and her illness,
I called whenever I could. Then I forgot about it. I arrived in
a place, I was welcomed with great courtesy, an intense program had been prepared for me, I tried to show that I was up
to it, I was celebrated at interminable dinners. Once I tried to
call, but the telephone rang unanswered, and I let it go; once
Enzo answered and said in his laconic way: Do what you have

to do, don't worry; once I talked to Dede, who said, in an adult voice, We're fine, Mamma, bye, have fun. But when I returned I discovered that Imma had been in hospital for three days. She had pneumonia, and had been admitted. Lila was with her, she had abandoned every commitment, had abandoned even Tina, had stayed in the hospital with my daughter. I was desperate, I protested that I had been kept in the dark. But she wouldn't give in, even when I returned, she continued to feel responsible for the child. Go, she said, you're always traveling, rest.

I was truly tired, but above all I was dazed. I regretted not having been with the child, of having deprived her of my presence just when she needed me. Because now I didn't know anything about how much and in what way she had suffered. Whereas Lila had in her head all the phases of my daughter's illness, her difficulty breathing, the suffering, the rush to the hospital. I looked at her, there in the corridor of the hospital, and she seemed more worn-out than I was. She had offered Imma the permanent and loving contact of her body. She hadn't been home for days, she had hardly slept, she had the blunted gaze of exhaustion. I, however, in spite of myself, felt inside—and maybe appeared outside—luminous. Even now that I knew about my daughter's illness, I couldn't get rid of the satisfaction for what I had become, the pleasure of feeling free, moving all over Italy, the pleasure of disposing of myself as if I had no past and everything were starting now.

As soon as the child was discharged, I confessed my state of mind to Lila. I wanted to find an order in the confusion of guilt and pride that I felt inside, I wanted to tell her how grateful I was but also hear from her in detail what Imma—since I hadn't been there to give it to her—had gotten from her. But Lila replied almost with irritation: Lenù, forget it, it's over, your daughter's fine, there are bigger problems now. I thought for a few seconds that she meant her problems at work but it wasn't

that, the problems had to do with me. She had found out, just
before Imma's illness, that a lawsuit was about to be brought
against me. The person who was bringing it was Carmen.

95.

I was frightened, and I felt distressed. Carmen? Carmen
had done a thing like that to me?

The thrilling phase of success ended at that moment. In a
few seconds the guilt at having neglected Imma was added to
the fear that by legal means everything would be taken away
from me, joy, prestige, money. I was ashamed of myself, of my
aspirations. I said to Lila that I wanted to talk to Carmen right
away, she advised me against it. But I had the impression that
she knew more than what she had said and I went to look for
Carmen anyway.

First I went to the gas pump, but she wasn't there. Roberto
was embarrassed in my presence. He was silent about the lawsuit, he said that his wife had gone with the children to
Giugliano, to some relatives, and would be there for a while.
I left him standing there and went to their house to see if he
had told me the truth. But Carmen either really had gone to
Giugliano or wouldn't open the door to me. It was very hot. I
walked for a while to calm myself, then I looked for Antonio,
I was sure he would know something. I thought it would be
hard to track him down, he was always out. But his wife told
me that he had gone to the barber and I would find him there.
I asked him if he had heard talk of legal actions against me, and
instead of answering he began to complain about the school,
he said that the teachers were annoyed with his children, they
complained that they spoke in German or in dialect, but meanwhile they didn't teach them Italian. Then out of the blue he
almost whispered:

"Let me take this moment to say goodbye."

"Where are you going."

"I'm going back to Germany."

"When?"

"I don't yet know."

"Why are you saying goodbye now?"

"You're never here, we hardly see each other."

"It's you who never come to see me."

"You don't come to see me, either."

"Why are you going?"

"My family isn't happy here."

"Is it Michele who's sending you away?"

"He commands and I obey."

"So it's he who doesn't want you in the neighborhood anymore."

He looked at his hands, he examined them carefully.

"Every so often my nervous breakdown returns," he said, and he began to talk to me about his mother, Melina, who wasn't right in the head.

"You'll leave her to Ada?"

"I'll take her with me," he muttered. "Ada already has too many troubles. And I have the same constitution, I want to keep her in sight to see what I'm going to become."

"She's always lived here, she'll suffer in Germany."

"One suffers everywhere. You want some advice?"

I understood from the way he looked at me that he had decided to get to the point.

"Let's hear it."

"You get out of here, too."

"Why?"

"Because Lina believes that the two of you are invincible but it's not true. And I can't help you any longer."

"Help us in what?"

He shook his head unhappily.

"The Solaras are furious. Did you see how people voted here in the neighborhood?"

"No."

"It turned out that they no longer control the votes they used to control."

"So?"

"Lina has managed to shift a lot of them to the Communists."

"And what do I have to do with it?"

"Marcello and Michele see Lina behind everything, especially behind you. There is a lawsuit, and Carmen's lawyers are their lawyers."

96.

I went home, I didn't look for Lila. I assumed that she knew all about the elections, about the votes, about the Solaras, enraged, who were waiting in ambush behind Carmen. She told me things a little at a time, for her own ends. Instead I called the publishing house, I told the editor in chief about the lawsuit and what Antonio had reported to me. For now it's only a rumor, I said, nothing certain, but I'm worried. He tried to reassure me, he promised that he would ask the legal department to investigate and as soon as he found out anything he would telephone me. He concluded: Why are you so agitated, this is good for the book. Not for me, I thought, I've been wrong about everything, I shouldn't have returned here to live.

Days passed, I didn't hear from the publisher, but the notification of the lawsuit arrived at my house like a stab. I read it and was speechless. Carmen demanded that the editor and I withdraw the book from circulation, plus enormous damages for having tarnished the memory of her mother, Giuseppina. I had never seen a document that summed up in itself, in the letterhead, in the quality of the writing, in the decorative stamps

and notarized seals, the power of the law. I discovered that what
had never made an impression on me as an adolescent, even as
a young woman, now terrified me. This time I hurried to see
Lila. When I told her what it was about she started teasing me:

"You wanted the law, the law has arrived."

"What should I do?"

"Make a scene."

"What do you mean?"

"Tell the newspapers what's happening to you."

"You're crazy. Antonio said that behind Carmen are the
Solaras' lawyers, and don't say you don't know."

"Of course I know."

"Then why didn't you tell me?"

"Because you see how nervous you are? But you don't have
to worry. You're afraid of the law and the Solaras are afraid of
your book."

"I'm afraid that with all the money they have they can ruin
me."

"But it's precisely their money you have to go for. Write.
The more you write about their disgusting affairs the more you
ruin their business."

I was depressed. Lila thought this? This was her project?
Only then did I understand clearly that she ascribed to me the
power that as children we had ascribed to the author of *Little
Women*. That was why she had wanted me to return to the
neighborhood at all costs? I left without saying anything. I
went home, I called the publisher again. I hoped that he was
exerting himself in some way, I wanted news that would calm
me, but I didn't reach him. The next day he called me. He
announced gaily that in the *Corriere della Sera* there was an
article by him—yes, by his hand—in which he gave an account
of the lawsuit. Go and buy it, he said, and let me know what
you think.

97.

I went to the newsstand more anxious than ever. There again was the photograph of me with Tina, this time in black-and-white. The lawsuit was announced in the headline; it was considered an attempt to muzzle one of the very few courageous writers et cetera, et cetera. The article didn't name the neighborhood, it didn't allude to the Solaras. Skillfully, it set the episode within a conflict that was taking place everywhere, "between the medieval remnants that are keeping this country from modernizing and the unstoppable advance, even in the South, of political and cultural renewal." It was a short piece, but it defended effectively, especially in the conclusion, the rights of literature, separating them from what were called "very sad local disputes."

I was relieved, I had the impression of being well protected. I telephoned, I praised the article, then I went to show the paper to Lila. I expected her to be be excited. That was what it seemed to me she wanted: a deployment of the power that she ascribed to me. Instead she said coolly:

"Why did you let this man write the article?"

"What's wrong? The publisher is standing behind me, they're attending to this mess, it seems a good thing."

"It's just talk, Lenù, this guy is only interested in selling the book."

"And isn't that good?"

"It's good, but you should have written the article."

I became nervous, I couldn't understand what she had in mind.

"Why?"

"Because you're smart and you know the situation well. You remember when you wrote the article against Bruno Soccavo?"

That reference, instead of pleasing me, upset me. Bruno was dead and I didn't like to remember what I had written. He wasn't very bright, ending up in the clutches of the Solaras and who knows how many others, given that they had killed him. I wasn't happy that I had been angry with him.

"Lila," I said, "the article wasn't against Bruno, it was an article about factory work."

"I know, and with this? You made them pay, and now that you're an even more important person you can do better. The Solaras shouldn't hide behind Carmen. You have to drag the Solaras out into the open, and they should no longer command."

I understood why she had disparaged the editor's article. She didn't care in the least about freedom of expression and the battle between backwardness and modernization. She was interested only in the sad local disputes. She wanted me, here, now, to contribute to the clash with real people, people we had known since childhood, and what they were made of. I said:

"Lila, the *Corriere* doesn't give a damn about Carmen, who sold herself, and the Solaras, who bought her. To be in a big newspaper, an article has to have a broad meaning, otherwise they won't publish it."

Her face fell.

"Carmen didn't sell herself," she said. "She's still your friend and she has brought the suit against you for one reason alone: they forced her."

"I don't understand, explain it."

She smiled at me, sneering, she was really angry.

"I'm not explaining anything to you: you write the books, you're the one who has to explain. I know only that here we don't have any publisher in Milan to protect us, no one who puts big articles in the newspaper for us. *We* are only a local matter and we fix things however we can: if *you* want to help us, good, and if not we'll do it alone."

98.

I went back to Roberto and harassed him until he gave me the address of the relatives in Giugliano, then I got in the car with Imma and left to look for Carmen.

The heat was suffocating. I had trouble locating the place, the relatives lived on the outskirts. At the door, a large woman answered who told me brusquely that Carmen had returned to Naples. Hardly persuaded, I went off with Imma, who, even though we had walked only a hundred meters, protested that she was tired. But as soon as I turned the corner to go back to the car I ran into Carmen, loaded with shopping bags. It was an instant, she saw me and burst into tears. I hugged her, Imma wanted to hug her, too. Then we found a café with a table in the shade and after ordering the child to play silently with her dolls I got Carmen to explain the situation. She confirmed what Lila had told me: she had been forced to bring a suit against me. And she also told me the reason: Marcello had made her believe that he knew where Pasquale was hiding.

"Is it possible?"

"It's possible."

"And do you know where he's hiding?"

She hesitated, she nodded.

"They said that they'll kill him whenever they want to."

I tried to soothe her. I told her that if the Solaras really knew where the person they believed had killed their mother was they would have seized him long ago.

"So you think they don't know?"

"Not that they don't know. But at this point for the good of your brother there's only one thing you can do."

"What?"

I told her that if she wanted to save Pasquale she should turn him in to the carabinieri.

The effect this produced on Carmen was not good. She

stiffened, I struggled to explain that it was the only way to protect him from the Solaras. But it was useless, I realized that my solution sounded to her like the worst of betrayals, something much more serious than her betrayal of me.

"This way you remain in their hands," I said. "They asked you to bring a suit against me, they can ask you any other thing."

"I'm his sister," she exclaimed.

"It's not a question of a sister's love," I said. "A sister's love in this case has harmed me, certainly won't save him, and risks ruining you, too."

But there was no way to convince her, in fact the more we talked, the more confused I got. Soon she began crying again: one moment she felt sorry for what she had done to me and asked my pardon, the next she felt sorry for what they could do to her brother and she despaired. I remembered how she had been as a girl, at the time I would never have imagined that she was capable of such stubborn loyalty. I left her because I wasn't able to console her, because Imma was all sweaty and I was afraid that she would get sick again, because it became increasingly less clear what I expected from Carmen. Did I want her to break off her long complicity with Pasquale? Why did I believe it was the right thing? Did I want her to choose the state over her brother? Why? To take her away from the Solaras and make her withdraw the suit? Did that count more than her anguish? I said to her:

"Do what you think is best, and remember that anyway I'm not mad at you."

But Carmen at that point had an unpredictable flash of anger in her eyes:

"And why should you be mad at me? What do you have to lose? You're in the newspapers, you're getting publicity, you'll sell more books. No, Lenù, you shouldn't say that, you advised me to give Pasquale up to the carabinieri, you were wrong."

I went away feeling bitter and already on the drive home I doubted that it had been a good idea to want to see her. I imagined that she would now go to the Solaras and that they would force her, after the editor's article in the *Corriere*, to take other actions against me.

99.

For days I expected new disasters, but nothing happened. The article created a certain sensation, the Neapolitan papers took it up and amplified it, I got phone calls and letters of support. The weeks passed, and I became used to the idea of being sued; I discovered that it had happened to many who did the same work I did and had been much more at risk than I was. Daily life asserted itself. For a while I avoided Lila, and I was especially careful not to let myself be drawn into making wrong moves.

The book never stopped selling. In August I went on vacation to Santa Maria di Castellabate; Lila and Enzo were also supposed to take a house at the sea, but work prevailed and it seemed natural for them to give Tina to me. The only pleasure, among the endless difficulties and tasks of that time (call this one, shout at that one, settle a quarrel, do the shopping, the cooking), was seeing a couple of readers sitting under their umbrella each with my book in their hands.

In the fall things started off better. I won a fairly important prize that came with a substantial sum, and I felt smart, skilled in public relations, with increasingly satisfying financial prospects. But the joy, the astonishment of the first weeks of success never returned. I felt the days as if the light had become opaque, and I perceived around me a widespread malaise. For a while there hadn't been a night when Enzo didn't raise his voice with Gennaro, something that had been very rare before.

When I stopped in at Basic Sight I found Lila plotting with Alfonso, and if I tried to approach she signaled me to wait a moment with a distracted gesture. She behaved the same way if she was talking to Carmen, who had returned to the neighborhood, or to Antonio, who for obscure reasons had put off his departure to some indeterminate time.

It was clear that things around Lila were getting worse, but she kept me out of it and I preferred to stay out of it. Then there were two terrible moments, one after the other. Lila happened to discover that Gennaro's arms were covered in needle marks. I heard her screaming as I had never heard her scream before. She incited Enzo, she drove him to give her son a beating: they were two strong men and they thrashed each other. The next day she threw her brother Rino out of Basic Sight, even though Gennaro begged her not to fire his uncle, he swore it wasn't Rino who had started him on heroin. That tragedy struck the girls deeply, especially Dede.

"Why does Aunt Lina treat her son like that?"

"Because he did something that he shouldn't do."

"He's grown-up, he can do what he wants."

"Not what can kill him."

"Why? It's his life, he has the right to do what he wants with it. You don't know what freedom is, and neither does Aunt Lina."

She, Elsa, and even Imma were as if stunned by that outburst of cries and curses that came from their beloved Aunt Lina. Gennaro was a prisoner in the house and he shouted all day. His Uncle Rino disappeared from Basic Sight after breaking a very expensive machine, and his curses could be heard throughout the neighborhood. Pinuccia came one evening with her children to beg Lila to rehire her husband and brought her mother-in-law, too. Lila treated both her mother and her sister-in-law rudely; the shouts and insults reached my house clearly. You are delivering us hand and foot to the

Solaras, Pinuccia cried desperately. And Lila replied: you deserve it, I'm fucking sick and tired of slaving for you without a drop of gratitude.

But that was petty compared to what happened a few weeks later. Things had scarcely calmed down when Lila began to quarrel with Alfonso, who was now indispensable to the operations of Basic Sight and yet had become increasingly unreliable. He missed important appointments, when he did make them his attitude was an embarrassment, he was heavily made up, he spoke of himself using the feminine. By now Lila had disappeared completely from his face and, in spite of his efforts, he was regaining his masculinity. In his nose, in his forehead, in his eyes something of his father, Don Achille, was appearing, and he himself was disgusted by it. As a result he seemed continuously in flight from his own body, which was putting on weight, and sometimes nothing was heard of him for days. When he reappeared he almost always showed signs of beatings. He went back to work but listlessly.

Then one day he disappeared for good. Lila and Enzo looked for him everywhere, without success. His body was found days later on the beach at Coroglio. He had been beaten to death somewhere else and then thrown into the sea. At the time I couldn't believe it. When I realized that it was all brutally true I was seized by a grief that wouldn't go away. I saw him again as he had been in our school days, gentle, attentive to others, beloved by Marisa, tormented by Gino, the pharmacist's son. Sometimes I even recalled him behind the counter at the grocery during his summer vacations, when he was obliged to do a job he detested. But I cut away the rest of his life, I knew little about it, I felt it as confused. I couldn't think of him as what he had become, every recent encounter faded, I even forgot the period when he worked in the shoe store in Piazza dei Martiri. Lila's fault, I thought in the heat of the moment: with her mania for forcing others by mixing everything up, she overwhelmed him. She had obscurely used him and then let him go.

But I changed my mind almost right away. Lila had learned the news several hours earlier. She knew that Alfonso was dead, but she couldn't get rid of the rage she had felt for days and kept insisting, rudely, on his unreliability. Then, right in the middle of a tirade like this, she collapsed on the floor of my house, evidently because her grief was unbearable. From that moment it seemed to me that she had loved him more than I did, even more than Marisa, and—as, besides, Alfonso had often told me—had helped him as no one else had. In the following hours she became listless, she stopped working, she lost interest in Gennaro, she left Tina with me. Between her and Alfonso there must have been a more complex relationship than I had imagined. She must have looked at him as at a mirror and seen herself in him and had wanted to draw out of his body a part of herself. The complete opposite, I thought uneasily, of what I had narrated in my second book. That work of Lila's must have pleased Alfonso very much, he had offered himself to her like a living material and she had molded him. Or at least so it seemed to me in the brief time in which I tried to put what had happened in order and calm myself. But, in the end, it was nothing but a vague impression of mine. In reality she never told me anything about their bond, not then or later. She was numbed by her suffering, harboring who knows what feelings, until the day of the funeral.

100.

There were very few of us at the funeral. None of Alfonso's friends from Piazza dei Martiri came, and his relatives didn't come, either. I was struck above all by the absence of Maria, his mother, even though none of his siblings came, neither Pinuccia nor Stefano, nor was Marisa there with the children, maybe his children, maybe not. Instead, surprisingly, the Solaras appeared. Michele was grim, very thin, he was constantly looking around with the eyes of a madman. Marcello, on the other hand, seemed contrite, an attitude that contrasted with the luxuriousness of every item of his clothing. They didn't limit themselves to the funeral service; they drove to the cemetery, and were present at the burial. The whole time I wondered why they had showed up at the service and I tried to catch Lila's eye. She never looked at me, she focused on them, she kept staring at them in a provocative manner. At the end, when she saw that they were leaving, she grabbed my arm, she was furious.

"Come with me."

"Where?"

"To talk to the two of them."

"I have the children."

"Enzo will take care of them."

I hesitated, I tried to resist, I said:

"Forget it."

"Then I'll go by myself."

I grumbled, it had always been like that: if I didn't agree to go with her she abandoned me. I nodded to Enzo to watch the girls—he seemed not to have noticed the Solaras—and in the same spirit with which I had followed her up the stairs to Don Achille's house or in the stone-throwing battles with the boys, I followed her through the geometry of whitish buildings, packed with burial niches.

Lila ignored Marcello, she stood in front of Michele:

"Why did you come? Do you feel some remorse?"

"Don't bother me, Lina."

"You two are finished, you'll have to leave the neighborhood."

"It's better if you go, while you still have time."

"Are you threatening me?"

"Yes."

"Don't you dare touch Gennaro, and don't touch Enzo.
Michè, do you understand me? Remember that I know enough
to ruin you, you and that other beast."

"You don't know anything, you have nothing in hand, and
above all you've understood nothing. Is it possible that you can
be so intelligent and you still don't know that by now I don't
give a fuck about you?"

Marcello pulled him by the arm, he said in dialect:

"Let's go, Michè, we're wasting time here."

Michele freed his arm forcefully, he turned to Lila:

"You think you scare me because Lenuccia is always in the
newspapers? Is that what you think? That I'm afraid of someone who writes novels? But this here is no one. You, however,
you are someone, even your shadow is better than any flesh-
and-blood person. But you would never understand, so much
the worse for you. I'll take away everything you have."

He said that last sentence as if he were suddenly sick to his
stomach, and then, as if reacting to the physical pain, before
his brother could stop him he punched Lila violently in the
face, knocking her to the ground.

101.

I was paralyzed by that utterly unpredictable gesture. Not
even Lila could have imagined it, we were now so used to the
idea that Michele not only would never touch her but would
kill anyone who did. I was unable to scream, not even a choked
sound came out of me.

Marcello dragged his brother away, but as he pulled and
pushed him, as Lila vomited in words dialect and blood (*I'll
kill you, by God, you are both dead already*), he said to me with
affectionate sarcasm: Put this in your next novel, Lenù, and tell

Lina, if she doesn't understand yet, that my brother and I have *truly* stopped loving her.

It was hard to convince Enzo that Lila's swollen face was due to the disastrous fall that, as we told him, had followed a sudden fainting fit. In fact I'm almost certain that he wasn't convinced at all, first because my version—agitated as I was—must have seemed anything but plausible, second because Lila didn't even make an effort to be persuasive. But when Enzo tried to object she said sharply that it was true, and he stopped discussing it. Their relationship was based on the idea that even an open lie from Lila was the only truth that could be uttered.

I went home with my daughters. Dede was frightened, Elsa incredulous, Imma asked questions like: Is there blood in a nose? I was disoriented, I was furious. Every so often I went down to see how Lila felt and to try and take Tina with me, but the child was alarmed by her mother's state and eager to help her. For both reasons she wouldn't leave her, even for a moment: she delicately spread an ointment, placed metal objects on her mother's forehead to cool it and make the headache go away. When I brought my daughters down as a lure to draw Tina up to my place, I merely made things more complicated. Imma tried every way she could to intervene in the treatment game, but Tina wouldn't yield at all and shrieked desperately even when Dede and Elsa attempted to take away her authority. The sick mamma was hers and she didn't want to give her up to anyone. Finally Lila sent everyone away, including me, and with such energy that it seemed to me she was already better.

She recovered quickly, in fact. Not me. My fury first became rage, then changed into contempt for myself. I couldn't forgive myself for remaining paralyzed in the face of violence. I said to myself: What have you become; why did you come back here to live, if you weren't capable of reacting against those two shits;

you're too well-meaning, you want to play the democratic lady who mixes with the working class, you like to say to the newspapers: I live where I was born, I don't want to lose touch with my reality; but you're ridiculous, you lost touch long ago, you faint at the stink of filth, of vomit, of blood. I had thoughts like that and meanwhile images came to my mind in which I let loose mercilessly against Michele. I hit him, scratched him, bit him, my heart pounding. Then the desire for violence died down and I said to myself: Lila is right, one writes not so much to write, one writes to inflict pain on those who wish to inflict pain. The pain of words against the pain of kicks and punches and the instruments of death. Not much, but enough. Of course, she still had in mind our dreams of childhood. She thought that if you gained fame, money, and power through writing, you became a person whose sentences were thunderbolts. Whereas I had long known that everything was more mediocre. A book, an article, could make noise, but ancient warriors before the battle also made noise, and if it wasn't accompanied by real force and immeasurable violence it was only theater. Yet I wished to redeem myself, the noise could do some damage. One morning I went downstairs, I asked her: What do you know that frightens the Solaras.

She looked at me with curiosity, she circled around reluctantly for a while, she answered: When I worked for Michele I saw a lot of documents, I studied them, some stuff he gave me himself. Her face was livid, she made a pained grimace, she added, in the crudest dialect: If a man wants pussy and he wants it so much that he can't even say I want it, even if you order him to stick his prick in boiling oil he does it. Then she held her head in her hands, she shook it hard as if it were a tin cup with dice in it, and I realized that she, too, at that moment despised herself. She didn't like the way she was forced to treat Gennaro, the way she had insulted Alfonso, the way she had thrown out her brother. She didn't like a single one of the very vulgar words that were coming out of her now. She couldn't bear herself, she couldn't bear anything. But at a certain point she must have felt that we were in the same mood and she asked me:

"If I give you things to write you'll write them?"

"Yes."

"And then what you write you'll get printed?"

"Maybe, I don't know."

"What does it depend on?"

"I have to be sure that it will do damage to the Solaras and not to me and my daughters."

She looked at me, unable to make up her mind. Then she said: Take Tina for ten minutes, and she left. She returned half an hour later with a floral-print bag full of documents.

We sat down at the kitchen table, while Tina and Imma chattered softly, moving dolls, horses, and carriages around the floor. Lila took out a lot of papers, her notes, also two notebooks with stained red covers. I immediately leafed through these with interest: graph-paper pages written in the calligraphy of the old elementary schools—account books, minutely annotated in a language full of grammatical mistakes and initialed on every page "M.S." I understood that they were part of what the neighborhood had always called Manuela Solara's red book. How the expression "red book" had echoed during our childhood and adolescence: evocative yet threatening—or perhaps evocative precisely because threatening. But whatever other word one might use in speaking of it—"register," for example—and no matter if the color was altered, Manuela Solara's book excited us like a secret document at the center of bloody adventures. Here it was, instead. It was a collection of school notebooks like the two I had before me: very ordinary dirty notebooks with the lower right edge raised like a wave. I realized in a flash that the memory was already literature and that perhaps Lila was right: my book—even though it was having

so much success—really was bad, and this was because it was
well organized, because it was written with obsessive care,
because I hadn't been able to imitate the disjointed, unaes-
thetic, illogical, shapeless banality of things.

While the children played—if they merely hinted at a quarrel we let out nervous cries to quiet them—Lila placed before
my eyes all the material in her possession, and explained the
meaning of it. We organized and summarized. It was a long
time since we had undertaken something together. She seemed
pleased, I understood that this was what she wanted and
expected from me. At the end of the day she disappeared again
with her bag and I returned to my apartment to study the
notes. Then, in the following days, she wanted us to meet at
Basic Sight. We locked ourselves in her office and sat at the
computer, a kind of television with a keyboard, very different
from what she had showed me and the children some time
before. She pressed the power button, she slid dark rectangles
into gray blocks. I waited, bewildered. On the screen luminous
tremors appeared. Lila began to type on the keyboard, I was
speechless. It was in no way comparable to a typewriter, even
an electric one. With her fingertips she caressed gray keys, and
the writing appeared silently on the screen, green like newly
sprouted grass. What was in her head, attached to who knows
what cortex of the brain, seemed to pour out miraculously and
fix itself on the void of the screen. It was power that, although
passing for act, remained power, an electrochemical stimulus
that was instantly transformed into light. It seemed to me like
the writing of God as it must have been on Sinai at the time of
the Commandments, impalpable and tremendous, but with a
concrete effect of purity. Magnificent, I said. I'll teach you, she
said. And she taught me, and dazzling, hypnotic segments
began to lengthen, sentences that I said, sentences that she
said, our volatile discussions were imprinted on the dark well
of the screen like wakes without foam. Lila wrote, I would

reconsider. Then with one key she erased, with others she made an entire block of light disappear, and made it reappear higher up or lower down in a second. But right afterward it was Lila who changed her mind, and everything was altered again, in a flash: ghostly moves, what's here now is no longer here or is there. And no need for pen, pencil, no need to change the paper, put another sheet in the roller. The page is the screen, unique, no trace of a second thought, it always seems the same. And the writing is incorruptible, the lines are all perfectly straight, they emit a sense of cleanliness even now that we are adding the filthy acts of the Solaras to the filthy acts of half of Campania.

We worked for days. The text descended from Heaven to earth through the noise of the printer, materialized in black dots laid on paper. Lila found it inadequate, we returned to pens, we labored to correct it. She was irritable: from me she expected more, she thought I could respond to all her questions, she got angry because she was convinced that I was a well of knowledge, while at every line she discovered that I didn't know the local geography, the tiny details of bureaucracies, how the communal councils functioned, the hierarchies of a bank, the crimes and the punishments. And yet, contradictorily, I hadn't felt her to be so proud of me and of our friendship in a long time. *We have to destroy them, Lenù, and if this isn't enough I'll murder them.* Our heads collided—for the last time, now that I think of it—one against the other, and merged until they were one. Finally we had to resign ourselves and admit that it was finished, and the dull period of what's done is done began. She printed it yet again, I put our pages in an envelope, and sent it to the publishing house and asked the editor to show it to the lawyers. I need to know—I explained on the telephone—if this stuff was sufficient to send the Solaras to jail.

102.

A week passed, two weeks. The editor telephoned one morning and was lavish in his praise.

"You're in a splendid period," he said.

"I worked with a friend of mine."

"It shows your hand at its best, it's an extraordinary text. Do me a favor: show these pages to Professor Sarratore, so he sees how anything can be transformed into passionate reading."

"I don't see Nino anymore."

"Maybe that's why you're in such good shape."

I didn't laugh, I needed to know urgently what the lawyers had said. The answer disappointed me. There's not enough material, the editor said, for even a day in jail. You can take some satisfaction, but these Solaras of yours aren't going to prison, especially if, as you recount, they're rooted in local politics and have money to buy whoever they want. I felt weak, my legs went limp, I lost conviction, I thought: Lila will be furious. I said, depressed: They're much worse than I've described. The editor perceived my disappointment, he tried to encourage me, he went back to praising the passion I had put into the pages. But the conclusion remained the same: with this you won't ruin them. Then, to my surprise, he insisted that I not put aside the text but publish it. I'll call *L'Espresso*, he suggested, if you come out with a piece like this right now, it'll be an important move for yourself, for your audience, for everyone, you'll show that the Italy we live in is much worse than the one we talk about. And he asked permission to submit the pages to the lawyers again to find out what legal risks I would run, what I would have to take out and what I could keep. I thought of how easy everything had been when it was a matter of scaring Bruno Soccavo, and I refused firmly. I said, I'll end up being sued again, I'd find myself in trouble for no reason, and I would be forced—

something I don't want to do, for the sake of my children—to think that the laws work for those who fear them, not for those who violate them.

I waited a while, then I gathered my strength and told Lila everything, word for word. She stayed calm, she turned on the computer, she scanned the text, but I don't think she reread it, she stared at the screen and meanwhile reflected. Then she asked me in a hostile tone:

"Do you trust this editor?"

"Yes, he's a smart person."

"Then why don't you want to publish the article?"

"What would be the point?"

"To clarify."

"It's already clear."

"To whom? To you, to me, to the editor?"

She shook her head, displeased, and said coldly that she had to work.

I said: "Wait."

"I'm in a hurry. Without Alfonso work's gotten complicated. Go on, please, go."

"Why are you angry at me?"

"Go."

We didn't see each other for a while. In the morning she sent Tina up to me, in the evening either Enzo came to get her or she shouted from the landing: Tina, come to Mamma. A couple of weeks passed, I think, then the editor telephoned me in a very cheerful mood.

"Good for you, I'm glad you made up your mind."

I didn't understand and he explained to me that his friend at *L'Espresso* had called, he urgently needed my address. From him he had learned that the text on the Solaras would come out in that week's issue, with some cuts. You could have told me, he said, that you changed your mind.

I was in a cold sweat, I didn't know what to say, I pretended nothing was wrong. But it took me a moment to realize that Lila had sent our pages to the weekly. I hurried to her to protest, I was indignant, but I found her especially affectionate and above all happy.

"Since you couldn't make up your mind, I did."

"I had decided not to publish it."

"Not me."

"You sign it alone, then."

"What do you mean? You're the writer."

It was impossible to communicate to her my disapproval and my anguish, every critical sentence of mine was blunted against her good humor. The article, six dense pages, was given great prominence, and naturally it had a single byline, mine.

When I saw that, we quarreled. I said to her angrily:

"I don't understand why you behave like that."

"I understand," she said.

Her face still bore the marks of Michele's fist, but certainly it hadn't been fear that kept her from putting her name to it. She was terrified by something else and I knew it, she didn't give a damn about the Solaras. But I felt so resentful that I threw it in her face just the same—*You removed your name because you like to stay hidden, because it's convenient to throw stones and hide your hand, I'm tired of your plots*—and she began to laugh, it seemed to her a senseless accusation. I don't like that you think that, she said. She became sullen, she muttered that she had sent the article to *L'Espresso* with only my name on it because hers didn't count, because I was the one who had studied, because I was famous, because now I could give anyone a beating without fear. In those words I found the confirmation that she ingenuously overestimated my role, and I told her so. But she was annoyed, she answered that it was I who underrated myself, so she wanted me to take on more and better, to have even greater success, all she wanted was for my merits to be recognized. You'll see, she exclaimed, what will happen to the Solaras.

I went home depressed. I couldn't drive out the suspicion that she was using me, just as Marcello had said. She had sent me out to risk everything and counted on that bit of fame I had to win her war, to complete her revenge, to silence all her feelings of guilt.

103.

In reality, having my name on that article was a further step up for me. As a result of its wide circulation, many of my fragments were connected. I proved that not only did I have a vocation as a fiction writer but, as in the past I had been involved in the union struggles, as I had engaged in criticizing the condition of women, so I fought against the degradation of my city. The small audience I had won in the late sixties merged with the one that, amid ups and downs, I had cultivated in the seventies and the new, larger one of now. That helped the first two books, which were reprinted, and the third, which continued to sell well, while the idea of making a film from it became more concrete.

Naturally the article caused a lot of bother. I was summoned by the carabinieri. I was bugged by the financial police. I was vilified by local papers on the right with labels like *divorcée, feminist, Communist, supporter of terrorists*. I received anonymous phone calls that threatened me and my daughters in a dialect full of obscenities. But, although I lived in anxiety—a state of anxiety now seemed to me inherent to writing—I was in the end not as agitated as at the time of the article in *Panorama* and Carmen's lawsuit. It was my job, I was learning to do it better and better. And then I felt protected by the legal support of the publisher, by the success I had in newspapers on the left, by the increasingly well attended public appearances, and by the idea that I was right.

But, if I have to be honest, it wasn't only that. I calmed down mainly when it became evident that the Solaras would do absolutely nothing to me. My visibility drove them to be as invisible as possible. Marcello and Michele not only didn't bring a second lawsuit but were completely silent, the whole time, and even when I encountered them before law-enforcement officers, both confined themselves to cold but respectful greetings. Thus the waters subsided. The only concrete thing that happened was that various investigations were opened, along with an equal number of files. But, as the lawyers of the publishing house had predicted, the first soon came to a halt, the second ended—I imagine—under thousands of other files, and the Solaras remained free. The only harm the article caused was of an emotional nature: my sister, my nephew Silvio, even my father—not in words but in deeds—cut me out of their lives. Only Marcello continued to be polite. One afternoon I met him along the *stradone*, and I looked away. But he stopped in front of me, he said: Lenù, I know that if you could you wouldn't have done it, I'm not angry with you, it's not your fault. So remember that my house is always open. I replied: Elisa hung up on me just yesterday. He smiled: Your sister is the boss, what can I do?

104.

But the outcome, which was in essence conciliatory, depressed Lila. She didn't hide her disappointment and yet she didn't put it into words. She carried on, pretending that nothing was wrong: she dropped off Tina at my house and shut herself in the office. But sometimes she stayed in bed all day; she said her head was bursting, and she dozed.

I was careful not to remind her that the decision to publish our pages had been hers. I didn't say: I warned you that the

Solaras would come out of it unharmed, the publisher told me, now it's pointless for you to suffer over it. But stamped on her face was also regret that she had been wrong in her assessment. In those weeks she felt humiliated at having always ascribed a power to things that in the current hierarchies were insignificant: the alphabet, writing, books. Only then—I think today—did she, who seemed so disillusioned, so adult, come to the end of her childhood.

She stopped helping me. More and more often she gave me charge of her daughter and sometimes, though rarely, even of Gennaro, who was forced to hang around my house. Yet my life had become increasingly busy and I didn't know how to manage. One morning when I asked her about the children she answered in annoyance: Call my mother, get her to help you. It was a novelty, I withdrew in embarrassment, I obeyed. So it was that Nunzia arrived at my house, much aged, submissive, uneasy, but efficient as in the days when she took care of the house in Ischia.

My older daughters immediately treated her with disdain, especially Dede, who was going through puberty and had lost any sense of tact. Her face was inflamed, her body was swelling, becoming shapeless, driving out, day by day, the image she was used to, and she felt ugly, she became mean. We began to bicker:

"Why do we have to stay with that old lady? It's disgusting what she cooks, you should cook."

"Stop it."

"She spits when she talks, did you see she doesn't have any teeth?"

"I don't want to hear another word, that's enough."

"We already have to live in this toilet, now we have to have that person in the house? I don't want her to sleep here when you're not here."

"Dede, I said that's enough."

Elsa was no better, but in her own way: she remained serious, assuming a tone that seemed to support me and yet was duplicitous.

"I like her, Mamma, you were right to have her come. She smells nice, just like a corpse."

"Now I'll slap you. You know she can hear you?"

The only one who was immediately fond of Lila's mother was Imma: she was Tina's slave and so she imitated her in everything, even in her attachments. The two of them followed Nunzia around as she worked in the apartment; they called her grandma. But Grandma was brusque, especially with Imma. She caressed her real grandchild, occasionally softening at her chatter and her affection, while she worked in silence when her pretend grandchild looked for attention. Meanwhile—I discovered—something was bothering her. At the end of the first week she said, looking down: Lenù, we haven't talked about how much you'll give me. I felt hurt: I had stupidly thought that she came because her daughter had asked her to; if I had known I had to pay I would have chosen a young person, whom my daughters would like and from whom I could have demanded what I needed. But I contained myself, we talked about money and fixed on an amount. Only then Nunzia cheered up a little. At the end of the negotiation she felt the need to justify herself: My husband is sick, she said, he no longer works, and Lina is crazy, she fired Rino, we don't have a cent. I muttered that I understood, I told her to be nicer to Imma. She obeyed. From then on, although she always favored Tina, she made an effort to be kind to my daughter.

Toward Lila, however, her attitude didn't change. Neither when she arrived nor when she left did Nunzia ever feel the need to stop by at her daughter's, although Lila had gotten the job for her. If they met on the stairs they didn't even greet each other. She was an old woman who had lost her former wary friendliness. But Lila, too, it must be said, was intractable, and visibly worsening.

105.

With me she was always spiteful, for no reason. It especially irritated me that she acted as if everything that happened to my daughters escaped me.

"Dede got the curse."

"Did she tell you?"

"Yes, you weren't here."

"Did you use that expression with her?"

"What word should I have used?"

"Something less vulgar."

"You know how your daughters speak to each other? And have you ever heard the things they say about my mother?"

I didn't like that tone. She, who in the past had appeared so fond of Dede, Elsa, and Imma, seemed determined to disparage them to me, and she took every opportunity to show me that, because I was always traveling around Italy, I neglected them, with serious consequences for their upbringing. I was especially upset when she began accusing me of not seeing Imma's problems.

"What's wrong," I asked her.

"She has a tic in her eye."

"Not very often."

"I've seen it a lot."

"What do you think it means?"

"I don't know. I only know that she feels fatherless and isn't even sure she has a mother."

I tried to ignore her but it was difficult. Imma, as I've said, had always worried me a little, and even when she stood up well to Tina's vivacity she still seemed to lack something. Also, some time earlier I had recognized in her features of mine that I didn't like. She was submissive, she gave in immediately out of fear of not being liked, it depressed her that she had given in. I would have preferred her to inherit Nino's bold capacity for seduction, his thoughtless vitality, but she wasn't like that. Imma was unhappily compliant, she wanted everything and pretended to want nothing. Children, I said, are the product of chance, she's got nothing of her father. Lila didn't agree; she was always finding ways of alluding to the child's resemblance to Nino, but she didn't see it as positive, she spoke as if it were a congenital defect. And then she kept repeating: I'm telling you these things because I love them and I'm worried.

I tried to explain to myself her sudden persecution of my daughters. I thought that, since I had disappointed her, she was withdrawing from me by separating first of all from them. I thought that since my book was increasingly successful, which sanctioned my autonomy from her and from her judgment, she was trying to belittle me by belittling my children and my capacity to be a good mother. But neither of those hypotheses soothed me and a third advanced: Lila saw what I, as a mother, didn't know how or didn't want to see, and since she appeared critical of Imma in particular, I had better find out if her comments had any foundation.

So I began to observe the child and was soon convinced that she really suffered. She was the slave of Tina's joyful expansiveness, of her elevated capacity for verbalization, of the way she aroused tenderness, admiration, affection in everyone, especially me. Although my daughter was pretty, and intelligent, beside Tina she turned dull, her virtues vanished, and she felt this deeply. One day I witnessed an exchange between them, in a good Italian, Tina's pronunciation very precise, Imma's still missing some syllables. They were coloring in the outlines of animals and Tina had decided to use green for a rhinoceros, while Imma added colors randomly for a cat. Tina said:

"Make it gray or black."

"You mustn't give me orders about the color."

"It's not an order, it's a suggestion."

Imma looked at her in alarm. She didn't know the difference between an order and a suggestion. She said:

"I don't want to follow the suggestion, either."

"Then don't."

Imma's lower lip trembled.

"All right," she said, "I'll do it but I don't like it."

I tried to be more attentive to her. To begin with, I stopped getting excited about everything Tina did, I reinforced Imma's skills, I praised her for every little thing. But I soon realized it wasn't enough. The two little girls loved each other. Dealing with each other helped them grow, some extra artificial praise was of no help in keeping Imma, looking at her reflection in Tina, from seeing something that wounded her and that her friend was certainly not the cause of.

At that point I began to turn over Lila's words: *she's fatherless and isn't even sure she has a mother.* I remembered the mistake in the *Panorama* caption. That caption, buttressed by Dede and Elsa's mean jokes (*You don't belong to this family: your name is Sarratore, not Airota*), must have done its damage. But was that really the core of the problem? I ruled it out. Her father's absence seemed to me something more serious and I was sure that her suffering came from that.

Once I had started down this road I began to notice how Imma sought Pietro's attention. When he called his daughters, she sat in a corner and listened to the conversation. If the sisters had a good time she pretended to be having fun, too, and when the conversation ended and they said goodbye to their father in turn, Imma shouted: Bye. Often Pietro heard her and said to Dede: Give me Imma so I can say hello. But in those cases either she became shy and ran away or took the receiver and remained mute. She behaved the same way when he came to Naples. Pietro never forgot to bring her a little present, and Imma hovered near him, played at being his daughter, was happy if he said something nice or picked her up. Once when my ex-husband came to get Dede and Elsa, the child's sadness must have seemed especially obvious, and as he left he said: Cuddle her, she's sorry that her sisters are leaving and she has to stay behind.

That observation increased my anxieties, I said to myself that I had to do something, I thought of talking to Enzo and asking him to be more present in Imma's life. But he was already very attentive. If he carried his daughter on his shoulders, after a while he put her down, picked up my daughter, and put her up there; if he got Tina a toy, he got an identical one for her; if he was pleased almost to the point of being moved at the intelligent questions his child asked, he managed to remember to show enthusiasm for the somewhat more prosaic questions of my child. But I spoke to him anyway, and sometimes Enzo admonished Tina, if she occupied the stage and didn't leave room for Imma. I didn't like that, it wasn't the child's fault. In those cases Tina was as if stunned, the lid that was suddenly lowered on her vivacity seemed an undeserved punishment. She didn't understand why the spell was broken, she struggled to regain her father's favor. At that point I would pull her to me, play with her.

In other words things were not going well. One morning I was in the office with Lila, I wanted her to teach me to write on the computer. Imma was playing with Tina under the desk and Tina was sketching in words imaginary places and characters with her usual brilliance. Monstrous creatures were pursuing their dolls, courageous princes were about to rescue them. But I heard my daughter exclaim with sudden rage:

"Not me."

"Not you?"

"I won't rescue myself."

"You don't have to rescue yourself, the prince rescues you."

"I don't have one."

"Then mine will rescue you."

"I said no."

The sudden leap with which Imma had gone from her doll to herself wounded me, even though Tina tried to keep her in the game. Because I was distracted, Lila became irritated, she said:

"Girls, either talk quietly or go outside and play."

106.

That day I wrote a long letter to Nino. I enumerated the problems that I thought were complicating our daughter's life: her sisters had a father who was attentive to them, she didn't; her playmate, Lila's daughter, had a very devoted father and she didn't; because of my work I was always traveling and often had to leave her. In other words, Imma was in danger of growing up feeling that she was continually at a disadvantage. I sent the letter and waited for him to respond. He didn't and so I decided to call his house. Eleonora answered.

"He's not here," she said listlessly. "He's in Rome."

"Would you please tell him that my daughter needs him?"

Her voice caught in her throat. Then she composed herself:

"Mine haven't seen their father, either, for at least six months."

"Has he left you?"

"No, he never leaves anyone. Either you have the strength to leave him yourself—and in this you were smart, I admire you—or he goes, comes, disappears, reappears, as it suits him."

"Will you tell him I called, and if he won't see the child I'll track him down, and take her to him wherever he is?"

I hung up.

It was a while before Nino made up his mind to call, but in the end he did. As usual he acted as if we had seen each other

a few hours earlier. He was energetic, cheerful, full of compliments. I cut him off, I asked:

"Did you get my letter?"

"Yes."

"Then why didn't you answer?"

"I've got no time."

"Find the time, as soon as possible, Imma's not well."

He said reluctantly that he would return to Naples for the
weekend, I insisted that he come to lunch on Sunday. I insisted
that he was not to talk to me, not joke with Dede or Elsa, but
focus the whole day on Imma. That visit, I said, has to become
a habit: it would be wonderful if you would come once a week,
but I won't ask that, I don't expect that from you; once a
month, however, is essential. He said in a serious tone that he
would come every week, he promised, and at that moment he
was surely sincere.

I don't remember the day of the phone call, but the day
when, at ten in the morning, Nino appeared in the neighborhood, elegantly dressed and driving a brand-new luxury car, I
will never forget. It was September 16, 1984. Lila and I had
just turned forty, Tina and Imma were almost four.

107.

I told Lila that Nino was coming to lunch at my house. I
said to her: I forced him, I want him to spend the whole day
with Imma. I hoped she would understand that for at least
that one day she shouldn't send Tina to my house, but she
didn't understand or didn't want to. Instead she acted helpful, she said: I'll tell my mother to cook for everyone and
maybe we'll eat here at my house where there's more room. I
was surprised, and annoyed. She hated Nino; what was that
intrusion all about? I refused, I said: I'll cook, and I repeated

that the day was dedicated to Imma, there would be no way and no time for anything else. But exactly at nine the next day Tina climbed the stairs with her toys and knocked at my door. She was tidy and neat, her black braids shiny, her eyes sparkling with affection.

I told her to come in, but I immediately had to fight with Imma, who was still in her pajamas, sleepy, she hadn't had breakfast, and yet she wanted to start playing immediately. Since she refused to obey me and kept making faces and laughing with her friend, I got mad and closed Tina—frightened by my tone—in a room to play by herself, then I made Imma wash. I don't want to, she screamed. I told her: You have to get dressed, Papa is coming. I had been announcing it for days, but she, hearing that word, became even more rebellious. I myself, in using it to signal to her the imminence of his arrival, became more anxious. The child writhed, screamed: I don't want Papa, as if Papa were a repellent medicine. I ruled out that she remembered Nino, she wasn't expressing a rejection of a definite person. I thought: Maybe I was wrong to make him come; when Imma says she doesn't want Papa, she means that she doesn't want just anyone, she wants Enzo, she wants Pietro, she wants what Tina and her sisters have.

At that point I remembered the other child. She hadn't protested, she hadn't poked her head out. I was ashamed of my behavior. Tina was not responsible for the day's tensions. I called her affectionately, she reappeared and sat happily on a stool in a corner of the bathroom giving me advice on how to braid Imma's hair. My daughter brightened, she let me dress her up without protesting. Finally they ran away to play and I went to get Dede and Elsa out of bed. Elsa jumped up very happily, she was glad to see Nino again and was ready in a short time. But Dede spent an infinite amount of time washing and came out of the bathroom only because I started yelling. She couldn't accept her transformation. I'm disgusting, she said, with tears in her eyes. She shut herself in the bedroom crying that she didn't want to see anyone.

I got myself ready in a hurry. I didn't care about Nino, but I didn't want him to find me neglected and aged. And I was afraid that Lila would show up and I was well aware that, if she wanted, she could focus a man's gaze totally on her. I was agitated and at the same time lethargic.

108.

Nino was exceedingly punctual, and he came up the stairs loaded with presents. Elsa ran to wait for him on the landing, immediately followed by Tina and then, cautiously, Imma. I saw the tic appear in her right eye. Here's Papa, I told her, and she feebly shook her head no.

But Nino behaved well. Already on the stairs he began to sing: Where's my little Imma, I have to give her three kisses and a little bite. When he reached the landing he said hi to Elsa, pulled one of Tina's braids absentmindedly, and grabbed his daughter, covered her with kisses, told her he had never seen such pretty hair, complimented her dress, her shoes, everything. He came in without even a greeting for me. Instead he sat down on the floor, lifted Imma onto his crossed legs, and only then gave some encouragement to Elsa, and warmly greeted Dede (*Good Lord, how you've grown, you're magnificent*), who had approached with a timid smile.

I saw that Tina was puzzled. Strangers, without exception, were dazzled by her and cuddled her as soon as they saw her, whereas Nino had begun to distribute the gifts and was ignoring her. She turned to him with her caressing little voice and tried to take a place on his knees next to Imma, but she couldn't and leaned against his arm, put her head with a languid expression on one shoulder. No, Nino gave Dede and Elsa each a book, then he focused on his daughter. He had bought her all kinds of things. He waited for her to unwrap one gift and immediately gave her another. Imma seemed charmed, moved. She looked at that man as if he were a wizard who had come to cast spells for her alone and when Tina tried to take a gift she cried: It's mine. Tina quickly drew back with her lower lip trembling, I picked her up, I said: Come with aunt. Only then did Nino seem to realize that he was overdoing it and he dug in his pocket, took out an expensive-looking pen, said: This is for you. I put the child down on the floor, she took the pen whispering thank you and he seemed to really see her for the first time. I heard him mutter in amazement:

"You look exactly like your mother."

"Shall I write my name for you?" Tina asked, serious.

"You already know how to write?"

"Yes."

Nino pulled a folded piece of paper out of his pocket, she put it on the floor and wrote: "Tina." Very good! he praised her. But a moment afterward he sought my gaze, afraid of being reprimanded, and to remedy the situation he turned to his daughter: I bet you're very good, too. Imma wanted to show him, and, snatching the pen away from her friend, scribbled on the page with intense concentration. He complimented her profusely, even as Elsa tormented her little sister (*No one can understand that, you don't know how to write*) and Tina tried in vain to get her pen back, saying: I know how to write other words, too. Finally, Nino, to cut it off, stood up with his daughter and said: Now let's go see the most beautiful car in the world, and he carried them all off, Imma in his arms, Tina trying to get him to take her hand, Dede pulling her away and keeping her close, Elsa taking possession of the expensive pen with a greedy gesture.

109.

The door closed behind them. I heard Nino's thick voice on the stairs—he was promising to buy sweets, to take them for a ride in the car—and Dede, Elsa, and the two little girls shouting their excitement. I imagined Lila on the floor below, shut in her apartment, in silence, while the same voices that reached me reached her, too. Separating us was only a layer of floor, and yet she could shorten the distance further or expand it according to her mood and convenience and the movements of her mind, which shifted like the sea when the moon seizes it whole and pulls it upward. I tidied, cooked, I thought Lila—below—was doing the same. We were both waiting to hear again the voices of our daughters, the steps of the man we had loved. It occurred to me that she must have recognized Nino's features in Imma countless times, as he had just now recognized hers in Tina. Had she always felt an aversion, all these years, or was her loving concern for the child a result of that resemblance? Did she still, in secret, like Nino? Was she observing him from the window? Had Tina managed to get him to take her hand and was she looking at her daughter beside that tall thin man, thinking: If things had gone differently she could be his. What was she planning? Would she come up to my house, in a moment, to wound me with a malicious comment? Or would she open the door of her house just as he was passing by, returning with the four girls, and would she invite him to come in and then call up from below, so that I would be compelled to invite her and Enzo to lunch, too?

The apartment was very silent, but outside there was a mixture of Sunday sounds: the pealing bells of midday, the cries of vendors in the stalls, the trains passing on the siding, the traffic of the trucks heading to work sites busy every day of the week. Nino would no doubt let the girls fill up on sweets, without thinking that they would not eat their lunch later. I knew him well: he granted every request, he bought everything without batting an eye, he overdid it. As soon as lunch was ready and the table set, I looked out the window onto the *stradone*. I wanted to call them to say it was time to come home. But the stalls impeded my view, all I could see was Marcello walking with my sister on one side and Silvio on the other. The image of the *stradone* from above gave me a sense of anguish. Sundays had always seemed to me a paint concealing the decay, but that day the impression was stronger. What was I doing in that place, why did I continue to live there, when I had enough money and could go anywhere. I had given Lila too much rope, I had let her retie too many knots, I myself had believed that, reassigning myself publicly to my origins, I would be able to write better. Everything struck me as ugly, I felt a strong repulsion for the food I had prepared. Then I pulled myself together, brushed my hair, made sure that I looked all right, and went out. I passed Lila's door almost on tiptoe; I didn't want her to hear me and decide to come with me.

Outside there was a strong odor of toasted almonds, I looked around. First I saw Dede and Elsa, eating cotton candy and examining a stall selling junk: bracelets, earrings, necklaces, hairpins. Not far away I could make out Nino, standing at the corner. Only after a fraction of a second did I discover that he was talking to Lila, beautiful the way she was when she wanted to be, and Enzo, serious, frowning.

She was holding Imma, who was tormenting one of her ears, as she usually did with mine when she felt neglected. Lila let the child twist it roughly, without stopping her, she was apparently so absorbed by Nino, who was talking in his pleasing way, smiling, gesturing with his long arms, his long hands.

I was enraged. That's why Nino had gone out and hadn't been seen again. Here was how he cared for his daughter. I called him, he didn't hear me. Dede turned, she laughed with Elsa at my faint voice, they always did when I shouted. I called again. I wanted Nino to come back right away, return home, *alone*, alone with my daughters. But there was the deafening whistle of the peanut seller and the din of a truck passing, every one of its parts rattling, raising clouds of dust. I grumbled, I joined them. Why was Lila holding my daughter in her arms, what need was there? And why was Imma not playing with Tina? I didn't say hello, I said to Imma: What are you doing being held, you're a big girl, come down, and I pulled her away from Lila. Then I turned to Nino: The children have to eat, it's ready. Meanwhile I realized that my daughter was attached to my skirt, she hadn't left me to run to her friend. I looked around, I asked Lila: Where is Tina?

She still had on her face the expression of cordial assent with which until a minute earlier she had been listening to Nino's conversation. She must be with Dede and Elsa, she said. I answered: She's not. And I wanted her to see about her daughter, together with Enzo, instead of inserting herself between mine and her father on the only day he had made himself available. But while Enzo looked around for Tina, Lila continued talking to Nino. She told him about the times Gennaro had disappeared. She laughed, saying: One morning he couldn't be found, everyone had gone to school and he wasn't there. I was terrified, I imagined the worst things, and instead he was sitting quietly in the gardens. But it was precisely as she remembered that episode that she lost color. Her eyes emptied, in a changed voice she asked Enzo:

"Did you find her, where is she?"

110.

We looked for Tina along the *stradone*, then throughout the whole neighborhood, then again along the *stradone*. Many people joined us. Antonio came, Carmen came, Roberto, Carmen's

332 · ELENA FERRANTE

husband, came, and even Marcello Solara mobilized some of his people, walking the streets himself, until late into the night. Lila now seemed like Melina, she ran here and there with no reason. But Enzo seemed even crazier than she was. He screamed, he got angry at the peddlers, he threatened terrible things, he wanted to look in their cars and vans and carts. The carabinieri had to intervene to calm him.

At every moment it seemed that Tina had been found and there was a sigh of relief. Everyone knew the child, there was no one who wouldn't swear to have seen her a moment before standing at this stall or that corner or in the courtyard or in the gardens over by the tunnel with a tall man, a short one. But every sighting turned out to be illusory, people lost faith and goodwill.

In the evening a rumor took hold that later prevailed. The child had left the sidewalk to chase a blue ball. But just at that moment a truck was passing. The truck was a mud-colored hulk, traveling at high speed, clattering and bouncing because of the holes in the *stradone*. No one had seen anything else, but the collision was heard, the collision that passed directly from the story into the memory of whoever was listening. The truck hadn't braked, or even tried to, and had disappeared at the end of the *stradone* along with Tina's body, her braids. On the asphalt not a drop of blood remained, nothing, nothing at all. In that nothing the vehicle was lost, the child was lost forever.

OLD AGE
THE STORY OF BAD BLOOD

1.

I left Naples definitively in 1995, when everyone said that the city was reviving. But I no longer believed in its resurrections. Over the years I had seen the advent of the new railway station, the dull tower of the skyscraper on Via Novara, the soaring structures of Scampia, the proliferation of tall, shining buildings above the gray stone of Arenaccia, of Via Taddeo da Sessa, of Piazza Nazionale. Those buildings, conceived in France or Japan and rising between Ponticelli and Poggioreale with the usual breakdowns and delays, had immediately, at high speed, lost all their luster and become dens for the desperate. So what resurrection? It was only cosmetic, a powder of modernity applied randomly, and boastfully, to the corrupt face of the city.

It happened like that every time. The scam of rebirth raised hopes and then shattered them, became crust upon ancient crusts. Thus, just as the obligation arose to stay in the city and support the revival under the leadership of the former Communist party, I decided to leave for Turin, drawn by the possibility of running a publishing house that at the time was full of ambition. Once I turned forty, time had begun to race, I couldn't keep up. The real calendar had been replaced by one of contract deadlines, the years leaped from one publication to the next; giving dates to the events that concerned me, and my daughters, cost me a lot, and I forced them into the writing, which took me more and more time. When had this or that happened? In an almost heedless way I oriented myself by the publication dates of my books.

I now had quite a few books behind me, and they had won me some authority, a good reputation, a comfortable life. Over time the weight of my daughters had greatly diminished. Dede and Elsa—first one, then the other—had gone to study in Boston, encouraged by Pietro, who for seven or eight years had had a professorship at Harvard. They were at ease with their father. Apart from the letters in which they complained about the cruel climate and the pedantry of the Bostonians, they were satisfied, with themselves and with escaping the choices that, in the past, I had compelled them to confront. At that point, since Imma was desperate to do what her sisters had, what was I doing in the neighborhood? If at first the image of the writer who, although able to live elsewhere, had stayed in a dangerous outlying neighborhood to continue to nourish herself on reality, had been useful to me, now there were many intellectuals who prided themselves on the same cliché. And my books had taken other paths, the material of the neighborhood had been set aside. Wasn't it therefore hypocritical to have a certain fame, and many advantages, and yet to limit myself, to live in a place where I could only record uneasily the deterioration of the lives of my siblings, my friends, their children and grand-children, maybe even of my last daughter?

Imma was then fourteen; I didn't deprive her of anything, and she studied hard. But if necessary she spoke in a harsh dialect, she had schoolmates I didn't like, I was so worried if she went out after dinner that often she decided to stay home. I, too, when I was in the city, had a limited life. I saw my friends from cultured Naples, I let myself be courted and embarked on relationships, but they never lasted. Even the most brilliant men sooner or later turned out to be disillu-sioned, raging at a cruel fate, witty and yet subtly malicious. At times I had the impression that they wanted me mainly so that they could give me their manuscripts to read, ask me about television or the movies, in some cases borrow money that they never paid back. I made the best of it, exerting myself to have a social and emotional life. But going out at night, dressed up, wasn't a pleasure, it was a cause of anxiety. On one occasion I didn't have time to close the street door behind me before I was beaten and robbed by two kids who were no more than thirteen. The taxi driver, who was waiting right out front, didn't even look out the window. So in the summer of 1995 I left Naples with Imma.

I rented an apartment on the Po, near the Isabella Bridge, and my life and that of my third daughter immediately improved. From there it became simpler to reflect on Naples, to write about it and let myself write about it with lucidity. I loved my city, but I uprooted from myself any dutiful defense of it. I was convinced, rather, that the anguish in which that love sooner or later ended was a lens through which to look at the entire West. Naples was the great European metropolis where faith in technology, in science, in economic development, in the kindness of nature, in history that leads of necessity to improvement, in democracy, was revealed, most clearly and far in advance, to be completely without foundation. To be born in that city—I went so far as to write once, thinking not of myself but of Lila's pessimism—is useful for only one thing: to have always known, almost instinctively, what today, with endless fine distinctions, everyone is beginning to claim: that the dream of unlimited progress is in reality a nightmare of savagery and death.

In 2000 I was left alone; Imma went to study in Paris. I tried to convince her that there was no need, but since many of her friends had decided to go, she didn't want to be left out. At first it didn't bother me, I had a busy life. But within a few years I began to feel old age, it was as if I were fading along with the world in which I had established myself. Although I had won, at various times and with various works, some prestigious prizes, my books were now hardly selling at all: in 2003, for example, the thirteen novels and two volumes of essays I had published earned altogether twenty-three hundred and twenty-three euros before taxes. I had to acknowledge, at that point, that my audience expected nothing more from me and that younger readers—it would be more accurate to say younger women readers; from the start it was mainly women who read my books—had other tastes, other interests. The newspapers were no longer a source of income, either. They weren't interested in me; they rarely asked for articles, and paid nothing or next to nothing. As for television, after some successful experiences in the nineties, I had tried to do an afternoon show devoted to classics of Greek and Latin literature, an idea that was accepted only thanks to the regard of some friends, including Armando Galiani, who had a show on Channel 5 but good relations with public television. It was an unquestionable fiasco and I had not had other opportunities. Things also deteriorated at the publishing house I had run for many years. In the fall of 2004 I was pushed out by a clever young man, scarcely over thirty, and reduced to an external consultant. I was sixty, I felt my journey was ending. In Turin the winters were too cold, the summers too hot, the cultured classes unwelcoming. I was anxious, I didn't sleep much. Men no longer noticed me. I looked out at the Po from my balcony, at the rowers, the hill, and I was bored.

I began to go more frequently to Naples, but I had no wish to see friends and relatives, and friends and relatives had no wish to see me. I saw only Lila, but often, by my choice, not even her. She made me uneasy. In recent years she had become passionate about the city with a chauvinism that seemed crude, so I preferred to walk alone on Via Caracciolo, or go up to the Vomero, or walk through the Tribunali. So it happened that in the spring of 2006, shut up in an old hotel on Corso Vittorio Emanuele during an incessant rain, I wrote, in a few days, to pass the time, a narrative of scarcely eighty pages that was set in the neighborhood and told the story of Tina. I wrote it rapidly in order not to give myself time to invent. The pages were terse, direct. The story took off imaginatively only at the end.

I published the book in the fall of 2007 with the title *A Friendship*. It was very well received, and it still sells well today; teachers recommend it to students as summer reading.

But I hate it.

Just two years earlier, when Gigliola's body was found in the gardens—she had died of a heart attack, in solitude, a death terrible in its bleakness—Lila had made me promise that I would never write about her. Instead, here, I had done it, and I had done it in the most direct way. For a few months I believed that I had written my best book, and my fame as a writer took off again; it was a long time since I'd had such success. But already by the end of 2007—during the Christmas season—when I went to Feltrinelli in Piazza dei Martiri to present *A Friendship*, I suddenly felt ashamed and was afraid of seeing Lila in the audience, maybe the front row, ready to interrupt and make trouble for me. But the evening went very well, I was much celebrated. When I returned to the hotel, a bit more confident, I tried to telephone her, first on the regular phone, then on the cell, then again on the other. She didn't answer, she hasn't answered me since.

2.

I don't know how to recount Lila's grief. What befell her, what had perhaps been lying in wait in her life forever, was not the death of a daughter through illness, an accident, an act of violence, but her daughter's sudden disappearance. The grief couldn't coagulate around anything. She had no lifeless body to cling to in despair, there was no one for whom to hold a funeral, she couldn't linger before a corpse that had walked, run, talked, hugged her, and had ended up a broken thing. Lila felt, I think, as if a limb, which until a moment before had been part of her body, had lost form and substance without undergoing any trauma. But I don't know the suffering that derived from it well enough, nor can I imagine it.

In the ten years that followed the loss of Tina, although I continued to live in the same building, although I met Lila every day, I never saw her cry, I never witnessed a crisis of despair. After at first rushing through the neighborhood, day and night, in that vain search for her daughter, she gave in as if she were too weary. She sat beside the kitchen window and didn't move for a long period, even though from there you could see only a slice of the railroad and a little sky. Then she pulled herself together and began normal life again, but without resignation. The years washed over her, her nasty character got even worse, she sowed uneasiness and fear, she grew old screeching, quarreling. At first she talked about Tina on every occasion and with anyone, she clung to the name of the child as if uttering it would serve to bring her back. But later it was impossible even to mention that loss in her presence, and even if it was I who did so she got rid of me rudely after a few seconds. She seemed to appreciate only a letter from Pietro, mainly—I think—because he managed to write to her lovingly without ever mentioning Tina. Even in 1995, before I left, except on very rare occasions she acted as if nothing had happened. Once Pinuccia spoke of the child as a little angel watching over us all. Lila said: Get out.

3.

No one in the neighborhood put faith in the forces of order or in the journalists. Men, women, even gangs of kids spent days and weeks looking for Tina, ignoring the police and television. All the relatives, all the friends were mobilized. The only one who turned up just a couple of times—and by telephone, with generic phrases that existed only to be repeated: I have no responsibility, I had just handed the child over to Lina and Enzo—was Nino. But I wasn't surprised, he was one of those adults who when they play with a child and the child falls and skins his knee behave like children themselves, afraid that someone will say: It was you who let him fall. Besides, no one gave him any importance, we forgot about him in a few hours. Enzo and Lila trusted Antonio above all, and he put off his departure for Germany yet again, to track down Tina. He did it out of friendship but also, as he himself explained, surprising us, because Michele Solara had ordered him to.

The Solaras undertook more than anyone else in that business of the child's disappearance and—I have to say—they made their involvement highly visible. Although they knew they would be treated with hostility they appeared one evening at Lila's house with the attitude of those who are speaking for an entire community, and they vowed they would do everything possible to return Tina safe and sound to her parents. Lila stared at them the whole time as if she saw them but didn't hear them. Enzo, extremely pale, listened for a few minutes and then cried that it was they who had taken his daughter. He said it then and on many other occasions, he shouted it everywhere: the Solaras had taken Tina away from them because he and Lila had refused to give them a percentage of the profits of Basic Sight. He wanted someone to object so that he could murder him. But no one ever objected in his presence. That evening not even the two brothers objected.

"We understand your grief," Marcello said. "If they had taken Silvio I would have gone mad, just like you."

They waited for someone to calm Enzo and they left. The next day they sent on a courtesy call their wives, Gigliola and Elisa, who were welcomed without warmth but more politely. And later they multiplied their initiatives. Probably it was the

Solaras who organized a sort of roundup of all the street peddlers who were usually present in the neighborhood on
Sundays and holidays and of all the Gypsies in the area. And
certainly they were at the head of a real surge of anger against
the police when they arrived, sirens blasting, to arrest Stefano,
who had his first heart attack at that time and ended up in the
hospital, and then Rino, who was released in a few days, and
finally Gennaro, who wept for hours, swearing that he loved his
little sister more than any other person in the world and would
never harm her. Nor can it be ruled out that they were the ones
responsible for surveillance of the elementary school—thanks
to which the "faggot seducer of children," who until then had
been only a popular fantasy, materialized. A slender man of
around thirty who, although he didn't have children to deliver
to the entrance and pick up at the exit, appeared just the same
at the school, was beaten, managed to escape, was pursued by
a furious mob to the gardens. There he would surely have been
murdered if he hadn't managed to explain that he wasn't what
they thought but a trainee at *Il Mattino* looking for news.

After that episode the neighborhood began to settle down,
people slowly slipped back into the life of every day. Since no
trace of Tina was found, the rumor of the truck hitting her
became increasingly plausible. Those who were tired of searching took it seriously, both police and journalists. Attention
shifted to the construction sites in the area and remained there
for a long time. It was at that point that I saw Armando Galiani,
the son of my high-school teacher. He had stopped practicing
medicine, had lost in the parliamentary elections of 1983, and
now, thanks to a scruffy local television station, he was attempting an aggressive type of journalism. I knew that his father had
died a little over a year earlier and that his mother lived in
France but wasn't in good health, either. He asked me to take
him to Lila's, I said Lila wasn't at all well. He insisted, I telephoned. Lila struggled to remember Armando, but when she did

she—who until that moment hadn't spoken to journalists—
agreed to see him. Armando explained that he had been inves-
tigating the aftermath of the earthquake and that traveling
around to the construction sites he had heard of a truck that
was scrapped in a hurry because of a terrible thing it had been
involved in. Lila let him speak, then said:

"You're making it all up."

"I'm saying what I know."

"You don't care a thing about the truck, the construction
sites, or my daughter."

"You're insulting me."

"No, I'll insult you now. You were disgusting as a doctor,
disgusting as a revolutionary, and now you're disgusting as a
journalist. Get out of my house."

Armando scowled, nodded goodbye to Enzo, and left. Out
on the street he looked annoyed. He said: Not even that great
sorrow has changed her, tell her I wanted to help. Then he did
a long interview with me and we said goodbye. I was struck by
his kind manners, by his attentiveness to words. He must have
been through some bad times both when Nadia made her decisions and when he separated from his wife. Now, though, he
seemed in good shape. His old attitude, of a know-it-all who
follows a strict anticapitalist line, had turned into a painful
cynicism.

"Italy has become a cesspool," he said in an aggrieved tone,
"and we've all ended up in it. If you travel around, you see that
the respectable people have understood. What a pity, Elena,
what a pity. The workers' parties are full of honest people who
have been left without hope."

"Why did you start doing this job?"

"For the same reason you do yours."

"What's that?"

"Once I was unable to hide behind anything, I discovered I
was vain."

"Who says I'm vain?"

"The comparison: your friend isn't. But I'm sorry for her, vanity is a resource. If you're vain you pay attention to yourself and your affairs. Lina is without vanity, so she lost her daughter."

I followed his work for a while, he seemed good at it. He tracked down the burned-out wreck of an old vehicle in the neighborhood of the Ponti Rossi, and connected it to Tina's disappearance. The news caused a certain sensation, it reverberated in the national dailies, and remained in the news for several days. Then it was ascertained that there was no possible connection between the burned vehicle and the child's disappearance. Lila said to me:

"Tina is alive, I never want to see that piece of shit again."

4.

I don't know how long she believed that her daughter was still alive. The more Enzo despaired, worn out by tears and rage, the more Lila said: You'll see, they'll give her back. Certainly she never believed in the hit-and-run truck, she said that she would have noticed right away, that before anyone else she would have heard the collision, or at least a cry. And it didn't seem to me that she gave credence to Enzo's thesis, either, she never alluded to involvement on the part of the Solaras. Instead for a long period she thought that one of her clients had taken Tina, someone who knew what Basic Sight earned and wanted money in exchange for the child. That was also Antonio's thesis, but it's hard to say what concrete facts inspired it. Of course the police were interested in that possibility, but since there were never any telephone calls asking for ransom they finally let it go.

The neighborhood was soon divided into a majority that believed Tina was dead and a minority that thought she was alive and a prisoner somewhere. We who loved Lila dearly were part of that minority. Carmen was so sure of it that she repeated it insistently to everyone, and if, as time passed, someone was persuaded that Tina was dead she became that person's enemy. I once heard her whisper to Enzo: Tell Lina that Pasquale is with you, he thinks the child will be found. But the majority prevailed, and those who kept on looking for Tina seemed to the majority either stupid or hypocritical. People also began to think that Lila's intelligence wasn't helping her.

Carmen was the first to intuit that the respect our friend had inspired before Tina's disappearance and the solidarity that arose afterward were both superficial, an old aversion toward her lurked underneath. Look, she said to me, once they treated her as if she were the Madonna and now they pass by her without even a glance. I began to pay attention and saw that it was true. Deep inside, people thought: we're sorry you lost Tina, but it means that if you had truly been what you wanted us to believe, nothing and no one would have touched you. On the street, when we were together, they began to greet me but not her. They were put off by her troubled expression and the cloud of misfortune they saw around her. In other words, the part of the neighborhood that had become used to thinking of Lila as an alternative to the Solaras withdrew in disappointment.

Not only that. An initiative was undertaken that at first seemed kind but then became malicious. In the early weeks, flowers, emotional notes addressed to Lila or directly to Tina, even poems copied from schoolbooks appeared at the entrance to the house, at the door of Basic Sight. Then there were old toys brought by mothers, grandmothers, and children. Then barrettes, colorful hair ribbons, old shoes. Then puppets sewed by hand, with ugly sneers, stained with red, and animal carcasses wrapped in dirty rags. Since Lila calmly picked everything up and threw it into the trash, but suddenly began screaming horrible curses at anyone who passed by, especially the children, who observed her from a distance, she went from being a mother who inspired pity to a madwoman who spread terror. When a girl she had been angry with because she had seen her writing with chalk on the doorway, *the dead are eating Tina*, became seriously ill, old rumors joined the new and people avoided Lila, as if just to look at her could bring misfortune.

Yet she seemed not to realize it. The certainty that Tina was still alive absorbed her completely and it was what, I think, pushed her toward Imma. In the first months I had tried to reduce the contact between her and my youngest daughter, I was afraid that seeing her would cause more suffering. But Lila soon seemed to want her around constantly, and I let her keep her even to sleep. One morning when I went to get her the door of the house was half open, I went in. My child was asking about Tina. After that Sunday I had tried to soothe her by telling her that Tina had gone to stay for a while with Enzo's relatives in Avellino, but she kept asking when she would return. Now she was asking Lila directly, but Lila seemed not to hear Imma's voice, and instead of answering was telling her in detail about Tina's birth, her first toy, how she attached herself to her breast and never let go, things like that. I stopped in the doorway for a few seconds, I heard Imma interrupt her impatiently:

"But when is she coming back?"

"Do you feel lonely?"

"I don't know who to play with."

"I don't, either."

"Then when is she coming back?"

Lila said nothing for a long moment, then scolded her:

"It's none of your business, shut up."

Those words, uttered in dialect, were so brusque, so harsh, so unsuitable that I was alarmed. I said something, brought my child home.

I had always forgiven Lila her excesses and in those circumstances I was inclined to do so even more than in the past.
She often went too far, and as much as possible I tried to get
her to be reasonable. When the police interrogated Stefano
and she was immediately convinced that he had taken Tina—
so that at first she refused even to visit him in the hospital after
the heart attack—I mollified her, and we went together to visit
him. And it was thanks to me that she hadn't attacked her
brother when the police questioned him. I had also done all I
could on the awful day when Gennaro was summoned to the
police station and, once at home, felt himself accused; there
was a quarrel, and he went to live at his father's house, shouting at Lila that she had lost forever not only Tina but also him.
The situation, in other words, was terrible and I could understand why she fought with everyone, even me. But with Imma,
no, I couldn't allow it. From then on, when Lila took the child
I became anxious, I pondered, I looked for ways out.

But there was little to do; the threads of her grief were tangled and Imma was for a time part of that tangle. In the general
chaos where we had all ended up, Lila, despite her weariness,
continued to tell me about my daughter's every little difficulty,
as she had done until I decided to insist that Nino visit. I felt
angry, I was irritated, and yet I tried *also* to see a positive aspect:
she's slowly shifting onto Imma—I thought—her maternal love,
she's saying to me: Since you've been lucky, and you still have
your daughter, you ought to take advantage of it, pay attention
to her, give her all the care you haven't given her.

But that was only the appearance of things. Soon I had a
different theory: that, more deeply, Imma—her body—must
be a symbol of guilt. I thought often of the situation in which
the little girl had been lost. Nino had handed her over to Lila
but *Lila hadn't attended to her.* She had said to her daughter,
You wait here, and to my daughter, *Come with your aunt.* She
had done it, perhaps, to show off Imma to her father, to praise

her to him, to stir his affection, who knows. But Tina was lively, or more simply she had felt neglected, offended, and had wandered off. As a result Lila's suffering had made a nest in the weight of Imma's body in her arms, in the contact, in the living warmth it still gave off. But my daughter was fragile, slow, different in every way from Tina, who was shining, vivacious. Imma could in no way become a substitute, she was only holding back time. I imagined, in other words, that Lila kept her nearby in order to stay within that terrible Sunday, and meanwhile thought: Tina is here, soon she'll pull on my skirt, she'll call me, and then I'll pick her up in my arms, and everything will return to its place. That was why she didn't want the child to upset everything. When the little girl kept asking for her friend, when she merely reminded Lila that in fact Tina wasn't there, Lila treated her with the same harshness with which she treated us adults. But I couldn't accept that. As soon as she came to get Imma, I found some excuse or other to send Dede or Elsa to watch her. If she had used that tone when I was present, what might happen when she took her away for hours?

5.

Every so often I escaped from the apartment, from the flight of stairs between my rooms and hers, from the gardens, the *stradone*, and left for work. These were moments when I sighed with relief: I put on makeup, stylish clothes, even the slight limp that remained from the pregnancy was a sort of pleasingly distinctive trait. Although I frequently made sarcastic remarks about the ill-humored behavior of literary people and artists, at the time everything having to do with publishing, cinema, television—every type of aesthetic display—seemed to me a fantastic landscape in which it was marvelous to appear. I liked being present in the extravagant, festive chaos of big conventions, big conferences, big theater productions, big exhibitions, big films, big operas, and I was flattered on the few occasions when I had a place in the front rows, the reserved seats, from which, sitting among famous people, I could observe the spectacle of powers large and small. Lila, on the other hand, remained at the center of *her* horror, without any distraction. Once I had an invitation to an opera at the San Carlo—a magnificent place where not even I had been—and I insisted on taking her; she didn't want to go, and persuaded Carmen to go instead. The only distraction, if that is the right word for it, she would allow was another reason for suffering. A new affliction acted on her as a sort of antidote. She became combative, determined, she was like someone who knows she has to drown but in spite of herself agitates her arms and legs to stay afloat.

One night she discovered that her son had started shooting up again. Without saying a word, without even telling Enzo, she went to get him from Stefano, in the house in the new neighborhood where decades earlier she had lived as a bride. But he wasn't there: Gennaro had quarreled with his father, too, and a few days earlier had moved to his uncle Rino's. She was greeted with open hostility by Stefano and Marisa, who now lived together. That once handsome man was now skin and bones, and very pale; his clothes seemed several sizes too big. The heart attack had crushed him, he was frightened, he scarcely ate, he didn't drink, he no longer smoked, he wasn't supposed to get upset, because of his bad heart. But on that occasion he became extremely upset and had reason to be. He had closed the grocery because of his illness. Ada demanded money for herself and their daughter. His sister Pinuccia and his mother, Maria, also demanded money. Marisa demanded it for herself and her children. Lila understood immediately that Stefano wanted that money from her and that the excuse for getting it was Gennaro. In fact, although he had thrown his son out of the house, he took his side; he said, and Marisa

supported him, that it would take a lot of money to get treatment for Gennaro. And since Lila replied that she would never
give a cent to anyone, she didn't give a damn about relatives,
friends, or the whole neighborhood, the quarrel became furious. With tears in his eyes, Stefano listed all he had lost over
the years—from the grocery stores to the house itself—and for
those losses he in some obscure way blamed Lila. But the worst
came from Marisa, who yelled at her: Alfonso was ruined
because of you, you've ruined us all, you're worse than the
Solaras, whoever stole your child did a good thing.

Only at that point did Lila become silent, she looked around
for a chair to sit on. She couldn't find one and leaned against
the living room wall, which, decades earlier, had been her living
room, a white room at the time, the furniture brand-new, nothing yet damaged by the havoc of the children who had grown
up there, by the carelessness of the adults. Let's go, Stefano said
to her, perhaps realizing that Marisa had gone too far, let's go
get Gennaro. And they left together; he took her by the arm,
and they went to Rino's house.

Once they were outside, Lila recovered, and freed herself.
They walked, she a few steps ahead. Her brother lived in the
Carraccis' old house, with his mother-in-law, Pinuccia, their
children. Gennaro was there and as soon as he saw his parents
he began shouting. So another fight broke out, first between
father and son, then between mother and son. For a while Rino
was silent, then, his eyes dull, he began whining about the harm
his sister had done since they were children. When Stefano
intervened Rino got angry at him, insulted him, insisted that all
the trouble had started when he wanted to make people think
he was someone and instead he had been cheated first by Lila
and then by the Solaras. They were about to come to blows and
Pinuccia had to restrain her husband, muttering, You're right,
but calm down, this isn't the moment, while the old lady, Maria,
had to restrain Stefano, wheezing: That's enough, son, pretend

you didn't hear him, Rino is sicker than you. At that point Lila grabbed her son forcefully by the arm and took him away.

But Rino followed them to the street, they heard him limping after them. He wanted money, he wanted it at all costs, right away. He said: You'll kill me if you leave me like this. Lila kept walking while he pushed her, laughed, moaned, held her back by the arm. Gennaro began to cry, he yelled at her: You have money, Ma, give it to him. But Lila drove her brother away and brought her son home, hissing: You want to become like that, you want to end up like your uncle?

6.

With the return of Gennaro the apartment below became an even worse inferno; at times I was compelled to go down because I was afraid they'd kill each other. Lila opened the door, said coldly: What do you want. I answered just as coldly: You're overdoing it, Dede's crying, she wants to call the police, and Elsa is scared. She answered: Stay in your own home and plug up your children's ears if they don't want to hear.

In that period she showed less and less interest in the two girls; with explicit sarcasm she called them the young ladies. But my daughters' attitude toward her changed as well. Dede especially stopped feeling her fascination, as if in her eyes, too, Tina's disappearance had taken away Lila's authority. One evening she asked me:

"If Aunt Lina didn't want another child why did she have one?"

"How do you know she didn't want one?"

"She told Imma."

"Imma?"

"Yes, I heard it with my own ears. She talks to her as if she weren't a child, I think she's insane."

"It's not insanity, Dede, it's grief."

"She's never shed a tear."

"Tears aren't grief."

"Yes, but without tears how can you be sure that the grief is there?"

"It's there and often it's an even greater suffering."

"That's not her case. You want to know what I think?"

"All right."

"She lost Tina on purpose. And now she also wants to lose Gennaro. Not to mention Enzo, don't you see how she treats him? Aunt Lina is just like Elsa, she doesn't love anyone."

Dede was like that, she wanted to be someone who is more perceptive than everyone else, and loved to formulate judgments without appeal. I forbade her to repeat those terrible words in Lila's presence and tried to explain to her that not all human beings react in the same way, Lila and Elsa had emotional strategies different from hers.

"Your sister, for example," I said, "doesn't confront emotional issues the way you do; she finds feelings that are too intense ridiculous, and she always stands back a step."

"By standing back a step she's lost any sensitivity."

"Why are you so annoyed with Elsa?"

"Because she's just like Aunt Lina."

A vicious circle: Lila was wrong because she was like Elsa, Elsa was wrong because she was like Lila. In reality at the center of this negative judgment was Gennaro. According to Dede, precisely in this crucial situation Elsa and Lila were making the same mistaken assessment and showed the same emotional disorder. Just as for Lila, for Elsa, too, Gennaro was worse than a beast. Her sister—Dede reported to me—often told her, to offend her, that Lila and Enzo were right to beat him as soon as he tried to stick his nose out of the house. Only someone as stupid as you—she taunted her—who doesn't know anything about men, could be dazzled by a mass of unwashed flesh without a crumb of intelligence. And Dede replied: Only a bitch like you could describe a human being that way.

Since they both read a lot, they quarreled in the language of books, so that, if they didn't slip suddenly into the most brutal dialect to insult each other, I would have listened to their squabbling almost with admiration. The positive side of the conflict was that Dede's rancor toward me diminished, but the negative side burdened me greatly: her sister and Lila became the object of all her malice. Dede was constantly reporting to me Elsa's disgraceful actions: she was hated by her schoolmates because she considered herself the best at everything and was always humiliating them; she boasted of having had relations with adult men; she skipped school and forged my signature on the absence slips. Of Lila she said: She's a fascist, how can you be her friend? And she took Gennaro's side with no equivocation. In her view drugs were a rebellion of sensitive people against the forces of repression. She swore that sooner or later she would find a way of getting Rino out—she always called him that, and only that, habituating us to call him that, too—from the prison in which his mother kept him.

I tried whenever I could to throw water on the flames, I reprimanded Elsa, I defended Lila. But sometimes it was hard to take Lila's part. The peaks of her bitter grief frightened me. On the other hand I was afraid that, as had happened in the past, her body wouldn't hold up, and so, even though I liked Dede's lucid and yet passionate aggression, even though I found Elsa's quirky impudence amusing, I was careful not to let my daughters set off crises with reckless words. (I knew that Dede would have been more than capable of saying: *Aunt Lina, tell things as they are, you wanted to lose Tina, it didn't happen by chance.*) But every day I feared the worst. The young ladies, as Lila called them, although they were immersed in the reality of the neighborhood, had a strong sense that they were different. Especially when they returned from Florence they

354 · ELENA FERRANTE

felt they were of superior quality and did all they could to demonstrate it. Dede was doing very well in high school and when her professor—a very cultivated man no more than forty, awestruck by the surname Airota—interrogated her he seemed more worried that he would make a mistake in the questions than that she would make a mistake in the answers. Elsa was less brilliant scholastically, and her midyear report cards were generally poor, but what made her intolerable was the ease with which at the end she shuffled the cards and came in among the top. I knew their insecurities and terrors, I felt them to be fearful girls, and so I didn't put much credence in their domineering attitudes. But others did, and seen from the outside they must surely have seemed odious. Elsa, for example, gleefully bestowed offensive nicknames in class and outside, she had no respect for anyone. She called Enzo the mute bumpkin; she called Lila the poisonous moth; she called Gennaro the laughing crocodile. But she was especially irked by Antonio, who went to Lila's almost every day, either to the office or to her house, and as soon as he arrived drew her and Enzo into a room to conspire. Antonio, after the episode of Tina, had become cantankerous. If I was present he more or less explicitly took his leave; if it was my daughters, he cut them off by closing the door. Elsa, who knew Poe well, called him the mask of yellow death, because Antonio had a naturally jaundiced complexion. It was obvious, therefore, that I should fear some blunder on their part. Which duly happened.

I was in Milan. Lila rushed into the courtyard, where Dede was reading, Elsa was talking to some friends, Imma was playing. They weren't children. Dede was sixteen, Elsa almost thirteen; only Imma was little, she was five. But Lila treated all three as if they had no autonomy. She dragged them into the house without explanation (they were used to hearing explanations), crying only that staying outside was dangerous. My oldest daughter found that behavior unbearable, she said:

"Mamma entrusted my sisters to me, it's up to me to decide whether to go inside or not."

"When your mother isn't here I'm your mother."

"A shit mother," Dede answered, moving to dialect. "You lost Tina and you haven't even cried."

Lila slapped her, crushing her. Elsa defended her sister and was slapped in turn, Imma burst into tears. You don't go out of the house, my friend repeated, gasping, outside it's dangerous, outside you'll die. She kept them inside for days, until I returned.

When I returned, Dede recounted the whole episode, and, honest as she was, on principle, she also reported her own ugly response. I wanted her to understand that what she had said was terrible, and I scolded her harshly: I warned you not to. Elsa sided with her sister, she explained to me that Aunt Lina was out of her mind, she was possessed by the idea that to escape danger you had to live barricaded in the house. It was hard to convince my daughters that it wasn't Lila's fault but the Soviet empire's. In a place called Chernobyl a nuclear power plant had exploded and emitted dangerous radiation that, since the planet was small, could be absorbed by anyone. Aunt Lina was protecting you, I said. But Elsa shouted: It's not true, she beat us, the only good thing is that she fed us only frozen food. Imma: I cried a lot, I don't like frozen food. And Dede: She treated us worse than she treats Rino. I said: Aunt Lina would have behaved the same way with Tina, think of what torture it must have been for her to protect you, imagining that her daughter is somewhere and no one's taking care of her. But it was a mistake to express myself like that in front of Imma. While Dede and Elsa looked skeptical, she was upset, and ran away to play.

A few days later Lila confronted me in her direct way:

"Is it you who tell your daughters that I lost Tina and never cried?"

"Stop it, do you think I would say a thing like that?"

"Dede called me a shit mother."

"She's a child."

"She's a very rude child."

At that point I committed errors no less serious than those of my daughters. I said:

"Calm down. I know how much you loved Tina. Try not to keep it all inside, you should let it out, you should say whatever comes into your mind. I know the birth was difficult, but you shouldn't elaborate on it."

I got everything wrong: the past tense of "you loved," the allusion to the birth, the fatuous tone. She answered curtly: Mind your own business. And then she cried, as if Imma were an adult: Teach your daughter that if someone tells her something, she shouldn't go around repeating it.

7.

Things got even worse when, one morning—I think it was in June of 1986—there was another disappearance. Nunzia arrived, grimmer than usual, and said that Rino hadn't returned home the previous night, that Pinuccia was looking for him all over the neighborhood. She gave me the news without looking at me, as she did when what she was telling me was really meant for Lila.

I went downstairs to report it. Lila immediately summoned Gennaro—she took it for granted that he would know where his uncle was. The boy resisted, he didn't want to reveal anything that might lead his mother to become even harsher. But when the entire day passed and Rino still couldn't be found, he decided to cooperate. The next morning he refused to let Enzo and Lila come with him on the search, but resigned himself to the company of his father. Stefano arrived out of breath, nervous because of yet another difficulty that his brother-in-law was causing, apprehensive because of his own ill health, and, continually touching his throat, said, ashen-faced: I can't breathe. Finally father and son—the boy large, the man looking like a stick in his oversized clothes—set off for the railroad.

They crossed the switching yard and walked along the old tracks where disused cars had been abandoned. In one of them they found Rino. He was seated, his eyes were open. His nose seemed enormous, his unshaved beard, still black, covered his face, up to the cheekbones, like an overgrown plant. Stefano, seeing his brother-in-law, forgot his health and had a real fit of rage. He shouted insults at the corpse, he wanted to kick it. You were a shit as a boy—he screamed—and a shit you've remained. You deserve this death, you died like a shit. He was angry because he had ruined his sister Pinuccia, because he had ruined his nephews, and because he had ruined his son. Look, he said to Gennaro, look what's waiting for you. Gennaro grabbed him from behind and gripped him hard to restrain him while, kicking and thrashing, Stefano tried to get free.

It was early morning but already starting to get hot. The car stank of shit and pee, the seats were broken, the windows so dirty you couldn't see out. Since Stefano continued to struggle and howl, the boy lost his temper and said ugly things to his father. He said that it disgusted him to be his son, that the only people in the whole neighborhood he respected were his mother and Enzo. At that point Stefano began to cry. They sat together for a while beside Rino's body, not to watch over him, only to calm down. They went home to deliver the news.

8.

Nunzia and Fernando were the only ones who felt the loss of Rino. Pinuccia mourned her husband only as much as was indispensable and then seemed to be reborn. Two weeks afterward she showed up at my house to ask if she could replace her mother-in-law, who was crushed by grief and didn't feel like working anymore: she would clean the house, cook, and take care of my daughters in my absence for exactly the same sum. She was less efficient than Nunzia but more talkative and above all more appealing to Dede, Elsa, and Imma. She was full of compliments for all three of them and for me as well. How well you look, she said, you're a lady: I see you've got beautiful dresses and a lot of shoes in the closet, it's obvious that you're important and you go out with important people: is it true that they're making a film out of your book?

At first she acted like a widow, but then she asked if there were dresses I didn't wear anymore, even if she was large and they didn't fit her. I'll let them out, she said, and I chose some for her. She altered them carefully and skillfully, and then she appeared at work as if she were going to a party, parading back and forth along the hall so that the girls and I could give her our opinion. She was very grateful to me; at times she was so content that she wanted to talk rather than work, and she recalled the days of Ischia. She often alluded to Bruno Soccavo, becoming emotional, and saying in a low voice: What a terrible end he had. A few times she made a remark that must have pleased her greatly: I was widowed twice. One morning she confided to me that Rino had been a real husband only for a few years, otherwise he had behaved like a boy: even in bed, one minute and off he got, sometimes not even the minute. Ah, yes, he was immature, he was a braggart, a liar, but also arrogant, arrogant like Lina. It's a characteristic of the race of the Cerullos—she grew angry—they're bigmouths and they've got no feelings. Then she began to speak ill of Lila, she said she had appropriated everything that was a product of her brother's intelligence and hard work. I replied: It's not true, Lina loved Rino, it was he who exploited her in every way. Pinuccia looked at me bitterly, out of the blue she began to praise her husband. Cerullo shoes, she pronounced, he invented, but then Lina took advantage, she cheated Stefano, she made him marry her, she stole a lot of money—Papa had left us millionaires—and then she made a deal with Michele Solara, she ruined us all. She added: Don't defend her, you know it perfectly well.

It wasn't true, naturally, I knew something quite different, Pinuccia spoke like that because of old resentments. And yet Lila's only real reaction to the death of her brother was that she confirmed many of those lies. I had long since realized that each of us organizes memory as it suits him, I'm still surprised when I do it myself. But it surprised me that one could go so far as to give the facts an arrangement that went against one's own interests. Lila began almost immediately to attribute to Rino all the merits of the business with the shoes. She said that her brother had had extraordinary imagination and skill since he was a boy, that if the Solaras hadn't interfered he might have surpassed Ferragamo. She strove to stop the flow of Rino's life at the exact moment when her father's workshop was transformed into a small factory, and from all the rest—everything that he had done and had done to her—she removed shape and form. She kept alive and solid only the figure of the boy who had defended her against a violent father, who had indulged the yearnings of a girl who sought outlets for her own intelligence.

This must have seemed to her a good remedy for grief, because in that same period she revived, and she began to do the same thing with Tina. She no longer spent her days as if the child might return at any moment, but tried to fill the void in the house and in herself with a luminous little figure, as if it were the product of a computer program. Tina became a sort of hologram, she was there and not there. Lila called her up rather than recalling her. She showed me the photos in which she looked best or made me listen to her voice that Enzo had recorded on a tape recorder at one year, at two, at three, or quoted her funny little questions, her extraordinary answers, taking care to speak of her always in the present: Tina has, Tina does, Tina says.

This didn't soothe her, naturally, in fact she yelled more than before. She yelled at her son, at her clients, at me, at Pinuccia, at Dede and Elsa, sometimes at Imma. She yelled at Enzo, in particular, if, while he was working, he burst into tears. But sometimes she sat down, as she had done in the first days, and talked to Imma about Rino and about the child, as if for some reason they had left together. If the little girl asked, when are they coming back, she answered without getting angry: They'll come back when they feel like it. But this, too, became less frequent. After our fight about my daughters she didn't seem to need Imma anymore. In fact, she gradually reduced Imma's visits, and, though with more affection, began to treat her like her sisters. One evening when we had just come into the shabby entranceway of our building—and Elsa complained because she had seen a cockroach, and Dede at the mere idea was disgusted, and Imma wanted me to pick her up—Lila said to all three, as if I weren't present: You're the daughters of a lady, what are you doing here, persuade your mother to take you away.

9.

Apparently, then, after Rino's death she seemed to improve. She stopped narrowing her eyes in alarm. The skin of her face, which seemed a pure white canvas sail flattened by a strong wind, softened. But it was a momentary improvement. Soon there was a jumble of wrinkles, on her forehead, at the edges of her eyes, even on her cheeks, where they looked like fake pleats. And her whole body began to age, her back was bent, her stomach swelled.

Carmen one day used an expression of her own, she said anxiously: Tina is encysted in her, we have to get her out. And she was right, we had to find a way to flush out the story of the child. But Lila refused, everything about her daughter was fixed. I think that something shifted, very painfully, only with Antonio and with Enzo but, out of necessity, in secret. And when suddenly Antonio left—without saying goodbye to anyone, taking his blond family and crazy Melina, now old—she no longer had even the mysterious reports he gave her. She was left alone to rage at Enzo and Gennaro, often setting one against the other. Or distracted, with her own thoughts, as if she were waiting.

I stopped by every day, even when I was pressed by deadlines, and did all I could to revive our intimacy. Since she was always idle, I asked her once:

"Do you still like your work?"

"I never liked it."

"You're lying, I remember you liked it."

"No, you don't remember anything: Enzo liked it and so I made myself like it."

"Then find something else to do."

"I'm fine like this. Enzo's head is in the clouds and if I don't help we'll go out of business."

"You both need to emerge from your suffering."

"What suffering, Lenù, we have to emerge from our rage."

"Then emerge from rage."

"We're trying."

"Try with more conviction. Tina doesn't deserve it."

"Forget Tina, think about your own daughters."

"I am thinking about them."

"Not enough."

She always found, in those years, cracks through which to turn a situation upside down and force me to look at the flaws of Dede, of Elsa, of Imma. You neglect them, she said. I accepted the criticisms, some were well-founded, I too often pursued my own life, neglecting theirs. But meanwhile I waited for an opportunity to shift the conversation back to her and Tina. At a certain point, I began to harass her about her pasty complexion.

"You're very pale."

"You're too red: look, you're purple."

"I'm talking about you: what's wrong?"

"Anemia."

"What anemia."

"My period comes when it likes, but then it doesn't go away."

"Since when?"

"Forever."

"Tell the truth, Lila."

"The truth."

I pressed her, often I provoked her, and she reacted but never to the point of losing control and letting go.

It occurred to me that it was now a linguistic question. She resorted to Italian as if to a barrier; I tried to push her toward dialect, our language of candor. But while her Italian was translated from dialect, my dialect was increasingly translated from Italian, and we both spoke a false language. She needed to explode, lose control of the words. I wanted her to say in the authentic Neapolitan of our childhood: What the fuck do you want, Lenù, I'm like this because I lost my daughter, and maybe she's alive, maybe she's dead, but I can't bear either of those possibilities, because if she's alive she's alive far away from me, she's in a place where horrible things are happening to her, which I see clearly, I see them all day and all night as if they were happening right before my eyes; but if she's dead I'm dead, too, dead here inside, a death more unbearable than real death, which is death without feeling, while this death forces you to feel everything, every day, to wake up, wash, dress, eat and drink, work, talk to you who don't understand or won't understand, to you who even if I just see you, all set, fresh from the hairdresser, with your daughters who do well in school, who always do everything perfectly, who aren't spoiled even by this place of shit, which, rather, seems to do them good—makes them even more confident, even more arrogant, even more sure they have the right to take everything—all this makes me more furious than I already was: so go, go, leave me in peace, Tina would have been better than all of you, and instead they took her, and I can't bear it anymore.

I would have liked to lead her into a conversation like that, jumbled, intoxicated. I felt that if she made up her mind she would extract from the tangled mass of her brain words of that sort. But it didn't happen. In fact, as I think back, in that phase she was less aggressive than in other periods of our story. Maybe the outburst I hoped for was made up of my own feelings, which therefore hindered me from seeing the situation clearly and made Lila even more elusive. Sometimes I wondered if she had in her mind something unutterable that I wasn't even capable of imagining.

10.

Sundays were the worst. Lila stayed home, she didn't work, and from outside came the holiday voices. I went down, I said: Let's go out, let's take a walk to the center, let's go to the sea. She refused, and got angry if I was too insistent. So, to make up for her rudeness, Enzo said: I'll go, come on. She shouted immediately: Yes, go, leave me in peace, I'll take a bath and wash my hair, let me breathe.

We would go out, my daughters came with us and sometimes also Gennaro—who, after the death of his uncle, we all called Rino. During those hours of our walks Enzo confided in me, in his laconic, sometimes obscure way. He said that without

Tina he didn't know what the point of making money was. He said that stealing children to make their parents suffer was a sign of the wretched times that were coming. He said that after the birth of his daughter it was as if a light had switched on in his head, and now the light had gone out. He said: You remember when right here, on this street, I carried her on my shoulders? He said: Thank you, Lenù, for the help you give us, don't be angry with Lina, this is a time of tribulation, but you know her better than I do, sooner or later she'll recover.

I listened, I asked him: She's very pale, physically how is she? I meant: I know she is tortured by grief, but tell me, is she healthy, have you noticed worrying symptoms? But in the face of "physically" Enzo was embarrassed. He knew almost nothing about Lila's body, he adored it as one adores an idol, warily and with respect. And he answered without conviction: fine. Then he grew nervous, he was in a hurry to get home, he said: Let's try to persuade her at least to take a short walk in the neighborhood.

Useless. Only very rarely could I get Lila outside on a Sunday. But it wasn't a good idea. She walked quickly, carelessly dressed, her hair loose and disheveled, flashing angry glances. My daughters and I followed haltingly behind her, supportive, like handmaidens more beautiful, more richly adorned than our mistress. Everyone knew her, even the peddlers, who remembered the troubles they had had because of Tina's disappearance and, afraid there could be others, avoided her. To everyone she was the terrifying woman who, stricken by a great misfortune, carried its potency with her, spreading it wherever she went. Lila walked along the *stradone* with her fierce gaze, toward the gardens, and people lowered their eyes, looked in another direction. But even if someone greeted her she paid no attention, and didn't respond. From the way she walked she seemed to have an urgent goal. The truth is, she was running from the memory of that Sunday two years earlier.

When we went out together we inevitably met the Solaras. Lately, they hadn't been straying from the neighborhood much; there had been a lengthy list of people murdered in Naples, and, at least on Sundays, they preferred to remain peacefully on the streets of their childhood that for them were as safe as a fortress. The two families always did the same things. They went to Mass, they walked amid the stalls, they brought their children to the neighborhood library, which by long tradition, since the days when Lila and I were young, was open on Sundays. I thought it must be Elisa or Gigliola who imposed that educated ritual, but once when I stopped to exchange a few words I discovered that it was Michele. He said, pointing to his children, who although they were grown obeyed him, evidently out of fear, while they had no respect for their mother:

"They know that if they don't read at least one book a month from the first page to the last I won't give them a lira. I'm doing the right thing, no, Lenù?"

I don't know if they really took out books, they had enough money to buy the entire Biblioteca Nazionale. But whether they did it out of real need or as a performance, they now had this habit: they went up the stairs, pushed open the glass door, a relic of the forties, went in, stayed for no more than ten minutes, and came out.

When I was alone with my daughters, Marcello, Michele, Gigliola, and the boys, too, were cordial; only my sister was cool. With Lila, on the other hand, things were complicated, and I was afraid that the tension would rise dangerously. But on those very rare Sunday walks she always pretended that they didn't exist. And the Solaras behaved the same way, and since I was with Lila they preferred to ignore me as well. Elsa, however, one Sunday morning, decided not to follow that unwritten rule and with her queen-of-hearts manners greeted the children of Michele and Gigliola, who responded uneasily.

As a result, although it was very cold, we were forced to stop for a few minutes. The two Solaras pretended to have urgent things to talk about with each other, I spoke to Gigliola, the girls to the boys, Imma studied her cousin Silvio attentively, since we saw him so infrequently. No one addressed a word to Lila, and Lila, for her part, was silent. Only Michele, when he broke off his conversation with his brother and spoke to me in his teasing way, referred to her without looking at her:

"Now, Lenù, we're going to look in at the library and then we're going to eat. Would you like to come with us?"

"No, thank you," I said, "we have to go. Another time, though, certainly."

"Good, then tell the boys what they should read and what they shouldn't. You are an example for us, you and your daughters. When we see you pass by on the street we always say: once Lenuccia was like us, and look how she is now. She doesn't know what pride is, she is democratic, she lives here with us, just like us, even though she's an important person. Ah, yes, those who study become good. Today everyone goes to school, everyone keeps his eyes on the books, and so in the future we'll have so much of that goodness it'll be coming out of our ears. But if you don't read and you don't study, which is what happened to Lina, it happened to all of us, you stay malicious, and malice is ugly. Isn't it true, Lenù?"

He grabbed me by the wrist, his eyes were shining. He repeated sarcastically: Isn't it true? and I nodded yes, but I freed my wrist too forcefully, my mother's bracelet remained in his hand.

"Oh," he exclaimed, and this time he sought Lila's gaze, but didn't find it. He said with feigned regret: "I'm sorry, I'll have it fixed for you."

"It's nothing."

"Absolutely not, it's my duty: you'll have it back like new. Marcè, you'll go by the jeweler's?"

Marcello nodded yes.

People were passing, eyes lowered; it was almost time for lunch. When we managed to get rid of the brothers Lila said to me:

"You're even more defenseless than you used to be: you'll never see that bracelet again."

11.

I was convinced that she was about to have one of her crises. I saw that she was debilitated and anguished, as if she expected something uncontrollable to break the building in two, the apartment, herself. For several days, knocked out by the flu, I didn't hear anything about her. Dede, too, had a cough and a fever, and I assumed that the virus would soon be transmitted to Elsa and to Imma. Also, I had an article to hand in urgently (I was supposed to do something for a magazine that was devoting an entire issue to the female body) and I didn't have the desire or the strength to write.

Outside a cold wind had arisen; it shook the windowpanes, blades of cold penetrated the loose frames. On Friday Enzo came to tell me that he had to go to Avellino because an old aunt of his was ill. As for Rino, he would be spending Saturday and Sunday with Stefano, who had asked him to help dismantle the fixtures in the grocery and take them to a man who was willing to buy them. Lila therefore would be alone, and Enzo said that she was a little depressed, he wanted me to keep her company. But I was tired, I barely had time to focus on a thought when Dede called me, Imma wanted me, Elsa protested, and the thought vanished. When Pinuccia came to clean the house I asked her to cook enough for Saturday and Sunday, then I shut myself in my bedroom, where I had a table to work at.

The next day, since I hadn't heard from Lila, I went down to invite her to lunch. She came to the door in sandals, an old green bathrobe over her pajamas, her hair disheveled. But to my amazement her eyes and mouth were heavily made up. The house was a mess, and there was an unpleasant smell. She said: If the wind blows any harder the neighborhood will fly away. Nothing but an overused hyperbole and yet I was alarmed: she had said it as if she were convinced that the neighborhood really could be torn from its foundations and carried off to shatter near Ponti Rossi. Once she realized that I had perceived how odd her tone was, she smiled in a forced way, whispered: I was joking. I nodded, I listed the good things there were for lunch. She became excited in an exaggerated way, but a moment later her mood abruptly changed, she said: Bring me lunch here, I don't want to come to your house, your daughters get on my nerves.

I brought her lunch and also dinner. The stairs were cold, I didn't feel well, and I didn't want to go up and down just to have unpleasant things said to me. But this time I found her surprisingly cordial, she said Wait, sit with me for a moment. She drew me into the bathroom, she brushed her hair carefully, and meanwhile spoke about my daughters with tenderness, with admiration, as if to convince me that she didn't seriously believe what she had said to me earlier.

"At first," she said, dividing the hair into two, and beginning to braid it without losing sight of her image in the mirror, "Dede resembled you, now instead she's becoming like her father. The opposite is happening with Elsa: she seemed identical to her father and now instead she's starting to look like you. Everything moves. A wish, a fantasy travels more swiftly than blood."

"I don't understand."

"You remember when I thought Gennaro was Nino's?"

"Yes."

"To me he really seemed so, he was identical to Nino, his exact image."

"You mean that a desire can be so strong as to seem fulfilled?"

"No, I mean that for a few years Gennaro was *truly* Nino's child."

"Don't exaggerate."

She stared at me spitefully for a moment, she took a few steps in the bathroom, limping, she burst out laughing in a slightly artificial way.

"So it seems to you that I'm exaggerating?"

I realized with some annoyance that she was imitating my walk.

"Don't make fun of me, my hip hurts."

"Nothing hurts, Lenù. You invented that limp in order not to let your mother die completely, and now you really do limp, and I've studied you, it's good for you. The Solaras took your bracelet and you said nothing, you weren't sorry, you weren't worried. At the time I thought it was because you don't know how to rebel, but now I understand it's not that. You're getting old properly. You feel strong, you stopped being a daughter, you truly became a mother."

I felt uneasy, I repeated:

"It's just a little pain."

"Even pain does you good. You just needed a slight limp and now your mother stays quietly inside you. Her leg is glad that you limp and so you, too, are glad. Isn't that true?"

"No."

She gave me an ironic look to reassert that she didn't believe me, and with her made-up eyes narrowed to cracks said:

"Do you think that when Tina is forty-two, she'll be like this?"

I stared at her. She had a provocative expression, her hands tight around the braids. I said:

"It's likely, yes, maybe so."

12.

My daughters had to fend for themselves, I stayed to eat with Lila, even though I felt cold in my bones. We talked the whole time about physical resemblances; I tried to understand what was happening in her mind. But I also mentioned to her the work I was doing. Talking to you helps, I said to give her confidence, you make me think.

The idea seemed to cheer her, she said: Knowing I'm useful to you I feel better. Right afterward, thanks to the effort involved in being useful to me, she moved on to contorted or illogical arguments. She had put on a lot of powder to hide her pallor, and she didn't seem herself but a Carnival mask with very red cheeks. At times I followed her with interest, at times I recognized only the signs of the illness that I was well acquainted with by now, and was alarmed. For example, she said, laughing: For a while I brought up Nino's child, just as you've done with Imma, a flesh and blood child; but when that child became Stefano's where did Nino's child go, does Gennaro still have him inside, do I have him? Remarks like that: she got lost. Then she started abruptly to praise my cooking, she said she had eaten with pleasure, something she hadn't done for a long time. When I said it wasn't mine but Pinuccia's, she darkened, she grumbled that she didn't want anything from Pinuccia. At that point Elsa called me from the landing, she shouted that I had to come home right away, Dede with a fever was even worse than Dede healthy. I urged Lila to call me whenever she needed me, I told her to rest, I hurried up to my apartment.

For the rest of the day I tried to forget about her; I worked late into the night. The children had grown up with the idea that when I really had my back to the wall they had to look after themselves and not disturb me. In fact they left me in peace, and I worked well. As usual a half sentence of Lila's was enough and my brain recognized her aura, became active, liberated my intelligence. By now I knew that I could do well especially when she, even just with a few disjointed words, assured the more insecure part of me that I was right. I gave to her digressive complaints a concise, elegant organization. I wrote about my hip, about my mother. Now that I was surrounded by admiration, I could admit without uneasiness that talking to her incited ideas, pushed me to make connections between distant things. In those years of being neighbors, I on the floor above, she below, it often happened. A slight push was enough and the seemingly empty mind discovered that it was full and lively. I attributed to her a sort of farsightedness, as I had all our lives, and I found nothing wrong with it. I said to myself that to be adult was to recognize that I needed her impulses. If once I had hidden, even from myself, that spark she induced in me, now I was proud of it, I had even written about it somewhere. *I was I* and for that very reason I could make space for her in me and give her an enduring form. *She instead didn't want to be her*, so she couldn't do the same. The tragedy of Tina, her weakened physical state, her drifting brain surely contributed to her crises. But *that* was the underlying cause of the illness that she called "dissolving boundaries." I went to bed around three, I woke at nine.

Dede's fever was gone, but in compensation Imma had a cough. I straightened the apartment, I went to see how Lila was. I knocked for a long time, she didn't open the door. I pressed the bell until I heard her dragging footsteps and her voice grumbling insults in dialect. Her braids were half undone, her makeup was smeared, even more than the day before it was a mask with a pained expression.

"Pinuccia poisoned me," she said with conviction. "I couldn't sleep, my stomach is splitting."

I went in, I had an impression of carelessness, of filth. On the floor, next to the sink, I saw toilet paper soaked with blood. I said:

"I ate the same things you ate and I'm fine."

"Then explain to me what's wrong with me."

"Menstruation?"

She got mad:

"I'm always menstruating."

"Then you should be examined."

"I'm not going to have my stomach examined by anyone."

"What do you think is wrong?"

"I know what it is."

"I'll go get you a painkiller at the pharmacy."

"You must have something in the house?"

"I don't need them."

"And Dede and Elsa?"

"They don't, either."

"Ah, you're perfect, you never need anything."

I was irked, it was starting up again.

"You want to quarrel?"

"You want to quarrel, since you say I have menstrual cramps. I'm not a child like your daughters, I know if I have that pain or something else."

It wasn't true, she knew nothing about herself. When it came to the workings of her body she was worse than Dede and Elsa. I realized that she was suffering, she pressed her stomach with her hands. Maybe I was wrong: certainly she was overwhelmed with anguish, but not because of her old fears—she really was ill. I made her some chamomile tea, forced her to drink it. I put on a coat and went to see if the pharmacy was open. Gino's father was a skilled pharmacist, he would surely give me good advice. But I had barely emerged onto the *stradone*, among the Sunday stalls, when I heard explosions—*pah, pah, pah, pah*—similar to the sound of the firecrackers that children set off at Christmastime. There were four close together, then came a fifth: *pah*.

I turned onto the street where the pharmacy was. People

seemed disoriented, Christmas was still weeks away, some walked quickly, some ran.

Suddenly the litany of sirens began: the police, an ambulance. I asked someone what had happened, he shook his head, he admonished his wife because she was slow and hurried off. Then I saw Carmen with her husband and two children. They were on the other side of the street, I crossed. Before I could ask a question Carmen said in dialect: They've killed both Solaras.

13.

There are moments when what exists on the edges of our lives, and which, it seems, will be in the background forever— an empire, a political party, a faith, a monument, but also simply the people who are part of our daily existence—collapses in an utterly unexpected way, and right when countless other things are pressing upon us. This period was like that. Day after day, month after month, task was added to task, tremor to tremor. For a long time it seemed to me that I was like certain figures in novels and paintings who stand firm on a cliff or on the prow of a ship in the face of a storm, which doesn't overwhelm them and in fact doesn't even touch them. My telephone rang continuously. The fact that I lived in the dominion of the Solaras compelled me to an infinite chain of words, written and spoken. After the death of her husband, my sister Elisa became a terrified child, she wanted me with her day and night, she was sure that the murderers would return to kill her and her son. And above all I had to tend to Lila, who that same Sunday was suddenly torn from the neighborhood, from her son, from Enzo, from her job, and ended up in the hands of the doctors, because she was weak, she saw things that seemed real but weren't, she was losing blood. They discovered a fibromatous uterus, they operated and took it out. Once—she was still in the hospital—she woke suddenly, exclaimed that Tina had come out of her belly again and now was taking revenge on everyone, even on her. For a fraction of a second she was sure that the killer of the Solaras was her daughter.

14.

Marcello and Michele died on a Sunday in December of 1986, in front of the church where they had been baptized. Just a few minutes after their murder the whole neighborhood knew the details. Michele had been shot twice, Marcello three times. Gigliola had run away, her sons had instinctively followed her. Elisa had grabbed Silvio and held him tight, turning her back on the murderers. Michele had died immediately, Marcello, no, he had sat down on a step and tried to button his jacket, but couldn't.

When it came to saying who had actually killed the Solara brothers, those who appeared to know everything about the murders realized they had seen almost nothing. It was a single man who fired the shots, then had got calmly into a red Ford Fiesta and left. No, there had been two, two men, and at the wheel of the yellow Fiat 147 in which they escaped there was a woman. Not at all, the murderers were three, men, faces covered by ski masks, and they had fled on foot. In some cases it seemed that no one had fired the shots. In the story Carmen told me, for example, the Solaras, my sister, my nephew, Gigliola, her children became agitated in front of the church as if they had been hit by effects without cause: Michele fell to the ground backward and hit his head hard on the lava stone; Marcello sat down cautiously on a step and since he couldn't close his jacket over the blue turtleneck sweater he cursed and lay down on one side; the wives, the children hadn't got even

a scratch and in a few seconds had gone into the church to
hide. It seemed that those present had looked only in the direction of the killed and not that of the killers.

Armando, in this situation, returned to interview me for his
television station. He wasn't the only one. At that moment I
said, and recounted in writing, in various places, what I knew.
But in the two or three days that followed I realized that in
particular the reporters for the Neapolitan papers knew much
more than I did. Information that until not long before could
be found nowhere was suddenly flooding in. An impressive
list of criminal enterprises I had never heard of were attributed to the Solara brothers. Equally impressive was the list of
their assets. What I had written with Lila, what I had published when they were still alive was nothing, almost nothing
in comparison with what appeared in the papers after their
death. On the other hand I realized that I knew other things,
things that no one knew and no one wrote, not even me. I
knew that the Solaras had always seemed very handsome to us
as girls, that they went around the neighborhood in their Fiat
1100 like ancient warriors in their chariots, that one night they
had defended us in Piazza dei Martiri from the wealthy youths
of Chiaia, that Marcello would have liked to marry Lila but
then had married my sister Elisa, that Michele had understood the extraordinary qualities of my friend long before that
and had loved her for years in a way so absolute that he had
ended up losing himself. Just as I realized that I knew these
things I discovered that they were important. They indicated
how I and countless other respectable people all over Naples
had been within the world of the Solaras, we had taken part
in the opening of their businesses, had bought pastries at their
bar, had celebrated their marriages, had bought their shoes,
had been guests in their houses, had eaten at the same table,
had directly or indirectly taken their money, had suffered their
violence and pretended it was nothing. Marcello and Michele

were, like it or not, part of us, just as Pasquale was. But while
in relation to Pasquale, even with innumerable distinctions, a
clear line of separation could immediately be drawn, the line
of separation in relation to people like the Solaras had been
and was, in Naples, in Italy, vague. The farther we jumped
back in horror, the more certain it was that we were behind
the line.

The concreteness that being behind the line assumed in the
reduced and overfamiliar space of the neighborhood depressed
me. Someone, to sling mud on me, wrote that I was related to
the Solaras and for a while I avoided going to see my sister and
my nephew. I even avoided Lila. Of course, she had been the
brothers' bitterest enemy, but hadn't she gotten the money to
start her little business working for Michele, maybe stealing it
from him? I wandered around that theme for a while. Then
time passed, the Solaras, too, joined the many who every day
ended up on the list of the murdered, and slowly what began
to worry us was only that people less familiar and more violent
would take their place. I forgot them to the point that when a
teenage boy delivered a package from a jeweler in Montesanto,
I didn't immediately guess what it contained. The red case
inside amazed me, the envelope addressed to Dottoressa Elena
Greco. I had to read the note to realize what it was. Marcello
had, in a laborious handwriting, written only "Sorry," and had
signed it with a swirling "M," of the type that used to be taught
in elementary school. In the case was my bracelet, so highly
polished that it seemed new.

15.

When I told Lila about that package and showed her the
polished bracelet she said: Don't wear it and don't even let
your daughters wear it. She had returned home very weak;

when she went up a flight of stairs you could hear the breath straining in her chest. She took pills and gave herself injections, but she was so pale that she seemed to have been in the kingdom of the dead and spoke of the bracelet as if she were sure that it had come from there.

The death of the Solaras overlapped with her emergency admission to the hospital, the blood she had shed was mixed—in my feeling of that chaotic Sunday—with theirs. But whenever I tried to talk to her about that execution, so to speak, in front of the church, she became irritated, she reacted with remarks like: They were shits, Lenù, who gives a damn about them, I'm sorry for your sister but if she had been a little smarter she wouldn't have married Marcello, everyone knows that people like him end up getting killed.

Sometimes I tried to draw her into the sense of contiguity that at that time embarrassed me, I thought she should feel it more than I did. I said something like:

"We'd known them since they were boys."

"All men were once boys."

"They gave you work."

"It was convenient for them and it was convenient for me."

"Michele was certainly a bastard but so were you sometimes."

"I should have done worse."

She made an effort to limit herself to contempt, but she had a malicious look, she entwined her fingers and gripped them, making her knuckles turn white. I saw that behind those words, fierce in themselves, there were even fiercer ones that she avoided saying, but that she had ready in her mind. I read them in her face, I heard them shouted: If it was the Solaras who took Tina away from me, then too little was done to them, they should have been drawn and quartered, their hearts ripped out, and their guts dumped on the street; if it wasn't them, whoever murdered them did a good thing just the same, they deserved that and more; if the assassins had whistled I would have hurried to give them a hand.

But she never expressed herself in that way. To all appearances the abrupt exit from the scene of the two brothers seemed to have little effect on her. Only it encouraged her to walk in the neighborhood more frequently, since there was no longer any chance of meeting them. She never mentioned returning to the activities of the time before Tina's disappearance, she never resumed the life of home and office. She made her convalescence last for weeks and weeks, as she wandered around the tunnel, the *stradone*, the gardens. She walked with her head down, she spoke to no one, and since, partly because of her neglected appearance, she continued to seem dangerous to herself and others, no one spoke to her.

Sometimes she insisted that I go with her, and it was hard to say no. We often passed the bar-pastry shop, which bore a sign saying "Closed for mourning." The mourning never ended, the shop never reopened, the time of the Solaras was over. But Lila glanced every time at the lowered shutters, the faded sign, and said with satisfaction: It's still closed. The fact seemed to her so positive that, as we passed by, she might even give a small laugh, just a small laugh, as if in that closure there was something ridiculous.

Only once did we stop at the corner as if to take in its ugliness, now that it was without the old embellishments of the bar. Once, there had been tables and colored chairs, the fragrance of pastries and coffee, the coming and going of people, secret trafficking, honest deals and corrupt deals. Now there was the chipped gray wall. When the grandfather died, Lila said, after their mother's murder, Marcello and Michele carpeted the neighborhood with crosses and Madonnas, they made endless lamentations; now that they're dead, zero. Then she remembered when she was still in the clinic and I had told her that, according to the reticent words of the people, the bullets that killed the Solaras hadn't been fired by anyone. No one killed them—she smiled—no one weeps for them. And she stopped, and was silent for a few seconds. Then, without any obvious connection, she told me that she didn't want to work anymore.

16.

It didn't seem like a random manifestation of a bad mood, surely she had thought about it for a long time, maybe since she had left the clinic. She said:

"If Enzo can do it by himself, good, and if not we'll sell it."

"You want to give up Basic Sight? And what will you do?"

"Does a person necessarily have to do something?"

"You have to use your life."

"The way you do?"

"Why not?"

She laughed, she sighed:

"I want to waste time."

"You have Gennaro, you have Enzo, you have to think of them."

"Gennaro is twenty-three years old, I've been too taken up with him. And I have to separate Enzo from me."

"Why?"

"I want to go back to sleeping alone."

"It's terrible to sleep alone."

"You do, don't you?"

"I don't have a man."

"Why should I have one?"

"Aren't you fond of Enzo anymore?"

"Yes, but I have no desire for him or anyone. I'm old and no one should disturb me when I sleep."

"Go to a doctor."

"Enough with doctors."

"I'll go with you, those are problems that can be solved."

She became serious.

"No, I'm fine like this."

"No one is fine like this."

"I am. Fucking is very overrated."

"I'm talking about love."

"I have other things on my mind. You've already forgotten Tina, not me."

I heard Enzo and her arguing more frequently. Rather, in the case of Enzo, only his heavy voice reached me, slightly more emphatic than usual, while Lila did nothing but scream. Only a few phrases of his reached me upstairs, filtered through the floor. He wasn't angry—he was never angry with Lila—he was desperate. In essence he said that everything had gotten worse—Tina, the work, their relationship—but she wasn't doing anything to redefine the situation; rather she wanted everything to continue getting worse. You talk to us, he said to me once. I answered that it was no use, she just needed more time to find an equilibrium. Enzo, for the first time, replied roughly: Lina has never had any equilibrium.

It wasn't true. Lila, when she wanted, could be calm, thoughtful, even in that phase of great tension. She had good days, when she was serene and very affectionate. She took care of me and my daughters, she asked about my trips, about what I was writing, about the people I met. She followed—often with amusement, sometimes with indignation—the stories Dede, Elsa, even Imma told about school failures, crazy teachers, quarrels, loves. And she was generous. One afternoon, with Gennaro's help, she brought me up an old computer. She taught me how it worked and said: I'm giving it to you.

The next day I began writing on it. I got used to it quickly, even though I was obsessed by the fear that a power outage would sweep away hours of work. Otherwise I was excited about the machine. I told my daughters, in Lila's presence: Imagine, I learned to write with a fountain pen, then moved on to a ballpoint pen, then the typewriter—and also an electric typewriter—and finally here I am, I tap on the keys and this miraculous writing appears. It's absolutely beautiful, I'll never go back, I'm finished with the pen, I'll always write on the computer, come, touch the callus I have here on my index finger, feel how hard it is: I've always had it but now it will disappear.

Lila enjoyed my satisfaction, she had the expression of someone who is happy to have made a welcome gift. Your mother, however, she said, has the enthusiasm of someone who understands nothing, and she drew them away to let me work. Although she knew she had lost their confidence, when she was in a good mood she often took them to the office to teach them what the newest machines could do, and how and why. She said, to win them back: Signora Elena Greco, I don't know if you know her, has the attention of a hippopotamus sleeping in a swamp, whereas you girls are very quick. But she couldn't regain their affection, in particular Dede and Elsa's. The girls said to me: It's impossible to understand what she has in mind, Mamma, first she urges us to learn and then she says that these machines are useful for making a lot of money by destroying all the old ways of making money. Yet, while I knew how to use the computer only for writing, my daughters, and even Imma to a small extent, soon acquired knowledge and skills that made me proud. Whenever I had a problem I began to depend especially on Elsa, who always knew what to do and then boasted to Aunt Lina: I fixed it like this and like that, what do you say, was I clever?

Things went even better when Dede began to involve Rino. He, who had never even wanted to touch one of those objects of Enzo and Lila's, began to show some interest, if only not to be admonished by the girls. One morning Lila said to me, laughing:

"Dede is changing Gennaro."
I answered:
"Rino just needs some confidence."
She replied with ostentatious vulgarity:
"I know what kind of confidence he needs."

17.

Those were the good days. But soon the bad ones arrived: she was hot, she was cold, she turned yellow, then she flared up, she yelled, she demanded, she broke out in a sweat, then she quarreled with Carmen, whom she called stupid and whiny. After the operation her body seemed even more confused. Suddenly she put an end to the kindnesses; she found Elsa unbearable, reprimanded Dede, treated Imma harshly; while I was speaking to her she abruptly turned her back and went off. In those dark periods she couldn't stand to be in the house and had even less tolerance for the office. She took a bus or the subway and off she went.

"What are you doing?" I asked.
"I'm traveling around Naples."
"Yes, but where?"
"Do I have to account for myself to you?"

Any occasion could provide a pretext for a fight; it took nothing. She quarreled mainly with her son but ascribed the cause of their disagreements to Dede and Elsa. In fact she was right. My oldest daughter happily spent time with Rino, and now her sister, in order not to feel excluded, made an effort to accept him, and was often with them. The result was that both were inoculating him with a sort of permanent insubordination, an attitude that, while in their case was only a passionate verbal exercise, for Rino became confused and self-indulgent chatter that Lila couldn't bear. Those two girls, she scolded her son, put intelligence into it, you repeat nonsense like a parrot. In those days she was intolerant, she wouldn't accept clichéd phrases, maudlin expressions, any form of sentimentality, or, especially, the spirit of rebellion fed by old slogans. And yet at the opportune moment she herself displayed an affected anarchism that to me seemed out of place now. We confronted each other harshly when, at the approach of the electoral campaign of '87, we read that Nadia Galiani had been arrested in Chiasso.

Carmen hurried to my house in the grip of a panic attack, she couldn't think, she said: Now they'll seize Pasquale, you'll see, he escaped the Solaras but the carabinieri will murder him. Lila answered: The carabinieri didn't arrest Nadia, she turned herself in to bargain for a lighter sentence. That hypothesis seemed sensible to me. There were a few lines in the papers, but no talk of pursuits, shooting, capture. To soothe Carmen I again advised her: Pasquale would do well to turn himself in, you know what I think. All hell broke loose, Lila became furious, she began to shout:

"Turn himself over to whom."

"To the state."

"To the state?"

She made a concise list of thefts and criminal collaborations old and new by ministers, simple parliamentarians, policemen, judges, secret services from 1945 until then, showing herself as usual more informed than I could have imagined. And she yelled:

"*That* is the state, why the fuck do you want to give it Pasquale?" Then she pushed me: "Let's bet that Nadia does a few months in jail and comes out, while, if they get Pasquale, they'll lock him in a cell and throw away the key?" She was almost on top of me, repeating aggressively: "Do you want to bet?"

I didn't answer. I was worried, this sort of conversation

384 · ELENA FERRANTE

wasn't good for Carmen. After the death of the Solaras she had immediately withdrawn the lawsuit against me, she had done endless nice things for me, she was always available to my daughters, even if she was burdened by obligations and worries. I was sorry that instead of soothing her we were tormenting her. She was trembling, she said, addressing me but invoking Lila's authority: If Nadia turned herself in, Lenù, it means that she's repented, that now she's throwing all the blame on Pasquale and will get herself off. Isn't it true, Lina? But then she spoke bitterly to Lila, invoking my authority: It's no longer a matter of principle, Lina, we have to think of what's right for Pasquale, we have to let him know that it's better to live in prison than to be killed: isn't it true, Lenù?

At that point Lila insulted us grossly and, although we were in her house, went out, slamming the door.

18.

For Lila, going out, wandering around, was now the solution to all the tensions and problems she struggled with. Often she left in the morning and returned in the evening, paying no attention to Enzo, who didn't know how to deal with the clients, or to Rino, or to the commitments she made to me, when I had to travel and left her my daughters. She was now unreliable, all it took was some small setback and she dropped everything, without a thought of the consequences.

Carmen maintained that Lila took refuge in the old cemetery on the Doganella, where she chose the grave of a child to think about Tina, who had no grave, and then she walked along the shaded paths, amid plants, old niches, stopping in front of the most faded photographs. The dead—Carmen said to me—are a certainty, they have stones, the dates of birth and death, while her daughter doesn't, her daughter will remain forever with only the date of birth, and that is terrible, that poor child will never have a conclusion, a fixed point where her mother can sit and be tranquil. But Carmen had a propensity for fantasies about death and so I took no notice. I imagined that Lila walked through the city paying no attention to anything, only to numb the grief that after years continued to poison her. Or I hypothesized that she really had decided, in her way, extreme as always, not to devote herself anymore to anything or anyone. And since I knew that her mind needed exactly the opposite, I feared that she would have a nervous breakdown, that at the first opportunity she would let loose against Enzo, against Rino, against me, against my daughters, against a passerby who annoyed her, against anyone who gave her an extra glance. At home I could quarrel, calm her down, control her. But on the street? Every time she went out I was afraid she'd get in trouble. But frequently, when I had something to do and heard the door below close and her steps on the stairs, then out in the street, I drew a sigh of relief. She wouldn't come up to me, she wouldn't drop in with provocative words, she wouldn't taunt the girls, she wouldn't disparage Imma, she wouldn't try in every possible way to hurt me.

I went back to thinking insistently that it was time to leave. Now it was senseless for me, for Dede, for Elsa, for Imma to remain in the neighborhood. Lila herself, besides, after her stay in the hospital, after the operation, after the imbalances of her body, had begun to say more often what she first said sporadically: Go away, Lenù, what are you doing here, look at you, it's as if you're staying only because you made a vow to the Madonna. She wanted to remind me that I hadn't met her expectations, that my living in the neighborhood was only an intellectual pretense, that in fact for her, for the place where we were born—with all my studies, with all my books—I had been useless, I was useless. I was irritated and I thought: she treats me as if she wanted to fire me for poor performance.

19.

A period began in which I racked my brains constantly over what to do. My daughters needed stability and I had to work hard to get their fathers to attend to them. Nino remained the bigger problem. Occasionally he telephoned, said some sweet thing to Imma on the telephone, she responded in monosyllables, that was it. Recently he had made a move that was, all in all, predictable, considering his ambitions: during the elections he had appeared on the socialist party lists. For the occasion he had sent me a letter in which he asked me to vote for him and get people to vote. In the letter, which ended with *Tell Lina, too!* he had enclosed a flyer that included an attractive photograph of him and a biographical note. Underlined in pen was a line in which he declared to the electors that he had three children: Albertino, Lidia, and Imma. Next to it he had written: *Please read this to the child.*

I hadn't voted and I had done nothing to get people to vote for him, but I had shown the flyer to Imma and she had asked if she could keep it. When her father was elected I explained briefly the meaning of people, elections, representation, parliament. Now he lived permanently in Rome. After his electoral success he had been in touch only once, with a letter as hasty as it was self-satisfied, which he asked me to read to his daughter, Dede, and Elsa. No telephone number, no address, only words whose meaning was an offer of protection at a distance (*Be sure that I will watch over you*). But Imma also wanted to keep that testimony to her father's existence. And when Elsa said to her things like, You're boring, that's why you're called Sarratore and we're Airota, she seemed less disoriented—perhaps less worried—by having a surname that was different from that of her sisters. One day the teacher had asked her: Are you the daughter of the Honorable Sarratore, and the next day she had brought in as proof the flyer, which she kept for

any eventuality. I was pleased with that pride and planned to
try to consolidate it. Nino's life was, as usual, crowded and turbulent? All right. But his daughter wasn't a rosette to use and
then put back in the drawer until the next occasion.

With Pietro in recent years I had never had any problems.
He contributed money for his daughters' maintenance punctually (from Nino I had never received a lira) and was as far as
possible a conscientious father. But not long ago he had broken up with Doriana, he was tired of Florence, he wanted to
go to the United States. And, stubborn as he was, he would
manage it. That alarmed me. I said to him: You'll abandon
your daughters, and he replied: it seems a desertion now but
you'll see, soon it will be an advantage for them especially. He
was probably right, in that his words had something in common with Nino's (*Be sure that I will watch over you*). In fact,
however, Dede and Elsa, too, would remain without a father.
And if Imma had always done without, Dede and Elsa clung to
Pietro, they were used to having recourse to him when they
wanted. His departure would sadden and limit them, that I
was sure of. Of course they were old enough, Dede was eighteen, Elsa almost fifteen. They were in good schools, they both
had good teachers. But was it enough? They had never become
assimilated, neither of them had close schoolmates or friends,
they seemed comfortable only with Rino. And what did they
really have in common with that large boy who was much older
and yet more childish than they?

No, I had to leave Naples. I could try to live in Rome, for
example, and for Imma's sake resume relations with Nino, only
on the level of friendship, of course. Or return to Florence, so
that Pietro could be closer to his daughters, and thus would
not move across the ocean. The decision seemed particularly
urgent when one night Lila came upstairs with a quarrelsome
look, evidently in a bad mood, and asked me:

"Is it true that you told Dede to stop seeing Gennaro?"

I was embarrassed. I had only explained to my daughter that she shouldn't be stuck to him all the time.

"See him—she can see him when she wants: I'm only afraid that Gennaro might be annoyed, he's grown-up, she's a girl."

"Lenù, be clear. You think my son isn't good for your daughter?"

I stared at her in bewilderment.

"Good how?"

"You know perfectly well she's in love."

I burst out laughing.

"Dede? Rino?"

"Why, don't you think it's possible that your child has lost her head over mine?"

20.

Until that moment I had paid little attention to the fact that Dede, unlike her sister, who happily changed suitors every month, had never had a declared and ostentatious passion. I had attributed that withdrawn attitude partly to the fact that she didn't feel pretty, partly to her rigor, and from time to time I had teased her (*Are all the boys in your school unappealing?*). She was a girl who didn't forgive frivolity in anyone, above all in herself, but especially in me. The times she had seen me, I wouldn't say flirt but even just laugh with a man—or, I don't know, give a warm welcome to some boy who had brought her home—she made her disapproval clear and on one unpleasant occasion some months earlier had even gone so far as to use a vulgarity in dialect to me, which had made me furious.

But maybe it wasn't a question of a war on frivolity. After Lila's words I began to observe Dede and I realized that her protective attitude toward Lila's son could not be reduced, as I had thought until then, to a long childhood affection or a heated adolescent defense of the humiliated and offended. I realized, rather, that her asceticism was the effect of an intense and exclusive bond with Rino that had endured since early childhood. That frightened me. I thought of the long duration of my love for Nino and I said to myself in alarm: Dede is setting off on the same path, but with the aggravating factor that if Nino was an extraordinary boy and had become a handsome, intelligent, successful man, Rino is an insecure, uneducated youth, without attractions, without any future, and, if I thought about it, more than Stefano he physically recalled his grandfather, Don Achille.

I decided to speak to her. It was a few months until her final exams, she was very busy, it would be easy for her to say to me: I've got a lot to do, let's put it off. But Dede wasn't Elsa, who was able to reject me, who could pretend. With my oldest daughter it was enough to ask and I was sure that she, at any moment, whatever she was doing, would answer with the greatest frankness. I asked:

"Are you in love with Rino?"

"Yes."

"And he?"

"I don't know."

"Since when have you had that feeling?"

"Forever."

"But if he doesn't reciprocate?"

"My life would no longer have meaning."

"What are you thinking of doing?"

"I'll tell you after the exams."

"Tell me now."

"If he wants me we'll go away."

"Where?"

"I don't know, but certainly away from here."

"He also hates Naples?"

"Yes, he wants to go to Bologna."

390 · ELENA FERRANTE

"Why?"

"It's a place where there's freedom."

I looked at her with affection.

"Dede, you know that neither your father nor I will let you go."

"There's no need for you to let me go. I'm going and that's it."

"What about money?"

"I'll work."

"And your sisters? And me?"

"Some day or other, Mamma, we'll have to separate anyway."

I emerged from that conversation drained of strength. Although she had presented unreasonable things in an orderly fashion, I tried to behave as if she were saying very reasonable things.

Later, anxiously, I tried to think what to do. Dede was only an adolescent in love, one way or another I would make her obey. The problem was Lila, I was afraid of her, I knew immediately that the fight with her would be bitter. She had lost Tina, Rino was her only child. She and Enzo had gotten him away from drugs in time, using very harsh methods; she wouldn't accept that I, too, would cause him suffering. All the more since the company of my two daughters was doing him good; he was even working a little with Enzo, and it was possible that separating him from them would send him off the rails again. Besides, any possible regression of Rino worried me, too. I was fond of him, he had been an unhappy child and was an unhappy youth. Certainly he had always loved Dede, certainly giving her up would be unbearable for him. But what to do. I became more affectionate, I didn't want any misunderstandings: I valued him, I would always try to help him in everything, he had only to ask; but anyone could see that he and Dede were very different and that any solution they came up with would in a short time be disastrous. Thus I proceeded, and Rino became in turn kinder, he fixed broken blinds, dripping faucets, with the three sisters acting as helpers. But Lila didn't appreciate her son's availability. If he spent too much time at our house she summoned him with an imperious cry.

21.

I didn't confine myself to that strategy, I telephoned Pietro. He was about to move to Boston; now he seemed determined. He was mad at Doriana, who—he said with disgust—had turned out to be an untrustworthy person, completely without ethics. Then he listened to me attentively. He knew Rino, he remembered him as a child and knew what he had become as an adult. He asked a couple of times, to be sure of not making a mistake: He has no drug problems? And once only: Does he work? Finally he said: It's preposterous. We agreed that between the two of them, taking account of our daughter's sensitivity, even a flirtation had to be ruled out.

I was glad that we saw things the same way, I asked him to come to Naples and talk to Dede. He promised he would, but he had endless commitments and appeared only near Dede's exams, in essence to say goodbye to his daughters before leaving for America. We hadn't seen each other for a long time. He had his usual distracted expression. His hair was by now grizzled, his body had become heavier. He hadn't seen Lila and Enzo since Tina's disappearance—when he came to see the girls he would stay only a few hours or take them off on a trip—and he devoted himself to them. Pietro was a kind man, careful not to cause embarrassment with his role as a prestigious professor. He talked to them at length, assuming that serious and sympathetic expression that I knew well and that in the past had irritated me, but that today I appreciated because it wasn't feigned, and was natural also to Dede. I don't know what he said about Tina, but while Enzo remained impassive Lila cheered up, she thanked him for his wonderful letter of years earlier, said it had helped her a lot. Only then did I learn that Pietro had written to her about the loss of her daughter, and Lila's genuine gratitude surprised me. He was modest; she excluded Enzo from the conversation completely and began to speak to my ex-husband about Neapolitan things. She dwelt at length on the Palazzo Cellamare, about which I knew nothing except that it was above Chiaia, while she—I discovered then—knew in minute detail the structure, the history, the treasures. Pietro listened with interest. I fumed, I wanted him to stay with his daughters and, especially, deal with Dede.

When Lila finally left him free and Pietro, after spending some time with Elsa and Imma, found a way of going off with Dede, father and daughter talked a lot, peacefully. I observed them from the window as they walked back and forth along the *stradone*. It struck me, I think for the first time, how similar they were physically. Dede didn't have her father's bushy hair but she had his large frame and also something of his clumsy walk. She was a girl of eighteen, she had a feminine softness, but at every gesture, every step, she seemed to enter and exit Pietro's body as if it were her ideal dwelling. I stayed at the window hypnotized by the sight. The time extended, they talked so long that Elsa and Imma began to get restless. I also have things to tell Papa, said Elsa, and if he leaves when will I tell him? Imma murmured: He said he'd talk to me, too.

Finally Pietro and Dede returned, they seemed in a good mood. In the evening all three girls gathered around to listen to him. He said he was going to work in a very big, very beautiful redbrick building that had a statue at the entrance. The statue represented a man whose face and clothes were dark, except for one shoe, which the students touched every day for good luck and so it had become highly polished, and sparkled in the sun like gold. They had a good time together, leaving me out. I thought, as always on those occasions: now that he doesn't have to be a father every day he's a very good father, even Imma adores him; maybe with men things can't go otherwise: live with them for a while, have children, and then they're gone. The superficial ones, like Nino, would go without feeling any type of obligation; the serious ones, like Pietro, wouldn't fail in any of their duties and would if necessary give the best of themselves. Anyway, the time of faithfulness and permanent relationships was over for men and for women. But then why did we look at poor Gennaro, called Rino, as a threat? Dede would live her passion, would use it up, would go on her way. Every so often she would see him again, they would exchange some affectionate words. The process was that: why did I want something different for my daughter?

The question embarrassed me, I announced in my best authoritarian tone that it was time to go to bed. Elsa had just finished vowing that in a few years, once she got her high school diploma, she would go and live in the United States with her father, and Imma was tugging on Pietro's arm, she wanted attention, she was no doubt about to ask if she could join him, too. Dede sat in uncertain silence. Maybe, I thought, things are already resolved, Rino has been put aside, now she'll say to Elsa: You have to wait four years, I'm finishing high school now and in a month at most I'm going to Papa's.

22.

But as soon as Pietro and I were alone I had only to look at his face to understand that he was very worried. He said:

"There's nothing to do."

"What do you mean?"

"Dede functions by theorems."

"What did she tell you?"

"It's not important what she said but what she will certainly do."

"She'll go to bed with him?"

"Yes. She has a very firm plan, with the stages precisely marked out. Right after her exams she'll make a declaration to Rino, lose her virginity, they'll leave together and live by begging, putting the work ethic in crisis."

"Don't joke."

"I'm not joking, I'm reporting her plan to you word for word."

"Easy for you to be sarcastic, since you can avoid it, leaving the role of the bad mother to me."

"She's counting on me. She said that as soon as that boy wants, she'll come to Boston, with him."

"I'll break her legs."

"Or maybe he and she will break yours."

We talked into the night, at first about Dede, then also about Elsa and Imma, finally everything: politics, literature, the books I was writing, the newspaper articles, a new essay he was working on. We hadn't talked so much for a long time. He teased me good-humoredly for always taking, in his view, a middle position. He made fun of my halfway feminism, my halfway Marxism, my halfway Freudianism, my halfway Foucault-ism, my halfway subversiveness. Only with me, he said in a slightly harsher tone, you never used half measures. He sighed: Nothing was right for you, I was inadequate in everything. That other man was perfect. But now? He acted like the rigorous person and he ended up in the socialist gang. Elena, Elena, how you have tormented me. You were angry with me even when those kids pointed a gun at me. And you brought to our house your childhood friends who were murderers. You remember? But so what, you're Elena, I loved you so much, we have two children, and of course I still love you.

I let him talk. Then I admitted that I had often held senseless positions. I even admitted that he was right about Nino, he

had been a great disappointment. And I tried to return to
Dede and Rino. I was worried, I didn't know how to manage
the issue. I said that to keep the boy away from our daughter
would cause, among other things, trouble with Lila and that I
felt guilty, I knew she would consider it an insult. He nodded.

"You have to help her."

"I don't know how to."

"She's trying everything possible to engage her mind and
emerge from her grief, but she's unable to."

"It's not true, she did before, now she's not even working,
she's not doing anything."

"You're wrong."

Lila had told him that she spent entire days in the Biblioteca
Nazionale: she wanted to learn all she could about Naples. I
looked at him dubiously. Lila again in a library, not the neighborhood library of the fifties but the prestigious, inefficient
Biblioteca Nazionale? That's what she was doing when she disappeared from the neighborhood? That was her new mania?
And why had she not told me about it? Or had she told Pietro
just so that he would tell me?

"She hid it from you?"

"She'll talk to me about it when she needs to."

"Urge her to continue. It's unacceptable that a person so
gifted stopped school in fifth grade."

"Lila does only what she feels like."

"That's how you want to see her."

"I've known her since she was six."

"Maybe she hates you for that."

"She doesn't hate me."

"It's hard to observe every day that you are free and she has
remained a prisoner. If there's an inferno it's inside her unsatisfied mind, I wouldn't want to enter it even for a few seconds."

Pietro used precisely the phrase "enter it," and his tone was
of horror, of fascination, of pity. I repeated:

"Lina doesn't hate me at all."

He laughed.

"All right, as you like."

"Let's go to bed."

He looked at me uncertainly. I hadn't made up the cot as I usually did.

"Together?"

It was a dozen years since we had even touched each other. All night I was afraid that the girls would wake up and find us in the same bed. I lay looking in the shadowy light at that large, disheveled man, snoring faintly. Rarely, when we were married, had he slept with me for long. Usually he tormented me for a long time with his sex and his arduous orgasm, he fell asleep, then he got up and went to study. This time lovemaking was pleasant, a farewell embrace, we both knew it wouldn't happen again and so we felt good. From Doriana Pietro had learned what I had been unable or unwilling to teach him, and he did all he could so that I would notice.

Around six I woke him, I said: It's time for you to go. I went out to the car with him, he urged me yet again to look after the girls, especially Dede. We shook hands, we kissed each other on the cheeks, he left.

I walked idly to the newsstand, the news dealer was unpacking the papers. I went home with, as usual, three dailies, whose headlines I would look at but no more. I was making breakfast, I was thinking about Pietro, and our conversation. I could have lingered on any subject—his bland resentment, Dede, his somewhat facile psychologizing about Lila—and yet sometimes a mysterious connection is established between our mental circuits and the events whose echo is about to reach us. His description of Pasquale and Nadia—the childhood friends he had polemically alluded to—as murderers had stayed with me. To Nadia—I realized—I by now applied the word "murderer" naturally, to Pasquale, no, I continued to reject it. Yet again, I was asking myself why when the telephone rang. It was Lila calling from downstairs. She had heard me when I went out with Pietro and when I returned. She wanted to know if I had bought the papers. She had just heard on the radio that Pasquale had been arrested.

23.

That news absorbed us entirely for weeks, and I was more involved—I admit—in the story of our friend than in Dede's exams. Lila and I hurried to Carmen's house, but she already knew everything, or at least the essentials, and she appeared serene. Pasquale had been arrested in the mountains of Serino, in the Avellinese. The carabinieri had surrounded the farmhouse where he was hiding and he had behaved in a reasonable way, he hadn't reacted violently, he hadn't tried to escape. Now—Carmen said—I only have to hope that they don't let him die in prison the way Papa did. She continued to consider her brother a good person, in fact on the wave of her emotion she went so far as to say that the three of us—she, Lila, and I—carried within us a quantity of wickedness much greater than his. We have been capable of attending only to our own affairs—she murmured, bursting into tears—not Pasquale, Pasquale grew up as our father taught him.

Owing to the genuine suffering in those words, Carmen managed, perhaps for the first time since we had known one another, to have the better of Lila and me. For example, Lila didn't make objections, and, as for me, I felt uneasy at her speech. The Peluso siblings, by their mere existence in the background of my life, confused me. I absolutely ruled out that their father the carpenter had taught them, as Franco had done with Dede, to challenge the silly moral fable of Menenius Agrippa, but both—Carmen less, Pasquale more—had always known instinctively that the limbs of a man are not nourished when he fills the belly of another, and that those who would make you believe it should sooner or later get what they deserve. Although they were different in every way, with their history they formed a block that I couldn't relate to me or to Lila, but that I couldn't distance us from, either. So maybe one day I said to Carmen: You should be happy, now that Pasquale is in the hands of the law we can understand better how to help him; and the next day I said to Lila, in complete agreement with her: Laws and guarantees count for nothing, whereas they should protect those who have no power—in prison they'll kill him. At times, I even admitted, with the two of them, that, although the violence we had experienced from birth now disgusted me, a modest amount was needed to confront the fierce world we lived in. Along those confusing lines I undertook to do everything possible for Pasquale. I didn't want him to feel—unlike his companion Nadia, who was treated with great consideration—like a nobody whom nobody cared about.

24.

I looked for reliable lawyers, I even decided, through telephone calls, to track down Nino, the only member of parliament I knew personally. I never managed to speak to him but a secretary, after lengthy negotiations, made an appointment for me. Tell him—I said coldly—that I'll bring our daughter. At the other end of the line there was a long moment of hesitation. I'll let him know, the woman said finally.

A few minutes later the telephone rang. It was the secretary again: the Honorable Sarratore would be very happy to meet us in his office in Piazza Risorgimento. But in the following days the place and hour of the appointment changed continuously: the Honorable had left, the Honorable had returned but was busy, the Honorable had an interminable sitting in parliament. I marveled at how difficult it was to have direct contact—in spite of my modest fame, in spite of my journalist's credentials, in spite of the fact that I was the mother of his child—with a representative of the people. When everything was finally set— the location was nothing less than Montecitorio, the parliament itself—Imma and I got dressed up and left for Rome. She asked if she could take her precious electoral flyer, I said yes. In the train she kept looking at it, as if to prepare for a comparison between the photograph and the reality. In the capital, we took a taxi, we presented ourselves at Montecitorio. At every obstacle I showed our papers and said, mainly so that Imma could hear: We're expected by the Honorable Sarratore, this is his daughter Imma, Imma Sarratore.

We waited a long time, the child at one point said, in the grip of anxiety: What if the people hold him up? I reassured her: They won't hold him up. Nino finally arrived, preceded by the secretary, a very attractive young woman. Well dressed, radiant, he hugged and kissed his daughter rapturously, picked her up and held her the whole time, as if she were still little. But what surprised me was the immediate assurance with which Imma clung to his neck and said to him happily, unfolding the leaflet: You're handsomer than in this photo, you know my teacher voted for you?

Nino was very attentive to her; he had her tell him about school, about her friends, about the subjects she liked best. He paid only the slightest attention to me, by now I belonged to another life—an inferior life—and it seemed pointless to waste his energies. I talked about Pasquale, he listened, but without neglecting his daughter, and nodded at the secretary to take notes. At the end of my account he asked seriously:

"What do you expect from me?"

"To find out if he's in good health and is getting the full protection of the law."

"Is he cooperating with the law?"

"No, and I doubt that he ever will."

"He'd be better off."

"Like Nadia?"

He gave a small, embarrassed laugh.

"Nadia is behaving in the only way possible, if she doesn't intend to spend the rest of her life in jail."

"Nadia is a spoiled girl, Pasquale isn't."

He didn't answer right away, he pressed Imma's nose as if it were a button and imitated the sound of a bell. They laughed together and then he said:

"I'll see what your friend's situation is, I'm here to be sure that the rights of everyone are protected. But I'll tell him that the relatives of the people he killed also have rights. You don't play at being a rebel, shed real blood, and then cry: we have rights. Do you understand, Imma?"

"Yes."

"Yes, Papa."

"Yes, Papa."

"And if the teacher mistreats you, call me."

I said:

"If the teacher mistreats her, she'll manage by herself."

"The way Pasquale Peluso managed?"

"Pasquale never asked anyone to protect him."

"And that vindicates him?"

"No, but it's significant that if Imma has to assert her right you tell her: call me."

"For your friend Pasquale aren't you calling me?"

I left very nervous and unhappy, but for Imma it was the most important day of her first seven years of life.

The days passed. I thought it had been a waste of time, but in fact Nino kept his word, he looked into Pasquale's situation. It was from him I learned, later, things that the lawyers either didn't know or didn't tell us about. The involvement of our friend in some notorious political crimes that had afflicted Campania was at the center of Nadia's detailed confession, but this had also been common knowledge for some time. The new information, instead, was that she now tended to ascribe everything to him, even acts of minor interest. Thus the long list of Pasquale's crimes included mentions of the murder of Gino, of Bruno Soccavo, the death of Manuela Solara, and, finally, that of her sons, Marcello and Michele.

"What agreement did your old girlfriend make with the carabinieri?" I asked Nino the last time I saw him.

"I don't know."

"Nadia is telling a pile of lies."

"I don't rule it out. But one thing I know for sure: she is ruining a lot of people who thought they were safe. So tell Lina to be careful, Nadia has always hated her."

25.

So many years had passed, and yet Nino didn't miss a chance to mention Lila, to show that he was solicitous of her even at a distance. I was there with him, I had loved him, I had beside me his daughter who was licking a chocolate ice-cream cone. But he considered me only a friend of his youth to whom he could show off the extraordinary path he had traveled, from his high school desk to a seat in parliament. In that last encounter of ours his greatest compliment was to put me on the same rung of the ladder. I don't remember in relation to what subject he said: The two of us climbed very high. But even as he uttered that sentence I read in his gaze that the declaration of equality was a sham. He considered himself much better than me and the proof was that, in spite of my successful books, I stood before him as a petitioner. His eyes smiled at me cordially, suggesting: Look what you lost by losing me.

I left in a hurry with the child. I was sure that he would have had quite a different attitude if Lila had been present. He would have mumbled, he would have felt mysteriously crushed, maybe even a little ridiculous with that preening. When we reached the garage where I had left the car—that time I had come to Rome by car—something occurred to me for the first time: only with Lila had Nino put at risk his own ambitions. On Ischia, and for the following year, he had given in to a romance that could have caused him nothing but trouble. An anomaly, in the journey of his life. At the time he was already a well-known and very promising university student. He had taken up with Nadia—that was clear to me now—because she was the daughter of Professor Galiani, because he had considered her the key to gaining access to what then appeared to us a superior class. His choices had always been consistent with his ambitions. Hadn't he married Eleonora out of self-interest? And I myself, when I had left Pietro for him, wasn't I in fact a well-connected woman, a writer of some success, with ties to an important publishing house—useful, in short, to his career? And all the other women who had helped him: didn't they come under the same logic? Nino loved women, certainly, but he was above all a cultivator of useful relations. What his intelligence produced would never, alone, have had sufficient energy to assert itself, without the web of power that he had been weaving since he was a boy. What about Lila? She had gone to school up to fifth grade, she was the very young wife of a shopkeeper, if Stefano had known of their relationship he could have killed them both. Why had Nino in that case gambled his entire future?

I put Imma in the car, I scolded her for letting the ice cream drip on the dress bought for the occasion. I started the car, I left Rome. Maybe what had attracted Nino was the impression of having found in Lila what he, too, presumed he had and that now, just by comparison, he discovered that he didn't have.

She possessed intelligence and didn't put it to use but, rather, wasted it, like a great lady for whom all the riches of the world are merely a sign of vulgarity. That was the fact that must have beguiled Nino: the gratuitousness of Lila's intelligence. *She stood out among so many because she, naturally, did not submit to any training, to any use, or to any purpose.* All of us had submitted and that submission had—through trials, failures, successes—reduced us. Only Lila, nothing and no one seemed to reduce her. Rather, even if over the years she became as stupid and intractable as anyone, the qualities that we had attributed to her would remain intact, maybe they would be magnified. Even when we hated her we ended by respecting her and fearing her. It didn't surprise me, when I thought about it, that Nadia, although she had met Lila only a few times, detested her and wanted to hurt her. Lila had taken Nino from her. Lila had humiliated her in her revolutionary beliefs. Lila was mean and could hit before being hit. Lila was from the proletariat but rejected any deliverance. In other words Lila was an honorable enemy and hurting her could be pure satisfaction, without the store of guilt that a designated victim like Pasquale would certainly arouse. Nadia could truly think of her in that way. How tawdry everything had become over the years: Professor Galiani, her house with a view of the bay, her thousands of books, her paintings, her cultured conversations, Armando, Nadia herself. She was so pretty, so well brought up, when I saw her beside Nino, outside the school, when she welcomed me to the party at her parents' beautiful house. And there was still something incomparable about her when she stripped herself of every privilege with the idea that, in a radically new world, she would have a more dazzling garment. But now? The noble reasons for that denuding had all dissolved. There remained the horror of so much blood stupidly shed and the villainy of unloading the blame on the former bricklayer, who had once seemed to her the avant-garde of a new humanity, and who now, along with so many others, served to reduce her own responsibilities almost to nothing.

I was upset. As I drove toward Naples I thought of Dede. I felt she was close to making a mistake similar to Nadia's, similar to all mistakes that take you away from yourself. It was the end of July. The day before Dede had got the highest grades on her graduation exam. She was an Airota, she was my daughter, her brilliant intelligence could only produce the best results. Soon she would be able to do much better than I had and even than her father. What I had gained by hard work and much luck, she had taken, and would continue to take, with ease, as if by birthright. Instead, what was her plan? To declare her love for Rino. To sink with him, to rid herself of every advantage, lose herself out of a spirit of solidarity and justice, out of fascination with what doesn't resemble us, because in the muttering of that boy she saw some sort of extraordinary mind. I asked Imma suddenly, looking at her in the rearview mirror:

"Do you like Rino?"

"No, but Dede likes him."

"How do you know?"

"Elsa told me."

"And who told Elsa?"

"Dede."

"Why don't you like Rino?"

"Because he's very ugly."

"And who do you like?"

"Papa."

I saw in her eyes the flame that in that moment she saw blazing around her father. A light—I thought—that Nino would never have had if he had sunk with Lila; the same light that Nadia had lost forever, sinking with Pasquale; and that would abandon Dede if she were lost following Rino. Suddenly I felt with shame that I could understand, and excuse, the irritation of Professor Galiani when she saw her daughter on

Pasquale's knees, I understood and excused Nino when, one way or another, he withdrew from Lila, and, why not, I understood and excused Adele when she had had to make the best of things and accept that I would marry her son.

26.

As soon as I was back in the neighborhood I rang Lila's bell. I found her listless, absent, but now it was typical of her and I wasn't worried. I told her in detail what Nino had said and only at the end did I report that threatening phrase that concerned her. I asked:

"Seriously, can Nadia hurt you?"

She assumed a look of nonchalance.

"You can be hurt only if you love someone. But I don't love anyone."

"And Rino?"

"Rino's gone."

I immediately thought of Dede and her intentions. I was frightened.

"Where?"

She took a piece of paper from the table, she handed it to me, muttering:

"He wrote so well as a child and now look, he's illiterate."

I read the note. Rino, very laboriously, said he was tired of everything, insulted Enzo heavily, announced that he had gone to Bologna to a friend he had met during his military service. Six lines in all. No mention of Dede. My heart was pounding in my chest. That writing, that spelling, that syntax, what did they have to do with my daughter? Even his mother considered him a failed promise, a defeat, perhaps even a prophecy: look what would have happened to Tina if they hadn't taken her.

"He left by himself?" I asked.

"Who would he have left with?"

I shook my head uncertainly. She read in my eyes the reason for my concern, she smiled:

"You're afraid he left with Dede?"

27.

I hurried home, trailed by Imma. I went in, I called Dede, I called Elsa. No answer. I rushed into the room where my older daughters slept and studied. I found Dede lying on the bed, her eyes burning with tears. I felt relieved. I thought that she had told Rino of her love and that he had rejected her.

I didn't have time to speak: Imma, maybe because she hadn't realized her sister's state, began talking enthusiastically about her father, but Dede rebuffed her with an insult in dialect, then sat up and burst into tears. I nodded to Imma not to get mad, I said to my oldest daughter gently: I know it's terrible, I know very well, but it will pass. The reaction was violent. As I was caressing her hair she pulled away with an abrupt movement of her head, crying: What are you talking about, you don't know anything, you don't understand anything, all you think about is yourself and the crap you write. Then she handed me a piece of graph paper—rather—she threw it in my face and ran away.

Once Imma realized that her sister was desperate, her eyes began to tear up in turn. I whispered, to keep her occupied: Call Elsa, see where she is, and I picked up the piece of paper. It was a day of notes. I immediately recognized the fine handwriting of my second daughter. Elsa had written at length to Dede. She explained to her that one can't control feelings, that Rino had loved her for a long time and that little by little she, too, had fallen in love. She knew, of course, that she was causing her pain and she was sorry, but she also knew that a possible renunciation of the loved person would not fix things. Then she addressed me in an almost amused tone. She wrote that she had decided to give up school, that my cult of study had always seemed to her foolish, that it wasn't books that made people good but good people who made some good books. She emphasized that Rino was good, and yet he had never read a book; she emphasized that her father was good and had made very good books. The connection between books, people, and goodness ended there: I wasn't cited. She said goodbye with affection and told me not to be too angry: Dede and Imma would give me the satisfactions that she no longer felt able to give me. To her younger sister she dedicated a little heart with wings.

I turned into a fury. I was angry with Dede, who hadn't realized how her sister, as usual, intended to steal what she valued. You should have known, I scolded her, you should have stopped her, you're so intelligent and you let yourself be tricked by a vain sly girl. Then I ran downstairs, I said to Lila:

"Your son didn't go alone, your son took Elsa with him."

She looked at me, disoriented:

"Elsa?"

"Yes. And Elsa is a minor. Rino is nine years older, I swear to God I'll go to the police and report him."

She burst out laughing. It wasn't a mean laugh but incredulous. She laughed and said, alluding to her son:

"But look how much damage he was able to do, I underrated him. He made both young ladies lose their heads, I can't believe it. Lenù, come here, calm down, sit down. If you think about it, there's more to laugh at than cry about."

I said in dialect that I found nothing to laugh at, that what Rino had done was very serious, that I really was about to go to the police. Then she changed her tone, she pointed to the door, she said:

"Go to the cops, go on, what are you waiting for?"

I left, but for the moment I gave up the idea of the police. I went home, taking the steps two at a time. I shouted at Dede: I want to know where the fuck they went, tell me immediately. She was frightened, Imma put her hands over her ears, but I wouldn't calm down until Dede admitted that Elsa had met Rino's Bolognese friend once when he came to the neighborhood.

"Do you know his name?"

"Yes."

"Do you have the address, the phone number?"

She trembled, she was on the point of giving me the information I wanted. Then, although by now she hated her sister even more than Rino, she must have thought it would be shameful to collaborate and was silent. I'll find it myself, I cried, and began to turn her things upside down. I rummaged through the whole house. Then I stopped. While I was looking for yet another piece of paper, a note in a school diary, I realized that a lot else was missing. All the money was gone from the drawer where I normally kept it, and all my jewelry was gone, even my mother's bracelet. Elsa had always been very fond of that bracelet. She said, partly joking and partly serious, that her grandmother, if she had made a will, would have left it to her and not to me.

28.

That discovery made me even more determined, and Dede finally gave me the address and telephone number I was looking for. When she made up her mind, despising herself for giving in, she shouted at me that I was just like Elsa, we didn't respect anything or anyone. I silenced her and went to the telephone. Rino's friend was called Moreno, I threatened him. I told him that I knew he sold heroin, that I would get him in such deep trouble that he would never get out of jail. I got nothing. He swore that he didn't know anything about Rino, that he remembered Dede, but that this daughter I was talking about, Elsa, he had never met.

I went back to Lila. She opened the door, but now Enzo was there, who made me sit down, and treated me kindly. I said I wanted to go to Bologna right away, I ordered Lila to go with me.

"There's no need," she said, "you'll see that when they run out of money they'll be back."

"How much money did Rino take?"

"Nothing. He knows that if he touches even ten lire I'll break his bones."

I felt humiliated. I muttered:

"Elsa took my money and my jewelry."

"Because you didn't know how to bring her up."

Enzo said to her:

"Stop it."

She turned against him sharply:

"I say what I like. My son is a drug addict, my son didn't study, my son speaks and writes poorly, my son is a good-for-nothing, my son has all the sins. But the one who steals is her daughter, the one who betrays her sister is Elsa."

Enzo said to me:

"Let's go, I'll go with you to Bologna."

We left in the car, we traveled at night. I had scarcely returned from Rome, the trip in the car had tired me. The sorrow and the fury that had arisen had absorbed all my remaining forces and now that the tension was easing I felt exhausted. Sitting next to Enzo, as we left Naples and got on the highway, what took hold was anxiety for the state in which I had left Dede, fear for what could happen to Elsa, some shame for the way I had frightened Imma, the way I had spoken to Lila, forgetting that Rino was her only child. I didn't know whether to telephone Pietro in America and tell him to come back right away, I didn't know if I really should go to the police. "We'll solve it ourselves," Enzo said, feigning confidence. "Don't worry, it's pointless to hurt the boy."

"I don't want to report Rino," I said. "I just want them to find Elsa."

It was true. I muttered that I wanted to recover my daughter, go home, pack my bags, not remain a minute longer in that house, in the neighborhood, in Naples. It makes no sense, I said, that now Lila and I start fighting about who brought up her children better, and if what happened is her fault or mine— I can't bear it.

Enzo listened to me at length, in silence, then, although I felt he had been angry at Lila for a long time, he began to make excuses for her. He didn't speak about Rino, about the problems he caused his mother, but about Tina. He said: If a being a few years old dies, she's dead, it's over, sooner or later you resign yourself. But if she disappears, if you no longer know anything about her, there's not a thing that remains in her place, in your life. Will Tina never return or will she return? And when she returns, will she be alive or dead? Every moment—he murmured—you're asking where she is. Is she a Gypsy on the street? Is she at home with rich people who have no children? Are people making her do horrible things and selling the photographs and films? Did they cut her up and sell her heart for a high price so it could be transplanted to another child's chest? Are the other pieces underground, or were they burned? Or is she under the ground intact, because she died accidentally after she was abducted? And if earth and fire didn't take her, and she is growing up who knows where, what does she look like now, what will she become later, if we meet her on the street will we recognize her? And if we recognize her who will give us back everything we lost of her, everything that happened when we weren't there and little Tina felt abandoned?

At a certain point, while Enzo spoke in his laborious but dense sentences, I saw his tears in the glow of the headlights, I knew he wasn't talking only about Lila but was trying to express his own suffering as well. That trip with him was important; I still find it hard to imagine a man with a finer sensibility than his. At first he told me what, every day, every night in those four years Lila had whispered or shouted. Then he urged me to talk about my work and my dissatisfactions. I told him about the girls, about books, about men, about resentments, about the need for approval. And I mentioned all my writing, which now had become obligatory, I struggled day and night to feel myself present, to not let myself be marginalized, to fight against those who considered me an upstart little woman without talent: persecutors—I muttered—whose only purpose is to make me lose my audience, and not because they're inspired by any elevated motives but, rather, for the enjoyment of keeping me from improvement, or to carve out for themselves or for their protégés some wretched power harmful to me. He let me vent, he praised the energy I put into things. You see—he said—how excited you get. The effort has anchored you to the world you've chosen, it's given you broad and detailed expertise in it, above all it has engaged your feelings. So life has dragged you along, and Tina, for you, is certainly an atrocious episode, thinking about it makes you sad, but it's also, by now, a distant fact. For Lila, on the other hand, in all these years, the world collapsed as if it were hearsay, and slid into the void left by her daughter, like the rain that rushes down a drainpipe. She remains frozen at Tina, and feels bitter toward everything that continues to be alive, that grows and prospers. Of course, he said, she is strong, she treats me terribly, she gets angry with you, she says ugly things. But you don't know how many times she has fainted just when she seemed tranquil, washing the dishes or staring out the window at the *stradone*.

29.

In Bologna we found no trace of Rino and my daughter, even though Moreno, frightened by Enzo's fierce calm, dragged us through streets and hangouts where, according to him, if they were in the city, the two would certainly have been welcomed. Enzo telephoned Lila often, I Dede. We hoped that there would be good news, but there wasn't. At that point I was seized by a new crisis, I no longer knew what to do. I said again:

"I'm going to the police."

Enzo shook his head.

"Wait a little."

"Rino has ruined Elsa."

"You can't say that. You have to try to look at your daughters as they really are."

"It's what I do continuously."

"Yes, but you don't do it well. Elsa would do anything to make Dede suffer and they are in agreement on a single point: tormenting Imma."

"Don't make me say mean things: it's Lila who sees them like that and you're repeating what she says."

"Lila loves you, admires you, is fond of your daughters. It's me who thinks these things, and I'm saying them to help you be reasonable. Calm down, you'll see, we'll find them."

We didn't find them, we decided to return to Naples. But as we were nearing Florence Enzo wanted to call Lila again to find out if there was any news. When he hung up he said, bewildered:

"Dede needs to talk to you but Lina doesn't know why."

"Is she at your house?"

"No, she's at yours."

I called immediately, I was afraid that Imma was sick. Dede didn't even give me a chance to speak, she said:

"I'm leaving tomorrow for the United States, I'm going to study there."

I tried not to shout:

"Now is not the moment for that conversation, as soon as possible we'll talk about it with Papa."

"One thing has to be clear, Mamma: Elsa will return to this house only when I am gone."

"For now the most urgent thing is to find out where she is."

She cried to me in dialect:

"That bitch telephoned a little while ago, she's at Grandma's."

30.

The grandma was, of course, Adele; I called my in-laws. Guido answered coldly and put his wife on. Adele was cordial, she told me that Elsa was there and added, Not only her.

"The boy's there, too?"

"Yes."

"Would you mind if I came to you?"

"We're expecting you."

I had Enzo leave me at the station in Florence. The journey was complicated, with delays, waits, annoyances of every type. I thought about how Elsa, with her sly capriciousness, had ended up involving Adele. If Dede was incapable of deception, Elsa was at her best when it came to inventing strategies that could protect her and perhaps let her win. She had planned, it was clear, to impose Rino on me in the presence of her grandmother, a person who—she and her sister knew well—had been very unwilling to accept me as a daughter-in-law. For the entire journey I felt relieved because I knew she was safe and hated her for the situation she was putting me in.

I arrived in Genoa ready for a hard battle. But I found Adele very welcoming and Guido polite. As for Elsa—dressed for a party, heavily made up, on her wrist my mother's bracelet, and on full display the ring that years earlier her father had given me—she was affectionate and relaxed, as if she found it inconceivable that I could be mad at her. The only silent one, eyes perpetually downcast, was Rino, so that I felt sorry for him and ended up more hostile toward my daughter than toward him. Maybe Enzo was right, the boy had had scant importance in that story. Of his mother's hardness, her insolence, he had no trace, it was Elsa who had dragged him along, beguiling him, and only to hurt Dede. The rare times he had the courage to look at me his glances were those of a faithful dog.

I quickly understood that Adele had received Elsa and Rino as a couple: they had their own room, their own towels, they slept together. Elsa had no trouble flaunting that intimacy authorized by her grandmother, maybe she even accentuated it for me. When the two withdrew after dinner, holding hands, my mother-in-law tried to push me to confess my aversion for Rino. She's a child, she said at a certain point, I really don't know what she sees in that young man, she has to be helped to get out of it. I tried, I said: He's a good kid, but even if he weren't, she's in love and there's little to be done. I thanked her for welcoming them with affection and broad-mindedness, and went to bed.

But I spent the whole night thinking about the situation. If I said the wrong thing, even just a wrong word, I would probably ruin both my daughters. I couldn't make a clean break between Elsa and Rino. I couldn't oblige the two sisters to live together at that impossible moment: what had happened was serious and for a while the two girls couldn't be under the same roof. To think of moving to another city would only complicate things, Elsa would make it her duty to stay with Rino. I quickly realized that if I wanted to take Elsa home and get her to graduate from high school I would have to lose Dede—actually send her to live with her father. So the next day, instructed by Adele about the best time to call (she and her son—I discovered—talked to each other constantly), I talked to Pietro. His mother had informed him in detail about what had happened and from his bad mood I deduced that Adele's true feelings were certainly not what she showed me. Pietro said gravely:

"We have to try to understand what sort of parents we've been and how we've failed our daughters."

"Are you saying that I haven't been and am not a good mother?"

"I'm saying that there's a need for continuity of affection and that neither you nor I have been able to insure that Dede and Elsa have that."

I interrupted him, announcing that he would have a chance to be a full-time father to at least one of the girls: Dede wanted to go and live with him immediately, she would leave as soon as possible.

He didn't take the news well, he was silent, he prevaricated, he said he was still adapting and needed time. I answered: You know Dede, you're identical, even if you tell her no you'll find her there.

The same day, as soon as I had a chance to talk to Elsa alone, I confronted her, ignoring her blandishments. I had her give back the money, the jewelry, my mother's bracelet, which I immediately put on, stating: You must never touch my things again.

She was conciliatory, I wasn't, I hissed that I wouldn't hesitate for a moment to report first of all Rino, and then her. As soon as she tried to answer I pushed her against a wall, I raised my hand to hit her. I must have had a terrible expression, she burst into terrified tears.

"I hate you," she sobbed. "I don't ever want to see you again, I will never go back to that shitty place where you made us live."

"All right, I'll leave you here for the summer, if your grandparents don't kick you out first."

"And then?"

"Then in September you'll come home, you'll go to school, you'll study, you'll live with Rino in our apartment until you've had enough of him."

She stared at me, stunned; there was a long instant of incredulity. I had uttered those words as if they contained the most terrible punishment, she took them as a surprising gesture of generosity.

"Really?"

"Yes."

"I'll never have enough of him."

"We'll see."

"And Aunt Lina?"

"Aunt Lina will agree."

"I didn't want to hurt Dede, Mamma, I love Rino, it happened."

"It will happen countless more times."

"It's not true."

"Worse for you. It means you'll love Rino your whole life."

"You're making fun of me."

I said no, I felt only all the absurdity of that verb in the mouth of a child.

31.

I returned to the neighborhood, I told Lila what I had proposed to the children. It was a cold exchange, almost a negotiation.

"You'll have them in your house?"

"Yes."

"If it's all right with you, it's all right with me, too."

"We'll split the expenses."

"I can pay it all."

"For now I have money."

"For now I do, too."

"We're agreed, then."

"How did Dede take it?"

"Fine. She's leaving in a couple of weeks, she's going to visit her father."

"Tell her to come and say goodbye."

"I don't think she will."

"Then tell her to say hello to Pietro for me."

"I'll do that."

Suddenly I felt a great sorrow, I said:

"In just a few days I've lost two daughters."

"Don't use that expression: you haven't lost anything, rather you've gained a son."

"It's you who pushed him in that direction."

She wrinkled her forehead, she seemed confused.

"I don't know what you're talking about."

"You always have to incite, shove, poke."

"Now you want to get mad at me, too, for what your children get up to?"

I muttered, I'm tired, and left.

For days, for weeks, in fact, I couldn't stop thinking that Lila couldn't bear the equilibrium in my life and so aimed at disrupting it. It had always been so, but after Tina's disappearance it had worsened: she made a move, observed the consequences, made another move. The objective? Maybe not even she knew. Of course the relationship of the two sisters was ruined, Elsa was in terrible trouble, Dede was leaving, I would remain in the neighborhood for an indeterminate amount of time.

32.

I was preoccupied with Dede's departure. Occasionally I said to her: Stay, you're making me very unhappy. She answered: You have so many things to do, you won't even notice I'm gone. I insisted: Imma adores you and so does Elsa, you'll clear things up, it will pass. But Dede didn't want to hear her sister's name, as soon as I mentioned it she assumed an expression of disgust and went out, slamming the door.

A few nights before her departure she suddenly grew very pale—we were having dinner—and began to tremble. She muttered: I can't breathe. Imma quickly poured her a glass of water. Dede took a sip, then left her place and came to sit on my lap. It was something she had never done. She was big, taller than me, she had long since cut off even the slightest contact between our bodies; if by chance we touched she sprang back as if by a force of repulsion. Her weight surprised me, her warmth, her full hips. I held her around the waist, she put her arms around my neck, she wept with deep sobs. Imma left her place at the table, came over and tried to be included in the embrace. She must have thought that her sister wouldn't leave, and for the next days she was happy, she behaved as if everything had been put right. But Dede did leave; rather, after that breakdown she seemed tougher and more determined. With Imma she was affectionate, she kissed her hundreds of times, she said: I want at least one letter a week. She let me hug and kiss her, but without returning it. I hovered around her, I struggled to predict her every desire, it was useless. When I complained of her coldness she said: It's impossible to have a real relationship with you, the only things that count are work and Aunt Lina; there's nothing that's not swallowed up inside them, the real punishment, for Elsa, is to stay here. Bye, Mamma.

On the positive side there was only the fact that she had gone back to calling her sister by name.

33.

When, in early September of 1988, Elsa returned home, I hoped that her liveliness would drive out the impression that

Lila really had managed to pull me down into her void. But it wasn't so. Rino's presence in the house, instead of giving new life to the rooms, made them bleak. He was an affectionate youth, completely submissive to Elsa and Imma, who treated him like their servant. I myself, I have to say, got into the habit of entrusting to him endless boring tasks—mainly the long lines at the post office—which left me more time to work. But it depressed me to see that big slow body around, available at the slightest nod and yet moping, always obedient except when it came to basic rules like remembering to raise the toilet seat when he peed, leaving the bathtub clean, not leaving his dirty socks and underwear on the floor.

Elsa didn't lift a finger to improve the situation, rather she purposely complicated it. I didn't like her coy ways with Rino in front of Imma, I hated her performance as an uninhibited woman when in fact she was a girl of fifteen. Above all I couldn't bear the state in which she left the room where once she had slept with Dede and which now she occupied with Rino. She got out of bed, sleepily, to go to school, had breakfast quickly, slipped away. After a while Rino appeared, ate for an hour, shut himself in the bathroom for at least another half hour, got dressed, hung around, went out, picked up Elsa at school. When they got back they ate cheerfully and immediately shut themselves in the room.

That room was like a crime scene, Elsa didn't want me to touch anything. But neither of them bothered to open the windows or tidy up a little. I did it before Pinuccia arrived; it annoyed me that she would smell the odor of sex, that she would find traces of their relations.

Pinuccia didn't like the situation. When it came to dresses, shoes, makeup, hairstyles, she admired what she called my modernity, but in this case she let me understand quickly and in every possible way that I had made a decision that was too modern, an opinion that must have been widespread in the neighborhood. It was very unpleasant, one morning, to find her there, as I was trying to work, with a newspaper on which lay a condom, knotted so that the semen wouldn't spill. I found it at the foot of the bed, she said disgusted. I pretended it was nothing. There's no need to show it to me, I remarked, continuing to type on the computer, there's the wastebasket for that.

In reality I didn't know how to behave. At first I thought that over time everything would improve. Every day there were clashes with Elsa, but I tried not to overdo it; I still felt wounded by Dede's departure and didn't want to lose her as well. So I went more and more often to Lila to say to her: Tell Rino, he's a good boy, try to explain that he has to be a little neater. But she seemed just to be waiting for my complaints to pick a quarrel.

"Send him back here," she raged one morning, "enough of that nonsense of staying at your house. Rather, let's do this: there's room, when your daughter wants to see him she comes down, knocks, and sleeps here if she wants."

I was annoyed. My child had to knock and ask if she could sleep with hers? I muttered:

"No, it's fine like this."

"If it's fine like this, what are we talking about?"

I fumed.

"Lila, I'm just asking you to talk to Rino: he's twenty-four years old, tell him to behave like an adult. I don't want to be quarreling with Elsa continuously, I'm in danger of losing my temper and driving her out of the house."

"Then the problem is your child, not mine."

On those occasions the tension rose rapidly but had no outlet; she was sarcastic, I went home frustrated. One evening we were having dinner when, from the stairs, her intransigent cry reached us, she wanted Rino to come to her immediately. He got agitated, Elsa offered to go with him. But as soon as Lila saw her she said: This is our business, go home. My daughter returned sullenly and meanwhile downstairs a violent quarrel erupted. Lila shouted, Enzo shouted, Rino shouted. I suffered for Elsa, who was anxiously wringing her hands, she said: Mamma, do something, what's happening, why do they treat him like that?

I said nothing, I did nothing. The quarrel stopped, some time passed, Rino didn't return. Elsa then insisted that I go see what had happened. I went down and Enzo, not Lila, opened the door. He was tired, depressed, he didn't invite me to come in. He said:

"Lila told me that the boy doesn't behave well, so from now on he's staying here."

"Let me talk to her."

I discussed it with Lila until late into the night; Enzo, gloomy, shut himself in another room. I understood almost immediately that she wanted to be thanked. She had intervened, she had taken back her son, had humiliated him. Now she wanted me to say to her: Your son is like a son of mine, it's fine with me that he's at my house, that he sleeps with Elsa, I won't come and complain anymore. I resisted for a long time, then I gave in and brought Rino back to my house. As soon as we left the apartment I heard her and Enzo start fighting again.

34.

Rino was grateful.

"I owe you everything, Aunt Lenù, you're the best person I know and I'll always love you."

"Rino, I'm not good at all. All you owe me is the favor of remembering that we have a single bathroom and, besides Elsa, Imma and I also use that bathroom."

"You're right, I'm sorry, sometimes I get distracted, I won't do it anymore."

He constantly apologized, he was constantly distracted. He was, in his way, in good faith. He declared endlessly that he wanted to find a job, that he wanted to contribute to the household expenses, that he would be very careful not to cause me trouble in any way, that he had an unbounded respect for me. But he didn't find a job, and life, in all the most dispiriting aspects of dailiness, continued as before, and perhaps worse. At any rate, I stopped going to Lila. I told her: Everything's fine.

It was becoming very clear to me that the tension between her and Enzo was increasing, and I didn't want to be the fuse for their rages. What had been upsetting me, for a while, was that the nature of their arguments had changed. In the past Lila yelled and Enzo for the most part was silent. But now it wasn't like that. She yelled, I often heard Tina's name, and her voice, filtered through the floor, seemed a kind of sick whine. Then suddenly Enzo exploded. He shouted and his shouting extended into a tumultuous torrent of exasperated words, all in violent dialect. Lila was silent then; while Enzo shouted she couldn't be heard. But as soon as he was silent you could hear the door slam. I strained my ears for the shuffling of Lila on the stairs, in the entrance. Then her steps vanished in the sounds of the traffic on the *stradone*.

Enzo used to run after her, but now he didn't. I thought: maybe I should go down, talk to him, tell him: You yourself told me how Lina continues to suffer, be understanding. But I gave up and hoped that she would return soon. But she stayed away the whole day and sometimes even the night. What was she doing? I imagined that she took refuge in some library, as Pietro had told me, or that she was wandering through Naples, noting every building, every church, every monument, every plaque. Or that she was combining the two things: first she explored the city, then she dug around in books to find information. Overwhelmed by events, I had never had the wish or the time to mention that new mania, nor had she ever talked to me about it. But I knew how she could become obsessively focused when something interested her, and it didn't surprise me that she could dedicate so much time and energy to it. I thought about it with some concern only when her disappearances followed the shouting, and the shadow of Tina joined the one vanishing into the city, even at night. Then the tunnels of tufa under the city came to mind, the catacombs with rows of death's-heads, the skulls of blackened bronze that led to the unhappy souls of the church of Purgatorio ad Arco. And sometimes I stayed awake until I heard the street door slam and her footsteps on the stairs.

On one of those dark days the police appeared. There had been a quarrel, she had left. I looked out at the window in alarm, I saw the police heading toward our building. I was frightened, I thought something had happened to Lila. I hurried onto the landing. The police were looking for Enzo, they had come to arrest him. I tried to intervene, to understand. I was rudely silenced, they took him away in handcuffs. As he went down the stairs Enzo shouted to me in dialect: When Lina gets back tell her not to worry, it's a lot of nonsense.

35.

For a long time it was hard to know what he was accused of. Lila stopped being hostile toward him, gathered her strength, and concerned herself only with him. In that new ordeal she was silent and determined. She became enraged only when she discovered that the state—since she had no official bond with Enzo and, furthermore, had never been separated from Stefano—wouldn't grant her a status equivalent to a wife or, as a result, the possibility of seeing him. She began to spend a lot of money so that, through unofficial channels, he would feel her closeness and her support.

Meanwhile I went back to Nino. I knew from Marisa that it was useless to expect help from him, he wouldn't lift a finger even for his own father, his mother, his siblings. But with me he again readily made an effort, maybe to make a good impression on Imma, maybe because it meant showing Lila, if indirectly, his power. Not even he, however, could understand precisely what Enzo's situation was and at different times he gave me different versions that he himself admitted were not reliable. What had happened? It was certain that Nadia, in the course of her sobbing confessions, had mentioned Enzo's name. It was certain that she had dug up the period when Enzo, with Pasquale, had frequented the worker-student collective in Via dei Tribunali. It was certain that she had implicated them both in small demonstrations, carried out, many years earlier, against the property of NATO officials who lived in Via Manzoni. It was certain that the investigators were trying to involve Enzo, too, in many of the crimes that they had attributed to Pasquale. But at this point certainties ended and suppositions began. Maybe Nadia had claimed that Enzo had had recourse to Pasquale for crimes of a nonpolitical nature. Maybe Nadia had claimed that some of those bloody acts—in particular the murder of Bruno Soccavo—had been carried out by Pasquale and planned by Enzo. Maybe Nadia had said she had learned from Pasquale himself that it was three men who killed the Solara brothers: him, Antonio Cappuccio, Enzo Scanno, childhood friends who, incited by a longtime solidarity and by an equally longstanding resentment, had committed that crime.

They were complicated years. The order of the world in which we had grown up was dissolving. The old skills resulting from long study and knowledge of the correct political line suddenly seemed senseless. Anarchist, Marxist, Gramscian, Communist, Leninist, Trotskyite, Maoist, worker were quickly becoming obsolete labels or, worse, a mark of brutality. The exploitation of man by man and the logic of maximum profit, which before had been considered an abomination, had returned to become the linchpins of freedom and democracy everywhere. Meanwhile, by means legal and illegal, all the accounts that remained open in the state and in the revolutionary organizations were being closed with a heavy hand. One might easily end up murdered or in jail, and among the common people a stampede had begun. People like Nino, who had a seat in parliament, and like Armando Galiani—who was now famous, thanks to television—had intuited for a while that the climate was changing and had quickly adapted to the new season. As for those like Nadia, evidently they had been well advised and were cleansing their consciences by informing. But not people like Pasquale and Enzo. I imagine that they continued to think, to express themselves, to attack, to defend, resorting to watchwords they had learned in the sixties and seventies. In truth, Pasquale carried on his war even in prison, and to the servants of the state said not a word, either to implicate or to exonerate himself. Enzo, on the other hand, certainly talked. In his usual laborious way, weighing every word with care, he displayed his feelings as a Communist but at the same time denied all the charges that had been brought against him.

Lila, for her part, focused her acute intelligence, her bad character, and very expensive lawyers on the battle to get him out of trouble. Enzo a strategist? A combatant? And when, if he had been working for years, from morning to night, at Basic Sight? How would it have been possible to kill the Solaras with Antonio and Pasquale if he was in Avellino at the time and Antonio was in Germany? Above all, even admitting that it was possible, the three friends were well known in the neighborhood and, masked or not, would have been recognized.

But there was little to do, the wheels of justice, as they say, advanced, and at a certain point I was afraid that Lila, too, would be arrested. Nadia named names upon names. They arrested some of those who had been part of the collective of Via dei Tribunali—one worked at the U.N., one at the F.A.O., one was a bank employee—and even Armando's former wife, Isabella, a peaceful housewife married to a technician at Enel, got her turn. Nadia spared only two people: her brother and, in spite of widespread fears, Lila. Maybe the daughter of Professor Galiani thought that by involving Enzo she had already struck her deeply. Or maybe she hated her and yet respected her, so that after much hesitation she decided to keep her out of it. Or maybe she was afraid of her, and feared a direct confrontation. But I prefer the hypothesis that she knew the story of Tina and took pity on her, or, better still, she had thought that if a mother has an experience like that, there is nothing that can truly hurt her.

Meanwhile, eventually, the charges against Enzo proved to be without substance, justice lost its grip, got tired. After many months, very little remained standing: his old friendship with Pasquale, militancy in the worker-student committee in the days of San Giovanni a Teduccio, the fact that the run-down farmhouse in the mountains of Serino, the one where Pasquale had been hiding, was rented to one of his Avellinese relations. Step by judicial step, he who had been considered a dangerous leader, the planner and executor of savage crimes, was demoted to sympathizer with the armed struggle. When finally even those sympathies proved to be generic opinions that had never been transmuted into criminal actions, Enzo returned home.

But by then almost two years had passed since his arrest, and in the neighborhood a reputation as a terrorist who was much more dangerous than Pasquale Peluso had solidified around him. Pasquale—said people on the streets and in the shops— we've all known him since he was a child, he always worked, his only crime was that he was always an upright man who, even after the fall of the Berlin Wall, didn't shed the uniform of a Communist his father sewed on him, who took on himself the sins of others and will never surrender. Enzo, on the other hand—they said—is very intelligent, he is well camouflaged by his silences and by the Basic Sight millions, above all he has behind him, directing him, Lina Cerullo, his black soul, more intelligent and more dangerous than he is: the two of them, yes, they must have done horrible things. Thus, as spiteful rumors accumulated, they were both marked out as people who not only had shed blood but had been clever enough to get away with it.

In that climate their business, already in trouble because of Lila's indifference and the money she had spent on lawyers and other things, couldn't get going again. By mutual consent they sold it, and although Enzo had often imagined that it was worth a billion lire, they barely got a couple of hundred million. In the spring of 1992, when they had stopped fighting, they separated both as business partners and as a couple. Enzo left a good part of the money to Lila and went to look for work in Milan. To me he said one afternoon: Stay near her, she's a woman who isn't comfortable with herself, she'll have a hard old age. For a while he wrote regularly, I did the same. A couple of times he called me. Then that was all.

36.

More or less around the same time another couple broke up, Elsa and Rino. Their love and complicity lasted for five or six months, at which point my daughter took me aside and confided that she felt attracted to a young mathematics teacher, a teacher in another section who didn't even know of her existence. I asked:

"And Rino?"

She answered:

"He is my great love."

I understood, as she added jokes to sighs, that she was making a distinction between love and attraction, and that her love for Rino wasn't affected in the least by her attraction to the teacher.

Since I was as usual stressed—I was writing a lot, publishing a lot, traveling a lot—it was Imma who became the confidante of both Elsa and Rino. My youngest daughter, who respected the feelings of both, gained the trust of both and became a reliable source of information for me. I learned from her that Elsa had succeeded in her intention of seducing the professor. I learned from her that Rino had eventually begun to suspect that things with Elsa weren't going well. I learned from her that Elsa had abandoned the professor so that Rino wouldn't suffer. I learned from her that, after a break of a month, she had started up again. I learned from her that Rino, suffering for almost a year, finally confronted her, weeping, and begged her to tell him if she still loved him. I learned from her that Elsa had shouted at him: I don't love you anymore, I love someone else. I learned from her that Rino had slapped her, but *only* with his fingertips, just to show he was a man. I learned from her that Elsa had run to the kitchen, grabbed the broom, and beaten him furiously, with no reaction from him.

From Lila, however, I learned that Rino—when I was absent and Elsa didn't come home from school and stayed out all night—had gone to her in despair. Pay some attention to your daughter, she said one evening, try to understand what she wants. But she said it indifferently, without concern for Elsa's future or for Rino's. In fact she added: Besides, look, if you have your commitments and you don't want to do anything it's all right just the same. Then she muttered: We weren't made for children. I wanted to respond that I felt I was a good mother and wore myself out trying to do my work without taking anything away from Dede, Elsa, and Imma. But I didn't, I perceived that at that moment she wasn't angry with me or my daughter, she was only trying to make her own indifference toward Rino seem normal.

Things were different when Elsa left the professor, and began going out with a classmate with whom she was studying for her final exams. She told Rino right away, so that he would understand that it was over. Lila then came up to my house, and, taking advantage of the fact that I was in Turin, made an ugly scene. What did your mother put in your head, she said in dialect, you have no sensitivity, you hurt people and don't realize it. Then she yelled at her: My dear, you think you're so important, but you're a whore. Or at least Elsa reported that, entirely confirmed by Imma, who said to me: It's true, Mamma, she called her a whore.

Whatever Lila had said, my second daughter was marked by it. She lost her lightness. She also gave up the schoolmate she was studying with, and became nice to Rino, but she left him alone in the bed and moved to Imma's room. When the exams were over she decided to visit her father and Dede, even though Dede had never given any sign of wanting to reconcile with her. She left for Boston, and there the two sisters, helped by Pietro, agreed on the fact that being in love with Rino had been a mistake. Once they made peace they had a good time, traveling around the United States, and when Elsa returned to Naples she seemed more serene. But she didn't stay with me for long. She enrolled in Physics, she became frivolous and sharp again, she changed boyfriends frequently. Since she was pursued by her schoolmate, by the young mathematics teacher, and naturally by Rino, she didn't take her exams, returned to her old loves, mixed them with new ones, accomplished nothing. Finally she flew off again to the United States, having decided to study there. She, like Dede, left without saying goodbye to Lila, but completely unexpectedly she spoke of her positively. She said that she understood why I had been her friend for so many years, and, without irony, called her the best person she had ever known.

37.

That was not Rino's opinion, however. Elsa's departure did
not stop him, surprising as it may seem, from continuing to live
with me. He was in despair for a long time, afraid of falling again
into the physical and moral wretchedness from which *I* had res-
cued him. Full of devotion he attributed that and many other
virtues to me. And he continued to occupy the room that had
been Dede and Elsa's. He naturally did many jobs for me. When
I left he drove me to the station and carried my suitcase, when I
returned he did the same. He became my driver, my errand boy,
my factotum. If he needed money he asked me for it politely,
affectionately, and without the least scruple.

At times, when he made me nervous, I reminded him that
he had some obligations toward his mother. He understood
and disappeared for a while. But sooner or later he returned
discouraged, muttering that Lila was never home, that the
empty apartment made him sad, or he grumbled: She didn't
even say hello, she sits at her computer and writes.

Lila was writing? What was she writing?

My curiosity at first was faint, the equivalent of an absent-
minded observation. I was nearly fifty at the time, I was in the
period of my greatest success, I was publishing two books a
year, and selling well. Reading and writing had become a
career, and, like all careers, it began to burden me. I remember
thinking: in her place I'd sit on a beach in the sun. Then I said
to myself: if writing helps her, good. And I went on to something else, I forgot about it.

38.

Dede's departure and then Elsa's grieved me. It depressed
me that both, in the end, preferred their father to me. Of

course they loved me, of course they missed me. I sent letters constantly, at moments of melancholy I telephoned without caring about the expense. And I liked Dede's voice when she said, I dream of you often; how moved I was if Elsa wrote, I'm looking everywhere for your perfume, I want to use it, too. But the fact was that they were gone, I had lost them. Every letter of theirs, every telephone call attested to the fact that, even if they suffered because of our separation, with their father they didn't have the conflicts they had had with me, he was the point of entry to their true world.

One morning Lila said to me in a tone that was hard to decipher: It makes no sense for you to keep Imma here in the neighborhood, send her to Rome to Nino, it's very clear that she wants to be able to say to her sisters, I've done what you did. Those words had an unpleasant effect on me. As if she were giving dispassionate advice, she was suggesting that I separate also from my third child. She seemed to be saying: Imma would be better off and so would you. I replied: If Imma leaves me, too, my life will no longer have meaning. But she smiled: Where is it written that lives should have a meaning? So she began to disparage all that struggle of mine to write. She said mockingly: Is the meaning that line of black markings that look like insect shit? She invited me to take a rest, she exclaimed: What need is there to work so hard. Enough.

I had a long period of uneasiness. On the one hand I thought: she wants to deprive me of Imma, too. On the other I said to myself: she's right, I should bring Imma and her father together. I didn't know whether to cling to the affection of the only child who remained or, for her sake, to try to reinforce her bond with Nino.

This last was not easy, and the recent elections had been proof of it. Imma was eleven—but she was inflamed by political passion. She wrote, I remember, to her father, she called him, she offered in every possible way to campaign for him and wanted me to help him, too. I hated the socialists even more than in the past. When I saw Nino I'd made remarks like: What's become of you, I no longer recognize you. I went so far as to say, with some rhetorical exaggeration: We were born in poverty and violence, the Solaras were criminals who stole everything, but you are worse, you are gangs of looters who make laws against the looting of others. He had answered lightheartedly: You've never understood anything about politics and you never will understand anything, play with literature and don't talk about things you don't know about.

But then the situation came to a head. Long-standing corruption—commonly practiced and commonly submitted to at every level as an unwritten rule but always in force among the most widely respected—came to the surface thanks to a sudden determination of the judiciary. The high-level crooks, who at first seemed few and so inexperienced that they were caught with their hands in the till, multiplied, became the true face of the management of the republic. As the elections approached I saw that Nino was less carefree. Since I had my fame and a certain reputation, he used Imma to ask me to stand behind him publicly. I said yes to the child in order not to upset her, but then in fact I withdrew. Imma was angry, she repeated her support for her father and when he asked her to stand next to him in a campaign ad she was enthusiastic. I rebelled and found myself in a terrible situation. On the one hand I didn't refuse Imma permission—it would have been impossible without a rift—on the other I scolded Nino on the telephone: Put Albertino, put Lidia in your ad, and don't dare use my daughter in this way. He insisted, he hesitated, finally he gave in. I forced him to tell Imma that he had inquired and that children weren't allowed in the ads. But she understood that I was the reason she had been deprived of the pleasure of standing publicly next to her father, and she said: You don't love me, Mamma, you send Dede and Elsa to Pietro, but I can't even spend five minutes with Papa. When Nino wasn't reelected Imma began to cry, she muttered between her sobs that it was my fault.

In other words, it was all complicated. Nino was bitter, he became intractable. For a while he seemed to be the only victim of those elections, but it wasn't so, soon the entire system of the parties was swept away and we lost track of him. The voters were angry with the old, the new, and the very new. If people had been horrified at those who wanted to overthrow the state, now they were disgusted by those who, pretending to serve it, had consumed it, like a fat worm in the apple. A black wave, which had lain hidden under gaudy trappings of power and a flow of words as impudent as it was arrogant, became increasingly visible and spread to every corner of Italy. The neighborhood of my childhood wasn't the only place untouched by any grace, Naples wasn't the only irredeemable city. I met Lila on the stairs one morning, she seemed cheerful. She showed me the copy of the *Repubblica* she had just bought. There was a photograph of Professor Guido Airota. The photographer had caught on his face, I don't know when, a frightened expression that made him almost unrecognizable. The article, full of theysays and perhaps, advanced the hypothesis that even the prestigious scholar, not to mention old political operator, might soon be summoned by the judges as one who was well informed about the corruption of Italy.

39.

Guido Airota never appeared before the judges, but for days dailies and weeklies drew maps of corruption in which even he played a part. I was glad, in that situation, that Pietro was in America, that Dede and Elsa, too, now had a life on the other side of the ocean. But I was worried about Adele, I thought I should at least telephone her. But I hesitated, I said to myself: she'll think that I'm enjoying it and it will be hard to convince her it's not true.

Instead I called Mariarosa, it seemed to me an easier path to take. I was wrong. It was years since I'd seen or spoken to her, she answered coldly. She said with a note of sarcasm: What a career you've had, my dear, now you're read everywhere, one can't open a newspaper or a journal without finding your name. Then she spoke in detail about herself, something she had never done in the past. She cited books, she cited articles, she cited travels. It struck me mainly that she had left the university.

"Why?" I asked.

"It disgusted me."

"And now?"

"Now what?"

"How do you live?"

"I have a rich family."

But she regretted that phrase as soon as she uttered it, she laughed uneasily, and it was she, right afterward, who spoke of her father. She said: It was bound to happen. And she quoted Franco, she said that he had been among the first to understand that either everything would change, and in a hurry, or even harder times would come and there would be no more hope. She was angry: My father thought you could change one thing here and one there, deliberately. But when you change almost nothing like that you're forced to enter into the system of lies and either you tell them, like the others, or they get rid of you. I asked her:

"Guido is guilty, he took money?"

She laughed nervously:

"Yes. But he is entirely innocent, in his whole life he never put a single lira that wasn't more than legal in his pocket."

Then she turned again to me, but in an almost offensive tone. She repeated: You write too much, you no longer surprise me. And although I had been the one to call, it was she who said goodbye and hung up.

The incongruous double judgment that Mariarosa had pronounced on her father was true. The media storm around Guido slowly faded and he returned to his study, but as an innocent who surely was guilty and, if you like, as a guilty man who surely was innocent. It seemed to me that at that point I could telephone Adele. She thanked me ironically for my concern, showed that she was better informed than I was regarding the life and studies of Dede and Elsa, uttered remarks like: This is a country where one is exposed to every insult, respectable people should be in a hurry to emigrate. When I asked if I could say hello to Guido she said: I'll say it for you, he's resting now. Then she exclaimed bitterly: His only crime was to be surrounded by newly literate types with no ethics, young arrivistes ready for anything, scum.

That very evening the television showed a particularly cheerful image of the former socialist deputy Giovanni Sarratore—who was not exactly a youth, at the time: he was fifty—and inserted him in the increasingly crowded list of corrupters and corrupt.

40.

That news especially upset Imma. In those first years of her conscious life she had seen her father very little, and yet had made him her idol. She boasted of him to her schoolmates, she boasted to her teachers, she showed everyone a photograph from the newspapers in which they were hand in hand right at the entrance to Montecitorio. If she had to imagine the man she would marry, she said: He will surely be very tall, dark, and handsome. When she learned that her father had ended up in jail like an ordinary inhabitant of the neighborhood—a place that she considered horrible: now that she was growing up she said in no uncertain terms that she was afraid of it, and, increasingly, she had reason to be—she lost the bit of serenity I had been able to guarantee her. She sobbed in her sleep, she woke in the middle of the night and wanted to get in bed with me.

Once we met Marisa, worn-out, shabby, angrier than usual. She said, paying no attention to Imma: Nino deserves it, he's always thought only of himself, and, as you well know, he never wanted to give us any help, he acted like an honest man only with his relatives, that piece of shit. My daughter couldn't bear even a word of it, she left us on the *stradone* and ran away. I quickly said goodbye to Marisa, I chased after Imma, I tried to console her: You mustn't pay any attention, your father and his sister never got along. But I stopped speaking critically of Nino in front of her. In fact I stopped speaking critically of him in front of anyone. I remembered when I went to him to find out about Pasquale and Enzo. You always needed some patron saint in Paradise to navigate the calculated opacity of the underworld, and Nino, although far from any sanctity, had helped me. Now that the saints were falling into the inferno, I had no one to ask to find out about him. Unreliable news came to me only from the infernal circle of his many lawyers.

41.

Lila, I have to say, never showed any interest in Nino's fate; she reacted to the news of his legal troubles as if it were something to laugh about. She said, with the expression of someone who has remembered a detail that explained everything: Whenever he needed money he got Bruno Soccavo to give it to him, and he certainly never paid it back. Then she muttered that she could imagine what had happened to him. He had smiled, he had shaken hands, he had felt he was the best of all, he had continuously wanted to demonstrate that he was equal to any possible situation. If he had done something wrong he had done it out of a desire to be more likable, to seem the most intelligent, to climb higher and higher. That's it. And later she acted as if Nino no longer existed. As much as she had exerted herself for Pasquale and Enzo, so she appeared completely indifferent to the problems of the former Honorable Sarratore. It's likely that she followed the proceedings in the papers and on television, where Nino appeared often, pale, suddenly grizzled, with the expression of a child who says: I swear it wasn't me. Certainly she never asked me what I knew about him, if I had managed to see him, what he expected, how his father, his mother, his siblings had reacted. Instead, for no clear reason, her interest in Imma was rekindled, she got involved with her again.

While she had abandoned her son Rino to me like a puppy who, having grown fond of another mistress, no longer greets the old one, she became very attached to my daughter again, and Imma, always greedy for affection, went back to loving her. I saw them talking, and they often went out together. Lila said to me: I showed her the botanic garden, the museum, Capodimonte.

In the last phase of our life in Naples, she guided Imma all over the city, transmitting an interest in it that remained with her. Aunt Lina knows so many things, Imma said in admiration. And I was pleased, because Lila, taking her around on her wanderings, managed to diminish her anguish about her father, the anger at the fierce insults of her classmates, prompted by their parents, and the loss of the attention she had received from her teachers thanks to her surname. But it wasn't only that. I learned from Imma's reports, and with greater and greater precision, that the object in which Lila's mind was engaged, and on which she was writing for perhaps hours and hours, bent over her computer, was not this or that monument but Naples in its entirety. An enormous project that she had never talked to me about. The time had passed in which she tended to involve me in her passions, she had chosen my daughter as her confidante. To her she repeated the things she learned, or dragged her to see what had excited or fascinated her.

42.

Imma was very receptive, and memorized everything rapidly. It was she who taught me about Piazza dei Martiri, so important for Lila and me in the past. I knew nothing about it, whereas Lila had studied its history and told her about it. She repeated it to me right in the piazza, one morning when we went shopping, mixing up, I think, facts, her fantasies, fantasies of Lila's. Here, Mamma, in the eighteenth century it was all countryside. There were trees, there were the peasants' houses, inns, and a road that went straight down to the sea called Calata Santa Caterina a Chiaia, from the name of the church there at the corner, which is old but quite ugly. After May 15, 1848, when, right in this spot, many patriots who wanted a constitution and a parliament were killed, the Bourbon King Ferdinando II, to show that peace had returned, decided to construct a Road of Peace and put up in the piazza a column with a Madonna at the top. But when the annexation of Naples by the Kingdom of Italy was proclaimed and the Bourbon was driven out, the mayor Giuseppe Colonna di Stigliano asked the sculptor Enrico Alvino to transform the column with the Madonna of Peace at the top into a column in memory of the Neapolitans who had died for freedom. So Enrico Alvino put at the base of the column these four lions, which symbolized the great moments of revolution in Naples: the lion of 1799, mortally wounded; the lion of the movements of 1820, pierced by the sword but still biting the air; the lion of

1848, which represents the force of the patriots subdued but not conquered; finally, the lion of 1859, threatening and avenging. Then, Mamma, up there, instead of the Madonna of Peace he put the bronze statue of a beautiful young woman, that is, Victory, who is balanced on the world: that Victory holds the sword in her left hand and in the right a garland for the Neapolitan citizens, martyrs for Freedom, who, fallen in battle and on the gallows, avenged the people with their blood, et cetera et cetera.

I often had the impression that Lila used the past to make Imma's tempestuous present normal. In the Neapolitan facts as she recounted them there was always something terrible, disorderly, at the origin, which later took the form of a beautiful building, a street, a monument, only to be forgotten, to lose meaning, to decline, improve, decline, according to an ebb and flow that was by its nature unpredictable, made of waves, flat calm, downpours, cascades. The essential, in Lila's scheme, was to ask questions. Who were the martyrs, what did the lions mean, and when had the battles and the gallows occured, and the Road of Peace, and the Madonna, and the Victory. The stories were a lineup of the befores, the afters, the thens. Before elegant Chiaia, the neighborhood for the wealthy, there was the *playa* cited in the letters of Gregory, the swamps that went down to the beach and the sea, the wild forest that crept up to the Vomero. Before the Risanamento, or cleanup, of the end of the nineteenth century, before the railroad cooperatives, there was an unhealthy area, polluted in every stone, but also with quite a few splendid monuments, swept away by the mania for tearing down under the pretense of cleaning up. And one of the areas to be cleaned up had, for a very long time, been called Vasto. Vasto was a place name that indicated the terrain between Porta Capuana and Porta Nolana, and the neighborhood, once cleaned up, had kept the name. Lila repeated that name—Vasto—she liked it, and Imma, too, liked it: Vasto and

Risanamento, waste and good health, a yearning to lay waste, sack, ruin, gut, and a yearning to build, order, design new streets or rename the old, for the purpose of consolidating new worlds and hiding old evils, which, however, were always ready to exact their revenge.

In fact, before the Vasto was called Vasto and was in essence wasteland—Aunt Lina recounted—there had been villas, gardens, fountains. In that very place the Marchese di Vico had built a palace, with a garden, called Paradise. The garden of Paradise was full of hidden water games, Mamma. The most famous was a big white mulberry tree, which had a system of almost invisible channels: water flowed through them, falling like rain from the branches or coursing like a waterfall down the trunk. Understand? From the Paradise of the Marchese di Vico to the Vasto of the Marchese del Vasto, to the Cleanup of Mayor Nicola Amore, to the Vasto again, to further renaissances and so on at that rate.

Ah, what a city, said Aunt Lina to my daughter, what a splendid and important city: here all languages are spoken, Imma, here everything was built and everything was torn down, here the people don't trust talk and are very talkative, here is Vesuvius which reminds you every day that the greatest undertaking of powerful men, the most splendid work, can be reduced to nothing in a few seconds by the fire, and the earthquake, and the ash, and the sea.

I listened, but at times I was baffled. Yes, Imma was consoled but only because Lila was introducing her to a permanent stream of splendors and miseries, a cyclical Naples where everything was marvelous and everything became gray and irrational and everything sparkled again, as when a cloud passes over the sun and the sun appears to flee, a timid, pale disk, near extinction, but now look, once the cloud dissolves it's suddenly dazzling again, so bright you have to shield your eyes with your hand. In Lila's stories the palaces with paradisiacal gardens fell into ruin, grew wild, and sometimes nymphs, dryads, satyrs, and fauns inhabited them, sometimes the souls of the dead, sometimes demons whom God sent to the castles and also the houses of common people to make them atone for their sins or to put to the test good-hearted inhabitants, to reward them after death. What was beautiful and solid and radiant was populated with nighttime imaginings, and they both liked stories of shades. Imma informed me that at the cape of Posillipo, a few steps from the sea, opposite Gajóla, just above the Grotta delle Fate, there was a famous building inhabited by spirits. The spirits, she told me, were also in the buildings of Vico San Mandato and Vico Mondragone. Lila had promised her that they would go together to look in the streets of Santa Lucia for a spirit called Faccione, called that because of his broad face, who was dangerous and threw big stones at anyone who disturbed him. Also—she had told her— many spirits of dead children lived in Pizzofalcone and other places. A child could often be seen at night in the neighborhood of Porta Nolana. Did they really exist, or did they not exist? Aunt Lina said that the spirits existed, but not in the palaces, or in the alleys, or near the ancient gates of the Vasto. They existed in people's ears, in the eyes when the eyes looked inside and not out, in the voice as soon as it begins to speak, in the head when it thinks, because words are full of ghosts but so are images. Is it true, Mamma?

Yes, I answered, maybe yes: if Aunt Lina says so, it could be. This city is full of events, both large and small—Lila had told her—you can even see spirits if you go to the museum, the painting gallery, and, especially, the Biblioteca Nazionale, there are a lot of them in the books. You open one and, for example, Masaniello jumps out. Masaniello is a funny and terrible spirit, he makes the poor laugh and the rich tremble. Imma liked it in particular when, with his sword, he killed not the duke of Maddaloni, not the father of the duke of Maddaloni, but their

portraits, *zac, zac, zac.* In fact, in her opinion, the most entertaining moment was when Masaniello cut off the heads of the
duke and his father in the portraits, or hanged the portraits of
other ferocious noblemen. *He cut off the heads in the portraits,*
Imma laughed, in disbelief, *he hanged the portraits.* And after
those decapitations and hangings Masaniello put on an outfit
of blue silk embroidered with silver, placed a gold chain
around his neck, stuck a diamond pin in his hat, and went to
the market. He went like that, Mamma, all decked out like a
marquis, a duke, a prince, he who was a workingman, a fisher-
man, and didn't know how to read or write. Aunt Lina had
said that in Naples that could happen and other things, openly,
without the pretense of making laws and decrees and entire
conditions better than the previous ones. In Naples one could
get carried away without subterfuges, with clarity and complete satisfaction.

The story of a minister had made a great impression on her.
It involved the museum of our city, and Pompeii. Imma told
me in a serious tone: You know, Mamma, that a Minister of
Education, Nasi, a representative of the people almost a hundred years ago, accepted as a gift from workers at the excava-
tions of Pompeii a small, valuable statue they had just dug up?
You know that he had models made of the best artworks found
at Pompeii to adorn his villa in Trapani? This Nasi, Mamma,
even though he was a Minister of the Kingdom of Italy, acted
instinctively: the workers brought him a beautiful little statue
as a gift and he took it, he thought it would make a very fine
impression at his house. Sometimes you make a mistake, but
when as a child you haven't been taught what the public good
is, you don't understand what a crime is.

I don't know if she said the last part because she was reporting the words of Aunt Lina, or because she had made her own
arguments. Anyway I didn't like those words and I decided to
intervene. I made a cautious speech, but explicit: Aunt Lina

tells you so many wonderful things, I'm pleased, when she gets excited no one can stop her. But you mustn't think that people carry out terrible acts lightly. You mustn't believe it, Imma, especially if it concerns members of parliament and ministers and senators and bankers and Camorrists. You mustn't believe that the world is chasing its tail—now it's going well, now badly, now it's going well again. We have to work with consistency, with discipline, step by step, no matter how things are going around us, and be careful not to make a mistake, because we pay for our mistakes.

Imma's lower lip trembled, she asked me:

"Papa won't go to parliament anymore?"

I didn't know what to say and she realized it. As if to encourage me to give a positive response, she said:

"Aunt Lina thinks so, that he'll return."

I hesitated, then made up my mind.

"No, Imma, I don't think so. But there's no need for Papa to be an important person for you to love him."

43.

It was the completely wrong answer. Nino, with his usual ability, slipped out of the trap he had ended up in. Imma found out and was very pleased. She asked to see him, but he disappeared for a while, it was difficult to track him down. When we made a date he took us to a pizzeria in Mergellina, but he didn't display his usual liveliness. He was nervous, distracted, to Imma he said one should never rely on political alignments, he described himself as the victim of a left that wasn't a left, in fact it was worse than the fascists. You'll see—he reassured her—Papa will fix everything up.

Later I read some very aggressive articles of his in which he returned to a thesis that he had espoused long ago: legal power had to be subject to executive power. He wrote indignantly: How can the judges one day be fighting against those who want to strike at the heart of the state and the next make the citizens believe that very same heart is sick and should be thrown out. He fought not to be thrown out. He passed through the old parties now out of commission, shifting further to the right, and in 1994, radiant, he regained a seat in parliament.

Imma was joyful when she learned that her father was again the Honorable Sarratore and that Naples had given him a very high number of preferences. As soon as she heard the news she came to tell me: You write books but you can't see the future the way Aunt Lina does.

44.

I didn't get angry with her, in essence my daughter wanted only to point out to me that I had been spiteful about her father, that I hadn't understood how great he was. But those words (*You write books but you can't see the future the way Aunt Lina does*) had an unexpected function: they pushed me to pay attention to the fact that Lila, the woman who in Imma's opinion could see the future, at fifty had returned officially to books, to studying, and was even writing. Pietro had imagined that with that decision she had self-prescribed a kind of therapy to fight the anguishing absence of Tina. But in my last year in the neighborhood I wasn't satisfied with Pietro's sensitivity or Imma's mediation: as soon as I could, I broached the subject, I asked questions.

"Why all this interest in Naples?"

"What's wrong with it?"

"Nothing, in fact I envy you. You're studying for your own pleasure, while I now read and write only for work."

"I'm not studying. I limit myself to seeing a building, a

street, a monument, and maybe I spend a little time looking for information, that's all."

"And that's studying."

"You think?"

She was evasive, she didn't want to confide in me. But sometimes she became excited, the way she could be, and began to speak of the city as if it were not made up of the usual streets, of the normality of everyday places, but had revealed only to her a secret sparkle. So in a few brief sentences she transformed it into the most memorable place in the world, into the place richest in meanings, and after a little conversation I returned to my things with my mind on fire. What a grave negligence it had been to be born and live in Naples without making an effort to know it. I was about to leave the city for the second time, I had been there altogether for thirty full years of my life, and yet of the place where I was born I knew almost nothing. Pietro, in the past, had admonished me for my ignorance, now I admonished myself. I listened to Lila and felt my insubstantiality.

Meanwhile, she, who learned with effortless speed, now seemed able to give to every monument, every stone, a density of meaning, a fantastic importance such that I would have happily stopped the nonsense that I was busy with to start studying in turn. But "the nonsense" absorbed all my energy, thanks to it I lived comfortably, I usually worked even at night. Sometimes in the silent apartment I stopped, I thought that perhaps at that moment Lila, too, was awake, maybe she was writing like me, maybe summarizing texts she'd read in the library, maybe putting down her reflections, maybe she moved on from there to recount episodes of her own, maybe the historic truth didn't interest her, she sought only starting points from which to let imagination wander.

Certainly she proceeded in her usual extemporaneous way, with unexpected interests that later weakened and vanished.

446 · ELENA FERRANTE

Now, as far as I could tell, she was concerned with the porcelain factory near the Palazzo Reale. Now she was gathering information on San Pietro a Majella. Now she sought testimonies of foreign travelers in which it seemed to her she could trace a mixture of attraction and repulsion. Everyone, she said, everyone, century after century, praised the great port, the sea, the ships, the castles, Vesuvius tall and black with its disdainful flames, the city like an amphitheater, the gardens, the orchards, the palaces. But then, century after century, they began to complain about the inefficiency, the corruption, the physical and moral poverty. No institution—behind the façade, behind the pompous name and the numerous employees—truly functioned. No decipherable order, only an unruly and uncontrollable crowd on streets cluttered with sellers of every possible type of merchandise, people speaking at the top of their lungs, urchins, beggars. Ah, there is no city that gives off so much noise and such a clamor as Naples.

Once she talked to me about violence. We believed, she said, that it was a feature of the neighborhood. We had it around us from birth, it brushed up against us, touched us all our lives, we thought: we were unlucky. You remember how we used words to cause suffering, and how many we invented to humiliate? You remember the beatings that Antonio, Enzo, Pasquale, my brother, the Solaras, and even I, and even you, gave and took? You remember when my father threw me out the window? Now I'm reading an old article on San Giovanni a Carbonara, where it explains what the Carbonara or Carboneto was. I thought that there was coal there once, and coal miners. But no, it was the place for the garbage, all cities have them. It was called Fosso Carbonario, dirty water ran in it, animal carcasses were tossed into it. And since ancient times the Fosso Carbonario of Naples was where the church of San Giovanni a Carbonara stands today. In the area called Piazza di Carbonara the poet Virgil in his time ordered that every year

the *ioco de Carbonara* take place, gladiator games that didn't
lead to the death of men, as they did later—*morte de homini
come de po è facto* (she liked that old Italian, it amused her, she
quoted it to me with visible pleasure)—but gave men practice
in deeds of arms: *li homini ali facti de l'arme*. Soon, however, it
wasn't a matter of *ioco* or practice. In that place where they
threw out beasts and garbage a lot of human blood was shed.
It seems that the game of throwing the *prete* was invented
there, the stone throwing that we did as girls, you remember,
when Enzo hit me in the forehead—I still have the scar—and
he was desperate and gave me a garland of sorb apples. But
then, in Piazza di Carbonara, from stones she moved on to
weapons, and it became the place where men fought to the last
drop of blood. Beggars and gentlemen and princes hurried to
see people killing each other in revenge. When some handsome youth fell, pierced by a blade beaten on the anvil of
death, immediately beggars, bourgeois citizens, kings and
queens offered applause that rose to the stars. Ah, the violence:
tearing, killing, ripping. Lila, between fascination and horror,
spoke to me in a mixture of dialect, Italian, and very educated
quotations that she had taken from who knows where and
remembered by heart. The entire planet, she said, is a big
Fosso Carbonario. And at times I thought that she could have
held crowded rooms fascinated, but then I brought her down
to size. She's a barely educated woman of fifty, she doesn't
know how to do research, she doesn't know what the documentary truth is: she reads, she is excited, she mixes truth and
falsehood, she imagines. No more. What seemed to interest
and absorb her most was that all that filth, all that chaos of
broken limbs and dug-out eyes and split heads was then covered—literally covered—by a church dedicated to San
Giovanni Battista and by a monastery of Augustinian hermits
who had a valuable library. Ah, ah—she laughed—underneath
there's blood and above, God, peace, prayer, and books. Thus

the coupling of San Giovanni and the Fosso Carbonario, that is to say the place name of San Giovanni a Carbonara: a street we've walked on thousands of times, Lenù, it's near the station, near Forcella and the Tribunali.

I knew where the street of San Giovanni a Carbonara was, I knew it very well, but I didn't know those stories. She talked about it at length. She talked so as to let me know—I suspected—that the things she was telling me orally she had in substance already written, and they belonged to a vast text whose structure, however, escaped me. I wondered: what does she have in mind, what are her intentions? Is she just organizing her wandering and readings or is she planning a book of Neapolitan curiosities, a book that, naturally, she'll never finish but that it's good for her to keep working on, day after day, now that not only Tina is gone but Enzo is gone, the Solaras are gone, I, too, am going, taking away Imma, who, one way and another, has helped her survive?

45.

Shortly before I left for Turin I spent a lot of time with her, we had an affectionate farewell. It was a summer day in 1995. We talked about everything, for hours, but finally she focused on Imma, who was now fourteen; she was pretty, and lively, and had just graduated from middle school. She praised her without sudden malice, and I listened to her praise, I thanked her for helping her at a difficult time. She looked at me in bafflement, she corrected me:

"I've always helped Imma, not just now."

"Yes, but after Nino's troubles you were really helpful to her."

She didn't like those words, either, it was a moment of confusion. She didn't want me to associate with Nino the attention she had devoted to Imma, she reminded me that she had taken care of the child from the start, she said she had done it because Tina loved her dearly, she added: Maybe Tina loved Imma even more than me. Then she shook her head in discontent.

"I don't understand you," she said.

"What don't you understand?"

She became nervous, she had something in mind that she wanted to tell me but restrained herself.

"I don't understand how it's possible that in all this time you never thought of it even once."

"Of what, Lila?"

She was silent for a few seconds, then spoke, eyes down.

"You remember the photograph in *Panorama*?"

"Which one?"

"The one where you were with Tina and the caption said that it was you and your daughter."

"Of course I remember."

"I've often thought that they might have taken Tina because of that photo."

"What?"

"They thought they were stealing your daughter, and instead they stole mine."

She said it, and that morning I had the proof that of all the infinite hypotheses, the fantasies, the obsessions that had tormented her, that still tormented her, I had perceived almost nothing. A decade hadn't served to calm her, her brain couldn't find a quiet corner for her daughter. She said:

"You were always in the newspapers and on television, beautiful, elegant, blond: maybe they wanted money from you and not from me, who knows, I don't know anything anymore, things go one way and then they change direction."

She said that Enzo had talked to the police, that she had talked about it with Antonio, but neither the police nor Antonio had taken the possibility seriously. Yet she spoke to me as if at that moment she were again sure that that was what had

450 · ELENA FERRANTE

happened. Who knows what else she had brooded over and was still brooding over that I hadn't realized. Nunziatina had been taken in place of my Immacolata? My success was responsible for the kidnapping of her daughter? And that bond of hers with Imma was an anxiety, a protection, a safeguard? She imagined that the kidnappers, having thrown away the wrong child, would return to get the right one? Or what else? What had passed and was passing through her mind? Why was she talking to me about this only now? Did she want to inject in me a final poison to punish me for leaving her? Ah, I understood why Enzo had left. Living with her had become too harrowing.

She realized that I was looking at her with concern and, as if to reach safety, began to speak about what she was reading. But now in a jumbled way; her unease contorted her features. She muttered, laughing, that evil took unpredictable pathways. You cover it over with churches, convents, books—they seem so important, the books, she said sarcastically, you've devoted your whole life to them—and the evil breaks through the floor and emerges where you don't expect it. Then she calmed down and began to speak again of Tina, Imma, me, but in a conciliatory way, as if apologizing for what she had said to me. When there's too much silence, she said, so many ideas come to mind, I don't pay attention. Only in bad novels people always think the right thing, always say the right thing, every effect has its cause, there are the likable ones and the unlikable, the good and the bad, everything in the end consoles you. She whispered: It might be that Tina will return tonight and then who gives a damn how it happened, the essential thing will be that she's here again and forgives me for the distraction. You forgive me, too, she said, and, embracing me, concluded: Go, go, do better things than you've done so far. I've stayed near Imma *also* out of fear that someone might take her, and you loved my son truly *also* when your daughter left him. How many things you've endured for him, thank you. I'm so glad we've been friends for so long and that we are still.

46.

The idea that Tina had been taken in the belief that she was
my daughter upset me, but not because I considered that it had
some foundation. I thought rather of the tangle of obscure
feelings that had generated it, and I tried to put them in order.
I even remembered, after so long, that for completely coinci-
dental reasons—under the most insignificant coincidences
expanses of quicksand lie hidden—Lila had given her daughter the name of my beloved doll, the one that, as a child, she
herself had thrown into a cellar. It was the first time, I recall,
that I fantasized about it, but I couldn't stand it for long, I
looked into a dark well with a few glimmers of light and drew
back. Every intense relationship between human beings is full
of traps, and if you want it to endure you have to learn to avoid
them. I did so then, and finally it seemed that I had only come
up against yet another proof of how splendid and shadowy our
friendship was, how long and complicated Lila's suffering had
been, how it still endured and would endure forever. But I
went to Turin convinced that Enzo was right: Lila was very far
from a quiet old age within the confines she had established for
herself. The last image she gave me of herself was that of a
woman of fifty-one who looked ten years older and who from
time to time, as she spoke, was hit by waves of heat, and turned
fiery red. There were patches on her neck, too, her gaze
dimmed, she grabbed the edge of her dress with her hands and
fanned herself, showing Imma and me her underwear.

47.

In Turin now everything was ready: I had found an apartment near the Isabella bridge and had worked hard to get most
of my things and Imma's moved. We departed. The train, I

remember, had just left Naples, my daughter was sitting across from me, and for the first time she seemed sad about what she was leaving behind. I was very tired from the traveling back and forth of the past months, from the thousands of things I had had to arrange, from what I had done, from what I had forgotten to do. I collapsed against the seat back, I looked out the window at the outskirts of the city and Vesuvius as they grew distant. Just at that moment the certainty sprang to mind that Lila, writing about Naples, would write about Tina, and the text—precisely because it was nourished by the effort of expressing an inexpressible grief—would be extraordinary.

That certainty took hold forcefully and never weakened. In the years of Turin—as long as I ran the small but promising publishing house that had hired me, as long as I felt much more respected, I would say in fact more powerful, than Adele had been in my eyes decades earlier—the certainty took the form of a wish, a hope. I would have liked Lila to call me one day and say: I have a manuscript, a notebook, a *zibaldone*, in other words a text of mine that I'd like you to read and help me arrange. I would have read it immediately. I would have worked to give it a proper form, probably, passage by passage, I would have ended up rewriting it. Lila, in spite of her intellectual liveliness, her extraordinary memory, the reading she must have done all her life, at times talking to me about it, more often hiding it from me, had an absolutely inadequate basic education and no skill as a narrator. I was afraid it would be a disorderly accumulation of good things badly formulated, splendid things put in the wrong place. But it never occurred to me—never—that she might write an inane little story, full of clichés, in fact I was absolutely sure that it would be a worthy text. In the periods when I was struggling to put together an editorial plan of a high standard, I even went so far as to urgently interrogate Rino, who, for one thing, showed up frequently at my house; he would arrive without calling, say I came to say hello, and stay at least a couple of weeks. I asked him: Is your mother still writing? Have you ever happened to take a look, to see what it is? But he said yes, no, I don't remember, it's her business, I don't know. I insisted. I fantasized about the series in which I would put that phantom text, about what I would do to give it the maximum visibility and get some prestige from it myself. Occasionally I called Lila, I asked how she was, I questioned her discreetly, sticking to generalities: Do you still have your passion for Naples, are you taking more notes? She automatically responded: What passion, what notes, I'm a crazy old woman like Melina, you remember Melina, who knows if she's still alive. Then I dropped the subject, we moved on to other things.

48.

In the course of those phone calls we spoke more and more frequently of the dead, which was an occasion to mention the living, too.

Her father, Fernando, had died, and a few months later Nunzia died. Lila then moved with Rino to the old apartment where she was born and that she had bought long ago with her own money. But now the other siblings claimed that it was the property of her parents and harassed her by claiming rights to a part of it.

Stefano had died after another heart attack—they hadn't had time even to call an ambulance, he had fallen facedown on the ground—and Marisa had left the neighborhood, with her children. Nino had finally done something for her. Not only had he found her a job as a secretary in a law firm on Via Crispi but he gave her money to support her children at the university.

A man I had never met but who was known to be the lover of my sister, Elisa, had died. She had left the neighborhood but neither she nor my father nor my brothers had told me. I found out from Lila that she had gone to Caserta, had met a lawyer who was also a city councilman, and had remarried, but hadn't invited me to the wedding.

We talked about things like this, she kept me updated on all the news. I told her about my daughters, about Pietro, who had married a colleague five years older than he, of what I was writing, of how my publishing experience was going. Only a couple of times did I go so far as to ask somewhat explicit questions on the subject important to me.

"If you, let's say, were to write something—it's a hypothesis—would you let me read it?"

"What sort of something?"

"Something. Rino says you're always at the computer."

"Rino talks nonsense. I'm going on the Internet. I'm finding out new information about electronics. That's what I'm doing when I'm at the computer."

"Really?"

"Of course. Do I never respond to your e-mails?"

"No, and you make me mad: I always write to you and you write nothing."

"You see? I write nothing to no one, not even to you."

"All right. but if you should write something, you'd let me read it, you'd let me publish it?"

"You're the writer."

"You didn't answer me."

"I did answer you, but you pretend not to understand. To write, you have to want something to survive you. I don't even have the desire to live, I've never had it strongly the way you have. If I could eliminate myself now, while we're speaking, I'd be more than happy. Imagine if I'm going to start writing."

She had often expressed that idea of eliminating herself, but, starting in the late nineties—and especially from 2000 on—it became a sort of teasing chorus. It was a metaphor, of course. She liked it, she had resorted to it in the most diverse circumstances, and it never occurred to me, in the many years of our friendship—not even in the most terrible moments following Tina's disappearance—that she would think of suicide. Eliminating herself was a sort of aesthetic project. One can't go on anymore, she said, electronics seems so clean and yet it dirties, dirties tremendously, and it obliges you to leave traces of yourself everywhere as if you were shitting and peeing on yourself continuously: I want to leave nothing, my favorite key is the one that deletes.

That yearning had been more true in some periods, in others less. I remember a malicious tirade that started with my fame. Eh, she said once, what a fuss for a name: famous or not, it's only a ribbon tied around a sack randomly filled with blood, flesh, words, shit, and petty thoughts. She mocked me at length on that point: I untie the ribbon—*Elena Greco*—and the sack stays there, it functions just the same, haphazardly, of course, without virtues or vices, until it breaks. On her darkest days she said with a bitter laugh: I want to untie my name, slip it off me, throw it away, forget it. But on other occasions she was more relaxed. It happened—let's say—that I called her hoping to persuade her to talk to me about her text and, although she forcefully denied its existence, continuing to be evasive, it sounded as if my phone call had surprised her in the middle of a creative moment. One evening I found her happily dazed. She made the usual speech about annihilating all hierarchies—*So much fuss about the greatness of this one and that one, but what virtue is there in being born with certain qualities, it's like admiring the bingo basket when you shake it and good numbers come out*—but she expressed herself with imagination and with precision, I perceived the pleasure of inventing images. Ah, how she could use words when she wanted to. She seemed to safeguard a secret meaning that took meaning away from everything else. Perhaps it was that which began to sadden me.

49.

The crisis arrived in the winter of 2002. At that time, in spite of the ups and downs, I again felt fulfilled. Every year Dede and Elsa returned from the United States, sometimes alone, sometimes with temporary boyfriends. The first was involved in the same things as her father, the second had precociously won a professorship in a very mysterious area of algebra. When her sisters returned Imma freed herself of every obligation and spent all her time with them. The family came together again, we were four women in the house in Turin, or out in the city, happy to be together at least for a short period, attentive to one another, affectionate. I looked at them and said to myself: How lucky I've been.

But at Christmas of 2002 something happened that depressed me. The three girls all returned for a long period. Dede had married a serious engineer of Iranian origin, she had a very energetic two-year-old named Hamid. Elsa came with one of her colleagues from Boston, also a mathematician, even more youthful, and rowdy. Imma returned from Paris, where she had been studying philosophy for two years, and brought a classmate, a tall, not very good-looking, and almost silent Frenchman. How pleasant that December was. I was fifty-eight, a grandmother, I cuddled Hamid. I remember that on Christmas evening I was in a corner with the baby and looking serenely at the young bodies of my daughters, charged with energy. They all resembled me and none of them did, their lives were very far from mine and yet I felt them as inseparable parts of me. I thought: how much work I've done and what a long road I've traveled. At every step I could have given in and yet I didn't. I left the neighborhood, I returned, I managed to leave again. Nothing, nothing pulled me down, along with these girls I produced. We're safe, I brought them all to safety. Oh, they now belong to other places and other languages.

They consider Italy a splendid corner of the planet and, at the same time, an insignificant and ineffectual province, habitable only for a short vacation. Dede often says to me: Leave, come and stay in my house, you can do your work from there. I say yes, sooner or later I will. They're proud of me and yet I know that none of them would tolerate me for long, not even Imma by now. The world has changed tremendously and belongs more and more to them, less and less to me. But that's all right—I said to myself, caressing Hamid—in the end what counts is these very smart girls who haven't encountered a single one of the difficulties I faced. They have habits, voices, requirements, entitlements, self-awareness that even today I wouldn't dare allow myself. Others haven't had the same luck. In the wealthier countries a mediocrity that hides the horrors of the rest of the world has prevailed. When those horrors release a violence that reaches into our cities and our habits we're startled, we're alarmed. Last year I was dying of fear and I made long phone calls to Dede, to Elsa, even to Pietro, when I saw on television the planes that set the towers in New York ablaze the way you light a match by gently striking the head. In the world below is the inferno. My daughters know it but only through words, and they become indignant, all the time enjoying the pleasures of existence, while it lasts. They attribute their well-being and their success to their father. But I—I who did not have privileges—am the foundation of their privileges.

While I was reasoning like this, something depressed me. I suppose it was when the three girls led the men playfully to the shelf that held my books. Probably none of them had ever read one, certainly I had never seen them do so, nor had they ever said anything to me about them. But now they were paging through them, they even read some sentences aloud. Those books originated in the climate in which I had lived, in what had influenced me, in the ideas that had impressed me. I had followed my time, step by step, inventing stories, reflecting. I had pointed out evils, I had staged them. Countless times I had anticipated redemptive changes that had never arrived. I had used the language of every day to indicate things of every day. I had stressed certain themes: work, class conflicts, feminism, the marginalized. Now I was hearing my sentences chosen at random and they seemed embarrassing. Elsa—Dede was more respectful, Imma more cautious—was reading in an ironic tone from my first novel, she read from the story about the invention of women by men, she read from books with many prizes. Her voice skillfully highlighted flaws, excesses, tones that were too exclamatory, the aged ideologies that I had supported as indisputable truths. Above all she paused with amusement on the vocabulary, she repeated two or three times words that had long since passed out of fashion and sounded foolish. What was I witnessing? An affectionate mockery in the Neapolitan manner—certainly my daughter had learned that tone there—which, however, line by line, was becoming a demonstration of the scant value of all those volumes, sitting there along with their translations?

Elsa's friend the young mathematician was the only one, I think, who realized that my daughter was hurting me and he interrupted her, took away the book, asked me questions about Naples as if it were a city of the imagination, similar to those which the most intrepid explorers brought news of. The holiday slipped away. But something inside me changed. Occasionally I took down one of my volumes, read a few pages, felt its fragility. My old uncertainties gained strength. I increasingly doubted the quality of my works. Lila's hypothetical text, in parallel, assumed an unforeseen value. If before I had thought of it as a raw material on which I could work with her, shaping it into a good book for my publishing house, now it was transformed into a completed work and so into a possible touchstone. I was surprised to ask myself: and if sooner or later a story much better than mine emerges from her files? If

I have never, in fact, written a memorable novel and she, she, on the other hand, has been writing and rewriting one for years? If the genius that Lila had expressed as a child in *The Blue Fairy*, disturbing Maestra Oliviero, is now, in old age, manifesting all its power? In that case her book would become—even only for me—the proof of my failure, and reading it I would understand how I should have written but had been unable to. At that point, the stubborn self-discipline, the laborious studies, every page or line that I had published successfully would vanish as when a storm arriving over the sea collides with the violet line of the horizon and blots out everything. My image as a writer who had emerged from a blighted place and gained success, esteem, would reveal its insubstantiality. My satisfactions would diminish: with my daughters who had turned out well, with my fame, even with my most recent lover, a professor at the Polytechnic, eight years younger than me, twice divorced, with a son, whom I saw once a week in his house in the hills. My entire life would be reduced merely to a petty battle to change my social class.

50.

I kept depression at bay, I called Lila less. Now I no longer hoped, but *feared*, feared she would say: Do you want to read these pages I've written, I've been working for years, I'll send them by e-mail. I had no doubts about how I would react if I discovered that she really had irrupted into my professional identity, emptying it. I would certainly remain admiring, as I had with *The Blue Fairy*. I would publish her text without hesitation. I would exert myself to make it successful in every way possible. But I was no longer that little being who had had to discover the extraordinary qualities of her classmate. Now I was a mature woman with an established profile. I was what

Lila herself, sometimes joking, sometimes serious, had often repeated: Elena Greco, the brilliant friend of Raffaella Cerullo. From that unexpected reversal of destinies I would emerge annihilated.

But in that phase things were still going well for me. A full life, a still youthful appearance, the obligations of work, a reassuring fame didn't leave much room for those thoughts, reduced them to a vague uneasiness. Then came the bad years. My books sold less. I no longer had my position in the publishing house. I gained weight, I lost my figure, I felt old and frightened by the possibility of an old age of poverty, without fame. I had to acknowledge that, while I was working according to the mental approach I had imposed decades earlier, everything was different now, including me.

In 2005 I went to Naples, I saw Lila. It was a difficult day. She was further changed, she tried to be sociable, she neurotically greeted everyone, she talked too much. Seeing Africans, Asians in every corner of the neighborhood, smelling the odors of unknown cuisines, she became excited, she said: I haven't traveled around the world like you, but, look, the world has come to me. In Turin by now it was the same, and I liked the invasion of the exotic, how it had been reduced to the everyday. Yet only in the neighborhood did I realize how the anthropological landscape had altered. The old dialect had immediately taken in, according to an established tradition, mysterious languages, and meanwhile it was dealing with different phonic abilities, with syntaxes and sentiments that had once been very distant. The gray stone of the buildings had unexpected signs, old trafficking, legal and illegal, was mixed with new, the practice of violence opened up to new cultures.

That was when the news spread of Gigliola's corpse in the gardens. At the time we still didn't know that she had died of a heart attack, I thought she had been murdered. Her body, supine on the ground, was enormous. How she must have suffered from that transformation, she who had been beautiful and had caught the handsome Michele Solara. I am still alive—I thought—and yet I can't feel any different from that big body lying lifeless in that sordid place, in that sordid way. It was so. Although I paid excessive attention to my appearance, I no longer recognized myself, either: I moved more hesitantly, my physical expression was not what I had been used to for decades. As a girl I had felt so different and now I realized that I was like Gigliola.

Lila, on the other hand, seemed not to notice old age. She moved with energy, she shouted, she greeted people with expansive gestures. I didn't ask her, yet again, about her possible text. Whatever she said I was certain that it wouldn't reassure me. I didn't know how to get out of this depression, what to hold on to. The problem was no longer Lila's work, or its quality, or at least I didn't need to be aware of that threat to feel that everything I had written, since the end of the sixties, had lost weight and force, no longer spoke to an audience as it seemed to me it had done for decades, had no readers. Rather, on that melancholy occasion of death, I realized that the very nature of my anguish had changed. Now I was distressed that nothing of me would endure through time. My books had come out quickly and with their minor success had for decades given me the illusion of being engaged in meaningful work. But suddenly the illusion faded, I could no longer believe in the importance of my work. On the other hand, for Lila, too, everything had passed by: she led an obscure life; shut up in her parents' small apartment, she filled the computer with impressions and thoughts. And yet, I imagined, there was the possibility that her name—whether it was just a ribbon or not—now that she was an old woman, or even after her death, would be bound to a single work of great significance: not the thousands of pages that I had written, but a book whose success she would never enjoy, as I instead had done with mine, yet that nevertheless would endure through time and would be read and reread for hundreds of years. Lila had that possibility, I had squandered it. My fate was no different from Gigliola's, hers might be.

51.

For a while I let myself go. I did very little work, but then again, neither the publisher nor anyone else asked me to work more. I saw no one, I only made long phone calls to my daughters, insisting that they put the children on, and I spoke to them in baby talk. Now Elsa, too, had a boy, named Conrad, and Dede had given Hamid a sister, whom she had called Elena.

Those childish voices which expressed themselves with such precision made me think of Tina again. In the moments of greatest darkness I was sure that Lila had written the detailed story of her daughter, sure that she had mixed it into the history of Naples with the arrogant naïveté of the uneducated person who, perhaps for that very reason, obtains tremendous results. Then I understood that it was a fantasy of mine. Without wanting to, I was adding apprehension to envy, bitterness, and affection. Lila didn't have that type of ambition, she had never had ambitions. To carry out any project to which you attach your own name you have to love yourself, and she had told me, she didn't love herself, she loved nothing about herself. On the evenings of greatest depression I went so far as to imagine that she had lost her daughter in order not to see herself reproduced, in all her antipathy, in all her malicious reactivity, in all her intelligence without purpose. She wanted to eliminate herself, cancel all the traces, because she couldn't tolerate herself. She had done it continuously, for her entire existence, ever since she had shut herself off within a suffocating perimeter, confining herself at a time when the planet wanted to eliminate borders. She had never gotten on a train, not even to go to Rome. She had never taken a plane. Her experience was extremely limited, and when I thought about it I felt sorry for her, I laughed, I got up with a groan, I went to the computer, I wrote yet another e-mail saying: Come and see me, we'll be together for a while. At those moments I took it for granted that there was not and never would be a manuscript of Lila's. I had always overestimated her, nothing memorable would emerge from her—something that reassured me and yet truly upset me. I loved Lila. I wanted her to last. But I wanted it to be I who made her last. I thought it was my task. I was convinced that she herself, as a girl, had assigned it to me.

52.

The story that I later called *A Friendship* originated in that mildly depressive state, in Naples, during a week of rain. Of course I knew that I was violating an unwritten agreement between Lila and me, I also knew that she wouldn't tolerate it. But I thought that if the result was good, in the end she would say: I'm grateful to you, these were things I didn't have the courage to say even to myself, and you said them in my name. There is this presumption, in those who feel destined for art and above all literature: we act as if we had received an investiture, but in fact no one has ever invested us with anything, it is we who have authorized ourselves to be authors and yet we are resentful if others say: This little thing you did doesn't interest me, in fact it bores me, who gave you the right. Within a few days I wrote a story that over the years, hoping and fearing that Lila was writing it, I had imagined in every detail. I did it because everything that came from her, or that I ascribed to her, had seemed to me, since we were children, more meaningful, more promising, than what came from me.

When I finished the first draft I was in a hotel room with a balcony that had a beautiful view of Vesuvius and the gray semicircle of the city. I could have called Lila on the cell phone, said to her: I've written about me, about you, about Tina, about Imma, do you want to read it, it's only eighty pages, I'll come by your house, I'll read it aloud. I didn't do that out of fear. She had explicitly forbidden me not only to write about her but also to use persons and episodes of the neighborhood. When I had, she always found a way of telling me—even if painfully—that the book was bad, that either one is capable of telling things just as they happened, in teeming chaos, or one works from imagination, inventing a thread, and I had been able to do neither the first thing nor the second. So I let it go, I calmed myself, saying: it will happen as it always does, she won't like the story, she'll pretend it doesn't matter, in a few years she'll make it known to me, or tell me clearly, that I have to try to achieve more. In truth, I thought, if it were up to her I would never publish a line.

The book came out, I was swept up by a success I hadn't felt for a long time, and since I needed it I was happy. *A Friendship* kept me from joining the list of writers whom everyone considers dead even when they're still alive. The old books began to sell again, interest in me was rekindled, in spite of approaching old age life became full again. But that book, which at first I considered the best I had written, I later did not love. It's Lila who made me hate it, by refusing in every possible way to see me, to discuss it with me, even to insult me and hit me. I called her constantly, I wrote endless e-mails, I went to the neighborhood, I talked to Rino. She was never there. And on the other hand her son never said: My mother is acting like this because she doesn't want to see you. As usual he was vague, he stammered: You know how she is, she's always out, she either turns off the cell phone or forgets it at home, sometimes she doesn't even come home to sleep. So I had to acknowledge that our friendship was over.

53.

In fact I don't know what offended her, a detail, or the whole story. *A Friendship* had the quality, in my opinion, of being linear. It told concisely, with the necessary disguises, the story of our lives, from the loss of the dolls to the loss of Tina. Where had I gone wrong? I thought for a long time that she was angry because, in the final part, although resorting to imagination more than at other points of the story, I related what in fact had happened in reality: Lila had given Imma more importance in Nino's eyes, in doing so had been distracted, and as a result lost Tina. But evidently what in the fiction of the story serves in all innocence to reach the heart of the reader becomes an abomination for one who feels the echo of the facts she has really lived. In other words I thought for a long time that what had assured the book's success was also what had hurt Lila most.

Later, however, I changed my mind. I'm convinced that the reason for her repudiation lay elsewhere, in the way I recounted the episode of the dolls. I had deliberately exaggerated the moment when they disappeared into the darkness of the cellar, I had accentuated the trauma of the loss, and to intensify the emotional effects I had used the fact that one of the dolls and the lost child had the same name. The whole led the reader, step by step, to connect the childhood loss of the pretend daughters to the adult loss of the real daughter. Lila must have found it cynical, dishonest, that I had resorted to an important moment of our childhood, to her child, to her sorrow, to satisfy my audience.

But I am merely piecing together hypotheses, I would have to confront her, hear her protests, explain myself. Sometimes I feel guilty, and I understand her. Sometimes I hate her for this decision to cut me off so sharply right now, in old age, when we are in need of closeness and solidarity. She has always acted like that: when I don't submit, see how she excludes me, punishes me, ruins even my pleasure in having written a good book. I'm exasperated. Even this staging of her own disappearance, besides worrying me, irritates me. Maybe little Tina has nothing to do with it, maybe not even her ghost, which continues to obsess Lila both in the more enduring form of the child of nearly four, and in the labile form of the woman who today, like Imma, would be thirty. It's only and always the two of us who are involved: she who wants me to give what her nature and circumstances kept her from giving, I who can't give what she demands; she who gets angry at my inadequacy and out of spite wants to reduce me to nothing, as she has done with herself, I who have written for months and months and months to give her a form whose boundaries won't dissolve, and defeat her, and calm her, and so in turn calm myself.

EPILOGUE
RESTITUTION

1.

I can't believe it myself. I've finished this story that I thought would never end. I finished it and patiently reread it not so much to improve the quality of the writing as to find out if there are even a few lines where it's possible to trace the evidence that Lila entered my text and decided to contribute to writing it. But I have had to acknowledge that all these pages are mine alone. What Lila often threatened to do—enter my computer—she hasn't done, maybe she wasn't even capable of doing, it was long a fantasy I had as an old woman inexperienced in networks, cables, connections, electronic spirits. Lila is not in these words. There is only what I've been able to put down. Unless, by imagining what she would write and how, I am no longer able to distinguish what's mine and what's hers.

Often, during this work, I telephoned Rino, I asked about his mother. He doesn't know anything, the police limited themselves to summoning him three or four times to show him the bodies of nameless old women—so many of them disappear. A couple of times I had to go to Naples, and I met him in the old apartment in the neighborhood, a space darker, more run-down than it had been. There really wasn't anything of Lila anymore, everything that had been hers was gone. As for the son, he seemed more distracted than usual, as if his mother had definitively gone out of his head.

I returned to the city for two funerals, first my father's, then Lidia's, Nino's mother. I missed the funeral of Donato, not out of bitterness, only because I was abroad. When I came to the neighborhood for my father there was a great uproar because a young man had just been murdered at the entrance to the library. That made me think that this story would continue forever, recounting now the efforts of children without privileges to improve themselves by getting books from the old shelves, as Lila and I had done as girls, and now the thread of seductive chatter, promises, deceptions, of blood that prevents any true improvement in my city or in the world.

The day of Lidia's funeral was overcast, the city seemed tranquil, I felt tranquil, too. Then Nino arrived and all he did was talk loudly, joke, even laugh, as if we were not at his mother's funeral. I found him large, bloated, a big ruddy man with thinning hair who was constantly celebrating himself. Getting rid of him, after the funeral, was difficult. I didn't want to listen to him or even look at him. He gave me an impression of wasted time, of useless labor, that I feared would stay in my mind, extending into me, into everything.

On the occasion of both funerals I made plans ahead of time to visit Pasquale. In those years I did that whenever I could. In prison he had studied a lot, had received his high school diploma, and, recently, a degree in astronomical geography.

"If I'd known that to get a diploma and a degree all you needed to have was free time, to be shut up in a place without worrying about earning a living, and, with discipline, learning by heart pages and pages of some books, I would have done it before," he said once, in a teasing tone.

Today he's an old man, he speaks serenely, he is much better preserved than Nino. With me he rarely resorts to dialect. But he hasn't moved even a hairsbreadth out of the space of generous ideas in which his father enclosed him as a boy. When I saw him after Lidia's funeral and told him about Lila he burst out laughing. She must be doing her intelligent and imaginative things somewhere, he muttered. And it moved him to remember the time in the neighborhood library when the teacher assigned prizes to the most diligent readers, and the most diligent was Lila, who took out books illegally with her relatives' cards. Ah, Lila the shoemaker, Lila who imitated Kennedy's wife, Lila the artist and designer, Lila the worker, Lila the programmer, Lila always in the same place and always out of place.

"Who took Tina from her?" I asked.

"The Solaras."

"Sure?"

He smiled, showing his bad teeth. I understood that he wasn't telling the truth—maybe he didn't know it and it didn't even interest him—but was proclaiming the unshakable faith, based on the primary experience of injustice, the experience of the neighborhood, that—in spite of the reading he had done, the degree he had taken, the clandestine journeys, the crimes he had committed or been accused of—remained the currency of every certainty he had. He answered:

"Do you also want me to tell you who murdered those two pieces of shit?"

Suddenly I read in his gaze something that horrified me— an inextinguishable rancor—and I said no. He shook his head, and continued to smile. He said:

"You'll see that when Lila decides to, she'll show up."

But there was not a trace of her. On those two occasions for mourning I walked through the neighborhood, I asked around out of curiosity: no one remembered her, or maybe they were pretending. I couldn't even talk about her with Carmen. Roberto died, she left the gas pump, went to live with one of her sons, in Formia.

What is the point of all these pages, then? I intended to capture her, to have her beside me again, and I will die without knowing if I succeeded. Sometimes I wonder where she vanished. At the bottom of the sea. Through a fissure or down some subterranean tunnel whose existence she alone knows. In an old bathtub filled with a powerful acid. In an ancient garbage pit, one of those she devoted so many words to. In the crypt of an abandoned church in the mountains. In one of the many dimensions that we don't know yet but Lila does, and now she's there with her daughter.

Will she return?

Will they return together, Lila old, Tina a grown woman?

This morning, sitting on the balcony that looks out over the Po, I'm waiting.

2.

I have breakfast every day at seven, I go to the newsstand with the Labrador I got recently, I spend a good part of the morning in the Valentino playing with the dog, leafing through the papers. Yesterday, when I got back, I found on top of my mailbox a package roughly wrapped in newspaper. I took it, perplexed. Nothing indicated that it had been left for me or for any other tenant. There was no note with it and it didn't even have my last name written in pen somewhere.

I cautiously opened one edge of the wrapping, and that was enough. Tina and Nu leaped out of memory even before I got them completely out of the newspaper. I immediately recognized the dolls that one after the other, almost six decades earlier, had been thrown—mine by Lila, Lila's by me—into a cellar in the neighborhood. They were the dolls we had never found, although we had descended underground to look for them. They were the ones that Lila had pushed me to go and retrieve from the house of Don Achille, ogre and thief, and Don Achille had claimed that he hadn't taken them, and maybe he had imagined that it was his son Alfonso who stole them, and so had compensated us with money to buy new ones. But we hadn't bought dolls with that money—how could we have replaced Tina and Nu?—instead we bought *Little Women*, the novel that had led Lila to write *The Blue Fairy* and me to become what I was today, the author of many books and, most important, of a remarkably successful story entitled *A Friendship*.

The lobby of the building was silent, no voices or other sounds came from the apartments. I looked around anxiously. I wanted Lila to emerge from stairway A or B or from the deserted porter's room, thin, gray, her back bent. I wished it more than any other thing, I wished it more than an unexpected visit from my daughters with their children. I expected that she would say in her usual mocking way: Do you like this gift? But it didn't happen and I burst into tears. Here's what she had done: she had deceived me, she had dragged me wherever she wanted, from the beginning of our friendship. All our lives she had told a story of redemption that was *hers*, using *my* living body and *my* existence.

Or maybe not. Maybe those two dolls that had crossed more than half a century and had come all the way to Turin meant only that she was well and loved me, that she had broken her confines and finally intended to travel the world by now no less small than hers, living in old age, according to a new truth, the life that in youth had been forbidden to her and that she had forbidden herself.

I went up in the elevator, I shut myself in my apartment. I examined the two dolls carefully, I smelled the odor of mold, I arranged them against the spines of my books. Seeing how cheap and ugly they were I felt confused. Unlike stories, real life, when it has passed, inclines toward obscurity, not clarity. I thought: now that Lila has let herself be seen so plainly, I must resign myself to not seeing her anymore.

Elena Ferrante is the author of *The Days of Abandonment* (Europa, 2005), *Troubling Love* (Europa, 2006), and *The Lost Daughter* (Europa, 2008), soon to be a film directed by Maggie Gyllenhaal and starring Olivia Colman, Dakota Johnson, and Paul Mescal. She is also the author of *Incidental Inventions* (Europa, 2019), illustrated by Andrea Ucini, *Frantumaglia: A Writer's Journey* (Europa, 2016) and *The Beach at Night* (Europa, 2016), a children's picture book illustrated by Mara Cerri. The four volumes known as the "Neapolitan quartet" (*My Brilliant Friend*, *The Story of a New Name, Those Who Leave and Those Who Stay*, and *The Story of the Lost Child*) were published by Europa Editions in English between 2012 and 2015. *My Brilliant Friend*, the HBO series directed by Saverio Costanzo, premiered in 2018. Ferrante's most recent novel is *The Lying Life of Adults*, published in 2020 by Europa Editions.

"[Ferrante's Neapolitan Novels] don't merely offer a teeming vision of working-class Naples, with its cobblers and professors, communists and mobbed-up businessmen, womanizing poets and downtrodden wives; they present one of modern fiction's richest portraits of a friendship."   —John Powers, Fresh Air, *NPR*

"The feverish speculation about the identity of Elena Ferrante betrays an understandable failure of imagination: it seems impossible that right now somewhere someone sits in a room and draws up these books. Palatial and heartbreaking beyond measure, the Neapolitan novels seem less written than they do revealed. One simply surrenders. When the final volume appears—may that day never come!—they're bound to be acknowledged as one of the most powerful works of art, in any medium, of our age."
                    —Gideon Lewis-Kraus, author of *A Sense of Direction*

"Ferrante tackles girlhood and friendship with amazing force."
                    —Gwyneth Paltrow, actor

"Ferrante draws an indelible picture of the city's mean streets and the poverty, violence and sameness of lives lived in the same place forever . . . She is a fierce writer."   —*Shelf Awareness*

"Ferrante transforms the love, separation and reunion of two poor urban girls into the general tragedy of their city."
                    —*The New York Times*

"Elena Ferrante: the best angry woman writer ever!"
                    —John Waters, director

"Beautifully translated by Ann Goldstein . . . Ferrante writes with a ferocious, intimate urgency that is a celebration of anger. Ferrante is terribly good with anger, a very specific sort of wrath harbored by women, who are so often not allowed to give voice to it. We are angry, a lot of the time, at the position we're in—whether it's as wife, daughter, mother, friend—and I can think of no other woman writing who is so swift and gorgeous in this rage, so bracingly fearless in mining fury."   —Susanna Sonnenberg, The *San Francisco Chronicle*

"Elena Ferrante's *The Story of a New Name*. Book two in her Naples trilogy. Two words: Read it."   —Ann Hood, writer (from Twitter)

"The through-line in all of Ferrante's investigations, for me, is nothing less than one long, mind-and-heart-shredding howl for the history of women (not only Neapolitan women), and its implicit *j'accuse* . . . Ferrante's effect, critics agree, is inarguable. 'Intensely, violently personal' and 'brutal directness, familial torment' is how James Wood ventures to categorize her—descriptions that seem mild after you've encountered the work."
                              —Joan Frank, The *San Francisco Chronicle*

"Lila, mercurial, unsparing, and, at the end of this first episode in a planned trilogy from Ferrante, seemingly capable of starting a full-scale neighborhood war, is a memorable character."
                                                        —*Publishers Weekly*

"Ferrante's own writing has no limits, is willing to take every thought forward to its most radical conclusion and backwards to its most radical birthing."   —*The New Yorker*

FROM THE UNITED KINGDOM

"*The Story of a New Name*, like its predecessor, is fiction of the very highest order."   —*Independent on Sunday*

"*My Brilliant Friend*, translated by Ann Goldstein, is stunning: an intense, forensic exploration of the friendship between Lila and the story's narrator, Elena. Ferrante's evocation of the working-class district of Naples where Elena and Lila first meet as two wiry eight-year-olds is cinematic in the density of its detail."
                                          —*The Times Literary Supplement*

"This is a story about friendship as a mass of roiling currents—love, envy, pity, spite, dependency and Schadenfreude coiling around one another, tricky to untangle."   —*Intelligent Life*

"Elena Ferrante may be the best contemporary novelist you have

never heard of. The Italian author has written six lavishly praised novels. But she writes under a pseudonym and will not offer herself for public consumption. Her characters likewise defy convention . . . Her prose is crystal, and her storytelling both visceral and compelling."
—*The Economist*

FROM ITALY

"*Those Who Leave and Those Who Stay* evokes the vital flux of a heartbeat, of blood flowing through our veins."   —*La Repubblica*

"We don't know who she is, but it doesn't matter. Ferrante's books are enthralling self-contained monoliths that do not seek friendship but demand silent, fervid admiration from her passionate readers . . . The thing most real in these novels is the intense, almost osmotic relationship that unites Elena and Lila, the two girls from a neighborhood in Naples who are the peerless protagonists of the Neapolitan novels."
—*Famiglia Cristiana*

"Today it is near impossible to find writers capable of bringing smells, tastes, feelings, and contradictory passions to their pages. Elena Ferrante, alone, seems able to do it. There is no writer better suited to composing the great Italian novel of her generation, her country, and her time."
—*Il Manifesto*

"Regardless of who is behind the name Elena Ferrante, the mysterious pseudonym used by the author of the Neapolitan novels, two things are certain: she is a woman and she knows how to describe Naples like nobody else. She does so with a style that recalls an enchanted spider web with its expressive power and the wizardry with which it creates an entire world."   —*Huffington Post* (Italy)

"A marvel that is without limits and beyond genre." —*Il Salvagente*

"Elena Ferrante is proving that literature can cure our present ills; it can cure the spirit by operating as an antidote to the nervous attempts we make to see ourselves reflected in the present-day of a country that is increasingly repellent."
—*Il Mattino*

"*My Brilliant Friend* flows from the soul like an eruption from Mount Vesuvio."   —*La Repubblica*

FROM AUSTRALIA

"No one has a voice quite like Ferrante's. Her gritty, ruthlessly frank novels roar off the page with a barbed fury, like an attack that is also a defense . . . Ferrante's fictions are fierce, unsentimental glimpses at the way a woman is constantly under threat, her identity submerged in marriage, eclipsed by motherhood, mythologised by desire. Imagine if Jane Austen got angry and you'll have some idea of how explosive these works are."   —John Freeman, *The Australian*

"One of the most astounding—and mysterious—contemporary Italian novelists available in translation, Elena Ferrante unfolds the tumultuous inner lives of women in her thrillingly menacing stories of lost love, negligent mothers and unfulfilled desires."   —*The Age*

"Ferrante bewitches with her tiny, intricately drawn world . . . *My Brilliant Friend* journeys fearlessly into some of that murkier psychological territory where questions of individual identity are inextricable from circumstance and the ever-changing identities of others."
—*The Melbourne Review*

"The Neapolitan novels move far from contrivance, logic or respectability to ask uncomfortable questions about how we live, how we love, how we singe an existence in a deeply flawed world that expects pretty acquiescence from its women. In all their beauty, their ugliness, their devotion and deceit, these girls enchant and repulse, like life, like our very selves."   —The *Sydney Morning Herald*

THOSE WHO LEAVE
AND THOSE WHO STAY

Elena Ferrante

THOSE WHO LEAVE
AND THOSE WHO STAY

Book Three, The Neapolitan Quartet
Middle Time

*Translated from the Italian
by Ann Goldstein*

Europa
editions

Europa Editions
1 Penn Plaza Suite 6282
New York, N. Y. 10019
www.europaeditions.com
info@europaeditions.com

Copyright © 2013 by Edizioni E/O
First Publication 2014 by Europa Editions
Twenty-fourth printing, 2021

Translation by Ann Goldstein
Original title: *Storia di chi fugge e di chi resta*
Translation copyright © 2014 by Europa Editions

Library of Congress Cataloging in Publication Data is available
ISBN 978-1-60945-233-9

Ferrante, Elena
Those Who Leave and Those Who Stay

Book design by Emanuele Ragnisco
www.mekkanografici.com

Cover photo © J Wheeler and V Laws/Corbis

Prepress by Grafica Punto Print – Rome

Printed in Italy

THOSE WHO LEAVE
AND THOSE WHO STAY

INDEX OF CHARACTERS AND NOTES ON THE EVENTS
OF THE EARLIER VOLUMES

The Cerullo family (the shoemaker's family):

Fernando Cerullo, shoemaker, Lila's father. He wouldn't send his daughter beyond elementary school.

Nunzia Cerullo, Lila's mother. Close to her daughter, but without sufficient authority to support her against her father.

Raffaella Cerullo, called Lina, or Lila. She was born in August, 1944, and is sixty-six when she disappears from Naples without a trace. A brilliant student, at the age of ten she writes a story titled *The Blue Fairy*. She leaves school after getting her elementary-school diploma and learns to be a shoemaker. She marries Stefano Carracci at a young age and successfully manages first the grocery store in the new neighborhood and then the shoe store in Piazza dei Martiri. During a vacation on Ischia she falls in love with Nino Sarratore, for whom she leaves her husband. After the shipwreck of her relationship with Nino and the birth of her son Gennaro (also called Rino), Lila leaves Stefano definitively when she discovers that he is expecting a child with Ada Cappuccio. She moves with Enzo Scanno to San Giovanni a Teduccio and begins working in the sausage factory belonging to Bruno Soccavo.

Rino Cerullo, Lila's older brother, also a shoemaker. With his father, Fernando, and thanks to Lila and to Stefano Carracci's money, he sets up the Cerullo shoe factory. He marries Stefano's sister, Pinuccia Carracci, with whom he has a son, Ferdinando, called Dino. Lila's son bears his name, Rino.

Other children.

The Greco family (the porter's family):

Elena Greco, called Lenuccia or Lenù. Born in August, 1944, she is the author of the long story we are reading. Elena begins to write it when she learns that her childhood friend Lina Cerullo, whom she calls Lila, has disappeared. After elementary school, Elena continues to study, with increasing success; in high school her abilities and Professor Galiani's protection allow her to survive unscathed a clash with the religion teacher about the role of the Holy Spirit. At the invitation of Nino Sarratore, with whom she has been secretly in love since childhood, and with valuable help from Lila, she writes an article about this clash, which, in the end, is not published in the magazine Nino contributes to. Elena's brilliant schoolwork is crowned by a degree from the Scuola Normale, in Pisa, where she meets and becomes engaged to Pietro Airota, and by the publication of a novel in which she reimagines the life of the neighborhood and her adolescent experiences on Ischia.

Peppe, *Gianni*, and *Elisa*, Elena's younger siblings.

The *father* is a porter at the city hall.

The *mother* is a housewife. Her limping gait haunts Elena.

The Carracci family (Don Achille's family):

Don Achille Carracci, the ogre of fairy tales, dealer in the black market, loan shark. He was murdered.

Maria Carracci, wife of Don Achille, mother of Stefano, Pinuccia, and Alfonso. She works in the family grocery store.

Stefano Carracci, son of Don Achille, husband of Lila. He manages the assets accumulated by his father and over time becomes a successful shopkeeper, thanks to two profitable grocery stores and the shoe store in Piazza dei Martiri, which he opens with the Solara brothers. Dissatisfied by his stormy marriage to Lila, he initiates a relationship with Ada Cappuccio. He and Ada start living together when she becomes pregnant and Lila moves to San Giovanni a Teduccio.

Pinuccia, daughter of Don Achille. She works in the family grocery store, and then in the shoe store. She is married to Lila's brother, Rino, and has a son with him, Ferdinando, called Dino.

Alfonso, son of Don Achille. He is Elena's schoolmate. He is the boyfriend of Marisa Sarratore and becomes the manager of the shoe store in Piazza dei Martiri.

The Peluso family (the carpenter's family):

Alfredo Peluso, carpenter. Communist. Accused of killing Don Achille, he was convicted and sent to prison, where he dies.

Giuseppina Peluso, wife of Alfredo. A worker in the tobacco factory, she is devoted to her children and her imprisoned husband. After his death, she commits suicide.

Pasquale Peluso, older son of Alfredo and Giuseppina, construction worker, militant Communist. He was the first to become aware of Lila's beauty and to declare his love for her. He detests the Solaras. He was the boyfriend of Ada Cappuccio.

Carmela Peluso, also called *Carmen,* sister of Pasquale. She is a salesclerk in a notions store but is soon hired by Lila to work in Stefano's new grocery store. She was the girlfriend of Enzo Scanno for a long time, but he leaves her without explanation at the end of his military service. She subsequently becomes engaged to the owner of the gas pump on the *stradone.*

Other children.

The Cappuccio family (the mad widow's family):

Melina, a relative of Nunzia Cerullo, a widow. She washes the stairs of the apartment buildings in the old neighborhood. She was the lover of Donato Sarratore, Nino's father. The Sarratores left the neighborhood because of that relationship, and Melina has nearly lost her mind.

Melina's husband, who unloaded crates in the fruit and vegetable market, and died in mysterious circumstances.

Ada Cappuccio, Melina's daughter. As a girl she helped her mother wash the stairs. Thanks to Lila, she is hired as a salesclerk in the Carraccis' grocery. She is the girlfriend of Pasquale Peluso, and becomes the lover of Stefano Carracci: when she gets pregnant she goes to live with him. From their relationship a girl, Maria, is born.

Antonio Cappuccio, her brother, a mechanic. He is Elena's boyfriend and is very jealous of Nino Sarratore. The prospect of leaving for military service worries him deeply, but when Elena turns to the Solara brothers to help him avoid it, he is humiliated, so much so that he breaks off their relationship. During his military service he has a nervous breakdown and is discharged early; back in the neighborhood, driven by poverty, he goes to work for Michele Solara, who at a certain point sends him to Germany on a long and mysterious job.

Other children.

The Sarratore family (the railway-worker poet's family):

Donato Sarratore, train conductor, poet, journalist. A great womanizer, he was the lover of Melina Cappuccio. When Elena goes on vacation to Ischia, and is a guest in the same house where the Sarratores are staying, she is compelled to leave in a hurry to escape Donato's sexual molestations. The following summer, however, Elena gives herself to him on the beach, driven by the suffering that the relationship between Nino and Lila has caused her. To exorcise this degrading experience, Elena writes about it in the book that is then published.

Lidia Sarratore, wife of Donato.

Nino Sarratore, the oldest of the five children of Donato and Lidia. He hates his father. He is an extremely brilliant student and has a long secret affair with Lila. They live together briefly when Lila becomes pregnant.

Marisa Sarratore, sister of Nino. The girlfriend of Alfonso Carracci.

Pino, *Clelia*, and *Ciro Sarratore,* younger children of Donato and Lidia.

The Scanno family (the fruit-and-vegetable seller's family):

Nicola Scanno, fruit-and-vegetable seller, died of pneumonia.

Assunta Scanno, wife of Nicola, died of cancer.

Enzo Scanno, son of Nicola and Assunta, also a fruit-and-vegetable seller. Lila has felt a liking for him since childhood. Enzo was for a long time the boyfriend of Carmen Peluso, whom he leaves without explanation upon his return from military service. During his military service he started to study again, and he earns an engineering diploma. When Lila finally decides to leave Stefano, he takes responsibility for her and her son, Gennaro, and the three of them go to live in San Giovanni a Teduccio.

Other children.

The Solara family (the family of the owner of the Solara bar-pastry shop):

Silvio Solara, owner of the bar-pastry shop, Monarchist-fascist and Camorrist tied to the illegal trafficking in the neighborhood. He opposed the Cerullo shoe factory.

Manuela Solara, wife of Silvio, moneylender: her red book is much feared in the neighborhood.

Marcello and Michele Solara, sons of Silvio and Manuela. Braggarts, arrogant, they are nevertheless loved by the neighborhood girls, except Lila and Elena. Marcello is in love with Lila but she rejects him. Michele, a little younger than Marcello, is colder, more intelligent, more violent. He is engaged to Gigliola, the daughter of the pastry maker, but over the years develops a morbid obsession with Lila.

The Spagnuolo family (the baker's family):
Signor Spagnuolo, pastry maker at the Solaras' bar-pastry shop.
Rosa Spagnuolo, wife of the pastry maker.
Gigliola Spagnuolo, daughter of the pastry maker, engaged to Michele Solara.
Other children.

The Airota family:
Guido Airota, professor of Greek literature.
Adele Airota, his wife. She works for the Milanese publishing house that publishes Elena's novel.
Mariarosa Airota, the older daughter, professor of art history in Milan.
Pietro Airota, university colleague of Elena's and her fiancé, destined for a brilliant academic career.

The teachers:
Maestro Ferraro, teacher and librarian. He gave both Lila and Elena prizes when they were young, because they were diligent readers.
Maestra Oliviero, teacher. She is the first to notice the potential of Lila and Elena. At the age of ten, Lila writes a story titled *The Blue Fairy*. Elena, who likes the story a lot, gives it to Maestra Oliviero to read. But the teacher, angry because Lila's parents wouldn't send their daughter beyond elementary school, never says anything about it. In fact, she stops

concerning herself with Lila and concentrates only on the success of Elena. She dies after a long illness soon after Elena graduates from the university.

Professor Gerace, high-school teacher.

Professor Galiani, high-school teacher. She is a very cultured woman and a Communist. She is immediately charmed by Elena's intelligence. She lends her books, protects her in the clash with the religion teacher, invites her to a party at her house given by her children. Their relations cool when Nino, overwhelmed by his passion for Lila, leaves her daughter Nadia.

Other characters:

Gino, son of the pharmacist. Elena's first boyfriend.

Nella Incardo, the cousin of Maestra Oliviero. She lives in Barano, on Ischia, and rents rooms during the summer to the Sarratore family. Elena stays with her for a vacation at the beach.

Armando, medical student, son of Professor Galiani.

Nadia, student, daughter of Professor Galiani, and girlfriend of Nino, who leaves her, sending her a letter from Ischia when he falls in love with Lila.

Bruno Soccavo, friend of Nino Sarratore and son of a rich industrialist in San Giovanni a Teduccio, near Naples. He gives Lila a job in his family's sausage factory.

Franco Mari, student and Elena's boyfriend during her first years at the university.

MIDDLE TIME

I saw Lila for the last time five years ago, in the winter of 2005. We were walking along the *stradone,* early in the morning and, as had been true for years now, were unable to feel at ease. I was the only one talking, I remember: she was humming, she greeted people who didn't respond, the rare times she interrupted me she uttered only exclamations, without any evident relation to what I was saying. Too many bad things, and some terrible, had happened over the years, and to regain our old intimacy we would have had to speak our secret thoughts, but I didn't have the strength to find the words and she, who perhaps had the strength, didn't have the desire, didn't see the use.

Yet I loved her, and when I came to Naples I always tried to see her, even though, I have to say, I was a little afraid of her. She had changed a great deal. Age had had the better of us both by then, but while I fought a tendency to gain weight she was permanently skin and bones. She had short hair that she cut herself; it was completely white, not by choice but from neglect. Her face was deeply lined, and increasingly recalled her father's. She laughed nervously, almost a shriek, and spoke too loudly. She was constantly gesturing, giving to each gesture such fierce determination that she seemed to want to slice in half the houses, the street, the passersby, me.

We had gone as far as the elementary school when a young man I didn't know overtook us, out of breath, and shouted to her that the body of a woman had been found in a flowerbed next to the church. We hurried to the gardens, and Lila dragged me into the knot of curious bystanders, rudely opening a path. The woman was lying on one side; she was extraordinarily fat, and was wearing an unfashionable dark-green raincoat. Lila recognized her immediately, but I did not: it was our childhood friend Gigliola Spagnuolo, the ex-wife of Michele Solara.

I hadn't seen her for several decades. Her beautiful face was ruined, and her ankles had become enormous. Her hair, once brown, was now fiery red, and long, the way she'd had it as a girl, but thin, and spread out on the loose dirt. One foot was shod in a worn, low-heeled shoe; the other was encased in a gray wool stocking, with a hole at the big toe, and the shoe was a few feet beyond, as if she had lost it kicking against some pain or fear. I burst into tears; Lila looked at me in annoyance.

Sitting on a bench nearby, we waited in silence until Gigliola was taken away. What had happened to her, how she had died, for the moment no one knew. We went to Lila's house, her parents' old, small apartment, where she now lived with her son Rino. We talked about our friend; Lila criticized her, the life she had led, her pretensions, her betrayals. But now it was I who couldn't listen. I thought of that face in profile on the dirt, of how thin the long hair was, of the whitish patches of skull. How many who had been girls with us were no longer alive, had disappeared from the face of the earth because of illness, because their nervous systems had been unable to endure the sandpaper of torments, because their blood had been spilled. For a while we sat in the kitchen listlessly, neither of us decisive enough to clear the table. Then we went out again.

The sun of the fine winter day gave things a serene aspect. The old neighborhood, unlike us, had remained the same. The low gray houses endured, the courtyard of our games, the dark mouths of the tunnel, and the violence. But the landscape around it had changed. The greenish stretch of the ponds was no longer there, the old canning factory had vanished. In their place was the gleam of glass skyscrapers, once signs of a radiant future that no one had ever believed in. I had registered the changes, all of them, over the years, at times with curiosity, more often carelessly. As a child I had imagined that, beyond the neighborhood, Naples was full of marvels. The skyscraper at the central station, for example, had made a great impression, decades earlier, as it rose, story by story, the skeleton of a building that seemed to us extremely tall, beside the ambitious railroad station. How surprised I was when I passed through Piazza Garibaldi: look how high it is, I said to Lila, to Carmen, to Pasquale, to Ada, to Antonio, to all the companions of those days, as we made our way to the sea, to the edges of the wealthy neighborhoods. At the top, I thought, live the angels, and surely they delight in the whole city. To climb up there, to ascend—how I would have liked that. It was *our* skyscraper, even if it was outside the neighborhood, a thing that we saw growing day by day. But the work had stopped. When I came back from Pisa, the station skyscraper no longer seemed the symbol of a community that was reviving but, rather, another nest of inefficiency.

During that period I was convinced that there was no great difference between the neighborhood and Naples, the malaise slid from one to the other without interruption. Whenever I returned I found a city that was spineless, that couldn't stand up to changes of season, heat, cold, and, especially, storms. Look how the station on Piazza Garibaldi was flooded, look how the Galleria opposite the museum had collapsed; there was a landslide, and the electricity didn't come back on. Lodged in my memory were dark streets full of dangers, unregulated traffic, broken pavements, giant puddles. The clogged sewers splattered, dribbled over. Lavas of water and sewage and garbage and bacteria spilled into the sea from the hills that were burdened with new, fragile structures, or eroded the world from below. People died of carelessness, of corruption, of abuse, and yet, in every round of voting, gave their enthusiastic approval to the politicians who made their life unbearable. As soon as I got off the train, I moved cautiously in the places where I had grown up, always careful to speak in dialect, as if to indicate *I am one of yours, don't hurt me.*

When I graduated from college, when, in a single burst, I wrote a story that in the space of a few months became, surprisingly, a book, the things of the world I came from seemed to me to deteriorate even further. In Pisa, in Milan, I felt good, at times even happy; upon every return to my own city I feared that some unexpected event would keep me from escaping, that the things I had gained would be taken away from me. I would be unable to reach Pietro, whom I was soon to marry; the tidy space of the publishing house would be barred to me; I would no longer enjoy the refinements of Adele, my future mother-in-law, a mother as mine had never been. Already in the past the city had seemed to me crowded, a crush from Piazza Garibaldi to Forcella, to Duchesca, to Lavinaio, to the Rettifilo. In the late sixties the crush seemed to intensify, while impatience, aggressiveness spread without restraint. One morning I ventured out to Via Mezzocannone, where some years earlier I had worked as a clerk in a bookstore. I went because I was curious to see the place where I had toiled, and also to see the university, where I had never been. I wanted to compare it with the university in Pisa, the Normale, I was even hoping I might run into the children of Professor Galiani—Armando, Nadia—and boast of what I had accomplished. But the street, the university buildings had distressed me. They were teeming with students from Naples and the province and the whole South, well-dressed, noisy, self-confident youths, and others, rough yet inferior. They thronged the entrances, the classrooms, stood in long, often quarrelsome lines in front of the secretaries. Without warning, three or four started hitting each other a few steps from me, as if the mere sight of one another were sufficient for an explosion of insults and blows, a fury of boys shouting their craving for blood in a dialect that I myself had difficulty understanding. I left in a hurry, as if something threatening had touched me in a place that I had imagined safe, inhabited only by good reasons.

Every year, in other words, it seemed to me worse. In that season of rains, the city had cracked yet again, an entire build-ing had buckled onto one side, like a person who, sitting in an old chair, leans on the worm-eaten arm and it gives way. Dead, wounded. And shouts, blows, cherry bombs. The city seemed to harbor in its guts a fury that couldn't get out and therefore eroded it from the inside, or erupted in pustules on the sur-face, swollen with venom against everyone, children, adults, old people, visitors from other cities, Americans from NATO, tourists of every nationality, the Neapolitans themselves. How could one endure in that place of disorder and danger, on the outskirts, in the center, on the hills, at the foot of Vesuvius? What a brutal impression San Giovanni a Teduccio had left on me, and the journey to get there. How brutal the factory where Lila was working, and Lila herself—Lila with her small child, Lila who lived in a run-down building with Enzo, although they didn't sleep together. She had said that he wanted to study computers, and that she was trying to help him. I still remem-ber her voice, as it tried to erase San Giovanni, the salami, the odor of the factory, her situation, by citing with false expertise abbreviations like: Cybernetics Center of the State University of Milan, Soviet Center for the Application of Computer Science to the Social Sciences. She wanted to make me believe that a center of that type would soon be established even in Naples. I had thought: in Milan maybe, certainly in the Soviet Union, but here no, here it is the folly of your uncontrollable mind, into which you are dragging even poor, devoted Enzo. Leave, instead. Get away for good, far from the life we've lived since birth. Settle in well-organized lands where everything really is possible. I had fled, in fact. Only to discover, in the decades to come, that I had been wrong, that it was a chain with larger and larger links: the neighborhood was connected to the city, the city to Italy, Italy to Europe, Europe to the whole planet. And this is how I see it today: it's not the neighborhood that's sick, it's not Naples, it's the entire earth, it's the universe, or universes. And shrewdness means hiding and hiding from oneself the true state of things.

I talked about it with Lila that afternoon, in the winter of 2005, emphatically and as if to make amends. I wanted to acknowledge openly that she had understood everything since she was a girl, without ever leaving Naples. But I was almost immediately ashamed, I heard in my words the irritable pessimism of someone who is getting old, a tone I knew she detested.

In fact, in a nervous grimace of a smile that showed her old teeth, she said: "Are you playing the know-it-all, the moralizer? What do you intend to do? You want to write about us? You want to write about me?"

"No."

"Tell the truth."

"It would be too complicated."

"You've thought about it, though, you're thinking about it."

"A little, yes."

"Let me be, Lenù. Let us all be. We ought to disappear, we deserve nothing, neither Gigliola nor me, no one."

"That's not true."

She had an ugly expression of discontent, and she scrutinized me, her pupils hardly visible, her lips half parted.

"All right," she said, "write, if you want, write about Gigliola, about whoever you want. But about me no, don't you dare, promise."

"I won't write about anyone, not even you."

"Careful, I've got my eye on you."

"Yes?"

"I'll come look in your computer, I'll read your files, I'll erase them."

"Come on."

"You think I'm not capable of it?"

"I know you're capable. But I can protect myself."

She laughed in her old mean way.

"Not from me."

2.

I have never forgotten those three words; it was the last thing she said to me: *Not from me.* For weeks now I've been writing at a good pace, without wasting time rereading. If Lila is still alive—I imagine as I sip my coffee and look out at the Po, bumping against the piers of the Principessa Isabella bridge—she won't be able to resist, she'll come and poke around in my computer, she'll read, and, cantankerous old woman that she is, she'll get angry at my disobedience, she'll want to interfere, correct, add, she'll forget her craving to disappear. Then I wash the cup, go back to the desk to write, starting from that cold spring evening in Milan, more than forty years ago, in the bookstore, when the man with the thick eyeglasses spoke derisively about me and my book in front of everyone, and I replied in confusion, shaking. Until suddenly Nino Sarratore stood up and, almost unrecognizable with his unruly black beard, harshly attacked the man who had attacked me. Right then my whole self began to silently shout his name—how long had it been since I'd seen him: four, five years—and although I was ice-cold with tension I felt myself blushing.

As soon as Nino stopped talking, the man, with a slight gesture, asked to respond. It was clear that he was offended, but I was too agitated by violent emotions to immediately understand why. I was aware, naturally, that Nino's words had shifted the conversation from literature to politics, and in an aggressive, almost disrespectful way. Yet at the moment I gave that little importance; I couldn't forgive myself for my failure to stand up to the challenge, for having been ineffectual in front of a sophisticated audience. And yet I was clever. In high school I had reacted to my disadvantages by trying to become like Professor Galiani, I had adopted her tones and her language. In Pisa that model of a woman hadn't been enough; I had had to deal with highly experienced people. Franco, Pietro, all the best students, and of course the renowned teachers at the Normale expressed themselves in a complex manner: they wrote with deliberate artifice, they had an ability to classify, a logical lucidity, that Professor Galiani didn't possess. But I had trained myself to be like them. And often I succeeded: it seemed to me that I had mastered words to the point of sweeping away forever the contradictions of being in the world, the surge of emotions, and breathless speech. In short, I now knew a method of speaking and writing that—by means of a refined vocabulary, stately and thoughtful pacing, a determined arrangement of arguments, and a formal orderliness that wasn't supposed to fail—sought to annihilate the interlocutor to the point where he lost the will to object. But that evening things didn't go as they should have. First, Adele and her friends, whom I imagined as very sophisticated readers, and then the man with the thick eyeglasses intimidated me. I had become again the eager little girl from the poor neighborhood of Naples, the daughter of the porter with the dialect cadence of the South, amazed at having ended up in that place, playing the part of the cultured young writer. So I had lost confidence and expressed myself in an unconvincing, disjointed manner. Not to mention Nino. His appearance had taken away any self-control, and the very quality of his speech on my behalf had confirmed to me that I had abruptly lost my abilities. We came from backgrounds that were not very different, we had both worked hard to acquire that language. And yet not only had he used it naturally, turning it easily against the speaker, but, at times, when it seemed to him necessary, he had even dared to insert disorder into that polished Italian with a bold nonchalance that rapidly managed to make the professorial tones of the other man sound out of date and perhaps a little ridiculous. As a result, when I saw that the man wished to speak again, I thought: he's really angry, and if he said bad things about my book before, now he'll say something even worse to humiliate Nino, who defended it.

But the man seemed to be gripped by something else: he did not return to my book; he didn't bring me into it at all. He focused instead on certain formulas that Nino had used incidentally but had repeated several times: things like *baronial arrogance, anti-authoritarian literature*. I understood only then that what had made him angry was the political turn of the discussion. He hadn't liked that vocabulary, and he emphasized this by inserting a sudden sarcastic falsetto into his deep voice (*And so pride in knowledge is today characterized as pretension, and so literature, too, has become anti-authoritarian?*). Then he began to play subtly with the word *authority*, thank God, he said, a barrier against the uncultured youths who make random pronouncements on everything by resorting to the nonsense of who knows what student-run course at the state university. And he spoke at length on that subject, addressing the audience, never Nino or me directly. In his conclusion, however, he focused first on the old critic who was sitting next to me and then directly on Adele, who was perhaps his true polemical objective from the beginning. I have no argument with the young people, he said, briefly, but with those educated adults who, out of self-interest, are always ready to ride the latest fashion in stupidity. Here at last he was silent, and he prepared to leave with quiet but energetic "Excuse me"s, "May I"s, "thank you"s.

The audience rose to let him pass, hostile and yet deferential. It was utterly clear to me by now that he was an important man, so important that even Adele answered his dark nod of greeting with a cordial *Thank you, goodbye*. Maybe for that reason Nino surprised everyone a little when, in an imperative and at the same time joking tone, evidence that he was aware who he was dealing with, he called him by the title of professor—*Professor, where are you going, don't run off*—and then, thanks to the agility of his long legs, cut off his path, confronted him, spoke to him in that new language of his that I couldn't really hear from where I was, couldn't really understand, but that must be like steel cables in a hot sun. The man listened without moving, showing no signs of impatience, and then he made a gesture with his hand that meant move aside, and headed toward the door.

3.

I left the table in a daze, struggling to take in the fact that Nino was really there, in Milan, in that room. And yet he was, already he was coming toward me, smiling, but at a restrained, unhurried pace. We shook hands, his was hot, mine cold, and we said how glad we were to see each other after so long. To know that finally the worst of the evening was over and that now he was before me, real, assuaged my bad mood but not my agitation. I introduced him to the critic who had generously praised my book, saying that he was a friend from Naples, that we had gone to high school together. The professor, although he, too, had received some jabs from Nino, was polite, praised the way he had treated that man, and spoke of Naples with fondness, addressing him as if he were a gifted student who was to be encouraged. Nino explained that he had lived in Milan for some years, his field was economic geography, he belonged—and he smiled—to the most wretched category in the academic pyramid, that is to say lecturer. He said it sweetly, without the almost sullen tones he had had as a boy, and it seemed to me that he wore a lighter armor than that which had fascinated me in high school, as if he had shed any excess weight in order to be able to joust more rapidly and with elegance. I noted with relief that he wasn't wearing a wedding ring.

Meanwhile some of Adele's friends had come over to have their books signed, which made me nervous: it was the first time I had done this. I hesitated: I didn't want to lose sight of Nino even for an instant, but I also wanted to mitigate the impression I must have made of a clumsy girl. So I left him with the old professor—his name was Tarratano—and greeted my readers politely. I intended to do this quickly, but the books were new, with an odor of ink, so different from the dog-eared, ill-smelling books that Lila and I took out from the library in the neighborhood, and I didn't feel like marring them carelessly with the pen. I displayed my best handwriting, from the time of Maestra Oliviero, I invented elaborate dedications that caused some impatience in the women who were waiting. My heart was pounding as I wrote, with an eye on Nino. I trembled at the idea that he would leave.

He didn't. Now Adele had gone up to him and Tarratano, and Nino spoke to her confidently and yet with deference. I remembered when he used to talk to Professor Galiani in the corridors of the high school, and it took me a while to consolidate in my mind the brilliant high school student of then with the young man of now. I vehemently discarded, on the other hand, as a pointless deviation that had made all of us suffer, the university student of Ischia, the lover of my married friend, the helpless youth who hid in the bathroom of the shop on Piazza dei Martiri and who was the father of Gennaro, a child he had never seen. Certainly Lila's irruption had thrown him off, but—it now seemed obvious—it was just a digression. However intense that experience must have been, however deep the marks it had left, it was over now. Nino had found himself again, and I was pleased. I thought: I have to tell Lila that I saw him, that he's well. Then I changed my mind: no, I won't tell her.

When I finished the dedications, the room was empty. Adele took me gently by the hand, she praised the way I had spoken of my book and the way I had responded to the terrible intrusion—so she called it—of the man with the thick eyeglasses. Since I denied having done well (I knew perfectly well that it wasn't true), she asked Nino and Tarratano to give their opinion, and both were profuse with compliments. Nino went so far as to say, looking at me seriously: *You don't know what that girl was like in high school, extremely intelligent, cultivated, very courageous, very beautiful.* And while I felt my face burning, he began to tell with exaggerated courtesy the story of my clash with the religion teacher years earlier. Adele laughed frequently as she listened. In our family, she said, we understood Elena's virtues right away, and then she said she had made a reservation for dinner at a place nearby. I was alarmed, I said in embarrassment that I was tired and not hungry, I would happily take a short walk with Nino before going to bed. I knew it was rude, the dinner was meant to celebrate me and thank Tarratano for his work on behalf of my book, but I couldn't stop myself. Adele looked at me for a moment with a sardonic expression, she replied that naturally my friend was invited, and added mysteriously, as if to compensate for the sacrifice I was making: I have a nice surprise in store for you. I looked at Nino anxiously: would he accept the invitation? He said he didn't want to be a bother, he looked at his watch, he accepted.

4.

We left the bookstore. Adele, tactfully, went ahead with Tarratano, Nino and I followed. But I immediately found that I didn't know what to say to him, I was afraid that every word would be wrong. He made sure there were no silences. He praised my book again, he went on to speak with great respect of the Airotas (he called them "the most civilized of the families who count for something in Italy"), he said he knew Mariarosa ("She's always on the front lines: two weeks ago we had a big argument"), he congratulated me because he had learned from Adele that I was engaged to Pietro, whose book on Bacchic rites he seemed to know, amazing me; but he spoke with respect especially of the father, Professor Guido Airota, "a truly exceptional man." I was a little annoyed that he already knew of my engagement, and it made me uneasy that the praise of my book had served as an introduction to the far more insistent praise of Pietro's entire family, Pietro's book. I interrupted him, I asked him about himself, but he was vague, with only a few allusions to a small volume coming out that he called boring but obligatory. I pressed him, I asked if he had had a hard time during his early days in Milan. He answered with a few generic remarks about the problems of coming from the South without a cent in your pocket. Then out of the blue he asked me:

"Are you living in Naples again?"

"For now, yes."

"In the neighborhood?"

"Yes."

"I've broken conclusively with my father, and I don't see anyone in my family."

"Too bad."

"It's better that way. I'm just sorry not to have any news of Lina."

For a moment I thought I'd been wrong, that Lila had never gone out of his life, that he had come to the bookstore not for me but only to find out about her. Then I said to myself: if he had really wanted to find out about Lila, in so many years he would have found a way, and I reacted violently, in the sharp tone of someone who wants to end the subject quickly:

"She left her husband and lives with someone else."

"Did she have a boy or a girl?"

"A boy."

He made a grimace of displeasure and said: "Lina is brave, even too brave. But she doesn't know how to submit to reality, she's incapable of accepting others and herself. Loving her was a difficult experience."

"In what sense?"

"She doesn't know what dedication is."

"Maybe you're exaggerating."

"No, she's really made badly: in her mind and in everything, even when it comes to sex."

Those last words—*even when it comes to sex*—struck me more than the others. So Nino's judgment on his relationship with Lila was negative? So he had just said to me, disturbingly, that that opinion included even the sexual arena? I stared for some seconds at the dark outlines of Adele and her friend walking ahead of us. The disturbance became anxiety, I sensed that *even when it comes to sex* was a preamble, that he wished to become still more explicit. Years earlier, Stefano, after his marriage, had confided in me, had told me about his problems with Lila, but he had done so without ever mentioning sex—

no one in the neighborhood would have in speaking of the woman he loved. It was unthinkable, for example, that Pasquale would talk to me about Ada's sexuality, or, worse, that Antonio would speak to Carmen or Gigliola about my sexuality. Boys might talk among themselves—and in a vulgar way, when they didn't like us girls or no longer liked us—but among boys and girls no. I guessed instead that Nino, the new Nino, considered it completely normal to discuss with me his sexual relations with my friend. I was embarrassed, I pulled back. Of this, too, I thought, I must never speak to Lila, and meanwhile I said with feigned indifference: water under the bridge, let's not be sad, let's go back to you, what are you working on, what are your prospects at the university, where do you live, by yourself? But I certainly overdid it; he must have felt that I had made a quick escape. He smiled ironically, and was about to answer. But we had arrived at the restaurant, and we went in.

5.

Adele assigned us places: I was next to Nino and opposite Tarratano, she next to Tarratano and opposite Nino. We ordered, and meanwhile the conversation had shifted to the man with the thick glasses, a professor of Italian literature—I learned—a Christian Democrat, and a regular contributor to the *Corriere della Sera*. Adele and her friend now lost all restraint. Outside of the bookstore ritual, they couldn't say enough bad things about the man, and they congratulated Nino for the way he had confronted and routed him. They especially enjoyed recalling what Nino had said as the man was leaving the room, remarks they had heard and I hadn't. They asked him what his exact words were, and Nino retreated, saying that he didn't remember. But then the words emerged, maybe reinvented for the occasion, something like: *In order to safeguard authority in all of its manifestations, you suspend democracy.* And from there the three of them took off, talking, with increasing ardor, about the secret services, about Greece, about torture in the Greek prisons, about Vietnam, about the unexpected uprising of the student movement not only in Italy but in Europe and the world, about an article in *Il Ponte* by Professor Airota—which Nino said that he agreed with, word for word—about the conditions of research and teaching in the universities.

"I'll tell my daughter that you liked it," Adele said. "Mariarosa thought it was terrible."

"Mariarosa gets passionate only about what the world can't give."

"Very good, that really is what she's like."

I knew nothing of that article by my future father-in-law. The subject made me uneasy, and I listened in silence. First my exams, then my thesis, then the book and its rapid publication had absorbed much of my time. I was informed about world events only superficially, and I had picked up almost nothing about students, demonstrations, clashes, the wounded, arrests, blood. Since I was now outside the university, all I really knew about that chaos was Pietro's grumblings, his complaints about what he called literally "the Pisan nonsense." As a result I felt around me a scene with confusing features: features that, however, my companions seemed able to decipher with great precision, Nino even more than the others. I sat beside him, I listened, I touched his arm with mine, a contact merely of fabrics which nevertheless agitated me. He had kept his fondness for figures: he was giving a list of numbers, of students enrolled in the university, a crowd by now, and of the capacity of the buildings; of the hours the tenured professors actually worked, and how many of them, rather than doing research and teaching, sat in parliament or on administrative committees or devoted themselves to lucrative consulting jobs and private practice. Adele agreed, and so did her friend; occasionally they interrupted, mentioning people I had never heard of. I felt excluded. The celebration for my book was no longer at the top of their thoughts, my mother-in-law seemed to have forgotten even the surprise she had announced for me. I said that I had to get up for a moment; Adele nodded absently, Nino continued to speak passionately. Tarratano must have thought that I was getting bored and said kindly, almost in a whisper:

"Hurry back, I'd like to hear your opinion."

"I don't have opinions," I said with a half smile.

He smiled in turn: "A writer always invents one."

"Maybe I'm not a writer."

"Yes, you are."

I went to the bathroom. Nino had always had the capacity, as soon as he opened his mouth, to demonstrate to me my backwardness. I have to start studying, I thought, how could I let myself go like this? Of course, if I want I can fake some expertise and some enthusiasm. But I can't go on like that, I've learned too many things that don't count and very few that do. At the end of my affair with Franco, I had lost the little curiosity about the world that he had instilled in me. And my engagement to Pietro hadn't helped, what didn't interest him lost interest for me. How different Pietro is from his father, his sister, his mother. And how different he is from Nino. If it had been up to him, I wouldn't ever have written my novel. He was almost irritated by it, as an infraction of the academic rules. Or maybe I'm exaggerating, it's just my problem. I'm so limited, I can only concentrate on one thing at a time, excluding everything else. But now I'll change. Right after this boring dinner I'll drag Nino with me, I'll make him walk all night, I'll ask him what books I should read, what films I should see, what music I should listen to. And I'll take him by the arm, I'll say: I'm cold. Confused intentions, incomplete proposals. I hid from myself the anxiety I felt, I said to myself only: It might be the only chance we have, tomorrow I'm leaving, I won't see him again.

Meanwhile I gazed angrily into the mirror. My face looked tired, small pimples on my chin and dark circles under my eyes announced my period. I'm ugly, short, my bust is too big. I should have understood long ago that he never liked me, it was no coincidence that he preferred Lila. But with what result? *She's made badly even when it comes to sex*, he said. I was wrong to avoid the subject. I should have acted curious, let him continue. If he talks about it again I'll be more open-minded, I'll say: what does it mean that a girl is made badly when it comes to sex? I'm asking you, I'll explain laughing, so that I can correct myself, if it seems necessary. Assuming that one can correct it, who knows. I remembered with disgust what had happened with his father on the beach at the Maronti. I thought of making love with Franco on the little bed in his room in Pisa—had I done something wrong that he had noticed but had tactfully not mentioned to me? And if that very evening, let's say, I had gone to bed with Nino, would I make more mistakes, so that he would think: she's made badly, like Lila, and would he speak of it behind my back to his girl-friends at the university, maybe even to Mariarosa?

I realized the offensiveness of those words; I should have rebuked him. From that mistaken sex, I should have said to him, from an experience of which you now express a negative opinion, came a child, little Gennaro, who is very intelligent: it's not nice for you to talk like that, you can't reduce the question to who is made badly and who is made well. Lila ruined herself for you. And I made up my mind: when I get rid of Adele and her friend, when he walks me to the hotel, I'll return to the subject and tell him.

I came out of the bathroom. I went back to the dining room and discovered that during my absence the situation had changed. As soon as my mother-in-law saw me, she waved and said happily, her cheeks alight: the surprise finally got here. The surprise was Pietro, he was sitting next to her.

6.

My fiancé jumped up, he embraced me. I had never told him anything about Nino. I had said a few words about Antonio, and had told him something about my relationship with Franco, which, besides, was well known in the student world of Pisa. Nino, however, I had never mentioned. It was a story that hurt me, it had painful moments that I was ashamed of. To tell it meant to confess that I had loved forever a person as I would never love him. And to give it an order, a sense, involved talking about Lila, about Ischia, maybe even going so far as to admit that the episode of sex with an older man, as it appeared in my book, was inspired by a true experience at the Maronti, by a decision that I had made as a desperate girl and which now, after so much time had passed, seemed to me repugnant. My own business, therefore. I had held on to my secrets. If Pietro had known, he would have easily understood why I was greeting him without pleasure.

He sat down again at the head of the table, between his mother and Nino. He ate a steak, drank some wine, but he looked at me in alarm, aware of my unhappiness. Certainly he felt at fault because he hadn't arrived in time and had missed an important event in my life, because his neglect could be interpreted as a sign that he didn't love me, because he had left me among strangers without the comfort of his affection. It would have been difficult to tell him that my dark face, my muteness, could be explained *precisely* by the fact that he hadn't remained completely absent, that he had intruded between me and Nino.

Nino, meanwhile, was making me even more unhappy. He

was sitting next to me but didn't address a word to me. He seemed happy about Pietro's arrival. He poured wine for him, offered him cigarettes, lighted one, and now they were both smoking, lips compressed, and talking about the difficult journey by car from Pisa to Milan, and the pleasure of driving. It struck me how different they were: Nino thin, lanky, his voice high and cordial; Pietro thick-set, with the comical tangle of hair over his large forehead, his broad cheeks scraped by the razor, his voice always low. They seemed pleased to have met, which was unusual for Pietro, who was generally reserved. Nino pressed him, showing a real interest in his studies (*I read an article somewhere in which you compare milk and honey to wine and every form of drunkenness*), and urging him to talk about them, so that my fiancé, who tended not to talk about his subject, gave in, he corrected good-humoredly, he opened up. But just when Pietro was starting to gain confidence, Adele interrupted.

"Enough talk," she said to her son. "What about the surprise for Elena?"

I looked at her uncertainly. There were other surprises? Wasn't it enough that Pietro had driven for hours without stopping, to arrive only in time for the dinner in my honor? I thought of my fiancé with curiosity, he had a sulky expression that I knew and that he assumed when circumstances forced him to speak about himself in public. He announced to me, but almost in a whisper, that he had become a tenured professor, a very young tenured professor, with a position at Florence. Like that, by magic, in his typical fashion. He never boasted of his brilliance, he was scarcely aware of his value as a scholar, he kept silent about the struggles he had endured. And now, look, he mentioned that news casually, as if he had been forced to by his mother, as if for him it meant nothing. In fact, it meant remarkable prestige at a young age, it meant economic security, it meant leaving Pisa, it meant escaping a political and cultural climate that for months, I don't know why, had exasperated him. It meant finally that in the fall, or at the beginning of the next year, we would get married and I would leave Naples. No one mentioned this last thing, instead they all congratulated Pietro and me. Even Nino, who right afterward looked at his watch, made some acerbic remarks on university careers, and exclaimed that he was sorry but he had to go.

We all got up. I didn't know what to do, I uselessly sought his gaze, as a great sorrow filled my heart. End of the evening, missed opportunity, aborted desires. Out on the street I hoped that he would give me a phone number, an address. He merely shook my hand and wished me all the best. From that moment it seemed to me that each of his gestures was deliberately cutting me off. As a kind of farewell I gave him a half smile, waving my hand as if I were holding a pen. It was a plea, it meant: you know where I live, write to me, please. But he had already turned his back.

7.

I thanked Adele and her friend for all the trouble they had taken for me and for my book. They both praised Nino at length, sincerely, speaking to me as if it were I who had contributed to making him so likable, so intelligent. Pietro said nothing, he merely nodded a bit nervously when his mother told him to return soon, they were both guests of Mariarosa. I said immediately: you don't have to come with me, go with your mother. It didn't occur to anyone that I was serious, that I was unhappy and would rather be alone.

All the way back I was impossible. I exclaimed that I didn't like Florence, and it wasn't true. I exclaimed that I didn't want to write anymore, I wanted to teach, and it wasn't true. I exclaimed that I was tired, I was very sleepy, and it wasn't true.

Not only that. When, suddenly, Pietro declared that he wanted to meet my parents, I yelled at him: you're crazy, forget my parents, you're not suitable for them and they aren't suitable for you. Then he was frightened, and asked:

"Do you not want to marry me anymore?"

I was about to say: *No, I don't want to*, but I restrained myself in time, I knew that that wasn't true, either. I said weakly, I'm sorry, I'm depressed, of course I want to marry you, and I took his hand, I interlaced my fingers in his. He was an intelligent man, extraordinarily cultured, and good. I loved him, I didn't mean to make him suffer. And yet, even as I was holding his hand, even as I was affirming that I wanted to marry him, I knew clearly that if he hadn't appeared that night at the restaurant I would have tried to sleep with Nino.

I had a hard time admitting it to myself. Certainly it would have been an offense that Pietro didn't deserve, and yet I would have committed it willingly and perhaps without remorse. I would have found a way to draw Nino to me, with all the years that had passed, from elementary school to high school, up to the time of Ischia and Piazza dei Martiri. I would have made love with him, even though I hadn't liked that remark about Lila, and was distressed by it. I would have slept with him and to Pietro I would have said nothing. Maybe I could have told Lila, but who knows when, maybe as an old woman, when I imagined that nothing would matter anymore to her or to me. Time, as in all things, was decisive. Nino would last a single night, he would leave me in the morning. Even though I had known him forever, he was made of dreams, and holding on to him forever would have been impossible: he came from childhood, he was constructed out of childish desires, he had no concreteness, he didn't face the future. Pietro, on the other hand, was of the present, massive, a boundary stone. He marked a land new to me, a land of good reasons, governed by rules that originated in his family and endowed everything with meaning. Grand ideals flourished, the cult of the reputation, matters of principle. Nothing in the sphere of the Airotas was perfunctory. Marriage, for example, was a contribution to a secular battle. Pietro's parents had had only a civil wedding, and Pietro, although as far as I knew he had a vast religious knowledge, would never get married in a church; rather, he would give me up. The same went for baptism. Pietro hadn't been baptized, nor had Mariarosa, so any children that might come wouldn't be baptized, either. Everything about him had that tendency, seemed always to be guided by a superior order that, although its origin was not divine but came from his family, gave him, just the same, the certainty of being on the side of truth and justice. As for sex, I don't know, he was wary. He knew enough of my affair with Franco Mari to deduce that I wasn't a virgin, and yet he had never mentioned the subject, not even an accusatory phrase, a vulgar comment, a laugh. I didn't think he'd had other girlfriends; it was hard to imagine him with a prostitute, I was sure he hadn't spent even a minute of his life talking about women with other men. He hated salacious remarks. He hated gossip, raised voices, parties, every form of waste. Although his circumstances were comfortable, he tended—in this unlike his parents and his sister—to a sort of asceticism amid the abundance. And he had a conspicuous sense of duty, he would never fail in his commitments to me, he would never betray me.

No, I did not want to lose him. Never mind if my nature, coarse in spite of the education I had had, was far from his rigor, if I honestly didn't know how I would stand up to all that geometry. He gave me the certainty that I was escaping the opportunistic malleability of my father and the crudeness of my mother. So I forced myself to repress the thought of Nino, I took Pietro by the arm, I murmured, yes, let's get married as soon as possible, I want to leave home, I want to get a driver's license, I want to travel, I want to have a telephone, a television, I've never had anything. And he at that point became cheerful, he laughed, he said yes to everything I randomly asked for. A few steps from the hotel he stopped, he whispered hoarsely: Can I sleep with you? That was the last surprise of the evening. I looked at him bewildered: I had been ready so many times to make love, he had always avoided it; but having him in the bed there, in Milan, in the hotel, after the traumatic discussion in the bookstore, after Nino, I didn't feel like it. I answered: We've waited so long, we can wait a little longer. I kissed him in a dark corner, I watched him from the hotel entrance as he walked away along Corso Garibaldi, and every so often turned and waved timidly. His clumsy gait, his flat feet, the tangle of his hair moved me.

8.

From that moment life began to pound me without respite, the months were rapidly grafted onto one another, there was no day when something good or bad didn't happen. I returned to Naples, thinking about Nino, and that encounter without consequences, and at times the wish to see Lila was strong, to go and wait for her to come home from work, tell her what could be told without hurting her. Then I convinced myself that merely mentioning Nino would wound her, and I gave it up. Lila had gone her way, he his. I had urgent things to deal with. For example, the evening of my return from Milan I told my parents that Pietro was coming to meet them, that probably we would be married within the year, that I was going to live in Florence.

They showed no joy, or even satisfaction. I thought that they had finally grown used to my coming and going as I liked, increasingly estranged from the family, indifferent to their problems of survival. And it seemed to me normal that only my father became somewhat agitated, always nervous at the prospect of situations he didn't feel prepared for.

"Does the university professor have to come to our house?" he asked, in irritation.

"Where else?" my mother said angrily. "How can he ask you for Lenuccia's hand if he doesn't come here?"

Usually she seemed more prepared than he, concrete, resolute to the point of indifference. But once she had silenced him, once her husband had gone to bed and Elisa and Peppe and Gianni had set up their beds in the dining room, I had to change my mind. She attacked me in very low but shrill tones, hissing with reddened eyes: We are nothing to you, you tell us nothing until the last minute, the young lady thinks she's somebody because she has an education, because she writes books, because she's marrying a professor, but my dear, you came out of this belly and you are made of this substance, so don't act superior and don't ever forget that if you are intelligent, I who carried you in here am just as intelligent, if not more, and if I had had the chance I would have done the same as you, understand? Then, on the crest of her rage, she first reproached me saying that because I had left, and thought only of myself, my siblings hadn't done well in school, and then asked me for money, or, rather, demanded it: she needed it to buy a decent dress for Elisa and to fix up the house a bit, since I was forcing her to receive my fiancé.

I passed over my siblings' lack of success in school. The money, on the other hand, I gave her right away, even if it wasn't true that she needed it for the house—she continually asked for money, any excuse would do. Although she had never said so explicitly, she still couldn't accept the fact that I kept my money in a post-office savings account, that I hadn't handed it over to her as I always had, ever since I first took the stationer's daughters to the beach, or worked in the bookstore on Via Mezzocannone. Maybe, I thought, by acting as if my money

belonged to her she wants to convince me that I myself belong
to her, and that, even if I get married, I will belong to her forever.

I remained calm, I told her as a sort of compensation that
I would have a telephone put in, that I would buy a television
on the installment plan. She looked at me uncertainly, with a
sudden admiration that clashed with what she had just been
saying.

"A television and telephone in this house here?"

"Yes."

"You'll pay for it?"

"Yes."

"Always, even after you're married?"

"Yes."

"The professor knows that there's not a cent for a dowry,
and not even for a reception?"

"He knows, and we're not having a reception."

Again her mood changed, her eyes became inflamed.

"What do you mean, no reception? Make him pay."

"No, we're doing without."

My mother became furious again, she provoked me in every
way she could think of, she wanted me to respond so that she
could get angrier.

"You remember Lila's wedding, you remember the reception she had?"

"Yes."

"And you, who are much better than she is, don't want to
do anything?"

"No."

We went on like that until I decided that, rather than taking her rage in doses, it would be better to have it all at once,
one grand fury:

"Ma," I said, "not only are we not having a party but I'm

not even getting married in church, I'm getting married at city hall."

At that point it was as if doors and windows had been blown open by a strong wind. Although she wasn't religious, my mother lost control and, leaning toward me, red in the face, began yelling insults at me. She shouted that the marriage was worthless if the priest didn't say that it was valid. She shouted that if I didn't get married before God I would never be a wife but only a whore, and, despite her lame leg, she almost flew as she went to wake my father, my siblings, to let them know what she had always feared, that too much education had ruined my brain, that I had had all the luck and yet I was treated like a whore, that she would never be able to go out of the house because of the shame of having a godless daughter.

My father, stunned, in his underwear, and my siblings sought to understand what other trouble they had to deal with because of me, and tried to calm her, but in vain. She shouted that she wanted to throw me out of the house immediately, before I exposed her, too, *her, too,* to the shame of having a concubine daughter like Lila and Ada. Meanwhile, although she wasn't actually hitting me, she struck the air as if I were a shadow and she had grabbed a real me, whom she was beating ferociously. It was some time before she quieted down, which she did thanks to Elisa. My sister asked cautiously:

"But is it you who want to get married at city hall or is it your fiancé?"

I explained to her, but as if I were explaining the matter to all of them, that for me the Church hadn't counted for a long time, but that whether I got married at city hall or at the altar was the same to me; while for my fiancé it was very important to have only a civil ceremony, he knew all about religious matters and believed that religion, however valuable, was ruined precisely when it interfered in the affairs of the state. In other words, I concluded, if we don't get married at city hall, he won't marry me.

At that point my father, who had immediately sided with my mother, suddenly stopped echoing her insults and laments.

"He won't marry you?"

"No."

"And what will he do, leave you?"

"We'll go and live together in Florence without getting married."

That information my mother considered the most intolerable of all. She completely lost control, vowing that in that case she would take a knife and cut my throat. My father instead nervously ruffled his hair, and said to her:

"Be quiet, don't get me mad, let's be reasonable. We know very well that someone can get married by the priest, have a fancy celebration, and still come to a bad end."

He, too, was obviously alluding to Lila, the ever-vivid scandal of the neighborhood, and my mother finally understood. The priest wasn't a guarantee, nothing was a guarantee in the brutal world we lived in. So she stopped shouting and left to my father the task of examining the situation and, if necessary, letting me have my way. But she didn't stop pacing, with her limp, shaking her head, insulting my future husband. What was he, the professor? Was he a Communist? Communist and professor? Professor of that shit, she shouted. What kind of professor is he, one who thinks like that? A shit thinks like that. No, replied my father, what do you mean shit, he's a man who's educated and knows better than anyone what disgusting things the priests do, that's why he wants to go and say "I do" only at city hall. Yes, you're right, a lot of Communists do that. Yes, you're right, like this our daughter doesn't seem married. But I would trust this university professor: he loves her. I can't believe that he would put Lenuccia in a situation where she seems like a whore. And anyway if we don't want to trust him—but I do trust him, even if I don't know him yet: he's an important person, the girls here dream of a match like that—at least we can trust the city hall. I work there, at the city hall, and a marriage there, I can assure you, is as valid as the one in church and maybe even more.

He went on for hours. My siblings at a certain point collapsed and went back to sleep. I stayed to soothe my parents and persuade them to accept something that for me, at that moment, was an important sign of my entrance into Pietro's world. Besides, it made me feel bolder than Lila. And most of all, if I met Nino again, I would have liked to be able to say to him, in an allusive way: See where that argument with the religion teacher led, every choice has its history, so many moments of our existence are shoved into a corner, waiting for an outlet, and in the end the outlet arrives. But I would have been exaggerating, in reality it was much simpler. For at least ten years the God of childhood, already fairly weak, had been pushed aside like an old sick person, and I felt no need for the sanctity of marriage. The essential thing was to get out of Naples.

9.

My family's horror at the idea of a civil union alone certainly was not exhausted that night, but it diminished. The next day my mother treated me as if anything she touched—the coffee pot, the cup with the milk, the sugar bowl, the fresh loaf of bread—were there only to lead her into the temptation to throw it in my face. Yet she didn't start yelling again. As for me I ignored her; I left early in the morning, and went to start the paperwork for the installation of the telephone. Having taken care of that business I went to Port'Alba and wandered through the bookstores. I was determined, within a short time, to enable myself to speak with confidence when situations like the one in

Milan arose. I chose journals and books more or less at random, and spent a lot of money. After many hesitations, influenced by that remark of Nino's that kept coming to mind, I ended up getting *Three Essays on the Theory of Sexuality*—I knew almost nothing of Freud and the little I knew irritated me—along with a couple of small books devoted to sex. I intended to do what I had done in the past with schoolwork, with exams, with my thesis, what I had done with the newspapers that Professor Galiani passed on to me or the Marxist texts that Franco had given me. I wanted to *study* the contemporary world. Hard to say what I had already taken in at that time. There had been the discussions with Pasquale, and also with Nino. There had been some attention paid to Cuba and Latin America. There was the incurable poverty of the neighborhood, the lost battle of Lila. There was school, which defeated my siblings because they were less stubborn than I was, less dedicated to sacrifice. There were the long conversations with Franco and occasional ones with Mariarosa, now jumbled together in a wisp of smoke. (*The world is profoundly unjust and must be changed, but both the peaceful coexistence between American imperialism and the Stalinist bureaucracies, on the one hand, and the reformist politics of the European, and especially the Italian, workers' parties, on the other, are directed at keeping the proletariat in a subordinate wait-and-see situation that throws water on the fire of revolution, with the result that if the global stalemate wins, if social democracy wins, it will be capital that triumphs through the centuries and the working class will fall victim to enforced consumerism.*) These stimuli had functioned, certainly they had been working in me for a long time, occasionally they excited me. But driving that decision to bring myself up to date by forced marches was, at least at first, I think, the old urgency to succeed. I had long ago convinced myself that one can train oneself to anything, even to political passion.

As I was paying, I glimpsed my novel on a shelf, and immediately looked in another direction. Whenever I saw the book in a window, among other novels that had just come out, I felt inside a mixture of pride and fear, a dart of pleasure that ended in anguish. Certainly, the story had come into being by chance, in twenty days, without struggle, as a sedative against depression. Moreover, I knew what great literature was, I had done a lot of work in the classics, and it never occurred to me, while I was writing, that I was making something of value. But the effort of finding a form had absorbed me. And the absorption had become *that* book, an object that contained me. Now *I* was there, *exposed*, and seeing myself caused a violent pounding in my chest. I felt that not only in my book but in novels in general there was something that truly agitated me, a bare and throbbing heart, the same that had burst out of my chest in that distant moment when Lila had proposed that we write a story together. It had fallen to me to do it seriously. But was that what I wanted? To write, to write with purpose, to write better than I had already? And to study the stories of the past and the present to understand how they worked, and to learn, learn everything about the world with the sole purpose of constructing living hearts, which no one would ever do better than me, not even Lila if she had had the opportunity?

I came out of the bookshop, I stopped in Piazza Cavour. The day was fine, Via Foria seemed unnaturally clean and solid in spite of the scaffolding that shored up the Galleria. I imposed on myself the usual discipline. I took out a notebook that I had bought recently, I wished to start acting like a real writer, putting down thoughts, observations, useful information. I read *l'Unità* from beginning to end, I took notes on the things I didn't know. I found the article by Pietro's father in *Il Ponte* and skimmed it with curiosity, but it didn't seem as important as Nino had claimed. Rather, it put me off for two reasons: first, Guido Airota used the same professorial language as the man with the thick eyeglasses but even more rigorously; second, in a passage in which he spoke about women students ("It's a new crowd," he wrote, "and by all the evidence they are not from well-off families, young ladies in modest dresses and of modest upbringing who justly expect from the immense labor of their studies a future not of domestic rituals alone"), it seemed to me that I saw an allusion to myself, whether deliberate or completely unconscious. I made a note of that in my notebook as well (*What am I to the Airotas, a jewel in the crown of their broad-mindedness?*) and, not exactly in a good mood, in fact with some irritation, I began to leaf through the *Corriere della Sera*.

I remember that the air was warm, and I've preserved an olfactory memory—invented or real—a mixture of printed paper and fried pizza. Page after page I looked at the headlines, until one took my breath away. There was a photograph of me, set amid four dense columns of type. In the background was a view of the neighborhood, with the tunnel. The headline said: *Salacious Memoirs of an Ambitious Girl: Elena Greco's Début Novel.* The byline was that of the man with the thick eyeglasses.

10.

I was covered in a cold sweat while I read; I had the impression that I was close to fainting. My book was treated as an occasion to assert that in the past decade, in all areas of productive, social, and cultural life, from factories to offices, to the university, publishing, and cinema, an entire world had collapsed under the pressure of a spoiled youth, without values. Occasionally he cited some phrase of mine, in quotation marks, to demonstrate that I was a fitting exponent of my badly brought-up generation. In conclusion he called me "a girl concerned with hiding her lack of talent behind titillating pages of mediocre triviality."

I burst into tears. It was the harshest thing I had read since the book came out, and not in a daily with a small circulation but in the most widely read newspaper in Italy. Most of all, the image of my smiling face seemed to me intolerable in the middle of a text so offensive. I walked home, not before getting rid of the *Corriere*. I was afraid my mother might read the review and use it against me. I imagined that she would have liked to put it, too, in her album, to throw in my face whenever I upset her.

I found the table set only for me. My father was at work, my mother had gone to ask a neighbor for something or other, and my siblings had already eaten. As I ate pasta and potatoes I reread at random some passages of my book. I thought desperately: Maybe it really is worthless, maybe it was published only as a favor to Adele. How could I have come up with such pallid sentences, such banal observations? And how sloppy, how many useless commas; I won't write anymore. Between disgust with the food and disgust with the book I was depressed, when Elisa arrived with a piece of paper. It came from Signora Spagnuolo, who had kindly agreed to let her telephone number be used by anyone who urgently needed to communicate with me. The piece of paper said that there had been three phone calls, one from Gina Medotti, who ran the press office at the publisher's, one from Adele, and one from Pietro.

The three names, written in Signora Spagnuolo's labored handwriting, had the effect of giving concreteness to a thought that until a moment before had remained in the background: the terrible words of the man with the thick eyeglasses were spreading rapidly, and in the course of the day they would be everywhere. They had already been read by Pietro, by his family, by the directors of the publishing house. Maybe they had reached Nino. Maybe they were before the eyes of my professors in Pisa. Certainly they had come to the attention of

Professor Galiani and her children. And who knows, even Lila might have read them. I burst into tears again, frightening Elisa.

"What's wrong, Lenù?"

"I don't feel well."

"Shall I make you some chamomile tea?"

"Yes."

But there wasn't time. Someone was knocking at the door, it was Rosa Spagnuolo. Cheerful, slightly out of breath from hurrying up the stairs, she said that my fiancé was again looking for me, he was on the telephone, what a lovely voice, what a lovely northern accent. I ran to answer, apologizing repeatedly for bothering her. Pietro tried to console me, he said that his mother urged me not to be upset, the main thing was that it talked about the book. But, surprising Signora Spagnuolo, who knew me as a meek girl, I practically screamed, What do I care if it talks about it if it says such terrible things? He urged me again to be calm and added: Tomorrow an article is coming out in *l'Unità*. I ended the call coldly, I said: It would be better if no one worried about me anymore.

I couldn't close my eyes that night. In the morning I couldn't contain myself and went out to get *l'Unità*. I leafed through it in a rush, still at the newsstand, a few steps from the elementary school. I was again confronted by a photograph of myself, the same that had been in the *Corriere*, not in the middle of the article this time but above it, next to the headline: *Young Rebels and Old Reactionaries: Concerning the Book by Elena Greco*. I had never heard of the author of the article, but it was certainly someone who wrote well, and his words acted as a balm. He praised my novel wholeheartedly and insulted the prestigious professor. I went home reassured, maybe even in a good mood. I paged through my book and this time it seemed to me well put together, written with mastery. My mother said sourly: Did you win the lottery? I left the paper on the kitchen table without saying anything.

In the late afternoon Signora Spagnuolo reappeared, I was wanted again on the telephone. In response to my embarrassment, my apologies, she said she was very happy to be able to be useful to a girl like me, she was full of compliments. Gigliola had been unlucky, she sighed on the stairs, her father had taken her to work in the Solaras' pastry shop when she was thirteen, and good thing she was engaged to Michele, otherwise she'd be slaving away her whole life. She opened the door and led me along the hall to the telephone that was attached to the wall. I saw that she had put a chair there so that I would be comfortable: what deference was shown to someone who is educated. Studying was considered a ploy used by the smartest kids to avoid hard work. How can I explain to this woman—I thought—that from the age of six I've been a slave to letters and numbers, that my mood depends on the success of their combinations, that the joy of having done well is rare, unstable, that it lasts an hour, an afternoon, a night?

"Did you read it?" Adele asked.

"Yes."

"Are you pleased?"

"Yes."

"Then I'll give you another piece of good news: the book is starting to sell, if it keeps on like this we'll reprint it."

"What does that mean?"

"It means that our friend in the *Corriere* thought he was destroying us and instead he worked for us. Bye, Elena, enjoy your success."

11.

The book was selling really well, I realized in the following days. The most conspicuous sign was the increasing number of phone calls from Gina, who reported a notice in such-and-such a newspaper, or announced some invitation from a book-store or cultural group, without ever forgetting to greet me with the kind words: The book is taking off, Dottoressa Greco, congratulations. Thank you, I said, but I wasn't happy. The articles in the newspapers seemed superficial, they confined themselves to applying either the enthusiastic matrix of *l'Unità* or the ruinous one of the *Corriere*. And although Gina repeated on every occasion that even negative reviews were good for sales, those reviews nevertheless wounded me and I would wait anxiously for a handful of favorable comments to offset the unfavorable ones and feel better. In any case, I stopped hiding the malicious reviews from my mother; I handed them all over, good and bad. She tried to read them, spelling them out with a stern expression, but she never managed to get beyond four or five lines before she either found a point to quarrel with or, out of boredom, took refuge in her mania for collecting. Her aim was to fill the entire album and, afraid of being left with empty pages, she complained when I had nothing to give her.

The review that at the time wounded me most deeply appeared in *Roma*. Paragraph by paragraph, it retraced the one in the *Corriere*, but in a florid style that at the end fanatically hammered at a single concept: women are losing all restraint, one has only to read Elena Greco's indecent novel to understand it, a novel that is a cheap version of the already vulgar *Bonjour Tristesse*. What hurt me, though, was not the content but the byline. The article was by Nino's father, Donato Sarratore. I thought of how impressed I had been as a girl by the fact that that man was the author of a book of poems; I thought of the glorious halo I had enveloped him in when I discovered that he wrote for the newspapers. Why that review? Did he wish to get revenge because he recognized himself in the obscene family man who seduces the protagonist? I was tempted to call him and insult him atrociously in dialect. I gave it up only because I thought of Nino, and made what seemed an important discovery: his experience and mine were similar. We had both refused to model ourselves on our families: I had been struggling forever to get away from my mother, he had burned his bridges with his father. This similarity consoled me, and my rage slowly diminished.

But I hadn't taken into account that, in the neighborhood, *Roma* was read more than any other newspaper. I found out that evening. Gino, the pharmacist's son, who lifted weights and had become a muscular young man, looked out from the doorway of his father's shop just as I was passing, in a white pharmacist's smock even though he hadn't yet taken his degree. He called to me, holding out the paper, and said, in a fairly serious tone, because he had recently moved up a little in the local section of the neo-fascist Italian Social Movement party: Did you see what they're writing about you? In order not to give him the satisfaction, I answered, they write all sorts of things, and went on with a wave. He was flustered, and stammered something, then he said, with explicit malice: I'll have to read that book of yours, I understand it's *very* interesting.

That was only the start. The next day Michele Solara came up to me on the street and insisted on buying me a coffee. We went into his bar and while Gigliola served us, without saying a word, in fact obviously annoyed by my presence and perhaps also by her boyfriend's, he began: Lenù, Gino gave me an article to read where it says you wrote a book that's banned for those under eighteen. Imagine that, who would have expected it. Is *that* what you studied in Pisa? Is *that* what they taught you at the university? I can't believe it. In my opinion you and Lina made a secret agreement: she does nasty things and you write them. Is that right? Tell me the truth. I turned red, I didn't wait for the coffee, I waved to Gigliola and left. He called after me, laughing: What's the matter, you're offended, come here, I was joking.

Soon afterward I had an encounter with Carmen Peluso.

My mother had obliged me to go to the Carraccis' new grocery, because oil was cheaper there. It was afternoon, there were no customers, Carmen was full of compliments. How well you look, she said, it's an honor to be your friend, the only good luck I've had in my whole life. Then she said that she had read Sarratore's article, but only because a supplier had left *Roma* behind in the shop. She described it as spiteful, and her indignation seemed genuine. On the other hand, her brother, Pasquale, had given her the article in *l'Unità*—really, really good, such a nice picture. You're beautiful, she said, in everything you do. She had heard from my mother that I was going to marry a university professor and that I was going to live in Florence in a luxurious house. She, too, was getting married, to the owner of the gas pump on the *stradone*, but who could say when, they had no money. Then, without a break, she began complaining about Ada. Ever since Ada had taken Lila's place with Stefano, things had gone from bad to worse. She acted like the boss in the grocery stores, too, and had it in for her, accused her of stealing, ordered her around, watched her closely. She couldn't take it anymore, she wanted to quit and go to work at her future husband's gas pump.

I listened closely, I remembered when Antonio and I wanted to get married and, similarly, have a gas pump. I told her about it, to amuse her, but she muttered, darkening: Yes, why not, just imagine it, you at a gas pump, lucky you who got yourself out of this wretchedness. Then she made some obscure comments: there's too much injustice, Lenù, too much, it has to end, we can't go on like this. And as she was talking she pulled out of a drawer my book, with the cover all creased and dirty. It was the first copy I'd seen in the hands of anyone in the neighborhood, and I was struck by how bulging and grimy the early pages were, how flat and white the others. I read a little at night, she said, or when there aren't any customers. But I'm still on page 32, I don't have time, I have to do everything, the Carraccis keep me shut up here from six in the morning to nine in the evening. Then suddenly she asked, slyly, how long does it take to get to the dirty pages? How much do I still have to read?

The dirty pages.

A little while later I ran into Ada carrying Maria, her daughter with Stefano. I struggled to be friendly, after what Carmen had told me. I praised the child, I said her dress was pretty and her earrings adorable. But Ada was aloof. She spoke of Antonio, she said they wrote to each other, it wasn't true that he was married and had children, she said I had ruined his brain and his capacity to love. Then she started on my book. She hadn't read it, she explained, but she had heard that it wasn't a book to have in the house. And she was almost angry: Say the child grows up and finds it, what can I do? I'm sorry, I won't buy it. But, she added, I'm glad you're making money, good luck.

12.

These episodes, one after the other, led me to suspect that the book was selling because both the hostile newspapers and the favorable ones had indicated that there were some risqué passages. I went so far as to think that Nino had alluded to Lila's sexuality only because he thought that there was no problem in discussing such things with someone who had written what I had written. And via that path the desire to see my friend returned. Who knows, I said to myself, if Lila had the book, as Carmen did. I imagined her at night, after the factory—Enzo in solitude in one room, she with the baby beside her in the other—exhausted and yet intent on reading me, her mouth half open, wrinkling her forehead the way she did when she was concentrating. How would she judge it? Would she, too, reduce the novel to the *dirty pages*? But maybe she wasn't reading it at all, I doubted that she had the money to buy a copy, I ought to take her one as a present. For a while it seemed to me a good idea, then I forgot about it. I still cared more about Lila than about any other person, but I couldn't make up my mind to see her. I didn't have time, there were too many things to study, to learn in a hurry. And then the end of our last visit—in the courtyard of the factory, she with that apron under her coat, standing in front of the bonfire where the pages of *The Blue Fairy* were burning—had been a decisive farewell to the remains of childhood, the confirmation that our paths by now diverged, and maybe she would say: I don't have time to read you, you see the life I have? I went my own way.

Whatever the reason, the book really was doing better and better. Once Adele telephoned and, with her usual mixture of irony and affection, said: If it keeps going like this you'll get rich and you won't know what to do with poor Pietro anymore. Then she passed me on to her husband, no less. Guido, she said, wants to talk to you. I was agitated, I had had very few conversations with Professor Airota and they made me feel awkward. But Pietro's father was very friendly, he congratulated me on my success, he spoke sarcastically about the sense of decency of my detractors, he talked about the extremely long duration of the dark ages in Italy, he praised the contribution I was making to the modernization of the country, and so on with other formulas of that sort. He didn't say anything specific about the novel; surely he hadn't read it, he was a very busy man. But it was nice that he wanted to give me a sign of approval and respect.

Mariarosa was no less affectionate, and she, too, was full of praise. At first she seemed on the point of talking in detail about the book, then she changed the subject excitedly, she said she wanted to invite me to the university: it seemed to her important that I should take part in what she called *the unstop-*

pable flow of events. Leave tomorrow, she urged, have you seen what's happening in France? I knew all about it, I clung to an old blue grease-encrusted radio that my mother kept in the kitchen, and said yes, it's magnificent, Nanterre, the barricades in the Latin Quarter. But she seemed much better informed, much more involved. She was planning to drive to Paris with some of her friends, and invited me to go with her. I was tempted. I said all right, I'll think about it. To go to Milan, and on to France, to arrive in Paris in revolt, face the brutality of the police, plunge with my whole personal history into the most incandescent magma of these months, add a sequel to the journey I'd made years earlier with Franco. How wonderful it would be to go with Mariarosa, the only girl I knew who was so open-minded, so modern, completely in touch with the realities of the world, almost as much a master of political speech as the men. I admired her, there were no women who stood out in that chaos. The young heroes who faced the violence of the reactions at their own peril were called Rudi Dutschke, Daniel Cohn-Bendit, and, as in war films where there were only men, it was hard to feel part of it; you could only love them, adapt their thoughts to your brain, feel pity for their fate. It occurred to me that among Mariarosa's friends there might also be Nino. They knew each other, it was possible. Ah, to see him, to be swept into that adventure, expose myself to dangers along with him. The day passed like that. The kitchen was silent now, my parents were sleeping, my brothers were still out wandering in the streets, Elisa was in the bathroom, washing. To leave, tomorrow morning.

13.

I left, but not for Paris. After the elections of that turbulent year, Gina sent me out to promote the book. I began with

Florence. I had been invited to teach by a woman professor friend of a friend of the Airotas, and I ended up in one of those student-run courses, widespread in that time of unrest in the universities, speaking to around thirty students, boys and girls. I was immediately struck by the fact that many of the girls were even worse than those described by my father-in-law in *Il Ponte:* badly dressed, badly made up, muddled, excitable, angry at the exams, at the professors. Urged by the professor who had invited me, I spoke out about the student demonstrations with manifest enthusiasm, especially the ones in France. I showed off what I was learning; I was pleased with myself. I felt that I was expressing myself with conviction and clarity, that the girls in particular admired the way I spoke, the things I knew, the way I skillfully touched on the complicated problems of the world, arranging them into a coherent picture. But I soon realized that I tended to avoid any mention of the book. Talking about it made me uneasy, I was afraid of reactions like those of the neighborhood, I preferred to summarize in my own words ideas from *Quaderni piacentini* or the *Monthly Review*. On the other hand I had been invited because of the book, and someone was already asking to speak. The first questions were all about the struggles of the female character to escape the environment where she was born. Then, near the end, a girl I remember as being tall and thin asked me to explain, breaking off her phrases with nervous laughs, why I had considered it necessary to write, in such a polished story, a *risqué part*.

I was embarrassed, I think I blushed, I jumbled together a lot of sociological reasons. Finally, I spoke of the necessity of recounting frankly every human experience, including—I said emphatically—what seems unsayable and what we do not speak of even to ourselves. They liked those last words, I regained respect. The professor who had invited me praised them, she said she would reflect on them, she would write to me.

Her approval established in my mind those few concepts, which soon became a refrain. I used them often in public, sometimes in an amusing way, sometimes in a dramatic tone, sometimes succinctly, sometimes developing them with elaborate verbal flourishes. I found myself especially relaxed one evening in a bookstore in Turin, in front of a fairly large audience, which I now faced with growing confidence. It began to seem natural that someone would ask me, sympathetically or provocatively, about the episode of sex on the beach, and my ready response, which had become increasingly polished, enjoyed a certain success.

On the orders of the publisher, Tarratano, Adele's old friend, had accompanied me to Turin. He said that he was proud of having been the first to understand the potential of my novel and introduced me to the audience with the same enthusiastic words he had used before in Milan. At the end of the evening he congratulated me on the great progress I had made in a short time. Then he asked me, in his usual good-humored way: why are you so willing to let your erotic pages be called "risqué," why do you yourself describe them that way in public? And he explained to me that I shouldn't: my novel wasn't simply the episode on the beach, there were more interesting and finer passages; and then, if here and there something sounded daring, that was mainly because it had been written by a girl; obscenity, he said, is not alien to good literature, and the true art of the story, even if it goes beyond the bounds of decency, is never risqué.

I was confused. That very cultured man was tactfully explaining to me that the sins of my book were venial, and that I was wrong to speak of them every time as if they were mortal. I was overdoing it, then. I was submitting to the public's myopia, its superficiality. I said to myself: Enough, I have to be less subservient, I have to learn to disagree with my readers, I shouldn't descend to their level. And I decided that at the first opportunity I would be more severe with anyone who wanted to talk about those pages.

At dinner, in the hotel restaurant where the press office had reserved a table for us, I listened, half embarrassed, half amused, as Tarratano quoted, as proof that I was essentially a chaste writer, Henry Miller, and explained, calling me dear child, that not a few very gifted writers of the twenties and thirties could and did write about sex in a way that I at the moment couldn't even imagine. I wrote down their names in my notebook, but meanwhile I began to think: This man, in spite of his compliments, doesn't consider that I have much talent; in his eyes I'm a girl who's had an undeserved success; even the pages that most attract readers he doesn't consider outstanding, they may scandalize those who don't know much but not people like him.

I said that I was a little tired and helped my companion, who had drunk too much, to get up. He was a small man but had the prominent belly of a gourmand. Tufts of white hair bristled over large ears, he had a red face interrupted by a narrow mouth, a big nose, and very bright eyes; he smoked a lot, and his fingers were yellowed. In the elevator he tried to kiss me. Although I wriggled out of his embrace I had a hard time keeping him away; he wouldn't give up. The touch of his stomach and his winey breath stayed with me. At the time, it would never have occurred to me that an old man, so respectable, so cultured, that man who was such a good friend of my future mother-in-law, could behave in an unseemly way. Once we were in the corridor he hastened to apologize, he blamed the wine, and went straight to his room.

14.

The next day, at breakfast and during the entire drive to Milan, he talked passionately about what he considered the

most exciting period of his life, the years between 1945 and
1948. I heard in his voice a genuine melancholy, which vanished, however, when he went on to describe with an equally
genuine enthusiasm the new climate of revolution, the
energy—he said—that was infusing young and old. I kept nodding yes, struck by how important it was for him to convince
me that my present was in fact the return of his thrilling past.
I felt a little sorry for him. A random biographical hint led me,
at a certain point, to make a quick calculation: the person with
me was fifty-eight years old.

Once in Milan I had the driver drop me near the publishing house, and I said goodbye to my companion. I had slept
badly and was in something of a daze. On the street I tried to
eradicate my disgust at that physical contact with Tarratano,
but I still felt the stain of it and a confusing continuity with a
kind of vulgarity I recognized from the neighborhood. At the
publisher's I was greeted warmly. It wasn't the courtesy of a
few months earlier but a sort of generalized satisfaction that
meant: how clever we were to guess that you were clever. Even
the switchboard operator, the only one there who had treated
me condescendingly, came out of her booth and embraced me.
And for the first time the editor who had done that punctilious
editing invited me to lunch.

As soon as we sat down in a half-empty restaurant near the
office, he returned to his emphasis on the fact that my writing
guarded a fascinating secret, and between courses he suggested that I would do well to plan a new novel, taking my time
but not resting too long on my laurels. Then he reminded me
that I had an appointment at the state university at three.
Mariarosa had nothing to do with it; the publishing house
itself, through its own channels, had organized something with
a group of students. Whom should I look for when I get there?
I asked. My authoritative lunch companion said proudly: My
son will be waiting for you at the entrance.

I retrieved my bag from the office, and went to the hotel. I stayed a few minutes and left for the university. The heat was unbearable. I found myself against a background of posters dense with writing, red flags, and struggling people, placards announcing activities, noisy voices, laughter, and a widespread sense of apprehension. I wandered around, looking for signs that had to do with me. I recall a dark-haired young man who, running, rudely bumped into me, lost his balance, picked himself up, and ran out into the street as if he were being pursued, even though no one was behind him. I recall the pure, solitary sound of a trumpet that pierced the suffocating air. I recall a tiny blond girl, who was dragging a clanking chain with a large lock at the end, and zealously shouting, I don't know to whom: I'm coming! I remember it because in order to seem purposeful, as I waited for someone to recognize me and come over, I took out my notebook and wrote down this and that. But half an hour passed, and no one arrived. Then I examined the placards and posters more carefully, hoping to find my name, or the title of the book. It was useless. I felt a little nervous, and decided not to stop one of the students: I was ashamed to cite my book as a subject of discussion in an environment where the posters pasted to the walls proclaimed far more significant themes. I found to my annoyance that I was poised between opposing feelings: on the one hand, a strong sympathy for all those young men and women who in that place were flaunting, gestures and voices, with an absolute lack of discipline, and, on the other, the fear that the disorder I had been fleeing since I was a child might, now, right here, seize me and fling me into the middle of the commotion, where an incontrovertible power—a Janitor, a Professor, the Rector, the Police—would quickly find me at fault, me, me who had always been good, and punish me.

I thought of sneaking away, what did I care about a handful of kids scarcely younger than me, to whom I would say the usual foolish things? I wanted to go back to the hotel, enjoy my situation as a successful author who was traveling all over, eating in restaurants and sleeping in hotels. But five or six busy-looking girls passed by, carrying bags, and almost against my will I followed them, the voices, the shouts, even the sound of the trumpet. Like that, walking and walking, I ended up outside a crowded classroom from which, just then, an angry clamor arose. And since the girls I was following went in, I, too, cautiously entered.

A sharp conflict involving various factions was under way, both in the packed classroom and in a small crowd that besieged the lectern. I stayed near the door, ready to leave, already repelled by a burning cloud of smoke and breath, by a strong odor of excitement.

I tried to orient myself. I think they were discussing procedural matters, in an atmosphere, however, in which no one—some were shouting, some were silent, some poking fun, some laughing, some moving rapidly like runners on a battlefield, some paying no attention, some studying—seemed to think that agreement was possible. I hoped that Mariarosa was there somewhere. Meanwhile I was getting used to the uproar, the smells. So many people: mostly males, handsome, ugly, well-dressed, scruffy, violent, frightened, amused. I observed the women with interest; I had the impression that I was the only one who was there alone. Some—for example the ones I had followed—stayed close together, even as they distributed leaflets in the crowded classroom: they shouted together, laughed together, and if they were separated by a few meters they kept an eye on each other so as not to get lost. Longtime friends or perhaps chance acquaintances, they seemed to draw from the group the authority to stay in that place of chaos, seduced by the lawless atmosphere, yes, but open to the experience only on the condition that they not separate, as if they had decided beforehand, in more secure places, that if one left they would all leave. Other women, however, by themselves or at most in pairs, had infiltrated the male groups, displaying a provocative intimacy, the lighthearted dissolution of safe distances, and they seemed to me the happiest, the most aggressive, the proudest.

I felt different, there illegally, without the necessary credentials to shout myself, to remain inside those fumes and those odors that brought to mind, now, the odors and fumes that came from Antonio's body, from his breath, when we embraced at the ponds. I had been too wretched, too crushed by the obligation to excel in school. I had hardly ever gone to the movies. I had never bought records, yet how I would have liked to. I wasn't a fan of any singers, hadn't rushed to concerts, collected autographs; I had never been drunk, and my limited sexual experiences had taken place uncomfortably, amid subterfuges, fearfully. Those girls, on the other hand, to varying degrees, must have grown up in easier circumstances, and were more prepared to change their skin; maybe they felt their presence in that place, in that atmosphere, not as a derailment but as a just and urgent choice. Now that I have some money, I thought, now that I'll earn who knows how much, I can have some of the things I missed. Or maybe not, I was now too cultured, too ignorant, too controlled, too accustomed to freezing life by storing up ideas and facts, too close to marriage and settling down, in short too obtusely fixed within an order that here appeared to be in decline. That last thought frightened me. Get out of this place right away, I said to myself, every gesture or word is an insult to the work I've done. Instead I slipped farther inside the crowded classroom.

I was struck immediately by a very beautiful girl, with delicate features and long black hair that hung over her shoulders, who was certainly younger than me. I couldn't take my eyes off her. She was standing in the midst of some combative young men, and behind her a dark man about thirty, smoking a cigar, stood glued to her like a bodyguard. What distinguished her in that environment, besides her beauty, was that she was holding in her arms a baby a few months old, she was nursing him and, at the same time, closely following the conflict, and occasionally even shouting something. When the baby, a patch of blue, with his little reddish-colored legs and feet uncovered, detached his mouth from the nipple, she didn't put her breast back in the bra but stayed like that, exposed, her white shirt unbuttoned, her breast swollen, her mouth half open, frowning, until she realized the child was no longer suckling and mechanically tried to reattach him.

That girl disturbed me. In the noisy smoke-filled classroom, she was an incongruous icon of maternity. She was younger than me, she had a refined appearance, responsibility for an infant. Yet she seemed determined to reject the persona of the young woman placidly absorbed in caring for her child. She yelled, she gesticulated, she asked to speak, she laughed angrily, she pointed to someone with contempt. And yet the child was part of her, he sought her breast, he lost it. Together they made up a fragile image, at risk, close to breaking, as if it had been painted on glass: the child would fall out of her arms or something would bump his head, an elbow, an uncontrolled movement. I was happy when, suddenly, Mariarosa appeared beside her. Finally: there she was. How lively, how bright, how cordial she was: she seemed to be friendly with the young mother. I waved my hand, she didn't see me. She whispered briefly in the girl's ear, disappeared, reappeared in the crowd that was gathered around the lectern. Meanwhile, through a side door, a small group burst in whose mere arrival calmed people down. Mariarosa signaled, waited for a signal in response, grabbed the megaphone, and spoke a few words that silenced the packed classroom. For a few seconds I had the impression that Milan, the tensions of that period, my own excitement had the power to let the shadows I had in my head emerge. How many times had I thought in those days of my early political education? Mariarosa yielded the megaphone to a young man beside her, whom I recognized immediately. It was Franco Mari, my boyfriend from the early years in Pisa.

15.

He had stayed the same: the same warm and persuasive tone of voice, the same ability to organize a speech, moving from general statements that led, step by step, in a logical sequence to ordinary, everyday experiences, revealing their meaning. As I write, I realize that I recall very little of his physical aspect, only his pale clean-shaven face, his short hair. And yet his was the only body that, so far, I had been close to as if we were married.

I went over to Franco after his speech, and his eyes lighted up with amazement, he embraced me. But it was hard to talk, someone pulled him by the arm, someone else had started to criticize, pointing at him insistently, as if he had to answer for terrible crimes. I stayed near the lectern, uneasy; in the crush I had lost Mariarosa. But this time it was she who saw me, and she tugged on my arm.

"What are you doing here?" she asked, pleased.

I avoided explaining that I had missed an appointment, that I had arrived by chance. I said, indicating Franco: "I know him."

"Mari?"

"Yes."

She spoke about Franco enthusiastically, then she whispered: They'll make me pay for it, I invited him, look what a hornets' nest. And since he was going to stay at her house and leave for Turin the following day, she immediately insisted that

I should come and stay with her, too. I accepted, too bad about the hotel.

The meeting dragged on, there were moments of extreme tension, and a permanent sensation of alarm. It was getting dark when we left the university. Besides Franco, Mariarosa was joined by the young mother, whose name was Silvia, and the man around thirty whom I had noticed in the classroom, the one who was smoking the cigar, a Venezuelan painter named Juan. We all went to dinner in a trattoria that my sister-in-law knew. I talked to Franco enough to find out that I was wrong, he hadn't stayed the same. Covering his face—and maybe he had placed it there himself—a mask, which, although it perfectly matched the features of before, had eliminated the generosity. Now he was pinched, restrained, he weighed his words. In the course of a short, apparently confidential exchange, he never alluded to our old relationship, and when I brought it up, complaining that he had never written to me, he cut me off, saying: It had to be like that. About the university, too, he was vague, and I understood that he hadn't graduated.

"There are other things to do," he said.

"What?"

He turned to Marirosa, as if irritated by the too private note of our exchange:

"Elena is asking what there is to do."

Mariarosa answered cheerfully: "The revolution."

So I assumed a mocking tone, I said: "And in your free time?"

Juan, who was sitting next to Silvia, broke in seriously, gently shaking the baby's closed fist. "In our free time we're getting ready for it."

After dinner we piled into Mariarosa's car; she lived in a large old apartment in Sant'Ambrogio. I discovered that the Venezuelan had a kind of studio there, a very untidy room where he brought Franco and me to show us his work: big canvases depicting crowded urban scenes, painted with an almost photographic skill, but he had spoiled them by nailing to the surface tubes of paint or brushes or palettes or bowls for turpentine and rags. Mariarosa praised him warmly, but addressing Franco in particular, whose opinion she seemed to value.

I observed, without comprehending. Certainly Juan lived there, certainly Silvia also lived there, since she moved through the house confidently with Mirko, the baby. But at first I thought that the painter and the young mother were a couple and lived as tenants in one of those rooms, but soon I changed my idea. The Venezuelan, in fact, all evening showed Silvia an abstracted courtesy, while he often put an arm around Mariarosa's shoulders and once he kissed her on the neck.

At first there was a lot of talk about Juan's work. Franco had always had an enviable expertise in the visual arts and a strong critical sensibility. We all listened eagerly, except Silvia, whose baby, until then very good, suddenly began to cry inconsolably. For a while I hoped that Franco would also talk about my book, I was sure he would say something intelligent, such as, with some severity, he was saying about Juan's paintings. Instead no one alluded to my novel, and, after a burst of impatience from the Venezuelan, who hadn't appreciated a remark of Franco's on art and society, we went on to discuss Italy's cultural backwardness, the political picture that emerged from the elections, the chain-reaction concessions of social democracy, the students and police repression, what was termed *the lesson of France*. The exchange between the two men immediately became contentious. Silvia couldn't understand what Mirko needed. She left the room and returned, scolding him harshly as if he were a grown child, and then, from the long hall where she was carrying him up and down or from the room where she had gone to change him, shouted out clichéd phrases of dissent. Mariarosa, after describing the nurseries organized at the Sorbonne for the children of the striking students, evoked a Paris of early June, rainy and cold, still paralyzed by the general strike—not at first hand (she regretted it, she hadn't managed to get there) but as a friend had described it to her in a letter. Franco and Juan both listened distractedly, and yet never lost the thread of their argument; rather, they confronted each other with increasing animosity.

The result was that we found ourselves, we three women, in the situation of drowsy heifers waiting for the two bulls to complete the testing of their powers. This irritated me. I waited for Mariarosa to intervene in the conversation again; I intended to do so myself. But Franco and Juan left us no space; the baby meanwhile was screaming and Silvia treated him even more aggressively. Lila—I thought—was even younger when she had Gennaro. And I realized that something had driven me, even during the meeting, to establish a connection between Silvia and Lila. Maybe it was the solitude as a mother that Lila had felt after the disappearance of Nino and the break with Stefano. Or her beauty: if she had been at that meeting with Gennaro she would have been an even more captivating, more determined mother than Silvia. But Lila was now cut off. The wave that I had felt in the classroom would reach as far as San Giovanni a Teduccio; but she, in that place where she had ended up, demeaning herself, would never be aware of it. A pity, I felt guilty. I should have carried her off, kidnapped her, made her travel with me. Or at least reinforced her presence in my body, mixed her voice with mine. As in that moment. I heard her saying: If you are silent, if you let only the two of them speak, if you behave like an apartment plant, at least give that girl a hand, think what it means to have a small child. It was a confusion of space and time, of distant moods. I jumped up, I took the child from Silvia gently and carefully, and she was glad to let me.

16.

What a handsome child: it was a memorable moment. Mirko charmed me immediately; he had folds of rosy flesh around his wrists, around his legs. How cute he was, what a nice shape his eyes had, how much hair, what long, delicate feet, what a good smell. I whispered all those compliments, softly, as I carried him around the house. The voices of the men faded, as did the ideas they defended and their hostility, and something happened that was new to me. I felt pleasure. I felt, like an uncontrollable flame, the child's warmth, his motility, and it seemed to me that all my senses became more vigilant, as if the perception of that perfect fragment of life that I had in my arms had become achingly acute, and I felt his sweetness and my responsibility for him, and was prepared to protect him from all the evil shadows lying in wait in the dark corners of the house. Mirko must have understood and he was quiet. This, too, gave me pleasure, I was proud of having been able to give him peace.

When I returned to the room, Silvia, who had settled herself on Mariarosa's lap and was listening to the discussion between the two men, joining in with nervous exclamations, turned to look at me and must have seen in my face the pleasure with which I was hugging the child to me. She jumped up, took him from me with a harsh thank you, and went to put him to bed. I had an unpleasant sensation of loss. I felt Mirko's warmth leaving me, I sat down again, in a bad mood, with my thoughts in confusion. I wanted the baby back, I hoped that he would start crying again, that Silvia would ask for my help. What's got into me? Do I want children? Do I want to be a mamma, nursing and singing lullabies? Marriage plus pregnancy? And if my mother should emerge from my stomach just now when I think I'm safe?

17.

It took me a while to focus on the lesson that was coming to us from France, on the tense confrontation between the two men. But I didn't want to be silent. I wanted to say something about what I had read and thought about the events in Paris, the speech was twisting around in sentences that remained incomplete in my mind. And it amazed me that Mariarosa, so clever, so free, said nothing, that she confined herself to agreeing always and only with what Franco said, with pretty smiles, which made Juan nervous and occasionally insecure. If she doesn't speak, I said to myself, I will, otherwise why did I agree to come here, why didn't I go to the hotel? Questions to which I had an answer. I wanted to show those who had known me in the past what I had become. I wanted Franco to realize that he couldn't treat me like the girl of long ago, I wanted him to realize that I had become a completely different person, I wanted him to say in front of Mariarosa that *this other person* had his respect. Therefore, since the baby was quiet, since Silvia had disappeared with him, since neither one had further need of me, I waited a little and finally found a way of disagreeing with my old boyfriend. It was an improvised disagreement: I wasn't moved by solid convictions, the goal was to express myself *against Franco* and I did it, I had certain formulas in my mind, I combined them with false confidence. I said more or less that I was puzzled by the development of the class struggle in France, that I found the student-worker alliance for the moment very abstract. I spoke with decision, I was afraid that one of the two men would interrupt me to say something that would rekindle the argument between them. Instead, they listened to me attentively, all of them, including Silvia, who had returned almost on tiptoe, without the baby. And neither Franco nor Juan gave signs of impatience while I spoke, in fact the Venezuelan agreed when, two or three times,

I uttered the word "people." This annoyed Mari. You're saying that the situation *isn't objectively* revolutionary, he said
emphatically, sarcastically, and I recognized that tone, it meant
that he would defend himself by making fun of me. So the sentences piled up, mine on top of his and vice versa: I don't know
what *objectively* means; it means that to act is inevitable; so if
it's not inevitable, you sit on your hands; no, the task of the revolutionary is always to do what's possible; in France the students have done the impossible, the mechanism of instruction
is broken and will never be fixed; admit that things have
changed and they will change; yes, but no one asked you or
anyone else for certification on official paper or for a guarantee that the situation is *objectively* revolutionary, the students
have acted and that's all; it's not true; it is true. And so on.
Until at the same moment we were silent.

It was an odd exchange, not in its content but in its heated
tones, the rules of etiquette abandoned. In Mariarosa's eyes I
glimpsed a flash of amusement: she understood that if Franco
and I talked to each other like that there had been something
more than a friendship between university colleagues. Come,
give me a hand, she said to Silvia and Juan. She had to get a
ladder, to find sheets for me, for Franco. The two followed her,
Juan whispered something in her ear.

Franco stared at the floor for a moment, he pressed his lips
together as if to restrain a smile, and said affectionately: "You've
remained the petit bourgeois you always were."

That was the way, years earlier, he had often made fun of me
when I was afraid of being caught in his room. In the absence
of the others, I said impetuously: "You're the petit bourgeois,
by origin, by education, by behavior."

"I didn't mean to offend you."

"I'm not offended."

"You've changed, you've become aggressive."

"I'm the same as ever."

"Everything all right at home?"

"Yes."

"And that friend of yours who was so important to you?"

The question came with a logical leap that disoriented me. Had I talked to him about Lila in the past? In what terms? And why did she come to mind now? Where was the connection that he had seen somewhere and I hadn't?

"She's fine," I said.

"What is she doing?"

"She works in a sausage factory on the outskirts of Naples."

"Didn't she marry a shopkeeper?"

"The marriage didn't work."

"When I come to Naples you must introduce me."

"Of course."

"Leave me a number, an address."

"All right."

He looked at me to assess what words would be least hurtful, and asked: "Has she read your book?"

"I don't know, did you read it?"

"Of course."

"How did it seem to you?"

"Good."

"In what way?"

"There are wonderful passages."

"Which ones?

"Those where you give the protagonist the capacity to put together the fragments of things in her own way."

"And that's all?"

"Isn't that enough?"

"No: it's clear that you didn't like it."

"I told you it's good."

I knew him, he was trying not to humiliate me. That exasperated me, I said:

"It's a book that's inspired discussion, it's selling well."

"So good, no?"

"Yes, but not for you. What is it that doesn't work?"

He compressed his lips again, and made up his mind: "There's not much depth, Elena. Behind the petty love affairs and the desire for social ascent you hide precisely what it would be valuable to tell."

"What?"

"Forget it, it's late, we should go to sleep." And he tried to assume an expression of benevolent irony, but in reality he had that new tone of someone who has an important task to complete and gives only sparingly to all the rest: "You did everything possible, right? But this, objectively, is not the moment for writing novels."

18.

Mariarosa returned just then along with Juan and Silvia, carrying clean towels and nightclothes. She certainly heard that last phrase, and surely she understood that we were talking about my book, but she didn't say a word. She could have said that she had liked the book, that novels can be written at any moment, but she didn't. From that I deduced that, beyond the declarations of liking and affection, in those circles that were so caught up and sucked in by political passions my book was considered an insignificant little thing, and the pages that were helping its circulation either were judged cheap versions of much more sensational texts that I had never read, or deserved that dismissive label of Franco's: *a story of petty love affairs*.

My sister-in-law showed me the bathroom and my room with a fleeting courtesy. I said goodbye to Franco, who was leaving early. I merely shook his hand, and he made no move to embrace me. I saw him disappear into a room with Mariarosa, and from Juan's dark expression and Silvia's unhappy look I understood that the guest and the mistress of the house would sleep together.

I withdrew into the room assigned to me. There was a strong smell of stale smoke, an unmade single bed, no night table, no lamp except the weak ceiling light, newspapers piled up on the floor, some issues of journals like *Menabò*, *Nuovo impegno*, *Marcatré*, expensive art books, some well-thumbed, others evidently never opened. Under the bed I found an ashtray overflowing with cigarette butts; I opened the window, and put it on the sill. I got undressed. The nightgown that Mariarosa had given me was too long, too tight. I went to the bathroom barefoot, along the shadowy corridor. The absence of a toothbrush didn't bother me: I hadn't grown up brushing my teeth, it was a recent habit, acquired in Pisa.

In bed I tried to erase the Franco I had met that night by superimposing the Franco of years earlier, the rich, generous youth who had loved me, who had helped me, who had bought everything for me, who had educated me, who had taken me to Paris for his political meetings and on vacation to Versilia, to his parents' house. But I was unsuccessful. The present, with its unrest, the shouting in the packed classroom, the political jargon that was buzzing in my head and spilling out onto my book, vilifying it, prevailed. Was I deluded about my literary future? Was Franco right, there were other things to do besides write novels? What impression had I made on him? What memory did he have of our love, if he even had one? Was he complaining about me to Mariarosa as Nino had complained to me about Lila? I felt wounded, disheartened. Certainly what I had imagined as a pleasant and perhaps slightly melancholy evening seemed to me sad. I couldn't wait for the night to pass so that I could return to Naples. I had to get up to turn out the light. I went back to bed in the dark.

I had trouble falling asleep. I tossed and turned, the bed and the room had the odors of other bodies, an intimacy similar to that of my house but in this case made up of the traces of possibly repulsive strangers. Then I fell asleep, but I woke suddenly: someone had come into the room. I whispered: Who's there? Juan answered. He said, straight out, in a pleading voice, as if he were asking an important favor, like some form of first aid:

"Can I sleep with you?"

The request seemed to me so absurd that, to wake myself completely, to understand, I asked: "Sleep?"

"Yes, lie next to you, I won't bother you, I just don't want to be alone."

"Absolutely not."

"Why?"

I didn't know what to say. I murmured: "I'm engaged."

"So what? We'll sleep, that's all."

"Go away, please, I don't even know you."

"I'm Juan, I showed you my work, what else do you want?"

I felt him sit down on the bed, I saw his dark profile, I felt his breath that smelled of cigars.

"Please," I said, "I'm sleepy."

"You're a writer, you write about love. Everything that happens to us feeds the imagination and helps us to create. Let me be near you, it's something you'll be able to write about."

He touched my foot with the tips of his fingers. I couldn't bear it, I leaped up and turned on the light. He was still sitting on the bed, in underpants and undershirt.

"Out," I hissed and in such a peremptory tone, so clearly close to shouting, so determined to attack and to fight with all my energy, that he got up, slowly, and said with disgust:

"You're a hypocrite."

He went out. I closed the door behind him, there was no key.

I was appalled, I was furious, I was frightened, a bloodthirsty dialogue was whirling in my head. I waited a while before going back to bed, and I didn't turn out the light. What had I intimated about myself, what sort of person did it seem that I was, what legitimatized Juan's request? Was it the reputation of a free woman that my book was giving me? Was it the political words I had uttered, which evidently were not only a dialectical jousting, a game to prove that I was as skillful as a man, but defined the entire person, sexual availability included? Was it a sort of membership in the same ranks that had led that man to show up in my room without scruples, and Mariarosa, also without scruples, to lead Franco into hers? Or had I been contaminated myself by the diffuse erotic excitement that I had felt in the university classroom, and that, unaware, I gave off? In Milan I always felt ready to make love with Nino, betraying Pietro. But that was an old passion, it justified sexual desire and betrayal, while sex in itself, that unmediated demand for orgasm, no, I couldn't be drawn into that. I was unprepared; it disgusted me. Why let myself be touched by Adele's friend in Turin, why in this house by Juan, what did I display, what did *they* want to display? Suddenly I thought of what had happened with Donato Sarratore. Not so much the evening on the beach in Ischia, which I had transformed into the episode in the novel, but the time he appeared in Nella's kitchen, when I had just gone to bed, and he had kissed me, touched me, causing a flow of pleasure against my very will. Between the girl of then, astonished, frightened, and the woman attacked in the elevator, the woman who had been subjected to that incursion now, was there a connection? The extremely cultured friend of Adele's Tarratano, the Venezuelan artist Juan, were they of the same clay as Nino's father, train conductor, bad poet, hack journalist?

19.

I couldn't get to sleep. Added to my strained nerves, to the contradictory thoughts, was Mirko, who had started crying again. I recalled the powerful emotion I had felt when I held the child in my arms and, since he didn't calm down, I couldn't restrain myself. I got up, and, following the trail of his wailing, reached a door through which light filtered. I knocked, Silvia answered rudely. The room was more welcoming than mine, it had an old armoire, a night table, a double bed on which the girl was sitting, in baby-doll pink, legs crossed, a spiteful expression on her face. Her arms flung wide, the backs of both hands on the sheet, she was holding Mirko on her bare thighs, like a votive offering: he, too, was naked, violet, the black hole of his mouth opened wide, his little eyes narrowed, his limbs agitated. At first she greeted me with hostility, then she softened. She said she felt she was an incompetent mother, she didn't know what to do, she was desperate. Finally she said: He always acts like this if he doesn't eat, maybe he's sick, he'll die here on the bed, and as she spoke she seemed very unlike Lila—ugly, disfigured by the nervous twisting of her mouth, by her staring eyes. Until she burst into tears.

The weeping of mother and child moved me, I would have liked to embrace them both, hold them tight, rock them. I whispered: Can I take him for a moment? She nodded yes between her sobs. So I took the child off her knees, brought him to my breast, and again felt the flood of odors, sounds, warmth, as if his vital energies were rushing joyfully to return to me, after the separation. I walked back and forth in the room murmuring a sort of ungrammatical litany that I invented on the spot, a long senseless declaration of love. Mirko miraculously calmed down, fell asleep. I laid him gently beside his mother, but with no desire to be separated from him. I was afraid to go back to my room, a part of me was sure of finding Juan there and wanted to stay here.

Silvia thanked me without gratitude, a thank you to which she coldly added a list of my virtues: You're intelligent, you know how to do everything, you know how to be respected, you're a real mother, your children will be lucky. I denied it, I said I'm going. But she had a jolt of anxiety, she took my hand, and begged me to stay: He listens to you, do it for him, he'll sleep peacefully. I accepted immediately. We lay down on the bed with the baby in the middle, and turned off the light. But we didn't sleep, we began to talk about ourselves.

In the dark Silvia became less hostile. She told me of the disgust she had felt when she discovered she was pregnant. She had hidden the pregnancy from the man she loved and also from herself, she was sure it would pass like an illness that has to run its course. Meanwhile, however, her body reacted, changing shape. She had had to tell her parents, wealthy professionals in Monza. There had been a scene, she had left home. But, instead of admitting that she had let months pass, waiting for a miracle, instead of confessing that physical fear had prevented her from considering abortion, she had claimed that she wanted the child, for love of the man who had made her pregnant. He had said to her: If you want him, for love of you I want him, too. Love her, love him: at that moment they were both serious. But after several months, even before the pregnancy reached its end, they had both fallen out of love. Silvia insisted over and over on this point, sorrowfully. Nothing remained, only bitterness. So she had found herself alone and if until now she had managed to get by, it was thanks to Mariarosa, whom she praised abundantly, she spoke of her rapturously, a wonderful teacher and truly on the side of the students, an invaluable companion.

I told her that the whole Airota family was admirable, that I was engaged to Pietro, that we would be married in the fall. She said impetuously: Marriage horrifies me and so does the family, it's all old stuff. Abruptly her tone became melancholy.

"Mirko's father also works at the university."

"Yes?"

"It all began because I took his course. He was so assured,

so competent, very intelligent, handsome. He had all the virtues. And even before the student struggles began he said: Re-educate your professors, don't be treated like beasts."

"Does he take any interest in the baby?"

She laughed in the darkness, she murmured bitterly:

"A male, apart from the mad moments when you love him and he enters you, always remains outside. So afterward, when you no longer love him, it bothers you just to think that you once wanted him. He liked me, I liked him, the end. It happens to me many times a day—I'm attracted to someone. That doesn't happen to you? It lasts a short time, then it passes. Only the child remains, he's part of you; the father, on the other hand, was a stranger and goes back to being a stranger. Even the name no longer has the sound it used to. Nino, I'd say, and I would repeat it, over and over in my head, as soon as I woke up, it was a magic word. Now, though, it's a sound that makes me sad."

I didn't say anything for a while, finally I whispered:

"Mirko's father is named Nino?"

"Yes, everyone knows him, he's very famous at the university."

"Nino what?"

"Nino Sarratore."

20.

I went out early, leaving Silvia sleeping with the child at her breast. Of the painter I found no trace. I managed to say goodbye only to Mariarosa, who had got up very early to take Franco to the station and had just returned. She looked sleepy, and seemed uneasy. She asked:

"Did you sleep well?"

"I talked to Silvia a lot."

"She told you about Sarratore?"

"Yes."

"I know you're friends."

"Did he tell you?"

"Yes. We gossiped a little about you."

"Is it true that Mirko is his son?"

"Yes." She repressed a yawn, she smiled. "Nino is fascinating, the girls fight over him, they drag him this way and that. And these, luckily, are happy times, you take what you want, all the more since he has a power that conveys joy and the desire to act."

She said that the movement needed people like him. She said that it was necessary, however, to look after him, let him grow, direct him. The very capable people, she said, should be guided: in them the bourgeois democrat, the technical manager, the modernizer is always lying in wait. We both regretted that we had spent so little time together and vowed to do better on the next occasion. I picked up my bag at the hotel, and left.

Only on the train, during the long journey to Naples, did I take in that second paternity of Nino's. A squalid desolation extended from Silvia to Lila, from Mirko to Gennaro. It seemed to me that the passion of Ischia, the night of love in Forio, the secret relationship of Piazza dei Martiri, and the pregnancy—all faded, were reduced to a mechanical device that Nino, upon leaving Naples, had activated with Silvia and who knows how many others. The thing offended me, as if Lila were squatting in a corner of my mind and I felt her feelings. I was bitter as she would have been if she had known, I was furious as if I had suffered the same wrong. Nino had betrayed Lila and me. We were, she and I, similarly humiliated, we loved him without ever being truly loved in return. And so, in spite of his virtues, he was a frivolous, superficial man, an animal organism who dripped sweat and fluids and left behind, like the residue of a careless pleasure, living material conceived, nourished, shaped within female bellies. I remembered when he had come to see me in the neighborhood, years earlier, and we had stayed talking in the courtyard, and Melina had seen him from the window and had taken him for his father. Donato's former lover had caught resemblances that had seemed nonexistent to me. But now it was clear, she was right and I was wrong. Nino was not fleeing his father out of fear of becoming like him: Nino *already was* his father and didn't want to admit it.

Yet I couldn't hate him. In the burning-hot train I not only reflected on the time I had seen him in the bookstore but inserted him into events, words, remarks of those days. Sex had pursued me, clawed me, foul and attractive, obsessively present in gestures, in conversations, in books. The dividing walls were crumbling, the shackles of good manners were breaking. And Nino was living that period intensely. He was part of the rowdy gathering at the university, with its intense odor, he was fit for the disorder of Mariarosa's house, surely he had been her lover. With his intelligence, with his desires, with his capacity for seduction, he moved confident, curious within those times. Maybe I was wrong to connect him to the obscene desires of his father; his behavior belonged to another culture, as Silvia and Mariarosa had pointed out; girls wanted him, he took them, there was no abuse of power, there was no guilt, only the rights of desire. Who knows, maybe Nino in telling me that Lila was made badly even when it comes to sex, wished to convey that the time for pretenses was over, that to load pleasure with responsibility was an error. Even if he had his father's nature, surely his passion for women told a different story.

With astonishment, with disappointment, I arrived in Naples at the moment when a part of me, at the thought of how much Nino was loved and how much he loved, had yielded and reached the point of admitting: what's wrong with it, he enjoys life with those who know how to enjoy it. And as I was returning to the neighborhood, I realized that precisely because all women wanted him and he took them all, I who had wanted him forever wanted him even more. So I decided that I would at all costs avoid meeting him again. As for Lila, I didn't know how to behave. Be silent, tell her everything? Whenever I see her, I would decide then.

21.

At home I didn't have, or didn't want to have, time to go back to the subject. Pietro telephoned, he said that he was coming to meet my parents the following week. I accepted it as an inevitable misfortune, I struggled to find a hotel, clean the house, lessen my family's anxiety. That last task was in vain, the situation had grown worse. In the neighborhood the malicious gossip had increased: about my book, about me, about my constant traveling alone. My mother had put up a defense by boasting that I was about to get married, but, to keep my decisions against God from complicating things further, she pretended that I was getting married not in Naples but in Genoa. As a result the gossip increased, which exasperated her.

One night she confronted me harshly, saying that people were reading my book, were outraged, and talking behind her back. My brothers—she cried—had had to beat up the butcher's sons, who had called me a whore, and not only that: they had punched in the face a classmate of Elisa's who had asked her to do nasty things like her older sister.

"What did you write?" she yelled.

"Nothing, Ma."

"Did you write the disgusting things that you go around doing?"

"What disgusting things. Read it."

"I can't waste time with your nonsense."

"Then leave me alone."

"If your father finds out what people are saying about you, he'll throw you out of the house."

"He won't have to, I'll go myself."

It was evening, and I went for a walk so as not to reproach her with things I would later regret. On the street, in the gardens, along the *stradone*, I had the impression that people stared at me insistently, spiteful shadows of a world I no longer inhabited. I ran into Gigliola, who was returning from work. We lived in the same building, we walked together, but I was afraid that sooner or later she would find a way of saying something irritating. Instead, to my surprise, she spoke timidly, she who was always aggressive if not malicious:

"I read your book, it's wonderful, how brave you were to write those things."

I stiffened.

"What things?"

"The things you do on the beach."

"I don't do them, the character does."

"Yes, but you wrote them really well, Lenù, just the way it happens, with the same filthiness. They are secrets that you know only if you're a woman." Then she took me by the arm, made me stop, said softly, "Tell Lina, if you see her, that she was right, I admit it to her. She was right not to give a shit about her husband, her mamma, her father, her brother, Marcello, Michele, all that shit. I should have escaped from here, too, following the example of you two, who are intelligent. But I was born stupid and I can't do anything about it."

We said nothing else important, she stopped on her landing, I went to my house. But those comments stayed with me. It struck me that she had arbitrarily put together Lila's fall and my rise, as if, compared with her situation, they had the same degree of positivity. But what was most clearly impressed in my mind was how she had recognized in the filthiness of my story her own experience of filthiness. It was a new fact, I didn't know how to evaluate it. Especially since Pietro arrived and for a while I forgot about it.

22.

I went to meet him at the station, and took him to Via Firenze, where there was a hotel that my father had recommended and which I had finally decided on. Pietro seemed even more anxious than my family. He got off the train, as unkempt as usual, his tired face red in the heat, dragging a large suitcase. He wanted to buy a bouquet for my mother, and contrary to his habits he was satisfied only when it seemed to him big enough, expensive enough. At the hotel he left me in the lobby with the flowers, swearing that he would return immediately, and reappeared half an hour later in a blue suit, white shirt, blue tie, and polished shoes. I burst out laughing, he asked: I don't look good? I reassured him, he looked very good. But on the street I felt men's gazes, their mocking laughter, maybe even more insistent than if I had been alone, as if to emphasize that my escort did not deserve respect. Pietro, with that big bunch of flowers that he wouldn't let me carry, so respectable in every detail, was not suited to my city. Although he put his free arm around my shoulders, I had the impression that it was I who had to protect him.

Elisa opened the door, then my father arrived, then my brothers, all in their best clothes, all too cordial. My mother appeared last, the sound of her crooked gait could be heard right after that of the toilet flushing. She had set her hair, she had put a little color on her lips and cheeks, and thought, She was once a pretty girl. She accepted the flowers with condescension, and we sat in the dining room, which for the occasion held no trace of the beds we made at night and unmade in the morning. Everything was tidy, the table had been set with care. My mother and Elisa had cooked for days, which made the dinner interminable. Pietro, amazing me, became very expansive. He questioned my father about his work at the city hall and encouraged him to the point where he forgot his labored Italian and began to tell in dialect witty stories about his fellow employees, which my fiancé, although he understood little, appeared to appreciate tremendously. Above all he ate as I had never seen him eat, and not only complimented my mother and sister on every course but asked—he, who was unable even to cook an egg—about the ingredients of every dish as if he intended to get to the stove right away. He showed such a liking for the potato *gattò* that my mother served him a second very generous portion and promised him, even if in her usual reluctant tone, that she would make it again before he left. In a short time the atmosphere became friendly. Even Peppe and Gianni stayed at the table, instead of running out to join their friends.

After dinner we came to the point. Pietro turned serious and asked my father for my hand. He used just that expression, in a voice full of emotion, which brought tears to my sister's eyes and amused my brothers. My father was embarrassed, he mumbled expressions of friendship for a professor so clever and serious who was honoring him with that question. And the evening finally seemed to be reaching its conclusion, when my mother interrupted. She said darkly:

"Here we don't approve of your not getting married in church: a marriage without a priest isn't a marriage."

Silence. My parents must have come to a secret agreement that my mother would take on the job of making this announcement. But my father couldn't resist, and immediately gave Pietro a half smile to indicate that, although he was included in that *we* invoked by his wife, he was ready to see reason. Pietro returned the smile, but this time he didn't consider him a valid interlocutor, he addressed himself only to my mother. I had told him of my family's hostility, and he was prepared. He began with a simple, affectionate, and, according to his usual habit, very clear speech. He said that he understood, but that he wished to be, in turn, understood. He said that he had the greatest respect for all those who sincerely believed in a god, but that he did not feel he could do so. He said that not being a believer didn't mean believing in nothing, he had his convictions and absolute faith in his love for me. He said it was love that would consolidate our marriage, not an altar, a priest, a city official. He said that the rejection of a religious service was for him a matter of principle and that surely I would stop loving him, or certainly I would love him less, if he proved to be a man without principles. He said finally that surely my mother herself would refuse to entrust her daughter to a person ready to knock down even a single one of the pillars on which he had based his existence.

At those words my father made broad nods of assent, my brothers were openmouthed, Elisa was moved again. But my mother remained impassive. For some moments she fiddled with her wedding ring, then she looked Pietro in the eye and instead of going back to the subject to say that she was persuaded, or to continue to argue, she began to sing my praises with cold determination. Ever since I was small I had been an unusual child. I had been capable of doing things that no girl of the neighborhood had been capable of doing. I had been and was her pride, the pride of the whole family. I had never disappointed her. I had won the right to be happy and if someone made me suffer she would make him suffer a thousand times more.

I listened in embarrassment. All the while I tried to understand if she was speaking seriously or if, as usual, she was intending to explain to Pietro that she didn't give a damn about the fact that he was a professor and all his talk, it wasn't he who was doing the Grecos a favor but the Grecos who were doing him one. I couldn't tell. My fiancé instead believed her absolutely and as my mother spoke he simply assented. When at last she was silent, he said that he knew very well how precious I was and that he was grateful to her for having brought me up as I was. Then he stuck a hand in a pocket of his jacket and took out a blue case that he gave me with a timid gesture. What is it, I thought, he's already given me a ring, is he giving me another? Meanwhile I opened the case. There was a very beautiful ring, of red gold, and in the setting an amethyst surrounded by diamonds. Pietro murmured: it was my grandmother's, my mother's mother, and in my family we would all like you to have it.

That gift was the signal that the ritual was over. We began to drink again, my father went back to telling funny stories of his private and work life, Gianni asked Pietro what team he rooted for, Peppe challenged him to arm wrestling. I helped my sister clear the table. In the kitchen I made the mistake of asking my mother:

"How is he?"

"The ring?"

"Pietro."

"He's ugly, he has crooked feet."

"Papa was no better."

"What do you have to say against your father?"

"Nothing."

"Then be quiet, you only know how to be bossy with us."

"It's not true."

"No? Then why do you let him order you? If he has principles, you don't have them? Make yourself respected."

Elisa intervened: "Ma, Pietro is a gentleman and you don't know what a real gentleman is."

"And you do? Be careful, you're small and if you don't stay in your place I'll hit you. Did you see that hair? A gentleman has hair like that?"

"A gentleman doesn't have normal handsomeness, Ma, a gentleman you can tell, he's a type."

My mother pretended she was going to hit her and my sister, laughing, pulled me out of the kitchen, saying cheerfully:

"Lucky you, Lenù. How refined Pietro is, how he loves you. He gave you his grandmother's antique ring, will you show it to me?"

We returned to the dining room. All the males of the house now wanted to arm-wrestle with my fiancé, they were eager to show that they were superior to the professor at least in tests of strength. He didn't back off. He removed his jacket, rolled up his sleeve, sat down at the table. He lost to Peppe, he lost to Gianni, he lost also to my father. But I was impressed by how seriously he competed. He turned red, a vein swelled on his forehead, he argued that his opponents were shamelessly violating the rules of the contest. He held out stubbornly against Peppe and Gianni, who lifted weights, and against my father, who was capable of unscrewing a screw with just his bare hand. All the while, I was afraid that, in order not to give in, he would break his arm.

23.

Pietro stayed for three days. My father and brothers quickly became attached to him. My brothers were pleased that he didn't give himself airs and was interested in them even though school had judged them incompetent. My mother on the other hand continued to treat him in an unfriendly manner and not until the day before he left did she soften. It was a Sunday, and my father said he wanted to show his son-in-law how beautiful

Naples was. His son-in-law agreed, and proposed that we should eat out.

"In a restaurant?" my mother asked, scowling.

"Yes, ma'am, we ought to celebrate."

"Better if I cook, we said we'd make you another *gattò*."

"No, thank you, you've already done too much."

While we were getting ready my mother drew me aside and asked: "Will he pay?"

"Yes."

"Sure?"

"Sure, Ma, he's the one who invited us."

We went into the city center early in the morning, dressed in our best clothes. And something happened that first of all amazed me. My father had taken on the task of tour guide. He showed our guest the Maschio Angioino, the royal palace, the statues of the kings, Castel dell'Ovo, Via Caracciolo, and the sea. Pietro listened attentively. But at a certain point he, who was coming to our city for the first time, began modestly to tell us about it, to make us discover our city. It was wonderful. I had never had a particular interest in the background of my childhood and adolescence, I marveled that Pietro could talk about it with such learned admiration. He showed that he knew the history of Naples, the literature, fables, legends, anecdotes, the visible monuments and those hidden by neglect. I imagined that he knew about the city in part because he was a man who knew everything, and in part because he had studied it thoroughly, with his usual rigor, because it was mine, because my voice, my gestures, my whole body had been subjected to its influence. Naturally my father soon felt deposed, my brothers were annoyed. I realized it, I hinted to Pietro to stop. He blushed, and immediately fell silent. But my mother, with one of her unpredictable twists, hung on his arm and said:

"Go on, I like it, no one ever told me those things."

We went to eat in a restaurant in Santa Lucia that according to my father (he had never been there but had heard about it) was very good.

"Can I order what I want?" Elisa whispered in my ear.

"Yes."

The time flew by pleasantly. My mother drank too much and made some crude remarks, my father and my brothers started joking again with each other and with Pietro. I didn't take my eyes off my future husband; I was sure that I loved him, he was a person who knew his value and yet, if necessary, he could forget himself with naturalness. I noticed for the first time his propensity to listen and his sympathetic tone of voice, like that of a lay confessor, and they pleased me. Maybe I should persuade him to stay another day and take him to see Lila, tell her: I'm marrying this man, I'm about to leave Naples with him, what do you say, am I doing well? And I was considering that possibility when at a nearby table five or six students began to look at us insistently and laugh. I immediately realized that they found Pietro funny-looking because of his thick eyebrows, the bushy hair over his forehead. After a few minutes my brothers, both at the same time, stood up, went over to the students' table, and started a quarrel in their usual violent manner. An uproar arose, shouting, some punches. My mother shrieked insults in support of her sons, my father and Pietro rushed to pull them away. Pietro was almost amused; he seemed not to have understood the reason for the fight. Once in the street he said ironically: Is this a local custom, you suddenly get up and start hitting the people at the next table? He and my brothers became livelier and friendlier than before. But as soon as possible my father drew Peppe and Gianni aside and rebuked them for the bad impression they had made in front of the professor. I heard Peppe justifying himself almost in a whisper: They were making fun of Pietro, Papa, what the hell were we supposed to do? I liked that he said Pietro and not the professor: it meant that Pietro was part of the family, at home, a friend with the best qualities, and that, even if he was rather odd-looking, no one could make fun of him in his presence. But the incident convinced me that it was better not to take Pietro to see Lila: I knew her, she was mean, she would find him ridiculous and would make fun of him like the young men in the restaurant.

In the evening, exhausted by the day outside, we ate at home and then we all went out again, taking my future husband to the hotel. As we parted, my mother, in high spirits, unexpectedly kissed him noisily on each cheek. But when we returned to the neighborhood, saying a lot of nice things about Pietro, she kept to herself, without saying a word. Before she went to her room she said to me bitterly:

"You are too fortunate—you don't deserve that poor boy."

24.

The book sold well all summer, and I continued to talk about it here and there around the country. I was careful now to defend it with a tone of detachment, at times chilling the more inquisitive audiences. Every so often I remembered Gigliola's words and I mixed them with my own, trying to give them a place.

In early September, Pietro moved to Florence, to a hotel near the station, and started looking for an apartment. He found a small place to rent in the neighborhood of Santa Maria del Carmine, and I went right away to see it. It was an apartment with two dingy rooms, in terrible condition. The kitchen was tiny, the bathroom had no window. When in the past I had gone to Lila's brand-new apartment to study, she would often let me stretch out in her spotless tub, enjoying the warm water and the dense bubbles. The bathtub in that apartment in Florence was cracked and yellowish, the type you had to sit upright in. But I smothered my unhappiness, I said it was all right: Pietro's course was starting, he had to work, he couldn't waste time. And, besides, it was a palace compared to my parents' house.

However, just as Pietro was getting ready to sign the lease, Adele arrived. She didn't have my timidity. She judged the apartment a hovel, completely unsuited to two people who were to spend a large part of their time at home working. So she did what her son hadn't done and what she, on the other hand, could do. She picked up the telephone and, paying no attention to Pietro's show of opposition, marshaled some Florentine friends, all influential people. In a short time she had found in San Niccolò, for a laughable rent, because it was a favor, five light-filled rooms, with a large kitchen and an adequate bathroom. She wasn't satisfied with that: she made some improvements at her own expense, she helped me furnish it. She listed possibilities, gave advice, guided me. But I often noted that she didn't trust either my submissiveness or my taste. If I said yes, she wanted to make sure I really agreed, if I said no she pressed me until I changed my mind. In general we always did as she said. On the other hand, I seldom opposed her; I had no trouble going along with her, and in fact made an effort to learn. I was mesmerized by the rhythm of her sentences, by her gestures, by her hair style, by her clothes, her shoes, her pins, her necklaces, her always beautiful earrings. And she liked my attitude of an attentive student. She persuaded me to cut my hair short, she urged me to buy clothes of her taste in an expensive shop that offered her big discounts, she gave me a pair of shoes that she liked and would have bought for herself but didn't consider suitable for her age, and she even took me to a friend who was a dentist.

Meanwhile, because of the apartment that, in Adele's opinion, constantly needed some new attention, because of Pietro, who was overwhelmed by work, the wedding was put off from autumn to spring, something that allowed my mother to prolong her war to get money from me. I tried to avoid serious conflicts by demonstrating that I hadn't forgotten my family. With the arrival of the telephone, I had the hall and kitchen repainted, I had new wine-colored flowered wallpaper put in the dining room, I bought a coat for Elisa, I got a television on the installment plan. And at a certain point I also gave myself something: I enrolled in a driving school, passed the exam easily, got my license. But my mother darkened:

"You like throwing away money? What's the use of a license if you don't have a car?"

"We'll see later."

"You want to buy a car? How much do you really have saved up?"

"None of your business."

Pietro had a car, and once we were married I intended to use it. When he returned to Naples, in the car, in fact, to bring his parents to meet mine, he let me drive a little, around the old neighborhood and the new one. I drove on the *stradone*, passing the elementary school, the library, I drove on the streets where Lila had lived when she was married, I turned back and skirted the gardens. That experience of driving is the only good thing I can remember. Otherwise it was a terrible afternoon, followed by an endless dinner. Pietro and I struggled to make our families less uncomfortable, but they were so many worlds apart that the silences were extremely long. When the Airotas left, loaded with an enormous quantity of leftovers pressed on them by my mother, it suddenly seemed to me that I was wrong about everything. I came from that family, Pietro from that other, each of us carried our ancestors in our body. How would our marriage go? What awaited me? Would the affinities prevail over the differences? Would I be capable of writing another book?

When? About what? And would Pietro support me? And Adele? And Mariarosa?

One evening, with thoughts like that in my head, I heard someone call me from the street. I rushed to the window—I had immediately recognized the voice of Pasquale Peluso. I saw that he wasn't alone, he was with Enzo. I was alarmed. At that hour shouldn't Enzo be in San Giovanni a Teduccio, at home, with Lila and Gennaro?

"Can you come down?" Pasquale shouted.

"What's happening?"

"Lina doesn't feel well and wants to see you."

I'm coming, I said, and ran down the stairs although my mother was shouting after me: Where are you going at this hour, come back here.

25.

I hadn't seen either Pasquale or Enzo for a long time, but they got right to the point—they had come for Lila and began talking about her immediately. Pasquale had grown a Che Guevara-style beard and it seemed to me that it had improved him. His eyes seemed bigger and more intense, and the thick mustache covered his bad teeth even when he laughed. Enzo, on the other hand, hadn't changed, as silent, as compact, as ever. Only when we were in Pasquale's old car did I realize how surprising it was to see them together. I had been sure that no one in the neighborhood wanted to have anything to do with Lila and Enzo. But it wasn't so: Pasquale often went to their house, he had come with Enzo to get me, Lila had sent them together.

It was Enzo who in his dry and orderly way told me what had happened: Pasquale, who was working at a construction site near San Giovanni a Teduccio, was supposed to stop for

dinner at their house. But Lila, who usually returned from the
factory at four-thirty, still hadn't arrived at seven, when Enzo
and Pasquale got there. The apartment was empty, Gennaro
was at the neighbor's. The two began cooking, Enzo fed the
child. Lila hadn't shown up until nine, very pale, very nervous.
She hadn't answered Enzo and Pasquale's questions. The only
thing she said, in a terrified tone of voice, was: They're pulling
out my nails. Not true, Enzo had taken her hands and
checked, the nails were in place. Then she got angry and shut
herself in her room with Gennaro. After a while she had yelled
at them to find out if I was at home, she wanted to speak to
me urgently.

I asked Enzo:

"Did you have a fight?"

"No."

"Did she not feel well, was she hurt at work?"

"I don't think so, I don't know."

Pasquale said to me:

"Now, let's not make ourselves anxious. Let's bet that as
soon as Lina sees you she'll calm down. I'm so glad we found
you—you're an important person now, you must have a lot to
do."

I denied it, but he cited as proof the old article in *l'Unità*
and Enzo nodded in agreement; he had also read it.

"Lila saw it, too," he said.

"And what did she say?"

"She was really pleased with the picture."

"But they made it sound like you were still a student,"
Pasquale grumbled. "You should write a letter to the paper
explaining that you're a graduate."

He complained about all the space that even *l'Unità* was
giving to the students. Enzo said he was right, and they held
forth with arguments not so different from those I had heard
in Milan, only the vocabulary was cruder. It was clear that

Pasquale especially wanted to entertain me with arguments worthy of someone who, though she was their friend, appeared in *l'Unità* with a photograph. But maybe they did it to dispel the anxiety, theirs and mine.

I listened. I quickly realized that their relationship had solidified precisely because of their political passion. They often met after work, at party or some sort of committee meetings. I listened to them, I joined in out of politeness, they replied, but meanwhile I couldn't get Lila out of my mind, Lila consumed by an unknown anguish, she who was always so resistant. When we reached San Giovanni they seemed proud of me, Pasquale in particular didn't miss a single word of mine, and kept checking on me in the rear-view mirror. Although he had his usual knowing tone—he was the secretary of the local section of the Communist Party—he ascribed to my agreement on politics the power to sanction his position. So that, when he felt clearly supported, he explained to me, in some distress, that, with Enzo and some others, he was engaged in a serious fight *within* the party, which—he said, frowning, pounding his hands on the wheel—preferred to wait for a whistle from Aldo Moro, like an obedient dog, rather than stop procrastinating and join the battle.

"What do you think?" he asked.

"It's as you say," I said.

"You're clever," he praised me then, solemnly, as we were going up the dirty stairs, "you always were. Right, Enzo?"

Enzo nodded yes, but I understood that his worry about Lila was increasing at every step, as it was in me, and he felt guilty for being distracted by that chatter. He opened the door, said aloud, We're here, and pointed to a door whose top half was of frosted glass, and through which a faint light shone. I knocked softly and went in.

26.

Lila was lying on a cot, fully dressed. Gennaro was sleeping next to her. Come in, she said, I knew you'd come, give me a kiss. I kissed her on the cheeks, I sat on the empty bed that must be her son's. How much time had passed since I'd last seen her? I found her even thinner, even paler, her eyes were red, the sides of her nose were cracked, her long hands were scarred by cuts. She continued almost without a pause, in a low voice so as not to wake the baby: I saw you in the newspapers, how well you look, your hair is lovely, I know everything about you, I know you're getting married, he's a professor, good for you, you're going to live in Florence, I'm sorry I made you come at this hour, my mind's no help to me, it's coming unglued like wallpaper, luckily you're here.

"What's happening?" I asked, and moved to caress her hand.

That question, that gesture were enough. She opened her eyes wide, clenched her hand, abruptly pulled it away.

"I'm not well," she said, "but wait, don't be scared, I'll calm down now."

She became calm. She said softly, enunciating the words:

"I've disturbed you, Lenù, because you have to make me a promise, you're the only person I trust: if something happens to me, if I end up in the hospital, if they take me to the insane asylum, if they can't find me anymore, you have to take Gennaro, you have to keep him with you, bring him up in your house. Enzo is good, he's smart, I trust him, but he can't give the child the things you can."

"Why are you talking like that? What's wrong? If you don't explain I can't understand."

"First promise."

"All right."

She became agitated again, alarming me.

"No, you mustn't say all right; you must say here, now, that you'll take the child. And if you need money, find Nino, tell him he has to help you. But promise: *I will bring up the child.*"

I looked at her uncertainly. But I promised. I promised and I sat and listened to her all night long.

27.

This may be the last time I'll talk about Lila with a wealth of detail. Later on she became more evasive, and the material at my disposal was diminished. It's the fault of our lives diverging, the fault of distance. And yet even when I lived in other cities and we almost never met, and she as usual didn't give me any news and I made an effort not to ask for it, her shadow goaded me, depressed me, filled me with pride, deflated me, giving me no rest.

Today, as I'm writing, that goad is even more essential. I wish she were here, that's why I'm writing. I want her to erase, add, collaborate in our story by spilling into it, according to her whim, the things she knows, what she said or thought: the time she confronted Gino, the fascist; the time she met Nadia, Professor Galiani's daughter; the time she returned to the apartment on Corso Vittorio Emanuele where long ago she had felt out of place; the time she looked frankly at her experience of sex. As for my own embarrassments as I listened, my sufferings, the few things I said during her long story, I'll think about them later.

28.

As soon as *The Blue Fairy* turned to ash in the bonfire of the courtyard, Lila went back to work. I don't know how strong an effect our meeting had on her—certainly she felt unhappy for days but managed not to ask herself why. She had learned that it hurt to look for reasons, and she waited for the unhappiness to become first a general discontent, then a kind of melancholy, and finally the normal labor of every day: taking care of Gennaro, making the beds, keeping the house clean, washing and ironing the baby's clothes, Enzo's, and her own, making lunch for the three of them, leaving little Rino at the neighbor's with a thousand instructions, hurrying to the factory and enduring the work and the abuses, coming home to devote herself to her son, and also to the children Gennaro played with, making dinner, the three of them eating again, putting Gennaro to bed while Enzo cleared up and washed the dishes, returning to the kitchen to help him study, something that was very important to him, and that, despite her weariness, she didn't want to deny him.

What did she see in Enzo? In essence, I think, the same thing she had wanted to see in Stefano and in Nino: a way of finally putting everything back on its feet in the proper way. But while Stefano, once the screen of money vanished, had turned out to be a person without substance and dangerous; while Nino, once the screen of intelligence vanished, had been transformed into a black smoke of pain, Enzo for now seemed incapable of nasty surprises. He was the boy whom, for obscure reasons, she had always respected in elementary school, and now he was a man so deeply compact in every gesture, so resolute toward the world, and so gentle with her that she could be sure he wouldn't abruptly change shape.

Of course, they didn't sleep together. Lila couldn't do it. They shut themselves in their rooms, and she heard him moving on the other side of the wall until every noise stopped and there remained only the sounds of the apartment, the building, the street. She had trouble falling asleep, in spite of her exhaustion. In the dark all the reasons for unhappiness that she had prudently left nameless got mixed up and were concentrated on Gennaro, little Rino. She thought: What will this child become? She thought: I mustn't call him Rinuccio, that would drive him to regress into dialect. She thought: I also have to help the children he plays with if I don't want him to be ruined by being with them. She thought: I don't have time, I myself am not what I once was, I never pick up a pen, I no longer read books.

Sometimes she felt a weight on her chest. She became alarmed and turned on the light in the middle of the night, looked at her sleeping child. She saw almost nothing of Nino; Gennaro reminded her, rather, of her brother. When he was younger, the child had followed her around, now instead he was bored, he yelled, he wanted to run off and play, he said bad words to her. I love him—Lila reflected—but do I love him just as he is? An ugly question. The more she observed her son, the more she felt that, even if the neighbor found him very intelligent, he wasn't growing up as she would have liked. She felt that the years she had dedicated to him had been in vain, now it seemed to her wrong that the quality of a person depends on the quality of his early childhood. You had to be constant, and Gennaro had no constancy, nor did she. My mind is always scattering, she said to herself, I'm made badly and he's made badly. Then she was ashamed of thinking like that, she whispered to the sleeping child: you're clever, you already know how to read, you already know how to write, you can do addition and subtraction, your mother is stupid, she's never satisfied. She kissed the little boy on the forehead and turned out the light.

But still she couldn't sleep, especially when Enzo came home late and went to bed without asking her to study. On these occasions, Lila imagined that he had met some prostitute or had a lover, a colleague in the factory where he worked, an activist from the Communist cell he had immediately joined.

Males are like that, she thought, at least the ones I've known: they have to have sex constantly, otherwise they're unhappy. I don't think Enzo is any different, why should he be. And besides I've rejected him, I've left him in the bed by himself, I can't make any demands. She was afraid only that he would fall in love and send her away. She wasn't worried about finding no roof over her head, she had a job at the sausage factory and felt strong, surprisingly, much stronger than when she had married Stefano and found herself with a lot of money but was subjugated by him. Rather, she was afraid of losing Enzo's kindness, the attention he gave to all her anxieties, the tranquil strength he emanated and thanks to which he had saved her first from Nino's absence, then from Stefano's presence. All the more because, in her present situation, he was the only one who gave her any gratification, who continued to ascribe to her extraordinary capabilities.

"You know what that means?"

"No."

"Look closely."

"It's German, Enzo, I don't know German."

"But if you concentrate, after a while you'll know it," he said to her, partly joking, partly serious.

Enzo had worked hard to get a diploma and had succeeded, but, even though she had stopped going to school in fifth grade, he believed that she had a much brighter intelligence than he did and attributed to her the miraculous quality of rapidly mastering any material. In fact, when, with very little to go on, he nevertheless became convinced that the languages of computer programming held the future of the human race, and that the élite who first mastered them would have a resounding part in the history of the world, he immediately turned to her.

"Help me."

"I'm tired."

"The life we lead is disgusting, Lina, we have to change."

"For me it's fine like this."

"The child is with strangers all day."

"He's big, he can't live in a bell jar."

"Look what bad shape your hands are in."

"They're my hands and I'll do as I like with them."

"I want to earn more, for you and for Gennaro."

"You take care of your things and I'll take care of mine."

Harsh reactions, as usual. Enzo enrolled in a correspondence course—it was expensive, requiring periodic tests to be sent to an international data processing center with headquarters in Zurich, which returned them corrected—and gradually he had involved Lila and she had tried to keep up. But she behaved in a completely different way than she had with Nino, whom she had assailed with her obsession to prove that she could help him in everything. When she studied with Enzo she was calm, she didn't try to overpower him. The evening hours that they spent on the course were a struggle for him, for her a sedative. Maybe that was why, the rare times he returned late and seemed able to do without her, Lila remained wakeful, anxious, as she listened to the water running in the bathroom, with which she imagined Enzo washing off his body every trace of contact with his lovers.

29.

In the factory—she had immediately understood—overwork drove people to want to have sex not with their wife or husband in their own house, where they returned exhausted and empty of desire, but there, at work, morning or afternoon. The men reached out their hands at every opportunity, they propositioned you if they merely passed by; and women, especially the ones who were not so young, laughed, rubbed against them with their big bosoms, fell in love, and love became a diversion that mitigated the labor and the boredom, giving an impression of real life.

From Lila's first days the men had tried to get close, as if to sniff her. Lila repulsed them, and they laughed or went off humming songs full of obscene allusions. One morning, to make things perfectly clear, she almost pulled off the ear of a man who passing by had made a lewd remark and pressed a kiss on her neck. He was a fairly attractive man in his forties, named Edo, who spoke to everyone in an allusive way and was good at telling dirty jokes. Lila grabbed the ear with one hand and twisted it, pulling with all her strength, her nails digging into the membrane, without letting go her grip even though the man was yelling, as he tried to parry the kicks she was giving him. After which, furious, she went to see Bruno Soccavo to protest.

Lila had seen him only a few times since he hired her—fleetingly, without paying him much attention. In that situation, however, she was able to observe him closely. He was standing behind the desk; he had risen deliberately, the way men do when a woman enters the room. Lila was amazed: Soccavo's face was bloated, his eyes shrouded by dissipation, his chest heavy, and his flushed complexion clashed like magma against his black hair and the white of his wolfish teeth. She wondered: what does this man have to do with the young man, the friend of Nino who was studying law? And she felt there was no continuity between the time on Ischia and the sausage factory: between them stretched a void, and in the leap from one space to the other Bruno—maybe because his father had been ill recently and the weight of the business (the debts, some said) had fallen suddenly on his shoulders—had changed for the worse.

She told him her complaints, he began to laugh.

"Lina," he warned her, "I did you a favor, but don't make

trouble for me. We all work hard here, don't always have your gun aimed: people have to relax every so often, otherwise it causes problems for me."

"The rest of you can relax with each other."

He ran his eyes over her with a look of amusement.

"I thought you liked to joke."

"I like it when I decide."

Lila's hard tone made him change his. He became serious, he said without looking at her: you're the same as ever—so beautiful in Ischia. Then he pointed to the door: go to work, go on.

But from then on, when he met her in the factory, he never failed to speak to her in front of everyone, and he always gave her a good-humored compliment. That familiarity in the end sanctioned Lila's situation in the factory: she was in the good graces of the young Soccavo, and so it was as well to leave her alone. This seemed to be confirmed when one afternoon, right after the lunch break, a large woman named Teresa stopped her and said teasingly: you're wanted in the seasoning room. Lila went into the big room where the salamis were drying, a rectangular space crammed with salamis hanging from the ceiling in the yellow light. There she found Bruno, who appeared to be doing an inspection but in reality wanted to chat.

While he wandered around the room poking and sniffing with the air of an expert, he asked her about Pinuccia, her sister-in-law, and—a thing that irritated Lila—said, without looking at her, in fact as he examined a soppressata: she was never happy with your brother, she fell in love with me that summer, like you and Nino. Then he passed by and, with his back to her, added: it was thanks to her that I discovered that pregnant women love to make love. Then, without giving her the time to comment or make a sarcastic remark or get angry, he stopped in the middle of the room and said that while the place as a whole had nauseated him ever since he was a child, here in the drying room he had always felt comfortable, there was something satisfying, solid, the product that was nearly finished, acquiring refinement, spreading its odor, being readied for the market. Look, touch it, he said to her, it's compact, hard, smell the fragrance it gives off: it's like the odor of man and woman when they embrace and touch—you like it?—if you knew how many girls I've brought here since I was a boy. And just then he grabbed her by the waist, slid his lips down her long neck, as he squeezed her bottom—he seemed to have a hundred hands, he was rubbing her on top of the apron, underneath it, at a frenetic and breathless speed, in an exploration without pleasure, a pure intrusive desire.

For Lila everything, except the smell of the salamis, reminded her of Stefano's violence and for several seconds she felt annihilated, she was afraid of being murdered. Then fury seized her, and she hit Bruno in the face and between the legs, she yelled him, you are a shit of a man, you've got nothing down there; come here, pull it out so I can cut it off, you shit.

Bruno let go, retreated. He touched his lip, which was bleeding, he snickered in embarrassment, he mumbled: I'm sorry, I thought there might be at least a little gratitude. Lila shouted at him: You mean I have to pay a penalty, or you'll fire me, is that it? He laughed again, shook his head: No, if you don't want to you don't want to, that's all, I apologized, what else should I do? But she was beside herself, only now did she begin to feel on her body the traces of his hands, and she knew it would last, it wasn't something she could wash off with soap. She backed up toward the door, she said to him: You were lucky right now, but whether you fire me or not, I swear I'll make you curse the moment you touched me. As she was leaving he muttered: What did I do to you, I didn't do anything, come here, as if these were real problems, let's make peace.

She went back to her job. At the time she was working in the steamy vat room, as a kind of attendant who among other things was supposed to keep the floor dry, a fruitless task. Edo, the one whose ear she had almost torn off, looked at her with curiosity. All of them, men and women, kept their eyes on her as she returned, enraged, from the drying room. Lila didn't exchange a glance with anyone. She grabbed a rag, slammed it down on the bricks, and began to wipe the floor, which was a swamp, uttering aloud, in a threatening tone: Let's see if some other son of a bitch wants to try. Her companions concentrated on their work.

For days she expected to be fired, but she wasn't. If she happened to run into Bruno, he smiled kindly, she responded with a cold nod. No consequences, then, except disgust at those short hands, and flashes of hatred. But since Lila continued to show the same contemptuous indifference toward the supervisors, they suddenly began to torment her again, by constantly changing her job, forcing her to work until she was worn out, making obscene remarks. A sign that they had been given permission.

She didn't tell Enzo anything about almost tearing off the ear, about Bruno's attack, about the everyday harassments and struggles. If he asked her how things were going at the sausage factory, she answered sarcastically: Why don't you tell me how it is where you work? And since he was silent, Lila teased him a little and then together they turned to the exercises for the correspondence course. They took refuge there for many reasons, the most important being to avoid questions about the future: what were they to each other, why was he taking care of her and Gennaro, why did she accept it, why had they been living together for so long while Enzo waited in vain every night for her to join him, tossing and turning in the bed, going to the kitchen with the excuse of getting a drink of water, glancing at the door with the frosted glass to see if she had turned off the light yet and to look at her shadow. Mute tensions—I knock, I let him enter—his doubts, hers. In the end they preferred to dull their senses by competing with block diagrams as if they were equipment for gymnastics.

"Let's do the diagram of the door opening," Lila said.

"Let's do the diagram of knotting the tie," Enzo said.

"Let's do the diagram of tying Gennaro's shoes," Lila said.

"Let's do the diagram of making coffee in the *napoletana*," Enzo said.

From the simplest actions to the most complicated, they racked their brains to diagram daily life, even if the Zurich tests didn't require it. And not because Enzo wanted to but because, as usual, Lila, who had begun diffidently, grew more and more excited each day, and now, in spite of the cold at night, she was frantic to reduce the entire wretched world they lived in to the truth of 0s and 1s. She seemed to aspire to an abstract linearity—the abstraction that bred all abstractions— hoping that it would assure her a restful tidiness.

"Let's diagram the factory," she proposed one evening.

"The whole process?" he asked, bewildered.

"Yes."

He looked at her, he said: "All right, let's start with your job."

An irritated scowl crossed her face; she said good night and went to her room.

30.

That equilibrium, already precarious, changed when Pasquale reappeared. He was working at a construction site in the area and had come to San Giovanni a Teduccio for a meeting of the local section of the Communist Party. He and Enzo met on the street, by chance, and immediately regained their old intimacy. They ended up talking about politics, and manifested the same dissatisfaction. Enzo expressed himself cautiously at first, but Pasquale, surprisingly, although he had an important local post—secretary of the section—proved to be anything but cautious, and he criticized the party, which was revisionist, and the union, which too often closed both eyes. The two spent so long talking that Lila found Pasquale in the house at dinnertime and had to feed him as well.

The evening began badly. She felt herself observed, and had to make an effort not to get angry. What did Pasquale want, to spy on her, report to the neighborhood how she was living? What right did he have to come there to judge her? He didn't speak a single friendly word, he brought no news of her family—of Nunzia, of her brother Rino, of Fernando. Instead he gave her male looks, the kind she got in the factory, appraising, and if she became aware of them he turned his eyes elsewhere. He must have found that she had grown ugly. Surely he was thinking, How could I, as a boy, have fallen in love with this woman, I was a fool. And without a doubt he considered her a terrible mother, since she could have brought up her son in the comfort of the Carracci grocery stores and instead she had dragged him into that poverty. At a certain point Lila said huffily to Enzo, you clean up, I'm going to bed. But Pasquale, to her surprise, assumed a grandiose tone and said to her, with some emotion: Lina, before you go I have to tell you one thing. There is no woman like you, you throw yourself into life with a force that, if we all had it, the world would have changed a long time ago. Then, having broken the ice in this way, he told her that Fernando had gone back to resoling shoes, that Rino had become Stefano's cross to bear, and was constantly begging him for money, that Nunzia he rarely saw, she never left the house. But you did well, he repeated: no one in the neighborhood has kicked the Carraccis and the Solaras in the face as much as you, and I'm on your side.

After that he showed up often, which cut into their studying. He would arrive at dinnertime with four hot pizzas, playing his usual role of someone who knows all about how the capitalist and anti-capitalist world functions, and the old friendship grew stronger. It was clear that he lived without emotional ties; his sister Carmen was engaged and had little time for him. But he reacted to his solitude with an angry activism that Lila liked, that interested her. Although crushed by hard labor at the construction sites, he was involved in union activities: he threw blood-red paint at the American consulate, if there were fascists to be beaten up he was always on the front lines, he was a member of a worker-student committee where he continuously quarreled with the students. Not to mention the Communist Party: because of his critical position he expected at any moment to lose his post as secretary of the section. With Enzo and Lila he spoke freely, mixing personal resentments and political arguments. They tell *me* I'm an enemy of the party, he complained, they tell *me* I make too much of a fuss, I should calm down. But *they* are the ones who are destroying the party, *they* are the ones turning it into a cog in the system, *they* are the ones who've reduced anti-fascism to democratic oversight. But do you know who's been installed as the head of the neighborhood fascists? The pharmacist's son, Gino, an idiot slave of Michele Solara. And must I put up with the fact that the fascists are raising their heads again in my neighborhood? My father—he said, with emotion—gave his entire self to the party, and why: for this watered-down anti-fascism, for this shit we have today? When that poor man ended up in jail, innocent, completely innocent, he got angry—he didn't murder Don Achille—the party abandoned him, even though he had been a loyal comrade, even though he had taken part in the Four Days of Naples, and fought at the Ponte della Sanità, even though after the war, in the neighborhood, he had been more exposed than anyone else. And Giuseppina, his mother? Had anyone helped her? As soon as he mentioned his mother, Pasquale picked up Gennaro and sat him on his lap, saying: See how pretty your mamma is, do you love her?

Lila listened. At times it occurred to her that she should have said yes to that youth, the first who had noticed her, rather than aiming Stefano and his money, rather than getting herself in trouble with Nino: stayed in her place, not committed the sin of pride, pacified her mind. But at other times, because of Pasquale's tirades, she felt gripped again by her childhood, by the ferocity of the neighborhood, by Don Achille, by his murder, which she, as a child, had recounted so often and with so many invented details that now it seemed to her that she had been present. So she remembered the arrest of Pasquale's father, and how much the carpenter had shouted, and his wife, and Carmen, and she didn't like that, true memories mingled with false ones, she saw the violence, the blood. Then she roused herself, uneasily, escaped from the flood of Pasquale's bitterness, and to soothe herself she urged him to recall, I don't know, Christmas and Easter in his family, his mother Giuseppina's cooking. He quickly realized what was going on and maybe he thought that Lila missed the affections of her family, as he missed his. The fact is that one day he showed up without warning and said gaily: Look who I brought you. He had brought her Nunzia.

Mother and daughter embraced, Nunzia cried for a long time, and gave Gennaro a Pinocchio ragdoll. But as soon as she started to criticize her daughter's decisions, Lila, who at first had appeared happy to see her, said: Ma, either we act as if nothing happened or it's better that you go. Nunzia was offended, she played with the child, and kept saying, as if she really were talking to the boy: If your mamma goes to work, what about you, poor thing, where does she leave you? At that point Pasquale realized he had made a mistake, he said it was late and they had to go. Nunzia got up and spoke to her daughter, partly threatening her, partly entreating her. You, she complained. First you had us living the life of rich people and then you ruined us: your brother felt abandoned and doesn't want to see you anymore, your father has effaced you; Lina, please, I'm not telling you to make peace with your husband, that's not possible, but at least clear things up with the Solaras; they've taken everything because of you, and Rino, your father, we Cerullos, now once again we're nothing.

Lila listened and then she practically pushed her out, saying: Ma, it's better if you don't come back. She shouted the same thing to Pasquale as well.

31.

Too many problems at once: the feelings of guilt toward Gennaro, toward Enzo; the cruel shifts at work, the overtime, Bruno's obscenities; her family, who wanted to return to burden her; and that presence of Pasquale, toward whom it was pointless to be aloof. He never got angry; he burst in cheerfully, sometimes dragging Lila, Gennaro, and Enzo out to a pizzeria, sometimes driving them in the car to Agerola so the child could have some fresh air. But mostly he tried to involve her in his activities. He pushed her to join the union, even though she didn't want to and did it only to slight Soccavo, who wouldn't like it. He brought her pamphlets of various kinds, very clear, concise, on subjects like the pay package, collective bargaining, wage differentials, knowing that even if he hadn't opened them Lila would sooner or later read them. He took her with Enzo and the child to Riviera di Chiaia, to a demonstration for peace in Vietnam that turned into a general stampede: rocks flying, fascists stirring things up, police charging, Pasquale punching, Lila shouting insults, and Enzo cursing the moment they had decided to take Gennaro into the middle of that fracas.

But there were two episodes in particular, in that period, that were significant for Lila. Once Pasquale insisted that she come to hear an important comrade, a woman. Lila accepted the invitation; she was curious. But she heard almost none of the speech—a speech more or less about the party and the working class—because the important comrade arrived late and when the meeting finally began Gennaro was fidgety, and she had to amuse him, taking him out to the street to play, bringing him back inside, taking him out again. Yet the little she heard was enough for her to understand how much dignity the woman had, and how distinct she was in every way from the working- and lower-middle-class audience. So when she noticed that Pasquale, Enzo, and some others weren't satisfied with what the speaker was saying, she thought that they were unfair, that they should be grateful to that educated woman who had come to waste her time with them. And when Pasquale made a speech so argumentative that the comrade delegate lost her temper and, her voice cracking, exclaimed, in irritation, That's enough, I'm going to get up and leave, that reaction pleased her, she took her side. But evidently her feelings were, as usual, muddled. When Enzo shouted, in support of Pasquale: Comrade, *without us* you don't even exist, so you stay as long as *we* want you to, and go only when *we* tell you, she changed her mind, with sudden sympathy for the violence of that *we*— it seemed to her that the woman deserved it. She went home angry at the child, who had ruined the evening for her.

Much more lively was a meeting of the committee that Pasquale, with his thirst for engagement, had joined. Lila went not only because it meant a lot to him but because it seemed to her that the restlessness that drove him to try and to understand was good. The committee met in Naples, in an old house on Via dei Tribunali. They arrived one night in Pasquale's car, and climbed up crumbling, monumental stairs. The place was large, and there weren't many people present. Lila noticed how easy it was to distinguish the faces of the students from those of the workers, the fluency of the leaders from the stuttering of the followers. And she quickly became irritated. The students made speeches that seemed to her hypocritical; they had a modest manner that clashed with their pedantic phrases. The refrain, besides, was always the same: We're here to learn from you, meaning from the workers, but in reality they were showing off ideas that were almost too obvious about capital, about exploitation, about the betrayal of social democracy, about the modalities of the class struggle. Furthermore—she discovered—the few girls, who were mostly silent, flirted eagerly with Enzo and Pasquale. Especially Pasquale, who was the more sociable, and was treated with great friendliness. He was a worker who—although he carried a Communist Party card, and was the head of a section—had chosen to bring his experience of the proletariat into a revolutionary meeting. When he and Enzo spoke, the students, who among themselves did nothing but quarrel, always registered approval. Enzo as usual said only a few, loaded words. Pasquale, on the other hand, recounted, with an inexhaustible patter, half in Italian, half in dialect, the progress that the political work was making at the construction sites around Naples, hurling small polemical darts at the students, who hadn't been very active. At the conclusion, without warning, he dragged her, Lila, into it. He introduced her by her name and last name, he called her a worker comrade who had a job in a small food factory, and he heaped praises on her.

Lila furrowed her brow and narrowed her eyes: she didn't like them all looking at her like a rare animal. And when, after Pasquale, a girl spoke—the first of the girls to speak—she became even more annoyed, first of all because the girl expressed herself like a book, second because she kept referring to her, calling her Comrade Cerullo, and, third, because Lila already knew her: it was Nadia, the daughter of Professor

Galiani, Nino's little girlfriend, who had written him love letters on Ischia.

For a moment she was afraid that Nadia had in turn recognized her, but although the girl addressed her as she spoke, she gave no sign of remembering her. Besides, why should she? Who could say how many rich people's parties she had gone to and what crowd of shadows inhabited her memory? For Lila, on the other hand, there had been that one long-ago occasion, and she remained struck by it. She recalled the apartment on Corso Vittorio Emanuele precisely, along with Nino and all those young people from good families, the books, the paintings, and her own agonizing experience of it, the unease it had inspired. She couldn't bear it, she got up while Nadia was still speaking and went out with Gennaro, carrying inside her an evil energy that, finding no precise outlet, writhed in her stomach.

After a while, however, she returned; she had decided to have her say, in order not to feel inferior. A curly-headed youth was speaking with great expertise about Italsider and piecework. Lila waited for him to finish and, ignoring Enzo's look of bewilderment, asked to speak. She spoke for a long time, in Italian, with Gennaro fussing in her arms. She began slowly, then she continued on amid a general silence, perhaps her voice was too loud. She said jokingly that she knew nothing about the working class. She said she knew only the workers, men and women, in the factory where she worked, people from whom there was absolutely nothing to learn except wretchedness. Can you imagine, she asked, what it means to spend eight hours a day standing up to your waist in the mortadella cooking water? Can you imagine what it means to have your fingers covered with cuts from slicing the meat off animal bones? Can you imagine what it means to go in and out of refrigerated rooms at twenty degrees below zero, and get ten lire more an hour—ten lire—for cold compensation? If you imagine this, what do you think you can learn from people who are forced to live like that? The women have to let their asses be groped by supervisors and colleagues without saying a word. If the owner feels the need, someone has to follow him into the seasoning room; his father used to ask for the same thing, maybe also his grandfather; and there, before he jumps all over you, that same owner makes you a tired little speech on how the odor of salami excites him. Men and women both are subjected to body searches, because at the exit there's something called the "partial," and if the red light goes on instead of the green, it means that you're stealing salamis or mortadellas. The "partial" is controlled by the guard, who's a spy for the owner, and turns on the red light not only for possible thieves but especially for shy pretty girls and for troublemakers. That is the situation in the factory where I work. The union has never gone in and the workers are nothing but poor victims of blackmail, dependent on the law of the owner, that is: I pay you and so I possess you and I possess your life, your family, and everything that surrounds you, and if you don't do as I say I'll ruin you.

At first no one breathed. Then other speakers followed, who all quoted Lila devotedly. At the end Nadia came to give her a hug. She was full of compliments, How pretty you are, how clever, you speak so well. She thanked her, and said seriously: You've made us understand how much work we still have to do. But in spite of her lofty, almost solemn tone, to Lila she seemed more childish than she remembered when, that night years earlier, she had seen her with Nino. What did they do, she and the son of Sarratore, did they dance, did they talk, did they stroke each other, did they kiss? She no longer knew. Certainly, the girl had a loveliness that was unforgettable. And now Lila thought, seeing Nadia right before her, she seemed even purer than she had then, pure and fragile and so genuinely open to the suffering of others that she appeared to feel their torments in her own body to an unendurable extent.

"Will you come back?"

"I have the child."

"You have to come back, we need you."

But Lila shook her head uneasily, she repeated to Nadia: I have the child, and pointed to him, and to Gennaro she said, Say hello to the lady, tell her you know how to read and write, let her hear how well you speak. And since Gennaro hid his face against her neck while Nadia smiled vaguely but didn't seem to notice him, she said again to her: I have the child, I work eight hours a day not counting overtime, people in my situation want only to sleep at night. She left in a daze, with the impression of having exposed herself too fully to people who, yes, were good-hearted but who, even if they understood it in the abstract, in the concrete couldn't understand a thing. *I know*—it stayed in her head without becoming sound—*I know what a comfortable life full of good intentions means, you can't even imagine what real misery is.*

Once she was on the street her uneasiness increased. As they went toward the car, she felt that Pasquale and Enzo were sulking, she guessed that her speech had wounded them. Pasquale took her gently by the arm, closing a physical gap that before that moment he had never tried to close, and asked her:

"You really work in those conditions?"

She, irritated by the contact, pulled her arm away, protesting: "And how do you work, the two of you, how do you work?"

They didn't answer. They worked hard, that was obvious. And at least Enzo in front of him, in the factory, women worn out by the work, by humiliations, by domestic obligations no less than Lila was. Yet now they were both angry because of the conditions *she* worked in; they couldn't tolerate it. You had to hide everything from men. They preferred not to know, they preferred to pretend that what happened at the hands of the boss miraculously didn't happen to the women important to

them and that—this was the idea they had grown up with—
they had to protect her even at the risk of being killed. In the
face of that silence Lila got even angrier. "Fuck off," she said,
"you and the working class."

They got in the car, exchanging only trite remarks all the way
to San Giovanni a Teduccio. But when Pasquale left them at
their house he said to her seriously: There's nothing to do, you're
always the best, and then he left again for the neighborhood.
Enzo, instead, with the child asleep in his arms, muttered darkly:

"Why didn't you say anything? People in the factory put
their hands on you?"

They were tired, she decided to soothe him. She said:

"With me they don't dare."

32.

A few days later the trouble began. Lila arrived at work
early in the morning, worn out by her innumerable tasks and
completely unprepared for what was about to happen. It was
very cold, she'd had a cough for days, it felt like flu coming on.
At the entrance she saw a couple of kids, they must have
decided to skip school. One of them greeted her with some
familiarity and gave her not a flyer as sometimes happened but
a pamphlet several pages long. She responded to his greeting
but she was bewildered; she had seen the boy at the committee meeting on Via dei Tribunali. Then she put the pamphlet
in her coat pocket and passed Filippo, the guard, without
deigning to look at him, so he shouted after her: Not even a
good morning, eh.

She worked extremely hard as usual—at that time she was
in the gutting section—and forgot about the boy. At lunchtime
she went into the courtyard with her lunchbox to find a sunny
corner, but as soon as Filippo saw her he left the guard booth

and joined her. He was a man of about fifty, short, heavy, full of the most disgusting obscenities but also inclined to a sticky sentimentality. He had recently had his sixth child, and he easily became emotional, pulling out his wallet to show off a picture of the baby. Lila thought he had decided to show it to her as well, but no. The man pulled the pamphlet out of his jacket pocket and said to her in an extremely aggressive tone:

"Cerù, listen carefully to what I'm telling you: if you said to these shits the things that are written here, you've got yourself in deep trouble, you know?"

She answered coldly:

"I don't know what the fuck you're talking about, let me eat."

Filippo, angrily throwing the pamphlet in her face, snapped:

"You don't know, eh? Read it, then. We were all happy and in harmony here, and only a whore like you could spread these things. I turn on the 'partial' as I please? I put my hands on the girls? I, the father of a family? Look out, or don Bruno will make you pay, and dearly, or by God I'll smash your face myself."

He turned and went back to the guard booth.

Lila calmly finished eating, then she picked up the pamphlet. The title was pretentious: "Investigation Into the Condition of Workers in Naples and the Provinces." She scanned the pages, and found one devoted entirely to the Soccavo sausage factory. She read word for word everything that had come out of her mouth at the meeting on Via dei Tribunali.

She pretended it was nothing. She left the pamphlet on the ground, she went inside without even looking at the guard booth and returned to work. But she was furious with whoever had gotten her into that mess, and without even warning her, especially saintly Nadia. Surely she had written that stuff, it was all tidily in order and full of maudlin emotion. As she worked the knife on the cold meat and the odor made her sick and her rage increased, she felt around her the hostility of the other workers, male and female. They had all known one another a long time, they knew they were complicit victims, and they had no doubt about who the whistleblower was: she, the only one who behaved from the start as if the need to work didn't go hand in hand with the need to be humiliated.

In the afternoon Bruno appeared and soon afterward he sent for her. His face was redder than usual, and he had the pamphlet in his hand.

"Was it you?"

"No."

"Tell me the truth, Lina: there are already too many people out there making trouble, you've joined them?"

"I told you no."

"No, eh? There is no one here, however, who has the ability and the impudence to make up all these lies."

"It must have been one of the office workers."

"The office workers least of all."

"Then what do you want from me, little birds sing, get mad at them."

He snorted, he seemed truly strained. He said:

"I gave you a job. I said nothing when you joined the union, my father would have kicked you out. All right, I did something foolish, there in the drying room, but I apologized, you can't say I persecuted you. And you, what do you do, you take revenge by casting a bad light on my factory and setting it down in black and white that I take my women workers into the drying room? For chrissake, when? Me, the workers, are you mad? You're making me regret the favor I did you."

"The favor? I work hard and you pay me a few cents. It's more the favor I do you than what you do for me."

"You see? You talk like those shits. Have the courage to admit that you wrote this crap."

"I didn't write anything."

Bruno twisted his mouth, he looked at the pages in front of him, and she understood that he was hesitating, he couldn't make up his mind: move to a harsher tone, threaten her, fire her, retreat and try to find out if there were other initiatives like that being prepared? She made up *her* mind, and said in a low voice—reluctantly but with a small charming expression that clashed with the memory of his violence, still vivid in her body—three conciliatory phrases:

"Trust me, I have a small child, I honestly didn't do this thing."

He nodded yes, but he also muttered, unhappily: "You know what you're forcing me to do?"

"No, and I don't want to know."

"I'll tell you just the same. If those are your friends, warn them: as soon as they come back and make a scene out front here, I'll have them beaten to a pulp. As for you, be careful: stretch the cord too far and it will snap."

But the day didn't end there. On the way out, when Lila passed, the red light of the partial went on. It was the usual ritual: every day the guard cheerfully chose three or four victims, the shy girls, eyes lowered, let him feel them up, the savvy older women laughed, saying: Filì, if you have to touch go on, but hurry up, I've got to go make dinner. This time, Filippo stopped only Lila. It was cold, a strong wind was blowing. The guard came out of his booth. Lila shivered, she said: "If you so much as brush me, by God I'll murder you or have you murdered."

Filippo, grim, pointed to a small café table that was always next to the booth.

"Empty your pockets one at a time, put the stuff there."

Lila found a fresh sausage in her coat, with disgust she felt the soft meat inside the casing. She pulled it out and burst into laughter, saying, "What shits you people are, all of you."

33.

Threats to report her for theft. Deductions from her salary, fines. And insults, Filippo's hurled at her, and hers at Filippo. Bruno didn't appear, and yet he was surely still in the factory, his car was in the courtyard. Lila guessed that from then on things would get even worse for her.

She went home wearier than usual; she got angry at Gennaro, who wanted to stay at the neighbor's; she made dinner. She told Enzo that he would have to study on his own and she went to bed early. Since she couldn't get warm under the covers, she got up and put on a wool sweater over her nightgown. She was getting back in bed when suddenly, for no obvious reason, her heart was in her throat and began pounding so hard that it seemed like someone else's.

She already knew those symptoms, they went along with the thing that later—eleven years later, in 1980—she called dissolving boundaries. But the signs had never manifested themselves so violently, and this was the first time it had happened when she was alone, without people around who for one reason or another set off that effect. Then she realized with a jolt of horror that she wasn't alone. From her unstuck head figures and voices of the day were emerging, floating through the room: the two boys from the committee, the guard, her fellow-workers, Bruno in the drying room, Nadia—all moving too rapidly, as in a silent film. Even the flashes of red light from the partial came at very narrow intervals, and Filippo who was tearing the sausage out of her hands and yelling threats. All a trick of the mind: except for Gennaro, in the cot beside her, with his regular breathing, there were no real persons or sounds in the room. But that didn't soothe her, in fact it magnified the fear. Her heartbeats were now so powerful that they seemed capable of exploding the interlocking solidity of objects. The tenacity of the grip that held the walls of the room together had weakened, the violent knocking in her throat was shaking the bed, cracking the plaster, unsoldering the upper part of her skull, maybe it would shatter the child, yes, it would shatter him like a plastic puppet, splitting open his chest and stomach and head to reveal his insides. I have to get him away, she thought; the closer he is to me, the more likely he'll break. But she remembered another baby that she had pushed out, the baby that had never taken shape in her womb, Stefano's child. I pushed him out, or at least that's what Pinuccia and Gigliola said behind my back. And maybe I really did, I expelled him deliberately. Why hasn't anything, so far, really gone well for me? And why should I keep the things that haven't worked? The beating showed no sign of diminishing, the figures of smoke pursued her with the sound of their voices, she got out of the bed again, and sat on the edge. She was soaked with a sticky sweat, it felt like frozen oil. She placed her bare feet against Gennaro's bed, pushed it gently, to move it away but not too far: if she kept him next to her she was afraid of breaking him, if she pushed him too far away she was afraid of losing him. She went into the kitchen, taking small steps and leaning on the furniture, the walls, but repeatedly looking behind her out of fear that the floor would cave in and swallow up Gennaro. She drank from the faucet, washed her face, and suddenly her heart stopped, throwing her forward as if it had braked abruptly.

Over. Objects were sticking together again, her body slowly settled, the sweat dried. Lila was trembling now, and so tired that the walls were spinning around her, she was afraid she would faint. I have to go to Enzo, she thought, and get warm: get in his bed now, press myself against his back while he sleeps, go to sleep myself. But she gave it up. She felt on her face the pretty little expression she had made when she said to Bruno: *Trust me, I have a small child, I didn't do this thing*, a charming affectation, perhaps seductive, the body of a woman acting autonomously in spite of disgust. She was ashamed: how could she behave like that, after what Soccavo had done to her in the drying room? And yet. Ah, to push men and drive them like obedient beasts toward goals that were not theirs. No, no, enough, in the past she had done it for different reasons, almost without realizing it, with Stefano, with Nino, with the Solaras, maybe even with Enzo. Now she didn't want to anymore, she would take care of things herself: with the guard, with her fellow workers, with the students, with Soccavo, with her own mind, which, full of demands, would not resign itself and, worn out by the impact of persons and things, was collapsing.

34.

Upon waking she discovered that she had a fever; she took an aspirin and went to work anyway. In the still dark sky there was a weak bluish light that licked the low buildings, the muddy weeds and refuse. Already as she skirted the puddles on the unpaved stretch of road that led to the factory, she noticed that there were four students, the two from the day before, a third about the same age, and a fat kid, decidedly obese, around twenty years old. They were pasting on the boundary wall placards that called on the workers to join the struggle, and had just begun to hand out a leaflet of the same type. But if, the day before, the workers, out of curiosity, out of courtesy, had taken the pamphlet, the majority now either kept going with their heads down or took the sheet and immediately crumpled it up and threw it away.

As soon as she saw that the youths were there, punctual as if what they called political work had a schedule stricter than hers, Lila was annoyed. The annoyance became hostility when the boy from the day before recognized her and hurried

toward her, with a friendly expression, and a large number of
leaflets in his hand.

"Everything all right, Comrade?"

Lila paid no attention, her throat was sore, her temples
pounding. The boy ran after her, said uncertainly:

"I'm Dario, maybe you don't remember, we met on Via dei
Tribunali."

"I know who the fuck you are," she snapped, "but I don't
want to have anything to do with you or your friends."

Dario was speechless, he slowed down, he said almost to
himself:

"You don't want the leaflet?"

Lila didn't answer, so that she wouldn't yell something hostile at him. But the boy's disoriented face, wearing the expression people have when they feel they are right and don't understand how it is that others don't share their opinion, stayed in
her mind. She thought that she ought to explain to him carefully why she had said the things she had said at the meeting,
and why she found it intolerable that those things had ended
up in the pamphlet, and why she judged it pointless and stupid
that the four of them, instead of still being in bed or about to
enter a classroom, were standing there in the cold handing out
a densely written leaflet to people who had difficulty reading,
and who, besides, had no reason to subject themselves to the
effort of reading, since they already knew those things, they
lived them every day, and could tell even worse: unrepeatable
sounds that no one would ever say, write, or read, and that nevertheless held as potential the real causes of their inferiority.
But she had a fever, she was tired of everything, it would cost
her too much effort. And anyway she had reached the gate,
and there the situation was becoming complicated.

The guard was yelling at the oldest boy, the fat one, shouting at him in dialect: You cross that line, cross it, shit, then
you're entering private property without permission and I'll

shoot. The student, also agitated, replied with a laugh, a broad aggressive laugh, accompanied by insults: he called him a slave, he shouted, in Italian, Shoot, show me how you shoot, this isn't private property, everything in there belongs to the people. Lila passed both of them—how many times had she witnessed bluster like that: Rino, Antonio, Pasquale, even Enzo were masters of it—and said to Filippo, seriously: Satisfy him, don't waste time chattering, someone who could be sleeping or studying and instead is here being a pain in the ass deserves to be shot. The guard saw her, heard her, and, openmouthed, tried to decide if she was really encouraging him to do some-thing crazy or making fun of him. The student had no doubts: he stared at her angrily, shouted: Go on, go in, go kiss the boss's ass, and he retreated a few steps, shaking his head, then he continued to hand out leaflets a few meters from the gate.

Lila headed toward the courtyard. She was already tired at seven in the morning, her eyes were burning, eight hours of work seemed an eternity. Meanwhile behind her there was a noise of screeching brakes and men shouting, and she turned. Two cars had arrived, one gray and one blue. Someone had got out of the first car and begun to tear off the placards that had just been pasted on the wall. It's getting bad, Lila thought, and instinctively went back, although she knew that, like the others, she ought to hurry in and start work.

She took a few steps, enough to identify the youth at the wheel of the gray car: it was Gino. She saw him open the door and, tall, muscular as he had become, get out of the car hold-ing a stick. The others, the ones who were tearing off the posters, the ones who, more slowly, were still getting out of the cars, seven or eight in all, were carrying chains and metal bars. Fascists, mostly from the neighborhood, Lila knew some of them. Fascists, as Stefano's father, Don Achille, had been, as Stefano had turned out to be, as the Solaras were, grandfather, father, grandsons, even if at times they acted like monarchists, at times Christian Democrats, as it suited them. She had hated them ever since, as a girl, she had imagined every detail of their obscenities, since she had discovered that there was no way to be free of them, to clear everything away. The connection between past and present had never really broken down, the neighborhood loved them by a large majority, pampered them, and they showed up with their filth whenever there was a chance to fight.

Dario, the boy from Via dei Tribunali, was the first to move, he rushed to protest the torn-down posters. He was holding the ream of leaflets, and Lila thought: Throw them away, you idiot, but he didn't. She heard him saying in Italian useless things like Stop it, you have no right, and at the same time saw him turn to his friends for help. He doesn't know anything about fighting: never lose sight of your adversary, in the neighborhood there'd be no talk, at most there'd be some yelling, wide-eyed, to inspire fear, and meanwhile you were the first to strike, causing as much injury as possible, without stopping—it was up to others to stop you if they could. One of the youths who were tearing down the posters acted just like that: he punched Dario in the face, with no warning, knocking him to the ground amid the leaflets he had dropped, and then he was on him, hitting him, while the pages flew around as if there were a fierce excitement in the things themselves. At that point the obese student saw that the boy was on the ground and hurried to help him, bare-handed, but he was blocked halfway by someone armed with a chain, who hit him on the arm. The youth grabbed the chain furiously, and started pulling on it, to tear it away from his attacker, and for several seconds they fought for it, screaming insults at one another. Until Gino came up behind the fat student and hit him with the stick, knocking him down.

Lila forgot her fever and her exhaustion, and ran to the gate, but without a precise purpose. She didn't know if she wanted to have a better view, if she wanted to help the students, if she was simply moved by an instinct she had always had, by virtue of which fighting didn't frighten her but, rather, kindled her fury. She wasn't in time to return to the street, she had to jump aside in order not to be run over by a group of workers who were rushing through the gate. A few had tried to stop the attackers, including Edo, certainly, but they hadn't been able to, and now they were escaping. Men and women were running, pursued by two youths holding iron bars. A woman named Isa, an office worker, ran toward Filippo yelling: Help, do something, call the police, and Edo, one of whose hands was bleeding, said aloud to himself: I'm going to get the hatchet and then we'll see. So by the time Lila reached the unpaved road, the blue car had already left and Gino was getting into the gray one, but he recognized her and paused, astonished, saying: Lina, you've ended up here? Then, pulled in by his comrades, he started the engine and drove off, but he shouted out window: You acted the lady, bitch, and look what the fuck you've become.

35.

The workday passed in an anxiety that, as usual, Lila contained behind an attitude that at one moment was contemptuous, the next threatening. They all made it clear that they blamed her for the tensions that had emerged suddenly in a place that had always been peaceful. But soon two parties formed: one, a small group, wanted to meet somewhere during the lunch break and take advantage of the situation to urge Lila to go to the owner with some cautious wage demands; the other, the majority, wouldn't even speak to Lila and was opposed to any undertaking that would complicate a work life that was already complicated. Between the two groups there was no way to reach agreement. In fact Edo, who belonged to the first party and was worried about the injury to his hand, went so far as to say to someone who belonged to the second: If my hand gets infected, if they cut it off, I'm coming to your house, I'll pour a can of gasoline on it, and set you and your family on fire. Lila ignored both factions. She kept to herself and worked, head down, with her usual efficiency, driving away the conversation, the insults, and the cold. But she reflected on what awaited her, a whirl of different thoughts passed through her feverish head: what had happened to the injured students, where had they gone, what trouble had they got her into; Gino would talk about her in the neighborhood, he would tell Michele Solara everything; it was humiliating to ask Bruno for favors, and yet there was no other way, she was afraid of being fired, she was afraid of losing a salary that, even though it was miserable, allowed her to love Enzo without considering him fundamental to her survival and that of Gennaro.

Then she remembered the terrible night. What had happened to her, should she go to a doctor? And if the doctor found some illness, how would she manage with work and the child? Careful, don't get agitated, she needed to put things in order. Therefore, during the lunch break, oppressed by her cares, she resigned herself to going to Bruno. She wanted to tell him about the nasty trick of the sausage, about Gino's fascists, reiterate that it wasn't her fault. First, however, despising herself, she went to the bathroom to comb her hair and put on a little lipstick. But the secretary said with hostility that Bruno wasn't there and almost certainly wouldn't be all week. Anxiety gripped her again. Increasingly nervous, she thought of asking Pasquale to keep the students from returning to the gate, she said to herself that, once the boys from the committee disappeared, the fascists, too, would disappear, the factory would settle back into its old ways. But how to find Peluso? She didn't know where he worked, she didn't want to look for him in the neighborhood—she was afraid of running into her mother, her father, and especially her brother, with whom she didn't want to fight. So, exhausted, she added up all her troubles and decided to turn directly to Nadia. At the end of her shift she hurried home, left a note for Enzo to prepare dinner, bundled Gennaro up carefully in coat and hat, and set off, bus after bus, to Corso Vittorio Emanuele.

The sky was pastel-colored, with not even a puff of a cloud, but the late-afternoon light was fading and a strong wind was blowing in the violet air. She remembered the house in detail, the entrance, all of it, and the humiliation of the past intensified the bitterness of the present. How brittle the past was, continually crumbling, falling on her. From that house where she had gone with me to a party that had made her suffer, Nadia, Nino's old girlfriend, had tumbled out to make her suffer even more. But she wasn't one to stay quiet, she walked up the hill, dragging Gennaro. She wanted to say to that girl: You and the others are making trouble for my son; for you it's only an amusement, nothing terrible will happen to you; for me, for him, no, it's a serious thing, so either do something to fix it or I'll bash your face in. That was what she intended to say, and she coughed and her rage mounted; she couldn't wait to explode.

She found the street door open. She climbed the stairs, she remembered herself and me, and Stefano, who had taken us to the party, the clothes, the shoes, every word that we had said to each other on the way and on the way back. She rang, Professor Galiani herself opened the door, just as she remembered her, polite, orderly, just like her house. In comparison Lila felt dirty, because of the odor of raw meat that clung to her, the cold that clogged her chest, the fever that confused her feelings, the child whose whining in dialect irritated her. She asked abruptly:

"Is Nadia here?"

"No, she's out."

"When will she be back?"

"I'm sorry, I don't know, in ten minutes, in an hour, she does as she likes."

"Could you tell her that Lina came to see her?"

"Is it urgent?"

"Yes."

"Do you want to tell me?"

Tell her what? Lila gave a start, she looked past the professor. She glimpsed the ancient nobility of furniture and lamps, the book-filled library that had captivated her, the precious paintings on the walls. She thought: This is the world that Nino aspired to before he got mixed up with me. She thought: What do I know of this other Naples, nothing; I'll never live there and neither will Gennaro. Let it be destroyed, then, let fire and ashes come, let the lava reach the top of the hills. Then finally she answered: No, thank you, I have to talk to Nadia. And she was about to leave, it had been a fruitless journey. But she liked the hostile attitude with which the professor had spoken of her daughter and she exclaimed in a suddenly frivolous tone:

"Do you know that years ago I was in this house at a party? I don't know what I expected, but I was bored, I couldn't wait to leave."

36.

Professor Galiani, too, must have seen something she liked, maybe a frankness verging on rudeness. When Lila mentioned our friendship, the professor seemed pleased, she exclaimed: Ah yes, Greco, we never see her anymore, success has gone to her head. Then she led mother and son to the living room, where she had left her grandson playing, a blond child whom she almost ordered: Marco, say hello to our new friend. Lila in turn pushed her son forward, she said, go on, Gennaro, play with Marco, and she sat in an old, comfortable green armchair, still talking about the party years ago. The professor was sorry she had no recollection of it, but Lila remembered everything. She said that it had been one of the worst nights of her life. She spoke of how out of place she had felt, she described in sarcastic tones the conversations she had listened to without understanding anything. I was very ignorant, she exclaimed, with an excessive gaiety, and today even more than I was then.

Professor Galiani listened and was impressed by her sincerity, by her unsettling tone, by the intense Italian of her sentences, by her skillfully controlled irony. She must have felt in Lila, I imagine, that elusive quality that seduced and at the same time alarmed, a siren power: it could happen to anyone, it happened to her, and the conversation broke off only when Gennaro slapped Marco, insulting him in dialect and grabbing a small green car. Lila got up quickly, and, seizing her son by the arm, forcefully slapped the hand that had hit the other child, and although Professor Galiani said weakly, Let it go, they're children, she rebuked him harshly, insisting that he return the toy. Marco was crying, but Gennaro didn't shed a tear; instead, he threw the toy at him with contempt. Lila hit him again, hard, on the head.

"We're going," she said, nervously.

"No, stay a little longer."

Lila sat down again.

"He's not always like that."

"He's a very handsome child. Right, Gennaro, you're a good boy?"

"He isn't good, he isn't at all good. But he's clever. Even though he's little, he can read and write all the letters, capitals and small. What do you say, Gennà, do you want to show the professor how you read?"

She picked up a magazine from a beautiful glass table, pointed to a word at random on the cover, and said: Go on, read. Gennaro refused. Lila gave him a pat on the shoulder, repeated in a threatening tone: Read, Gennà. The child reluctantly deciphered, *d-e-s-t*, then he broke off, staring angrily at Marco's little car. Marco hugged it to his chest, gave a small smile, and read confidently: *destinazione*.

Lila was disappointed, she darkened, she looked at Galiani's grandson with annoyance.

"He reads well."

"Because I devote a lot of time to him. His parents are always out."

"How old is he?"

"Three and a half."

"He seems older."

"Yes, he's sturdy. How old is your son?"

"He's five," Lila admitted reluctantly.

The professor caressed Gennaro, and said to him:

"Mamma made you read a difficult word, but you're a clever boy, I can see that you know how to read."

Just then there was a commotion, the door to the stairs opened and closed, the sound of footsteps scurrying through the house, male voices, female voices. Here are my children, Professor Galiani said, and called out: Nadia. But it wasn't Nadia who came into the room; instead a thin, very pale, very blond girl, with eyes of a blue so blue that it looked fake, burst in noisily. The girl opened wide her arms and cried to Marco: Who's going to give his mamma a kiss? The child ran to her and she embraced him, kissed him, followed by Armando, Professor Galiani's son. Lila remembered him, too, immediately, and looked at him as he practically tore Marco from his mother's arms, crying: Immediately, at least thirty kisses for papa. Marco began to kiss his father on the cheek, counting: One, two, three, four.

"Nadia," Professor Galiani called again in a suddenly irritated tone, "are you deaf? Come, there's someone here to see you."

Nadia finally looked into the room. Behind her was Pasquale.

37.

Lila's bitterness exploded again. So Pasquale, when work was over, rushed to the house of those people, amid mothers and fathers and grandmothers and aunts and happy babies, all affectionate, all well educated, all so broad-minded that they welcomed him as one of them, although he was a construction worker and still bore the dirty traces of his job?

Nadia embraced her in her emotional way. Lucky you're here, she said, leave the child with my mother, we have to talk. Lila replied aggressively that yes, they had to talk, right away, that's why she was there. And since she said emphatically that she had only a minute, Pasquale offered to take her home in the car. So they left the living room, the children, the grandmother, and met—also Armando, also the blond girl, whose name was Isabella—in Nadia's room, a large room with a bed, a desk, shelves full of books, posters showing singers, films, and revolutionary struggles that Lila knew little about. There were three other young men, two whom she had never seen, and Dario, banged up from the beating he'd had, sprawled on Nadia's bed with his shoes on the pink quilt. All three were smoking, the room was full of smoke. Lila didn't wait, she didn't even respond to Dario's greeting. She said that they had got her in trouble, that their lack of consideration had put her at risk of being fired, that the pamphlet had caused an uproar, that they shouldn't come to the gate anymore, that because of them the fascists had showed up and everyone was now angry with both the reds and the blacks. She hissed at Dario: As for you, if you don't know how to fight stay home, you know they could kill you? Pasquale tried to interrupt her a few times, but she cut him off contemptuously, as if his mere presence in that house were a betrayal. The others instead listened in silence. Only when Lila had finished, did Armando speak. He had his mother's delicate features, and thick black eyebrows; the violet trace of his carefully shaved beard rose to his cheekbones, and he spoke in a warm, thick voice. He introduced himself, he said that he was very happy to meet her, that he regretted he hadn't been there when she spoke at the meeting, that, however, what she had told them they had discussed among themselves and since they had considered it an important contribution they had decided to put everything in writing. Don't worry, he concluded calmly, we'll support you and your comrades in every way.

Lila coughed, the smoke in the room irritated her throat.

"You should have informed me."

"It's true, but there wasn't time."

"If you really want the time you find it."

"We are few and our initiatives are more every day."

"What work do you do?"

"In what sense?"

"What do you do for a living?"

"I'm a doctor."

"Like your father?"

"Yes."

"And at this moment are you risking your job? Could you end up in the street at any moment along with your son?"

Armando shook his head unhappily and said:

"Competing for who is risking the most is wrong, Lina."

And Pasquale:

"He's been arrested twice and I have eight charges against me. Nobody here risks more or less than anyone else."

"Oh, no?"

"No," said Nadia, "we're all in the front lines and ready to assume our responsibilities."

Then Lila, forgetting that she was in someone else's house, cried:

"So if I should lose my job, I'll come and live here, you'll feed me, you'll assume responsibility for my life?"

Nadia answered placidly:

"If you like, yes."

Four words only. Lila understood that it wasn't a joke, that Nadia was serious, that even if Bruno Soccavo fired his entire work force she, with that sickly-sweet voice of hers, would give the same senseless answer. She claimed that she was in the service of the workers, and yet, from her room in a house full of books and with a view of the sea, she wanted to command you, she wanted to tell you what you should do with your work, she decided for you, she had the solution ready even if you ended up in the street. I—it was on the tip of Lila's tongue—if I want, can smash everything much better than you: I don't need you to tell me, in that sanctimonious tone, how I should think, what I should do. But she restrained herself, and said abruptly to Pasquale:

"I'm in a hurry, are you going to take me or are you staying here?"

Silence. Pasquale glanced at Nadia, muttered, I'll take you, and Lila started to leave the room, without saying goodbye. The girl rushed to lead the way, saying to her how unacceptable it was to work in the conditions that Lila herself had described so well, how urgent it was to kindle the spark of the struggle, and other phrases like that. Don't pull back, she urged, finally, before they went into the living room. But she got no response.

Professor Galiani, sitting in the armchair, was reading, a frown on her face. When she looked up she spoke to Lila, ignoring her daughter, ignoring Pasquale, who had just arrived, embarrassed.

"You're leaving?"

"Yes, it's late. Let's go, Gennaro, leave Marco his car and put your coat on."

Professor Galiani smiled at her grandson, who was pouting.

"Marco gave it to him."

Lila narrowed her eyes, reduced them to cracks.

"You're all so generous in this house, thank you."

The professor watched as she struggled with her son to get his coat on.

"May I ask you something?"

"Go ahead."

"What did you study?"

The question seemed to irritate Nadia, who broke in:

"Mamma, Lina has to go."

For the first time Lila noticed some nervousness in the child's voice, and it pleased her.

"Will you let me have two words?" Professor Galiani snapped, in a tone no less nervous. Then she repeated to Lila, but kindly: "What did you study?"

"Nothing."

"To hear you speak—and shout—it doesn't seem so."

"It's true, I stopped after fifth grade."

"Why?"

"I didn't have the ability."

"How did you know?"

"Greco had it, I didn't."

Professor Galiani shook her head in a sign of disagreement, and said:

"If you had studied you would have been as successful as Greco."

"How can you say that?"

"It's my job."

"You professors insist so much on education because that's how you earn a living, but studying is of no use, it doesn't even improve you—in fact it makes you even more wicked."

"Has Elena become more wicked?"

"No, not her."

"Why not?"

Lila stuck the wool cap on her son's head. "We made a pact when we were children: I'm the wicked one."

38.

In the car she got mad at Pasquale (*Have you become the servant of those people?*) and he let her vent. Only when it seemed to him that she had come to the end of her recriminations did he start off with his political formulas: the condition of workers in the South, the condition of slavery in which they lived, the permanent blackmail, the weakness if not absence of unions, the need to force situations and reach the point of struggle. Lina, he said in dialect, his tone heartfelt, you're afraid of losing the few cents they give you and you're right, Gennaro has to grow up. But I know that you are a true comrade, I know that you understand: here we workers have never even been within the regular wage scales, we're outside all the rules, we're less than zero. So, it's blasphemy to say: leave me alone, I have my own problems and I want to mind my own business. Each of us, in the place assigned to us, has to do what he can.

Lila was exhausted; fortunately Gennaro was sleeping on the back seat with the little car clutched in his right hand. Pasquale's speech came to her in waves. Every so often the beautiful apartment on Corso Vittorio Emanuele came into her mind, along with the professor and Armando and Isabella and Nino, who had gone off to find a wife somewhere of Nadia's type, and Marco, who was three and could read much better than her son. What a useless struggle to make Gennaro become smart. The child was already losing, he was being pulled back and she couldn't hold on to him. When they reached the house and she saw that she had to invite Pasquale in she said: I don't know what Enzo's made, he's a terrible cook, maybe you don't feel like it, and hoped he would leave. But he answered: I'll stay ten minutes, then go, so she touched his arm with her fingertips and murmured:

"Don't tell him anything."

"Anything about what?"

"About the fascists. If he knows, he'll go and beat up Gino tonight."

"Do you love him?"

"I don't want to hurt him."

"Ah."

"That's the way it is."

"Remember that Enzo knows better than you and me what needs to be done."

"Yes, but don't say anything to him just the same."

Pasquale agreed with a scowl. He picked up Gennaro, who wouldn't wake up, and carried him up the stairs, followed by Lila, who was mumbling unhappily: What a day, I'm dead tired, you and your friends have got me in huge trouble. They told Enzo that they had gone to Nadia's house for a meeting, and Pasquale gave him no chance to ask questions, he talked without stopping until midnight. He said that Naples, like the whole world, was churning with new life, he praised Armando, who, good doctor that he was, instead of thinking of his career treated the poor for nothing, he took care of the children in the Quartieri and with Nadia and Isabella was involved in countless projects that served the people—a nursery school, a clinic. He said that no one was alone any longer, comrades helped comrades, the city was going through a wonderful time. You two, he said, shouldn't stay shut up here in the house, you should go out, we should be together more. And finally he announced that he was finished with the Communist Party: too many ugly things, too many compromises, national and international, he couldn't stand that dreariness anymore. Enzo was deeply disturbed by his decision, they argued about it for a long time: the party is the party, no, yes, no, enough with the politics of stabilization, we need to attack the institutional structures of the system. Lila quickly became bored, and she went to put Gennaro to bed—he was sleepy, whining as he ate his supper—and didn't return.

But she stayed awake even when Pasquale left and the evidence of Enzo's presence in the house had been extinguished. She took her temperature, it was 100. She recalled the moment when Gennaro had struggled to read. What sort of word had she put in front of him: destination. Certainly it was a word that Gennaro had never heard. It's not enough to know the alphabet, she thought, there are so many difficulties. If Nino had had him with Nadia, that child would have had a completely different destiny. She felt she was the wrong mother. And yet I wanted him, she thought, it was with Stefano that I didn't want children, with Nino yes. She had truly loved Nino. She had desired him deeply, she had desired to please him and for his pleasure had done willingly everything that with her husband she had had to do by force, overcoming disgust, in order not to be killed. But she had never felt what it was said she was supposed to feel when she was penetrated, that she was sure of, and not only with Stefano but also with Nino. Males were so attached to their penis, they were so proud of it, and they were convinced that you should be even more attached to it than they were. Even Gennaro was always playing with his; sometimes it was embarrassing how much he jiggled it in his hands, how much he pulled it. Lila was afraid he would hurt himself; and even to wash it, or get him to pee, she had had to make an effort, get used to it. Enzo was so discreet, never in his underwear in the house, never a vulgar word. For that reason she felt an intense affection for him, and was grateful to him for his devoted wait in the other room, which had never been interrupted by a wrong move. The control he exercised over things and himself seemed to her the only consolation. But then a sense of guilt emerged: what consoled her surely made him suffer. And the thought that Enzo was suffering because of her was added to all the terrible things of that day. Events and conversations whirled chaotically in her head for a long time. Tones of voice, single words. How should she act the next day in the factory? Was there really all that fervor in Naples and the world, or were Pasquale and Nadia and Armando imagining it to allay their anxieties, out of boredom, to give themselves courage? Should she trust them, with the risk of becoming captive to fantasies? Or was it better to look for Bruno again to get her out of trouble? But would it really be any use trying to placate him, with the risk that he might jump on her again? Would it help to give in to the abuses of Filippo and the supervisors? She didn't make much progress. In the end, in a waking sleep, she landed on an old principle that we two had assimilated since we were little. It seemed to her that to save herself, to save Gennaro, she had to intimidate those who wished to intimidate her, she had to inspire fear in those who wished to make her fear. She fell asleep with the intention of doing harm, to Nadia by showing her that she was just a girl from a good family, all sugary chatter, to Soccavo by ruining the pleasure he got in sniffing salamis and women in the drying room.

39.

She woke at five in the morning, in a sweat; she no longer had a fever. At the factory gate she found not the students but the fascists. Same automobiles, same faces as the day before:

they were shouting slogans, handing out leaflets. Lila felt that more violence was planned and she walked with her head down, hands in pockets, hoping to get into the factory before the fighting started. But Gino appeared in front of her.

"You still know how to read?" he asked in dialect, holding out a leaflet. Keeping her hands in her pockets, she replied:

"I do, yes, but when did you learn?"

Then she tried to go by, in vain. Gino obstructed her, he jammed the leaflet into her pocket with a gesture so violent that he scratched her hand with his nail. Lila crumpled it up calmly.

"It's not even good for wiping your ass," she said and threw it away.

"Pick it up," the pharmacist's son ordered her, grabbing her by the arm. "Pick it up now and you listen to me: yesterday afternoon I asked that cuckold your husband for permission to beat you up and he said yes."

Lila looked him straight in the eye:

"You went to ask my husband for permission to beat me up? Let go of my arm right now, you shit."

At that moment Edo arrived, and instead of pretending not to notice, as was to be expected, he stopped.

"Is he bothering you, Cerù?"

It was an instant. Gino punched him in the face, Edo ended up on the ground. Lila's heart jumped to her throat, and everything began to speed up. She picked up a rock and gripping it solidly struck the pharmacist's son right in the chest. There was a long moment. While Gino shoved her back against a light pole, while Edo tried to get up, another car appeared on the unpaved road, raising dust. Lila recognized Pasquale's broken-down car. Here, she thought, Armando listened to me, maybe Nadia, too, they're well-brought-up people, but Pasquale couldn't resist, he's coming to make war. In fact the doors opened, and five men got out, including him. They were men from the construction sites, carrying knotty clubs, and they began hitting the fascists with a methodical ferocity; they didn't get angry, they planted a single, precise blow intended to knock down the adversary. Lila immediately saw that Pasquale was heading toward Gino, and since Gino was still a few steps away from her she grabbed one of his arms with both hands and said, laughing: You'd better go or they'll kill you. But he didn't go; rather, he pushed her away again and rushed at Pasquale. Lila helped Edo get up, and tried to drag him into the courtyard, but it was difficult; he was heavy, and he was writhing, shouting insults, bleeding. He calmed down a little only when he saw Pasquale hit Gino with his stick and knock him to the ground. The confusion increased: debris the men picked up along the side of the street flew like bullets, men were spitting and screaming insults. Pasquale, leaving Gino unconscious, had rushed into the courtyard, with a man wearing only an undershirt and loose blue pants streaked with cement. Both were now bludgeoning Filippo's booth; he was locked inside, terrorized. Shouting obscenities, they smashed the windows, while the wail of a police siren grew louder. Lila noticed yet again the anxious pleasure of violence. Yes, she thought, you have to strike fear into those who wish to strike fear into you, there is no other way, blow for blow, what you take from me I take back, what you do to me I do to you. But while Pasquale and his people were getting back in the car, while the fascists did the same, carrying off Gino bodily, while the police siren got closer, she felt, terrified, that her heart was becoming like the too tightly wound spring of a toy, and she knew that she had to find a place to sit down as soon as possible. Once she was inside, she collapsed in the hallway, her back against the wall, and tried to calm down. Teresa, the large woman in her forties who worked in the gutting room, was looking after Edo, wiping the blood off his face, and she teased Lila.

"First you pull off his ear, then you help him? You should have left him outside."

"He helped me and I helped him."

Teresa turned to Edo, incredulous:

"*You* helped her?"

He stammered:

"I didn't like to see a stranger beating her up, I want to do it myself."

The woman said:

"Did you see how Filippo shat himself?"

"Serves him right," Edo muttered, "too bad all they broke was the booth."

Teresa turned to Lila and asked her, with a hint of malice:

"Did you call the Communists? Tell the truth."

Is she joking, Lila wondered, or is she a spy, who'll go running to the owner.

"No," she answered, "but I know who called the fascists."

"Who?"

"Soccavo."

40.

Pasquale appeared that evening, after dinner, with a grim expression, and invited Enzo to a meeting at the San Giovanni a Teduccio section. Lila, alone with him for a few minutes, said:

"That was a shitty thing to do, this morning."

"I do what's necessary."

"Did your friends agree with you?"

"Who are my friends?"

"Nadia and her brother."

"Of course they agreed."

"But they stayed home."

Pasquale muttered:

"And who says they stayed home?"

He wasn't in a good mood, in fact he seemed emptied of energy, as if the practice of violence had swallowed up his craving for action. Further, he hadn't asked her to go to the meeting, he had invited only Enzo, something that never happened, even when it was late, and cold, and unlikely that she would take Gennaro out. Maybe they had other male wars to fight. Maybe he was angry with her because, with her resistance to the struggle, she had caused him to look bad in front of Nadia and Armando. Certainly he was bothered by the critical tone she had used in alluding to the morning's expedition. He's convinced, Lila thought, that I don't understand why he hit Gino like that, why he wanted to beat up the guard. Good or bad, all men believe that after every one of their undertakings you have to put them on an altar as if they were St. George slaying the dragon. He considers me ungrateful, he did it to avenge me, he would like me to at least say thank you.

When the two left, she got in bed and read the pamphlets on work and unions that Pasquale had given her long ago. They helped to keep her anchored to the dull things of every day, she was afraid of the silence of the house, of sleep, of her unruly heartbeats, of the shapes that threatened to break apart at any moment. In spite of her weariness, she read for a long time, and in her usual way became excited, and learned a lot of things quickly. To feel safe, she made an effort to wait for Enzo to return. But he didn't, and finally the sound of Gennaro's regular breathing became hypnotic and she fell asleep.

The next morning Edo and the woman from the gutting room, Teresa, began to hang around her with timid, friendly words and gestures. And Lila not only didn't rebuff them but treated the other workers courteously as well. She showed herself available to those who were complaining, understanding to those who were angry, sympathetic toward those who cursed the abuses. She steered the trouble of one toward the trouble of another, joining all together with eloquent words. Above all, in the following days, she let Edo and Teresa and their tiny group talk, transforming the lunch break into a time for secret meeting. Since she could, when she wanted, give the impression that it wasn't she who was proposing and disposing but the others, she found more and more people happy to hear themselves say that their general complaints were just and urgent necessities. She added the claims of the gutting room to those of the refrigerated rooms, and those of the vats, and discovered to her surprise that the troubles of one department depended on the troubles of another, and that all together were links in the same chain of exploitation. She made a detailed list of the illnesses caused by the working conditions: damage to the hands, the bones, the lungs. She gathered enough information to demonstrate that the entire factory was in terrible shape, that the hygienic conditions were deplorable, that the raw material they handled was sometimes spoiled or of uncertain origin. When she was able to talk to Pasquale in private she explained to him what in a very short time she had started up, and he, in his peevish way, was astonished, then said beaming: I would have sworn that you would do it, and he set up an appointment with a man named Capone, who was secretary of the union local.

Lila copied down on paper in her fine handwriting everything she had done and brought the copy to Capone. The secretary examined the pages, and he, too, was enthusiastic. He said to her things like: Where did you come from, Comrade, you've done really great work, bravo. And besides, we've never managed to get into the Soccavo plant; they're all fascists in there, but now that you've arrived things have changed.

"How should we start?" she asked.

"Form a committee."

"We already are a committee."

"Good: the first thing is to organize all this."

"In what sense *organize*?"

Capone looked at Pasquale, Pasquale said nothing.

"You're asking for too many things at once, including things that have never been asked for anywhere—you have to establish priorities."

"In that place everything is a priority."

"I know, but it's a question of tactics: if you want everything at once you risk defeat."

Lila narrowed her eyes to cracks; there was some bickering. It emerged that, among other things, the committee couldn't go and negotiate directly with the owner, the union had to mediate.

"And am I not the union?" she flared up.

"Of course, but there are times and ways."

They quarreled again. Capone said: You look around a little, open the discussion, I don't know, about the shifts, about holidays, about overtime, and we'll take it from there. Anyway—he concluded—you don't know how happy I am to have a comrade like you, it's a rare thing; let's coordinate, and we'll make great strides in the food industry—there aren't many women who get involved. At that point he put his hand on his wallet, which was in his back pocket, and asked:

"Do you want some money for expenses?"

"What expenses?"

"Mimeographing, paper, the time you lose, things like that."

"No."

Capone put the wallet back in his pocket.

"But don't get discouraged and disappear, Lina, let's keep in touch. Look, I'm writing down here your name and surname, I want to talk about you at the union, we have to use you."

Lila left dissatisfied, she said to Pasquale: Who did you bring me to? But he calmed her, assured her that Capone was an excellent person, said he was right, you had to understand, there was strategy and there were tactics. Then he became excited, almost moved, he was about to embrace her, had second thoughts, said: Move ahead, Lina, screw the bureaucracy, meanwhile I'll inform the committee.

Lila didn't choose among the objectives. She confined herself to compressing the first draft, which was very long, into one densely written sheet, which she handed over to Edo: a list of requests that had to do with the organization of the work, the pace, the general condition of the factory, the quality of the product, the permanent risk of being injured or sick, the wretched compensations, wage increases. At that point the problem arose of who was to carry that list to Bruno.

"You go," Lila said to Edo.

"I get angry easily."

"Better."

"I'm not suitable."

"You're very suitable."

"No, you go, you're a member of the union. And then you're a good speaker, you'll put him in his place right away."

41.

Lila had known from the start that it would be up to her. She took her time; she left Gennaro at the neighbor's, and went with Pasquale to a meeting of the committee on Via dei Tribunali, called to discuss *also* the Soccavo situation. There were twelve this time, including Nadia, Armando, Isabella, and Pasquale. Lila circulated the paper she had prepared for Capone; in that first version all the demands were more carefully argued. Nadia read it attentively. In the end she said: Pasquale was right, you're one of those people who don't hold anything back, you've done a great job in a very short time.

And in a tone of sincere admiration she praised not only the political and union substance of the document but the writing: You're so clever, she said, I've never seen this kind of material written about in this way! Still, after that beginning, she advised her not to move to an immediate confrontation with Soccavo. And Armando was of the same opinion.

"Let's wait to get stronger and grow," he said. "The situation concerning the Soccavo factory needs to develop. We've got a foot in there, which is already a great result, we can't risk getting swept away out of pure recklessness."

Dario asked:

"What do you propose?"

Nadia answered, addressing Lila: "Let's have a wider meeting. Let's meet as soon as possible with your comrades, let's consolidate your structure, and maybe with your material prepare another pamphlet."

Lila, in the face of that sudden cautiousness, felt a great, aggressive satisfaction. She said mockingly: "So in your view I've done this work and am putting my job at risk to allow *all of you* to have a bigger meeting and another pamphlet?"

But she was unable to enjoy that feeling of revenge. Suddenly Nadia, who was right opposite her, began to vibrate like a window loose in its frame, and dissolved. For no evident reason, Lila's throat tightened, and the slightest gestures of those present, even a blink, accelerated. She closed her eyes, leaned against the back of the broken chair she was sitting on, felt she was suffocating.

"Is something wrong?" asked Armando.

Pasquale became upset.

"She gets overtired," he said. "Lina, what's wrong, do you want a glass of water?"

Dario hurried to get some water, while Armando checked her pulse and Pasquale, nervous, pressed her:

"What do you feel, stretch your legs, breathe."

Lila whispered that she was fine and abruptly pulled her wrist away from Armando, saying she wanted to be left in peace for a minute. But when Dario returned with the water she drank a small mouthful, murmured it was nothing, just a little flu.

"Do you have a fever?" Armando asked calmly.

"Today, no."

"Cough, difficulty breathing?"

"A little, I can feel my heart beating in my throat."

"Is it a little better now?"

"Yes."

"Come into the other room."

Lila didn't want to, and yet she felt a vast sense of anguish. She obeyed, she struggled to get up, she followed Armando, who had picked up a black leather bag with gold clasps. They went into a large, cold room that Lila hadn't seen before, with three cots covered by dirty-looking old mattresses, a wardrobe with a corroded mirror, a chest of drawers. She sat down on one of the beds, exhausted: she hadn't had a medical examination since she was pregnant. When Armando asked about her symptoms, she mentioned only the weight in her chest, but added: It's nothing.

He examined her in silence and she immediately hated that silence, it seemed a treacherous silence. That detached, clean man, although he was asking questions, did not seem to trust the answers. He examined her as if only her body, aided by instruments and expertise, were a reliable mechanism. He listened to her chest, he touched her, he peered at her, and meanwhile he forced her to wait for a conclusive opinion on what was happening in her chest, in her stomach, in her throat, places apparently well known that now seemed completely unknown. Finally Armando asked her:

"Do you sleep well?"

"Very well."

"How much?"

"It depends."

"On what?"

"On my thoughts."

"Do you eat enough?"

"When I feel like it."

"Do you ever have difficulty breathing?"

"No."

"Pain in your chest?"

"A weight, but light."

"Cold sweats?"

"No."

"Have you ever fainted or felt like fainting?"

"No."

"Are you regular?"

"In what?"

"Menstruation."

"No."

"When did you last have a period?"

"I don't know."

"You don't keep track?"

"Should I keep track?"

"It's better. Do you use contraceptives?"

"What do you mean?"

"Condoms, coil, the Pill."

"What Pill?"

"A new medicine: you take it and you can't get pregnant."

"Is that true?"

"Absolutely true. Your husband has never used a condom?"

"I don't have a husband anymore."

"He left you?"

"I left him."

"When you were together did he use one?"

"I don't even know how a condom is made."

"Do you have a regular sex life?"

"What's the use of talking about these things?"

"If you don't want to we won't."

"I don't want to."

Armando put his instruments back in the case, sat down on a half-broken chair, sighed.

"You should slow down, Lina: you've pushed your body too far."

"What does that mean?"

"You're undernourished, anxious, you've seriously neglected yourself."

"And so?"

"You have a little catarrh, I'll give you a syrup."

"And so?"

"You should have a series of tests, your liver is a little enlarged."

"I don't have time for tests, give me some medicine."

Armando shook his head discontentedly.

"Listen," he said. "I understand that with you it's better not to beat around the bush: you have a murmur."

"What's that?"

"A problem with the heart, and it could be something that's not benign."

Lila made a grimace of anxiety.

"What do you mean? I might die?"

He smiled and said:

"No, only you should get checked by a cardiologist. Come see me in the hospital tomorrow, and I'll send you to someone good."

Lila furrowed her brow, got up, said coldly: "I have a lot to do tomorrow, I'm going to see Soccavo."

42.

Pasquale's worried tone exasperated her. As he was driving home he asked her:

"What did Armando say, how are you?"

"Fine, I should eat more."

"You see, you don't take care of yourself."

Lila burst out: "Pasquà, you're not my father, you're not my brother, you're no one. Leave me alone, get it?"

"I can't be worried about you?"

"No, and be careful what you do and say, especially with Enzo. If you tell him I was ill—and it's not true, I was only dizzy—you risk ruining our friendship."

"Take two sick days and don't go to Soccavo: Capone advised you against it and the committee advised against it, it's a matter of political expediency."

"I don't give a damn about political expediency: you're the one who got me in trouble and now I'll do as I like."

She didn't invite him to come in and he went away angry. Once at home, Lila cuddled Gennaro, made dinner, waited for Enzo. Now it seemed to her that she was constantly short of breath. Since Enzo was late, she fed Gennaro; she was afraid it was one of those evenings when he was seeing women and would return in the middle of the night. When the child spilled a glass of water, the caresses stopped, and she yelled at him as if he were an adult, in dialect: Will you hold still a moment, I'll hit you, why do you want to ruin my life?

Just then Enzo returned, and she tried to be nice. They ate, but Lila had the impression that the food was struggling to get to her stomach, that it was scratching her chest. As soon as Gennaro fell asleep, they turned to the installments of the Zurich course, but Enzo soon got tired, and tried, politely, to go to bed. His attempts were vain, Lila kept going until it was late, she was afraid of shutting herself in her room, she feared that as soon as she was alone in the dark the symptoms she hadn't admitted to Armando would appear, all together, and kill her. He asked her softly:

"Will you tell me what's wrong?"

"Nothing."

"You come and go with Pasquale, why, what secrets do you have?"

"It's things to do with the union, he made me join and now I have to take care of them."

Enzo looked disheartened, and she asked:

"What's wrong?"

"Pasquale told me what you're doing in the factory. You told him and you told the people on the committee. Why am I the only one who doesn't deserve to know?"

Lila became agitated, she got up, she went to the bathroom. Pasquale hadn't held out. What had he told? Only about the union seed that she wanted to plant at Soccavo or also about Gino, about her not feeling well at Via dei Tribunali? He hadn't been able to stay silent—friendship between men had its unwritten but inviolable pacts, not like that between women. She flushed the toilet, returned to Enzo and said:

"Pasquale is a spy."

"Pasquale is a friend. Whereas you, what are you?"

His tone hurt, she gave in unexpectedly, suddenly. Her eyes filled with tears and she tried in vain to push them back, humiliated by her own weakness.

"I don't want to make more trouble for you than I already have," she sobbed, "I'm afraid you'll send me away." Then she blew her nose and added in a whisper: "Can I sleep with you?"

Enzo stared at her, in disbelief.

"Sleep how?"

"However you want."

"And do you want it?"

Lila gazed at the water pitcher in the middle of the table, with its comical rooster's head: Gennaro liked it. She whispered:

"The crucial thing is for you to hold me close."

Enzo shook his head unhappily.

"You don't want me."

"I want you, but I don't feel anything."

"You don't feel anything *for me?*"

"What do you mean, I love you, and every night I wish you would call me and hold me close. *But beyond that I don't want anything.*"

Enzo turned pale, his handsome face was contorted as if by an intolerable grief, and he observed:

"I disgust you."

"No, no, no, let's do what you want, right away, I'm ready."

He had a desolate smile, and was silent for a while. Then he couldn't bear her anxiety, he muttered: "Let's go to bed."

"Each in our own room?"

"No, in my bed."

Lila, relieved, went to get undressed. She put on her nightgown, went to him trembling with cold. He was already in bed.

"I'll go here?"

"All right."

She slid under the covers, rested her head on his shoulder, put an arm around his chest. Enzo remained motionless; she felt immediately that he gave off a violent heat.

"My feet are cold," she whispered, "can I put them near yours?"

"Yes."

"Can I caress you a little?"

"Leave me alone."

Slowly the cold disappeared. The pain in her chest dissolved, she forgot the grip on her throat, she gave in to the respite of his warmth.

"Can I sleep?" she asked, dazed by weariness.

"Sleep."

43.

At dawn she started: her body reminded her that she had to wake up. Immediately, the terrible thoughts arrived, all very clear: her sick heart, Gennaro's regressions, the fascists from the neighborhood, Nadia's self-importance, Pasquale's untrustworthiness, the list of demands. Only afterward did she realize that she had slept with Enzo, but that he was no longer in the bed. She rose quickly, in time to hear the door closing. Had he arisen as soon as she fell asleep? Had he been awake all night? Had he slept in the other room with the child? Or had he fallen asleep with her, forgetting every desire? Certainly he had had breakfast alone and had left the table set for her and Gennaro. He had gone to work, without a word, keeping his thoughts to himself.

Lila, too, after taking her son to the neighbor, hurried to the factory.

"So did you make up your mind?" Edo asked, a little sulkily.

"I'll make up my mind when I like," Lila answered, returning to her old tone of voice.

"We're a committee, you have to inform us."

"Did you circulate the list?"

"Yes."

"What do the others say?"

"Silence means consent."

"No," she said, "silence means they're shitting in their pants."

Capone was right, also Nadia and Armando. It was a weak initiative, a forced effort. Lila worked at cutting the meat furiously, she had a desire to hurt and be hurt. To jab her hand with the knife, let it slip, now, from the dead flesh to her own living flesh. To shout, hurl herself at the others, make them all pay for her inability to find an equilibrium. Ah, Lina Cerullo, you are beyond correction. Why did you make that list? You don't want to be exploited? You want to improve your condition and the condition of these people? You're convinced that you, and they, starting from here, from what you are now, will join the victorious march of the proletariat of the whole world? No way. March to become what? Now and forever workers? Workers who slave from morning to night but are empowered? Nonsense. Hot air to sweeten the pill of toil. You know that it's a terrible condition, it shouldn't be improved but eliminated, you've known it since you were a child. Improve, improve yourself? You, for example, are you improved, have you become like Nadia or Isabella? Is your brother improved, has he become like Armando? And your son, is he like Marco? No, we remain us and they are they. So why don't you resign yourself? Blame the mind that can't settle down, that is constantly seeking a way to function. Designing shoes. Getting busy setting up a shoe factory. Rewriting Nino's articles, tormenting him until he did as you said. Using for your own purposes the installments from Zurich, with Enzo. And now demonstrating to Nadia that if she is making the revolution, you are even more. The mind, ah yes, the evil is there, it's the mind's discontent that causes the body to get sick. I've had it with myself, with everything. I've even had it with Gennaro: his fate, if all goes well, is to end up in a place like this, crawling to some boss for another five lire. So? So, Cerullo, take up your responsibilities and do what you have always had in mind: frighten Soccavo, eliminate his habit of fucking the workers in the drying room. Show the student with the wolf face what you've prepared. That summer on Ischia. The drinks, the house in Forio, the luxurious bed where I was with Nino. The money came from this place, from this evil smell, from these days spent in disgust, from this poorly paid labor. What did I cut, here? A revolting yellowish pulp spurted out. The world turns but, luckily, if it falls it breaks.

Right before the lunch break she made up her mind, she said to Edo: I'm going. But she didn't have time to take off her apron, the owner's secretary appeared in the gutting room to tell her:

"Dottor Soccavo wants you urgently in the office."

Lila thought that some spy had told Bruno what was coming. She stopped work, took the sheet of demands from the closet and went up. She knocked on the door of the office, and went in. Bruno was not alone in the room. Sitting in a chair, cigarette in his mouth, was Michele Solara.

44.

She had always known that Michele would sooner or later reappear in her life, but finding him in Bruno's office frightened her like the spirits in the dark corners of the house of her childhood. What is he doing here, I have to get out of here. But Solara, seeing her, stood up, spread his arms wide, seemed genuinely moved. He said in Italian: Lina, what a pleasure, how happy I am. He wanted to embrace her, and would have if she hadn't stopped him with an unconscious gesture of revulsion. Michele stood for some instants with his arms outstretched, therefore, in confusion, with one hand he caressed his cheekbone, his neck, with the other he pointed to Lila, this time speaking in an artificial tone:

"But really, I can't believe it: right in the middle of the salamis, you were hiding Signora Carracci?"

Lila turned to Bruno abruptly: "I'll come back later."

"Sit down," he said, darkly.

"I prefer to stand."

"Sit, you'll get tired."

She shook her head, remained standing, and Michele gave Bruno a smile of understanding:

"She's made like that, resign yourself, she never obeys."

To Lila it seemed that Solara's voice had more power than in the past, he stressed the end of every word as if he had been practicing his pronunciation. Maybe to save her strength, maybe just to contradict him, she changed her mind and sat down. Michele also changed position, but so that he was turned completely toward her, as if Bruno were no longer in the room. He observed her carefully, affectionately, and said, in a tone of regret: your hands are ruined, too bad, as a girl you had such nice ones. Then he began to talk about the shop in Piazza dei Martiri in the manner of one imparting information, as if Lila were still his employee and they were having a work meeting. He mentioned new shelves, new light fixtures, and how he had had the bathroom door that opened onto the courtyard walled up again. Lila remembered that door and said softly, in dialect:

"I don't give a fuck about your shop."

"You mean *our:* we invented it together."

"Together with you I never invented anything."

Michele smiled again, shaking his head in a sign of mild dissent. Those who put in the money, he said, do and undo just the way those who work with their hands and their head do. Money invents scenarios, situations, people's lives. You don't know how many people I can make happy or ruin just by signing a check. And then he began chatting again, placidly; he seemed eager to tell her the latest news, as if they were two friends catching up. He began with Alfonso, who had done his job in Piazza dei Martiri well and now earned enough to start a family. But he had no wish to marry, he preferred to keep poor Marisa in the condition of fiancée for life and continued to do as he liked. So he, as his employer, had encouraged him, a regular life is good for one's employees, and had offered to pay for the wedding celebration; thus, finally, in June the marriage would take place. You see, he said, if you had continued to work for me, rather than Alfonso, I would have given you everything you asked for, you would have been a queen. Then, without giving her time to answer, he tapped the ashes of his cigarette into an old bronze ashtray and announced that he, too, was getting married, also in June, and to Gigliola, naturally, the great love of his life. Too bad I can't invite you, he complained, I would have liked to, but I don't want to embarrass your husband. And he began to talk about Stefano, Ada, and their child, first saying nice things about all three, then pointing out that the two grocery stores weren't doing as well as they used to. As long as his father's money lasted, he explained, Carracci kept afloat, but commerce is a rough sea now, Stefano's been shipping water for quite some time, he can't manage things anymore. Competition, he said, had increased, new stores were constantly opening. Marcello himself, for example, had got it into his head to expand the late Don Carlo's old store and transform it into one of those places where you can get anything, from soap to light bulbs, mortadella, and candy. And he had done it, the business was booming, it was called Everything for Everyone.

"You're saying that you and your brother have managed to ruin Stefano, too?"

"What do you mean ruin, Lina, we do our job and that's all, in fact, when we can help our friends we help them happily. Guess who Marcello has working in the new store?"

"I don't know."

"Your brother."

"You've reduced Rino to being your clerk?"

"Well, you abandoned him, and that fellow is carrying all of them on his shoulders: your father, your mother, a child,

Pinuccia, who's pregnant again. What could he do? He turned
to Marcello for help and Marcello helped him. Doesn't that
please you?"

Lila responded coldly:

"No, it doesn't please me, nothing you do pleases me."

Michele appeared dissatisfied, and he remembered Bruno:

"You see, as I was telling you, her problem is that she has a
bad character."

Bruno gave an embarrassed smile that was meant to be conspiratorial.

"It's true."

"Did she hurt you, too?"

"A little."

"You know that she was still a child when she held a shoemaker's knife to my brother's throat, and he was twice her size?
And not as a joke, it was clear that she was ready to use it."

"Seriously?"

"Yes. That girl has courage, she's determined."

Lila clenched her fists tightly. She detested the weakness
she felt in her body. The room was undulating, the bodies of
the dead objects and the living people were expanding. She
looked at Michele, who was extinguishing the cigarette in the
ashtray. He was putting too much energy into it, as if he, too,
in spite of his placid tone, were giving vent to an uneasiness.
Lila stared at his fingers, which went on squashing the butt, the
nails were white. Once, she thought, he asked me to become
his lover. But that's not what he really wants, there's something
else, something that doesn't have to do with sex and that not
even he can explain. He's obsessed, it's like a superstition.
Maybe he thinks that I have a power and that that power is
indispensable to him. He wants it but he can't get it, and it
makes him suffer, it's a thing he can't take from me by force.
Yes, maybe that's it. Otherwise he would have crushed me by
now. But why me? What has he recognized in me that's useful

to him? I mustn't stay here, under his eyes, I mustn't listen to him, what he sees and what he wants scares me. Lila said to Soccavo:

"I've got something to leave for you and then I'll go."

She got up, ready to give him the list of demands, a gesture that seemed to her increasingly pointless and yet necessary. She wished to place the piece of paper on the table, next to the ashtray, and leave that room. But Michele's voice stopped her. Now it was definitely affectionate, almost caressing, as if he had intuited that she was trying to get away from him and wanted to do everything possible to charm her and keep her. He continued speaking to Soccavo:

"You see, she really has a bad character. I'm speaking, but she doesn't give a damn, she pulls out a piece of paper, says she wants to leave. But you forgive her, because she has many good qualities that make up for her bad character. You think you hired a worker? It's not true. This woman is much, much more. If you let her, she'll change shit into gold for you, she's capable of reorganizing this whole enterprise, taking it to levels you can't even imagine. Why? Because she has the type of mind that normally no woman has but also that not even we men have. I've had an eye on her since she was a child and it's true. She designed shoes that I still sell today in Naples and outside, and I make a lot of money. And she renovated a shop in Piazza dei Martiri with such imagination that it became a salon for the rich people from Via Chiaia, from Posillipo, from the Vomero. And there are many—very many—other things she could do. But she has a crazy streak, she thinks she can always do what she wants. Come, go, fix, break. You think I fired her? No, one day, as if it were nothing, she didn't come to work. Just like that, vanished. And if you catch her again, she'll slip away again, she's an eel. This is her problem: even though she's extremely intelligent, she can't understand what she can do and what she can't. That's because she hasn't yet found a real man. A real man puts the woman in her place. She's not capable of cooking? She learns. The house is dirty? She cleans it. A real man can make a woman do everything. For example: I met a woman a while ago who didn't know how to whistle. Well, we were together for two hours only—hours of fire—and afterward I said to her: Now whistle. She—you won't believe it—whistled. If you know how to train a woman, good. If you don't know how to train her, forget about her, you'll get hurt." He uttered these last words in a very serious tone, as if they summed up an irrefutable commandment. But even as he was speaking, he must have realized that he hadn't been able, and was still unable, to respect his own law. So suddenly his expression changed, his voice changed, he felt an urgent need to humiliate her. He turned toward Lila with a jolt of impatience and said emphatically, in a crescendo of obscenities in dialect: "But with her it's difficult, it's not so easy to kiss her off. And yet you see what she looks like, she has small eyes, small tits, a small ass, she's just a broomstick. With someone like that what can you do, you can't even get it up. But an instant is enough, a single instant: you look at her and you want to fuck her."

It was at that point that Lila felt a violent bump inside her head, as if her heart, instead of hammering in her throat, had exploded in her skull. She yelled an insult at him no less obscene than the words he had uttered, she grabbed from the desk the bronze ashtray, spilling out butts and ashes, and tried to hit him. But the gesture, in spite of her fury, was slow, powerless. And even Bruno's voice—*Lina, please, what are you doing*—passed through her slowly. So maybe for that reason Solara stopped her easily and easily took away the ashtray, saying to her angrily:

"You think you work for Dottor Soccavo? You think I'm no one here? You are mistaken. Dottor Soccavo has been in my mother's red book for quite some time, and that book is a lot more important than Mao's little book. So you don't work for him, you work for me, you work for me and only me. And so far I've let you, I wanted to see what the fuck you were driving at, you and that shit you sleep with. But from now on remember that I have my eyes on you and if I need you, you better come running, got that?"

Only then Bruno jumped to his feet nervously and exclaimed: "Leave her, Michè, you're going too far."

Solara let go of Lila's wrist, then he muttered, addressing Soccavo, again in Italian:

"You're right, sorry. But Signora Carracci has this ability: one way or another she always compels you to go too far."

Lina repressed her fury, she rubbed her wrist carefully, with the tip of her finger she wiped off some ash that had fallen on it. Then she unfolded the piece of paper with the demands, she placed it in front of Bruno, and as she was going to the door she turned to Solara, saying:

"I've known how to whistle since I was five years old."

45.

When she came back down, her face very pale, Edo asked her how it went, but Lila didn't answer, she pushed him away with one hand and shut herself in the bathroom. She was afraid that Bruno would call her back, she was afraid of being forced to have a confrontation in Michele's presence, she was afraid of the unaccustomed fragility of her body—she couldn't get used to it. From the little window she spied on the courtyard and drew a sigh of relief when she saw Michele, tall, in a black leather jacket and dark pants, going bald at the temples, his handsome face carefully shaved, walk nervously to his car, and leave. Then she returned to the gutting room and Edo asked her again:

"So?"

"I did it. But from now on the rest of you have to take care of it."

"In what sense?"

She couldn't answer: Bruno's secretary had appeared, breathless, the owner wanted her right away. She went like that saint who, although she still has her head on her shoulders, is carrying it in her hands, as if it had already been cut off. Bruno, as soon as he saw her, almost screamed:

"You people want to have coffee in bed in the morning? What is this latest thing, Lina? Do you have any idea? Sit down and explain. I can't believe it."

Lila explained to him, demand by demand, in the tone she used with Gennaro when he refused to understand. She said emphatically that he had better take that piece of paper seriously and deal with the various points in a constructive spirit, because if he behaved unreasonably, the office of the labor inspector would soon come down on him. Finally she asked him what sort of trouble he'd got into, to end up in the hands of dangerous people like the Solaras. At that point Bruno lost control completely. His red complexion turned purple, his eyes grew bloodshot, he yelled that he would ruin her, that a few extra lire for the four dickheads she had set against him would be enough to settle everything. He shouted that for years his father had been bribing the inspector's office and she was dreaming if she thought he was afraid of an inspection. He cried that the Solaras would eliminate her desire to be a union member, and finally, in a choked voice, he said: Out, get out immediately, out.

Lila went to the door. On the threshold she said:

"This is the last time you'll see me. I'm done working here, starting now."

At those words Soccavo abruptly returned to himself. He had an expression of alarm, he must have promised Michele that he wouldn't fire her. He said: "Now you're insulted? Now you're being difficult? What do you say, come here, let's discuss it, I'll decide if I should fire you or not. Bitch, I said come here."

For a fraction of a second Ischia came to mind, the morning we waited for Nino and his rich friend, the boy who had a house in Forio, who was always so polite and patient, to arrive. She went out and closed the door behind her. Immediately afterward she began to tremble violently, she was covered with sweat. She didn't go to the gutting room, she didn't say goodbye to Edo and Teresa, she passed by Filippo, who looked at her in bewilderment and called to her: Cerù, where are you going, come back inside. But she ran along the unpaved road, took the first bus for the Marina, reached the sea. She walked for a long time. There was a cold wind, and she went up to the Vomero in the funicular, walked through Piazza Vanvitelli, along Via Scarlatti, Via Cimarosa, took the funicular again to go down. It was late when she realized that she had forgotten about Gennaro. She got home at nine, and asked Enzo and Pasquale, who were anxiously questioning her to find out what had happened to her, to come and look for me in the neighborhood.

And now here we are, in the middle of the night, in this bare room in San Giovanni a Teduccio. Gennaro is sleeping, Lila talks on and on in a low voice, Enzo and Pasquale are waiting in the kitchen. I feel like the knight in an ancient romance as, wrapped in his shining armor, after performing a thousand astonishing feats throughout the world, he meets a ragged, starving herdsman, who, never leaving his pasture, subdues and controls horrible beasts with his bare hands, and with prodigious courage.

46.

I was a tranquil listener, and I let her talk. Some moments

of the story, especially when the expression of Lila's face and the pace of her sentences underwent a sudden, painful nervous contraction, disturbed me deeply. I felt a powerful sense of guilt, I thought: this is the life that could have been mine, and if it isn't it's partly thanks to her. Sometimes I almost hugged her, more often I wanted to ask questions, comment. But in general I held back, I interrupted two or three times at most.

For example, I certainly interrupted when she talked about Professor Galiani and her children. I would have liked her to explain better what the professor had said, what precise words she had used, if my name had ever come up with Nadia and Armando. But I realized in time the pettiness of the questions and restrained myself, even though a part of me considered the curiosity legitimate—they were acquaintances of mine, after all, who were important to me.

"Before I go to Florence for good, I should pay a visit to Professor Galiani. Maybe you'd come with me, do you want to?" and I added: "My relationship with her cooled a little, after Ischia, she blamed me for Nino's leaving Nadia." Since Lila looked at me as if she didn't see me, I said again: "The Galianis are good people, a little stuck up, but this business of the murmur should be checked."

This time she reacted.

"The murmur is there."

"All right," I said, "but even Armando said you'd need a cardiologist."

She replied:

"He heard it, anyway."

But I felt involved above all when it came to sexual matters. When she told me about the drying room, I almost said: an old intellectual jumped on me, in Turin, and in Milan a Venezuelan painter I'd known for only a few hours came to my room to get in bed as if it were a favor I owed him. Yet I held back, even with that. What sense was there in speaking of my affairs at that moment? And then really what could I have told her that had any resemblance to what she was telling me?

That last question presented itself clearly when, from a simple recitation of the facts—years before, when she told me about her wedding night, we had talked only of the most brutal facts—Lila proceeded to talk generally about her sexuality. It was a subject completely new for us. The coarse language of the environment we came from was useful for attack or self-defense, but, precisely because it was the language of violence, it hindered, rather than encouraged, intimate confidences. So I was embarrassed, I stared at the floor, when she said, in the crude vocabulary of the neighborhood, that fucking had never given her the pleasure she had expected as a girl, that in fact she had almost never felt anything, that after Stefano, after Nino, to do it really annoyed her, so that she had been unable to accept inside herself even a man as gentle as Enzo. Not only that: using an even more brutal vocabulary, she added that sometimes out of necessity, sometimes out of curiosity, sometimes out of passion, she had done everything that a man could want from a woman, and that even when she had wanted to conceive a child with Nino, and had become pregnant, the pleasure you were supposed to feel, particularly at that moment of great love, had been missing.

Before such frankness I understood that I could not be silent, that I had to let her feel how close I was, that I had to react to her confidences with equal confidences. But at the idea of having to speak about myself—the dialect disgusted me, and although I passed for an author of racy pages, the Italian I had acquired seemed to me too precious for the sticky material of sexual experiences—my uneasiness grew, I forgot how difficult her confession had been, that every word, however vulgar, was set in the weariness in her face, in the trembling of her hands, and I was brief.

"For me it's not like that," I said.

I wasn't lying, and yet it wasn't the truth. The truth was more complicated and to give it a form I would have needed practiced words. I would have had to explain that, in the time of Antonio, rubbing against him, letting him touch me had always been very pleasurable, and that I still desired that pleasure. I would have had to admit that being penetrated had disappointed me, too, that the experience was spoiled by the sense of guilt, by the discomfort of the conditions, by the fear of being caught, by the haste arising from that, by the terror of getting pregnant. But I would have had to add that Franco—the little I knew of sex was largely from him—before entering me and afterward let me rub against one of his legs, against his stomach, and that this was nice and sometimes made the penetration nice, too. As a result, I would have had to tell her, I was now waiting for marriage, Pietro was a very gentle man, I hoped that in the tranquility and the legitimacy of marriage I would have the time and the comfort to discover the pleasure of coitus. There, if I had expressed myself like that, I would have been honest. But the two of us, at nearly twenty-five, did not have a tradition of such articulate confidences. There had been only small general allusions when she was engaged to Stefano and I was with Antonio, bashful phrases, hints. As for Donato Sarratore, as for Franco, I had never talked about either one. So I kept to those few words—*For me it's not like that*—which must have sounded to her as if I were saying: *Maybe you're not normal.* And in fact she looked at me in bewilderment, and said as if to protect herself:

"In the book you wrote something else."

So she had read it. I murmured defensively:

"I don't even know anymore what ended up in there."

"Dirty stuff ended up in there," she said, "stuff that men don't want to hear and women know but are afraid to say. But now what—are you hiding?"

She used more or less those words, certainly she said *dirty*.

She, too, then, cited the risqué pages and did it like Gigliola, who had used the word *dirt*. I expected that she would offer an evaluation of the book as a whole, but she didn't, she used it only as a bridge to go back and repeat what she called several times, insistently, *the bother of fucking*. That is in your novel, she exclaimed, and if you told it you know it, it's pointless for you to say: For me it's not like that. And I mumbled Yes, maybe it's true, but I don't know. And while she with a tortured lack of shame went on with her confidences—the great excitement, the lack of satisfaction, the sense of disgust—I thought of Nino, and the questions I had so often turned over and over reappeared. Was that long night full of tales a good moment to tell her I had seen him? Should I warn her that for Gennaro she couldn't count on Nino, that he already had another child, that he left children behind him heedlessly? Should I take advantage of that moment, of those admissions of his, to let her know that in Milan he had said an unpleasant thing about her: *Lila is made badly even when it comes to sex*? Should I go so far as to tell her that in those agitated confidences of hers, even in that way of reading the *dirty* pages of my book, now, while she was speaking I seemed to find confirmation that Nino was, in essence, right? What in fact had Sarratore's son intended if not what she herself was admitting? Had he realized that for Lila being penetrated was only a duty, that she couldn't enjoy the union? He, I said to myself, is experienced. He has known many women, he knows what good female sexual behavior is and so he recognizes when it's bad. *To be made badly when it comes to sex* means, evidently, not to be able to feel pleasure in the male's thrusting; it means twisting with desire and rubbing yourself to quiet that desire, it means grabbing his hands and placing them against your sex as I sometimes did with Franco, ignoring his annoyance, the boredom of the one who has already had his orgasm and now would like to go to sleep. My uneasiness increased, I thought: I wrote *that* in my novel, is *that* what Gigliola and Lila recognized, was *that* what Nino recognized, perhaps, and the reason he wanted to talk about it? I let everything go and whispered somewhat randomly:

"I'm sorry."

"What?"

"That your pregnancy was without joy."

She responded with a flash of sarcasm:

"Imagine how I felt."

My last interruption came when it had begun to get light, and she had just finished telling me about the encounter with Michele. I said: That's enough, calm down, take your temperature. It was 101. I hugged her tight, I whispered: now I'll take care of you, and until you're better we'll stay together, and if I have to go to Florence you and the child will come with me. She refused energetically, she made the final confession of that night. She said she had been wrong to follow Enzo to San Giovanni a Teduccio, she wanted to go back to the neighborhood.

"To the neighborhood?"

"Yes."

"You're crazy."

"As soon as I feel better I'll do it."

I rebuked her, I told her it was a thought induced by the fever, that the neighborhood would exhaust her, that to set foot there was stupid.

"I can't wait to leave," I exclaimed.

"You're strong," she answered, to my astonishment. "I have never been. The better and truer you feel, the farther away you go. If I merely pass through the tunnel of the *stradone*, I'm scared. Remember when we tried to get to the sea but it started raining? Which of us wanted to keep going and which of us made an about-face, you or me?"

"I don't remember. But, anyway, don't go back to the neighborhood."

I tried in vain to make her change her mind. We discussed it for a long time.

"Go," she said finally, "talk to the two of them, they've been waiting for hours. They haven't closed their eyes and they have to go to work."

"What shall I tell them?"

"Whatever you want."

I pulled the covers up, I also covered Gennaro, who had been tossing in his sleep all night. I realized that Lila was already falling asleep. I whispered:

"I'll be back soon."

She said: "Remember what you promised."

"What?"

"You've already forgotten? If something happens to me, you've got to take Gennaro."

"Nothing will happen to you."

As I went out of the room Lila started in her half-sleep, she whispered: "Watch me until I fall asleep. Watch me always, even when you leave Naples. That way I'll know that you see me and I'm at peace."

47.

In the time that passed between that night and the day of my wedding—I was married on May 17, 1969, in Florence, and, after a honeymoon of just three days in Venice, enthusiastically began my life as a wife—I tried to do all I could for Lila. At first, in fact, I thought simply that I would help her until she got over the flu. I had things to do about the house in Florence, I had a lot of engagements because of the book—the telephone rang constantly, and my mother grumbled that she had given the number to half the neighborhood but no one called her, to have that thingamajig in the house, she said, is just a bother, since the calls were almost always for me—I wrote notes for hypothetical new novels, I tried to fill the gaps in my literary and political education. But my friend's general state of weakness soon led me to neglect my own affairs and occupy myself with her. My mother realized right away that we had resumed our friendship: she found it shameful, she flew into a rage, she was full of insults for both of us. She continued to believe that she could tell me what to do and what not to, she limped after me, criticizing me. Sometimes she seemed determined to insert herself into my body, simply to keep me from being my own master. What do you have in common with her anymore, she insisted, think of what you are and of what she is, isn't that disgusting book you wrote enough, you want to go on being friends with a whore? But I behaved as if I were deaf. I saw Lila every day and from the moment I left her sleeping in her room and went to face the two men who had waited all night in the kitchen I devoted myself to reorganizing her life.

I told Enzo and Pasquale that Lila was ill, she couldn't work at the Soccavo factory anymore, she had quit. With Enzo I didn't have to waste words, he had understood for a while that she couldn't go on at the factory, that she had gotten into a difficult situation, that something inside her was giving in. Pasquale, instead, driving back to the neighborhood on the early-morning streets, still free of traffic, objected. Let's not overdo it, he said, it's true that Lila has a hard life, but that's what happens to all the exploited of the world. Then, following a tendency he had had since he was a boy, he went on to speak about the peasants of the south, the workers of the north, the populations of Latin America, of northeastern Brazil, of Africa, about the Negroes, the Vietnamese, American imperialism. I soon stopped him, saying: Pasquale, if Lina goes on as she has she'll die. He wouldn't concede, he continued to object, and not because he didn't care about Lila but because the struggle at Soccavo seemed to him important, he considered our friend's role crucial, and deep down he was convinced that all those stories about a little flu came not so much from her as from me, a bourgeois intellectual more worried about a slight fever than about the nasty political consequences of a workers' defeat. Since he couldn't make up his mind to say these things to me explicitly but spoke in sentence fragments, I summed it up for him with soothing clarity, to show him I had understood. That made him even more anxious and as he left me at the gate he said: I have to go to work now, Lenù, but we'll talk about it again. As soon as I returned to the house in San Giovanni a Teduccio I took Enzo aside and said: Keep Pasquale away from Lina if you love her, she mustn't hear any talk of the factory.

In that period I always carried in my purse a book and a notebook: I read on the bus or when Lila was sleeping. Sometimes I discovered her with her eyes open, staring at me, maybe she was peeking to see what I was reading, but she never asked me the title of the book, and when I tried to read her some passages—from scenes at the Upton Inn, I remember—she closed her eyes as if I were boring her. The fever passed in a few days, but the cough didn't, so I forced her to stay in bed. I cleaned the house, I cooked, I took care of Gennaro. Maybe because he was already big, somewhat aggressive, willful, he didn't have the defenseless charm of Mirko, Nino's other child. But sometimes in the midst of violent games he would turn unexpectedly sad, and fall asleep on the floor; that softened me, and I grew fond of him, and when that became clear to him he attached himself to me, keeping me from doing chores or reading.

Meanwhile I tried to get a better understanding of Lila's situation. Did she have money? No. I lent her some and she accepted it after swearing endlessly that she would pay me back. How much did Bruno owe her? Two months' salary. And severance pay? She didn't know. What was Enzo's job, how much did he earn? No idea. And that correspondence course in Zurich—what concrete possibilities did it offer? Who knows. She coughed constantly, she had pains in her chest, sweats, a vise in her throat, her heart would suddenly go crazy. I wrote down punctiliously all the symptoms and tried to convince her that another medical examination was necessary, more thorough than the one Armando had done. She didn't say yes but she didn't oppose it. One evening before Enzo returned, Pasquale looked in, he said very politely that he, his comrades on the committee, and some workers at the Soccavo factory wanted to know how she was. I replied that she wasn't well, she needed rest, but he asked to see her just the same, to say hello. I left him in the kitchen, I went to Lila, I advised her not to see him. She made a face that meant: I'll do as you want. I was moved by the fact that she gave in to me—she who had always commanded, done and undone—without arguing.

48.

At home that same night I made a long call to Pietro, telling him in detail all Lila's troubles and how important it was to me to help her. He listened patiently. At a certain point he even exhibited a spirit of collaboration: he remembered a young Pisan Greek scholar who was obsessed with computers and imagined that they would revolutionize philology. I was touched by the fact that, although he was a person who was always buried in his work, on this occasion, for love of me, he made an effort to be useful.

"Find him," I begged him, "tell him about Enzo, you never know, maybe some job prospects might turn up."

He promised he would and added that, if he remembered correctly, Mariarosa had had a brief romance with a young

Neapolitan lawyer: maybe he could find him and ask if he could help.

"To do what?"

"To get your friend's money back."

I was excited.

"Call Mariarosa."

"All right."

I insisted: "Don't just promise, call her, please."

He was silent for a moment, then he said: "Just then you sounded like my mother."

"In what sense?"

"You sounded like her when something is very important to her."

"I'm very different, unfortunately."

He was silent again.

"You're different, fortunately. But in these types of things there's no one like her. Tell her about that girl and you'll see, she'll help you."

I telephoned Adele. I did it with some embarrassment, which I overcame by reminding myself of all the times I had seen her at work, for my book, in the search for the apartment in Florence. She was a woman who liked to be busy. If she needed something, she picked up the telephone and, link by link, put together the chain that led to her goal. She knew how to ask in such a way that saying no was impossible. And she crossed ideological borders confidently, she respected no hier-archies, she tracked down cleaning women, bureaucrats, industrialists, intellectuals, ministers, and she addressed all with cordial detachment, as if the favor she was about to ask she was in fact already doing for them. Amid a thousand awkward apologies for disturbing her, I told Adele in detail about my friend, and she became curious, interested, angry. At the end she said:

"Let me think."

"Of course."

"Meanwhile, can I give you some advice?"

"Of course."

"Don't be timid. You're a writer, use your role, test it, make something of it. These are decisive times, everything is turning upside down. Participate, be present. And begin with the scum in your area, put their backs to the wall."

"How?"

"By writing. Frighten Soccavo to death, and others like him. Promise you'll do it?"

"I'll try."

She gave me the name of an editor at *l'Unità*.

49.

The telephone call to Pietro and, especially, the one to my mother-in-law released a feeling that until that moment I had kept at bay, that in fact I had repressed, but that was alive and ready to advance. It had to do with my changed status. It was likely that the Airotas, especially Guido but perhaps Adele herself, considered me a girl who, although very eager, was far from the person they would have chosen for their son. It was just as likely that my origin, my dialectal cadence, my lack of sophistication in everything, had put the breadth of their views to a hard test. With just a slight exaggeration I could hypothesize that even the publication of my book was part of an emergency plan intended to make me presentable in their world. But the fact remained, incontrovertible, that they had accepted me, that I was about to marry Pietro, with their consent, that I was about to enter a protective family, a sort of well-fortified castle from which I could proceed without fear or to which I could retreat if I were in danger. So it was urgent that I get used to that new membership, and above all I had to be conscious of it. I was no longer a small match-seller almost down to the last match; I had won for myself a large supply of matches. And so—I suddenly understood—I could do for Lila much more than I had calculated on doing.

It was with this perspective that I had my friend give me the documentation she had collected against Soccavo. She handed it over passively, without even asking what I wanted to do with it. I read with increasing absorption. How many terrible things she had been able to say precisely and effectively. How many intolerable experiences could be perceived behind the description of the factory. I turned the pages in my hands for a long time, then suddenly, almost without coming to a decision, I looked in the telephone book, I called Soccavo. I subdued my voice to the right tone, I asked for Bruno. He was cordial— *What a pleasure to talk to you*—I cold. He said: You've done so many great things, Elena, I saw a picture of you in *Roma*, bravo, what a wonderful time we had on Ischia. I answered that it was a pleasure to talk to him, too, but that Ischia was far away, and for better and worse we had all changed, that in his case, for example, I had heard some nasty rumors that I hoped were not true. He understood immediately and protested. He spoke harshly of Lila, of her ungratefulness, of the trouble she had caused him. I changed my tone, I said that I believed Lila more than him. Take a pencil and paper, I said, write down my number, got it? Now give instructions for her to be paid down to the last lira you owe her, and let me know when I can come and get the money: I wouldn't like to see your picture in the papers, too.

I hung up before he could object, feeling proud of myself. I hadn't shown the least emotion, I had been curt, a few remarks in Italian, polite first, then aloof. I hoped that Pietro was right: was I really acquiring Adele's tone, was I learning, without realizing it, her way of being in the world? I decided to find out whether I was capable, if I wanted, of carrying out the threat I had ended the phone call with. Agitated—as I had not been when I called Bruno, still the boring boy who had tried to kiss me on the beach of Citara—I dialed the number of the editorial offices of *l'Unità*. While the telephone rang, I hoped that the voice of my mother yelling at Elisa in dialect in the background wouldn't be heard. My name is Elena Greco, I said to the switchboard operator, and I didn't have time to explain what I wanted before the woman exclaimed: Elena Greco the writer? She had read my book, and was full of compliments. I thanked her, I felt happy, strong, I explained, unnecessarily, that I had in mind an article about a factory on the outskirts, and I gave the name of the editor Adele had suggested. The operator congratulated me again, then she resumed a professional tone. Hold on, she said. A moment later a very hoarse male voice asked me in a teasing tone since when practitioners of literature had been willing to dirty their pens on the subject of piece work, shifts, and overtime, very boring subjects that young, successful novelists in particular stayed away from.

"What's the angle?" he asked. "Construction, longshoremen, miners?"

"It's a sausage factory," I said. "Not a big deal."

The man continued to make fun of me: "You don't have to apologize, it's fine. If Elena Greco, to whom this newspaper devoted no less than half a page of profuse praise, decides to write about sausages, can we poor editors possibly say: that it doesn't interest us? Are thirty lines enough? Too few? Let's be generous, make it sixty. When you've finished, will you bring it to me in person or dictate it?"

I began working on the article right away. I had to squeeze out of Lila's pages my sixty lines, and for love of her I wanted to do a good job. But I had no experience of newspaper writing, apart from when, at the age of fifteen, I had tried to write about the conflict with the religion teacher for Nino's journal: with terrible results. I don't know, maybe it was that memory that complicated things. Or maybe it was the editor's sarcastic tone that rang in my ears, especially when, at the end of the call, he asked me to give his best to my mother-in-law. Certainly I took a lot of time, I wrote and rewrote stubbornly. But even when the article seemed to be finished I wasn't satisfied and I didn't take it to the newspaper. I have to talk to Lila first, I said to myself, it's a thing that should be decided together; I'll turn it in tomorrow.

The next day I went to see Lila; she seemed particularly unwell. She complained that when I wasn't there certain presences took advantage of my absence and emerged from objects to bother her and Gennaro. Then she realized that I was alarmed and, in a tone of amusement, said it was all nonsense, she just wanted me to be with her more. We talked a lot, I soothed her, but I didn't give her the article to read. What held me back was the idea that if *l'Unità* rejected the piece I would be forced to tell her that they hadn't found it good, and I would feel humiliated. It took a phone call from Adele that night to give me a solid dose of optimism and make up my mind. She had consulted her husband and also Mariarosa. She had moved half the world in a few hours: luminaries of medicine, socialist professors who knew about the union, a Christian Democrat whom she called a bit foolish but a good person and an expert in workers' rights. The result was that I had an appointment the next day with the best cardiologist in Naples—a friend of friends, I wouldn't have to pay—and that the labor inspector would immediately pay a visit to the Soccavo factory, and that to get Lila's money I could go to that friend of Mariarosa's whom Pietro had mentioned, a young socialist lawyer who had an office in Piazza Nicola Amore and had already been informed.

"Happy?"

"Yes."

"Did you write your article?"

"Yes."

"You see? I was sure you wouldn't do it."

"In fact it's ready, I'll take it to *l'Unità* tomorrow."

"Good. I run the risk of underestimating you."

"It's a risk?"

"Underestimating always is. How's it going with that poor little creature my son?"

50.

From then on everything became fluid, almost as if I possessed the art of making events flow like water from a spring. Even Pietro had worked for Lila. His colleague the Greek scholar turned out to be extremely talkative but useful just the same: he knew someone in Bologna who really was a computer expert—the reliable source of his philological fantasies—and he had given him the number of an acquaintance in Naples, judged to be equally reliable. He gave me the name, address, and telephone number of the Neapolitan, and I thanked him warmly, commenting with affectionate irony on his forced entrepreneurship—I even sent him a kiss over the phone.

I went to see Lila immediately. She had a cavernous cough, her face was strained and pale, her gaze excessively watchful. But I was bringing good news and was happy. I shook her, hugged her, held both her hands tight, and meanwhile told her about the phone call I had made to Bruno, read her the article I had written, enumerated the results of the painstaking efforts of Pietro, of my mother-in-law, of my sister-in-law. She listened as if I were speaking from far away—from another world into which I had ventured—and could hear clearly only half the things I was saying. Besides, Gennaro was constantly tugging on her to play with him, and, as I spoke, she was attending to him, but without warmth. I felt content just the same. In the past Lila had opened the miraculous drawer of the grocery store and had bought me everything, especially books. Now I opened my drawers and paid her back, hoping that she would feel safe, as I now did.

"So," I asked her finally, "tomorrow morning you'll go to the cardiologist?"

She reacted to my question in an incongruous way, saying with a small laugh: "Nadia won't like this way of doing things. And her brother won't, either."

"What way, I don't understand."

"Nothing."

"Lila," I said, "please, what does Nadia have to do with it, don't give her more importance than she already gives herself. And forget Armando, he's always been superficial."

I surprised myself with those judgments, after all I knew very little about Professor Galiani's children. And for a few seconds I had the impression that Lila didn't recognize me but saw before her a spirit who was exploiting her weakness. In fact, rather than criticizing Nadia and Armando, I only wanted her to understand that the hierarchies of power were different, that compared to the Airotas the Galianis didn't count, that people like Bruno Soccavo or that thug Michele counted even less, that in other words she should do as I said and not worry. But as I was speaking I realized I was in danger of boasting and I caressed her cheek, saying that, of course, I admired Armando and Nadia's political engagement, and then I added, laughing: but trust me. She muttered:

"O.K., we'll go to the cardiologist."

I persisted:

"And for Enzo what appointment should I make, what time, what day?"

"Whenever you want, but after five."

As soon as I got home I went back to the telephone. I called the lawyer, I explained Lila's situation in detail. I called the cardiologist, I confirmed the appointment. I telephoned the computer expert, he worked at the Department of Public Works: he said that the Zurich courses were useless, but that I could send Enzo to see him on such and such a day at such an address. I called *l'Unità*, the editor said: You're certainly taking your sweet time—are you bringing me this article, or are we waiting for Christmas? I called Soccavo's secretary and asked her to tell her boss that, since I hadn't heard from him, my article would be out soon in *l'Unità*.

That last phone call provoked an immediate, violent reaction. Soccavo called me two minutes later and this time he wasn't friendly; he threatened me. I answered that, momentarily, he would have the inspector on his back and a lawyer who would take care of Lila's interests. Then, that evening, pleasantly overexcited—I was proud of fighting against injustice, out of affection and conviction, in spite of Pasquale and Franco, who thought they could still give me lessons—I hurried to *l'Unità* to deliver my article.

The man I had talked to was middle-aged, short, and fat, with small, lively eyes that permanently sparkled with a benevolent irony. He invited me to sit down on a dilapidated chair and he read the article carefully.

"And this is sixty lines? To me it seems like a hundred and fifty."

I reddened, I said softly: "I counted several times, it's sixty."

"Yes, but written by hand and in a script that couldn't be read with a magnifying glass. But the piece is very good, Comrade. Find a typewriter somewhere and cut what you can."

"Now?"

"And when? For once I've got something people will actually look at if I put it on the page, and you want to make me wait for doomsday?"

51.

What energy I had in those days. We went to the cardiologist, a big-name professor who had a house and office in Via Crispi. I took great care with my appearance for the occasion. Although the doctor was from Naples, he was connected with Adele's world and I didn't want to make a bad impression. I brushed my hair, wore a dress that she had given me, used a subtle perfume that resembled hers, put on light makeup. I wanted the professor, if he spoke to my mother-in-law on the telephone, or if by chance they met, to speak well of me. Lila instead looked as she did every day at home, careless of her appearance. We sat in a grand waiting room, with nineteenth-century paintings on the walls: a noblewoman in an armchair with a Negro servant in the background, a portrait of an old lady, and a large, lively hunting scene. There were two other people waiting, a man and a woman, both old, both with the tidy, elegant look of prosperity. We waited in silence. Lila, who on the way had repeatedly praised my appearance, said only, in a low voice: You look like you came out of one of these paintings—you're the lady and I'm the maid.

We didn't wait long. A nurse called us; for no obvious reason, we went ahead of the patients who were waiting. Now Lila became agitated, she wanted me to be present at the examination, she swore that alone she would never go in, and she pushed me forward as if I were the one being examined. The doctor was a bony man in his sixties, with thick gray hair. He greeted me politely, he knew everything about me, and chatted for ten minutes as if Lila weren't there. He said that his son had also graduated from the Normale, but six years before me. He noted that his brother was a writer and had a certain reputation, but only in Naples. He was full of praise for the Airotas, he knew a cousin of Adele's very well, a famous physicist. He asked me:

"When is the wedding?"

"May 17th."

"The seventeenth? That's bad luck, please change the date."

"It's not possible."

Lila was silent the whole time. She paid no attention to the professor, I felt her curiosity on me, she seemed amazed by my every gesture and word. When, finally, the doctor turned to her, questioning her at length, she answered unwillingly, in dialect or in an ugly Italian that imitated dialect patterns. Often I had to interrupt to remind her of symptoms that she had reported to me or to stress those which she minimized. Finally she submitted to a thorough examination and exhaustive tests, with a sullen expression, as if the cardiologist and I were doing her a wrong. I looked at her thin body in a threadbare pale blue slip that was too big for her. Her long neck seemed to be struggling to hold up her head, the skin was stretched over her bones like tissue paper that might tear at any moment. I realized that the thumb of her left hand every so often had a small, reflexive twitch. It was a good half hour before the professor told her to get dressed. She kept her eyes on him as she did so; now she seemed frightened. The cardiologist went to the desk, sat down, and finally announced that everything was in order, he hadn't found a murmur. Signora, he said, you have a perfect heart. But the effect of the verdict on Lila was apparently dubious, she didn't seem pleased, in fact she seemed irritated. It was I who felt relieved, as if it were my heart, and it was I who showed signs of worry when the professor, again addressing me and not Lila, as if her lack of reaction had offended him, added, with a frown, that, however, given the general state of my friend, urgent measures were necessary. The problem, he said, isn't the cough: the signora has a cold, has had a slight flu, and I'll give her some cough syrup. The problem, according to him, was that she was exhausted, run down. Lila had to take better care of herself, eat regularly, have a tonic treatment, get at least eight hours of sleep a night. The majority of your friend's symptoms, he said, will vanish when she regains her strength. In any case, he concluded, I would advise a neurological examination.

It was the penultimate word that roused Lila. She scowled, leaned forward, said in Italian: "Are you saying that I have a nervous illness?"

The doctor looked at her in surprise, as if the patient he had just finished examining had been magically replaced by another person.

"Not at all: I'm only advising an examination."

"Did I say or do something I shouldn't have?"

"No, madam, there's no need to worry. The examination serves only to get a clear picture of your situation."

"A relative of mine," said Lila, "a cousin of my mother's, was unhappy, she'd been unhappy her whole life. In the summer, when I was little, I would hear her through the open window, shouting, laughing. Or I would see her on the street doing slightly crazy things. But it was unhappiness, and so she never went to a neurologist, in fact she never went to any doctor."

"It would have been useful to go."

"Nervous illnesses are for ladies."

"Your mother's cousin isn't a lady?"

"No."

"And you?"

"Even less so."

"Do you feel unhappy?"

"I'm very well."

The doctor turned to me again, irritably: "Absolute rest. Have her do this treatment, regularly. If you have some way of taking her to the country, it would be better."

Lila burst out laughing, she returned to dialect: "The last

time I went to a doctor he sent me to the beach and it brought me a lot of grief."

The professor pretended not to hear, he smiled at me as if to elicit a conspiratorial smile, gave me the name of a friend who was a neurologist, and telephoned himself so that the man would see us as soon as possible. It wasn't easy to drag Lila to the new doctor's office. She said she didn't have time to waste, she was already bored enough by the cardiologist, she had to get back to Gennaro, and above all she didn't have money to throw away nor did she want me to throw away mine. I assured her that the examination would be free and in the end, reluctantly, she gave in.

The neurologist was a small lively man, completely bald, who had an office in an old building in Toledo and displayed in his waiting room an orderly collection of philosophy books. He liked to hear himself talk, and he talked so much that, it seemed to me, he paid more attention to the thread of his own discourse than to the patient. He examined her and addressed me, he asked her questions and propounded to me his observations, taking no notice of the responses she gave. In the end, he concluded abstractedly that Lila's nervous system was in order, just like her cardiac muscle. But—he said, continuing to address me—my colleague is right, dear Dottoressa Greco, the body is weakened, and as a result both the irascible and the concupiscible passions have taken advantage of it to get the upper hand over reason: let's restore well-being to the body and we'll restore health to the mind. Then he wrote out a prescription, in indecipherable marks, but pronouncing aloud the names of the medicines, the doses. Then he moved on to advice. He advised, for relaxation, long walks, but avoiding the sea: better, he said, the woods of Capodimonte or Camaldoli. He advised reading, but only during the day, never at night. He advised keeping the hands employed, even though a careful glance at Lila's would have been enough to realize that they had been too much employed. When he began to insist on the neurological benefits of crochet work, Lila became restless in her chair, and without waiting for the doctor to finish speaking, she asked him, following the course of her own secret thoughts:

"As long as we're here, could you give me the pills that prevent you from having children?"

The doctor frowned, and so, I think, did I. The request seemed out of place.

"Are you married?"

"I was, not now."

"In what sense not now?"

"I'm separated."

"You're still married."

"Well."

"Have you had children?"

"I have one."

"One isn't much."

"It's enough for me."

"In your condition pregnancy would help, there is no better medicine for a woman."

"I know women who were destroyed by pregnancy. Better to have the pills."

"For that problem of yours you'll have to consult a gynecologist."

"You only know about nerves, you don't know about pills?"

The doctor was irritated. He chatted a little more and then, in the doorway, gave me the address and telephone number of a doctor who worked in a clinic in Ponte di Tappia. Go to her, he said, as if it were I who had asked for the contraceptives, and he said goodbye. On the way out the secretary asked us to pay. The neurologist, I gathered, was outside the chain of favors that Adele had set in motion. I paid.

Once we were in the street Lila almost shouted, irately: I

will not take a single one of the medicines that shit gave me, since my head is falling off just the same, I already know it. I answered: I disagree, but do as you like. Then she was confused, she said quietly: I'm not angry with you, I'm angry with the doctors, and we walked in the direction of Ponte di Tappia, but without saying so, as if we were strolling aimlessly, just to stretch our legs. First she was silent, then she imitated in annoyance the neurologist's tone and his babble. It seemed to me that her impatience signaled a return of vitality. I asked her:

"Is it going a little better with Enzo?"

"It's the same as always."

"Then what do you want with the pills?"

"Do you know about them?"

"Yes."

"Do you take them?"

"No, but I will as soon as I'm married."

"You don't want children?"

"I do, but I have to write another book first."

"Does your husband know you don't want them right away?"

"I'll tell him."

"Shall we go see this woman and have her give both of us pills?"

"Lila, it's not candy you can take whenever you like. If you're not doing anything with Enzo forget it."

She looked at me with narrowed eyes, cracks in which her pupils were scarcely visible: "I'm not doing anything now but later who knows."

"Seriously?"

"I shouldn't, in your opinion?"

"Yes, of course."

At Ponte di Tappia we looked for a phone booth and called the doctor, who said she could see us right away. On the way to the clinic I made it clear to Lila that I was glad she was getting close to Enzo, and she seemed encouraged by my approval. We went back to being the girls of long ago, we began joking, partly serious, partly pretending, saying to each other: You do the talking, you're bolder, no you, you're dressed like a lady, I'm not in a hurry, I'm not, either, then why are we going.

The doctor was waiting for us at the entrance, in a white coat. She was a cordial woman, with a shrill voice. She invited us to the café and treated us like old friends. She emphasized repeatedly that she wasn't a gynecologist, but she was so full of explanations and advice that, while I kept to myself, somewhat bored, Lila asked increasingly explicit questions, made objections, asked new questions, offered ironic observations. They became very friendly. Finally, along with many recommendations, she gave each of us a prescription. The doctor refused to be paid because, she said, it was a mission she and her friends had. As she left—she had to go back to work—instead of shaking hands she embraced us. Lila, once we were in the street, said seriously: Finally a good person. She was cheerful then— I hadn't seen her like that for a long time.

52.

In spite of the editor's enthusiasm, *l'Unità* put off publishing my article. I was anxious, afraid that it wouldn't come out at all. But the day after the neurological exam I went out early to the newsstand and scanned the paper, jumping rapidly from page to page, until, at last, I found it. I expected that it would run, heavily cut, amid the local items, but instead it was in the national news, complete, with my byline, which pierced me like a long needle when I saw it in print. Pietro called me, happy about it, and Adele, too, was pleased; she said that her husband had liked the article very much and so had Mariarosa. But the surprising thing was that the head of my publishing house, along with two well-known intellectuals who had been connected to the firm for years, and Franco, Franco Mari, telephoned to congratulate me. Franco had asked Mariarosa for my number, and he spoke with respect, he said that he was pleased, that I had provided an example of a thorough investigation into the condition of workers, that he hoped to see me soon to talk about it. I expected at that point that through some unforeseen channel Nino would communicate his approval. But in vain—I was disappointed. There was no word from Pasquale, either, but then out of political disgust he had long ago stopped reading the party newspaper. The editor from *l'Unità,* however, consoled me, seeking me out to tell me how much the editorial office had liked the piece, and encouraging me, in his usual teasing way, to buy a typewriter and write more good articles.

I have to say that the most disorienting phone call was from Bruno Soccavo. He had his secretary call me, then he got on the phone. He spoke in a melancholy tone, as if the article, which he didn't even mention at first, had hit him so hard that it had sapped his energy. He said that in our time on Ischia, and our beautiful walks on the beach, he had loved me as he had never loved. He declared his utter admiration for the direction that, although I was very young, I had given to my life. He swore that his father had handed over to him a business in a lot of trouble, beset by evil practices, and that he was merely the blameless inheritor of a situation that in his eyes was deplorable. He stated that my article—finally he mentioned it—had been illuminating and that he wished to correct as soon as possible the many defects inherited from the past. He was sorry about the misunderstandings with Lila and told me that the administration was arranging everything with my lawyer. He concluded softly: you know the Solaras, in this difficult situation they're helping me give the Soccavo factory a new face. And he added: Michele sends you warm greetings. I exchanged the greetings, I took note of his good intentions, and I hung up. But right away I called Mariarosa's lawyer friend to tell him about that phone call. He confirmed that the money question had been resolved, and I met him a few days later in the office where he worked. He wasn't much older than me, well dressed, and likable, except for unpleasantly thin lips. He wanted to take me out for coffee. He was full of admiration for Guido Airota, he remembered Pietro well. He gave me the sum that Soccavo had paid for Lila, he urged me to be careful not to have my purse snatched. He described the chaos of students and union members and police he had found at the gates, he said that the labor inspector had also showed up at the factory. And yet he didn't seem satisfied. Only when we were saying goodbye, he asked me at the door:

"You know the Solaras?"

"They're from the neighborhood where I grew up."

"You know that they are behind Soccavo?"

"Yes."

"And you're not worried?"

"I don't understand."

"I mean: the fact that you've known them forever and that you studied outside Naples—maybe you can't see the situation clearly."

"It's very clear."

"In recent years the Solaras have expanded, in this city they're important."

"And so?"

He pressed his lips together, shook my hand.

"And so nothing: we've got the money, everything's in order. Say hello to Mariarosa and Pietro. When's the wedding? Do you like Florence?"

53.

I gave the money to Lila, who counted it twice with satisfaction and wanted to give me back immediately the amount I had lent her. Enzo arrived soon afterward, he had just been to see the person who knew about computers. He seemed pleased, naturally within the bounds of his impassiveness, which, maybe even against his own wishes, choked off emotions and words. Lila and I struggled to get the information out of him, but finally a fairly clear picture emerged. The expert had been extremely kind. At first he had repeated that the Zurich course was a waste of money, but then he had realized that Enzo, in spite of the uselessness of the course, was smart. He had told him that IBM was about to start producing a new computer in Italy, in the Vimercate factory, and that the Naples branch had an urgent need for operators, keypunch operators, programmer-analysts. He had assured him that, as soon as the company started training courses, he would let Enzo know. He had written down all his information.

"Did he seem serious?" Lila asked.

Enzo, to give proof of the man's seriousness, nodded at me, said: "He knew all about Lenuccia's fiancé."

"Meaning?"

"He told me he's the son of an important person."

Annoyance showed in Lila's face. She knew, obviously, that the appointment had been arranged by Pietro and that the name Airota counted in the positive outcome of the meeting, but she seemed put out by the fact that Enzo should notice it. I thought she was bothered by the idea that he, too, owed me something, as if that debt, which between her and me could have no consequence, not even the subordination of gratitude, might instead be harmful to Enzo. I said quickly that the prestige of my father-in-law didn't count that much, that the computer expert had explained even to me that he would help only if Enzo was good. And Lila, making a slightly excessive gesture of approval, said emphatically:

"He's really good."

"I've never seen a computer," Enzo said.

"So? That guy must have understood anyway that you know what you're doing."

He thought about it, and turned to Lila with an admiration that for an instant made me jealous: "He was impressed by the exercises you made me do."

"Really?"

"Yes. Especially diagramming things like ironing, and hammering a nail."

Then they began joking with one another, resorting to a jargon that I didn't understand and that excluded me. And suddenly they seemed to me a couple in love, very happy, with a secret so secret that it was unknown even to them. I saw again the courtyard when we were children. I saw her and Enzo competing to be first in arithmetic as the principal and Maestra Olivieri looked on. I saw Lila, who never cried, in despair because she had thrown a rock and injured him. I thought: their way of being together comes from something better in the neighborhood. Maybe Lila is right to want to go back.

54.

I began to pay attention to the "For rent" signs fixed to the building entrances, indicating apartments available. Meanwhile, an invitation to the wedding of Gigliola Spagnuolo and Michele Solara arrived, not for my family but for me. And a few hours later, by hand, came another invitation: Marisa Sarratore and Alfonso Carracci were getting married, and both the Solara family and the Carracci family addressed me with deference: *egregia dottoressa* Elena Greco. Almost immedi-

ately, I considered the two wedding invitations an opportunity
to find out if it was a good idea to encourage Lila's return to
the neighborhood. I planned to go and see Michele, Alfonso,
Gigliola, and Marisa, apparently to offer congratulations and
to explain that I would not be in Naples when the weddings
took place but in fact to discover if the Solaras and the
Carraccis still wanted to torture Lila. It seemed to me that
Alfonso was the only person capable of telling me in a dispassionate way how resentful Stefano still was. And with Michele,
even though I hated him—perhaps above all because I hated
him—I thought I could speak with composure about Lila's
health problems, letting him know that, even though he
thought he was a big shot and teased me as if I were still a little girl, I now had sufficient power to complicate his life, and
his affairs, if he continued to persecute my friend. I put both
cards in my purse, I didn't want my mother to see them and be
offended at the respect shown to me and not to my father and
her. I set aside a day to devote to these visits.

The weather wasn't promising, so I carried an umbrella,
but I was in a good mood, I wanted to walk, reflect, give a sort
of farewell to the neighborhood and the city. Out of the habit
of a diligent student, I started with the more difficult meeting,
the one with Solara. I went to the bar, but neither he nor
Gigliola nor even Marcello was there; someone said that they
might be at the new place on the *stradone*. I stopped in and
looked around with the attitude of someone with nothing better to do. Any memory of Don Carlo's shop had been utterly
erased—the dark, deep cave where as a child I had gone to
buy liquid soap and other household things. From the windows of the building's third floor an enormous vertical sign
hung down over the wide entrance: Everything for Everyone.
The store was brightly lit, even though it was day, and offered
merchandise of every type, the triumph of abundance. I saw
Lila's brother, Rino, who had grown very fat. He treated me

coldly, saying that he was the boss there, he didn't know anything about the Solaras. If you're looking for Michele, go to his house, he said bitterly, and turned his back as if he had something urgent to do.

I started walking again, and reached the new neighborhood, where I knew that the entire Solara family had, years earlier, bought an enormous apartment. The mother, Manuela, the loan shark, opened the door; I hadn't seen her since the time of Lila's wedding. I felt that she had been observing me through the spyhole. She looked for a long time, then she drew back the bolt and appeared in the frame of the door, her figure partly contained by the darkness of the apartment, partly eroded by the light coming from the large window on the stairs. She was as if dried up. The skin was stretched over her large bones, one of her pupils was very bright and the other as if dead. In her ears, around her neck, against the dark dress that hung loosely, gold sparkled, as if she were getting ready for a party. She treated me politely, inviting me to come in, have coffee. Michele wasn't there, did I know that he had another house, on Posillipo, where he was to go and live after his marriage. He was furnishing it with Gigliola.

"They're going to leave the neighborhood?" I asked.

"Yes, certainly."

"For Posillipo?"

"Six rooms, Lenù, three facing the sea. I would have preferred the Vomero, but Michele does as he likes. Anyway, there's a breeze, in the morning, and a light that you can't imagine."

I was surprised. I would never have believed that the Solaras would move away from the area of their trafficking, from the den where they hid their booty. But here was Michele, the shrewdest, the greediest of the family, going to live somewhere else, up, on the Posillipo, facing the sea and Vesuvio. The brothers' craving for greatness really had increased, the lawyer was right. But at the moment the fact cheered me, I was glad that Michele was leaving the neighborhood. I found that this favored Lila's possible return.

55.

I asked Signora Manuela for the address, said goodbye, and crossed the city, first by subway to Mergellina, then on foot, and by bus up Posillipo. I was curious. I now felt that I belonged to a legitimate power, universally admired, haloed by a high level of culture, and I wanted to see what garish guise was being given to the power I had had before my eyes since childhood—the vulgar pleasure of bullying, the unpunished practice of crime, the smiling tricks of obedience to the law, the display of profligacy—as embodied by the Solara brothers. But Michele escaped me again. On the top floor of a recent structure I found only Gigliola, who greeted me with obvious amazement and an equally obvious bitterness. I realized that as long as I had used her mother's telephone at all hours I had been cordial, but ever since I'd had the phone installed at home the entire Spagnuolo family had gone out of my life, and I'd scarcely noticed. And now without warning, at noon, on a dark day that threatened rain, I showed up here, in Posillipo, bursting into the house of a bride where everything was still topsy-turvy? I was ashamed, and greeted her with artificial warmth so that she would forgive me. For a while Gigliola remained sullen, and perhaps also alarmed, then her need to boast prevailed. She wanted me to envy her, she wanted to feel in a tangible way that I considered her the most fortunate of us all. And so, observing my reactions, enjoying my enthusiasm, she showed me the rooms, one by one, the expensive furniture, the gaudy lamps, two big bathrooms, the huge hot-water heater, the refrigerator, the washing machine, three telephones, unfortunately not yet hooked up, the I don't know how many-inch television, and finally the terrace, which wasn't a terrace but a hanging garden filled with flowers, whose multicolored variety the ugly day kept me from appreciating.

"Look, have you ever seen the sea like that? And Naples? And Vesuvius? And the sky? In the neighborhood was there ever all that sky?"

Never. The sea was of lead and the gulf clasped it like the rim of a crucible. A dense churning mass of black clouds was rolling toward us. But in the distance, between sea and clouds, there was a long gash that collided with the violet shadow of Vesuvius, a wound from which a dazzling whiteness dripped. We stood looking at it for a long time, our clothes pasted to us by the wind. I was as if hypnotized by the beauty of Naples; not even from the terrace of the Galianis, years before, had I seen it like this. The defacement of the city provided high-cost observatories of concrete from which to view an extraordinary landscape; Michele had acquired a memorable one.

"Don't you like it?"

"Marvelous."

"There's no comparison with Lina's house in the neighbor-hood, is there?"

"No, no comparison."

"I said Lina, but now Ada's there."

"Yes."

"Here it's much more upper-class."

"Yes."

"But you made a face."

"No, I'm happy for you."

"To each his own. You're educated, you write books, and I have this."

"Yes."

"You're not sure."

"I'm very sure."

"If you look at the nameplates in this building, you'll see, only professionals, lawyers, big professors. The view and the luxuries are expensive. If you and your husband save, in my opinion you could buy a house like this."

"I don't think so."

"He doesn't want to come and live in Naples?"

"I doubt it."

"You never know. You're lucky: I've heard Pietro's voice on the telephone quite a few times, and I saw him from the window—it's obvious that he's a clever man. He's not like Michele, he'll do what you want."

At that point she dragged me inside, she wanted us to eat something. She unwrapped prosciutto and provolone, she cut slices of bread. It's still camping, she apologized, but sometime when you're in Naples with your husband come and see me, I'll show you how I've arranged everything. Her eyes were big and shining, she was excited by the effort of leaving no doubts about her prosperity. But that improbable future—Pietro and I coming to Naples and visiting her and Michele—must have appeared perilous. For a moment she was distracted, she had bad thoughts, and when she resumed her boasting she had lost faith in what she was saying, she began to change. I've been lucky, too, she repeated, yet she spoke without satisfaction—rather, with a kind of sarcasm addressed to herself. Carmen, she enumerated, ended up with the gas pump attendant on the *stradone*, Pinuccia is poisoned by that idiot Rino, Ada is Stefano's whore. Instead, I have Michele, lucky me, who is handsome, intelligent, bosses everybody, is finally making up his mind to marry me and you see where he's put me, you don't know what a celebration he's prepared—not even the Shah of Persia when he married Soraya had a wedding like ours. Yes, lucky I grabbed him as a child, I was the sly one. And she went on, but taking a self-mocking turn. She wove the praises of her own cleverness, slipping slowly from the luxuries that she had acquired by winning Solara to the solitude of her duties as a bride. Michele, she said, is never here, it's as if I were getting married by myself. And she suddenly asked me, as if she really wanted an opinion: Do you think I exist? Look at me, in your view do I exist? She hit her full breasts with her open hand, but she did it as if to demonstrate physically that the hand went right through her, that her body, because of Michele, wasn't there. He had taken everything of her, immediately, when she was almost a child. He had consumed her, crumpled her, and now that she was twenty-five he was used to her, he didn't even look at her anymore. He fucks here and there as he likes. The revulsion I feel, when someone asks how many children do you want and he brags, he says: Ask Gigliola, I already have children, I don't even know how many. Does your husband say such things? Does your husband say: With Lenuccia I want three, with the others I don't know? In front of everyone he treats me like a rag for wiping the floor. And I know why. He's never loved me. He's marrying me to have a faithful servant, that's the reason all men get married. And he keeps saying to me: What the fuck am I doing with you, you don't know anything, you have no intelligence, you have no taste, this beautiful house is wasted, with you everything becomes disgusting. She began to cry, saying between her sobs:

"I'm sorry, I'm talking like this because you wrote that book I liked, and I know you've suffered."

"Why do you let him say those things to you?"

"Because otherwise he won't marry me."

"But after the wedding make him pay for it."

"How? He doesn't give a damn about me: even now I never see him, imagine afterward."

"Then I don't understand you."

"You don't understand me because you're not me. Would you take someone if you knew very well that he was in love with someone else?"

I looked at her in bewilderment: "Michele has a lover?"

"Lots of them, he's a man, he sticks it in wherever he can. But that's not the point."

"What is?"

"Lenù, if I tell you you mustn't repeat it to anyone, otherwise Michele will kill me."

I promised, and I kept the promise: I write it here, now, only because she's dead. She said:

"He loves Lina. And he loves her in a way he never loved me, in a way he'll never love anyone."

"Nonsense."

"You mustn't say it's nonsense, Lenù, otherwise it's better that you go. It's true. He's loved Lina since the terrible day when she put the shoemaker's knife to Marcello's throat. I'm not making it up, he told me."

And she told me things that disturbed me profoundly. She told me that not long before, in that very house, Michele had gotten drunk one night and told her how many women he had been with, the precise number: a hundred and twenty-two, paying and free. You're on that list, he said emphatically, but you're certainly not among those who gave me the most pleasure. You know why? Because you're an idiot, and even to fuck well it takes a little intelligence. For example you don't know how to give a blow job, you're hopeless, and it's pointless to explain it to you, you can't do it, it's too obvious that it disgusts you. And he went on like that for a while, making speeches that became increasingly crude; with him vulgarity was normal. Then he wanted to explain clearly how things stood: he was marrying her because of the respect he felt for her father, a skilled pastry maker he was fond of; he was marrying her because one had to have a wife and even children and even an official house. But there should be no mistake: she was nothing to him, he hadn't put her on a pedestal, she wasn't the one he loved best, so she had better not be a pain in the ass, believ-

ing she had some rights. Brutal words. At a certain point
Michele himself must have realized it, and he became gripped
by a kind of melancholy. He had murmured that women for
him were all games with a few holes for playing in. All. All
except one. Lina was the only woman in the world he loved—
love, yes, as in the films—and respected. He told me, Gigliola
sobbed, that she would have known how to furnish this house.
He told me that giving her money to spend, yes, that would be
a pleasure. He told me that with her he could have become
truly important, in Naples. He said to me: You remember what
she did with the wedding photo, you remember how she fixed
up the shop? And you, and Pinuccia, and all the others, what
the fuck are you, what the fuck do you know how to do? He
had said those things to her and not only those. He had told
her that he thought about Lila night and day, but not with normal desire, his desire for her didn't resemble what he knew. *In
reality he didn't want her.* That is, he didn't want her the way
he generally wanted women, to feel them under him, to turn
them over, turn them again, open them up, break them, step on
them, and crush them. He didn't want her in order to have sex
and then forget her. He wanted the subtlety of her mind with
all its ideas. He wanted her imagination. And he wanted her
without ruining her, to make her last. He wanted her not to
screw her—that word applied to Lila disturbed him. He
wanted to kiss her and caress her. He wanted to be caressed,
helped, guided, commanded. He wanted to see how she
changed with the passage of time, how she aged. He wanted
to talk with her and be helped to talk. You understand? He
spoke of her in way that to me, to me—when we are about to
get married—he has never spoken. I swear it's true. He whispered: My brother Marcello, and that dickhead Stefano, and
Enzo with his cheeky face, what have they understood of
Lina? Do they know what they've lost, what they might lose?
No, they don't have the intelligence. I alone know what she is,

who she is. *I recognized her.* And I suffer thinking of how she's wasted. He was raving, just like that, unburdening himself. And I listened to him without saying a word, until he fell asleep. I looked at him and I said: how is it possible that Michele is capable of that feeling—it's not him speaking, it's someone else. And I hated that someone else, I thought: Now I'll stab him in his sleep and take back my Michele. Lila no, I'm not angry with her. I wanted to kill her years ago, when Michele took the shop on Piazza dei Martiri away from me and sent me back behind the counter in the pastry shop. Then I felt like shit. But I don't hate her anymore, she has nothing to do with it. She always wanted to get out of it. She's not a fool like me, I'm the one marrying him, she'll never take him. In fact, since Michele will grab everything there is to grab, but not her, I've loved her for quite a while: at least there's someone who can make him shit blood.

I listened, now and then I tried to play it down, to console her. I said: If he's marrying you it means that, whatever he says, you're important to him, don't feel hopeless. Gigliola shook her head energetically, she dried her cheeks with her fingers. You don't know him, she said, no one knows him like me. I asked:

"Could he lose his head, do you think, and hurt Lina?"

She uttered a kind exclamation, between a laugh and a cry.

"Him? Lina? Haven't you seen how he's behaved all these years? He could hurt me, you, anyone, even his father, his mother, his brother. He could hurt all the people Lina is attached to, her son, Enzo. And he could do it without a qualm, coldly. But to her, her person, he will never do anything."

56.

I decided to complete my exploratory tour. I walked to Mergellina and when I reached Piazza dei Martiri the black sky was so low that it seemed to be resting on the buildings. I hurried into the elegant Solara shoe store certain that the storm would burst at any moment. Alfonso was even more handsome than I remembered, with his big eyes and long lashes, his sharply drawn lips, his slender yet strong body, his Italian made slightly artificial by the study of Latin and Greek. He was genuinely happy to see me. The arduous years of middle school and high school we'd spent together had created an affectionate bond, and even though we hadn't seen each other for a long time, we picked up again right away. We started joking. We talked easily, the words tumbling out, about our academic past, the teachers, the book I had published, his marriage, mine. It was I, naturally, who brought up Lila, and he became flustered, he didn't want to speak ill of her, or of his brother, or Ada. He said only:

"It was predictable that it would end like this."

"Why?"

"You remember when I told you that Lina scared me?"

"Yes."

"It wasn't fear, I understood much later."

"What was it?"

"Estrangement and belonging, an effect of distance and closeness at the same time."

"Meaning what?"

"It's hard to say: you and I became friends immediately, you I love. With her that always seemed impossible. There was something tremendous about her that made me want to go down on my knees and confess my most secret thoughts."

I said ironically: "Great, an almost religious experience."

He remained serious: "No, only an admission of inferiority. But when she helped me study, that was great, yes. She would read the textbook and immediately understand it, then she'd summarize it for me in a simple way. There have been, and still are today, moments when I think: If I had been born a woman

I would have wanted to be like her. In fact, in the Carracci family we were both alien bodies, neither she nor I could endure. So her faults never mattered to me, I always felt on her side."

"Is Stefano still angry with her?"

"I don't know. Even if he hates her, he has too many problems to be aware of it. Lina is the least of his troubles at the moment."

The statement seemed sincere and, above all, well founded. I put Lina aside. I went back instead to asking him about Marisa, the Sarratore family, finally Nino. He was vague about all of them, especially Nino, whom no one—by Donato's wishes, he said—had dared to invite to the intolerable wedding that was in store for him.

"You're not happy to be getting married?" I ventured.

He looked out the window: there was lightning and thunder but still no rain. He said: "I was fine the way I was."

"And Marisa?"

"No, she wasn't fine."

"You wanted her to be your fiancée for life?"

"I don't know."

"So finally you've satisfied her."

"She went to Michele."

I looked at him uncertainly. "In what sense?"

He laughed, a nervous laugh.

"She went to him, she set him against me."

I was sitting on a pouf, he was standing, against the light. He had a tense, compact figure, like the toreador in a bull-fighting film.

"I don't understand: you're marrying Marisa because she asked Solara to tell you that you had to do it?"

"I'm marrying Marisa in order not to upset Michele. He put me in here, he trusted my abilities, I'm fond of him."

"You're crazy."

"You say that because you all have the wrong idea about Michele, you don't know what he's like." His face contracted, he tried vainly to hold back tears. He added, "Marisa is pregnant."

"Ah."

So that was the real reason. I took his hand, in great embarrassment I tried to soothe him. He became quiet with a great effort, and said:

"Life is a very ugly business, Lenù."

"It's not true: Marisa will be a good wife and a fine mother."

"I don't give a damn about Marisa."

"Now don't overdo it."

He fixed his eyes on me, I felt he was examining me as if to understand something about me that left him bewildered. He asked: "Lina never said anything even to you?"

"What should she have said?"

He shook his head, suddenly amused.

"You see I'm right? She is an unusual person. Once I told her a secret. I was afraid and I needed to tell someone the reason for my fear. I told her and she listened attentively, and I calmed down. It was important for me to talk to her, it seemed to me that she listened not with her ears but with an organ that she alone had and that made the words acceptable. At the end I didn't ask her, as one usually does: swear, please, not to betray me. But it's clear that if she hasn't told you she hasn't told anyone, not even out of spite, not even in the period that was hardest for her, when my brother hated her and beat her."

I didn't interrupt him. I felt only that I was sorry because he had confided something to Lila and not to me, although I had been his friend forever. He must have realized that and he decided to make up for it. He hugged me tight, and whispered in my ear:

"Lenù, I'm a queer, I don't like girls."

When I was about to leave, he said softly, embarrassed: I'm

sure you already knew. This increased my unhappiness; in fact it had never occurred to me.

57.

The long day passed in that way, without rain but dark. And then began a reversal that rapidly changed a phase of apparent growth in the relationship between Lila and me into a desire to cut it off and return to taking care of my own life. Or maybe it had begun before that, in tiny details that I scarcely noticed as they struck me, and now instead were starting to add up. The trip had been useful, and yet I came home unhappy. What sort of friendship was mine and Lila's, if she had been silent about Alfonso for years, though she knew I had a close relationship with him? Was it possible that she hadn't realized Michele's absolute dependence on her, or for her own reasons had she decided not to say anything? On the other hand, I—how many things had I kept hidden from her?

For the rest of the day I inhabited a chaos of places, times, various people: the haunted Signora Manuela, the vacuous Rino, Gigliola in elementary school, Gigliola in middle school, Gigliola seduced by the potent good looks of the Solara boys, Gigliola dazzled by the Fiat 1100, and Michele who attracted women like Nino but, unlike him, was capable of an absolute passion, and Lila, Lila who had aroused that passion, a rapture that was fed not only by a craving for possession, by thuggish bragging, by revenge, by low-level desire, as she might say, but was an obsessive form of appreciation of a woman, not devotion, not subservience, but rather a sought-after form of male love, a complex feeling that was capable—with determination, with a kind of ferocity—of making a woman the chosen among women. I felt close to Gigliola, I understood her humiliation.

That night I went to see Lila and Enzo. I didn't say anything about that exploration I had made for love of her and also to protect the man she lived with. I took advantage instead of a moment when Lila was in the kitchen feeding the child to tell Enzo that she wanted to go back to the neighborhood. I decided not to hide my opinion. I said it didn't seem like a good idea to me, but that anything that could help stabilize her—she was healthy, she had only to regain some equilibrium—or that she considered such, should be encouraged. All the more since time had passed and, as far as I knew, in the neighborhood they wouldn't be worse off than in San Giovanni a Teduccio. Enzo shrugged.

"I have nothing against it. I'll have to get up earlier in the morning, return a little later in the evening."

"I saw that Don Carlo's old apartment is for rent. The children have gone to Caserta and the widow wants to join them."

"What's the rent?"

I told him: in the neighborhood the rents were lower than in San Giovanni a Teduccio.

"All right," Enzo agreed.

"You realize you'll have some problems anyway."

"There are problems here, too."

"The irritations will increase, and also the claims."

"We'll see."

"You'll stay with her?"

"As long as she wants, yes."

We joined Lila in the kitchen. She had just had a fight with Gennaro. Now that the child spent more time with his mother and less with the neighbor he was disoriented. He had less freedom, he was forced to give up a set of habits, and he rebelled by insisting, at the age of five, on being fed with a spoon. Lila had started yelling, he had thrown the plate, which shattered on the floor. When we went into the kitchen she had just slapped him. She said to me aggressively:

"Was it you who pretended the spoon was an airplane?"

"Just once."

"You shouldn't."

I said: "It won't happen again."

"No, never again, because you're going to be a writer and I have to waste my time like this."

Slowly she grew calmer, I wiped up the floor. Enzo told her that looking for a place in the neighborhood was fine with him, and I told her about Don Carlo's apartment, smothering my resentment. She listened unwillingly as she comforted the child, then she reacted as if it were Enzo who wanted to move, as if I were the one encouraging that choice. She said: All right, I'll do as you like.

The next day we all went to see the apartment. It was in poor condition, but Lila was enthusiastic: she liked that it was on the edge of the neighborhood, almost near the tunnel, and that from the windows you could see the gas pump of Carmen's fiancé. Enzo observed that at night they would be disturbed by the trucks that passed on the *stradone* and by the trains at the shunting yard. But since she found pleasure even in the sounds that had been part of our childhood, they came to an agreement with the widow for a suitable rent. From then on, every evening Enzo, instead of returning to San Giovanni a Teduccio, went to the neighborhood to carry out a series of improvements that would transform the apartment into a worthy home.

It was now almost May, the date of my wedding was approaching, and I was going back and forth to Florence. But Lila, as if she considered that deadline irrelevant, drew me into shopping for the finishing touches for the apartment. We bought a double bed, a cot for Gennaro, we went together to apply for a telephone line. People saw us on the street, some greeted only me, some both, others pretended not to have seen either of us. Lila seemed in any case relaxed. Once we ran into Ada; she was alone, she nodded cordially, and kept going as if she were in a hurry. Once we met Maria, Stefano's mother, Lila and I greeted her, she turned her head. Once Stefano himself passed in the car and stopped of his own initiative; he got out of the car, spoke only to me, cheerfully, asked about my wedding, praised Florence, where he had been recently with Ada and the child; finally patted Gennaro, gave a nod to Lila, and left. Once we saw Fernando, Lila's father: bent and very aged, he was standing in front of the elementary school, and Lila became agitated, she told Gennaro that she wanted him to meet his grandfather. I tried to restrain her, but she wanted to go anyway, and Fernando, behaving as if his daughter weren't present, looked at his grandson for a few seconds and said plainly, If you see your mother, tell her she's a whore, and went off.

But the most disturbing encounter, even if at the time it seemed the least significant, was a few days before she finally moved to the new apartment. Just as we came out of the house, we ran into Melina, who was holding by the hand her granddaughter Maria, the child of Stefano and Ada. She had her usual absent-minded air but she was nicely dressed, she had peroxided her hair, her face was heavily made up. She recognized me but not Lila, or maybe at first she chose to speak only to me. She talked to me as if I were still the girlfriend of her son, Antonio: she said that he would be back soon from Germany and that in his letters he always asked about me. I complimented her warmly on her dress and her hair, she seemed pleased. But she was even more pleased when I praised her granddaughter, who timidly clung to her grandmother's skirt. At that point she must have felt obliged to say something nice about Gennaro, and she turned to Lila: Is he your son? Only then did she seem to remember her. Until that moment she had stared at her without saying a word, and it must have occurred to her that here was the woman whose husband her own daughter Ada had taken. Her eyes were sunk deep in the large sockets, she said seriously: Lina, you've gotten ugly and thin, of course Stefano left you, men like flesh, otherwise they don't know where to put their hands and they leave. Then with a rapid jerk of her head she turned to Gennaro, and pointing to the little girl almost screamed: You know that's your sister? Give each other a kiss, come on, my goodness how cute you are. Gennaro immediately kissed the girl, who let herself be kissed without protesting, and Melina, seeing the two faces next to each other, exclaimed: They both take after their father, they're identical. After that statement, as if she had urgent things to do, she tugged her granddaughter and left without another word.

Lila had stood mute the whole time. But I understood that something extremely violent had happened to her, like the time when, as a child, she had seen Melina walking on the *stradone* eating soap flakes. As soon as the woman and the child were some distance away, she started, she ruffled her hair with one hand, she blinked, she said: I'll become like that. Then she tried to smooth her hair, saying:

"Did you hear what she said?"

"It's not true that you're ugly and skinny."

"Who gives a damn if I'm ugly and skinny, I'm talking about the resemblance."

"What resemblance?"

"Between the two children. Melina's right, they're both identical to Stefano."

"Come on, the girl is, but Gennaro is different."

She burst out laughing: after a long time her old, mean laugh was back.

She repeated: "They're two peas in a pod."

58.

I absolutely had to go. What I could do for her I had done, now I was in danger of getting caught up in useless reflections

218 - ELENA FERRANTE

on who the real father of Gennaro was, on how far-seeing
Melina was, on the secret motions of Lila's mind, on what she
knew or didn't know or supposed and didn't say, or was convenient for her to believe, and so on, in a spiral that was damaging to me. We discussed that encounter, taking advantage of
the fact that Enzo was at work. I used clichés like: A woman
always knows who the father of her children is. I said: You
always felt that child was Nino's, in fact you wanted him for
that reason, and now you're sure it's Stefano's just because
crazy Melina said so? But she sneered, she said: What an idiot,
how could I not have known, and—something incomprehensible to me—she seemed pleased. So in the end I was silent. If
that new conviction helped her to feel better, good. And if it
was another sign of her instability, what could I do? Enough.
My book had been bought in France, Spain, and Germany, it
would be translated. I had published two more articles on
women working in factories in Campania, and *l'Unità* was content. From the publisher came solicitations for a new novel. In
other words, I had to take care of countless things of my own;
for Lila I had done all I could, and I couldn't continue to get
lost in the tangles of her life. In Milan, encouraged by Adele, I
bought a cream-colored suit for the wedding, it looked good
on me, the jacket was fitted, the skirt short. When I tried it on
I thought of Lila, of her gaudy wedding dress, of the photograph that the dressmaker had displayed in the shop window
on the Rettifilo, and the contrast made me feel definitively different. Her wedding, mine: worlds now far apart. I had told
her earlier that I wasn't getting married in a church, that I
wouldn't wear a traditional wedding dress, that Pietro had
barely agreed to the presence of close relatives.

"Why?" she had asked, but without particular interest.

"Why what?"

"Why aren't you getting married in church."

"We aren't believers."

"And the finger of God, the Holy Spirit?" she had quoted, reminding me of the article we had written together as girls.

"I'm grown up."

"But at least have a party, invite your friends."

"Pietro doesn't want to."

"You wouldn't invite even me?"

"Would you come?"

She laughed, shaking her head.

"No."

That was it. But in early May, when I had decided on a final venture before leaving the city for good, things took an unpleasant turn concerning my wedding, but not only that. I decided to go and see Professor Galiani. I looked for her number, I called. I said I was about to get married, I was going to live in Florence, I wanted to come and say goodbye to her. She, without surprise, without joy, but politely, invited me for five o'clock the next day. Before hanging up she said: Bring your friend, Lina, if you want.

Lila in that case didn't have to be asked twice, and she left Gennaro with Enzo. I put on makeup, I fixed my hair, I dressed according to the taste I had developed from Adele, and helped Lila to at least look respectable, since it was difficult to persuade her to dress up. She wanted to bring pastries, I said it wasn't suitable. Instead I bought a copy of my book, although I assumed that Professor Galiani had read it: I did it so that I would have a way of inscribing it to her.

We arrived punctually, rang the bell, silence. We rang again. Nadia opened the door, breathless, half dressed, without her usual courtesy, as if we had introduced disorder not only into her appearance but also into her manners. I explained that I had an appointment with her mother. She's not here, she said, but make yourselves comfortable in the living room. She disappeared. We remained mute, but exchanged little smiles of uneasiness in the silent house. Perhaps five minutes passed, finally steps could be heard in the hall. Pasquale appeared, slightly disheveled. Lila didn't show the least surprise, but I exclaimed, in real astonishment: What are you doing here? He answered seriously, unfriendly: What are *you two* doing here. And the phrase reversed the situation, I had to explain to him, as if that were his house, that I had an appointment with my professor.

"Ah," he said, and asked Lila, teasingly, "Are you recovered?"

"Pretty much."

"I'm glad."

I got angry, I answered for her, I said that Lila was only now beginning to get better and that anyway the Soccavo factory had been taught a lesson—the inspectors had paid a visit, the business had had to pay Lila everything she was owed.

"Yes?" he said just as Nadia reappeared, now immaculate, as if she were going out. "You understand, Nadia? Dottoressa Greco says she taught Soccavo a lesson."

I exclaimed: "Not me."

"Not her, God Almighty taught Soccavo a lesson."

Nadia gave a slight smile, crossed the room and although there was a sofa free she sat on Pasquale's lap. I felt ill at ease.

"I only tried to help Lina."

Pasquale put his arm around Nadia's waist, leaned toward me, said:

"Excellent. You mean that in all the factories, at all the construction sites, in every corner of Italy and the world, as soon as the owner kicks up a fuss and the workers are in danger, we'll call Elena Greco: she telephones her friends, the labor authority, her connections in high places, and resolves the situation."

He had never spoken to me like that, not even when I was a girl and he seemed to me already adult, and acted like a political expert. I was offended, and was about to answer, but Nadia interrupted, ignoring me. She spoke to Lila, in her slow little voice, as if it were not worth the trouble to speak to me.

"The labor inspectors don't count for anything, Lina. They went to Soccavo, they filled out their forms, but then? In the factory everything is the same as before. And meanwhile those who spoke out are in trouble, those who were silent got a few lire under the counter, the police charged us, and the fascists came right here and beat up Armando."

She hadn't finished speaking when Pasquale started talking to me more harshly than before, this time raising his voice:

"Explain to us what the fuck you thought you resolved," he said, with genuine pain and disappointment. "You know what the situation is in Italy? Do you have any idea what the class struggle is?"

"Don't shout, please," Nadia asked him, then she turned again to Lila, almost whispering: "Comrades do not abandon one another."

She answered: "It would have failed anyway."

"What do you mean?"

"In that place you don't win with leaflets or even by fighting with the fascists."

"How do you win?"

Lila was silent, and Pasquale, now turning to her, hissed:

"You win by mobilizing the good friends of the owners? You win by getting a little money and screwing everyone else?"

Then I burst out: "Pasquale, stop it." Involuntarily I, too, raised my voice. "What kind of tone is that? It wasn't like that."

I wanted to explain, silence him, even though I felt an emptiness in my head, I didn't know what arguments to resort to, and the only concept that occurred to me readily was malicious and politically useless: You treat me like this because, now that you've got your hands on this young lady from a good family, you're full of yourself? But Lila, here, stopped me with a completely unexpected gesture of irritation, which confused me. She said:

"That's enough, Lenù, they're right."

I was upset. They were right? I wanted to respond, to get angry at her. What did she mean? But just then Professor Galiani arrived: her footsteps could be heard in the hall.

59.

I hoped that the professor hadn't heard me shouting. But at the same time I wanted to see Nadia jump off Pasquale's lap and hurry over to the sofa, I wished to see both of them humiliated by the need to pretend an absence of intimacy. I noticed that Lila, too, looked at them sardonically. But they stayed where they were; Nadia, in fact, put an arm around Pasquale's neck, as if she were afraid of falling, and said to her mother, who had just appeared in the doorway: Next time, tell me if you're having visitors. The professor didn't answer, she turned to us coldly: I'm sorry I was late, let's sit in my study. We followed her, while Pasquale moved Nadia off him, saying in a tone that seemed to me suddenly depressed: Come on, let's go.

Professor Galiani led us along the hall muttering irritably: What really bothers me is the boorishness. We entered an airy room with an old desk, a lot of books, sober, cushioned chairs. She assumed a polite tone, but it was clear that she was struggling with a bad mood. She said she was happy to see me and to see Lila again; yet at every word, and between the words, I felt her rage increasing, and I wanted to leave as quickly as possible. I apologized for not having come to see her, and went on somewhat breathlessly about studying, the book, the innumerable things that had overwhelmed me, my engagement, my approaching marriage.

"Are you getting married in church or only in a civil service?"

"Only a civil service."

"Good for you."

She turned to Lila, to draw her into the conversation: "You were married in church?"

"Yes."

"Are you a believer?"

"No."

"Then why did you get married in church?"

"That's what's done."

"You don't always have to do things just because they're done."

"We do a lot of them."

"Will you go to Elena's wedding?"

"She didn't invite me."

I was startled, I said right away:

"It's not true."

Lila laughed harshly: "It's true, she's ashamed of me."

Her tone was ironic, but I felt wounded anyway. What was happening to her? Why had she said earlier, in front of Nadia and Pasquale, that I was wrong, and now was making that hostile remark in front of the professor?

"Nonsense," I said, and to calm down I took the book out of my bag and handed it to Professor Galiani, saying: I wanted to give you this. She looked at it for a moment without seeing it, perhaps following her own thoughts, then she thanked me, and saying that she already had a copy, gave it back:

"What does your husband do?"

"He's a professor of Latin literature in Florence."

"Is he a lot older than you?"

"He's twenty-seven."

"So young, already a professor?"

"He's very smart."

"What's his name?"

"Pietro Airota."

Professor Galiani looked at me attentively, like when I was at school and I gave an answer that she considered incomplete.

"Relative of Guido Airota?"

"He's his son."

She smiled with explicit malice.

"Good marriage."

"We love each other."

"Have you already started another book?"

"I'm trying."

"I saw that you're writing for *l'Unità*."

"A bit."

"I don't write for it anymore, it's a newspaper of bureaucrats."

She turned again to Lila, she seemed to want to let her know how much she liked her. She said to her:

"It's remarkable what you did in the factory."

Lila grimaced in annoyance.

"I didn't do anything."

"That's not true."

The professor got up, rummaged through the papers on the desk, and showed her some pages as if they were an incontrovertible truth.

"Nadia left this around the house and I took the liberty of reading it. It's a courageous, new work, very well written. I wanted to see you so that I could tell you that."

She was holding in her hand the pages that Lila had written, and from which I had taken my first article for *l'Unità*.

60.

Oh yes, it was really time to get out. I left the Galiani house embittered, my mouth dry, without the courage to say to the professor that she didn't have the right to treat me like that. She hadn't said anything about my book, although she'd had it for some time and surely had read it or at least skimmed it. She hadn't asked for a dedication in the copy I had brought for that reason and when, before leaving—out of weakness, out of a need to end that relationship affectionately—I had offered anyway, she hadn't answered, she had smiled, and continued to talk to Lila. Above all, she had said nothing about my articles, rather she had mentioned them only to include them in her negative opinion of *l'Unità*, and then pulled out Lila's pages and began to talk to her as if my opinion on the subject didn't count, as if I were no longer in the room. I would have liked to yell: Yes, it's true, Lila has a tremendous intelligence, an intelligence that I've always recognized, that I love, that's influenced everything I've done; but I've worked hard to develop mine and I've been successful, I'm valued everywhere, I'm not a pretentious nobody like your daughter. Instead, I listened silently while they talked about work and the factory and the workers demands. They kept talking, even on the landing, until Professor Galiani absently said goodbye to me, while to Lila she said, now using the familiar *tu*, Stay in touch, and embraced her. I felt humiliated. Moreover, Pasquale and Nadia hadn't returned, I hadn't had a chance to refute them and my anger at them was still raging inside me: why was it wrong to help a friend, to do it I had taken a risk, how could they dare to criticize what I'd done. Now, on the stairs, in the lobby, on the sidewalk of Corso Vittorio Emanuele, it was only Lila and me. I was ready to shout at her: Do you really think I'm ashamed of you, what were you thinking, why did you say those two were right, you're ungrateful, I did all I could to stay close to you, to be useful to you, and you treat me like that, you really have a sick mind. But as soon as we were outside, even before I could open my mouth (and on the other hand what would have changed if I had?), she took me by the arm and began to defend me against Professor Galiani.

I couldn't find a single opening in order to reproach her for aligning herself with Pasquale and Nadia, or for the senseless accusation that I didn't want her at my wedding. She behaved as if it had been another Lila who said those things, a Lila of whom she herself knew nothing and whom it was pointless to ask for explanations. What terrible people—she began, and spoke without stopping all the way to the subway at Piazza Amedeo—did you see how the old woman treated you, she wanted to get revenge, she can't bear that you write books and articles, she can't bear that you're about to marry well, she especially can't bear that Nadia, brought up precisely to be the best of all, Nadia who was to give her so much satisfaction, isn't up to anything good, is sleeping with a construction worker and acting like a whore right in front of her: no, she can't bear it, but you're wrong to be upset, forget about it, you shouldn't have left her your book, you shouldn't have asked if she wanted it inscribed, you especially shouldn't have done that, those are people who should be treated with a kick in the ass, your weakness is that you're too good, you swallow everything that educated people say as if they're the only ones who had a mind, but it's not true, relax, go, get married, have a honeymoon, you were too worried about me, write another novel, you know that I expect great things from you, I love you.

I simply listened, overwhelmed. With her, there was no way to feel that things were settled; every fixed point of our relationship sooner or later turned out to be provisional; something shifted in her head that unbalanced her and unbalanced me. I couldn't understand if those words were in fact intended to apologize to me, or if she was lying, concealing feelings that she had no intention of confiding to me, or if she was aiming at a final farewell. Certainly she was false, and she was ungrateful, and I, in spite of all that had changed for me, continued to feel inferior. I felt that I would never free myself from that inferiority, and that seemed to me intolerable. I wished—and I couldn't keep the wish at bay—that the cardiologist had been wrong, that Armando had been right, that she really was ill and would die.

For years after that, we didn't see each other, we only talked on the phone. We became for each other fragments of a voice, without any visual corroboration. But the wish that she would die remained in a far corner, I tried to get rid of it but it wouldn't go away.

61.

The night before I left for Florence I couldn't sleep. Of all the painful thoughts the most persistent had to do with Pasquale. His criticisms burned me. At first I had rejected them altogether, now I was wavering between the conviction that they were undeserved and the idea that if Lila said he was right maybe I really had been mistaken. Finally I did something I had never done: I got out of bed at four in the morning and left the house by myself, before dawn. I felt very unhappy; I wished something terrible would happen to me, an event that, punishing me for my mistaken actions and my wicked thoughts, would as a result punish Lila, too. But nothing happened. I walked for a long time on the deserted streets, which were much safer than when they were crowded. The sky turned violet. I reached the sea, a gray sheet under a pale sky with scattered pink-edged clouds. The mass of Castel dell'Ovo was cut sharply in two by the light, a shining ochre shape on the Vesuvius side, a brown stain on the Mergellina and Posillipo side. The road along the cliff was empty, the sea made no sound but gave off an intense odor. Who knows what feeling I would have had about Naples, about myself, if I had waked every morning not in my neighborhood but in one of those buildings along the shore. What am I seeking? To change my origins? To change, along with myself, others, too? Repopulate this now deserted city with citizens not assailed by poverty or greed, not bitter or angry, who could delight in the splendor of the landscape like the divinities who once inhabited it? Indulge my demon, give him a good life and feel happy? I had used the power of the Airotas, people who for generations had been fighting for socialism, people who were on the side of men and women like Pasquale and Lila, not because I thought I would be fixing all the broken things of the world but because I was in a position to help a person I loved, and it seemed wrong not to do so. Had I acted badly? Should I have left Lila in trouble? Never again, never again would I lift a finger for anyone. I departed, I went to get married.

62.

I don't remember anything about my wedding. A few photographs, acting as props, rather than inspiring memory, have frozen it around a few images: Pietro with an absent-minded expression, me looking angry, my mother, who is out of focus but manages nevertheless to appear unhappy. Or not. It's the ceremony itself that I can't remember, but I have in mind the long discussion I had with Pietro a few days before we got married. I told him that I intended to take the Pill in order not to have children, that it seemed to me urgent to try first of all to write another book. I was sure that he would immediately agree. Instead, surprisingly, he was opposed. First he made it a problem of legality, the Pill was not yet officially for sale; then he said there were rumors that it ruined one's health; then he made a complicated speech about sex, love, and reproduction; finally he stammered that someone who really has to write will write anyway, even if she is expecting a baby. I was unhappy, I was angry, that reaction seemed to me not consistent with the educated youth who wanted only a civil marriage, and I told him so. We quarreled. Our wedding day arrived and we were not reconciled: he was mute, I cold.

There was another surprise, too, that hasn't faded: the

reception. We had decided to get married, greet our relatives, and go home without any sort of celebration. That decision had developed through the combination of Pietro's ascetic tendency and my intention to demonstrate that I no longer belonged to the world of my mother. But our line of conduct was secretly undone by Adele. She dragged us to the house of a friend of hers, for a toast, she said; and there, instead, Pietro and I found ourselves at the center of a big reception, in a very aristocratic Florentine dwelling, among a large number of relatives of the Airotas and famous and very famous people who lingered until evening. My husband became taciturn, I wondered, bewildered, why, since in fact it was a celebration for *my* wedding, I had had to be limited to inviting only my immediate family. I said to Pietro:

"Did you know this was happening?"

"No."

For a while we confronted the situation together. But soon he evaded the attempts of his mother and sister to introduce him to this man, to that woman; he entrenched himself in a corner with my relatives and talked to them the whole time. At first I resigned myself, somewhat uneasily, to inhabiting the trap we had fallen into, then I began to find it exciting that well-known politicians, prestigious intellectuals, young revolutionaries, even a well-known poet and a famous novelist showed interest in me, in my book, and spoke admiringly of my articles in *l'Unità*. The time flew by, I felt more and more accepted in the world of the Airotas. Even my father-in-law wanted to detain me, questioning me kindly on my knowledge of labor matters. A small group formed, of people engaged in the debate, in newspapers and journals, over the tide of demands that was rising in Italy. And me, here I was, with them, and it was my celebration, and I was at the center of the conversation.

At some point, my father-in-law warmly praised an essay,

published in *Mondo Operaio,* that in his view laid out the problem of democracy in Italy with crystalline intelligence. Drawing on a large number of facts, the piece demonstrated that, as long as the state television, the big papers, the schools, the universities, the judiciary worked day after day to solidify the dominant ideology, the electoral system would in fact be rigged, and the workers' parties would never have enough votes to govern. Nods of assent, supporting citations, references to this article and that one. Finally, Professor Airota, with all his authority, mentioned the name of the author of the article, and I knew even before he uttered it—Giovanni Sarratore—that it was Nino. I was so happy that I couldn't contain myself, I said I knew him, I called Adele over to confirm to her husband and the others how brilliant my Neapolitan friend was.

Nino was present at my wedding even if he wasn't present, and speaking of him I felt authorized to talk also about myself, about the reasons I had become involved in the workers' struggle, about the need to provide the parties and parliamentary representatives on the left with hard data so that they could address the delays in their understanding of the current political and economic period, and so on with other stock phrases I had learned only recently but used with assurance. I felt clever. My mood brightened; I enjoyed being with my in-laws and feeling admired by their friends. At the end, when my relatives timidly said goodbye and hurried off somewhere to wait for the first train to take them back to Naples, I no longer felt irritated with Pietro. He must have realized it, because he, in turn, softened, and the tension vanished.

As soon as we got to our apartment and closed the door we began to make love. At first it was very pleasurable, but the day reserved for me yet another surprising fact. Antonio, my first boyfriend, when he rubbed against me was quick and intense; Franco made great efforts to contain himself but at a certain point he pulled away with a gasp, or when he had a condom stopped suddenly and seemed to become heavier, crushing me under his weight and laughing in my ear. Pietro, on the other hand, strained for a time that seemed endless. His thrusting was deliberate, violent, so that the initial pleasure slowly diminished, overwhelmed by the monotonous insistence and the hurt I felt in my stomach. He was covered with sweat from his long exertions, maybe from suffering, and when I saw his damp face and neck, touched his wet back, desire disappeared completely. But he didn't realize it, he continued to withdraw and then sink into me forcefully, rhythmically, without stopping. I didn't know what to do. I caressed him, I whispered words of love, and yet I hoped that he would stop. When he exploded with a roar and collapsed, finally exhausted, I was content, even though I was hurting and unsatisfied.

He didn't stay in bed long; he got up and went to the bathroom. I waited for him for a few minutes, but I was tired, I fell asleep. I woke with a start after an hour and realized that he hadn't come back to bed. I found him in his study, at the desk.

"What are you doing?"

He smiled at me.

"I'm working."

"Come to bed."

"You go, I'll join you later."

I'm sure that I became pregnant that night.

63.

As soon as I discovered that I was expecting a child I was overwhelmed by anxiety and I called my mother. Although our relationship had always been contentious, in that situation the need to talk to her prevailed. It was a mistake: she immediately started nagging. She wanted to leave Naples, settle in with me, help me, guide me, or, vice versa, bring me to the neighborhood, have me back in her house, entrust me to the old midwife who had delivered all her children. I had a hard time putting her off, I said that a gynecologist friend of my mother-in-law was looking after me, a great professor, and I would give birth in his clinic. She was offended. She hissed: you prefer your mother-in-law to me. She didn't call again.

After a few days, on the other hand, I heard from Lila. We had had some telephone conversations after I left, but brief, a few minutes, we didn't want to spend too much, she cheerful, I aloof, she asking ironically about my life as a newlywed, I inquiring seriously about her health. This time I realized that something wasn't right.

"Are you angry with me?" she asked.

"No, why should I be?"

"You don't tell me anything. I got the news only because your mother is bragging to everyone that you're pregnant."

"I just got the confirmation."

"I thought you were taking the Pill."

I was embarrassed.

"Yes, but then I decided not to."

"Why?"

"The years are passing."

"And the book you're supposed to write?"

"I'll see later."

"You'd better."

"I'll do what I can."

"You have to do the maximum."

"I'll try."

"I'm taking the Pill."

"So with Enzo it's going well?"

"Pretty well, but I don't ever want to be pregnant again."

She was silent, and I didn't say anything, either. When she began talking once more, she told me about the first time she had realized she was expecting a baby, and the second. She described both as terrible experiences: the second time, she said, I was sure the baby was Nino's and even though I felt sick I was happy. But, happy or not, you'll see, the body suffers, it doesn't like losing its shape, there's too much pain. From there she went on in a crescendo that got darker and darker, telling me things she had told me before but never with the same desire to pull me into her suffering, so that I, too, would feel it. She seemed to want to prepare me for what awaited me, she was very worried about me and my future. This life of another, she said, clings to you in the womb first and then, when it finally comes out, it takes you prisoner, keeps you on a leash, you're no longer your own master. With great animation she sketched every phase of my maternity, tracing it over hers, expressing herself with her habitual effectiveness. It's as if you fabricated your very own torture, she exclaimed, and I realized then that she wasn't capable of thinking that she was her self and I was my self; it seemed to her inconceivable that I could have a pregnancy different from hers, and a different feeling about children. She so took it for granted that I would have the same troubles that she seemed ready to consider any possible joy I found in motherhood a betrayal.

I didn't want to listen to her anymore, I held the receiver away from my ear, she was scaring me. We said goodbye coolly.

"If you need me," she said, "let me know."

"All right."

"You helped me, now I want to help you."

"All right."

That phone call didn't help me at all; rather, it left me unsettled. I lived in a city I knew nothing about, even if thanks to Pietro I now was acquainted with every corner of it, which I could not say of Naples. I loved the path along the river, I took beautiful walks, but I didn't like the color of the houses, it put me in a bad mood. The teasing tone of the inhabitants—the porter in our building, the butcher, the baker, the mailman—incited me to become teasing, too, and a hostility with no motivation emerged from it. And then the many friends of my in-laws, so available on the day of the wedding, had never showed up again, nor did Pietro have any intention of seeing them. I felt alone and fragile. I bought some books on how to become a perfect mother and prepared with my usual diligence.

Days passed, weeks, but, surprisingly, the pregnancy didn't weigh on me at all; in fact it made me feel light. The nausea was negligible, I felt no breakdown in my body, in my mood, in the wish to be active. I was in the fourth month when my book received an important prize that brought me greater fame and a little more money. I went to the prize ceremony in spite of the political climate, which was hostile to that type of recognition, feeling that I was in a state of grace; I was proud of myself, with a sense of physical and intellectual fullness that made me bold, expansive. In the thank-you speech I went overboard, I said I felt as happy as the astronauts on the white expanse of the moon. A couple of days later, since I felt strong, I telephoned Lila to tell her about the prize. I wanted to let her know that things were not going as she had predicted, that in fact they were going smoothly, that I was satisfied. I felt so pleased with myself that I wanted to skip over the unhappiness she had caused me. But Lila had read in *Il Mattino*—only the Naples papers had devoted a few lines to the prize—that phrase of mine about the astronauts, and, without giving me time to speak, she criticized me harshly. The white expanse of the moon, she said ironically, sometimes it's better to say nothing than to talk nonsense. And she added that the moon was a rock among billions of other rocks, and that, as far as rocks go, the best thing was to stand with your feet planted firmly in the troubles of the earth.

I felt a viselike grip in my stomach. Why did she continue to wound me? Didn't she want me to be happy? Or maybe she hadn't recovered and her illness had heightened her mean side? Bitter words came to me, but I couldn't utter them. As if she didn't even realize she had hurt me, or as if she felt she had the right, she went on to tell me what was happening to her, in a very friendly tone. She had made peace with her brother, with her mother, even with her father; she had quarreled with Michele Solara on the old matter of the label on the shoes and the money he owed Rino; she had been in touch with Stefano to claim that, at least from the economic point of view, he should act as Gennaro's father, too, and not just Maria's. Her remarks were irascible, sometimes vulgar: against Rino, the Solaras, Stefano. And at the end she asked, as if she had an urgent need for my opinion: Did I do the right thing? I didn't answer. I had won an important prize and she had mentioned only that phrase about the astronauts. I asked her, maybe to offend her, if she still had those symptoms that unglued her head from her body. She said no, she repeated a couple of times that she was very well, she said with a mocking laugh: Only, sometimes out of the corner of my eye I see people coming out of the furniture. Then she asked me: Is everything all right with the pregnancy? Good, very good, I said, never felt better.

I traveled a lot in those months. I was invited here and there not only because of my book but also because of the articles I was writing, which in turn forced me to travel to see close up the new kinds of strike, the reactions of the owners. I never thought of trying to become a freelance journalist. I did it because doing it I was happy. I felt disobedient, in revolt and inflated with such power that my meekness seemed a disguise. In fact it enabled me to join the pickets in front of the factories, to talk to workers, both men and women, and to union officials, to slip out among the policemen. Nothing frightened me. When the Banca di Agricoltura in Milan was bombed I was in the city, at the publisher's, but I wasn't alarmed, I didn't have dark presentiments. I thought of myself as part of an unstoppable force,

I thought I was invulnerable. No one could hurt me and my child. We two were the only enduring reality, I visible and he (or she: but Pietro wanted a boy) for now invisible. The rest was a flow of air, an immaterial wave of images and sounds that, whether disastrous or beneficial, constituted material for my work. It passed by or it loomed so that I could put it into magic words in a story, an article, a speech, taking care that nothing ended up outside the frame, and that every concept pleased the Airotas, the publishing house, Nino, who surely somewhere was reading me, even Pasquale, why not, and Nadia, and Lila, all of whom would finally have to think: Look, we were wrong about Lena, she's on our side, see what she's writing.

It was a particularly intense time, that period of the pregnancy. It surprised me that being pregnant made me more eager to make love. It was I who initiated it, embraced Pietro, kissing him, even though he had no interest in kissing and began almost immediately to make love in that prolonged, painful way of his. Afterward he got up and worked until late. I slept for an hour or two, then I woke up, found him gone, turned on the light, and read until I was tired. Then I went to his room, insisted that he come to bed. He obeyed, but he got up early: sleep seemed to frighten him. Whereas I slept until midday.

There was only one event that distressed me. I was in my seventh month and my belly was heavy. I was outside the Nuovo Pignone factory when scuffles broke out, and I hurried away. Maybe I made a wrong movement, I don't know, I felt a painful spasm in the center of my right buttock that extended along my leg like a hot wire. I limped home, went to bed, and it passed. But every so often the pain reappeared, radiating through my thigh toward my groin. I learned to respond by finding positions that alleviated it, but when I realized that I was starting to limp all the time I was terrified, and I went to the gynecologist. He reassured me, saying that everything was in order, the weight I was carrying in my womb tired me out, causing this slight sciatica. Why are you so worried, he asked in an affectionate tone, you're such a serene person. I lied, I said I didn't know. In reality I knew perfectly well: I was afraid that my mother's gait had caught up with me, that she had settled in my body, that I would limp forever, like her.

I was soothed by the reassurances of the gynecologist; the pain lasted for a while longer, then disappeared. Pietro forbade me to do other foolish things, no more running around. I admitted that he was right, and spent the last weeks of my pregnancy reading; I wrote almost nothing. Our daughter was born on February 12, 1970, at five-twenty in the morning. We called her Adele, even though my mother-in-law kept repeating, poor child, Adele is a terrible name, give her any other name, but not that. I had atrocious labor pains, but they didn't last long. When the baby emerged and I saw her, black-haired, a violet organism that, full of energy, writhed and wailed, I felt a physical pleasure so piercing that I still know no other pleasure that compares to it. We didn't baptize her; my mother screamed terrible things on the telephone, she swore she would never come to see her. She'll calm down, I thought, sadly, and anyway if she doesn't it's her loss.

As soon as I was back on my feet I telephoned Lila, I didn't want her to be angry that I hadn't told her anything.

"It was a wonderful experience," I told her.

"What?"

"The pregnancy, the birth. Adele is beautiful, and very good."

She answered: "Each of us narrates our life as it suits us."

64.

What a tangle of threads with untraceable origins I discovered in myself in that period. They were old and faded, very new, sometimes bright-colored, sometimes colorless, extremely thin, almost invisible. That state of well-being ended suddenly, just when it seemed to me that I had escaped Lila's prophecies. The baby became troublesome, and the oldest parts of that jumble surfaced as if stirred by a distracted gesture. At first, when we were still in the clinic, she attached herself easily to my breast, but once we were home something went wrong and she didn't want me anymore. She sucked for a few seconds, then shrieked like a furious little animal. I felt weak, vulnerable to old superstitions. What was happening to her? Were my nipples too small, did they slip out? Did she not like my milk? Or was it an aversion toward me, her mother, had she been inoculated remotely with an evil spell?

An ordeal began, as we went from doctor to doctor, she and I alone; Pietro was always busy at the university. My bosom, swollen uselessly, hurt; I had burning stones in my breasts; I imagined infections, amputations. To empty them, to get enough milk to nourish the baby with a bottle, to alleviate the pain, I tortured myself with a breast pump. I whispered, coaxing her: come on, sweetie, suck, such a good baby, so sweet, what a dear little mouth, what dear little eyes, what's the matter. In vain. First I decided, regretfully, to try mixed feeding, then I gave up on that, too. I tried artificial milk, which required lengthy preparations night and day, a tiresome system of sterilizing nipples and bottles, an obsessive check of her weight before and after feeding, a sense of guilt every time she had diarrhea. Sometimes I thought of Silvia, who, in the turbulent atmosphere of the student gathering in Milan, breast-fed Nino's child, Mirko, so easily. Why not me? I suffered long secret crying spells.

For a few days the baby settled down. I was relieved, hoping the moment had arrived to get my life back in order. But the reprieve lasted less than a week. In her first year of life the baby barely closed her eyes; her tiny body writhed and screamed for hours, with an unsuspected energy and endurance. She was quiet only if I carried her around the house, holding her tight in my arms, speaking to her: Now mamma's splendid creature is good, now she's quiet, now she's resting, now she's sleeping. But the splendid creature wouldn't sleep, she seemed to fear sleep, like her father. What was wrong: a stomach ache, hunger, fear of abandonment because I hadn't breast-fed her, the evil eye, a demon that had entered her body? And what was wrong with me? What poison had polluted my milk? And the leg? Was it imagination or was the pain returning? My mother's fault? Did she want to punish me because I had been trying all my life not to be like her? Or was there something else?

One night I seemed to hear the sound of Gigliola's voice, faint, repeating throughout the neighborhood that Lila had a tremendous power, that she could cast an evil spell by fire, that she smothered the creatures in her belly. I was ashamed of myself, I tried to resist, I needed rest. So I tried leaving the baby to Pietro, who thanks to his habit of studying at night wasn't so tired. I said: I'm exhausted, call me in a couple of hours, and I went to bed and fell asleep as if I had lost consciousness. But once I was wakened by the baby's desperate wailing, I waited; it didn't stop. I got up. I discovered that Pietro had dragged the crib into his study and, paying no attention to his daughter's cries, was bent over his books, taking notes as if he were deaf. I lost all my manners, and regressed, insulting him in my dialect. You don't give a damn about anything, that stuff is more important than your daughter? My husband, distant, cool, asked me to leave the room, take away the crib. He had an important article to finish for an English journal, the deadline was very near. From then on I stopped asking him for help and if he offered I said: Go on, thanks, I know you have things to do. After dinner he hung around me uncertain, awkward, then he closed himself in his study and worked until late at night.

65.

I felt abandoned but with the impression that I deserved it: I wasn't capable of providing tranquility for my daughter. Yet I kept going, doggedly, even though I was more and more frightened. My organism was rejecting the role of mother. And no matter how I denied the pain in my leg by doing everything possible to ignore it, it had returned, and was getting worse. But I persisted, I wore myself out taking charge of everything. Since the building had no elevator, I carried the stroller with the baby in it up and down, I did the shopping, came home loaded down with bags, I cleaned the house, I cooked, I thought: I'm becoming ugly and old before my time, like the women of the neighborhood. And naturally, just when I was particularly desperate, Lila telephoned.

As soon as I heard her voice I felt like yelling at her: What have you done to me, everything was going smoothly and now, suddenly, what you said is happening, the baby is sick, I'm limping, it's impossible, I can't bear it anymore. But I managed to restrain myself in time, I said quietly, everything's fine, the baby's a little fussy and right now she's not growing much, but she's wonderful, I'm happy. Then, with feigned interest, I asked about Enzo, Gennaro, her relations with Stefano, her brother, the neighborhood, if she had had other problems with Bruno Soccavo and Michele. She answered in an ugly, obscene, aggressive dialect, but mostly without rage. Soccavo, she said, has to bleed. And when I run into Michele I spit in his face. As for Gennaro, she now referred to him explicitly as Stefano's son, saying, he's stocky like his father, and she laughed when I said he's such a nice little boy. She said: You're such a good little mamma, you take him. In those phrases I heard the sarcasm of someone who knew, thanks to some mysterious secret power, what was really happening to me, and I felt rancor, but I became even more insistent with my charade—listen to what a sweet voice Dede has, it's really pleasant here in Florence, I'm reading an interesting book by Baran—and I kept going until she forced me to end it by telling me about the IBM course that Enzo had started.

Only of him did she speak with respect, at length, and right afterward she asked about Pietro.

"Everything's going well with your husband?"

"Very well."

"And for me with Enzo."

When she hung up, her voice left a trail of images and sounds of the past that stayed in my mind for hours: the court-yard, the dangerous games, the doll she had thrown into the cel-lar, the dark stairs we climbed to Don Achille's to retrieve it, her wedding, her generosity and her meanness, how she had taken Nino. She can't tolerate my good fortune, I thought fearfully, she wants me with her again, under her, supporting her in her affairs, in her wretched neighborhood wars. Then I said to myself: How stupid I've been, what use has my education been, and I pretended everything was under control. To my sister Elisa, who called frequently, I said that being a mother was wonderful. To Carmen Peluso, who told me about her marriage to the gas-pump owner on the *stradone*, I responded: What good news, I wish you every happiness, say hello to Pasquale, what's he up to. With my mother, the rare times she called, I pretended I was ecstatic, but once I broke down and asked her: What happened to your leg, why do you limp. She answered: What does it matter to you, mind your own business.

I struggled for months, trying to keep at bay the more opaque parts of myself. Occasionally I surprised myself by praying to the Madonna, even though I considered myself an atheist, and was ashamed. More often, when I was alone in the house with the baby, I let out terrible cries, not words, only breath spilling out along with despair. But that difficult period wouldn't end; it was a grueling, tormented time. At night, I carried the baby up and down the hall, limping. I no longer whispered sweet nonsense phrases, I ignored her and tried to think of myself. I was always holding a book, a journal, even though I hardly managed to read anything. During the day, when Adele slept peacefully—at first I called her Ade, without realizing how it sounded like Hades, a hell summed up in two syllables, so that when Pietro pointed it out I was embarrassed and began calling her Dede—I tried to write for the newspaper. But I no longer had time—and certainly not the desire— to travel around on behalf of *l'Unità*. So the things I wrote had no energy, they were merely demonstrations of my formal skill, flourishes lacking substance. Once, having written an article, I had Pietro read it before dictating it to the editorial office. He said: "It's empty."

"In what sense?"

"It's just words."

I felt offended, and dictated it just the same. It wasn't published. And from then on, with a certain embarrassment, both the local and the national editorial offices began to reject my texts, citing problems of space. I suffered, I felt that everything that up to a short time earlier I had taken as an unquestioned condition of life and work was rapidly collapsing around me, as if violently jolted from inaccessible depths. I read just to keep my eyes on a book or a newspaper, but it was as if I had stopped at the signs and no longer had access to the meanings. Two or three times I came across articles by Nino, but reading them didn't give me the usual pleasure of imagining him, of hearing his voice, of enjoying his thoughts. I was happy for him, certainly: if he was writing it meant that he was well, he was living his life who knows where, with who knows whom.

But I stared at the signature, I read a few lines, I retreated, as if every one of his sentences, black on white, made my situation even more unbearable. I lost interest in things, I couldn't even bother with my appearance. And besides, for whom would I bother? I saw no one, only Pietro, who treated me courteously, but I perceived that for him I was a shadow. At times I seemed to think with his mind and I imagined I felt his unhappiness. Marrying me had only complicated his existence as a scholar, and just when his fame was growing, especially in England and the United States. I admired him, and yet he irritated me. I always spoke to him with a mixture of resentment and inferiority.

Stop it, I ordered myself one day, forget *l'Unità*, it will be enough if I can find the right approach for a new book: as soon as it's done, everything will be in order. But what book? To my mother-in law, to the publisher, I claimed that I was at a good point, but I was lying, I lied on every occasion in the friendliest tones. In fact all I had was notebooks crammed with idle notes, nothing else. And when I opened them, at night or during the day, according to the schedule that Dede imposed on me, I fell asleep without realizing it. One late afternoon Pietro returned from the university and found me in a condition worse than the one I had surprised him in some time earlier: I was in the kitchen, fast sleep, with my head resting on the table; the baby had missed her feeding and was screaming, off in the bedroom. Her father found her in the crib, half naked, forgotten. When Dede calmed down, greedily attached to the bottle, Pietro said in despair: "Is it possible that you don't have anyone who could help you?"

"Not in this city, and you know that perfectly well."

"Have your mother come, your sister."

"I don't want to."

"Then ask your friend in Naples: you did so much for her, she'll do the same for you."

I started. For a fraction of a second, part of me had the clear sensation that Lila was in the house already, present: if once she had been hiding inside me, now, with her narrow eyes, her furrowed brow, she had slipped into Dede. I shook my head energetically. Get rid of that image, that possibility, what was I looking onto?

Pietro resigned himself to calling his mother. Reluctantly he asked her if she could come and stay with us for a little while.

66.

I entrusted myself to my mother-in-law with an immediate sense of relief, and here, too, she showed herself to be the woman I would have liked to resemble. In the space of a few days she found a big girl named Clelia, barely twenty, and originally from the Maremma, to whom she gave detailed instructions about taking care of the house, the shopping, the cooking. When Pietro found Clelia in the house without even having been consulted he made a gesture of annoyance.

"I don't want slaves in my house," he said.

Adele answered calmly: "She's not a slave, she's a salaried employee."

And I, fortified by the presence of my mother-in-law, stammered: "Do you think I should be a slave?"

"You're a mother, not a slave."

"I wash and iron your clothes, I clean the house, I cook for you, I've given you a daughter, I bring her up in the midst of endless difficulties, I'm worn out."

"And who makes you do that, have I ever asked you for anything?"

I couldn't bear to argue, but Adele did, she crushed her son with a sometimes ferocious sarcasm, and Clelia remained. Then she took the child away from me, carried the crib into the room I had given her, managed with great precision the schedule of bottles both at night and during the day. When she noticed that I was limping, she took me to a doctor, a friend of hers, who prescribed various injections. She herself appeared every morning and every evening with the syringe and the vials, to blithely stick the needle into my buttocks. I felt better right away, the pain in my leg disappeared, my mood improved, I was happier. But Adele didn't stop there. She politely insisted that I attend to myself, she sent me to the hairdresser, made me go back to the dentist. And above all she talked to me constantly about the theater, the cinema, a book she was translating, another she was editing, what her husband or other famous people whom she called familiarly by name had written in this or that journal. From her I heard for the first time about the new radical feminist tracts. Mariarosa knew the women who were writing them; she was infatuated with them, admired them. Not Adele. She said with her usual ironic attitude that they went on and on about the feminist question as if it could be dealt with separately from the class conflict. Read them anyway, she advised me, and left me a couple of those little volumes with a final cryptic phrase: Don't miss anything, if you want to be a writer. I put them aside, I didn't want to waste time with writings that Adele herself disparaged. But I also felt, just then, that in no way did my mother-in-law's cultivated conversation arise from a true need to exchange ideas with me. Adele intended to systematically pull me out of the desperate state of an incompetent mother, she was rubbing words together to strike a spark and rekindle my frozen mind, my frozen gaze. But the truth was that she liked saving me more than listening to me.

And yet. Yet Dede, in spite of everything, continued to cry at night, I heard her and became agitated, she gave off a sense of unhappiness that undid the beneficial action of my mother-in-law. And though I had more time I still couldn't write. And

Pietro, who was usually controlled, in the presence of his mother became uninhibited to the point of rudeness; his return home was almost always followed by an aggressive exchange of sarcastic remarks, and this only increased the sense of breakdown I felt around me. My husband—I soon realized—found it natural to consider Adele ultimately responsible for all his problems. He got angry with her for everything, even what happened to him at work. I knew almost nothing about the wearing tensions that he was experiencing at the university; in general to my *how are things* he responded *fine*, he tended to spare me. But with his mother the barriers broke down; he assumed the recriminatory tone of the child who feels neglected. He poured out onto Adele everything he hid from me, and if I was present he acted as if I weren't, as if I, his wife, were to act only as silent witness.

Thus many things became clear to me. His colleagues, all older than him, attributed his dazzling career, as well as the small reputation that he was starting to develop abroad, to the name he bore, and had isolated him. The students considered him unnecessarily rigid, a pedantic bourgeois who tended his own plot without making any concession to the chaos of the present, in other words a class enemy. And he, as usual, neither defended himself nor attacked, but kept straight on his path, offering—of this I was sure—lectures of acute intelligence, assessing students' abilities with equal acuity, failing them. But it's hard, he almost shouted at Adele, one evening, in a tone of complaint. Then he immediately lowered his voice, said that he needed tranquility, that the job was a struggle, that no small number of his colleagues set the students against him, that groups of youths often erupted into the classroom where he was teaching and forced him to break off the classes, that despicable slogans had appeared on the walls. At that point, even before Adele could speak, I lost control. If you were a little less reactionary, I said, those things wouldn't happen to you. And he, for the first time since I'd known him, answered rudely, hissing: Shut up, you always speak in clichés.

I locked myself in the bathroom and I suddenly realized that I scarcely knew him. What *did* I know about him? He was a peaceful man but determined to the point of stubbornness. He was on the side of the working class and the students, but he taught and gave exams in the most traditional way. He was an atheist, he hadn't wanted to get married in a church, he had insisted that Dede not be baptized, but he admired the early Christian communities of the Oltrarno and he spoke on religious matters with great expertise. He was an Airota, but he couldn't bear the privileges and comforts that came from that. I calmed down, I tried to be closer to him, more affectionate. He's my husband, I said to myself, we ought to talk more. But Adele's presence became increasingly problematic. There was something unexpressed between them that drove Pietro to set aside manners and Adele to speak to him as if he were a fool with no hope of redemption.

We lived now like that, amid constant battles: he quarreled with his mother, he ended up saying something that made me angry, I attacked him. Until the point came when my mother-in-law, at dinner, in my presence, asked him why he was sleeping on the sofa. He answered: It's better if you leave tomorrow. I didn't intervene, and yet I knew why he slept on the sofa: he did it for me, so that he wouldn't disturb me when, around three, he stopped working and allowed himself some rest. The next day Adele returned to Genoa. I felt lost.

67.

Nevertheless, the months passed and both the baby and I made it. Dede started walking by herself the day of her first birthday: her father squatted in front of her, encouraged her warmly, she smiled, left me, and moved unsteadily toward him, arms outstretched, mouth half open, as if it were the happy goal of her year of crying. From then on, her nights became tranquil, and so did mine. She spent more time with Clelia, her anxieties diminished, I carved out some space for myself. But I discovered that I had no desire for demanding activities. As after a long illness, I couldn't wait to go outside, enjoy the sun and the colors, walk on the crowded streets, look in the shop windows. And since I had some money of my own, in that period I bought clothes for myself, for the baby, and for Pietro, I crowded the house with furniture and knickknacks, I squandered money as I never had before. I felt the need to be pretty, to meet interesting people, have conversations, but I hadn't made any friends, and Pietro, for his part, rarely brought guests home.

I tried gradually to resume the satisfying life I had had until a year before, and only then noticed that the telephone hardly ever rang, that the calls for me were rare. The memory of my novel was fading and, with it, interest in my name was diminishing. That period of euphoria was followed by a phase of anxiety and, occasionally, depression, as I wondered what to do; I began reading contemporary literature again, and was often ashamed of my novel, which in comparison seemed frivolous and very traditional; I put aside the notes for the new book, which tended to repeat the old one, and made an effort to think of a story with more political engagement, one that would contain the tumult of the present.

I made a few timid phone calls to *l'Unità* and tried again to write articles, but I soon realized that my pieces no longer appealed to the editors. I had lost ground, I wasn't well informed, I didn't have time to go and examine particular situations and report on them, I wrote elegant sentences of an abstract rigor to announce—in that particular newspaper, to whom I'm not sure—my support of the harshest criticisms of the Communist Party and the unions. Today it's hard to explain why I insisted on writing that stuff or, rather, why, although I scarcely took part in the city's political life, and in spite of my meekness, I felt increasingly drawn to extreme positions. Maybe I did it out of insecurity. Or maybe out of distrust in every form of mediation, a skill that, from early childhood, I associated with the intrigues of my father, who operated shrewdly in the inefficiency of the city hall. Or out of the vivid knowledge of poverty, which I felt an obligation not to forget; I wanted to be on the side of those who remained downtrodden and were fighting to turn everything upside down. Or because everyday politics, the demands that I myself had scrupulously written about, didn't matter to me, I wished that *something great*—I had used and often did use that formulation—would break out, which I could experience, and report on. Or because—and this was hard to admit—my model remained Lila, with her stubborn unreasonableness that refused to accept half measures, so that although I was now distant from her in every way, I wanted to say and do what I imagined she would say and do if she had had my tools, if she had not confined herself within the space of the neighborhood.

I stopped buying *l'Unità*, I began to read *Lotta Continua* and *Il Manifesto*. In the latter, I discovered, Nino's name sometimes appeared. His articles were, as usual, well documented, and shaped with cogent logic. As I had when I talked to him as a girl, I, too, felt the need to contain myself in a network of deliberately formulated general propositions that would keep me from breaking down. I noticed that I no longer thought of him with desire, or even with love. He had become, it seemed to me, a figure of regret, the synthesis of what I was at risk of not becoming, even though I had had the opportunity. We were born in the same environment, both had brilliantly got out of it. Why then was I sliding into despair? Because of marriage? Because of motherhood and Dede? Because I was a woman, because I had to take care of house and family and clean up shit and change diapers? Every time I came upon an article by Nino, and the article seemed well done, I was resentful. And the person who paid for it was Pietro, in fact the only person I had to talk to. I got angry at him, I accused him of abandoning me in the most terrible period of my life, of caring only about his career and forgetting me. Our relations—I had trouble admitting it because it frightened me, but that was the reality—got worse and worse. I knew that he suffered because of his problems at work, and yet I couldn't forgive him, rather I criticized him, often starting from political positions no different from those of the students who made things so hard for him. He listened to me uneasily, scarcely responding. I suspected, in those moments, that the words he had shouted before (*shut up, you speak in clichés*) hadn't been an accidental loss of temper but indicated that in general he didn't consider me capable of a serious discussion. It exasperated me, depressed me, my rancor increased, especially because I myself knew that I wavered between contradictory feelings whose essence could be summed up like this: it was inequality that made school laborious for some (me, for example), and almost a game for others (Pietro, for example); on the other hand, inequality or not, one had to study, and do well, in fact very well—I was proud of my journey, of the intelligence I had demonstrated, and I refused to believe that my labor had been in vain, if in certain ways obtuse. And yet, for obscure reasons, with Pietro I gave expression only to the injustice of inequality. I said to him: You act as if all your students were the same, but it's not like that, it's a form of sadism to insist on the same results from kids who haven't had the same opportunities. And I even criticized him when he reported that he'd had a violent discussion with a colleague some twenty years his senior, an acquaintance of his sister's, who had thought he would find in him an ally against the most conservative part of the faculty. It happened that that man had in a friendly way advised him to be less severe with the students. Pietro had replied in his polite but un-nuanced way that he didn't think he was severe but only demanding. Well, the other had said, be less demanding, especially with the ones who are generously spending a lot of their time changing the current situation. At that point things came to a head, although I don't know exactly how or based on what arguments. Pietro, whose account was as usual minimal, first maintained that he had said only, in self-defense, that it was his habit always to treat all students with the respect that they deserved; then he admitted he had accused his colleague of using a double standard, of accommodating the students who were more aggressive and ruthless and even humiliating the more fearful ones. The man had taken offense, had gone so far as to say that only the fact that he knew his sister well prevented him from telling Pietro—and meanwhile, however, he had told him—that he was a fool unworthy of the professorship he held.

"Couldn't you be more cautious?"

"I am cautious."

"It doesn't seem that way to me."

"Well, I have to say what I think."

"Maybe you should find out who are your friends and who are your enemies."

"I don't have enemies."

"Or friends, either."

One thing leads to another—I overdid it. The result of your behavior, I hissed at him, is that no one in this city, least of all the friends of your parents, invites us to dinner or a concert or for a visit to the country.

68.

It was evident to me now that Pietro, at the university, was considered a dull man, very remote from the keen activism of his family, an unsuccessful Airota. And I shared that opinion, something that did not help our life in common or our intimate relations. When Dede finally settled down and began to sleep regularly, he returned to our bed, but as soon as he approached me I felt irritated, I was afraid of getting pregnant again, I wanted him to let me sleep. So I pushed him away, wordlessly, or simply turned my back, and if he insisted and pressed his sex against my nightgown, I hit his leg gently with my heel, a signal: I don't want to, I'm sleepy. Pietro retreated unhappily, he got up and went to his study.

One night we argued yet again about Clelia. There was always some tension when we had to pay her, but on that occasion it was clear that Clelia was an excuse. He said somberly: Elena, we have to examine our relationship and take stock. I agreed immediately. I told him that I adored his intelligence and his civility, that Dede was marvelous, but I added that I didn't want more children, I found the isolation I had ended up in unbearable, I wanted to return to an active life, I hadn't slaved since childhood just to be imprisoned in the roles of wife and mother. We talked, I bitterly, he with courtesy. He stopped protesting about Clelia, he gave in. He decided to buy condoms, he began to invite friends or, rather, acquaintances—he didn't have any friends—to dinner, he resigned himself to my going sometimes with Dede to meetings and demonstrations, in spite of the increasingly frequent violence in the streets.

But that new course, rather than improving my life, complicated it. Dede became more attached to Clelia and when I took her out she was bored, she got upset, she pulled my ears, my hair, my nose, tearfully begging for her. I was convinced that she was happier with the girl from the Maremma than with me, and the suspicion returned that because I hadn't breast-fed her and her first year of life had been hard, I was now a dark figure in her eyes, the mean woman who was constantly scolding her, and who, out of jealousy, mistreated her cheerful nanny, a playmate, a storyteller. She pushed me away even when with a mechanical gesture I wiped the snot off her nose with a handkerchief or the remains of food off her mouth. She cried, she said I was hurting her.

As for Pietro, the condoms dulled his sensitivity even more, and it took him even longer to reach orgasm, which made him suffer, and made me suffer. Sometimes I made him take me from behind, I had the impression that it was less painful, and while he dealt those violent blows I grabbed his hand and brought it to my sex hoping he would understand that I wanted to be caressed. But he seemed incapable of doing both things, and since he preferred the first he almost immediately forgot the second, nor, once satisfied, did he seem to understand that I wanted some part of his body to consummate, in turn, my desire. After he had had his pleasure he caressed my hair, and whispered, I'll work a little. When he left, the solitude seemed to me a consolation prize.

Sometimes, at the demonstrations, I observed with curiosity the young men who exposed themselves fearlessly to every danger, who were charged with a joyful energy even when they felt threatened and became threatening. I felt their fascination, I was attracted by that fever heat. But I considered myself remote in every way from the bright girls who surrounded them, I was too cultured, wore glasses, was married, my time was always limited. I returned home unhappy, I treated my husband coldly, I felt I was already old. A few times I daydreamed that one of those young men—he was well known in Florence, very popular—noticed me and dragged me away, as when, in adolescence, I felt clumsy and wouldn't dance, but Antonio or Pasquale would take me by the arm and force me.

Naturally it never happened. Rather, it was the acquaintances Pietro began to bring home who created complications. I labored to prepare dinners, I played the wife who can keep the conversation interesting, and I didn't complain, I had asked my husband to invite people. But I soon perceived, uneasily, that that ritual was not complete in itself: I was attracted by any man who gave me the slightest encouragement. Tall, short, thin, fat, ugly, handsome, old, married or a bachelor, if the guest praised an observation of mine, if he had nice things to say about my book, if he grew excited by my intelligence, I looked at him cordially and in a brief exchange of phrases and glances my availability communicated itself. Then the man, bored at the start, became lively, ignoring Pietro, redoubling his attentions to me. His words grew more allusive, and his gestures, his attitude in the course of conversation gained intimacy. With his fingertips he grazed my shoulder, my hand, looked into my eyes formulating sentimental phrases, touched my knees with his, the tips of my shoes with his shoes.

At those moments I felt good, I forgot the existence of Pietro and Dede, the wake of boring obligations they trailed. I feared only the moment when the guest would leave and I would fall back into the dreariness of my house: pointless days, idleness, rage concealed behind meekness. So I went overboard: excitement goaded me to talk too much and too loudly, I crossed my legs, hiking up my skirt as far as possible, with a careless gesture I unfastened a button on my shirt. It was I who shortened the distances, as if a part of me were convinced that, if in some way I clung to that stranger, some of the well-being I felt at that moment would remain in my body, and when he had left the apartment, along with his wife or companion, I would feel the depression, the emptiness behind the display of feelings and ideas, the anguish of failure.

In reality, afterward, alone in bed while Pietro studied, I felt simply stupid and despised myself. But however I tried I couldn't change myself. Especially because those men were convinced they had made an impression and generally called the next day, invented excuses to see me again. I accepted. But as soon as I arrived at the appointment I was frightened. The simple fact that they were excited, although they were, let's say, thirty years older or were married, canceled their authority, canceled the savior role I had assigned them, and the very pleasure I had felt during the game of seduction was a shameful mistake. I asked myself in bewilderment: Why did I behave like that, what's happening to me? I paid more attention to Dede and Pietro.

But at the first chance it all started again. I fantasized, I listened at high volume to the music I had been ignorant of as a girl, I didn't read, I didn't write. And I felt increasingly regretful that, because of my self-discipline in everything, I had missed the joy of letting go that the women of my age, of the milieu I now lived in, made a show of having enjoyed and enjoying. Whenever Mariarosa, for example, appeared in Florence, sometimes for research, sometimes for political meetings, she came to stay with us, always with different men, sometimes with girlfriends, and she took drugs, and offered them to her companions and to us, and if Pietro darkened and shut himself in his study, I was fascinated, and though hesitant to try smoking or LSD—I was afraid I would feel sick—I stayed to talk to her and her friends until late into the night.

They talked about everything; often the exchanges were violent, and I had the impression that the good language I had struggled to acquire had become inadequate. Too neat, too clean. Look how Mariarosa's language has changed, I thought, she's broken with her upbringing, she's got a dirty mouth. Pietro's sister now expressed herself more vulgarly than Lila and I had as girls. She didn't utter a noun that wasn't preceded by "fucking." *Where did I put that fucking match, where are the fucking cigarettes.* Lila had never stopped talking like that; so what was I supposed to do, become like her again, go back to the starting point? Then why had I worn myself out?

I observed my sister-in-law. I liked how she displayed solidarity with me and embarrassed her brother, instead, and the men she brought home. One night she abruptly interrupted the conversation to say to the young man with her: enough, let's go fuck. *Fuck*. Pietro had invented a well-mannered child's jargon for sexual things, I had acquired it and used it in place of the vulgar dialect vocabulary I had known since early childhood. But now, if one truly wanted to feel part of the changing world, was it necessary to bring back the obscene words, to say: I want to screw, fuck me this way and that way? Unimaginable with my husband. But the few men I saw, all highly educated, willingly pretended to be lower-class, were amused by women who acted like sluts, and seemed to enjoy treating a woman like a whore. At first these men were very formal, they controlled themselves. But they couldn't wait to start a skirmish that moved from the unsaid to the said, to the more explicitly said, in a game of freedom where female shyness was considered a sign of hypocritical foolishness. Candor, rather, immediacy: these were the qualities of the liberated woman, and I made an effort to live up to them. But the more I did, the more I felt enthralled by my interlocutor. A couple of times it seemed to me that I was falling in love.

69.

It happened first with a lecturer in Greek literature, a man of my age, originally from Asti, who had in his home town a fiancée with whom he said he was unhappy; then with the husband of a temporary lecturer in papyrology, a couple with two small children, she from Catania, he from Florence, an engineer who taught mechanics, named Mario, who was seven years older than me. He had an extensive political education, a lot of authority in public, long hair, and in his spare time he played drums in a rock band. With both, the routine was the same: Pietro invited them to dinner, I began to flirt. Phone calls, carefree participation in demonstrations, many walks, sometimes with Dede, sometimes alone, and occasional movies. With the Greek lecturer I retreated as soon as he became explicit. But Mario trapped me in a tightening net and one evening, in his car, he kissed me, he kissed me for a long time and, putting his hands in my bra, caressed my breasts. I pushed him away with difficulty, I said I didn't want to see him anymore. But he called, he called again, I missed him, I gave in. Since he had kissed me and touched me, he was sure he had some rights and behaved immediately as if we were starting up again from the point where we had left off. He insisted, proposed, demanded. When I, on the one hand, led him on and, on the other, dodged him, laughing, he got offended, he offended me.

One morning I was walking with him and Dede, who, if I remember, was a little over two and was completely absorbed by a beloved doll, Tes, a name she had invented. In the circumstances, I was paying scarcely any attention to her, carried away by the verbal game, and sometimes I forgot about her completely. As for Mario, he gave no importance to the child's presence, he was interested only in keeping after me, with his uninhibited talk, and he turned to Dede to whisper playfully in her ear things like: Please, will you tell your mamma to be nice to me? The time flew, we parted, Dede and I headed home. But after a few steps the child said harshly: Tes told me she has a secret to tell Papa. My heart stopped in my chest. Tes? And what will she tell Papa? Tes knows. Something good or bad? Bad. I threatened her: You explain to Tes that if she reports that thing to Papa you will lock her up in the storeroom, in the dark. She burst into tears, and I had to carry her home: she who, to please me, would walk and walk, pretending that she never got tired. Dede understood, therefore, or at least perceived, that between that man and me there was something that her father wouldn't tolerate.

I again broke off the meetings with Mario. What was he, in the end? A middle-class man who liked pornographic wordplay. But I couldn't control my restlessness, an eagerness for violation was growing in me, I wanted to break the rules, as the entire world seemed to be breaking the rules. I wanted, even just once, to break out of marriage, or, why not, everything in my life, what I had learned, what I had written, what I was trying to write, the child I had brought into the world. Ah yes, marriage was a prison: Lila, who had courage, had escaped at risk of her very life: and what risks did I run with Pietro, so distracted, so absent? None. So? I called Mario. I left Dede to Clelia, I went to his office. We kissed, he sucked my nipples, he touched me between the legs as Antonio had at the ponds years before. But when he pulled down his pants and, with his underpants at his knees, grabbed me by the neck and tried to push me against his sex I wriggled free, said no, put myself in order, and rushed away.

I returned home in great agitation, filled with guilt. I made love with Pietro passionately, I had never felt so rapt, it was I who said no to the condom. What am I worried about, I said to myself, I'm near my period, nothing will happen. But it did happen. Within a few weeks I found that I was pregnant again.

70.

With Pietro I didn't even hint at abortion—he was very happy that I was giving him another child—and, besides, I myself was afraid of trying that route, the very word made my stomach hurt. Adele mentioned abortion on the telephone, but

I immediately avoided the subject with stock phrases like: Dede needs company, growing up alone is hard, it's better for her to have a little brother or sister.

"The book?"

"It's going well," I lied.

"Will you let me read it?"

"Of course."

"We're all waiting."

"I know."

I was panic-stricken, almost without thinking I made a move that astounded Pietro, maybe even me. I telephoned my mother, I said I was expecting another child, I asked if she wanted to come and stay in Florence for a while. She muttered that she couldn't, she had to take care of my father, of my siblings. I shouted at her: It'll be your fault if I don't write anymore. Who gives a damn, she answered, isn't it enough for you to lead the life of a lady? And she hung up. But five minutes later Elisa telephoned. I'll take care of the household, she said, Mamma will leave tomorrow.

Pietro picked up my mother at the station in the car, which made her proud, made her feel loved. As soon as she set foot in the house I listed a series of rules: Don't move anything around in Pietro's study or mine; don't spoil Dede; don't interfere between me and my husband; supervise Clelia without fighting with her; stay in the kitchen or your room if I have guests. I was resigned to the idea that she wouldn't respect any of those rules, but instead, as if the fear of being sent away had modified her nature, she became within a few days a devoted servant who provided for every necessity of the house and resolved every problem decisively and efficiently without ever disturbing me or Pietro.

From time to time she went to Naples and her absence immediately made me feel exposed to chance, I was afraid she would never return. But she always did. She told me the news of the neighborhood (Carmen was pregnant, Marisa had had a boy, Gigliola was giving Michele Solara a second child; she said nothing about Lila, to avoid conflict) and then she became a kind of invisible household spirit who insured for all of us clean, ironed clothes, meals that tasted of childhood, an apartment that was always tidy, an orderliness that, as soon as it was disturbed, was put back in order with a maniacal punctuality. Pietro thought of trying again to get rid of Clelia and my mother was in agreement. I got angry, but instead of raging at my husband I lost my temper with her, and she withdrew into her room without responding. Pietro reproached me and made an effort to reconcile us quickly. He adored her, he said she was a very intelligent woman, and he would sit in the kitchen with her after dinner, chatting. Dede called her Grandma and grew so attached to her that she was irritated when Clelia appeared. Now, I said to myself, everything is in order, now you have no excuses. And I forced myself to focus on the book.

I looked at my notes again. I was absolutely convinced that I had to change course. I wanted to leave behind me what Franco had called *petty love affairs* and write something suited to a time of demonstrations, violent deaths, police repression, fears of a coup d'état. I couldn't get beyond a dozen inert pages. What was missing, then? It was hard to say. Naples, maybe, the neighborhood. Or an image like the Blue Fairy. Or a passion. Or an authoritative voice that would direct me. I sat at the desk for hours, in vain, I leafed through novels, I never went out of the room for fear of being captured by Dede. How unhappy I was. I heard the voice of the child in the hall, Clelia's, my mother's limping step. I lifted my skirt, I looked at the belly that was already starting to grow, spreading an undesired well-being through my whole organism. I was for the second time pregnant and yet empty.

71.

It was then that I began telephoning Lila, not sporadically, as I had until then, but almost every day. I made the expensive intercity calls with the sole purpose of crouching in her shadow, letting my pregnancy run its course, hoping that, in line with an old habit, she would set my imagination in motion. Naturally I was careful not to say the wrong things, and I hoped that she wouldn't, either. I knew clearly, now, that our friendship was possible only if we controlled our tongues. For example, I couldn't confess to her that a dark part of me feared that she was casting an evil spell on me from afar, that that part still hoped that she was really sick and would die. For example, she couldn't tell me the real reasons that motivated the rough, often offensive, tone in which she treated me. So we confined ourselves to talking about Gennaro, who was one of the smartest children in the elementary school, about Dede, who already knew how to read, and we did it like two mothers doing the normal boasting of mothers. Or I mentioned my attempt to write, but without making a big deal of it, I said only: I'm working, it's not easy, being pregnant makes me tired. Or I tried to find out if Michele was still hanging around her, to somehow capture her and keep her. Or, sometimes, I would ask if she liked certain movie or television actors, and urge her to tell me if men unlike Enzo attracted her, and perhaps confide to her that it happened to me, too, that I was attracted to men unlike Pietro. But this last subject didn't seem to interest her. When I mentioned an actor she always said: Who's he, I've never seen him in the movies or on television. And if I merely uttered the name of Enzo she began updating me on the computer story, bewildering me with an incomprehensible jargon.

Her accounts were enthusiastic, and occasionally, on the hypothesis that they might be useful to me in the future, I took notes while she spoke. Enzo had made it, now he worked in an underwear factory fifty kilometers from Naples. The company had rented an IBM machine and he was the systems engineer. You know what kind of work that is? He diagrams manual processes by transforming them into flow charts. The central unit of the machine is as big as a wardrobe with three doors and it has a memory of 8 kilobytes. You can't imagine how hot it is, Lenù: the computer is worse than a stove. Maximum abstraction along with sweat and a terrible stink. She talked to me about ferrite cores, rings traversed by an electrical cable whose tension determined the rotation, 0 or 1, and a ring was a bit, and the total of eight rings could represent a byte, that is a character. Enzo was the singular protagonist of Lila's monologues. He dominated all that material like a god, he manipulated the vocabulary and the substance inside a large room with big air-conditioners, a hero who could make the machine do everything that people did. Is that clear? she asked me every so often. I answered yes, weakly, but I didn't know what she was talking about. I perceived only that she noticed that nothing was clear to me, and I was ashamed of this.

Her enthusiasm grew with every phone call. Enzo was now earning a hundred and forty-eight thousand lire a month, exactly, *a hundred and forty-eight*. Because he was so smart, the most intelligent man she had ever met. So smart, so clever, that he had soon become indispensable and had managed to get her hired, as an assistant. Here, this was the news: Lila was working again, and this time she liked it. He's the boss, Lenù, and I'm the deputy. I leave Gennaro with my mother—sometimes even with Stefano—and I go to the factory every morning. Enzo and I study the company point by point. We do everything the employees do so we know what we have to put into the computer. We check off, I don't know, the transactions, we attach the stamps to the invoices, we check the trainees' cards, the time cards, and then we transform everything into diagrams and holes in cards. Yes, yes, I'm also a punch-card operator: I'm there with three other women, and I'm getting eighty thousand lire. A hundred and forty-eight plus eighty is two hundred and twenty-eight, Lenù. Enzo and I are rich, and it will be even better in a few months, because the owner realized that I'm very capable and wants me to take a course. You see what sort of life I have, are you pleased?

72.

One night she was the one who telephoned, she said she had just had some bad news: Dario, the student she had told me about some time earlier, the kid from the committee who handed out leaflets in front of the Soccavo factory, had been beaten to death, right outside of school, in Piazza del Gesù.

She seemed worried. She spoke of a black cloud that lay oppressively on the neighborhood and the whole city, attacks and more attacks. Behind many of these beatings, she said, were Gino's fascists, and behind Gino was Michele Solara, names that, in uttering, she charged with old disgust, new rage, as if beneath what she said there was much else about which she was silent. I thought: How can she be so sure that they're the ones responsible? Maybe she's stayed in touch with the students of Via dei Tribunali, maybe Enzo's computers are not the only thing in her life. I listened without interrupting while she let the words flow in her usual gripping way. She told me in great detail about a number of expeditions by the fascists, who started at the party headquarters opposite the elementary school, spread up the Rettifilo, through Piazza Municipio, up the Vomero, and attacked comrades with iron bars and knives. Even Pasquale had been beaten a couple of times, his front teeth had been broken. And Enzo, one night, had fought with Gino himself right in front of their house.

Then she stopped, she changed her tone. Do you remember,

she asked, the atmosphere of the neighborhood when we were little? It's worse, or rather no, it's the same. And she mentioned her father-in-law, Don Achille Carracci, the loan shark, the Fascist, and Peluso, the carpenter, the Communist, and the war taking place right before our eyes. We slipped slowly back into those times, I remembered one detail, she another. Until Lila accentuated the visionary quality of her phrases and began to tell the story of the murder of Don Achille the way she had as a girl, with many fragments of reality and many of imagination. The knife to the neck, the spurting blood that had stained a copper pot. She ruled out, as she had at the time, that it was the carpenter who killed him. She said, with adult conviction: justice then, and today, for that matter, settled for the most obvious trail, the one that led to the Communist. Then she exclaimed: Who says it was really Carmen and Pasquale's father? And who says it was a man and not a woman? As in one of our childhood games, when it seemed to us that we were in all ways complementary, I followed her step by step, adding my voice excitedly to hers, and I had the impression that together—the girls of the past and the adults of the present—we were arriving at a truth that for two decades had been unspeakable. *Think about it*, she said, *who really gained from that murder, who ended up with the money-lending market that Don Achille controlled?* Yes, who? We found the answer in unison: the person who had gotten something out of it was the woman with the red book, Manuela Solara, the mother of Marcello and Michele. She killed Don Achille, we said excitedly, and then, turning melancholy, said softly, first I, then she: but what are we talking about, that's enough, we're still children, we'll never grow up.

73.

Finally the moment seemed auspicious, it was a long time

since we'd had our old harmony. Only this time the harmony really was confined to a tangle of vibrating breaths along the telephone wires. We hadn't seen each other for a long time. She didn't know what I looked like after two pregnancies, I didn't know if she was still pale and very thin, or had changed. For several years I had been speaking to a mental image that the voice was slowly reviving. Maybe for that reason, the murder of Don Achille suddenly seemed like an invention, the core of a possible story. And once I got off the telephone I tried to put order into our conversation, reconstructing the passages on the basis of which Lila, fusing past and present, had led me from the murder of poor Dario to that of the loan shark, up to Manuela Solara. I had trouble sleeping, I pondered for a long time. I felt with increasing lucidity that that material might be a shore from which to lean out and grasp a story. In the following days I mixed Florence with Naples, the tumults of the present with distant voices, the comfort of now and the struggle I had had to pull myself out of my origins, the anxiety of losing everything and the fascination of regression. As I thought about it I became convinced that I could make a book out of it. With great effort, with constant, painful second thoughts, I filled a graph-paper notebook, constructing a web of violence that welded together the past twenty years. Sometimes Lila telephoned, she asked:

"Why don't you call anymore, aren't you well?"

"I'm very well, I'm writing."

"And when you write I no longer exist?"

"You exist but I'm distracted."

"If I'm ill, if I need you?"

"Call."

"And if I don't telephone you stay inside your novel?"

"Yes."

"I envy you, lucky you."

I worked with growing anxiety that I wouldn't be able to

get to the end of the story before the baby was born, I was afraid I might die while I was giving birth, leaving the book unfinished. It was hard, nothing like the happy unconsciousness in which I had written the first novel. Once I had sketched out the story, I decided to give the text a more thoughtful pace. I wanted the writing to be lively, new, deliberately chaotic, and I didn't hold back. So I worked on a second, detailed draft. I went back and rewrote every line even when, thanks to a Lettera 32 that I had bought when I was expecting Dede, thanks to carbon paper, I had transformed the notebooks into a solid typescript in triplicate, almost two hundred pages, with not a single typing mistake.

It was summer, it was very hot, my belly was enormous. The pain in my buttock had reappeared, it came and went, and my mother's step in the hall got on my nerves. I stared at the pages, I discovered that I was afraid of them. For days I couldn't make up my mind, I worried about giving it to Pietro to read. Maybe, I thought, I should send it directly to Adele, this isn't the type of story for him. And besides, with the persistence that distinguished him, he continued to make life difficult for himself at the university, coming home in a state of agitation, making abstract speeches about the value of law—in other words, he wasn't in the right state of mind to read a novel about workers, bosses, struggles, blood, camorrists, loan sharks. What's more, *my* novel. He keeps me separate from the confusion inside him, he's never been interested in what I was and what I've become, what's the point of giving him the book? He'll just discuss this or that choice of word, and the punctuation, and if I insist on an opinion he'll say something vague. I sent Adele a copy of the manuscript, then I called her.

"I've finished."

"I'm so pleased. Will you let me read it?"

"I sent it to you this morning."

"Good, I can't wait to read it."

74.

I settled myself to wait, a wait that became much more anxious than that for the child who was kicking in my belly. I counted five days, one after another, no word from Adele. On the sixth day, at dinner, while Dede was making an effort to eat by herself in order not to displease me, and her grandmother was desperate to help her but didn't, Pietro asked me:

"Did you finish your book?"

"Yes."

"And why did you give it to my mother to read and not me?"

"You're busy, I didn't want to bother you. But if you want to read it, there's a copy on my desk."

He didn't answer. I waited, I asked:

"Adele told you I sent it to her?"

"Who else would it have been?"

"Did she finish it?"

"Yes."

"What does she think?"

"She'll tell you, it's between you two."

He was offended. After dinner I moved the manuscript from my desk to his, I put Dede to bed, I watched television without seeing or hearing anything, and finally I went to bed. I couldn't close my eyes: Why had Adele talked to Pietro about the book but hadn't yet called me? The next day, July 30, 1973, I went to see if my husband had started reading: the typescript was under the books he had been working on for most of the night, it was clear that he hadn't even looked through it. I became nervous, I shouted at Clelia to take care of Dede, not to sit around and let my mother to do everything. I was very harsh with her, and my mother evidently took it as a sign of affection. She touched my belly as if to calm me, she asked:

"If it's another girl what will you call her?"

I had other things on my mind, my leg hurt, I answered without thinking:

"Elsa."

She darkened, I realized too late that she was expecting me to say: We gave Dede the name of Pietro's mother, and if it's another girl this time we'll give her your name. I tried to justify it, but reluctantly. I said: Ma, try to understand, your name is Immacolata, I can't give my daughter a name like that, I don't like it. She grumbled: Why, is Elsa nicer? I replied: Elsa is like Elisa, if I give her the name of my sister you should be pleased. She didn't say another word. Oh, how tired I was of everything. The heat was getting worse, I was dripping with sweat, I couldn't stand my heavy belly, I couldn't stand my limping, I couldn't stand anything, not a thing.

Finally, a little before lunchtime, Adele telephoned. Her voice lacked its usual ironic inflection. She spoke slowly and seriously, I felt that every word was a struggle: she said, with a lot of euphemistic phrases and many fine distinctions, that the book wasn't good. But when I tried to defend it, she stopped looking for formulations that wouldn't hurt me and became explicit. The protagonist was unlikable. The characters were caricatures. Situations and dialogues were mannered. The writing tried to be modern and was only confused. All that hatred was unpleasant. The ending was crude, like a spaghetti Western, it was an insult to my intelligence, my education, my talent. I resigned myself to silence, I listened to her criticisms to the end. She concluded by saying: The earlier novel was vivid, innovative, this, however, is old in its contents and so pretentiously written that the words seem empty. I said quietly: Maybe at the publisher they'll be kinder. She stiffened and replied: If you want to send it, go ahead, but I would assume

they'll judge it unpublishable. I didn't know what to say, I said:
All right, I'll think about it, goodbye. She kept me on the line,
however, and, rapidly changing her tone, began to speak affectionately of Dede, of my mother, my pregnancy, of Mariarosa,
who enraged her. Then she asked:

"Why didn't you give the novel to Pietro?"

"I don't know."

"He could have advised you."

"I doubt it."

"You don't respect him?"

"No."

Afterward, shut in my study, I despaired. It had been
humiliating, intolerable. I could hardly eat, I fell asleep with
the window closed despite the heat. At four in the afternoon I
had my first labor pains. I said nothing to my mother, I took
the bag I had prepared, I got in the car, and drove to the clinic,
hoping to die on the way, I and my second child. Instead everything went smoothly. The pain was excruciating, but in a few
hours I had another girl. Pietro insisted the next morning that
our second daughter should be given the name of my mother,
it seemed to him a necessary tribute. I replied bitterly that I
was tired of following tradition, I repeated that she was to be
called Elsa. When I came home from the clinic, the first thing
I did was call Lila. I didn't tell her I had just given birth, I
asked if I could send her the novel.

I heard her breathing lightly for a few seconds, then she
said: "I'll read it when it comes out."

"I need your opinion right away."

"I haven't opened a book for a long time, Lenù, I don't
know how to read anymore, I'm not capable."

"I'm asking you as a favor."

"The other you just published, period; why not this one?"

"Because the other one didn't even seem like a book to
me."

"I can only tell you if I like it."
"All right, that's enough."

75.

While I was waiting for Lila to read, we learned that there
was a cholera outbreak in Naples. My mother became excessively agitated, then distracted, finally she broke a soup tureen
I was fond of, and announced that she had to go home. I imagined that if the cholera figured heavily in that decision, my
refusal to give her name to my new daughter wasn't secondary.
I tried to make her stay but she abandoned me anyway, when
I still hadn't recovered from the birth and my leg was hurting.
She could no longer bear to sacrifice months and months of
her life to me, a child of hers without respect and without gratitude, she would rather go and die of the cholera bacterium
with her husband and her good children. Yet even in the doorway she maintained the impassiveness that I had imposed on
her: she didn't complain, she didn't grumble, she didn't
reproach me for anything. She was happy for Pietro to take her
to the station in the car. She felt that her son-in-law loved her
and probably—I thought—she had controlled herself not to
please me so that she wouldn't make a bad impression on him.
She became emotional only when she had to part from Dede.
On the landing she asked the child in her effortful Italian: Are
you sorry that grandma is leaving? Dede, who felt that departure as a betrayal, answered grimly: No.

I was angry with myself, more than with her. Then I was
seized by a self-destructive frenzy and a few hours later I fired
Clelia. Pietro was amazed, alarmed. I said to him rancorously
that I was tired of fighting with Dede's Maremman accent,
with my mother's Neapolitan one. I wanted to go back to being
mistress of my house and my children. In reality I felt guilty

and had a great need to punish myself. With desperate pleasure I surrendered to the idea of being overwhelmed by the two children, by my domestic duties, by my painful leg.

I had no doubt that Elsa would compel me to a year no less terrible than the one I'd had with Dede. But maybe because I was more experienced with newborns, maybe because I was resigned to being a bad mother and wasn't anxious about perfection, the infant attached herself to my breast with no trouble and devoted herself to feeding and sleeping. As a result I, too, slept a lot, those first days at home, and Pietro surprisingly cleaned the house, did the shopping and cooking, bathed Elsa, played with Dede, who was as if dazed by the arrival of a sister and the departure of her grandmother. The pain in my leg suddenly disappeared. And I was in a generally peaceful state when, one late afternoon, as I was napping, my husband came to wake me: Your friend from Naples is on the phone, he said. I hurried to answer.

Lila had talked to Pietro for a long time, she said she couldn't wait to meet him in person. I listened reluctantly— Pietro was always amiable with people who didn't belong to the world of his parents—and since she dragged it out in a tone that seemed to me nervously cheerful, I was ready to shout at her: I've given you the chance to hurt me as much as possible, hurry up, speak, you've had the book for thirteen days, let me know what you think. But I confined myself to breaking in abruptly:

"Did you read it or not?"

She became serious.

"I read it."

"And so?"

"It's good."

"Good how? Did it interest you, amuse you, bore you?"

"It interested me."

"How much? A little? A lot?"

"A lot."

"And why?"

"Because of the story: it makes you want to read."

"And then?"

"Then what?"

I stiffened, and said:

"Lila, I absolutely have to know how this thing that I wrote is and I have no one else who can tell me, only you."

"I'm doing that."

"No, it's not true, you're cheating me: you've never talked about anything in such a superficial way."

There was a long silence. I imagined her sitting, legs crossed, next to an ugly little table on which the telephone stood. Maybe she and Enzo had just returned from work, maybe Gennaro was playing nearby. She said:

"I told you I don't know how to read anymore."

"That's not the point: it's that I need you and you don't give a damn."

Another silence. Then she muttered something I didn't understand, maybe an insult. She said harshly, resentful: I do one job, you do another, what do you expect from me, you're the one who had an education, you're the one who knows what books should be like. Then her voice broke, she almost cried: You mustn't write those things, Lenù, you aren't that, none of what I read resembles you, it's an ugly, ugly book, and the one before it was, too.

Like that. Rapid and yet strangled phrases, as if her breath, light, a whisper, had suddenly become solid and couldn't move in and out of her throat. I felt sick to my stomach, a sharp pain above my belly, which grew sharper, but not because of what she said but rather because of *how* she said it. Was she sobbing? I exclaimed anxiously: Lila, what's wrong, calm down, come on, breathe. She didn't calm down. They were really sobs, I heard them in my ear, burdened with such suffering that I couldn't feel the wound of that *ugly, Lenù, ugly, ugly*, nor was I offended that she reduced my first book, too—the book that had sold so well, the book of my success, but of which she had never told me what she thought—to a failure. What hurt me was her weeping. I wasn't prepared, I hadn't expected it. I would have preferred the mean Lila, I would have preferred her treacherous tone. But no, she was sobbing, and she couldn't control herself.

I felt bewildered. All right, I thought, I've written two bad books, but what does it matter, this unhappiness is much more serious. And I said softly: Lila, why are you crying, I should be crying, stop it. But she shrieked: Why did you make me read it, why did you force me to tell you what I think, I should have kept it to myself. And I: No, I'm glad you told me, I swear. I wanted her to quiet down but she couldn't, she poured out on me a confusion of words: Don't make me read anything else, I'm not fit for it, I expect the best from you, I'm too certain that you can do better, *I want* you to do better, it's what I want most, because who am I if you aren't great, who am I? I whispered: Don't worry, always tell me what you think, that's the only way you can help me, you've helped me since we were children, without you I'm not capable of anything. And finally she smothered her sobs, she said, sniffling: Why did I start crying, I'm an idiot. She laughed: I didn't want to upset you, I had prepared a positive speech, imagine, I wrote it, I wanted to make a good impression. I urged her to send it, I said, it could be that you know better than I do what I should write. And at that point we forgot the book, I told her that Elsa was born, we talked about Florence, Naples, the cholera. What cholera, she said sarcastically, there's no cholera, there's only the usual mess and the fear of dying in shit, more fear than facts, we eat a bag of lemons and no one shits anymore.

Now she talked continuously, without a break, almost cheerful, a weight had been lifted. As a result I began again to feel the bind I was in—two small daughters, a husband generally absent, the disaster of the writing—and yet I didn't feel anxious; rather, I felt light, and I brought the conversation back to my failure. I had in mind phrases like: the thread is broken, that fluency of yours that had a positive effect on me is gone, now I'm truly alone. But I didn't say it. I confessed instead in a self-satirizing tone that behind the labor of that book was the desire to settle accounts with the neighborhood, that it seemed to me to represent the great changes that surrounded me, that what had in some way suggested it, encouraging me, was the story of Don Achille and the mother of the Solaras. She burst out laughing. She said that the disgusting face of things alone was not enough for writing a novel: without imagination it would seem not a true face but a mask.

76.

I don't really know what happened to me afterward. Even now, as I sort out that phone call, it's hard to relate the effects of Lila's sobs. If I look closely, I have the impression of seeing mainly a sort of incongruous gratification, as if that crying spell, in confirming her affection and the faith she had in my abilities, had ultimately cancelled out the negative judgment of both books. Only much later did it occur to me that the sobs had allowed her to destroy my work without appeal, to escape my resentment, to impose on me a purpose so high—*don't disappoint her*—that it paralyzed every other attempt to write. But I repeat: however much I try to decipher that phone call, I can't say that it was at the origin of this or that, that it was an exalted moment of our friendship or one of the most wretched. Certainly Lila reinforced her role as a mirror of my inabilities. Certainly I was more willing to accept failure, as if Lila's opinion were much more authoritative—but also more persuasive and more affectionate—than that of my mother-in-law.

In fact a few days later I called Adele and said to her: Thank you for being so frank, I realized that you're right, and it strikes me now that my first book, too, had a lot of flaws. Maybe I ought to think about it, maybe I'm not a good writer, or I simply need more time. My mother-in-law hastily drowned me in compliments, praised my capacity for self-criticism, reminded me that I had an audience and that that audience was waiting. I said yes, of course. And right afterward I put the last copy of the novel in a drawer, I also put away the notebooks full of notes, I let myself be absorbed by daily life. The irritation at that useless labor extended to my first book, too, perhaps even to the literary purposes of writing. If an image or an evocative phrase came to mind, I felt a sense of uneasiness, and moved on to something else.

I devoted myself to the house, to the children, to Pietro. Not once did I think of having Clelia back or of replacing her with someone else. Again I took on everything, and certainly I did it to put myself in a stupor. But it happened without effort, without bitterness, as if I had suddenly discovered that this was the right way of spending one's life, and a part of me whispered: Enough of those silly notions in your head. I organized the household tasks rigidly, and I took care of Elsa and Dede with an unexpected pleasure, as if besides the weight of the womb, besides the weight of the manuscript, I had rid myself of another, more hidden weight, which I myself was unable to name. Elsa proved to be a placid creature—she took long happy baths, she nursed, she slept, she smiled even in her sleep—but I had to be very attentive to Dede, who hated her sister. She woke in the morning with a wild expression, recounting how she had saved the baby from fire, from a flood, from a wolf, but mostly she pretended to be a newborn herself, and asked to suck on my nipples, imitated infant wails, refused to act as what she now was, a child of almost four with highly developed language, perfectly independent in her primary functions. I was careful to give her a lot of affection, to praise her intelligence and her ability, to persuade her that I needed her help with everything, the shopping, the cooking, keeping her sister out of trouble.

Meanwhile, since I was terrified by the possibility of getting pregnant again, I began to take the Pill. I gained weight, I felt as if I'd swelled up, yet I didn't dare stop: a new pregnancy frightened me more than any other thing. And then my body didn't matter to me the way it used to. The two children seemed to have confirmed that I was no longer young, that the signs of my labors—washing them, dressing them, the stroller, the shopping, cooking, one in my arms and one by the hand, both in my arms, wiping the nose of one, cleaning the mouth of the other—testified to my maturity as a woman, that to become like the mammas of the neighborhood wasn't a threat but the order of things. It's fine this way, I told myself.

Pietro, who had given in on the Pill after resisting for a long time, examined me, preoccupied. You're getting fat. What are those spots on your skin? He was afraid that the children, and he, and I were getting sick, but he hated doctors. I tried to reassure him. He had gotten very thin lately: he always had circles under his eyes and white strands had appeared in his hair; he complained of pain in his knee, in his right side, in his shoulder, and yet he wouldn't have an examination. I forced him to go, I went with him, along with the children, and, apart from the need for some sleeping pills, he turned out to be very healthy. That made him euphoric for a few hours, and all his symptoms vanished. But in a short time, in spite of the sedatives, he felt ill again. Once Dede wouldn't let him watch the news—it was right after the coup in Chile—and he spanked her much too hard. And as soon as I began to take the Pill he developed a desire to make love even more frequently than before, but only in the morning or the afternoon, because—he said—it was the evening orgasm that made him sleepless; then he was compelled to study for a good part of the night, which made him feel chronically tired and consequently ill.

Nonsensical talk: working at night had always been for him a habit and a necessity. Yet I said: Let's not do it at night anymore, anything was fine with me. Of course, sometimes I was exasperated. It was hard to get help from him even in small things: the shopping when he was free, washing the dishes after dinner. One evening I lost my temper: I didn't say anything terrible, I just raised my voice. And I made an important discovery: if I merely shouted, his stubbornness disappeared and he obeyed me. It was possible, by speaking harshly, to make even his unpredictable pains go away, even his neurotic wish to make love constantly. But I didn't like doing it. When I behaved like that, I was sorry, it seemed to cause a painful tremor in his brain. Besides, the results weren't lasting. He gave in, he adjusted, he took on tasks with a certain gravity, but then he really was tired, he forgot agreements, he went back to thinking only about himself. In the end I let it go, I tried to make him laugh, I kissed him. What did I gain from a few washed dishes, poorly washed at that? Better to leave him tranquil, I was glad when I could avoid tension.

In order not to upset him I also learned not to say what I thought. He didn't seem to care, anyway. If he talked, I don't know, about the government measure in response to the oil crisis, if he praised the rapprochement of the Communist Party to the Christian Democrats, he preferred me to be only an approving listener. And when I appeared to disagree he assumed an absent-minded expression, or said in a tone that he obviously used with his students: you were badly brought up, you don't know the value of democracy, of the state, of the law, of mediation between established interests, balance between nations— you like apocalypse. I was his wife, an educated wife, and he expected me to pay close attention when he spoke to me about politics, about his studies, about the new book he was working on, filled with anxiety, wearing himself out, but the attention had to be affectionate; he didn't want opinions, especially if they caused doubts. It was as if he were thinking out loud, explaining to himself. And yet his mother was a completely different type of woman. And so was his sister. Evidently he didn't want me to be like them. During that period of weakness, I understood from certain vague remarks that he wasn't happy about not only the success of my first book but its very publication. As for the second, he never asked me what had happened to the manuscript and what future projects I had. The fact that I no longer mentioned writing seemed to be a relief to him.

That Pietro every day revealed himself to be worse than I had expected did not, however, drive me again toward others. At times I ran into Mario, the engineer, but I quickly discovered that the desire to seduce and be seduced had disappeared and in fact that former agitation seemed to me a rather ridiculous phase; luckily it had passed. The craving to get out of the house, participate in the public life of the city also diminished. If I decided to go to a debate or a demonstration, I always took the children, and I was proud of the bags I toted, stuffed with everything they might need, of the cautious disapproval of those who said: They're so little, it might be dangerous.

But I went out every day, in whatever weather, so that my daughters could have air and sun. I never went without taking a book. Out of a habit that I had never lost, I continued to read wherever I was, even if the ambition of making a world for myself had vanished. I generally took a short walk and then sat on a bench not far from home. I paged through complicated essays, I read the newspaper, I yelled: Dede, don't go far, stay close to Mamma. I was that, I had to accept it. Lila, whatever turn her life might take, was different.

77.

It happened that around that time Mariarosa came to Florence to present the book of a university colleague of hers on the *Madonna del Parto*. Pietro swore he wouldn't miss it, but at the last minute he made an excuse and hid somewhere. My sister-in-law arrived by car, alone this time, a bit tired but affectionate as always and loaded with presents for Dede and Elsa. She never mentioned my aborted novel, even though Adele had surely told her about it. She talked volubly about trips she'd taken, about books, with her usual enthusiasm. She pursued energetically the many novelties of the planet. She would assert one thing, get tired of it, go on to another that a little earlier, out of distraction, blindness, she had rejected. When she spoke about her colleague's book, she immediately gained the admiration of the art historians in the audience. And the evening would have run smoothly along the usual academic tracks if at a certain point, with an abrupt swerve, she hadn't uttered remarks, occasionally vulgar, of this type: children shouldn't be given to any father, least of all God the Father, children should be given to themselves; the moment has arrived to study as women and not as men; behind every discipline is the penis and when the penis feels impotent it resorts to the iron bar, the police, the prisons, the army, the concentration camps; and if you don't submit, if, rather, you continue to turn everything upside down, then comes slaughter. Shouts of discontent, of agreement: at the end she was surrounded by a dense crowd of women. She called me over with welcoming gestures, proudly showed off Dede and Elsa to her Florentine friends, said nice things about me. Some remembered my book, but I avoided it, as if I hadn't written it. The evening was nice, and brought an invitation, from a small, varied group of girls and adult women, to go to the house of one of them, once a week, to talk—they said—about us.

Mariarosa's provocative remarks and the invitation of her friends led me to fish out from under a pile of books those pamphlets Adele had given me long before. I carried them around in my purse, I read them outside, under the gray sky of late winter. First, intrigued by the title, I read an essay entitled *We Spit on Hegel*. I read it while Elsa slept in her carriage and Dede, in coat, scarf, and woolen hat, talked to her doll in a low voice. Every sentence struck me, every word, and above all the bold freedom of thought. I forcefully underlined many of the sentences, I made exclamation points, vertical strokes. Spit on Hegel. Spit on the culture of men, spit on Marx, on Engels, on Lenin. And on historical materialism. And on Freud. And on psychoanalysis and penis envy. And on marriage, on family. And on Nazism, on Stalinism, on terrorism. And on war. And on the class struggle. And on the dictatorship of the proletariat. And on socialism. And on Communism. And on the trap of equality. And on *all* the manifestations of patriarchal culture. And on *all* its institutional forms. Resist the waste of female intelligence. Deculturate. Disacculturate, starting with maternity, don't *give* children to anyone. Get rid of the master-slave dialectic. Rip inferiority from our brains. Restore women to themselves. Don't create antitheses. Move on another plane in the name of one's own difference. The university doesn't free women but completes their repression. Against wisdom. While men devote themselves to undertakings in space, life for women on this planet has yet to begin. Woman is the other face of the earth. Woman is the Unpredictable Subject. Free oneself from subjection here, now, in this present. The author of those pages was called Carla Lonzi. How is it possible, I wondered, that a woman knows how to think like that. I worked so hard on books, but I endured them, I never actually used them, I never turned them against themselves. This is thinking. This is thinking against. I—after so much exertion—don't know how to think. Nor does Mariarosa: she's read pages and pages, and she rearranges them with flair, putting on a show. That's it. Lila, on the other hand, knows. It's her nature. If she had studied, she would know how to think like this.

That idea became insistent. Everything I read in that period ultimately drew Lila in, one way or another. I had come upon a female model of thinking that, given the obvious differences, provoked in me the same admiration, the same sense of inferiority that I felt toward her. Not only that: I read thinking of her, of fragments of her life, of the sentences she would agree with, of those she would have rejected. Afterward, impelled by that reading, I often joined the group of Mariarosa's friends, but it wasn't easy: Dede asked me continuously when we were leaving, Elsa would suddenly let out cries of joy. But it wasn't just my daughters who were the problem. It was that there I found only women who, resembling me, couldn't help me. I was bored when the discussion became a sort of inelegant summary of what I already knew. And it seemed to me I knew well enough what it meant to be born female, I wasn't interested in the work of consciousness-raising. And I had no intention of speaking in public about my relationship with Pietro, or with men in general, to provide testimony about what men are, of every class and of every age. And no one knew better than I did what it meant to make your own head masculine so that it would be accepted by the culture of men; I had done it, I was doing it. Furthermore I remained completely outside the tensions, the explosions of jealousy, the authoritarian tones, weak, submissive voices, intellectual hierarchies, struggles for primacy in the group that ended in desperate tears. But there was one new fact, which naturally led me to Lila. I was fascinated by the way people talked, confronted each other—explicit to the point of being disagreeable. I didn't like the amenability that yielded to gossip: I had known enough of that since childhood. What seduced me instead was an urge for authenticity that I had never felt and that perhaps was not in my nature. I never said a single word, in that circle, that was equal to that urgency. But I felt that I should do something like that with Lila, examine our connection with the same inflexibility, that we should tell each other fully what we had been silent about, starting perhaps from the unaccustomed lament for my mistaken book.

That need was so strong that I imagined going to Naples with the children for a while, or asking her to come to me with Gennaro, or to write to each other. I talked about it with her once on the phone but it was a fiasco. I told her about the books by women I was reading, about the group I went to. She listened but then she laughed at titles like *The Clitoral Woman and the Vaginal Woman,* and did her best to be vulgar: What the fuck are you talking about, Lenù, pleasure, pussy, we've got plenty of problems here already, you're crazy. She wanted to prove that she didn't have the tools to put into words the things that interested me. And in the end she was scornful, she said: Work, do the nice things you have to do, don't waste time. She got angry. Evidently it's not the right moment, I thought, I'll try again later on. But I never found the time or the courage to try again. I concluded that first of all I had to understand better what I was. Investigate my nature as a woman. I had been excessive, I had striven to give myself male capacities. I thought I had to know everything, be concerned with everything. What did I care about politics, about struggles. I wanted to make a good impression on men, be at their level. At the level of what, of their reason, most unreasonable. Such persistence in memorizing fashionable jargon, wasted effort. I had been conditioned by my education, which had shaped my mind, my voice. To what secret pacts with myself had I consented, just to excel. And now, after the hard work of learning, what must I unlearn. Also, I had been forced by the powerful presence of Lila to imagine myself as I was not. I was added to her, and I felt mutilated as soon as I removed myself. Not an idea, without Lila. Not a thought I trusted, without the support of her thoughts. Not an image. I had to accept myself outside of her. The gist was that. Accept that I was an average person. What should I do. Try again to write. Maybe I didn't have the passion, I merely limited myself to carrying out a task. So don't write anymore. Find some job. Or act the lady, as my mother said. Shut myself up in the family. Or turn everything upside down. House. Children. Husband.

78.

I consolidated my relations with Mariarosa. I called her frequently, but when Pietro noticed he began to speak more and more contemptuously of his sister. She was frivolous, she was empty, she was dangerous to herself and others, she had been the cruel tormenter of his childhood and adolescence, she was the great worry of her parents. One evening he came out of his study disheveled, his face tired, while I was talking to my sister-in-law on the phone. He walked around the kitchen, ate something, joked with Dede, eavesdropping on our conversation. Then all of a sudden he shouted: Doesn't that idiot know it's time for dinner? I apologized to Mariarosa and hung up. It's all ready, I said, we can eat right away, there's no need to shout. He complained that spending money on phone calls to listen to his sister's nonsense seemed stupid to him. I didn't answer, I set the table. He realized I was angry, and said, in a tone of apprehension: I'm mad at Mariarosa, not you. But after that night he began to look through the books I was reading, to make sarcastic comments on the sentences I had underlined. He said, Don't be taken in, it's nonsense. And he tried to demonstrate the weak logic of feminist manifestos and pamphlets.

On this very subject we ended up arguing one evening and

maybe I overdid it, going so far as to say to him: You think you're so great but everything you are you owe to your father and mother, just like Mariarosa. His reaction was completely unexpected: he slapped me, and in Dede's presence.

I took it well, better than he did: I had had many blows in the course of my life, Pietro had never given any and almost certainly had never received any. I saw in his face the revulsion for what he had done; he stared at his daughter for an instant, and left the house. My anger cooled. I didn't go to bed, I waited for him, and when he didn't return I became anxious, I didn't know what to do. Did he have some nervous illness, from too little sleep? Or was that his true nature, buried under thousands of books and a proper upbringing? I realized yet again that I knew little about him, that I wasn't able to predict his moves: he might have jumped into the Arno, be lying drunk somewhere, even left for Genoa to find comfort and complain in his mother's arms. Oh enough, I was frightened. I realized that I was leaving what I was reading, and what I knew, on the edges of my personal life. I had two daughters, I didn't want to draw conclusions too hastily.

Pietro came home at around five in the morning and the relief of seeing him safe and sound was so great that I hugged him, I kissed him. He mumbled: You don't love me, you've never loved me. And he added: Anyway, I don't deserve you.

79.

The fact was that Pietro couldn't accept the disorder that was by now spreading into every aspect of existence. He would have liked a life ruled by unquestioned habits: studying, teaching, playing with the children, making love, contributing every day, in his small way, to resolving by democratic means the vast confusion of Italian affairs. Instead he was exhausted by the conflicts at the university, his colleagues disparaged his work, and although he was gaining a reputation abroad, he felt constantly vilified and threatened, he had the impression that because of my restlessness (but what restlessness, I was an opaque woman) our very family was exposed to constant risks. One afternoon Elsa was playing on her own, I was making Dede practice reading, he was shut in his study, the house was still. Pietro, I thought anxiously, is looking for a fortress where he works on his book, I take care of the household, and the children grow up serenely. Then the doorbell rang, I went to open the door, and to my surprise Pasquale and Nadia entered.

They carried large military knapsacks; he wore a cap over a thick mass of curly hair that fell into an equally thick and curly beard, while she looked thin and tired, her eyes enormous, like a frightened child who is pretending not to be afraid. They had asked for the address from Carmen, who in turn had asked my mother. They were both affectionate, and I was, too, as if there had never been tensions or disagreements between us. They took over the house, leaving their things everywhere. Pasquale talked a lot, in a loud voice, almost always in dialect. At first they seemed a pleasant break in my flat daily existence. But I soon realized that Pietro didn't like them. It bothered him that they hadn't telephoned to announce themselves, that they brazenly made themselves at home. Nadia took off her shoes and stretched out on the sofa. Pasquale kept his cap on, handled objects, leafed through books, took a beer from the refrigerator for himself and one for Nadia without asking permission, drank from the bottle and burped in a way that made Dede laugh. They said they had decided to take a trip, they said just that, a *trip*, without specifying. When had they left Naples? They were evasive. When would they return? They were equally evasive. Work? I asked Pasquale. He laughed: Enough, I've worked too much, now I'm resting. And he showed Pietro his hands, he demanded that he show him his,

286 · ELENA FERRANTE

he rubbed their palms together saying: You feel the difference? Then he grabbed *Lotta Continua* and brushed his right hand over the first page, proud of the sound of the paper scraping over his rough skin, as pleased as if he had invented a new game. Then he added, in an almost threatening tone: Without these rasping hands, professor, not a chair would exist, or a building, a car, nothing, not even you; if we workers stopped working everything would stop, the sky would fall to earth and the earth would shoot up to the sky, the plants would take over the cities, the Arno would flood your fine houses, and only those who have always worked would know how to survive, and as for you two, you with all your books, the dogs would tear you to pieces.

It was a speech in Pasquale's style, fervent and sincere, and Pietro listened without responding. As did Nadia, who, while her companion was speaking, lay on the sofa with a serious expression, staring at the ceiling. She almost never interrupted the two men's talk, nor did she say anything to me. But when I went to make coffee she followed me into the kitchen. She noticed that Elsa was always attached to me, and she said gravely:

"She really loves you."

"She's little."

"You're saying that when she grows up she won't love you?"

"No, I hope she'll love me when she's grown up, too."

"My mother used to talk about you all the time. You were only her student, but it seemed as if you were her daughter more than me."

"Really?"

"I hated you for that and because you had taken Nino."

"It wasn't for me that he left you."

"Who cares, I don't even remember what he looked like now."

"As a girl I would have liked to be like you."

"Why? You think it's nice to be born with everything all ready-made for you?"

"Well, you don't have to work so hard."

"You're wrong—the truth is that it seems like everything's been done already and you've got no good reason to do anything. All you feel is the guilt of what you are and that you don't deserve it."

"Better that than to feel the guilt of failure."

"Is that what your friend Lina tells you?"

"No."

"I prefer her to you. You're two pieces of shit and nothing can change you, two examples of underclass filth. But you act all friendly and Lina doesn't."

She left me in the kitchen, speechless. I heard her shout to Pasquale: I'm taking a shower, and you could use one, too. They shut themselves in the bathroom. We heard them laughing, she letting out little cries that—I saw—worried Dede. When they came out their hair was wet, they were half-naked, and gay. They went on joking and laughing with each other as if we weren't there. Pietro tried to intervene with questions like: How long have you been together? Nadia answered coldly: We're not together, maybe *you two* are together. In the finicky tone he displayed in situations where people appeared to him extremely superficial: What does that mean? You can't understand, Nadia responded. My husband objected: When someone can't understand, you try to explain. And at that point Pasquale broke in laughing: There's nothing to explain, prof: you better believe you're dead and you don't know it—everything is dead, the way you live is dead, the way you speak, your conviction that you're very intelligent, and democratic, and on the left. How can you explain a thing to someone who's dead?

There were other tense moments. I said nothing, I couldn't get Nadia's insults out of my mind, the way she spoke, as if it were nothing, in my house. Finally they left, almost without warning, as they had arrived. They picked up their things and disappeared. Pasquale said only, in the doorway, in a voice that was unexpectedly sorrowful:

"Goodbye, Signora Airota."

Signora Airota. Even my friend from the neighborhood was judging me in a negative way? Did it mean that for him I was no longer Lenù, Elena, Elena Greco? For him and for how many others? Even for me? Did I myself not almost always use my husband's surname, now that mine had lost that small luster it had acquired? I tidied the house, especially the bathroom, which they had left a mess. Pietro said: I never want those two in my house; someone who talks like that about intellectual work is a Fascist, even if he doesn't know it; as for her, she's a type I'm very familiar with, there's not a thought in her head.

80.

As if to prove Pietro right, the disorder began to take concrete form, touching people who had been close to me. I learned from Mariarosa that Franco had been attacked in Milan by the fascists, he was in bad shape, and had lost an eye. I left immediately, with Dede and little Elsa. I took the train, playing with the girls and feeding them, but saddened by another me—the poor, uneducated girlfriend of the wealthy and hyperpoliticized student Franco Mari: how many me's were there by now?—who had been lost somewhere and was now re-emerging.

At the station I met my sister-in-law, who was pale and worried. She took us to her house, which this time was deserted, yet even more untidy than when I had stayed there after the meeting at the university. While Dede played and Elsa slept, she told me more than she had on the telephone. The episode had happened five days earlier. Franco had spoken at a demonstration of Avanguardia Operaia, in a packed theater. Afterward he had gone off with Silvia, who now lived with an editor at *Giorno* in a beautiful apartment near the theater: he was to sleep there and leave the next day for Piacenza. They were almost at the door, Silvia had just taken the keys out of her purse, when a white van pulled up and the fascists had jumped out. He had been severely beaten, Silvia had been beaten and raped.

We drank a lot of wine, Mariarosa took out the drug: that's what she called it, in other situations she used the plural. This time I decided to try it, but only because, in spite of the wine, I felt I hadn't a single solid thing to hold on to. My sister-in-law became furious, then stopped talking and burst into tears. I couldn't find a single word of comfort. *I felt* her tears, it seemed to me that they made a sound sliding from her eyes down her cheeks. Suddenly I couldn't see her, I couldn't even see the room, everything turned black. I fainted.

When I came to, I apologized, hugely embarrassed, I said it was tiredness. I didn't sleep much that night: my body weighed heavily because of an excess of discipline, and the lexicon of books and journals dripped anguish as if suddenly the signs of the alphabet could no longer be combined. I held the two little girls close as if they were the ones who had to comfort and protect me.

The next day I left Dede and Elsa with my sister-in-law and went to the hospital. I found Franco in a sickly-green ward that had an intense odor of breath, urine, and medicine. He was as if shortened and distended, I can still see him in my mind's eye, because of the white bandages, the violet color of part of his face and neck. He didn't seem glad to see me, he seemed ashamed of his condition. I talked, I told him about my children. After a few minutes he said: Go away, I don't want you here. When I insisted on staying, he was irritated, and whispered: I'm not myself, go away. He was very ill; I learned from a small group of his companions that he might have to have another operation. When I came back from the hospital Mariarosa saw that I was upset. She helped with the children, and as soon as Dede fell asleep she sent me to bed, too. The next day, however, she wanted me to come with her to see Silvia. I tried to avoid it, I had found it unbearable to see Franco and feel not only that I couldn't help him but that I made him feel more fragile. I said I preferred to remember her as I had seen her during the meeting at the university. No, Mariarosa insisted, she wants us to see her as she is now, it's important to her. We went.

A very well-groomed woman, with blond hair that fell in waves over her shoulders, opened the door. It was Silvia's mother, and she had Mirko with her; he, too, was blond, a child of five or six by now, whom Dede, in her sulky yet bossy way, immediately insisted play a game with Tes, the old doll she carried everywhere. Silvia was sleeping but had left word that she wanted to be awakened when we got there. We waited awhile before she appeared. She was heavily made up, and had put on a pretty long green dress. I wasn't struck so much by the bruises, the cuts, the hesitant walk—Lila had seemed in even worse shape when she returned from her honeymoon—as by her expressionless gaze. Her eyes were blank, and completely at odds with the frenetic talking, broken by little laughs, with which she began to recount *to me*, only to me, who still didn't know, what the fascists had done to her. She spoke as if she were reciting a horrendous nursery rhyme that was for now the way in which she deposited the horror, repeating it to anyone who came to see her. Her mother kept trying to make her stop, but each time she pushed her away with a gesture of irritation, raising her voice, uttering obscenities and predicting a time soon, very soon, of violent revenge. When I burst into tears she stopped abruptly. But other people arrived, mostly family friends and comrades. Then Silvia began again, and I quickly retreated to a corner, hugging Elsa, kissing her lightly. I remembered details of what Stefano had done to Lila, details that I imagined while Silvia was narrating, and it seemed to me that the words of both stories were animal cries of terror.

At a certain point I went to look for Dede. I found her in the hall with Mirko and her doll. They were pretending to be a mother and father with their baby, but it wasn't peaceful: they were pretending to have a fight. I stopped. Dede instructed Mirko: *You have to hit me, understand?* The new living flesh was replicating the old in a game, we were a chain of shadows who had always been on the stage with the same burden of love, hatred, desire, and violence. I observed Dede carefully; she seemed to resemble Pietro. Mirko, on the other hand, was just like Nino.

81.

Not long afterward, the underground war that occasionally erupted into the newspapers and on television—plans for coups, police repression, armed bands, firefights, woundings, killings, bombs and slaughters I was struck again by in the cities large and small. Carmen telephoned, she was extremely worried, she hadn't heard from Pasquale in weeks.

"Did he by any chance visit you?"

"Yes, but at least two months ago."

"Ah. He asked for your phone number and address: he wanted to get your advice, did he?"

"Advice about what?"

"I don't know."

"He didn't ask me for advice."

"What did he say?"

"Nothing, he was fine, he was happy."

Carmen had asked everywhere, even Lila, even Enzo, even the people in the collective on Via dei Tribunali. Finally she had called Nadia's house, but the mother had been rude and Armando had told her only that Nadia had moved without leaving any address.

"They must have gone to live together."

"Pasquale and that girl? Without leaving an address or phone number?"

We talked about it for a long time. I said maybe Nadia had broken with her family because of Pasquale, who knows, maybe they had gone to live in Germany, in England, in France. But Carmen wasn't persuaded. Pasquale is a loving brother, she said, he would never disappear like that. She had instead a terrible presentiment: there were now daily clashes in the neighborhood, anyone who was a comrade had to watch his back, the fascists had even threatened her and her husband. And they had accused Pasquale of setting fire to the fascist headquarters and to the Solaras' supermarket. I hadn't known either of those things, I was astonished: This had happened in the neighborhood, and the fascists blamed Pasquale? Yes, he was at the top of the list, he was considered someone to get out of the way. Maybe, Carmen said, Gino had him killed.

"You went to the police?"

"Yes."

"What did they say?"

"They nearly arrested me, they're more fascist than the fascists."

I called Professor Galiani. She said to me sarcastically: What happened, I don't see you in the bookshops anymore or even in the newspapers, have you already retired? I said that I had two children, that for now I was taking care of them, and then I asked her about Nadia. She became unfriendly. Nadia is a grownup, she's gone to live on her own. Where, I asked. Her business, she answered, and, without saying goodbye, just as I was asking if she would give me her son's telephone number, she hung up.

I spent a long time finding a number for Armando, and had an even harder time finding him at home. When he finally answered, he seemed happy to hear from me, and even too eager for confidences. He worked a lot in the hospital, his marriage was over, his wife had left, taking the child, he was alone and eccentric. He stumbled when he talked about his sister. He said quietly: I don't have any contact with her. Political differences, differences about everything. Ever since she's been with Pasquale you can't talk to her. I asked: Did they go to live together? He broke off: Let's say that. And as if the subject seemed too frivolous, he avoided it, moved on, making harsh comments on the political situation, talking about the slaughter in Brescia, the bosses who bankrolled the parties and, as soon as things looked bad, the fascists.

I called Carmen again to reassure her. I told her that Nadia had broken with her family to be with Pasquale and that Pasquale followed her like a puppy.

"You think?" Carmen asked.

"I'm sure, love is like that."

She was skeptical. I insisted, I told her in greater detail about the afternoon they had spent at my house and I exaggerated a little about how much they loved each other. We said goodbye. But in mid-June Carmen called again, desperate. Gino had been murdered in broad daylight in front of the pharmacy, shot in the face. I thought first that she was giving me that news because the son of the pharmacist was part of our early adolescence and, fascist or not, certainly that event would upset me. But the reason was not to share with me the horror of that violent death. The carabinieri had come and searched the apartment from top to bottom, even the gas pump. They were looking for any information that might lead them to

Pasquale, and she had felt much worse than when they had come to arrest her father for the murder of Don Achille.

82.

Carmen was overwhelmed by anxiety, she wept because of what seemed to her the revival of persecution. I, on the other hand, couldn't get out of my mind the small barren square the pharmacy faced, and the shop's interior, which I had always liked for its odor of candies and syrups, the dark-wood shelves with their rows of colored jars, and, above all, Gino's parents, who were so kind, leaning out from behind the counter as if from a balcony: surely they had been there, had been startled by the sound of the shots, from there, perhaps, had watched, eyes wide, as their son fell in the doorway, had seen the blood. I wanted to talk to Lila. But she appeared completely indifferent, she dismissed the episode as one of many, she said only: Of course the carabinieri would go after Pasquale. Her voice knew how to grip me immediately, to persuade me; she emphasized that even if Pasquale had murdered Gino—which she ruled out—she would be on his side, because the carabinieri should have gone after the dead man for all the terrible things he had done, rather than our friend, a construction worker and Communist. After which, in the tone of someone who is going on to more important things, she asked if she could leave Gennaro with me until school began. Gennaro? How would I manage? I already had Dede and Elsa, who wore me out. I said:

"Why?"

"I have to work."

"I'm about to go to the beach with the girls."

"Take him, too."

"I'm going to Viareggio and staying till the end of August.

He barely knows me, he'll want you. If you come, too, that's fine, but alone I don't know."

"You swore you'd take care of him."

"Yes, but if you were ill."

"And how do you know I'm not ill?"

"Are you ill?"

"No."

"So why can't you leave him with your mother or Stefano?"

She was silent for a few seconds, she became rude.

"Will you do me this favor or not?"

I gave in immediately.

"All right, bring him here."

"Enzo will bring him."

Enzo arrived on a Saturday night in a bright white Fiat 500 that he had just bought. Merely seeing him from the window, hearing the dialect in which he said something to the boy who was still in the car—it was him, identical, the same composed gestures, the same physical compactness—gave solidity back to Naples, to the neighborhood. I opened the door with Dede hanging on my dress, and a single glance at Gennaro was enough to know that Melina, five years earlier, had seen correctly: the child, now that he was ten, showed plainly that he had in him not only nothing of Nino but nothing of Lila; he was, rather, a perfect replica of Stefano.

The observation provoked an ambiguous sentiment, a mixture of disappointment and satisfaction. I had thought that, since the boy would be with me for so long, it would be nice to have in the house, along with my daughters, a child of Nino; and yet I noted with pleasure that Nino had left Lila nothing.

83.

Enzo wanted to start off again right away, but Pietro welcomed him courteously and obliged him to stay for the night. I tried to get Gennaro to play with Dede, even if there was almost six years' difference between them, but while she was clearly eager he refused, shaking his head decisively. I was struck by the way Enzo cared for the son who wasn't his, indicating that he knew his habits, his tastes, his needs. Although Gennaro protested because he was sleepy, Enzo gently insisted that he pee and brush his teeth before going to bed, and, when the child collapsed, he delicately undressed him and put his pajamas on.

While I washed the dishes and cleaned up, Pietro entertained the guest. They were sitting at the kitchen table; they had nothing in common. They tried politics, but when my husband made a positive reference to the progressive rapprochement of the Communists and the Christian Democrats, and Enzo said that if that strategy prevailed Berlinguer would be giving a hand to the worst enemies of the working class, they ended the discussion in order to avoid a quarrel. Pietro then politely asked him about his job, and Enzo must have found his interest sincere, because he was less laconic than usual and started on a dry, perhaps slightly too technical account. IBM had just decided to send Lila and him to a bigger company, a factory near Nola that had three hundred technical workers and forty clerical employees. The financial offer had left them stunned: three hundred and fifty thousand lire a month for him, who was the department head, and a hundred thousand for her, as his assistant. They had accepted, naturally, but now they had to earn all that money, and the work to be done was really tremendous. We are responsible, he explained—and from then on he used "we"—for a System 3 Model 10, and we have at our disposal two operators and five punch-card operators, who are also checkers. We have to collect and put into the System 3 a huge quantity of information, which is necessary so that the machine can do things like—I don't know—the accounting, wages, invoicing, the warehousing, management of the salespeople, orders to suppliers, production, and shipping. For this purpose we use little cards—that is, the punch cards. The holes are everything, the effort is concentrated there. I'll give you an example of the work it takes to program a simple operation like issuing invoices. You begin with the paper invoices, on which the warehouseman has marked both the products and the client they've been delivered to. The client has a code, his personal information has a code, and so do the products. The punch-card operators sit at the machines, press a key to release the cards, then by typing on the keys reduce the bill number, the client code, the personal-data code, the product-quantity code, to holes in the cards. To help you understand, a thousand bills for ten products make ten thousand punch cards with holes like the ones a needle would make: is it clear, do you follow?

So the evening passed. Pietro every so often nodded to show that he was following and even tried to ask some questions (*The holes count but do the unperforated parts also count?*). I confined myself to a half smile while I washed and polished. Enzo appeared pleased to be able to explain to a university professor, who listened to him like a disciplined student, and an old friend who had her degree and had written a book, and now was tidying up the kitchen, things that they knew nothing about. But in truth I was quickly distracted. An operator took ten thousand cards and inserted them in a machine that was called a sorter. The machine put them in order according to the product code. Then there were two readers, not in the sense of people but in the sense of machines programmed to read the holes and the non-holes in the cards. And then? There I got lost. I got lost amid codes and the enormous packets of cards and the holes that compared holes, that sorted holes, that read holes, that did the four operations, that printed names, addresses, totals. I got lost following a word I'd never heard before, *file*, which Enzo kept using, pronouncing it *fi-le,* this *file*, that *file*, continually. I got lost following Lila, who knew everything about those words, those machines, that work, and was doing that work now in a big company in Nola, even if with the salary her companion was earning she could be more of a lady than me. I got lost following Enzo, who could say proudly: *Without her I wouldn't be able to do it.* Thus he conveyed to us his love and devotion, and it was clear that he liked to remind himself and others of the extraordinary quality of his woman, whereas my husband never praised me but, rather, reduced me to the mother of his children; even though I had had an education he did not want me to be capable of independent thought, he demeaned me by demeaning what I read, what interested me, what I said, and he appeared willing to love me only provided that I continually demonstrate my nothingness.

Finally I, too, sat down at the table, depressed because neither of the two had made a move to say: Can we help you set the table, clear, wash the dishes, sweep the floor. An invoice, Enzo was saying, is a simple document, what does it take to do by hand? Nothing, if I have to create ten a day. But if I have to do a thousand? The readers read two hundred cards a minute, so two thousand in ten minutes, and ten thousand in fifty. The speed of the machine is an enormous advantage, especially if it's enabled to do complex operations, which require a lot of time. And that's what Lila's and my work is: to prepare the System 3 to do complex operations. The development phases of the programs are really wonderful. The operational phases a little less. The cards often jam and break in the sorters. Very often a container in which the cards have just been sorted falls and the cards scatter on the floor. But it's great, it's great even then.

Just to feel that I was present, I interrupted, saying: "Can he make a mistake?"

"He who?"

"The computer."

"There's no he, Lenù, he is me. If he makes a mistake, if he gets in trouble, I've made a mistake, I've gotten in trouble."

"Oh," I said, and then, "I'm tired."

Pietro nodded in agreement and seemed ready to end the evening. He turned to Enzo:

"It's certainly exciting, but if it's as you say, these machines will take the place of men, and skills will disappear; at Fiat robots already do the welding. A lot of jobs will be lost."

Enzo at first agreed, then he seemed to have second thoughts, and finally he resorted to the only person whose authority he credited:

"Lina says it's all a good thing: humiliating and stultifying jobs should disappear."

Lina, Lina, Lina. I asked teasingly: if Lina is so good, why do they give you three hundred and fifty thousand lire and her a hundred thousand, why are you the boss and she's the assistant? Enzo hesitated again, he seemed on the point of saying something pressing, which he then decided to abandon. He mumbled: What do you want from me, private ownership of the means of production should be abolished. In the kitchen the hum of the refrigerator could be heard for a few seconds. Pietro stood up and said: Let's go to bed.

84.

Enzo wanted to leave by six, but already at four in the morning I heard him moving in his room and I got up to make him some coffee. In private, in the silent house, the language of computers disappeared, along with the Italian suited to Pietro's position, and we moved to dialect. I asked about his relationship with Lila. He said it was good, even though she never sat still. Now she was chasing after work problems, now she was squabbling with her mother, her father, her brother, now she was helping Gennaro with his homework and, one way or another, she ended up helping Rino's children, too, and all the children who happened to be around. Lila didn't look after herself, and so she was overworked, she always seemed close to collapse, as she once had; she was tired. I quickly understood that their harmony as a couple, working side by side, blessed by good salaries, should be set within a more complicated sequence. I ventured:

"Maybe the two of you have to impose some order: Lina shouldn't get overtired."

"I tell her that constantly."

"And then there's the separation, divorce: it makes no sense for her to stay married to Stefano."

"She doesn't give a damn about that."

"But Stefano?"

"He doesn't even know that you can divorce now."

"And Ada?"

"Ada has survival problems. The wheel turns, those who were on top end up on the bottom. The Carraccis don't have even a lira left, only debts with the Solaras, and Ada is taking care to get what she can before it's too late."

"And you? You don't want to get married?"

It was clear that he would happily get married, but Lila was against it. Not only did she not want to waste time with divorce—who cares if I'm still married to him, I'm with you, I sleep with you, that's the essential—but the mere idea of another wedding made her laugh. She said: You and I? You and I get married? Why, we're fine like this, and as soon as we get fed up with each other we go our own way. The prospect of another marriage didn't interest Lila, she had other things to think about.

"What?"

"Forget it."

"Tell me."

"She never talked to you about it?"

"What?"

"Michele Solara."

He told me in brief, tense phrases that in all these years Michele had never stopped asking Lila to work for him. He had proposed that she manage a new shop on the Vomero. Or the accounting and the taxes. Or be a secretary for a friend of his, an important Christian Democratic politician. He had even gone so far as to offer her a salary of two hundred thousand lire a month just to invent things, crazy notions, anything that came into her head. Even though he lived on Posillipo, he still kept the headquarters of all his businesses in the neighborhood, at his mother and father's house. So Lila found him around her constantly, on the street, in the market, in the shops. He stopped her, always very friendly, he joked with Gennaro, gave him little gifts. Then he became very serious, and even when she refused the jobs he offered, he wasn't impatient, he said goodbye, joking as usual: I'm not giving up, I'll wait for you for eternity, call me when you want and I'll come running. Until he found out she was working for IBM. That had angered him, and he had gone so far as to get people he knew to remove Enzo from the market for consultants, and hence Lila, too. He hadn't had any success, IBM urgently needed technicians and there weren't many good technicians like Enzo and Lila. But the climate had changed. Enzo had found Gino's fascists outside the house and he escaped because he managed to reach the front door in time and lock it behind him. But shortly afterward an alarming thing had happened to Gennaro. Lila's mother had gone to pick him up at school as usual. All the students had come out and the child was nowhere to be seen. The teacher: He was here a minute ago. His classmates: He was here and then he disappeared.

Nunzia, terribly frightened, had called her daughter at work; Lila returned right away and went to look for Gennaro. She found him on a bench in the gardens. The child was sitting quietly, with his smock, his ribbon, his schoolbag, and he laughed at the questions—where did you go, what did you do—with expressionless eyes. She wanted to go and kill Michele right away, both for the attempted beating of Enzo and the kidnapping of her son, but Enzo restrained her. The fascists now went after anyone on the left and there was no proof that it was Michele who ordered the kidnapping. As for Gennaro, he himself had admitted that his brief absence was only an act of disobedience. In any case, once Lila calmed down, Enzo had decided on his own to go and talk to Michele. He had showed up at the Bar Solara and Michele had listened without batting an eye. Then he had said, more or less: I don't know what the fuck you're talking about, Enzù: I'm fond of Gennaro, anyone who touches him is dead, but among all the foolish things you've said the only true thing is that Lina is smart and it's a pity that she's wasting her intelligence, I've been asking her to work with me for years. Then he continued: That irritates you? Who gives a damn. But you're wrong, if you love her you should encourage her to use her capabilities. Come here, sit down, have a coffee and a pastry, tell me what those computers of yours do. And it hadn't ended there. They had met two or three times, by chance, and Michele had demonstrated increasing interest in the System 3. One day he even said, amused, that he had asked someone at IBM who was smarter, him or Lila, and that person had said that Enzo was certainly smart, but the best in the business was Lila. After that, he had stopped her on the street again and made her a significant offer. He intended to rent the System 3 and use it in all his commercial activities. Result: he wanted her as the chief technician, at four hundred thousand lire a month.

"She didn't even tell you that?" Enzo asked me warily.

"No."

"You see she didn't want to bother you, you have your life. but you understand that for her personally it would be a significant step up, and for the two of us it would be a fortune: we'd have seven hundred and fifty thousand lire a month altogether, I don't know if that's clear."

"But Lina?"

"She has to answer by September."

"And what will she do?"

"I don't know. Have you ever been able to figure out what's in her mind ahead of time?"

"No. But what do you think she should do?"

"I think what she thinks."

"Even if you don't agree?"

"Even then."

I went out to the car with him. On the stairs it occurred to me that maybe I should tell him what he surely didn't know, that Michele harbored for Lila a love like a spiderweb, a dangerous love that had nothing to do with physical possession or even with a loyal subservience. And I was about to do it, I was fond of him, I didn't want him to believe that he was merely dealing with a quasi-camorrist who had been planning for a long time to buy the intelligence of this woman. When he was already behind the wheel I asked him:

"And if Michele wants to sleep with her?"

He was impassive.

"I'll kill him. But anyway he doesn't want her, he already has a lover and everybody knows it."

"Who's that?"

"Marisa, he's got her pregnant again."

For a moment it seemed to me that I hadn't understood.

"Marisa Sarratore?"

"Marisa, the wife of Alfonso."

I recalled my conversation with my schoolmate. He had

tried to tell me how complicated his life was and I had retreated, struck more by the surface of his revelation than by the substance. And to me his uneasiness seemed confused—to get things straight I would have had to talk to him again, and maybe not even then would I have understood—and yet it pierced me unpleasantly, painfully. I asked:

"And Alfonso?"

"He doesn't give a damn, they say he's a fag."

"Who says?"

"Everyone."

"Everyone is very general, Enzo. What else does everyone say?"

He looked at me with a flash of conspiratorial irony:

"A lot of things, the neighborhood is always gossiping."

"Like?"

"Old stories have come back to the surface. They say it was the mother of the Solaras who murdered Don Achille."

He left, and I hoped he would take away his words, too. But what I had learned stayed with me, worried me, made me angry. In an attempt to get rid of it I went to the telephone and talked to Lila, mixing anxieties and reproaches: Why didn't you say anything about Michele's job offers, especially the last one; why did you tell Alfonso's secret; why did you start that story about the mother of the Solaras, it was a game of ours; why did you send me Gennaro, are you worried about him, tell me plainly, I have the right to know; why, once and for all, don't you tell me what's really in your mind? It was an outburst, but, sentence by sentence, deep inside myself, I hoped that we wouldn't stop there, that the old desire to confront our entire relationship and re-examine it, to elucidate and have full consciousness of it, would be realized. I hoped to provoke her and draw her in to other, increasingly personal questions. But Lila was annoyed, she treated me coldly, she wasn't in a good mood. She answered that I had been gone for years, that I now had a life in which the Solaras, Stefano, Marisa, Alfonso meant nothing, counted for less than zero. Go on vacation, she said, abruptly, write, act the intellectual, here we've remained too crude for you, stay away; and please, make Gennaro get some sun, otherwise he'll come home stunted like his father.

The sarcasm in her voice, the belittling, almost rude tone, removed any weight from Enzo's story and eliminated any possibility of drawing her into the books I was reading, the vocabulary I had learned from Mariarosa and the Florentine women, the questions that I was trying to ask myself and that, once I had provided her with the basic concepts, she would surely know how to take on better than all of us. But yes, I thought, I'll mind my own business and you mind yours: if you like, don't grow up, go on playing in the courtyard even now that you're about to turn thirty; I've had enough, I'm going to the beach. And so I did.

85.

Pietro took the three children and me in the car to an ugly house in Viareggio that we had rented, then he returned to Florence to try to finish his book. Look, I said to myself, now I'm a vacationer, a well-off lady with three children and a pile of toys, a beach umbrella in the front row, soft towels, plenty to eat, five bikinis in different colors, menthol cigarettes, the sun that darkens my skin and makes me even blonder. I called Pietro and Lila every night. Pietro reported on people who had called for me, remnants of a distant time, and, more rarely, talked about some hypothesis having to do with his work that had just come to mind. I handed Lila to Gennaro, who reluctantly recounted what he considered important events of his day and said good night. I said almost nothing to either one or the other. Lila especially seemed reduced to voice alone.

But I realized after a while that it wasn't exactly so: part of her existed in flesh and blood in Gennaro. The boy was certainly very like Stefano and didn't resemble Lila at all. Yet his gestures, the way he talked, some words, certain interjections, a kind of aggressiveness were those of Lila as a child. So sometimes if I was distracted I jumped at hearing his voice, or was spellbound as I observed him gesticulating, explaining a game to Dede.

Unlike his mother, however, Gennaro was devious. Lila's meanness when she was a child had always been explicit, no punishment ever drove her to hide it. Gennaro, on the other hand, played the role of the well-brought-up, even timid child, but as soon as I turned my back he teased Dede, he hid her doll, he hit her. When I threatened him, saying that as a punishment we wouldn't call his mamma to say good night he assumed a contrite expression. In reality, that possible punishment didn't worry him at all; the ritual of the evening phone call had been established by me, and he could easily do without it. What worried him, rather, was the threat that I wouldn't buy him ice cream. Then he began to cry; between his sobs he said he wanted to go back to Naples, and I immediately gave in. But that didn't soothe him. He took revenge on me by secretly being mean to Dede.

I was sure that she feared him, hated him. But no. As time passed, she responded less and less to Gennaro's harassments: she fell in love with him. She called him Rino or Rinuccio, because he had told her that was what his friends called him, and she followed him, paying no attention to my commands, in fact it was she who urged him to wander away from our umbrella. My day was made up of shouting: Dede where are you going, Gennaro come here, Elsa what are you doing, don't put sand in your mouth, Gennaro stop it, Dede if you don't stop it I'm coming over and we'll see. A pointless struggle: Elsa ate sand no matter what and, no matter what, Dede and Gennaro disappeared.

Their refuge was a nearby expanse of reeds. Once I went with Elsa to see what they were up to and discovered that they had taken off their bathing suits and Dede was touching, with fascination, the erect penis that Gennaro was showing her. I stopped a short distance away, I didn't know what to do. Dede—I knew, I had seen her—often masturbated lying on her stomach. But I had read a lot about infant sexuality—I had even bought for my daughter a little book of colored illustrations that explained in very short sentences what happened between man and woman, words I had read her but which aroused no interest—and, although I felt uneasy, I had not only forced myself not to stop her, not to reproach her, but, assuming that her father would, I had been careful to keep him from surprising her.

Now, though? Should I let them play together? Should I retreat, slip away? Or approach without giving the thing any importance, talk nonchalantly about something else? And if that violent boy, much bigger than Dede, forced on her who knows what, hurt her? Wasn't the difference in age a danger? Two things precipitated the situation: Elsa saw her sister, shouted with joy, calling her name; and at the same time I heard the dialect words that Gennaro was saying to Dede, coarse words, the same horribly vulgar words I had learned as a child in the courtyard. I couldn't control myself, everything I had read about pleasures, latencies, neurosis, polymorphous perversions of children and women vanished, and I scolded the two severely, especially Gennaro, whom I seized by the arm and dragged away. He burst into tears, and Dede said to me coldly, fearless: You're very mean.

I bought them both ice cream, but a period began in which a certain alarm at how Dede's language was absorbing obscene words of Neapolitan dialect was added to a wary supervision, intended to keep the episode from being repeated. At night, while the children slept, I got into the habit of making an effort to remember: had I played games like that with my friends in the courtyard? And had Lila had experiences of that type? We had never talked about it. At the time we had uttered repulsive words, certainly, but they were insults that served, among other things, to ward off the hands of obscene adults, bad words that we shouted as we fled. For the rest? With difficulty I reached the point of asking myself: had she and I ever touched each other? Had I ever wished to, as a child, as a girl, as an adult? And her? I hovered on the edge of those questions for a long time. I answered slowly: I don't know, I don't want to know. And then I admitted that there had been a kind of admiration for her body, maybe that, yes, but I ruled out anything ever happening between us. Too much fear, if we had been seen we would have been beaten to death.

In any case, on the days when I faced that problem, I avoided taking Gennaro to the public phone. I was afraid he would tell Lila that he didn't like being with me anymore, that he would even tell her what had happened. That fear annoyed me: why should I be concerned? I let it all fade. Even my vigilance toward the two children slowly diminished, I couldn't oversee them continuously. I devoted myself to Elsa, I forgot about them. I shouted nervously from the shore, towels ready, only if, despite purple lips and wrinkled fingertips, they wouldn't get out of the water.

The days of August slipped away. House, shopping, preparing the overflowing beach bags, beach, home again, dinner, ice cream, phone call. I chatted with other mothers, all older than me, and I was pleased if they praised *my* children, and my patience. They talked about husbands, about the husbands' jobs. I talked about mine, I said: He's a Latin professor at the university. On the weekend Pietro arrived, just as, years earlier, on Ischia, Stefano and Rino had. My acquaintances shot him respectful looks and seemed to appreciate, thanks to his professorship, even his bushy hair. He went swimming with the girls and Gennaro, he drew them into make-believe dangerous adventures that they all hugely enjoyed, then he sat studying under the umbrella, complaining from time to time about his lack of sleep—he often forgot the sleeping pills. In the kitchen, when the children were sleeping, we had sex standing up to avoid the creaking of the bed. Marriage by now seemed to me an institution that, contrary to what one might think, stripped coitus of all humanity.

86.

It was Pietro who, one Saturday, picked out, in the crowd of headlines that for days had been devoted to the 'fascists' bombing of the Italicus express train, a brief news item in the *Corriere della Sera* that concerned a small factory on the out-skirts of Naples.

"Wasn't Soccavo the name of the company where your friend worked?" he asked me.

"What happened?"

He handed me the paper. A commando group made up of two men and a woman had burst into a sausage factory on the outskirts of Naples. The three had first shot the legs of the guard, Filippo Cara, who was in very serious condition; then they had gone up to the office of the owner, Bruno Soccavo, a young Neapolitan entrepreneur, and had killed him with four shots, three to the chest and one to the head. I saw, as I read, Bruno's face ruined, shattered, along with his gleaming white teeth. Oh God, God, I was stunned. I left the children with Pietro, I rushed to telephone Lila, the phone rang for a long time with no answer. I tried again in the evening, nothing. I got her the next day, she asked me in alarm: What's the matter, is Gennaro ill? I reassured her, then told her about Bruno. She knew nothing about it, she let me speak, finally she said tonelessly: This is really bad news you're giving me. And nothing else. I goaded her: Telephone someone, find out, ask where I can send a telegram of condolence. She said she no longer had any contact with anyone at the factory. What telegram, she muttered, forget it.

I forgot it. But the next day I found in *Il Manifesto* an article signed by Giovanni Sarratore, that is, Nino, which had a lot of information about the small Campanian business, underlining the political tensions present in those backward places, and referring affectionately to Bruno and his tragic end. I followed the development of the news for days, but to no purpose: it soon disappeared from the papers. Besides, Lila refused to talk about it. At night I called her with the children and she cut me off, saying, Give me Gennaro. She became especially irritated when I quoted Nino to her. Typical of him, she grumbled. He always has to interfere: What does politics have to do with it, there must be other matters, here people are murdered for a thousand reasons, adultery, criminal activity, even just one too many looks. So the days passed and of Bruno there remained an image and that was all. It wasn't the image of the factory owner I had threated on the phone using the authority of the Airotas but that of the boy who had tried to kiss me and whom I had rudely rejected.

87.

I began to have some ugly thoughts on the beach. Lila, I said to myself, deliberately pushes away emotions, feelings. The more I sought tools to try to explain myself to myself, the more she, on the contrary, hid. The more I tried to draw her into the open and involve her in my desire to clarify, the more she took refuge in the shadows. She was like the full moon when it crouches behind the forest and the branches scribble on its face.

In early September I returned to Florence, but the ugly thoughts rather than dissolving grew stronger. Useless to try to talk to Pietro. He was unhappy about the children's and my return, he was late with his book and the idea that the academic year would soon begin made him short-tempered. One night when, at the table, Dede and Gennaro were quarreling about something or other he jumped up suddenly and left the kitchen, slamming the door so violently that the frosted glass shattered. I called Lila, I told her straight off that she had to take her child back, he'd been living with me for a month and a half.

"You can't keep him till the end of the month?"

"No."

"It's bad here."

"Here, too."

Enzo left in the middle of the night and arrived in the morning, when Pietro was at work. I had already packed Gennaro's bag. I explained to him that the tensions between the children had become unbearable, I was sorry but three was too many, I couldn't handle it anymore. He said he understood, he thanked me for all I had done. He said only, by way of apology: You know what Lina is like. I didn't answer, because Dede was yelling, desperate at Gennaro's departure, and because, if I had, I might have said—beginning precisely with what Lila was like—things I would later regret.

I had in my head thoughts I didn't want to formulate even to myself; I was afraid that the facts would magically fit the words. But I couldn't cancel out the sentences; in my mind I heard their syntax all ready, and I was frightened by it, fascinated, horrified, seduced. I had trained myself to find an order by establishing connections between distant elements, but here it had got out of hand. I had added Gino's violent death to Bruno Soccavo's (Filippo, the factory guard, had survived). And I had arrived at the idea that each of these events led to Pasquale, maybe also to Nadia. This hypothesis was extremely distressing. I had thought of telephoning Carmen, to ask if she had news of her brother; then I changed my mind, frightened by the possibility that her telephone was bugged. When Enzo came to get Gennaro I said to myself: Now I'll talk to him about it, let's see how he responds. But then, too, I had said nothing, out of fear of saying too much, out of fear of uttering the name of the figure who was behind Pasquale and Nadia: Lila, that is. Lila, as usual: Lila who doesn't say things, she does them; Lila who is steeped in the culture of the neighborhood and takes no account of police, the law, the state, but believes there are problems that can be resolved only with the shoemaker's knife; Lila who knows the horror of inequality; Lila who, at the time of the collective of Via dei Tribunali, found in revolutionary theory and action a way of applying her hyperactive mind; Lila who has transformed into political objectives her rages old and new; Lila who moves people like characters in a story; Lila who has connected, is connecting, our personal knowledge of poverty and abuse to the armed struggle against the fascists, against the owners, against capital. I admit it here, openly, for the first time: in those September days I suspected that not only Pasquale—Pasquale driven by his history toward the necessity of taking up arms—not only Nadia, but Lila herself had spilled that blood. For a long time, while I cooked, while I took care of my daughters, I saw her, with the other two, shoot Gino, shoot Filippo, shoot Bruno Soccavo. And if I had trouble imagining Pasquale and Nadia in every detail—I considered him a good boy, something of a braggart, capable of fierce fighting but of murder no; she seemed to me a respectable girl who could wound at most with verbal treachery—about Lila I had never had doubts: she would know how to devise the most effective plan, she would reduce the risks to a minimum, she would keep fear under control, she would be able to give murderous intentions an abstract purity, she knew how to remove human substance from bodies and blood, she would have no scruples and no remorse, she would kill and feel that she was in the right.

So there she was, clear and bright, along with the shadow of Pasquale, of Nadia, of who knows what others. They drove through the piazza in a car and, slowing down in front of the pharmacy, fired at Gino, at his thug's body in the white smock. Or they drove along the dusty road to the Soccavo factory, garbage of every type piled up on either side. Pasquale went through the gate, shot Filippo's legs, the blood spread through the guard booth, screams, terrified eyes. Lila, who knew the way well, crossed the courtyard, entered the factory, climbed the stairs, burst into Bruno's office, and, just as he said cheerfully: Hi, what in the world are you doing around here, fired three shots at his chest and one at his face.

Ah yes, militant anti-fascism, new resistance, proletarian justice, and other formulas to which she, who instinctively knew how to avoid rehashing clichés, was surely able to give depth. I imagined that those actions were necessary in order to join, I don't know, the Red Brigades, Prima Linea, Nuclei Armati Proletari. Lila would disappear from the neighborhood as Pasquale had. Maybe that's why she had tried to leave Gennaro with me, apparently for a month, in reality intending to give him to me forever. We would never see each other again. Or she would be arrested, like the leaders of the Red Brigades, Curcio and Franceschini. Or she would evade every policeman and prison, imaginative and bold as she was. And when the *big thing* was accomplished, she would reappear triumphant, admired for her achievements, in the guise of a revolutionary leader, to tell me: You wanted to write novels, I created a novel with real people, with real blood, in reality.

At night every imagining seemed a thing that had happened or was still happening, and I was afraid for her, I saw her cap-

tured, wounded, like so many women and men in the chaos of
the world, and I felt pity for her, but I also envied her. The
childish conviction that she had always been destined for
extraordinary things was magnified. And I regretted that I had
left Naples, detached myself from her, the need to be near her
returned. But I was also angry that she had set out on that road
without consulting me, as if she hadn't considered me up to it.
And yet I knew a lot about capital, exploitation, class struggle,
the inevitability of the proletarian revolution. I could have
been useful, participated. And I was unhappy. I lay in bed, discontent with my situation as a mother, a married woman, the
whole future debased by the repetition of domestic rituals in
the kitchen, in the marriage bed.

By day I felt more lucid, and the horror prevailed. I imagined a capricious Lila who provoked hatred deliberately and in
the end found herself more deeply involved in violent acts.
Certainly she had had the courage to push ahead, to take the
lead with the crystalline determination, the generous cruelty of
one who is spurred by just reasons. But with what purpose? To
start a civil war? Transform the neighborhood, Naples, Italy
into a battlefield, a Vietnam in the Mediterranean? Hurl us all
into a pitiless, interminable conflict, squeezed between the
Eastern bloc and the Western? Encourage its fiery spread
throughout Europe, throughout the entire planet? Until victory, always? What victory? Cities destroyed, fire, the dead in
the streets, the shame of violent clashes not only with the class
enemy but also within the front itself, among the revolutionary
groups of various regions and with various motivations, all in
the name of the proletariat and its dictatorship. Maybe even
nuclear war.

I closed my eyes in terror. The children, the future. And I
hung on to formulas: the unpredictable subject, the destructive
logic of patriarchy, the feminine value of survival, compassion.
I have to talk to Lila, I said to myself. She has to tell me every-

thing she's doing, what she plans, so that I can decide whether to be her accomplice or not.

But I never called nor did she call me. I was convinced that the long voice thread that had been our only contact for years hadn't helped us. We had maintained the bond between our two stories, but by subtraction. We had become for each other abstract entities, so that now I could invent her for myself both as an expert in computers and as a determined and implacable urban guerrilla, while she, in all likelihood, could see me both as the stereotype of the successful intellectual and as a cultured and well-off woman, all children, books, and highbrow conversation with an academic husband. We both needed new depth, body, and yet we were distant and couldn't give it to each other.

88.

Thus September passed, then October. I didn't talk to anyone, not even Adele, who had a lot of work, or even Mariarosa, who had brought Franco to her house—an invalid Franco, in need of help, changed by depression—and who greeted me warmly, promised to say hello to him for me, but then broke off because she had too many things to do. Not to mention Pietro's muteness. The world outside books burdened him increasingly, he went reluctantly into the regulated chaos of the university, and often said he was ill. He said he did it in order to work, but he couldn't get to the end of his book, he rarely went into his study, and, as if to forgive himself and be forgiven, he took care of Elsa, cooked, swept, washed, ironed. I had to treat him rudely to get him to go back to teaching, but I immediately regretted it. Ever since the violence had struck people I knew, I was afraid for him. He had never given in, even though he got into dangerous situations, opposing publicly what, in a term that he preferred, he called the load of nonsense of his students and many of his colleagues. Although I was worried about him, in fact maybe just because I was worried, I never admitted he was right. I hoped that if I criticized him he would understand, would stop his reactionary reformism (I used that phrase), become more flexible. But, in his eyes, that drove me yet again to the side of the students who were attacking him, the professors who were plotting against him.

It wasn't like that, the situation was more complicated. On the one hand I vaguely wanted to protect him, on the other I wanted to be on Lila's side, defend the choices I secretly attributed to her. To the point where every so often I thought of telephoning her and, starting with Pietro, with our conflicts, get her to tell me what she thought about it and, step by step, bring her out into the open. I didn't to it, naturally, it was absurd to expect sincerity on these subjects on the phone. But one night she called me, sounding really happy.

"I have some good news."

"What's happening?"

"I'm the head of technology."

"In what sense?"

"Head of the IBM data-processing center that Michele rented."

It seemed incredible to me. I asked her to repeat it, to explain carefully. She had accepted Solara's proposal? After so much resistance she had gone back to working for him, as in the days of Piazza dei Martiri? She said yes, enthusiastically, and became more and more excited, more explicit: Michele had entrusted to her the System 3 that he had rented and placed in a shoe warehouse in Acerra; she would employ operators and punch-card workers; the salary was four hundred and twenty-five thousand lire a month.

I was disappointed. Not only had the image of the guerrilla

vanished in an instant but everything I thought I knew of Lila wavered. I said:

"It's the last thing I would have expected of you."

"What was I supposed to do?"

"Refuse."

"Why?"

"We know what the Solaras are."

"And so what? It's already happened, and I'm better off working for Michele than for that shit Soccavo."

"Do as you like."

I heard her breathing. She said:

"I don't like that tone, Lenù. I'm paid more than Enzo, who is a man: What's wrong with that?"

"Nothing."

"The revolution, the workers, the new world, and that other bullshit?"

"Stop it. If you've unexpectedly decided to make a truthful speech I'm listening, otherwise let's forget it."

"May I point out something? You always use *true* and *truthfully*, when you speak and when you write. Or you say: *unexpectedly*. But when do people ever speak *truthfully* and when do things ever happen *unexpectedly*? You know better than I that it's all a fraud and that one thing follows another and then another. I don't do anything *truthfully* anymore, Lenù. And I've learned to pay attention to things. Only idiots believe that they happen *unexpectedly*."

"Bravo. What do you want me to believe, that you have everything under control, that it's you who are using Michele and not Michele you? Let's forget it, come on. Bye."

"No, speak, say what you have to say."

"I have nothing to say."

"Speak, otherwise I will."

"Then speak, let me listen."

"You criticize me but you say nothing to your sister?"

I was astonished.

"What does my sister have to do with anything?"

"You don't know anything about Elisa?"

"What should I know?"

She laughed maliciously.

"Ask your mother, your father, and your brothers."

89.

She wouldn't say anything else, she hung up, furious. I anxiously called my parents' house, my mother answered.

"Every so often you remember we exist," she said.

"Ma, what's happening to Elisa?"

"What happens to girls today."

"What?"

"She's with someone."

"She's engaged?"

"Let's put it like that."

"Who is she with?"

The answer went right through my heart.

"Marcello Solara."

That's what Lila wanted me to know. Marcello, the handsome Marcello of our early adolescence, her stubborn, desperate admirer, the young man she had humiliated by marrying Stefano Carracci, had taken my sister Elisa, the youngest of the family, my good little sister, the woman whom I still thought of as a magical child. And Elisa had let herself be taken. And my parents and my brothers had not lifted a finger to stop him. And my whole family, and in some way I myself, would end up related to the Solaras.

"Since when?" I asked.

"How do I know, a year."

"And you two gave your consent?"

"Did you ask our consent? You did as you liked. And she did the same thing."

"Pietro isn't Marcello Solara."

"You're right: Marcello would never let himself be treated by Elisa the way Pietro is treated by you."

Silence.

"You could have told me, you could have consulted me."

"Why? You left. 'I'll take care of you, don't worry.' Hardly. You've only thought of your own affairs, you didn't give a damn about us."

I decided to leave immediately for Naples with the children. I wanted to go by train, but Pietro volunteered to drive us, passing off as kindness the fact that he didn't want to work. As soon as we came down from the Doganella and were in the chaotic traffic of Naples, I felt gripped by the city, ruled by its unwritten laws. I hadn't set foot there since the day I left to get married. The noise seemed unbearable, I was irritated by the constant honking, by the insults the drivers shouted at Pietro when, not knowing the way, he hesitated, slowed down. A little before Piazza Carlo III I made him pull over. I got into the driver's seat, and drove aggressively to Via Firenze, to the same hotel he had stayed in years before. We left our bags. I carefully dressed the two girls and myself. Then we went to the neighborhood, to my parents' house. What did I think I could do, impose on Elisa my authority as the older sister, a university graduate, well married? Persuade her to break her engagement? Tell her: I've known Marcello since he grabbed my wrist and tried to pull me into the Fiat 1100, breaking Mamma's silver bracelet, so trust me, he's a vulgar, violent man? Yes. I felt determined, my job was to pull Elisa out of that trap.

My mother greeted Pietro affectionately and, in turn—*This is for Dede from Grandma, this is for Elsa*—she gave the two girls many small gifts that, in different ways, excited them. My father's voice was hoarse with emotion, he seemed thinner, even more subservient. I waited for my brothers to appear, but I discovered that they weren't home.

"They're always at work," my father said without enthusiasm.

"What do they do?"

"They work," my mother broke in.

"Where?"

"Marcello arranged jobs for them."

I remembered how the Solaras had *arranged a job* for Antonio, what they had made him into.

"Doing what?" I asked.

My mother answered in irritation:

"They bring money home and that's enough. Elisa isn't like you, Lenù, Elisa thinks of all of us."

I pretended not to hear: "Did you tell her I was coming today? Where is she?"

My father lowered his gaze, my mother said curtly: "At her house."

I became angry: "She doesn't live here anymore?"

"No."

"Since when?"

"Almost two months. She and Marcello have a nice apartment in the new neighborhood," my mother said coldly.

90.

He was more than just a boyfriend, then. I wanted to go to Elisa's house right away, even though my mother kept saying: What are you doing, your sister is preparing a surprise for you, stay here, we'll all go together later. I paid no attention. I telephoned Elisa, she answered happily and yet embarrassed. I said: Wait for me, I'm coming. I left Pietro and the girls with my parents and set off on foot.

The neighborhood seemed to me more run-down: the build-

ings dilapidated, the streets and sidewalks full of holes, littered
with garbage. From black-edged posters that carpeted the
walls—I had never seen so many—I learned that the old man
Ugo Solara, Marcello and Michele's grandfather, had died. As
the date attested, the event wasn't recent—it went back at least
two months—and the high-flown phrases, the faces of grieving
Madonnas, the very name of the dead man were faded,
smudged. Yet the death notices persisted on the streets as if the
other dead, out of respect, had decided to disappear from the
world without letting anyone know. I saw several even at the
entrance to Stefano's grocery. The shop was open, but it
seemed to me a hole in the wall, dark, deserted, and Carracci
appeared in the back, in his white smock, and disappeared like
a ghost.

I climbed up toward the railroad, passing what we used to
call the new grocery. The lowered shutter, partly off its tracks,
was rusty and defaced by obscene words and drawings. That
whole part of the neighborhood appeared abandoned, the
shiny white of long ago had turned gray, the plaster had flaked
off in places, revealing the bricks. I walked by the building
where Lila had lived. Few of the stunted trees had survived.
Packing tape held together the crack in the glass of the front
door. Elisa lived farther on, in a better maintained area, more
pretentious. The porter, a small bald man with a thin mustache, appeared, and stopped me, asking with hostility who I
was looking for. I didn't know what to say. I muttered, Solara.
He became deferential and let me go.

Only in the elevator did I realize that my entire self had in a
sense slid backward. What would have seemed to me acceptable in Milan or Florence—a woman's freedom to dispose of
her own body and her own desires, living with someone outside
of marriage—there in the neighborhood seemed inconceivable:
at stake was my sister's future, I couldn't control myself. Elisa
had set up house with a dangerous person like Marcello? And

my mother was pleased? She who had been enraged because I was married in a civil and not a religious ceremony; she who considered Lila a whore because she lived with Enzo, and Ada a prostitute because she had become Stefano's lover: *she* allowed her young daughter to sleep with Marcello Solara—a bad person—outside of marriage? I had thoughts of that sort as I went up to Elisa's, and a rage that I felt was justified. But my mind—my disciplined mind—was confused, I didn't know what arguments I would resort to. Those my mother would have asserted until a few years before, if I had made such a choice? Would I therefore regress to a level that she had left behind? Or should I say: Go and live with whoever you like but not with Marcello Solara? Should I say that? But what girl, today, in Florence, in Milan, would I ever force to leave a man, whoever he was, if she was in love with him?

When Elisa opened the door, I hugged her so hard that she said, laughing: You're hurting me. I felt her alarm as she invited me to sit down in the living room—a showy room full of flowered sofas and chairs with gilded backs—and began to speak quickly, but of other things: how well I looked, what pretty earrings I was wearing, what a nice necklace, how chic I was, she was so eager to meet Dede and Elsa. I described her nieces in detail, I took off my earrings, made her try them at the mirror, gave them to her. I saw her brighten; she laughed and said:

"I was afraid you'd come to scold me, to say you were opposed to my relationship with Marcello."

I stared at her for a long moment, I said:

"Elisa, I *am* opposed to it. And I made this trip purposely to tell you, Mamma, Papa, and our brothers."

Her expression changed; her eyes filled with tears.

"Now you're upsetting me: why are you against it?"

"The Solaras are terrible people."

"Not Marcello."

She began to tell me about him. She said it had started when I was pregnant with Elsa. Our mother had left to stay with me and she had found all the weight of the family on her. Once when she had gone to do the shopping at the Solaras' supermarket, Rino, Lila's brother, had said that if she left the list of what she needed he would have it delivered. And while Rino was talking, she noticed that Marcello gave her a nod of greeting as if to let her know that that order had been given by him. From then on he had begun to hang around, doing kind things for her. Elisa had said to herself: He's old, I don't like him. But he had become increasingly present in her life, always courteous, there hadn't been a word or a gesture that recalled the hateful side of the Solaras. Marcello was really a respectable person, with him she felt safe, he had a strength, an authority, that made him seem ten meters tall. Not only that. From the moment it became clear that he was interested in her, Elisa's life had changed. Everyone, in the neighborhood and outside it, had begun to treat her like a queen, everyone had begun to consider her important. It was a wonderful feeling, she wasn't yet used to it. Before, she said, you're nobody, and right afterward even the mice in the sewer grates know you: of course, you've written a book, you're famous, you're used to it, but I'm not, I was astonished. It had been thrilling to discover that she didn't have to worry about anything. Marcello took care of it all, every desire of hers was a command for him. So as time passed she fell in love. In the end she had said yes. And now if a day went by and she didn't see or hear from him, she was awake all night crying.

Elisa was convinced that she had had an unimaginable stroke of luck and I knew that I wouldn't have the strength to spoil all that happiness. Especially since she didn't offer me any opportunity: Marcello was capable, Marcello was responsible, Marcello was handsome, Marcello was perfect. With every word she uttered she was careful either to keep him separate from the Solara family or to speak with cautious liking for

324 · ELENA FERRANTE

his mother, or his father, who had a stomach disease, and almost never left the house, or of the deceased grandfather, sometimes even of Michele, who, if you spent time with him, also seemed different from the way people judged him; he was very affectionate. So believe me, she said, I've never been so happy since I was born, and even Mamma, and you know what she's like, is on my side, even Papa, and Gianni and Peppe, who until a short time ago spent their days doing nothing, now Marcello employs them, paying them really well.

"If that's really the way things are, get married," I said.

"We will. But now isn't a good time, Marcello says he has to settle some complicated business affairs. And then there's the mourning for his grandfather, poor man, he lost his mind, he couldn't remember how to walk, or even how to speak, by taking him God set him free. But as soon as things calm down we'll get married, don't worry. And then, before you get married, it's better to see if you get along, isn't it?"

She began to speak in words that weren't hers, the words of a modern girl picked up from the comic books she read. I compared them with the ones I would have uttered on those same subjects and I realized that they weren't very different, Elisa's words only seemed a little coarser. How to respond? I didn't know at the start of that visit, and I don't know now. I could have said: There's not much to say, Elisa, it's all clear: Marcello will consume you, he'll get used to your body, he'll leave you. But they were words that sounded old, not even my mother had dared to say them. So I resigned myself. I had gone away, Elisa had stayed. What would I have been if I, too, had stayed, what choices would I have made? Hadn't I, too, liked the Solara boys when I was a girl? And besides, what had I gained by leaving? Not even the capacity to find words of wisdom to persuade my sister not to ruin herself. Elisa had a pretty face with delicate features, an unremarkable body, a caressing voice. Marcello I remembered as tall, handsome, muscular, he had a square face with a healthy complexion, and was capable of intense feelings of love: he had demonstrated that when he was in love with Lila, it didn't seem that he'd had other loves since. What to say, then? In the end she went to get a box and showed me all the jewelry Marcello had given her, objects compared to which the earrings I had given her were what they were, small things.

"Be careful," I said. "Don't lose yourself. And if you need to, call me."

I was about to get up, but she stopped me, laughing.

"Where are you going, didn't Mamma tell you? They're all coming here for dinner. I've made a huge amount of food."

I showed my annoyance:

"All who?"

"Everyone: it's a surprise."

91.

The first to arrive were my father and mother, with the two little girls and Pietro. Dede and Elsa received more presents from Elisa, who fussed over them (*Dede, sweetie, give me a big kiss here; Elsa, how nice and plump you are, come to your aunt, you know we have the same name?*). My mother disappeared immediately into the kitchen, head down, without looking at me. Pietro tried to pull me aside to tell me I don't know what serious thing but with the air of one who wants to declare his innocence. Instead, my father dragged him over to sit on a couch in front of the television and turned it on at high volume.

Soon afterward Gigliola appeared with her children, two fierce boys who immediately ganged up with Dede, while Elsa, bewildered, took refuge with me. Gigliola was fresh from the hairdresser, her extremely high heels clacked on the floor, she sparkled with gold, in her ears, around her neck, on her arms. A bright green dress, with a very low décolletage, barely contained her, and she wore heavy makeup that was already cracking. She turned to me and said without preamble, sarcastically:

"Here we are, we've come to honor you professors. Everything good, Lenù? Is that the genius of the university? My goodness, what nice hair your husband has."

Pietro freed himself from my father, who had an arm around his shoulders, jumped up with a timid smile, and couldn't restrain himself, his gaze instinctively rested on the large wave of Gigliola's breasts. She noted it with satisfaction.

"Easy, easy," she said to him, "or I'll be embarrassed. Here no one ever gets up to greet a lady."

My father pulled my husband back, worried that someone would take him away, and started talking to him again about something or other, in spite of the booming television. I asked Gigliola how she was, trying to convey to her with my gaze, my tone of voice, that I hadn't forgotten her confidences and was close to her. The idea must not have pleased her, she said:

"Listen, sweetheart, I'm fine, you're fine, we're all fine. But if my husband hadn't ordered me to come here and bore my ass off, I'd be much better off at my house. Just to be clear."

I couldn't answer, someone was ringing the doorbell. My sister moved lightly, she seemed to glide on a breath of wind, she hurried to open the door. I heard her exclaim: How happy I am, come, Mamma, come in. And she reappeared, holding by the hand her future mother-in-law, Manuela Solara, who was dressed for a party, a fake flower in her dyed reddish hair, sorrowful eyes set in deep sockets, even thinner than the last time I'd seen her—almost skin and bone. Behind her was Michele, well dressed, carefully shaved, with a brusque power in his gaze and in his calm movements. And a moment afterward appeared a big man I had trouble recognizing, everything about him was enormous: he was tall, with big feet, long large powerful legs, his stomach and chest and shoulders inflated by some heavy, compact material; he had a large head with a broad forehead, his long brown hair was combed back, his beard was coal-black. It was Marcello: Elisa confirmed it by offering her lips as if to a god to whom one owes respect and gratitude. He bent over, brushing hers with his, while my father rose, pulling up Pietro, too, with an embarrassed air, and my mother hurried limping from the kitchen. I realized that the presence of Signora Solara was considered exceptional, a thing to be proud of. Elisa whispered to me with emotion: Today my mother-in-law is sixty. Ah, I said, and meanwhile I was surprised to see Marcello, as soon as he came in, turn directly to my husband as if they already knew each other. He gave him a bright smile, shouting: Everything's taken care of, Prof. *What everything was taken care of?* Pietro responded with an uncertain smile, then he looked at me, shaking his head in distress, as if to say: I did everything I could. I would have liked him to explain, but already Marcello was introducing Manuela: Come, Mamma, this is the professor husband of Lenuccia, sit down here next to him. Pietro made a half bow, and I, too, felt compelled to greet Signora Solara, who said: How pretty you are Lenù, you're pretty like your sister, and then she asked me with some anxiety: It's warm in here, don't you feel it? I didn't answer, Dede was whining, calling me, Gigliola—the only one who appeared to give no importance to the presence of Manuela—shouted something vulgar in dialect to her children who had hit mine. I realized that Michele was studying me silently, without even saying hello. I greeted him, in a loud voice, then tried to soothe Dede and Elsa, who, seeing her sister distressed, was about to start crying in turn. Marcello said to me: I'm so happy to have you as a guest in my house, it's a great honor for me, believe me. He turned to Elisa as if to speak directly to me were beyond his powers: You tell her how pleased I am, your sister intimidates me. I said something to put him at ease, but at that moment the doorbell rang again.

Michele went to the door, and he returned shortly afterward with a look of amusement. He was followed by an old man who was carrying suitcases, *my suitcases*, the suitcases we had left in the hotel. Michele gestured toward me, the man placed them in front of me as if he had performed a magic trick for my entertainment. No, I exclaimed, oh no, you're making me angry. But Elisa embraced me, kissed me, said: We have room, you can't stay in a hotel, we have so much space here, and two bathrooms. Anyway, Marcello said emphatically, I asked your husband for permission, I wouldn't have dared take the initiative: Prof, please talk to your wife, defend me. I gasped, furious but smiling: Good Lord, what a mess, thank you Marcè, you're very kind, but we really can't accept. And I tried to send the suitcases back to the hotel. But I also had to attend to Dede, I said to her: Let me see what the boys did, it's nothing, a little kiss will make it go away, go play, take Elsa. And I called Pietro, already caught in the coils of Manuela Solara: Pietro, come here, please, what did you say to Marcello, we can't sleep here. And I realized that my voice was taking on the tones of the dialect, out of nervousness, that words were coming to me in the Neapolitan of the neighborhood, that the neighborhood—from the courtyard to the *stradone* and the tunnel—was imposing its language on me, its mode of acting and reacting, its figures, those which in Florence seemed faded images and here were flesh and blood.

There was another ring at the door, Elisa went to open it. Who else was still to arrive? A few seconds passed and Gennaro rushed into the room. He saw Dede, Dede saw him, incredulous. She immediately stopped whining, and they stared at each other, overwhelmed by that unexpected reunion. Right afterward Enzo appeared, the only blond among so many dark-haired people and bright colors, and yet he was grim. Finally Lila entered.

92.

A long period of words without body, of voice alone that ran in waves over an electric sea, suddenly shattered. Lila wore a knee-length blue dress. She was thin, all sinews, which made her seem taller than usual in spite of her low heels. She had deep wrinkles at the sides of her mouth and her eyes, otherwise the pale skin of her face was stretched over the forehead, the cheekbones. Her hair, combed into a ponytail, showed threads of white over her ears, which were almost without lobes. As soon as she saw me she smiled, she narrowed her eyes. I didn't smile and was so surprised I said nothing, not even hello. Although we were both thirty years old, she seemed older, more worn than I imagined I was. Gigliola shouted: Finally the other little queen is here, the children are hungry, I can't control them anymore.

We ate. I felt as if I were being squeezed in an uncomfortable device; I couldn't swallow. I thought angrily of the suitcases, which I had unpacked in the hotel and which had been arbitrarily repacked by one or more strangers, people who had touched my things, Pietro's, the children's, making a mess. I couldn't accept the evidence—that I would sleep in the house of Marcello Solara to please my sister, who shared his bed. I watched, with a hostility that grieved me, Elisa and my mother, the first, overwhelmed by an anxious happiness, talking on and on as she played the part of mistress of the house, the second appearing content, so content that she even filled Lila's plate politely. I observed Enzo, who ate with his head down, annoyed by Gigliola, who pressed her enormous bosom against his arm and talked in loud, flirtatious tones. I looked

330 · ELENA FERRANTE

with irritation at Pietro, who, although assailed by my father, by Marcello, by Signora Solara, paid attention only to Lila, who sat opposite him and was indifferent to everyone, even to me—maybe especially to me—but not to him. And the children got on my nerves, the five new lives who had arranged themselves into two groups: Gennaro and Dede, well-behaved and devious, against Gigliola's children, who, drinking wine from their distracted mother's glass, were becoming intolerable, and now appealing to Elsa, who had joined them, even if they took no notice of her.

Who had put on this show? Who had mixed together different reasons to celebrate? Elisa obviously, but pushed by whom? Maybe by Marcello. But Marcello had surely been directed by Michele, who was sitting next to me, and who, at his ease, ate, drank, pretended to ignore the behavior of his wife and children, but stared ironically at my husband, who seemed fascinated by Lila. What did he want to prove? That this was the territory of the Solaras? That even if I had escaped I belonged to that place and therefore to them? That they could force on me anything by mobilizing affections, vocabulary, rituals, but also by destroying them, by making at their convenience the ugly beautiful and the beautiful ugly? He spoke to me for the first time since he had arrived. Did you see Mamma, he said, imagine, she's sixty, but who would ever say so, look how pretty she is, she carries it well, no? He raised his voice on purpose, so that everyone could hear not so much his question as the answer that I was now obliged to give. I had to speak in praise of Mamma. Here she was, sitting next to Pietro, an old woman who was a little vague, polite, apparently innocuous, with a long bony face, a massive nose, that crazy flower in her thinning hair. And yet she was the loan shark who had founded the family fortunes; the caretaker and guardian of the red book in which were the names of so many in the neighborhood, the city, and the province; the woman of the crime without punishment, a ruthless and dangerous woman, according to the telephonic fantasy I had indulged in, along with Lila, and according to the pages of my aborted novel: Mamma who had killed Don Achille, to replace him and gain a monopoly on loan-sharking, and who had brought up her two sons to seize everything, trampling on everyone. And now I had the obligation to say to Michele: Yes, it's true, how pretty your mother looks, how well she carries her years, congratulations. And I saw out of the corner of my eye that Lila had stopped talking to Pietro and expected nothing else, already she was turning to look at me, her full lips parted, her eyes cracks, her brow furrowed. I read the sarcasm in her face, it occurred to me that maybe she had suggested to Michele that he put me in that cage: *Mamma's just turned sixty, Lenù, the mamma of your brother-in-law, your sister's mother-in-law, let's see what you say now, let's see if you continue to play the schoolmistress.* I responded, turning to Manuela, *Happy Birthday*, nothing else. And immediately Marcello broke in, as if to help me, he exclaimed, with emotion: Thank you, thank you, Lenù. Then he turned to his mother; her face was pained, sweaty, and red blotches had appeared on her skinny neck: Lenuccia has congratulated you, Mamma. And immediately Pietro said to the woman who was sitting next to him: Happy Birthday also from me, Signora. And so everyone—everyone except Gigliola and Lila—paid respects to Signora Solara, even the children, in chorus: Many happy returns, Manuela, many happy returns, Grandma. And she shied away, saying, I'm old, and, taking out of her purse a blue fan with the image of the gulf and a smoking Vesuvio, she began to fan herself, slowly at first, then more energetically.

Michele, although he had turned to me, seemed to give my husband's good wishes more importance. He spoke to him politely: too kind, Prof, you aren't from here and you can't know the good qualities of our mother. He assumed a confidential tone: We're good folk, my late grandfather, rest his soul, started out with the bar here at the corner, started from nothing, and my father expanded it, he made a pastry shop that's famous in all Naples, thanks also to the skill of Spagnuolo, my wife's father, an extraordinary artisan—right, Gigliò? But, he added, it's to my mother, to *our* mother, that we owe everything. In recent times envious people, people who wish us harm, have spread odious rumors about her. But we are tolerant people, life has taught us to stay in business and to be patient. So the truth always prevails. And the truth is that this woman is extremely intelligent, she has a strong character; there has never been a moment when it would even cross your mind that she has the desire to do nothing. She has always worked, always, and she has done it only for the family, she never enjoyed anything for herself. What we have today is what she built for us children, what we do today is only the continuation of what she did.

Manuela fanned herself with a more deliberate gesture, she said aloud to Pietro: Michele is a wonderful son. When he was a child, at Christmas, he would climb up on the table and recite poetry beautifully; but his flaw is that he likes to talk and when he talks he has to exaggerate. Marcello interrupted: No, Mamma, what exaggeration, it's all true. And Michele continued to sing Manuela's praises, how beautiful she was, how generous, he wouldn't stop. Until suddenly he turned to me. He said seriously, in fact solemnly: There's only one other woman who is *almost* like our mother. *Another woman? A woman almost comparable to Manuela Solara?* I looked at him in bewilderment. The phrase, in spite of that *almost*, was out of place, and for a few instants the noisy dinner became soundless. Gigliola stared at her husband with nervous eyes, the pupils dilated by wine and unhappiness. My mother, too, assumed an expression that was unsuitable, watchful: Maybe she hoped that that woman was Elisa, that Michele was about to assign to her daughter a sort of right of succession to the most elevated seat among the Solaras. And Manuela stopped fanning herself for a moment, she dried with her index finger the sweat on her lips, she waited for her son to upend those words in a mocking remark.

But, with the audacity that had always distinguished him, not giving a damn about his wife or Enzo or even his mother, he stared at Lila while his face turned a greenish color and his gestures became more agitated and his words served as a rope, dragging her attention away from Pietro. Tonight, he said, we're all here, at my brother's house, first to welcome as they deserve these two esteemed professors and their beautiful children; second to celebrate my mother, the most blessed woman, third to wish Elisa great happiness and, soon, a fine marriage; fourth, if you will allow me, to toast an agreement that I was afraid would never be made. Lina, please, come here.

Lina. Lila.

I sought her gaze and she looked back for a fraction of a second, a look that said: Now do you understand the game, you remember how it works? Then, to my great surprise, while Enzo stared at an indeterminate point on the tablecloth, she rose meekly and came over to Michele.

He didn't touch her. He didn't touch a hand, an arm, nothing, as if between them hung a blade that could wound him. Instead he placed his fingers for several seconds on my shoulder and turned to me again: You mustn't be offended, Lenù, you're smart, you've gone so far, you've been in the newspapers, you're the pride of us all who have known you since you were a child. But—and I'm sure you agree, and you'll be pleased if I say it now, because you love her—Lina has something alive in her mind that no one else has, something strong, that jumps here and there and nothing can stop it, a thing that not even the doctors can see and that I think not even she knows, even though it's been there since she was born—she doesn't know it and doesn't want to recognize it, look what a mean face she's making right now—a thing that, if it doesn't like you can cause you a lot of problems but, if it does, leaves everyone astonished. Well, for a long time I've wanted to buy this distinctive aspect of her. Yes, buy, there's nothing wrong, buy the way you buy pearls, diamonds. But until now, unfortunately, it was impossible. We've made just a small step forward, and it's this small step that I wish to celebrate tonight: I've hired Signora Cerullo to work in the data-processing center that I've set up in Acerra, a very modern thing that if it interests you, Lenù, if it interests the professor, I'll take you to visit tomorrow, or anyway before you leave. What do you say, Lina?

Lila made an expression of disgust. She shook her head unhappily and said, staring at Signora Solara: Michele doesn't understand anything about computers and I don't know what he thinks that I do, but it's nonsense, it just takes a correspondence course, I learned it even though I only went up to fifth grade in school. And she said nothing else. She didn't mock Michele, as I expected she would, because of that tremendous image he had invented, the living thing that flowed in her mind. She didn't mock him for the pearls, the diamonds. Above all, she didn't evade the compliments. In fact she allowed us to toast her hiring as if she really had been assumed into Heaven, she allowed Michele to continue to praise her, justifying with his praise the salary he was paying her. And all while Pietro, with that capacity of his for feeling at ease with people he considered inferior, was already saying, without consulting me, that he would very much like to visit the center in Acerra and he wanted to hear about it from Lila, who had sat down again. I thought for a moment that if I gave her time she would take away my husband as she had taken Nino from me. But I didn't feel jealous: if it happened it would happen only out of a desire to dig a deeper furrow between us, I took it for granted that she couldn't like Pietro and that Pietro would never be capable of betraying me out of desire for someone else.

Another feeling, however, came over me, a more tangled one. I was in the place where I was born, I had always been considered the girl who had been most successful, I was convinced that it was, at least in that place, an indisputable fact. Instead Michele, as if he had deliberately organized my demotion in the neighborhood and in particular in the midst of the family I came from, had contrived to make Lila overshadow me, he had even wanted me to comply with my overshadowing by publicly recognizing the incomparable power of my friend. And she had willingly agreed to it. In fact, maybe she had even had a hand in the result, planning and organizing it. If a few years earlier, when I had had my little success as a writer, the thing wouldn't have wounded me, in fact would have pleased me, now that that was over I realized that I was suffering. I exchanged a look with my mother. She was frowning, she had the expression she assumed when she was struggling not to hit me. She wanted me not to pretend my usual meekness, she wanted me to react, to show how much I knew, all the high-quality stuff, not that nonsense of Acerra. She was saying it to me with her eyes, like a mute command. But I said nothing. Suddenly Manuela Solara, darting glances of impatience, exclaimed: I feel hot, don't you all, too?

93.

Elisa, like my mother, could not tolerate my loss of prestige. But while my mother remained silent, she turned to me, radiant, affectionate, to let me know that I remained her extraordinary older sister, whom she would always be proud of. I have something to give you, she said, and added, jumping lightheartedly, as was her way, from one subject to another: Have you ever been in an airplane? I said no. Possible? Possible. It turned out that of those present only Pietro had flown, several times, but he spoke of it as if it were nothing much. Instead for Elisa it had been a wonderful experience, and also for Marcello. They had gone to Germany, a long flight, for reasons of work and pleasure. Elisa had been afraid at first, because of the jolting and shaking, and a jet of cold air struck her right in the head as if it were going to drill a hole. Then through the window she had seen white clouds below and blue sky above. So she had discovered that above the clouds there was always fine weather, and from high up the earth was all green and blue and violet and shining with snow when they flew over the mountains. She asked me:

"Guess who we met in Düsseldorf."

I said, unhappy with everything:

"I don't know, Elisa, tell me."

"Antonio."

"Ah."

"He was very eager for me to send his greetings."

"Is he well?"

"Very well. He gave me a gift for you."

So that was the thing she had for me, a gift from Antonio. She got up and went to get it. Marcello looked at me with a smile, Pietro asked:

"Who is Antonio?"

"An employee of ours," said Marcello.

"A boyfriend of your wife," said Michele, laughing. "Times have changed, Professò, today women have a lot of boyfriends and they boast about it much more than men. How many girlfriends have you had?"

Pietro said seriously:

"None, I've loved only my wife."

"Liar," Michele exclaimed, in great amusement. "Can I whisper to you how many girlfriends I've had?"

He got up and, followed by Gigliola's look of disgust, stood behind my husband, whispered to him.

"Incredible," Pietro exclaimed, cautiously ironic. They laughed together.

Meanwhile Elisa returned, she handed me a package wrapped in packing paper.

"Open it."

"Do you know what's in it?" I asked, puzzled.

"We both know," said Marcello, "but we hope you don't."

I unwrapped the package. I realized, as I did, that they were all watching me. Lila looked at me sideways, intent, as if she expected a snake to dart out. When they saw that Antonio, the son of crazy Melina, the illiterate and violent servant of the Solaras, my boyfriend in adolescence, had sent me as a gift nothing wonderful, nothing moving, nothing that alluded to times past, but only a book, they seemed disappointed. Then they noticed that I had changed color, that I was looking at the cover with a joy I couldn't control. It wasn't just any book. It was *my* book. It was the German translation of my novel, six years after its publication in Italy. For the first time I was present at the spectacle—yes, a spectacle—of my words dancing before my eyes in a foreign language.

"You didn't know about it?" Elisa asked, happy.

"No."

"And you're pleased?"

"Very pleased."

My sister announced to everyone proudly:

"It's the novel Lenuccia wrote, but with German words."

And my mother, reddening in return, said:

"You see how famous she is?"

Gigliola took the book, paged through it, said admiringly: the only thing I can understand is *Elena Greco*. Lila then reached out her hand in an imperative way, indicating that she wanted it. I saw in her eyes curiosity, the desire to touch and look at and read the unknown language that contained me and had transported me far away. I saw in her the urgency for that object, an urgency that I recognized, she had had it as a child, and it softened me. But Gigliola started angrily, she pulled the book away so that Lila couldn't take it, and said:

"Wait, I have it now. What is it, you know German?" And Lila withdrew her hand, shook her head no, and Gigliola exclaimed: "Then don't be a pain in the ass, let me look: I want to see what Lenuccia was able to do." In the general silence, she turned the book over and over in her hands with satisfaction. She leafed through the pages one after another, slowly, as if she were reading a few lines here, a few there. Finally, her voice thickened by the wine, she said, handing it to me: "Bravo, Lenù, compliments for everything, the book, the husband, the children. You might think that we're the only ones who know you and instead even the Germans do. What you have, you deserve, you got it with hard work, without hurting anyone, without bullshitting with other people's husbands. Thank you, now I really have to go, good night."

She struggled to get up, sighing, she had become even heavier, because of the wine. She yelled at the children: Hurry up, and they protested, the older said something vulgar in dialect, she slapped him and dragged him toward the door. Michele shook his head with a smile on his face, he muttered: I've had a rough time with that bitch, she always has to ruin my day. Then he said calmly: Wait, Gigliò, what's your hurry, first we have to eat your father's dessert, then we'll go. And the children, in a flash, fortified by their father's words, slipped away and returned to the table. Gigliola, instead, continued with her heavy tread toward the door, saying in irritation: I'll go by myself, I don't feel well. But at that point Michele shouted at her in a loud voice, charged with violence: Sit down right now, and she stopped as if the words had paralyzed her legs. Elisa jumped up and said softly, Come, help me get the cake. She took her by the arm, pulled her toward the kitchen. I reassured Dede with a look, she was frightened by Michele's shouting. Then I held out the book to Lila, saying: Do you want to see? She shook her head with an expression of indifference.

94.

"Where have we ended up?" Pietro asked, half outraged and half amused, when, once the children had been put to bed, we closed the door of the room that Elisa had given us. He wanted to joke about the more incredible moments of the evening, but I attacked him, we quarreled in low voices. I was angry with him, with everyone, with myself. From the chaotic feeling I had inside, the desire that Lila would get sick and die was re-emerging. Not out of hatred, I loved her more and more, I wouldn't have been capable of hating her. But I couldn't bear the emptiness of her evasion. How could you possibly, I asked Pietro, agree to let them take our bags, bring them here, give them the authority to move us to this house? And he: I didn't know what sort of people they were. No, I hissed, it's that you've never listened to me, I've always told you where I come from.

We talked for a long time, he tried to soothe me, I berated him. I said he had been too timid, that he had been put upon, that he knew how to insist only with the well-brought-up people of his world, that I no longer trusted him, that I didn't even trust his mother, how could it be that my book had come out in Germany two years ago and the publisher had said nothing about it, what other countries had it been published in without my knowing, I wanted to get to the bottom of it, et cetera et cetera. To make me feel better, he agreed, and urged me to telephone his mother and the publisher the next morning. Then he declared a great liking for what he called the working-class environment I had been born and brought up in. He whispered that my mother was a generous and very intelligent person, he had kind words for my father, for Elisa, for Gigliola, for Enzo. But his tone changed abruptly when he came to the Solaras: he called them crooks, vicious scoundrels, smooth-talking criminals. And finally he came to Lila. He said softly: It's she who disturbed me most. I noticed, I snapped, you talked to her the whole evening. Pietro shook his head ener-getically, he explained, surprisingly, that Lila had seemed to him the worst person. He said that she wasn't at all my friend, that she hated me, that she was extraordinarily intelligent, that she was very fascinating, but her intelligence had been put to bad use—it was the evil intelligence that sows discord and hates life—and her fascination was the more intolerable, the fascination that enslaves and drives a person to ruin. Just like that.

At first I pretended to disagree, but in fact I was pleased. I had been wrong then, Lila hadn't affected him, Pietro was a man practiced in perceiving the subtext of every text and had easily picked up her unpleasant aspects. But soon it seemed to me that he was overdoing it. He said: I don't understand how your relationship could have lasted so long, obviously you've carefully hidden from each other anything that could rupture it. And he added: either I haven't understood anything about her—and it's likely, I don't know her—or I haven't understood anything about you, and that is more upsetting. Finally he said the ugliest words: She and that Michele are made for each other, if they aren't already lovers they will be. Then I revolted. I hissed that I couldn't bear his pedantic overeducated bour-geois tone, that he must never again speak of my friend in that way, that he hadn't understood anything. And as I was speak-ing I seemed to perceive something that at that moment not even he knew: Lila had affected him, seriously; Pietro had grasped her exceptionality so well that he was frightened by it and now felt the need to vilify her. He was afraid not for himself, I think, but for me and for our relationship. He was afraid that, even at a distance, she would tear me away from him, destroy us. And to protect me he overdid it, he slandered her, in a confused way he wanted me to be disgusted by her and expel her from my life. I whispered good night, and turned the other way.

95.

The next day I got up very early and packed the suitcases, I wanted to return to Florence right away. But I couldn't. Marcello said he had promised his brother to take us to Acerra and since Pietro, although I let him know in every possible way that I wanted to leave, was willing, we left the children with Elisa and agreed to let that big man drive us to a long, low yellow building, a large shoe warehouse. The whole way I was silent, while Pietro asked questions about the Solaras' business in Germany and Marcello equivocated, with disjointed phrases like: Italy, Germany, the world, Professò, I'm more Communist than the Communists, more revolutionary than the revolutionaries, for me if you could flatten everything and build it all again from the beginning I'd be in the first row. Anyway, he added, looking at me in the rear-view mirror in search of agreement, love for me comes before everything.

When we got there, he led us into a low-ceilinged room, illuminated by neon lights. There was a strong odor of ink, of dust, of overheated insulators, mixed with that of uppers and shoe polish. Look, Marcello said, here's the contraption Michele rented. I looked around, there was no one at the machine. The System 3 was completely unremarkable, an unin-

342 · ELENA FERRANTE

teresting piece of furniture backed up to a wall: metal panels, control knobs, a red switch, a wooden shelf, keyboards. I don't understand anything about it, said Marcello, this is stuff that Lina knows, but she doesn't have a schedule, she's always in and out. Pietro carefully examined the panels, the control knobs, everything, but it was clear that modernity was disappointing him, all the more since Marcello answered every question with: This is my brother's business, I have other problems on my mind.

Lila showed up when we were about to leave. She was with two young women who were carrying metal containers. She seemed irritated, and ordered them around. As soon as she noticed us she changed her tone, she became polite but in a forced way, as if a part of her brain had broken free and were reaching toward urgent things to do with the job. She ignored Marcello, and addressed Pietro but as if she were also speaking to me. What do you care about this stuff, she said, teasing, if you're really interested in it let's make a deal: You work here and I'll take up your things, novels, paintings, antiquities. Again I had the impression that she had aged before me, not only in her appearance but in her movements, her voice, her choice of a dull, vaguely bored manner in which to explain to us not only how the System 3 and the various machines worked but also the magnetic cards, the tapes, the five-inch disks, and other innovations that were on the way, like desktop computers that one could have at home for one's personal use. She was no longer the Lila who on the telephone talked about the new job in childish tones, and she seemed far removed from Enzo's enthusiasm. She acted like a super-competent employee on whom the boss has dumped one of the many headaches, the tourist visit. She wasn't friendly toward me, she never joked with Pietro. Finally she ordered the girls to show my husband how the punch-card machine worked, then she pushed me into the hall, and said:

"So? Did you congratulate Elisa? Does one sleep well in Marcello's house? Are you glad the old witch is sixty?"

I replied nervously: "If my sister wants it, what can I do, beat her over the head?"

"You see? In the fairy tales one does as one wants, and in reality one does what one can."

"That's not true. Who forced you to be used by Michele?"

"I'm using him, not him me."

"You're deceiving yourself."

"Wait and you'll see."

"What do you want me to see, Lila, forget it."

"I repeat, I don't like it when you act like that. You don't know anything about us anymore, so it's better if you say nothing."

"You mean I can criticize you only if I live in Naples?"

"Naples, Florence: you aren't doing anything anywhere, Lenù."

"Who says so?"

"The facts."

"I know my facts, not you."

I was tense, she realized it. She gave me a conciliatory look.

"You make me mad and I say things I don't think. You did well to leave Naples, you did very well. But you know who's back?"

"Who?"

"Nino."

The news burned my chest.

"How do you know?"

"Marisa told me. He got a professorship at the university."

"He didn't like Milan?"

Lila narrowed her eyes.

"He married someone from Via Tasso who is related to half the Banco di Napoli. They have a child a year old."

I don't know if I suffered, certainly I had trouble believing it.

"He's really married?"

"Yes."

I looked at her to see what she had in mind.

"Do you intend to see him?"

"No. But if I happen to run into him, I want to tell him that Gennaro isn't his."

96.

She said to me this and some other fragmented things: *Congratulations, you have an intelligent and handsome husband, he speaks as if he were religious even if he's not a believer, he knows ancient and modern facts, in particular he knows a lot of things about Naples, I'm ashamed, I'm Neapolitan but I don't know anything. Gennaro is growing up, my mother takes care of him more than I do, he's smart in school. With Enzo things are good, we work a lot, we rarely see each other. Stefano has ruined himself with his own hands: the carabinieri found stolen goods in the back of the shop, I don't know what, he was arrested; now he's out but he has to be careful, he has nothing anymore, I give him money, not the other way around. You see how things change: if I had remained Signora Carracci I would be ruined, I would have ended up with my ass on the ground like all the Carraccis; instead I am Raffaella Cerullo and I'm the technical director for Michele Solara at four hundred and twenty thousand lire a month. The result is that my mother treats me like a queen, my father has forgiven me for everything, my brother sucks money out of me, Pinuccia says she loves me so much, their children call me Auntie. But it's a boring job, completely the opposite of what it seemed at first: still too slow, you waste a lot of time, let's hope that the new machines get here soon—they're a lot faster. Or no. Speed consumes everything, as when photographs come out blurry. Alfonso used that expression, he used it*

*in fun, he said that he came out blurry, without clear outlines.
Lately he's been talking to me constantly about friendship. He
wants to be my friend, he would like to copy me on copying
paper, he swears that he would like to be a girl like me. What
sort of girl, I said to him, you're a male, Alfò, you don't know
anything about what I'm like, and even if we're friends and you
study me and spy on me and copy me, you'll never know anything. So—he was having a good time—what do I do, I suffer
being the way I am. And he confessed to me that he has always
loved Michele—yes, Michele Solara—and he wishes Michele
would like him the way he thinks Michele likes me. You understand, Lenù, what happens to people: we have too much stuff
inside and it swells us, breaks us. All right, I said, we're friends,
but get out of your mind that you can be a woman like me, all
you'd succeed in being is what a woman is according to you men.
You can copy me, make a portrait as precise as an artist, but my
shit will always remain mine, and yours will be yours. Ah, Lenù,
what happens to us all, we're like pipes when the water freezes,
what a terrible thing a dissatisfied mind is. You remember what
we did with my wedding picture? I want to continue on that
path. The day will come when I reduce myself to diagrams, I'll
become a perforated tape and you won't find me anymore.*

Nonsense, that's all. That talk in the hall confirmed to me
that our relationship no longer had any intimacy. It had been
reduced to succinct information, scant details, mean remarks,
hot air, no revelation of facts and thoughts for me alone. Lila's
life was now hers and that was all, it seemed that she didn't
want to share it with anyone. Pointless to persist with questions like: What do you know about Pasquale, where did he end
up, what do you have to do with Soccavo's death, the kneecapping of Filippo, what led you to accept Michele's offer, what do
you make of his dependence on you. Lila had retreated into the
unconfessable, any questions of mine could not become conversation, she would say: What are you thinking, you're crazy,

Michele, dependence, Soccavo, what are you talking about? Even now, as I write, I realize that I don't have enough information to move on to *Lila went, Lila did, Lila met, Lila planned*. And yet, as I was returning in the car to Florence, I had the impression that there in the neighborhood, between backwardness and modernity, she had more history than I did. How much I had lost by leaving, believing I was destined for who knows what life. Lila, who had remained, had a very new job, she earned a lot of money, she acted in absolute freedom and according to schemes that were indecipherable. She was very attached to her son, she had been extremely devoted to him in the first years of his life, and she still kept an eye on him; but she seemed capable of being free of him as and when she wanted, he didn't cause her the anxieties my daughters caused me. She had broken with her family, and yet she took on their burden and the responsibility for them whenever she could. She took care of Stefano who was in trouble, but without getting close to him. She hated the Solaras and yet she submitted to them. She was ironic about Alfonso and was his friend. She said she didn't want to see Nino again, but I knew it wasn't so, that she would see him. Hers was a life in motion, mine was stopped. While Pietro drove in silence and the children quarreled, I thought a lot about her and Nino, about what might happen. Lila will take him back, I fantasized, she'll manage to see him again, she'll influence him the way she knows how, she'll get him away from his wife and son, she'll use him in her war I no longer know against whom, she'll induce him to get divorced, and meanwhile she'll escape from Michele after taking a lot of money from him, and she'll leave Enzo, and finally she'll make up her mind to divorce Stefano, and maybe she'll marry Nino, maybe not, but certainly they'll put their intelligences together and who can say what they will become.

Become. It was a verb that had always obsessed me, but I realized it for the first time only in that situation. *I wanted to become*, even though I had never known what. And I had *become*, that was certain, but without an object, without a real passion, without a determined ambition. I had wanted to become something—here was the point—only because I was afraid that Lila would become someone and I would stay behind. *My becoming was a becoming in her wake.* I had to start again to *become*, but for myself, as an adult, outside of her.

97.

I telephoned Adele as soon as I got home, to find out about the German translation that Antonio had sent me. It had come out of the blue, she didn't know anything about it, either. She called the publisher. She called me back after a while to tell me that the book had been published not only in Germany but in France and Spain. So, I asked, what should I do? Adele answered in bewilderment: Nothing, be satisfied. Of course, I said, I'm *very* pleased, but from the practical point of view, I don't know, should I go promote it abroad? She said affectionately: You don't have to do anything, Elena, the book unfortunately didn't sell anywhere.

My mood got worse. I nagged the publisher, I asked for precise information about the translations, I was angry because no one cared to keep me informed, I ended up saying to an indifferent secretary: I found out about the German edition not from you but from a semiliterate friend: can you do your job or not? Then I apologized, I felt stupid. One after the other the French copy and the Spanish arrived, a copy in German without the crumpled look of the one sent by Antonio. They were ugly books: on the cover were women in black dresses, men with drooping mustaches and a cloth cap on their head, laundry hung out to dry. I leafed through them, I showed them to Pietro, I placed them on a bookshelf among other novels. Mute paper, useless paper.

A time of weary discontent began. I called Elisa every day to find out if Marcello was still kind, if they had decided to get married. She responded to my apprehensions with carefree laughter and stories of a happy life, of trips by car or plane, of prosperity for our brothers, of well-being for our father and mother. Now, at times, I envied her. I was tired, irritable. Elsa was constantly getting sick, Dede required attention, Pietro lingered over his book without finishing it. I lost my temper for no reason. I scolded the children, I quarreled with my husband. The result was that all three were afraid of me. The girls, if I merely passed by their room, stopped playing and looked at me in alarm, and Pietro increasingly preferred the university library to our house. He went out early in the morning and came home at night. When he returned he seemed to have on him signs of the conflicts that I, now left out of all public activity, read about only in the newspapers: the fascists who knifed and killed, the comrades who did no less, the police who had by law a broad mandate to shoot and did so even here in Florence. Until what I had long been expecting happened: Pietro found himself at the center of a nasty episode that got a lot of attention in the papers. He failed a youth with an important surname, who was very active in the struggles. The young man insulted him in front of everyone and aimed a gun at him. Pietro, according to the story that an acquaintance told me, not him—nor was it a first-hand version, she wasn't present— calmly recorded the failure, handed the exam book to the boy, and said more or less: Either be serious and shoot or you'd best get rid of that weapon immediately, because in a moment I'm going to go and report you. The boy aimed the gun at his face for long minutes, then he put it in his pocket, took the exam book, and fled. Pietro went to the carabinieri and the student was arrested. But it didn't end there. The young man's family went not to Pietro but to his father to persuade him to withdraw the charges. Professor Guido Airota tried to convince his son, and there were long phone calls, in the course of which, with some amazement, I heard the old man lose his temper, raise his voice. But Pietro wouldn't give in. In great agitation, I confronted him, I asked:

"Do you realize how you're behaving?"

"What should I do?"

"Reduce the tension."

"I don't understand you."

"You don't *want* to understand me. You're just like our professors in Pisa, the most intolerable."

"I don't think so."

"But you are. Have you forgotten how we struggled in vain to keep up with stupid courses and pass exams that were even more stupid?"

"My course isn't stupid."

"You might ask your students."

"One asks for an opinion from those who are competent to give it."

"Would you ask me, if I were your student?"

"I have very good relations with the ones who study."

"So you like the ones who suck up to you?"

"You like the ones who brag, like your friend in Naples?"

"Yes."

"And is that why you were always the most dutiful?"

I was confused.

"Because I was poor and it seemed a miracle to have gone so far."

"Well, that boy has nothing in common with you."

"You don't have anything in common with me, either."

"What do you mean?"

I didn't answer, I avoided it out of prudence. But then my rage increased again, I went back to criticizing his intransigence, I said to him: You'd already failed him, what was the point of pressing charges? He said: He committed a crime. I: He was playing at frightening you, he's a boy. He answered coldly: That gun is a weapon, not a toy, and it was stolen with other weapons seven years ago, from a carabinieri barracks in Rovezzano. I said: The boy didn't shoot. He muttered: The weapon was loaded, what if he had? He didn't, I cried. He, too, raised his voice: I should have waited for him to shoot me and then reported him? I yelled: Don't shout, your nerves are shattered. He answered: Think of your own nerves. And it was pointless to explain to him, anxiously, that even if my words and tone were argumentative, the situation actually seemed very dangerous and I was worried. I'm afraid for you, I said, for the children, for me. But he didn't console me. He went to his study and tried to work on his book. Only weeks later he told me that two plainclothes policemen had come to see him and asked for information about certain students, had showed him some photographs. The first time he had greeted them politely and politely sent them away without giving them any information. The second time he had asked:

"Have these youths committed crimes?"

"No, for now no."

"Then what do you want from me?"

He had seen them to the door with all the contemptuous courtesy he was capable of.

98.

For months Lila never called; she must have been very busy. Nor did I seek her out, although I felt the need. To diminish the feeling of emptiness I tried to strengthen my connection with Mariarosa, but there were many obstacles. Franco now lived permanently at my sister-in-law's house, and Pietro didn't like me getting too close to his sister or seeing my former boyfriend. If I stayed in Milan for more than a day his mood darkened, imaginary illnesses multiplied, tension increased. Also, Franco himself, who in general never went out except for the medical treatments he constantly needed, didn't welcome my presence; he was impatient with the children's voices, which he found too loud, and at times he disappeared, alarming both Mariarosa and me. My sister-in-law, besides, had endless engagements and was permanently surrounded by women. Her apartment was a sort of gathering place, she welcomed everyone, intellectuals, middleclass women, working-class women fleeing abusive companions, runaway girls, so that she had little time for me, and anyway she was too much a friend to all for me to feel sure of our bond. And yet in her house the desire to study was rekindled, and even to write. Or, rather, it seemed to me that I would be capable of it.

We discussed ourselves a lot. But although we were all women—Franco, if he hadn't fled, stayed shut in his room— we struggled to understand what a woman was. Our every move or thought or conversation or dream, once analyzed in depth, seemed not to belong to us. And this excavation seemed to exasperate those who were weaker, who couldn't tolerate such an excess of self-reflection and believed that to embark on the road of freedom it was enough simply to cut off men. These were unstable times, arcing in waves. Many of us feared a return to the flat calm and stayed on the crest, holding on to extreme formulations and looking down with fear and rage. When we learned that the security force of Lotta Continua had attacked a separatist women's demonstration, we grew bitter to the point where, if one of the more rigid participants discovered that Mariarosa had a man in the house—which she didn't declare but didn't hide, either—the discussion became fierce, the ruptures dramatic.

I hated those moments. I was looking for inspiration, not

conflict, subjects for research, not dogmas. Or at least so I said to myself, and sometimes also to Mariarosa, who listened to me in silence. On one of those occasions I told her about my relationship with Franco in the days of the Normale, and what he had meant to me. I'm grateful to him, I said, I learned so much from him, and I'm sorry that he now treats me and the children coldly. I thought about it for a moment, and continued: Maybe there's something mistaken in this desire men have to instruct us; I was young at the time, and I didn't realize that in his wish to transform me was the proof that he didn't like me as I was, he wanted me to be different, or, rather, he didn't want just a woman, he wanted the woman he imagined he himself would be if he were a woman. For Franco, I said, I was an opportunity for him to expand into the feminine, to take possession of it: I constituted the proof of his omnipotence, the demonstration that he knew how to be not only a man in the right way but also a woman. And today when he no longer senses me as part of himself, he feels betrayed.

I expressed myself exactly like that. And Mariarosa listened with genuine interest, not the slightly feigned curiosity she displayed with the women in general. Write something on that subject, she urged me. She was moved, she said that she had been too late to know the Franco I was talking about. Then she added: Maybe it was a good thing, I would never have been in love with him, I hate men who are too intelligent and tell me how I should be; I prefer this suffering and reflective man I've taken in and am caring for. Then she insisted: Put it in writing, what you've said.

I nodded somewhat nervously, pleased with the praise but also embarrassed, I said something about my relationship with Pietro, about how he tried to impose his views on me. This time Mariarosa burst out laughing, and the almost solemn tone of our conversation changed. Franco associated with Pietro? You're joking, she said, Pietro has trouble keeping together his own virility, imagine if he has the energy to impose on you his feeling for what a woman is. You want to know something? I would have sworn that you wouldn't marry him. I would have sworn that, if you had, you would leave him in a year. I would have sworn that you would be careful not to have children. The fact that you're still together seems to me a miracle. You're really a good girl, poor you.

99.

We were therefore at this point: my husband's sister considered my marriage a mistake and said it to me frankly. I didn't know whether to laugh or cry, it seemed to me the ultimate and unbiased confirmation of my conjugal unease. Besides, what could I do about it? I said to myself that maturity consisted in accepting the turn that existence had taken without getting too upset, following a path between daily practices and theoretical achievements, learning to see oneself, know oneself, in expectation of great changes. Day by day I grew calmer. My daughter Dede went to first grade early, already knowing how to read and write; my daughter Elsa was happy to stay alone with me all morning in the still house; my husband, although he was the dullest of academics, seemed finally close to finishing a second book that promised to be even more important than the first; and I was Signora Airota, Elena Airota, a woman depressed by submissiveness who nevertheless, urged by her sister-in-law but also in order to fight discouragement, had begun to study almost in secret the invention of woman by men, mixing the ancient and modern worlds. I didn't have an objective; only to be able to say to Mariarosa, to my mother-in-law, to this or that acquaintance: I'm working.

And so I pushed on, in my speculations, from the first and

second Biblical creations to Defoe-Flanders, Flaubert-Bovary, Tolstoy-Karenina, *La dernière mode*, Rose Sélavy, and beyond, and still further, in a frenzy of revelation. Slowly I began to feel some satisfaction. I discovered everywhere female automatons created by men. There was nothing of ourselves, and the little there was that rose up in protest immediately became material for their manufacturing. When Pietro was at work and Dede was at school and Elsa was playing next to my desk and I, at last, felt alive, digging into words and among words, I sometimes imagined what my life and Lila's would have been if we had both taken the test for admission to middle school and then high school, if together we had studied to get our degree, elbow to elbow, allied, a perfect couple, the sum of intellectual energies, of the pleasures of understanding and the imagination. We would have written together, we would have been authors together, we would have drawn power from each other, we would have fought shoulder to shoulder because what was ours was inimitably ours. The solitude of women's minds is regrettable, I said to myself, it's a waste to be separated from each other, without procedures, without tradition. Then I felt as if my thoughts were cut off in the middle, absorbing and yet defective, with an urgent need for verification, for development, yet without conviction, without faith in themselves. Then the wish to telephone her returned, to tell her: Listen to what I'm thinking about, please let's talk about it together, you remember what you said about Alfonso? But the opportunity was gone, lost decades ago. I had to learn to be satisfied with myself.

Then one day, just as I was preoccupied with that need, I heard the key turn in the lock. It was Pietro, coming home for lunch after picking up Dede at school. I closed books and notebooks as the child burst into the room, greeted enthusiastically by Elsa. She was starving, I knew she would cry: Mamma, what is there to eat? Instead, even before throwing down her book bag, she exclaimed: a friend of Papa's is coming to lunch with us. I remember the date precisely: March 9, 1976. I pulled myself out of my bad mood, Dede grabbed me by the hand and drew me into the hallway. Meanwhile Elsa, because of the announced presence of a stranger, was keeping prudent hold of my skirt. Pietro said gaily: Look who I brought you.

100.

Nino no longer had the thick beard I had seen years earlier in the bookstore, but his hair was long and disheveled. Otherwise he had remained the boy of years ago, tall, skinny, his eyes bright, his appearance unkempt. He embraced me, he knelt to greet the two girls, he stood up, apologizing for the intrusion. I murmured some cool words: Come in, sit down, what on earth are you doing in Florence? I felt as if I had hot wine in my brain, I couldn't give concreteness to what was happening: Nino, Nino himself, in my house. And it seemed to me that something was no longer functioning in the organization of internal and external. What was I imagining and what was happening, who was the shadow and who the living body? Meanwhile Pietro explained: We met at the university, I invited him to lunch. And I smiled, I said Yes, it's all ready, where there's enough for four there's enough for five, keep me company while I set the table. I seemed tranquil but I was extremely agitated, my face hurt with the effort of smiling. How is it that Nino is here, and what is *here*, what is *is*? I surprised you, Pietro said, with some apprehension, as when he was afraid of having been wrong about something. And Nino, laughing: I told him a hundred times to call you, I swear, but he didn't want to. Then he explained that it was my father-in-law who had told him to introduce himself. He had met Professor Airota in Rome, at the Socialist Party congress, and

there, one thing leading to another, he had said that he had
work to do in Florence and the professor had mentioned
Pietro, the new book his son was writing, a volume that he
had just obtained for him and that he needed urgently. Nino
had offered to take it in person and now here we were at
lunch, the girls fighting for his attention, he who was charming to both of them, obliging to Pietro, and had a few serious
words for me.

"Think," he said to me, "I've come so often to this city for
work, but I didn't know you were living here, that you had two
lovely young ladies. Luckily there was this opportunity."

"Are you still teaching in Milan?" I asked, knowing perfectly well that he no longer lived in Milan.

"No, I'm teaching now in Naples."

"What subject?"

He made a grimace of displeasure.

"Geography."

"Meaning?"

"Urban geography."

"How in the world did you decide to go back?"

"My mother's not well."

"I'm sorry, what's wrong?"

"Her heart."

"And your brothers and sisters?"

"Fine."

"Your father?"

"The usual. But time passes, one grows up, and recently
we've reconciled. Like everyone, he has his flaws and his
virtues." He turned to Pietro: "How much trouble we've made
for fathers and for the family. Now that it's our turn, how are
we doing?"

"I'm doing well," my husband said, with a touch of irony.

"I have no doubt. You married an extraordinary woman
and these two little princesses are perfect, very well brought

up, very stylish. What a pretty dress, Dede, it looks very nice on you. And Elsa, who gave you the barrette with the stars?"

"Mamma," said Elsa.

Slowly I calmed down. The seconds regained their orderly rhythm, I took note of what was happening to me. Nino was sitting at the table next to me, he ate the pasta I had prepared, carefully cut Elsa's meat into small pieces, ate his with a good appetite, mentioned with disgust the bribes that Lockheed had paid to Tanassi and to Gui, praised my cooking, discussed with Pietro the socialist option, peeled an apple in a single coil that sent Dede into ecstasies. Meanwhile a fluid benevolence spread through the apartment that I hadn't felt for a long time. How nice it was that the two men agreed with one another, liked one another. I began to clear the table in silence. Nino jumped up and offered to do the dishes, provided the girls helped him. Sit down, he said, and I sat, while he got Dede and Elsa busy, eager, every so often he asked where he should put something or other, and continued to chat with Pietro.

It was really him, after so long, and he was there. I looked without wanting to at the ring he wore on his ring finger. He never mentioned his marriage, I thought, he spoke of his mother, his father, but not of his wife and child. Maybe it wasn't a marriage of love, maybe he had married for convenience, maybe he was *forced* to get married. Then the flutter of hypotheses ceased. Nino out of the blue began to tell the girls about his son, Albertino, and he did it as if the child were a character in a fable, in tones that were comical and tender by turns. Finally he dried his hands, took out of his wallet a picture, showed it to Elsa, then Dede, then Pietro, who handed it to me. Albertino was very cute. He was two and sat in his mother's arms with a sulky expression. I looked at the child for a few seconds, and immediately went on to examine her. She seemed magnificent, with big eyes and long black hair, she could hardly be more than twenty. She was smiling, her teeth were sparkling, even, her gaze seemed to me that of someone in love. I gave him back the photograph, I said: I'll make coffee. I stayed alone in the kitchen, the four of them went into the living room.

Nino had an appointment for work, and with profuse apologies left immediately after coffee and a cigarette. I'm leaving tomorrow, he said, but I'll be back soon, next week. Pietro urged him repeatedly to let him know, he promised he would. He said goodbye to the girls affectionately, shook hands with Pietro, nodded to me, and disappeared. As soon as the door closed behind him I was overwhelmed by the dreariness of the apartment. I waited for Pietro, although he had been so at ease with Nino, to find something hateful about his guest, he almost always did. Instead he said contentedly: Finally a person it's worthwhile spending time with. That remark, I don't know why, hurt me. I turned on the television, and watched it with the girls for the rest of the afternoon.

101.

I hoped that Nino would call right away, the next day. I started every time the phone rang. Instead, an entire week slipped by without news from him. I felt as if I had a terrible cold. I became idle, I stopped my reading and my notes, I got angry at myself for that senseless expectation. Then one afternoon Pietro returned home in an especially good mood. He said that Nino had come by the department, that they had spent some time together, that there was no way to persuade him to come to dinner. He invited us to go out tomorrow evening, he said, the children, too: he doesn't want you to go to the trouble of cooking.

The blood began to flow more quickly, I felt an anxious tenderness for Pietro. As soon as the girls went to their room I embraced him, I kissed him, I whispered words of love. I hardly slept that night, or rather I slept with the impression of being awake. The next day, as soon as Dede came home from school, I put her in the bathtub with Elsa and washed them thoroughly. Then I moved on to myself. I took a long pleasant bath, I shaved my legs, I washed my hair and dried it carefully. I tried on every dress I owned, but I was getting more and more nervous, nothing looked right, and I didn't like the way my hair had turned out. Dede and Elsa were right there, pretending to be me. They posed in front of the mirror, they expressed dissatisfaction with clothes and hairdos, they shuffled around in my shoes. I resigned myself to being what I was. After I scolded Elsa too harshly for getting her dress dirty at the last minute, we got in the car and drove to pick up Pietro and Nino, who were at the university. I drove apprehensively, constantly reprimanding the girls, who were singing nursery rhymes of their own invention based on shit and pee. The closer I got to the place where we were to meet, the more I hoped that some last-minute engagement would keep Nino from coming. Instead I saw the two men right away, talking. Nino had enveloping gestures, as if he were inviting his interlocutor to enter into a space designed just for him. Pietro seemed as usual clumsy, the skin of his face flushed, he alone was laughing and in a deferential way. Neither of the two showed particular interest in my arrival.

My husband sat in the back seat with the two girls, Nino sat beside me to direct me to a place where the food was good and— he said, turning to Dede and Elsa—they made delicious *frittelle*. He described them in detail, getting the girls excited. A long time ago, I thought, observing him out of the corner of my eye, we held hands as we walked, and twice he kissed me. What nice fingers. To me he said only *Here go right, then right again, then left at the intersection*. Not an admiring look, not a compliment.

360 · ELENA FERRANTE

At the trattoria we were greeted in a friendly but respectful way. Nino knew the owner, the waiters. I ended up at the head of the table between the girls, the two men sat opposite each other, and my husband began talking about the difficulties of life in the university. I said almost nothing, attending to Dede and Elsa, who usually at the table were very well behaved but that night kept causing trouble, laughing, to attract Nino's attention. I thought uneasily: Pietro talks too much, he's boring him, he doesn't leave him space. I thought: We've lived in this city for seven years and we have no place of our own where we could take him in return, a restaurant where the food is good, as it is here, where we're recognized as soon as we enter. I liked the owner's courtesy, he came to our table often, and even went so far as to say to Nino: Tonight I won't give you that, it's not fit for you and your guests, and he advised something else. When the famous *frittelle* arrived, the girls were elated, and so was Pietro, they fought over them. Only then Nino turned to me.

"Why haven't you had anything else published?" he asked, without the frivolity of dinner conversation, and an interest that seemed genuine.

I blushed, I said indicating the children:

"I did something else."

"That book was really good."

"Thank you."

"It's not a compliment, you've always known how to write. You remember the article about the religion teacher?"

"Your friends didn't publish it."

"There was a misunderstanding."

"I lost faith."

"I'm sorry. Are you writing now?"

"In my spare time."

"A novel?"

"I don't know what it is."

"But the subject?"

"Men who fabricate women."

"Nice."

"We'll see."

"Get busy, I'd like to read you soon."

And, to my surprise, he turned out to be very familiar with the works by women I was concerned with: I had been sure that men didn't read them. Not only that: he cited a book by Starobinski that he had read recently, and said there was something that might be useful to me. He knew so much; he had been like that since he was a boy, curious about everything. Now he was quoting Rousseau and Bernard Shaw, I broke in, he listened attentively. And when the children, nerve-rackingly, began tugging at me to order more *frittelle*, he signaled to the owner to make us some more. Then, turning to Pietro, he said:

"You should leave your wife more time."

"She has all day available."

"I'm not kidding. If you don't, you're guilty not only on a human level but also on a political one."

"What's the crime?"

"The waste of intelligence. A community that finds it natural to suffocate with the care of home and children so many women's intellectual energies is its own enemy and doesn't realize it."

I waited in silence for Pietro to respond. My husband reacted with sarcasm.

"Elena can cultivate her intelligence when and how she likes, the essential thing is that she not take time from me."

"If she doesn't take it from you, then who can she take it from?"

Pietro frowned.

"When the task we give ourselves has the urgency of passion, there's nothing that can keep us from completing it."

I felt wounded, I whispered with a false smile:

"My husband is saying that I have no true interest."

Silence. Nino asked:

"And is that true?"

I answered in a rush that I didn't know, I didn't know anything. But while I was speaking, with embarrassment, with rage, I realized that my eyes were filled with tears. I lowered my gaze. That's enough *fritelle*, I said to the children in a scarcely controlled voice, and Nino came to my aid, he exclaimed: I'll eat just one more, Mamma also, Papa, too, and you can have two, but then that's it. He called over the owner and said solemnly: I'll be back here with these two young ladies in exactly thirty days and you'll make us a mountain of these exquisite *fritelle*, all right?

Elsa asked: "When is a month, when is thirty days?"

And I, having managed to repress my tears, stared at Nino and said:

"Yes, when is a month, when is thirty days?"

We laughed—Dede more than us adults—at Elsa's vague idea of time. Then Pietro tried to pay, but he discovered that Nino had already done it. He protested. He drove, I sat in the back between the two girls, who were half asleep. We took Nino to the hotel and all the way I listened to their slightly tipsy conversation. Once we were there Pietro, euphoric, said:

"It doesn't make sense to throw away money: we have a guest room, next time you can come and stay with us, don't stand on ceremony."

Nino smiled:

"Less than an hour ago we said that Elena needs time, and now you want to burden her with my presence?"

I interrupted wearily: "It would be a pleasure for me, and also for Dede and Elsa."

But as soon as we were alone I said to my husband:

"Before making certain invitations you might at least consult me."

He started the car, looked at me in the rearview mirror, stammered:

"I thought it would please you."

102.

Oh of course it pleased me, it pleased me *greatly*. But I also felt as if my body had the consistency of eggshell, and a slight pressure on my arm, on my forehead, on my stomach would be enough to break it and dig out all my secrets, in particular those which were secrets even to me. I avoided counting the days. I concentrated on the texts I was studying, but I did it as if Nino had commissioned that work and on his return would expect first-rate results. I wanted to tell him: I followed your advice, I kept going, here's a draft, tell me what you think.

It was a good expedient. The thirty days of waiting went by too quickly. I forgot about Elisa, I never thought of Lila, I didn't telephone Mariarosa. And I didn't read the newspapers or watch television. I neglected the children and the house. Of arrests and clashes and assassinations and wars, in the permanent agon of Italy and the planet, only an echo reached me; I was scarcely aware of the heavy tensions of the electoral campaign. All I did was write, with great absorption. I racked my brains over a pile of old questions, until I had the impression that I had found, at least in writing, a definitive order. At times I was tempted to turn to Pietro. He was much smarter than me, he would surely save me from writing hasty or crude or stupid things. But I didn't do it, I hated the moments when he intimidated me with his encyclopedic knowledge. I worked hard, I remember, especially on the first and second Biblical creations. I put them in order, taking the first as a sort of synthesis of the divine creative act, the second as a sort of more expansive account. I made up a lively story, without ever feeling imprudent. God—I wrote, more or less—creates man, *Ish*, in his image. He creates a masculine and a feminine version. How? First, with the dust of the earth, he forms Ish, and blows into his nostrils the breath of life. Then he makes *Isha'h*, the woman, from the already formed male material, material no longer raw but living, which he takes from Ish's side, and immediately closes up the flesh. The result is that Ish can say: This thing is not, like the army of all that has been created, *other* than me, but is flesh of *my* flesh, bone of *my* bones. God produced it from me. He made me fertile with the breath of life and extracted it from *my* body. I am Ish and she is Isha'h. In the word above all, in the word that names her, she derives from me. I am in the image of the divine spirit. I carry within me his Word. She is therefore a pure suffix applied to my verbal root, she can express herself *only* within *my* word.

And I went on like that and lived for days and days in a state of pleasurable intellectual overexcitement. My only pressure was to have a readable text in time. Every so often I was surprised at myself: I had the impression that striving for Nino's approval made the writing easier, freed me.

But the month passed and he didn't appear. At first it helped me: I had more time and managed to complete my work. Then I was alarmed, I asked Pietro. I discovered that they often talked in the office, but that he hadn't heard from him for several days.

"You often talk?" I said annoyed.

"Yes."

"Why didn't you tell me?"

"What?"

"That you often talked."

"They were calls about work."

"Well, since you've become so friendly, call and see if he'll deign to tell us when he's coming."

"Is that necessary?"

"Not for you, but the effort is mine: I'm the one who has to take care of everything and I'd like to be warned in time."

He didn't call him. I responded by saying to myself: All right, let's wait, Nino promised the girls he'd be back, I don't think he'll disappoint them. And it was true. He called a week late, in the evening. I answered, he seemed embarrassed. He uttered a few generalities, then he asked: Is Pietro not there? I was embarrassed in turn, I gave the phone to Pietro. They talked for a long time, I felt with increasing uneasiness that my husband was using unfamiliar tones: exclamations, laughter, his voice too loud. I understood only then that the relationship with Nino reassured him, made him feel less isolated, he forgot his troubles and worked more eagerly. I went into my study, where Dede was reading and Elsa playing, both waiting for dinner. But even there his voice reached me, he seemed drunk. Then he was silent, I heard his steps in the house. He peeked in, and said gaily to his daughters:

"Girls, tomorrow night we're going to eat *frittelle* with uncle Nino."

Dede and Elsa shouted with excitement, I asked:

"What's he doing, is he coming to stay here?"

"No," he answered, "he's with his wife and son, they're at the hotel."

103.

It took me a long time to absorb the meaning of those words. I burst out:

"He could have warned us."

"They decided at the last minute."

"He's a boor."

"Elena, what is the problem?"

So Nino had come with his wife; I was terrified by the comparison. I knew what I was like, I knew the crude physicality of my body, but for a good part of my life I had given it little importance. I had grown up with one pair of shoes at a time, ugly dresses sewed by my mother, makeup only on rare occasions. In recent years I had begun to be interested in fashion, to educate my taste under Adele's guidance, and now I enjoyed dressing up. But sometimes—especially when I had dressed not only to make a good impression in general but for a man—preparing myself (this was the word) seemed to me to have something ridiculous about it. All that struggle, all that time spent camouflaging myself when I could be doing something else. The colors that suited me, the ones that didn't, the styles that made me look thinner, those that made me fatter, the cut that flattered me, the one that didn't. A lengthy, costly preparation. Reducing myself to a table set for the sexual appetite of the male, to a well-cooked dish to make his mouth water. And then the anguish of not succeeding, of not *seeming* pretty, of not managing to conceal with skill the vulgarity of the flesh with its moods and odors and imperfections. But I had done it. I had done it also for Nino, recently. I had wanted to show him that I was different, that I had achieved a refinement of my own, that I was no longer the girl at Lila's wedding, the student at the party of Professor Galiani's children, and not even the inexperienced author of a single book, as I must have appeared in Milan. But now, enough. He had brought his wife and I was angry, it seemed to me a mean thing. I hated competing in looks with another woman, especially under the gaze of a man, and I suffered at the thought of finding myself in the same place with the beautiful girl I had seen in the photograph, it made me sick to my stomach. She would size me up, study every detail with the pride of a woman of Via Tasso taught since birth to attend to her body; then, at the end of the evening, alone with her husband, she would criticize me with cruel lucidity.

I hesitated for hours and finally decided that I would invent an excuse, my husband would go alone with the children. But the next day I couldn't resist. I dressed, I undressed, I combed my hair, I uncombed it, I nagged Pietro. I went to his room constantly, now with one dress, now another, now with one hairdo, now another, and I asked him, tensely: How do I look? He gave me a distracted glance, he said: You look nice. I answered: And if I put on the blue dress? He agreed. But I put on the blue dress and I didn't like it, it was tight across the hips. I went back to him, I said, It's too tight. Pietro replied patiently Yes, the green one with the flowers looks better. But I didn't want the green one with the flowers to simply look better, I wanted it to look great, and my earrings to look great, and my hair to look great, and my shoes to look great. In other words I couldn't rely on Pietro, he looked at me without seeing me. And I felt more and more ungainly, too much bosom, too much ass, wide hips, and that dirty-blond hair, that big nose. I had the body of my mother, a graceless body, all I needed was for the sciatica to return and start limping. Nino's wife, instead, was very young, beautiful, rich, and surely knew how to be in the world, as I would never manage to learn. So I returned a thousand times to my first decision: I won't go, I'll send Pietro with the children, I'll have him say I don't feel well. I did go. I put on a white shirt over a cheerful flowered skirt, the only jewel I wore was my mother's old bracelet, in my purse I put the text I had written. I said who gives a damn about her, him, all of them.

104.

Because of all my hesitations we arrived late at the restaurant. The Sarratore family was already at the table. Nino introduced his wife, Eleonora, and my mood changed. Oh yes, she had a pretty face and beautiful black hair, just as in the photograph. But she was shorter than I, and I wasn't very tall. She had no bosom, though she was plump. And she wore a bright-red dress that didn't suit her at all. And she was wearing too much jewelry. And from the first words she spoke she revealed a shrill voice with the accent of a Neapolitan brought up by canasta players in a house with a picture window on the gulf. But mainly, in the course of the evening, she proved to be une-ducated, even though she was studying law, and inclined to speak ill of everything and everyone with the air of one who feels she is swimming against the tide and is proud of it. Wealthy, in other words, capricious, vulgar. Even her pleasing features were constantly spoiled by an expression of irritation followed by a nervous laugh, *ih ih ih*, which broke up her con-versation, even the individual sentences. She was irritated by Florence—*What does it have that Naples doesn't*—by the restaurant—*terrible*—by the owner—*rude*—by whatever Pietro said—*What nonsense*—by the girls—*My goodness, you talk so much, let's have a little quiet, please*—and naturally me—*You studied in Pisa, but why, literature in Naples is much better, I've never heard of that novel of yours, when did it come out, eight years ago I was fourteen*. She was sweet only with her son and with Nino. Albertino was sweet, round, with a happy expres-sion, and Eleonora did nothing but praise him. The same hap-pened with her husband: no one was better than he, she agreed with everything he said, and she touched him, hugged him, kissed him. What did that girl have in common with Lila, even with Silvia? Nothing. Why then had Nino married her?

I observed her all evening. He was nice to her, he let him-self be hugged and kissed, he smiled at her affectionately when she said rude and foolish things, he played distractedly with the child. But he didn't change his attitude toward my daugh-ters, giving them a lot of attention; he continued to talk pleas-antly to Pietro, and even spoke a few words to me. His wife—I wished to think—did not absorb him. Eleonora was one of the many pieces of his busy life, but had no influence on him,

Nino went forward on his own path without attaching any importance to her. And so I felt increasingly at ease, especially when he held my wrist for a few seconds, and almost caressed it, showing that he recognized my bracelet; especially when he kidded my husband, asking him if he had left me a little more time for myself; especially when, right afterward, he asked if I had made progress with my work.

"I finished a first draft," I said.

Nino turned to Pietro seriously: "Have you read it?"

"Elena never lets me read anything."

"It's you who don't want to," I replied, but without bitterness, as if it were a game between us.

Eleonora at that point interrupted, she didn't want to be left out.

"What sort of thing is it?" she asked. But just as I was about to answer, her flighty mind carried her away and she asked me blithely: "Tomorrow will you take me to see the shops, while Nino works?"

I smiled with false cordiality and she began with a detailed list of things that she meant to buy. Only when we left the restaurant I managed to approach Nino and whisper:

"Do you feel like looking at what I've written?"

He looked at me with genuine amazement: "Would you really let me read it?"

"If it wouldn't bore you, yes."

I handed him my pages furtively, my heart pounding, as if I didn't want Pietro, Eleonora, or the children to notice.

105.

I didn't close my eyes. In the morning I resigned myself to the date with Eleonora; we were to meet at ten at the hotel. Don't do the stupid thing—I ordered myself—of asking her if her husband began to read it: Nino is busy, it will take time; you mustn't think about it, at least a week will go by.

But at precisely nine, when I was about to leave, the phone rang and it was him.

"I'm sorry," he said, "but I'm on my way to the library and I can't telephone until tonight. Sure I'm not bothering you?"

"Absolutely not."

"I read it."

"Already?"

"Yes, and it's really excellent. You have a great capacity for research, an admirable rigor, and astonishing imagination. But what I envy most is your ability as a narrator. You've written something hard to define, I don't know if it's an essay or a story. But it's extraordinary."

"Is that a flaw?"

"What?"

"That it's not classifiable."

"Of course not, that's one of its merits."

"You think I should publish it as it is?"

"Absolutely yes."

"Thank you."

"Thank you, now I have to go. Be patient with Eleonora, she seems aggressive but it's only timidity. Tomorrow morning we return to Naples, but I'll be back after the elections and if you want we can talk."

"It would be a pleasure. Will you come and stay with us?"

"You're sure I won't bother you?"

"Not at all."

"All right."

He didn't hang up, I heard him breathing.

"Elena."

"Yes."

"Lina, when we were children, dazzled us both."

I felt an intense uneasiness.

"In what sense?"

"You ended up attributing to her capacities that are only yours."

"And you?"

"I did worse. What I had seen in you, I then stupidly seemed to find in her."

I was silent for several seconds. Why had he felt the need to bring up Lila, like that, on the telephone? And what was he saying to me? Was it merely compliments? Or was he trying to communicate to me that as a boy he would have loved me but that on Ischia he had attributed to one what belonged to the other?

"Come back soon," I said.

106.

I went out with Eleonora and the three children in a state of such well-being that even if she had stuck a knife in me I would not have felt bad. Nino's wife, besides, in the face of my euphoria and the many kindnesses I showed her, stopped being hostile, praised Dede and Elsa's good behavior, confessed that she admired me. Her husband had told her everything about me, my studies, my success as a writer. But I'm a little jealous, she admitted, and not because you're clever but because you've known him forever and I haven't. She, too, would like to have met him as a girl, and know what he was like at ten, at fourteen, his voice before it changed, his laughter as a boy. Luckily I have Albertino, she said, he's just like his father.

I observed the child, but it didn't seem to me that I saw signs of Nino, maybe they would appear later. I look like Papa, Dede exclaimed suddenly, proudly, and Elsa added: I'm more like my mamma. I thought of Silvia's son, Mirko, who had seemed identical to Nino. What pleasure I had felt holding him in my arms, soothing his cries in Mariarosa's house. What had I been looking for at that time, in that child, when I was still far from the experience of motherhood? What had I sought in Gennaro, before I knew that his father was Stefano. What was I looking for in Albertino, now that I was the mother of Dede and Elsa, and why did I examine him so closely? I dismissed the idea that Nino remembered Mirko from time to time. Nor did I think he had ever demonstrated any interest in Gennaro. Men, dazed by pleasure, absent-mindedly sow their seed. Overcome by their orgasm, they fertilize us. They show up inside us and withdraw, leaving, concealed in our flesh, their ghost, like a lost object. Was Albertino the child of will, of attention? Or did he, too, exist in the arms of this woman-mother without Nino's feeling that he had had anything to do with it? I roused myself, I said to Eleonora that her son was the image of his father and was content with that lie. Then I told her in detail, with affection, with tenderness, about Nino at the time of elementary school, at the time of the contests organized by Maestra Oliviero and the principal to see who was smartest, Nino at the time of high school, about Professor Galiani and the vacation we had had on Ischia, with other friends. I stopped there, even though she kept childishly asking: And then?

The more we talked, the more she liked me; she became attached to me. If we went into a shop and I liked something, tried it on but then decided against it, I discovered on leaving that Eleonora had bought it, as a present for me. She also wanted to buy clothes for Dede and Elsa. At the restaurant she paid. And she paid for the taxi in which she took me home with the children, and then had herself driven to the hotel, loaded with packages. We said goodbye, the children and I waved until the car turned the corner. She's another piece of my city, I thought. Outside my field of experience. She used money as if it had no value. I ruled out that it was Nino's money. Her father was a lawyer, also her grandfather, her mother was from a banking family. I wondered what difference there was between their bourgeois wealth and that of the Solaras. I thought of how many hidden turns money takes before becoming high salaries and lavish fees. I remembered the boys from the neighborhood who were paid by the day unloading smuggled goods, cutting trees in the parks, working at the construction sites. I thought of Antonio, Pasquale, Enzo. Ever since they were boys they had been scrambling for a few lire here, a few there to survive. Engineers, architects, lawyers, banks were another thing, but their money came, if through a thousand filters, from the same shady business, the same destruction, a few crumbs had even mutated into tips for my father and had contributed to allowing me an education. What therefore was the threshold beyond which bad money became good and vice versa? How clean was the money that Eleonora had heedlessly spent in the heat of a Florentine day; and the checks with which the gifts that I was taking home had been bought, how different were they from those with which Michele paid Lila for her work? All afternoon, the girls and I paraded in front of the mirror in the clothes we had been given as presents. They were nice things, pretty and cheerful. There was a pale red, forties-style dress that looked especially good on me, I would have liked Nino to see me in it.

But the Sarratore family returned to Naples without our having a chance to see them again. Unpredictably, time didn't collapse; rather, it began to flow lightly. Nino would return, that was certain. And he would talk about my writing. To avoid unnecessary friction I put a copy of my work on Pietro's desk. Then I called Mariarosa with the pleasant certainty that I had worked well and told her I had managed to put in order that tangle I had talked to her about. She wanted me to send it immediately. A few days later she called me excitedly, asked if she could translate it herself into French and send it to a friend of hers in Nanterre who had a small publishing house. I agreed enthusiastically, but it didn't end there. A few hours later my mother-in-law called pretending to be offended.

"How is it that now you give what you write to Mariarosa and not to me?"

"I'm afraid it wouldn't interest you. It's just seventy pages, it's not a novel, I don't even know what it is."

"When you don't know what you've written it means you've worked well. And anyway let me decide if it interests me or not."

I sent her a copy. I did it almost casually. The same morning Nino, around midday, called me by surprise from the station, he had just arrived in Florence.

"I'll be at your house in half an hour, I'll leave my bag and go to the library."

"You won't eat something?" I asked with naturalness. It seemed to me normal that he—arriving after a long journey—should come to sleep at my house, that I should prepare something for him to eat while he took a shower in my bathroom, that we should have lunch together, he and I and the children, while Pietro was giving exams at the university.

107.

Nino stayed for ten days. Nothing of what happened in that time had anything to do with the yearning for seduction I had experienced years earlier. I didn't joke with him; I didn't act flirtatious; I didn't assail him with all sorts of favors; I didn't play the part of the liberated woman, modeling myself on my sister-in-law; I didn't tenderly seek his gaze; I didn't contrive to sit next to him at the table or on the couch, in front of the television; I didn't go around the house half-dressed; I didn't try to be alone with him; I didn't graze his elbow with mine, his arm with my arm or breast, his leg with my leg. I was timid, restrained, spoke concisely, making sure only that he ate well, that the girls didn't bother him, that he felt comfortable. And it wasn't a choice, I couldn't have behaved differently. He joked a lot with Pietro, with Dede, with Elsa, but as soon as he spoke to me he became serious, he seemed to measure his words as if there were not an old friendship between us. And it seemed right to me to do the same. I was very happy to have him in the house, and yet I felt no need for confidential tones and gestures; in fact, I liked staying on the edge and avoiding contact between us. I felt like a drop of rain in a spiderweb, and I was careful not to slide down.

We had a single long exchange, focused entirely on my writing. He spoke about it immediately, upon arriving, with precision and acuteness. He had been struck by the story of Ish and Isha'h, he questioned me, he asked: for you, the woman, in the Biblical story, is no different from the man, is the man himself? Yes, I said. Eve can't, doesn't know how, doesn't have the material to be Eve outside of Adam. *Her* evil and *her* good are evil and good according to Adam. Eve is Adam as a woman. And the divine work was so successful that she herself, in herself, doesn't know what she is, she has pliable features, she doesn't possess her own language, she doesn't have a spirit or a logic of her own, she loses her shape easily. A terrible condition, Nino commented, and I nervously looked at him out of the corner of my eye to see if he was making fun of me. No, he wasn't. Rather, he praised me without the slightest sarcasm, he cited some books I didn't know on relevant subjects, he repeated that he considered the work ready to be published. I listened without showing any satisfaction, I said only, at the end: Mariarosa also liked it. Then he asked about my sister-in-law, he spoke well of her both as a scholar and for her devotion to Franco, and went off to the library.

Otherwise he left every morning with Pietro and returned at

night after him. On very rare occasions we all went out together. Once, for example, he wanted to take us to the movies to see a comedy chosen just for the girls. Nino sat next to Pietro, I between my daughters. When I realized that I was laughing hard as soon as he laughed, I stopped laughing completely. I scolded him mildly because during the intermission he wanted to buy ice cream for Dede, Elsa, and naturally for the adults, too. For me no, I said, thank you. He joked a little, said that the ice cream was good and I didn't know what I was missing, he offered me a taste, I tasted. Small things, in other words. One afternoon we took a long walk, Dede, Elsa, he and I. We didn't say much, Nino let the children talk. But the walk made a deep impression, I could point out every street, the places where we stopped, every corner. It was hot, the city was crowded. He constantly greeted people, some called to him by his last name, I was introduced to this person and that, with exaggerated praise. I was struck by his notoriety. One man, a well-known historian, complimented him on the children, as if they were our children. Nothing else happened, apart from a sudden, inexplicable change in the relations between him and Pietro.

108.

It all began one evening at dinner. Pietro spoke to him with admiration of a professor from Naples, at the time quite respected, and Nino said: I would have bet that you liked that asshole. My husband was disoriented, he gave an uncertain smile, but Nino piled it on, making fun of him for how easily he had let himself be deceived by appearances. The next morning after breakfast there was another incident. I don't remember in relation to what, Nino referred to my old clash with the religion professor about the Holy Spirit. Pietro, who didn't know about that episode, wanted to know, and Nino, addressing not him but the girls, immediately began to tell the story as if it were some grandiose undertaking of their mother as a child.

My husband praised me, he said: You were very courageous. But then he explained to Dede, in the tone he took when stupid things were being said on television and he felt it his duty to explain to his daughter how matters really stood, what had happened to the twelve apostles on the morning of Pentecost: a noise as of wind, flames like fire, the gift of being understood by anyone, in any language. Then he turned to me and Nino speaking with passion of the *virtus* that had pervaded the disciples, and he quoted the prophet Joel, *I will spread my spirit over every flesh*, adding that the Holy Spirit was an indispensable symbol for reflecting on how the multitudes find a way of confronting each other and organizing into a community. Nino let him speak, but with an increasingly ironic expression. At the end he exclaimed: I bet there's a priest hiding in you. And to me, in amusement: Are you a wife or a priest's housekeeper? Pietro turned red, he was confused. He had always loved those subjects, I felt that he was upset. He stammered: I'm sorry, I'm wasting your time, let's go to work.

Such moments increased and for no obvious reason. While relations between Nino and me remained the same, attentive to form, courteous and distant, between him and Pietro the dikes broke. At both breakfast and dinner, the guest began to speak to the host in a crescendo of mocking remarks, just bordering on the offensive, humiliating but expressed in a friendly way, offered with a smile, so that you couldn't object without seeming petulant. I recognized that tone; in the neighborhood the swifter party often used it to dominate the slower one and push him wordlessly into the middle of the joke. Mainly, Pietro appeared disoriented: he liked Nino, he appreciated him, and so he didn't react, he shook his head, pretending to be amused, while at times he seemed to wonder where he had gone wrong and waited for him to return to the old, affectionate tone. But Nino continued, implacable. He turned to me, to the children, he exaggerated in order to receive our approval. And the girls approved, laughing, and I, too, a little. Yet I thought: Why is he acting like this, if Pietro gets mad their relations will be ruined. But Pietro didn't get mad, he simply didn't understand, and as the days passed his old nervousness returned. His face was tired, the strain of those years reappeared in his worried eyes and his lined forehead. I have to do something, I thought, and as soon as possible. But I did nothing; rather, I struggled to expel not the admiration, but the excitement—maybe yes, it was excitement—that gripped me in seeing, in hearing, how an Airota, an extremely well-educated Airota, lost ground, was confused, responded feebly to the swift, brilliant, even cruel aggressions of Nino Sarratore, my schoolmate, my friend, born in the neighborhood, like me.

109.

A few days before he returned to Naples, there were two especially unpleasant episodes. One afternoon Adele telephoned; she, too, was very pleased with my work. She told me to send the manuscript right away to the publisher—they could make a small volume to publish simultaneously with the publication in France or, if it couldn't be done in time, right afterward. I spoke of it at dinner in a tone of detachment and Nino was full of compliments, he said to the girls:

"You have an exceptional mamma." Then he turned to Pietro: "Have you read it?"

"I haven't had time."

"Better for you not to read it."

"Why?"

"It's not stuff for you."

"That is?"

"It's too intelligent."

"What do you mean?"

"That you're less intelligent than Elena."

And he laughed. Pietro said nothing, Nino pressed him:

"Are you offended?"

He wanted him to react, in order to humiliate him again. But Pietro got up from the table, he said:

"Excuse me, I have work to do."

I murmured:

"Finish eating."

He didn't answer. We were eating in the living room, it was a big room. For a few seconds it seemed that he wished to cross it and go to his study. Instead he made a half turn, sat down on the couch, and turned on the television, raising the volume. The atmosphere was intolerable. In the space of a few days it had all become complicated. I felt very unhappy.

"Lower it a bit?" I asked him.

He answered simply:

"No."

Nino gave a little laugh, finished eating, helped me clear. In the kitchen I said to him:

"Excuse him, Pietro works a lot and doesn't sleep much."

He answered with a burst of rage:

"How can you stand him?"

I looked at the door in alarm, luckily the volume of the television was still loud.

"I love him," I answered. And since he insisted on helping me wash the dishes I added: "Go, please, otherwise you're in the way."

The other episode was even uglier, but decisive. I no longer knew what I truly wanted: now I hoped that this period would be over quickly, I wished to return to familiar habits, watch over my little book. Yet I liked going into Nino's room in the morning, tidying up the mess he left, making the bed, thinking as I cooked that he would have dinner with us that evening. And it distressed me that it was all about to end. At certain hours of the afternoon I felt mad. I had the impression that the house was empty in spite of the girls, I myself was emptied, I felt no interest in what I had written, I perceived its superficiality, I lost faith in the enthusiasm of Mariarosa, of Adele, of the French publisher, the Italian. I thought: As soon as he goes, nothing will make sense.

I was in that state—life was slipping away with an unbearable sensation of loss—when Pietro returned from the university with a grim look. We were waiting for him for dinner, Nino had been back for half an hour but had immediately been kidnapped by the children. I asked him kindly:

"Did something happen?"

He muttered:

"Don't ever again bring to this house people from your home."

I froze, I thought he was referring to Nino. And Nino, too, who had come in trailed by Dede and Elsa, must have thought the same thing, because he looked at him with a provocative smile, as if he expected a scene. But Pietro had something else in mind. He said in his contemptuous tone, the tone he used well when he was convinced that basic principles were at stake and he was called to defend them:

"Today the police returned and they named some names, they showed me some photographs."

I breathed a sigh of relief. I knew that, after he refused to withdraw the charges against the student who had pointed a gun at him, the visits of the police—even more than the scorn of many militant youths and not a few professors—weighed on him, as they treated him as an informer. I was sure that was why he was angry and I interrupted him, bitterly:

"Your fault. You shouldn't have acted like that, I told you. Now you'll never get rid of them."

Nino intervened, he asked Pietro, mockingly:

"Who did you report?"

Pietro didn't even turn to look at him. He was angry with me, it was with me he wanted to quarrel. He said:

"I did what was necessary then and I should have done what was necessary today. But I was silent because you were in the middle of it."

At that point I realized that the problem was not the police but what he had learned from them. I said:

"What do I have to do with it?"

His voice changed:

"Aren't Pasquale and Nadia your friends?"

I repeated obtusely:

"Pasquale and Nadia?"

"The police showed me photographs of terrorists and they were among them."

I didn't react, words failed. What I had imagined was true, then; Pietro in fact was confirming it. For a few seconds the images returned, of Pasquale firing the gun at Gino, kneecapping Filippo, while Nadia—Nadia, not Lila—went up the stairs, knocked on Bruno's door, went in and shot him in the face. Terrible. And yet at that moment Pietro's tone seemed out of place, as if he were using the information to make trouble for me in Nino's eyes, to start a discussion that I had no wish to have. In fact Nino immediately interrupted again, continuing to make fun of him:

"So are you an informer for the police? What are you doing? Informing on comrades? Does your father know? Your mother? Your sister?"

I said weakly: Let's go and eat. But right afterward I said to Nino, politely making light of it, and to get him to stop goading Pietro by bringing up his family: Stop it, what do you mean, informer. Then I alluded vaguely to the fact that some time ago Pasquale Peluso, maybe he remembered him, from the neighborhood, a good kid who had ended up getting together with Nadia, he remembered her, naturally, Professor Galiani's daughter. And there I stopped because Nino was already laughing. He exclaimed: Nadia, oh good Lord, Nadia, and he turned again to Pietro, even more mockingly: only you and a couple of idiot police could think that Nadia Galiani is part of the armed struggle, it's madness. Nadia, the best and nicest person I've ever known, what have we come to in Italy, let's go and eat, come on, the defense of the established order can do without you for now. And he went to the table, calling Dede and Elsa, as I began to serve, sure that Pietro was about to join us.

But he didn't. I thought he had gone to wash his hands, that he was delaying in order to calm down, and I sat in my place. I was agitated, I would have liked a nice calm evening, a quiet ending to that shared life. But he didn't come, the children were already eating. Now even Nino seemed bewildered.

"Start," I said, "it's getting cold."

"Only if you eat, too."

I hesitated. Maybe I should go and see how my husband was, what he was doing, if he had calmed down. But I didn't want to, I was annoyed by his behavior. Why hadn't he kept to himself that visit from the police, usually he did with everything of his, he never told me anything. Why had he spoken like that in Nino's presence: *Don't ever again bring to this house people from your home.* What urgency was there to make that subject public, he could wait, he could have an outburst later, once we were in the bedroom. He was angry with me, that was the point. He wanted to ruin the evening for me, he didn't care what I did or what I wanted.

I began to eat. The four of us ate, first course, second, and even the dessert I had made. Pietro didn't appear. At that point

I became furious. Pietro didn't want to eat? All right, he didn't have to eat, evidently he wasn't hungry. He wanted to mind his own business? Very well, the house was big, without him there would be no tension. Anyway, now it was clear that the problem was not simply that two people who had once showed up at our house were suspected of being part of an armed gang. The problem was that he didn't have a sufficiently quick intelligence, that he didn't know how to sustain the skirmishes of men, that he suffered from it and was angry with me. But what do I care about you and your pettiness. I'll clean up later, I said aloud, as if I were issuing an order to myself, to my confusion. Then I turned on the television and sat on the sofa with Nino and the girls.

A long time passed, filled with tension. I felt that Nino was uneasy and yet amused. I'm going to call Papa, said Dede, who, with her stomach full, was now worried about Pietro. Go, I said. She came back almost on tiptoe, she whispered in my ear: He went to bed, he's sleeping. Nino heard her anyway, he said:

"I'm leaving tomorrow."

"Did you finish your work?"

"No."

"Stay a little longer."

"I can't."

"Pietro is a good person."

"You defend him?"

Defend him from what, from whom? I didn't understand, I was on the point of getting mad at him, too.

110.

The children fell asleep in front of the television, I put them to bed. When I came back Nino wasn't there, he had gone to his room. Depressed, I cleaned up, washed the dishes. How

384 · ELENA FERRANTE

foolish to ask him to stay longer, it would be better if he left. On the other hand, how to endure the dreariness of life without him. I would have liked him at least to leave with the promise that sooner or later he would return. I wished that he would sleep again in my house, have breakfast with me in the morning and eat at the same table in the evening, that he would talk about this and that in his playful tone, that he would listen to me when I wanted to give shape to an idea, that he would be respectful of my every sentence, that with me he would never resort to irony, to sarcasm. Yet I had to admit that if the situation had so quickly deteriorated, making our living together impossible, it was his fault. Pietro was attached to him. It gave him pleasure to see him around, the friendship that had arisen was important to him. Why had Nino felt the need to hurt him, to humiliate him, to take away his authority? I took off my makeup, I washed, I put on my nightgown. I locked the house door, I turned off the gas, I lowered all the blinds. I checked on the children. I hoped that Pietro wasn't pretending to sleep, that he wasn't waiting for me in order to quarrel. I looked at his night table, he had taken a sleeping pill, he had collapsed. It made me feel tender toward him, I kissed him on the cheek. What an unpredictable person: extremely intelligent and stupid, sensitive and dull, courageous and cowardly, highly educated and ignorant, well brought up and rude. A failed Airota, he had stumbled on the path. Could Nino, so sure of himself, so determined, have gotten him going again, helped him improve? Again I asked myself why that nascent friendship had changed to hostility in one direction. And this time it seemed to me that I understood. Nino wanted to help me see my husband for what he really was. He was convinced that I had an idealized image that I had submitted to on both the emotional and the intellectual level. He had wanted to reveal to me the lack of substance behind this very young professor, the author of a thesis that had become a highly regarded book, the scholar who had been working for a long time on a new publication that was to secure his reputation. It was as if in these last days he had done nothing but scold me: You live with a dull man, you've had two children with a nobody. His project was to liberate me by disparaging him, restore me to myself by demolishing him. But in doing so did he realize that he had proposed himself, like it or not, as an alternative model of virility?

That question made me angry. Nino had been reckless. He had thrown confusion into a situation that for me constituted the only possible equilibrium. Why sow disorder without even consulting me? Who had asked him to open my eyes, to save me? From what had he deduced that I needed it? Did he think he could do what he wanted with my life as a couple, with my responsibility as a mother? To what end? What did he think he was driving at? It's he—I said to myself—who ought to clarify his ideas. Doesn't our friendship interest him? The holidays are close. I'll go to Viareggio, he said he's going to Capri to his in-laws' house. Must we wait until the end of the vacations to see each other again? And why? Now, during the summer, it would be possible to consolidate the relation between our families. I could telephone Eleonora, invite her, her husband, the child to spend a few days with us in Viareggio. And I would like to be invited, in turn, to Capri, where I've never been, with Dede, Elsa, and Pietro. But if that doesn't happen, why not write each other, exchange ideas, titles of books, talk about our work?

I couldn't quiet myself. Nino was wrong. If he really was attached to me, he had to take everything back to the starting point. He had to regain the liking and friendship of Pietro, my husband asked nothing else. Did he really think he was doing me good by causing those tensions? No, no, I had to talk to him, tell him it was foolish to treat Pietro that way. I got out of bed cautiously, I left the room. I went down the hall barefoot, knocked on Nino's door. I waited a moment, I went in. The room was dark.

"You've decided," I heard him say.

I was startled, I didn't ask *decided what*. I knew only that he was right, I had decided. I quickly took off my nightgown, I lay down beside him in spite of the heat.

111.

I returned to my bed around four in the morning. My husband started, he murmured in his sleep: What's happening? I said in a peremptory way: Sleep, and he became quiet. I was stunned. I was happy about what had happened, but no matter how great an effort I made I couldn't comprehend it *inside* of my situation, *inside* of what I was in that house, in Florence. It seemed to me that everything between Nino and me had been sealed in the neighborhood, when his parents were moving and Melina was throwing things out the window and yelling, racked by suffering; or on Ischia, when we went for a walk and held hands; or the night in Milan, after the meeting in the bookstore, when he had defended me against the fierce critic. That for a while gave me a sense of irresponsibility, maybe even of innocence, as if the friend of Lila, the wife of Pietro, the mother of Dede and Elsa had nothing to do with the child-girl-woman who loved Nino and finally had made love with him. I felt the trace of his hands and his kisses in every part of my body. The craving for pleasure wouldn't be soothed, the thoughts were: the day is far off, what am I doing here, I'll go back to him, again.

Then I fell asleep. I opened my eyes suddenly, the room was light. What had I done? Here, in my own house, how foolish. Now Pietro would wake up. Now the children would wake up. I had to make breakfast. Nino would say goodbye, he would return to Naples to his wife and child. I would become myself again.

I got up, took a long shower, dried my hair, carefully put on my makeup, chose a nice dress, as if I were going out. Oh, of course, Nino and I had sworn in the middle of the night that we would never lose each other, that we would find a way to continue to love each other. But how, and when? Why should he have to look for me again? Everything that could happen between us had happened, the rest was only complications. Enough, I set the table carefully for breakfast. I wanted to leave him with a beautiful image of that permanence, the house, the customary objects, me.

Pietro appeared disheveled, in his pajamas.

"Where are you going?"

"Nowhere."

He looked at me in bewilderment—I never dressed that carefully as soon as I got up.

"You look nice."

"No thanks to you."

He went to the window, looked out, then muttered:

"I was very tired, last night."

"Also very rude."

"I'll apologize to him."

"You should apologize to me."

"I'm sorry."

"He's leaving today."

Dede appeared, barefoot. I went to get her slippers and woke Elsa, who, as usual, her eyes still closed, covered me with kisses. What a good smell she had, how soft she was. Yes, I said to myself, it happened. Fortunately, it could never happen. But now I had to discipline myself. Telephone Mariarosa to find out about France, talk to Adele, go in person to the publishers to find out what they intend to do with my book, if they are thinking about it seriously or just want to please my mother-in-law. Then I heard noises in the hall. It was Nino, I was overwhelmed by the signs of his presence, he was here, for a short time still. I disentangled myself from the child's hug, I said: sorry, Elsa, Mamma will be right back, and I hurried out.

Nino was coming sleepily out of his room, I pushed him into the bathroom, I closed the door. We kissed each other, again I lost awareness of place and time. I was amazed at how much I wanted him: I was good at hiding things from myself. We embraced with a fury that I had never known, as if our bodies were crashing against each other with the intention of breaking. So pleasure was this: breaking, mixing, no longer knowing what was mine and what was his. Even if Pietro had appeared, if the children had looked in, they would have been unable to recognize us. I whispered in his mouth:

"Stay longer."

"I can't."

"Then come back, swear you'll come back."

"Yes."

"And call me."

"Yes."

"Tell me you won't forget me, tell me you won't leave me, tell me you love me."

"I love you."

"Say it again."

"I love you."

"Swear that it's not a lie."

"I swear."

112.

He left an hour later, even though Pietro sullenly insisted that he stay, even though Dede burst into tears. My husband went to wash, and reappeared soon afterward ready to go out.

Looking down he said: I didn't tell the police that Pasquale and Nadia were in our house; and I did it not to protect you but because I think dissent now is being confused with crime. I didn't understand right away what he was talking about. Pasquale and Nadia had completely vanished from my mind, and they had a hard time re-entering. Pietro waited for a few seconds in silence. Maybe he wanted me to show that I agreed with his observation, and wished to face this day of heat and exams knowing that we were close again, that for once, at least, we thought in the same way. But I merely gave him a distracted nod. What did I care anymore about his political opinions, about Pasquale and Nadia, about the death of Ulrike Meinhof, the birth of the Socialist Republic of Vietnam, the electoral advances of the Communist Party? The world had retreated. I felt sunk inside myself, inside my flesh, which seemed to me not only the sole dwelling possible but also the only material for which it was worthwhile to struggle. It was a relief when he, the witness to order and disorder, closed the door behind him. I couldn't bear to be under his gaze, I feared that lips raw from kissing, the night's weariness, the body hypersensitive, as if burned, all would suddenly become visible.

As soon as I was alone, the certainty returned that I would never again see or hear from Nino. And along with it was another certainty: I could no longer live with Pietro, it seemed intolerable that we should continue to sleep in the same bed. What to do? I'll leave him, I thought. I'll go away with the children. But what procedure should I follow, do I simply leave? I knew nothing about separations and divorces, what was the practical part, how much time did it take to be free again. And I knew no couple who had taken that path. What happened to the children? How did one agree about their maintenance? Could I take the children to another city, for example Naples? And then why Naples, why not Milan? If I leave Pietro, I said to myself, I'll sooner or later need a job. Times are hard, the

economy is bad, and Milan is the right place, there's the publisher. But Dede and Elsa? Their relations with their father?
Must I stay in Florence, then? Never, ever. Better Milan, Pietro
could come and see his daughters whenever he could and
wanted to. Yes. And yet my head led me to Naples. Not to the
neighborhood, I would not return there. I imagined going to
live in the dazzling Naples where I had never lived, near Nino's
house, on Via Tasso. See him from the window when he was
going to and from the university, meet him on the street, speak
to him every day. Without disturbing him. Without causing
trouble to his family, rather, intensifying my friendship with
Eleonora. That nearness would be enough. In Naples, then, not
Milan. Besides, Milan, if I were separated from Pietro, would
no longer be so hospitable. My relations with Mariarosa would
cool, and also with Adele. Not cut off, no, they were civilized
people, but, still, they were Pietro's mother and sister, even if
they didn't have much respect for him. Not to mention Guido,
the father. No, certainly I would no longer be able to count on
the Airotas in the same way, maybe not even on the publishing
house. Help could come only from Nino. He had strong friendships everywhere, certainly he would find a way to support me.
Unless my being close made his wife nervous, made him nervous. For him I was a married woman who lived in Florence with
her family. Far from Naples, therefore, and not free. To break
up my marriage in a rush, run after him, go and live right near
him—really. He would think me mad; I would look like a silly
woman, out of her mind, the type of woman, dependent on a
man, who horrified Mariarosa's friends. And, above all, not
suitable for him. He had loved many women, he went from one
bed to the next, he sowed children carelessly, he considered
marriage a necessary convention but one that couldn't keep
desires in a cage. I would make myself ridiculous. I had done
without so many things in my life, I could do without Nino as
well. I would go my own way with my daughters.

But the telephone rang and I hurried to answer. It was him, in the background I could hear a loudspeaker, noise, confusion, it was hard to hear the voice. He had just arrived in Naples, he was calling from the station. Only a hello, he said, I wanted to know how you are. Fine, I said. What are you doing? I'm about to eat with the children. Is Pietro there? No. Did you like making love with me? Yes. A lot? Really a lot. I don't have any more phone tokens. Go, goodbye, thanks for calling. We'll talk again. Whenever you like. I was pleased with myself, with my self-control. I kept him at a proper distance, I said to myself, to a polite phone call I responded politely. But three hours later he called again, again from a public telephone. He was nervous. Why are you so cold? I'm not cold. This morning you insisted that I say I loved you and I said it, even if on principle I don't say it to anyone, not even to my wife. I'm glad. And do you love me? Yes. Tonight you'll sleep with him? Who should I sleep with? I can't bear it. Don't you sleep with your wife? It's not the same thing. Why? I don't care about Eleonora. Then come back here. How can I? Leave her. And then? He began to call obsessively. I loved those phone calls, especially when we said goodbye and I had no idea when we would talk again, but then he called back half an hour later, sometimes even ten minutes later, and began to rave, he asked if I had made love with Pietro since we had been together, I said no, he made me swear, I swore, I asked if he had made love to his wife, he shouted no, I insisted that he swear, and oath followed oath, and so many promises, above all the solemn promise to stay home, to be findable. He wanted me to wait for his phone calls, so that if by chance I went out—I had to, to do the shopping—he let the telephone ring and ring in the emptiness, he let it ring until I returned and dropped the children, dropped the bags, didn't even close the door to the stairs, ran to answer. I found him desperate at the other end: I thought you would never answer me again. Then he added, relieved: but I would have telephoned forever, in your absence I would have loved the sound of the telephone, that sound in the void, it seemed the only thing that remained to me. And he recalled our night in detail—do you remember this, do you remember that—he recalled it constantly. He listed everything he wanted to do with me, not only sex: a walk, a journey, go to the movies, a restaurant, talk to me about the work he was doing, listen to how it was going with my book. Then I lost control. I whispered yes yes yes, everything, everything you want, and I cried to him: I'm about to go on vacation, in a week I'll be at the sea with the children and Pietro, as if it were a deportation. And he: Eleonora is going to Capri in three days, as soon as she leaves I'll come to Florence, even just for an hour. Meanwhile Elsa looked at me, she asked: Mamma, who are you talking to all the time, come and play. One day Dede said: Leave her alone, she's talking to her boyfriend.

113.

Nino traveled at night, he reached Florence around nine in the morning. He called, Pietro answered, he hung up. He called again, I went to answer. He had parked downstairs. Come down. I can't. Come down immediately, or I'll come up. We were leaving in a few days for Viareggio, Pietro by now was on vacation. I left the children with him, I said I had some urgent shopping to do for the beach. I rushed to Nino.

Seeing each other was a terrible idea. We discovered that, instead of waning, desire had flared up and made a thousand demands with brazen urgency. If at a distance, on the telephone, words allowed us to fantasize, constructing glorious prospects but also imposing on us an order, containing us, frightening us, finding ourselves together, in the tiny space of the car, careless of the terrible heat, gave concreteness to our delirium, gave it the cloak of inevitability, made it a tile in the great subversive season under way, made it consistent with the forms of realism of that era, those which asked for the impossible.

"Don't go home."

"And the children, Pietro?"

"And us?"

Before he left again for Naples he said he didn't know if he could tolerate not seeing me for all of August. We were desperate as we said goodbye. I didn't have a telephone in the house we had rented in Viareggio, he gave me the number of the house in Capri. He made me promise to call every day.

"If your wife answers?"

"Hang up."

"If you're at the beach?"

"I have to work, I'll almost never go to the beach."

In our fantasy, telephoning was to serve also to set a date, sometime in August, and find a way of seeing each other at least once. He urged me to invent an excuse and return to Florence. He would do the same with Eleonora and would join me. We would see each other at my house, we would have dinner together, we would sleep together. More madness. I kissed him, I caressed him, I bit him, and I tore myself away from him in a state of unhappy happiness. I went to buy, at random, towels, a couple of bathing suits for Pietro, a shovel and pail for Elsa, a blue bathing suit for Dede. At the time blue was her favorite color.

114.

We went on vacation. I paid little attention to the children, I left them with their father most of the time. I was constantly running around to find a telephone, if only to tell Nino that I loved him. Eleonora answered a couple of times, and I hung up. But her voice was enough to irritate me, I found it unjust that she should be beside him day and night, what did she have to do with him, with us. That annoyance helped me overcome my fear, the plan of seeing each other in Florence seemed increasingly feasible. I said to Pietro, and it was true, that while the Italian publisher, with all the will in the world, couldn't bring out my book before January, it would come out in France at the end of October. I therefore had to clarify some urgent questions, a couple of books would be helpful, I needed to go home.

"I'll go get them for you," he offered.

"Stay with the girls, you're never with them."

"I like to drive, you don't."

"Leave me alone. Can't I have a day off? Maids get one, why not me?"

I left early in the morning in the car; the sky was streaked with white, and through the window came a cool breeze that carried the odors of summer. I went into the empty house with my heart pounding. I undressed, I washed, I looked at myself in the mirror, dismayed by the white stain of stomach and breast, I got dressed, I undressed, I dressed again until I felt pretty.

Nino arrived around three in the afternoon; I don't know what nonsense he had told his wife. We made love until evening. For the first time he had the luxury of dedicating himself to my body with a devotion, an idolatry that I wasn't prepared for. I tried to be his equal, I wanted at all costs to seem good to him. But when I saw him exhausted and happy, something suddenly went bad in my mind. *For me that was a unique experience, for him a repetition.* He loved women, he adored their bodies as if they were fetishes. I didn't think so much of the other women of his I knew about, Nadia, Silvia, Mariarosa, or his wife, Eleonora. I thought instead of what I knew well, the crazy things he had done for Lila, the frenzy that had brought him close to destroying himself. I recalled how she had believed in that passion and had clung to him, to the complicated books he read, his thoughts, his ambitions, to affirm herself and give herself the chance for change. I remembered how she had collapsed when Nino abandoned her. Did he know how to love and induce one to love only in that excessive way, did he not know others? Was this mad love of ours the repeat of other mad loves? Was he exploiting a prototype: wanting me in this way, without caring about anything, was it the same way he had wanted Lila? Didn't even his coming to my and Pietro's house resemble Lila's taking him to the house where she and Stefano lived? Were we not doing but redoing?

I pulled back, he asked: what's wrong? Nothing, I didn't know what to say, they weren't thoughts that could be spoken. I pressed against him, I kissed him and I tried to get out of my heart the feeling of his love for Lila. But Nino insisted and finally I couldn't escape, I seized a relatively recent echo— *Here, maybe this I can say to you*—and asked him in a tone of feigned amusement:

"Do I have something wrong when it comes to sex, like Lina?"

His expression changed. In his eyes, in his face, a different person appeared, a stranger who frightened me. Even before he answered I quickly whispered:

"I was joking, if you don't want to answer forget it."

"I don't understand what you said."

"I was only quoting your words."

"I've never said anything like that."

"Liar, you did in Milan, when we were going to the restaurant."

"It's not true, and anyway I don't want to talk about Lina."

"Why?"

He didn't answer. I felt bitter, I turned away. When he touched my back with his fingers I whispered coldly: Leave me alone. We were motionless for a while, without speaking. Then he began to caress me again, he kissed me lightly on the shoulder, I gave in. Yes, I admitted to myself, he's right, I should never ask him about Lila.

In the evening the telephone rang; it must be Pietro, with the girls. I nodded to Nino not to breathe, I left the bed and went to answer. I prepared in my throat an affectionate, reassuring tone, but without realizing it I kept my voice too low, an unnatural murmur, I didn't want Nino to hear and later make fun of me or even get angry.

"Why are you whispering like that?" Pietro asked. "Everything all right?"

I raised my voice immediately, and now it was excessively loud. I sought loving words, I made much of Elsa, I urged Dede not to make her father's life difficult and to brush her teeth before going to bed. Nino said, when I came back to bed:

"What a good wife, what a good mamma."

I answered: "You are no less."

I waited for the tension to diminish, for the echo of the voices of my husband and children to fade. We took a shower together. It was a new, enjoyable experience, a pleasure to wash him and be washed. Afterward I got ready to go out. Again I was trying to look nice for him, but this time I was doing it in front of him and suddenly without anxiety. He watched, fascinated, as I tried on dresses in search of the right one, as I put on my makeup, and from time to time—even though I said, joking, don't you dare, you're tickling me, you'll ruin the makeup and I'll have to start over, careful of the dress, it will tear, leave me alone—he came up behind me, kissed me on the neck, put his hands down the front and under the dress.

I made him go out alone, I told him to wait for me in the car. Although people were on vacation and the building was half deserted, I was afraid that someone would see us together.

We went to dinner, we ate a lot, talked a lot, drank a lot. When we got back we went to bed but didn't sleep. He said:

"In October I'll be in Montpellier for five days, I have a conference."

"Have fun. You'll go with your wife?"

"I want to go with you."

"Impossible."

"Why?"

"Dede is six, Elsa three. I have to think of them."

We began to discuss our situation, for the first time we uttered words like *married, children*. We went from despair to sex, from sex to despair. Finally I whispered:

"We shouldn't see each other anymore."

"If for you it's possible, fine. For me it's not."

"Nonsense. You've known me for decades and yet you've had a full life without me. You'll forget about me before you know it."

"Promise that you'll keep calling me every day."

"No, I won't call you anymore."

"If you don't I'll go mad."

"I'll go mad if I go on thinking of you."

We explored with a sort of masochistic pleasure the dead end we felt ourselves in, and, exasperated by the obstacles we ourselves were piling up, we ended by quarreling. He left, anxiously, at six in the morning. I cleaned up the house, had a cry, drove all the way to Viareggio hoping never to arrive. Halfway there I realized that I hadn't taken a single book capable of justifying that trip. I thought: better this way.

115.

When I returned I was warmly welcomed by Elsa, who said sulkily: Papa isn't good at playing. Dede defended Pietro, she

398 · ELENA FERRANTE

exclaimed that her sister was small and stupid, and ruined every game. Pietro examined me, in a bad mood.

"You didn't sleep."

"I slept badly."

"Did you find the books?"

"Yes."

"Where are they?"

"Where do you think they are? At home. I checked what I had to check and that was it."

"Why are you angry?"

"Because you make me angry."

"We called you again last night. Elsa wanted to say good night but you weren't there."

"It was hot, I took a walk."

"Alone?"

"With whom?"

"Dede says you have a boyfriend."

"Dede has a strong bond with you and she's dying to replace me."

"Or she sees and hears things that I don't see or hear."

"What do you mean?"

"What I said."

"Pietro, let's try to be clear: to your many maladies do you want to add jealousy, too?"

"I'm not jealous."

"Let's hope not. Because if it weren't so I'm telling you right away: jealousy is too much, I can't bear it."

In the following days clashes like that became more frequent. I kept him at bay, I reproached him, and at the same time I despised myself. But I was also enraged: what did he want from me, what should I do? I loved Nino, I had always loved him: how could I tear him out of my breast, my head, my belly, now that he wanted me, too? Ever since I was a child I had constructed for myself a perfect self-repressive mechanism. Not one of my true desires had ever prevailed, I had always found a way of channeling every yearning. Now enough, I said to myself, let it all explode, me first of all.

But I wavered. For several days I didn't call Nino, as I had sagely declared in Florence. Then suddenly I started calling three or four times a day, heedless. I didn't even care about Dede, standing a few steps from the phone booth. I talked to him in the unbearable heat of that sun-struck cage, and occasionally, soaked with sweat, exasperated by my daughter's spying look, I opened the glass door and shouted: What are you doing standing there like that, I told you to look after your sister. At the center of my thoughts now was the conference in Montpellier. Nino harassed me; he made it into a sort of definitive proof of the genuineness of my feelings, so that we went from violent quarrels to declarations of how indispensable we were to each other, from long, costly complaints to the urgent spilling of our desire into a river of incandescent words. One afternoon, exhausted, as Dede and Elsa, outside the phone booth, were chanting, Mamma, hurry up, we're getting bored, I said to him:

"There's only one way I could go with you to Montpellier."

"What."

"Tell Pietro everything."

There was a long silence.

"You're really ready to do that?"

"Yes, but on one condition: you tell Eleonora everything."

Another long silence. Nino murmured:

"You want me to hurt Eleonora and the child?"

"Yes. Won't I be hurting Pietro and my daughters? To decide means to do harm."

"Albertino is very small."

"So is Elsa. And for Dede it will be intolerable."

"Let's do it after Montpellier."

"Nino, don't play with me."

"I'm not playing."

"Then if you're not playing behave accordingly: you speak to your wife and I'll speak to my husband. Now. Tonight."

"Give me some time, it's not easy."

"For me it is?"

He hesitated, tried to explain. He said that Eleonora was a very fragile woman. He said she had organized her life around him and the child. He said that as a girl she had twice tried to kill herself. But he didn't stop there, I felt that he was forcing himself to the most absolute honesty. Step by step, with the lucidity that was customary with him, he reached the point of admitting that breaking up his marriage meant not only hurting his wife and child but also saying goodbye to many comforts—*only living comfortably makes life in Naples acceptable*—and to a network of relationships that guaranteed he could do what he wanted at the university. Then, overwhelmed by his own decision to be silent about nothing, he concluded: Remember that your father-in-law has great respect for me and that to make our relationship public would cause both for me and for you an irremediable breach with the Airotas. It was this last point of his, I don't know why, that hurt me.

"All right," I said, "let's end it here."

"Wait."

"I've already waited too long, I should have made up my mind earlier."

"What do you want to do?"

"Understand that my marriage no longer makes sense and go my way."

"You're sure?"

"Yes."

"And you'll come to Montpellier?"

"I said my way, not yours. Between you and me it's over."

116.

I hung up in tears and left the phone booth. Elsa asked: Did you hurt yourself, Mamma? I answered: I'm fine, it's Grandma who doesn't feel well. I went on sobbing under the worried gaze of Dede and Elsa.

During the final part of the vacation I did nothing but weep. I said I was tired, it was too hot, I had a headache, and I sent Pietro and the children to the beach. I stayed in bed, soaking the pillow with tears. I hated that excessive fragility, I hadn't been like that even as a child. Both Lila and I had trained ourselves never to cry, and if we did it was in exceptional moments, and for a short time: the shame was tremendous, we stifled our sobs. Now, instead, as in Ariosto's Orlando, in my head a fountain had opened and it flowed from my eyes without ever drying up; it seemed to me that even when Pietro, Dede, Elsa were about to return and with an effort I repressed the tears and hurried to wash my face under the tap, the fountain continued to drip, waiting for the right moment to return to the egress of my eyes. Nino didn't really want me, Nino pretended a lot and loved little. He had wanted to fuck me—yes, fuck me, as he had done with who knows how many others—but to have me, have me forever by breaking the ties with his wife, well, that was not in his plans. Probably he was still in love with Lila. Probably in the course of his life he would love only her, like so many who had known her. And as a result he would remain with Eleonora forever. Love for Lila was the guarantee that no woman—no matter how much he wanted her, in his passionate way—would ever put that fragile marriage in trouble, I least of all. That was how things stood. Sometimes I got up in the middle of lunch or dinner and went to cry in the bathroom.

Pietro treated me cautiously, sensing that I might explode at any moment. At first, a few hours after the break with Nino, I had thought of telling him everything, as if he were not only a husband to whom I had to explain myself but also a confessor. I felt the need of it; and especially when he approached me in bed and I put him off, whispering: No, the children will wake up, I was on the point of pouring out to him every detail. But I always managed to stop myself in time, it wasn't necessary to tell him about Nino. Now that I no longer called the person I loved, now that I felt truly lost, it seemed to me useless to be cruel to Pietro. It was better to close the subject with a few clear words: I can't live with you anymore. And yet I was unable to do even that. Just when, in the shadowy light of the bedroom, I felt ready to take that step, I pitied him, I feared for the future of the children, I caressed his shoulder, his cheek, I whispered: Sleep.

On the last day of the vacation, things changed. It was almost midnight, Dede and Elsa were sleeping. For at least ten days I hadn't called Nino. I had packed the bags, I was worn out by sadness, by effort, by the heat, and I was sitting with Pietro on the balcony, each in our own lounge chair, in silence. There humidity was debilitating, soaking our hair and clothes, and our smell of the sea and of resin. Pietro suddenly said:

"How's your mother?"

"My mother?"

"Fine."

"Dede told me she's ill."

"She recovered."

"I called her this afternoon. Your mother has always been in good health."

I said nothing.

How inopportune that man was. Here, already, the tears were returning. Oh good God, I was fed up, fed up. I heard him say calmly:

"You think I'm blind and deaf. You think I didn't realize it when you flirted with those imbeciles who came to the house before Elsa was born."

"I don't know what you're talking about."

"You know perfectly well."

"No, I don't know. Who are you talking about? People who came to dinner a few times years ago? And I flirted with them? Are you crazy?"

Pietro shook his head, smiling to himself. He waited a few seconds, then he asked me, staring at the railing: "You didn't even flirt with the one who played the drums?"

I was alarmed. He wasn't retreating, he wasn't giving in. I snorted.

"Mario?"

"See, you remember?"

"Of course I remember, why shouldn't I? He's one of the few interesting people you brought home in seven years of marriage."

"Did you find him interesting?"

"Yes, and so what? What's got into you tonight?"

"I want to know. Can't I know?"

"What do you want to know? All that I know, you do, too. It must be at least four years since we saw that man, and you come out now with this foolishness?"

He stopped staring at the railing, he turned to look at me, serious.

"Then let's talk about more recent events. What is there between you and Nino?"

117.

It was a blow as violent as it was unexpected. *He wanted to know what there was between Nino and me.* That question, that name were enough to make the fountain flow again in my head. I was blinded by tears, I shouted at him, beside myself, forgetting we were outside, that people tired out by a day of

404 · ELENA FERRANTE

sun and sea were sleeping: Why did you ask that question, you should have kept it to yourself, now you've spoiled everything and there's nothing to do, it would have been enough for you to keep silent, instead you couldn't, and now I have to go, now I have *no choice* but to go.

I don't know what happened to him. Maybe he was convinced he had made a mistake that now, for obscure reasons, risked ruining our relationship forever. Or he saw me suddenly as a crude organism that cracked the fragile surface of discourse and appeared in a pre-logical way, a woman in her most alarming manifestation. Certainly I must have seemed to him an intolerable spectacle: he jumped up, and went inside. But I ran after him and continued shouting all manner of things: my love for Nino since I was a child, the new possibilities of life that he revealed to me, the unused energy I felt inside me, and the dreariness in which he, Pietro, had plunged me for years, his responsibility for having kept me from living fully.

When I had exhausted my strength and collapsed in a corner, I found him in front of me with hollow cheeks, his eyes sunk into violet stains, his tan a crust of mud. I understood only then that I had shocked him. The questions he had asked didn't admit even hypothetical affirmative answers like: Yes, I flirted with the drummer and even more; Yes, Nino and I have been lovers. Pietro had formulated them only to be denied, to silence the doubts that had come to him, to go to bed more serene. Instead I had imprisoned him in a nightmare from which, now, he no longer knew how to escape. He asked, almost whispering, in search of safety:

"Have you made love?"

Again I felt pity for him. If I had answered affirmatively I would have started shouting again, I would have said: Yes, once while you were sleeping, a second time in his car, a third in our bed in Florence. And I would have uttered those sen-

THOSE WHO LEAVE AND THOSE WHO STAY · 405

tences with the pleasure that that list provoked in me. Instead I shook my head no.

118.

We returned to Florence. We reduced the communication between us to what was indispensable and to friendly tones in the presence of the children. Pietro went to sleep in his study as he had in the time when Dede never closed her eyes, I in the bedroom. I thought and thought about what to do. The way Lila and Stefano's marriage had ended didn't constitute a model, it was something from other times, managed without the law. I counted on a civil procedure, according to the law, suited to the times and to our situation. But in fact I continued not to know what to do and so I did nothing. Especially since I had just returned and already Mariarosa was telephoning me to tell me that the French volume was progressing, she would send me the proofs, while the serious, punctilious editor at the Italian publishing house was raising various questions about the text. For a while I was pleased I tried to become interested again in my work. But I couldn't, it seemed to me that I had problems much more serious than a passage interpreted incorrectly, or some awkward sentences.

Then, one morning, the telephone rang, Pietro answered. He said hello, he repeated hello, he hung up. My heart began to beat madly, I got ready to rush to the phone ahead of my husband. It didn't ring again. Hours passed, I tried to distract myself by rereading my book. It was a terrible idea: it seemed to me utter nonsense, and made me so weary that I fell asleep with my head on the desk. But then the phone rang again, my husband answered again. He shouted, frightening Dede: Hello, and slammed down the receiver as if he wanted to break it.

It was Nino, I knew it, Pietro knew it. The date of the conference was approaching, surely he wanted to insist again that I come with him. He would aim at pulling me inside the materiality of desires. He would show me that our only chance was a secret relationship lived to exhaustion, amid evil actions and pleasures. The way was to betray, invent lies, leave together. I would fly in a plane for the first time, I would be next to him as it took off, as in films. And why not, after Montpellier we would go to Nanterre, we would see Mariarosa's friend, I would talk to her about my book, I would agree on initiatives, I would introduce them to Nino. Ah yes, to be accompanied by a man I loved, who had a power, a force that no one failed to notice. The hostile feeling softened. I was tempted.

The next day Pietro went to the university, I waited for Nino to telephone. He didn't, and so, in an unreasonable outburst, I called him. I waited many seconds, I was very agitated, in my mind there was nothing but the urgent need to hear his voice. Afterward, I didn't know. Maybe I would attack him, I would start crying again. Or I would shout: All right, I'll come with you, I will be your lover, I will be until you're tired of me. At that moment, however, I only needed him to answer.

Eleonora answered. I snatched back my voice in time before it addressed the ghost of Nino, running breathlessly down the telephone line with who knows what compromising words. I subdued it to a cheerful tone: Hello, it's Elena Greco, are you well, how was the vacation, and Albertino? She let me speak in silence, then she screamed: You're Elena Greco, eh, the whore, the hypocritical whore, leave my husband alone and don't dare telephone ever again, because I know where you live and as God is my witness I'll come there and smash your face. After which she hung up.

119.

I don't know how long I stayed beside the phone. I was filled with hatred, my head was spinning with phrases like: Yes, come, come right now, bitch, it's just what I'd expect, where the fuck are you from, Via Tasso, Via Filangieri, Via Crispi, the Santarella, and you're angry with me, you piece of garbage, you stinking nonentity, you don't know who you're dealing with, you are nothing. Another me wanted to rise up from the depths, where she had been buried under a crust of meekness; she struggled in my breast, mixing Italian and words from childhood, I was a turmoil. If Eleonora dared to show up at my door I would spit in her face, throw her down the stairs, drag her out to the street by the hair, shatter that head full of shit on the sidewalk. I had evil in my heart, my temples were pounding. Some work was being done outside our building, and from the window came the heat and the jangle of drilling and the dust and the irritating noise of some machine or other. Dede was quarreling with Elsa in the other room: You mustn't do everything I do, you're a monkey, only monkeys act like that. Slowly I understood. Nino had decided to speak to his wife and that was why she had attacked me. I went from rage to an uncontainable joy. *Nino wanted me* so much that he had told his wife about us. He had ruined his marriage, he had given it up in full awareness of the advantages that came from it, he had upset his whole life, choosing to make Eleonora and Albertino suffer rather than me. So it was true, he loved me. I sighed with contentment. The telephone rang again, I answered right away.

Now it was Nino, his voice. He seemed calm. He said that his marriage was over, he was free. He asked me:

"Did you talk to Pietro?"

"I started to."

"You haven't told him yet?"

"Yes and no."

"You want to back out?"

"No."

"Then hurry up, we have to go."

He had already assumed that I would go with him. We would meet in Rome, it was all arranged, hotel, tickets.

"I have the problem of the children," I said, but softly, without conviction.

"Send them to your mother."

"Don't even say that."

"Then take them with you."

"Are you serious?"

"Yes."

"You would take me with you anyway, even with my daughters?"

"Of course."

"You really love me," I whispered.

"Yes."

120.

I discovered that I was suddenly invulnerable and invincible, as in a past stage of my life, when it had seemed to me that I could do anything. I had been born lucky. Even when fate seemed adverse, it was working for me. Of course, I had some good qualities. I was orderly, I had a good memory, I worked stubbornly, I had learned to use the tools perfected by men, I knew how to give logical consistency to any jumble of fragments, I knew how to please. But luck counted more than anything, and I was proud of feeling it next to me like a trusted friend. To have it again on my side reassured me. I had married a respectable man, not a person like Stefano Carracci or, worse, Michele Solara. I would fight with him, he would suffer, but in the end we would come to an agreement. Certainly breaking up the marriage, the family, would be traumatic. And since for different reasons we had no wish to tell our relatives, and would in fact keep it hidden as long as possible, we couldn't even count, at first, on Pietro's family, which in every situation knew what to do and whom to turn to in handling complex situations. But I felt at peace, finally. We were two reasonable adults, we would confront each other, we would discuss, we would explain ourselves. In the chaos of those hours one single thing, now, appeared irrevocable: I would go to Montpellier.

I talked to my husband that evening, I confessed to him that Nino was my lover. He did everything possible not to believe it. When I convinced him that it was the truth, he wept, he entreated, he got angry, he lifted up the glass top of the coffee table and hurled it against the wall under the terrified gaze of the children, who had been awakened by the shouts and stood in disbelief in the living room doorway. I put Dede and Elsa back to bed, I soothed them, I waited for them to go to sleep. Then I returned to confront my husband: every minute became a wound. Meanwhile, Eleonora began to batter us with phone calls, day and night, insulting me, insulting Pietro because he didn't know how to act like a man, telling me that her relatives would find a way of leaving us and our daughters with nothing, not even eyes to cry with.

But I didn't get discouraged. I was in a state of such exaltation that I couldn't feel that I was wrong. In fact, it seemed to me that even the pain I caused, the humiliation and attacks I endured, were working in my favor. That unbearable experience not only would help me to *become* something I would be satisfied with but in the end, by inscrutable means, would also be useful to those who now were suffering. Eleonora would understand that with love there is nothing to be done, that it's senseless to say to a person who wants to go away: No, you must stay. And Pietro, who surely in theory already knew that precept, would only need time to assimilate it and change it to wisdom, to the practice of tolerance.

Only with the children did I feel that everything was difficult. My husband insisted that we tell them the reason we were quarreling. I was against it: They're small, I said, what can they understand. But at a certain point he reproached me: If you have decided to go, you have to give your daughters an explanation, and if you don't have the courage then stay, it means you yourself don't believe in what you want to do. I said: Let's talk to a lawyer. He answered: There's time for lawyers. And treacherously he summoned Dede and Elsa, who as soon as they heard us shouting would shut themselves in their room, in a close alliance.

"Your mother has something to tell you," Pietro began, "sit down and listen."

The two girls sat quietly on the sofa and waited. I started:

"Your father and I love each other, but we no longer get along and we have decided to separate."

"That's not true," Pietro interrupted calmly, "it's your mother who has decided to leave. And it's not true, either, that we love each other: she doesn't love me anymore."

I became agitated:

"Girls, it's not so simple. People can continue to love one another even though they no longer live together."

He interrupted again.

"That's also not true: either we love each other, and then we live together and are a family; or we don't love each other, and so we leave each other and are no longer a family. If you tell lies, what can they understand? Please, explain truthfully, clearly why we are leaving each other."

I said:

"I am not leaving you, you are the most important thing I have, I couldn't live without you. I only have problems with your father."

"What?" he pressed me. "Explain what those problems are."

I sighed, I said softly:

"I love someone else and I wish to live with him."

Elsa glanced at Dede to understand how she should react to that news, and since Dede remained impassive, she, too, remained impassive. But my husband lost his composure, he shouted:

"The name, say what this other person is called. You don't want to? Are you ashamed? I'll say it: you know that other person, it's Nino, you remember him? Your mother wants to go and live with him."

Then he began to cry desperately, while Elsa, alarmed, whispered: Will you take me with you, Mamma? But she didn't wait for my response. When her sister got up and almost ran out of the room, she immediately followed her.

That night Dede cried out in her sleep, I woke with a jolt, hurried to her. She was sleeping, but she had wet her bed. I had to wake her, change her, change the sheets. When I put her back to bed, she whispered that she wanted to come to mine. I agreed, I held her next to me. Every so often she started in her sleep, and made certain I was there.

121.

Now the date of the departure was approaching, but things with Pietro didn't improve, any agreement, even just for that trip to Montpellier, seemed impossible. If you go, he said, I'll never let you see the children again. Or: If you take the children I'll kill myself. Or: I'll report you for abandonment of the conjugal home. Or: let's the four of us go on a trip, let's go to Vienna. Or: Children, your mother prefers Signor Nino Sarratore to you.

I began to weaken. I recalled the resistance that Antonio had put up when I left him. But Antonio was a boy, he had inherited Melina's unstable mind, and he had not had an upbringing like Pietro's: he hadn't been trained since childhood to distinguish rules in chaos. Maybe, I thought, I've given too much weight to the cultivated use of reason, to good reading, to well controlled language, to political affiliation; maybe, in the face of abandonment, we are all the same; maybe not even a very orderly mind can endure the discovery of not being loved. My husband—there was nothing to be done—was convinced that he had to protect me at all costs from the poisonous bite of my desires, and so, to remain my husband, he was ready to resort to any means, even the most abject. He who had wanted a civil marriage, he who had always been in favor of divorce, demanded because of an uncontrolled internal movement that our bond should endure eternally, as if we had been married before God. And since I insisted on wanting to put an end to our relationship, first he tried all the paths of persuasion, then he broke things, he slapped himself, suddenly he began to sing.

When he overdid it like that he made me angry. I insulted him. And he, as usual, changed suddenly, like a frightened beast, sat beside me, apologized, said he wasn't upset with me, it was his mind that wasn't functioning. Adele—he revealed one night amid tears—had always betrayed his father, it was a discovery he had made as a child. At six he had seen her kiss an enormous man, dressed in blue, in the big living room in Genoa that looked out on the sea. He remembered all the details: the man had a large mustache that was like a dark blade; his pants showed a bright stain that seemed like a hundred-lire coin; his mother, against that man, seemed a bow so tensed that it was in danger of breaking. I listened in silence, I tried to console him: Be calm, those are false memories, you know it, I don't have to tell you. But he insisted: Adele wore a pink sundress, one strap had slid off her tan shoulder; her long nails seemed like glass; she had a black braid that hung down her back like a snake. He said, finally, moving from suffering to anger: Do you understand what you've done to me, do you understand the horror you've plunged me into? And I thought: Dede, too, will remember, Dede, too, will cry out something similar, as an adult. But then I pulled away, I convinced myself that Pietro was telling me about his mother only now, after so many years, deliberately to lead me to that thought and wound me and hold me back.

I kept going, exhausted, day and night; I no longer slept. If my husband tormented me, Nino in his way did no less. When he heard me worn out by tension and worries, instead of consoling me he became irritable, he said: You think it's easier for me, but it's an inferno here, just as much as for you, I'm afraid for Eleonora, I'm afraid for what she could do, so don't think that I'm not in as much trouble as you, maybe even worse. And he exclaimed: But you and I together are stronger than anyone else, our union is an inevitable necessity, is that clear, tell me, I want to hear it, is it clear. It was clear to me. But those words weren't much help. I drew all my strength, rather, from imagining the moment when I would finally see him again and we would fly to France. I had to hold out until then, I said to myself, afterward we'll see. For now I aspired only to a suspension of the torture, I couldn't stand it anymore. I said to Pietro, at the end of a violent quarrel in front of Dede and Elsa:

"That's enough. I'm leaving for five days, just five days, then I'll return and we'll see what to do. All right?"

He turned to the children:

"Your mother says she will be absent for five days, but do you believe it?"

Dede shook her head no, and so did Elsa.

"They don't believe you, either," Pietro said then. "We all know that you will leave us and never return."

And meanwhile, as if by an agreed-on signal, both Dede and Elsa hurled themselves at me, throwing their arms around my legs, begging me not to leave, to stay with them. I couldn't bear it. I knelt down, I held them around the waist, I said: All right, I won't go, you are my children, I'll stay with you. Those words calmed them, slowly Pietro, too, calmed down. I went to my room.

Oh God, how out of order everything was: they, I, the world around us: a truce was possible only by telling lies. It was only a couple of days until the departure. I wrote first a long letter to Pietro, then a short one to Dede with instructions to read it to Elsa. I packed a suitcase, I put it in the guest room, under the bed. I bought all sorts of things, I loaded the refrigerator. I prepared for lunch and dinner the dishes that Pietro loved, and he ate gratefully. The children, relieved, began again to fight about everything.

122.

Nino, meanwhile, now that the day of departure was approaching, had stopped calling. I tried to call him, hoping that Eleonora wouldn't answer. The maid answered and at the moment I felt relieved, I asked for Professor Sarratore. The answer was sharp and hostile: I'll give you the signora. I hung up, I waited. I hoped that the telephone call would become an occasion for a fight between husband and wife and Nino would find out that I was looking for him. Minutes later the phone rang. I rushed to answer, I was sure it was him. Instead it was Lila.

We hadn't talked for a long time and I didn't feel like talking to her. Her voice annoyed me. In that phase even just her name, as soon as it passed through my mind, serpentlike, confused me, sapped my strength. And then it wasn't a good moment to talk: if Nino had telephoned he would find the line busy and communication was already very difficult.

"Can I call you back?" I asked.

"Are you busy?"

"A little."

She ignored my request. As usual it seemed to her that she could enter and leave my life without any worries, as if we were still a single thing and there was no need to ask how are you, how are things, am I disturbing you. She said in a weary tone that she had just heard some terrible news: the mother of the Solaras had been murdered. She spoke slowly, attentive to every word, and I listened without interrupting. And the words drew behind them, as if in a procession, the loan shark all dressed up, sitting at the newlyweds' table at Lila and Stefano's wedding, the haunted woman who had opened the door when I was looking for Michele, the shadow woman of our childhood who had stabbed Don Achille, the old woman who had a fake flower in her hair and fanned herself with a blue fan as she said, bewildered: I'm hot, aren't you, too? But I felt no emotion, even when Lila mentioned the rumors that had reached her and she listed them in her efficient way. They had killed Manuela by slitting her throat with a knife; or she had been shot five times with a pistol, four in the chest and once in the neck; or they had beaten and kicked her, dragging her through the apartment; or the killers—she called them that—hadn't even entered the house, they had shot her as soon as she opened the door, Manuela had fallen face down on the landing and her husband, who was watching television, hadn't even realized it. What is certain—Lila said—is that the Solaras have gone crazy, they are competing with the police to find the killer, they've called people from Naples and outside, all their activities have stopped, I myself today am not working, and it's frightening here, you can't even breathe.

How intensely she was able to give importance and depth to what was happening to her and around her: the murdered loan shark, the children undone, their henchmen ready to spill more blood, and her watchful person amid the surging tide of events. Finally she came to the real reason for her phone call:

"Tomorrow I'm sending you Gennaro. I know I'm taking advantage, you have your daughters, your things, but here, now, I can't and don't want to keep him. He'll miss a little school, too bad. He's attached to you, he's fine with you, you're the only person I trust."

I thought for a few seconds about that last phrase: *You're the only person I trust.* I felt like smiling, she still didn't know that I had become untrustworthy. So that, faced with her request, which took for granted the immobility of my existence amid the most serene reasonableness, which seemed to assign to me the life of a red berry on the leafy branch of butcher's broom, I had no hesitation, I said to her:

"I'm about to go, I'm leaving my husband."

"I don't understand."

"My marriage is over, Lila. I saw Nino again and we discovered that we have always loved each other, ever since we were young, without realizing it. So I'm leaving, I'm starting a new life."

There was a long silence, then she asked me:

"Are you kidding?"

"No."

It must have seemed impossible to her that I was inserting disorder into my house, my well-organized mind, and now she was pressing me by mechanically grasping at my husband. Pietro, she said, is an extraordinary man, good, extremely intelligent, you're crazy to leave him, think of the harm you're doing to your children. She talked, making no mention of Nino, as if that name had stopped in her eardrum without reaching her brain. It must have been I who uttered it again, saying: No, Lila, I can't live with Pietro anymore because I can't do without Nino, whatever happens I'll go with him; and other phrases like that, displayed as if they were badges of honor. Then she began to shout:

"You're throwing away everything you are for Nino? You're ruining your family for him? You know what will happen to you? He'll use you, he'll suck your blood, he'll take away your will to live and abandon you. Why did you study so much? What fucking use has it been for me to imagine that you would enjoy a wonderful life for me, too? I was wrong, you're a fool."

123.

I put down the receiver as if it were burning hot. She's jealous, I said to myself, she's envious, she hates me. Yes, that was the truth. A long procession of seconds passed; the mother of the Solaras didn't return to my mind, her body marked by death vanished. Instead I wondered anxiously: Why doesn't Nino call, is it possible that now that I've told everything to Lila, he'll retreat and make me ridiculous? For an instant I saw myself exposed to her in all my possible pettiness as a person who had ruined herself for nothing. Then the telephone rang again. When I grabbed the receiver, I had words on my tongue ready for Lila: Don't ever concern yourself with me again, you have no right to Nino, let me make my own mistakes. But it wasn't her. It was Nino and I overwhelmed him with broken phrases, happy to hear him. I told him how things had been arranged with Pietro and the children, I told him that it was impossible to reach an agreement with calm and reason, I told him that I had packed my suitcase and couldn't wait to hold him. He told me of furious quarrels with his wife, the last hours had been intolerable. He whispered: Even though I'm very frightened, I can't think of my life without you.

The next day, while Pietro was at the university, I asked the neighbor if she would keep Dede and Elsa for a few hours. I put on the kitchen table the letters I had written and I left. I thought: Something great is happening that will dissolve the old way of living entirely and I'm part of that dissolution. I joined Nino in Rome, we met in a hotel near the station. Holding him tight, I said to myself: I'll never get used to that nervous body, it's a constant surprise, long bones, skin with an exciting smell, a mass, a force, a mobility completely different from what Pietro is, the habits we had.

The next morning, for the first time in my life, I boarded an airplane. I didn't know how to fasten my seat belt, Nino helped me. How thrilling it was to squeeze his hand while the sound of the engines grew louder, louder, and louder, and the plane began its takeoff. How exciting it was to lift off from the ground with a jerk and see the houses that became parallelopipeds and the streets that changed into strips and the countryside that was reduced to a green patch, and the sea that inclined like a compact paving stone, and the clouds that fell below in a landslide of soft rocks, and the anguish, the pain, the very happiness that became part of a unique, luminous motion. It seemed to me that flying subjected everything to a process of simplification, and I sighed, I tried to lose myself. Every so often I asked Nino: Are you happy? And he nodded yes, kissed me. At times I had the impression that the floor under my feet—the only surface I could count on—was trembling.

ABOUT THE AUTHOR

Elena Ferrante is the author of *The Days of Abandonment* (Europa, 2005), *Troubling Love* (Europa, 2006), and *The Lost Daughter* (Europa, 2008), soon to be a film directed by Maggie Gyllenhaal and starring Olivia Colman, Dakota Johnson, and Paul Mescal. She is also the author of *Incidental Inventions* (Europa, 2019), illustrated by Andrea Ucini, *Frantumaglia: A Writer's Journey* (Europa, 2016) and *The Beach at Night* (Europa, 2016), a children's picture book illustrated by Mara Cerri. The four volumes known as the "Neapolitan quartet" (*My Brilliant Friend*, *The Story of a New Name*, *Those Who Leave and Those Who Stay*, and *The Story of the Lost Child*) were published by Europa Editions in English between 2012 and 2015. *My Brilliant Friend*, the HBO series directed by Saverio Costanzo, premiered in 2018. Ferrante's most recent novel is *The Lying Life of Adults*, published in 2020 by Europa Editions.

THE NEAPOLITAN QUARTET
by Elena Ferrante

"Imagine if Jane Austen got angry and you'll have
some idea how explosive these works are."
—John Freeman

"Ferrante's novels are intensely, violently personal,
and because of this they seem to dangle bristling key
chains of confession before the unsuspecting reader."
—James Wood, *The New Yorker*

978-1-60945-078-6 • September 2012

"Stunning . . . cinematic in the density of its detail."
—The *Times Literary Supplement*

978-1-60945-134-9 • September 2013

"Everyone should read anything with Ferrante's
name on it."—Eugenia Williamson, *The Boston Globe*

978-1-60945-233-9 • September 2014

"One of modern fiction's richest portraits of a friendship."
—John Powers, *NPR's Fresh Air*

978-1-60945-286-5 • September 2015

Elena Ferrante's New Novel
The Lying Life of Adults

"Another spellbinding coming-of-age tale from a master."
—*People Magazine*

978-1-60945-715-0 • Available now

"To imbue fiction with the undiluted energy of life—to make it not words upon a page but a visceral force—is the greatest artistic achievement . . . Ferrante has done this."
—Claire Messud, author of *The Woman Upstairs*

"An unconditional masterpiece . . . I was totally enthralled. There was nothing else I wanted to do except follow the lives of Lila and Lenù to the end."
—Pulitzer Prize-winning author Jhumpa Lahiri

"One of modern fiction's richest portraits of a friendship."
—John Powers, NPR's Fresh Air

"Dazzling . . . stunning . . . an extraordinary epic."
—Michiko Kakutani, *The New York Times*

"Reading *My Brilliant Friend* reminded me of that child-like excitement when you can't look up from the page."
—Elizabeth Strout, Pulitzer Prize-winning author of *My Name Is Lucy Barton*

"An engrossing, wildly original contemporary epic."
—*The Los Angeles Times*

"The depth of perception Ferrante shows about her characters' conflicts and psychological states is astonishing . . . Her novels ring so true."—*The Wall Street Journal*

"To imbue fiction with the undiluted energy of life—to make it not words upon a page but a visceral force—is the greatest artistic achievement . . . Ferrante has done this."
—Claire Messud, author of *The Woman Upstairs*

"An unconditional masterpiece . . . I was totally enthralled. There was nothing else I wanted to do except follow the lives of Lila and Lenù to the end."
—Pulitzer Prize-winning author Jhumpa Lahiri

"One of modern fiction's richest portraits of a friendship."
—John Powers, NPR's Fresh Air

"Dazzling . . . stunning . . . an extraordinary epic."
—Michiko Kakutani, *The New York Times*

"Reading *My Brilliant Friend* reminded me of that child-like excitement when you can't look up from the page."
—Elizabeth Strout, Pulitzer Prize-winning author of *My Name Is Lucy Barton*

"An engrossing, wildly original contemporary epic."
—*The Los Angeles Times*

"The depth of perception Ferrante shows about her characters' conflicts and psychological states is astonishing . . . Her novels ring so true."—*The Wall Street Journal*

ALSO BY

ELENA FERRANTE

The Days of Abandonment
Troubling Love
The Lost Daughter
The Beach at Night
Frantumaglia: A Writer's Journey
Incidental Inventions
The Lying Life of Adults

MY BRILLIANT FRIEND
(The Neapolitan Quartet)

My Brilliant Friend
The Story of a New Name
Those Who Leave and Those Who Stay
The Story of the Lost Child

THE STORY
OF A NEW NAME

Elena Ferrante

THE STORY
OF A NEW NAME

Book Two, The Neapolitan Quartet
Youth

*Translated from the Italian
by Ann Goldstein*

Europa
editions

Europa Editions
1 Penn Plaza Suite 6282
New York, N.Y. 10019
www.europaeditions.com
info@europaeditions.com

Copyright © 2012 by Edizioni E/O

First Publication 2013 by Europa Editions

Thirty-fifth printing, 2021

Translation by Ann Goldstein
Original title: *Storia del nuovo cognome*
Translation copyright © 2013 by Europa Editions

Library of Congress Cataloging in Publication Data is available
ISBN 978-1-60945-134-9

Ferrante, Elena
The Story of a New Name

Book design by Emanuele Ragnisco
www.mekkanografici.com

Cover photo © Ismo Holtto/Getty Images

Prepress by Grafica Punto Print – Rome

Printed in Italy

The *father* is a porter at the city hall.

The *mother* is a housewife. Her limping gait haunts Elena.

The Carracci family (Don Achille's family):

Don Achille Carracci, the ogre of fairy tales, dealer in the black market, loan shark. He was murdered.

Maria Carracci, wife of Don Achille, mother of Stefano, Pinuccia, and Alfonso. She works in the family grocery store.

Stefano Carracci, son of the deceased Don Achille, husband of Lila. He manages the property accumulated by his father and is the proprietor, along with his sister Pinuccia, Alfonso, and his mother, Maria, of a profitable grocery store.

Pinuccia, the daughter of Don Achille. She works in the grocery store. She is engaged to Rino, Lila's brother.

Alfonso, son of Don Achille. He is the schoolmate of Elena. He is the boyfriend of Marisa Sarratore.

The Peluso family (the carpenter's family):

Alfredo Peluso, carpenter. Communist. Accused of killing Don Achille, he has been convicted and is in prison.

Giuseppina Peluso, wife of Alfredo. A former worker in the tobacco factory, she is devoted to her children and her imprisoned husband.

Pasquale Peluso, older son of Alfredo and Giuseppina, construction worker, militant Communist. He was the first to become aware of Lila's beauty and to declare his love for her. He detests the Solaras. He is engaged to Ada Cappuccio.

Carmela Peluso, also called *Carmen,* sister of Pasquale. She is a sales clerk in a notions store. She is engaged to Enzo Scanno.

Other children.

The Cappuccio family (the mad widow's family):

Melina, a relative of Nunzia Cerullo, a widow. She washes the stairs of the apartment buildings in the old neighborhood.

She was the lover of Donato Sarratore, Nino's father. The Sarratores left the neighborhood precisely because of that relationship, and Melina has nearly lost her reason.

Melina's *husband*, who unloaded crates in the fruit and vegetable market, and died in mysterious circumstances.

Ada Cappuccio, Melina's daughter. As a girl she helped her mother wash the stairs. Thanks to Lila, she will be hired as salesclerk in the Carracci's grocery. She is engaged to Pasquale Peluso.

Antonio Cappuccio, her brother, a mechanic. He is Elena's boyfriend and is very jealous of Nino Sarratore.

Other children.

The Sarratore family (the railway-worker poet's family):

Donato Sarratore, conductor, poet, journalist. A great womanizer, he was the lover of Melina Cappuccio. When Elena went on vacation to Ischia, she is compelled to leave in a hurry to escape Donato's sexual molestations.

Lidia Sarratore, wife of Donato.

Nino Sarratore, the oldest of the five children of Donato and Lidia. He hates his father. He is a brilliant student.

Marisa Sarratore, sister of Nino. She is studying, with mediocre success, to be a secretary.

Pino, Clelia, and *Ciro Sarratore*, younger children of Donato and Lidia.

The Scanno family (the fruit-and-vegetable seller's family):

Nicola Scanno, fruit-and-vegetable seller.

Assunta Scanno, wife of Nicola.

Enzo Scanno, son of Nicola and Assunta, also a fruit-and-vegetable seller. Lila has felt a liking for him since childhood. Their friendship begins when Enzo, during a school competition, shows an unsuspected ability in mathematics. Enzo is engaged to Carmen Peluso.

Other children.

The Solara family (the family of the owner of the Solara bar-pastry shop):

Silvio Solara, owner of the bar-pastry shop, a Camorrist tied to the illegal trafficking of the neighborhood. He was opposed to the Cerullo shoe factory.

Manuela Solara, wife of Silvio, moneylender: her red book is much feared in the neighborhood.

Marcello and Michele Solara, sons of Silvio and Manuela. Braggarts, arrogant, they are nevertheless loved by the neighborhood girls, except Lila, of course. Marcello is in love with Lila but she rejects him. Michele, a little younger than Marcello, is colder, more intelligent, more violent. He is engaged to Gigliola, the daughter of the pastry maker.

The Spagnuolo family (the baker's family):

Signor Spagnuolo, pastry maker at the Solaras' bar-pastry shop.

Rosa Spagnuolo, wife of the pastry maker.

Gigliola Spagnuolo, daughter of the pastry maker, engaged to Michele Solara.

Other children.

The Airota family:

Airota, professor of Greek literature.

Adele, his wife.

Mariarosa Airota, the older daughter, professor of art history in Milan.

Pietro Airota, student.

The teachers:

Maestro Ferraro, teacher and librarian.

Maestra Oliviero, teacher. She is the first to notice the potential of Lila and Elena. When Lila writes *The Blue Fairy*, Elena, who likes the story a lot, and gives it to Maestra Oliviero to read. But the teacher, angry because Lila's parents decided not to send their daughter to middle school, never says anything about the story. In fact, she stops concerning herself with Lila and concentrates only on the success of Elena.

Professor Gerace, high-school teacher.

Professor Galiani, high-school teacher. She is a very cultured woman and a Communist. She is immediately charmed by Elena's intelligence. She lends her books, protects her in the clash with the religion teacher.

Other characters:

Gino, son of the pharmacist.

Nella Incardo, the cousin of Maestra Oliviero. She lives in Barano, on Ischia, and Elena stayed with her for a vacation at the beach.

Armando, medical student, son of Professor Galiani.

Nadia, student, daughter of Professor Galiani.

Bruno Soccavo, friend of Nino Sarratore and son of a rich industrialist in San Giovanni a Teduccio, near Naples.

Franco Mari, student.

YOUTH

1.

In the spring of 1966, Lila, in a state of great agitation, entrusted to me a metal box that contained eight notebooks. She said that she could no longer keep them at home, she was afraid her husband might read them. I carried off the box without comment, apart from some ironic allusions to the excessive amount of string she had tied around it. At that time our relationship was terrible, but it seemed that only I considered it that way. The rare times we saw each other, she showed no embarrassment, only affection; a hostile word never slipped out.

When she asked me to swear that I wouldn't open the box for any reason, I swore. But as soon as I was on the train I untied the string, took out the notebooks, began to read. It wasn't a diary, although there were detailed accounts of the events of her life, starting with the end of elementary school. Rather, it seemed evidence of a stubborn self-discipline in writing. The pages were full of descriptions: the branch of a tree, the ponds, a stone, a leaf with its white veinings, the pots in the kitchen, the various parts of a coffeemaker, the brazier, the coal and bits of coal, a highly detailed map of the courtyard, the broad avenue of *stradone*, the rusting iron structure beyond the ponds, the gardens and the church, the cut of the vegetation alongside the railway, the new buildings, her parents' house, the tools her father and her brother used to repair shoes, their gestures when they worked, and above all colors, the colors of every object at different times of the day. But there were not only pages of description. Isolated words appeared, in dialect and in Italian, sometimes circled, without comment. And Latin and Greek translation exercises. And entire passages in English on the neighborhood shops and their wares, on the cart loaded with fruit and vegetables that Enzo Scanno took through the streets every day, leading the mule by the halter. And many observations on the books she read, the films she saw in the church hall. And many of the ideas that she had asserted in the discussions with Pasquale, in the talks she and I used to have. Of course, the progress was sporadic, but whatever Lila captured in writing assumed importance, so that even in the pages written when she was eleven or twelve there was not a single line that sounded childish.

Usually the sentences were extremely precise, the punctuation meticulous, the handwriting elegant, just as Maestra Oliviero had taught us. But at times, as if a drug had flooded her veins, Lila seemed unable to bear the order she had imposed on herself. Everything then became breathless, the sentences took on an overexcited rhythm, the punctuation disappeared. In general it didn't take long for her to return to a clear, easy pace. But it might also happen that she broke off abruptly and filled the rest of the page with little drawings of twisted trees, humped, smoking mountains, grim faces. I was entranced by both the order and the disorder, and the more I read, the more deceived I felt. How much practice there was behind the letter she had sent me on Ischia years earlier: that was why it was so well written. I put everything back in the box, promising myself not to become inquisitive again.

But I soon gave in—the notebooks exuded the force of seduction that Lila had given off since she was a child. She had treated the neighborhood, her family, the Solaras, Stefano, every person or thing with ruthless accuracy. And what to say of the liberty she had taken with me, with what I said, with what I thought, with the people I loved, with my very physical appearance. She had fixed moments that were decisive for her without worrying about anything or anyone. Here vividly was the pleasure she had felt when at ten she wrote her story, *The Blue Fairy*. Here just as vivid was what she had suffered when our teacher Maestra Oliviero hadn't deigned to say a single word about that story, in fact had ignored it. Here was the suffering and the fury because I had gone to middle school, neglecting her, abandoning her. Here the excitement with which she had learned to repair shoes, the desire to prove herself that had induced her to design new shoes, and the pleasure of completing the first pair with her brother Rino. Here the pain when Fernando, her father, had said that the shoes weren't well made. There was everything, in those pages, but especially hatred for the Solara brothers, the fierce determination with which she had rejected the love of the older, Marcello, and the moment when she had decided, instead, to marry the gentle Stefano Carracci, the grocer, who out of love had wanted to buy the first pair of shoes she had made, vowing that he would keep them forever. Ah, the wonderful moment when, at fifteen, she had felt herself a rich and elegant lady, on the arm of her fiancé, who, all because he loved her, had invested a lot of money in her father and brother's shoe business: Cerullo shoes. And how much satisfaction she had felt: the shoes of her imagination in large part realized, a house in the new neighborhood, marriage at sixteen. And what a lavish wedding, how happy she was. Then Marcello Solara, with his brother Michele, had appeared in the middle of the festivities, wearing on his feet the very shoes that her husband had said were so dear to him. Her husband. What sort of man had she married? Now, when it was all over, would the false face be torn off, revealing the horribly true one underneath? Questions, and the facts, without embellishment, of our poverty. I devoted myself to those pages, for days, for weeks. I studied them. I ended up learning by heart the passages I liked, the ones that thrilled me, the ones that hypnotized me, the ones that humiliated me. Behind their naturalness was surely some artifice, but I couldn't discover what it was.

Finally, one evening in November, exasperated, I went out carrying the box. I couldn't stand feeling Lila on me and in me, even now that I was esteemed myself, even now that I had a life outside of Naples. I stopped on the Solferino bridge to look at the lights filtered through a cold mist. I placed the box on the parapet, and pushed it slowly, a little at a time, until it fell into the river, as if it were her, Lila in person, plummeting, with her thoughts, words, the malice with which she struck back at anyone, the way she appropriated me, as she did every person or thing or event or thought that touched her: books and shoes, sweetness and violence, the marriage and the wedding night, the return to the neighborhood in the new role of Signora Raffaella Carracci.

2.

I couldn't believe that Stefano, so kind, so in love, had given Marcello Solara the vestige of the child Lila, the evidence of her work on the shoes she had designed.

I forgot about Alfonso and Marisa, who, sitting at the table, were talking to each other, eyes shining. I paid no more attention to my mother's drunken laughter. The music faded, along with the voice of the singer, the dancing couples, and Antonio, who had gone out to the terrace and, overwhelmed by jealousy, was standing outside the glass door staring at the violet city, the sea. Even the image of Nino, who had just left the room like an archangel without annunciations, grew faint. Now I saw only Lila, speaking animatedly into Stefano's ear, she very pale in her wedding dress, he unsmiling, a white patch of unease running over his flushed face from his forehead to his eyes like a Carnival mask. What was happening, what would happen? My friend tugged her husband's arm with both hands. She used all her strength, and I who knew her thoroughly felt that if she could she would have wrenched it from his body, crossed the room holding it high above her head, blood dripping in her train, and she would have used it as a club or a donkey's jawbone to crush Marcello's face with a solid blow. Ah yes, she would have done it, and at the idea my heart pounded furiously, my throat became dry. Then she would have dug out the eyes of both men, she would have torn the flesh from the bones of their faces, she would have bitten them. Yes, yes, I felt that I wanted that, I wanted it to happen. An end of love and of that intolerable celebration, no embraces in a bed in Amalfi. Immediately shatter everything and every person in the neighborhood, tear them to pieces, Lila and I, go and live far away, lightheartedly descending together all the steps of humiliation, alone, in unknown cities. It seemed to me the just conclusion to that day. If nothing could save us, not money, not a male body, and not even studying, we might as well destroy everything immediately. Her rage expanded in my breast, a force that was mine and not mine, filling me with the pleasure of losing myself. I wished that that force would overflow. But I realized that I was also afraid of it. I understood only later that I can be quietly unhappy, because I'm incapable of violent reactions, I fear them, I prefer to be still, cultivating resentment. Not Lila. When she left her seat, she got up so decisively that the table shook, along with the silverware on the dirty plates; a glass was overturned. As Stefano hurried mechanically to cut off the tongue of wine that was heading toward Signora Solara's dress, Lila went out quickly through a side door, jerking her dress away whenever it got caught.

I thought of running after her, grabbing her hand, whispering to her let's get out, out of here. But I didn't move. Stefano moved, after a moment of uncertainty, and, making his way among the dancing couples, joined her.

I looked around. Everyone realized that something had upset the bride. But Marcello continued to chat in a conspiratorial way with Rino, as if it were normal for him to have those shoes on his feet. The increasingly lewd toasts of the metal merchant continued. Those who felt at the bottom of the hierarchy of tables and guests went on struggling to put a good face on things. In other words, no one except me seemed to realize that the marriage that had just been celebrated—and that would probably last until the death of the spouses, among the births of many children, many more grandchildren, joys and sorrows, silver and gold wedding anniversaries—that for Lila, no matter what her husband did in his attempt to be forgiven, that marriage was already over.

3.

At first the events disappointed me. I sat with Alfonso and Marisa, paying no attention to their conversation. I waited for signs of revolt, but nothing happened. To be inside Lila's head was, as usual, difficult: I didn't hear her shouting, I didn't hear her threatening. Stefano reappeared half an hour later, very friendly. He had changed his clothes; the white patch on his forehead and around his eyes had vanished. He strolled about among friends and relatives waiting for his wife to arrive, and when she returned to the hall not in her wedding dress but in her traveling outfit, a pastel-blue suit, with very pale buttons, and a blue hat, he joined her immediately. Lila distributed sugared almonds to the children, taking them from a crystal bowl with a silver spoon, then she moved among the tables handing out the wedding favors, first to her relatives, then to Stefano's. She ignored the entire Solara family and even her brother

Rino, who asked her with an anxious half-smile: Don't you love me anymore? She didn't answer, but gave the wedding favor to Pinuccia. She had an absent gaze, her cheekbones appeared more prominent than usual. When she got to me, she distractedly handed me, without even a smile of complicity, the white tulle-wrapped ceramic basket full of sugared almonds.

The Solaras were irritated by that discourtesy, but Stefano made up for it, embracing them one by one, with a pleasant, soothing expression, and murmuring, "She's tired, be patient."

He kissed Rino, too, on the cheeks, but his brother-in-law gave a sign of displeasure, and I heard him say, "It's not tiredness, Ste', she was born twisted and I'm sorry for you."

Stefano answered seriously, "Twisted things get straightened out."

Afterward I saw him hurry after his wife, who was already at the door, while the orchestra spewed drunken sounds and people crowded around for the final goodbyes.

No rupture, then, we would not run away together through the streets of the world. I imagined the newlyweds, handsome, elegant, getting into the convertible. Soon they would be on the Amalfi coast, in a luxurious hotel, and every bloodcurdling insult would have changed into a bad mood that was easily erased. No second thoughts. Lila had detached herself from me definitively and—it suddenly seemed to me—the distance was in fact greater than I had imagined. She wasn't *only* married, her submission to conjugal rites would not be limited merely to sleeping with a man every night. There was something I hadn't understood, which at that moment seemed to me obvious. Lila—bowing to the fact that some business arrangement or other between her husband and Marcello had been sealed by her girlish labors—had admitted that she cared about him more than any other person or thing. If she had *already* yielded, if she had *already* swallowed that insult, her bond with Stefano must truly be strong. She loved him, she loved him like the girls in the photonovels. For her whole life she would sacrifice to him every quality of her own, and he wouldn't even be aware of the sacrifice, he would be surrounded by the wealth of feeling, intelligence, imagination that were hers, without knowing what to do with them, he would ruin them. I, I thought, am not capable of loving anyone like that, not even Nino, all I know is how to get along with books. And for a fraction of a second I saw myself identical to a dented bowl in which my sister Elisa used to feed a stray cat, until he disappeared, and the bowl stood empty, gathering dust on the landing. At that point, with a sharp sense of anguish, I felt sure that I had ventured too far. I must go back, I said to myself, I should be like Carmela, Ada, Gigliola, Lila herself. Accept the neighborhood, expel pride, punish presumption, stop humiliating the people who love me. When Alfonso and Marisa went off to meet Nino, I, making a large detour to avoid my mother, joined my boyfriend on the terrace.

My dress was too light: the sun had gone, it was beginning to get cold. As soon as he saw me, Antonio lit a cigarette and pretended to look at the sea again.

"Let's go," I said.

"Go yourself, with Sarratore's son."

"I want to go with you."

"You're a liar."

"Why?"

"Because if he wanted you, you would leave me here without so much as a goodbye."

It was true, but it enraged me that he said it so openly, heedless of the words. I hissed, "If you don't understand that I'm here running the risk that at any moment my mother might show up and start hitting me because of you, then it means that you're thinking only of yourself, that I don't matter to you at all."

He heard scarcely any dialect in my voice, he noted the long sentence, the subjunctives, and he lost his temper. He threw away the cigarette, grabbed me by the wrist with a barely controlled force and cried—a cry locked in his throat—that he was there for me, only for me, that it was I who had told him to stay near me in the church and at the celebration, yes, I, and you made me swear, he gasped, swear, you said, that you won't ever leave me alone, and so I had a suit made, and I'm deep in debt to Signora Solara, and to please you, to do as you asked, I didn't spend even a minute with my mother or my sisters and brothers: and what is my reward, my reward is that you treat me like shit, you talk the whole time to the poet's son and humiliate me in front of my friends, you make me look ridiculous, because to you I'm no one, because you're so educated and I'm not, because I don't understand the things you say, and it's true, it's very true that I don't understand you, but God damn it, Lenù, look at me, look me in the face: you think you can order me around, you think I'm not capable of saying That's enough, and yet you're wrong, you know everything, but you don't know that if you go out of that door with me now, if now I tell you O.K. and we go out, but then I discover that you see that jerk Nino Sarratore at school, and who knows where else, I'll kill you, Lenù, so think about it, leave me here this minute, he said in despair, leave me, because it's better for you, and meanwhile he looked at me, his eyes red and very large, and uttered the words with his mouth wide open, shouting at me without shouting, his nostrils flaring, black, and in his face such suffering that I thought Maybe he's hurting himself inside, because the words, shouted in his throat like that, in his chest, but without exploding in the air, are like bits of sharp iron piercing his lungs and his pharynx.

I had a confused need for that aggression. The vise on my wrist, the fear that he would hit me, that river of painful words ended by consoling me: it seemed to me that at least he valued me.

"You're hurting me," I muttered.

He slowly relaxed his grip, but remained staring at me with his mouth open. The skin of my wrist was turning purple, giving him weight and authority, anchoring me to him.

"What do you choose?" he asked.

"I want to stay with you," I said, but sullenly.

He closed his mouth, his eyes filled with tears, he looked at the sea to give himself time to suppress them.

Soon afterward we were in the street. We didn't wait for Pasquale, Enzo, the girls, we didn't say goodbye to anyone. The most important thing was not to be seen by my mother, so we slipped away on foot; by now it was dark. For a while we walked beside each other without touching, then Antonio hesitantly put an arm around my shoulders. He wanted me to understand that he expected to be forgiven, as if he were the guilty one. Because he loved me, he had decided to consider the hours that, right before his eyes, I had spent with Nino, seducing and seduced, a time of hallucinations.

"Did I leave a bruise?" he asked, trying to take my wrist.

I didn't answer. He grasped my shoulder with his broad hand, I made a movement of annoyance that immediately caused him to relax his grip. He waited, I waited. When he tried again to send out that signal of surrender, I put an arm around his waist.

4.

We kissed without stopping, behind a tree, in the doorway of a building, along dark alleys. We took a bus, then another, and reached the station. We went toward the ponds on foot, still kissing each other on the nearly deserted street that skirted the railroad tracks.

I was hot, even though my dress was light and the cold of the evening pierced the heat of my skin with sudden shivers.

Every so often Antonio clung to me in the shadows, embracing me with such ardor that it hurt. His lips were burning, and the heat of his mouth kindled my thoughts and my imagination. Maybe Lila and Stefano, I said to myself, are already in the hotel. Maybe they're having dinner. Maybe they're getting ready for the night. Ah, to sleep next to a man, not to be cold. I felt Antonio's tongue moving around my mouth and while he pressed my breasts through the material of my dress, I touched his sex through the pocket of his pants.

The black sky was stained with pale clouds of stars. The ponds' odor of moss and putrid earth was yielding to the sweeter scents of spring. The grass was wet, the water abruptly hiccupped, as if an acorn had fallen in it, a rock, a frog. We took a path we knew well, which led to a stand of dead trees, with slender trunks and broken branches. A little farther on was the old canning factory, with its caved-in roof, all iron beams and fragments of metal. I felt an urgency of pleasure, something that drew me from inside like a smooth strip of velvet. I wanted desire to find a violent satisfaction, capable of shattering that whole day. I felt it rubbing, caressing and pricking at the base of my stomach, stronger than it had ever been. Antonio spoke words of love in dialect, he spoke them in my mouth, on my neck, insisting. I was silent, I was always silent during those encounters, I only sighed.

"Tell me you love me," he begged.

"Yes."

"Tell me."

"Yes."

I said nothing else. I embraced him, I clasped him to me with all my strength. I would have liked to be caressed and kissed over every inch of my body, I felt the need to be rubbed, bitten, I wanted my breath to fail. He pushed me a little away from him and slid a hand into my bra as he continued to kiss me. But it wasn't enough for me, that night it was too little. All the contact that we had had up to that minute, that he had imposed on me with caution and that I had accepted with equal caution, now seemed to me inadequate, uncomfortable, too quick. Yet I didn't know how to tell him that I wanted more, I didn't have the words. In each of our secret meetings we celebrated a silent rite, stage by stage. He caressed my breasts, he lifted my skirt, he touched me between the legs, and meanwhile he pushed against me, like a signal, the convulsion of tender flesh and cartilage and veins and blood that vibrated in his pants. But that night I delayed pulling out his sex; I knew that as soon as I did he would forget about me, he would stop touching me. Breasts, hips, bottom, pubis would no longer occupy him, he would be concentrated only on my hand, in fact he would tighten his around it to encourage me to move it with the right rhythm. Then he would get out his handkerchief and keep it ready for the moment when a light rattling sound would come from his mouth and from his penis his dangerous liquid. Finally he would draw back, slightly dazed, perhaps embarrassed, and we would go home. A habitual conclusion, which I now felt a confused need to change: I didn't care about being pregnant without being married, I didn't care about the sin, the divine overseers nesting in the cosmos above us, the Holy Spirit or any of his stand-ins, and Antonio felt this and was disoriented. While he kissed me, with growing agitation, he tried repeatedly to bring my hand down, but I pulled it away, I pushed my pubis against his fingers, I pushed hard and repeatedly, with drawn-out sighs. Then he withdrew his hand, he tried to unbutton his pants.

"Wait," I said.

I drew him toward the skeleton of the canning factory. It was darker there, more sheltered, but I could hear the wary rustling of scampering mice. My heart began to beat hard, I was afraid of the place, of myself, of the craving that possessed me to obliterate from my manners and from my voice the sense of alienation that I had discovered a few hours earlier. I wanted to return, and sink into that neighborhood, to be as I had been. I wanted to throw away studying, the notebooks full of exercises. Exercising for what, after all. What I could become outside of Lila's shadow counted for nothing. What was I compared with her in her wedding dress, with her in the convertible, the blue hat and the pastel suit? What was I, here with Antonio, secretly, in this rusting ruin, with the scurrying rats, my skirt raised over my hips, my underpants lowered, yearning and anguished and guilty, while she lay naked, with languid detachment, on linen sheets, in a hotel that looked out on the sea, and let Stefano violate her, enter her completely, give her his seed, impregnate her legitimately and without fear? What was I as Antonio fumbled with his pants and placed his gross male flesh between my legs, against my naked sex, and clutching my buttocks rubbed against me, moving back and forth, panting? I didn't know. I knew only that I was not what I wanted at that moment. It wasn't enough for him to rub against me. I wanted to be penetrated, I wanted to tell Lila when she returned: I'm not a virgin, either, what you do I do, you can't leave me behind. So I held Antonio tight around his neck and kissed him, I stood on tiptoe, I sought his sex with mine, I sought it wordlessly, by trial and error. He realized it and helped me with his hand, I felt him entering just a little, I trembled with curiosity and fear. But I also felt the effort he was making to stop, to keep from pushing with all the violence that had been smoldering for an entire afternoon and surely was still. He was about to stop, I realized, and I pressed against him to persuade him to continue.

But with a deep breath Antonio pushed me away and said in dialect, "No, Lenù, I want to do it the way it's done with a wife, not like this."

He grabbed my right hand, brought it to his sex with a kind of repressed sob, and I resigned myself to masturbating him.

Afterward, as we were leaving the ponds, he said uneasily that he respected me and didn't want to make me do something that I would later regret, not in that place, not in that dirty and careless way. He spoke as if it were he who had gone too far, and maybe he believed that. I didn't utter a single word the whole way, and said goodbye with relief. When I knocked on the door, my mother opened it and, in vain restrained by my brothers and sister, without yelling, without a word of reproach, began hitting me. My glasses flew to the floor and immediately I shouted with bitter joy, and not a hint of dialect, "See what you've done? You've broken my glasses and now because of you I can't study, I'm not going to school anymore."

My mother froze, even the hand she had struck me with remained still in the air, like the blade of an axe.

Elisa, my little sister, picked up the glasses and said softly, "Here, Lenù, they're not broken."

5.

I was overcome by an exhaustion that, no matter how much I rested, wouldn't go away. For the first time, I skipped school. I was absent, I think, for some two weeks, and not even to Antonio did I say that I couldn't stand it anymore, I wanted to stop. I left home at the usual time, and wandered all morning through the city. I learned a lot about Naples in that period. I rummaged among the used books in the stalls of Port'Alba, unwillingly absorbing titles and authors' names, and continued toward Toledo and the sea. Or I climbed the Vomero on Via Salvator Rosa, went up to San Martino, came back down by the Petraio. Or I explored the Doganella, went to the cemetery, wandered on the silent paths, read the names of the dead. Sometimes idle young men, stupid old men, even respectable middle-aged men pursued me with obscene offers. I quickened my pace, eyes lowered, I escaped, sensing danger, but didn't stop. In fact the more I skipped school the bigger the hole that those long mornings of wandering made in the net of scholastic obligations that had imprisoned me since I was six years old. At the proper time I went home and no one suspected that I, *I*, had not gone to school. I spent the afternoon reading novels, then I hurried to the ponds, to Antonio, who was very happy that I was so available. He would have liked to ask if I had seen Sarratore's son. I read the question in his eyes, but he didn't dare ask, he was afraid of a quarrel, he was afraid that I would get angry and deny him those few minutes of pleasure. He embraced me, to feel me compliant against his body, to chase away any doubt. At those moments he dismissed the possibility that I could insult him by also seeing that other.

He was wrong: in reality, although I felt guilty, I thought only of Nino. I wanted to see him, talk to him, and on the other hand I was afraid to. I was afraid that he would humiliate me with his superiority. I was afraid that one way or another he would return to the reasons that the article about my quarrel with the religion teacher hadn't been published. I was afraid that he would report to me the cruel judgments of the editors. I couldn't have borne it. While I drifted through the city, and at night, in bed, when I couldn't sleep and felt my inadequacy with utter clarity, I preferred to believe that my text had been rejected for pure and simple lack of space. Let it diminish, fade. But it was hard. I hadn't been equal to Nino's brilliance, and so I couldn't stay with him, be listened to, tell him my thoughts. What thoughts, after all? I didn't have any. Better to eliminate myself—no more books, grades, praise. I hoped to forget everything, slowly: the notions that crowded my head, the languages living and dead, Italian itself that rose now to my lips even with my sister and brothers. It's Lila's fault, I thought, if I started down this path, I have to forget her, too: Lila always knew what she wanted and got it; I don't want anything, I'm made of nothing. I hoped to wake in the morning without desires. Once I was emptied—I imagined—the affection of Antonio, my affection for him will be enough.

Then one day, on the way home, I met Pinuccia, Stefano's sister. I learned from her that Lila had returned from her honeymoon and had had a big lunch to celebrate the engagement of her sister-in-law and her brother.

"You and Rino are engaged?" I asked, feigning surprise.

"Yes," she said, radiant, and showed me the ring he had given her.

I remember that while Pinuccia was talking I had a single, twisted thought: Lila had a party at her new house and didn't invite me, but it's better that way, I'm glad, stop comparing myself to her, I don't want to see her anymore. Only when every detail of the engagement had been examined did I ask, hesitantly, about my friend. With a treacherous half smile, Pinuccia offered a formula in dialect: *she's learning.* I didn't ask what. When I got home I slept for the whole afternoon.

The next morning I went out at seven as usual to go to school, or, rather, to pretend to go to school. I had just crossed the *stradone*, when I saw Lila get out of the convertible and enter our courtyard without even turning to say goodbye to Stefano, who was at the wheel. She had dressed with care, and wore large dark glasses, even though there was no sun. I was struck by a scarf of blue voile that she had knotted in such a way that it covered her lips, too. I thought resentfully that this was her new style—not Jackie Kennedy but, rather, the mysterious lady we had imagined we would become ever since we were children. I kept going without calling to her.

After a few steps, however, I turned back, not with a clear intention but because I couldn't help it. My heart was pounding, my feelings were confused. Maybe I wanted to ask her to tell me to my face that our friendship was over. Maybe I wanted to cry out that I, too, had decided to stop studying and get married—to go and live at Antonio's house with his mother and his brothers and sisters, wash the stairs like Melina the madwoman. I crossed the courtyard quickly, I saw her go in the entranceway that led to her mother-in-law's apartment. I started up the stairs, the same ones we had climbed together as children when we went to ask Don Achille to give us our dolls. I called her, she turned.

"You're back," I said.

"Yes."

"Why didn't you tell me?"

"I didn't want you to see me."

"Others can see you and not me?"

"I don't care about others, I do care about you."

I looked at her uncertainly. What was I not supposed to see? I climbed the stairs that separated us and delicately pulled aside the scarf, raised the sunglasses.

6.

I do it again now, in my imagination, as I begin to tell the story of her honeymoon, not only as she told it to me there on the landing but as I read it later, in her notebooks. I had been unjust to her, I had wished to believe in an easy surrender on her part to be able to humiliate her as I felt humiliated when Nino left the reception; I had wished to diminish her in order not to feel her loss. There she is, instead, the reception now over, shut up in the convertible, the blue hat, the pastel suit. Her eyes were burning with rage and as soon as the car started she blasted Stefano with the most intolerable words and phrases of our neighborhood.

He swallowed the insults in his usual way, with a faint smile, not saying a word, and finally she was silent. But the silence didn't last. Lila started again calmly, but panting slightly. She told him that she wouldn't stay in that car a minute longer, that it disgusted her to breathe the air that he breathed, that she wanted to get out, immediately. Stefano saw the disgust in her face, yet he continued to drive, without saying anything, so she raised her voice again to make him stop. Then he pulled over, but when Lila tried to open the door he grabbed her firmly by the wrist.

"Now listen to me," he said softly. "There are serious reasons for what happened."

He explained to her in placid tones how it went. To keep the shoe factory from closing down before it even opened its doors, he had found it necessary to enter into a partnership with Silvio Solara and his sons, who alone could insure not only that the shoes were placed in the best shops in the city but that in the fall a shop selling Cerullo shoes exclusively would open in Piazza dei Martiri.

"What do I care about your necessities," Lila interrupted him, struggling to get free.

"My necessities are yours, you're my wife."

"I? I'm nothing to you, nor are you to me. Let go of my arm."

Stefano let go of her arm.

"Your father and brother are nothing, either?"

"Wash your mouth out when you talk about them, you're not fit to even mention their names."

But Stefano did mention their names. He said that it was Francesco himself who had wanted to make the agreement with Silvio Solara. He said that the biggest obstacle had been Marcello, who was extremely angry at Lila, at the whole Cerullo family, and, especially, at Pasquale, Antonio, and Enzo, who had smashed his car and beaten him up. He said that Rino had calmed him down, that it had taken a lot of patience, and so when Marcello had said, then I want the shoes that Lina made, Rino had said O.K., take the shoes.

It was a bad moment, Lila felt as if she'd been stabbed in the chest. But just the same she cried, "And you, what did you do?"

Stefano had a moment of embarrassment.

"What was I supposed to do? Fight with your brother, ruin your family, start a war against your friends, lose all the money I invested?"

To Lila, every word, in both tone and content, seemed a hypocritical admission of guilt. She didn't even let him finish, but began hitting him on the shoulder with her fists, yelling, "So even you, you said O.K., you went and got the shoes, you gave them to him?"

Stefano let her go on, but when she tried again to open the door and escape he said to her coldly, Calm down. Lila turned suddenly: calm down after he had thrown the blame on her father and brother, calm down when all three had treated her like an old rag, a rag for wiping up the floor. I don't want to calm down, she shouted, you piece of shit, take me home right now, repeat what you just said in front of those two other shit men. And only when she uttered that expression in dialect, shit men, *uommen'e mmerd*, did she notice that she had broken the barrier of her husband's measured tones. A second afterward Stefano struck her in the face with his strong hand, a violent slap that seemed to her an explosion of truth. She winced, startled by the painful burning of her cheek. She looked at him, incredulous, while he started the car and said, in a voice that for the first time since he had begun to court her was not calm, that in fact trembled, "See what you've made me do? See how you go too far?"

"We've been wrong about everything," she murmured.

But Stefano denied it decisively, as if he refused even to consider that possibility, and he made a long speech, part threatening, part didactic, part pathetic.

He said, more or less, "We haven't been wrong about anything, Lina, we just have to get a few things straight. Your name is no longer Cerullo. You are Signora Carracci and you must do as I say. I know, you're not practical, you don't know what business is, you think I find money lying on the ground. But it's not like that. I have to make money every day, I have to put it where it can grow. You designed the shoes, your father and brother are good workers, but the three of you together aren't capable of making money grow. The Solaras are, and so—please listen to me—I don't give a damn if you don't like those people. Marcello is repulsive to me, too, and when he looks at you, even so much as out of the corner of his eye, when I think of the things he said about you, I feel like sticking a knife in his stomach. But if he is useful for making money, then he becomes my best friend. And you know why? Because if we don't make money we don't have this car, I can't buy you that dress, we lose the house with everything in it, in the end you can't act the lady, and our children grow up like the children of beggars. So just try saying again what you said tonight and I will ruin that beautiful face of yours so that you can't go out of the house. You understand? Answer me."

Lila's eyes narrowed to cracks. Her cheek had turned purple, but otherwise she was very pale. She didn't answer him.

7.

They reached Amalfi in the evening. Neither had ever been to a hotel, and they were embarrassed and ill at ease. Stefano was especially intimidated by the vaguely mocking tones of the receptionist and, without meaning to, assumed a subservient attitude. When he realized it, he covered his discomfiture with brusque manners, and his ears flushed merely at the request to show his documents. Meanwhile the porter appeared, a man in his fifties with a thin mustache, but Stefano refused his help, as if he were a thief, then, thinking better of it, disdainfully gave him a large tip, even though he didn't take advantage of his services. Lila followed her husband as he carried the suitcases up the stairs and—she told me—for the first time had the impression that somewhere along the way she had lost the youth she had married that morning, and was in the company of a stranger. Was Stefano really so broad, his legs short and fat, his arms long, his knuckles white? To whom had she bound herself forever? The rage that had overwhelmed her during the journey gave way to anxiety.

Once they were in the room he made an effort to be affectionate again, but he was tired and still unnerved by the slap he had had to give her. He assumed an artificial tone. He praised the room, it was very spacious, opened the French window, went out on the balcony, said to her, Come and smell the fragrant air, look how the sea sparkles. But she was seeking a way out of that trap, and, distracted, shook her head no, she was cold. Stefano immediately closed the window, and remarked that if they wanted to take a walk and eat outside they'd better put on something warmer, saying, Just in case get me a vest, as if they had already been living together for many years and she knew how to dig expertly in the suitcases, to pull out a vest for him exactly as she would have found a sweater for herself. Lila seemed to agree, but in fact she didn't open the suitcases, she took out neither sweater nor vest. She immediately went out into the corridor, she didn't want to stay in the room a minute longer. He followed her muttering: I'm also fine like this, but I'm worried about you, you'll catch cold.

They wandered around Amalfi, to the cathedral, up the steps and back down again, to the fountain. Stefano now tried to amuse her, but being amusing had never been his strong point, sentimental tones suited him better, or the sententious phrases of the mature man who knows what he wants. Lila barely responded, and in the end her husband confined himself to pointing out this and that, exclaiming, Look. But she, who in other times would have appreciated every stone, wasn't interested in the beauty of the narrow streets or the scents of the gardens or the art and history of Amalfi, or, especially, the voice of her husband, who kept saying, tiresomely, Beautiful, isn't it?

Soon Lila began to tremble, but not because she was particularly cold; it was nerves. He realized it and proposed that they return to the hotel, even venturing a remark like: Then we can hug each other and get warm. But she wanted to keep walking, on and on, until, overcome by weariness, and though she wasn't at all hungry, she entered a restaurant, without consulting him. Stefano followed her patiently.

They ordered all kinds of things, ate almost nothing, drank a lot of wine. At a certain point he could no longer hold back, and asked if she was still angry. Lila shook her head no, and it was true. At that question, she herself was amazed not to feel the least rancor toward the Solaras, or her father and brother, or Stefano. Everything had rapidly changed in her mind. Suddenly, she didn't care at all about the shoes; in fact she couldn't understand why she had been so enraged at seeing them on Marcello's feet. Now, instead, the broad wedding band that gleamed on her ring finger frightened and distressed her. In disbelief, she retraced the day: the church, the ceremony, the celebration. What have I done, she thought, dazed by wine, and what is this gold circle, this glittering zero I've stuck my finger in. Stefano had one, too, and it shone amid the black hairs, hairy fingers, as the books said. She remembered him in his bathing suit, as she had seen him at the beach. The broad chest, the large kneecaps, like overturned pots. There was not the smallest detail that, once recalled, revealed to her any charm. He was a being, now, with whom she felt she could share nothing and yet there he was, in his jacket and tie, he moved his fat lips and scratched the fleshy lobe of an ear and kept sticking his fork in something on her plate to taste it. He had little or nothing to do with the seller of cured meats who had attracted her, with the ambitious, self-confident, but well-mannered youth, with the bridegroom of that morning in church. He revealed white jaws, a red tongue in the dark hole of his mouth: something in and around him had broken. At that table, amid the coming and going of the waiters, everything that had brought her here to Amalfi seemed without any logical coherence and yet unbearably real. Thus, while the face of that unrecognizable being lighted up at the idea that the storm had passed, that she had understood his reasons, that she had accepted them, that he could finally talk to her about his big plans, she suddenly had the idea of stealing a knife from the table to stick in his throat when, in the room, he tried to deflower her.

In the end she didn't do it. Since in that restaurant, at that table, to her wine-fogged mind, her entire marriage, from the wedding dress to the ring, had turned out to make no sense, it also seemed to her that any possible sexual demand on Stefano's part would make no sense, above all to him. So at first she contemplated how to get the knife (she took the napkin off her lap, covered the knife with it, placed both back on her lap, prepared to drop the knife in her purse, and put the napkin back on the table), then she gave it up. The screws holding together her new condition of wife, the restaurant, Amalfi, seemed to her so loose that at the end of dinner Stefano's voice no longer reached her, in her ears there was only a clamor of objects, living beings, and thoughts, without definition.

On the street, he started talking again about the good side of the Solaras. They knew, he told her, important people in the city government, they had ties to the parties, the monarchists, the Fascists. He liked to speak as if he really understood something about the Solaras' dealings, he took a knowing tone, he said emphatically: Politics is ugly but it's important for making money. Lila remembered the discussions she had had with Pasquale in earlier times, and even the ones she'd had with Stefano during their engagement, the plan to separate themselves completely from their parents, from the abuses and hypocrisies and cruelties of the past. He said yes, she thought, he said he agreed, but he wasn't listening to me. Who did I talk to. I don't know this person, I don't know who he is.

And yet when he took her hand and whispered that he loved her, she didn't pull away. Maybe she planned to make him think that everything was in order, that they really were bride and groom on their honeymoon, in order to wound him more profoundly when she told him, with all the disgust she felt in her stomach: to get into bed with the hotel porter or with you—you both have smoke-yellowed fingers—it's the same revolting thing to me. Or maybe—and this I think is more likely—she was too frightened and by now was striving to delay every reaction.

As soon as they were in the room, he tried to kiss her, and she recoiled. Gravely, she opened the suitcase, took out her nightgown, gave her husband his pajamas. That attention made him smile happily at her, and he tried again to grab her. But she shut herself in the bathroom.

Alone, she washed her face for a long time to get rid of the stupor from the wine, the impression of a world that had lost its contours. She didn't succeed; rather, the feeling that her very gestures lacked coordination intensified. What can I do, she thought. Stay locked in here all night. And then.

She was sorry that she hadn't taken the knife: for a moment, in fact, she believed that she had, then was forced to admit she hadn't. Sitting on the edge of the bathtub, she compared it appreciatively with the one in the new house, thinking that hers was nicer. Her towels, too, were of a higher quality. Hers? To whom, in fact, did the towels, the tub—everything—

belong? She was bothered by the idea that the ownership of the nice new things was guaranteed by the last name of that particular individual who was waiting for her out there. Carracci's possessions, she, too, was Carracci's possession. Stefano knocked on the door.

"What are you doing, do you feel all right?"

She didn't answer.

Her husband waited a little and knocked again. When nothing happened, he twisted the handle nervously and said in a tone of feigned amusement, "Do I have to break down the door?"

Lila didn't doubt that he would have been capable of it—the stranger who waited for her outside was capable of anything. I, too, she thought, am capable of anything. She undressed, she washed, she put on the nightgown, despising herself for the care with which she had chosen it months earlier. Stefano—purely a name that no longer coincided with the habits and affections of a few hours earlier—was sitting on the edge of the bed in his pajamas and he jumped to his feet as soon as she appeared.

"You took your time."

"The time needed."

"You look beautiful."

"I'm very tired, I want to sleep."

"We'll sleep later."

"Now. You on your side, I on mine."

"O.K., come here."

"I'm serious."

"I am, too."

Stefano uttered a little laugh, tried to take her by the hand. She drew back, he darkened.

"What's wrong with you?"

Lila hesitated. She sought the right expression, said softly, "I don't want you."

Stefano shook his head uncertainly, as if the three words were in a foreign language. He murmured that he had been waiting so long for that moment, day and night. Please, he said, in a pleading tone, and, with an expression almost of dejection, he pointed to his wine-colored pajama pants, and mumbled with a crooked smile: See what happens to me just when I look at you. She looked without wanting to and, with a spasm of disgust, averted her gaze.

At that point Stefano realized that she was about to lock herself in the bathroom again and with an animal leap he grabbed her by the waist, picked her up, and threw her on the bed. What was happening. It was clear that he didn't want to understand. He thought they had made peace at the restaurant, now he was wondering: Why is Lina behaving like this, she's too young. In fact he was laughing, on top of her, trying to soothe her.

"It's a beautiful thing," he said, "you mustn't be afraid. I love you more than my mother and my sister."

But no, she was already pulling herself up to get away from him. How difficult it is to keep up with this girl: she says yes and means no, she says no and means yes. Stefano muttered: No more of these whims, and he stopped her again, sat astride her, pinned her wrists against the bedspread.

"You said that we should wait and we waited," he said, "even though being near you without touching you was terrible and I suffered. But we're married now—behave yourself, don't worry."

He leaned over to kiss her on the mouth, but she avoided him, turning her face forcefully to right and left, struggling, twisting, as she repeated, "Leave me alone, I don't want you, I don't want you, I don't want you."

At that point, almost against his will, the tone of Stefano's voice rose: "Now you're really pissing me off, Lina."

He repeated that remark two or three times, each time

louder, as if to assimilate fully an order that was coming to him from very far away, perhaps even from before he was born. The order was: be a man, Ste'; either you subdue her now or you'll never subdue her; your wife has to learn right away that she is the female and you're the male and therefore she has to obey. And Lila hearing him—you're pissing me off, you're pissing me off, you're pissing me off—and seeing him, broad, heavy above her narrow pelvis, his sex erect, holding up the material of his pajamas like a tent support, remembered when, years before, he had wanted to grab her tongue with his fingers and prick it with a pin because she had dared to humiliate Alfonso in a school competition. He was never Stefano, she seemed to discover suddenly, he was always the oldest son of Don Achille. And that thought, immediately, brought to the young face of her husband, like a revival, features that until that moment had remained prudently hidden in his blood but that had always been there, waiting for their moment. Oh yes, to please the neighborhood, to please her, Stefano had striven to be someone else, softening his features with courteousness, adapting his gaze to meekness, modeling his voice on the tones of conciliation; his fingers, his hands, his whole body had learned to restrain their force. But now the limits that he had imposed for so long were about to give way, and Lila was seized by a childish terror, greater than when we had gone down into the cellar to get our dolls. Don Achille was rising from the muck of the neighborhood, feeding on the living matter of his son. The father was cracking his skin, changing his gaze, exploding out of his body. And in fact look at him, he tore the nightgown off her chest, bared her breasts, clasped her fiercely, leaned over to bite her nipples. And when she, as she had always been able to do, repressed her horror and tried to tear him off her by pulling his hair, groping with her mouth as she sought to bite him until he bled, he drew back, seized her arms, pinned them under his huge bent legs, said to her contemptuously: What are you doing, be quiet, you're just a twig, if I want to break you I'll break you. But Lila wouldn't calm down, she bit the air, she arched to get his weight off of her. In vain. He now had his hands free and leaning over her he slapped her lightly with the tips of his fingers and kept telling her, pressing her: see how big it is, eh, say yes, say yes, say yes, until he took out of his pajamas his stubby sex that, extended over her, seemed like a puppet without arms or legs, congested by mute stirrings, in a frenzy to uproot itself from that other, bigger puppet that was saying, hoarsely, Now I'll make you feel it, Lina, look how nice it is, nobody's got one like this. And since she was still writhing, he hit her twice, first with the palm of his hand, then with the back, and so hard that she understood that if she continued to resist he would certainly kill her—or at least Don Achille would: who frightened the neighborhood because you knew that with his strength he could hurl you against a wall or a tree—and she emptied herself of all rebellion, yielding to a soundless terror, while he drew back, pulled up her nightgown, whispered in her ear: you don't realize how much I love you, but you will know, and tomorrow it will be you asking me to love you as I am now, and more, in fact you will go down on your knees and beg me, and I will say yes but only if you are obedient, and you will be obedient.

When, after some awkward attempts, he tore her flesh with passionate brutality, Lila was absent. The night, the room, the bed, his kisses, his hands on her body, every sensation was absorbed by a single feeling: she hated Stefano Carracci, she hated his strength, she hated his weight on her, she hated his name and his surname.

8.

They returned to the neighborhood four days later. That

same evening Stefano invited his parents-in-law and his brother-in-law to the new house. With a humbler expression than usual, he asked Fernando to tell Lila what had happened with Silvio Solara. Fernando confirmed to his daughter, in unhappy, disjointed sentences, Stefano's version. As for Rino, Carracci asked him, right afterward, to tell why, in the end, they had made the mutual but painful decision to give Marcello the shoes he insisted on. Rino, in the manner of a man who knows what's what, declared pompously: There are situations in which certain choices are obligatory, then he started in with the serious trouble Pasquale, Antonio, and Enzo had got into when they beat up the Solara brothers and wrecked their car.

"You know who was more at risk?" he said, leaning toward his sister and raising his voice. "Them, your friends, those knights in shining armor. Marcello recognized them and was convinced that you had sent them. Stefano and I—what were we supposed to do? You wanted those three idiots to get a beating a lot worse than the one they gave? You wanted to ruin them? And for what, anyway? For a pair of size 43 shoes that your husband can't wear because they're too narrow for him and when it rains the water gets in? We made peace, and, since those shoes were so important to Marcello, we gave them to him."

Words: with them you can do and undo as you please. Lila had always been good with words, but on that occasion, contrary to expectations, she didn't open her mouth. Relieved, Rino reminded her spitefully that it was she who, ever since she was a child, had been harassing him, telling him they had to get rich. Then, she said, laughing, make us rich without complicating our life, which is already too complicated.

At that point—a surprise for the mistress of the house, though certainly not for the others—the doorbell rang, and Pinuccia, Alfonso, and their mother, Maria, appeared, with a tray of pastries freshly made by Spagnuolo himself, the Solaras' pastry maker.

At first it seemed that they had come to celebrate the new-lyweds' return from their honeymoon, since Stefano passed around the wedding pictures, which he had just picked up from the photographer (for the movie, he explained, it would take a little longer). But it soon became clear that the wedding of Stefano and Lila was already old news, the pastries were intended to mark a new happy event: the engagement of Rino and Pinuccia. All the tension was set aside. Rino replaced the violent tones of a few minutes earlier with tender modulations in dialect, exaggerated pronouncements of love, the wonderful idea of having the engagement party right away, in his sister's lovely house. Then, with a theatrical gesture, he took a package out of his pocket; the package, when it was unwrapped, revealed a dark rounded case; and the case, when it was opened, revealed a diamond ring.

Lila noted that it wasn't that different from the one she wore on her finger, next to the wedding ring, and wondered where her brother had got the money. There were hugs and kisses. There was a lot of talk of the future, speculation about who would manage the Cerullo shoe store in Piazza dei Martiri when the Solaras opened it, in the fall. Rino supposed that Pinuccia would manage it, maybe by herself, maybe with Gigliola Spagnuolo, who was officially engaged to Michele and so was making claims. The family reunion became livelier and full of hope.

Lila remained standing most of the time, it hurt to sit down. No one, not even her mother, who was silent during the entire visit, seemed to notice her swollen, black right eye, the cut on her lower lip, the bruises on her arms.

9.

She was still in that state when, there on the stairs that led to the house of her mother-in-law, I took off her glasses, unwound her scarf. The skin around her eye had a yellowish color, and her lower lip was a purple stain with fiery red stripes.

To her friends and relatives she said that she had fallen on the rocks in Amalfi on a beautiful sunny morning, when she and her husband had taken a boat to a beach just at the foot of a yellow wall. During the engagement lunch for her brother and Pinuccia she had used, in telling that lie, a sarcastic tone and they had all sarcastically believed her, especially the women, who knew what had to be said when the men who loved them and whom they loved beat them severely. Besides, there was no one in the neighborhood, especially of the female sex, who did not think that she had needed a good thrashing for a long time. So the beatings did not cause outrage, and in fact sympathy and respect for Stefano increased—there was someone who knew how to be a man.

But when I saw her so battered, my heart leaped to my throat, I embraced her. And when she said she hadn't come to visit because she didn't want me to see her in that state, tears came to my eyes. The story of her honeymoon, as the photonovels put it, although stripped down, almost cold, made me angry, pained me. And yet, I have to admit, I also felt a tenuous pleasure. I was content to discover that Lila now needed help, maybe protection, and that admission of fragility not toward the neighborhood but toward me moved me. I felt that the distances had unexpectedly gotten shorter again and I was tempted to tell her right away that I had decided to quit school, that school was useless, that I didn't have the right qualities. It seemed to me that the news would comfort her.

But her mother-in-law looked out over the banister on the top floor and called her. Lila ended her story with a few hurried sentences, she said that Stefano had tricked her, that he was just like his father.

"You remember that Don Achille gave us money instead of the dolls?" she asked.

"Yes."

"We shouldn't have taken it."

"We bought *Little Women*."

"We were wrong: ever since that moment I've been wrong about everything."

She wasn't upset, she was sad. She put her dark glasses back on, she reknotted the scarf. I was pleased about that *we* (*we* shouldn't have taken it, *we* were wrong), but the abrupt transition to the *I* annoyed me: *I* have been wrong about everything. *We*, I would have liked to correct her, *always we*, but I didn't. It seemed to me that she was trying to comprehend her new condition, and that she urgently needed to know what she could hold on to in order to confront it. Before starting up the flight of stairs she asked, "Would you like to come and study at my house?"

"When?"

"This afternoon, tomorrow, every day."

"Stefano will be annoyed."

"If he is the master, I am the master's wife."

"I don't know, Lila."

"I'll give you a room, I'll shut you in."

"What's the point?"

She shrugged.

"To know that you're there."

I didn't say yes or no. I went off, and wandered through the city as usual. Lila was sure that I would never quit school. She had assigned me the role of the friend with glasses and pimples, always bent over her books, smart in school, and she couldn't even imagine that I might change. But I didn't want that role anymore. It seemed to me that, thanks to the humiliation of the unpublished article, I had thoroughly understood my inadequacy. Even though Nino was born and had grown up like Lila and me in that wretched outlying neighborhood, he was able to use school with intelligence, I was not. So stop deluding myself, stop striving. Accept your lot, as Carmela, Ada, Gigliola, and, in her way, Lila herself have long since done. I didn't go to her house that afternoon or the following ones, and I continued to skip school, tormenting myself.

One morning I went wandering not far from the school, along Via Veterinaria, behind the Botanic Garden. I thought of the conversations I had had recently with Antonio: he was hoping to avoid military service, as the son of a widowed mother and the sole support of the family; he wanted to ask for a raise in the shop, and also save so that he could take over the management of a gas pump along the *stradone*; we would get married, I would help out at the pump. The choice of a simple life, my mother would approve. I can't always please Lila, I said to myself. But how hard it was to erase from my mind the ambitions inspired by school. At the time when classes were over, I went, almost without intending it, to the neighborhood of the school, and walked around there. I was afraid of being seen by the teachers, and yet, I realized, I wished them to see me. I wanted to be either branded irremediably as a no longer model student or recaptured by the rhythms of school and submit to the obligation to go back.

The first groups of students appeared. I heard someone calling me, it was Alfonso. He was waiting for Marisa, but she was late.

"Are you going together?" I asked, teasing.

"No, she's the one who's got a crush."

"Liar."

"You're the liar, telling me you were sick, and look at you, you're fine. Professor Galiani is always asking about you, I told her you had a bad fever."

"I did, in fact."

"Obviously."

He was carrying his books, tied up with elastic, under his arm, his face was strained by the tension of the hours of school.

Did Alfonso also conceal Don Achille, his father, in his breast, despite his delicate appearance? Is it possible that our parents never die, that every child inevitably conceals them in himself? Would my mother truly emerge from me, with her limping gait, as my destiny?

I asked him, "Did you see what your brother did to Lina?"

Alfonso was embarrassed. "Yes."

"And you didn't say anything to him?"

"You have to see what Lina did to him."

"Would you be able to act the same way with Marisa?"

He laughed timidly. "No."

"You're sure?"

"Yes."

"Why?"

"Because I know you, because we talk, because we go to school together."

At the moment, I didn't understand: what did "I know you" mean, what did "we talk" and "we go to school together" mean? I saw Marisa at the end of the street, she was running because she was late.

"Your girlfriend's coming," I said.

He didn't turn, he shrugged, he mumbled, "Come back to school, please."

"I'm sick," I repeated, and left.

I didn't want to exchange even a hello with Nino's sister, any sign that evoked him made me anxious. But Alfonso's obscure words did me good, I turned them over in my mind as I walked. He had said that because he knew me, we talked to each other, we sat at the same desk, he would never impose his authority on a possible wife by beating her. He had expressed himself with a frank sincerity, he wasn't afraid of attributing to me, even if in a confused way, the capacity to influence him, a male, to change his behavior. I was grateful to him for that tangled message, which consoled me and set in motion a reconciliation between me and myself. It doesn't take much for a conviction that has become fragile to weaken to the point of giving way. The next day I forged my mother's signature and returned to school. That evening, at the ponds, clinging to Antonio to escape the cold, I promised him: I'll finish the school year and we'll get married.

10.

But I had a hard time making up the ground I had lost, especially in science, and I tried to reduce my meetings with Antonio so that I could concentrate on my books. When I missed a date because I had to study, he became gloomy, he asked me, in alarm, "Is something wrong?"

"I've got a lot of homework."

"How is it that all of a sudden you've got more homework?"

"I've always had a lot."

"Before you didn't have any."

"It was a coincidence."

"What are you hiding from me, Lenù?"

"Nothing."

"Do you still love me?"

I reassured him, but meanwhile the time moved quickly by us and I went home angry at myself because I still had so much studying to do.

Antonio's fixation was always the same: Sarratore's son. He was afraid that I would talk to him, even that I would see him. Naturally, to prevent him from suffering, I concealed the fact that I ran into Nino entering school, coming out, in the corridors. Nothing particular happened, at most we exchanged a nod of greeting and went on our way: I could have talked to my boyfriend about it without any problems if he had been a reasonable person. But Antonio was not reasonable and in truth I wasn't, either. Although Nino gave me no encouragement, a mere glimpse of him left me distracted during class. His presence a few classrooms away—real, alive, better educated than the professors, and courageous, and disobedient—drained meaning from the teachers' lectures, the pages of books, the plans for marriage, the gas pump on the *stradone*.

Even at home I couldn't study. Added to my confusing thoughts about Antonio, about Nino, about the future was my mother's irritability, as she yelled at me to do this or that, and my siblings, who came one by one to have me look at their homework. That permanent turmoil wasn't new, I had always studied in disorder. But the old determination that had allowed me to do my best even in those conditions seemed to be used up, I couldn't or didn't want to reconcile school with everyone's needs anymore. So I would let the afternoon go by helping my mother, correcting my sister's and brothers' exercises, and studying little or not at all for myself. And if once I had sacrificed sleep to books, now, since I was still exhausted and sleep seemed to me a respite, at night I forgot about homework and went to bed.

And so I began to show up in class not only inattentive but unprepared, and I lived in fear that the teachers would call on me. Which soon happened. Once, in the same day, I got low marks in chemistry, art history, and philosophy, and my nerves were so frayed that right after the last bad grade I burst into tears in front of everyone. It was a terrible moment: I felt the horror and the pleasure of losing myself, the fear and the pride in going off the rails.

As we were leaving school Alfonso told me that his sister-in-law had asked him to tell me to go and see her. Go on, he urged me anxiously, surely you'll study better there than at your house. So that afternoon I made up my mind and walked to the new neighborhood. But I didn't go to Lila's house to find a solution to my problems with school, I took it for granted that we would talk the whole time and that my situation as a former model student would get even worse. I said to myself, rather: better to go off the rails talking to Lila than in the midst of my mother's yelling, the petulant demands of my siblings, the yearnings for Nino, Antonio's recriminations; at least I would learn something about married life, a life that soon—I now assumed—would be mine.

Lila greeted me with obvious pleasure. Her eye was no longer swollen, her lip was healing. She was nicely dressed, her hair was carefully combed, she wore lipstick, yet she moved through the apartment as if her house were alien to her and she herself felt like a visitor. The wedding presents were still piled up near the door, the rooms had a smell of plaster and fresh paint mixed with the vaguely alcoholic scent that emanated from the new furniture in the dining room, the table, the sideboard with a mirror framed by dark-wood foliage, the silver chest full of silver, the plates, glasses, and bottles of colored liquors.

Lila made coffee: it was pleasant to sit with her in the spacious kitchen and play at being ladies, as we had done as children in front of the cellar air vent. It's relaxing, I thought, I was wrong not to come sooner. I had a friend of my age with her own house, full of opulent, orderly things. That friend, who had nothing to do all day, seemed happy for my company. Although we had changed and the changes were still occurring, the warmth between us endured intact. Why, then, not give in to it? For the first time since her wedding day I felt at ease.

"How's it going with Stefano?" I asked.

"Fine."

"You've cleared things up?"

She smiled in amusement.

"Yes, it's all clear."

"And so?"

"Disgusting."

"The same as Amalfi?"

"Yes."

"Did he beat you again?"

She touched her face.

"No, this is old stuff."

"Then?"

"It's the humiliation."

"And you?"

"I do what he wants."

I thought for a moment, I asked her, suggestively, "But at least when you sleep together, isn't it nice?"

She made a grimace of discomfort, became serious. She began to speak of her husband with a sort of loathing acceptance. It wasn't hostility, it wasn't a need for retaliation, it wasn't even disgust, but a placid disdain, a contempt that invested Stefano's entire person like polluted water in the ground.

I listened, I understood and I didn't understand. Long ago she had threatened Marcello with the shoemaker's knife simply because he had dared to grab my wrist and break the bracelet. From that point on, I was sure that if Marcello had just brushed against her she would have killed him. But toward Stefano, now, she showed no explicit aggression. Of course, the explanation was simple: we had seen our fathers beat our mothers from childhood. We had grown up thinking that a stranger must not even touch us, but that our father, our boyfriend, and our husband could hit us when they liked, out of love, to educate us, to reeducate us. As a result, since Stefano was not the hateful Marcello but the young man to whom she had declared her love, whom she had married, and with whom she had decided to live forever, she assumed complete responsibility for her choice. And yet it didn't add up. In my eyes Lila was Lila, not an ordinary girl of the neighborhood. Our mothers, after they were slapped by their husbands, did not have that expression of calm disdain. They despaired, they wept, they confronted their man sullenly, they criticized him behind his back, and yet, more and less, they continued to respect him (my mother, for example, plainly admired my father's devious deals). Lila instead displayed an acquiescence without respect.

I said, "I feel comfortable with Antonio, even though I don't love him."

And I hoped that, in accord with our old habits, she would be able to grasp in that statement a series of hidden questions. Although I love Nino—I was saying without saying it—I feel pleasantly excited just thinking of Antonio, of our kisses, of holding and touching each other at the ponds. Love in my case is not indispensable to pleasure, nor is respect. Is it possible, therefore, that *the disgust, the humiliation* begin *afterward*, when a man subdues you and violates you at his pleasure solely because now you belong to him, love or not, respect or not? What happens when you're in a bed, crushed by a man? She had experienced that and I would have liked her to talk about it. Instead she confined herself to saying, sarcastically, Better for you if you're comfortable, and she led me to a small room that looked out onto the railroad tracks. It was a bare space, there was only a desk, a chair, a cot, nothing on the walls.

"Do you like it here?"

"Yes."

"Then study."

She left, closing the door behind her.

The room smelled of damp plaster more than the rest of the house. I looked out the window, I would have preferred to go on talking. But it was immediately clear to me that Alfonso had told her about my absence from school, maybe even about my bad grades, and that she wanted to restore to me the wisdom she had always attributed to me, even at the cost of imposing it on me. Better that way. I heard her moving through the house, making a phone call. It struck me that she didn't say *Hello, it's Lina*, or, I don't know, *It's Lina Cerullo*, but *Hello, this is Signora Carracci*. I sat down at the desk, opened my history book, and forced myself to study.

11.

The close of the school year was inauspicious. The building that housed the high school was crumbling, rain leaked into the classrooms, after one violent storm a street nearby caved in. There followed a period when we went to school on alternate days, homework began to count more than the normal lessons, the teachers loaded it on to the point where it was unbearable. Despite my mother's protests, I got in the habit of going to Lila's right after school.

I arrived at two in the afternoon, I dropped my books somewhere. She made me a sandwich with prosciutto, cheese, salami—anything I wanted. Such abundance was never seen at my parents' house: how good the smell of the fresh bread was, and the taste of the fillings, especially the prosciutto, bright red edged with white. I ate greedily and Lila made me coffee. After we'd had some intense conversation, she closed me in the little room and seldom looked in, except to bring me a snack and to eat or drink with me. Since I had no wish to run into Stefano, who generally returned from the grocery around eight at night, I always left right at seven.

I became familiar with the apartment, with its light, with the sounds that came from the railroad. Every space, every thing was new and clean, but especially the bathroom, which had a sink, a bidet, a bathtub. One afternoon when I felt particularly lazy I asked Lila if I could have a bath, I who still washed under the tap or in a copper tub. She said I could do what I wanted and went to bring me towels. The water came out hot from the tap and I let it run. I undressed, I sank in up to my neck.

That warmth was an unexpected pleasure. After a while I tried out the numerous little bottles that crowded the corners of the tub: a steamy foam arose, as if from my body, and almost overflowed. Ah, how many wonderful things Lila possessed. It was no longer just a matter of a clean body, it was play, it was abandon. I discovered the lipsticks, the makeup, the wide mirror that reflected an image without deformities, the hair dryer. Afterward, my skin was smoother than I had ever felt it, and my hair was full, luminous, blonder. Maybe the wealth we wanted as children is this, I thought: not strongboxes full of diamonds and gold coins but a bathtub, to immerse yourself like this every day, to eat bread, salami, prosciutto, to have a lot of space even in the bathroom, to have a telephone, a pantry and icebox full of food, a photograph in a silver frame on the sideboard that shows you in your wedding dress—to have *this entire* house, with the kitchen, the bedroom, the dining room, the two balconies, and the little room where I am studying, and where, even though Lila hasn't said so, soon, when it comes, a baby will sleep.

That evening I hurried to the ponds, I couldn't wait for Antonio to caress me, smell me, marvel, enjoy that luxurious cleanliness that highlighted beauty. It was a gift that I wanted to give him. But he had his anxieties: he said, I'll never be able to offer you these things, and I answered, Who says that I want them, and he replied, You always want to do what Lila does. I was offended, we quarreled. I was independent. I did only what I liked, I did what he and Lila didn't and couldn't do, I went to school, I studied hard, was going blind over my books. I cried that he didn't understand me, that all he did was disparage and insult me, and I ran away.

But Antonio understood me too well. Day by day my friend's

house charmed me more, it became a magical place where I could have everything, far from the wretched gray of the old buildings where we had grown up, the flaking walls, the scratched doors, the same objects always, dented and chipped. Lila was careful not to disturb me, I would call out: I'm thirsty, I'm kind of hungry, let's turn on the television, can I see this, can I see that. I was bored by studying, I struggled. Sometimes I asked her to listen to me while I repeated the lessons aloud. She sat on the cot, I at the desk. I showed her the pages I had to repeat, I recited, Lila checked me line for line.

It was on those occasions that I realized how her relationship with books had changed. Now she was intimidated by them. She no longer wanted to impose on me an order, her own rhythm, as if just a few sentences were enough to get a picture of the whole and master it so that she could tell me: This is the important concept, start here. When, following me in the textbook, she had the impression that I was mistaken, she corrected me with a thousand apologies, such as: Maybe I didn't understand it, maybe you should check. She seemed not to realize that her capacity to learn effortlessly remained intact. But I knew. I saw, for example, that chemistry, so boring for me, provoked in her that narrow look, and her few observations awakened me from my apathy, excited me. I saw that after half a page of the philosophy textbook she was able to find surprising connections between Anaxagoras, the order that the intellect imposes on the chaos of things, and Mendeleev's tables. But more often I had the impression that she was aware of the inadequacy of her tools, of the naïveté of her observations, and she restrained herself on purpose. As soon as she realized that she had let herself get too involved, she retreated as if before a trap, and mumbled: Lucky you who understand, I don't know what you're talking about.

Once, she closed the book abruptly and said with annoyance, "That's enough."

"Why?"

"Because I've had it, it's always the same story: inside something small there's something even smaller that wants to leap out, and outside something large there's always something larger that wants to keep it a prisoner. I'm going to cook."

And yet I wasn't studying anything that had to do in an obvious way with the small and the large. Her own capacity to learn had irritated her, or perhaps frightened her, and she had retreated.

Where?

To make dinner, to clean the house, to watch television with the volume low in order not to disturb me, to look at the tracks, the train traffic, the fleeting outline of Vesuvius, the streets of the new neighborhood, still without trees and without shops, the rare car traffic, the women with their shopping bags, small children attached to their skirts. Occasionally, and only on Stefano's orders, or because he asked her to go with him, she went out to the place—it was less than five hundred meters from the house; once I went with her—where the new grocery was to be built. There she took measurements with a carpenter's measuring tape to plan shelves and furnishings.

That was it, she had nothing else to do. I soon realized that, being married, she was more alone than before. I sometimes went out with Carmela, with Ada, even with Gigliola, and at school I had made friends with girls in my class and other classes, so that sometimes I met them for ice cream on Via Foria. But she saw only Pinuccia, her sister-in-law. As for the boys, if during the period of her engagement they still stopped to exchange a few words, now, after her marriage, they gave a nod of greeting, at most, when they met on the street. And yet she was beautiful and she dressed like the pictures in the women's magazines that she bought in great numbers. But the condition of wife had enclosed her in a sort of glass container, like a sailboat sailing with sails unfurled in an inaccessible place, without the sea. Pasquale, Enzo, Antonio himself would never have ventured onto the unshaded white streets of newly built houses, to her doorway, to her apartment, to talk a little or invite her to take a walk. And even the telephone, a black object attached to the kitchen wall, seemed a useless ornament. The whole time I studied at her house, it seldom rang and when it did it was usually Stefano, who had put one in the grocery as well, to take orders from customers. Their conversations as newlyweds were brief, she answered listlessly, yes, no.

She used the telephone mainly for making purchases. In that period she hardly ever went out of the house, as she waited for the signs of the beating to completely disappear from her face, but she bought things just the same. For example, after my joyous bath, after my enthusiasm about the way my hair had turned out, I heard her order a new hair dryer, and when it was delivered she wanted to give it to me. She uttered that sort of magic formula (*Hello, this is Signora Carracci*) and then she negotiated, discussed, gave up, bought. She didn't pay, the shopkeepers were all from the neighborhood, they knew Stefano well. She merely signed, *Lina Carracci*, name and last name, as Maestra Oliviero had taught us, and she wrote the signature as if it were an assignment, with an intent half-smile, never even checking the merchandise, as if those marks on paper mattered more to her than the objects that were being delivered.

She also bought some big albums with green covers decorated with floral motifs, in which she arranged the wedding photographs. She had printed just for me copies of I don't know how many of them, all the ones in which I, my parents, my sister and brothers, even Antonio appeared. She telephoned and ordered the photographs. I found one in which Nino could be seen: there was Alfonso, there was Marisa, and he was at the right, cut off by the edge of the frame, only his hair, his nose, his mouth.

"Can I have this, too?" I asked without much enthusiasm.

"You're not in it."

"I'm here, from the back."

"All right, if you want it I'll have it printed for you."

I abruptly changed my mind.

"No, forget it."

"Really, go ahead."

"No."

But the acquisition that most impressed me was the projector. The movie of the wedding had finally been developed; the photographer came one night to show it to the newlyweds and their relatives. Lila found out how much the machine cost, she had one delivered to her house and invited me to watch the film. She put the projector on the dining-room table, took a painting of a stormy sea off the wall, expertly inserted the film, lowered the blinds, and the images began to flow over the white wall. It was a marvel: the movie was in color, just a few minutes long. I was astonished. Again I saw her enter the church on Fernando's arm, come out into the church square with Stefano, their happy walk through the Parco delle Rimembranze, ending with a long kiss, the entrance into the restaurant, the dance that followed, the relatives eating or dancing, the cutting of the cake, the handing out of the favors, the goodbyes addressed to the lens, Stefano happy, she grim, both in their traveling clothes.

The first time I saw it I was struck most of all by myself. I appeared twice. First in the church square, beside Antonio: I looked awkward, nervous, my face taken up by my glasses. The second time, I was sitting at the table with Nino, and was barely recognizable: I was laughing, hands and arms moved with casual elegance, I adjusted my hair, toyed with my mother's bracelet—I seemed to myself refined and beautiful.

Lila in fact exclaimed, "Look how well you came out."

"Not really," I lied.

"You look the way you do when you're happy."

The second time we watched (I said to her, Play it again, she didn't have to be asked twice), what struck me instead was the Solaras' entrance into the restaurant. The cameraman had caught the moment that had registered most profoundly in me: the moment Nino left the room and Marcello and Michele burst in. The two brothers entered side by side, in their dress clothes; they were tall and muscular, thanks to the time they spent in the gym lifting weights; meanwhile Nino, slipping out, head lowered, just bumped Marcello's arm, and as Marcello abruptly turned, with a mean, bullying look, he vanished, indifferent, without looking back.

The contrast seemed violent. It wasn't so much the poverty of Nino's clothes, which clashed with the opulence of the Solaras', with the gold they wore on their necks and their wrists and their fingers. It wasn't even his extreme thinness, which was accentuated by his height—he was at least three inches taller than the brothers, who were tall, too—and which suggested a fragility opposed to the virile strength that Marcello and Michele displayed with smug satisfaction. Rather, it was the indifference. While the Solaras' arrogance could be considered normal, the haughty carelessness with which Nino had bumped into Marcello and kept going was not at all normal. Even those who detested the Solaras, like Pasquale, Enzo, or Antonio, had, one way or another, to reckon with them. Nino, on the other hand, not only didn't apologize but didn't so much as glance at Marcello.

The scene provided documentary proof of what I had intuited as I was experiencing it in reality. In that sequence Sarratore's son—who had grown up in the run-down buildings of the old neighborhood just like us, and who had seemed so frightened when it came to defeating Alfonso in the school competitions—now appeared completely outside the scale of values at whose peak stood the Solaras. It was a hierarchy that visibly did not interest him, that perhaps he no longer understood.

Looking at him, I was seduced. He seemed to me an ascetic prince who could intimidate Michele and Marcello merely by means of a gaze that didn't see them. And for an instant I hoped that now, in the image, he would do what he had not done in reality: take me away.

Lila noticed Nino only then, and said, curious, "Is that the same person you sat with at the table with Alfonso?"

"Yes. Didn't you recognize him? It's Nino, the oldest son of Sarratore."

"He's the one who kissed you when you were on Ischia?"

"It was nothing."

"Just as well."

"Why just as well?"

"He's a person who thinks he's somebody."

As if to excuse that impression I said, "This year he graduates and he's the best in the whole school."

"You like him because of that?"

"No."

"Forget him, Lenù, Antonio is better."

"You think?"

"Yes. He's skinny, ugly, and most of all really arrogant."

I heard the three adjectives like an insult and was on the point of saying: it's not true, he's handsome, his eyes sparkle, and I'm sorry you don't realize it, because a boy like that doesn't exist in the movies or on television or even in novels, and I'm happy that I've loved him since I was little, and even if he's out of my reach, even if I'm going to marry Antonio and spend my life pumping gas, I will love him more than myself, I'll love him forever.

Instead, unhappy again, I said, "I used to like him, in elementary school: I don't anymore."

12.

The months that followed were packed with small events that tormented me a great deal, and even today I find it difficult to put them in order. Although I imposed on myself an appearance of self-assurance and an iron discipline, I gave in continuously, with painful pleasure, to waves of unhappiness. Everything seemed to be against me. At school I couldn't get the grades I used to, even though I had begun to study again. The days passed without even a moment during which I felt alive. The road to school, the one to Lila's house, the one to the ponds were colorless backdrops. Tense, discouraged, I ended up, almost without realizing it, blaming Antonio for a good part of my troubles.

He, too, was very upset. He wanted to see me continuously, sometimes he left work and I found him waiting for me, self-conscious, on the sidewalk across from the school entrance. He was worried about the crazy behavior of his mother, Melina, and was frightened by the possibility that he wouldn't be exempted from military service. He had submitted, in time, application after application to the recruiting office documenting the death of his father, the condition of his mother's health, his role as the sole support of his family, and it seemed that the Army, overwhelmed by the papers, had decided to forget about him. But now he had learned that Enzo Scanno was to leave in the autumn and he was afraid that his turn would come, too. "I can't leave my mother and Ada and the other children with no money and no protection," he said in despair.

One day he appeared at school out of breath: he had learned that the carabinieri had come to get information about him.

"Ask Lina," he said anxiously, "ask her if Stefano had an exemption because his mother is widowed or for some other reason."

I soothed him, tried to distract him. I organized an evening

THE STORY OF A NEW NAME · 63

for him at the pizzeria with Pasquale and Enzo and their girl-friends, Ada and Carmela. I hoped that, seeing his friends, he would calm down, but it didn't help. Enzo, as usual, showed not the least emotion about his departure, he was sorry only because, while he was in the Army, his father would have to go back to walking the streets with the cart, and his health wasn't good. As for Pasquale, he revealed somewhat morosely that he had been rejected for military service because of an old tuber-cular infection. But he said that he regretted it, one ought to be a soldier, though not to serve the country. People like us, he muttered, have a duty to learn to use weapons, because soon the time will come when those who should pay will pay. From there we went on to discuss politics, or, to be exact, Pasquale did, and in a very intolerant way. He said that the Fascists wanted to return to power with the help of the Christian Democrats. He said that the police and the Army were on their side. He said that we had to be prepared, and he spoke in par-ticular to Enzo, who nodded assent and, though he was gener-ally silent, said, with a little laugh, don't worry, when I get back I'll show you how to shoot.

Ada and Carmela appeared very impressed by that conver-sation, and pleased to be the girlfriends of such dangerous men. I would have liked to speak, but I knew little or nothing of alliances between Fascists, Christian Democrats, and police, in my head I had not even a thought. Every so often I looked at Antonio, hoping that he would get excited about the subject, but he didn't, he just kept trying to go back to what was tor-turing him. He asked over and over what it was like in the Army, and Pasquale, even though he hadn't been there, answered: a real shithole, if you don't knuckle under they break you. Enzo was silent, as if the question didn't concern him. Antonio, on the other hand, stopped eating, and, playing with the pizza on his plate, kept saying things like: They don't know who they're dealing with, let them just try, I'll break them.

When we were alone he said to me, all of a sudden, in a depressed tone of voice, "I know if I leave you won't wait for me, you'll go with someone else."

At that point I understood. The problem wasn't Melina, wasn't Ada, wasn't his other brothers and sisters, who would be left without a means of support, and it wasn't even the harassments of Army life. The problem was me. He didn't want to leave me, even for a minute, and it seemed that no matter what I said or did to reassure him he wouldn't believe me. I decided to take the offensive. I told him to follow the example of Enzo: He's confident, I whispered, if he has to go he goes, he doesn't whine, even if he's just gotten engaged to Carmela. Whereas you're complaining for no reason, yes, for no reason, Antò, especially since you won't go, because if Stefano Carracci got an exemption as the son of a widowed mother, certainly you will, too.

That slightly aggressive, slightly affectionate tone eased him. But before saying goodbye he repeated, in embarrassment, "Ask your friend."

"She's your friend, too."

"Yes, but you ask."

The next day I talked to Lila about it, but she didn't know anything about her husband's military service; reluctantly she promised that she would find out.

She didn't do it immediately, as I'd hoped. There were constant tensions with Stefano and with Stefano's family. Maria had told her son that his wife spent too much money. Pinuccia made trouble about the new grocery, she said that she wasn't going to be involved, if anyone it should be her sister-in-law. Stefano silenced his mother and sister, but in the end he reproached his wife for her excessive spending, and tried to find out whether she might if necessary be willing to work in the new store.

Lila in that period became, even in my eyes, particularly evasive. She said that she would spend less, she readily agreed to work in the grocery, but meanwhile she spent more than before and if previously she had stopped in at the new shop out of curiosity or duty she no longer did even that. Now that the bruises on her face were gone, she had an urgent desire to go out, especially in the morning, when I was at school.

She would go for a walk with Pinuccia, and they vied to see who was better dressed, who could buy more useless things. Usually Pina won, mainly because, with a lot of coyly childish looks, she managed to get money from Rino, who felt obliged to prove that he was more generous than his brother-in-law.

"I work all day," said the fiancé to the fiancée. "Have fun for me, too."

And proudly casual, in front of the workers and his father, he pulled out of his pants pocket a crumpled fistful of money, offered it to Pina, and immediately afterward made a teasing gesture of giving some to his sister, too.

His behavior irritated Lila, like a gust of wind that causes a door to slam and knocks objects off a shelf. But she also saw signs that the shoe factory was finally taking off, and all in all she was pleased that Cerullo shoes were now displayed in many shops in the city, the spring models were selling well, the reorders were increasing. As a result Stefano had taken over the basement under the factory and had transformed it into a warehouse and workshop, while Fernando and Rino had had to hire another assistant in a hurry and sometimes even worked at night.

Naturally there were disputes. The shoe store that the Solaras had undertaken to open in Piazza dei Martiri had to be furnished at Stefano's expense, and he, alarmed by the fact that no written contract had ever been drawn up, squabbled a lot with Marcello and Michele. But now it seemed that they were arriving at a private agreement that would set out in black and white the figure (slightly inflated) that Carracci intended to invest in the furnishings. And Rino was very satisfied with the result: while his brother-in-law put down the money, he acted like the boss, as if he had done it himself.

"If things continue like this, next year we'll get married," he promised his fiancée, and one morning Pina decided to go to the same dressmaker who had made Lila's dress, just to look.

The dressmaker welcomed them cordially, then, since she was crazy about Lila, asked her to describe the wedding in detail, and insisted on having a large photograph of her in the wedding dress. Lila had one printed for her and she and Pina went to give it to her.

As they were walking on the Rettifilo, Lila asked her sister-in-law how it happened that Stefano hadn't done his military service: if the carabinieri had come to verify his status as the son of a widowed mother, if the exemption had been communicated by mail from the recruiting office or if he had had to find out in person.

Pinuccia looked at her ironically.

"Son of a widowed mother?"

"Yes, Antonio says that if you're in that situation they don't make you go."

"I know that the only certain way not to go is to pay."

"Pay whom?"

"The people in the recruiting office."

"Stefano paid?"

"Yes, but you mustn't tell anyone."

"And how much did he pay?"

"I don't know. The Solaras took care of everything."

Lila froze.

"Meaning?"

"You know, don't you, that neither Marcello nor Michele served in the Army. They got out of it owing to thoracic insufficiency."

"Them? How is that possible?"

"Contacts."

"And Stefano?"

"He went to the same contacts as Marcello and Michele. You pay and the contacts do you a favor."

That afternoon my friend reported everything to me, but it was as if she didn't grasp how bad the information was for Antonio. She was electrified—yes, electrified—by the discovery that the alliance between her husband and the Solaras did not originate in the obligations imposed by business but were of long standing, preceding even their engagement.

"He deceived me from the start," she repeated, with a kind of satisfaction, as if the story of military service were the definitive proof of Stefano's true nature and now she felt somehow liberated. It took time before I was able to ask her, "Do you think that if the recruiting office doesn't give Antonio an exemption the Solaras would do a favor for him, too?"

She gave me her mean look, as if I had said something hostile, and cut me off: "Antonio would never go to the Solaras."

13.

I did not report a single word of that conversation to my boyfriend. I avoided meeting him, I told him I had too much homework and a lot of class oral exams coming up.

It wasn't an excuse, school was really hell. The local authority harassed the principal, the principal harassed the teachers, the teachers harassed the students, the students tormented each other. A large number of us couldn't stand the load of homework, but we were glad that there was class on alternate days. There was a minority, however, who were angry about the decrepit state of the school building and the loss of class time, and who wanted an immediate return to the normal schedule. At the head of this faction was Nino Sarratore, and this was to further complicate my life.

I saw him whispering in the hall with Professor Galiani; I passed by hoping that the professor would call me over. She didn't. So then I hoped that he would speak to me, but he didn't, either. I felt disgraced. I'm not able to get the grades I used to, I thought, and so in no time I've lost the little respect I had. On the other hand—I thought bitterly—what do I expect? If Nino or Professor Galiani asked my opinion on this business of the unused classrooms and too much homework, what would I say? I didn't have opinions, in fact, and I realized it when Nino appeared one morning with a typewritten sheet of paper and asked abruptly, "Will you read it?"

My heart was beating so hard that I said only, "Now?"

"No, give it back to me after school."

I was overwhelmed by my emotions. I ran to the bathroom and read in great agitation. The page was full of figures and discussed things I knew nothing of: plan for the city, school construction, the Italian constitution, certain fundamental articles. I understood only what I already knew, which was that Nino was demanding an immediate return to the normal schedule of classes.

In class I showed the paper to Alfonso.

"Forget it," he advised me, without even reading it. "We're at the end of the year, we've got final examinations, that would get you in trouble."

But it was as if I had gone mad, my temples were pounding, my throat was tight. No one else, in the school, exposed himself the way Nino did, without fear of the teachers or the principal. Not only was he the best in every subject but he knew things that were not taught, that no student, even a good one, knew. And he had character. And he was handsome. I counted the hours, the minutes, the seconds. I was in a hurry to give him back his page, to praise it, to tell him that I agreed with everything, that I wanted to help him.

I didn't see him on the stairs, in the crush of students, and in the street I couldn't find him. He was among the last to come out, and his expression was more morose than usual. I went to meet him, cheerfully waving the paper, and I poured out a profusion of words, all exaggerated. He listened to me frowning, then he took the piece of paper, angrily crumpled it up, and threw it away.

"Galiani said it's no good," he mumbled.

I was confused.

"What's no good about it?"

He scowled unhappily and made a gesture that meant forget about it, it's not worth talking about.

"Anyway, thank you," he said in a somewhat forced manner, and suddenly he leaned over and kissed me on the cheek.

Since the kiss on Ischia we had had no contact, not even a handshake, and that way of parting, utterly unusual at the time, paralyzed me. He didn't ask me to walk a little distance with him, he didn't say goodbye: everything ended there. Without energy, without voice, I watched him walk away.

At that point two terrible things happened, one after the other. First, a girl came out of a narrow street, a girl certainly younger than me, at most fifteen, whose pure beauty was striking: she had a nice figure, and smooth black hair that hung down her back; every gesture or movement had a gracefulness, every item of her spring outfit had a deliberate restraint. She met Nino, he put an arm around her shoulders, she lifted her face, offering him her mouth, and they kissed: a kiss very different from the one he had given me. Right afterward I realized that Antonio was at the corner. He was supposed to be at work and instead he had come to get me. Who knew how long he had been there.

14.

It was hard to convince him that what he had seen with his

own eyes was not what he had for a long time imagined but only a friendly gesture, with no other purpose. "He's already got a girlfriend," I said, "you saw it yourself." But he must have caught a trace of suffering in those words, and he threatened me, his lower lip and his hands began to tremble. Then I muttered that I was tired of this, I wanted to leave him. He gave in, and we made up. But from that moment on he trusted me even less, and the anxiety of departure for military service was welded conclusively to the fear of leaving me to Nino. More and more often he abandoned his job to be in time, he said, to meet me. In reality his aim was to catch me in the act and prove, to himself above all, that I really was unfaithful. What he would do then not even he knew.

One afternoon his sister Ada saw me passing the grocery, where she now worked, to her great satisfaction and to Stefano's. She ran out to see me. She wore a greasy white smock that covered her to below the knees, but she was still very pretty and it was clear from her lipstick, her made-up eyes, the pins in her hair that, under the smock, she was dressed as if for a party. She said she wanted to talk to me, and we agreed to meet in the courtyard before dinner. She arrived breathless from the grocery, along with Pasquale, who had picked her up.

They spoke to me together, an embarrassed phrase from one, an embarrassed phrase from the other. I understood that they were worried: Antonio lost his temper for no reason, he no longer had patience with Melina, he was absent without warning from work. And even Gallese, the owner of the shop, was upset, because he had known him since he was a boy and had never seen him like this.

"He's afraid of military service," I said.

"So if they call him, of course he has to go," Pasquale said, "otherwise he becomes a deserter."

"When you're around, it all goes away," said Ada.

"I don't have much time," I said.

"People are more important than school," said Pasquale.

"Spend less time with Lina, and you'll see, you'll find the time," said Ada.

"I do what I can," I said, offended.

"His nerves are fragile," Pasquale said.

Ada concluded abruptly, "I've been taking care of a crazy person since I was a child—two would really be too much, Lenù."

I was annoyed, and scared. Filled with a sense of guilt, I went back to seeing Antonio often, even though I didn't want to, even though I had to study. It wasn't enough. One night at the ponds he began to cry, he showed me a card. He hadn't received an exemption, he was to leave with Enzo, in the fall. And at a certain point he did something extremely upsetting. He fell on the ground and in a frenzy began sticking handfuls of dirt in his mouth. I had to hold him tight, say that I loved him, wipe the dirt out of his mouth with my fingers.

What kind of mess am I getting myself into, I thought later, in bed, unable to sleep, and I discovered that suddenly the wish to leave school—to accept myself for what I was, to marry him, to live at his mother's house with his siblings, pumping gas—had faded. I decided that I had to do something to help him and, when he recovered, get myself out of that relationship.

The next day I went to Lila's, really frightened. I found her overly cheerful; during that period we were both unsettled. I told her about Antonio, and the card, and I told her that I had made a decision: in secret from him, because he would never give me permission, I intended to go to Marcello or even Michele to ask if they could get him out of his predicament.

I was exaggerating my determination. In reality I was confused: on the one hand it seemed to me that I was obliged to try, since I was the cause of Antonio's suffering; on the other, I was consulting Lila precisely because I took it for granted that she would tell me not to. But I was so absorbed by my own emotional chaos that I hadn't taken into account hers.

Her reaction was equivocal. First she teased me, she said I was a liar, she said I must really love my boyfriend if I was willing to go in person and humble myself with the Solaras, even though I knew that, given all that had happened, they would not lift a finger for him. Immediately afterward, however, she began nervously going in circles, she laughed, became serious, laughed again. Finally she said: all right, go, let's see what happens. And then she added:

"After all, Lenù, where's the difference between my brother and Michele Solara or, let's say, between Stefano and Marcello?"

"What do you mean?"

"I mean that maybe I should have married Marcello."

"I don't understand you."

"At least Marcello isn't dependent on anyone, he does as he likes."

"Are you serious?"

She quickly denied that she was, laughing, but she didn't convince me. She can't possibly be reconsidering Marcello, I thought: all that laughter isn't real, it's just a sign of ugly thoughts, of suffering because things aren't going well with her husband.

I had proof of that immediately. She became thoughtful, she narrowed her eyes to cracks, she said, "I'm going with you."

"Where."

"To the Solaras."

"To do what?"

"To see if they can help Antonio."

"No."

"Why?"

"You'll make Stefano angry."

"Who gives a damn. If he goes to them, I can, too, I'm his wife."

15.

I couldn't stop her. One Sunday—on Sundays Stefano slept until noon—we were going out for a walk and she pressed me to go to the Bar Solara. When she appeared on the new street, still white with lime, I was astonished. She was extravagantly dressed and made up: she was neither the shabby Lila of long ago nor the Jackie Kennedy of the glossy magazines but, based on the films we liked, maybe Jennifer Jones in *Duel in the Sun*, maybe Ava Gardner in *The Sun Also Rises*.

Walking next to her I felt embarrassment and also a sense of danger. It seemed to me that she was risking not only gossip but ridicule, and that both reflected on me, a sort of colorless but loyal puppy who served as her escort. Everything about her—the hair, the earrings, the close-fitting blouse, the tight skirt, the way she walked—was unsuitable for the gray streets of the neighborhood. Male gazes, at the sight of her, seemed to start, as if offended. The women, especially the old ones, didn't limit themselves to bewildered expressions: some stopped on the edge of the sidewalk and stood watching her, with a laugh that was both amused and uneasy, as when Melina did odd things on the street.

And yet when we entered the Bar Solara, which was crowded with men buying the Sunday pastries, there was only a respectful ogling, some polite nods of greeting, the truly admiring gaze of Gigliola Spagnuolo behind the counter, and a greeting from Michele, at the cash register—an exaggerated hello that was like an exclamation of joy. The verbal exchanges that followed were all in dialect, as if tension prevented any engagement with the laborious filters of Italian pronunciation, vocabulary, syntax.

"What would you like?"

"A dozen pastries."

Michele shouted at Gigliola, this time with a slight hint of sarcasm:

"Twelve pastries for Signora Carracci."

At that name, the curtain that opened onto the bakery was pushed aside and Marcello looked out. At the sight of Lila right there, in his bar and pastry shop, he grew pale and retreated. But a few seconds later he came out again and greeted her. He mumbled, to my friend, "It's a shock to hear you called Signora Carracci."

"To me, too," Lila said, and her amused half-smile, her total absence of hostility, surprised not only me but the two brothers as well.

Michele examined her carefully, his head inclined to one side, as if he were looking at a painting.

"We saw you," he said, and called to Gigliola. "Right, Gigliò, didn't we see her yesterday afternoon?"

Gigliola nodded yes, unenthusiastically. And Marcello agreed—*saw, yes saw*—but without Michele's sarcasm, rather as if he had been hypnotized at a magic show.

"Yesterday afternoon?" Lila asked.

"Yesterday afternoon," Michele confirmed, "on the Rettifilo."

Marcello came to the point, irritated by his brother's tone of voice. "You were on display in the dressmaker's window—there's a photograph of you in your wedding dress."

They talked a little about the photograph, Marcello with devotion, Michele with irony, both asserting in different ways how perfectly it captured Lila's beauty on her wedding day. She seemed annoyed, but playfully: the dressmaker hadn't told her she would put the picture in the window, otherwise she would never have given it to her.

"I want *my* picture in the window," Gigliola cried from behind the counter, imitating the petulant voice of a child.

"If someone marries you," said Michele.

"You're marrying me," she replied darkly, and went on like that until Lila said seriously:

"Lenuccia wants to get married, too."

The attention of the Solara brothers shifted reluctantly to me; until then I had felt invisible, and hadn't said a word.

"No." I blushed.

"Why not, I'd marry you, even if you are four-eyed," said Michele, catching another black look from Gigliola.

"Too late, she's already engaged," said Lila. And slowly she managed to lead the two brothers around to Antonio, evoking his family situation, including a vivid picture of how much worse it would be if he had to go into the Army. It wasn't just her skill with words that struck me, that I knew. What struck me was a new tone, a shrewd dose of impudence and assurance. There she was, her mouth flaming with lipstick. She made Marcello believe that she had put a seal on the past, made Michele believe that his sly arrogance amused her. And, to my great amazement, toward both she behaved like a woman who knows what men are, who has nothing more to learn on the subject and in fact would have much to teach: and she wasn't playing a part, the way we had as girls, imitating novels in which fallen ladies appeared; rather, it was clear that her knowledge was true, and this did not embarrass her. Then abruptly she became aloof, she sent out signals of refusal, I know you want me but I don't want you. Thus she retreated, throwing them off balance, so that Marcello became self-conscious and Michele darkened, irresolute, with a hard gaze that meant: Watch it, because, Signora Carracci or not, I'm ready to slap you in the face, you whore. At that point she changed her tone again, again drew them toward her, appeared to be amused and amused them. The result? Michele didn't commit himself, but Marcello said: "Antonio doesn't deserve it, but Lenuccia's a good girl, so to make her happy I can ask a friend and find out if something can be done."

I felt satisfied, I thanked him.

Lila chose the pastries, was friendly toward Gigliola and also toward her father, the pastry maker, who poked his head out of the bakery to say: Hello to Stefano. When she tried to pay, Marcello made a clear gesture of refusal, and his brother, if less decisively, seconded him. We were about to leave when Michele said to her seriously, in the slow tone he assumed when he wanted something and ruled out any disagreement:

"You look great in that photograph."

"Thank you."

"The shoes are very conspicuous."

"I don't remember."

"I remember and I want to ask you something."

"You want a photo, too, you want to put it up here in the bar?"

Michele shook his head with a cold little laugh.

"No. But you know that we're getting the shop ready in Piazza dei Martiri."

"I don't know anything about your affairs."

"Well, you should find out, because our affairs are important and we all know that you're not stupid. I think that if that photograph is useful to the dressmaker as an advertisement for a wedding dress, we can make much better use of it as an advertisement for Cerullo shoes."

Lila burst out laughing, she said, "You want to put that photograph in the window in Piazza dei Martiri?"

"No, I want it enlarged, huge, in the shop."

She thought about it for a moment, then made a gesture of indifference.

"Don't ask me, ask Stefano, he's the one who decides."

I saw the brothers exchange a puzzled glance, and I understood that they had already discussed the idea and had assumed that Lila would never agree, so they couldn't believe that she hadn't been indignant, that she hadn't immediately said no, but had surrendered without argument to the authority of her husband. They didn't recognize her, and, right then, even I didn't know who she was.

Marcello went to the door with us. Outside, he became solemn, and said, "This is the first time in a long while that we've spoken, Lina, and it's disturbing. You and I didn't go with each other—all right, that's the way it is. But I don't want anything between us to remain unclear. And especially I don't want blame that I don't deserve. I know that your husband goes around saying that as an insult I claimed those shoes. But I swear to you in front of Lenuccia: he and your brother gave me the shoes to demonstrate that there was no more bad feeling. I had nothing to do with it."

Lila listened without interrupting, a sympathetic expression on her face. Then, as soon as he had finished, she became herself again. She said with contempt, "You're like children, accusing each other."

"You don't believe me?"

"No, Marcè, I believe you. But what you say, what they say, I don't give a damn about it anymore."

16.

I dragged Lila into our old courtyard, I couldn't wait to tell Antonio what I had done for him. I confided to her, trembling with excitement: as soon as he calms down a little, I'll leave him, but she had no comment, she seemed distracted.

I called. Antonio looked out, came down, serious. He said hello to Lila, apparently without noticing how she was dressed, how she was made up, in fact trying to look at her as little as possible, maybe because he was afraid that I would read in his face some male agitation. I told him that I couldn't stay, I had only time to give him some good news. He listened, but as I was speaking I realized that he was pulling back as if before the point of a knife. He promised he'll help you, I said anyway, emphatically, enthusiastically, and asked Lila to confirm it.

"Marcello said so, right?"

Lila confined herself to assenting. But Antonio had turned very pale, he lowered his eyes. He muttered, in a strangled voice:

"I never asked you to talk to the Solaras."

Lila said right away, lying, "It was my idea."

Antonio answered without looking at her. "Thank you, it wasn't necessary."

He said goodbye to her—said goodbye to her, not to me—turned his back, and vanished into the doorway.

I felt sick to my stomach. Where was my mistake, why had he gotten angry like that? On the street I exploded, saying to Lila that Antonio was worse than his mother, Melina, the same unstable blood, I couldn't take it anymore. She let me speak and meanwhile wanted me go to her house with her. When we got there, she asked me to come in.

"Stefano's there," I objected, but that wasn't the reason. I was upset by Antonio's reaction and wanted to be alone, to figure out where I had made the mistake.

"Five minutes and you can go."

I went up. Stefano was in his pajamas, disheveled, unshaved. He greeted me politely, glanced at his wife, at the package of pastries.

"You were at the Bar Solara?"

"Yes."

"Dressed like that?"

"I don't look nice?"

Stefano shook his head ill-humoredly, opened the package.

"Would you like a pastry, Lenù?"

"No, thank you, I have to go and eat."

He bit into a pastry, turned to his wife. "Who did you see at the bar?"

"Your friends," said Lila. "They paid me a lot of compliments. Isn't that true, Lenù?"

She recounted every word the Solaras had said to her, except the matter of Antonio, that is to say the real reason we had gone to the bar, the reason that, I thought, she had decided to go with me. Then she concluded, in a tone of deliberate satisfaction, "Michele wants to put an enlargement of the photograph in the store in Piazza dei Martiri."

"And you told him it was all right?"

"I told him they had to speak to you."

Stefano finished the pastry in a single bite, then licked his fingers. He said, as if this were what had upset him most, "See what you force me to do? Tomorrow, because of you, I have to go and waste time with the dressmaker on the Rettifilo." He sighed, he turned to me: "Lenù, you who are a respectable girl, try to explain to your friend that I have to work in this neighborhood, that she shouldn't make me look like a jerk. Have a good Sunday, and say hello to Papa and Mamma for me."

He went into the bathroom.

Lila behind his back made a teasing grimace, then went with me to the door.

"I'll stay if you want," I said.

"He's a son of a bitch, don't worry."

She repeated, in a heavy male voice, words like *try to explain to your friend, she shouldn't make me look like a jerk*, and the caricature made her eyes light up.

"If he beats you?"

"What can beatings do to me? A little time goes by and I'm better than before."

On the landing she said again, again in a masculine voice:

Lenù, I have to work in this neighborhood, and then I felt obliged to do Antonio, I whispered, *Thank you, but there was no need*, and suddenly it was as if we saw ourselves from the outside, both of us in trouble with our men, standing there on the threshold, actors in a recital of women, and we started laughing. I said: The minute we move we've done something wrong, who can understand men, ah, how much trouble they are. I hugged her warmly, and left. But I hadn't even reached the bottom of the stairs when I heard Stefano shouting odious curses. Now he had the voice of an ogre, like his father's.

17.

Already on the way home I began to worry both about her and about me. If Stefano killed her? If Antonio killed me? I was racked by anxiety, I walked quickly, in the dusty heat, along Sunday streets that were beginning to empty as lunchtime approached. How difficult it was to find one's way, how difficult it was not to violate any of the incredibly detailed male regulations. Lila, perhaps based on secret calculations of her own, perhaps only out of spite, had humiliated her husband by going to flirt in front of everyone—she, Signora Carracci—with her former wooer Marcello Solara. I, without intending to, in fact convinced that I was doing good, had gone to argue the case of Antonio with those who years before had insulted his sister, who had beaten him up, whom he in turn had beaten up. When I entered the courtyard, I heard someone calling me, I started. It was him, he was at the window waiting for me to return.

He came down and I was afraid. I thought: he must have a knife. Instead, the whole time he spoke with his hands sunk in his pockets as if to keep them prisoner, calmly, his gaze distant. He said that I had humiliated him in front of the people he despised most in the world. He said I had made him look like someone who sends his woman to ask a favor. He said that he would not go down on his knees to anyone and that he would be a soldier not once but a hundred times, that in fact he would die in the Army rather than go and kiss the hand of Marcello Solara. He said that if Pasquale and Enzo should find out, they would spit in his face. He said that he was leaving me, because he had had the proof, finally, that I cared nothing about him and his feelings. He said that I could say and do with the son of Sarratore what I liked, he never wanted to see me again.

I couldn't reply. Suddenly he took his hands out of his pockets, pulled me inside the doorway and kissed me, pressing his lips hard against mine, searching my mouth desperately with his tongue. Then he pulled away, turned his back, and left.

I went up the stairs in confusion. I thought that I was more fortunate than Lila, Antonio wasn't like Stefano. He would never hurt me, the only person he could hurt was himself.

18.

I didn't see Lila the next day, but, surprisingly, I was compelled to see her husband.

That morning I had gone to school depressed: it was hot, I hadn't studied, I had scarcely slept. The school day had been a disaster. I had looked for Nino outside, I would have liked to talk just a little, but I didn't see him, maybe he was wandering through the city with his girlfriend, maybe he was in one of the movie theaters that were open in the morning, kissing her in the dark, maybe he was in the woods at Capodimonte having her do to him the things I had done to Antonio for months. In the first class I had been interrogated in chemistry and had given muddled or inadequate answers; who knows what grade I had received, and there wasn't time to make it up, I was in danger of having to retake the exam in September. I had met Professor Galiani in the hall and she had given me a gentle speech whose meaning was: What is happening to you, Greco, why aren't you studying anymore? And I had been unable to say anything but: Professor, I am studying, I'm studying all the time, I swear; she listened to me for a bit and then walked away and went into the teachers' lounge. I had had a long cry in the bathroom, a cry of self-pity for how wretched my life was. I had lost everything: success in school; Antonio, whom I had always wanted to leave, and who in the end had left me, and already I missed him; Lila, who since she had become Signora Carracci was more removed every day. Worn out by a headache, I had walked home thinking of her, of how she had used me—yes, used—to provoke the Solaras, to get revenge on her husband, to show him to me in his misery as a wounded male, and the whole way I wondered: Is it possible that a person can change like that, that now there's nothing to distinguish her from someone like Gigliola?

But at home there was a surprise. My mother didn't attack me the way she usually did because I was late and she suspected I had been seeing Antonio, or because I had neglected one of the thousands of household tasks. She said to me instead, with a sort of gentle annoyance, "Stefano asked me if you could go with him this afternoon to the dressmaker's on the Rettifilo."

Befuddled by tiredness and discouragement, I thought I hadn't understood. Stefano? Stefano Carracci? He wanted me to go with him to the Rettifilo?

"Why doesn't he go with his wife?" my father joked from the other room. Formally he was taking a sick day but in reality he had to keep an eye on some of his indecipherable deals. "How do those two pass the time? Do they play cards?"

My mother made a gesture of annoyance. She said maybe Lila was busy, she said we ought to be nice to the Carraccis, she said some people were never satisfied with anything. In reality my father was more than satisfied: to have good relations with the grocer meant that one could buy food on credit and put off paying indefinitely. But he liked to be witty. Lately, whenever the occasion arose, he had found it amusing to make allusions to Stefano's presumed sexual laziness. At the table every so often he would ask: What's Carracci doing, he only likes television? And he laughed and it didn't take much to guess the meaning of his question: how is it that the two of them don't have any children, does Stefano function or not? My mother, who in those matters understood him immediately, answered seriously: It's early, leave them alone, what do you expect? But in fact she enjoyed as much as or more than he the idea that the grocer Carracci, in spite of the money he had, didn't function.

The table was already set; they were waiting for me. My father continued to joke, with a half-sly expression, saying to my mother: "Have I ever said to you, I'm sorry, tonight I'm tired, let's play cards?"

"No, because you are not a respectable person."

"And would you like me to become a respectable person?"

"A little, but don't exaggerate."

"So starting tonight I'll be a respectable person like Stefano."

"I said don't exaggerate."

How I hated those duets. They talked as if they were sure that my brothers and sister and I couldn't understand; or maybe they took it for granted that we caught every nuance, but they considered that it was the proper way to teach us how to be males and how to be females. Exhausted by my problems, I felt like screaming—throw away the plate, run out, never see my family again, the dampness in the corners of the ceiling, the flaking walls, the odor of food, any of it. Antonio:

how foolish I had been to lose him, I was already sorry, I wished he would forgive me. If they make me retake the exams in September, I said to myself, I won't show up, I'll fail, I'll marry him right away. Then I thought of Lila, how she had dressed, the tone she had taken with the Solaras, what she had in mind, how spiteful humiliation and suffering were making her. My mind wandered like that all afternoon, with disconnected thoughts. A bath in the tub of the new house, anxiety about that request of Stefano's, how to tell my friend, what her husband wanted from me. And chemistry. And Empedocles. And school. And quitting school. And finally a cold sadness. There was no escape. No, neither Lila nor I would ever become like the girl who had waited for Nino after school. We both lacked something intangible but fundamental, which was obvious in her even if you simply saw her from a distance, and which one possessed or did not, because to have that thing it was not enough to learn Latin or Greek or philosophy, nor was the money from groceries or shoes of any use.

Stefano called from the courtyard. I hurried down and immediately saw in his face an expression of despair. He said he wanted me to go with him to retrieve the photograph that the dressmaker had displayed in her window without permission. Do me this kindness, he muttered, in a sentimental tone of voice. Then without a word he opened the door of the convertible, and we drove off, assailed by the hot wind.

As soon as we were out of the neighborhood he started talking and he didn't stop until we got to the dressmaker's. He spoke in a mild dialect, without cursing or joking. He began by saying that I must do him a favor, but he didn't immediately explain what the favor was, he said only, stumbling over his words, that if I did it for him, it would be as if I were doing it for my friend. Then he went on to talk to me about Lila, how intelligent, how beautiful she was. But she is rebellious by nature, he added, and either you do things the way she says or she torments you. Lenù, you don't know what I'm suffering, or maybe you do know, but all you know is what she tells you. Now, listen to me, too. Lina has a fixed idea that all I think about is money, and maybe it's true, but I'm doing it for the family, for her brother, for her father, for all her relatives. Am I wrong? You are very educated, tell me if I'm wrong. What does she want from me—the poverty she comes from? Should only the Solaras make money? Do we want to leave the neighborhood in their hands? If you tell me I'm wrong, I won't argue with you, I will immediately admit that I'm wrong. But with her I have to argue whether I want to or not. She doesn't want me, she told me, she repeats it to me. Making her understand that I'm her husband is a battle, and ever since I got married life has been unbearable. To see her in the morning, in the evening, to sleep next to her and not be able to make her feel how much I love her, with the strength I'm capable of, is a terrible thing.

I looked at his broad hands gripping the steering wheel, his face. With tears in his eyes, he admitted that on their wedding night he had had to beat her, that he had been forced to do it, that every morning, every evening she drew slaps from his hands on purpose to humiliate him, forcing him to act in a way that he never, ever, ever would have wanted. Here he assumed an almost frightened tone: I had to beat her again, she shouldn't have gone to the Solaras' dressed like that. But she has a force inside that I can't subdue. It's an evil force that makes good manners—everything—useless. A poison. You see she's not pregnant? Months pass and nothing happens. Relatives, friends, customers ask, and you can see the mockery on their faces: any news? And I have to say, what news, pretending not to understand. Because if I understood I would have to answer. And what can I answer? There are things you know that can't be said. With that force she has, she murders the children inside, Lenù, and she does it on purpose to make people think

I don't know how to be a man, to show me up in front of every-one. What do you think? Am I exaggerating? You don't know what a favor you're doing to listen to me.

I didn't know what to say. I was stunned, I had never heard a man talk about himself like that. The whole time, even when he spoke of his own brutality, he used a dialect full of feeling, defenseless, like the language of certain songs. I still don't know why he behaved that way. Of course, afterward he revealed what he wanted. He wanted me to ally myself with him for the good of Lila. He said that she had to be helped to understand how necessary it was to behave like a wife and not like an enemy. He asked me to persuade her to help out in the second grocery and with the accounts. But for that purpose he didn't have to confess to me in that way. Probably he thought that Lila had kept me minutely informed and therefore he had to give me his version of the facts. Or maybe he hadn't counted on opening himself up so frankly to his wife's best friend, and had done so only on the wave of emotion. Or he hypothesized that, if he moved me, I would then move Lila by reporting everything to her. Certainly I listened to him with increasing sympathy. I was pleased by that free flow of intimate confi-dences. But above all, I have to admit, what pleased me was the importance he attached to me. When in his own words he articulated a suspicion that I myself had always had, that is, that Lila harbored a force that made her capable of anything, even of keeping her body from conceiving children, it seemed that he was attributing to me a beneficent power, one that could win over Lila's maleficent one, and this flattered me. We got out of the car, and arrived at the dressmaker's shop. I felt consoled by that acknowledgment. I went so far as to say pompously, in Italian, that I would do everything possible to help them to be happy.

But as soon as we were in front of the dressmaker's window I became nervous again. We both stopped to look at the framed photograph of Lila amid fabrics of many colors. She was seated, her legs crossed, her wedding dress pulled up a little to reveal her shoes, an ankle. She rested her chin on the palm of one hand, her gaze was solemn, intense, turned boldly toward the lens, and in her hair shone a crown of orange blossoms. The photographer had been fortunate. I felt that he had caught the force Stefano had talked about; it was a force—I seemed to grasp—against which not even Lila could prevail. I turned as if to say to him, in admiration and at the same time dismay, here's what we were talking about, but he pushed open the door and let me go in first.

The tones he had used with me disappeared, and he was harsh with the dressmaker. He said that he was Lina's husband, he used that precise construction. He explained that he, too, was in business, but that it would never occur to him to get publicity in that way. He went so far as to say: You are a good-looking woman, what would your husband say if I took a photograph of you and stuck it in amid the provolone and the salami? He asked for the photograph back.

The dressmaker was bewildered; she tried to defend herself, and finally she gave in. But she appeared very unhappy, and to demonstrate the effectiveness of her initiative and the basis of her regret, she told three or four anecdotes that later, over the years, became a small legend in the neighborhood. Among those who had stopped in to ask for information about the young woman in the wedding dress during the period in which the photograph was in the window were the famous singer Renato Carosone, an Egyptian prince, Vittorio De Sica, and a journalist from the paper *Roma*, who wanted to talk to Lila and send a photographer to do a story on bathing suits like the ones worn at beauty contests. The dressmaker swore that she had refused to give Lila's address to anyone, even though, especially in the case of Carosone and of De Sica, the refusal had seemed to her very rude, given the status of those persons.

I noticed that the more the dressmaker talked the more Stefano softened again. He became sociable, he wanted the woman to tell him in more detail about those episodes. When we left, taking with us the photograph, his mood had changed, and the monologue of the return did not have the anguished tone of the earlier one. Stefano was cheerful, he began to speak of Lila with the pride of someone possessing a rare object whose ownership confers great prestige. Of course, he asked again for my help. And before leaving me at my house he made me swear over and over that I would try to make Lila understand what was the right path and what was wrong. Yet Lila, in his words, was no longer a person who couldn't be controlled but a sort of precious fluid stored in a container that belonged to him. In the following days Stefano told everyone, even in the grocery, about Carosone and De Sica, so that the story spread and Lila's mother, Nunzia, as long as she lived, went around repeating to everyone that her daughter would have had the opportunity of becoming a singer and actress, appearing in the film *Marriage Italian Style*, going on television, even becoming an Egyptian princess, if the dressmaker of the Rettifilo had not been so reticent and if fate had not let her marry, at the age of sixteen, Stefano Carracci.

19.

The chemistry teacher was generous with me (or maybe it was Professor Galiani who went to the trouble to get her to be generous), and gave me a pass. I was promoted with average grades in literary subjects, low passing grades in scientific ones, a narrow pass in religion and, for the first time, a less than perfect grade in behavior, a sign that the priest and a great many of the teachers had never really forgiven me. I was sorry about it; I felt that my old dispute with the religion teacher on the role of the Holy Spirit had been presumptuous, and I regretted not having listened to Alfonso, who at the time had tried to restrain me. Naturally I did not get a scholarship, and my mother was enraged, saying that it was all because of the time I had wasted with Antonio. Her words infuriated me. I said I didn't want to go to school anymore. She raised her hand to slap me, feared for my glasses, and hurried to get the carpet beater. Terrible days, in other words, and they got worse. The only thing that seemed positive was that, the morning I went to see the grades, the janitor came up and handed me a package left by Professor Galiani. It was books, but not novels: books full of arguments, a subtle sign of trust that still was not enough to bring me relief.

I had too many worries and, whatever I did, the feeling of always being in the wrong. I looked for my old boyfriend at home and at his job, but he always managed to avoid me. I stuck my head in the grocery to ask Ada for help. She treated me coldly, said that her brother didn't want to see me anymore, and from then on, if we met, she looked the other way. Now that there was no school, waking up in the morning became traumatic, a kind of painful blow to the head. At first I tried to read Professor Galiani's books, but I was bored, I could scarcely understand them. I started to borrow novels from the circulating library, and read one after the other. But in the long run they didn't help. They presented intense lives, profound conversations, a phantom reality more appealing than my real life. So, in order to feel as if I were not real, I sometimes went all the way to school in the hope of seeing Nino, who was taking the graduation exams. The day of the written Greek test I waited for hours, patiently. But just as the first candidates began to emerge, with Rocci under their arms, the pretty, pure girl I had seen raising her lips to him appeared. She settled herself to wait not far from me, and in a second I was imagining the two of us—models displayed in a catalogue—as we would appear to the eyes of Sarratore's son the moment he came out the door. I felt ugly, shabby, and I left.

I went to Lila's house in search of comfort. But I knew I had made a mistake with her, too. I had done something stupid: I hadn't told her about going with Stefano to get the photograph. Why had I been silent? Was I pleased with the role of peacemaker that her husband had proposed and did I think I could exercise it better by being silent about the visit to the Rettifilo? Had I been afraid of betraying Stefano's confidence and as a result, without realizing it, betrayed her? I didn't know. Certainly it hadn't been a real decision: rather, an uncertainty that first became a feigned carelessness, then the conviction that not having said right away what had happened made remedying the situation complicated and perhaps vain. How easy it was to do wrong. I sought excuses that might seem convincing to her, but I wasn't able to make them even to myself. I sensed that the foundations of my behavior were flawed, I was silent.

On the other hand, she had never indicated that she knew the encounter had taken place. She always welcomed me kindly, let me take a bath in her bathtub, use her makeup. But she made few comments on the plots of the novels that I recounted to her, preferring to give me frivolous information about the lives of actors and singers she read about in the magazines. And she no longer told me any of her thoughts or secret plans. If I saw a bruise, if I took that as a starting point to get her to examine the reasons for Stefano's ugly reaction, if I said that maybe he had been cruel because he would like her to help him, support him in his difficulties, she looked at me ironically, she shrugged, she was evasive. In a short time I understood that although she didn't want to break off her relationship with me, she had decided not to confide in me anymore. Did she in fact know, and no longer considered me a trustworthy friend? I even went so far as to make my visits less frequent, hoping that she would feel my absence, ask the reason for it, and we would explain things to each other. But she didn't seem to notice. Then I couldn't stand it and went back to visiting constantly, which seemed to make her neither happy nor unhappy.

That very hot day in July I was especially depressed when I arrived at her house and yet I said nothing about Nino, about Nino's girlfriend, because without intending to—it's the way these things go—I had ended up reducing the play of confidences almost to nothing myself. She was welcoming as usual. She made an orzata. I curled up on the couch in the dining room to drink the cold almond syrup, irritated by the clatter of the trains, by the sweat, by everything.

I observed her silently as she moved through the house; I was enraged by her capacity to travel through the most depressing labyrinths, holding on to the thread of her declaration of war without showing it. I thought of what her husband had told me, his words about the power that Lila held back like the spring of a dangerous device. I looked at her stomach and imagined that truly inside it, every day, every night, she was fighting a battle to destroy the life that Stefano wanted to insert there by force. How long will she resist, I wondered, but I didn't dare to ask explicit questions, I knew she would consider them disagreeable.

A little later Pinuccia arrived, apparently to visit her sister-in-law. But in fact ten minutes afterward Rino showed up, and he and Pina began kissing, practically right in front of us, in a way so excessive that Lila and I exchanged looks. When Pina said she wanted to see the view, he followed her, and they shut themselves in a room for a good half hour.

This happened often. Lila talked about it with a mixture of irritation and sarcasm, and I was envious of the couple's ease: no fear, no misery, when they reappeared they were more contented than before. Rino went to the kitchen to get something to eat;

returning, he talked about shoes with his sister, he said that things were constantly improving, and tried to get suggestions from her that he could later take credit for with the Solaras.

"You know that Marcello and Michele want to put your picture in the store in Piazza dei Martiri?" he asked suddenly, in an appealing tone.

"It doesn't seem appropriate," Pinuccia immediately interrupted.

"Why not?" Rino asked.

"What sort of question is that? If she wants, Lina can put the picture in the new grocery: she's going to run it, no? If I'm getting the shop in Piazza dei Martiri, will you let me decide what goes in it?"

She spoke as if she were defending Lila's rights against her brother's intrusiveness. In fact, we all knew that she was defending herself and her own future. She was tired of depending on Stefano, she wanted to quit the grocery store, and she liked the idea of being the proprietor of a store in the center of the city. So a small war had been going on for some time between Rino and Michele, whose object was the management of the shoe store, a war inflamed by pressure from their respective fiancées: Rino insisted that Pinuccia should do it, Michele that Gigliola should. But Pinuccia was the more aggressive and had no doubt that she would get the best of it; she knew that she could add the authority of her brother to that of her fiancé. And so at every opportunity she put on airs, like someone who has already made the leap, has left behind the old neighborhood and now decrees what is suitable and what is not for the sophisticated customers in the center.

I realized that Rino was afraid his sister would take the offensive, but Lila displayed complete indifference. Then he checked his watch to let us all know that he was very busy, and said in the tone of one who sees into the future, "In my opinion that photograph has great commercial possibilities." Then he kissed Pina, who immediately drew back, to signal disapproval, and left.

We girls remained. Pinuccia, hoping to use my authority to settle the question, asked me, sulkily, "Lenù, what do you think? Do you think the photo of Lina should stay in Piazza dei Martiri?"

I said, in Italian, "It's Stefano who should decide, and since he went to the dressmaker purposely to get it removed from her window, I consider it out of the question that he'll give permission."

Pinuccia glowed with satisfaction, and almost shouted, "My goodness, how smart you are, Lenù."

I waited for Lila to have her say. There was a long silence, then she spoke just to me: "How much do you want to bet you're wrong? Stefano will give his permission."

"No."

"Yes."

"What do you want to bet?"

"If you lose, you must never again pass with anything less than the best grades."

I looked at her in embarrassment. We hadn't spoken about my difficulties, I didn't even think she knew, but she was well informed and now was reproaching me. You weren't up to it, she was saying, your grades fell. She expected from me what she would have done in my place. She really wanted me fixed in the role of someone who spends her life with books, while she had money, nice clothes, a house, television, a car, took everything, granted everything.

"And if you lose?" I asked, with a shade of bitterness.

That look of hers returned instantly, shot through dark slits.

"I'll enroll in a private school, start studying again, and I swear I'll get my diploma along with you and do better than you."

Along with you and do better than you. Was that what she had in mind? I felt as if everything that was roiling inside me in that terrible time—Antonio, Nino, the unhappiness with the nothing that was my life—had been sucked up by a broad sigh.

"Are you serious?"

"When is a bet ever made as a joke?"

Pinuccia interrupted, aggressively.

"Lina, don't start acting crazy the way you always do: you have the new grocery store, Stefano can't manage it alone." Immediately, however, she controlled herself, adding with false sweetness, "Besides, I'd like to know when you and Stefano are going to make me an aunt."

She used that sweet-sounding formula but her tone seemed resentful to me, and I felt the reasons for that resentment irritatingly mixed with mine. Pinuccia meant: you're married, my brother gives you everything, now do what you're supposed to do. And in fact what's the sense of being Signora Carracci if you're going to shut all the doors, barricade yourself, obstruct, guard a poisoned fury in your stomach? Is it possible that you must always do harm, Lila? When will you stop? Will your energy diminish, will you be distracted, will you finally collapse, like a sleepy sentinel? When will you grow wide and sit at the cash register in the new neighborhood, with your stomach swelling, and make Pinuccia an aunt, and me, me, leave me to go my own way?

"Who knows," Lila answered, and her eyes grew large and deep again.

"Am I going to become a mamma first?" said her sister-in-law, smiling.

"If you're always pasted to Rino like that, it's possible."

They had a little skirmish; I didn't stay to listen.

20.

To placate my mother, I had to find a summer job. Naturally

I went to the stationer. She welcomed me the way you'd welcome a schoolteacher or the doctor, she called her daughters,
who were playing in the back of the shop, and they embraced
me, kissed me, wanted me to play with them. When I mentioned that I was looking for a job, she said that she was ready
to send her daughters to the Sea Garden right away, without
waiting for August, just so that they could spend their days
with a good, intelligent girl like me.

"Right away when?" I asked.

"Next week?"

"Wonderful."

"I'll give you a little more money than last year."

That, finally, seemed to be good news. I went home satisfied, and my mood didn't change even when my mother said
that as usual I was lucky, going swimming and sitting in the sun
wasn't a job.

Encouraged, the next day I went to see Maestra Oliviero. I
was upset about having to tell her that I hadn't particularly distinguished myself in school that year, but I needed to see her;
I had to tactfully remind her to get me the books for the next
school year. And then I thought it would please her to know
that Lila, now that she had made a good marriage and had so
much free time, might start studying again. Reading in her eyes
the reaction to that would help soothe the unease it had provoked in me.

I knocked and knocked, the teacher didn't come to the
door. I asked the neighbors, and around the neighborhood, and
returned an hour later, but still she didn't answer. And yet no
one had seen her go out, nor had I met her on the streets or in
the shops. Since she was a woman alone, old, and not well, I
went back to the neighbors. The woman who lived next door
decided to ask her son for help. The young man got into the
apartment by climbing from the balcony of his mother's apartment into one of the teacher's windows. He found her on the

kitchen floor, in her nightgown—she had fainted. The doctor was called and he thought that she should be admitted to the hospital immediately. They carried her downstairs. I saw her as she emerged from the entrance, in disarray, her face swollen, she who always came to school carefully groomed. Her eyes were frightened. I gave her a nod of greeting, and she lowered her gaze. They settled her in a car that took off blasting its horn.

The heat that year must have had a cruel effect on frailer bodies. In the afternoon Melina's children could be heard in the courtyard calling their mother in increasingly worried voices. When the cries didn't stop, I went to see what was happening and ran into Ada. She said anxiously, her eyes shiny with tears, that Melina couldn't be found. Right afterward Antonio arrived, out of breath and pale; he didn't even look at me but hurried off. Soon half the neighborhood was looking for Melina, even Stefano, who, still in his grocer's smock, got in the convertible, with Ada beside him, and drove slowly along the streets. I followed Antonio, and we ran here and there, without saying a word. We ended up near the ponds, and made our way through the tall grass, calling his mother. His cheeks were hollow, he had dark circles under his eyes. I took his hand, wanting to be of comfort, but he repulsed me, with an odious phrase, he said: Leave me alone, you're no woman. I felt a sharp pain in my chest, but just then we saw Melina. She was sitting in the water, cooling off. Her face and neck were sticking out from the greenish surface, her hair was soaked, her eyes red, her lips matted with leaves and mud. She was silent: she whose attacks of madness had for ten years taken the form of shouting or singing.

We brought her home, Antonio supporting her on one side, I on the other. People seemed relieved, called to her, she waved weakly. I saw Lila next to the gate; isolated in her house in the new neighborhood, she must have heard the news late, and hadn't taken part in the search. I knew that she felt a strong bond with Melina, but it struck me that, while everyone was showing signs of sympathy, and here was Ada running toward her, crying mamma, followed by Stefano—who had left the car in the middle of the *stradone* with the doors open, and had the happy expression of someone who has had ugly thoughts but now discovers that all is well—she stood apart with an expression that was hard to describe. She seemed to be moved by the pitiful sight of the widow: dirty, smiling faintly, her light clothes soaked and muddy, the outline of her wasted body visible under the material, the feeble wave of greeting to friends and acquaintances. But Lila also seemed to be wounded by it, and frightened, as if she felt inside the same disruption. I nodded to her, but she didn't respond. I gave up Melina to her daughter, then, and tried to join Lila, I also wanted to tell her about Maestra Oliviero, about the terrible thing Antonio had said to me. But I couldn't find her; she was gone.

21.

When I saw Lila again, I realized immediately that she felt bad and tended to make me feel bad, too. We spent a morning at her house in an atmosphere that seemed to be playful. In fact she insisted, with growing spitefulness, that I try on all her clothes, even though they didn't fit me. The game became torture. She was taller and thinner; everything of hers that I put on made me look ridiculous. But she wouldn't admit it, she said all you need is an adjustment here or there, and yet her mood darkened as she gazed at me, as if my appearance offended her.

At a certain point she exclaimed that's enough: she looked as if she had seen a ghost. Then she pulled herself together, and, assuming a frivolous tone, told me that a couple of nights earlier she had gone to have ice cream with Pasquale and Ada.

I was in my slip, helping her put the clothes back on the hangers.

"With Pasquale and Ada?"

"Yes."

"And Stefano, too?"

"Just me."

"Did they invite you?"

"No, I asked them."

And, as though she wanted to surprise me, she added that she hadn't confined herself to that brief visit to the old world of her girlhood: the next day she had gone to have a pizza with Enzo and Carmela.

"Also by yourself?"

"Yes."

"And what does Stefano say?"

She made a grimace of indifference. "Being married doesn't mean leading the life of an old lady. If he wants to come with me, fine; if he's too tired in the evening, I go out by myself."

"How was it?"

"I had fun."

I hoped she couldn't read the disappointment in my face. We saw each other frequently, she could have said: Tonight I'm going out with Ada, Pasquale, Enzo, Carmela, do you want to come? Instead she had said nothing, she had arranged and managed those outings by herself, in secret, as if they had been not *our* friends forever but only hers. And now she was telling me in detail, with an air of satisfaction, everything they had said: Ada was worried, Melina ate almost nothing and threw up whatever she did eat, Pasquale was anxious about his mother, Giuseppina, who couldn't sleep, felt a heaviness in her legs, had palpitations, and when she returned from visiting her husband in prison wept inconsolably. I listened. I noticed that, more than usual, she had an involved way of talking. She chose emotionally charged words, she described Melina Cappuccio and Giuseppina Peluso as if their bodies had seized hers, imposing on it the same contracted or inflated forms, the same bad feelings. As she spoke, she touched her face, her breast, her stomach, her hips as if they were no longer hers, and showed that she knew everything about those women, down to the tiniest details, in order to prove that no one told me anything but told her everything, or, worse, in order to make me feel that I was wrapped in a fog, unable to see the suffering of the people around me. She spoke of Giuseppina as if she had kept up with her, despite the vortex of her engagement and marriage; she spoke of Melina as if the mother of Ada and Antonio had always been in her mind and she were thoroughly familiar with her madness. Then she went on to enumerate many other people in the neighborhood, people whom I hardly knew but whose histories she seemed to know, as if she had a sort of long-distance involvement in their lives. Finally she announced:

"I also had ice cream with Antonio."

That name was a punch in the stomach.

"How is he?"

"Fine."

"Did he say anything about me?"

"No, nothing."

"When does he leave?"

"In September."

"Marcello did nothing to help him."

"It was predictable."

Predictable? If it was predictable, I thought, that the Solaras would do nothing, why did you take me there? And why do you, who are married, now want to see your friends again, like that, by yourself? And why did you have ice cream with Antonio without telling me, knowing that he is my old boyfriend and that though he doesn't want to see me anymore I would like to see him? Do you want revenge because I went

driving with your husband and didn't report to you a word of
what we said to each other? I dressed nervously, mumbled that
I had things to do, had to go.

"I have something else to tell you."

In a serious voice she said that Rino, Marcello, and Michele
had wanted Stefano to go to Piazza dei Martiri to see how well
the shop was coming along, and that the three of them, amid
sacks of cement and cans of paint and brushes, had pointed
out the wall opposite the entrance and told him they were
thinking of putting the enlargement of the photograph of her
in her wedding dress there. Stefano had listened, then he had
answered that certainly it would be a good advertisement for
the shoes, but that it didn't seem to him suitable. The three
had insisted, he had said no to Marcello, no to Michele, and no
to Rino as well. In other words I had won the bet: her husband
had not given in to the Solaras.

I said, making an effort to appear enthusiastic, "See?
Always saying mean things about poor Stefano. And instead I
was right. Now you have to start studying."

"Wait."

"Wait for what? A bet is a bet and you lost."

"Wait," Lila repeated.

My bad mood got worse. She doesn't know what she wants,
I thought. She's unhappy that she was wrong about her husband. Or, I don't know, maybe I'm exaggerating, maybe she
appreciated Stefano's refusal, but she expects a more ferocious
clash of men around her image, and she's disappointed
because the Solaras weren't insistent enough. I saw that she
was lazily running a hand over her hip and along one leg, like
a caress of farewell, and in her eyes appeared for a moment
that mixture of suffering, fear, and disgust that I had noticed
the night of Melina's disappearance. I thought: and if, instead,
she secretly wants her picture to be on display, enlarged, in the
center of the city, and is sorry that Michele didn't succeed in

forcing it on Stefano? Why not, she wants to be first in everything, she's made like that: the most beautiful, the most elegant, the wealthiest. Then I said to myself: above all, the most intelligent. And at the idea that Lila would really start studying again I felt a regret that discouraged me. Of course she would make up for all the years of school she had missed. Of course I would find her beside me, elbow to elbow, taking the high-school graduation exam. And I realized that the prospect was intolerable. But it was even more intolerable to discover that feeling in myself. I was ashamed and immediately started telling her how wonderful it would be if we studied together again, and insisting that she should find out how to proceed. She shrugged, so I said, "Now I really have to go."

This time she didn't stop me.

22.

As usual, once I was on the stairs I began to sympathize with her reasons, or so it seemed to me: she was isolated in the new neighborhood, shut up in her modern house, beaten by Stefano, engaged in some mysterious struggle with her own body in order not to conceive children, envious of my success in school to the point of indicating to me with that crazy bet that she would like to study again. Besides, it was likely that she saw me as much freer than she was. The breakup with Antonio, my troubles with school seemed like nonsense compared to hers. Step by step, without realizing it, I felt driven to a grudging support, then renewed admiration. Yes, it would be wonderful if she started studying again. To return to the time of elementary school, when she was always first and I second. To give meaning back to studying because she knew how to give it meaning. To stay in her shadow and therefore feel strong and secure. Yes, yes, yes. Start again.

At some point, on the way home, the mixture of suffering, fear, and disgust I had seen in her face returned to my mind. Why. I thought back to the teacher's body in disarray, to Melina's uncontrolled body. For no obvious reason, I began to look closely at the women on the *stradone*. Suddenly it seemed to me that I had lived with a sort of limited gaze: as if my focus had been only on us girls, Ada, Gigliola, Carmela, Marisa, Pinuccia, Lila, me, my schoolmates, and I had never really paid attention to Melina's body, Giuseppina Pelusi's, Nunzia Cerullo's, Maria Carracci's. The only woman's body I had studied, with ever-increasing apprehension, was the lame body of my mother, and I had felt pressed, threatened by that image, and still feared that it would suddenly impose itself on mine. That day, instead, I saw clearly the mothers of the old neighborhood. They were nervous, they were acquiescent. They were silent, with tight lips and stooping shoulders, or they yelled terrible insults at the children who harassed them. Extremely thin, with hollow eyes and cheeks, or with broad behinds, swollen ankles, heavy chests, they lugged shopping bags and small children who clung to their skirts and wanted to be picked up. And, good God, they were ten, at most twenty years older than me. Yet they appeared to have lost those feminine qualities that were so important to us girls and that we accentuated with clothes, with makeup. They had been consumed by the bodies of husbands, fathers, brothers, whom they ultimately came to resemble, because of their labors or the arrival of old age, of illness. When did that transformation begin? With housework? With pregnancies? With beatings? Would Lila be misshapen like Nunzia? Would Fernando leap from her delicate face, would her elegant walk become Rino's, legs wide, arms pushed out by his chest? And would my body, too, one day be ruined by the emergence of not only my mother's body but my father's? And would all that I was learning at school dissolve, would the neighborhood prevail again, the cadences, the manners, everything be confounded in a black mire, Anaximander and my father, Folgóre and Don Achille, valences and the ponds, aorists, Hesiod, and the insolent vulgar language of the Solaras, as, over the millenniums, had happened to the chaotic, debased city itself?

I was suddenly sure that, without being aware of it, I had intercepted Lila's feelings and was adding them to mine. Why did she have that expression, that ill humor? Had she caressed her leg, her hip, as a sort of farewell? Had she touched herself, speaking, as if she felt the edges of her body besieged by Melina, by Giuseppina, and was frightened, disgusted by it? Had she turned to our friends out of a need to react?

I remembered how, as a child, she had looked at Maestra Oliviero when she fell off the platform like a broken puppet. I remembered how she had looked at Melina on the *stradone,* eating the soft soap she had just bought. I remembered when she told the rest of us about the murder, and the blood on the copper pot, and claimed that the killer of Don Achille was not a man but a woman, as if, in the story she was telling us, she had heard and seen the form of a female body break, from the need for hatred, the urgency for revenge or justice, and lose its substance.

23.

Starting in the last week of July, I went with the stationer's daughters to the Sea Garden every day, including Sunday. Along with the thousand things that the children might need, I brought in a canvas bag the books that Professor Galiani had lent me. They were small volumes that examined the past, the present, the world as it was and as it ought to become. The writing resembled that of textbooks, but was more difficult and more interesting. I wasn't used to that sort of reading, and got tired quickly. Besides, the girls required a lot of attention. And then there was the lazy sea, the leaden sun that bore down on the gulf and the city, stray fantasies, desires, the ever-present wish to undo the order of the lines—and, with it, every order that required an effort, a wait for fulfillment yet to come—and yield, instead, to what was within reach, immediately gained, the crude life of the creatures of the sky, the earth, and the sea. I approached my seventeenth birthday with one eye on the daughters of the stationer and one on *Discourse on the Origins of Inequality*.

One Sunday I felt someone putting fingers over my eyes and a female voice asked, "Guess who?"

I recognized Marisa's voice and hoped that she was with Nino. How I would have liked him to see me made beautiful by the sun, the salt water, and intent on reading a difficult book. I exclaimed happily, "Marisa!" and immediately turned around. But Nino wasn't there; it was Alfonso, with a blue towel over his shoulder, cigarette, wallet, and lighter in his hand, a black bathing suit with a white stripe, he himself pale as one who has never had a ray of sun in his entire life.

I marveled at seeing them together. Alfonso had to retake exams in two subjects in October, and, since he was busy in the grocery, I imagined that on Sundays he studied. As for Marisa, I was sure that she would be at Barano with her family. Instead she told me that her parents had quarreled with Nella the year before and, with some friends from *Roma*, had taken a small villa at Castelvolturno. She had returned to Naples just for a few days: she needed some school books—three subjects to do again—and, then, she had to see a person. She smiled flirtatiously at Alfonso. The person was him.

I couldn't contain myself, I asked right away how Nino had done on his graduation exams. She made a face of disgust.

"All A's and A-minuses. As soon as he found out the results

he went off on his own to England, without a lira. He says he'll find a job there and stay until he learns English."

"Then?"

"Then I don't know, maybe he'll enroll in economy and business."

I had a thousand other questions, I even looked for a way to ask who the girl was who waited outside school, and if he had really gone alone or in fact with her, when Alfonso said, embarrassed, "Lina's here, too." Then he added, "Antonio brought us in the car."

Antonio?

Alfonso must have noticed how my expression changed, the flush that was spreading over my face, the jealous amazement in my eyes. He smiled, and said quickly, "Stefano had some work to do about the counters in the new grocery and couldn't come. But Lina was extremely eager to see you, she has something to tell you, and so she asked Antonio if he would take us."

"Yes, she has something urgent to tell you," Marisa said emphatically, clapping her hands gleefully to let me know that she already knew the thing.

What thing? Judging from Marisa, it seemed good. Maybe Lila had soothed Antonio and he wanted to be with me again. Maybe the Solaras had finally roused their acquaintances at the recruiting office and Antonio didn't have to go. These hypotheses came to mind immediately. But when the two appeared I eliminated both right away. Clearly Antonio was there only because obeying Lila gave meaning to his empty Sunday, only because to be her friend seemed to him a piece of luck and a necessity. But his expression was still unhappy, his eyes frightened, and he greeted me coldly. I asked about his mother, but he gave me scarcely any news. He looked around uneasily and immediately dived into the water with the girls, who welcomed him warmly. As for Lila, she was pale, without lipstick, her gaze hostile. She didn't seem to have anything urgent to tell me. She sat on the concrete, picked up the book I was reading, leafed through it without a word.

Marisa, in the face of those silences, became ill at ease; she tried to make a show of enthusiasm for everything in the world, then she got flustered and she, too, went to swim. Alfonso chose a place as far from us as possible and, sitting motionless in the sun, concentrated on the bathers, as if the sight of naked people going in and out of the water were utterly absorbing.

"Who gave you this book?" Lila asked.

"My professor of Latin and Greek."

"Why didn't you tell me?"

"I didn't think it would interest you."

"Do you know what is of interest to me and what isn't?"

I immediately resorted to a conciliatory tone, but I also felt a need to brag.

"As soon as I finish I'll lend it to you. These are books that the professor gives the good students to read. Nino reads them, too."

"Who is Nino?"

Did she do it on purpose? Did she pretend not even to remember his name in order to diminish him in my eyes?

"The one in the wedding film, Marisa's brother, Sarratore's oldest son."

"The ugly guy you like?"

"I told you that I don't like him anymore. But he does great things."

"What?"

"Now, for instance, he's in England. He's working, traveling, learning to speak English."

I was excited merely by summarizing Marisa's words. I said to Lila, "Imagine if you and I could do things like that. Travel. Work as waiters to support ourselves. Learn to speak English better than the English. Why can he be free to do that and we can't?"

"Did he finish school?"

"Yes, he got his diploma. Afterward, though, he's going to do a difficult course at the university."

"Is he smart?"

"As smart as you."

"I don't go to school."

"Yes, but: you lost the bet and now you have to go back to books."

"Stop it, Lenù."

"Stefano won't let you?"

"There's the new grocery, I'm supposed to manage it."

"You'll study in the grocery."

"No."

"You promised. You said we'd get our diploma together."

"No."

"Why?"

Lila ran her hand back and forth over the cover of the book, ironing it.

"I'm pregnant," she said. And without waiting for me to react she muttered, "It's so hot," left the book, went to the edge of the concrete, hurled herself without hesitation into the water, yelling at Antonio, who was playing and splashing with Marisa and the children, "Tonì, save me!"

She flew for a few seconds, arms wide, then clumsily hit the surface of the water. She didn't know how to swim.

24.

In the days that followed, Lila started on a period of feverish activity. She began with the new grocery, involving herself as if it were the most important thing in the world. She woke up early, before Stefano. She threw up, made coffee, threw up again. He had become very solicitous, he wanted to drive her, but Lila refused, she said she wanted to walk, and she went out in the cool air of the morning, before the heat exploded, along the deserted streets, past the newly constructed buildings, most of them still empty, to the store that was being fitted out. She pulled up the shutter, washed the paint-splattered floor, waited for the workers and suppliers who were delivering scales, slicers, and furnishings, gave orders on where to place them, moved things around herself, trying out new, more efficient arrangements. Large threatening men, rough-mannered boys were ordered about and submitted to her whims without protesting. Since she had barely finished giving an order when she undertook some other heavy job, they cried in apprehension: Signora Carracci, and did all they could to help her.

Lila, in spite of the heat, which sapped her energy, did not confine herself to the shop in the new neighborhood. Sometimes she went with her sister-in-law to the small work site in Piazza dei Martiri, where Michele generally presided, but often Rino, too, was there, feeling he had the right to monitor the work both as the maker of Cerullo shoes and as the brother-in-law of Stefano, who was the Solaras' partner. Lila would not stay still in that space, either. She inspected it, she climbed the workmen's ladders, she observed the place from high up, she came down, she began to move things. At first she hurt everybody's feelings, but soon, one after the other, they reluctantly gave in. Michele, although the most sarcastically hostile, seemed to grasp most readily the advantages of Lila's suggestions.

"*Signó*," he said teasing, "come and rearrange the bar, too, I'll pay you."

Naturally she wouldn't think of laying a hand on the Bar Solara, but when she had brought enough disorder to Piazza dei Martiri she moved on to the kingdom of the Carracci family, the old grocery, and installed herself there. She made Stefano keep Alfonso at home because he had to study for his makeup exams, and urged Pinuccia to go out more and more often, with her mother, to poke into the shop in Piazza dei Martiri. So, little by little, she reorganized the two adjacent spaces in the old neighborhood to make the work easier and more efficient. In a short time she demonstrated that both Maria and Pinuccia were substantially superfluous; she gave Ada a bigger job, and got Stefano to increase her pay.

When, in the late afternoon, I returned from the Sea Garden and delivered the girls to the stationer, I almost always stopped at the grocery to see how Lila was doing, if her stomach had started to swell. She was nervous, and her complexion wasn't good. To cautious questions about her pregnancy she either didn't respond or dragged me outside the store and said nonsensical things like: "I don't want to talk about it, it's a disease, I have an emptiness inside me that weighs me down." Then she started to tell me about the new grocery and the old one, and Piazza dei Martiri, with her usual exhilarating delivery, just to make me believe that these were places where marvelous things were happening and I, poor me, was missing them.

But by now I knew her tricks, I listened but didn't believe her, although I always ended up hypnotized by the energy with which she played both servant and mistress. Lila was able to talk to me, talk to the customers, talk to Ada, all at the same time, while continuing to unwrap, cut, weigh, take money, and give change. She erased herself in the words and gestures, she became exhausted, she seemed truly engaged in an unrelenting struggle to forget the weight of what she still described, incongruously, as "an emptiness inside."

What impressed me most, though, was her casual behavior with money. She went to the cash register and took what she wanted. Money for her was that drawer, the treasure chest of childhood that opened and offered its wealth. In the (rare) case that the money in the drawer wasn't enough, she had only to glance at Stefano. He, who seemed to have reacquired the generous solicitude of their engagement, pulled up his smock, dug in the back pocket of his pants, took out a fat wallet, and asked, "How much do you need?" Lila made a sign with her fingers, her husband reached out his right arm with the fist closed, she extended her long, thin hand.

Ada, behind the counter, looked at her the way she looked at the movie stars in the pages of magazines. I imagine that in that period Antonio's sister felt as if she were living in a fairy tale. Her eyes sparkled when Lila opened the drawer and gave her money. She handed it out freely, as soon as her husband turned his back. She gave Ada money for Antonio, who was going into the Army, she gave money to Pasquale, who urgently needed three teeth extracted. In early September she took me aside, too, and asked if I needed money for books.

"What books?"

"The ones for school but also the ones not for school."

I told her that Maestra Oliviero was still not out of the hospital, that I didn't know if she would help me get the textbooks, as usual, and here already Lila wanted to stick the money in my pocket. I withdrew, I refused, I didn't want to seem a kind of poor relative forced to ask for money. I told her I had to wait till school started, I told her that the stationer had extended the Sea Garden job until mid-September, I told her that I would therefore earn more than expected and would manage by myself. She was sorry, she insisted that I come to her if the teacher couldn't help me out.

It wasn't just me; certainly all of us, faced with that generosity of hers, had some difficulties. Pasquale, for example, didn't want to accept the money for the dentist, he felt humiliated, and finally took it only because his face was disfigured, his eye was inflamed, and the lettuce compresses were of no use. Antonio, too, was offended, to the point where to take money that our friend gave Ada in addition to her regular pay he had to be persuaded that it was making up for the disgraceful pay that Stefano had given her before. We had never had a lot of money, and we attached great importance even to ten lire; if we found a coin on the street it was a celebration. So it seemed to us a mortal sin that Lila handed out money as if it were a worthless metal, waste paper. She did it silently, with an imperious gesture resembling those with which as a child she had organized games, assigned parts. Afterward, she talked about other things, as if that moment hadn't existed. On the other hand—Pasquale said to me one evening, in his obscure way—mortadella sells, so do shoes, and Lina has always been our friend, she's on our side, our ally, our companion. She's rich now, but by her own merit: yes, by her own merit, because the money didn't come to her from the fact that she is Signora Carracci, the future mother of the grocer's child, but because it's she who invented Cerullo shoes, and even if no one seemed to remember that now, we, her friends, remembered.

All true. How many things Lila had made happen in the space of a few years. And yet now that we were seventeen the substance of time no longer seemed fluid but had assumed a gluelike consistency and churned around us like a yellow cream in a confectioner's machine. Lila herself confirmed this bitterly when, one Sunday when the sea was smooth and the sky white, she appeared, to my surprise, at the Sea Garden around three in the afternoon, by herself: a truly unusual event. She had taken the subway, a couple of buses, and now was here, in a bathing suit, with a greenish complexion and an outbreak of pimples on her forehead. "Seventeen years of shit," she said in dialect, with apparent cheer, her eyes full of sarcasm.

She had quarreled with Stefano. In the daily exchanges with the Solaras the truth came out about the management of the store in Piazza dei Martiri. Michele had tried to insist on

Gigliola, had harshly threatened Rino, who supported Pinuccia, had finally launched into a tense negotiation with Stefano, in which they had come close to blows. And in the end what happened? Neither winners nor losers, it seemed. Gigliola and Pinuccia would manage the store *together*. Provided that Stefano reconsider an old decision.

"What?" I asked.

"See if you can guess."

I couldn't guess. Michele had asked Stefano, in his teasing tone of voice, to concede on the photograph of Lila in her wedding dress. And this time her husband had done so.

"Really?"

"Really. I told you you just had to wait. They're going to display me in the shop. In the end I've won the bet, not you. Start studying—this year you'll have to get top marks."

Here she changed her tone, became serious. She said that she hadn't come because of the photograph, since she had known for a long time that as far as that shit was concerned she was merchandise to barter. She had come because of the pregnancy. She talked about it for a long time, nervously, as if it were something to be crushed in a mortar, and she did it with cold firmness. It has no meaning, she said, not concealing her anguish. Men insert their thingy in you and you become a box of flesh with a living doll inside. I've got it, it's here, and it's repulsive to me. I throw up continuously, it's my very stomach that can't bear it. I know I'm supposed to think beautiful things, I know I have to resign myself, but I can't do it, I see no reason for resignation and no beauty. Besides the fact, she added, that I feel incapable of dealing with children. You, yes, you are, just look how you take care of the stationer's children. Not me, I wasn't born with that gift.

These words hurt me, what could I say?

"You don't know if you have a gift or not, you have to try," I sought to reassure her, and pointed to the daughters of the stationer who were playing a little distance away. "Sit with them for a while, talk to them."

She laughed. She said maliciously that I had learned to use the sentimental voice of our mothers. But then, uneasily, she ventured to say a few words to the girls, retreated, began talking to me again. I equivocated, pressed her, urged her to take care of Linda, the smallest of the stationer's daughters. I said to her, "Go on, let her play her favorite game, drinking from the fountain next to the bar or spraying the water by putting your thumb over it."

She led Linda away unwillingly, holding her hand. Time passed and they didn't come back. I called the other two girls and went to see what was happening. Everything was fine, Lila had been happily made a prisoner by Linda. She held the child suspended over the jet, letting her drink or spray water. They were both laughing, and their laughter sounded like cries of joy.

I was relieved. I left Linda's sisters with her, too, and went to sit at the bar, in a place where I could keep an eye on all four and also read. She'll become that, I thought, looking at her. What seemed insupportable before is cheering her up now. Maybe I should tell her that things without meaning are the most beautiful ones. It's a good sentence, she'll like it. Lucky her, she's got everything that counts.

For a while I tried to follow, line by line, the arguments of Rousseau. Then I looked up, I saw that something was wrong. Shouts. Maybe Linda had leaned over too far, maybe one of her sisters had given her a shove, certainly she had escaped Lila's grasp and had hit her chin on the edge of the basin. I ran over in fear. Lila, as soon as she saw me, cried immediately, in a childish voice that I had never heard from her, not even when she was a child:

"It was her sister who made her fall, not me."

She was holding Linda, who was bleeding, screaming, crying, as her sisters looked elsewhere with small nervous movements and tight smiles, as if the thing had nothing to do with them, as if they couldn't hear, couldn't see.

I tore the child from Lila's arms and tilted her toward the jet of water, washing her face with resentful hands. There was a horizontal cut under her chin. I'll lose the money from the stationer, I thought, my mother will be angry. Meanwhile I ran for the attendant, who somehow cajoled Linda into calming down, surprised her with an inundation of rubbing alcohol, making her shriek again, then stuck a gauze bandage on her chin and went back to soothing her. Nothing serious, in other words. I bought ice cream for the three girls and went back to the concrete platform.

Lila had left.

25.

The stationer didn't seem especially upset by Linda's wound, but when I asked if I should come the next day at the usual time to pick up the girls, she said that her daughters had had too much swimming that summer and there was no need for me anymore.

I didn't tell Lila that I had lost my job. She on the other hand never asked me how things had turned out, she didn't even ask about Linda and her cut. When I saw her again she was extremely busy with the opening of the new grocery store and gave me the impression of an athlete in training, jumping rope more and more frantically.

She dragged me to the printer, from whom she had ordered a large number of flyers announcing the opening of the new store. She wanted me to go to the priest to set a time to come by for the blessing of the place and the stock. She announced that she had hired Carmela Peluso, at a salary a lot higher than what she was making at the notions store, but first of all she told me that in everything, truly everything, she was waging a serious war against her husband, Pinuccia, her mother-in-law, her brother Rino. She didn't seem especially aggressive, however. She spoke in a low voice, in dialect, doing a thousand other things that seemed more important than what she was saying. She enumerated the wrongs that her relatives, by marriage and by birth, had done and were doing to her. "They have placated Michele," she said, "just as they placated Marcello. They used me—to them I'm not a person but a thing. Let's give him Lina, let's stick her on a wall, since she's a zero, an absolute zero." As she spoke her eyes shone, full of movement, within dark circles, her skin was stretched over the cheekbones, her teeth flashed white, in quick nervous smiles. But she didn't convince me. It seemed to me that behind that raucous activity was a person who was exhausted and looking for a way out.

"What do you intend to do?" I asked.

"Nothing. All I know is they'll have to kill me to do what they want with my photograph."

"Forget it, Lila. Ultimately it's a nice thing, think about it: they only put actresses on billboards."

"And am I an actress?"

"No."

"So? If my husband has decided to sell himself to the Solaras, do you think he can sell me as well?"

I tried to soothe her, I was afraid that Stefano would lose patience and hit her. I said so, she started laughing: since she'd been pregnant her husband hadn't dared to give her even a slap. But now, just as she uttered that remark, the suspicion dawned on me that the photograph was an excuse, that really she wanted to infuriate all of them, to be massacred by Stefano, by the Solaras, by Rino, provoke them to the point where their blows would help her to crush the impatience, the pain, the living thing she had in her belly.

My hypothesis found support the night the grocery opened.

She seemed to be wearing her shabbiest clothes. In front of everyone she treated her husband like a servant. She sent away the priest she had had me call on before he could bless the store, contemptuously sticking some money in his hand. She went on to slice prosciutto and stuff sandwiches, handing them out free to anyone, along with a glass of wine. And this last move was so successful that the store had scarcely opened when it was jammed with customers; she and Carmela were besieged, and Stefano, who was elegantly dressed, had to help them deal with the situation as he was, without an apron, so that his good clothes got all greasy.

When they came home, exhausted, her husband made a scene and Lila did her best to provoke his fury. She shouted that if he wanted someone who obeyed, and that's all, he was out of luck; she was not his mother or his sister, she would always make life difficult for him. And she started with the Solaras, with the business of the photograph, insulting him grossly. First he let her have her say, then he responded with even worse insults. But he didn't beat her. When, the next day, she told me what had happened, I said that although Stefano had his faults, certainly he loved her. She denied it. "He understands only this," she replied, rubbing together thumb and index finger. And in fact the grocery was already popular throughout the new neighborhood, and was crowded from the moment it opened. "The cash drawer is already full. Thanks to me. I bring him wealth, a son, what more does he want?"

"What more do you want?" I asked, with a stab of rage that surprised me, and immediately I smiled, hoping she hadn't noticed.

I remember that she looked bewildered; she touched her forehead with her fingers. Maybe she didn't even know what she wanted, she felt only that she couldn't find peace.

As the other opening, that of the shop on Piazza dei Martiri, approached, she became unbearable. But maybe that adjective is excessive. Let's say that she poured out onto all of us, even me, the confusion that she felt inside. On the one hand, she made Stefano's life hell, she squabbled with her mother-in-law and her sister-in-law, she went to Rino and quarreled with him in front of the workers and Fernando, who, more hunched than usual, labored over his bench, pretending not to hear; on the other, she herself perceived that she was spinning around in her unhappiness, unresigned, and at times I caught her in the new grocery store, in a rare moment when it was empty or she wasn't dealing with suppliers, with a vacant look, one hand on her forehead, in her hair, as if to stanch a wound, and the expression of someone who is trying to catch her breath.

One afternoon I was at home; it was still very hot, although it was the end of September. School was about to begin, I felt at the mercy of the days. My mother reproached me for wasting time. Nino—who knows where he was, in England or in that mysterious space that was the university. I no longer had Antonio, or even the hope of getting back together with him; he had left, along with Enzo Scanno, for his military service, saying goodbye to everyone except me. I heard someone calling me from the street. It was Lila. Her eyes were shining, as if she had a fever, and she said she had found a solution.

"Solution to what?"

"The photograph. If they want to display it, they have to do it the way I say."

"And what do you say?"

She didn't tell me, maybe at that moment it wasn't clear to her. But I knew what sort of person she was, and I recognized in her face the expression she got when, from the dark depths of herself, a signal arrived that fired her brain. She asked me to go with her that evening to Piazza dei Martiri. There we would find the Solaras, Gigliola, Pinuccia, her brother. She wanted me to help her, support her, and I realized that what she had in mind would ferry her beyond her permanent war: a violent but conclusive outlet for the accumulated tensions; or a way of freeing her head, her body, from pent-up energies.

"All right," I said, "but promise not to be crazy."

"Yes."

After the stores closed she and Stefano came to get me in the car. From the few words they exchanged I understood that not even her husband knew what she had in mind and that this time my presence, rather than reassuring him, alarmed him. Lila had finally appeared to be accommodating. She had told him that, if there was no possibility of abandoning the photograph, she wanted at least to have her say on how it was displayed.

"A question of frame, wall, lighting?" he had asked.

"I have to see."

"But then that's it, Lina."

"Yes, that's it."

It was a beautiful warm evening; the brilliant lights of the shop's interior spread their glow into the square. The gigantic image of Lila in her wedding dress could be seen at a distance, leaning against the center wall. Stefano parked, we went in, making our way among the boxes of shoes, piled up haphazardly, cans of paint, ladders. Marcello, Rino, Gigliola, and Pinuccia were visibly irritated: for varying reasons they had no wish to submit yet again to Lila's caprices. The only one who greeted us cordially was Michele, who turned to my friend with a mocking laugh.

"Lovely signora, will you let us know, at last, what you have in mind or do you just want to ruin the evening?"

Lila looked at the panel leaning against the wall, asked them to lay it on the floor. Marcello said cautiously, with the dark timidity that he always showed toward Lila, "What for?"

"I'll show you."

Rino interrupted: "Don't be an idiot, Lina. You know how much this thing cost? If you ruin it, you're in trouble."

The Solaras laid the image on the floor. Lila looked around, with her brow furrowed, her eyes narrowed. She was looking for something that she knew was there, that perhaps she had bought herself. In a corner she spied a roll of black paper, and she took a pair of big scissors and a box of drawing pins from a shelf. Then, with that expression of extreme concentration which enabled her to isolate herself from everything around her, she went back to the panel. Before our astonished and, in the cases of some, openly hostile eyes, she cut strips of black paper, with the manual precision she had always possessed, and pinned them here and there to the photograph, asking for my help with slight gestures or quick glances.

I joined in with the devotion that I had felt ever since we were children. Those moments were thrilling, it was a pleasure to be beside her, slipping inside her intentions, to the point of anticipating her. I felt that she was seeing something that wasn't there, and that she was struggling to make us see it, too. I was suddenly happy, feeling the intensity that invested her, that flowed through her fingers as they grasped the scissors, as they pinned the black paper.

Finally, she tried to lift the canvas, as if she were alone in that space, but she couldn't. Marcello readily intervened, I intervened, we leaned it against the wall. Then we all backed up toward the door, some sneering, some grim, some appalled. The body of the bride Lila appeared cruelly shredded. Much of the head had disappeared, as had the stomach. There remained an eye, the hand on which the chin rested, the brilliant stain of the mouth, the diagonal stripe of the bust, the line of the crossed legs, the shoes.

Gigliola began, scarcely containing her rage: "I cannot put a thing like that in *my* shop."

"I agree," Pinuccia exploded. "We have to sell here, and with that grotesque thing people will run away. Rino, say something to your sister, please."

Rino pretended to ignore her, but he turned to Stefano as if his brother-in-law were to blame for what was happening. "I told you, you can't reason with her. You have to say yes, no, and that's it, or you see what happens? It's a waste of time."

Stefano didn't answer, he stared at the panel leaning against the wall and it was evident that he was looking for a way out. He asked me, "What do you think, Lenù?"

I said in Italian, "To me it seems very beautiful. Of course, I wouldn't want it in the neighborhood, that's not the right place for it. But here it's something else, it will attract attention, it will please. In *Confidenze* just last week I saw that in Rossano Brazzi's house there is a painting like this."

Hearing that, Gigliola got even angrier. "What do you mean? That Rossano Brazzi knows what's what, that you two know everything, and Pinuccia and I don't?"

At that point I felt the danger. I had only to glance at Lila to realize that, if when we arrived at the shop she had really felt willing to give in should the attempt prove fruitless, now that the attempt had been made and had produced that image of disfigurement she wouldn't yield an inch. Those minutes of work on the picture had broken ties: at that moment she was overwhelmed by an exaggerated sense of herself, and it would take time for her to retreat into the dimension of the grocer's wife, she wouldn't accept a sigh of dissent. In fact, while Gigliola was speaking, she was already muttering: Like this or not at all. And she wanted to quarrel, she wanted to break, shatter, she would have happily hurled herself at Gigliola with the scissors.

I hoped for a word of support from Marcello. But Marcello remained silent, head down: I understood that his residual feelings for Lila were vanishing at that moment, his old depressed passion couldn't carry them forward any longer. It was his brother who broke in, lashing Gigliola, his fiancée, in his most aggressive voice. "Shut up," he told her. And as soon as she tried to protest he became threatening, without even looking at her, staring, rather, at the panel: "Shut up, Gigliò." Then he turned to Lila.

"I like it, *signò*. You've erased yourself deliberately and I see why: to show the thigh, to show how well a woman's thigh goes with those shoes. Excellent. You're a pain in the ass, but when you do a thing you do it right."

Silence.

With her fingertips Gigliola dried silent tears that she couldn't hold back. Pinuccia stared at Rino, she stared at her brother, as if she wanted to say to them: Speak, defend me, don't let that bitch walk all over me.

Stefano instead murmured softly, "Yes, it convinces me, too."

And Lila said suddenly, "It's not finished."

"What do you still have to do?" Pinuccia shot back.

"I have to add a little color."

"Color?" Marcello mumbled, even more disoriented. "We're supposed to open in three days."

Michele laughed: "If we have to wait another little bit, we'll wait. Get to work, *signò*, do what you like."

That masterful tone, of one who makes and unmakes as he wishes, Stefano didn't like.

"There's the new grocery," he said, to let it be understood that he needed his wife there.

"Figure it out," Michele answered. "We have more interesting things to do here."

26.

We spent the last days of September shut up in the shop, the two of us and three workmen. They were magnificent hours of play, of invention, of freedom, such as we hadn't experienced together perhaps since childhood. Lila drew me into her frenzy.

We bought paste, paint, brushes. With extreme precision (she was demanding) we attached the black paper cutouts. We traced red or blue borders between the remains of the photograph and the dark clouds that were devouring it. Lila had always been good with lines and colors, but here she did something more, though I wouldn't have been able to say what it was; hour after hour it engulfed me.

For a while it seemed to me that she had fashioned that occasion to bring to an effective end the years that had begun with the designs for the shoes, when she was still the girl Lina Cerullo. And I still think that much of the pleasure of those days was derived from the resetting of the conditions of her, or our, life, from the capacity we had to lift ourselves above ourselves, to isolate ourselves in the pure and simple fulfillment of that sort of visual synthesis. We forgot about Antonio, Nino, Stefano, the Solaras, my problems with school, her pregnancy, the tensions between us. We suspended time, we isolated space, there remained only the play of glue, scissors, paper, paint: the play of shared creation.

But there was something else. I was soon reminded of the word Michele had used: *erase*. Likely, yes, very likely the black stripes did set the shoes apart and make them more visible: young Solara wasn't stupid, he knew how to look. But at times, and with growing intensity, I felt that that wasn't the true goal of our pasting and painting. Lila was happy, and she was drawing me deeper and deeper into her fierce happiness, because she had suddenly found, perhaps without even realizing it, an opportunity that allowed her to *portray* the fury she directed against herself, the insurgence, perhaps for the first time in her life, of the need—and here the verb used by Michele was appropriate—to erase herself.

Today, in the light of many subsequent events, I'm quite sure that that is really what happened. With the black paper, with the green and purple circles that Lila drew around certain parts of her body, with the blood-red lines with which she sliced and said she was slicing it, she completed her own self-destruction *in an image*, presented to the eyes of all in the space bought by the Solaras to display and sell *her* shoes.

It's likely that it was she who provoked in me that impression, who motivated it. While we worked, she began to talk about when she had begun to realize that she was now Signora Carracci. At first I didn't really understand what she was saying, her observations seemed to me banal. When, as girls, of course, we were in love, we would try out the sound of our name joined to the last name of the beloved. I, for example, still have a notebook from the first year of high school in which I practiced signing myself Elena Sarratore, and I clearly remember how I would very faintly whisper that name. But it wasn't what Lila meant. I soon realized that she was confessing exactly the opposite, a game like mine had never occurred to her. Nor, she said, had the formula of her new designation at first made much of an impression: *Raffaella Cerullo Carracci.* Nothing exciting, nothing serious. In the beginning, that "Carracci" had been no more absorbing than an exercise in logical analysis, of the sort that Maestra Oliviero had hammered into us in elementary school. What was it, an indirect object of place? Did it mean that she now lived not with her parents but with Stefano? Did it mean that the new house where she was going to live would have on the door a brass plate that said "Carracci"? Did it mean that if I were to write to her I would no longer address the letter to Raffaella Cerullo but to Raffaella Carracci? Did it mean that in everyday usage *Cerullo* would soon disappear from *Raffaella Cerullo Carracci,* and that she herself would define herself, and sign, only as Raffaella Carracci, and that her children would have to make an effort to recall their mother's surname, and that her grandchildren would be completely ignorant of their grandmother's surname?

Yes. A custom. Everything according to the rules, then. But

Lila, as usual, hadn't stopped there, she had soon gone further. As we worked with brushes and paints, she told me that she had begun to see in that formula an indirect object of place to which, as if *Cerullo Carracci* somehow indicated that Cerullo *goes toward Carracci, falls into it, is sucked up by it, is dissolved in it*. And, from the abrupt assignment of the role of speech maker at her wedding to Silvio Solara, from the entrance into the restaurant of Marcello Solara, wearing on his feet, no less, the shoes that Stefano had led her to believe he considered a sacred relic, from her honeymoon and the beatings, up until that installation—in the void that she felt inside, the living thing determined by Stefano—she had been increasingly oppressed by an unbearable sensation, a force pushing down harder and harder, crushing her. That impression had been getting stronger, had prevailed. Raffaella Cerullo, overpowered, had lost her shape and had dissolved inside the outlines of Stefano, becoming a subsidiary emanation of him: *Signora Carracci*. It was then that I began to see in the panel the traces of what she was saying. "It's a thing that's still going on," she said in a whisper. And meanwhile we pasted paper, laid on color. But what were we really doing, what was I helping her do?

The workmen, in great bewilderment, attached the panel to the wall. We were sad but we didn't say so; the game was over. We cleaned the shop thoroughly. Lila changed her mind once again about the position of a sofa, of an ottoman. Finally we withdrew together to the door and contemplated our work. She burst out laughing as I had never heard her laugh, a free, self-mocking laugh. I, on the other hand, was so enthralled by the upper part of the panel, where Lila's head no longer was, that I couldn't take in the whole. All you could see, at the top, was a very vivid eye, encircled by midnight blue and red.

27.

The day of the opening Lila arrived in Piazza dei Martiri sitting in the convertible next to her husband. When she got out, I saw in her the uncertain gaze of someone who is afraid something bad is going to happen. The overexcitement of the days of the panel had dissipated; she had again taken on the sickly look of a woman who is unwillingly pregnant. Yet she was carefully dressed, she seemed to have stepped out of a fashion magazine. She immediately left Stefano and dragged me off to look at the shopwindows of Via dei Mille.

We walked for a while. She was tense, she kept asking me if anything was out of place.

"Do you remember," she said suddenly, "the girl dressed all in green, the one with the derby?"

I remembered. I remembered the uneasiness we had felt when we saw her, on that same street, years before, and the fight between our boys and the local boys, and the intervention of the Solaras, and Michele with the iron bar, and the fear. I realized that she wanted to hear something soothing, I said:

"It was just a matter of money, Lila. Today it's all changed, you're much prettier than the girl in green."

But I thought: It's not true, I'm lying to you. There was something malevolent in the inequality, and now I knew it. It acted in the depths, it dug deeper than money. The cash of two grocery stores, and even of the shoe factory and the shoe store, was not sufficient to hide our origin. Lila herself, even if she had taken from the cash drawer more money than she had taken, even if she had taken millions, thirty, even fifty, couldn't do it. I had understood this, and finally there was something that I knew better than she did, I had learned it not on those streets but outside the school, looking at the girl who came to meet Nino. She was superior to us, just as she was, unwittingly. And this was unendurable.

We returned to the shop. The afternoon went on like a kind of marriage feast: food, sweets, a lot of wine; all the guests in the clothes they had worn to Lila's wedding, Fernando, Nunzia, Rino, the entire Solara family, Alfonso, we girls, Ada, Carmela, and I. There was a crowd of cars haphazardly parked, there was a crowd in the shop, the clamor of voices grew louder. The entire time, Gigliola and Pinuccia competed to act like the proprietor, each striving harder than the other, and both worn out by the strain. The panel with Lila's picture loomed over everything. Some paused to look at it with interest, some gave it a skeptical glance or even laughed. I couldn't take my eyes off it. Lila was no longer recognizable. What remained was a seductive, tremendous form, the image of a one-eyed goddess who thrust her beautifully shod feet into the center of the room.

In the crush I was amazed by Alfonso, who was lively, cheerful, elegant. I had never seen him like that, at school or in the neighborhood or in the grocery, and Lila herself pondered him for a long time, perplexed. I said to her, laughing, "He's not himself anymore."

"What happened to him?"

"I don't know."

Alfonso was the true good news of that afternoon. Something that had been silent in him awakened, in the brightly lit shop. It was as if he had unexpectedly discovered that this part of the city made him feel good. He became unusually active. We saw him arrange this object and that, start up conversations with the stylish people who came in out of curiosity, who examined the shoes or grabbed a pastry and a glass of vermouth. At a certain point he joined us and in a self-assured tone praised effusively the work we had done on the photograph. He was in a state of such mental freedom that he overcame his timidity and said to his sister-in-law, "I've always known you were dangerous," and he kissed her on both cheeks.

I stared at him perplexed. Dangerous? What had he perceived, in the panel, that had escaped me? Was Alfonso capable of seeing beyond appearances? Did he know how to look with imagination? Is it possible, I wondered, that his real future is not in studying but in this affluent part of the city, where he'll be able to use the little he's learning in school? Ah yes, he concealed inside himself another person. He was different from all the boys of the neighborhood, and mainly he was different from his brother, Stefano, who, sitting on an ottoman in a corner, was silent but ready to respond with a tranquil smile to anyone who spoke to him.

Evening fell. Suddenly a bright light flared outside. The Solaras, grandfather, father, mother, sons, rushed out to see, gripped by a noisy familial enthusiasm. We all went out into the street. Above the windows and the entrance shone the word "SOLARA."

Lila grimaced, she said to me, "They gave in on that, too."

She pushed me reluctantly toward Rino, who seemed happiest of all, and said to him, "If the shoes are Cerullo, why is the shop Solara?"

Rino took her by the arm and said in a low voice, "Lina, why do you always want to be a pain in the ass? You remember the mess you got me into in this very square? What am I supposed to do, you want another mess? Be satisfied for once. We are here, in the center of Naples, and we are the masters. Those shits who wanted to beat us up less than three years ago—do you see them now? They stop, they look in the windows, they go in, they take a pastry. Isn't that enough for you? Cerullo shoes, Solara shop. What do you want to see up there, Carracci?"

Lila was evasive, saying to him, without aggression, "I'm perfectly calm. Enough to tell you that you'd better not ask me for anything ever again. What do you think you're doing? Do you borrow money from Signora Solara? Does Stefano borrow money from her? Are you both in debt to her, and so you always say yes? From now on, every man for himself, Rino."

She abandoned us, headed straight toward Michele Solara, in a playfully flirtatious way. I saw that she went off with him to the square, they walked around the stone lions. I saw that her husband followed her with his gaze. I saw that he didn't take his eyes off her all the while she and Michele walked, talking. I saw that Gigliola grew furious, she whispered in Pinuccia's ear and they both stared at her.

Meanwhile the shop emptied, someone turned off the large, luminous sign. The square darkened for a few seconds, then the street lamps regained their strength. Lila left Michele laughing, but as she entered the shop her face was suddenly drained of life, she shut herself in the back room where the toilet was.

Alfonso, Marcello, Pinuccia, and Gigliola began to straighten up. I went to help.

Lila came out of the bathroom and Stefano, as if he had been waiting in ambush, immediately grabbed her by the arm. She wriggled free, irritated, and joined me. She was very pale. She whispered, "I've had some blood. What does it mean, is the baby dead?"

28.

Lila's pregnancy lasted scarcely more than ten weeks; then the midwife came and scraped away everything. The next day she went back to work in the new grocery with Carmen Peluso. This marked the beginning of a long period in which, sometimes gentle, sometimes fierce, she stopped running around, having apparently decided to compress her whole life into the orderliness of that space fragrant with mortar and cheese, filled with sausages, bread, mozzarella, anchovies in salt, hunks of *cicoli*, sacks overflowing with dried beans, bladders stuffed with lard.

This behavior was greatly appreciated in particular by Stefano's mother, Maria. As if she had recognized in her daughter-in-law something of herself, she suddenly became more affectionate, and gave her some old earrings of red gold. Lila accepted them with pleasure and wore them often. For a while her face remained pale, she had pimples on her forehead, her eyes were sunk deep into the sockets, the skin was stretched so tight over her cheekbones that it seemed transparent. Then she revived and put even more energy into promoting the shop. Already by Christmastime the profits had risen and within a few months surpassed those of the grocery in the old neighborhood.

Maria's appreciation grew. She went more and more often to give her daughter-in-law a hand, rather than her son, whose failed paternity—along with the pressures of business—had made him surly, or her daughter, who had started working in the store in Piazza dei Martiri and had strictly forbidden her mother to appear, so as not to make a bad impression with the clientele. The old Signora Carracci even took the young Signora Carracci's side when Stefano and Pinuccia blamed her for her inability, or unwillingness, to keep a baby inside her.

"She doesn't want children," Stefano complained.

"Yes," Pinuccia supported him, "she wants to stay a girl, she doesn't know how to be a wife."

Maria reproached them both harshly: "Don't even think such things, Our Lord gives children and Our Lord takes them away, I don't want to hear that nonsense."

"You be quiet," her daughter cried, in annoyance. "You gave that bitch the earrings I liked."

Their arguments, Lila's reactions, soon became neighborhood gossip, which spread, and even I heard it. But I didn't pay much attention, the school year had begun.

It started right off in a way that amazed me most of all. I did well from the first days, as if, with the departure of Antonio, the disappearance of Nino, maybe even Lila's decisive commitment to managing the grocery, something in my head had relaxed. I found that I remembered with precision everything I had learned badly in my first year; I answered the teachers' questions with ready intelligence. Not only that. Professor Galiani, maybe because she had lost Nino, her most brilliant student, redoubled her interest in me and said that it would be stimulating and instructive for me to go to a march for world peace that started in Resina and continued on to Naples. I decided to have a look, partly out of curiosity, partly out of fear that Professor Galiani would be offended, and partly because the march went along the *stradone*, skirting the neighborhood, and it wouldn't take much effort. But my mother wanted me to take my brothers. I argued, I protested, and was late. I arrived with them at the railway bridge, and down below saw the people marching; they occupied the whole street, preventing the cars from passing. They were normal people and weren't really marching but walking, carrying banners and signs. I wanted to find Professor Galiani, to be seen, and I ordered my brothers to wait on the bridge. It was a terrible idea: I couldn't find the professor, and, as soon as I turned my back, they joined some other children who were throwing stones at the demonstrators and yelling insults. In a sweat I rushed to get them, and hurried them away, terrified by the idea that the far-sighted Professor Galiani had picked them out and recognized that they were my brothers.

Meanwhile the weeks passed, there were new classes and the textbooks to buy. It seemed pointless to show the list of books to my mother so that she would negotiate with my father and get money from him, I knew that there was no money. In addition, there was no news of Maestra Oliviero. Between August and September, I had gone twice to visit her in the hospital, but the first time I had found her asleep and the second I discovered that she had been discharged but had not returned home. Feeling desperate, in early November I went to ask the neighbor about her, and learned that, because of her health, she had gone to a sister in Potenza, and who knew if she would ever return to Naples, to the neighborhood, to her job. At that point I decided to ask Alfonso if, when his brother had bought the books for him, we could somehow arrange things so that I could use his. He was enthusiastic and proposed that we should study together, maybe at Lila's house, which, ever since she had started working at the grocery, was empty from seven in the morning until nine at night. We resolved to do that.

But one morning Alfonso said to me, somewhat annoyed, "Go and see Lila in the grocery today, she wants to see you." He knew why, but she had sworn him to silence and it was impossible to get the secret out of him.

In the afternoon I went to the new grocery. Carmen, with a mixture of sadness and joy, wanted to show me a card from some city in Piedmont that Enzo, her fiancé, had sent her. Lila had also received a card, from Antonio, and for a moment I thought she had wanted me to come there just to show it to me. But she didn't show it to me or tell me what he had written. She dragged me into the back of the shop and asked, in a tone of amusement:

"You remember our bet?"

I nodded yes.

"You remember that you lost?"

I nodded yes.

"You remember that you now have to pass with the best grades?"

I nodded yes.

She pointed to two large packages tied up in wrapping paper. In them were the school books.

29.

They were very heavy. At home, I was very excited to discover that they were not the used, often ill-smelling volumes that in the past the teacher had got for me but were brand-new, fragrant with fresh ink, and conspicuous among them were the dictionaries—Zingarelli, Rocci, and Calonghi-Georges—which the teacher had never been able to acquire.

My mother, who had a word of contempt for anything that happened to me, burst into tears as she watched me unwrap the packages. Surprised, intimidated by that unusual reaction, I went to her, caressed her arm. It's difficult to say what had moved her: maybe her sense of impotence in the face of our poverty, maybe the generosity of the grocer's wife, I don't know. She calmed down quickly, muttered something incomprehensible, and became engrossed in her duties.

In the little room where I slept with my sister and brothers I had a small, rough table, riddled with worm holes, where I usually did my homework. On it I arranged all the books, and, seeing them lined up there, against the wall, I felt charged with energy.

The days began to fly by. I gave back to Professor Galiani the books she had lent me for the summer, she gave me others, which were even more difficult. I read them diligently on Sundays, but I didn't understand much. I ran my eyes along the lines, I turned the pages, and yet the style annoyed me, the meaning escaped me. That year, my fourth year of high school, between studying and difficult readings, I was exhausted, but it was the exhaustion of contentment.

One day Professor Galiani asked me, "What newspaper do you read, Greco?"

That question provoked the same uneasiness I had felt talking to Nino at Lila's wedding. The professor took it for granted that I normally did something that at my house, in my envi-

ronment, was not at all normal. How could I tell her that my
father didn't buy the newspaper, that I had never read one? I
didn't have the heart, and my mind raced to remember if
Pasquale, who was a Communist, read one. A useless effort.
Then I thought of Donato Sarratore and I remembered Ischia,
the Maronti, I remembered that he wrote for *Roma*. I
answered:

"I read *Roma*."

The professor gave an ironic half smile, and the next day
began handing on her newspapers. She bought two, sometimes three, and after school she would give me one. I thanked
her and went home upset by what seemed to me still more
homework.

At first I left the paper around the house, and put off reading it until I had finished my homework, but at night it had disappeared, my father had grabbed it to read in bed or in the
bathroom. So I got in the habit of hiding it among my books,
and took it out only at night, when everyone was sleeping.
Sometimes it was *Unità*, sometimes *Il Mattino*, sometimes
Corriere della Sera, but all three were difficult for me, it was
like having to follow a comic strip whose preceding episodes
you didn't know. I hurried from one column to the next, more
out of duty than out of real curiosity, hoping, as in all things
imposed by school, that what I didn't understand today I
would, by sheer persistence, understand tomorrow.

In that period I saw little of Lila. Sometimes, right after
school, before I rushed off to do my homework, I went to the
new grocery. I was starving, she knew it, and would make me
a generously stuffed sandwich. While I devoured it, I would
articulate, in good Italian, statements I had memorized from
Professor Galiani's books and newspapers. I would mention,
let's say, "the atrocious reality of the Nazi extermination camps,"
or "what men were able to do and what they can do today as
well," or "the atomic threat and the obligation to peace," or the

fact that "as a result of subduing the forces of nature with the tools that we invent, we find ourselves today at the point where the force of our tools has become a greater concern than the forces of nature," or "the need for a culture that combats and eliminates suffering," or the idea that "religion will disappear from men's consciousness when, finally, we have constructed a world of equals, without class distinctions, and with a sound scientific conception of society and of life." I talked to her about these and other things because I wanted to show her that I was sailing toward passing with high marks, and because I didn't know who else to say them to, and because I hoped she would respond so that we could resume our old habit of discussion. But she said almost nothing, in fact she seemed embarrassed, as if she didn't really understand what I was talking about. Or if she made a remark, she concluded by digging up an old obsession that now—I didn't know why—had started working inside her again. She began to talk about the origin of Don Achille's money, and of the Solaras', even in the presence of Carmen, who immediately agreed. But as soon as a customer came in she stopped, she became very polite and efficient, she sliced, weighed, took money.

Once, she left the cash drawer open and, staring at the money, said, angrily, "I earn this with my labor and Carmen's. But nothing in there is mine, Lenù, it's made with Stefano's money. And Stefano to make money started with his father's money. Without what Don Achille put under the mattress, working the black market and loan-sharking, today there would not be this and there would not be the shoe factory. Not only that. Stefano, Rino, my father would not have sold a single shoe without the money and the connections of the Solara family, who are also loan sharks. Is it clear what I've got myself into?"

Clear, but I didn't understand the point of those discussions.

"It's water under the bridge," I said, and reminded her of the conclusions she had come to when she was engaged to Stefano. "What you're talking about is what's behind us, we are something else."

But although she had invented that theory, she did not seem convinced by it. She said to me, and I have a vivid memory of the phrase, which was in dialect:

"I don't like what I've done and what I'm doing."

I thought that she must be spending time with Pasquale, who had always had opinions like that. I thought that maybe their relationship had been strengthened by the fact that Pasquale was engaged to Ada, who worked in the old grocery, and was the brother of Carmen, who worked with her in the new one. I went home dissatisfied, struggling to hold off an old childhood feeling, from the period when I suffered because Lila and Carmela had become friends and tried to exclude me. I calmed myself down by studying until very late.

One night as I was reading *Il Mattino*, my eyes heavy with sleep, a short, unsigned article jolted me awake like an electric charge. I couldn't believe it—the article was about the shop in Piazza dei Martiri and it praised the panel that Lila and I had created.

I read and reread it, I can still recall a few lines: "The young women who manage the friendly shop in Piazza dei Martiri did not want to reveal the name of the artist. A pity. Whoever invented that anomalous mixture of photography and color has an avant-garde imagination that, with sublime ingenuity but also with unusual energy, subdues the material to the urgent needs of an intimate, potent grief." Otherwise, it had generous praise for the shoe store, "an important sign of the dynamism that, in recent years, has invested Neapolitan entre-preneurial endeavors."

I didn't sleep a wink.

After school I hurried to find Lila. The shop was empty,

Carmen had gone home to her mother, Giuseppina, who wasn't well, Lila was on the phone with a local supplier who had not delivered mozzarella or provolone or I don't remember what. I heard her shout, curse, I was upset. I thought maybe the man at the other end was old, he would be insulted, he would send one of his sons to take revenge. I thought: Why does she always overdo it? When she got off the phone she gave a snort of contempt and turned to me to apologize: "If I don't act like that, they won't even listen to me."

I showed her the newspaper. She gave it a distracted glance, said, "I know about it." She explained that it had been an initiative of Michele Solara's, carried out as usual without consulting anyone. Look, she said, and went to the cash register, took out of the drawer a couple of creased clippings, handed them to me. Those, too, were about the shop in Piazza dei Martiri. One was a small article in *Roma*, whose author lavished praise on the Solaras, but made not the slightest mention of the panel. The other was an article spread over three columns, in *Napoli Notte*, and in it the shop sounded like a royal palace. The space was described in an extravagant Italian that praised the furnishings, the splendid illumination, the marvelous shoes, and, above all, "the kindness, the sweetness, and the grace of the two seductive Nereids, Miss Gigliola Spagnuolo and Miss Giuseppina Carracci, marvelous young women upon whom rests the fate of an enterprise that stands high among the flourishing commercial activities of our city." You had to get to the end to find a mention of the panel, which was dismissed in a few lines. The author of the article called it "a crude mess, an out-of-tune note in a place of majestic refinement."

"Did you see the signature?" Lila asked, teasingly.

The article in *Roma* was signed "d.s." and the article in *Napoli Notte* bore the signature of Donato Sarratore, Nino's father.

"Yes."

"And what do you say?"

"What should I say?"

"Like father like son, you should say."

She laughed mirthlessly. She explained that, seeing the growing success of Cerullo shoes and the Solara shop, Michele had decided to publicize the business and had distributed a few gratuities here and there, thanks to which the city newspapers had promptly come out with admiring articles. Advertising, in other words. Paid for. Pointless even to read. In those articles, she said, there was not a single true word.

I was disappointed. I didn't like the way she belittled the newspapers, which I was diligently trying to read, sacrificing sleep. And I didn't like her emphasis on the relationship between Nino and the author of the two articles. What need was there to associate Nino with his father, a pompous fabricator of factitious phrases?

30.

Yet it was thanks to those phrases that in a short time the Solaras' shop and Cerullo shoes became more successful. Gigliola and Pinuccia boasted a lot about how they had been quoted in the papers, but the success did not diminish their rivalry and each went on to give herself the credit for the shop's fortunes, and began to consider the other an obstacle to further successes. On a single point they continued to agree: Lila's panel was an abomination. They were rude to anyone who, in a refined little voice, stopped in just to have a look at it. And they framed the articles from *Roma* and *Napoli Notte*, but not the one from *Il Mattino*.

Between Christmas and Easter, the Solaras and the Carraccis made a lot of money. Stefano, especially, drew a sigh of relief. The new grocery and the old one were prospering, the Cerullo shoe factory was working at full capacity. In addition, the shop in Piazza dei Martiri revealed what he had always known, and that is that the shoes Lila had designed years before sold well not only on the Rettifilo, Via Foria, and Corso Garibaldi but were coveted by the wealthy, those who casually reached for their wallets. An important market, therefore, which had to be consolidated and expanded.

As proof of that success, in the spring some good imitations of Cerullo shoes began to appear in the shopwindows of the outlying neighborhoods. These shoes were essentially identical to Lila's, but slightly modified by a fringe, a stud. Protests, threats immediately blocked their circulation: Michele Solara straightened things out. But he didn't stop there, he soon reached the conclusion that new models had to be designed. For that reason, one evening in the shop in Piazza dei Martiri, he summoned his brother Marcello, the Carraccis, Rino, and, naturally, Gigliola and Pinuccia. Surprisingly, Stefano showed up without Lila, he said that his wife was sorry, she was tired.

Her absence did not please the Solara brothers. If Lila isn't here, Michele said, making Gigliola nervous, what the fuck are we talking about. But Rino immediately interrupted. He asserted, lying, that he and his father had begun some time ago to think of new models and planned to introduce them at a trade show that was to be held in Arezzo in September. Michele didn't believe him, and became still more irritable. He said that they had to come out with products that were really innovative and not with normal stuff. Finally he turned to Stefano:

"Your wife is necessary, you've got to make her come."

Stefano answered with startling hostility: "My wife works hard all day in the grocery store and at night she has to stay home, she has to think of me."

"All right," Michele said, with a grimace, spoiling for a moment his handsome boy's face. "But see if she can think of us, too, a little."

The evening left everyone unhappy, but Pinuccia and Gigliola in particular. For different reasons, they found the importance that Michele gave Lila intolerable, and in the following days their disgruntlement became a dark mood that at the slightest opportunity gave rise to a quarrel.

At that point—I think it was March—an accident happened; I don't really know how. One afternoon, during one of their daily disagreements, Gigliola slapped Pinuccia. Pinuccia complained to Rino, who, believing at the time that he was riding the crest of a wave as high as a house, came to the shop with a proprietary air and told Gigliola off. Gigliola reacted aggressively and he went so far as to threaten to fire her.

"Starting tomorrow," he said to her, "you can go and stuff ricotta in the cannoli again."

Then Michele showed up. Smiling, he led Rino outside, to the square, to indicate the sign over the door.

"My friend," he said, "the shop is called Solara and you have no right to come here and tell my girlfriend: I'm firing you."

Rino retaliated by reminding him that everything in the shop belonged to his brother-in-law, and that he made the shoes himself, so he certainly did have the right. Inside, meanwhile, Gigliola and Pinuccia, each feeling protected by her own fiancé, had already started fighting again. The two young men hurried back inside, tried to calm them down, and couldn't. Michele lost patience and cried that he would fire them both. Not only that: he let slip that he would have Lila manage the shop.

Lila?

The shop?

The two girls were silent and the idea left even Rino speechless. Then the discussion started up again, this time focused on that outrageous statement. Gigliola, Pinuccia, and Rino were allied against Michele—what's wrong, what use to you is Lina, we're making money here, you can't complain, I thought up all the shoe styles, she was a child, what could she invent—and the tension increased. Who knows how long the quarreling would have gone on if the accident I mentioned hadn't happened. Suddenly, and it's unclear how, the panel—the panel with the strips of black paper, the photograph, the thick patches of color—let out a rasping sound, a kind of sick breath, and burst into flame. Pinuccia had her back to the photograph when it happened. The fire blazed up behind her as if from a secret hearth and licked her hair, which crackled and would have burned completely if Rino hadn't quickly extinguished it with his bare hands.

31.

Both Rino and Michele blamed Gigliola for the fire, because she smoked secretly and so had a tiny lighter. According to Rino, Gigliola had done it on purpose: while they were all occupied by their wrangling, she had set fire to the panel, which, loaded with paper, glue, paint, had instantly burst into flames. Michele was more circumspect: Gigliola, he knew, continuously toyed with the lighter and so, unintentionally, caught up in the argument, hadn't realized that the flame was too close to the photograph. But the girl couldn't bear either the first hypothesis or the second, and with a fiercely combative look blamed Lila herself, that is, she blamed the disfigured image, which had caught fire spontaneously, like the Devil, who, attempting to corrupt the saints, assumed the features of a woman, but the saints called on Jesus, and the demon was transformed into flames. She added, in confirmation of her version, that Pinuccia herself had told her that her sister-in-law had the ability not to stay pregnant, and, in fact, if she was unsuccessful she would let the child drain out, rejecting the gifts of the Lord.

This gossip grew worse when Michele Solara began to go regularly to the new grocery store. He spent a lot of time joking with Lila, joking with Carmen, so that Carmen hypothesized that he came for her and on the one hand was afraid that someone would tell Enzo, doing his military service in Piedmont, while on the other she was flattered and began to flirt. Lila instead made fun of the young Solara. She heard the rumors spread by his fiancée and so she said to him: "You'd better go, we're witches here, we're very dangerous."

But when I went to see her, during that period, I never found her truly cheerful. She assumed an artificial tone and was sarcastic about everything. Did she have a bruise on her arm? Stefano had caressed her too passionately. Were her eyes red from crying? Those were tears of happiness, not grief. Be careful of Michele, he liked to hurt people? No, she said, all he has to do is touch me and he'll burn: it's I who hurt people.

On that last point there had always been modest agreement. But Gigliola especially had no doubts by now: Lila was a witch-whore, she had cast a spell on her fiancé; that's why he wanted her to manage the shop in Piazza dei Martiri. And for days, jealous, desperate, she wouldn't go to work. Then she decided to talk to Pinuccia, they became allies, and moved to the offensive. Pinuccia worked on her brother, insisting that he was a happy cuckold, and then she attacked Rino, her fiancé, telling him that he wasn't a boss but Michele's servant. So one evening Stefano and Rino waited for Michele outside the bar, and when he appeared they made a very general speech that in substance, however, meant: leave Lila alone, you're making her waste time, she has to work. Michele immediately got the message and replied coldly:

"What the fuck are you saying?"

"If you don't understand it means you don't want to understand."

"No, my fine friends, it's you who don't want to understand

our commercial needs. And if you won't understand them, I necessarily have to see to them."

"Meaning?" Stefano asked.

"Your wife is wasted in the grocery."

"In what sense?"

"In Piazza dei Martiri she would make in a month what your sister and Gigliola couldn't make in a hundred years."

"Explain yourself."

"Lina needs to command, Ste'. She needs to have a responsibility. She should invent things. She ought to start thinking right away about the new shoe styles."

They argued and finally, amid a thousand fine distinctions, came to an agreement. Stefano absolutely refused to let his wife go and work in Piazza dei Martiri: the new grocery was going well and to take Lila out of there would be foolish; but he agreed to have her design new models right away, at least for winter. Michele said that not to let Lila run the shoe store was stupid, and with a vaguely threatening coolness he put off the discussion until after the summer; he considered it a done deal that she would start designing new shoes.

"They have to be chic," he urged, "you have to insist on that point."

"She'll do what she wants, as usual."

"I can advise her, she'll listen to me," said Michele.

"There's no need."

I went to see Lila shortly after that agreement, and she spoke to me about it herself. I had just come from school, the weather was already getting hot, and I was tired. She was alone in the grocery and for the moment she seemed as if relieved. She said that she wouldn't design anything, not even a sandal, not even a slipper.

"They'll get mad."

"What can I do about it?"

"It's money, Lila."

"They already have enough."

It was her usual sort of obstinacy, I thought. She was like that, as soon as someone told her to focus on something the wish to do so vanished. But I soon realized that it wasn't a matter of her character or even of disgust with the business affairs of her husband, Rino, and the Solaras, reinforced by the Communist arguments of Pasquale and Carmen. There was something more and she spoke slowly, seriously, about it.

"Nothing comes to mind," she said.

"Have you tried?"

"Yes. But it's not the way it was when I was twelve."

The shoes—I understood—had come out of her brain only that one time and they wouldn't again, she didn't have any others. That game was over, she didn't know how to start it again. The smell of leather repelled her, of skins, what she had done she no longer knew how to do. And then everything had changed. Fernando's small shop had been consumed by the new spaces, by the workers' benches, by three machines. Her father had as it were grown smaller, he didn't even quarrel with his oldest son, he worked and that was all. Even affections were as if deflated. If she still felt tender toward her mother when she came to the grocery to fill her shopping bags, free, as if they still lived in poverty, if she still gave little gifts to her younger siblings, she could no longer feel the bond with Rino. Ruined, broken. The need to help and protect him had diminished. Thus the motivations for the fantasy of the shoes had vanished, the soil in which they had germinated was arid. It was most of all, she said suddenly, a way of showing you that I could do something well even if I had stopped going to school. Then she laughed nervously, glancing obliquely at me to see my reaction.

I didn't answer, prevented by a strong emotion. Lila was like that? She didn't have my stubborn diligence? She drew out of herself thoughts, shoes, words written and spoken, complicated plans, rages and inventions, only to show *me* something of herself? Having lost that motivation, she was lost? Even the treatment to which she had subjected her wedding photograph—even that she would never be able to repeat? Everything, in her, was the result of the chaos of an occasion?

I felt that in some part of me a long painful tension was relaxing, and her wet eyes, her fragile smile moved me. But it didn't last. She continued to speak, she touched her forehead with a gesture that was customary with her, she said, regretfully, "I always have to prove that I can be better," and she added darkly, "When we opened this place, Stefano showed me how to cheat on the weight; and at first I shouted you're a thief, that's how you make money, and then I couldn't resist, I showed him that I had learned and immediately found my own ways to cheat and I showed him, and I was constantly thinking up new ones: I'll cheat you all, I cheat you on the weight and a thousand other things, I cheat the neighborhood, don't trust me, Lenù, don't trust what I say and do."

I was uneasy. In the space of a few seconds she had changed, already I no longer knew what she wanted. Why was she speaking to me like this now? I didn't know if she had decided to or if the words came out of her mouth unwittingly, an impetuous stream in which the intention of reinforcing the bond between us—a real intention—was immediately swept away by the equally real need to deny it specificity: you see, with Stefano I behave the way I do with you, I act like this with everyone, I'm beauty and the beast, good and evil. She interlaced her long thin fingers, clasped them tight, asked, "Did you hear that Gigliola says the photograph caught fire by itself?"

"It's stupid, Gigliola is mad at you."

She gave a little laugh that was like a shock, something in her twisted too abruptly.

"I have something that hurts here, behind the eyes, something is pressing. You see the knives there? They're too sharp—

I just gave them to the knife grinder. While I'm slicing salami I think how much blood there is in a person's body. If you put too much stuff in things, they break. Or they catch fire and burn. I'm glad the wedding picture burned. The marriage should burn, too, the shop, the shoes, the Solaras, everything."

I realized that, no matter how she struggled, worked, proclaimed, she couldn't get out of it: since the day of her wedding she had been pursued by an ever greater, increasingly ungovernable unhappiness, and I felt pity. I told her to be calm, she nodded yes.

"You have to try to relax."

"Help me."

"How."

"Stay near me."

"That's what I'm doing."

"It's not true. I tell you all my secrets, even the worst, you tell me hardly anything about yourself."

"You're wrong. The only person I don't hide anything from is you."

She shook her head no energetically, she said, "Even if you're better than me, even if you know more things, don't leave me."

32.

They pressured her, wearing her down, and so she pretended to give in. She told Stefano that she would design the new shoes, and at the first opportunity she also told Michele. Then she summoned Rino and spoke to him exactly as he had always wanted her to: "You design them, I can't. Design them with papa, you're in the business, you know how to do it. But until you put them on the market and sell them, don't tell anyone that I didn't do them, not even Stefano."

"And if they don't go well?"

"It will be my fault."

"And if they do well?"

"I'll say how things are and you'll get the credit you deserve."

Rino was very pleased with that lie. He set to work with Fernando, but every so often he went to Lila in complete secrecy to show her what he had in mind. She examined the styles and at first pretended to admire them, partly because she couldn't tolerate his anxious expression, partly to get rid of him quickly. But soon she herself marveled at how genuinely good the new shoes were—they resembled the ones now selling and yet were different. "Maybe," she said to me one day, in an unexpectedly lighthearted tone, "I really didn't think up those shoes, they really are my brother's work." And at that point she truly did seem to be rid of a weight. She rediscovered her affection for Rino, or rather she realized that she had exaggerated: that bond couldn't be dissolved, it would never be dissolved, whatever he did, even if a rat came out of his body, a skittish horse, any sort of animal. The lie—she hypothesized—has relieved Rino of the anxiety of being inadequate, and that has taken him back to the way he was as a boy, and now he is discovering that he knows his job, that he's good at it. As for Rino himself, he was increasingly satisfied with his sister's praise. At the end of every consultation, he asked in a whisper for the house key and, also in complete secrecy, went to spend an hour there with Pinuccia.

For my part, I tried to show her that I would always be her friend, and on Sundays I often invited her to go out with me. Once we ventured as far as the Mostra d'Oltremare neighborhood with two of my schoolmates, who were intimidated, however, when they found out that she had been married for more than a year, and behaved respectfully, sedately, as if I had compelled them to go out with my mother. One asked her hesitantly:

"Do you have a child?"

Lila shook her head no.

"They haven't come?"

She shook her head no.

From that moment on the evening was more or less a failure.

In mid-May I dragged her to a cultural club where, because Professor Galiani had urged me to, I felt obliged to go to a talk by a scientist named Giuseppe Montalenti. It was the first time we had had an experience of that type: Montalenti gave a kind of lesson, not for children but, rather, for the adults who had come to hear him. We sat at the back of the bare room and I was quickly bored. The professor had sent me but she hadn't shown up. I murmured to Lila, "Let's go." But Lila refused, she whispered that she wasn't bold enough to get up, she was afraid of disrupting the lecture. But it wasn't her type of worry; it was the sign of an unexpected submissiveness, or of an interest that she didn't want to admit. We stayed till the end. Montalenti talked about Darwin; neither of us knew who Darwin was. As we left, I said jokingly, "He said a thing that I already knew: you're a monkey."

But she didn't want to joke: "I don't want to ever forget it," she said.

"That you're a monkey?"

"That we're animals."

"You and I?"

"Everyone."

"But he said there are a lot of differences between us and the apes."

"Yes? Like what? That my mother pierced my ears and so I've worn earrings since I was born, but the mothers of monkeys don't, so their offspring don't wear earrings?"

A fit of laughter possessed us, as we listed differences, one after the other, each more ridiculous than the last: we were enjoying ourselves. But when we returned to the neighborhood our good mood vanished. We met Pasquale and Ada taking a walk on the *stradone* and learned from them that Stefano was looking everywhere for Lila, very upset. I offered to go home with her, she refused. Instead she agreed to let Pasquale and Ada take her in the car.

I found out the next day why Stefano had been looking for her. It wasn't because we were late. It wasn't even because he was annoyed that his wife sometimes spent her free time with me and not with him. It was something else. He had just learned that Pinuccia was often seen with Rino at his house. He had just learned that the two were together in his bed, that Lila gave them the keys. He had just learned that Pinuccia was pregnant. But what had most infuriated him was that when he slapped his sister because of the disgusting things she and Rino had done, Pinuccia shouted at him, "You're jealous because I'm a woman and Lina isn't, because Rino knows how to behave with women and you don't." Lila, seeing him so upset, listening to him—and recalling the composure he had always shown when they were engaged—had burst out laughing, and Stefano had gone for a drive, so as not to murder her. According to her, he had gone to look for a prostitute.

33.

The preparations for Rino and Pinuccia's wedding were carried out in a rush. I was not much concerned with it, I had my final class essays, the final oral exams. And then something else happened that caused me great agitation. Professor Galiani, who was in the habit of violating the teachers' code of behavior with indifference, invited me—me and no one else in the school—to her house, to a party that her children were giving. It was unusual enough that she lent me books and newspapers, that she had directed me to a march for peace and a demanding lecture. Now she had gone over the limit: she had taken me aside and given me that invitation. "Come as you like," she had said, "alone or with someone, with your boyfriend or without: the important thing is to come." Like that, a few days before the end of the school year, without worrying about how much I had to study, without worrying about the earthquake that it set off inside me.

I had immediately said yes, but I quickly discovered that I would never have the courage to go. A party at any professor's house was unthinkable, imagine at the house of Professor Galiani. For me it was as if I were to present myself at the royal palace, curtsey to the queen, dance with the princes. A great pleasure but also an act of violence, like a yank: to be dragged by the arm, forced to do a thing that, although it appeals to you, you know is not suitable—you know that, if circumstances did not oblige you, you would happily avoid doing it. Probably it didn't even occur to Professor Galiani that I had nothing to wear. In class I wore a shapeless black smock. What did she expect there was, the professor, under that smock: clothes and slips and underwear like hers? There was inadequacy, rather, there was poverty, poor breeding. I possessed a single pair of worn-out shoes. My only nice dress was the one I had worn to Lila's wedding, but now it was hot, the dress was fine for March but not for the end of May. And yet the problem was not just what to wear. There was the solitude, the awkwardness of being among strangers, kids with ways of talking among themselves, joking, with tastes I didn't know. I thought of asking Alfonso if he would go with me, he was always kind to me. But—I recalled—Alfonso was a schoolmate and Professor Galiani had addressed the invitation to me alone. What to do? For days I was paralyzed by anxiety, I thought of talking to the professor and coming up with some excuse. Then it occurred to me to ask Lila's advice.

She was as usual in a difficult period, she had a yellow bruise under one cheekbone. She didn't welcome the news.

"Why are you going there?"

"She invited me."

"Where does this professor live?"

"Corso Vittorio Emanuele."

"Can you see the sea from her house?"

"I don't know."

"What does her husband do?"

"A doctor at the Cotugno."

"And the children are still in school?"

"I don't know."

"Do you want one of my dresses?"

"You know they don't fit me."

"You just have a bigger bust."

"Everything of me is bigger, Lila."

"Then I don't know what to tell you."

"I shouldn't go?"

"It's better."

"O.K., I won't go."

She was visibly satisfied with that decision. I said goodbye, left the grocery, turned onto a street where stunted oleander bushes grew. But I heard her calling me, I turned back.

"I'll go with you," she said.

"Where?"

"To the party."

"Stefano won't let you."

"We'll see. Tell me if you want to take me or not."

"Of course I want to."

She became at that point so pleased that I didn't dare try to make her change her mind. But already on the way home I felt that my situation had become worse. None of the obstacles that prevented me from going to the party had been removed, and that offer of Lila's confused me even more. The reasons

were tangled and I had no intention of enumerating them, but
if I had I would have been confronted by contradictory statements. I was afraid that Stefano wouldn't let her come. I was
afraid that Stefano would let her. I was afraid that she would
dress in an ostentatious fashion, the way she had when she
went to the Solaras. I was afraid that, whatever she wore, her
beauty would explode like a star and everyone would be eager
to grab a fragment of it. I was afraid that she would express herself in dialect, that she would say something vulgar, that it
would become obvious that school for her had ended with an
elementary-school diploma. I was afraid that, if she merely
opened her mouth, everyone would be hypnotized by her intelligence and Professor Galiani herself would be entranced. I
was afraid that the professor would find her both presumptuous and naïve and would say to me: Who is this friend of yours,
stop seeing her. I was afraid she would understand that I was
only Lila's pale shadow and would be interested not in me any
longer but in her, she would want to see her again, she would
undertake to make her go back to school.

For a while I avoided the grocery. I hoped that Lila would
forget about the party, that the day would come and I would
go almost secretly, and then I would tell her: you didn't let me
know. Instead she soon came to see me, which she hadn't done
for a long time. She had persuaded Stefano not only to take us
but also to come and get us, and she wanted to know what time
we were to be at the professor's house.

"What are you going to wear?" I asked anxiously.

"Whatever you wear."

"I'm going to wear a blouse and skirt."

"Then I will, too."

"And Stefano is sure that he'll take us and then come and
get us?"

"Yes."

"How did you persuade him?"

She made a face, cheerfully, saying that by now she knew how to handle him. "If I want something," she whispered, as if she herself didn't want to hear, "I just have to act a little like a whore."

She said it like that, in dialect, and added other crude, self-mocking expressions, to make me understand the revulsion her husband provoked in her, the disgust she felt at herself. My anxiety increased. I should tell her, I thought, that I'm not going to the party, I should tell her that I changed my mind. I knew, naturally, that behind the appearance of the disciplined Lila, at work from morning to night, there was a Lila who was anything but submissive; yet, in particular now that I was assuming the responsibility of introducing her into the house of Professor Galiani, the recalcitrant Lila frightened me, seemed to me increasingly spoiled by her very refusal to surrender. What would happen if, in the presence of the professor, something made her rebel? What would happen if she decided to use the language she had just used with me? I said cautiously:

"There, please, don't talk like that."

She looked at me in bewilderment. "Like what?"

"Like now."

She was silent for a moment, then she asked, "Are you ashamed of me?"

34.

I wasn't ashamed of her, I swore it, but I hid from her the fact that I was afraid of having to be ashamed of myself for it.

Stefano took us in the convertible to the professor's house. I sat in the back, the two of them in front, and for the first time I was struck by the massive wedding rings on their hands, his and hers. While Lila wore a skirt and blouse, as she had promised, nothing excessive, and no makeup except some lipstick, he was dressed up, with a lot of gold, and a strong odor of shaving soap, as if he expected that at the last moment we would say to him: You come, too. We didn't. I confined myself to thanking him warmly several times, Lila got out of the car without saying goodbye. Stefano drove off with a painful screeching of tires.

We were tempted by the elevator, but then decided against it. We had never taken an elevator, not even Lila's new building had one, we were afraid of getting in trouble. Professor Galiani had said that her apartment was on the fourth floor, that on the door it said "Dott. Prof. Frigerio," but just the same we checked the name plates on every floor. I went ahead, Lila behind, in silence, flight after flight. How clean the building was, the doorknobs and the brass nameplates gleamed. My heart was pounding.

We identified the door first of all by the loud music coming from it, by the din of voices. We smoothed our skirts, I pulled down the slip that tended to rise up my legs, Lila straightened her hair with her fingertips. Both of us, evidently, were afraid of escaping ourselves, of erasing in a moment of distraction the mask of self-possession we had given ourselves. I pressed the bell. We waited, no one came to the door. I looked at Lila, I pressed the button again, longer. Quick footsteps, the door opened. A dark young man appeared, small in stature, with a handsome face and a lively gaze. He appeared to be around twenty. I said nervously that I was a student of Professor Galiani, and without even letting me finish, he laughed, exclaimed, "Elena?"

"Yes."

"In this house we all know you, our mother never misses a chance to torment us by reading us your papers."

The boy's name was Armando and that remark of his was decisive, it gave me a sudden sense of power. I still remember him fondly, there in the doorway. He was absolutely the first person to show me in a practical sense how comfortable it is to arrive in a strange, potentially hostile environment, and discover that you have been preceded by your reputation, that you don't have to do anything to be accepted, that your name is known, that everyone knows about you, and it's the others, the strangers, who must strive to win your favor and not you theirs. Used as I was to the absence of advantages, that unforeseen advantage gave me energy, an immediate self-confidence. My anxieties disappeared, I no longer worried about what Lila could or couldn't do. In the grip of my unexpected centrality, I even forgot to introduce my friend to Armando, nor, on the other hand, did he seem to notice her. He led me in as if I were alone, enthusiastically insisting on how much his mother talked about me, on how she praised me. I followed, self-deprecatingly, Lila closed the door.

The apartment was big, the rooms open and bright, the ceilings high and decorated with floral motifs. What struck me most was the books everywhere, there were more books in that house than in the neighborhood library, entire walls covered by floor-to-ceiling shelves. And music. And young people dancing freely in a large, brilliantly lighted room. And others talking, smoking. All of whom obviously went to school, and had parents who had gone to school. Like Armando: his mother a teacher, his father a surgeon, though he wasn't there that evening. The boy led us onto a small terrace: warm air, large sky, an intense odor of wisteria and roses mixed with that of vermouth and marzipan. We saw the city sparkling with lights, the dark plane of the sea. The professor called my name in greeting, it was she who reminded me of Lila behind me.

"Is she a friend of yours?"

I stammered something, I realized that I didn't know how to make introductions. "My professor. Her name is Lina. We went to elementary school together," I said. Professor Galiani spoke approvingly of long friendships, they're important, an anchorage, generic phrases uttered as she stared at Lila, who responded self-consciously in monosyllables, and who, when she realized that the professor's gaze had come to rest on the wedding ring, immediately covered it with her other hand.

"Are you married?"

"Yes."

"You're the same age as Elena?"

"I'm two weeks older."

Professor Galiani looked around, turned to her son: "Have you introduced them to Nadia?"

"No."

"What are you waiting for?"

"Take it easy, Mamma, they just got here."

The professor said to me, "Nadia is really eager to meet you. This fellow here is a rascal, don't trust him, but she's a good girl, you'll see, you'll be friends, she'll like you."

We left her alone to smoke. Nadia, I understood, was Armando's younger sister: sixteen years of being a pain in the ass—he described her with feigned animosity—she ruined my childhood. I jokingly alluded to the trouble that my younger sister and brothers had always given me, and I turned to Lila for confirmation, smiling. But she remained serious, she said nothing. We returned to the room with the dancers, which had darkened. A Paul Anka song, or maybe "What a Sky," who can remember anymore. The dancers held each other close, faint flickering shadows. The music ended. Even before someone reluctantly switched on the lights, I felt an explosion in my chest, I recognized Nino Sarratore. He was lighting a cigarette, the flame leaped up into his face. I hadn't seen him for almost a year, he seemed to me older, taller, more disheveled, more handsome. Meanwhile the electric light flooded the room and I also recognized the girl he had just stopped dancing with. She was the same girl I had seen long ago outside school, the refined, luminous girl, who had compelled me to comprehend my dullness.

"Here she is," said Armando.

It was Nadia, the daughter of Professor Galiani.

35.

Odd as it may seem, that discovery did not spoil the pleasure of finding myself there, in that house, among respectable people. I loved Nino, I had no doubt, I never had any doubt about that. And of course I should have suffered in the face of further proof that I would never have him. But I didn't. That he had a girlfriend, that the girlfriend was in every way better than me, I already knew. The novelty was that it was the daughter of Professor Galiani, who had grown up in that house, among those books. I immediately felt that the thing, instead of grieving me, calmed me, further justified their choosing each other, made it an inevitable movement, in harmony with the natural order of things. In other words, I felt as if suddenly I had before my eyes an example of symmetry so perfect that I had to enjoy it in silence.

But it wasn't only that. As soon as Armando said to his sister, "Nadia, this is Elena, mamma's student," the girl blushed and impetuously threw her arms around my neck, murmuring, "Elena, how happy I am to meet you." Then, without giving me time to say a single word, she went on to praise, without her brother's mocking tone, what I had written and how I wrote, in tones of such enthusiasm that I felt the way I did when her mother read a theme of mine in class. Or maybe it was even better, because there, present, listening to her, were the people I most cared about, Nino and Lila, and both could observe that in that house I was loved and respected.

I adopted a friendly demeanor that I had never considered

myself capable of, I immediately engaged in casual conversation, I came out with a fine, cultured Italian that didn't feel artificial, like the language I used at school. I asked Nino about his trip to England, I asked Nadia what books she was reading, what music she liked. I danced with Armando, with others, without a pause, even to a rock-and-roll song, during which my glasses flew off my nose but didn't break. A miraculous evening. At one point I saw that Nino exchanged a few words with Lila, invited her to dance. But she refused; she left the dancing room, and I lost sight of her. A long time passed before I remembered my friend. It took the slow waning of the dances, a passionate discussion between Armando, Nino, and a couple of other boys their age, a move, along with Nadia, to the terrace, partly because of the heat and partly to bring into the discussion Professor Galiani, who had stayed by herself, smoking and enjoying the cool air. "Come on," Armando said, taking me by the hand. I said, "I'll get my friend," and I freed myself. All hot, I went through the rooms looking for Lila. I found her alone in front of a wall of books.

"Come on, let's go out on the terrace," I said.

"To do what?"

"Cool off, talk."

"You go."

"Are you bored?"

"No, I'm looking at the books."

"See how many there are?"

"Yes."

I felt she was unhappy. Because she had been neglected. Fault of the wedding ring, I thought. Or maybe her beauty isn't recognized here, Nadia's counts more. Or perhaps it's she who, although she has a husband, has been pregnant, had a miscarriage, designed shoes, can make money—she who doesn't know who she is in this house, doesn't know how to be appreciated, the way she is in the neighborhood. I do. Suddenly I felt that the state of suspension that had begun the day of her wedding was over. I knew how to be with these people, I felt more at ease than I did with my friends in the neighborhood. The only anxiety was what Lila was provoking now by her withdrawal, by remaining on the margins. I drew her away from the books, dragged her onto the terrace.

While many of the guests were still dancing, a small group had formed around the professor, three or four boys and two girls. Only the boys talked. The sole woman who took part, and she did so with irony, was the professor. I saw right away that the older boys, Nino, Armando and one called Carlo, found it somehow improper to argue with her. They wished mainly to challenge each other, considering her the authority, bestower of the palm of victory. Armando expressed opinions contrary to his mother's but in fact he was addressing Nino. Carlo agreed with the professor but in refuting the others he strove to separate his arguments from hers. And Nino, politely disagreeing with the professor, contradicted Armando, contradicted Carlo. I listened spellbound. Their words were buds that blossomed in my mind into more or less familiar flowers, and then I flared up, mimicking participation; or they manifested forms unknown to me, and I retreated, to hide my ignorance. In this second case, however, I became nervous: I don't know what they're talking about, I don't know who this person is, I don't understand. They were sounds without sense, they demonstrated that the world of persons, events, ideas was endless, and the reading I did at night had not been sufficient, I would have to work even harder in order to be able to say to Nino, to Professor Galiani, to Carlo, to Armando: Yes, I understand, I know. The entire planet is threatened. Nuclear war. Colonialism, neocolonialism. The pieds-noirs, the O.A.S. and the National Liberation Front. The fury of mass slaughters. Gaullism, Fascism. France, Armée, Grandeur, Honneur. Sartre is a pessimist, but he counts on the Communist workers in Paris. The wrong direction taken by

France, by Italy. Opening to the left. Saragat, Nenni. Fanfani in London, Macmillan. The Christian Democratic congress in our city. The followers of Fanfani, Moro, the Christian Democratic left. The socialists have ended up in the jaws of power. We will be Communists, we with our proletariat and our parliamentarians, to get the laws of the center left passed. If it goes like that, a Marxist-Leninist party will become a social democracy. Did you see how Leone behaved at the start of the academic year? Armando shook his head in disgust: Planning isn't going to change the world, it will take blood, it will take violence. Nino responded calmly: Planning is an indispensable tool. The talk was tense, Professor Galiani kept the boys at bay. How much they knew, they were masters of the earth. At some point Nino mentioned America favorably, he said words in English as if he were English. I noticed that in the space of a year his voice had grown stronger, it was thick, almost hoarse, and he used it less rigidly than he had at Lila's wedding and, later, at school. He even spoke of Beirut as if he had been there, and Danilo Dolci and Martin Luther King and Bertrand Russell. He appeared to support an organization he called the World Brigade for Peace and rebuked Armando when he referred to it sarcastically. Then he grew excited, his voice rose. Ah, how handsome he was. He said that the world had the technical capability to eliminate colonialism, hunger, war from the face of the earth. I was overwhelmed by emotion as I listened, and, although I felt lost in the midst of a thousand things I didn't know—what were Gaullism, the O.A.S., social democracy, the opening to the left; who were Danilo Dolci, Bertrand Russell, the pieds-noirs, the followers of Fanfani; and what had happened in Beirut, what in Algeria—I felt the need, as I had long ago, to take care of him, to tend to him, to protect him, to sustain him in everything that he would do in the course of his life. It was the only moment of the evening when I felt envious of Nadia, who stood beside him like a minor but radiant divinity. Then I heard myself utter sentences as if it were not I who had decided to do so, as if another person, more assured, more informed, had decided to speak through my mouth. I began without knowing what I would say, but, hearing the boys, fragments of phrases read in Galiani's books and newspapers stirred in my mind, and the desire to speak, to make my presence felt, became stronger than timidity. I used the elevated Italian I had practiced in making translations from Greek and Latin. I was on Nino's side. I said I didn't want to live in a world at war. We mustn't repeat the mistakes of the generations that preceded us, I said. Today we should make war on the atomic arsenals, should make war on war itself. If we allow the use of those weapons, we will all become even guiltier than the Nazis. Ah, how moved I was, as I spoke: I felt tears coming to my eyes. I concluded by saying that the world urgently needed to be changed, that there were too many tyrants who kept peoples enslaved. But it should be changed by peaceful means.

I don't know if everyone appreciated me. Armando seemed unhappy and a blond girl whose name I didn't know stared at me with a small, mocking smile. But as I was speaking Nino nodded at me in agreement. And when Professor Galiani, just afterward, gave her opinion, she referred to me twice, and it was thrilling to hear, "As Elena rightly said." It was Nadia, though, who did the most wonderful thing. She left Nino and came over and whispered in my ear: "How clever you are, how brave." Lila, who was next to me, didn't say a word. But while the professor was still talking to me she gave me a tug and whispered, in dialect, "I'm falling asleep on my feet, find out where the telephone is and call Stefano?"

36.

How much that evening had hurt her I learned later from

her notebooks. She admitted that she had asked to go with me. She admitted she had thought she could at least for one evening get away from the grocery and be comfortable with me, share in that sudden widening of my world, meet Professor Galiani, talk to her. She admitted she thought she would find a way of making a good impression. She admitted she had been sure she would be attractive to the males, she always was. Instead she immediately felt voiceless, graceless, deprived of movement, of beauty. She listed details: even when we were next to each other, people chose to speak only to me; they had brought me pastries, a drink, no one had done anything for her; Armando had shown me a family portrait, something from the seventeenth century, he had talked to me about it for a quarter of an hour; she had been treated as if she weren't capable of understanding. They didn't want her. They didn't want to know anything about what sort of person she was. That evening for the first time it had become clear to her that her life would forever be Stefano, the grocery stores, the marriage of her brother and Pinuccia, the conversations with Pasquale and Carmen, the petty war with the Solaras. This she had written, and more, maybe that very night, maybe in the morning, in the store. There, for the entire evening, she had felt irrefutably lost.

But in the car, as we returned to the neighborhood, she didn't allude in the slightest to her feeling, she just became mean, treacherous. She began as soon as she got in the car, when her husband asked resentfully if we had had a good time. I let her answer, I was dazed by the effort, by excitement, by pleasure. And then she went on slowly to hurt me. She said in dialect that she had never been so bored in her life. It would have been better if we'd gone to a movie, she apologized to her husband, and—it was unusual, done evidently on purpose to wound me, to remind me: See, good or bad I have a man, while you've got nothing, you're a virgin, you know everything but

you don't know anything about this—she caressed the hand
that he kept on the gear shift. Even watching television, she
said, would have been more entertaining than spending time
with those disgusting people. There's not a thing there, an
object, a painting, that was acquired by them directly. The furniture is from a hundred years ago. The house is at least three
hundred years old. The books yes, some are new, but others
are very old, they're so dusty they haven't been opened since
who knows when, old law books, history, science, politics.
They've read and studied in that house, fathers, grandfathers,
great-grandfathers. For hundreds of years they've been, at the
least, lawyers, doctors, professors. So they all talk just so, so
they dress and eat and move just so. They do it because they
were born there. But in their heads they don't have a thought
that's their own, that they struggled to think. They know everything and they don't know a thing. She kissed her husband on
the neck, she smoothed his hair with her fingertips. If you were
up there, Ste', all you'd see is parrots going *cocorico, cocorico*.
You couldn't understand a word of what they were saying and
they didn't even understand each other. You know what the
O.A.S. is, you know what the opening to the left is? Next time,
Lenù, don't take me, take Pasquale, I'll show you, he'll put
them in their place in a flash. Chimpanzees that piss and shit
in the toilet instead of on the ground, and that's why they give
themselves a lot of airs, and they say they know what should be
done in China and in Albania and in France and in Katanga.
You, too, Lenù, I have to tell you: Look out, or you'll be the
parrots' parrot. She turned to her husband, laughing. You
should have heard her, she said. She made a little voice,
cheechee, cheechee. Show Stefano how you speak to those people? You and Sarratore's son: the same. *The world brigade for
peace; we have the technical capability; hunger, war.* But do you
really work that hard in school so you can say things just like
he does? *Whoever finds a solution to the problems is working*

for peace. Bravo. Do you remember how the son of Sarratore was able to find a solution: Do you remember, do you—and you pay attention to him? You, too, you want to be a puppet from the neighborhood who performs so you can be welcomed into the home of those people? You want to leave us alone in our own shit, cracking our skulls, while all of you go *cocorico cocorico*, hunger, war, working class, peace?

She was so spiteful, all the way home along Corso Vittorio Emanuele, that I was silent, and felt the poison that was transforming what had seemed to me an important moment of my life into a false step that had made me ridiculous. I struggled not to believe her. I felt she was truly hostile and capable of anything. She knew how to set the nerves of good people alight, in their breasts she kindled the fire of destruction. I felt that Gigliola and Pinuccia were right: it was she herself who in the photograph had blazed up like the devil. I hated her, and even Stefano noticed, and when he stopped at the gate and let me out on his side he said, "Bye, Lenù, good night, Lina's joking," and I muttered "Bye," and went in. Only when the car had left did I hear Lila shouting at me, re-creating the voice that in her view I had deliberately assumed at the Galiani house: "Bye, hey, bye."

37.

That night began the long, painful period that led to our first break and a long separation.

I had trouble recovering. There had been a thousand causes of tension up until that moment; her unhappiness and, at the same time, her yearning to dominate were constantly surfacing. But never, ever, ever had she so explicitly set out to humiliate me. I stopped dropping in at the grocery. Although she had paid for my schoolbooks, although we had made that bet, I didn't tell her that I had passed with all A's and two A-pluses. Just after school ended, I started working in a bookstore on Via Mezzocannone, and I disappeared from the neighborhood without telling her. The memory of the sarcastic tone of that night, instead of fading, became magnified, and my resentment, too, increased. It seemed to me that nothing could justify what she had done to me. It never occurred to me, as, in fact, it had on other occasions, that she had felt the need to humiliate me in order to better endure her own humiliation.

I soon had confirmation that I really had made a good impression at the party, and that made the separation easier. I was wandering along Via Mezzocannone during my lunch break when I heard someone call me. It was Armando, on his way to take an exam. I learned that he was studying medicine and that the exam was difficult but, just the same, before vanishing in the direction of San Domenico Maggiore, he stopped to talk, piling on compliments and starting in again on politics. In the evening he showed up in the bookstore, he'd gotten a high mark, and was happy. He asked for my telephone number, I said I didn't have a telephone; he asked if we could go for a walk the following Sunday, I said that on Sunday I had to help my mother in the house. He started talking about Latin America, where he intended to go right after graduating, to treat the destitute, and persuade them to take up arms against their oppressors, and he went on for so long that I had to send him away before the owner got irritated. In other words, I was pleased because he obviously liked me, and I was polite, but not available. Lila's words had indeed done damage. My clothes were wrong, my hair was wrong, my tone of voice was false, I was ignorant. Besides, with the end of school, and without Professor Galiani, I had lost the habit of reading the newspapers and, partly because money was tight, I didn't want to buy them out of my own pocket. Thus Naples, Italy, the world quickly went back to being a foggy terrain in which I could no longer orient myself. Armando talked, I nodded yes, but I understood little of what he was saying.

The next day there was another surprise. While I was sweeping the floor of the bookstore, Nino and Nadia appeared. They had heard from Armando where I worked and had come just to say hello. They invited me to go to the movies with them the following Sunday. I had to answer as I had answered Armando: it wasn't possible, I worked all week, and my mother and father wanted me home on my day off.

"But a little walk in the neighborhood—you could do that?"

"That, yes."

"So we'll come see you."

Since the owner was calling for me more impatiently than usual—he was a man of around sixty, the skin on his face seemed dirty, he was irascible, and had a dissolute look—they left right away.

Late in the morning on the following Sunday, I heard someone calling from the courtyard and I recognized Nino's voice. I looked out, he was alone. I quickly tried to make myself presentable and, without even telling my mother, happy and at the same time anxious, I ran down. When I found myself before him I could hardly breathe. "I only have ten minutes," I said, and we didn't go out to walk along the *stradone*, but wandered among the houses. Why had he come without Nadia? Why had he come all the way here if she couldn't? He answered my questions without my asking. Some relatives of Nadia's father were visiting and she had been obliged to stay home. He had wanted to see the neighborhood again but also to bring me something to read, the latest issue of a journal called *Cronache Meridionali*. He handed me the issue with a petulant gesture, I thanked him, and he started, incongruously, to criticize the review, and so I asked why he had decided to give it to me. "It's rigid," he said, and added, laughing, "Like Professor Galiani and Armando." Then he turned serious, he assumed a tone that was like an old man's. He said that he owed a great deal to our professor, that without her the period of high school would have been a waste of time, but that you had to be on guard, keep her at a distance. "Her greatest defect," he said emphatically, "is that she can't bear for someone to have an opinion different from hers. Take from her everything she can give you, but then go your own way." Then he returned to the review, he said that Galiani also wrote for it and suddenly, with no connection, he mentioned Lila: "Then, if possible, have her read it, too." I didn't tell him that Lila no longer read anything, that now she was Signora Carracci, that she had kept only her meanness from when she was a child. I was evasive, and asked about Nadia, he told me that she was taking a long car trip with her family, to Norway, and then would spend the rest of the summer in Anacapri, where her father had a family house.

"Will you go and see her?"

"Once or twice—I have to study."

"How's your mother?"

"Very well. She's going back to Barano this year, she's made up with the woman who owns the house."

"Will you go on vacation with your family?"

"I? With my father? Never ever. I'll be on Ischia but on my own."

"Where are you going?"

"I have a friend who has a house in Forio: his parents leave it to him for the whole summer, and we'll stay there and study. You?"

"I'm working at Mezzocannone until September."

"Even during the mid-August holiday?"

"No, for the holiday, no."

He smiled. "Then come to Forio, the house is big. Maybe Nadia will come for two or three days."

I smiled, nervously. To Forio? To Ischia? To a house without adults? Did he remember the Maronti? Did he remember that we had kissed there? I said I had to go in. "I'll stop by again," he promised. "I want to know what you think of the review." He added, in a low voice, his hands stuck in his pockets, "I like talking to you."

He had talked a lot, in fact. I was proud, thrilled, that he had felt comfortable. I murmured, "Me, too," although I had said little or nothing, and was about to go in when something happened that disturbed us both. A cry cut the Sunday quiet of the courtyard and I saw Melina at the window, waving her arms, trying to attract our attention. When Nino also turned to look, perplexed, Melina cried even louder, a mixture of joy and anguish. She cried, Donato.

"Who is it?" Nino asked.

"Melina," I said, "do you remember?"

He made a grimace of uneasiness. "Is she angry with me?"

"I don't know."

"She's saying Donato."

"Yes."

He turned again to look toward the window where the widow was leaning out, repeatedly calling that name.

"Do you think I look like my father?"

"No."

"Sure?"

"Yes."

He said nervously, "I'll go."

"You'd better."

He left quickly, shoulders bent, while Melina cried louder and louder, increasingly agitated: Donato, Donato, Donato.

I also escaped, I went home with my heart pounding, and a thousand tangled thoughts. Not a single feature of Nino's connected him to Sarratore: not his height, not his face, not his manners, not even his voice or his gaze. He was an anomalous, sweet fruit. How fascinating he was with his long, untidy hair.

How different from any other male form: in all Naples there was no one who resembled him. And he had respect for me, even if I still had my last year of high school to do and he was going to the university. He had come all the way to the neighborhood on a Sunday. He had been worried about me, he had come to put me on my guard. He had wanted to warn me that Professor Galiani was all well and good but even she had her flaws, and meanwhile he had brought me that journal in the conviction that I had the capacity to read it and discuss it, and he had even gone so far as to invite me to Ischia, to Forio, for the August holiday. Something impractical, not a real invitation, he himself knew perfectly well that my parents were not like Nadia's, they would never let me go; and yet he had invited me just the same, because in the words he said I heard other words, unsaid, like *I care a lot about seeing you, how I'd like to return to our talks at the Port, at the Maronti.* Yes, yes, I heard myself shouting in my head, I'd like it, too, I'll join you, in August I'll run away, no matter what.

I hid the review among my books. But at night, as soon as I was in bed, I looked at the table of contents and was startled. There was an article by Nino. An article by him in that very serious-looking magazine: almost a book, not the faded gray student magazine in which, two years earlier, he had suggested publishing my account of the priest, but important pages written by adults for adults. And yet there he was, Antonio Sarratore, name and last name. And I knew him. And he was only two years older than me.

I read, I didn't understand much, I reread. The article talked about Planning with a capital "P," Plan with a capital "P," and it was written in a complicated style. But it was a piece of his intelligence, a piece of his person, that, without boasting, quietly, he had given to me.

To me.

Tears came to my eyes, it was late when I put the magazine

down. Talk about it to Lila? Lend it to her? No, it was mine. I didn't want to have a real friendship with her anymore, just hello, trite phrases. She didn't know how to appreciate me. Whereas others did: Armando, Nadia, Nino. They were my friends, to them I owed my confidences. They had immediately seen in me what she had hastened not to see. Because she had the gaze of the neighborhood. She was able to see only the way Melina did, who, locked in her madness, saw Donato in Nino, took him for her former lover.

38.

At first I didn't want to go to Pinuccia and Rino's wedding, but Pinuccia came herself to bring me the invitation and since she treated me with exaggerated affection, and in fact asked my advice about many things, I didn't know how to say no, even though she didn't extend the invitation to the rest of my family. It's not me who's discourteous, she apologized, but Stefano. Not only had her brother refused to give her any of the family's money so that she could buy a house (he had told her that the investments he had made in the shoes and in the new grocery had left him broke) but, since it was he who had to pay for the wedding dress, the photographer, and the refreshments, he had personally removed half the neighborhood from the guest list. It was extremely rude behavior, and Rino was even more embarrassed than she was. His bride would have liked a wedding as lavish as his sister's and a new house, like hers, with a view of the railroad. Although he was by now the proprietor of a shoe factory, he couldn't manage with his own resources, but it was partly because he was a spendthrift; he had just bought a Fiat 1100, he didn't have a lira left. And so, after a lot of resistance, they had agreed to go and live in Don Achille's old house, evicting Maria from the bedroom. They intended to save as much as possible and, as soon as they could, buy an apartment nicer than Stefano and Lila's. My brother is a shit, Pinuccia said in conclusion, bitterly: when it comes to his wife he throws his money around, while for his sister he doesn't have a cent.

I avoided any comment. I went to the wedding with Marisa and Alfonso; he seemed to be just waiting for these worldly occasions to become someone else, not my usual classmate but a young man graceful in manner and appearance, with black hair, a heavy bluish beard showing on his cheeks, languid eyes, a suit that wasn't ill-fitting, as happened to other men, but showed off his slender yet sculpted body.

In the hope that Nino would be obliged to take his sister, I had very carefully studied his article and all of *Cronache Meridionali*. But by now Alfonso was Marisa's knight, he went to pick her up, he brought her home, and Nino didn't appear. I stayed close to the two of them, I wanted to avoid being alone with Lila.

In the church I glimpsed her in the first row, between Stefano and Maria; she was so beautiful, it was impossible to avoid looking at her. Later, at the wedding lunch, in the same restaurant on Via Orazio where her own reception was held, scarcely more than a year earlier, we met just once and exchanged wary words. Then I ended up at a table over on the side, with Alfonso, Marisa, and a fair-haired boy around thirteen, while she sat with Stefano at the bride and bridegroom's table, with the important guests. How many things had changed in a short time. Antonio wasn't there, Enzo wasn't there, both still doing their military service. The clerks from the groceries, Carmen and Ada, had been invited, but not Pasquale, or maybe he had chosen not to come, in order not to mix with people whom, as local gossip had it, partly joking, partly serious, he planned to murder with his own hands. His mother, Giuseppina Peluso, was also absent, as were Melina and her children. Instead, the Carraccis, the Cerullos, and the Solaras, business partners in various combinations, all sat together at the head table, along with the relatives from Florence, that is to say the metal merchant and his wife. I saw Lila talking to Michele, laughing in an exaggerated fashion. Every so often she looked in my direction, but I immediately turned away, with a mixture of irritation and distress. How much she laughed, too much. I thought of my mother: the way Lila was playing the married woman, the vulgarity of her manners, her dialect. She held Michele's attention completely, though next to him was his fiancée, Gigliola, pale and furious at being neglected. Only Marcello from time to time spoke soothingly to his future sister-in-law. Lila, Lila: she wanted to exceed and with her excesses make us all suffer. I noticed that Nunzia and Fernando also gave their daughter long, apprehensive looks.

The day went smoothly, apart from two episodes that apparently had no repercussions. Here's the first. Among the guests was Gino, the pharmacist's son, because he had recently become engaged to a second cousin of the Carraccis, a thin girl with brown hair worn close to her head and violet shadows under her eyes. As he got older he had become more detestable; I couldn't forgive myself for having been his girl-friend when I was younger. He had been devious then, and he remained devious, and, besides, he was in a situation that made him even more untrustworthy: he had failed his exams again. He hadn't even said hello to me for a long time, but he had continued to hang around Alfonso, at times he was friendly, at others he teased him with insults that always had sexual over-tones. That day, maybe out of envy (Alfonso had passed with good marks and, besides, was with Marisa, who was pretty, whose eyes sparkled), he was particularly unbearable. The fair-haired boy seated at our table, who was nice-looking and very shy, was the son of a relative of Nunzia's who had emigrated to

Germany and married a German. I was very nervous and didn't give him much encouragement to talk, but both Alfonso and Marisa had tried to put him at his ease. Alfonso in particular engaged him in conversation, did all he could if the waiters neglected him, and even took him out to the terrace for a view of the sea. Just as they came in and returned to the table, joking, Gino, with a laugh, left his fiancée, who tried to restrain him, and came to sit with us. He spoke to the boy in a low voice, indicating Alfonso:

"Watch out for that guy, he's a fag: this time he took you out to the terrace, next time it'll be the bathroom."

Alfonso turned fiery red but didn't react, he half-smiled, helplessly, and said nothing. It was Marisa who got angry:

"How dare you say such a thing!"

"I dare because I know."

"Tell me what you know."

"You're sure?"

"Yes."

"Then listen to what I'm telling you."

"Go ahead."

"My fiancée's brother stayed at the Carraccis' house once and had to sleep in the same bed with him."

"So?"

"He touched him."

"He who?"

"Him."

"Where's your fiancée?"

"Here she is."

"Tell that bitch I can prove that Alfonso likes girls, and I certainly don't know if she can say the same about you."

And at that point she turned to her boyfriend and kissed him on the lips: a passionate, public kiss—I would never have dared to do a thing like that in front of all those people.

Lila, who continued to look in my direction as if she were

monitoring me, was the first to see that kiss and she clapped her hands with spontaneous enthusiasm. Michele, too, applauded, laughing, and Stefano gave his brother a vulgar compliment, which was immediately expanded on by the metal merchant. All sorts of banter, in other words, but Marisa pretended not to notice. Squeezing Alfonso's hand tightly—her knuckles were white—she hissed at Gino, who had stared at the kiss with a blank expression, "Now get out of here, or I'll smack you."

The pharmacist's son got up without saying a word and went back to his table, where his girlfriend immediately whispered in his ear with an aggressive look. Marisa gave them both a last glance of contempt.

From that moment my opinion of her changed. I admired her courage, the stubborn capacity for love, the seriousness of her attachment to Alfonso. Here was another person I've neglected, I thought with regret, and wrongly so. How much my dependence on Lila had closed my eyes. How frivolous her applause had been, how it fit with the boorish amusement of Michele, of Stefano, of the metal merchant.

The second episode had as its protagonist Lila herself. The reception was now almost over. I had gotten up to go to the bathroom and was passing the bridal table when I heard the wife of the metal merchant laughing loudly. I turned. Pinuccia was standing and was shielding herself, because the woman was pulling up her wedding dress, baring her large, strong legs, and saying to Stefano, "Look at your sister's thighs, look at that butt and that stomach. You men of today like girls who resemble toilet brushes, but it's the ones like our Pinuccia whom God made just for bearing you children."

Lila, who was bringing a glass to her mouth, without a second's hesitation threw the wine in her face and on her silk dress. As usual, I thought, immediately anxious, she thinks she's entitled to do anything, and now all hell's going to break loose. I went out to the bathroom, locked myself in, stayed there as long as possible. I didn't want to see Lila's fury, I didn't want to hear it. I wanted to stay outside it, I was afraid of being dragged into her suffering, I was afraid of feeling obligated, out of long habit, to ally myself with her. Instead, when I came out, everything was calm. Stefano was chatting with the metal merchant and his wife, who was sitting stiffly in her stained dress. The orchestra played, couples danced. Only Lila wasn't there. I saw her outside the glass doors, on the terrace. She was looking at the sea.

39.

I was tempted to join her, I immediately changed my mind. She must be very upset and would surely be mean to me, which would make things even worse between us. I decided to return to my table when Fernando, her father, came up to me and asked timidly if I'd like to dance.

I didn't dare refuse, we danced a waltz in silence. He led me confidently around the room, among the tipsy couples, holding my hand too tight with his sweaty hand. His wife must have entrusted him with the task of telling me something important, but he couldn't get up his courage. Finally, at the end of the waltz, he muttered, addressing me, surprisingly, with formality: "If it's not too much trouble for you, talk to Lina a little, her mother is worried." Then he added awkwardly, "When you need shoes, come by, don't stand on ceremony," and he returned quickly to his table.

That hint at a kind of reward for my possibly devoting time to Lila bothered me. I asked Alfonso and Marisa to go, which they were happy to do. I felt Nunzia's gaze on me right up until we left the restaurant.

As the days passed, I began to lose confidence. I had thought that working in a bookstore meant having a lot of books available to me and time to read them, but I was unlucky. The owner treated me like a servant, he couldn't stand my being still for a moment: he forced me to unload boxes, pile them up, empty them, arrange the new books, rearrange the old ones, dust them, and he sent me up and down a ladder just so he could look under my skirt. Besides, Armando, after that first foray when he had seemed so friendly, hadn't showed up again. And Nino hadn't reappeared, either with Nadia or by himself. Had their interest in me been so short-lived? I began to feel solitude, boredom. The heat, the work, disgust at the bookseller's looks and his coarse remarks depressed me. The hours dragged. What was I doing in that dark cave, while along the sidewalk boys and girls filed past on their way to the mysterious university building, a place where I would almost certainly never go? Where was Nino? Had he gone to Ischia to study? He had left me the review, his article, and I had studied them as if for an examination, but would he ever come back to examine me? Where had I gone wrong? Had I been too reserved? Was he expecting me to seek him out and for that reason did not look for me? Should I talk to Alfonso, get in touch with Marisa, ask her about her brother? And why? Nino had a girlfriend, Nadia: What point was there in asking his sister where he was, what he was doing. I would make myself ridiculous.

Day by day the sense of myself that had so unexpectedly expanded after the party diminished, I felt dispirited. Get up early, hurry to Mezzocannone, slave all day, go home tired, the thousands of words learned in school packed into my head, unusable. I got depressed not only when I recalled conversations with Nino but also when I thought of the summers at the Sea Garden with the stationer's daughters, with Antonio. How stupidly our affair had ended, he was the only person who had truly loved me, there would never be anyone else. In bed at night, I recalled the odor of his skin, the meetings at the ponds, our kissing and petting at the old canning factory.

I was in this state of discouragement when, one evening, after dinner, Carmen, Ada, and Pasquale, who had one hand bandaged because he had injured it at work, came looking for me. We got ice cream, and ate it in the gardens. Carmen, coming straight to the point, asked me, somewhat aggressively, why I never stopped by the grocery anymore. I said I was working at Mezzocannone and didn't have time. Ada said, coldly, that if one is attached to a person one finds the time, but if that's how I was going to be, never mind. I asked, "Be how?" and she answered, "You have no feelings, just look how you treated my brother." I reminded her with an angry snap that it was her brother who had left me, and she replied, "Yes, anyone who believes that is lucky: there are people who leave and people who know how to be left." Carmen agreed: "Also friendships," she said. "You think they break off because of one person and instead, if you look hard, it's the other person's fault." At that point I got upset, I declared, "Listen, if Lina and I aren't friends anymore, it's not my fault." Here Pasquale intervened, he said, "Lenù, it's not important whose fault it is, it's important for us to support Lina." He brought up the story of his bad teeth, of how she had helped him, he talked about the money she still gave Carmen under the counter, and how she also sent money to Antonio, who, even if I didn't know and didn't want to know, was having a bad time in the Army. I tried cautiously to ask what was happening to my old boyfriend and they told me, in different tones of voice, some hostile, some less, that he had had a nervous breakdown, that he was ill, but that he was tough, he wouldn't give in, he would make it. *Lina, on the other hand.*

"What's wrong with Lina?"

"They want to take her to a doctor."

"Who wants to take her?"

"Stefano, Pinuccia, relatives."

"Why?"

"To find out why she's only gotten pregnant once and then never again."

"And she?"

"She acts like a madwoman, she doesn't want to go."

I shrugged my shoulders. "What can I do?"

"You take her."

40.

I talked to Lila. She started laughing, she said she would go to the doctor only if I swore that I wasn't angry with her.

"All right."

"Swear."

"I swear."

"Swear on your brothers, swear on Elisa."

I said that going to the doctor wasn't a big deal, but that if she didn't want to go I didn't care, she should do as she liked. She became serious.

"You don't swear, then."

"No."

She was silent for a moment, then she admitted, eyes lowered, "All right, I was wrong."

I made a grimace of irritation. "Go to the doctor and let me know."

"You won't come?"

"If I don't go in the bookseller will fire me."

"I'll hire you," she said ironically.

"Go to the doctor, Lila."

Maria, Nunzia, and Pinuccia took her to the doctor. All three insisted on being present at the examination. Lila was obedient, disciplined: she had never submitted to that type of examination, and the whole time she kept her lips pressed together, eyes wide. When the doctor, a very old man who had been recommended by the neighborhood obstetrician, said knowingly that everything was in order, her mother and mother-in-law were relieved, but Pinuccia darkened, asked:

"Then why don't children come and if they come why aren't they born?"

The doctor noticed her spiteful tone and frowned.

"She's very young," he said. "She needs to get a little stronger."

Get stronger. I don't know if the doctor used exactly that verb, yet that was reported to me and it made an impression. It meant that Lila, in spite of the strength she displayed at all times, was weak. It meant that children didn't come, or didn't last in her womb, not because she possessed a mysterious power that annihilated them but because, on the contrary, she was an inadequate woman. My resentment faded. When, in the courtyard, she told me about the torture of the medical examination, using vulgar expressions for both the doctor and the three who accompanied her, I gave no signs of annoyance but in fact took an interest: no doctor had ever examined me, not even the obstetrician. Finally she said, sarcastically:

"He tore me with a metal instrument, I gave him a lot of money, and to reach what conclusion? That I need strengthening."

"Strengthening of what sort?"

"I'm supposed to go to the beach and go swimming."

"I don't understand."

"The beach, Lenù, sun, salt water. It seems that if you go to the beach you get stronger and children come."

We said goodbye in a good mood. We had seen each other again and all in all we had felt good.

She came back the next day, affectionate toward me, irritated with her husband. Stefano wanted to rent a house at Torre Annunziata and send her there for all July and all August with Nunzia and Pinuccia, who also wanted to get stronger, even though she didn't need to. They were already thinking how to manage with the shops. Alfonso would take care of Piazza dei Martiri, with Gigliola, until school began, and Maria would replace Lila in the new grocery. She said to me, desperate, "If I have to stay with my mother and Pinuccia for two months I'll kill myself."

"But you'll go swimming, lie in the sun."

"I don't like swimming and I don't like lying in the sun."

"If I could get stronger in your place, I'd leave tomorrow."

She looked at me with curiosity, and said softly, "Then come with me."

"I have to work at Mezzocannone."

She became agitated, she repeated that she would hire me, but this time she said it without irony. "Quit," she began to press me, "and I'll give you what the bookseller gives you." She wouldn't stop, she said that if I agreed, it would all become tolerable, even Pinuccia, with that bulging stomach that was already showing. I refused politely. I imagined what would happen in those two months in the burning-hot house in Torre Annunziata: quarrels with Nunzia, tears; quarrels with Stefano when he arrived on Saturday night; quarrels with Rino when he appeared with his brother-in-law, to join Pinuccia; quarrels especially with Pinuccia, continuous, muted or dramatic, sarcastic, malicious, and full of outrageous insults.

"I can't," I said firmly. "My mother wouldn't let me."

She went away angrily, our idyll was fragile. The next morning, to my surprise, Nino appeared in the bookstore, pale, thinner. He had had one exam after another, four of them. I, who fantasized about the airy spaces behind the walls of the university where well-prepared students and old sages discussed Plato and Kepler all day, listened to him spellbound, saying only, "How clever you are." And as soon as the moment seemed apt, I volubly if somewhat inanely praised his article in *Cronache Meridionali*. He listened to me seriously, without interrupting, so that at a certain point I no longer knew what to say to show him that I knew his text thoroughly. Finally he seemed content, he exclaimed that not even Professor Galiani, not even Armando, not even Nadia had read it with such attention. And he started to talk to me about other essays he had in mind on the same subject. I stood listening to him in the doorway of the bookshop, pretending not to hear the owner calling me. After a shout that was sharper than the others, Nino muttered, What does that shit want; he stayed a little longer, with his insolent expression, and, saying that he was leaving for Ischia the next day, held out his hand to me. I shook it—it was slender, delicate—and he immediately drew me toward him, just slightly, leaned over, brushed my lips with his. It was a moment, then he left me with a light gesture, a caress on the palm with his fingers, and went off toward the Rettifilo. I stood watching as he walked away without turning, walked like a distracted chieftain who feared nothing in the world because the world existed only to submit to him.

That night I didn't close my eyes. In the morning I got up early, I hurried to the new grocery. I found Lila just as she was pulling up the gate, Carmen hadn't yet arrived. I said nothing about Nino, I said only, in the tone of someone who is asking the impossible and knows it:

"If you go to Ischia instead of Torre Annunziata, I'll quit and come with you."

41.

We disembarked on the island the second Sunday in July, Stefano and Lila, Rino and Pinuccia, Nunzia and I. The two men, loaded down with bags, were apprehensive, like ancient heroes in an unknown land, uneasy without the armor of their cars, unhappy that they had had to rise early and forgo the neighborhood leisureliness of their day off. The wives, dressed in their Sunday best, were annoyed with them but in different ways: Pinuccia because Rino was too encumbered to pay attention to her, Lila because Stefano pretended to know what he was doing and where he was going, when it was clear that he didn't. As for Nunzia, she had the appearance of someone who feels that she is barely tolerated, and she was careful not to say anything inappropriate that might annoy the young people. The only one who was truly content was me, with a bag over my shoulder that held my few things, excited by the smells of Ischia, the sounds, the colors that, as soon as I got off the boat, corresponded precisely to the memories of that earlier vacation.

We arranged ourselves in two mini cabs, jammed-in bodies, sweat, luggage. The house, rented in a hurry with the help of a *salumi* supplier of Ischian origin, was on the road that led to a place called Cuotto. It was a simple structure and belonged to a cousin of the supplier, a thin woman, over sixty, unmarried, who greeted us with brusque efficiency. Stefano and Rino dragged the suitcases up a narrow staircase, joking but also cursing because of the effort. The owner led us into shadowy rooms stuffed with sacred images and small, glowing lamps. But when we opened the windows we saw, beyond the road, beyond the vineyards, beyond the palms and pine trees, a long strip of the sea. Or rather: the bedrooms that Pinuccia and Lila took—after some friction of the *yours is bigger; no, yours is bigger* type—faced the sea, while the room that fell to Nunzia had a sort of porthole, high up, so that we never discovered what was outside it, and mine, which was very small, and barely had space for the bed, looked out on a chicken coop sheltered by a forest of reeds.

There was nothing to eat in the house. On the advice of the owner we went to a trattoria, which was dark and had no other customers. We sat down dubiously, just to get fed, but in the end even Nunzia, who was distrustful of all cooking that was not her own, found that it was good and wanted to take something home so that she could prepare dinner that evening. Stefano didn't make the slightest move to ask for the check, and, after a mute hesitation, Rino resigned himself to paying for everyone. At that point we girls proposed going to see the beach, but the two men resisted, yawned, said they were tired. We insisted, especially Lila. "We ate too much," she said, "it'll do us good to walk, the beach is right here, do you feel like it, Mamma?" Nunzia sided with the men, and we returned to the house.

After a bored stroll through the rooms, both Stefano and Rino, almost in unison, said that they wanted to have a little nap. They laughed, whispered to each other, laughed again, and then nodded at their wives, who followed them unwillingly into the bedrooms. Nunzia and I remained alone for a couple of hours. We inspected the state of the kitchen, and found it dirty, which led Nunzia to start washing everything carefully: plates, glasses, silverware, pots. It was a struggle to get her to let me help. She asked me to keep track of a number of urgent requests for the owner, and when she herself lost count of the things that were needed, she marveled that I was able to remember everything, saying, "That's why you're so clever at school."

Finally the two couples reappeared, first Stefano and Lila, then Rino and Pinuccia. I again proposed going to see the beach, but there was coffee, joking, chatting, and Nunzia who began to cook, and Pinuccia who was clinging to Rino, making him feel her stomach, murmuring, stay, leave tomorrow morning, and so the time flew and yet again we did nothing. In the end the men had to rush, afraid of missing the ferry, and, cursing because they hadn't brought their cars, had to find someone to take them to the Port. They disappeared almost without saying goodbye. Pinuccia burst into tears.

In silence we girls began to unpack the bags, to arrange our things, while Nunzia insisted on making the bathroom shine. Only when we were sure that the men had not missed the ferry and would not return, did we relax, begin to joke. We had ahead of us a long week and only ourselves to worry about. Pinuccia said she was afraid of being alone in her room—there was an image of a grieving Madonna with knives in her heart that sparkled in the lamplight—and went to sleep with Lila. I shut myself in my little room to enjoy my secret: *Nino was in Forio, not far away, and maybe even the next day I would meet him on the beach.* I felt wild, reckless, but I was glad about it. There was a part of me that was sick of being a sensible person.

It was hot, I opened the window. I listened to the chickens pecking, the rustle of the reeds, then I became aware of the mosquitoes. I closed the window quickly and spent at least an hour going after them and crushing them with one of the books that Professor Galiani had lent me, *Complete Plays*, by a writer named Samuel Beckett. I didn't want Nino to see me on the beach with red spots on my face and body; I didn't want him to catch me with a book of plays—for one thing, I had never set foot in a theater. I put aside Beckett, stained by the black or bloody silhouettes of the mosquitoes, and began to read a very complicated text on the idea of nationhood. I fell asleep reading.

42.

In the morning Nunzia, who felt committed to looking after us, went in search of a place to do the shopping and we headed to the beach, the beach of Citara, which for that entire long vacation we thought was called Cetara.

What pretty bathing suits Lila and Pinuccia displayed when

they took off their sundresses: one-piece, of course. The husbands, who as fiancés had been indulgent, especially Stefano,
now were against the two-piece; but the colors of the new fabrics were shiny, and the shape of the neckline, front and back,
ran elegantly over their skin. I, under an old long-sleeved blue
dress, wore the same faded bathing suit, now shapeless, that
Nella Incardo had made for me years earlier, at Barano. I
undressed reluctantly.

We walked a long way in the sun, until we saw steam rising
from some thermal baths, then turned back. Pinuccia and I
stopped often to swim, Lila didn't, although she was there for
that purpose. Of course, there was no Nino, and I was disappointed, I had been convinced that he would show up, as if by
a miracle. When the other two wanted to go back to the house,
I stayed on the beach, and walked along the shore toward
Forio. That night I was so sunburned that I felt I had a high
fever; the skin on my shoulders blistered and for the next few
days I had to stay in the house. I cleaned, cooked, and read,
and my energy pleased Nunzia, who couldn't stop praising me.
Every night, with the excuse that I had been in the house all
day to stay out of the sun, I made Lila and Pina walk to Forio,
which was some distance away. We wandered through the
town, had some ice cream. It's pretty here, Pinuccia complained, it's a morgue where we are. But for me Forio was also
a morgue: Nino did not appear.

Toward the end of the week I proposed to Lila that we
should visit Barano and the Maronti. Lila agreed enthusiastically, and Pinuccia didn't want to stay and be bored with
Nunzia. We left early. Under our dresses we wore our bathing
suits, and in a bag I carried our towels, sandwiches, a bottle of
water. My stated purpose was to take advantage of that trip to
say hello to Nella, Maestra Oliviero's cousin, whom I had stayed
with during my summer on Ischia. The secret plan, instead, was
to see the Sarratore family and get from Marisa the address of

the friend with whom Nino was staying in Forio. I was naturally afraid of running into the father, Donato, but I hoped that he was at work; and, in order to see the son, I was ready to run the risk of having to endure some obscene remark from him.

When Nella opened the door and I stood before her, like a ghost, she was stunned, tears came to her eyes. "It's happiness," she said, apologizing.

But it wasn't only that. I had reminded her of her cousin, who, she told me, wasn't comfortable in Potenza, was ill and wasn't getting better. She led us out to the terrace, offered us whatever we wanted, was very concerned with Pinuccia, and her pregnancy. She made her sit down, wanted to touch her stomach, which protruded a little. Meanwhile I made Lila go on a sort of pilgrimage: I showed her the corner of the terrace where I had spent so much time in the sun, the place where I sat at the table, the corner where I made my bed at night. For a fraction of a second I saw Donato leaning over me as he slid his hand under the sheets, touched me. I felt revulsion but this didn't keep me from asking Nella casually, "And the Sarratores?"

"They're at the beach."

"How's it going this year?"

"Ah, well . . . "

"They're too demanding?"

"Ever since he became more the journalist than the railroad worker, yes."

"Is he here?"

"He's on sick leave."

"And is Marisa here?"

"No, not Marisa, but except for her they're all here."

"All?"

"You understand."

"No, I swear, I don't understand anything."

She laughed heartily.

"Nino's here today, too, Lenù. When he needs money he shows up for half a day, then he goes back to stay with a friend who has a house in Forio."

43.

We left Nella, and went down to the beach with our things. Lila teased me mildly the whole way. "You're sneaky," she said, "you made me come to Ischia just because Nino's here, admit it." I wouldn't admit it, I defended myself. Then Pinuccia joined her sister-in-law, in a coarser tone, and accused me of having compelled her to make a long and tiring journey to Barano for my own purposes, without taking her pregnancy into account. From then on I denied it even more firmly, and in fact I threatened them both. I promised that if they said anything improper in the presence of the Sarratores I would take the boat and return to Naples that night.

I immediately picked out the family. They were in exactly the same place where they used to settle years before, and had the same umbrella, the same bathing suits, the same bags, the same way of basking in the sun: Donato belly up in the black sand, leaning on his elbows; his wife, Lidia, sitting on a towel and leafing through a magazine. To my great disappointment Nino wasn't under the umbrella. I scanned the water, and glimpsed a dark dot that appeared and disappeared on the rocking surface of the sea: I hoped it was him. Then I announced myself, calling aloud to Pino, Clelia, and Ciro, who were playing on the shore.

Ciro had grown; he didn't recognize me, and smiled uncertainly. Pino and Clelia ran toward me excitedly, and the parents turned to look, out of curiosity. Lidia jumped up, shouting my name and waving, Sarratore hurried toward me with a big welcoming smile and open arms. I avoided his embrace, saying only Hello, how are you. They were very friendly, I introduced

Lila and Pinuccia, mentioned their parents, said whom they had married. Donato immediately focused on the two girls. He began addressing them respectfully as Signora Carracci and Signora Cerullo, he remembered them as children, he began, with fatuous elaboration, to speak of time's flight. I talked to Lidia, asked politely about the children and especially Marisa. Pino, Clelia, and Ciro were doing well and it was obvious; they immediately gathered around me, waiting for the right moment to draw me into their games. As for Marisa, her mother said that she had stayed in Naples with her aunt and uncle, she had to retake exams in four subjects in September and had to go to private lessons. "Serves her right," she said darkly. "She didn't work all year, now she deserves to suffer."

I said nothing, but I doubted that Marisa was suffering: she would spend the whole summer with Alfonso in the store in Piazza dei Martiri, and I was happy for her. I noticed instead that Lidia bore deep traces of grief: in her face, which was losing its contours, in her eyes, in her shrunken breast, in her heavy stomach. All the time we talked she was glancing fearfully at her husband, who, playing the role of the kindly man, was devoting himself to Lila and Pinuccia. She stopped paying attention to me and kept her eyes glued to him when he offered to take them swimming, promising Lila that he would teach her to swim. "I taught all my children," we heard him say, "I'll teach you, too."

I never asked about Nino, nor did Lidia ever mention him. But now the black dot in the sparkling blue of the sea stopped moving out. It reversed direction, grew larger, I began to distinguish the white of the foam exploding beside it.

Yes, it's him, I thought anxiously.

Nino emerged from the water looking with curiosity at his father, who was holding Lila afloat with one arm and with the other was showing her what to do. Even when he saw me and recognized me, he continued to frown.

"What are you doing here?" he asked.

"I'm on vacation," I answered, "and I came by to see Signora Nella."

He looked again with annoyance in the direction of his father and the two girls.

"Isn't that Lina?"

"Yes, and that's her sister-in-law Pinuccia, I don't know if you remember her."

He rubbed his hair with the towel, continuing to stare at the three in the water. I told him almost breathlessly that we would be staying on Ischia until September, that we had a house not far from Forio, that Lila's mother was there, too, that on Sunday the husbands of Lila and Pinuccia would come. As I spoke it seemed to me that he wasn't even listening, but still I said, and in spite of Lidia's presence, that on the weekend I had nothing to do.

"Come see us," he said, and then he spoke to his mother: "I have to go."

"Already?"

"I have things to do."

"Elena's here."

Nino looked at me as if he had become aware of my presence only then. He rummaged in his shirt, which was hanging on the umbrella, took out a pencil and a notebook, wrote something, tore out the page, and handed it to me.

"I'm at this address," he said.

Clear, decisive as a movie actor. I took the page as if it were a holy relic.

"Eat something first," his mother begged him.

He didn't answer.

"And at least wave goodbye to Papa."

He changed out of his bathing suit, wrapping a towel around his waist, and went off along the shore without saying goodbye to anyone.

44.

We spent the entire day at the Maronti, I playing and swimming with the children, Pinuccia and Lila completely occupied by Donato, who took them for a walk all the way to the thermal baths. At the end Pinuccia was exhausted, and Sarratore showed us a convenient and pleasant way of going home. We went to a hotel that was built practically over the water, as if on stilts, and there, for a few lire, we got a boat, entrusting ourselves to an old sailor.

As soon as we set out, Lila said sarcastically, "Nino didn't give you much encouragement."

"He had to study."

"And he couldn't even say hello?"

"That's how he is."

"How he is is rude," Pinuccia interjected. "He's as rude as the father is nice."

They were both convinced that Nino hadn't been polite or pleasant, and I let them think it, I preferred prudently to keep my secrets. And it seemed to me that if they thought he was disdainful of even a really good student like me, they would more easily put up with the fact that he had ignored them and maybe they would even forgive him. I wanted to protect him from their rancor, and I succeeded: they seemed to forget about him right away, Pinuccia was enthusiastic about Sarratore's graciousness, and Lila said with satisfaction, "He taught me to float, and even how to swim. He's great."

The sun was setting. I thought of Donato's molestations, and shuddered. From the violet sky came a chilly dampness. I said to Lila, "He's the one who wrote that the panel in the Piazza dei Martiri shop was ugly."

Pinuccia had a smug expression of agreement.

Lila said, "He was right."

I became upset. "And he's the one who ruined Melina."

Lila answered, with a laugh, "Or maybe he made her feel good for once."

That remark wounded me. I knew what Melina had endured, what her children endured. I also knew Lidia's sufferings, and how Sarratore, behind his fine manners, hid a desire that respected nothing and no one. Nor had I forgotten that Lila, since she was a child, had witnessed the torments of the widow Cappuccio and how painful it had been for her. So what was this tone, what were those words—a signal to me? Did she want to say to me: you're a girl, you don't know anything about a woman's needs? I abruptly changed my mind about the secrecy of my secrets. I wanted immediately to show that I was a woman like them and knew.

"Nino gave me his address," I said to Lila. "If you don't mind, when Stefano and Rino come I'm going to see him."

Address. Go see him. Bold formulations. Lila narrowed her eyes, a sharp line crossed her forehead. Pinuccia had a malicious look, she touched Lila's knee, she laughed: "You hear? Lenuccia has a date tomorrow. And she has the address."

I flushed.

"Well, if you're with your husbands, what am I supposed to do?"

For a long moment there was only the noise of the engine and the mute presence of the sailor at the helm.

Lila said coldly, "Keep Mamma company. I didn't bring you here to have fun."

I restrained myself. We had had a week of freedom. That day, besides, both she and Pinuccia, on the beach, in the sun, during long swims, and thanks to the words that Sarratore knew how to use to inspire laughter and to charm, had forgotten themselves. Donato had made them feel like girl-women in the care of an unusual father, the rare father who doesn't punish you but encourages you to express your desires without guilt. And now that the day was over I, in declaring that I would have a Sunday to myself with a university student—what was I doing, was I reminding them both that that week in which their condition as wives was suspended was over and that their husbands were about to reappear? Yes, I had overdone it. Cut out your tongue, I thought.

45.

The husbands, in fact, arrived early. They were expected Sunday morning, but they appeared Saturday evening, very excited, with Lambrettas that they had, I think, rented at the Ischia Port. Nunzia prepared a lavish dinner. There was talk of the neighborhood, of the stores, of how the new shoes were coming along. Rino was full of self-praise for the models that he was perfecting with his father, but at an opportune moment he thrust some sketches under Lila's nose, and she examined them reluctantly, suggesting some modifications. Then we sat down at the table, and the two young men gorged themselves, competing to see who could eat more. It wasn't even ten when they dragged their wives to the bedrooms.

I helped Nunzia clear and wash the dishes. Then I shut myself in my room, I read a little. The heat in the closed room was suffocating, but I was afraid of the blotches I'd get from the mosquito bites, and I didn't open the window. I tossed and turned in the bed, soaked with sweat: I thought of Lila, of how, slowly, she had yielded. Certainly, she didn't show any particular affection for her husband; and the tenderness that I had sometimes seen in her gestures when they were engaged had disappeared. During dinner she had frequently commented with disgust at the way Stefano gobbled his food, the way he drank; but it was evident that some equilibrium, who knows how precarious, had been reached. When he, after some allusive remarks, headed toward the bedroom, Lila followed without delay, without saying go on, I'll join you later; she was resigned to an inevitable routine. Between her and her husband there was not the carnival spirit displayed by Rino and Pinuccia, but there was no resistance, either. Deep into the night I heard the noise of the two couples, the laughter and the sighs, the doors opening, the water coming out of the tap, the whirlpool of the flush, the doors closing. Finally I fell asleep.

On Sunday I had breakfast with Nunzia. I waited until ten for any of them to emerge; they didn't, I went to the beach. I stayed until noon and no one came. I went back to the house, Nunzia told me that the two couples had gone for a tour of the island on the Lambrettas, advising us not to wait for them for lunch. In fact they returned around three, slightly drunk, sunburned, all four full of enthusiasm for Casamicciola, Lacco Ameno, Forio. The two girls had shining eyes and immediately glanced at me slyly.

"Lenù," Pinuccia almost shouted, "guess what happened."

"What."

"We met Nino on the beach," Lila said.

My heart stopped.

"Oh."

"My goodness, he is really a good swimmer," Pinuccia said excitedly, cutting the air with exaggerated arm strokes.

And Rino: "He's not unlikable: he was interested in how shoes are made."

And Stefano: "He has a friend named Soccavo and he's the mortadella Soccavo: his father owns a sausage factory in San Giovanni a Teduccio."

And Rino again: "That guy's got money."

And again Stefano: "Forget the student, Lenù, he doesn't have a lira: aim for Soccavo, you'd be better off."

After a little more joking (*Would you look at that, Lenuccia is about to be the richest of all, She seems like a good girl and yet*), they withdrew again into the bedrooms.

I was incredibly disappointed. They had met Nino, gone swimming with him, talked to him, and without me. I put on my best dress—the same one, the one I'd worn to the wedding, even though it was hot—I carefully combed my hair, which had become very blond in the sun, and told Nunzia I was going for a walk.

I walked to Forio, uneasy because of the long, solitary distance, because of the heat, because of the uncertain result of my undertaking. I tracked down the address of Nino's friend, I called several times from the street, fearful that he wouldn't answer.

"Nino, Nino."

He looked out.

"Come up."

"I'll wait here."

I waited, I was afraid that he would treat me rudely. Instead he came out of the doorway with an unusually friendly expression. How disturbing his angular face was. And how pleasantly crushed I felt confronted by his long profile, his broad shoulders and narrow chest, that taut skin, the sole, dark covering of his thinness, merely bones, muscles, tendons. He said his friend would join us later; we walked through the center of Forio, amid the Sunday market stalls. He asked me about the bookstore on Mezzocannone. I told him that Lila had asked me to go with her on vacation and so I had quit. I didn't mention the fact that she was giving me money, as if going with her were a job, as if I were her employee. I asked him about Nadia, he said only: "Everything's fine." "Do you write to each other?" "Yes." "Every day?" "Every week." That was our conversation, already we had nothing more of our selves to share. We don't know anything about each other, I thought. Maybe I could ask how relations are with his father, but in what tone? And, besides, didn't I see with my own eyes that they're bad? Silence: I felt awkward.

But he promptly shifted onto the only terrain that seemed to justify our meeting. He said that he was glad to see me, all he could talk about with his friend was soccer and exam subjects. He praised me. Professor Galiani perceived it, he said, you're the only girl in the school who has any curiosity about things that aren't useful for exams and grades. He started to speak about serious subjects, we resorted immediately to a fine, impassioned Italian in which we knew we excelled. He started off with the problem of violence. He mentioned a peace demonstration in Cortona and related it skillfully to the beatings that had taken place in a piazza in Turin. He said he wanted to understand more about the link between immigration and industry. I agreed, but what did I know about those things? Nothing. Nino realized it, and he told me in great detail about an uprising of young southerners and the harshness with which the police had repressed them. "They call them *napoli*, they call them Moroccans, they call them Fascists, provocateurs, anarcho-syndicalists. But really they are boys whom no institution cares about, so neglected that when they get angry they destroy everything." Searching for something to say that would please him, I ventured, "If you don't have a solid knowledge of the problems and if you don't find lasting solutions, then naturally violence breaks out. But the people who rebel aren't to blame, it's the ones who don't know how to govern." He gave me an admiring look, and said, "That's exactly what I think."

I was really pleased. I felt encouraged and cautiously went on to some reflections on how to reconcile individuality and universality, drawing on Rousseau and other memories of the readings imposed by Professor Galiani. Then I asked, "Have you read Federico Chabod?"

I mentioned that name because he was the author of the book on the idea of nationhood that I had read a few pages of. I didn't know anything else, but at school I had learned to give the impression that I knew a lot. *Have you read Federico Chabod?* It was the only moment when Nino seemed to be annoyed. I realized that he didn't know who Chabod was and from that I got an electrifying sensation of fullness. I began to summarize the little I had learned, but I quickly realized that to know, to compulsively display what he knew, was his point of strength and at the same time his weakness. He felt strong if he took the lead and weak if he lacked words. He darkened, in fact he stopped me almost immediately. He sidetracked the conversation, he started talking about the Regions, about how urgent it was to get them approved, about autonomy and decentralization, about economic planning on a regional basis, all things I had never heard a word about. No Chabod, then: I left him the field. And I liked to hear him talk, read the passion in his face. His eyes brightened when he was excited.

We went on like that for at least an hour. Isolated from the shouting around us, its coarse dialect, we felt exclusive, he and I alone, with our vigilant Italian, with those conversations that mattered to us and no one else. What were we doing? A discussion? Practicing for future confrontations with people who had learned to use words as we had? An exchange of signals to prove to ourselves that such words were the basis of a long and fruitful friendship? A cultivated screen for sexual desire? I don't know. I certainly had no particular passion for those subjects, for the real things and people they referred to. I had no training, no habit, only the usual desire not to make a bad showing. It was wonderful, though—that is certain. I felt the way I did at the end of the year when I saw the list of my grades and read: passed. But I also understood that there was no comparison with the exchanges I had had with Lila years earlier, which ignited my brain, and in the course of which we tore the words from each other's mouth, creating an excitement that seemed like a storm of electrical charges. With Nino it was different. I felt that I had to pay attention to say what he wanted me to say, hiding from him both my ignorance and the few things that I knew and he didn't. I did this, and felt proud that he was trusting me with his convictions. But now something else happened. Suddenly he said, That's enough, grabbed my hand, exclaimed, like a fluorescent caption, *Now I'll take you to see a landscape that you'll never forget*, and dragged me to Piazza del Soccorso, without letting go, rather, he entwined his fingers in mine, so that, overwhelmed as I was by his clasp, I preserve no memory of the arc of the deep blue sea.

It truly overwhelmed me. Once or twice he disentangled his fingers to smooth his hair, but he immediately took my hand again. I wondered for a moment how he reconciled that intimate gesture with his bond with Professor Galiani's daughter. Maybe for him, I answered, it's merely how he thinks of the friendship between male and female. But the kiss on Via Mezzocannone? That, too, was nothing, new customs, new habits of youth; and anyway so slight, just the briefest contact. I should be satisfied with the happiness of right now, the chance of this vacation that I wanted: later I'll lose him, he'll leave, he has a destiny that can in no way be mine, too.

I was absorbed by these throbbing thoughts when I heard a roar behind me and noisy cries of my name. Rino and Stefano passed us at full speed on their Lambrettas, with their wives behind. They slowed down, turned back with a skillful maneuver. I let go of Nino's hand.

"And your friend?" Stefano asked, revving his engine.

"He'll be here soon."

"Say hello from me."

"Yes."

Rino asked, "Do you want to take Lenuccia for a spin?"

"No, thanks."

"Come on, you see she'd like to."

Nino flushed, he said, "I don't know how to ride a Lambretta."

"It's easy, like a bicycle."

"I know, but it's not for me."

Stefano laughed: "Rinù, he's a guy who studies, forget it."

I had never seen him so lighthearted. Lila sat close against him, with both arms around his waist. She urged him, "Let's go, if you don't hurry you'll miss the boat."

"Yes, let's go," cried Stefano, "tomorrow we have to work: not like you people who sit in the sun and go swimming. Bye, Lenù, bye, Nino, be good boys and girls."

"Nice to meet you," Rino said cordially.

They went off, Lila waved goodbye to Nino, shouting, "Please, take her home."

She's acting like my mother, I thought with a little annoyance, she's playing grownup.

Nino took me by the hand again and said, "Rino is nice, but why did Lina marry that moron?"

46.

A little later I also met his friend, Bruno Soccavo, who was around twenty, and very short, with a low forehead, black curly hair, a pleasant face but scarred by what must have been severe acne.

They walked me home, beside the wine-colored sea of twilight. Nino didn't take my hand again, even though Bruno left us practically alone: he went in front or lingered behind, as if he didn't want to disturb us. Since Soccavo never said a word to me, I didn't speak to him, either, his shyness made me shy. But when we parted, at the house, it was he who asked suddenly, "Will we meet tomorrow?" And Nino found out where we were going to the beach, he insisted on precise directions. I gave them.

"Are you going in the morning or the afternoon?"

"Morning and afternoon. Lina is supposed to swim a lot."

He promised they would come and see us.

I ran happily up the stairs of the house, but as soon as I came in Pinuccia began to tease me.

"Mamma," she said to Nunzia during dinner, "Lenuccia's going out with the poet's son, a skinny fellow with long hair, who thinks he's better than everybody."

"It's not true."

"It's very true, we saw you holding hands."

Nunzia didn't understand the teasing and took the thing with the earnest gravity that characterized her.

"What does Sarratore's son do?"

"University student."

"Then if you love each other you'll have to wait."

"There's nothing to wait for, Signora Nunzia, we're only friends."

"But if, let's say, you should happen to become engaged, he'll have to finish his studies first, then he'll have to find a job that's worthy of him, and only when he's found something will you be able to get married."

Here Lila interrupted, amused: "She's telling you you'll get moldy."

But Nunzia reproached her: "You mustn't speak like that to Lenuccia." And to console me she said that she had married Fernando at twenty-one, that she had had Rino at twenty-three. Then she turned to her daughter, and said, without malice, only to point out how things stood, "You, on the other hand, were married too young." That comment infuriated Lila and she went to her room. When Pinuccia knocked on the door, to go in to sleep, she yelled not to bother her, "you have your room." How in that atmosphere could I say: Nino and Bruno promised they'll come and see me on the beach? I gave it up. If it happens, I thought, fine, and if it doesn't why tell them. Nunzia, meanwhile, patiently invited her daughter-in-law into her bed, telling her not to be upset by her daughter's nerves.

The night wasn't enough to soothe Lila. On Monday she got up in a worse mood than when she had gone to bed. It's the absence of her husband, Nunzia said apologetically, but neither Pinuccia nor I believed it. I soon discovered that she was angry mainly at me. On the road to the beach she made me carry her bag, and once we were at the beach she sent me back twice, first to get her a scarf, then because she needed some nail scissors. When I gave signs of protest she nearly reminded me of the money she was giving me. She stopped in time, but not so that I didn't understand: it was like when someone is about to hit you and then doesn't.

It was a very hot day; we stayed in the water. Lila practiced hard to keep afloat, and made me stand next to her so that I could hold her up if necessary. Yet her spitefulness continued. She kept reproaching me, she said that it was stupid to trust me: I didn't even know how to swim, how could I teach her. She missed Sarratore's talents as an instructor, she made me swear that the next day we would go back to the Maronti. Still, by trial and error, she made a lot of progress. She learned every movement instantly. Thanks to that ability she had learned to make shoes, to dexterously slice salami and provolone, to cheat on the weight. She was born like that, she could have learned the art of engraving merely by studying the gestures of a goldsmith, and then been able to work the gold better than he. Already she had stopped gasping for breath, and was forcing composure on every motion: it was as if she were drawing her body on the transparent surface of the sea. Long, slender arms and legs hit the water in a tranquil rhythm, without raising foam like Nino, without the ostentatious tension of Sarratore the father.

"Is this right?"

"Yes."

It was true. In a few hours she could swim better than I could, not to mention Pinuccia, and already she was making fun of our clumsiness.

That bullying air dissipated abruptly when, around four in the afternoon, Nino, who was very tall, and Bruno, who came up to his shoulders, appeared on the beach, just as a cool wind rose, taking away the desire to swim.

Pinuccia was the first to make them out as they advanced along the shore, among the children playing with shovels and pails. She burst out laughing in surprise and said: Look who's coming, the long and the short of it. Nino and his friend, towels over their shoulder, cigarettes and lighters, advanced deliberately, looking for us among the bathers.

I had a sudden sense of power, I shouted, I waved to signal our presence. So Nino had kept his promise. So he had felt, already, the next day, the need to see me again. So he had come purposely from Forio, dragging along his mute companion, and since he had nothing in common with Lila and Pinuccia, it was obvious that he had taken that walk just for me, who alone was not married, or even engaged. I felt happy, and the more my happiness seemed justified—Nino spread his towel next to me, he sat down, he pointed to an edge of the blue fabric, and I, who was the only one sitting on the sand, quickly moved over—the more cordial and talkative I became.

Lila and Pinuccia instead were silent. They stopped teasing me, they stopped squabbling with each other; they listened to Nino as he told funny stories about how he and his friend had organized their life of study.

It was a while before Pinuccia ventured a few words, in a mixture of dialect and Italian. She said the water was nice and warm, that the man who sold fresh coconut hadn't come by yet, that she had a great desire for some. But Nino paid little attention, absorbed in his witty stories, and it was Bruno, more attentive, who felt it his duty not to ignore what a pregnant woman was saying: worried that the child might be born with a craving for coconut, he offered to go in search of some. Pinuccia liked his voice, choked by shyness but kind, the voice of a person who doesn't want to hurt anyone, and she eagerly began chatting with him, in a low voice, as if not to disturb.

Lila, however, remained silent. She took little interest in the platitudes that Pinuccia and Bruno were exchanging, but she didn't miss a word of what Nino and I were saying. That attention made me uneasy, and a few times I said I would be glad to take a walk to the fumaroles, hoping that Nino would say: let's go. But he had just begun to talk about the construction chaos on Ischia, so he agreed mechanically, then continued talking anyway. He dragged Bruno into it, maybe upset by the fact that he was talking to Pinuccia, and called on him as a witness to certain eyesores right next to his parents' house. Nino had a great need to express himself, to summarize his reading, to give shape to what he had himself observed. It was his way of putting his thoughts in order—talk, talk, talk—but certainly, I thought, also a sign of solitude. I proudly felt that I was like him, with the same desire to give myself an educated identity, to impose it, to say: Here's what I know, here's what I'm going to be. But Nino didn't leave me space to do it, even if occasionally, I have to say, I tried. I sat and listened to him, like the others, and when Pinuccia and Bruno exclaimed, "All right, we're going for a walk now, we're going to look for coconut," I gazed insistently at Lila, hoping that she would go with her sister-in-law, leaving me and Nino finally alone to face each other, side by side, on the same towel. But she didn't breathe, and when Pina realized that she was compelled to go for a walk by herself with a young man who was polite but nevertheless unknown, she asked me, in annoyance, "Lenù, come on, don't you want to walk?" I answered, "Yes, but let us finish our conversation, then maybe we'll join you." And she, displeased, went with Bruno toward the fumaroles: they were exactly the same height.

We continued to talk about how Naples and Ischia and all Campania had ended up in the hands of the worst people, who acted like the best people. "Marauders," Nino called them, his voice rising, "destroyers, bloodsuckers, people who steal suitcases of money and don't pay taxes: builders, lawyers for builders, Camorrists, monarcho-fascists, and Christian Democrats who behave as if cement were mixed in Heaven, and God himself, with an enormous trowel, were throwing blocks of it on the hills, on the coasts." But that the three of us were talking is an exaggeration. It was mainly he who talked, every so often I threw in some fact I had read in *Cronache Meridionali*. As for Lila, she spoke only once, and cautiously, when in the list of villains he included shopkeepers.

She asked, "Who are shopkeepers?"

Nino stopped in the middle of a sentence, looked at her in astonishment.

"Tradesmen."

"And why do you call them shopkeepers?"

"That's what they're called."

"My husband is a shopkeeper."

"I didn't mean to offend you."

"I'm not offended."

"Do you pay taxes?"

"I've never heard of them till now."

"Really?"

"Yes."

"Taxes are important for planning the economic life of a community."

"If you say so. You remember Pasquale Peluso?"

"No."

"He's a construction worker. Without all that cement he would lose his job."

"Ah."

"But he's a Communist. His father, also a Communist, in the court's opinion murdered my father-in-law, who had made money on the black market and as a loan shark. And Pasquale is like his father, he has never agreed on the question of peace, not even with the Communists, his comrades. But, even though my husband's money comes directly from my father-in-law's money, Pasquale and I are close friends."

"I don't understand what you're getting at."

Lila made a self-mocking face.

"I don't, either, I was hoping to understand by listening to the two of you."

That was it, she said nothing else. But in speaking she hadn't used her normal aggressive tone of voice, she seriously seemed to want us to help her understand, since the life of the neighborhood was a tangled skein. She had spoken in dialect most of the time, as if to indicate, modestly: I don't use tricks, I speak as I am. And she had summarized disparate things frankly, without seeking, as she usually did, a thread that would hold them together. And in fact neither she nor I had ever heard that word-formula loaded with cultural and political contempt: shopkeepers. And in fact neither she nor I knew anything about taxes: our parents, friends, boyfriends, husbands, relatives acted as if they didn't exist, and school taught nothing that had to do even vaguely with politics. Yet Lila still managed to disrupt what had until that moment been a new and thrilling afternoon. Right after that exchange, Nino tried to return to his subject but he faltered, he went back to telling funny anecdotes about life with Bruno. He said they ate only fried eggs and salami, he said that they drank a lot of wine. Then he seemed embarrassed by his own stories and appeared relieved when Pinuccia and Bruno, their hair wet, came back, eating coconut.

"That was really fun," Pina exclaimed, but with the air of

one who wants to say: You two bitches, you sent me off by myself with someone I don't even know.

When the two boys left I walked with them a little way, just to make it clear that they were my friends and had come because of me.

Nino said moodily, "Lina really got lost, what a shame."

I nodded yes, said goodbye, stood for a while with my feet in the water to calm myself.

When we got home, Pinuccia and I were lively, Lila thoughtful. Pinuccia told Nunzia about the visit of the two boys and appeared unexpectedly pleased with Bruno, who had taken the trouble to make sure that her child wasn't born with a craving for coconut. He's well brought up, she said, a student but not too boring: he seems not to care about how he's dressed but everything he has on, from his bathing suit to his shirt and his sandals, is expensive. She appeared curious about the fact that someone could be wealthy in a fashion different from that of her brother, Rino, the Solaras. She made a remark that struck me: At the bar on the beach he bought me this and that without showing off.

Her mother-in-law, who, for the entire length of that vacation, never went to the beach but took care of the shopping, the house, preparing dinner and also the lunch that we carried to the beach the next day, listened as if her daughter-in-law were recounting to her an enchanted world. Naturally she noticed immediately that her daughter was preoccupied, and kept glancing at her questioningly. But Lila was just distracted. She caused no trouble of any type, she allowed Pinuccia to sleep with her again, she wished everyone good night. Then she did something completely unexpected. I had just gone to bed when she appeared in the little room.

"Will you give me one of your books?" she asked.

I looked at her in bewilderment. She wanted to read? How long since she had opened a book, three, four years? And why now had she decided to start again? I took the volume of Beckett, the one I used to kill the mosquitoes, and gave it to her. It seemed the most accessible text I had.

47.

The week passed, between long waits and encounters that ended too quickly. The two boys kept to a rigorous schedule. They woke at six in the morning, they studied until lunchtime, at three they set out for their date with us, at seven they went home, had dinner, and resumed studying. Nino never came by himself. He and Bruno, although so different in every way, got along well, and especially when it came to us they seemed to gain confidence from each other's presence.

Pinuccia from the start did not share the hypothesis of their companionship. She claimed that they were neither particularly friendly nor particularly close. In her view it was a relationship that was sustained completely by the patience of Bruno, who was good-natured and so accepted without complaint the fact that Nino talked his head off from morning till night with all that nonsense that was constantly coming out of his mouth. "Nonsense, yes," she repeated, but then apologized, with a touch of sarcasm, for having described in that way the talk that I, too, liked so much. "You're students," she said, "and it's logical that you're the only ones who understand what you're saying; but wouldn't you agree, at least, that the rest of us get a little fed up?"

Those words pleased me greatly. They ratified in the presence of Lila, a mute witness, that between Nino and me there was a sort of exclusive relationship, in which it was hard to interfere. But one day Pinuccia said to Bruno and to Lila, in a disparaging tone, "Let's leave those two to act like intellectuals and go swimming, the water is lovely." *Act like intellectuals* was clearly a way of saying that the things we talked about didn't interest us seriously, it was an attitude, a performance. And while I didn't particularly mind that formulation, it annoyed Nino a lot, and he broke off in the middle of a sentence. He jumped to his feet, ran off and dived into the water, paying no attention to the temperature, splashed us as we started in, shivering and begging him to stop, then went on to fight with Bruno as if he wanted to drown him.

There, I thought, he's full of grand thoughts, but if he wants to he can also be lighthearted and fun. So why does he only show me his serious side? Has Professor Galiani convinced him that all I'm interested in is studying? Or is it me, do I create that impression, with my glasses, the way I speak?

From that moment I noticed with increasing bitterness that the afternoons slipped away, leaving words burdened with his anxiety to express himself and mine to anticipate a concept, to hear him say that he agreed with me. He never took me by the hand, never invited me to sit on the edge of his towel. When I saw Bruno and Pinuccia laughing at silly things I envied them, I thought: How much I would like to laugh with Nino like that—I don't want anything, I don't expect anything, I'd just like a little intimacy, even if it's polite, the way it is between Pinuccia and Bruno.

Lila seemed to have other problems. For the whole week she seemed tranquil. She spent a great part of the morning in the water, swimming back and forth, following a line parallel to the shore and a few meters away from it. Pinuccia and I kept her company, insisting on instructing her even though by now she swam much better than we did. But soon we got cold and went to lie on the hot sand, while she continued to exercise with steady arm strokes, feet kicking lightly, rhythmic mouthfuls of air as Sarratore the father had taught her. She always has to overdo it, Pinuccia grumbled in the sun, caressing her belly. And often I got up and shouted, "Enough swimming, you've been in the water too long, you'll catch cold." But Lila paid no attention and came out only when she was livid, her eyes white, her lips blue, her fingertips wrinkled. I waited for her on the shore with her towel, warmed in the sun; I put it around her shoulders and rubbed her energetically.

When the two boys, who didn't skip a single day, arrived, either we took another swim together—though Lila generally refused, she stayed on her towel, watching us from the shore—or we all went for a walk and she lagged behind, picking up shells, or, if Nino and I started talking about the world, she listened attentively but rarely said anything. In the meantime, small habits became established, and I was struck by her insistence that they be respected. For example, Bruno always arrived with cold drinks that he bought on the way, at a bar on the beach, and one day she pointed out to him that he had brought me a soda whereas usually I had orangeade; I said, "Thanks, Bruno, this is fine," but she made him go and exchange it. For example, Pinuccia and Bruno at a certain point in the afternoon went to get fresh coconut, and although they invited us to go with them, it never occurred to Lila to do so, or to me or Nino: it thus became completely normal for them to go off dry, return wet from a swim, and bring coconut, with the whitest flesh, and so if it seemed that they might forget Lila would say, "And where's the coconut today?"

Also, she was very interested in Nino's and my conversations. When there was too much talk about nothing in particular she would say to him, "Didn't you read anything interesting today?" Nino smiled, pleased, rambled a bit, then started on the subjects he cared about. He talked and talked, but there were never real frictions between us: I found myself almost always in agreement with him, and if Lila interrupted to make an objection she did it briefly, with tact, without ever accentuating the disagreement.

One afternoon he was quoting an article that was very critical of the functioning of the public schools, and he went on without a break to speak disparagingly of the elementary school in our neighborhood. I agreed, I recalled how Maestra Oliviero rapped us on the knuckles when we made a mistake and also the brutal competitions to see who was smartest that she subjected us to. But Lila, surprising me, said that elementary school for her had been extremely important, and she praised our teacher in an Italian I hadn't heard from her in a long time, so precise, so intense, that Nino didn't interrupt her to say what he thought, but listened to her attentively, and in the end made some generic remarks about the different requirements we have and about how the same experience can satisfy the needs of one and be insufficient for the needs of someone else.

There was also another case where Lila revealed a disagreement politely and in a cultivated Italian. I felt increasingly drawn to arguments based on the theory that the right kind of interventions, carried out over time, would resolve problems, eliminate injustices, and prevent conflicts. I had quickly learned that system of reasoning—I was always very good at that—and I applied it every time Nino brought up subjects about which he had read here and there: colonialism, neocolonialism, Africa. But one afternoon Lila said softly that there was nothing that could eliminate the conflict between the rich and the poor.

"Why?"

"Those who are on the bottom always want to be on top, those who are on top want to stay on top, and one way or another they always reach the point where they're kicking and spitting at each other."

"That's exactly why problems should be resolved before violence breaks out."

"And how? Putting everyone on top, putting everyone on the bottom?"

"Finding a point of equilibrium between the classes."

"A point where? Those from the bottom meet those from the top in the middle?"

"Let's say yes."

"And those on top will be willing to go down? And those on the bottom will give up on going any higher?"

"If people work to solve all the problems well, yes. You're not convinced?"

"No. The classes aren't playing cards, they're fighting, and it's a fight to the death."

"That's what Pasquale thinks," I said.

"I think so, too, now," she said calmly.

Apart from those few one-on-one exchanges, there were rarely, between Nino and Lila, words that were not mediated by me. Lila never addressed him directly, nor did Nino address her, they seemed embarrassed by one another. She appeared much more comfortable with Bruno, who, though quiet, managed, with his kindness, and the pleasant tone in which he would call her Signora Carracci, to establish a certain familiarity. For example, once when we all went in the water together—and Nino, surprisingly, did not go on one of the long swims that made me anxious—she turned to Bruno, and not to him, to show her after how many strokes she should take her head out of the water to breathe. He promptly gave her a demonstration. But Nino was annoyed that he hadn't been asked, given his mastery of swimming, and he interrupted, making fun of Bruno's short arms, his lack of rhythm. Then he showed Lila the right way. She observed him with attention and immediately imitated him. In the end Lila's swimming led Bruno to call her the Esther Williams of Ischia.

When the end of the week arrived—I remember it was a splendid Saturday morning, the air was still cool and the sharp odor of the pines accompanied us all the way to the beach—Pinuccia reasserted categorically, "Sarratore's son is really unbearable."

I defended Nino warily. I said in the tone of an expert that when a person studies, when he becomes interested in things, he feels the need to communicate those interests to others, and for Nino it was like that. Lila didn't seem convinced, she made a remark that sounded offensive to me: "If you removed from Nino's head the things he's read, you wouldn't find anything there."

I snapped, "It's not true. I know him and he has a lot of good qualities."

Pinuccia, on the other hand, agreed enthusiastically. But Lila, maybe because she didn't like that approval, said she hadn't explained well and reversed the meaning of the remark, as if she had formulated it only as a trial and now, hearing it, regretted it, and was grasping at straws to make up for it. He, she clarified, is habituating himself to the idea that only the big questions are important, and if he succeeds he will live his whole life only for those, without being disturbed by anything else: not like us, who think only of our own affairs—money, house, husband, children.

I didn't like that version, either. What was she saying? That for Nino feelings for individual persons would not count, that his fate was to live without love, without children, without marriage? I forced myself to say:

"You know he has a girlfriend he's very attached to? They write once a week."

Pinuccia interrupted: "Bruno doesn't have a girlfriend, but he's looking for his ideal woman and as soon as he finds her he'll get married and he wants to have a lot of children." Then, without obvious connection, she sighed: "This week has really flown by."

"Aren't you glad? Now your husband will be back," I replied.

She seemed almost offended by the possibility that I could imagine her feeling any annoyance at Rino's return.

She exclaimed, "Of course I'm glad."

Lila then asked me, "And are you glad?"

"That your husbands are returning?"

"No, you know what I meant."

I did know but I wouldn't admit it. She meant that the next day, Sunday, while they were involved with Stefano and Rino, I would be able to see the boys by myself, and in fact, almost certainly, Bruno, as he had the week before, would be minding his own business, and I would spend the afternoon with Nino. And she was right, that was what I was hoping. For days, before going to sleep, I had been thinking of the weekend. Lila and Pinuccia would have their conjugal pleasures, I would have the small happinesses of the unmarried girl in glasses who spends her life studying: a walk, being taken by the hand. Or who knows, maybe even more. I said, laughing, "What should I understand, Lila? You're the lucky ones, who are married."

48.

The day slid by slowly. While Lila and I sat calmly in the sun waiting until the time when Nino and Bruno would arrive with cool drinks, Pinuccia's mood began, for no reason, to darken. She kept uttering nervous remarks. Now she was afraid that they wouldn't come, now she exclaimed that we couldn't waste our time waiting for them to show up. When, punctually, the boys appeared with the drinks, she was surly, and said she felt tired. But a few minutes later, though still in a bad mood, she changed her mind and agreed, grumbling, to go get the coconut.

As for Lila, she did something I didn't like. For the whole week she had never said anything about the book I had lent her, and so I had forgotten about it. But as soon as Pinuccia and Bruno left, she didn't wait for Nino to start talking, and immediately asked him, "Have you ever been to the theater?"

"A few times."

"Did you like it?"

"It was all right."

"I've never been, but I've seen it on television."

"It's not the same thing."

"I know, but better than nothing."

And at that point she took out of her bag the book I had given her, the volume of Beckett's plays, and showed it to him.

"Have you read this?"

Nino took the book, examined it, admitted uneasily, "No."

"So there *is* something you haven't read."

"Yes."

"You should read it."

Lila began to talk to us about the book. To my surprise she was very deliberate, she talked the way she used to, choosing the words so as to make us see people and things, and also the emotion she gave them, portraying them anew, keeping them there, present, alive. She said that we didn't have to wait for nuclear war, in the book it was as if it had already happened. She told us at length about a woman named Winnie who at a certain point announced, *another happy day*, and she herself declaimed the phrase, becoming so upset that, in uttering it, her voice trembled slightly: *another happy day*, words that were insupportable, because nothing, nothing, she explained, in Winnie's life, nothing in her gestures, nothing in her head, was *happy*, not that day or the preceding days. But, she added, the biggest impression had been made on her by a Dan Rooney. Dan Rooney, she said, is blind but he's not bitter about it, because he believes that life is better without sight, and in fact he wonders whether, if one became deaf and mute, life would not be still more life, life without anything but life.

"Why did you like it?" Nino asked.

"I don't know yet if I liked it."

"But it made you curious."

"It made me think. What does it mean that life is more life without sight, without hearing, even without words?"

"Maybe it's just a gimmick."

"No, what gimmick. There's a thing here that suggests a thousand others, it's not a gimmick."

Nino didn't reply. He said only, staring at the cover of the book as if that, too, needed to be deciphered, "Have you finished it?"

"Yes."

"Will you lend it to me?"

That request disturbed me, I felt pained. Nino had said, I remembered it clearly, that he had little interest in literature, what he read was different. I had given that Beckett to Lila just because I knew that I couldn't use it in conversation with him. And now that she was talking about it he was not only listening but asked to borrow it.

I said, "It's Professor Galiani's, she gave it to me."

"Have you read it?" he asked me.

I had to admit that I hadn't, but I added right away, "I was thinking of starting tonight."

"When you're finished will you give it to me?"

"If it interests you so much," I said quickly, "you read it first."

Nino thanked me, scratched away with his nail the trace of a mosquito from the cover, said to Lila, "I'll read it overnight and tomorrow we can talk about it."

"Not tomorrow, we won't see each other."

"Why?"

"I'll be with my husband."

"Oh."

He seemed annoyed. I waited fearfully for him to ask me if the two of us would see each other. But he had a burst of impatience, he said, "I can't tomorrow, either. Bruno's parents arrive tonight and I have to go sleep in Barano. I'll be back on Monday."

Barano? Monday? I hoped that he would ask me to join him at the Maronti. But he was distracted, maybe his mind was still on Dan Rooney, who, not content with being blind, wished to become deaf and mute, too. He didn't ask me anything.

49.

On the way home I said to Lila, "If I lend you a book, which, besides, isn't mine, please don't take it to the beach. I can't give it back to Professor Galiani with sand in it."

"I'm sorry," she said, and cheerfully gave me a kiss on the cheek. She wanted to carry both my bag and Pinuccia's, maybe to ask forgiveness.

Slowly my mood cleared. I thought that Nino hadn't randomly alluded to the fact that he was going to Barano: he wanted me to know, and I decided independently to go and see him there. He's like that, I said to myself, with growing relief, he needs to be pursued: tomorrow I'll get up early and go. Pinuccia's ill humor, on the other hand, continued. Usually she was quick to get angry but quick to get over it, too, especially now that pregnancy had softened not only her body but also the rough edges of her character. Instead she became increasingly fretful.

"Did Bruno say something unpleasant?" I asked her.

"No."

"Then what happened?"

"Nothing."

"Do you not feel well?"

"I'm fine, I don't even know what's wrong with me."

"Go and get ready, Rino will be here."

"Yes."

But she continued to sit in her damp bathing suit, leafing distractedly through a photonovel. Lila and I got dressed up,

Lila especially decked herself out as if she were going to a party, and still Pinuccia did nothing. Then even Nunzia, who was laboring silently over the dinner preparations, said softly, "Pinù, what's the matter, sweetie, aren't you going to get dressed?" No answer. Only when we heard the roar of the Lambrettas and the voices of the two young men calling did Pina jump up and run to her room, crying, "Don't let them come in, please."

The evening was bewildering, for the husbands, too. Stefano, by now used to permanent conflict with Lila, found himself unexpectedly in the company of a girl who was very affectionate, yielding to caresses and kisses without her usual irritation; while Rino, accustomed to Pinuccia's clingy coquettishness, intensified by her pregnancy, was disappointed that his wife didn't come down the stairs to greet him, that he had to look for her in the bedroom, and when finally he embraced her, he immediately noticed the effort she made to act as if she were pleased. Not only that. While Lila laughed heartily when, after a few glasses of wine, the two men started in with the lively sexual allusions that indicated desire, Pinuccia, at a whispered remark from Rino, laughing, jerked away and hissed, in a half Italian, "Stop it, you're a boor." He got angry: "You call me a boor? Boor?" She resisted for a few minutes, then her lower lip trembled and she took refuge in her room.

"It's the pregnancy," Nunzia said, "you have to be patient."

Silence. Rino finished eating, then, fuming, went to his wife. He didn't come back.

Lila and Stefano decided to go out on the Lambretta to see the beach at night. They left laughing together, kissing. I cleared the table, as usual struggling with Nunzia, who didn't want me to lift a finger. We talked about when she had met Fernando and they fell in love, and she said something that made a deep impression. She said, "For your whole life you love people and you never really know who they are." Fernando was both good and bad, and she had loved him very much but she had also hated him. "So," she emphasized, "there's nothing to worry about: Pinuccia is in a bad mood but she'll get over it; and you remember how Lina came back from her honeymoon? Well, look at them now. Life is like that: one day you're getting hit, the next kissed."

I went to my room, I tried to finish Chabod, but I recalled how Nino had been charmed by the way Lila talked about that Rooney, and the desire to waste time with the idea of nationhood vanished. Even Nino is evasive, I thought, even with Nino it's hard to understand who he is. He seemed not to care about literature and yet Lila randomly picks up a book of plays, says two foolish things, and he becomes ardent about it. I rummaged among the books in search of other literary things, but I had none. I realized that a book was missing. Was that possible? Professor Galiani had given me six. Nino now had one, one I was reading, on the marble windowsill there were three. Where was the sixth?

I looked everywhere, even under the bed, and while I was looking I remembered that it was a book about Hiroshima. I was upset—surely Lila must have taken it while I was in the bathroom. What was happening to her? After years of shoes, engagement, love, grocery store, dealings with the Solaras, had she decided to revert to the person she had been in elementary school? Certainly there had already been a sign: she had wanted to make that bet, which, whatever its outcome, had surely been a way of demonstrating to me her wish to study. But had she followed up on that desire, had she actually done it? No. Yet had Nino's conversation been enough—six afternoons of sun on the sand—to revive in her the desire to learn, maybe compete again to be the best? Was that why she had sung the praises of Maestra Oliviero? Why had she found it wonderful that someone should become passionate for his whole life only about important things and not those of daily life? I left my room on tiptoe, opening the door carefully, so that it wouldn't squeak.

The house was silent,, Nunzia had gone to sleep, Stefano and Lila weren't back yet. I went into their room: a chaos of clothes, shoes, suitcases. On a chair I found the volume, it was titled *Hiroshima the Day After*. She had taken it without asking my permission, as if my things were hers, as if what I was I owed to her, as if even Professor Galiani's attention to my education resulted from the fact that she, with a distracted gesture, with a tentative phrase, had put me in the position of gaining that privilege for myself. I thought of taking the book. But I was ashamed, I changed my mind, and left it there.

50.

It was a dull Sunday. I suffered from the heat all night, I didn't dare open the window for fear of the mosquitoes. I fell asleep, woke up, fell asleep again. Go to Barano? With what result? Spend the day playing with Ciro, Pino, and Clelia, while Nino took long swims or sat in the sun without saying a word, in mute conflict with his father. I woke up late, at ten, and as soon as I opened my eyes a sensation of loss, as if from a great distance, came over me and pained me.

I learned from Nunzia that Pinuccia and Rino had already gone to the beach, while Stefano and Lila were still sleeping. I soaked my bread in the caffelatte without wanting it, I conclusively gave up going to Barano. I went to the beach, anxious and sad.

I found Rino sleeping in the sun, his hair wet, his heavy body lying, stomach down, on the sand, and Pinuccia walking back and forth on the shore. I invited her to go toward the fumaroles, she refused rudely. I walked for a long time alone in the direction of Forio to calm myself.

The morning passed slowly. When I came back I went swimming, then lay in the sun. I had to listen to Rino and Pinuccia, who, as if I weren't there, were murmuring to each other phrases such as:

"Don't go."

"I have to work: the shoes have to be ready for the fall. Did you see them, do you like them?"

"Yes, but the things Lina made you add are ugly, take them off."

"No, they look good."

"You see? What I say counts for nothing with you."

"That's not true."

"It's very true, you don't love me anymore."

"I do love you, and you know how much I want you."

"No way, look at the belly I have."

"I'd give that belly ten thousand kisses. For the whole week all I do is think about you."

"Then don't go to work."

"I can't."

"Then I'll leave tonight, too."

"We've already paid our share, you have to have your vacation."

"I don't want it anymore."

"Why?"

"Because as soon as I fall asleep I have terrible dreams and I'm awake all night."

"Even when you sleep with my sister?"

"Even more, if your sister could kill me, she would."

"Go sleep with my mamma."

"Your mamma snores."

Pinuccia's tone of voice was unbearable. All day I tried to figure out the reasons for her complaints. That she didn't sleep much or very well was true. But that she wanted Rino to stay, or that she really wanted to leave with him, seemed to me a lie.

At one point I was convinced that she was trying to tell him something that she herself didn't know and so could express only in the form of peevishness. But then I forgot about it, I had other things to think about. Lila's exuberance, first of all.

When she appeared at the beach with her husband, she seemed happier than the night before. She wanted to show him how she had learned to swim, and together they headed away from the shore—out where it's deep, Stefano said, even though it was really only a few meters from the shore. With her elegant and precise strokes, and the rhythmic turn of the head to breathe that she had by now learned, moving her mouth away from the water, she immediately left him behind. Then she stopped to wait for him, laughing, until he caught up, clumsily flailing his arms, his head straight up, as he snorted at the water that sprayed in his face.

She was even livelier in the afternoon, when they went for a ride on the Lambretta. Rino wanted to drive around, too, and since Pinuccia refused—she was afraid of falling and losing the baby—he said to me, "You come, Lenù." It was my first such experience, with Stefano in the lead, Rino following, and the wind, and the fear of falling or crashing, and the increasing excitement, the strong odor that came from the sweaty back of Pinuccia's husband, and the swaggering self-confidence that pushed him to violate every rule and to respond to any protests according to the habits of the neighborhood, braking suddenly, threatening, always ready to fight to assert his right to do as he pleased. It was fun, a return to those feelings of a bad girl, very different from the ones Nino inspired in me when he appeared on the beach, in the afternoon, with his friend.

In the course of that Sunday I named the two boys often: I especially liked saying the name of Nino. I quickly noticed that both Pinuccia and Lila acted as if it hadn't been the three of us who spent time with Bruno and Nino, but only me. As a result, when their husbands said goodbye, hurrying off to catch the ferry, Stefano asked me to say hello to Soccavo's son for him, as if I were the only one who would have the opportunity to see him, and Rino teased me, with remarks like: Who do you like more, the son of the poet or the son of the mortadella maker? Who do you think is handsomer? as if his wife and sister had no basis for forming their own opinions.

Finally, the reactions of both to the departure of their husbands annoyed me. Pinuccia became cheerful, she wanted to wash her hair, which—she said aloud—was full of sand. Lila lounged about the house listlessly, then she lay down on her unmade bed, paying no attention to the mess in the room. When I went to say good night I saw that she hadn't even undressed: she was reading the book about Hiroshima, frowning, eyes narrowed. I didn't reproach her, I said only, perhaps a little sharply:

"How is it that you suddenly feel like reading again?"

"It's none of your business," she answered.

51.

On Monday Nino appeared, like a ghost evoked by my desire, not at four in the afternoon, as usual, but, surprisingly, at ten in the morning. We three girls had just arrived at the beach, resentful, each convinced that the others had spent too much time in the bathroom, Pinuccia particularly upset about how her hair had been ruined by her sleeping on it. It was she who spoke first, stern, almost aggressive. She asked Nino, even before he could explain to us, why in the world he had turned his schedule upside down:

"Why didn't Bruno come, he had better things to do?"

"His parents are still here, they're leaving at noon."

"Then he'll come?"

"I think so."

"Because if he's not coming I'm going back to sleep, with just the three of you I'll be bored."

And while Nino was telling us how terrible his Sunday in Barano had been, and so he had left early and, since he couldn't go to Bruno's, had come straight to the beach, she interrupted once or twice, asking in a whine: Who's going to go swimming with me? Since both Lila and I ignored her, she went into the water angrily by herself.

Never mind. We preferred to listen attentively to the list of wrongs that Nino suffered at the hands of his father. A cheater, he called him, a malingerer. He had settled himself in Barano, extending his leave from work on the ground of some feigned illness, which had been properly certified, however, by a health-service doctor who was a friend of his. "My father," he said in disgust, "is in everything and for everything the negation of the general interest." And then, without a break, he did something unpredictable. With a sudden movement that made me jump he leaned over and gave me a big, noisy kiss on the cheek, followed by the remark: "I'm really glad to see you." Then, slightly embarrassed, as if he had realized that with that effusiveness toward me he might be acting rudely toward Lila, he said: "May I also give you a kiss?"

"Of course," Lila answered, affably, and he gave her a light kiss, with no sound, a barely perceptible contact. After that he began to talk excitedly about the plays of Beckett: Ah, how he liked those guys buried in the ground up to their necks; and how beautiful the statement was about the fire that the present kindles inside you; and, even though among the thousand evocative things that Maddy and Dan Rooney said he had had a hard time picking out the precise point cited by Lila, well, the concept that life is felt more when you are blind, deaf, mute, and maybe without taste or touch was objectively interesting in itself. In his view it meant: Let's get rid of all the filters that prevent us from fully savoring our being here and now, real.

Lila appeared bewildered, she said that she had thought about it and that life in the pure state frightened her. She expressed herself with some emphasis, she exclaimed, "Life without seeing and without speaking, without speaking and listening, life without a covering, without a container, is shapeless." She didn't use exactly those words, but certainly she said "shapeless" and she said it with a gesture of revulsion. Nino repeated reluctantly, "shapeless," as if it were a curse word. Then he started talking again, even more overwrought, until, with no warning, he took off his shirt, revealing himself in all his dark thinness, grabbed us both by the hand, and dragged us into the water, as I cried happily, "No, no, no, I'm cold, no," and he answered, "*Here finally another happy day,*" and Lila laughed.

So, I thought contentedly, Lila is wrong. So there certainly exists another Nino: not the gloomy boy, not the one who gets excited only when he's thinking about the general state of the world, but *this boy*, this boy who plays, who drags us furiously into the water, who mocks us, grips us, pulls us toward him, swims away, lets us reach him, lets us grab him, lets us push him under the water and pretends to be overpowered, pretends that we're drowning him.

When Bruno arrived things got even better. We all took a walk together and Pinuccia's good humor slowly returned. She wanted to swim again, she wanted to eat coconut. Starting then, and for the whole week that followed, we found it completely natural that the boys should join us on the beach at ten in the morning and remain until sunset, when we said, "We have to go or Nunzia will get mad," and they resigned themselves to going off to do some studying.

How intimate we were now. If Bruno called Lila Signora Carracci to tease her, she punched him playfully on the shoulder, chased him, threatening. If he showed too much reverence toward Pinuccia because she was carrying a child, Pinuccia linked arms with him, said, "Come on, let's run, I want a soda."

As for Nino, now he often took my hand, put an arm around my shoulders, and then put an arm around Lila's, too, he took her index finger, her thumb. The wary distances receded. We became a group of five friends who were having a good time doing little or nothing. We played games, whoever lost paid a fine. The fines were almost always kisses, but joke kisses, obviously: Bruno had to kiss Lila's sandy feet, Nino my hand, and then cheeks, forehead, ear, with a pop in the auricle. We also had long games of *tamburello*. The ball flew through the air and was sent back with a sharp crack against the taut hide of the tambourines; Lila was good, Nino, too. But most agile of all, most precise, was Bruno. He and Pinuccia always won, against Lila and me, against Lila and Nino, against Nino and me. They won partly because we had all developed a sort of automatic tenderness toward Pina. She ran, she jumped, she tumbled on the sand, forgetting her condition, and so we ended by letting her win, sometimes just to soothe her. Bruno reproached her gently, made her sit down, said, that's enough and cried, "Point for Pinuccia, excellent."

A thread of happiness thus began to extend through the hours and days. I no longer minded that Lila took my books, in fact it seemed to me a good thing. I didn't mind that, when the discussions got going, she more and more often said what she thought and Nino listened attentively and seemed to lack the words for a response. I found it thrilling, in fact, that in those circumstances he would suddenly stop talking to her and start up with me, as if that helped him rediscover his convictions.

That was what happened the time Lila showed off her reading on Hiroshima. A tense discussion arose, because Nino, I saw, was so critical of the United States and didn't like the fact that the Americans had a military base in Naples, but he was also attracted by their way of life, he said he wanted to study it, and he was disappointed when Lila said, more or less, that dropping atomic bombs on Japan had been a war crime, in fact more than a war crime—the war had scarcely anything to do with it—it had been a crime of pride.

"Can I remind you of Pearl Harbor?" he said hesitantly.

I didn't know what Pearl Harbor was but I discovered that Lila did. She told him that Pearl Harbor and Hiroshima were two things that couldn't be compared, that Pearl Harbor was a vile act of war and Hiroshima was an idiotic, fierce, vindictive horror, worse, much worse, than the Nazi massacres. And she concluded: the Americans should be tried like the worst criminals, those who do terrible things to terrorize the living and keep them on their knees. She was so passionate that Nino, instead of moving to the counterattack, was silent, very thoughtful. Then he turned to me, as if she weren't there. He said that the problem wasn't ferocity or revenge but the urgency to bring an end to the most atrocious of wars and, at the same time, by using that terrible new weapon, to all wars. He spoke in a low tone, looking me straight in the eyes, as if he were interested only in my agreement. It was a wonderful moment. He himself was wonderful, when he was like that. I was so filled with emotion that tears rose to my eyes and I had trouble repressing them.

Then Friday came again, a very hot day that we spent mostly in the water. And suddenly something went bad again.

We had just left the two boys and were going back to the house, the sun was low, the sky pinkish-blue, when Pinuccia, unexpectedly silent after many long hours of extravagant play-fulness, threw her bag on the ground, sat down on the side of road, and began to cry with rage, small thin cries, almost a moaning.

Lila narrowed her eyes, stared at her as if she saw not her sister-in-law but something ugly for which she wasn't pre-pared. I went back, frightened, asked, "Pina, what's the matter, don't you feel well?"

"I can't bear this wet bathing suit."

"We all have wet bathing suits."

"It bothers me."

"Calm down, come on, aren't you hungry?"

"Don't tell me to calm down. You irritate me when you tell me to calm down. I can't stand you anymore, Lenù, you and your calm down."

And she started moaning again, and hitting her thighs.

I sensed that Lila was going on without waiting for us. I sensed that she had decided to do so not out of annoyance or indifference but because there was something in that behavior, something scorching, and if she got too close it would burn her. I helped Pinuccia get up, I carried her bag.

52.

Eventually she became quieter, but she spent the evening sulking, as if we had somehow offended her. When she was rude even to Nunzia, brusquely criticizing the way the pasta was cooked, Lila flared up and, breaking into a fierce dialect, dumped on her all the fantastic insults she was capable of. Pina decided to sleep with me that night.

She tossed and turned in her sleep. And with two people in the room the heat made it almost impossible to breathe. Soaked with sweat, I resigned myself to opening the window and was tormented by the mosquitoes. Then I couldn't sleep at all, I waited for dawn, I got up.

Now I, too, was in a bad mood, I had three or four disfiguring bites on my face. I went to the kitchen, Nunzia was washing our dirty clothes. Lila, too, was already up, she had had her bread-and-milk, and was reading another of my books, who knows when she had stolen it from me. As soon as she saw me, she gave me a searching glance and asked, with a genuine concern that I didn't expect: "How is Pinuccia?"

"I don't know."

"Are you angry?"

"Yes, I didn't sleep a wink, and look at my face."

"You can't see anything."

"*You* can't see anything."

"Nino and Bruno won't see anything, either."

"What does that have to do with it?"

"You still like Nino?"

"I've told you no a hundred times."

"Calm down."

"I am calm."

"Let's think about Pinuccia."

"You think about her, she's your sister-in-law, not mine."

"You're angry."

"Yes, I am."

The day was even hotter than the one before. We went to the beach apprehensively, the bad mood traveled from one to the other like an infection.

Halfway there Pinuccia realized she had forgotten her towel and had another attack of nerves. Lila kept going, head down, without even turning around.

"I'll go get it," I offered.

"No, I'm going back to the house, I don't feel like the beach."

"Do you feel sick?"

"I'm perfectly fine."

"Then what?"

"Look at the belly I've got."

I looked at her belly, I said to her without thinking: "What about me? Don't you see these bites on my face?"

She started yelling, she called me an idiot, and ran away to catch up with Lila.

Once at the beach she apologized, muttering, You're so good that sometimes you make me mad.

"I'm not good."

"I meant that you're clever."

"I'm not clever."

Lila, who was trying in any case to ignore us, staring at the sea in the direction of Forio, said coldly, "Stop it, they're coming."

Pinuccia started. "The long and the short of it," she murmured, with a sudden softness in her voice, and she put on some lipstick even though she already had enough.

The boys' mood was just as bad as ours. Nino had a sarcastic tone, he said to Lila, "Tonight the husbands arrive?"

"Of course."

"And what nice things will you do?"

"We'll eat, drink, and sleep."

"And tomorrow?"

"Tomorrow we'll eat, drink, and sleep."

"Do they stay Sunday night, too?"

"No, on Sunday we eat, drink, and sleep only in the afternoon."

Hiding behind a tone of self-mockery, I forced myself to say, "I'm free: I'm not eating or drinking or going to sleep."

Nino looked at me as if he were becoming aware of something he had never noticed, so that I passed a hand over my right cheek, where I had an especially big mosquito bite. He said to me seriously, "Good, we'll meet here tomorrow morning at seven and then climb the mountain. When we get back, the beach till late. What do you say?"

I felt in my veins the warmth of elation, I said with relief, "All right, at seven, I'll bring food."

Pinuccia asked, unhappily, "And us?"

"You have husbands," he said, and pronounced "husbands" as if he were saying toads, snakes, spiders, so that she got up abruptly and went to the water's edge.

"She's a little oversensitive at the moment," I said in apology, "but it's because of her interesting condition, usually she's not like that."

Bruno said in his patient voice, "I'll take her to get some coconut."

We watched him as, small but well proportioned, his chest powerful, his thighs strong, he moved over the sand at a steady pace, as if the sun had neglected to burn the grains he walked on. When Bruno and Pina set off for the beach bar, Lila said, "Let's go swimming."

53.

The three of us moved together toward the sea, me in the middle, between them. It's hard to explain the sudden sense of fullness that had possessed me when Nino said: We'll meet here tomorrow morning at seven. Of course I was sorry about the swings in Pinuccia's moods, but it was a weak sorrow, it couldn't dent my state of well-being. I was finally content with myself, with the long, exciting Sunday that awaited me; and at the same time I felt proud to be there, at that moment, with the people who had always been important in my life, whose importance couldn't be compared even to that of my parents, my siblings. I took them both by the hand, I gave a shout of happiness, I dragged them into the cold water, spraying icy splinters of foam. We sank as if we were a single organism.

As soon as we were underwater we let go of the chain of our fingers. I've never liked the cold of the water in my hair, on my head, in my ears. I re-emerged immediately, spluttering. But I saw that they were already swimming and I began to swim, in order not to lose them. I had trouble right away: I wasn't capable of swimming straight, head in the water, with steady strokes; my right arm was stronger than the left, and I veered right; I had to be careful not to swallow the salt water. I tried to keep up by not losing sight of them, in spite of my myopic vision. They'll stop, I thought. My heart was pounding, I slowed down, I finally stopped and floated, admiring their confident progress toward the horizon, side by side.

Maybe they were going too far. I, too, in the grip of enthusiasm, had ventured beyond the reassuring imaginary line that normally allowed me to return to the shore in a few strokes, and beyond which Lila herself had never gone. Now there she was, competing with Nino. Despite her inexperience she wouldn't give in, she wanted to stay even, she pushed on, farther and farther.

I began to worry. If her strength failed. If she felt ill. Nino is expert, he'll help her. But if he gets a cramp, if he collapses, too. I looked around, the current was dragging me to the left. I can't wait for them here, I have to go back. I glanced down, and it was a mistake. The azure immediately turned bluer, darkened like night, even though the sun was shining, the surface of the sea sparkled, and pure white shreds of cloud were stretching across the sky. I perceived the abyss, I sensed its liquidness, with nothing to hold on to, I felt it as a pit of the dead from which anything might rise up in a flash, touch me, grab me, sink its teeth into me, drag me to the bottom.

I tried to calm myself: I shouted Lila. My eyes without glasses were of no use, defeated by the sparkle of the water. I thought of my outing with Nino the following day. Slowly I turned around, on my back, paddling with legs and arms until I reached the shore.

I sat there, half in the water, half on the beach, I could just make out their heads, black dots like abandoned buoys on the surface of the sea, I felt relieved. Lila not only was safe but she had done it, she had stayed with Nino. How stubborn she is, how she overdoes it, how courageous she is. I got up, joined Bruno, who was sitting beside our things.

"Where's Pinuccia?" I asked.

He gave a timid smile that seemed to conceal a worry.

"She left."

"Where did she go?"

"Home, she says she has to pack her bags."

"Her bags?"

"She wants to go, she doesn't feel she can leave her husband alone for so long."

I took my things and, after insisting that he not lose sight of Nino and especially Lila, I left, still dripping wet, to try to find out what else was happening to Pina.

54.

It was a disastrous afternoon followed by an even more disastrous evening. I found that Pinuccia was really packing her bags and that Nunzia was unable to quiet her.

"You mustn't worry," she said to her soothingly, "Rino knows how to wash his underwear, he knows how to cook, and then there is his father, his friends. He doesn't think you're here to have fun, he understands that you're here to rest so that you'll have a fine healthy baby. Come, I'll help you tidy up everything. I never went on vacation, but today there's money, thank God, and although you mustn't waste it, a little comfort isn't a sin, you can afford it. So Pinù, please, child: Rino worked all week, he's tired, he's about to arrive. Don't let him find you like this, you know him, he'll worry, and when he worries he gets angry, and if he gets angry what's the result? The result is that you want to leave to stay with him, he has left to be with you, and now when you'll be together, and you ought to be happy, instead you're torturing each other. Does that seem nice to you?"

But Pinuccia was impervious to the arguments that Nunzia rattled off. Then I began to enumerate them, too, since we had reached the point where we were taking her many things out of the suitcases and she was putting them in, she cried, she calmed down, she started again.

Eventually Lila returned. She leaned against the doorpost and stood looking, with a frown, a long horizontal crease across her brow, at that disheveled image of Pinuccia.

"Everything all right?" I asked her.

She nodded yes.

"You're such a good swimmer now."

She said nothing.

She had the expression of someone who is forced to repress joy and fear at the same time. It was evident that the spectacle of Pinuccia was becoming increasingly intolerable to her. Her sister-in-law was again displaying her intention to depart, farewells, regret that she had forgotten this object or that, sighs for her Rinuccio, all interwoven, in a contradictory fashion, with regret for the sea, the smells of the gardens, the beach. And yet Lila said nothing, not one of her mean statements or even a sarcastic remark. Finally, the words came out of her mouth, not a call to order but the announcement of an imminent event that threatened us all: "They're about to arrive."

At that point Pinuccia collapsed disconsolate on the bed, next to the closed suitcases. Lila grimaced, went off to dress. She returned soon afterward in a clinging red dress, her black hair pulled back. She was the first to recognize the sound of the Lambrettas, she looked out the window, waved enthusiastically. Then, becoming serious, she turned to Pinuccia and in her most scornful voice hissed: "Go wash your face and take off that bathing suit."

Pinuccia looked at her without reacting. Something passed rapidly between the two girls, their secret feelings darted invisibly, infinitesimal particles shot at each other from the depths of themselves, a jolt and a trembling that lasted a long second;

I caught it, bewildered, but couldn't understand, while they did, they understood, in something they recognized each other, and Pinuccia knew that Lila knew, understood and wished to help her, even with contempt. So she obeyed.

55.

Stefano and Rino burst in. Lila was even more affectionate than the week before. She embraced Stefano, let him embrace her, gave a cry of joy when he took a case out of his pocket and she opened it and found a gold necklace with a pendant in the shape of a heart.

Naturally Rino, too, had brought a present for Pinuccia, who did her best to react as her sister-in-law had, but her painful fragility was visible in her eyes. So Rino's kisses and embraces and the gift had soon swept away the form of the happy wife within which she had so hastily enclosed herself. Her mouth started to tremble, the fountain of tears erupted, and she said, in a choked voice, "I've packed my bags. I don't want to stay here a minute longer, I want to be with you and only you, always."

Rino smiled, he was moved by all that love, he laughed. Then he said, "I also want to be with you and only you, always." Finally he understood that his wife was not just communicating how much she missed him, and how much she would always miss him, but that she really wanted to leave, that everything was ready for departure, and she was insisting on that decision with a real, unbearable grief.

They shut themselves in the bedroom to discuss it, but the discussion didn't last long, Rino came out, shouting at his mother, "Mamma, I want to know what happened." And without waiting for an answer, he turned aggressively to his sister: "If it's your fault by God I'll smash your face." Then he shouted at his wife, "That's enough, you're a pain in the ass, come out now, I'm tired, I want to eat."

Pinuccia reappeared with swollen eyes. When Stefano saw her, he made a playful attempt to defuse the situation, embracing his sister, and sighing, "Ah, love, you women drive us crazy for it." Then, as if suddenly recalling the primary cause of his own craziness, he kissed Lila on the lips, and in observing the unhappiness of the other couple he felt happy at how unexpectedly happy they were.

We all sat down at the table and Nunzia served us, one by one, in silence. But this time it was Rino who couldn't bear it, he yelled that he wasn't hungry anymore, he hurled the plate of spaghetti and clams into the middle of the kitchen. I was frightened, Pinuccia began to cry again. And even Stefano lost his composure and said to his wife, sharply: "Let's go, I'll take you to a restaurant." Amid the protests of Nunzia and even of Pinuccia they left the kitchen. In the silence that followed we heard the Lambretta setting off.

I helped Nunzia clean the floor. Rino got up, went to the bedroom. Pinuccia locked herself in the bathroom, but then she came out and joined her husband. She closed the door. Only then did Nunzia explode, forgetting her role of tolerant mother-in-law.

"Do you see how that bitch is making Rinuccio suffer? What's happened to her?"

I said I didn't know, and it was true, but I spent the evening consoling her by romanticizing Pinuccia's feelings. I said that if I were carrying a child in my belly I, like her, would have wanted to be with my husband always, to feel protected, to be sure that my responsibility as a mother was shared by his as a father. I said that if Lila was there to have a child, and it was clear that the cure was right, that the sea was doing her good—you had only to look at the happiness that lighted up her face when Stefano arrived—Pinuccia instead was already full of love and wished to give all that love to Rino every minute of the day and night, otherwise it weighed on her and she suffered.

It was a sweet hour, Nunzia and I in the kitchen that was tidy now, the dishes and the pots shining because of the care with which they had been washed. She said to me, "How well you speak, Lenù, it's clear that you'll have a wonderful future." Tears came to her eyes, she murmured that Lila should have gone to school, it was her destiny. "But my husband didn't want it," she added, "and I didn't know how to oppose him: there wasn't the money then, and yet she could have done as you did; instead she got married, she chose a different path and one can't go back, life takes us where it wants." She wished me happiness, "with a fine young man who has studied like you." She asked if I really liked the son of Sarratore. I denied it, but I confided to her that I was going the next day to climb the mountain with him. She was glad, she helped me make some sandwiches with salami and provolone. I wrapped them in paper, put them in the bag with my towel for swimming, and everything else I needed. She urged me to be prudent as always and we said good night.

I went to my room, read a little, but I was distracted. How lovely it would be to go out early in the morning, with the cool air, the scents. How much I loved the sea, and even Pinuccia, her tears, the evening's quarrel, the conciliatory love that, week by week, was increasing between Lila and Stefano. And how much I desired Nino. And how pleasant it was to have there with me, every day, him and my friend, the three of us content despite misunderstandings, despite the bad feelings that did not always remain silent in the dark depths.

I heard Stefano and Lila return. Their voices and laughter were muffled. Doors opened, closed, opened again. I heard the tap, the flush. Then I turned off the light, I listened to the faint rustle of the reeds, the scurrying in the henhouse, I fell asleep.

But I woke immediately, there was someone in my room.

"It's me," Lila whispered.

I felt her sitting on the edge of the bed, I was about to turn on the light.

"No," she said, "I'll stay only a moment."

I turned it on anyway, I sat up.

She was wearing a pale pink nightgown. Her skin was so darkened by the sun that her eyes seemed white.

"Did you see how far I went?"

"You were great, but I was worried."

She shook her head proudly and gave a little smile as if to say that the sea now belonged to her. Then she became serious.

"I have to tell you something."

"What?"

"Nino kissed me," she said, and she said it in one breath, like someone who, making a spontaneous confession, is trying to hide, even from herself, something more unconfessable. "He kissed me but I kept my lips closed."

56.

The account was detailed. She, exhausted by the long swim and yet satisfied that she had proved how proficient she was, had leaned against him so that it would be less effort to float. But Nino had taken advantage of her closeness and had pressed his lips hard against hers. She had immediately compressed her mouth and although he had tried to open it with the tip of his tongue he hadn't been able to. "You're crazy," she had said, pushing him away, "I'm married." But Nino had answered, "I've loved you long before your husband, ever since we had that competition in class." Lila had ordered him never to try it again and they had started swimming again toward the shore. "He pressed so hard he hurt my lips," she concluded, "and they still hurt."

She waited for me to react, but I managed not to ask questions or comment. When she told me not to go to the mountain with him unless Bruno came, too, I said coldly that if Nino had kissed me, I wouldn't have found anything bad about it, I wasn't married and didn't even have a boyfriend. "Only it's a pity," I added, "that I don't like him: kissing him would be like putting my mouth on a dead rat." Then I pretended to be unable to repress a yawn and she, after a look that seemed to be of affection and also of admiration, went to bed. I wept from the moment she left until dawn.

Today I feel some uneasiness in recalling how much I suffered, I have no sympathy for myself of that time. But in the course of that night it seemed to me that I had no reason to live. Why did Nino behave in that way? He kissed Nadia, he kissed me, he kissed Lila. How could he be the same person I loved, who was so serious, so thoughtful. The hours passed, but it was impossible for me to accept that he was as profound in confronting the great problems of the world as he was superficial in feelings of love. I began to question myself, I had made a mistake, I was deluded. Was it possible that I—short, too full-figured, wearing glasses, I diligent but not intelligent, I who pretended to be cultured, informed, when I wasn't— could have believed that he would like me even just for the length of a vacation? And, besides, had I ever really thought that? I examined my behavior scrupulously. No, I wasn't able to tell myself what my desires were with any clarity. Not only was I careful to hide them from others but I admitted them to myself in a skeptical way, without conviction. Why had I never told Lila plainly what I felt for Nino? And now, why had I not cried to her the pain she had caused me with that confidence in the middle of the night, why hadn't I revealed to her that, before kissing her, Nino had kissed me? What drove me to act like that? Did I keep my feelings muted because I was frightened by the violence with which, in fact, in my innermost self,

I wanted things, people, praise, triumphs? Was I afraid that that violence, if I did not get what I wanted, would explode in my chest, taking the path of the worst feelings—for example, the one that had driven me to compare Nino's beautiful mouth to the flesh of a dead rat? Why, then, even when I advanced, was I so quick to retreat? Why did I always have ready a gracious smile, a happy laugh, when things went badly? Why, sooner or later, did I always find plausible excuses for those who made me suffer?

Questions and tears. It was daybreak when I felt that I understood what had happened. Nino had sincerely believed that he loved Nadia. Of course, aware of my reputation with Professor Galiani, he had looked at me for years with sincere respect and liking. But now, at Ischia, he had met Lila and had understood that she had been since childhood—and would be in the future—his only true love. Ah yes, surely it had happened that way. And how could one reproach him? Where was the fault? In their history there was something intense, sublime: elective affinities. I called on poems and novels as tranquilizers. Maybe, I thought, studying has been useful to me just for this: to calm myself. She had kindled the flame in his breast, he had preserved it for years without realizing it: now that that flame had flared up, what could he do but love her. Even if she was married and therefore inaccessible, forbidden: marriage lasts forever, beyond death. Unless one violates it, condemning oneself to the infernal whirlwind until Judgment Day. It seemed to me, when dawn broke, that I had gained some clarity. Nino's love for Lila was an impossible love. Like mine for him. And only within that frame of unattainability did the kiss he had given her in the middle of the sea begin to seem utterable.

The kiss.

It hadn't been a choice, it had happened: especially since Lila knew how to make things happen. Whereas I don't, what will I do now. I'll go to our meeting. We'll climb Epomeo. Or no. I'll leave tonight with Stefano and Rino. I'll say that my mother wrote and needs me. How can I go climbing with him when I know that he loves Lila, that he kissed her. And how will I be able to see them together every day, swimming, going farther and farther out. I was exhausted, I fell asleep. I woke with a start, and found that the formulas running through my head really had tamed the suffering a little. I hurried to the meeting.

57.

I was sure that he wouldn't come, but when I got to the beach he was already there, and without Bruno. But I realized that he had no desire to look for the road to the mountain, to set out on unknown paths. He said that he was ready to go, if I really wanted to, but he predicted that in this heat we'd get unbearably exhausted and dismissed the idea that we'd ever find anything as worthwhile as a good swim. I began to worry, I thought he was on the verge of saying that he was going to go back and study. Instead, to my surprise, he proposed renting a boat. He counted and recounted the money he had, I took out my few cents. He smiled, he said gently, "You've taken care of the sandwiches, I'll do this." A few minutes later we were on the sea, he at the oars, I sitting in the stern.

I felt better. I thought maybe Lila had lied to me, that he hadn't kissed her. But in some part of myself I knew very well that it wasn't so: I sometimes lied, yes, even (or especially) to myself; she, on the other hand, as far as I could remember, had never done so. Besides, I had only to wait a while and it was Nino himself who explained things. When we were out on the water he let go of the oars and dived in, I did the same. He didn't swim the way he usually did, mingling with the undulating surface of the sea. Instead he dropped toward the bottom, disappeared, reappeared farther on, sank again. I was alarmed by the depth, and swam around the boat, not daring to go too far, until I got tired and clumsily pulled myself in. After a while he joined me, grabbed the oars, began to row energetically, following a line parallel to the coast, toward Punta Imperatore. So far we had remarked on the sandwiches, the heat, the sea, how wise we had been not to take the mule paths up Epomeo. To my increasing wonder he hadn't yet resorted to the subjects he was reading about in books, in journals, in newspapers, even though every so often, afraid of the silence, I threw out some remark that might set off his passion for the things of the world. But no, he had something else on his mind. And eventually he put down the oars, stared for a moment at a rock face, a flight of seagulls, then he said:

"Did Lina say anything to you?"

"About what?"

He pressed his lips together uneasily, and said, "All right, I'm going to tell you what happened. Yesterday I kissed her."

That was the beginning. We spent the rest of the day talking about the two of them. We went swimming again, he explored cliffs and caves, we ate the sandwiches, drank all the water I had brought, he wanted to teach me to row, but as for talking we couldn't talk about anything else. And what most struck me was that he didn't try even once, as he normally tended to do, to transform his particular situation into a general situation. Only he and Lila, Lila and he. He said nothing about love. He said nothing about the reasons one ends up being in love with one person rather than another. He questioned me, instead, obsessively about her and her relationship with Stefano.

"Why did she marry him?"

"Because she was in love with him."

"It can't be."

"I assure you it is."

"She married him for money, to help her family, to settle herself."

"If that was all she could have married Marcello Solara."

"Who's that?"

"A guy who has more money than Stefano and was crazy about her."

"And she?"

"Didn't want him."

"So you think she married the grocer out of love."

"Yes."

"And what's this business about going swimming to have children?"

"The doctor told her."

"But does she want them?"

"At first no, now I don't know."

"And he?"

"He yes."

"Is he in love with her?"

"Very much."

"And you, from the outside, do you think that everything's fine between them?"

"With Lina things are never fine."

"Meaning?"

"They had problems from the first day of their marriage, but it was because of Lina, who couldn't adjust."

"And now?"

"Now it's going better."

"I don't believe it."

He went around and around that point with growing skepticism. But I insisted: Lila never had loved her husband as in that period. And the more incredulous he appeared the more I piled it on. I told him plainly that between them nothing could happen, I didn't want him to delude himself. This, however, was of no use in exhausting the subject. It became increasingly clear that the more I talked to him in detail about Lila the more pleasant for him that day between sea and sky would be. It didn't matter to him that every word of mine made him suffer. It mattered that I should tell him everything I knew, the good and the bad, that I should fill our minutes and our hours with her name. I did, and if at first this pained me, slowly it changed. I felt, that day, that to speak of Lila with Nino could in the weeks to come give a new character to the relationship between the three of us. Neither she nor I would ever have him. But both of us, for the entire time of the vacation, could gain his attention, she as the object of a passion with no future, I as the wise counselor who kept under control both his folly and hers. I consoled myself with that hypothesis of centrality. Lila had come to me to tell me about Nino's kiss. He, starting out from the confession of that kiss, talked to me for an entire day. I would become necessary to both.

In fact Nino already couldn't do without me.

"You think she'll never be able to love me?" he asked at one point.

"She made a decision, Nino."

"What?"

"To love her husband, to have a child with him. She's here just for that."

"And my love for her?"

"When one is loved one tends to love in return. It's likely that she'll feel gratified. But if you don't want to suffer more, don't expect anything else. The more Lina is surrounded by affection and admiration, the crueler she can become. She's always been like that."

We parted at sunset and for a while I had the impression of having had a good day. But as soon as I was on the road home the anguish returned. How could I even think of enduring that torture, talking about Lila with Nino, about Nino with Lila, and, from tomorrow, witnessing their flirtations, their games, the clasps, the touching? I reached the house determined to announce that my mother wanted me back home. But as soon as I came in Lila assailed me harshly.

"Where have you been? We came to look for you. We need you, you've got to help us."

I discovered that they had not had a good day. It was Pinuccia's fault, she had tormented everyone. In the end she had cried that if her husband didn't want her at home it meant that he didn't love her and so she preferred to die with the child. At that point Rino had given in and taken her back to Naples.

58.

I understood only the next day what Pinuccia's departure meant. That evening her absence struck me as positive: no more whining, the house quieted down, time slithered away silently. When I withdrew into my little room and Lila followed me, the conversation was apparently without tension. I held my tongue, careful to say nothing of what I truly felt.

"Do you understand why she wanted to leave?" Lila asked me, speaking of Pinuccia.

"Because she wants to be with her husband."

She shook her head no, she said seriously, "She was becoming afraid of her own emotions."

"Which means?"

"She fell in love with Bruno."

I was amazed, I had never thought of that possibility.

"Pinuccia?"

"Yes."

"And Bruno?"

"He had no idea."

"You're sure?"

"Yes."

"How do you know?"

"Bruno's interested in you."

"Nonsense."

"Nino told me yesterday."

"He didn't say anything to me today."

"What did you do?"

"We rented a boat."

"You and he alone?"

"Yes."

"What did you talk about?"

"Everything."

"Even about the thing I told you about?"

"What thing?"

"You know."

"The kiss?"

"Yes."

"No, he didn't tell me anything."

Although I was dazed by the hours of sun and swimming, I managed not to say the wrong thing. When Lila went to bed I felt that I was floating on the sheet and that the dark little room was full of blue and reddish lights. Pinuccia had left in a hurry because she was in love with Bruno? Bruno wanted not her but me? I thought back to the relationship between Pinuccia and Bruno, I listened again to remarks, tones of voice, I saw again gestures, and I was sure that Lila was right. I suddenly felt great sympathy for Stefano's sister, for the strength she had shown in forcing herself to leave. But that Bruno was interested in me I wasn't convinced. He had never even looked at me. Beyond the fact that, if he had had the intention that Lila said, he would have come to the appointment and not Nino. Or at least they would have come together. And anyway, true or not, I didn't like him: too short, too curly-haired, no forehead, wolflike teeth. No and no. Stay in the middle, I thought. That's what I'll do.

The next day we arrived at the beach at ten and discovered that the boys were already there, walking back and forth along the shore. Lila explained Pinuccia's absence in a few words: she had to work, she had left with her husband. Neither Nino nor Bruno showed the least regret and this disturbed me. How could someone vanish like that, without leaving a void? Pinuccia had been with us for two weeks. We had all five walked together, we had talked, joked, gone swimming. In those fifteen days something had certainly happened that had marked her, she would never forget that first vacation. But we? We, who in different ways had meant a lot to her, in fact didn't feel her absence. Nino, for example, made no comment on that sudden departure. And Bruno confined himself to saying, gravely, "Too bad, we didn't even say goodbye." A minute later we were already speaking of other things, as if she had never come to Ischia, to Citara.

Nor did I like a sort of rapid readjustment of roles. Nino, who had always talked to me and Lila together (in fact very often to me alone), immediately began talking only to her, as if it were no longer necessary, now that we were four, to take on the burden of entertaining both of us. Bruno, who until the preceding Saturday had been occupied with Pinuccia and nothing else, now focused on me, in the same timid and solicitous way, as if nothing distinguished us from each other, not even the fact that she was married and pregnant and I was not.

For the first walk that we took along the shore, we left as four, side by side. But soon Bruno spotted a shell turned up by a wave, said, "How pretty," and bent down to pick it up. Out of politeness I stopped to wait for him, and he gave me the shell, which was nothing special. Meanwhile Nino and Lila continued to walk, which transformed us into two couples taking a walk on the water's edge, the two of them ahead, the two of us behind, they talking animatedly, I trying to make conver-

sation with Bruno while Bruno struggled to talk to me. I tried
to hurry, he held me back, against my will. It was difficult to
establish a real connection. His conversation was banal, I don't
know, about the sea, the sky, the seagulls, but it was evident
that he was playing a role, the one that he thought was right for
me. With Pinuccia he must have talked about other things,
otherwise it was hard to know how they had enjoyed spending
so much time together. Besides, even if he had touched on
more interesting subjects, it would have been hard to know
what he was saying. If he was asking the time or for a cigarette
or a drink of water, he had a direct tone of voice, clear pronunciation. But when he started with that role of the devoted
young man (*the shell, do you like it, look how pretty it is, I'll
give it to you*), he got tangled up, he spoke neither in Italian
nor in dialect, but in an awkward language that came to him in
an undertone, mumbled, as if he were ashamed of what he was
saying. I nodded my head yes but I didn't understand much,
and meanwhile I strained my ears to catch what Nino and Lila
were saying.

I imagined that he was talking about the serious subjects he
was studying, or that she was showing off the ideas she got
from the books she had taken from me, and I often tried to
catch up to join in their conversations. But every time I managed to get close enough to pick up some phrase, I was disoriented. He seemed to be telling her about his childhood in the
neighborhood, using intense, even dramatic tones; she listened
without interrupting. I felt intrusive, retreated, resolved to stay
behind to be bored by Bruno.

Even when we all decided to go swimming, I wasn't in time
to restore the old trio. Bruno without warning pushed me into
the water, I went under, got my hair wet when I didn't want to
get my hair wet. When I re-emerged, Nino and Lila were floating a few meters farther out and were continuing to talk, seriously. They stayed in the water much longer than we did, but

without going too far from the shore. They must have been so involved in what they were talking about that they gave up even the luxury of the long swim.

In the late afternoon Nino spoke to me for the first time. He asked roughly, as if he himself expected a negative answer: "Why don't we meet after dinner? We'll come and get you and take you home."

They had never asked us to go out in the evening. I gave Lila a questioning glance, but she looked away. I said, "Lila's mamma is at home, we can't leave her alone all the time."

Nino didn't answer nor did his friend intervene to help him out. But after the last swim, before parting, Lila said, "We're going to Forio tomorrow night to telephone my husband. We could get an ice cream together."

That remark of hers irritated me, but I was even more irritated by what happened next. As soon as the two boys had set off for Forio, and she was gathering up her things, she began to reproach me, as if I bore the blame for the entire day, hour by hour, micro-event upon micro-event, including that request of Nino's, and the clear contradiction between my answer and hers, in some indecipherable yet indisputable way.

"Why were you always with Bruno?"

"I?"

"Yes, you. Don't ever dare to leave me alone with that guy again."

"What are you talking about? It was you two who rushed ahead without stopping to wait for us."

"We? It was Nino who was rushing."

"You could have said that you had to wait for me."

"And you could have said to Bruno: Get going, otherwise we'll lose them. Do me a favor: since you like him so much, go out on your own business at night. Then you're free to say and do what you like."

"I'm here for you, not for Bruno."

"It doesn't look as though you're here for me, you're always doing what you please."

"If you don't want me here anymore I'll leave tomorrow morning."

"Yes? And tomorrow night I have to go and get ice cream with those two by myself?"

"Lila, it was you who said you wanted to get ice cream with them."

"Of necessity, I have to telephone Stefano, and what an impression we'd make if we meet them in Forio?"

We continued in this vein even at the house, after dinner, in Nunzia's presence. It wasn't a real quarrel, but an ambiguous exchange with spikes of malice in which we both tried to communicate something without understanding each other. Nunzia, who was listening in bewilderment, at a certain point said, "Tomorrow we'll have dinner and then I'll come, too, to get ice cream."

"It's a long way," I said. But Lila interrupted abruptly: "We don't have to walk. We'll take a mini cab, we're rich."

59.

The next day, to adjust to the boys' new schedule, we arrived at the beach at nine instead of ten, but they weren't there. Lila became anxious. We waited, they didn't appear at ten or later. Finally, in the early afternoon, they showed up, with a light-hearted conspiratorial air. They said that since they were going to spend the evening with us, they had decided to do their studying early. Lila's reaction stunned me in particular: she sent them away. Slipping into a violent dialect, she hissed that they could go and study when they liked, afternoon, evening, night, no one was holding them back. And since Nino and Bruno made an effort not to take her seriously and continued to smile as if those words had been just a witty remark, she put on her sundress, impetuously grabbed her bag, and set off toward the road with long strides. Nino ran after her but returned soon afterward with a grim face. Nothing to do, she was really enraged and wouldn't listen to reason.

"It will pass," I said, pretending to be calm, and I went swimming with them. I dried in the sun eating a sandwich, I chattered weakly, then I announced that I, too, had to go home.

"And tonight?" Bruno asked.

"Lina has to call Stefano, we'll be there."

But the outburst had upset me greatly. What did that tone, that behavior mean? What right had she to get angry at an appointment not kept? Why couldn't she control herself and treat the two young men as if they were Pasquale or Antonio or even the Solaras? Why did she behave like a capricious girl and not like Signora Carracci?

I got to the house out of breath. Nunzia was washing towels and bathing suits, Lila was in her room, sitting on the bed and, something that was also unusual, she was writing. The notebook was resting on her knees, her eyes narrowed, her brow furrowed, one of my books lying on the sheets. How long it was since I had seen her write.

"You overdid it," I said.

She shrugged. She didn't raise her eyes from the notebook, she continued to write all afternoon.

At night she decked herself out the way she did when her husband was arriving, and we drove to Forio. I was surprised that Nunzia, who never went out in the sun and was very white, had borrowed her daughter's lipstick to give a little color to her lips and her cheeks. She wanted to avoid—she said—seeming dead already.

We immediately ran into the two boys, who were standing in front of the bar like sentries beside a sentry box. Bruno was still in shorts, he had only changed his shirt. Nino was wearing long pants, a shirt of a dazzling white, and his unruly hair so forcibly tamed that he seemed less handsome to me. When they noticed Nunzia's presence, they stiffened. We sat under a canopy, at the entrance to the bar, and ordered spumoni. Nunzia, marveling at it, started talking and wouldn't stop. She spoke only to the boys. She praised Nino's mother, recalling how pretty she was; she told several stories of wartime, neighborhood events, and asked Nino if he remembered; when he said no, she replied, with absolute certainty, "Ask your mother, you'll see that she remembers." Lila soon gave signs of impatience, announced that it was time to telephone Stefano, and went into the bar, where the phone booths were. Nino grew silent and Bruno readily replaced him in the conversation with Nunzia. I noted, with annoyance, that he wasn't awkward the way he was when he talked to me alone.

"Excuse me a moment," Nino said suddenly. He got up, went into the bar.

Nunzia became agitated. She whispered in my ear, "He's not going to pay is he? I'm the oldest, so it's up to me."

Bruno heard her and said that it was already paid for, he was hardly going to let a lady pay. Nunzia resigned herself, went on to inquire about his father's sausage factory, bragged about her husband and son, who also had a factory—they had a shoe factory.

Lila didn't return. I was worried. I left Nunzia and Bruno chatting, and I, too, went into the bar. When had a telephone call to Stefano ever lasted so long? The two telephone booths were empty. I looked around me, but, standing still like that, I just bothered the owner's sons, who were waiting on the tables. I glimpsed a door left ajar to let in the air, opening onto a courtyard. I went out hesitantly, an odor of old tires mingled with the smell of the chicken coop. The courtyard was empty, but I noticed that on one side of the boundary wall there was an opening and, beyond it, a garden. I crossed the space, cluttered with rusty scrap iron, and before I entered the garden I saw Lila and Nino. The brightness of the summer night licked the plants. They were holding each other tight, they were kissing. He had one hand under her skirt, she was trying to push it away, but she went on kissing him.

I retreated quickly, trying not to make any noise. I went back to the bar, I told Nunzia that Lila was still on the telephone.

"Are they quarreling?"

"No."

I felt as if I were burning up, but the flames were cold and I felt no pain. She is married, I said to myself, she's been married scarcely more than a year.

Lila returned without Nino. She was impeccable, and yet I felt the disorder, in her clothes, in her body.

We waited a while, he didn't show up, I realized that I hated them both. Lila got up, said, "Let's go, it's late." When we were already in the cab that would take us back to the house, Nino arrived, running, and said goodbye cheerfully. "See you tomorrow," he cried, friendly as I had never seen him. I thought: the fact that Lila is married isn't an obstacle for him or for her, and that observation seemed to me so odiously true that it turned my stomach, and I brought a hand to my mouth.

Lila went to bed right away, I waited in vain for her to come and confess what she had done and what she proposed to do. Today, I believe that she didn't know herself.

60.

The days that followed clarified the situation further. Usually Nino arrived with a newspaper, a book: no more. Animated conversations about the human condition faded, were reduced to distracted phrases that sought an opening for more private words. Lila and Nino got in the habit of swimming far out together, until they were indistinguishable from the shore. Or they compelled us to long walks that consolidated the division into couples. And never, absolutely never, was I beside Nino, nor was Lila with Bruno. It became natural for the two of them to be behind. Whenever I turned around suddenly I had the impression of having caused a painful laceration: hands, mouths springing backward as if because of some nervous tic.

I suffered but, I have to admit, with a permanent undercurrent of disbelief that caused the suffering to come in waves. It seemed to me that I was watching a performance without substance: they were playing at being together, both knowing well that they were not and couldn't be: the one already had a girlfriend, the other was actually married. I looked at them at times like fallen divinities: once so clever, so intelligent, and now so stupid, involved in a stupid game. I planned to say to Lila, to Nino, to both of them: who do you think you are, come back to earth.

I couldn't do it. In the space of two or three days things changed further. They began to hold hands without hiding it, with an offensive shamelessness, as if they had decided that with us it wasn't worth pretending. They often quarreled jokingly, then grabbed each other, hit each other, held each other tight, tumbled on the sand together. When we were walking, if they spotted an abandoned hut, an old bath house reduced to its foundations, a path that got lost among the wild vegetation, they decided like children to go exploring and didn't invite us to follow. They went off with him in the lead, she behind, in silence. When they lay in the sun, they lessened the distance between them as much as possible. At first they were satisfied with the slight contact of shoulders, their arms, legs, feet just grazing. Later, returning from that interminable daily swim, they lay beside each other on Lila's towel, which was bigger, and soon, with a natural gesture, Nino put his arm around her shoulders, she rested her head on his chest. They even, once, went so far as to kiss on the lips, a light, quick kiss. I thought: she's mad, they're mad. If someone from Naples who knows Stefano sees them? If the supplier who got the house for us passes by? Or if Nunzia, now, should decide to make a visit to the beach?

I couldn't believe such recklessness, and yet time and time again they crossed the limit. Seeing each other during the day no longer seemed sufficient; Lila decided that she had to call Stefano every night, but she rudely rejected Nunzia's offer to go with us. After dinner she obliged me to go to Forio. She made a quick phone call to her husband and then we went walking, she with Nino, I with Bruno. We never returned home before midnight and the two boys came with us along the dark beach.

On Friday night, that is, the day before Stefano returned, she and Nino argued, unexpectedly, not in fun but seriously. We were eating ice cream at the table, Lila had gone to telephone. Nino, grim-faced, took out of his pocket a number of pages with writing on both sides and began to read, giving no explanation, but isolating himself from the dull conversation between Bruno and me. When she returned, he didn't even glance at her, he didn't put the pages back in his pocket, but went on reading. Lila waited half a minute, then asked in a lighthearted tone:

"Is it so interesting?"

"Yes," Nino said, without looking up.

"Then read aloud, we want to hear it."

"It's my business, it has nothing to do with the rest of you."

"What is it?" Lila asked, but it was clear that she knew already.

"A letter."

"From whom?"

"From Nadia."

With a sudden, lightning-like move, she reached out and

tore the pages from his grasp. Nino started, as if a giant insect had stung him, but he made no effort to get the letter back, even when Lila began to read it to us in declamatory tones, in a loud voice. It was a rather childish love letter, carrying on from line to line with sentimental variations on the theme of missing. Bruno listened silently, with an embarrassed smile, and I, seeing that Nino showed no sign of taking the thing as a joke, but was staring darkly at his sandaled, suntanned feet, whispered to Lila, "That's enough, give it back to him."

As soon as I spoke she stopped reading, but her expression of amusement lingered, and she didn't give the letter back.

"You're embarrassed, eh?" she asked. "You're the one to blame. How can you have a girlfriend who writes like that?"

Nino said nothing, he went on staring at his feet. Bruno interrupted, also lightheartedly: "Maybe, when you fall in love with someone, you don't make her take an exam to see if she can write a love letter."

But Lila didn't even turn to look at him, she spoke to Nino as if they were continuing in front of us one of their secret conversations:

"Do you love her? And why? Explain it to us. Because she lives on Corso Vittorio Emanuele in a house full of books and old paintings? Because she speaks in a simpering little voice? Because she's the daughter of the professor?"

Finally Nino roused himself and said abruptly, "Give me back those pages."

"I'll only give them back if you tear them up immediately, here, in front of us."

Countering Lila's tone of amusement Nino uttered grave monosyllables, with obvious aggressive undertones. "And then?"

"Then we'll all write Nadia a letter together in which you tell her you're leaving her."

"And then?"

"We'll mail it tonight."

He said nothing for a moment, then he agreed. "Let's do it."

Lila pointed to the pages in disbelief.

"You're really going to tear them up?"

"Yes."

"And you'll leave her?"

"Yes. But on one condition."

"Let's hear it."

"That you leave your husband. Now. Let's all of us go together to the phone and you'll tell him."

Those words provoked in me a violent emotion. At the time I didn't know why. As he spoke he raised his voice so unexpectedly that it cracked. And Lila's eyes, as she listened to him, suddenly narrowed to slits, following a mode of behavior that I knew well. Now she would change her tone. Now, I thought, she'll turn mean. She said to him, in fact: How dare you. She said to him: To whom do you think you're speaking. She said to him: "How can you think of putting this letter, your foolishness with that whore from a good family, on the same plane as me, my husband, my marriage and everything that is my life? You really think you're something, but you don't get the joke. In fact you don't understand a thing. Nothing, you heard me, and don't make that face. Let's go to bed, Lenù."

61.

Nino did nothing to restrain us, Bruno said, "See you tomorrow." We took a mini cab and returned to the house. But during the journey Lila began to tremble, she grabbed my hand and gripped it hard. She began to confess to me in a chaotic way everything that had happened between her and Nino. She had yearned for him to kiss her, she had let herself be kissed. She had wanted to feel his hands on her, she had let him. "I can't sleep. If I fall asleep I wake with a start, I look at the clock, I hope it's already day, that we have to go to the beach. But it's night, I can't sleep anymore, I have in my head all the words he said, all the ones that I can't wait to tell him. I resisted. I said: I'm not like Pinuccia, I can do what I like, I can start and stop, it's a game. I kept my lips pressed together, then I said to myself well, really, what's a kiss, and I discovered what it was, I didn't know—I swear to you that I didn't know—and now I can't do without it. I gave him my hand, I entwined my fingers with his, tight, and it seemed to me painful to let go. How many things I've missed that now are landing on me all at once. I go around like a girlfriend, when I'm married. I'm frantic, my heart is pounding here in my throat and in my temples. And I like everything. I like that he drags me into secluded places, I like the fear that someone might see us, I like the idea that they might see us. Did you do those things with Antonio? Did you suffer when you had to leave him and you couldn't wait to see him again? Is it normal, Lenù? Was it like that for you? I don't know how it began and when. At first I didn't like him: I liked how he talked, what he said, but physically no. I thought: How many things he knows, this man, I should listen, I should learn. Now, when he speaks, I can't even concentrate. I look at his mouth and I'm ashamed of looking at it, I turn my eyes in another direction. In a short time I've come to love everything about him: his hands, the delicate fingernails, that thinness, the ribs under his skin, his slender neck, the beard that he shaves badly so it's always rough, his nose, the hair on his chest, his long, slender legs, his knees. I want to caress him. And I think of things that disgust me, they really disgust me, Lenù, but I would like to do them to give him pleasure, to make him be happy."

I listened to her for a good part of the night, in her room, the door closed, the light out. She was lying on the window side and in the moon's glow the hair on her neck gleamed, and the curve of her hip. I was lying on the door side, Stefano's side, and I thought: Her husband sleeps here, every weekend, on this side of the bed, and draws her to him, in the afternoon, at night, and embraces her. And yet here, in this bed, she is telling me about Nino. The words for him take away her memory, they erase from these sheets every trace of conjugal love. She speaks of him and in speaking of him she calls him here, she imagines him next to her, and since she has forgotten herself she perceives no violation or guilt. She confides, she tells me things that she would do better to keep to herself. She tells me how much she desires the person I've desired forever, and she does so convinced that I— through insensitivity, through a less acute vision, through incapacity to grasp what she, instead, is able to grasp—have never truly understood that same person, never realized his qualities. I don't know if it's in bad faith or if she's really convinced—it's my fault, my tendency to conceal myself—that since elementary school I've been deaf and blind, so that it took her to discover, here on Ischia, the power unleashed by the son of Sarratore. Ah, how I hate this presumption of hers, it poisons my blood. Yet I don't know how to say to her, That's enough, I can't go to my room to cry in silence, but I stay here, and now and then I interrupt her, I try to calm her.

I pretended a detachment I didn't have. "It's the sea," I said to her, "the fresh air, the vacation. And Nino knows how to confuse you; the way he talks he makes everything look easy. But, unfortunately, tomorrow Stefano arrives and you'll see, Nino will seem like a boy to you. Which he really is, I know him well. To us he seems like somebody, but if you think how Professor Galiani's son treats him—you remember?—you understand immediately that we overestimate him. Of course, compared to Bruno he seems extraordinary, but after all he's only the son of a railroad worker who got it in his head to study. Remember that Nino was from the neighborhood, he comes from there. Remember that at school you were smarter, even if he was older. And then you see how he takes advantage of his friend, makes him pay for everything, drinks, ice cream."

It cost me to say those things, I considered them lies. And it was of little use: Lila grumbled, she objected hesitantly, I refuted her. Until she really got mad and began to defend Nino in the tone of someone who says: I'm the only one who knows what sort of person he is. She asked why I was always disparaging him. She asked me what I had against him. "He helped you," she said, "he even wanted to publish that nonsense of yours in a review. Sometimes I don't like you, Lenù, you diminish everything and everyone, even people who are lovable if you just look at them."

I lost control, I couldn't bear it anymore. I had spoken ill of the person I loved in order to do something to make her feel better and now she insulted me. Finally I managed to say, "Do what you like, I'm going to bed." But she immediately changed her tone, she embraced me, she hugged me tight, to keep me there, she whispered, "Tell me what to do." I pushed her away with annoyance, I whispered that she had to decide herself, I couldn't decide in her place. "Pinuccia," I said, "how did she do it? In the end she behaved better than you."

She agreed, we sang the praises of Pinuccia and abruptly she sighed: "All right, tomorrow I won't go to the beach and the day after I'll go back to Naples with Stefano."

62.

It was a terrible Saturday. She really didn't go to the beach, and I didn't go, either, but I thought only of Nino and Bruno, who were waiting for us in vain. And I didn't dare say: I'll make a quick trip to the sea, time for a swim and then I'll come back. Nor did I dare ask: What should I do, pack the suitcases, are we going, are we staying? I helped Nunzia clean the house, cook lunch and dinner, every so often checking on Lila, who didn't even get up. She stayed in bed reading and writing in her notebook, and when her mother called her to eat she didn't answer, and when she called her again she slammed the door of her room so violently that the whole house shook.

"Too much sea makes one nervous," Nunzia said, as we ate lunch alone.

"Yes."

"And she's not even pregnant."

"No."

In the late afternoon Lila left her bed, ate something, spent hours in the bathroom. She washed her hair, put on her makeup, chose a pretty green dress, but her face remained sullen. Still, she greeted her husband affectionately and he, seeing her, gave her a movie kiss, a long intense kiss, with Nunzia and I as embarrassed spectators. Stefano brought greetings from my family, said that Pinuccia had made no more scenes, recounted in minute detail how happy the Solaras were with the new shoe styles that Rino and Fernando were working on. Lila wasn't pleased by Stefano's reference to the new styles, and things between them were spoiled. Until that moment she had kept a forced smile on her face, but as soon as she heard the name of the Solaras she became aggressive, and said she didn't give a damn about those two, she wouldn't live her life according to what they thought about this or that. Stefano was disappointed, he frowned. He realized that the enchantment of the previous weeks was over, but he answered her with his usual agreeable half smile, he said that he was only telling her what had happened in the neighborhood, there was no need to take that tone. It was little use. Lila rapidly transformed the evening into a relentless conflict. Stefano couldn't say a word without hostile criticism from her. They went to bed squabbling and I heard them quarreling until I fell asleep.

I woke at dawn. I didn't know what to do: gather my things,

wait for Lila to make a decision; go to the beach, with the risk of running into Nino, something that Lila would not have forgiven; rack my brains all day as I was already doing, shut in my room. I decided to leave a note saying that I was going to the Maronti but would be back in the early afternoon. I wrote that I couldn't leave Ischia without seeing Nella. I wrote in good faith, but today I know what was going on in my mind: I wanted to trust myself to chance; Lila couldn't reproach me if I ran into Nino when he had gone to ask his parents for money.

The result was a muddled day and a modest waste of money. I hired a boat, to take me to the Maronti. I went to the place where the Sarratores usually camped and found only the umbrella. I looked around, and saw Donato, who was swimming, and he saw me. He waved in greeting, hurried out of the water, told me that his wife and children had gone to spend the day in Forio, with Nino. I was extremely disappointed, the situation was not only ironic, it was contemptuous; it had taken away the son and delivered me to the sickening patter of the father.

When I tried to get away to go and see Nella, Sarratore wouldn't let me go, he gathered up his things and insisted on coming with me. On the road he assumed a sentimental tone and without any embarrassment began to speak of what had happened between us years earlier. He asked me to forgive him, he murmured that one cannot command one's heart, he spoke in a melancholy tone of my beauty then and above all of my present beauty.

"What an exaggeration," I said, and, while I knew I should be serious and aloof, I began to laugh out of nervousness.

And though he was encumbered by the umbrella and his things, he would not relinquish a somewhat breathless, rambling discourse. He said that in substance the problem of youth was the lack of eyes to see oneself and feelings to feel about oneself with objectivity.

"There's the mirror," I replied, "and that is objective."

"The mirror? The mirror is the last thing you can trust. I'll bet that you feel less pretty than your two friends."

"Yes."

"And yet you are much, much more beautiful than they are. Trust me. Look what lovely blond hair you have. And what a bearing. You need to confront and resolve two problems only: the first is your bathing suit, it's not adequate to your potential; the second is the style of your glasses. This is really wrong, Elena: too heavy. You have such a delicate face, so remarkably shaped by the things you study. What you need is daintier glasses."

As I listened my irritation diminished; he was like a scientist of female beauty. Mainly he spoke with such detached expertise that at a certain point he led me to think: and if it's true? Maybe I don't know how to value myself. On the other hand where is the money to buy suitable clothes, a suitable bathing suit, suitable glasses? I was about to yield to a complaint about poverty and wealth when he said to me with a smile, "Besides, if you don't trust my judgment, you'll be aware, I hope, of how my son looked at you the time you came to see us."

Only then did I realize that he was lying to me. His words were intended to appeal to my vanity, to make me feel good and drive me toward him in the need for gratification. I felt stupid, wounded not by him, with his lies, but by my own stupidity. I cut him short with an increasing rudeness that froze him.

At the house I talked to Nella for a while, I told her that we might all be returning to Naples that night and I wanted to say goodbye.

"A pity that you're going."

"Ah yes."

"Eat with me."

"I can't, I have to go."

"But if you don't go, swear that you'll come again and not so short next time. Stay with me for a day, or even overnight, since you know there's the bed. I have so many things to tell you."

"Thanks."

Sarratore interrupted, he said, "We count on it, you know how much we love you."

I fled, also because there was a relative of Nella's who was going to the Port in a car and I didn't want to miss the ride.

Along the way Sarratore's words, surprisingly, even if I only rejected them, began to dig into me. No, maybe he hadn't lied. He knew how to see beyond appearances. He had really had a means of observing his son's gaze on me. And if I was pretty, if Nino seriously found me attractive—and I knew it was so: in the end he had kissed me, he had held my hand—it was time I looked at the facts for what they were: Lila had taken him from me; Lila had separated him from me to win him for herself. Maybe she hadn't done it on purpose, but still she had done it.

I decided suddenly that I had to find him, see him at all costs. Now that our departure was imminent, now that the force of seduction that Lila had exercised over him would no longer have a chance to fascinate him, now that she herself had decided to return to the life that was hers, the relationship between him and me could begin again. In Naples. In the form of friendship. At least we could meet to talk about her. And then we would return to our conversations, to our reading. I would demonstrate that I could get interested in his interests better than Lila, certainly, maybe even better than Nadia. Yes, I had to speak to him right away, tell him I'm leaving, tell him: let's see each other in the neighborhood, in Piazza Nazionale, in Mezzocannone, wherever you want, but as soon as possible.

I found a minicab, I took it to Forio, to Bruno's house. I called, no one looked out. I wandered through the town feeling more and more depressed, then I set out to walk along the beach. And this time chance apparently decided in my favor. I had been walking for a long time when I saw before me Nino: he was happy we had met, a barely controlled happiness. His eyes were too bright, his gestures excited, his voice over-wrought.

"I looked for the two of you yesterday and today. Where's Lina?"

"With her husband."

He took an envelope out of his pants pocket, he shoved it into my hand too forcefully.

"Can you give her this?"

I was annoyed. "It's pointless, Nino."

"Give it to her."

"Tonight we're leaving, we'll go back to Naples."

He had an expression of suffering, he said hoarsely, "Who decided?"

"She did."

"I don't believe it."

"It's true, she told me last night."

He thought for a moment, pointed to the envelope.

"Please, give her that anyway, right away."

"All right."

"Swear that you will."

"I told you, yes."

He walked with me for a long way, saying spiteful things about his mother and his brothers and sister. They tormented me, he said, luckily they went back to Barano. I asked him about Bruno. He made a gesture of irritation, he was studying, he said mean things about him as well.

"And you're not studying?"

"I can't."

His head sank between his shoulders, he grew melancholy. He began to talk about the mistakes one makes because a pro-fessor, as a result of his own problems, leads you to believe

THE STORY OF A NEW NAME · 263

you're smart. He realized that the things he wanted to learn had never really interested him.

"What do you mean? Suddenly?"

"A moment is enough to change the direction of your life completely."

What was happening to him, with these banal words, I no longer recognized him. I vowed I would help him return to himself.

"You're upset now, and you don't know what you're saying," I said in my best sensible tone. "But as soon as you return to Naples we can see each other, if you want, and talk."

He nodded yes, but right afterward cried angrily, "I'm finished with the university, I want to find a job."

63.

He came with me almost to the house, so that I was afraid of meeting Stefano and Lila. I said goodbye in a hurry and went up the stairs.

"Tomorrow morning at nine," he shouted.

I stopped.

"If we leave I'll see you in the neighborhood. Look for me there."

Nino made a sign of no, decisively.

"You won't leave," he said, as if he were giving a threatening order to fate.

I gave him a final wave and hurried up the stairs sorry that I hadn't had a chance to examine what was in the envelope.

In the house I found an unpleasant atmosphere. Stefano and Nunzia were whispering together. Lila must be in the bathroom or the bedroom. When I went in they both looked at me resentfully. Stefano said grimly, without preamble, "Will you tell me what you and she are getting up to?"

"In what sense?"

"She says she's tired of Ischia, she wants to go to Amalfi."

"I don't know anything about it."

Nunzia intervened but not in her usual motherly way.

"Lenù, don't put wrong ideas in her head, you can't throw money out the window. What does Amalfi have to do with anything? We've paid to stay here until September."

I got mad, I said, "You are both mistaken: it's I who do what Lina wants, not the opposite."

"Then go and tell her to be reasonable," Stefano muttered. "I'll be back next week, we'll be together for the mid-August holiday and you'll see, I'll show you a good time. But now I don't want to hear any nonsense. Shit. You think I'll take you to Amalfi? And if you don't like Amalfi, where do I take you, to Capri? And then? Cut it out, Lenù."

His tone intimidated me.

"Where is she?" I asked.

Nunzia indicated the bedroom. I went to Lila sure that I would find the suitcases packed and her determined to leave, even at the risk of a beating. Instead she was in her slip, and was sleeping on the unmade bed. All around was the usual disorder, but the suitcases were piled in a corner, empty. I shook her.

"Lila."

She started, asked me right away with a look veiled by sleep: "Where have you been, did you see Nino?"

"Yes. This is for you."

I gave her the envelope reluctantly. She opened it, took out a sheet of paper. She read it and in a flash became radiant, as if an injection of stimulants had swept away drowsiness and despair.

"What does it say?" I asked cautiously.

"To me nothing."

"So?"

"It's for Nadia, he's leaving her."

She put the letter back in the envelope and gave it to me, urging me to keep it carefully hidden.

I stood, confused, with the envelope in my hands. Nino was leaving Nadia? And why? Because Lila had asked him to? So she would win? I was disappointed. He was sacrificing the daughter of Professor Galiani to the game that he and the wife of the grocer were playing. I said nothing, I stared at Lila while she got dressed, put on her makeup. Finally I said, "Why did you ask Stefano that absurd thing, to go to Amalfi? I don't understand you."

She smiled.

"I don't, either."

We left the room. Lila kissed Stefano affectionately, rubbing against him happily, and we decided to go with him to the Port, Nunzia and I in the minicab, he and Lila on the Lambretta. We had some ice cream while we waited for the boat. Lila was nice to her husband, gave him a thousand bits of advice, promised to telephone every night. Before he started up the gangplank he put an arm around my shoulders and whispered in my ear:

"I'm sorry, I was really angry. Without you I don't know how it would have ended, this time."

It was a polite statement, and yet I felt in it a sort of ultimatum that meant: Tell your friend, please, that if she goes too far again, it's all over.

64.

At the head of the letter was Nadia's address in Capri. As soon as the boat left the shore carrying Stefano away, Lila propelled us cheerfully to the tobacconist, bought a stamp, and, while I kept Nunzia busy, recopied the address onto the envelope and mailed it.

We wandered through Forio, but I was too nervous, and kept talking to Nunzia. When we returned to the house I drew Lila into my room and spoke plainly to her. She listened to me in silence, but with a distracted air, as if on the one hand she felt the gravity of the things I was saying and on the other had abandoned herself to thoughts that made every word meaningless. I said to her, "Lila, I don't know what you have in mind, but in my view you're playing with fire. Now Stefano has left happy and if you telephone him every night he'll be even happier. But be careful: he'll be back in a week and will stay until August 20th. Do you think you can go on like this? Do you think you can play with people's lives? Do you know that Nino doesn't want to study anymore, he wants to find a job? What have you put in his head? And why did you make him leave his girlfriend? Do you want to ruin him? Do you want to ruin both of you?"

At that last question she roused herself and burst out laughing, but somewhat artificially. She sounded amused, but who knows. She said I ought to be proud of her, she had made me look good. Why? Because she had been considered in every way finer than the very fine daughter of my professor. Because the smartest boy in my school and maybe in Naples and maybe in Italy and maybe in the world—according to what I said, naturally—had just left that very respectable young lady, no less, to please her, the daughter of a shoemaker, elementary-school diploma, wife of Carracci. She spoke with increasing sarcasm and as if she were finally revealing a cruel plan of revenge. I must have looked angry, she realized it, but for several minutes she continued in that tone, as if she couldn't stop herself. Was she serious? Was that her true state of mind at that moment? I exclaimed:

"Who are you putting on this show for? For me? Do you want to make me believe that Nino is ready to do anything, however crazy, to please you?"

The laughter disappeared from her eyes, she darkened, abruptly changed her tone.

"No, I'm lying, it's completely the opposite. I'm the one who's prepared to do anything, and it's never happened to me with anyone, and I'm glad that it's happening now."

Then, overcome by embarrassment, she went to bed without even saying goodnight.

I fell into a nervous half sleep, during which I convinced myself that the last little trickle of words was truer than the torrent that had preceded it.

During the week that followed I had the proof. First of all, as early as Monday I realized that Bruno, after Pinuccia's departure, really had begun to focus on me, and he now considered that the moment had arrived to behave toward me as Nino behaved with Lila. While we were swimming he clumsily pulled me toward him to kiss me, so that I swallowed a mouthful of water and had to return to the shore coughing. I was annoyed, he saw it. When he came to lie down in the sun next to me, with the air of a beaten dog, I made a kind but firm little speech, whose sense was: Bruno, you're very nice, but between you and me there can't be anything but a fraternal feeling. He was sad but he didn't give up. The same night, after the phone call to Stefano, we all went to walk on the beach and then we sat on the cold sand and stretched out to look at the stars, Lila resting on her elbows, Nino with his head on her stomach, I with my head on Nino's stomach, Bruno with his head on my stomach. We gazed at the constellations, praising the portentous architecture of the sky with trite formulas. Not all of us, Lila didn't. She was silent, but when we had exhausted the catalogue of worshipful wonder, she said that the spectacle of night frightened her, she saw no structure but only random shards of glass in a blue pitch. This silenced us all, and I was vexed: she had that habit of speaking last, which gave her time to reflect and allowed her to disrupt with a single remark everything that we had more or less thoughtlessly said.

"How can you be afraid," I exclaimed. "It's beautiful."

Bruno immediately agreed. Nino instead encouraged her: with a slight movement he signaled me to free his stomach, he sat up and began to talk to her as if they were alone. The sky, the temple, order, disorder. Finally they got up and, still talking, disappeared into the darkness.

I was lying down but leaning on my elbows. I no longer had Nino's warm body as a pillow, and the weight of Bruno's head on my stomach was irritating. I said excuse me, touching his hair. He sat up, grabbed me by the waist, pressed his face against my chest. I muttered no, but he pushed me down on the sand and searched for my mouth, pressing one hand hard against my breast. Then I shoved him away, forcefully, crying, Stop it, and this time I was unpleasant, I hissed, "I don't like you, how do I have to tell you?" He stopped, embarrassed, sat up. He said in a low voice: "Is it possible that you don't like me even a little?" I tried to explain that it wasn't a thing that could be measured, saying, "It's not a matter of more beauty or less, more liking or less; it's that some people attract me and others don't, it's nothing to do with how they are really."

"You don't like me?"

I said impatiently, "No."

But as soon as I uttered that monosyllable I burst into tears, while stammering things like "See, I'm crying for no reason, I'm an idiot, I'm not worth wasting time on."

He touched my cheek with his fingers and tried again to embrace me, murmuring: I want to give you so many presents, you deserve them, you're so pretty. I pulled away angrily, and shouted into the darkness, my voice cracking, "Lila, come back right now, I want to go home."

The two friends went with us to the foot of the stairs, then they left. As Lila and I went up I said in exasperation, "Go where you like, do what you like, I'm not going with you anymore. It's the second time Bruno has put his hands on me: I don't want to be alone with him anymore, is that clear?"

65.

There are moments when we resort to senseless formulations and advance absurd claims to hide straightforward feelings. Today I know that in other circumstances, after some resistance, I would have given in to Bruno's advances. I wasn't attracted to him, certainly, but I hadn't been especially attracted to Antonio, either. One becomes affectionate toward men slowly, whether they coincide or not with whomever in the various phases of life we have taken as the model of a man. And Bruno Soccavo, in that phase of his life, was courteous and generous; it would have been easy to harbor some affection for him. But the reasons for rejecting him had nothing to do with anything really disagreeable about him. The truth was that I wanted to restrain Lila. I wanted to be a hindrance to her. I wanted her to be aware of the situation she was getting into and getting me into. I wanted her to say to me: Yes, you're right, I'm making a mistake, I won't go off in the dark with Nino anymore, I won't leave you alone with Bruno; starting now I will behave as befits a married woman.

Naturally it didn't happen. She confined herself to saying, "I'll talk to Nino about it and you'll see, Bruno won't bother you anymore." So day after day we continued to meet the boys at nine in the morning and separated at midnight. But on Tuesday night after the call to Stefano, Nino said, "You've never been to see Bruno's house. You want to come over?"

I immediately said no, I pretended I had a stomachache and wanted to go home. Nino and Lila looked uncertainly at each other, Bruno said nothing. I felt the weight of their discontent and added, embarrassed, "Maybe another night."

Lila said nothing but when we were alone she exclaimed, "You can't make my life unhappy, Lenù." I answered, "If Stefano finds out that we went alone to their house, he'll be angry not just at you but also at me." And I didn't stop there. At home I stirred up Nunzia's displeasure and used it to urge her to reproach her daughter for too much sun, too much sea, staying out till midnight. I even went so far as to say, as if I wished to make peace between mother and daughter, "Signora Nunzia, tomorrow night come and have ice cream with us, you'll see we're not doing anything wrong." Lila became furious, she said that she had had a miserable life all year, always shut up in the grocery, and now she had the right to a little freedom. Nunzia also lost her temper: "Lina, what are you saying? Freedom? What freedom? You are married, you must be accountable to your husband. Lenuccia can want a little freedom, you can't." Her daughter went to her room and slammed the door.

But the next day Lila won: her mother stayed home and we went to telephone Stefano. "You must be here at eleven on the dot," Nunzia said, grumpily, addressing me, and I answered, "All right." She gave me a long, questioning look. By now she was alarmed: she was our guard but she wasn't guarding us; she was afraid we were getting into trouble, but she thought of her own sacrificed youth and didn't want to keep us from some innocent amusement. I repeated to reassure her: "At eleven."

The phone call to Stefano lasted a minute at most. When Lila came out of the booth Nino asked, "Are you feeling well tonight, Lenù? Come see the house?"

"Come on," Bruno urged me. "You can have a drink and then go."

Lila agreed, I said nothing. On the outside the building was old, shabby, but inside it had been renovated: the cellar white and well lighted, full of wine and cured meats; a marble staircase with a wrought-iron banister; sturdy doors on which gold han-

dles shone; windows with gilded fixtures. There were a lot of
rooms, yellow couches, a television; in the kitchen, cupboards
painted aquamarine and in the bedrooms wardrobes that were
like gothic churches. I thought, for the first time clearly, that
Bruno really was rich, richer than Stefano. I thought that if ever
my mother had known that the student son of the owner of
Soccavo mortadella had courted me, and that I had been, no
less, a guest at his house, and that instead of thanking God for
the good fortune he had sent me and seeking to marry him I had
rejected him twice, she would have beaten me. On the other
hand it was precisely the thought of my mother, of her lame leg,
that made me feel unfit even for Bruno. In that house I was
intimidated. Why was I there, what was I doing there? Lila acted
nonchalant, she laughed often; I felt as if I had a fever, a nasty
taste in my mouth. I began to say yes to avoid the embarrassment of saying no. Do you want a drink of this, do you want to
put on this record, do you want to watch television, do you want
some ice cream. When, finally, I realized that Nino and Lila had
disappeared, I was worried. Where had they gone? Was it possible that they were in Nino's bedroom? Possible that Lila was
willing to cross even that limit? Possible that—I didn't want to
think about it. I jumped up, I said to Bruno:

"It's late."

He was kind, but with an undertone of sadness. He murmured, "Stay a little longer." He said that the next day he had to
leave very early, to attend a family celebration. He announced
that he would be gone until Monday and those days without
me would be a torment. He took my hand delicately, said that
he loved me and other things like that. I gently took my hand
away, he didn't try for any other contact. Instead, he spoke at
length about his feelings for me, he who in general said little,
and I had trouble interrupting him. When I did I said, "I really
have to go," then, in a louder voice, "Lila, please come, it's
quarter after ten."

Some minutes passed, the two reappeared. Nino and Bruno took us to a taxi, Bruno said goodbye as if he were going not to Naples for a few days but to America for the rest of his life. On the way home Lila, her tone pointed, as if she were delivering important news: "Nino told me that he has a lot of admiration for you."

"Not me," I answered right away, in a rude voice. And then I whispered: "What if you get pregnant?"

She said in my ear: "There's no danger. We're just kissing and holding."

"Oh."

"And anyway I don't stay pregnant."

"It happened once."

"I told you, I don't stay pregnant. He knows how to manage."

"He who?"

"Nino. He would use a condom."

"What's that?"

"I don't know, he called it that."

"You don't know what it is and you trust it?"

"It's something that he puts over it."

"Over where?"

I wanted to force her to name things. I wanted her to understand what she was saying. First she assured me that they were only kissing, then she spoke of him as someone who knew how not to get her pregnant. I was enraged, I expected that she would be ashamed. Instead she seemed pleased with everything that had happened to her and that would happen to her. So much so that when we got home she was nice to Nunzia, pointed out that we had returned early, got ready for bed. But she left her door open and when she saw me going to my room she called me, she said, "Stay here a minute, close the door."

I sat on the bed, but trying to make it clear that I was tired of her and everything.

"What do you have to tell me?"

She whispered, "I want to go and sleep at Nino's."

I was astonished.

"And Nunzia?"

"Wait, don't get mad. There's not much time left, Lenù. Stefano will arrive on Saturday, he'll stay for ten days, then we go back to Naples. And everything will be over."

"Everything what?"

"This, these days, these evenings."

We discussed it for a long time, she seemed very lucid. She murmured that nothing like this would ever happen to her again. She whispered that she loved him, that she wanted him. She used that verb, *amare*, that we had found only in books and in the movies, that no one used in the neighborhood, I would say it at most to myself, we all preferred *voler bene*. She no, she *loved*. She loved Nino. But she knew very well that that love had to be suffocated, every occasion for it to breathe had to be removed. And she would do it, she would do it starting Saturday night. She had no doubts, she would be capable of it, and I had to trust her. But the very little time that remained she wished to devote to Nino.

"I want to stay in a bed with him for a whole night and a whole day," she said. "I want to sleep holding him and being held, and kiss him when I feel like it, caress him when I feel like it, even while he's sleeping. Then that's it."

"It's impossible."

"You have to help me."

"How?"

"You have to convince my mother that Nella has invited us to spend two days at Barano and that we'll spend the night there."

I was silent for a moment. So she already had a project, she had a plan. Clearly she had worked it out with Nino, maybe he had even sent Bruno away on purpose. For how long had they been deciding the how, the where? No more speeches on neocapitalism, on neocolonialism, on Africa, on Latin America, on Beckett, on Bertrand Russell. Mere doodles. Nino no longer talked about anything. Their brilliant minds now were exercised only on how to deceive Nunzia and Stefano, using me.

"You're out of your mind," I said, furiously, "even if your mother believes you your husband never will."

"You persuade her to send us to Barano and I'll persuade her not to tell Stefano."

"No."

"Aren't we friends anymore?"

"No."

"You're not Nino's friend anymore?"

"No."

But Lila knew how to draw me in. And I was unable to resist: on the one hand I said that's enough, on the other I was depressed at the idea of not being part of her life, of the means by which she invented it for herself. What was that deception but another of her fantastic moves, which were always full of risks? The two of us together, allied with each other, in the struggle against all. We would devote the next day to overcoming Nunzia's opposition. The day after that we would leave early, together. At Forio we would separate. She would go to Bruno's house with Nino, I would take the boat for the Maronti. She would spend the whole day and the whole night with Nino, I would be at Nella's and sleep in Barano. The next day I would return to Forio for lunch, we would see each other at Bruno's, and together would return home. Perfect. The more her mind was ignited as, in minute detail, she planned how to make every part of the ruse add up, the more skillfully she ignited mine, too, and she hugged me, begged me. Here was a new adventure, *together*. Here was how *we* would take what life didn't want to give us. Here. Or would I rather that she be deprived of that joy, that Nino should suffer, that both should lose the light of reason and end up not capably managing their desire but being dangerously overwhelmed by it? There was a moment, that night, when, by following her along the thread of her arguments, I came to think that to support her in this undertaking, besides being an important milestone for our long sisterhood, was also the way of manifesting my love—she said friendship, but I desperately thought: love, love love—for Nino. And it was at that point that I said:

"All right, I'll help you."

66.

The next day I told Nunzia many lies that were so disgraceful I was ashamed. At the center of the lies I placed Maestra Oliviero, who was in Potenza, in goodness knows what terrible conditions, and it was my idea, not Lila's. "Yesterday," I said to Nunzia, "I met Nella Incardo, and she told me that her cousin, who is convalescing, has come to stay with her for a vacation at the seaside that will finally restore her health. Tomorrow night Nella's having a party for the teacher and she invited me and Lila, who were her best students. We would really like to go, but it will be late and so impossible. But Nella has said that we can sleep at her house."

"In Barano?" Nunzia asked, frowning.

"Yes, the party is there."

"You go, Lenù, Lila can't, her husband will get mad."

Lila threw in, "Let's not tell him."

"What do you mean?"

"Mamma, he's in Naples and I'm here, he'll never find out."

"One way or another things are always found out."

"Well, no."

"Yes, and that's enough. Lina, I don't want to discuss it further: if Lenuccia wants to go, fine, but you stay here."

We went on for a good hour, I making the point that the

276 · ELENA FERRANTE

teacher was very sick and this might be our last chance to show her our gratitude, and Lila pressing her like this: "How many lies have you told Papa, admit it, and not for bad reasons but for good ones, to have a moment to yourself, to do a just thing that he would never allow." Wavering, Nunzia first said that she had never told the tiniest lie to Fernando; then she admitted that she had told one, two, many; finally she cried with rage and at the same time maternal pride, "What happened when I conceived you, an accident, a hiccup, a convulsion, the lights went out, a bulb blew, the basin of water fell off the night table? Certainly there must have been something, if you were born so intolerable, so different from the others." And here she grew sad, she seemed to soften. But soon she was indignant again, she said you don't tell lies to a husband just to see a schoolteacher. And Lila exclaimed, "To Maestra Oliviero I owe the little I know, the only school I had was with her." And in the end Nunzia gave in. But she insisted on a precise timetable: Saturday at exactly two o'clock we were to be home again. Not a minute later. "If Stefano arrives early and doesn't find you? Really, Lina, don't put me in an ugly situation. Clear?"

"Clear."

We went to the beach. Lila was radiant, she embraced me, she kissed me, she said that she would be grateful for her whole life. But I already felt guilty about that evocation of Maestra Oliviero, whom I had placed at the center of a party, in Barano, imagining her as she was when, full of energy, she taught us, and not as, instead, she must be now, worse than when she was taken away in the ambulance, worse than when I had seen her in the hospital. My satisfaction in having invented an effective lie vanished, I lost the frenzy of complicity, I became resentful again. I asked myself why I supported Lila, why I covered for her: in fact she wanted to betray her husband, she wanted to violate the sacred bond of marriage, she wanted to tear off her condition of wife, she wanted to do a thing that would provoke Stefano, if he should find out, to bash her head in. Suddenly I remembered what she had done to the wedding-dress photograph and I felt sick to my stomach. Now, I thought, she is behaving in the same way, and not with a photograph but with the very person of Signora Carracci. And in this case, too, she pulls me in to help her. Nino is a tool, yes, yes. Like the scissors, the paste, the paint, he is being used to disfigure her. Toward what terrible act is she driving me? And why do I let myself be driven?

We found him waiting for us at the beach. He asked anxiously: "So?"

She said, "Yes."

They ran off to swim without even inviting me, and, besides, I wouldn't have gone. I felt chilled by anxiety, and then why swim, to stay near the shore alone, with my fear of the deep water?

There was some wind, some strips of cloud, the sea was a little rough. They dived in without hesitation, Lila with a long cry of joy. They were happy, full of their own romance, they had the energy of those who successfully seize what they desire, no matter the cost. Moving with determined strokes, they were immediately lost amid the waves.

I felt chained to an intolerable pact of friendship. How tortuous everything was. It was I who had dragged Lila to Ischia. I had used her to pursue Nino, hopelessly. I had relinquished the money from the bookstore on Via Mezzocannone for the money that she gave me. I had put myself in her service and now I was playing the role of the servant who comes to the aid of her mistress. I was covering for her adultery. I was preparing it. I was helping her take Nino, take him in my place, be fucked—yes, fucked—fucked by him for a whole day and a whole night, give him blow jobs. My temples began to throb, I kicked the sand with my heel once, twice, three times, it was a

278 - ELENA FERRANTE

thrill to hear echoing in my head childhood words, overloaded with sex imagined in ignorance. High school disappeared, the wonderful sonority of the books disappeared, of the translations from Greek and Latin. I stared at the sparkling sea, and the long livid array of clouds that was moving from the horizon toward the blue sky, toward the white streak of condensation, and I could barely see them, Nino and Lila, black dots. I couldn't tell if they were swimming toward the mass of clouds on the horizon or turning back. I wished that they would drown and that death would take from them the joys of the next day.

67.

I heard someone calling me, I turned suddenly.

"So I had good eyesight," said a teasing male voice.

"I told you it was her," said a female voice.

I recognized them immediately, I sat up. It was Michele Solara and Gigliola, along with her brother, a boy of twelve called Lello.

I welcomed them warmly, even though I never said: Sit down. I hoped that for some reason they were in a hurry, that they would leave right away, but Gigliola spread her towel, along with Michele's, carefully on the sand, placed her purse on it, cigarettes, lighter, said to her brother: lie down on the hot sand, because the wind's blowing, your bathing suit's wet and you'll catch cold. What to do. I made an effort not to look toward the sea, as if in that way it wouldn't occur to them to look at it, and I paid happy attention to Michele, who started talking in his usual unemotional, careless tone. They had taken a holiday, it was too hot in Naples. Boat in the morning, boat in the evening, good air. Since Pinuccia and Alfonso were in the shop on Piazza dei Martiri, or, rather, no, Alfonso and Pinuccia, because Pinuccia didn't do much, while Alfonso was

great. It was on Pina's recommendation that they had decided
to come to Forio. You'll find them, she had said, just walk
along the beach. And in fact, they had walked and walked,
Gigliola had shouted: Isn't that Lenuccia? And here we are. I
kept saying what a pleasure, and meanwhile Michele got up
absent-mindedly, with his sandy feet on Gigliola's towel, so she
reproached him—"Pay a little attention"—but in vain. Now
that he had finished the story of why they were on Ischia, I
knew that the real question was about to arrive, I read it in his
eyes even before he said it:

"Where's Lina?"

"She's swimming."

"In this sea?"

"It's not too rough."

It was inevitable, both he and Gigliola turned to look at the
sea, with its curls of foam. But they did it distractedly, they were
settling themselves on the towels. Michele argued with the boy,
who wanted to go swimming again. "Stay here," he said, "you
want to drown?" He stuck a comic book in his hand, adding, to
his girlfriend, "We're never taking him again."

Gigliola complimented me profusely: "How well you look,
all tanned, and your hair is even lighter."

I smiled, I was self-deprecating, but I was thinking only:
I've got to find a way to get them out of here.

"Come rest at the house," I said. "Nunzia's there, she'll be
very happy."

They refused, they had to catch the boat in a couple of
hours, they preferred to have a little more sun and then they
would head off on their walk.

"So let's go to the bath house, we'll get something to eat
there," I said.

"Yes, but let's wait for Lina."

As always in tense situations, I undertook to blot out the time
with words, and I started off with a flurry of questions, anything

that came into my head: How was Spagnuolo the pastry maker, how was Marcello, if he'd found a girlfriend, what did Michele think of the shoe designs, and what did his father think and what did his mamma think of them, and what did his grandfather think. At one point I got up, I said, "I'll call Lina," and I went down to the water's edge, I began to shout: "Lina, come back, Michele and Gigliola are here," but it was useless, she didn't hear me. I went back, and started talking again to distract them. I hoped that Lila and Nino, returning to shore, would become aware of the danger before Gigliola and Michele saw them and avoid any intimate attitude. But though Gigliola listened to me, Michele wasn't even polite enough to pretend. He had come to Ischia purposely to see Lila and talk to her about the new shoes, I was sure of it, and he cast long glances at the sea, which was getting rougher.

Finally he saw her. He saw her as she came out of the water, her hand entwined in Nino's, a handsome couple who would not pass unobserved, both tall, both naturally elegant, shoulders touching, smiles exchanged. They were so entranced with themselves that they didn't immediately realize I had company. When Lila recognized Michele and pulled her hand away, it was too late. Maybe Gigliola didn't notice, and her brother was reading the comic book, but Michele saw and turned to look at me as if to read on my face the verification of what he had just had before his eyes. He must have found it, in the form of fear. He said gravely, in the slow voice that he assumed when he had to deal with something that required speed and decisiveness: "Ten minutes, just the time to say hello, and we'll go."

In fact they stayed more than an hour. Michele, when he heard Nino's last name—introducing him I placed great emphasis on the fact that he was our schoolmate in elementary school as well as my classmate in high school—asked the most irritating question:

"You're the son of the guy who writes for *Roma* and for *Napoli Notte*?"

Nino nodded unwillingly, and Michele stared at him for a long instant, as if he wanted to find in his eyes confirmation of that relationship. Then he did not speak to him again, he spoke only and always to Lila.

Lila was friendly, ironic, at times deceitful.

Michele said to her, "That blowhard your brother swears he thought up the new shoes."

"It's the truth."

"So that's why they're garbage."

"You'll see, that garbage will sell even better than the preceding."

"Maybe, but only if you come to the store."

"You already have Gigliola, who's doing great."

"I need Gigliola in the pastry shop."

"Your problem, I have to stay in the grocery."

"You'll see, you'll move to Piazza dei Martiri, *signò,* and you'll have carte blanche."

"Carte blanche, carte noir, get it out of your head, I'm fine where I am."

And so on in this tone, they seemed to be playing *tamburello* with their words. Every so often Gigliola or I tried to say something, mainly Gigliola, who was furious at the way her fiancé talked about her fate without even consulting her. As for Nino, he was—I realized—stunned, or perhaps astonished at how Lila, skillful and fearless, found the phrases, in dialect, to match Michele's.

Finally the young Solara announced that they had to go, they had an umbrella with their belongings quite far away. He said goodbye to me, he said goodbye warmly to Lila, repeating that he would expect her in the store in September. To Nino he said seriously, as if to a subordinate whom one asks to go and buy a pack of Nationals, "Tell your papa that he was wrong to write that he didn't like the way the store looked. When you take money, you have to write that everything's great, otherwise no more money."

Nino was caught by surprise, perhaps by humiliation, and didn't answer. Gigliola held out her hand, he gave her his mechanically. The couple went off, dragging the boy, who was reading the comic book as he walked.

68.

I was enraged, frightened, unhappy with my every word or gesture. As soon as Michele and Gigliola were far enough away I said to Lila, so that Nino could also hear me: "He saw you."

Nino asked uneasily, "Who is he?"

"A shit Camorrist who thinks he's God's gift," said Lila contemptuously.

I corrected her immediately, Nino should know: "He's one of her husband's partners. He'll tell Stefano everything."

"What everything," Lila protested, "there's nothing to tell."

"You know perfectly well that they'll tell on you."

"Yes? And who gives a damn."

"I give a damn."

"Don't worry. Because even if you won't help me, things will go as they should go."

And as if I weren't present, she went on to make arrangements with Nino for the next day. But while she, precisely because of that encounter with Michele Solara, seemed to have multiplied her energies, he seemed like a windup toy that has run down. He murmured:

"Are you sure you won't get yourself in trouble because of me?"

Lila caressed his cheek. "You don't want to anymore?"

The caress seemed to revive him. "I'm just worried for you."

We soon left Nino, we returned home. Along the way I sketched catastrophic scenarios—"Michele will talk to Stefano tonight, Stefano will rush over here tomorrow morning, he won't find you at home, Nunzia will send him to Barano, he won't find you at Barano, either, you'll lose everything, Lila, listen to me, you'll ruin not only yourself but you'll ruin me, too, my mother will kill me"—but she confined herself to listening absent-mindedly, smiling, repeating in varying formulations a single idea: I love you, Lenù, and I will always love you; so I hope that you feel at least once in your life what I'm feeling at this moment.

Then I thought: so much the worse for you. We stayed home that night. Lila was nice to her mother, she wanted to cook, she wanted her to be served, she cleared, washed the dishes, sat on her lap, put her arms around her neck, resting her forehead against hers with an unexpected sadness. Nunzia, who wasn't used to those kindnesses and must have found them embarrassing, at a certain point burst into tears and amid her tears uttered a phrase convoluted by anxiety: "Please, Lina, no mother has ever had a daughter like you, don't make me die of sorrow."

Lila made fun of her affectionately and took her to her room. In the morning she dragged me out of bed; part of me was so anguished that it didn't want to get up and be conscious of the day. In the mini cab to Forio, I laid out other terrible scenarios that left her completely indifferent. "Nella's gone"; "Nella really has guests and has no room for me"; "The Sarratores decide to come here to Forio to visit their son." She continued to reply in a joking tone: "If Nella's gone, Nino's mother will welcome you"; "If there's no room you'll come back and sleep at our house"; "If the whole Sarratore family knocks at the door of Bruno's house we won't open it." And we went on like that until, a little before nine, we arrived at our destination. Nino was at the window waiting, he hurried to open the door. He gave me a nod of greeting, he drew Lila inside.

What until that door could still be avoided from that moment became an unstoppable mechanism. In the same cab, at Lila's expense, I was taken to Barano. On the way I realized that I couldn't truly hate them. I felt bitterness toward Nino, I certainly had some hostile feelings toward Lila, I could even wish death on both of them, but almost as a kind of incantation that was capable, paradoxically, of saving all three of us. Hatred no. Rather, I hated myself, I despised myself. I was there, I was there on the island, the air stirred by the cab's movement assailed me with the intense odors of the vegetation from which night was evaporating. But it was a mortified presence, submissive to the demands of others. I was living in them, unobtrusively. I couldn't cancel out the images of the embraces, kisses in the empty house. Their passion invaded me, disturbed me. I loved them both and so I couldn't love myself, feel myself, affirm myself with a need for life of *my own*, one that had the same blind, mute force as theirs. So it seemed to me.

69.

I was greeted by Nella and the Sarratore family with the usual enthusiasm. I assumed my humblest mask, the mask of my father when he collected tips, the elaborate mask of my forebears—always fearful, always subordinate, always pleasingly willing—by which to avoid danger, and I went from lie to lie in a pleasant manner. I said to Nella that if I had decided to come and disturb her it wasn't by choice but necessity. I said that the Carraccis had guests, that there was no room for me that night. I said that I hoped I hadn't presumed too much in showing up like this, unexpectedly, and that if there were difficulties I would return to Naples for a few days.

Nella embraced me, fed me, swearing that to have me in the house was an immense pleasure for her. I refused to go to the beach with the Sarratores, although the children protested. Lidia insisted that I join them soon and Donato declared that he would wait for me so we could swim together. I stayed with Nella, helped her straighten the house, cook lunch. For a moment everything weighed on me less: the lies, the images of the adultery that was taking place, my complicity, a jealousy that couldn't be defined because I felt at the same time jealous of Lila who was giving herself to Nino, of Nino who was giving himself to Lila. In the meantime, Nella, talking about the Sarratores, seemed less hostile. She said that husband and wife had found an equilibrium and since they were getting along they gave her less trouble. She told me about Maestra Oliviero: she had telephoned her in order to tell her that I had come to see her, and she had been very tired but more optimistic. For a while, in other words, there was a tranquil flow of news. But a few remarks were enough, an unexpected detour, and the weight of the situation I was involved in returned forcefully.

"She praised you a lot," Nella said, speaking of Maestra Oliviero, "but when she found out that you came to see me with your two married friends she asked a lot of questions, especially about Signora Lina."

"What did she say?"

"She said that in her entire career as a teacher she never had such a good student."

The evocation of Lila's old primacy disturbed me.

"It's true," I admitted.

But Nella made a grimace of absolute disagreement, her eyes lit up.

"My cousin is an exceptional teacher," she said, "and yet in my view this time she is wrong."

"No, she's not wrong."

"Can I tell you what I think?"

"Of course."

"It won't upset you?"

"No."

"I didn't like Signora Lina. You are much better, you're prettier and more intelligent. I talked about it with the Sarratores, too, and they agree with me."

"You say that because you love me."

"No. Pay attention, Lenù. I know that you are good friends, my cousin told me. And I don't want to interfere in things that have nothing to do with me. But a glance is enough for me to judge people. Signora Lina knows that you're better than her and so she doesn't love you the way you love her."

I smiled, pretending skepticism. "Does she hate me?"

"I don't know. But she knows how to wound, it's written in her face, it's enough to look at her forehead and her eyes."

I shook my head, I repressed my satisfaction. Ah, if it were all so straightforward. But I already knew—although not the way I do today—that between the two of us everything was more tangled. And I joked, laughed, made Nella laugh. I told her that Lila never made a good impression the first time. Since she was little she had seemed like a devil, and she really was, but in a good way. She had a quick mind and did well in whatever she happened to apply herself to: if she could have studied she would have become a scientist like Madame Curie or a great novelist like Grazia Deledda, or even like Nilde Iotti, the lover of Togliatti. And hearing those last two names, Nella exclaimed, oh Madonna, and ironically made the sign of the cross. Then she gave a little laugh, then another, and she couldn't contain herself, she wanted to whisper a secret, a very funny thing that Sarratore had said to her. Lila, according to him, had an almost ugly beauty, a type that males are, yes, enchanted by but also fear.

"What fear?" I asked, also in a low voice.

And she, in an even lower voice, "The fear that their thingy won't function or it will fall off or she'll pull out a knife and cut it off."

She laughed, her chest heaved, her eyes became teary. She couldn't contain herself for quite some time and I felt an unease I had never felt with her before. It wasn't my mother's laughter, the obscene laughter of the woman who knows. In Nella's there was something chaste and yet vulgar, it was the laugh of an aging virgin that assailed me and pushed me to laugh, too, but in a forced way. A smart woman like her, I said to myself, why does this amuse her? And meanwhile I saw myself growing old, with that laugh of malicious innocence in my breast. I thought: I'll end up laughing like that, too.

70.

The Sarratores arrived for lunch. They left a trail of sand on the floor, an odor of sea and sweat, a lighthearted reproach because the children had waited for me in vain. I set the table, cleared, washed the dishes, followed Pino, Clelia, and Ciro to the edge of a thicket to help them cut reeds to make a kite. With the children I was happy. While their parents rested, while Nella napped on a lounge chair on the terrace, the time slipped by, the kite absorbed me completely, I scarcely thought of Nino and Lila.

In the late afternoon we all went to the beach, even Nella, to fly the kite. I ran back and forth on the beach followed by the three children, who were silent, amazed, when the kite appeared to rise and they cried out when they saw it hit the sand after an unexpected pirouette. I kept trying but I couldn't make it fly, in spite of the instructions that Donato shouted to me from under the umbrella. Finally, all sweaty, I gave up, and said to Pino, Clelia, and Ciro, "Ask Papa." Dragged by his children, Sarratore came and checked the weave of the reeds, the blue tissue paper, the thread, then he studied the wind and began to run backward, leaping energetically despite his heavy body. The children ran beside him in their excitement, and I also revived, I began to run along with them, until their expanding happiness was transmitted to me, too. Our kite traveled higher and higher, it flew, there was no need to run, you had only to hold the string. Sarratore was a good father. He demonstrated that with his help Ciro could hold it, and Clelia, and Pino, and even me. He handed it to me, in fact, but he stood behind me, he breathed on my neck and said, "Like that, good, pull a little, let it go," and it was evening.

We had dinner, the Sarratore family went for a walk in the town, husband, wife, and three children, sunburned and dressed up. Although they urged me to come, I stayed with Nella. We cleaned up, she helped me make the bed in the usual corner of the kitchen, we sat on the terrace in the cool air. The moon wasn't visible, in the dark sky there were swells of white clouds. We talked about how pretty and intelligent the Sarratore children were, and Nella fell asleep. Then, suddenly, the day, the night that was beginning, fell on me. I left the house on tiptoe, I went toward the Maronti.

Who knows if Michele Solara had kept to himself what he had seen. Who knows if everything was going smoothly. Who knows if Nunzia was already asleep in the house on the road in Cuotto or was trying to calm her son-in-law who had arrived unexpectedly on the last boat, hadn't found his wife and was furious. Who knows if Lila had telephoned her husband and, reassured that he was in Naples, far away, in the apartment in the new neighborhood, was now in bed with Nino, without fear, a secret couple, a couple intent on enjoying the night. Everything in the world was in precarious balance, pure risk, and those who didn't agree to take the risk wasted away in a corner, without getting to know life. I understood suddenly why I hadn't had Nino, why Lila had had him. I wasn't capable of entrusting myself to true feelings. I didn't know how to be drawn beyond the limits. I didn't possess that emotional power that had driven Lila to do all she could to enjoy that day and that night. I stayed behind, waiting. She, on the other hand, seized things, truly wanted them, was passionate about them, played for all or nothing, and wasn't afraid of contempt, mockery, spitting, beatings. She deserved Nino, in other words, because she thought that to love him meant to try to have him, not to hope that he would want her.

I made the dark descent. Now the moon was visible amid scattered pale-edged clouds; the evening was very fragrant, and you could hear the hypnotic rhythm of the waves. On the beach I took off my shoes, the sand was cold, a gray-blue light extended as far as the sea and then spread over its tremulous expanse. I thought: yes, Lila is right, the beauty of things is a trick, the sky is the throne of fear; I'm alive, now, here, ten steps from the water, and it is not at all beautiful, it's terrifying; along with this beach, the sea, the swarm of animal forms, I am part of the universal terror; at this moment I'm the infinitesimal particle through which the fear of every thing becomes conscious of itself; I; I who listen to the sound of the sea, who feel the dampness and the cold sand; I who imagine all Ischia, the entwined bodies of Nino and Lila, Stefano sleeping by himself in the new house that is increasingly not so new, the furies who indulge the happiness of today to feed the violence of tomorrow. Ah, it's true, my fear is too great and so I hope that everything will end soon, that the figures of the nightmares will consume my soul. I hope that from this darkness packs of mad dogs will emerge, vipers, scorpions, enormous sea serpents. I hope that while I'm sitting here, on the edge of the sea, assassins will arrive out of the night and torture my body. Yes, yes, let me be punished for my insufficiency, let the worst happen, something so devastating that it will prevent me from facing tonight, tomorrow, the hours and days to come, reminding me with always more crushing evidence of my unsuitable constitution. Thoughts like that I had, the frenzied thoughts of girlish discouragement. I gave myself up to them, for I don't know how long. Then someone said, "Lena," and touched my shoulder with cold fingers. I started, an icy grip seized my heart and when I turned suddenly and recognized Donato Sarratore, the breath burst in my throat like the sip of a magic potion, the kind that in poems revives strength and the urge to live.

71.

Donato told me that Nella had awakened, found that I wasn't in the house, and was worried. Lidia, too, was a little alarmed, so she had asked him to go and look for me. The only one who had found it normal that I wasn't in the house was him. He had reassured the two women, he had said, "Go to sleep, surely she's gone to enjoy the moon on the beach." Yet to please them, out of prudence, he had come on a reconnaissance. And in fact here I was, sitting and listening to the sea's breath, contemplating the divine beauty of the sky.

He spoke like that, more or less. He sat beside me, he murmured that he knew me as he knew himself. We had the same sensitivity to beautiful things, the same need to enjoy them, the same need to search for the right words to say how sweet the night was, how magical the moon, how the sea sparkled, how two souls were able to meet and recognize each other in the darkness, in the fragrant air. As he spoke I heard clearly the ridiculousness of his trained voice, the crudeness of his poeticizing, the sleazy lyricizing behind which he concealed his eagerness to put his hands on me. But I thought: Maybe we really are made of the same clay, maybe we really are condemned, blameless, to the same, identical mediocrity. So I rested my head on his shoulder, I murmured, "I'm cold." And he quickly put an arm around my waist, pulled me slowly closer to him, asked me if it was better like that. I answered, "Yes," a whisper, and Sarratore lifted my chin with thumb and index finger, placed his lips lightly on mine, asked, "How's that?" Then he pressed me with little kisses that grew in intensity as he continued to murmur: "And like that, and like that, are you still cold, is it better like that, is it better?" His mouth was warm and wet, I welcomed it on mine with increasing gratitude, so that the kiss lasted longer and longer, his tongue grazed mine, collided with it, sank into my mouth. I felt better. I realized that I was regaining ground, that the ice was ceding, melting, that the fear was forgetting itself, that his hands were taking away the cold but slowly, as if it were made of very thin layers and Sarratore had the ability to peel them away with cautious precision, one by one, without tearing them, and that his mouth, too, had that capacity, and his teeth, his tongue, and he therefore knew much more about me than Antonio had ever learned, that in fact he knew what I myself didn't know. I had a hidden me—I realized—that fingers, mouth, teeth, tongue were able to discover. Layer after layer, that me lost every hiding place, was shamelessly exposed, and Sarratore showed that he knew how to keep it from fleeing, from being ashamed, he knew how to hold it as if it were the absolute reason for his affectionate motility, for his sometimes gentle, sometimes fevered pressures. The entire time, I didn't once regret having accepted what was happening. I had no second thoughts and I was proud of myself, I wanted it to be like that, I imposed it on myself. I was helped, perhaps, by the fact that Sarratore progressively forgot his flowery language, that, unlike Antonio, he claimed no intervention from me, he never took my hand to touch him, but confined himself to convincing me that he liked everything about me, and he applied himself to my body with the care, the devotion, the pride of the man absorbed in demonstrating how thoroughly he knows women. I didn't even hear him say *you're a virgin*, probably he was so sure of my condition that he would have been surprised by the opposite. When I was overwhelmed by a need for pleasure so demanding and so egocentric that it canceled out not only the entire world of sensation but also his body, in my eyes old, and the labels by which he could be classified—*father of Nino, railway worker-poet-journalist, Donato Sarratore*—he was aware of it and penetrated me. I felt that he did it delicately at first, then with a clear and decisive thrust that caused a rip in my stomach, a stab of pain immediately erased by a rhythmic oscillation, a sliding, a thrusting, an emptying and filling me with jolts of eager desire. Until suddenly he withdrew, turned over on his back on the sand and emitted a sort of strangled roar.

We were silent, the sea returned, the tremendous sky, I felt stunned. That impelled Sarratore again toward his coarse lyricism, he thought he had to lead me back to myself with tender words. But I managed to tolerate at most a couple of phrases. I got up abruptly, shook the sand out of my hair, off my whole body, straightened myself. When he ventured, "Where can we meet tomorrow?" I answered in Italian, in a calm voice, self-assured, that he was mistaken, he must never look for me again, not at Cetara or in the neighborhood. And when he smiled skeptically, I told him that what Antonio Cappuccio, Melina's son, could do to him was nothing in comparison to what Michele Solara, a person I knew well, would do. I need only say a word and Solara would make things very hard for him. I told him that Michele was eager to bash his face in, because he had taken money to write about the shop on Piazza dei Martiri but hadn't done his job well.

All the way back I continued to threaten him, partly because he had returned to his sugary-sweet little phrases and I wanted him to understand clearly my feelings, partly because I was amazed at how the tonality of threat, which since I was a

child I had used only in dialect, came easily to me also in the
Italian language.

72.

I was afraid I would find the two women awake but they
were both asleep. They weren't so worried that they would lose
sleep, they considered me sensible, they trusted me. I slept
deeply.

The next day I woke up cheerful and even when Nino, Lila,
and what had happened at the Maronti came back to me, in
fragments, I still felt good. I chatted a long time with Nella,
had breakfast with the Sarratores, didn't mind the falsely
paternal kindness with which Donato treated me. Not for a
moment did I think that sex with that rather conceited, vain,
garrulous man had been a mistake. Yet to see him there at the
table, to listen to him, and recognize that it was he who had
deflowered me, disgusted me. I went to the beach with the
whole family, I went swimming with the children, I left behind
me a wake of fondness. I arrived punctually at Forio.

I called Nino, he appeared immediately. I refused to go in,
partly because we had to leave as soon as possible, partly
because I did not want to preserve images of rooms that Nino
and Lila had inhabited by themselves for almost two days. I
waited, Lila didn't come. Suddenly my anxiety returned, I imagined that Stefano had been able to leave in the morning, that he
was disembarking several hours earlier than expected, and in
fact was already on his way to the house. I called again, Nino
returned, he indicated that I had to wait just another minute.
They came down a quarter of an hour later, they embraced and
kissed for a long time in the entrance. Lila ran toward me, but
she stopped suddenly, as if she had forgotten something, and
went back and kissed him again. I looked away uneasily and the

idea that there was something wrong with me, that I lacked a true capacity for involvement, regained strength. Yet the two of them again seemed to me so handsome, perfect in every movement, that to cry, "Lina, hurry up," was almost to disfigure a fantastical image. She seemed drawn away by a cruel force, her hand ran slowly from his shoulder, along the arm, to the fingers, as if in the movement of a dance. Finally she joined me.

We hardly spoke during the ride in the mini cab.

"Everything all right?"

"Yes. And you?"

"Fine."

I said nothing about myself, nor did she about herself. But the reasons for that reticence were very different. I had no intention of putting into words what had happened to me: it was a bare fact, it had to do with my body, its physiological reactivity. That for the first time a tiny part of another body had entered it seemed to me irrelevant: the nighttime mass of Sarratore communicated to me nothing except a sensation of alienness, and it was a relief that it had vanished like a storm that never arrives. It seemed to me clear, instead, that Lila was silent because she didn't have words. I felt she was in a state without thoughts or images, as if in detaching herself from Nino she had forgotten in him everything of herself, even the capacity to say what had happened to her, what was happening. This difference between us made me sad. I tried to search in my experience on the beach for something equivalent to her sorrowful-happy disorientation. I also realized that at the Maronti, in Barano, I had left nothing, not even that new self that had been revealed. I had taken everything with me, and so I didn't feel the urgency, which I read in Lila's eyes, in her half-closed mouth, in her clenched fists, to go back, to be reunited with the person I had had to leave. And if on the surface my condition might seem more solid, more compact, here instead, beside Lila, I felt sodden, earth too soaked with water.

73.

Fortunately I didn't read her notebooks until later. There were pages and pages about that day and night with Nino, and what those pages said was exactly what I hadn't had and couldn't say. Lila wrote not even a word about sexual pleasures, nothing that might be useful in comparing her experience with mine. She talked instead about love and she did so in a surprising way. She said that from the day of her marriage until those days on Ischia she had been, without realizing it, on the point of dying. She described minutely a sensation of imminent death: lack of energy, lethargy, a strong pressure in the middle of her head, as if between the brain and the skull there was an air bubble that was continually expanding, the impression that everything was moving in a hurry to leave, that the speed of every movement of persons and things was excessive and hit her, wounded her, caused her physical pain in her stomach and in her eyes. She said that all this was accompanied by a dulling of the senses, as if they had been wrapped in cotton wool, and her wounds came not from the real world but from a hollow space between her body and the mass of cotton wool in which she felt she was wrapped. She admitted on the other hand that imminent death seemed to her so assured that it took away her respect for everything, above all for herself, as if nothing counted anymore and everything deserved to be ruined. At times she was overwhelmed by a mania to express herself with no mediation: express herself for the last time, before becoming like Melina, before crossing the *stradone* just as a truck was coming, and be hit, dragged away. Nino had changed that state, he had snatched her away from death. And he had done it when he had asked her to dance, at Professor Galiani's house, and she had refused, frightened by that offer of salvation. Then, on Ischia, day by day, he had assumed the power of the savior. He had restored to her the capacity to feel. He had above all brought back to life her sense of herself. Yes, brought to life. Lines and lines and lines had at their center the concept of resurrection: an ecstatic rising, the end of every bond and yet the inexpressible pleasure of a new bond, a revival that was also a revolt: he and she, she and he together learned life again, banished its poison, reinvented it as the pure joy of thinking and living.

This, more or less. Her words were very beautiful, mine are only a summary. If she had confided it to me then, in the taxi, I would have suffered even more, because I would have recognized in her fulfillment the reverse of my emptiness. I would have understood that she had come to something that I thought I knew, that I had believed I felt for Nino, and that, instead, I didn't know, and perhaps would never know, except in a weak, muted form. I would have understood that she wasn't playing a summer game for fun but that a violent feeling was growing inside her and would overwhelm her. Instead, as we were returning to Nunzia after our violations, I couldn't get away from the usual confused sense of disparity, the impression—recurrent in our story—that I was losing something and she was gaining. So occasionally I felt the need to even the score, to tell her how I had lost my virginity between sea and sky, at night, on the beach at the Maronti. I couldn't tell her the name of Nino's father, I thought, I could invent a sailor, a smuggler of American cigarettes, and tell her what had happened to me, tell her how good it had been. But I realized that to tell her about me and my pleasure didn't matter to me, I would tell my story only to induce her to tell hers and find out how much pleasure she had had with Nino and compare it with mine and feel—I hoped—in the lead. Luckily I sensed that she would never do it and that I would only have stupidly exposed myself. I remained silent, as she did.

74.

Once we were home Lila found words again, along with an overexcited expansiveness. Nunzia welcomed us, greatly relieved by our return and yet hostile. She said she hadn't closed an eye, she had heard inexplicable noises in the house, had been afraid of ghosts and murderers. Lila embraced her and Nunzia almost pushed her away.

"Did you have fun?" she asked.

"A lot of fun, I want to change everything."

"What do you want to change?"

Lila laughed. "I'll think about it and let you know."

"Let your husband know first of all," Nunzia said, in an unexpectedly sharp tone.

Her daughter looked at her in amazement, a pleased, and perhaps slightly moved, amazement, as if the suggestion seemed to her right and urgent.

"Yes," she said, and went to her room, then to the bathroom.

She came out after a while and, still in her slip, motioned me to come to her room. I went reluctantly. She gazed at me with feverish eyes, she spoke rapidly, almost breathlessly: "I want to study what he studies."

"He's at the university, the subjects are difficult."

"I want to read the same books as him, I want to understand the things he thinks, I want to learn not for the university but for him."

"Lila, don't act crazy: we said that you would see him this time and that's all. What's wrong with you, calm down, Stefano is about to get here."

"Do you think, if I work hard, I can understand the things he understands?"

I couldn't take it anymore. What I already knew and what I nevertheless was hiding from myself became at that moment perfectly clear: she, too, now saw in Nino the only person able to save her. She had taken possession of my old feeling, had made it her own. And, knowing what she was like, I had no doubts: she would knock down every obstacle and continue to the end. I answered harshly.

"No. It's complicated stuff, you're too behind in everything, you don't read a newspaper, you don't know who's in the government, you don't even know who runs Naples."

"And do you know those things?"

"No."

"He thinks you know them, I told you, he thinks a lot of you."

I felt myself flushing, I muttered, "I'm trying to learn, and when I don't know I pretend to know."

"Even pretending to know, one gradually learns. Can you help me?"

"No, and no, Lila, it's not something you should do. Leave him alone, because of you he's already saying that he wants to stop going to the university."

"He'll study, he was born for that. And yet there are a lot of things that even he doesn't know. If I study the things he doesn't know, I'll tell him when he needs them and so I'll be useful to him. I have to change, Lenù, immediately."

I burst out again: "You're married, you have to get him out of your head, you're not right for what he needs."

"Who is right?"

I wanted to wound her, I said, "Nadia."

"He left her for me."

"So everything's fine? I don't want to listen to you anymore, you're both out of your minds, do what you like."

I went to my room, consumed by unhappiness.

75.

Stefano arrived at the usual time. We all three greeted him

with false cheerfulness, and he was polite but a little tense, as
if behind his benign expression he had a worry. Since his vacation was to begin that day, I was surprised that he hadn't
brought any luggage. Lila didn't seem to notice, but Nunzia
did and asked him, "You look preoccupied, Ste', is something
worrying you? Is your mamma well? And Pinuccia? And how
are things with the shoes? What do the Solaras say, are they
pleased?" He said that everything was fine, and we had dinner,
but the conversation was forced. First Lila made an effort to
seem in a good mood, but when Stefano responded with
monosyllables and no sign of affection she became annoyed
and was silent. Only Nunzia and I tried every possible means
to keep the silence from becoming permanent. When we got to
the fruit Stefano, with a half smile, said to his wife:

"You go swimming with Sarratore's son?"

My breath failed. Lila answered with irritation:
"Sometimes. Why?"

"How many times? One, two three, five, how many? Lenù,
do you know?"

"Once," I said, " he came by two or three days ago and we
all went swimming together."

Stefano, still with the half smile on his face, turned to his
wife.

"And you and the son of Sarratore are so intimate that
when you come out of the water you hold hands?"

Lila stared straight into his face: "Who told you that?"

"Ada."

"And who told Ada?"

"Gigliola."

"And Gigliola?"

"Gigliola saw you, bitch. She came here with Michele, they
came to visit you. And it's not true that you and that piece of
shit went swimming with Lenuccia, you went by yourselves
and you were holding hands."

Lila got up, she said calmly, "I'm going out, I'm going for a walk."

"You're not going anywhere: sit down and answer."

Lila remained standing. She said suddenly, in Italian and with an expression that looked like weariness but which—I realized—was contempt: "How stupid I was to marry you, you're worthless. You know that Michele Solara wants me in his shop, you know that for that reason Gigliola would kill me if she could, and what do you do, you believe her? I don't want to listen to you anymore, you let yourself be manipulated like a puppet. Lenù, will you come with me?"

She was about to move toward the door and I started to get up, but Stefano leaped up and grabbed her by the arm, said to her, "You're not going anywhere. You will tell me if it's true or not that you went swimming by yourself with the son of Sarratore, if it's true or not that you go around holding hands."

Lila tried to free herself, but she couldn't. She whispered, "Let go of my arm, you make me sick."

Nunzia at that point intervened. She reproached her daughter, said she could not allow herself to say that terrible thing to Stefano. But right afterward, with a surprising energy, she nearly shouted at her son-in-law to stop it, Lila had already answered, it was envy that made Gigliola say those things, the daughter of the pastry maker was treacherous, she was afraid of losing her place in Piazza dei Martiri, she wanted to get rid of Pinuccia, too, and be the sole mistress of the shop, she who knew nothing about shoes, who didn't even know how to make pastries, while everything—everything, everything—was due to Lila, including the success of the new grocery store, and so her daughter didn't deserve to be treated like that, no, she didn't deserve it.

She was truly enraged: her face was alight, wide-eyed, at a one point she seemed to be suffocating, as she added point to point without taking a breath. But Stefano didn't listen to a word. His mother-in-law was still speaking when he yanked Lila toward the bedroom, yelling: "You will now answer me, immediately," and when she insulted him grossly and grabbed the door of a cupboard to resist, he pulled her with such force that the door opened, the cupboard tottered dangerously, with a sound of plates and glasses rattling, and Lila almost flew through the kitchen and hit the wall of the hall that led to their room. A moment later her husband had grabbed her again and, holding her by the arm, but as if he were steadying a cup by the handle, pushed her into the bedroom and closed the door.

I heard the key turn in the lock, that sound terrified me. I had seen with my own eyes, in those long moments, that Stefano really was inhabited by the ghost of his father, that the shadow of Don Achille could swell the veins of his neck and the blue network under the skin of his forehead. But, although I was frightened, I felt that I couldn't stay still, sitting at the table, like Nunzia. I grabbed the doorknob and began to shake it, to pound the wooden door with my fist, begging, "Stefano, please, it's not true, leave her alone. Stefano, don't hurt her." But by now he was sealed within his rage, I could hear him yelling that he wanted the truth, and since Lila didn't respond—in fact, it was as if she were no longer in the room— he seemed to be talking to himself and meanwhile hitting himself, striking himself, breaking things.

"I'm going to call the landlady," I said to Nunzia, and I ran down the stairs. I wanted to ask the woman if she had another key or if her grandson was there, a large man who could have broken down the door. But I knocked in vain, the woman wasn't there, or if she was she didn't open the door. Meanwhile Stefano's shouts shattered the walls, spread through the street, through the reeds, toward the sea, and yet they seemed to find no ears but mine, no one looked out of the neighboring houses, no one came running. All that came was Nunzia's pleas, in a low tone, alternating with the threat that if Stefano continued to hurt her daughter she would tell Fernando and Rino everything, and they, as God was her witness, would kill him.

I ran back, I didn't know what to do. I hurled myself with all the weight of my body against the door, I cried that I had called the police, they were coming. Then, since Lila still showed no signs of life, I shrieked: "Lila, are you all right? Please, Lila, tell me you're all right." Only then did we hear her voice. She spoke not to us but to her husband, coldly:

"You want the truth? Yes, the son of Sarratore and I go swimming and we hold hands. Yes, we go into the deep sea and kiss each other and touch each other. Yes, I've been fucked by him a hundred times and so I discovered that you're a shit, that you're worthless, that you only demand disgusting things that make me throw up. Is that what you want? Are you happy?"

Silence. After those words Stefano didn't take a breath, I stopped pounding on the door, Nunzia stopped crying. Outside noises returned, the cars passing, some distant voices, the hens beating their wings.

Some minutes passed and it was Stefano who began speaking again, but so softly that we couldn't hear what he was saying. I realized, though, that he was looking for a way to calm down: short, disconnected phrases, show me that you're done, be good, stop it. Lila's confession must have seemed so unbearable that he had ended by taking it as a lie. He had seen in it something she resorted to in order to hurt him, an exaggeration equivalent to a solid punch to bring his feet back to the ground, words that in short meant: if you still don't realize what groundless things you're accusing me of, now I'm going to make it clear to you, you just listen.

But to me Lila's words seemed as terrible as Stefano's blows. I felt that if the excessive violence he repressed behind his polite manners and his meek face terrified me, I now couldn't bear her courage, that audacious impudence that allowed her to cry out the truth as if it were a lie. Every single word that she had addressed to Stefano had returned him to his senses, because he considered it a lie, but had pierced me painfully, because I knew the truth. When the voice of the grocer reached us more clearly, both Nunzia and I felt that the worst had passed, Don Achille was withdrawing from his son and returning him to his gentle, pliable side. And Stefano, restored to the part of himself that had made him a successful shop-keeper, was bewildered, he didn't understand what had happened to his voice, his hands, his arms. Even though the image of Lila and Nino holding hands probably persisted in his mind, what Lila had evoked for him with that hail of words could not help but have the flashing features of unreality.

The door didn't open, the key didn't turn in the lock until it was day. But Stefano's voice became sad, a depressed plead-ing, and Nunzia and I waited outside for hours, keeping each other company with despondent, barely heard remarks. Whispered words inside, whispered words outside. "If I tell Rino," Nunzia murmured, "he'll kill him, surely he'll kill him." And I whispered, as if I believed her: "Please, don't tell him." But meanwhile I thought: Rino, and even Fernando, after the wedding never moved a finger for Lila; not to mention that ever since she was born they've hit her whenever they wanted. And then I said to myself: men are all made of the same clay, only Nino is different. And I sighed, while my resentment grew stronger: now it's absolutely clear that Lila will have him, even if she's married, and together they'll get out of this filth, while I will be here forever.

76.

At the first light of dawn Stefano came out of his bedroom, Lila didn't. He said, "Pack your bags, we're leaving."

Nunzia couldn't contain herself and bitterly pointed out the damage he had done to the landlady's things, saying that he would have to compensate her. He answered—as if many of the words she had shouted at him hours earlier had stayed in his mind and he felt the need to dot the "i"s—that he always paid and would continue to pay. "I paid for this house," he enumerated in a tired voice, "I paid for your vacation, every-thing you, your husband, your son have I've given you: so don't be a pain in the neck, pack the bags and let's go."

Nunzia didn't say another word. A little later Lila came out of the room in a yellow dress with long sleeves and big dark glasses, like a movie star. She didn't say a word to us. She didn't at the Port, or on the boat, or even when we reached the neigh-borhood. She went home with her husband without saying goodbye.

As for me, I decided that from that moment on I would live for myself only, and as soon as we returned to Naples that was what I did, I imposed on myself an attitude of absolute detach-ment. I didn't look for Lila, I didn't look for Nino. I accepted without argument the scene that my mother made, as she accused me of having gone to play the lady on Ischia without thinking about how we needed money at home. Even my father, although he praised my healthy appearance, the golden blond of my hair, did the same: as soon as my mother attacked me in his presence, he backed her up. "You're a grownup," he said, "you see what you have to do."

Earning money was, in fact, an urgent necessity. I could have demanded from Lila what she had promised me in com-pensation for my coming to Ischia, but after that decision to cut myself off from her, and especially after the brutal words that Stefano had addressed to Nunzia (and in some way also to me), I didn't do it. For the same reason I absolutely ruled out the idea of her buying my school books, as she had the year before. When I saw Alfonso I asked him to tell her that I had already taken care of the books, and closed the discussion.

But after the August holiday I presented myself again at the bookstore on Mezzocannone, and partly because I had been an efficient and disciplined salesclerk, partly because of my looks, which had been improved by the sun and the sea, the owner, after some resistance, gave me back my job. He insisted, however, that I should not quit when school started but continue to work, if only in the afternoons, for the entire period of schoolbook sales. I agreed and spent long hours in the bookstore greeting teachers who came with bags full of books they had received free from publishing houses, to sell for a few lire, and students who sold their tattered used books for even less.

I lived through a week of pure anguish when my period didn't come. Afraid that Sarratore had made me pregnant, I was in despair; I was polite on the outside, grim inside. I spent sleepless nights, but didn't ask advice or comfort from anyone, I kept it all to myself. Finally, one afternoon in the bookstore I went to the dirty toilet and found the blood. It was one of the rare moments of well-being during that time. My period seemed a sort of symbolic cancellation of Sarratore's incursion into my body.

In early September it occurred to me that Nino must have returned from Ischia and I began to fear and hope that he would come by at least to say hello. But he didn't show up on Via Mezzocannone or in the neighborhood. As for Lila, I saw her only a couple of times, on Sunday, when, beside her husband in the car, she drove by on the *stradone*. Those few seconds were enough to enrage me. What had happened. How she had arranged things for herself. She continued to have everything, to keep everything: the car, Stefano, the house with the bathroom and the telephone and the television, the nice clothes, the prosperity. And who could say what plans she was devising in the secrecy of her mind. I knew how she was made and I said to myself that she wouldn't give up Nino even if Nino gave up her. But I chased away those thoughts and forced myself to respect the pact I had made with myself: to plan my life without them and learn not to suffer for it. To that end I concentrated on training myself to react little or not at all. I learned to reduce my emotions to the minimum: if the owner reached out his hands I repulsed him without indignation; if the customers were rude I made the best of it; even with my mother I managed to stay submissive. I said to myself every day: I am what I am and I have to accept myself; I was born like this, in this city, with this dialect, without money; I will give what I can give, I will take what I can take, I will endure what has to be endured.

77.

Then school began again. Only when I entered the class-room on the first of October did I realize that I was in my last year of high school, that I was eighteen years old, that the years of school, in my case already miraculously long, were about to end. So much the better. Alfonso and I talked a lot about what we would do after we graduated. He knew as much as I did. We'll take a civil-service exam, he said, but in fact we didn't have clear ideas on what the exams entailed; we said *sit the exam, pass the exam*, but the concept was vague: did you have to do a written exercise, take an oral test? And what did you get once you'd taken it, a salary?

Alfonso confided that he was thinking of getting married, once he had taken the exam and gained a post.

"To Marisa?"

"Yes, of course."

Sometimes I asked him warily about Nino, but he didn't like Nino, they didn't even say hello to each other. He had never understood what I found in him. He's ugly, he said, all out of proportion, skin and bone. Marisa, on the other hand, seemed pretty to him. But he immediately added, careful not to wound me, "You're pretty, too." He liked beauty, and especially appreciated care for one's body. He himself was attentive to his appearance, he smelled of the barber, he bought clothes, he lifted weights every day. He told me that he had a good time at the shop in Piazza dei Martiri. It wasn't like the grocery. There you could be elegant, in fact you had to be. There you could speak Italian, the people were respectable, had gone to school. There, even when you were on your knees in front of the customers, men and women, trying on the shoes, you could do it with pleasant manners, like the knight in a courtly love story. But unfortunately he wouldn't be able to stay in the shop.

"Why?"

"Well . . . "

At first he was vague and I didn't insist. Then he told me that Pinuccia was staying home now because she didn't want to get tired, she had a belly like a torpedo; and anyway it was clear that once she had the baby she wouldn't have time to work. This in theory should have cleared a path for him, the Solaras were pleased with him, maybe he would be able to establish himself there after he graduated. But it wasn't possible, and here suddenly the name of Lila came up. Just hearing it my stomach flared up.

"What does she have to do with it?"

I knew she had returned from the vacation like a madwoman. She still wasn't pregnant, the swimming had been of no use, she was behaving oddly. Once she had broken all the flowerpots on her balcony. She said she was going to the grocery, instead she left Carmen alone and went walking around. Stefano woke up at night and she wasn't in bed: she was wandering through the house, she read and wrote. Then suddenly she calmed down. Or rather she focused her entire capacity to spoil Stefano's life on a single objective: for Gigliola to work in the new grocery, and she in Piazza dei Martiri.

I was amazed.

"It's Michele who wants her in the shop," I said, "but she doesn't want to go."

"Once. Now she's changed her mind, she's moving heaven and earth to get herself there. The only obstacle is Stefano, he's against it. But of course in the end my brother does what she wants."

I asked no other questions, I wanted in no way to be reabsorbed into Lila's affairs. But for a while I surprised myself by wondering: what could she have in mind, why all of a sudden does she want to go and work in the city? Then I forgot about it, taken up by other problems: the bookstore, school, the class interrogations, the textbooks. Some I bought, most I stole from the bookstore without too many scruples. I began studying rigorously again, mainly at night. In the afternoon, in fact, until Christmas vacation, when I quit, I was busy at the bookstore. And right after that Professor Galiani herself arranged a couple of private pupils for me, and I worked hard for them. Between school, lessons, and study, there was no room for anything else.

When at the end of the month I gave my mother the money I earned, she put it in her pocket without saying anything, but in the morning she got up early to make breakfast for me, sometimes even a beaten egg, which she devoted such care to—while I was still in bed half asleep, I heard the *clack clack* of the spoon against the cup as she beat in the sugar—that it melted in my mouth like a cream, the sugar completely dissolved. As for the teachers at school, it seemed that they couldn't help considering me a brilliant student, as if the sluggish operation of the entire dusty scholastic machine had decided it. I had no trouble defending my position as first in the class and, with Nino gone, I ranked among the best in the whole school. But I soon realized that although Professor Galiani continued to be very generous, she blamed me for some offense that kept her from being as friendly as she had been in the past. For example, when I gave her back her books she was annoyed, because they were sandy, and took them away without promising to give me others. For example, she no longer offered me her newspapers, and for a while I forced myself to buy *Il Mattino*, then I stopped, it bored me, it was a waste of money. For example, she never invited me to her house, although I would have liked to see her son Armando again. Yet she continued to praise me publicly, to give me high grades, to advise me about important lectures and even films that were shown in a parish hall in Port'Alba. Until once, near Christmas vacation, she called as school was letting out and we walked some way together. Bluntly she asked what I knew about Nino.

"Nothing," I said.

"Tell me the truth."

"It's the truth."

It slowly emerged that Nino, after the summer, had not been in touch either with her or with her daughter.

"He broke up with Nadia in a very unpleasant way," she said, with the resentment of a mother. "He sent her a few lines in a letter from Ischia and caused her a lot of suffering." Then she contained herself and added, resuming her role as a professor again: "Never mind, you're all young, suffering helps one grow."

I nodded yes, she asked me: "Did he leave you, too?"

I turned red. "Me?"

"Didn't you see each other on Ischia?"

"Yes, but there was nothing between us."

"Really?"

"Absolutely."

"Nadia is convinced that he left her for you."

I denied it forcefully, I said I would be happy to see Nadia and tell her that between me and Nino there had never been anything and never would be. She was pleased, she assured me that she would report that. I didn't mention Lila, naturally, and not only because I had decided to mind my own business but also because to talk about it would have depressed me. I tried to change the subject, but she returned to Nino. She said that various rumors were circulating about him. There were some who said that not only had he not taken his exams in the autumn but he had stopped studying; and there were some who swore they had seen him one afternoon on Via Arenaccia, alone, completely drunk, lurching along, and every so often taking a swig from a bottle. But not everyone, she concluded, found him likable and maybe there were people who enjoyed spreading nasty rumors about him. If, however, they were true, what a pity.

"Surely they're lies," I said.

"Let's hope so. But it's hard to keep up with that boy."

"Yes."

"He's very smart."

"Yes."

"If you have a way of finding out what's happening, let me know."

We parted. I hurried off to give a Greek lesson to a girl in middle school who lived in Parco Margherita. But it was difficult. The large, permanently semi-dark room where I was greeted respectfully held heavy furniture, rugs with hunting scenes, old photographs of high-ranking soldiers, and various other signs of a long history of authority and ease that produced in my pale fourteen-year-old pupil a dullness of body and intelligence, and in me a feeling of impatience. That day I had to struggle to supervise declensions and conjugations. The picture of Nino as Professor Galiani had evoked him kept returning to my mind: worn jacket, tie flying, long legs staggering, the empty bottle that after the last swallow shattered on the stones of Via Arenaccia. What had happened between him and Lila, after Ischia? Contrary to my predictions, she had evidently seen her mistake, it was all over, she had returned to herself. Nino hadn't: from a studious youth with a well-formulated response to everything he had become a vagrant, undone by the pain of love for the grocer's wife. I thought of asking Alfonso again if he had news. I thought of going to Marisa myself and asking her about her brother. But soon I forced the idea out of my mind. It will pass, I said to myself. Has he come to see me? No. Has Lila come to see me? No. Why should I worry about him, or her, when they don't care about me? I continued the lesson and went on my way.

78.

After Christmas I found out from Alfonso that Pinuccia had given birth, she had had a boy, named Fernando. I went to see her, thinking that I would find her in bed, happy, with the baby at her breast. Instead, she was up, but in nightgown and slippers, sulking. She rudely sent away her mother, who said to her, "Get in bed, don't tire yourself," and when she led me to the cradle she said grimly, "Nothing ever works out for me, look how ugly he is, it upsets me just to look at him, let alone touch him." And although Maria, standing in the doorway, murmured, like a soothing formula, "What are you talking about, Pina, he's beautiful," she continued to repeat angrily, "He's ugly, he's uglier than Rino, that whole family is ugly." Then she drew in her breath and exclaimed desperately, with tears in her eyes, "It's my fault, I made a bad choice of a husband, but when you're a girl you don't think about it, and now look at what a child I've had, he has a pug nose just like Lina." Then, with no interruption, she began to insult her sister-in-law grossly.

I learned from her that Lila, the whore, had already in two weeks done and redone as she liked the shop in Piazza dei Martiri. Gigliola had had to give in, she had returned to the Solaras' pastry shop; she herself, Pinuccia, had had to give in, chained to the child until goodness knows when; they had all had to give in, Stefano above all, as usual. And now, every day, Lila was up to something new: she went to work dressed up as if she were Mike Bongiorno's assistant, and if her husband wouldn't take her in the car she had no scruples about getting Michele to drive her; she had spent who knows how much for two paintings that you couldn't understand what they were of, and had hung them in the shop for who knows what purpose; she had bought a lot of books and, instead of shoes, she put those on the shelf; she had fitted out a sort of living room, with couches, chairs, ottomans, and a crystal bowl where she kept chocolates from Gay Odin, available to whoever wanted them, free, as if she were there not to notice the stink of the customers' feet but to play the great lady in her castle.

"And it's not only that," she said, "there's something even worse."

"What?"

"You know what Marcello Solara did?"

"No."

"You remember the shoes that Stefano and Rino gave him?"

"The ones made exactly the way Lina designed them?"

"Yes, a wretched shoe, Rino always said that the water got in."

"Well, what happened?"

Pina overwhelmed me with a laborious, sometimes confused story, involving money, treacherous plots, deception, debts. Marcello, dissatisfied with the new models made by Rino and Fernando—and certainly in agreement with Michele—had had shoes like those manufactured, but not in the Cerullo factory, in another factory, in Afragola. Then, at Christmas, he had distributed them under the Solara name in the stores, including the one on Piazza dei Martiri.

"And he could do that?"

"Of course, they're his: my brother and my husband, those two shits, gave them to him, he can do what he likes."

"So?"

"So," she said, "now there are Cerullo shoes and Solara shoes circulating in Naples. And the Solara shoes are selling really well, better than the Cerullos. And all the profit is the Solaras'. So Rino is extremely upset, because he expected some competition, of course, but not from the Solaras themselves, his partners, and with a shoe he made with his own hands and then stupidly threw away."

I remembered Marcello when Lila threatened him with the shoemaker's knife. He was slower than Michele, more timid. What need had he to be so offensive? The Solaras had numerous businesses, some legitimate, others not, and they were getting bigger every day. They had had powerful friendships since the days of their grandfather, they did favors and received them. Their mother was a loan shark and had a book that struck fear into half the neighborhood, maybe now the Cerullos and the Carraccis, too. For Marcello, then, and for his brother, the shoes and the shop on Piazza dei Martiri were only one of the many wells into which their family dipped, and surely not among the most important. So why?

Pinuccia's story began to disturb me. Behind the appearance of money I felt something depressing. Marcello's love for Lila was over, but the wound had remained and become infected. No longer dependent, he felt free to hurt those who had humiliated him in the past. "Rino," Pinuccia in fact said, "went with Stefano to protest, but it was pointless." The Solaras had treated them contemptuously, they were people used to doing what they wanted, her brother and husband might as well have been talking to themselves. Finally Marcello had said vaguely that he and his brother were thinking of an entire Solara line that would repeat, with variations, the features of the shoe that had been made as a trial. And then he had added, without a clear connection, "Let's see how your new products go and if it's worth the trouble to keep them on the market." Understood? Understood. Marcello wanted to eliminate the Cerullo brand, replace it with Solara, and thus cause not insignificant economic damage to Stefano. I have to get out of the neighborhood, out of Naples, I said to myself, what do I care about their quarrels? But in the meantime I asked:

"And Lina?"

Pinuccia's eyes blazed.

"She's the real problem."

Lina had laughed at that story. When Rino and her husband got angry she made fun of them: "You gave him those shoes, not me; you did business with the Solaras, not me. If you two are idiots, what can I do?" She wouldn't cooperate, you couldn't tell where she stood, with the family or with the Solaras. So when Michele again insisted that he wanted her in Piazza dei Martiri, she had suddenly said yes, and had tormented Stefano to let her go.

"And why in the world did Stefano give in?" I asked.

Pinuccia let out a long sigh of impatience. Stefano had given in because he hoped that Lila, seeing that Michele valued her so much, and seeing that Marcello had always had a weakness for her, would manage to settle things. But Rino didn't trust his sister, he was frightened, he couldn't sleep at night. He liked the old shoe that he and Fernando had thrown away and that Marcello had had made in its original form; it sold well. What would happen if the Solaras began to deal with Lila directly and if she, a bitch since the day she was born, after refusing to design new shoes for the family, went on to design shoes for them?

"It won't happen," I said to Pinuccia.

"Did she tell you?"

"No, I haven't seen her since the summer."

"So?"

"I know what she's like. Lina gets curious about a thing and she's utterly caught up in it. But once she's done it, the desire goes away, she doesn't care about it anymore."

"You're sure?"

"Yes."

Maria was content with those words of mine, she clung to them to soothe her daughter.

"You hear?" she said. "Everything is fine, Lenuccia knows what she's talking about."

But in fact I knew nothing, the less pedantic part of me was well aware of Lila's unpredictability, so I couldn't wait to get out of that house. What do I have to do with it, I thought, with these wretched stories, with the petty vendetta of Marcello Solara, with this struggle and worry over money, cars, houses, furniture and knickknacks and vacations? And how could Lila, after Ischia, after Nino, go back to jousting with those thugs? I'll get my diploma, I'll take the entrance exams, I'll win. I'll get out of this muck, go as far away as possible. I said, softening toward the baby, whom Maria was now holding in her arms: "How cute he is."

79.

But I couldn't resist. I put it off for a long time and finally I gave in: I asked Alfonso if one Sunday we could go for a walk, he and Marisa and I. Alfonso was pleased, we went to a pizzeria on Via Foria. I asked about Lidia, the children, especially Ciro, and then I asked what Nino was up to. She answered reluctantly, talking about her brother upset her. She said that he had gone through a long period of madness, and her father, whom she adored, had had a difficult time with him; Nino had gone so far as to lay hands on him. What the cause of the madness was they never found out: he didn't want to study anymore, he wanted to leave Italy. Then suddenly it was over: he returned to himself and had just begun to take his exams.

"So he's all right?"

"Who knows."

"He's happy?"

"As far as somebody like him is capable of being happy, yes."

"And all he does is study?"

"You mean does he have a girlfriend?"

"No, of course not, I mean does he go out, does he have fun, does he go dancing."

"How should I know, Lenù? He's always out. Now he's obsessed with movies, novels, art, and the rare times he comes by the house he starts arguing with Papa, just to insult him and quarrel with us."

I felt relieved that Nino had come to his senses, but I was also bitter. Movies, novels, art? How quickly people changed, with their interests, their feelings. Well-made phrases replaced by well-made phrases, time is a flow of words coherent only in appearance, the one who piles up the most is the one who wins. I felt stupid, I had neglected the things I liked to conform to what Nino liked. Yes, yes, resign yourself to what you are, each on his own path. I only hoped that Marisa would not tell him that she had seen me and that I had asked about him. Not even to Alfonso, after that evening, did I mention Nino or Lila.

I withdrew even more into my duties, I multiplied them in order to cram my days and nights. That year I studied obsessively, punctiliously, and I even took on a new private lesson, for a lot of money. I imposed on myself an iron discipline, much harsher than what I had enforced since childhood. A marking of time, a straight line that went from dawn until late at night. In the past there had been Lila, a continuous happy detour into surprising lands. Now everything I was I wanted to get from myself. I was almost nineteen, I would never again depend on someone, and I would never again miss someone.

The last year of high school slipped by like a single day. I struggled with astronomical geography, with geometry, with trigonometry. It was a sort of race to know everything, when in fact I took it for granted that my inadequacy was constitutional and so couldn't be eliminated. Yet I liked to do my best. I didn't have time to go to the movies? I learned titles and plots. Hadn't been to the archeological museum? I ran through it in half a day. Hadn't been to the picture gallery of Capodimonte? I made a flying visit, two hours and done. I had too much to do, in short. What did I care about shoes and the shop on Piazza dei Martiri? I never went there.

Sometimes I met Pinuccia, disheveled-looking, as she pushed Fernando in his carriage. I stopped a moment, listened absent-mindedly to her complaints about Rino, Stefano, Lila, Gigliola, everyone. Sometimes I ran into Carmen, who was increasingly bitter about how badly things had been going in the new grocery since Lila left, abandoning her to the oppression of Maria and Pinuccia, and I let her vent for a few minutes about how she missed Enzo Scanno, how she counted the days as she waited for him to finish his military service, how her brother Pasquale slaved, between his construction work and his Communist activities. Sometimes I ran into Ada, who had begun to hate Lila, while she was very pleased with Stefano, and spoke of him tenderly, and not only because he had recently increased her salary but also because he was a hard worker, available to everyone, and didn't deserve that wife who treated him like dirt.

It was she who told me that Antonio had been discharged early because of a severe nervous breakdown.

"What happened?"

"You know what he's like, he already had a breakdown with you."

It was a mean statement that wounded me, I tried not to think about it. One Sunday in winter I ran into Antonio and scarcely recognized him, he was so thin. I smiled at him, expecting him to stop, but he seemed not to notice me and kept going. I called him, he turned, with a disoriented smile.

"Hello, Lenù."

"Hello, I'm so glad to see you."

"Me, too."

"What are you doing?"

"Nothing."

"You're not going back to the workshop?"

"There's no job."

"You're good, you'll find something somewhere else."

"No, if I don't get better I can't work."

"What's wrong with you?"

"Fear."

He said it just like that: fear. In Cordenons, one night, while he was on guard duty, he had remembered a game that his father played when he was still alive and he himself was very small: with a pen his father would draw eyes and mouths on the five fingers of his left hand, and then he would move them and make them talk as if they were people. It was such a sweet game that, as he remembered it, tears came to his eyes. But that night, during his shift, he had had the impression that his father's hand had entered his and that now he had real people inside his fingers, tiny but fully formed, who were laughing and singing. That was the source of the fear. He banged his hand against the sentry box until it bled, but the fingers went on laughing and singing, without stopping, not for an instant. He recovered only when his shift was over and he went to sleep. A little rest and the next morning it was gone. But the terror that the illness in his hand would return remained. In fact it did return, and, with increasing frequency, his fingers began to laugh and sing even in the daytime. Until he had gone mad and they had sent him to the doctor.

"It's gone now," he said, "but it could always start again."

"Tell me how I can help you."

He thought for a while, as if he were really evaluating a series of possibilities. He muttered, "No one can help me."

I immediately understood that he no longer felt anything for me, I had definitively gone out of his mind. So after that encounter I got in the habit of going every Sunday to his windows and calling. We would take a walk around the courtyard, talking about this and that, and when he said he was tired we said goodbye. Sometimes Melina came down with him, garishly made up, and he and his mother and I walked. Sometimes we met Ada and Pasquale and took a longer walk, but then it was generally the three of us who talked, Antonio was silent. In other words it became a peaceful routine. I went with him to the funeral of Nicola Scanno, the fruit-and-vegetable seller, who died suddenly of pneumonia; Enzo came home on leave but wasn't in time to see him alive. We also went together to console Pasquale, Carmen, and their mother, Giuseppina, when they learned that their father, the former carpenter who had killed Don Achille, had died in prison from a heart attack. And we were together also when we learned that Don Carlo Resta, the seller of soap and various household items, had been beaten to death in his cellar. We talked about it for a long time, the whole neighborhood talked about it, the talk spread truths and cruel rumors, someone said that the beating wasn't enough and they had stuck a file in his nose. Some vagrants were blamed for the crime, people who had stolen the day's cash. But Pasquale, later, told us he had heard rumors that in his view were well founded: Don Carlo was in debt to the mother of the Solaras, because he had the vice of gambling and went to her so that he could pay his debts.

"So what?" asked Ada, who was always skeptical when her fiancé came up with reckless hypotheses.

"So he wouldn't pay what he owed the loan shark and they had him murdered."

"Come on, you always talk such nonsense."

It's likely that Pasquale was exaggerating, but, first of all, no one knew who had killed Don Carlo Resta, and, second, it was, precisely, the Solaras who took over the shop, along with its stock, for very little money, even though they left Don Carlo's wife and oldest son there to manage it.

"Out of generosity," said Ada.

"Because they're bastards," said Pasquale.

I don't remember if Antonio made comments on that episode. He was crushed by his illness, which Pasquale's speeches in some way made more acute. It seemed to him that the dysfunction of his body was spreading to the whole neighborhood and was manifested in the bad things that happened.

The worst thing for us happened on a warm Sunday in the spring, when Pasquale and Ada and he and I were waiting in the courtyard for Carmela, who had gone up to get a pullover. Five minutes passed; Carmen looked out the window, shouted to her brother: "Pasquà, I can't find mamma. The door of the bathroom is locked from the inside but she doesn't answer."

Pasquale took the stairs two at a time and we followed. We found Carmela standing anxiously in front of the bathroom door, and Pasquale knocked, politely, again and again, but no one answered. Antonio then said to his friend, indicating the door: don't worry, I'll put it back in place, and, grabbing the handle, he practically tore it off.

The door opened. Giuseppina Peluso had been a radiant woman, energetic, hardworking, kindly, capable of confronting all adversities. She had continued, without fail, to occupy herself with her imprisoned husband, whose arrest—I remembered—she had opposed with all her strength, when he

was accused of killing Don Achille Carracci. She had thought-
fully accepted Stefano's invitation to spend New Year's Eve
together four years earlier, pleased with that reconciliation
between the families. And she had been happy when her
daughter found work, thanks to Lila, in the grocery in the new
neighborhood. But now, with her husband dead, evidently she
was worn out, she had become in a short time a tiny woman,
skin and bone, without her old vigor. She had unfastened the
lamp in the bathroom, a metal plate hanging on a chain, and
had attached a clothesline to the hook set in the ceiling. Then
she had hanged herself by the neck.

Antonio saw her first and burst into tears. It was easier to
calm Giuseppina's children, Carmen and Pasquale, than him.
He repeated to me, horrified: Did you see that her feet were
bare and that the nails were long and that on one foot there
was fresh red nail polish and not on the other? I hadn't noticed
but he had. He had returned from military service more convinced than before, in spite of his nervous breakdown, that his
job was to be the man in every situation, the one who hurls
himself into danger, fearlessly, and resolves every problem. But
he was fragile. For weeks after that episode, he saw Giuseppina
in every dark corner of the house, and he got worse, so I neglected some of my obligations to help him calm down. He was
the only person in the neighborhood I saw more or less regularly until I took my graduation exams. I had just a glimpse of
Lila, next to her husband, at Giuseppina's funeral, while she
hugged Carmen, who was sobbing. She and Stefano had sent a
large wreath on whose violet ribbon the condolences of the
Carracci spouses could be read.

80.

It wasn't because of the exams that I stopped seeing Antonio.

The two things happened to coincide, because just then he came to see me, rather relieved, to tell me that he had accepted a job from the Solara brothers. I didn't like it, it seemed to me another sign of his illness. He hated the Solaras. He had scuffled with them as a boy to defend his sister. He, Pasquale, and Enzo had beaten up Marcello and Michele and destroyed their car. But the main thing was that he had left me because I went to ask Marcello for his help in getting Antonio out of military service. Why, then, had he succumbed like that? He gave me confused explanations. He said that in the Army he had learned that if you are a simple soldier you owe obedience to anyone who wears stripes. He said that order is better than disorder. He said he had learned how you come up behind a man and kill him before he has even heard you arrive. I understood that the illness had something to do with it but that the real problem was poverty. He had presented himself at the bar to ask for work. And Marcello had treated him a little roughly but then had offered him a fixed amount each month—he put it like that—without, however, a precise duty, only to be available.

"Available?"

"Yes."

"Available for what?"

"I don't know."

"Forget it, Antò."

He didn't. And because of that job he ended up quarreling with both Pasquale and Enzo, who had returned from military service more taciturn than before, more inflexible. Illness or not, neither of them could forgive Antonio for that decision. Pasquale, although he was engaged to Ada, went so far as to threaten him, he said that, brother-in-law or not, he didn't want to see him anymore.

I quickly got away from these problems and concentrated on my graduation exam. While I studied day and night, some-

times, overwhelmed by the heat, I thought again about the previous summer, before Pinuccia left, when Lila, Nino, and I were
a happy trio, or at least so it seemed to me. But I repressed
every image, and even the faintest echo of a word: I allowed no
distractions.

The exam was a crucial moment of my life. In a couple of
hours I wrote an essay on the role of Nature in the poetry of
Giacomo Leopardi, putting in, along with lines I knew by heart,
finely written reworkings from the textbook of Italian literary
history; but, most important, I handed in my Latin and Greek
tests when my schoolmates, including Alfonso, had barely
started on it. This attracted the attention of the examiners, in
particular of an old, extremely thin teacher, with a pink suit
and freshly coiffed, pale-blue hair, who kept smiling at me. But
the real turning point took place during the oral exams. I was
praised by all the professors, but in particular I gained the
approval of the examiner with the blue hair. She had been
struck by my essay not only because of what I said but because
of how I said it.

"You write very well," she said, with an accent I didn't recognize, but anyway far from Neapolitan.

"Thank you."

"Do you really think that nothing is fated to last, not even
poetry?"

"That's what Leopardi thinks."

"You're sure?"

"Yes."

"And what do you think?"

"I think that beauty is a sham."

"Like the Leopardian garden?"

I didn't know anything about Leopardian gardens, but I
answered, "Yes. Like the sea on a calm day. Or like a sunset.
Or like the sky at night. It's like face powder patted on over the
horror. If you take it away, we are left alone with our fear."

The sentences came easily, I uttered them with an inspired cadence. And, besides, I wasn't improvising, it was an adaptation of what I had written in the essay.

"What faculty do you intend to choose?"

I didn't know much about faculties, that meaning of the term was barely familiar to me. I was evasive:

"I'll sit the civil-service exam."

"You won't go to the university?"

My cheeks burned, as if I were unable to hide a sin.

"No."

"You need to work?"

"Yes."

I was dismissed, I returned to Alfonso and the others. But a little later the professor came up to me in the hallway, and talked for a long time about a kind of college in Pisa, where, if you passed an exam like the one I had already done, you studied free.

"If you come back here in a couple of days, I'll give you all the necessary information."

I listened, but the way you do when someone is talking to you about something that will never really concern you. And when, two days later, I went back to school, only out of fear that the professor would be offended and give me a low grade, I was struck by the very precise information that she had transcribed for me on a sheet of foolscap. I never met her again, I don't even know her name, and yet I owe her a great deal. Continuing to address me formally, she unaffectedly gave me a dignified farewell embrace.

The exams were over, I passed with an A average. Alfonso also did well, with a B average. Before leaving forever, with no regrets, the run-down gray building whose only merit, in my eyes, was that Nino, too, had been there, I caught sight of Professor Galiani and went to say goodbye. She congratulated me on my results but without enthusiasm. She didn't offer me books for the summer, she didn't ask what I would do now that

I had my high-school diploma. Her distant tone upset me, I thought that things between us had been settled. What was the trouble? Once Nino had left her daughter and had fallen out of touch, was I to be associated with him forever, the same clay: insubstantial, unserious, unreliable? I was used to being liked by everyone, to wrapping that liking around me like shining armor; I was disappointed, and I think that her indifference had an important role in the decision I then made. Without talking about it to anyone (who could I ask advice from, anyway, if not Professor Galiani?) I applied for admission to the Pisa Normale. I immediately started doing everything I possibly could to earn money. Since the upper-class families whose children I had given lessons to all year were happy with me and my reputation as a good teacher had spread, I was able to fill the August days with new students who had to retake, in September, their exams in Latin, Greek, history, philosophy, and even mathematics. At the end of the month I found myself rich, I had amassed seventy thousand lire. I gave fifty to my mother, who reacted with a violent gesture, she almost tore the money from my hand and stuffed it in her bra, as if we were not in the kitchen of our house but on the street and she was afraid of being robbed. I didn't tell her that I had kept twenty thousand lire for myself.

Not until the day before my departure did I tell my family that I was going to Pisa to take exams. "If they accept me," I announced, "I'll go there to study and I won't have to spend a lira for anything." I spoke with great decisiveness, in Italian, as if it were not a subject that could be reduced to dialect, as if my father, my mother, my siblings shouldn't and couldn't understand what I was about to do. In fact they confined themselves to listening uneasily, it seemed to me that in their eyes I was no longer me but a stranger who had come to visit at an inconvenient time. Finally my father said, "Do what you have to do but be careful, we can't help you." And he went to bed. My little sister asked if she could come with me. My mother, instead, said nothing, but before she vanished she left five thousand lire on the table for me. I stared at it for a long time, without touching it. Then, overcoming my scruples about how I wasted money to satisfy my whims, I thought, it's my money, and I took it.

For the first time, I left Naples, left Campania. I discovered that I was afraid of everything: afraid of taking the wrong train, afraid of having to pee and not knowing where to do it, afraid that it would be night and I wouldn't be able to orient myself in an unfamiliar city, afraid of being robbed. I put all my money in my bra, as my mother did, and spent hours in a state of wary anxiety that coexisted seamlessly with a growing sense of liberation.

Everything went well. Except the exam, it seemed. The professor with the blue hair hadn't told me that it would be much more difficult than the graduation exam. The Latin, especially, seemed complex, but really that was only the beginning: every test was the occasion for an extremely painstaking investigation of my skills. I held forth, I stammered, I often pretended to have the answer on the tip of my tongue. The professor of Italian treated me as if even the sound of my voice irritated him: *You, miss, do not make a logical argument when you write but flit from one thing to another; I see, miss, that you launch recklessly into subjects in which you are completely ignorant of the issues of critical method.* I was depressed, I quickly lost confidence in what I was saying. The professor realized it and, looking at me ironically, asked me to talk about something I had read recently. I suppose he meant something by an Italian writer, but I didn't understand and clung to the first support that seemed to me secure, that is to say the conversation we had had the summer before, on Ischia, on the beach of Citara, about Beckett and about Dan Rooney, who, although he was blind, wanted to become deaf and mute as well. The professor's ironic expression changed slowly to bewilderment. He cut me off me quickly and delivered me to the history professor. He was just as bad. He subjected me to an endless and exhausting list of questions formulated with the utmost precision. I had never felt so ignorant as I did at that moment, not even in the worst years of school, when I had done so badly. I was able to answer everything, dates, events, but only in an approximate way. As soon as he pressed me with even more exacting questions I gave up. Finally he asked me, disgusted, "Have you ever read something that is not simply the school textbook?"

I said, "I've studied the idea of nationhood."

"Do you remember the name of the author of the book?"

"Federico Chabod."

"Let's hear what you understood."

He listened to me attentively for several minutes, then abruptly dismissed me, leaving me with the certainty that I had said a lot of nonsense.

I cried and cried, as if I had carelessly lost somewhere the most promising part of myself. Then I said that despair was stupid, I had always known that I wasn't really smart. Lila, yes, she was smart, Nino, yes, he was smart. I was only presumptuous and had been justly punished.

Instead I found out that I had passed the exam. I would have a place of my own, a bed that I didn't have to make at night and unmake in the morning, a desk and all the books I needed. I, Elena Greco, the daughter of the porter, at nineteen years old was about to pull myself out of the neighborhood, I was about to leave Naples. By myself.

81.

A series of whirlwind days began. A few things to wear, a very few books. My mother's sullen words: "If you earn money, send it to me by mail; now who's going to help your brothers with their homework? They'll do badly at school because of you. But go, leave, who cares: I've always known that you thought you were better than me and everybody else." And then my father's hypochondriac words: "I have a pain here, who knows what it is, come to your papa, Lenù, I don't know if you'll find me alive when you get back." And then my brothers' and sister's insistent words: "If we come to see you can we sleep with you, can we eat with you?" And Pasquale, who said to me, "Be careful where all this studying leads, Lenù. Remember who you are and which side you're on." And Carmen, who couldn't get over the death of her mother, and was fragile, started crying as she said good-bye. And Alfonso, who was stunned and murmured, "I knew you'd keep studying." And Antonio, who instead of listening to what I was saying about where I was going, and what I was going to do, kept repeating, "I'm really feeling good now, Lenù, it's all gone, it was going into the Army that made me ill." And then Enzo, who confined himself to taking my hand and squeezing it so hard that it hurt for days. And finally Ada, who said only, "Did you tell Lina, did you tell her?" and she gave a little laugh, and insisted, "Tell her, she'll die of envy."

I imagined that Lila had already heard from Alfonso, from Carmen, from her husband, whom Ada had certainly told, that I was going to Pisa. If she didn't come to congratulate me, I thought, it's likely that the news really has disturbed her. On the other hand, if she didn't know, to go deliberately to tell her, when for more than a year we had scarcely said hello, seemed to me out of place. I didn't want to flaunt the good fortune that she hadn't had. So I set aside the question and devoted myself to the last preparations. I wrote to Nella to tell her what had happened and ask for the address of Maestra Oliviero, so that I could give her the news. I visited a cousin of my father, who had promised me an old suitcase. I made the rounds of some of the houses where I had taught and where I had to collect my final payment.

It seemed to me an occasion to give a kind of farewell to Naples. I crossed Via Garibaldi, went along the Tribunali, at Piazza Dante took a bus. I went up to the Vomero, first to Via Scarlatti, then to the Santarella. Afterward I descended in the funicular to Piazza Amedeo. I was greeted with regret and, in some cases, affection by the mothers of my students. Along with the money they gave me coffee and almost always a small gift. When my rounds were over, I realized that I was a short distance from Piazza dei Martiri.

I turned onto Via Filangieri, uncertain what to do. I recalled the opening of the shoe store, Lila all dressed up like a rich lady, how she was gripped by the anxiety of not having truly changed, of not having the same refinement as the girls of that neighborhood. I, on the other hand, I thought, really have changed. I'm still wearing the same shabby clothes, but I've got my high-school diploma and I'm about to go and study in Pisa. I've changed not in appearance but deep inside. The appearance will come soon and it won't be just appearance.

I felt pleased with that thought, that observation. I stood in front of an optician's window, I studied the frames. Yes, I'll have to change my glasses, the ones I have overwhelm my face, I need lighter frames—I picked out a pair with large, round thin rims. Put up my hair. Learn to use makeup. I left the window and arrived at Piazza dei Martiri.

Many shops at that hour had their shutters lowered halfway; the Solaras' was three-quarters down. I looked around. What did I know of Lila's new habits? Nothing. When she worked in the new grocery she didn't go home for lunch, even though the house was nearby. She stayed in the shop and ate something with Carmen or talked to me when I came by after school. Now that she worked in Piazza dei Martiri, it was even more unlikely that she would go home for lunch: it would be pointless, besides the fact that there wasn't enough time. Maybe she was in a café, maybe walking along the sea with the assistant she surely had. Or maybe she was inside resting. I knocked on the shutter with my open hand. No answer. I knocked again. Nothing. I called, I heard steps inside, Lila's voice asked, "Who is it?"

"Elena."

"Lenù," I heard her exclaim.

She pulled up the shutter, she appeared before me. It was a long time since I'd seen her, even from a distance, and she seemed changed. She wore a white blouse and a tight blue skirt, her hair and makeup were done with the usual care. But her face was as if broadened and flattened, her entire body seemed to me broader and flatter. She pulled me inside, lowered the shutter. The place, gaudily illuminated, had changed, it really did seem not like a shoe store but like a living room. She said with a tone of such genuineness that I believed her: "What a wonderful thing has happened to you, Lenù, and how happy I am that you came to say goodbye." She knew about Pisa, of course. She embraced me warmly, she kissed me on both cheeks, her eyes filled with tears, she repeated, "I'm really happy." Then she called, turning to the door of the bathroom: "Come, Nino, you can come out, it's Lenuccia."

My breath failed. The door opened and Nino appeared, in his usual pose, head lowered, hands in pockets. But his face was furrowed by tension. "Hello," he murmured. I didn't know what to say and offered him my hand. He shook it without energy. Lila meanwhile went on to tell me many important things in a brief series of sentences: they had been secretly seeing each other for almost a year; she had decided for my good not to involve me further in a deception that, if discovered, would cause trouble for me as well; she was two months pregnant, she was about to confess everything to Stefano, she wanted to leave him.

82.

Lila spoke in a tone I knew well, of determination, with which she strove to eliminate emotion, and she confined herself to rapidly and almost disdainfully summarizing events and actions, as if she were afraid that allowing herself merely a tremor in her voice or lower lip would cause everything to lose its outlines and overflow, inundating her. Nino sat on the couch looking down, making at most a nod of assent. They held hands.

She said that their meetings there in the shop, amid all the anxieties, had ended the moment she had the urine analysis and discovered the pregnancy. Now she and Nino needed their own house, their own life. She wanted to share with him friendships, books, lectures, movies, theater, music. "I can't bear living apart anymore," she said. She had hidden some money and was negotiating for a small apartment in Campi Flegrei, twenty thousand lire a month. They would hide there, waiting for the baby to be born.

How? Without a job? With Nino who had to study? I couldn't control myself, I said:

"What need is there to leave Stefano? You're good at telling lies, you've told him so many, you can perfectly well continue."

She looked at me with narrow eyes. She had clearly perceived the sarcasm, the bitterness, even the contempt that those words contained behind the appearance of friendly advice. She also noticed that Nino had abruptly raised his head, that his mouth was half open as if he wanted to say something, but he contained himself in order to avoid an argument. She replied, "Lying was useful in order not to be killed. But now I would prefer to be killed rather than continue like this."

When I said goodbye, wishing them well, I hoped for *my* sake that I wouldn't see them again.

332 · ELENA FERRANTE

83.

The years at the Normale were important, but not for the story of our friendship. I arrived at the university very timid and awkward. I immediately realized I spoke a bookish Italian that at times was almost absurd, especially when, right in the middle of a much too carefully composed sentence, I needed a word and transformed a dialect word into Italian to fill the gap: I began to struggle to correct myself. I knew almost nothing about etiquette, I spoke in a loud voice, I chewed noisily; I became aware of other people's embarrassment and tried to restrain myself. In my anxiety to appear friendly I interrupted conversations, gave opinions on things that had nothing to do with me, assumed manners that were too familiar: so I endeavored to be polite but distant. Once a girl from Rome, answering a question of mine I don't remember what about, parodied my inflections and everyone laughed. I felt wounded, but I laughed, too, and gaily emphasized the dialectal accent as if I were the one making fun of myself.

In the first weeks I fought the desire to go home by burrowing inside my usual meek diffidence. But from within that I began to distinguish myself and gradually became liked. Students male and female, janitors, professors liked me, and though it might have appeared effortless, in fact I worked hard. I learned to subdue my voice and gestures. I assimilated rules of behavior, written and unwritten. I kept my Neapolitan accent as much under control as possible. I managed to demonstrate that I was smart and deserving of respect by never appearing arrogant, by being ironic about my ignorance, by pretending to be surprised at my good results. Above all I avoided making enemies. When one of the girls appeared hostile, I would focus my attention on her, I was friendly yet restrained, obliging but tactful, and my attitude didn't change even when she softened and was the one who sought me out. I did the same with the professors. Naturally with them I behaved more circumspectly, but my goal was the same: to be appreciated, to gain approval and affection. I approached the most aloof, the most severe, with serene smiles and an air of devotion.

I took the exams as scheduled, studying with my usual fierce self-discipline. I was terrified by the idea of failing, of losing what immediately seemed to me, in spite of the difficulties, paradise on earth: a space of my own, a bed of my own, a desk, a chair, books and more books, a city a world away from the neighborhood and Naples, around me only people who studied and who tended to discuss what they studied. I applied myself with such diligence that no professor ever gave me less than an A, and within a year I became one of the most promising students, whose polite greetings could be met with kindness.

There were only two difficult moments, both in the first few months. The girl from Rome who had made fun of my accent assailed me one morning, yelling at me in front of other girls that money had disappeared from her purse, and I must give it back immediately or she would report me to the dean. I realized that I couldn't respond with an accommodating smile. I slapped her violently and heaped insults on her in dialect. They were all frightened. I was classified as a person who always made the best of things, and my reaction disoriented them. The girl from Rome was speechless, she stopped up her nose, which was bleeding, a friend took her to the bathroom. A few hours later they both came to see me and the one who had accused me of being a thief apologized—she had found her money. I hugged her, said that her apologies seemed genuine, and I really thought so. The way I had grown up, I would never have apologized, even if I had made a mistake.

The other serious difficulty had to do with the opening party, which was to be held before Christmas vacation. It was a sort of dance for the first-year students that everyone essentially had to attend. The girls talked about nothing else: the boys, who lived in Piazza dei Cavalieri, would come, it was a great moment of intimacy between the university's male and female divisions. I had nothing to wear. It was cold that autumn; it snowed a lot, and the snow enchanted me. But then I discovered how troublesome the ice in the streets could be, hands that, without gloves, turned numb, feet with chilblains. My wardrobe consisted of two winter dresses made by my mother a couple of years earlier, a worn coat inherited from an aunt, a big blue scarf that I had made myself, a single pair of shoes, with a half heel, that had been resoled many times. I had enough problems with my clothes, I didn't know how to deal with that party. Ask my classmates? Most of them were having dresses made just for the occasion, and it was likely that they had something among their everyday clothes that would have been fine for me. But after my experience with Lila I couldn't bear the idea of trying on someone else's clothes and discovering that they didn't fit. Pretend to be sick? I was tempted by that solution but it depressed me: to be healthy, and desperate to be a Natasha at the ball with Prince Andrei or Kuryagin, and instead to be sitting alone, staring at the ceiling, while listening to the echo of the music, the sound of voices, the laughter. In the end I made a choice that was probably humiliating but that I was sure I wouldn't regret: I washed my hair, put it up, put on some lipstick, and wore one of my two dresses, the one whose only merit was that it was dark blue.

I went to the party, and at first I felt uncomfortable. But my outfit had the advantage of not arousing envy; rather, it produced a sense of guilt that encouraged camaraderie. In fact many sympathetic girls kept me company and the boys often asked me to dance. I forgot how I was dressed and even the state of my shoes. Besides, that night I met Franco Mari, a rather ugly but very amusing boy with a quick intelligence, insolent and profligate. He was a year older than me, and from a wealthy family in Reggio Emilia, a militant Communist but critical of the Party's social-democratic leanings. I happily spent a lot of my little free time with him. He gave me everything: clothes, shoes, a new coat, glasses that didn't obscure my eyes and my whole face, books about politics, because that was the subject dearest to him. I learned from him terrible things about Stalinism and he urged me to read Trotsky; as a result I developed an anti-Stalinist sensibility and the conviction that in the U.S.S.R. there was neither socialism nor even Communism: the revolution had been truncated and needed to be started up again.

He took me on my first trip abroad. We went to Paris, to a conference of young Communists from all over Europe. I hardly saw Paris: we spent all our time in smoky places. I was left with an impression of streets much more colorful than those of Naples and Pisa, irritation at the sound of the police sirens, and amazement at the widespread presence of blacks on the streets and in the meeting rooms; Franco gave a long speech, in French, that was much applauded. When I told Pasquale about my political experience, he wouldn't believe that I—*really, you*, he said—had done a thing like that. Then he was silent, embarrassed, when I showed off my reading, declaring that I was now a Trotskyite.

From Franco I also got many habits that were later reinforced by the instructions and conversations of some of the professors: to use the word "study" even if I was reading a book of science fiction; to compile very detailed note cards on every text I studied; to get excited whenever I came upon passages in which the effects of social inequality were well described. He was very attached to what he called my reeducation and I willingly let myself be reeducated. But to my great regret I couldn't fall in love. I loved him, I loved his restless body, but I never felt that he was indispensable. The little that I felt was gone in a short time, when he lost his place at the

Normale: he failed an exam and had to leave. For several months we wrote to each other. He tried to reenter the Normale; he said that he was doing it only to be near me. I encouraged him to take the exam, he failed. We wrote occasionally, and then for a long time I had no news of him.

84.

This is more or less what happened to me between the end of 1963 and the end of 1965. How easy it is to tell the story of myself without Lila: time quiets down and the important facts slide along the thread of the years like suitcases on a conveyor belt at an airport; you pick them up, put them on the page, and it's done.

It's more complicated to recount what happened to her in those years. The belt slows down, accelerates, swerves abruptly, goes off the tracks. The suitcases fall off, fly open, their contents scatter here and there. Her things end up among mine: to accommodate them, I am compelled to return to the narrative concerning me (and that had come to me unobstructed), and expand phrases that now sound too concise. For example, if Lila had gone to the Normale in my place would she ever have decided simply to make the best of things? And the time I slapped the girl from Rome, how much did her behavior influence me? How did she manage—even at a distance—to sweep away my artificial meekness, how much of the requisite determination did she give me, how much did she dictate even the insults? And the audacity, when, amid a thousand doubts and fears, I brought Franco to my room—where did that come from if not from her example? And the sense of unhappiness, when I realized that I didn't love him, when I observed the coldness of my feelings, what was its origin if not, by comparison, the capacity to love that she had demonstrated and was demonstrating?

Yes, it's Lila who makes writing difficult. My life forces me to imagine what hers would have been if what happened to me had happened to her, what use she would have made of my luck. And her life continuously appears in mine, in the words that I've uttered, in which there's often an echo of hers, in a particular gesture that is an adaptation of a gesture of hers, in my *less* which is such because of her *more*, in my *more* which is the yielding to the force of her *less*. Not to mention what she never said but let me guess, what I didn't know and read later in her notebooks. Thus the story of the facts has to reckon with filters, deferments, partial truths, half lies: from it comes an arduous measurement of time passed that is based completely on the unreliable measuring device of words.

I have to admit, for example, that everything about Lila's sufferings escaped me. Because she had taken Nino, because with her secret arts she had become pregnant by him and not by Stefano, because for love she was on the point of carrying out an act inconceivable in the environment we had grown up in—abandoning her husband, throwing away the comfort so recently acquired, running the risk of being murdered along with her lover and the child she carried in her womb—I considered her happy, with that tempestuous happiness of novels, films, and comic strips, the only kind that at that time truly interested me, that is to say not conjugal happiness but the happiness of passion, a furious confusion of evil and good that had befallen her and not me.

I was mistaken. Now I return to the moment when Stefano took us away from Ischia, and I know for certain that the moment the boat pulled out from the shore and Lila realized that she would no longer find Nino waiting for her on the beach in the morning, would no longer debate, talk, whisper with him, that they would no longer swim together, no longer kiss and caress and love each other, she was violently scarred by suffering. Within a few days the entire life of Signora Carracci—

balances and imbalances, strategies, battles, wars and alliances, troubles with suppliers and customers, the art of cheating on the weight, the devotion to piling up money in the drawer of the cash register—dematerialized, lost truth. Only Nino was concrete and true, and she who wanted him, who desired him day and night, who clung to her husband in the darkness of the bedroom to forget the other even for a few moments. A terrible fraction of time. It was in those very moments that she felt most strongly the need to have him, and so clearly, with such a precision of detail, that she pushed Stefano away like a stranger and took refuge in a corner of the bed, weeping and shouting insults, or she ran to the bathroom and locked herself in.

85.

At first she thought of sneaking out at night and returning to Forio, but she realized that her husband would find her right away. Then she thought of asking Alfonso if Marisa knew when her brother would return from Ischia, but she was afraid that her brother-in-law would tell Stefano she had asked that question and she let it go. She found in the telephone book the number of the Sarratore house and she telephoned. Donato answered. She said she was a friend of Nino, he cut her off in an angry tone, hung up. Out of desperation she returned to the idea of taking the boat, and had nearly made up her mind, when, one afternoon in early September, Nino appeared in the doorway of the crowded grocery, unshaved and totally drunk.

Lila restrained Carmen, who had jumped up to chase out the disorderly youth, in her eyes a crazy stranger. "I'll take care of it," she said, and dragged him away. Precise gestures, cold voice, the certainty that Carmen Peluso hadn't recognized the son of Sarratore, now very different from the child who had gone to elementary school with them.

She acted fast. She appeared normal, like a woman who knows how to solve every problem. In truth, she no longer knew where she was. The shelves stacked with goods had faded, the street had lost every definition, the pale façades of the new apartment buildings had dissolved; but most of all she didn't feel the risk she was running. Nino Nino Nino: she felt only joy and desire. He was before her again, finally, and his every feature loudly proclaimed that he had suffered and was suffering, had looked for her and wanted her, so much that he tried to grab her, kiss her on the street.

She took him to her house, it seemed to her the safest place. Passersby? She saw none. Neighbors? She saw none. They began to make love as soon as she closed the door of the apartment behind her. She felt no scruple. She felt only the need to grab Nino, immediately, hold him, keep him. That need didn't diminish even when they calmed down. The neighborhood, the neighbors, the grocery, the streets, the sounds of the trains, Stefano, Carmen waiting, perhaps anxious, slowly returned, but only as objects to be arranged hastily, so that they would not get in the way, but with enough care so that, piled up haphazardly, they would not suddenly fall.

Nino reproached her for having left without warning him, he held her tight, he still wanted her. He demanded that they go away immediately, together, but then he didn't know where. She answered yes yes yes, and shared his madness in everything, although, unlike him, she felt the time, the real seconds and minutes that, slipping by, magnified the danger of being surprised. So, lying with him on the floor, she looked at the lamp hanging from the ceiling just above them, like a threat, and if before she had been preoccupied only with having Nino right away, no matter what might come crashing down, now she thought about how to keep him close to her without the lamp detaching itself from the ceiling, without the floor cleaving in two, with him forever on one side, her on the other.

"Go."

"No."

"You're mad."

"Yes."

"Please, I'm begging you, go."

She convinced him. She waited for Carmen to say something, for the neighbors to gossip maliciously, for Stefano to return from the other grocery and beat her. It didn't happen, and she was relieved. She increased Carmen's pay, she became affectionate toward her husband, she invented excuses that allowed her to meet Nino secretly.

86.

At first the larger problem was not the possibility of gossip that would ruin everything but him, the beloved. Nothing mattered to him except to clutch her, kiss her, bite her, penetrate her. It seemed that he wanted, that he needed, to live his whole life with his mouth on her mouth, inside her body. And he couldn't tolerate the separations, he was frightened by them, he feared that she would vanish again. So he stupefied himself with alcohol, he didn't study, he smoked constantly. It was as if for him there was nothing in the world but the two of them, and if he resorted to words he did it only to cry to her his jealousy, to tell her obsessively how intolerable he found it that she continued to live with her husband.

"I've left everything," he murmured wearily, "and you don't want to leave anything."

"What are you thinking of doing?" she then asked him.

Nino was silent, disoriented by the question, or he became enraged, as if the situation offended him. He said desperately, "You don't want me anymore."

But Lila wanted him, wanted him again and again, but she

also wanted something else, and right away. She wanted him to return to studying, she wanted him to continue to stimulate her mind the way he had on Ischia. The phenomenal child of elementary school, the girl who had charmed Maestra Oliviero, who had written *The Blue Fairy*, had reappeared and was stirring with new energy. Nino had found her under the pile of dirt where she had ended up and pulled her out. That girl was now urging him to be once more the studious youth he had been and allow her to develop the power to sweep away Signora Carracci. Which she gradually did.

I don't know what happened: Nino must have perceived that in order not to lose her he had to be something more than a furious lover. Or maybe not, maybe he simply felt that passion was emptying him. The fact is that he began studying again. And Lila at first was content: he slowly recovered, became as she had known him on Ischia, which made him even more essential to her. She had again not only Nino but also something of his words, his ideas. He read Smith unhappily, she, too, tried to do it; he read Joyce even more unhappily, she tried, too. She bought the books that he mentioned to her the rare times they managed to meet. She wanted to talk about them, there was never a chance.

Carmen, who was increasingly bewildered, didn't understand what could be so urgent when Lila, with one excuse or another, was absent for several hours. She observed her frowning, so immersed in reading a book or writing in her notebooks that she seemed not to see or hear anything, as she left the burden of the customers to Carmen, even during the grocery's busiest hours. Carmen had to say, "Lina, please, can you help me?" Only then did she look up, run a fingertip over her lips, say yes.

As for Stefano, he fluctuated between anxiety and acquiescence. While he quarreled with his brother-in-law, his father-in-law, the Solaras, and was upset because, in spite of all that swimming in the sea, children didn't come, here was his wife being sarcastic about the troubles with the shoes, and wrapped up in novels, journals, newspapers until late into the night: this mania had returned, as if real life no longer interested her. He observed her, he didn't understand or didn't have the time or the wish to understand. After Ischia, a part of him, the most aggressive, in the face of those alternating attitudes of rejection and peaceful estrangement, was inciting him to a new clash and a definitive explanation. But another part, more prudent, perhaps afraid, restrained the first, pretended not to notice, thought: better like this than when she's being a pain in the ass. And Lila, who had grasped that thought, tried to make it last in his mind. At night, when they both returned home from work, she was not hostile toward her husband. But after dinner and some talk she withdrew cautiously into reading, a mental space inaccessible to him, inhabited only by her and Nino.

What did he become for her in that period? A sexual yearning that kept her in a state of permanent erotic fantasy; a blazing up of her mind that wanted to be at the same level as his; above all an abstract plan for a secret couple, hiding in a kind of refuge that was to be part bungalow for two hearts, part workshop of ideas on the complexity of the world, he present and active, she a shadow glued to his footsteps, cautious prompter, fervent collaborator. The rare times that they were able to be together not for a few minutes but for an hour, that hour was transformed into an inexhaustible flow of sexual and verbal exchanges, a complete well-being that, at the moment of separation, made the return to the grocery and to Stefano's bed unbearable.

"I can't take it anymore."

"Me neither."

"What can we do?"

"I don't know."

"I want to be with you always."

Or at least, she added, for a few hours every day.

But how to carve out time, safe and regular? Seeing Nino at home was extremely dangerous, seeing him in the street even more so. Not to mention that at times Stefano telephoned the grocery and she wasn't there, and to come up with a plausible explanation was difficult. So, caught between Nino's impatience and her husband's complaints, instead of regaining a sense of reality and telling herself clearly that she was in a situation with no way out, Lila began to act as if the real world were a backdrop or a chessboard, and you had only to shift a painted screen, move a pawn or two, and you would see that the game, the only thing that really counted, *her* game, *the game of the two of them*, could continue to be played. As for the future, the future became the day after and then the next and then the one after that. Or sudden images of massacre and blood, which were very frequent in her notebooks. She never wrote *I will die murdered*, but she noted local crime news, sometimes she reinvented it. In these stories of murdered women she emphasized the murderer's rage, the blood everywhere. And she added details that the newspapers didn't report: eyes dug out of their sockets, injuries caused by a knife to the throat or internal organs, the blade that pierced a breast, nipples cut off, the stomach ripped open from the bellybutton down, the blade that scraped across the genitals. It was as if she wanted to take the power away even from the realistic possibility of violent death by reducing it to words, to a form that could be controlled.

87.

It was in that perspective of a game with possibly mortal outcomes that Lila inserted herself into the conflict between her brother, her husband, and the Solara brothers. She used

Michele's conviction that she was the most suitable person to manage the commercial situation in Piazza dei Martiri. She abruptly stopped saying no and after quarrelsome negotiations as a result of which she obtained absolute autonomy and a substantial weekly salary, as if she were not Signora Carracci, she agreed to go and work in the shoe store. She didn't care about her brother, who felt threatened by the new Solara brand and saw her move as a betrayal; or about her husband, who at first was furious, threatened her, then drove her to complicated mediations in his name with the two brothers concerning debts contracted with their mother, sums of money to receive and to give. She also ignored the sugary words of Michele, who constantly hovered around her, to supervise, without appearing to, the reorganization of the shop, and at the same time pressed to get new shoe models directly from her, passing over Rino and Stefano.

Lila had perceived for a long time that her brother and her father would be swept away, that the Solaras would appropriate everything, that Stefano would stay afloat only if he became more dependent on their dealings. But if before that prospect made her indignant, now, she wrote in her notebooks, the situation left her completely indifferent. Of course, she was sad about Rino, she was sorry that his role as a boss was already declining, especially since he was married and had a child. But in her eyes the bonds of the past now had little substance, her capacity for affection had taken a single path, every thought, every feeling had Nino at its center. If before her motivation was to make her brother rich, now it was only to please Nino.

The first time she went to the shop in Piazza dei Martiri to see what to do with it she was struck by the fact that on the wall where the panel with her wedding photograph had been you could still see the yellowish-black stain from the flames that had destroyed it. That trace upset her. I don't like any part of what happened to me and what I did before Nino, she thought. And it suddenly occurred to her that there, in that space at the center of the city, and for reasons that were obscure to her, every crucial development in her war had occurred. There, the evening of the fight with the youths of Via dei Mille, she had decided conclusively that she had to escape poverty. There she had repented of that decision and had defaced her wedding photograph and had insisted that the defacement, as defacement, should be featured in the shop as a decoration. There she had discovered the signs that her pregnancy was about to end. There, now, the shoe enterprise was failing, swallowed up by the Solaras. And there, too, her marriage would end, she would tear off Stefano and his name, along with all that derived from it. What a mess, she said to Michele Solara, pointing out the burn marks. Then she went out to the sidewalk to look at the stone lions in the center of the square, and was afraid of them.

She had it all painted. In the bathroom, which had no windows, she reopened a walled-up door that had once led to an interior courtyard and installed a half window of frosted glass that could let in some light. She bought two paintings that she had seen in a gallery in Chiatamone and had liked. She hired a salesgirl, not from the neighborhood but a girl from Materdei who had studied to be a secretary. She arranged that the afternoon closing hours, from one until four, should be for her and for the assistant a period of absolute repose, for which the girl was always grateful. She held off Michele, who, although he supported every innovation sight unseen, nonetheless insisted on knowing the details of what she was doing, what she spent.

In the neighborhood, meanwhile, the decision to go to work in Piazza dei Martiri isolated her more than she already had been. A girl who had made a good marriage and had gained, out of nowhere, a comfortable life, a pretty girl who could be mistress of her own house, a house owned by her husband—why did she jump out of bed in the morning and remain far from home all day, in the city, employed by others, complicating Stefano's life, and her mother-in-law's, who because of her had to go back to work in the new grocery? Pinuccia and Gigliola especially, each in her way, threw on Lila all the mud they were capable of, and this was predictable. Less predictable was Carmen, who adored Lila for all she had done for her, but who, as soon as Lila left the grocery, withdrew her affection as if she were pulling back a hand grazed by an animal's claws. She didn't like the abrupt change from friend-colleague to servant in the clutches of Stefano's mother. She felt betrayed, abandoned to fate, and couldn't control her resentment. She even began to argue with her fiancé, Enzo, who didn't approve of her bitterness, he shook his head and, in his laconic way, rather than defend Lila, assigned her, in a few words, a sort of inviolability, the privilege of having reasons that were always just and indisputable.

"Everything I do is no good, everything she does is good," Carmen hissed bitterly.

"Who said so?"

"You: Lina thinks, Lina does, Lina knows. And I? I whom she went off and left there? But naturally she was right to leave and I am wrong to complain. Is it true? Is that what you think?"

"No."

But in spite of that pure and simple monosyllable, Carmen wasn't convinced, she suffered. She sensed that Enzo was tired of everything, even of her, and this enraged her even more: ever since his father died, since he had returned from the Army, he did what he had to do, led his usual life, but meanwhile he was studying at night—he had started during his military service—to get some sort of diploma. Now he was shut up in his head, roaring like a beast—roaring inside, outside silent—and Carmen couldn't bear it, she especially couldn't stand that he became a little animated only when he talked about that bitch, and she shouted at him, and began to cry, screaming:

"Lina makes me sick, because she doesn't give a damn about anyone, but you like that, I know. While if I acted the way she acts, you'd smash my face."

Ada, on the other hand, had long since aligned herself with her employer, Stefano, against the wife who harassed him, and when Lila went to the center of town to be the luxury saleswoman she simply became more treacherous. She said bad things about her to anyone, openly, straight out, but she was angry mainly with Antonio and Pasquale. "She has always taken you in, you men," she said, "because she knows how to get you, she's a whore." She said it just like that, irately, as if Antonio and Pasquale were the representatives of all the insufficiency of the male sex. She insulted her brother, who didn't side with her, she screamed at him: "You're silent because you take money from the Solaras, too, you're both employees of the company, and I know you're ordered around by a woman, you help her put the shop in order, she says move this and move that and you obey." And she was even worse with her fiancé, Pasquale, with whom she was increasingly at odds, constantly criticizing him, saying, "You're dirty, you stink." He apologized, he had just finished work, but Ada continued to attack him, every chance she got, so that Pasquale, to live in peace, gave in on the subject of Lila; the alternative was to break the engagement, although—it should be said—that was not the only reason. He had often been angry with both his fiancée and his sister for having forgotten all the benefits they had gained from Lila's rise, but when, one morning, he saw our friend in the Giulietta with Michele Solara, who was driving her to Piazza dei Martiri, dressed like a high-class prostitute, all made up, he admitted that he couldn't understand how, without a real economic need, she could sell herself to a man like that.

348 - ELENA FERRANTE

Lila, as usual, paid no attention to the hostility that was growing around her; she devoted herself to the new job. And soon sales rose sharply. The shop became a place where people went to buy, but also to chat with that lively, very pretty young woman, whose conversation sparkled, who kept books among the shoes, who read those books, who offered you little chocolates along with the intelligent talk, and who, moreover, never seemed to want to sell Cerullo shoes or Solara shoes to the wife or daughters of the lawyer or the engineer, to the journalist for *Mattino*, to the young or old dandy who was wasting time and money at the Club; rather, she wanted them to make themselves comfortable on the couch and the ottomans and chat about this and that.

The only obstacle, Michele. He was often in the way during work hours and once he said in that ironic, insinuating tone he had, "You have the wrong husband, Lina. I was right: look how well you move among the people who can be useful to us. You and I together in a few years would take over Naples and do what we like with it."

At that point he tried to kiss her.

She pushed him away, he wasn't offended. He said, in amusement, "That's all right, I know how to wait."

"Wait where you like, but not here," she said, "because if you wait here I'll go back to the grocery tomorrow."

Michele's visits diminished while Nino's secret visits increased. For months he and Lila had, finally, in the shop on Piazza dei Martiri, a life of their own, which lasted for three hours a day, except Sundays and holidays, and those were unbearable. He came in through the door of the bathroom at one o'clock, as soon as the assistant pulled the gate three-quarters of the way down and went off, and he left by that same door at four, exactly, before the assistant returned. On the rare occasions that there was some problem—a couple of times Michele arrived with Gigliola and there were particularly tense situations when Stefano showed up—Nino shut himself in the bathroom and sneaked out by the door that opened to the courtyard.

I think for Lila that was a tumultuous trial period for a happy existence. On the one hand she enthusiastically played the part of the young woman who gave the shoe store an eccentric touch, on the other she read for Nino, studied for Nino, reflected for Nino. And even the people of some prominence with whom she became acquainted in the shop seemed to her mainly connections to be used to help him.

During that period, Nino published an article in *Il Mattino* on Naples that gave him modest fame in university circles. I didn't know about it, and luckily: if they had included me in their story as they had on Ischia I would have been so severely scarred that I would never have managed to recover. And it wouldn't have taken me long to figure out that many of the lines in that article—not the most erudite, but those few intuitions that did not require great expertise, only an inspired moment of contact between things that were very distant from one another—were Lila's, and that the tonality of the writing in particular belonged to her. Nino had never been able to write in such a fashion nor was he able to later. Only she and I could write like that.

88.

Then she discovered that she was pregnant and decided to put an end to the deception of Piazza dei Martiri. One Sunday in the late autumn of 1963 she refused to go to lunch at her mother-in-law's, as they usually did, and devoted herself to cooking with great care. While Stefano went to get pastries at the Solaras', bringing some to his mother and sister to be forgiven for his Sunday desertion, Lila put in the suitcase bought for her honeymoon some underwear, a few dresses, a pair of winter shoes, and hid it behind the door of the living room. Then she washed all the pots that she had gotten dirty, set the table in the kitchen, took a carving knife out of a drawer and put it on the sink, covered by a towel. Finally, waiting for her husband to return, she opened the window to get rid of the cooking smells, and stood there looking at the trains and the shining tracks. The cold dissipated the warmth of the apartment, but it didn't bother her, it gave her energy.

Stefano returned, they sat down at the table. Irritated because he had been deprived of his mother's good cooking, he didn't say a single word in praise of the lunch but was harsher than usual toward his brother-in-law, Rino, and more affectionate than usual toward his nephew. He kept calling him *my sister's son*, as if Rino's contribution had been of little account. When they got to the pastries, he ate three, she none. Stefano carefully wiped the cream off his mouth and said, "Let's go to bed for a while."

Lila answered, "Starting tomorrow I'm not going to the shop anymore."

Stefano immediately understood that the afternoon was taking a bad turn. "Why?"

"Because I don't feel like it."

"Did you fight with Michele and Marcello?"

"No."

"Lina, don't talk nonsense, you know very well that your brother and I are just one step from a violent clash with them, don't complicate things."

"I'm not complicating anything. But I'm not going there anymore."

Stefano was silent and Lila saw that he was worried, that he wanted to escape without examining the matter. Her husband was afraid she was about to reveal to him some insult on the part of the Solaras, an unforgivable offense to which, once he knew about it, he would have to react, leading to an irrevocable rupture. Which he couldn't afford.

"All right," he said, when he made up his mind to speak, "don't go, go back to the grocery."

She answered, "I don't feel like the grocery, either."

Stefano looked at her in bewilderment. "You want to stay home? Good. You wanted to work, I never asked you. Is that true or not?"

"It's true."

"Then stay home, I'd be glad to have you at home."

"I don't want to stay home, either."

He was close to losing his calm, the only way he knew to expel anxiety.

"If you don't want to stay home, either, am I allowed to know what the fuck you want?"

Lila answered, "I want to go."

"Go where?"

"I don't want to stay with you anymore, I want to leave you."

The only thing Stefano could do was start laughing. Those words seemed to him so enormous that for a few minutes he seemed relieved. He pinched her cheek, he said with his usual half smile that they were husband and wife and that husband and wife don't leave each other, he promised that the following Sunday he would take her to the Amalfi Coast, so they could relax a little. But she answered calmly that there was no reason to stay together, that she had been wrong from the start, that even when they were engaged she had liked him only a little, that she now knew clearly that she had never loved him and that to be supported by him, to help him make money, to sleep with him were things that she could no longer tolerate. It was at the end of that speech that she received a blow that knocked her off her chair. She got up while Stefano moved to grab her, she ran to the sink, seized the knife that she had put under the dishtowel. She turned to him just when he was about to hit her again.

"Do it and I'll kill you the way they killed your father," she said.

Stefano stopped, stunned by that reference to the fate of his father. He muttered things like "All right, kill me, do what you want." And he made a gesture of boredom and yawned, an uncontrollable yawn, his mouth wide open, that left his eyes bright and shining. He turned his back on her and, still muttering resentfully—"Go on, go, I've given you everything, I've yielded in every way, and you repay me like this, me, who raised you out of poverty, who made your brother rich, your father, and your whole shitty family"—went to the table and ate another pastry.

Then he left the kitchen, retreated to the bedroom, and from there he cried suddenly, "You can't even imagine how much I love you."

Lila placed the knife on the sink, she thought: he doesn't believe that I'm leaving him; he wouldn't even believe that I have someone else, he can't. Yet she got up her courage and went to the bedroom to confess to him about Nino, to tell him she was pregnant. But her husband was sleeping, he had fallen asleep as if wrapped in a magic cape. So she put on her coat, took the suitcase, and left the apartment.

89.

Stefano slept all day. When he woke up and realized that his wife wasn't there he pretended not to notice. He had behaved like that since he was a boy, when his father terrorized him by his mere presence and he, in reaction, had trained himself to that half smile, to slow, tranquil gestures, to a controlled distance from the world around him, to keep at bay both fear and the desire to tear open his chest with his bare hands and, pulling it apart, rip out the heart.

In the evening he went out and did something rash: he went to Ada's windows, and though he knew she was supposed to be at the movies or somewhere with Pasquale, he called her, kept calling her. Ada looked out, both happy and alarmed. She had stayed home because Melina was raving more than usual and Antonio, ever since he had gone to work for the Solaras, was always out, he didn't have a schedule. Her fiancé was there keeping her company. Stefano went up just the same, and, without ever mentioning Lila, spent the evening at the Cappuccio house talking politics with Pasquale and about matters connected to the grocery with Ada. When he got home he pretended that Lila had gone to her parents' and before he went to bed he shaved carefully. He slept heavily all night.

The trouble began the next day. The assistant at Piazza dei Martiri told Michele that Lila hadn't shown up. Michele telephoned Stefano and Stefano told him that his wife was sick. The illness lasted for days, so Nunzia stopped by to see if her daughter needed her. No one opened the door, she went back in the evening, Stefano had just returned from work and was sitting in front of the television, which was at high volume. He swore, he went to open the door, invited her in. As soon as Nunzia said, "How is Lina?" he answered that she had left him, then he burst into tears.

Both families hurried over: Stefano's mother, Alfonso, Pinuccia with the baby, Rino, Fernando. For one reason or another they were all frightened, but only Maria and Nunzia were openly worried about Lila's fate and wondered where she had gone. The others quarreled for reasons that had little to do with her. Rino and Fernando, who were angry at Stefano because he had done nothing to prevent the closing of the shoe factory, accused him of having never understood Lila and said he had been very wrong to send her to the Solaras' shop.

Pinuccia got angry and yelled at her husband and her father-in-law that Lila had always been a hothead, that she wasn't Stefano's victim, Stefano was hers. When Alfonso ventured that they should turn to the police, ask at the hospitals, feelings flared up even more, they all criticized him as if he had insulted them: Rino in particular cried that the last thing they needed was to become the laughingstock of the neighborhood. It was Maria who said softly, "Maybe she's gone to stay with Lenù for a while." That hypothesis caught on. They continued to quarrel, but they all pretended, except Alfonso, to believe that Lila, because of Stefano, and the Solaras, had decided to go to Pisa. "Yes," Nunzia said, calming down, "she always does that, as soon as she has a problem she goes to Lenù." At that point, they all started to get angry about that reckless journey, all by herself, on the train, far away, without telling anyone. And yet that Lila was with me seemed so plausible and at the same time so reassuring that it immediately became a fact. Only Alfonso said, "I'll leave tomorrow and go see," but he was immediately checked by Pinuccia, "Where are you going when you have to work," and by Fernando, who muttered, "Leave her alone, let her calm down."

The next day that was the version that Stefano gave to anyone who asked about Lila: "She went to Pisa to see Lenù, she wants to rest." But that afternoon Nunzia was gripped again by anxiety, she went to see Alfonso and asked if he had my address. He didn't have it, no one did, only my mother. So Nunzia sent Alfonso to her, but my mother, out of her natural hostility toward everyone or to safeguard my studies from distraction, gave him an incomplete version (it's likely that she herself had it that way: writing was hard for my mother, and we both knew that she would never use that address). In any case Nunzia and Alfonso together wrote me a letter in which they asked in a very roundabout way if Lila was with me. They addressed it to the University of Pisa, nothing else, only my name and surname, and its arrival was much delayed. I read it, I became even angrier with Lila and Nino, I didn't answer.

Meanwhile, the day after Lila's so-called departure, Ada, in addition to working in the old grocery store, in addition to attending to her entire family and the needs of her fiancé, also began to tidy up Stefano's house and to cook for him, which put Pasquale in a bad mood. They quarreled, he said to her, "You're not paid to be a servant," and she answered, "Better to be a servant than waste time arguing with you." On the other hand, to keep the Solaras happy Alfonso was quickly sent to Piazza dei Martiri, where he felt at his ease: he left early in the morning dressed as if he were going to a wedding and returned at night very pleased: he liked spending the day in the center. As for Michele, who with the disappearance of Signora Carracci had become intractable, he called Antonio and said to him: "Find her for me."

Antonio muttered, "Naples is big, Michè, and so is Pisa, and even Italy. Where do I begin?"

Michele answered, "With Sarratore's oldest son." Then he gave him the look he reserved for people he considered worth less than nothing and said, "Don't you dare tell anyone about this search or I'll put you in the insane asylum at Aversa and you'll never get out. Everything you know, everything you see, you will tell me alone. Is that clear?"

Antonio nodded yes.

90.

That people, even more than things, lost their boundaries and overflowed into shapelessness is what most frightened Lila in the course of her life. The loss of those boundaries in her brother, whom she loved more than anyone in her family, had frightened her, and the disintegration of Stefano in the passage from fiancé to husband terrified her. I learned only from her notebooks how much her wedding night had scarred her and how she feared the potential distortion of her husband's body, his disfigurement by the internal impulses of desire and rage or, on the contrary, of subtle plans, base acts. Especially at night she was afraid of waking up and finding him formless in the bed, transformed into excrescences that burst out because of too much fluid, the flesh melted and dripping, and with it everything around, the furniture, the entire apartment and she herself, his wife, broken, sucked into that stream polluted by living matter.

When she closed the door behind her and, as if she were inside a white cloud of steam that made her invisible, took the metro to Campi Flegrei, Lila had the impression that she had left a soft space, inhabited by forms without definition, and was finally heading toward a structure that was capable of containing her fully, all of her, without her cracking or the figures around her cracking. She reached her destination along desolate streets. She dragged the suitcase to the third floor of a working-class apartment building, and into a shoddy, dark two-room apartment furnished with old, cheap furniture, a bathroom where there was only a toilet and sink. She had done it all herself, Nino had to prepare for his exams and he was also working on a new article for *Il Mattino* and on transforming the other into an essay that had been rejected by *Cronache Meridionali*, but that a journal called *Nord e Sud* said it was eager to publish. She had seen the apartment, had rented it, had given three payments in advance. Now, as soon as she entered, she felt enormously cheerful. She discovered with surprise the pleasure of having abandoned those she thought would have to be part of her forever. Pleasure, yes, she wrote just that. She didn't feel in the least the loss of the new neighborhood's comforts, she didn't smell the odor of mold, didn't see the stain of dampness in a corner of the bedroom, didn't notice the gray light that struggled to enter through the window, wasn't depressed by a place that immediately foretold a return to the poverty of her childhood. Instead, she felt as if she had magically disappeared from a place where she suffered, and had reappeared in a place that promised happiness. She was again fascinated, I think, by erasing herself: enough with everything she had been; enough with the *stradone*, shoes, groceries, husband, Solaras, Piazza dei Martiri; enough even with me, bride, wife, gone elsewhere, lost. All that remained of her self was the lover of Nino, who arrived that evening.

He was visibly overcome by emotion. He embraced her, kissed her, looked around disoriented. He barred doors and windows as if he feared sudden incursions. They made love, in a bed for the first time after the night in Forio. Then he got up, he started studying, he complained often about the weak light. She also got out of bed and helped him review. They went to sleep at three in the morning, after revising together the new article for *Il Mattino*, and they slept in an embrace. Lila felt safe, although it was raining outside, the windows shook, the house was alien to her. How new Nino's body was, long, thin, so different from Stefano's. How exciting his smell was. It seemed to her that she had come from a world of shadows and had arrived in a place where finally life was real. In the morning, as soon as she put her feet on the floor, she had to run to the toilet to throw up. She closed the door so that Nino wouldn't hear.

91.

They lived together for twenty-three days. The relief at having left everything increased from moment to moment. She didn't miss any of the comforts she had enjoyed after her marriage, and separation from her parents, her younger siblings, Rino, her nephew didn't sadden her. She never worried that the money would run out. The only thing that seemed to matter was that she woke up with Nino and fell asleep with him, that she was beside him when he studied or wrote, that they had lively discussions in which the jumble of thoughts in her head poured out. At night they went to a movie together, or chose a book presentation, or a political debate, and often they stayed out late, returning home on foot, clinging to one another to protect themselves from the cold or the rain, squabbling, joking.

Once they went to hear a writer named Pasolini, who also made films. Everything that had to do with him caused an uproar and Nino didn't like him, he twisted his mouth, said, "He's a fairy, all he does is make a lot of noise," so he had resisted, he would have preferred to stay home and study. But Lila was curious and she dragged him there. The talk was held in the same club where I had gone once, in obedience to Professor Galiani. Lila was enthusiastic when she came out, she pushed Nino toward the writer, she wanted to talk to him. But Nino was nervous and did his best to get her away, especially when he realized that on the sidewalk across the street there were youths shouting insults. "Let's go," he said, worried, "I don't like him and I don't like the fascists, either." But Lila had grown up amid violence, she had no intention of sneaking off; he tried to pull her toward an alley and she wriggled free, she laughed, she responded to the insults with insults. She gave in abruptly when, just as a real fight was starting, she recognized Antonio. His eyes and his teeth shone as if they were made of metal, but unlike the others he wasn't shouting. He seemed too busy hitting people to be aware of her, but the thing ruined the evening for her anyway. On the way home she felt some tension with Nino: they didn't agree about what Pasolini had said, they seemed to have gone to different places to hear different people. But it wasn't only that. That night he regretted the long exciting period of the furtive meetings in the shop on Piazza dei

Martiri and at the same time perceived that something about Lila disturbed him. She noticed his distraction, his irritation, and to avoid further tension did not say that among the attackers she had seen a friend of hers from the neighborhood, Melina's son.

From then on Nino seemed less and less inclined to take her out. First he said that he had to study, and it was true, then he let slip that on various public occasions she had been excessive.

"In what sense?"

"You exaggerate."

"Meaning?"

He made a resentful list: "You make comments out loud; if someone tells you to be quiet you start arguing; you bother the speakers with your own monologues. It's not done."

Lila had known that it wasn't done, but she had believed that now, with him, everything was possible, bridging gaps with a leap, speaking face to face with people who counted. Hadn't she been able to talk to influential types, in the Solaras' shop? Hadn't it been thanks to one of the customers that he had published his first article in *Il Mattino*? And so? "You're too timid," she said. "You still don't understand that you're better than they are and you'll do much more important things." Then she kissed him.

But the following evenings Nino, with one excuse or another, began to go out alone. And if he stayed home instead and studied, he complained of how much noise there was in the building. Or he grumbled because he had to go and ask his father for money, and Donato would torment him with questions like: Where are you sleeping, what are you doing, where are you living, are you studying? Or, in the face of Lila's ability to make connections between very different things, instead of being excited as usual he shook his head, became irritable.

After a while he was in such a bad mood, and so behind

with his exams, that in order to keep studying he stopped going to bed with her. Lila said, "It's late, let's go to sleep," he answered with a distracted, "You go, I'll come later." He looked at the outline of her body under the covers and desired its warmth but was also afraid of it. I haven't yet graduated, he thought, I don't have a job; if I don't want to throw my life away I have to apply myself; instead I'm here with this person who is married, who is pregnant, who vomits every morning, who prevents me from being disciplined. When he found out that *Il Mattino* wouldn't publish the article he was really upset. Lila consoled him, told him to send it to other newspapers. But then she added, "Tomorrow I'll call."

She wanted to call the editor she had met in the Solaras' shop and find out what was wrong. He stammered, "You won't telephone anyone."

"Why?"

"Because that shit was never interested in me but in you."

"It's not true."

"It's very true, I'm not a fool, you just make problems for me."

"What do you mean?"

"I shouldn't have listened to you."

"What did I do?"

"You confused my ideas. Because you're like a drop of water, *ting ting ting*. Until it's done your way, you won't stop."

"You thought of the article and wrote it."

"Exactly. And so why did you make me redo it four times?"

"*You* wanted to rewrite it."

"Lina, let's be very clear: choose something of your own that you like, go back to selling shoes, go back to selling salami, but don't desire to be something you're not by ruining me."

They had been living together for twenty-three days, a cloud in which the gods had hidden them so that they could enjoy each other without being disturbed. Those words wounded her deeply, she said, "Get out."

He quickly pulled his coat on over his sweater and slammed the door behind him.

Lila sat on the bed and thought: he'll be back in ten minutes, he left his books, his notes, his shaving cream and razor. Then she burst into tears: how could I have thought of living with him, of being able to help him? It's my fault: to free my head, I even made him write something wrong.

She went to bed and waited. She waited all night, but Nino didn't come back, not the morning after or the one after that.

92.

What I am now recounting I learned from various people at various times. I begin with Nino, who left the house in Campi Flegrei and took refuge with his parents. His mother treated him better, much better, than the prodigal son. With his father, on the other hand, he was quarreling within an hour, the insults flew. Donato yelled at him in dialect that he could either leave home or stay there, but the thing he absolutely could not do was to disappear for a month without telling anyone and then return only to swipe some money as if he had earned it himself.

Nino retreated to his room and had many arguments with himself. Although he already wanted to run back to Lina, ask her pardon, cry to her that he loved her, he assessed the situation and became convinced that he had fallen into a trap, not his fault, not Lina's fault, but the fault of desire. Now, for example, he thought, I can't wait to go back to her, cover her with kisses, assume my responsibilities; but a part of me knows perfectly well that what I did today on a wave of disappointment is true and right: Lina isn't right for me, Lina is pregnant, what's in her womb scares me; so I must absolutely not return, I have to go to Bruno, borrow some money, leave Naples as Elena did, study somewhere else.

He deliberated all night and all the next day, now pierced by a need for Lila, now clinging to chilling thoughts that evoked her crude ingenuousness, her too intelligent ignorance, the force with which she drew him into her thoughts, which seemed like insights but were, instead, muddled.

In the evening he telephoned Bruno and, in a frenzy, left to go see him. He ran through the rain to the bus stop, barely caught the right bus before it left. But suddenly he changed his mind and got off at Piazza Garibaldi. He took the metro to Campi Flegrei, he couldn't wait to embrace Lila, take her standing up, right away, as soon as he was in the house, against the entrance wall. That now seemed the most important thing, then he would think what to do.

It was dark, he walked with long strides in the rain. He didn't even notice the dark silhouette coming toward him. He was shoved so violently that he fell down. A long series of blows began, punching and kicking, kicking and punching. The person who hit him kept repeating, but not angrily:

"Leave her, don't see her and don't touch her again. Repeat: I will leave her. Repeat: I won't see her and I won't touch her again. You piece of shit: you like it, eh, taking other men's wives. Repeat: I was wrong, I'll leave her."

Nino repeated obediently, but his attacker didn't stop. He fainted more out of fear than out of pain.

93.

It was Antonio who beat up Nino, but he reported almost none of this to his boss. When Michele asked if he had found Sarratore's son he answered yes. When he asked with evident anxiety if that track had led to Lila he said no. When he asked him if he had had information about Lila he said he couldn't find her and the only thing he could absolutely rule out was that Sarratore's son had anything to do with Signora Carracci.

He was lying, of course. He had found Nino and Lila fairly soon, by chance, the night he had had the job of brawling with the Communists. He had smashed a few faces and then had left the fight to follow the two who had fled. He had discovered where they lived, he had understood that they were living together, and in the following days he had studied everything they did, how they lived. Seeing them he had felt both admiration and envy. Admiration for Lila. How is it possible, he had said to himself, that she abandoned her house, a beautiful house, and left her husband, the groceries, the cars, the shoes, the Solaras, for a student without a cent who keeps her in a place almost worse than the old neighborhood? What is it with that girl: courage, or madness? Then he concentrated on his envy of Nino. What hurt him most was that Lila and I both liked the skinny, ugly bastard. What was it about the son of Sarratore, what was his advantage? He had thought about it night and day. He was gripped by a kind of morbid obsession that affected his nerves, especially in his hands, so that he was constantly interlacing them, pressing them together as if he were praying. Finally he had decided that he had to free Lila, even if at that moment, perhaps, she had no desire to be freed. But—he had said to himself—it takes time for people to understand what's good and what's bad, and helping them means doing for them what in a particular moment of their life they aren't capable of doing. Michele Solara hadn't ordered him to beat up Sarratore's son, no: he had not told Michele the most important thing and so there was no reason to go that far; beating him up had been his own decision, and he had made it partly because he wanted to get Nino away from Lila and give her back what she had incomprehensibly thrown away, and partly for his own enjoyment, because of an exasperation he felt not toward Nino, an insignificant limp agglomerate of

effeminate flesh and bone, too long and breakable, but toward
what we two girls had attributed and did attribute to him.

I have to admit that when, some time afterward, he told me
that story I seemed to understand his motivations. It moved
me, I caressed his cheek to console him for his savage feelings.
And he reddened, he was flustered; to show me that he wasn't
a beast he said, "Afterward I helped him." He had picked up
Sarratore's son, taken him, half dazed, to a pharmacy, left him
at the entrance, and returned to the neighborhood to talk to
Pasquale and Enzo.

They had agreed to meet him reluctantly. They no longer
considered him a friend, especially Pasquale, even though he
was his sister's fiancé. But Antonio didn't care, he pretended
not to notice, he behaved as if their hostility because he had
sold himself to the Solaras were a gripe that made no dent in
their friendship. He said nothing about Nino, he focused on
the fact that he had found Lila and that they had to help her.

"Do what?" Pasquale had asked, aggressively.

"Go home to her own house: she didn't go to see Lenuccia,
she's living in a shitty place in Campi Flegrei."

"By herself?"

"Yes."

"And why in the world did she decide to do that?"

"I don't know, I didn't talk to her."

"Why?"

"I found her on behalf of Michele Solara."

"You're a shit fascist."

"I'm nothing, I did a job."

"Bravo, now what do you want?"

"I haven't told Michele that I found her."

"And so?"

"I don't want to lose my job, I have to think of earning a living. If Michele finds out that I lied to him he'll fire me. You go
get her and bring her home."

Pasquale had insulted him grossly again, but even then Antonio scarcely reacted. He became upset only when his future brother-in-law said that Lila had done well to leave her husband and all the rest: if she had finally gotten out of the Solaras' shop, if she realized that she had made a mistake in marrying Stefano, he certainly wouldn't be the one who brought her back.

"You want to leave her in Campi Flegrei by herself?" Antonio asked, bewildered. "Alone and without a lira?"

"Why, are we rich? Lina is a grownup, she knows what life is: if she made that decision she has her reasons, let's leave her in peace."

"But she helped us whenever she could."

At that reminder of the money Lila had given them Pasquale was ashamed. He had stammered some trite stuff about rich and poor, about the condition of women in the neighborhood and outside it, about the fact that if it was a matter of giving her money he was ready. But Enzo, who until then had been silent, broke in with a gesture of annoyance, and said to Antonio, "Give me the address, I'm going to see what she intends to do."

94.

He did go, the next day. He took the metro, got out at Campi Flegrei, and looked for the street, the building.

Of Enzo at that time I knew only that he couldn't tolerate anything anymore: the whining of his mother, the burden of his siblings, the Camorra in the fruit-and-vegetable market, the rounds with the cart, which earned less and less, Pasquale's Communist talk, and even his engagement to Carmen. None of it. But since he was reserved by nature, it was difficult to get an idea of what type of person he was. From Carmen I had learned

366 - ELENA FERRANTE

that he was secretly studying on his own, he wanted to get an engineering diploma. It must have been on the same occasion—Christmas?—that Carmen told me he had kissed her only four times since he returned from military service, in the spring. She added, with irritation, "Maybe he's not a man."

That was what we often said, we girls, when someone didn't care much about us: that he wasn't a man. Enzo was, wasn't he? I didn't know anything about the dark depths that men could have, none of us did, and so for any confusing manifestation we had recourse to that formula. Some, like the Solaras, like Pasquale, Antonio, Donato Sarratore, even Franco Mari, my boyfriend at the Normale, wanted us in ways that were different—aggressive, subordinate, heedless, attentive—but that they wanted us there was no doubt. Others, like Alfonso, Enzo, Nino, had—according to equally diverse attitudes—an aloof self-possession, as if between us and them there were a wall and the work of scaling it were our job. In Enzo, after the Army, this characteristic had become accentuated, and he not only did nothing to please women but did nothing to please the entire world. He was short, and yet his body seemed to have become even smaller, as if through a sort of self-compression: it had become a compact block of energy. The skin over the bones of his face was stretched like an awning, and he had reduced motion to the pure compass of his legs, no other part of him moved, not arms or neck or head, not even his hair, which was a reddish-blond helmet. When he decided to go and see Lila he told Pasquale and Antonio, not in order to discuss it but in the form of a brief statement that served to cut off any discussion. Nor when he arrived at Campi Flegrei did he display any uncertainty. He found the street, found the doorway, went up the stairs, and rang with determination at the right door.

95.

When Nino did not return in ten minutes or an hour or even the next day, Lila turned spiteful. She felt not abandoned but humiliated, and although she had admitted to herself that she wasn't the right woman for him, she still found it unbearable that he, disappearing from her life after only twenty-three days, had brutally confirmed it. In a rage she threw away everything he had left: books, underwear, socks, a sweater, even a pencil stub. She did it, she regretted it, she burst into tears. When finally the tears stopped, she felt ugly, swollen, stupid, cheapened by the bitter feelings that Nino, Nino whom she loved and by whom she believed she was loved in return, was provoking. The apartment seemed suddenly what it was, a squalid place through whose walls all the noises of the city reached her. She became aware of the bad smell, of the cockroaches that came in under the stairwell door, the stains of dampness on the ceiling, and felt for the first time that childhood was clutching at her again, not the childhood of dreams but the childhood of cruel privations, of threats and beatings. In fact suddenly she discovered that one fantasy that had comforted us since we were children—to become rich—had evaporated from her mind. Although the poverty of Campi Flegrei seemed to her darker than in the neighborhood of our games, although her situation was worse because of the child she was expecting, although in a few days she had used up the money she had brought, she discovered that wealth no longer seemed a prize and a compensation, it no longer spoke to her. The creased and evil-smelling paper money—piling up in the drawer of the cash register when she worked in the grocery, or in the colored metal box of the shop in Piazza dei Martiri— that in adolescence replaced the strongboxes of our childhood, overflowing with gold pieces and precious stones, no longer functioned: any remaining glitter was gone. The relationship between money and the possession of things had disappointed her. She wanted nothing for herself or for the child she would have. To be rich for her meant having Nino, and since Nino was gone she felt poor, a poverty that no money could obliterate. Since there was no remedy for that new condition—she had made too many mistakes since she was a child, and they had all converged in that last mistake: to believe that the son of Sarratore couldn't do without her as she couldn't without him, and that theirs was a unique, exceptional fate, and that the good fortune of loving each other would last forever and would extinguish the force of any other necessity—she felt guilty and decided not to go out, not to look for him, not to eat, not to drink, but to wait for her life and that of the baby to lose their outlines, any possible definition, and she found that there was nothing left in her mind, not even a trace of the thing that made her spiteful, that is to say the awareness of abandonment.

Then someone rang at the door.

She thought it was Nino: she opened it. It was Enzo. Seeing him didn't disappoint her. She thought he had come to bring her some fruit—as he had done many years earlier, as a child, after he was defeated in the competition created by the principal and Maestra Oliviero, and had thrown a stone at her—and she burst out laughing. Enzo considered the laughter a sign of illness. He went in, but left the door open out of respect, he didn't want the neighbors to think she was receiving men like a prostitute. He looked around, he glanced at her disheveled state, and although he didn't see what still didn't show, that is, the pregnancy, he deduced that she really needed help. In his serious way, completely without emotion, he said, even before she managed to calm down and stop laughing:

"We're going now."

"Where?"

"To your husband."

"Did he send you?"

"No."

"Who sent you?"

"No one sent me."

"I'm not coming."

"Then I'll stay here with you."

"Forever?"

"Until you're persuaded."

"And your job?"

"I'm tired of it."

"And Carmen?"

"You are much more important."

"I'll tell her, then she'll leave you."

"I'll tell her, I've already decided."

From then on he spoke distantly, in a low voice. She answered him laughing, in a teasing way, as if none of their words were real, as if they were speaking in fun of a world, of people, of feelings that hadn't existed for a long time. Enzo realized that, and for a while he said nothing more. He went through the house, found Lila's suitcase, filled it with the things in the drawers, in the closet. Lila let him do it, because she considered him not the flesh-and-blood Enzo but a shadow, in color, as in the movies, who although he spoke was nevertheless an effect of the light. Having packed the suitcase, Enzo confronted her again and made a very surprising speech. He said, in his concentrated yet detached way,

"Lina, I've loved you since we were children. I never told you because you are very beautiful and very intelligent, and I am short, ugly, and worthless. Now return to your husband. I don't know why you left him and I don't want to know. I know only that you can't stay here, you don't deserve to live in filth. I'll take you to the entrance of the building and wait: if he treats you badly, I'll come up and kill him. But he won't, he'll be glad you've come back. But let's make a pact: in the case that you can't come to an agreement with your husband, I brought you back to him and I will come and get you. All right?"

Lila stopped laughing, she narrowed her eyes, she listened to him attentively for the first time. Interactions between Enzo and her had been very rare until that moment, but the times I had been present they had always amazed me. There was something indefinable between them, originating in the confusion of childhood. She trusted Enzo, I think, she felt she could count on him. When the young man took the suitcase and headed toward the door, which had remained open, she hesitated a moment, then followed him.

96.

Enzo did wait under Lila and Stefano's windows the night he took her home, and, if Stefano had beaten her, he probably would have gone up and killed him. But Stefano didn't beat her; he welcomed her into her home, which was clean and tidy. He behaved as if his wife really had gone to stay with me in Pisa, even if there was no evidence that that was what had happened. Lila, on the other hand, did not take refuge in that excuse or any other. The following day, when she woke up, she said reluctantly, "I'm pregnant," and he was so happy that when she added, "The baby isn't yours," he burst out laughing, with genuine joy. When she angrily repeated that phrase, once, twice, three times, and even tried to hit him with clenched fists, he cuddled her, kissed her, murmuring, "Enough, Lina, enough, enough, I'm too happy. I know that I've treated you badly but now let's stop, don't say mean things to me," and his eyes filled with tears of joy.

Lila knew that people tell themselves lies to defend against the truth of the facts, but she was amazed that her husband was able to lie to himself with such joyful conviction. On the other hand she didn't care, by now, about Stefano or about herself, and after again repeating for a while, without emotion, "The baby isn't yours," she withdrew into the lethargy of pregnancy. He prefers to put off the pain, she thought, and all right, let him do as he likes: if he doesn't want to suffer now, he'll suffer later.

She went on to make a list of what she wanted and what she didn't want: she didn't want to work in the shop in Piazza dei Martiri or in the grocery; she didn't want to see anyone, friends, relatives, especially the Solaras; she wished to stay home and be a wife and mother. He agreed, sure that she would change her mind in a few days. But Lila secluded herself in the apartment, without showing any interest in Stefano's business, or that of her brother and her father, or in the affairs of his relatives or of her own relatives.

A couple of times Pinuccia came with her son, Fernando, whom they called Dino, but she didn't open the door.

Once Rino came, very upset, and Lila let him in, listened to all his chatter about how angry the Solaras were about her disappearance from the shop, about how badly things were going with Cerullo shoes, because Stefano thought only of his own affairs and was no longer investing. When at last he was silent, she said, "Rino, you're the older brother, you're a grownup, you have a wife and son, do me a favor: live your life without constantly turning to me." He was hurt and he went away depressed, after a complaint about how everyone was getting richer while he, because of his sister, who didn't care about the family, the blood of the Cerullos, but now felt she was a Carracci, was in danger of losing the little he had gained.

It happened that even Michele Solara went to the trouble of coming to see her—in the beginning even twice a day—at times when he was sure that Stefano wouldn't be there. But she never let him in, she sat silently in the kitchen, almost without breathing, so that once, before he left, he shouted at her from the street: "Who the fuck do you think you are, whore, you had an agreement with me and you didn't keep it."

Lila welcomed willingly only Nunzia and Stefano's mother, Maria, both of whom followed her pregnancy closely. She stopped throwing up but her complexion remained gray. She had the impression of having become large and inflated inside rather than outside, as if within the wrapping of her body every organ had begun to fatten. Her stomach seemed a bubble of flesh that was expanding because of the baby's breathing. She was afraid of that expansion, she feared that the thing she was most afraid of would happen: she would break apart, overflow. Then suddenly she felt that the being she had inside, that absurd modality of life, that expanding nodule that at a certain point would come out of her sex like a puppet on a string—suddenly she loved it, and through it the sense of herself returned. Frightened by her ignorance, by the mistakes she could make, she began to read everything she could find about what pregnancy is, what happens inside the womb, how to prepare for the birth. She hardly went out at all in those months. She stopped buying clothes or objects for the house, she got in the habit instead of having her mother bring at least a couple of newspapers and Alfonso some journals. It was the only money she spent. Once Carmen showed up to ask for money and she told her to ask Stefano, she had none; the girl went away discouraged. She didn't care about anyone anymore, only the baby.

The experience wounded Carmen, who became even more resentful. She still hadn't forgiven Lila for breaking up their alliance in the new grocery. Now she couldn't forgive her for not opening her purse. But mainly she couldn't forgive her because—as she began to gossip to everyone—she had done as she liked: she had vanished, she had returned, and yet she continued to play the part of the lady, to have a nice house, and now even had a baby coming. The more of a slut you are, the better off you are. She, on the other hand, who labored from morning to night with no gratification—only bad things happened to her, one after the other. Her father died in jail. Her mother died in that way she didn't even want to think about. And now Enzo as well. He had waited for her one night outside the grocery and told her that he didn't want to continue the engagement. Just like that, very few words, as usual, no explanation. She had run weeping to her brother, and Pasquale had met Enzo to ask for an explanation. But Enzo had given none, so now they didn't speak to each other.

When I returned from Pisa for Easter vacation and met Carmen in the gardens, she vented. "I'm an idiot," she wept, "waiting for him the whole time he was a soldier. An idiot slaving from morning to night for practically nothing." She said she was tired of everything. And with no obvious connection she began to insult Lila. She went so far as to ascribe to her a relationship with Michele Solara, who had often been seen wandering around the Carracci house. "Adultery and money," she hissed, "that's how she gets ahead."

Not a word, however, about Nino. Miraculously, the neighborhood knew nothing of that. During the same period, Antonio told me about beating him up, and about how he had sent Enzo to retrieve Lila, but he told only me, and I'm sure that for his whole life he never spoke a word to anyone else. But I learned something from Alfonso: insistently questioned, he told me he had heard from Marisa that Nino had gone to study in Milan. Thanks to them, when on Holy Saturday I ran into Lila on the *stradone*, completely by chance, I felt a subtle pleasure at the idea that I knew more than she about the facts of her life, and that from what I knew it was easy to deduce how little good it had done her to take Nino away from me.

Her stomach was already quite big, it was like an excrescence on her thin body. Even her face didn't show the florid beauty of pregnant women; it was ugly, greenish, the skin stretched over the prominent cheekbones. We both tried to pretend that nothing had happened.

"How are you?"

"Well."

"Can I touch your stomach?"

"Yes."

"And that matter?"

"Which?"

"The one on Ischia."

"It's over."

"Too bad."

"What are you doing?"

"I study, I have a place of my own and all the books I need. I even have a sort of boyfriend."

"A sort?"

"Yes."

"What's his name?"

"Franco Mari."

"What does he do?"

"He's also a student."

"Those glasses really suit you."

"Franco gave them to me."

"And the dress?"

"Also him."

"He's rich?"

"Yes."

"I'm glad."

"And how is the studying going?"

"I work hard, otherwise they'll send me away."

"Be careful."

"I'm careful."

"Lucky you."

"Well."

She said her due date was in July. She had a doctor, the one who had sent her to bathe in the sea. A doctor, not the obstetrician in the neighborhood. "I'm afraid for the baby," she said. "I don't want to give birth at home." She had read that it was better to go to a clinic. She smiled, she touched her belly. Then she said something that wasn't very clear.

"I'm still here just for this."

"Is it nice to feel the baby inside?"

"No, it repulses me, but I'm pleased to carry it."

"Was Stefano angry?"

"He wants to believe what's convenient for him."

"That is?"

"That for a while I was a little crazy and ran away to you in Pisa."

I pretended not to know anything, feigning amazement: "In Pisa? You and me?"

"Yes."

"And if he asks, should I say that's what happened?"

"Do as you like."

We said goodbye, promising to write. But we never wrote and I did nothing to find out about the birth. Sometimes a feeling stirred in me that I immediately repressed to keep it from becoming conscious: I wanted something to happen to her, so the baby wouldn't be born.

97.

In that period I often dreamed of Lila. Once she was in bed in a lacy green nightgown, her hair was braided, which was something she had never done, she held in her arms a little girl dressed in pink, and she kept saying, in a sorrowful voice, "Take a picture but only of me, not of the child." Another time she greeted me happily and then called her daughter, who had my name. "Lenù," she said, "come and say hello to your aunt." But a fat old giantess appeared, and Lila ordered me to undress her and wash her and change her diaper and swaddling. On waking I was tempted to look for a telephone and try to call Alfonso to find out if the baby had been born without any problems, if she was happy. But I had to study or maybe I had exams, and I forgot about it. When, in August, I was free of both obligations, it happened that I didn't go home. I wrote some lies to my parents and went with Franco to Versilia, to an apartment belonging to his family. For the first time I wore a two-piece bathing suit: it fit in one fist and I felt very bold.

It was at Christmas that I heard from Carmen how difficult Lila's delivery had been.

"She almost died," she said, "so in the end the doctor had to cut open her stomach, otherwise the baby couldn't be born."

"She had a boy?"

"Yes."

"Is he well?"

"He's lovely."

"And she?"

"She's lost her figure."

I learned that Stefano wanted to give his son the name of his father, Achille, but Lila was opposed to it, and the yelling of husband and wife, which hadn't been heard for a long time, echoed throughout the clinic, so that the nurses had reprimanded them. In the end the child was called Gennaro, that is, Rino, like Lila's brother.

I listened, I didn't say anything. I felt unhappy, and to cope with my unhappiness I imposed on myself an attitude of reserve. Carmen noticed:

"I'm talking and talking, but you don't say a word, you make me feel like the TV news. Don't you give a damn about us anymore?"

"Of course I do."

"You've gotten pretty, even your voice has changed."

"Did I have an ugly voice?"

"You had the voice that we have."

"And now?"

"You have it less."

I stayed in the neighborhood for ten days, from December 24, 1964, to January 3, 1965, but I never went to see Lila. I didn't want to see her son, I was afraid of recognizing in his mouth, in his nose, in the shape of his eyes or ears something of Nino.

At my house now I was treated like an important person who had deigned to stop by for a quick hello. My father observed me with pleasure. I felt his satisfied gaze on me, but if I spoke to him he became embarrassed. He didn't ask what I was studying, what was the use of it, what job I would have afterward, and not because he didn't want to know but out of fear that he wouldn't understand my answers. My mother instead moved angrily through the house, and, hearing her unmistakable footsteps, I thought of how I had been afraid of becoming like her. But, luckily, I had outdistanced her, and she felt it, she resented me for it. Even now, when she spoke to me, it was as if I were guilty of terrible things: in every situation I perceived in her voice a shadow of disapproval, but, unlike in the past, she never wanted me to do the dishes, clean up, wash the floors. There was some uneasiness also with my sister and brothers. They tried to speak to me in Italian and often corrected their own mistakes, ashamed. But I tried to show them that I was the same as ever, and gradually they were persuaded.

At night I didn't know how to pass the time, my old friends were no longer a group. Pasquale had terrible relations with Antonio and avoided him at all costs. Antonio didn't want to see anyone, partly because he didn't have time (he was constantly being sent here and there by the Solaras), partly

because he didn't know what to talk about: he couldn't talk
about his work and he didn't have a private life. Ada, after the
grocery, either hurried home to take care of her mother and
siblings or was tired and depressed, and went to bed, so that
she hardly ever saw Pasquale, and this made him very anxious.
Carmen now hated everything and everyone, maybe even me:
she hated the job in the new grocery, the Carraccis, Enzo, who
had left her, her brother, who had confined himself to quarreling about it and hadn't beaten him up. Yes, Enzo. Enzo,
finally—whose mother, Assunta, was now seriously ill, and
who, when he wasn't laboring to earn money during the day,
was taking care of her, and at night, too, and yet, surprisingly,
had managed to get his engineer's diploma—Enzo was never
around. I was curious at the news that he had accomplished
that very difficult goal of getting a diploma by studying on his
own. Who would have imagined, I thought. Before returning
to Pisa I made a big effort and persuaded him to take a short
walk. I was full of congratulations for his achievement, but he
had only a disparaging expression. He had reduced his vocabulary so far that I did all the talking, he said almost nothing. I
remember only one phrase, which he uttered before we separated. I hadn't mentioned Lila until that moment, not even a
word. And yet, as if I had talked exclusively about her, he said
suddenly,

"Anyway, Lina is the best mother in the whole neighborhood."

That *anyway* put me in a bad mood. I had never thought of
Enzo as particularly sensitive, but on that occasion I was sure
that, walking beside me, he had *felt*—felt as if I had proclaimed it aloud—the long mute list of wrongs that I attributed
to our friend, as if my body had angrily articulated it without
my knowing.

98.

For love of little Gennaro, Lila began to go out again. She put the baby, dressed in blue or white, in the cumbersome, enormous, and expensive carriage that her brother had given her and walked alone through the new neighborhood. As soon as Rinuccio cried, she went to the grocery and nursed him, amid the enthusiasm of her mother-in-law, the tender compliments of the customers, and the annoyance of Carmen, who lowered her head, and said not a word. Lila fed the baby as soon as he cried. She liked feeling him attached to her, she liked feeling the milk that ran out of her into him, pleasantly emptying her breast. It was the only bond that gave her a sense of well-being, and she confessed in her notebooks that she feared the moment when the baby would separate from her.

When the weather turned nice, she started going to the gardens in front of the church, since in the new neighborhood there were only bare streets with a few bushes or sickly saplings. Passersby stopped to look at the baby and praised him, which pleased her. If she had to change him, she went to the old grocery, where, as soon as she entered, the customers greeted Gennaro warmly. Ada, however, with her smock that was too tidy, the lipstick on her thin lips, her pale face, her neat hair, her commanding ways even toward Stefano, was increasingly impudent, acting like a servant-mistress, and, since she was busy, she did everything possible to let Lila understand that she, the carriage, and the baby were in the way. But Lila took little notice. The surly indifference of her husband confused her more: in private, inattentive but not hostile to the baby, in public, in front of the customers who spoke in tender childish voices and wanted to hold him and kiss him, he didn't even look at him, in fact he made a show of disinterest. Lila went to the rear of the shop, washed Gennaro, quickly dressed him again, and went back to the gardens. There she examined her son lovingly, searching for signs of Nino in his face, and wondering if Stefano had seen what she couldn't.

But soon she forgot about it. In general the days passed over her without provoking the least emotion. She mostly took care of her son, the reading of a book might last weeks, two or three pages a day. In the gardens, if the baby was sleeping, every so often she let herself be distracted by the branches of the trees that were putting out new buds, and she wrote in one of her battered notebooks.

Once she noticed that there was a funeral in the church, and when, with the baby, she went to see, she discovered that it was the funeral of Enzo's mother. She saw him, stiff, pale, but she didn't offer her condolences. Another time she was sitting on a bench with the carriage beside her, bent over a large volume with a green spine, when a skinny old woman appeared before her, leaning on a cane; her cheeks seemed to be sucked into her throat by her very breathing.

"Guess who I am."

Lila had trouble recognizing her, but finally the woman's eyes, in a flash, recalled the imposing Maestra Oliviero. She jumped up full of emotion, about to embrace her, but the teacher drew back in annoyance. Lila then showed her the baby, said proudly, "His name is Gennaro," and since everyone praised her son she expected that the teacher would, too. But Maestra Oliviero completely ignored the child, she seemed interested only in the heavy book that her former pupil was holding, a finger in the pages to mark her place.

"What is it?"

Lila became nervous. The teacher's looks had changed, her voice, everything about her, except her eyes and the sharp tones, the same tones as when she had asked her a question in the classroom. So she, too, showed that she hadn't changed, she answered in a lazy yet aggressive way: "The title is *Ulysses*."

"Is it about the Odyssey?"

"No, it's about how prosaic life is today."

"And so?"

"That's all. It says that our heads are full of nonsense. That we are flesh, blood, and bone. That one person has the same value as another. That we want only to eat, drink, fuck."

The teacher reproached her for that last word, as in school, and Lila posed as an insolent girl, and laughed, so that the old woman became even sterner, asked her how the book was. She answered that it was difficult and she didn't completely understand it.

"Then why are you reading it?"

"Because someone I knew read it. But he didn't like it."

"And you?"

"I do."

"Even if it's difficult?"

"Yes."

"Don't read books that you can't understand, it's bad for you."

"A lot of things are bad for you."

"You're not happy?"

"So-so."

"You were destined for great things."

"I've done them: I'm married and I've had a baby."

"Everyone can do that."

"I'm like everyone."

"You're wrong."

"No, you are wrong, and you always were wrong."

"You were rude as a child and you're rude now."

"Clearly you weren't much of a teacher as far as I'm concerned."

Maestra Oliviero looked at her carefully and Lila read in her face the anxiety of being wrong. The teacher was trying to find in her eyes the intelligence she had seen when she was a child, she wanted confirmation that she hadn't been wrong.

She thought: I have to remove from my face every sign that makes her right, I don't want her to preach to me how I'm wasted. But meanwhile she felt exposed to yet another examination, and, contradictorily, she feared the result. She is discovering that I am stupid, she said to herself, her heart pounding harder, she is discovering that my whole family is stupid, that my forebears were stupid and my descendants will be stupid, that Gennaro will be stupid. She became upset, she put the book in her bag, she grabbed the handle of the carriage, she said nervously that she had to go. Crazy old lady, she still believed she could rap me on the knuckles. She left the teacher in the gardens, small, clutching her cane, consumed by an illness that she would not give in to.

99.

Lila began to be obsessed with stimulating her son's intelligence. She didn't know what books to buy and asked Alfonso to find out from the booksellers. Alfonso brought her a couple of volumes and she dedicated herself to them. In her notebooks I found notes on how she was reading the difficult texts: she struggled to advance, page by page, but after a while she lost the thread, she thought of something else; yet she forced her eye to keep gliding along the lines, her fingers turned the pages automatically, and by the end she had the impression that, even though she hadn't understood, the words had nevertheless entered her brain and inspired thoughts. Starting there, she reread the book and, reading, corrected her thoughts or amplified them, until the text was no longer useful, she looked for others.

Her husband came home at night and found that she hadn't cooked dinner, that she had the baby playing games she had invented herself. He got angry, but she, as had happened for a long time, didn't react. It was as if she didn't hear him, as if the house were inhabited only by her and her son, and when she got up and started cooking she did it not because Stefano was hungry but because she was.

In those months their relationship, after a long period of mutual tolerance, began to deteriorate again. Stefano told her one night that he was tired of her, of the baby, of everything. Another time he said that he had married too young, without understanding what he was doing. But once she answered, "I don't know what I'm doing here, either, I'll take the baby and go," and he, instead of telling her to get out, lost his temper, as he hadn't for a long time, and hit her in front of the child, who stared at her from the blanket on the floor, dazed by the uproar. Her nose dripping blood and Stefano shouting insults at her, Lila turned to her son laughing, told him in Italian (she had been speaking to him only in Italian for a long time), "Papa's playing, we're having fun."

I don't know why, but at a certain point she began to take care of Dino, her nephew. It's possible that it began because she needed to compare Gennaro to another child. Or maybe not, maybe she felt a qualm that she was devoting all her attention only to her own son and it seemed right to take care of her nephew as well. Pinuccia, although she still considered Dino the living proof of the disaster that her life was, and was always yelling at him, and sometimes hit him ("Will you stop it, will you stop it? What do you want from me, you want to make me crazy?"), was resolutely opposed to having Lila take him to her house to play mysterious games with little Gennaro. She said to her angrily: "You take care of raising your son and I'll take care of mine, and instead of wasting time take care of your husband, otherwise you'll lose him." But here Rino intervened.

It was a terrible time for Lila's brother. He fought constantly with his father, who wanted to close the shoe factory because he was sick of working only to enrich the Solaras and, not understanding that it was necessary to go on at all costs, regretted his old workshop. He fought constantly with Michele and Marcello, who treated him like a petulant boy and when the problem was money spoke directly to Stefano. And mainly he fought with Stefano, shouting and insulting, because his brother-in-law wouldn't give him a cent and, according to him, was now negotiating secretly to deliver the whole shoe business into the hands of the Solaras. He fought with Pinuccia, who accused him of having led her to believe he was a big shot when really he was a puppet who could be manipulated by anyone, by his father, by Stefano, by Marcello and Michele. So, when he realized that Stefano was mad at Lila because she was being too much a mamma and not enough a wife, and that Pinuccia wouldn't entrust the child to her sister-in-law for even an hour, he began, defiantly, to take the baby to his sister himself, and since there was less and less work at the shoe factory, he got in the habit of staying, sometimes for hours, in the apartment in the new neighborhood to see what Lila did with Gennaro and Dino. He was fascinated by her maternal patience, by the way the children played, by the way his son, who at home was always crying or sat listlessly in his playpen like a sad puppy, with Lila became eager, quick, seemed happy.

"What do you do to them?" he asked admiringly.

"I make them play."

"My son played before."

"Here he plays and learns."

"Why do you spend so much time on it?"

"Because I read that everything we are is decided now, in the first years of life."

"And is mine doing well?"

"You see him."

"Yes, I see, he's better than yours."

"Mine is younger."

"Do you think Dino is intelligent?"

"All children are, you just have to train them."

"Then train them, Lina, don't get tired of it immediately the way you usually do. Make him very intelligent for me."

But one evening Stefano came home early and especially irritable. He found his brother-in-law sitting on the kitchen floor and, instead of confining himself to a harsh look because of the mess, his wife's lack of interest, the attention given to the children instead of to him, said to Rino that this was his house, that he didn't like seeing him around every day wasting time, that the shoe factory was failing precisely because he was so idle, that the Cerullos were unreliable—in other words, Get out immediately or I'll kick your ass.

There was a commotion. Lila cried that he mustn't speak like that to her brother, Rino threw in his brother-in-law's face everything that until that moment he had only hinted at or had prudently kept to himself. Gross insults flew. The two children, abandoned in the confusion, began grabbing each other's toys, crying, especially the smaller one, who was over-powered by the bigger one. Rino shouted at Stefano, his neck swollen, his veins like electric cables, that it was easy to be the boss with the goods that Don Achille had stolen from half the neighborhood, and added, "You're nothing, you're just a piece of shit, your father at least knew how to commit a crime, you don't even know that."

It was a terrible moment, which Lila watched in terror. Stefano seized Rino by the hips with both hands, like a ballet dancer with his partner, and although they were of the same height, the same build, although Rino struggled and yelled and spit, Stefano picked him up with a prodigious force and hurled him against a wall. Right afterward he took him by the arm and dragged him across the floor to the door, opened it, pulled him to his feet and threw him down the stairs, even though Rino tried to resist, even though Lila had roused herself and was clinging to Stefano, begging him to calm down.

It didn't end there. Stefano whirled around, and she realized that he wanted to do to Dino the same thing he had done to his father, throw him like an object down the stairs. So she flew at him, from behind, and, grabbing his face, scratched him, crying, "He's a child, Ste', he's a child." He froze, and said softly, "I'm fucking fed up with everything, I can't take it anymore."

100.

A complicated period began. Rino stopped going to his sister's house, but Lila didn't want to give up keeping Rinuccio and Dino together, so she got in the habit of going to her brother's house, but in secret from Stefano. Pinuccia endured it, sullenly, and at first Lila tried to explain to her what she was doing: exercises in reactivity, games of skill, she went so far as to confide in her that she would have liked to involve all the neighborhood children. But Pinuccia said simply, "You're a lunatic and I don't give a damn what nonsense you get up to. You want to take the child? You want to kill him, you want to eat him like the witches? Go ahead, I don't want him and I never did, your brother has been the ruin of my life and you are the ruin of my brother's life." Then she cried, "That poor devil is perfectly right to cheat on you."

Lila didn't react.

She didn't ask what that remark meant, in fact she made a careless gesture, one of those gestures that you make to brush away a fly. She took Rinuccio and, although she was sorry to be deprived of her nephew, she did not return.

But in the solitude of her apartment she discovered that she was afraid. She absolutely didn't care if Stefano was paying some whore, in fact she was glad—she didn't have to submit at night when he approached her. But after that remark of

Pinuccia's she began to worry about the baby: if her husband had taken another woman, if he wanted her every day and every hour, he might go mad, he might throw her out. Until that moment the possibility of a definitive break in her marriage had seemed to her a liberation; now instead she was afraid of losing the house, the money, the time, everything that allowed her to bring up the child in the best way.

She hardly slept. Maybe Stefano's rages were not only the sign of a constitutional lack of equilibrium, the bad blood that blew the lid off good-natured habits: maybe he really was in love with someone else, as had happened to her with Nino, and he couldn't stand to stay in the cage of marriage, of paternity, even of groceries and other dealings. She felt she had to make up her mind to confront the situation, if only to control it, and yet she delayed, she gave it up, she counted on the fact that Stefano enjoyed his lover and left her in peace. Ultimately, she thought, I just have to hold out for a couple of years, long enough for the child to grow up and be educated.

She organized her day so that he would always find the house in order, dinner ready, the table set. But, after the scene with Rino, he did not return to his former mildness, he was always disgruntled, always preoccupied.

"What's wrong?"

"Money."

"Money and that's all?"

Stefano got angry: "What does *and that's all* mean?"

For him there was no other problem, in life, but money. After dinner he did the accounts and cursed the whole time: the new grocery wasn't taking in cash as it used to; the Solaras, especially Michele, were acting as if the shoe business were all theirs and the profits weren't to be shared anymore; without saying anything to him, Rino, and Fernando, they were having the old Cerullo models made by cheap shoemakers on the outskirts, and meanwhile they were having new Solara styles

designed by artisans who in fact were simply making tiny variations in Lila's; in this way the small enterprise of his father-in-
law and brother-in-law really was being ruined, dragging him
down with it, the one who had invested in it.

"Understand?"

"Yes."

"So try not to be a pain in the ass."

But Lila wasn't convinced. She had the impression that her
husband was deliberately amplifying problems that were real
but old, in order to hide from her the true, new reasons for his
outbursts and his increasingly explicit hostility toward her. He
blamed her for all sorts of things, and especially for having
complicated his relations with the Solaras. Once he yelled at
her, "What did you do to that bastard Michele, I'd like to
know?"

And she answered, "Nothing."

And he: "It can't be, in every discussion he brings you up
but he screws me: try to talk to him and find out what he
wants, otherwise I ought to smash your faces, both of you."

And Lila, impulsively: "If he wants to fuck me what should
I do, let him fuck me?"

A moment later she was sorry she had said that—sometimes
contempt prevailed over prudence—but now she had done it
and Stefano hit her. The slap counted little, it wasn't even with
his hand open, as usual, he hit her with the tips of his fingers.
Rather, what he said right afterward, disgusted, carried more
weight:

"You read, you study, but you're vulgar: I can't bear people
like you, you make me sick."

From then on he came home later and later. On Sunday,
instead of sleeping until midday as usual, he went out early and
disappeared for the whole day. At the least hint from her of
concrete family problems, he got angry. For example, on the
first hot days she was preoccupied about a vacation at the

beach for Rinuccio, and she asked her husband how they should organize it. He answered: "You take the bus and go to Torregaveta."

She ventured: "Isn't it better to rent a house?"

He: "Why, so you can be a whore from morning to night?"

He left, and didn't return that night.

Everything became clear soon afterward. Lila went to the city with the child, she was looking for a book that she had found quoted in another book, but she couldn't find it. After much searching she went on to Piazza dei Martiri, to ask Alfonso, who was still happily managing the shop, if he could find it. She ran into a handsome young man, very well dressed, one of the handsomest men she had ever seen, his name was Fabrizio. He wasn't a customer, he was a friend of Alfonso's. Lila stayed to talk to him, she discovered that he knew a lot. They discussed literature, the history of Naples, how to teach children, something about which Fabrizio, who worked at the university, was very knowledgeable. Alfonso listened in silence the whole time and when Rinuccio began to whine he calmed him. Then some customers arrived, Alfonso went to take care of them. Lila talked to Fabrizio a little more; it was a long time since she had felt the pleasure of a conversation that excited her. When the young man had to leave, he kissed her with childish enthusiasm, then did the same with Alfonso, two big smacking kisses. He called to her from the doorway: "It was lovely talking to you."

"For me, too."

Lila was sad. While Alfonso continued to wait on customers, she remembered the people she had met in that place, and Nino, the lowered shutter, the shadowy light, the pleasant conversations, the way he arrived secretly, exactly at one, and disappeared at four, after they made love. It seemed to her an imaginary time, a bizarre fantasy, and she looked around uneasily. She didn't feel nostalgia for it, she didn't feel nostalgia for Nino. She felt only that time had passed, that what had been important was important no longer, that the tangle in her head endured and wouldn't come untangled. She took the child and was about to leave when Michele Solara came in.

He greeted her enthusiastically, he played with Gennaro, he said that the baby was just like her. He invited her to a bar, bought her a coffee, decided to take her home in his car. Once they were in the car he said to her, "Leave your husband, right away, today. I'll take you and your son. I've bought a house on the Vomero, in Piazza degli Artisti. If you want I'll drive you there now, I'll show it to you, I took it with you in mind. There you can do what you like: read, write, invent things, sleep, laugh, talk, and be with Rinuccio. I'm interested only in being able to look at you and listen to you."

For the first time in his life Michele expressed himself without his teasing tone of voice. As he drove and talked he glanced at her obliquely, slightly anxious, to see her reactions. Lila stared at the street in front of her the whole way, trying, meanwhile, to take the pacifier out of Gennaro's mouth, she thought he used it too much. But the child pushed her hand away energetically. When Michele stopped—she didn't interrupt him—she asked:

"Are you finished?"

"Yes."

"And Gigliola?"

"What does Gigliola have to do with it? You say yes or no, and then we'll see."

"No, Michè, the answer is no. I didn't want your brother and I don't want you, either. First, because I don't like either of you; and second because you think you can do anything and take anything without regard."

Michele didn't react right away, he muttered something about the pacifier, like: Give it to him, don't let him cry. Then he said, threateningly, "Think hard about it, Lina. Tomorrow you may be sorry and you'll come begging to me."

"I rule it out."

"Yes? Then listen to me."

He revealed to her what everyone knew ("Even your mother, your father, and that shit your brother, but they tell you nothing in order to keep the peace"): Stefano had taken Ada as a lover, and not recently. The thing had begun before the vacation on Ischia. "When you were on vacation," he said, "she went to your house every night." With Lila's return the two had stopped for a while. But they hadn't been able to resist: they had started again, had left each other again, had gone back together when Lila disappeared from the neighborhood. Recently Stefano had rented an apartment on the Rettifilo, they saw each other there.

"Do you believe me?"

"Yes."

"And so?"

So what. Lila was disturbed not so much by the fact that her husband had a lover and that the lover was Ada but by the absurdity of every word and gesture of his when he came to get her on Ischia. The shouts, the blows, the departure returned to her mind.

She said to Michele: "You make me sick, you, Stefano, all of you."

101.

Lila suddenly felt that she was in the right and this calmed her. That evening she put Gennaro to bed and waited for Stefano to come home. He returned a little after midnight, and found her sitting at the kitchen table. Lila looked up from the book she was reading, said she knew about Ada, she knew how long it had been going on, and that it didn't matter to her at all. "What you have done to me I did to you," she said clearly, smiling, and repeated to him—how many times had she said it in the past, two, three?—that Gennaro wasn't his son. She concluded that he could do what he liked, sleep where and with whom he wanted. "The essential thing," she cried suddenly, "is that you don't touch me again."

I don't know what she had in mind, maybe she just wanted to get things out in the open. Or maybe she was prepared for anything and everything. She expected that he would confess, that then he would beat her, chase her out of the house, make her, his wife, be a servant to his lover. She was prepared for every possible aggression and the arrogance of a man who feels that he is the master and has money to buy whatever he wants. Instead, getting to words that would clarify and sanction the failure of their marriage was impossible. Stefano denied it. He said, menacing, but calm, that Ada was merely the clerk in his grocery, that whatever gossip circulated about them had no basis. Then he got mad and told her that if she said that ugly thing about his son again, as God was his witness he would kill her: Gennaro was the image of him, identical, and everyone confirmed it, to keep provoking him on this point was useless. Finally—and this was the most surprising thing—he declared to her, as he had done at other times in the past, without varying the formulas, his love. He said that he would love her forever, because she was his wife, because they had been married before the priest and nothing could separate them. When he came over to kiss her and she pushed him away, he grabbed her, lifted her up, carried her to the bedroom, where the baby's cradle was, tore off everything she had on and entered her forcibly, while she begged him in a low voice, repressing sobs: "Rinuccio will wake up, see us, hear us, please let's go in there."

102.

After that night Lila lost many of the small freedoms that remained to her. Stefano's behavior was completely contradictory. Since his wife now knew of his relationship with Ada, he abandoned all caution. Often he didn't come home to sleep; every other Sunday he went out in the car with his lover. In August, he went on a vacation with her: they went to Stockholm in the sports car, even though officially Ada had gone to Turin, to visit a cousin who worked at Fiat. At the same time, a sick form of jealousy exploded in him: he didn't want his wife to leave the house, he obliged her to do the shopping by phone and if she went out for an hour so that the baby could get some air he interrogated her on whom she had met, whom she had talked to. He felt more a husband than ever and he watched her. It was as if he feared that his betrayal of her authorized her to betray him. What he did in his encounters with Ada on the Rettifilo stirred his imagination and led him to detailed fantasies in which Lila did even more with her lovers. He was afraid of being made ridiculous by a possible unfaithfulness on her part, while he did nothing to hide his own.

He wasn't jealous of all men, he had a hierarchy. Lila quickly understood that in particular he was preoccupied by Michele, by whom he felt cheated in everything and as if kept in a position of permanent subjugation. Although she had never said anything about the time Solara had tried to kiss her, or of his proposal that she become his lover, Stefano had perceived that to insult him by taking his wife was an important move in the process of ruining him in business. But on the other hand the logic of business meant that Lila should behave at least a little cordially. As a result whatever she did he didn't like. At times he pressed her obsessively: "Did you see Michele, did you talk to him, did he ask you to design new shoes?" Sometimes he shouted at her: "You are not even to say hello to that shit, is that clear?" And he opened all her drawers, rummaged through them in search of evidence of her nature as a whore.

To further complicate the situation first Pasquale interfered, then Rino.

Pasquale naturally was the last to know, even after Lila, that his fiancée was Stefano's lover. No one told him, he saw them with his own eyes, late on a Sunday afternoon in September, coming out of a doorway on the Rettifilo embracing. Ada had told him that she had things to do with Melina and couldn't see him. Besides, he was always out at work or at his political meetings, and took little notice of his fiancée's distortions and evasions. Seeing them caused him terrible pain, complicated by the fact that, while his immediate impulse would have been to kill them both, his education as a militant Communist prohibited him. Pasquale had recently become secretary of the neighborhood section of the Party and although in the past, like all the boys we had grown up with, he had classified us when necessary as whores, he now felt—since he kept himself up to date, read *l'Unità*, studied booklets, presided over debates in the section—that he could no longer do that, in fact he made an effort to consider us women not inferior, generally speaking, to men, with our feelings, our ideas, our freedoms. Caught, therefore, between rage and broad-mindedness, the next night, still dirty from work, he went to Ada and told her that he knew everything. She appeared relieved and admitted it, cried, begged forgiveness. When he asked if she had done it for money, she answered that she loved Stefano and that she alone knew what a good and generous and kind person he was. The result was that Pasquale punched the kitchen wall in the Cappuccio house, and returned home weeping, his knuckles sore. Afterward he talked to Carmen all night, the sister and brother suffered together, one because of Ada, the other because of Enzo, whom she couldn't forget. Things really took a bad turn when Pasquale, although he had been betrayed,

decided that he had to defend the dignity of both Ada and
Lila. First he wanted to clarify things, and went to talk to
Stefano; he made a complicated speech whose essence was that
he should leave his wife and set up a household with his lover.
Then he went to Lila and reproached her because she let
Stefano trample on her rights as a wife and her feelings as a
woman. One morning—it was six-thirty—Stefano confronted
him just as he was leaving to go to work and good-naturedly
offered him money so that he would stop bothering him, his
wife, and Ada. Pasquale took the money, counted it, and threw
it away, saying, "I've worked since I was a child, I don't need
you," then, as if to apologize, he added that he had to go, otherwise he would be late and would be fired. But when he had
gone some distance he had a second thought, he turned and
shouted at the grocer, who was picking up the money scattered
on the street: "You are worse than that fascist pig your father."
They fought, savagely, they had to be separated or they would
have murdered each other.

Then came the trouble from Rino. He couldn't bear the fact
that his sister had stopped trying to make Dino a very intelligent child. He couldn't bear the fact that his brother-in-law not
only wouldn't give him a cent but had even laid hands on him.
He couldn't bear the fact that the relation between Stefano and
Ada had become public knowledge, with all the humiliating
consequences for Lila. And he reacted in an unexpected way.
Since Stefano beat Lila, he began to beat Pinuccia. Since
Stefano had a lover, he found a lover. He started, that is, on a
persecution of Stefano's sister that mirrored what his sister was
subjected to by Stefano.

This threw Pinuccia into despair: with tears, with entreaties,
she begged him to end it. But no. If she merely opened her
mouth Rino, blinded by rage, and frightening even Nunzia,
shouted at her: "I should end it? I should calm down? Then go
to your brother and tell him that he should leave Ada, that he

should respect Lina, that we have to be a united family and that
he should give me the money that he and the Solaras have
cheated me of and are cheating me of." The result was that
Pinuccia very often ran out of the house, looking battered, and
went to the grocery, to her brother, and sobbed in front of Ada
and the customers. Stefano dragged her into the rear of the shop
and she listed all her husband's demands, but concluded, "Don't
give that bastard anything, come home now and kill him."

103.

This was more or less the situation when I returned to the
neighborhood for the Easter vacation. I had been living in Pisa
for two and a half years, I was a very brilliant student, and
returning to Naples for the holidays had become an ordeal that
I submitted to in order to avoid arguments with my parents,
especially with my mother. As soon as the train entered the station I became nervous. I feared that some accident would prevent me from returning to the Normale at the end of the vacation: a serious illness that obliged me to enter the chaos of a
hospital, some dreadful event that forced me to stop studying
because the family needed me.

I had been home for a few hours. My mother had just given
me a malicious report on the ugly affairs of Lila, Stefano, Ada,
Pasquale, Rino, on the shoe factory that was about to close, on
how these were times when one year you had money, you
thought you were somebody, you bought a sports car, and the
next year you had to sell everything, you ended up in Signora
Solara's red book and stopped acting like a big shot. And here
she cut off her litany and said to me, "Your friend thought she
really had arrived, the wedding of a princess, the big car, the
new house, and yet today you are much smarter and much
prettier than she is." Then she frowned, to repress her satis-

faction, and handed me a note that, naturally, she had read, even though it was for me. Lila wanted to see me, she invited me to lunch the next day, Holy Friday.

That was not the only invitation I had, the days were full. Soon afterward Pasquale called me from the courtyard and, as if I were descending from an Olympus instead of from my parents' dark house, wanted to expound to me his ideas about women, to tell me how much he was suffering, find out what I thought of his behavior. Pinuccia did the same in the evening, furious with both Rino and Lila. Ada, unexpectedly, did the same the next morning, burning with hatred and a sense of injury.

With all three I assumed a distant tone. I urged Pasquale to be calm, Pinuccia to concern herself with her son, and Ada to try to understand if it was true love. In spite of the superficiality of the words, I have to say that she interested me most. While she spoke, I stared at her as if she were a book. She was the daughter of Melina the madwoman, the sister of Antonio. In her face I recognized her mother, and many features of her brother. She had grown up without a father, exposed to every danger, used to working. She had washed the stairs of our buildings for years, with Melina, whose brain had suddenly stopped functioning. The Solaras had picked her up in their car when she was a girl and I could imagine what they had done to her. It seemed therefore normal that she should fall in love with Stefano, the courteous boss. She loved him, she told me, they loved each other. "Tell Lina," she said, her eyes shining with passion, "that one cannot command one's heart, and that if she is the wife I am the one who has given and gives Stefano everything, every attention and feeling that a man could want, and soon children, too, and so he is mine, he no longer belongs to her."

I understood that she wanted to get everything possible for herself, Stefano, the grocery stores, the money, the house, the cars. And I thought it was her right to fight that battle, which we were all fighting, one way or another. I tried to make her calm down, because she was very pale, her eyes were inflamed. And I was happy to hear how grateful she was to me, I was pleased to be consulted like a seer, handing out advice in a good Italian that confused her, as it did Pasquale and Pinuccia. Here, I thought sarcastically, is the use of history exams, classical philology, linguistics, and the thousands of file cards with which I drill myself rigorously: to soothe them for a few hours. They considered me impartial, without malicious feelings or passions, sterilized by study. And I accepted the role that they assigned me without mentioning my own suffering, my audaciousness, the times I had risked everything by letting Franco come to my room or sneaking into his, the vacation we had taken by ourselves in Versilia, living together as if we were married. I felt pleased with myself.

But as the time for lunch approached, the pleasure gave way to uneasiness, I went to Lila's unwillingly. I was afraid that she would find a way to restore in a flash the old hierarchy, causing me to lose faith in my choices. I feared that she would point out Nino's features in little Gennaro to remind me that the toy that was supposed to be mine had fallen to her. But it wasn't like that. Rinuccio—so she called him more and more frequently—touched me immediately: he was a handsome dark boy, and Nino hadn't yet emerged in his face and body, his features recalled Lila and even Stefano, as if all three had produced him. As for her, I felt that she had rarely been more fragile than she was then. At the mere sight of me her eyes shone with tears and her whole body trembled, I had to hold her tight to quiet her.

I noticed that in order not to make a bad impression she had combed her hair in a hurry, in a hurry had put on a little lipstick and a dress of pearl-gray rayon from the time of her engagement, that she wore shoes with a heel. She was still beautiful, but it was as if the bones of her face had become larger, her eyes smaller, and under the skin blood no longer circulated but an opaque liquid. She was very thin, embracing her I felt her bones, the clinging dress showed her swollen stomach.

At first she pretended that everything was fine. She was happy that I was enthusiastic about the baby, she liked the way I played with him, she wanted to show me all the things that Rinuccio could say and do. She began, in an anxious way that was unfamiliar, to pour out the terminology she had picked up from the chaotic reading she had done. She cited authors I had never heard of, made her son show off in exercises that she had invented for him. I noticed that she had developed a sort of tic, an expression of her mouth: she opened it suddenly and then pressed her lips together as if to contain the emotion produced by the things she was saying. Usually the expression was accompanied by a reddening of her eyes, a rosy light that the contraction of her lips, like a spring mechanism, promptly helped to reabsorb. She kept repeating that if she had dedicated herself assiduously to every child in the neighborhood, in a generation everything would change, there would no longer be the smart and the incompetent, the good and the bad. Then she looked at her son and again burst out crying. "He's ruined the books," she said between her tears, as if it were Rinuccio who had done it, and she showed them to me, torn, ripped in half. I had trouble understanding that the guilty person was not the little boy but her husband. "He's got in the habit of rummaging among my things," she murmured, "he doesn't want me to have even a thought of my own and if he discovers that I've hidden even some insignificant thing he beats me." She climbed up on a chair and took from on top of the wardrobe in the bedroom a metal box, and handed it to me. "Here's everything that happened with Nino," she said, "and so many thoughts that have gone through my head in these years, and also things of mine and yours that we haven't said.

Take it away, I'm afraid that he'll find it and start reading. But I don't want him to, they aren't things for him, they aren't for anyone, not even for you."

104.

I took the box unwillingly, I thought: where will I put it, what can I do with it. We sat at the table. I marveled that Rinuccio ate by himself, that he used his own small set of wooden implements, that, after his initial shyness passed, he spoke to me in Italian without mangling the words, that he answered each of my questions directly, with precision, and asked me questions in turn. Lila let me talk to her son, she ate almost nothing, she stared at her plate, absorbed. At the end, when I was about to go, she said:

"I don't remember anything about Nino, about Ischia, about the shop in Piazza dei Martiri. And yet it seemed to me that I loved him more than myself. It doesn't even interest me to know what happened to him, where he went."

I thought she was sincere, and said nothing of what I knew.

"Infatuations," I said, "have this good thing about them: after a while they pass."

"Are you happy?"

"Pretty much."

"How beautiful your hair is."

"Oh well."

"You have to do me another favor."

"What?"

"I have to leave this house before Stefano, without even realizing it, kills me and the child."

"You're worrying me."

"You're right to be worried, I'm afraid."

"Tell me what to do."

"Go to Enzo. Tell him that I tried but I couldn't make it."

"I don't understand."

"It's not important for you to understand: you have to go back to Pisa, you have your things. Tell him this, that's all: *Lina tried but she couldn't make it.*"

She went with me to the door with the child in her arms. She said to her son, "Rino, say goodbye to Aunt Lenù."

The baby smiled, waved his hand goodbye.

105.

Before I left I went to see Enzo. When I said to him, "*Lina told me to tell you that she tried but she couldn't make it,*" not even the shadow of an emotion crossed his face, so I thought that the message left him completely indifferent. "Things are bad," I added. "On the other hand I don't really know what can be done." He pressed his lips together, assumed a grave expression. We said goodbye.

On the train I opened the metal box, even though I had sworn not to. There were eight notebooks. From the first lines I began to feel bad. In Pisa, the bad feeling increased, over days, over months. Every word of Lila's diminished me. Every sentence, even sentences written when she was still a child, seemed to empty out mine, not the ones of that time but the ones now. And yet every page ignited my thoughts, my ideas, my pages as if until that moment I had lived in a studious but ineffectual stupor. Those notebooks I memorized, and in the end they made me feel that the world of the Normale—the friends, male and female, who respected me, the affectionate looks of those professors who encouraged me to constantly do more—was part of a universe that was too protected and thus too predictable, compared with that tempestuous world that, in the conditions of life in the neighborhood, Lila had been able to explore in her hurried lines, on pages that were crumpled and stained. Every past effort of mine seemed without meaning. I was frightened, for months school went badly. I was alone, Franco Mari had lost his place at the Normale, I couldn't pull myself out of the feeling of pettiness that had overwhelmed me. At a certain point it became clear that soon I, too, would get a bad mark and be sent home. So one evening in late autumn, without a precise plan, I went out carrying the metal box. I stopped on the Solferino bridge and threw it into the Arno.

106.

During my last year in Pisa the perspective from which I had experienced the first three changed. I was possessed by an ungrateful dislike of the city, my classmates, the teachers, the exams, the frigid days, the political meetings on warm evenings near the Baptistery, the films at the film forum, the entire unchanging urban space: the Timpano, the Lungarno Pacinotti, Via XXIV May, Via San Frediano, Piazza dei Cavalieri, Via Consoli del Mare, Via San Lorenzo, routes that were the same and yet alien even when the baker said hello and the newspaper seller chatted about the weather, alien in the voices that I had nevertheless forced myself to imitate from the start, alien in the color of the stone and the plants and the signs and the clouds or sky.

I don't know if it was because of Lila's notebooks. Certainly, right after reading them and long before throwing away the box that contained them, I became disenchanted. My first impression, that of finding myself part of a fearless battle, passed. The trepidation at every exam and the joy of passing it with the highest marks had faded. Gone was the pleasure of re-educating my voice, my gestures, my way of dressing and walking, as if I were competing for the prize of best disguise, the mask worn so well that it was *almost* a face.

Suddenly I was aware of that *almost*. Had I made it? Almost. Had I torn myself away from Naples, the neighborhood? Almost. Did I have new friends, male and female, who came from cultured backgrounds, often more cultured than the one that Professor Galiani and her children belonged to? Almost. From one exam to the next, had I become a student who was well received by the solemn professors who questioned me? Almost. Behind the *almost* I seemed to see how things stood. I was afraid. I was afraid as I had been the day I arrived in Pisa. I was scared of anyone who had that culture without the *almost*, with casual confidence.

There were many people at the Normale who did. It wasn't just students who passed the exams brilliantly, in Latin or Greek or history. They were youths—almost all male, as were the outstanding professors and the illustrious names who had passed through that institution—who excelled because they knew, without apparent effort, the present and future use of the labor of studying. They knew because of the families they came from or through an instinctive orientation. They knew how a newspaper or a journal was put together, how a publishing house was organized, what a radio or television office was, how a film originates, what the university hierarchies were, what there was beyond the borders of our towns or cities, beyond the Alps, beyond the sea. They knew the names of the people who counted, the people to be admired and those to be despised. I, on the other hand, knew nothing, to me anyone whose name was printed in a newspaper or a book was a god. If someone said to me with admiration or with resentment: that's so-and-so, that's the son of so-and-so, that's that other so-and-so's granddaughter, I was silent or I pretended to know. I perceived, of course, that they were *truly* important names, and yet I had never heard them, I didn't know what they had done that was important, I didn't know the map of prestige. For example, I came to my exams very well prepared, but if the professor were suddenly to ask me, "Do you know from what works I derive the authority on the basis of which I teach this subject in this university?" I wouldn't know what to answer. But the others knew. So I moved among them fearful of saying and doing the wrong things.

When Franco Mari fell in love with me, that fear diminished. He instructed me, I learned to move in his wake. Franco was lively, attentive to others, insolent, bold. He felt so sure of having read the right books and thus of being right that he always spoke with authority. I had learned to express myself in private and, more rarely, in public, relying on his reputation. And I was successful, or at least was becoming so. Strengthened by his certainties, I was at times bolder than he, at times more effective. But, although I had made a lot of progress, I still worried that I wasn't up to it, that I would say the wrong thing, reveal how ignorant and inexperienced I was in precisely the things that everyone knew. And as soon as Franco, in spite of himself, went out of my life, the fear regained power. I had had the proof of what, deep down, I already knew. His wealth, his upbringing, his reputation, well known among the students, as a young militant on the left, his sociability, even his courage when he delivered carefully measured speeches against powerful people within and outside the university—all this had given him an aura that automatically extended to me, as his fiancée or girlfriend or companion, as if the pure and simple fact that he loved me were the public sanctioning of my talents. But as soon as he lost his place at the Normale his merits faded, and no longer shone on me. The students from good families stopped inviting me to Sunday outings and parties. Some began making fun of my Neapolitan accent again. The things he had given me were no longer in fashion, looked dated. I had quickly understood that Franco, his presence in my life, had masked my true condition but hadn't changed it, I hadn't really succeeded in fitting in. I was one of those who labored day and night, got excellent results, were even treated with congeniality and respect, but would never carry off with the proper manner the high level of those studies. I would always be afraid: afraid of saying the wrong thing, of using an exaggerated tone, of dressing unsuitably, of revealing petty feelings, of not having interesting thoughts.

107.

I have to say that it was a depressing period for other reasons as well. Everyone knew, in Piazza dei Cavalieri, that I went to Franco's room at night, that I had gone alone with him to Paris, to Versilia, and this had given me the reputation of an easy girl. It's complicated to explain what it cost me to adapt to the idea of sexual freedom that Franco ardently supported; I myself hid the difficulty to seem free and open-minded to him. Nor could I repeat in public the ideas that he had instilled in me as if they were gospel, that is to say that half virgins were the worst kind of woman, petit bourgeois who preferred to give you their ass than to do things properly. And I couldn't say that I had a friend, in Naples, who at sixteen was already married, who at eighteen had taken a lover, who had become pregnant by him, who had returned to her husband, who would do God knows what else—that, in other words, going to bed with Franco seemed to me a small thing, compared with Lila's turbulent affairs. I had had to put up with malicious remarks from the girls, crude ones from the boys, their persistent looks at my large bosom. I had had to reject bluntly the bluntness with which some offered to replace my former boyfriend. I had to resign myself to the fact that the youths responded to my rejections with vulgar remarks. I kept on with clenched teeth, I said to myself: it will end.

Then, one afternoon, as I was leaving a crowded café on Via

San Frediano with two girlfriends, one of my rejected suitors shouted at me, seriously, in front of everyone, "Hey, Naples, remember to bring me the blue sweater I left in your room." Laughter, I went out without responding. But I soon realized that I was being followed by a boy I had already noticed in classes because of his peculiar appearance. He was neither a shadowy young intellectual like Nino nor an easygoing youth like Franco. He wore glasses, was very shy, solitary, with a tangled mass of black hair, a clearly solid body, crooked feet. He followed me to the college, then finally he called to me: "Greco."

Whoever he was, he knew my surname. I stopped out of politeness. The young man introduced himself, Pietro Airota, and made an embarrassed, confused speech. He said that he was ashamed of his companions but that he also hated himself because he had been cowardly and hadn't intervened.

"Intervened to do what?" I asked sarcastically, but at the same time amazed that someone like him, stooping, with thick glasses, that ridiculous hair, and the aura, the language of someone who is always at his books, felt it his duty to be the knight in shining armor like the boys of the neighborhood.

"To defend your good name."

"I don't have a good name."

He stammered something that seemed to me a mixture of apology and goodbye, and went off.

The next day I looked for him, I began to sit next to him in classes, we took long walks together. He surprised me: he had already begun to work on his thesis, for example, and like me he was doing it in Latin literature; unlike me, he didn't say "thesis," he said "work"; and once or twice he said "book," a book that he was finishing and that he would publish right after graduating. Work, book? What was he saying? Although he was twenty-two he had a thoughtful tone, he resorted continuously to the most refined quotations, he acted as if he already had a position at the Normale or some other university.

"Will you really publish your thesis?" I asked once, in disbelief.

He looked at me with equal amazement: "If it's good, yes."

"Are all theses that come out well published?"

"Why not."

He was studying Bacchic rites, I the fourth book of the Aeneid. I said, "Maybe Bacchus is more interesting than Dido."

"Everything is interesting if you know how to work on it."

We never talked about everyday things, or the possibility that the U.S.A. would give nuclear arms to West Germany, or whether Fellini was better than Antonioni, as Franco had accustomed me to do, but only about Latin literature, Greek literature. Pietro had a prodigious memory: he knew how to connect texts that were very unlike one another and he quoted them as if he were looking at them, but without being pedantic, without pretension, as if it were the most natural thing between two people who were devoted to their studies. The more time I spent with him, the more I realized that he was really smart, smart in a way that I would never be, because where I was cautious only out of fear of making a mistake, he demonstrated a sort of easy inclination to deliberate thought, to assertions that were never rash.

Even after I'd been walking with him a couple of times on Corso Italia or between the Duomo and the Camposanto, I saw that things around me changed again. One morning a girl I knew said to me, with friendly resentment, "What do you do to men? Now you've conquered the son of Airota."

I didn't know who Airota the father was, but certainly my classmates became respectful again: I was invited to parties or dinner. At a certain point I even had the suspicion that they talked to me because I brought Pietro out with me, since he generally kept to himself, absorbed in his work. I began to ask questions, all directed toward finding out what the merits of my new friend's father were. I discovered that he taught Greek literature at the university in Genoa but was also a prominent figure in the socialist party. This information constrained me, I was afraid of saying or having said in Pietro's presence things that were naïve or wrong. While he went on talking to me about his thesis-book, I, fearful of saying something stupid, talked less about mine.

One Sunday he arrived at the college out of breath, he wanted me to have lunch with his family, father, mother, and sister, who had come to see him. I was immediately apprehensive, I dressed up as well as I could. I thought: I'll make a mistake with subjunctives, they'll find me clumsy, they're grand people, they'll have a big car and a driver, what will I say, I'll look like an idiot. But as soon as I saw them I relaxed. Professor Airota was a man of medium height in a rather rumpled gray suit, he had a broad face that showed signs of weariness, large eyeglasses: when he took off his hat I saw that he was completely bald. Adele, his wife, was a thin woman, not pretty but refined, elegant without pretension. The car was like the Solaras' Fiat 1100, before they bought the Giulietta, and, I discovered, it was not a chauffeur who drove it from Genoa to Pisa but Mariarosa, Pietro's sister, who was attractive, with intelligent eyes, and who immediately hugged and kissed me as if we had been friends for a long time.

"Do you always drive here from Genoa?" I asked.

"Yes, I like driving."

"Was it hard to get a license?"

"Not at all."

She was twenty-four and was working for a professor in the art-history department at the University of Milan, she was studying Piero della Francesca. She knew everything about me, that is, everything her brother knew, my scholarly interests and that was all. Professor Airota and his wife knew the same things.

I spent a wonderful morning with them; they put me at my

ease. Unlike Pietro, his father, mother, and sister conversed on a wide variety of subjects. At lunch, in the restaurant of the hotel where they were staying, Professor Airota and his daughter had, for example, affectionate skirmishes on political subjects that I had heard about from Pasquale, from Nino, and from Franco but of whose substance I knew almost nothing. Arguments like: you've been trapped by inter-class collaboration; you call it a trap, I call it mediation; mediation in which the Christian Democrats always and only win; the politics of the center left is difficult; if it's difficult, go back to being socialists; you're not reforming a thing; in our place what would you do; revolution, revolution, and revolution; revolution is taking Italy out of the Middle Ages, without us socialists in the government, the students who talk about sex in school would be in jail and so would those who distribute pacifist leaflets; I want to see how you'd manage with the Atlantic Pact; we were always against the war and against all imperialism; you govern with the Christian Democrats, but will you stay anti-American?

Like that, a swift back and forth: a polemical exercise that they both obviously enjoyed, maybe a friendly habit of long standing. I recognized in them, father and daughter, what I had never had and, I now knew, would always lack. What was it? I wasn't able to say precisely: the training, perhaps, to feel that the questions of the world were deeply connected to me; the capacity to feel them as crucial and not purely as information to display at an exam, in view of a good grade; a mental conformation that didn't reduce everything to my own individual battle, to the effort to be successful. Mariarosa was kind, and so was her father; their tones were controlled, without a trace of the verbal excesses of Armando, Professor Galiani's son, or of Nino; and yet they injected warmth into political formulas that on other occasions had seemed to me cold, remote, to be used only in an attempt not to make a bad impression. Following each other in rapid succession, they moved on, without interruption, to the bombing of North Vietnam, to the student revolts on various campuses, to the many breeding grounds of anti-imperialist struggle in Latin America and Africa. And the daughter now seemed to be more up to date than the father. How many things Mariarosa knew, she talked as if she had first-hand information, so that Airota at a certain point looked at his wife ironically, and Adele said to her, "You're the only one who hasn't chosen a dessert yet."

"I'll have chocolate cake," she said, breaking off with a graceful frown.

I looked at her in admiration. She drove a car, lived in Milan, taught at the university, stood up to her father without resentment. I, instead: I was frightened by the idea of opening my mouth, and, at the same time, humiliated by staying silent. I couldn't contain myself, I said hyperbolically, "The Americans, after Hiroshima and Nagasaki, should be brought to trial for crimes against humanity."

Silence. The whole family looked at me. Mariarosa exclaimed Bravo!, she took my hand, shook it. I felt encouraged and immediately bubbled over with words, scraps of old phrases memorized at various times. I talked about planning and rationalization, the socialist-Christian Democratic precipice, about neocapitalism, about organizational structures, about Africa, Asia, primary school, Piaget, collusion of the police and the courts, fascist rot in every manifestation of the state. I was muddled, breathless. My heart was pounding, I forgot who I was with and where I was. Yet I felt around me an atmosphere of increasing approval, and I was happy to have expressed myself, I seemed to have made a good impression. I was also glad that no one in that nice little family had asked me, as happened frequently, where I came from, what my father did, and my mother. I was I, I, I.

I stayed with them, talking, in the afternoon, too. And in the evening we all went for a walk, before going to dinner. At every step Professor Airota met people he knew. Even two of the university professors, with their wives, stopped to greet him warmly.

108.

But already the next day I felt bad. The time spent with Pietro's family had given me further proof that the hard work of the Normale was a mistake. Merit was not enough, something else was required, and I didn't have it nor did I know how to learn it. How embarrassing that jumble of agitated words was, without logical rigor, without composure, without irony, things that Mariarosa, Adele, Pietro were capable of. I had learned the methodical persistence of the researcher who checks even the commas, that, yes, and I proved it during exams, or with the thesis that I was writing. But in fact I remained naïve, even if almost too cultured, I didn't have the armor to advance serenely as they did. Professor Airota was an immortal god who had given his children magical weapons before the battle. Mariarosa was invincible. And Pietro perfect in his overcultivated courtesy. I? I could only remain near them, shine in their radiance.

Anxiety not to lose Pietro seized me. I sought him out, I clung to him, I was affectionate. But I waited in vain for him to declare himself. One night I kissed him, on the cheek, and finally he kissed me on the mouth. We began to meet in secluded places, at night, waiting for darkness. I touched him, he touched me, he didn't want to penetrate me. It was as if I had returned to the time of Antonio, and yet the difference was enormous. There was the excitement of going out in the evening with Airota's son, getting strength from him. Every so often I thought of calling Lila from a public telephone: I wanted to tell her that I had this new boyfriend and that almost certainly our graduation theses would be published, they would become books, just like real books, with the cover, the title, the name. I wanted to tell her it was possible that both he and I would teach in the university, his sister Mariarosa at twenty-four was already doing so. I also wanted to tell her: you're right, Lila, if they teach you properly from childhood, as an adult you have less trouble with everything, you are someone who seems to have been born already knowing. But in the end I gave it up. Why telephone her? To listen silently to her story? Or, if she let me speak, what would I tell her? I knew very well that what would surely happen to Pietro would never happen to me. Most important, I knew that, like Franco, he would soon disappear, and that after all it was better that way, because I didn't love him, I was with him in the dark alleys, in the meadows, only so that I would feel the fear less.

109.

Around Christmas vacation in 1966 I got a very bad flu. I telephoned a neighbor of my parents—finally even in the old neighborhood many people had a telephone—and told them I wasn't coming home for the vacation. Then I sank into desolate days of fever and coughing, while the college emptied, became silent. I ate nothing, I even had trouble drinking. One morning when I had fallen into an exhausted half-sleep, I heard loud voices, in my dialect, as when in the neighborhood the women leaned out the windows, arguing. From the darkest depths of my mind came the known footsteps of my mother. She didn't knock, she opened the door, she entered, loaded down with bags.

It was unimaginable. She had hardly ever left the neighborhood, at most to go to the center of the city. Outside of Naples, as far as I knew, she had never been. And yet she had got on the train, had traveled all night, and had come to my room to heap on me Christmas food that she had prepared ahead of time, quarrelsome gossip in a loud voice, orders that were supposed, as if by magic, to bring me back to health and allow me to leave with her in the evening: because she had to go, at home she had other children and my father.

She depleted me more than the fever. She shouted so much, moving objects, carelessly rearranging things, that I was afraid the dean would come. At one point I felt I was fainting, I closed my eyes, hoping she wouldn't follow me into the nauseating darkness I was being dragged into. But she didn't stop at anything. Always in motion through the room, helpful and aggressive, she told me about my father, my siblings, the neighbors, friends, and, naturally, about Carmen, Ada, Gigliola, Lila.

I tried not to listen but she pursued me: *Do you understand what she did, do you understand what happened?* And she shook me, touching an arm or a foot buried under the covers. I discovered that, in the state of fragility caused by the illness, I was more sensitive to everything I couldn't stand about her. I got angry—and I told her this—at how, with every word, she wanted to demonstrate that all my contemporaries, compared to me, had failed. "Stop it," I muttered. She paid no attention, she kept repeating, *You, on the other hand.*

But what wounded me most was to sense behind her pride as a mother the fear that things would suddenly change and I would again lose points, no longer give her occasion to boast. She did not much trust the stability of the world. So she force-fed me, dried the sweat, made me take my temperature I don't know how many times. Was she afraid I would die, depriving her of my trophy existence? Was she afraid that, being ill, I would give in, be in some way demoted, have to return home without glory? She spoke obsessively about Lila. She was so insistent that I suddenly perceived how highly she had regarded her since she was a child. Even she, I thought, even my mother, realized that Lila is better than me and now she is surprised that I've left her behind, she believes and doesn't believe it, she's afraid of losing her position as *luckiest mother in the neighborhood*. Look how combative she is, look at the arrogance in her eyes. I felt the energy she gave off, and I thought that her lameness had required her to have greater strength than normal, in order to survive, imposing on her the ferocity with which she moved inside and outside the family. What, on the other hand, was my father? A weak little man, trained to be obliging, to hold out his hand discreetly to pocket small tips: certainly he would never have managed to overcome all the obstacles and arrive at this austere building. She had done it.

When she left and the silence returned, on the one hand I felt relieved, on the other, because of the fever, I was moved. I thought of her alone, asking every passerby if this was the right direction for the train station, her, walking, with her lame leg, in an unknown city. She would never spend the money for a bus, she was careful not to waste even five lire. But she would make it: she would buy the right ticket and take the right trains, traveling overnight on the uncomfortable seats, or even standing, all the way to Naples. There, after another long walk, she would arrive in the neighborhood, and start polishing and cooking, she would cut up the eel, and prepare the *insalata di rinforzo*, and the chicken broth, and the *struffoli*, without resting for a moment, filled with rage, but consoling herself by saying, in some part of her brain, "Lenuccia is better than Gigliola, than Carmen, than Ada, than Lina, than all of them."

110.

It was because of Gigliola, according to my mother, that Lila's situation had become even more intolerable. Everything

began on a Sunday in April when the daughter of Spagnuolo
the pastry maker invited Ada to the parish cinema. The following evening, after the stores closed, she again went to her
and said, "What are you doing all alone? Come watch television at my parents' house and bring along Melina." One thing
led to another, and she ended up dragging her along on
evening outings with Michele Solara, her boyfriend. Five of
them often went to the pizzeria: Gigliola, her younger brother,
Michele, Ada, Antonio. The pizzeria was in the center, at Santa
Lucia. Michele drove, Gigliola sat beside him, all dressed up,
and in the back seat were Lello, Antonio, and Ada.

Antonio didn't like spending his free time with his boss,
and at first he tried to tell Ada that he was busy. But when
Gigliola reported that Michele was angry that he didn't show
up, he sank his head between his shoulders and obeyed. The
conversation was almost always between the two girls; Michele
and Antonio didn't exchange a word, in fact Solara often left
the table and went to talk to the owner of the pizzeria, with
whom he had various dealings. Gigliola's brother ate pizza and
was quietly bored.

The girls' preferred subject was the love between Ada and
Stefano. They talked about the presents he had given her and
was giving her, of the wonderful trip to Stockholm in August
the year before (how many lies Ada had had to tell poor
Pasquale), how in the grocery he treated her better than if she
had been the owner. Ada softened, she talked and talked.
Gigliola listened and every so often said things like "The
Church, if you want, can annul a marriage."

Ada interrupted, scowling, "I know, but it's difficult."

"Difficult, not impossible. You have to go to the Sacra
Rota."

"What's that?"

"I don't know exactly, but the Sacra Rota can wipe out
everything."

416 · ELENA FERRANTE

"You're sure?"

"I read it."

Ada was very happy about that unexpected friendship. She had been living her story in silence, among many fears and much remorse. Now she discovered that talking about it did her good, proved she was right, erased her guilt. The only thing that spoiled her relief was her brother's hostility, and in fact when they got home all they did was quarrel. Once Antonio nearly hit her, he shouted at her, "Why the fuck do you tell your business to everybody? Do you realize you look like a whore and I'm the pimp?"

She said in the most antagonistic tone she was capable of: "You know why Michele Solara comes to dinner with us?"

"Because he's my boss."

"Oh yes, sure."

"Then why?"

"Because I'm with Stefano, who's important. If I waited for you, the daughter of Melina I would be and the daughter of Melina I would remain."

Antonio lost control, he said: "You're not *with* Stefano, you're Stefano's *whore*."

Ada burst into tears. "It's not true, Stefano loves only me."

One night things got even worse. They were at home, dinner was over. Ada was doing the dishes, Antonio was staring into space, their mother was humming an old song while she swept the floor too energetically. At some point Melina accidentally swept the broom over her daughter's feet. It was terrible. There was at the time a superstition—I don't know if it still exists—that if you sweep the broom over the feet of an unmarried girl she'll never get married. Ada saw her future in a flash. She leaped back as if she had been touched by a cockroach and the plate she was holding fell to the floor.

"You swept over my feet," she shrieked, leaving her mother astonished.

"She didn't do it on purpose," Antonio said.

"She did do it on purpose. You don't want me to get married, it's too useful for you to have me work for you, you want to keep me here my whole life."

Melina tried to embrace her daughter, saying no no, but Ada repulsed her rudely, so that she retreated, bumped into a chair, and fell on the floor amid the fragments of the broken plate.

Antonio rushed to help his mother, but Melina now was screaming in fear, fear of her son, of her daughter, of the things around her. And Ada screamed louder in return, saying, "I'll show you who I'm going to marry, and soon, because if Lina doesn't get out of the way by herself, I'll get her out, and off the face of the earth."

Antonio left the house, slamming the door. More desperate than usual, in the following days he tried to escape from that new tragedy in his life, he made an effort to be deaf and dumb, he avoided going past the old grocery, and if by chance he ran into Stefano Carracci he looked in another direction before the wish to beat him up overpowered him. His mind was troubled, he couldn't understand what was right and what wasn't. Had it been right not to hand Lila over to Michele? Had it been right to tell Enzo to take her home? If Lila hadn't returned to her husband, would his sister's situation be different? Everything happens by chance, he reasoned, without good and without ill. But at that point his brain got stuck and on the first occasion, as if to free himself from bad dreams, he went back to quarreling with Ada. He shouted at her, "He is a married man, bitch: he has a small child, you are worse than our mother, you don't have any sense of things." Ada then went to Gigliola, confided to her: "My brother is crazy, my brother wants to kill me."

So it was that one afternoon Michele called Antonio and sent him to do a long-term job in Germany. He didn't object, in fact he obeyed willingly, he left without saying goodbye to

his sister or even to Melina. He took it for granted that in a foreign country, among people who spoke like the Nazis at the
church cinema, he would be stabbed, or shot, and he was content. He considered it more tolerable to be murdered than to
continue to observe the suffering of his mother and Ada without being able to do anything.

The only person he wanted to see before setting off on the
train was Enzo. He found him busy: at the time he was trying
to sell everything, the mule, the cart, his mother's little shop, a
garden near the railroad. He wanted to give part of the proceeds
to a maiden aunt who had offered to take care of his siblings.

"And you?" Antonio asked.

"I'm looking for a job."

"You want to change your life?"

"Yes."

"It's a good thing."

"It's a necessity."

"I, on the other hand, am what I am."

"Nonsense."

"It's true, but it's all right. Now I have to leave and I don't
know when I'll be back. Every so often, please, could you cast
an eye on my mother, my sister, and the children?"

"If I stay in the neighborhood, yes."

"We were wrong, Enzù, we shouldn't have taken Lina
home."

"Maybe."

"It's all a mess, you never know what to do."

"Yes."

"Bye."

"Bye."

They didn't even shake hands. Antonio went to Piazza
Garibaldi and got the train. He had a long, difficult journey,
night and day, with many angry voices running through his
veins. He felt extremely tired after just a few hours, his feet

were tingling; he hadn't traveled since he returned from military service. Every so often he got out to get a drink of water from a fountain, but he was afraid the train would leave. Later he told me that at the station in Florence he felt so depressed that he thought: I'll stop here and go to Lenuccia.

111.

With the departure of Antonio the bond between Gigliola and Ada became very tight. Gigliola suggested to her what the daughter of Melina had had in mind for some time, that is, that she shouldn't wait any longer, the matrimonial situation of Stefano should be resolved. "Lina has to get out of that house," she said, "and you have to go in: if you wait too long, the enchantment will be broken and you'll lose everything, even the job in the grocery, because she'll regain ground and force Stefano to get rid of you." Gigliola went so far as to confide to her that she was speaking from experience, she had the same problem with Michele. "If I wait for him to make up his mind to marry me," she whispered, "I'll get old; so I'm tormenting him: either we marry by the spring of 1968 or I'm leaving and fuck him."

Thus Ada went on to envelop Stefano in a net of true, sticky desire that made him feel special, and meanwhile she murmured between kisses, "You have to decide, Ste', either me or her; I'm not saying you have to throw her out in the street with the child, that's your son, you have responsibilities; but do what lots of actors and important people do today: give her some money and that's it. Everybody in the neighborhood knows that I'm your real wife, so I want to stay with you, always."

Stefano said yes and hugged her tight in the uncomfortable narrow bed on the Rettifilo, but then he didn't do much, except return home to Lila and yell, because there were no clean socks, or because he had seen her talking to Pasquale or someone else.

At that point Ada began to despair. One Sunday morning she ran into Carmen, who spoke to her in accusatory tones of the working conditions in the two groceries. One thing led to another, they began to talk venomously about Lila, whom both of them, for different reasons, considered the origin of their troubles. Finally Ada couldn't resist and recounted her romantic situation, forgetting that Carmen was the sister of her former fiancé. And Carmen, who couldn't wait to be part of the network of gossip, listened willingly, often interrupted to fan the flames, tried with her advice to do as much damage to Ada, who had betrayed Pasquale, and to Lila, who had betrayed her. But, I should say, apart from the resentments, there was the pleasure of having something to do with a person, her childhood friend, who found herself in the role of lover of a married man. And although since childhood we girls of the neighborhood had wanted to become wives, growing up we had almost always sympathized with the lovers, who seemed to us more spirited, more combative, and, especially, more modern. On the other hand we hoped that the legitimate wife would get gravely ill and die (in general she was a very wicked or at least unfaithful woman), and that the lover would stop being a lover and crown her dream of love by becoming a wife. We were, in short, on the side of the violation, but only because it reaffirmed the value of the rule. As a result Carmen, although amid much devious advice, ended up by passionately taking Ada's side, her feelings were genuine, and one day she said to her, in all honesty: "You can't go on like this, you have to get rid of that bitch, marry Stefano, give him your own children. Ask the Solaras if they know anyone in the Sacra Rota."

Ada immediately added Carmen's suggestions to Gigliola's and one night, in the pizzeria, she turned directly to Michele: "Can you get to this Sacra Rota?"

He answered ironically, "I don't know, I can ask, one always finds a friend. But just take what's yours, that's the most urgent thing. And don't worry about anything: if someone gives you trouble, send him to me."

Michele's words were very important, Ada felt supported, never in her life had she felt so surrounded by approval. Yet Gigliola's hammering, Carmen's advice, that unexpected promise of protection on the part of an important male authority, and even her anger at the fact that in August Stefano wouldn't take a trip abroad as he had the year before but had only gone to the Sea Garden a few times, were not enough to push her to attack. It took a true, concrete new fact: the discovery that she was pregnant.

The pregnancy made Ada furiously happy, but she kept the news to herself, she didn't speak of it even to Stefano. One afternoon she took off her smock, left the grocery as if to go out for some fresh air, and instead went to Lila's house.

"Did something happen?" Signora Carracci asked in bewilderment as she opened the door.

Ada answered, "Nothing has happened that you don't already know."

She came in and told her everything, in the presence of the child. She began calmly, she talked about actors and also cyclists, she called herself a kind of "white lady"—like the lover of the famous cyclist Fausto Coppi—but more modern, and she mentioned the Sacra Rota to demonstrate that even the Church and God in certain cases where love is very strong would dissolve a marriage. Since Lila listened without interrupting, something that Ada would never have expected—rather, she hoped that she would say just half a word, so that she could beat her bloody—she got nervous and began to walk around the apartment, first to demonstrate that she had been in the house often and knew it well, and, second, to reproach her: "Look at this mess, dirty dishes, the dust, socks and underwear on the floor, it's not possible that that poor man has to live like this." Finally, in an uncontrollable frenzy, she began to pick the dirty clothes up off the bedroom floor, shrieking, "Starting tomorrow I'm coming here to tidy up. You don't even know how to make the bed, look here, Stefano can't bear the sheet to be folded like this, he told me he's explained it to you a thousand times and you pay no attention."

Here she stopped suddenly, confused, and said in a low voice, "You have to go, Lina, because if you don't I'll kill the child."

Lila managed to respond only, "You're behaving like your mother, Ada."

Those were the words. I imagine her voice now: she wasn't capable of emotional tones, she must have spoken as usual with cold malice, or with detachment. And yet years later she told me that, seeing Ada in the house in that state, she had remembered the cries of Melina, the abandoned lover, when the Sarratore family left the neighborhood, and she had seen again the iron that flew out the window and almost killed Nino. The long flame of suffering, which then had much impressed her, was flickering again in Ada; only now it wasn't the wife of Sarratore feeding it but her, Lila. A cruel game of mirrors that at the time escaped us all. But not her, and so it's likely that instead of resentment, instead of her usual determination to do harm, bitterness was triggered in her, and pity. Certainly she tried to take her hand, she said, "Sit down, I'll make you a cup of chamomile tea."

But Ada, in all Lila's words, from first to last, and above all in that gesture, saw an insult. She withdrew abruptly, she rolled her eyes in a striking way, showing the white, and when the pupils reappeared she shouted, "Are you saying that I'm mad? That I'm mad like my mother? Then you had better pay atten-tion, Lina. Don't touch me, get out of the way, make yourself a chamomile. I'm going to clean up this disgusting house."

She swept, she washed the floors, she remade the bed, and she didn't say another word.

Lila followed her with her gaze, afraid that she would break, like an artificial body subjected to excessive acceleration. Then she took the child and went out, she walked around the new neighborhood for a long time, talking to Rinuccio, pointing out things, naming them, inventing stories. But she did it more to keep her anguish under control than to entertain the child. She went back to the house only when, from a distance, she saw Ada go out the front door and hurry off as if she were late.

112.

When Ada returned to work, out of breath and extremely agitated, Stefano, menacing but calm, asked her, "Where have you been?" She answered, in the presence of the customers waiting to be served, "To clean up your house, it was disgusting." And addressing the audience on the other side of the counter: "There was so much dust on the night table you could write in it."

Stefano said nothing, disappointing the customers. When the shop emptied and it was time to close, Ada cleaned, swept, always watching her lover out of the corner of her eye. Nothing happened, he did the accounts sitting at the cash register, smoking heavily aromatic American cigarettes. Once the last butt was out, he grabbed the handle to lower the shutter, but he lowered it from the inside.

"What are you doing?" Ada asked, alarmed.

"We'll go out on the courtyard side."

After that, he struck her in the face so many times, first with the palm of his hand, then the back, that she leaned against the counter in order not to faint. "How dare you go to my house?" he said in a voice strangled by the will not to scream. "How dare you disturb my wife and my son?" Finally he realized that his heart was nearly bursting and he tried to calm down. It was the first time he had hit her. He stammered, trembling, "Don't ever do it again." And he went out, leaving her bleeding in the shop.

The next day Ada didn't go to work. Battered as she was, she appeared at Lila's house, and Lila, when she saw the bruises on her face, told her to come in.

"Make me the chamomile," said Melina's daughter.

Lila made it for her.

"The baby is cute."

"Yes."

"Just like Stefano."

"No."

"He has the same eyes and the same mouth."

"No."

"If you have to read your books, go ahead, I'll take care of the house and Rinuccio."

Lila stared at her, this time almost amused, then she said, "Do what you like, but don't go near the baby."

"Don't worry, I won't do anything to him."

Ada set to work: she straightened, washed the clothes, hung them in the sun, cooked lunch, prepared dinner. At one point she stopped, charmed by the way Lila was playing with Rinuccio.

"How old is he?"

"Two years and four months."

"He's little, you push him too much."

"No, he does what he can do."

"I'm pregnant."

"What?"

"It's true."

"With Stefano?"

"Of course."

"Does he know?"

"No."

Lila then understood that her marriage really was almost over, but, as usual when she became aware that change was imminent, she felt neither resentment nor anguish nor worry. When Stefano arrived, he found his wife reading in the living room, Ada playing with the baby in the kitchen, the apartment full of good smells and shining like a large, single precious object. He realized that the beating had been of no use, he turned white, he couldn't breathe.

"Go," he said to Ada in a low voice.

"No."

"What's got into your head?"

"I'm staying here."

"You want me to go mad?"

"Yes, that makes two of us."

Lila closed the book, took the baby without saying anything and withdrew into the room where, a long time earlier, I had studied, and where Rinuccio now slept. Stefano whispered to his lover, "You'll ruin me, like this. It's not true that you love me, Ada, you want me to lose all my customers, you want to reduce me to a pauper, and you know that circumstances are already not good. Please, tell me what you want and I'll give it to you."

"I want to be with you always."

"Yes, but not here."

"Here."

"This is my house, there's Lina, there's Rinuccio."

"From now on I'm here, too: I'm pregnant."

Stefano sat down. In silence he gazed at Ada's stomach as she stood before him, as if he were seeing through her dress, her underpants, her skin, as if he were seeing the baby already formed, a living being, all ready, about to jump out. Then there was a knock at the door.

It was a waiter from the Bar Solara, a boy of sixteen who had just been hired. He told Stefano that Michele and Marcello wanted to see him right away. Stefano roused himself, at that moment he considered the demand a salvation, given the storm he had in the house. He said to Ada, "Don't move." She smiled, she nodded yes. He went out, got in the Solaras' car. What a mess I've got myself into, he thought. What should I do? If my father were alive he would break my legs with an iron bar. Women, debts, Signora Solara's red book. Something hadn't worked. Lina. She had ruined him. What the fuck do Marcello and Michele want, at this hour, so urgently?

They wanted, he discovered, the old grocery. They didn't say it but they let him understand it. Marcello spoke merely of another loan that they were willing to give him. But, he said, the Cerullo shoes have to come definitively to us, we're finished with that lazy brother-in-law of yours, he's not reliable. And we need a guarantee, an activity, a property, you think about it. That said, he left, he said he had things to do. At that point Stefano was alone with Michele. They talked for a long time to see if Rino and Fernando's factory could be saved, if he could do without what Marcello had called the guarantee.

But Michele shook his head, he said, "We need guarantees, scandals aren't good for business."

"I don't know what you mean."

"*I* know what I mean. Who do you love more, Lina or Ada?"

"It's none of your business."

"No, Ste', when it's a question of money your business is my business."

"What can I tell you: we're men, you know how it works. Lina is my wife, Ada is another thing."

"So you love Ada more?"

"Yes."

"Resolve the situation and then we'll talk."

Many very dark days passed before Stefano found a way of getting out of that chokehold. Quarrels with Ada, quarrels with Lila, work gone to hell, the old grocery often closed, the neighborhood that watched and committed to memory and still remembers. The handsome engaged couple. The convertible. Soraya is going by with the Shah of Persia, Jack and Jackie are going by. Finally Stefano resigned himself and said to Lila, "I've found you a nice place, suitable for you and Rinuccio."

"How generous you are."

"I'll come twice a week to see the baby."

"As far as I'm concerned you don't have to come see him, since he's not your son."

"You're a bitch, you're going to make me smash your face."

"Smash my face when you want, I've got a callus there. But you take care of your child and I'll take care of mine."

He fumed, he got angry, he really tried to hit her. Finally he said, "The place is on the Vomero."

"Where?"

"I'll take you tomorrow and show it to you, in Piazza degli Artisti."

Lila remembered in a flash the proposal Michele Solara had made long ago: "I've bought a house on the Vomero, in Piazza degli Artisti. If you want I'll drive you there now, I'll show it to you, I took it with you in mind. There you can do what you like: read, write, invent things, sleep, laugh, talk, and be with Rinuccio. I'm interested only in being able to look at you and listen to you."

She shook her head in disbelief, she said to her husband, "You really are a piece of shit."

113.

Now Lila is barricaded in Rinuccio's room, thinking what to do. She'll never go back to her mother and father's house: the weight of her life belongs to her, she doesn't want to become a child again. She can't count on her brother: Rino is beside himself, he's angry with Pinuccia in order to get revenge on Stefano, and has begun to quarrel also with his mother-in-law, Maria, because he's desperate, he has no money and a lot of debts. She can count only on Enzo: she trusted and trusts him, even though he never showed up and in fact he seems to have disappeared from the neighborhood. She thinks: he promised that he'll get me out of here. But sometimes she hopes he won't keep his promise, she's afraid of making trouble for him. She's not worried about a possible fight with Stefano, her husband has now given her up, and then he's a coward, even if he has the strength of a wild beast. But she is afraid of Michele Solara. Not today, not tomorrow, but when I'm not even thinking about it anymore he'll appear and if I don't submit he'll make me pay, and he'll make anyone who's helped me pay. So it's better for me to go away without involving anyone. I have to find a job, anything, enough to earn what I need to feed him and give him a roof.

Just thinking of her son saps her strength. What ended up in Rinuccio's head: images, words. She worries about the voices that reach him, unmonitored. I wonder if he heard mine, while I carried him in my womb. I wonder how it was imprinted in his nervous system. If he felt loved, if he felt rejected, was he aware of my agitation. How does one protect a child. Nourishing him. Loving him. Teaching him things. Acting as a filter for every sensation that might cripple him forever. I've lost his real father, who doesn't know anything about him and will never love him. Stefano, who isn't his father and yet loved him a little, sold us for love of another woman and a more genuine son. What will happen to this child. Now Rinuccio knows that when I go into another room he won't lose me, I am still there. He maneuvers with objects and fantasies of objects, the outside and the inside. He knows how to eat with a fork and spoon. He handles things and forms them, transforms them. From words he has moved on to sentences. In Italian. He no longer says "he," he says "I." He recognizes the letters of the alphabet. He puts them together so as to write his name. He loves colors. He's happy. But all this rage. He has seen me insulted and beaten. He's seen me break things and shout insults. In dialect. I can't stay here any longer.

114.

Lila came cautiously out of the room only when Stefano wasn't there, when Ada wasn't. She made something to eat for Rinuccio, she ate something herself. She knew that the neighborhood gossiped, that rumors were spreading. One late afternoon in November the telephone rang.

"I'll be there in ten minutes."

She recognized him and without much surprise she answered, "All right." Then: "Enzo."

"Yes."

"You're not obliged."

"I know."

"The Solaras are involved."

"I don't give a fuck about the Solaras."

He arrived exactly ten minutes later. He came up, she had put her things and the child's in two suitcases and had left on the night table in the bedroom all her jewelry, including her engagement ring and her wedding ring.

"It's the second time I've left," she said, "but this time I'm not coming back."

Enzo looked around, he had never been in that house. She pulled him by the arm. "Stefano might arrive suddenly, sometimes he does that."

"Where's the problem?" he answered.

He touched objects that looked expensive to him, a vase for flowers, an ashtray, the sparkling silver. He leafed through a pad where Lila had written down what she needed for the baby and for the house. Then he gave her an inquiring glance, asked her if she was sure of her choice. He said he had found work in a factory in San Giovanni a Teduccio and had taken an apartment there, three rooms, the kitchen was a little dark. "But the things Stefano gave you," he added, "you won't have anymore: I can't give you those."

He said to her: "Maybe you're afraid, because you're not completely sure."

"I'm sure," she said, picking up Rinuccio with a gesture of impatience, "and I'm not afraid of anything. Let's go."

He still delayed. He tore a piece of paper off the shopping list and wrote something. He left the piece of paper on the table.

"What did you write?"

"The address in San Giovanni."

"Why?"

"We're not playing hide-and-seek."

Finally he picked up the suitcases and started down the stairs. Lila locked the door, left the key in the lock.

115.

I knew nothing about San Giovanni a Teduccio. When they told me that Lila had gone to live in that place with Enzo, the only thing that came to mind was the factory owned by the family of Bruno Soccavo, Nino's friend, which produced sausages, and was in that area. The association of ideas annoyed me. I hadn't thought of the summer on Ischia for a long time: and it made me realize that the happy phase of that vacation had faded, while its unpleasant side had expanded. I discovered that every sound from that time, every scent was repugnant to me, but what in memory, surprisingly, seemed most insupportable, and caused me long crying spells, was the night at the Maronti with Donato Sarratore. Only my suffering for what was happening between Lila and Nino could have driven me to consider it pleasurable. At this distance I understood that that first experience of penetration, in the dark, on the cold sand, with that banal man who was the father of the person I loved had been degrading. I was ashamed of it and that shame was added to other shames, of a different nature, that I was experiencing.

I was working night and day on my thesis, I harassed Pietro, reading aloud to him what I had written. He was kind, he shook his head, he fished in his memory of Virgil and other authors for passages that might be useful to me. I noted down every word he uttered, I worked hard, but in a bad mood. I went back and forth between two feelings. I sought help and it humiliated me to ask for it, I was grateful and at the same time hostile, in particular I hated that he did his best not to let his generosity weigh on me. What caused me the greatest anxiety was to find myself— together with him, before him, after him—submitting my research to the assistant professor who was following the progress of both of us, a man of around forty, earnest, attentive, sometimes even sociable. I saw that Pietro was treated as if he already had a professorship, I as a normal brilliant student. Often I decided not to talk to the teacher, out of rage, out of pride, out of fear of having to be aware of my constitutional inferiority. I have to do better than Pietro, I thought, he knows so many more things than I do, but he's gray, he has no imagination. His way of proceeding, the way that he gently tried to suggest to me, was too cautious. So I undid my work, I started again, I pursued an idea that seemed to me original. When I returned to the professor I was listened to, yes, I was praised, but without seriousness, as if my struggle were only a game well played. I soon grasped that Pietro Airota had a future and I didn't.

Then, there was my naiveté. The assistant professor treated me in a friendly way, one day he said, "You're a student of great sensitivity. Do you think you'll teach, after your degree?"

I thought he meant teach at the university and my heart jumped for joy, my cheeks turned red. I said that I loved both teaching and research, I said that I would like to continue to work on the fourth book of the Aeneid. He immediately realized that I had misunderstood and was embarrassed. He strung together some trite phrases on the pleasure of studying for one's whole life and suggested a civil-service exam that would take place in the fall, for a few positions to be won in the teaching institutes.

"We need," he urged me, his tone rising, "excellent professors who will train excellent teachers."

That was it. Shame, shame, shame. This overconfidence that had grown in me, this ambition to be like Pietro. The only thing I had in common with him was the small sexual exchanges in the dark. He panted, he rubbed against me, he asked nothing that I wouldn't give him spontaneously.

I felt blocked. For a while I couldn't work on my thesis, I looked at the pages of the books without seeing the lines of type. I lay in bed staring at the ceiling, I interrogated myself on what to do. Give up right at the end, return to the neighborhood. Get my degree, teach in middle school. Professor. Yes. More than Oliviero. Equal to Galiani. Or maybe not, maybe a little less. Professor Greco. In the neighborhood I would be considered an important person, the daughter of the porter who since she was a child had known everything. I alone, who had been to Pisa, who had met important professors, and Pietro, Mariarosa, their father—I would have understood very clearly that I hadn't gone very far. A great effort, many hopes, wonderful moments. I would miss the time with Franco Mari my whole life. How lovely the months, the years with him had been. At the moment I hadn't understood their importance, and now here I was, growing sad. The rain, the cold, the snow, the scents of spring along the Arno and on the flowering streets of the city, the warmth we gave each other. Choosing a dress, glasses. His pleasure in changing me. And Paris, the exciting trip to a foreign country, the cafés, the politics, the literature, the revolution that would soon arrive, even though the working class was becoming integrated. And him. His room at night. His body. All finished. I tossed nervously in my bed, unable to sleep. I'm lying to myself, I thought. Had it really been so wonderful? I knew very well that at that time, too, there had been shame. And uneasiness, and humiliation, and disgust: accept, submit, force yourself. Is it possible that even happy moments of pleasure never stand up to a rigorous examination? Possible. The blackness of the Maronti quickly extended to Franco's body and then to Pietro's. I escaped from my memories.

At a certain point I began to see Pietro less frequently, with the excuse that I was behind and was in danger of not finishing my thesis in time. One morning I bought a graph-paper notebook and began to write, in the third person, about what had happened to me that night on the beach near Barano. Then, still in the third person, I wrote what had happened to me on Ischia. Then I wrote a little about Naples and the neighborhood. Then I changed names and places and situations. Then I imagined a dark force crouching in the life of the protagonist, an entity that had the capacity to weld the world around her, with the colors of the flame of a blowtorch: a blue-violet dome where everything went well for her, shooting sparks, but that soon came apart, breaking up into meaningless gray fragments. I spent twenty days writing this story, a period during which I saw no one, I went out only to eat. Finally I reread some pages, I didn't like them, and I forgot about it. But I found that I was calmer, as if the shame had passed from me to the notebook. I went back into the world, I quickly finished my thesis, I saw Pietro again.

His kindness, his thoughtfulness moved me. When he graduated the whole family came, along with many Pisan friends of his parents. I was surprised to find that I no longer felt resentful of what awaited Pietro, of the plan of his life. In fact I was happy that he had such a good future and was grateful to the whole family, who invited me to the party afterward. Mariarosa in particular looked after me. We had a heated discussion of the fascist coup in Greece.

I graduated in the following session. I avoided telling my parents, I was afraid that my mother would feel it her duty to come and celebrate me. I presented myself to the professors in one of the dresses that Franco had given me, the one that still seemed acceptable. After such a long time, I really was pleased with myself. I wasn't yet twenty-three and I had obtained a degree in literature with the highest grade. My father hadn't gone beyond fifth grade in elementary school, my mother had stopped at second, none of my forebears, as far as I knew, had learned to read and write fluently. It had been an astonishing effort.

Besides some of my schoolmates, I found that Pietro had come to congratulate me. I remember that it was very hot. After the usual student rituals, I went to my room to freshen up and leave my thesis there. He was waiting for me downstairs, he wanted to take me to dinner. I looked at myself in the mirror, I had the impression that I was pretty. I took the notebook with the story I had written and put it in my purse.

It was the first time that Pietro had taken me to a restaurant. Franco had often done so, and had taught me everything about the arrangement of the silverware, the glasses.

He asked me, "Are we engaged?"

I smiled, I said, "I don't know."

He took a package out of his pocket, gave it to me. He murmured, "For this whole year I thought so. But if you have a different opinion consider it a graduation present."

I unwrapped the package, and there was a green case. Inside was a ring with little diamonds.

"It's beautiful," I said.

I tried it on, the size was right. I thought of the rings that Stefano had given Lila, much more elaborate than that. But it was the first jewel I had received, Franco had given me many gifts but never jewelry, the only jewelry I had was my mother's silver bracelet.

"We're engaged," I said, and, leaning across the table, kissed him on the lips. He turned red, he said, "I have another present."

He gave me an envelope, it was the proofs of his thesis-book. How fast, I thought, with affection and even some joy.

"I also have a little present for you."

"What is it?"

"Something foolish, but I don't know what else to give you that is truly mine."

I took the notebook out, I gave it to him.

"It's a novel," I said, "a one of a kind: only copy, only attempt, only capitulation. I'll never write another one." I added, laughing, "There are even some rather racy parts."

He seemed bewildered. He thanked me, he placed the notebook on the table. I was immediately sorry I had given it to him. I thought: he's a serious student, he has great traditions behind him, he's about to publish an essay on the Bacchic rites that will be the basis of a career; it's my fault, I shouldn't have embarrassed him with a little story that's not even typewritten. And yet even then I didn't feel uneasy, he was he, I was I. I told him that I had applied to enter teachers' training college, I told him that I would return to Naples, I told him, laughing, that our engagement would have a difficult life, I in a city in the south, he in one in the north. But Pietro remained serious, he had everything clear in his mind, he laid out his plan: two years to establish himself at the university and then he would marry me. He even set the date: September, 1969. When we went out he forgot the notebook on the table. I pointed it out in amusement: "My gift?" He was confused, he ran back to get it.

We walked for a long time. We kissed, we embraced on the Lungarno, I asked him, half serious, half joking, if he wanted to sneak into my room. He shook his head, he went back to kissing me passionately. There were entire libraries separating him and Antonio, but they were similar.

116.

My return to Naples was like having a defective umbrella that suddenly closes over your head in a gust of wind. I arrived in the middle of summer. I would have liked to look for a job right away, but my condition as a graduate meant that it was unsuitable for me to go looking for little jobs like the ones I used to have. On the other hand I had no money, and it was humiliating to ask my father and mother, who had already sacrificed enough for me. I became nervous. Everything irritated me, the streets, the ugly façades of the houses, the *stradone*, the gardens, even though at first every stone, every smell had moved me. If Pietro finds someone else, I thought, if I don't get in to the teachers' college, what will I do? It's not possible that I could remain forever a prisoner of this place and these people.

My parents, my siblings were very proud of me, but, I realized, they didn't know why: what use was I, why had I returned, how could they demonstrate to the neighbors that I was the pride of the family? If you thought about it I only complicated their life, further crowding the small apartment, making more arduous the arrangement of beds at night, getting in the way of a daily routine that by now didn't allow for me. Besides, I always had my nose in a book, standing up, sitting in one corner or another, a useless monument to study, a self-important, serious person whom they all made it their duty not to disturb, but about whom they also wondered: What are her intentions?

My mother resisted for a while before questioning me about my fiancé, whose existence she had deduced more from the ring that I wore on my finger than from my confidences. She wanted to know what he did, how much he earned, when he would introduce himself at our house with his parents, where I would live when I was married. At first I gave her some information: he was a professor at the university, for now he earned nothing, he was publishing a book that was considered very important by the other professors, we would get married in a couple of years, his parents were from Genoa, probably I would go to live in that city or anyway wherever he established himself. But from her intent look, from the way she kept asking the same questions, I had the impression that, too much in the grip of her preconceptions, she wasn't listening. I was engaged to someone who hadn't come and wasn't coming to ask for my hand, who lived very far away, who taught but wasn't paid, who was publishing a book but wasn't famous? She became upset as usual, even though she no longer got angry at me. She tried to contain her disapproval, maybe she didn't even feel capable of communicating it to me. Language itself, in fact, had become a mark of alienation. I expressed myself in a way that was too complex for her, although I made an effort to speak in dialect, and when I realized that and simplified the sentences, the simplification made them unnatural and therefore confusing. Besides, the effort I had made to get rid of my Neapolitan accent hadn't convinced the Pisans but was convincing to her, my father, my siblings, the whole neighborhood. On the street, in the stores, on the landing of our building, people treated me with a mixture of respect and mockery. Behind my back they began to call me the Pisan.

In that period I wrote long letters to Pietro, who answered

with even longer ones. At first I expected that he would make at least some reference to my notebook, then I forgot about it myself. We said nothing concrete, I still have those letters: there is not a single useful detail for reconstructing the daily life of the time, what was the price of bread or a ticket to the movies, how much a porter or a professor earned. We focused, let's say, on a book he had read, on an article of interest for our studies, on some reflection of his or mine, on unrest among certain university students, on the neo-avant-garde, which I didn't know anything about but which he was surprisingly well acquainted with, and which amused him to the point of inspiring him to write: "I would like to make a book out of crumpled-up pieces of paper: you start a sentence, it doesn't work, and you throw the page away. I'm collecting a few, I would have the pages printed just as they are, crumpled, so the random pattern of the creases is interwoven with the tentative, broken-off sentences. Maybe this is, in fact, the only literature possible today." That last note struck me. I suspected, I remember, that that was his way of communicating to me that he had read my notebook and that that literary gift of mine seemed to him a product that had arrived too late.

In those weeks of enervating heat I felt as if the weariness of years had poisoned my body, and I had no energy. Here and there I picked up news of Maestra Oliviero's state of health, I hoped that she was well, that I might see her and gain some strength from her satisfaction in my scholastic success. I knew that her sister had come to get her and had taken her back to Potenza. I felt very alone. I even missed Lila, and our turbulent meeting. I felt a desire to find her and measure the distance between us now. But I didn't. I confined myself to an idle, petty investigation into what people in the neighborhood thought of her, into the rumors that were circulating.

In particular I looked for Antonio. He wasn't there, it was said that he had remained in Germany, some claimed that he had married a beautiful German, a fat, blue-eyed platinum blonde, and that he was the father of twins.

So I talked to Alfonso. I went often to the shop on Piazza dei Martiri. He had grown really handsome, he looked like a refined Spanish nobleman, he spoke in a cultivated Italian, with pleasing inserts of dialect. The Solaras' shop, thanks to him, was thriving. His salary was satisfactory, he had rented a house in Ponte di Tappia, and he didn't miss the neighborhood, his siblings, the odor and grease of the grocery stores. "Next year I'll get married," he announced, without too much enthusiasm. The relationship with Marisa had lasted, had become stable, there was only the final step. I went out sometimes with them, they got along well; she had lost her old liveliness, her effusiveness, and now seemed above all careful not to say anything that might annoy him. I never asked her about her father, her mother, her brothers and sister. I didn't even ask about Nino nor did she mention him, as if he were gone forever out of her life, too.

I also saw Pasquale and Carmen: he still worked on construction jobs around Naples and the provinces, she continued to work in the new grocery. But the thing they were eager to tell me was that both had new loves: Pasquale was secretly seeing the oldest, though very young, daughter of the owner of the notions shop; Carmen was engaged to the gas-station man on the *stradone*, a nice man of forty who loved her dearly.

I also went to see Pinuccia, who was almost unrecognizable: slovenly, nervous, extremely thin, resigned to her fate, she bore the marks of the beatings that Rino continued to give her, taking revenge on Stefano, and, in her eyes and in the deep creases around her mouth, even more obvious traces of an unhappiness with no outlet.

Finally I got up my courage and tracked down Ada. I imagined I'd find her more distressed than Pina, humiliated by her situation. Instead she lived in the house that had been Lina's and was beautiful, and apparently serene; she had just given birth to a girl she had named Maria. Even during my pregnancy I didn't stop working, she said proudly. And I saw with my own eyes that she was the real mistress of the two groceries, she hurried from one to the other, she took care of everything.

Each of my childhood friends told me something about Lila, but Ada seemed to be the best informed. And it was she who spoke of her with greater understanding, almost sympathy. Ada was happy, happy with her baby, her comforts, her work, Stefano, and it seemed to me that for all that happiness she was sincerely grateful to Lila.

She exclaimed, admiringly, "I did things like a madwoman, I realize it. But Lina and Enzo behaved in an even crazier way. They were so careless of everything, even of themselves, that they frightened me, Stefano, and even that piece of shit Michele Solara. You know that she took nothing with her? You know that she left me all her jewelry? You know that they wrote on a piece of paper where they were going, the precise address, number, everything, as if to say: come find us, do what you like, who gives a damn?"

I wanted the address, I took it down. While I was writing she said, "If you see her, tell her that I'm not the one keeping Stefano from seeing the child: he has too much to do and although he's sorry, he can't. Also tell her that the Solaras don't forget anything, especially Michele. Tell her not to trust anyone."

117.

Enzo and Lila moved to San Giovanni a Teduccio in a used Fiat 600 that he had just bought. During the whole journey they said nothing, but battled the silence by talking to the child, Lila as if she were addressing an adult, and Enzo with monosyllables like *well, what, yes.* She scarcely knew San

Giovanni. She had gone there once with Stefano, they had stopped in the center for coffee and she had had a good impression. But Pasquale, who often came there for construction work and for political activities had once talked to her about it with great dissatisfaction, both as a worker and as a militant. "It's a filthy place," he had said, "a sewer: the more wealth it produces, the more poverty increases, and we can't change anything, even if we're strong." But Pasquale was always critical of everything and so not very reliable. Lila, as the car traveled along bumpy streets, past crumbling buildings and big, newly constructed apartment houses, preferred to tell herself that she was taking the child to a pretty little town near the sea and thought only of the speech that, to clarify things, out of honesty, she wanted to make to Enzo right away.

But because she was thinking about it she didn't do it. Later, she said to herself. So they arrived at the apartment that Enzo had rented, on the third floor of a new building that was already shabby. The rooms were half-empty, he said he had bought what was indispensable but that starting the next day he would get everything she needed. Lila reassured him, he had already done too much. Only when she saw the double bed she decided that it was time to speak: she said in an affectionate tone: "I've had great respect for you, Enzo, since we were children. You've done a thing I admire: you studied by yourself, you got a diploma, and I know the determination it takes, I've never had it. You're also the most generous person I know, no one would have done what you're doing for Rinuccio and for me. But I can't sleep with you. It's not because we've seen each other alone at most two or three times. And it's not that I don't like you. It's that I have no feelings, I'm like this wall or that table. So if you can live in the same house with me without touching me, good; if you can't I understand and tomorrow morning I'll look for another place. Know that I'll always be grateful for what you've done for me."

Enzo listened without interrupting. At the end he said, pointing to the bed: "You go there, I'll settle on the cot."

"I prefer the cot."

"And Rinuccio?"

"I saw there's another cot."

"He sleeps by himself?"

"Yes."

"You can stay as long as you like."

"You're sure?"

"Very sure."

"I don't want ugly things that could ruin our friendship."

"Don't worry."

"I'm sorry."

"It's fine like this. If by chance feeling returns to you, you know where I am."

118.

Feeling did not return to her; rather, a sense of alienation increased. The heavy air of the rooms. The dirty clothes. The bathroom door that didn't close properly. I imagine that San Giovanni seemed to her an abyss on the edge of our neighborhood. Although she had reached safety, she hadn't been careful where she put her feet down, and had fallen into a deep hole.

Rinuccio immediately worried her. The child, in general serene, began to have tantrums during the day, calling for Stefano, and to wake up crying at night. The attentions of his mother, her way of playing, calmed him, yes, but no longer fascinated him, in fact began to annoy him. Lila invented new games, his eyes lighted up, the child kissed her, he wanted to put his hands on her chest, he shrieked with joy. But then he pushed her away, he played by himself or napped on a blanket on the floor. And on the street he got tired after ten steps, he said his knee hurt, he demanded to be picked up, and if she refused he fell on the ground screaming.

At first Lila resisted, then slowly she began to give in. Since at night he would quiet down only if she let him come into her bed, she let him sleep with her. When they went out to do the shopping she carried him, even though he was a well nourished, heavy child: on one side the bags, on the other him. She returned exhausted.

She rediscovered what life without money was. No books, no journals or newspapers. Rinuccio grew before her eyes, and the things she had brought no longer fit him. She herself had very few clothes. But she pretended it was nothing. Enzo worked all day, he gave her the money she needed, but he didn't earn much, and besides he had to give money to the relatives who were taking care of his siblings. So they barely managed to pay the rent, the electricity, and the gas. But Lila didn't seem worried. The money she had had and had wasted were all one, in her imagination, with the poverty of childhood, it was without substance when it was there and when it wasn't. She was much more worried about the possible undoing of the education she had given her son and she devoted herself to making him energetic, eager, receptive, as he had been until recently. But Rinuccio now seemed to be content only when she left him on the landing to play with the neighbor's child. He fought, got dirty, laughed, ate junk, appeared happy. Lila observed him from the kitchen, from there she could see him and his friend framed by the door to the stairs. He's smart, she thought, he's smarter than the other child, who's a little older: maybe I should accept that I can't coddle him, that I've given him what's necessary but from now on he'll manage by himself, now he needs to hit, take things away from other children, get dirty.

One day, Stefano appeared on the landing. He had left the grocery and decided to come and see his son. Rinuccio greeted him joyfully, Stefano played with him for a while. But Lila saw that her husband was bored, he couldn't wait to leave. In the past it had seemed that he couldn't live without her and the child; instead here he was, looking at his watch, yawning, almost certainly he had come because his mother or even Ada had sent him. As for love, jealousy, it had all passed, he wasn't agitated anymore.

"I'll take the child for a walk."

"Watch out, he always wants to be picked up."

"I'll carry him."

"No, make him walk."

"I'll do as I like."

They went out, he returned half an hour later, he said he had to hurry back to the grocery. He swore that Rinuccio hadn't complained, hadn't asked to be picked up. Before he left he said, "I see that here you're known as Signora Cerullo."

"That's what I am."

"I didn't kill you and I won't kill you only because you're the mother of my son. But you and that shit friend of yours are taking a big risk."

Lila laughed, she provoked him, saying, "You're only tough with people who can't crack your head open, you bastard."

Then she realized that her husband was alluding to Solara and she yelled at him from the landing, as he was going down the stairs: "Tell Michele that if he shows up here I'll spit in his face."

Stefano didn't answer, he disappeared into the street. He returned, I think, at most four or five more times. That last time he met his wife he yelled at her, furiously, "You are the shame of your family. Even your mother doesn't want to see you anymore."

"It's clear that they never understood what a life I had with you."

"I treated you like a queen."

"Better a beggar, then."

"If you have another child you'd better abort it, because you have my surname and I don't want it to be my child."

"I'm not going to have any more children."

"Why? Have you decided not to screw anymore?"

"Fuck off."

"Anyway, I warned you."

"Rinuccio isn't your son, and yet he has your surname."

"Whore, you keep saying it so it must be true. I don't want to see you or him anymore."

He never really believed her. But he pretended, because it was convenient. He preferred a peaceful life that would vanquish the emotional chaos she caused him.

119.

Lila told Enzo in detail about her husband's visits. He listened attentively and almost never made comments. He continued to be restrained in every expression of himself. He didn't even tell her what sort of work he did in the factory and if it suited him or not. He went out at six in the morning and returned at seven in the evening. He ate dinner, he played a little with the boy, he listened to her conversation. As soon as Lila mentioned some urgent need of Rinuccio's, the next day he brought the necessary money. He never told her to ask Stefano to contribute to the maintenance of his child, he didn't tell her to find a job. He simply looked at her as if he lived only to get to those evening hours, to sit with her in the kitchen, listening to her talk. At a certain point he got up, said goodnight, and went into the bedroom.

One afternoon Lila had an encounter that had significant consequences. She went out alone, having left Rinuccio with the neighbor. She heard an insistent horn behind her. It was a fancy car, someone was signaling to her from the window.

"Lina."

She looked closely. She recognized the wolfish face of Bruno Soccavo, Nino's friend.

"What are you doing here?" he asked.

"I live here."

She said almost nothing about herself, since at that time such things were difficult to explain. She didn't mention Nino, nor did he. She asked instead if he had graduated, he said he had decided to stop studying.

"Are you married?"

"Of course not."

"Engaged?"

"One day yes, the next no."

"What do you do?"

"Nothing, there are people who work for me."

It occurred to her to ask him, almost as a joke: "Would you give me a job?"

"You? What do you need a job for?"

"To work."

"You want to make salami and mortadella?"

"Why not."

"And your husband?"

"I don't have a husband anymore. But I have a son."

Bruno looked at her attentively to see if she was joking. He seemed confused, evasive. "It's not a nice job," he said. Then he talked volubly about the problems of couples in general, about his mother, who was always fighting with his father, about a violent passion he himself had had recently for a married woman, but she had left him. Bruno was unusually talkative, he invited her to a café, continuing to tell her about himself. Finally, when Lila said she had to go, he asked, "Did you really leave your husband? You really have a child?"

"Yes."

He frowned, wrote something on a napkin.

"Go to this man, you'll find him in the morning after eight. And show him this."

Lila smiled in embarrassment.

"The napkin?"

"Yes."

"It's enough?"

He nodded yes, suddenly made shy by her teasing tone. He murmured, "That was a wonderful summer."

She said, "For me, too."

120.

All this I found out later. I would have liked to use the address in San Giovanni that Ada had given me right away, but something crucial happened to me as well. One morning I was lazily reading a long letter from Pietro and at the end of the last page I found a few lines in which he told me that he had had his mother read my text (that's what he called it). Adele had found it so good that she had typed it and had sent it to a publisher in Milan for whom she had done translations for years. They had liked it and wanted to publish it.

It was a late autumn morning, I remember a gray light. I sat at the kitchen table, the same one on which my mother was ironing the clothes. The old iron slid over the material with energy, the wood vibrated under my elbows. I looked at those lines for a long time. I said softly, in Italian, only to convince myself that the thing was real: "Mamma, here it says that they are going to publish a novel I wrote." My mother stopped, lifted the iron off the material, set it down upright.

"You wrote a novel?" she asked in dialect.

"I think so."

"Did you write it or not?"

"Yes."

"Will they pay you?"

"I don't know."

I went out, ran to the Bar Solara, where you could make long-distance phone calls in some comfort. After several attempts—Gigliola called from the bar, "Go on, talk"—Pietro answered but he had to work and was in a hurry. He said that he didn't know anything more about the business than he had written me.

"Did you read it?" I asked, in agitation.

"Yes."

"But you never said anything."

He stammered something about lack of time, studying, responsibilities.

"How is it?"

"Good."

"Good and that's all?"

"Good. Talk to my mother, I'm a philologist, not a literary person."

He gave me the number of his parents' house.

"I don't want to telephone, I'm embarrassed."

I sensed some irritation, rare in him who was always so courteous. He said, "You've written a novel, you take responsibility for it."

I scarcely knew Adele Airota, I had seen her four times and we had exchanged only a few formal remarks. In all that time I had been sure she was a wealthy, cultivated wife and mother—the Airotas never said anything about themselves, they acted as if their activities in the world were of scant interest, yet took it for granted that these activities were known to everyone—and only now began to realize that she had a job, that she was able to exercise power. I telephoned anxiously, the maid answered, gave her the phone. I was greeted cordially, but she used the formal *lei* and I did, too. She said that at the publishing house they were all very excited about how good the book was and, as far as she knew, a draft of the contract had already been sent.

"Contract?"

"Of course. Have you dealt with other publishers?"

"No. But I haven't even reread what I wrote."

"You wrote only a single draft, all at once?" she asked, vaguely ironic.

"Yes."

"I assure you that it's ready for publication."

"I still need to work on it."

"Trust yourself: don't touch a comma, there is sincerity, naturalness, and a mystery in the writing that only true books have."

She congratulated me again, although she accentuated the irony. She said that, as I knew, even the Aeneid wasn't polished. She ascribed to me a long apprenticeship as a writer, asked if I had other things, appeared amazed when I confessed that it was the first thing I had written. "Talent and luck," she exclaimed. She told me that there was an unexpected opening in the editorial list and my novel had been considered not only very good but lucky. They thought of bringing it out in the spring.

"So soon?"

"Are you opposed?"

I quickly said no.

Gigliola, who was behind the bar and had listened to the phone call, finally asked me, inquisitively, "What's happening?"

"I don't know," I said and left.

I wandered around the neighborhood overwhelmed by an incredulous joy, my temples pounding. My answer to Gigliola hadn't been a hostile way of cutting her off, I really didn't know. What was that unexpected announcement: a few lines from Pietro, long-distance words, nothing certainly true? And what was a contract, it meant money, it meant rights and duties, was I in danger of getting in some trouble? In a few days I'll find out that they've changed their mind, I thought, the book won't be published. They'll reread the story, those who found it good will find it pointless, those who haven't read it will be angry with those who were eager to publish it, they'll all be angry with Adele Airota, and Adele Airota herself will change her mind, she'll feel humiliated, she'll blame me for disgracing her, she'll persuade her son to leave me. I passed the building where the old neighborhood library was: how long it had been since I'd set foot in it. I went in, it was empty, it smelled of dust and boredom. I moved absentmindedly along the shelves, I touched tattered books without looking at title or author, just to feel them with my fingers. Old paper, curled cotton threads, letters of the alphabet, ink. Volumes, a dizzying word. I looked for *Little Women*, I found it. Was it possible that it was really about to happen? Possible that what Lila and I had planned to do together was happening to me? In a few months there would be printed paper sewn, pasted, all covered with my words, and on the cover the name, Elena Greco, me, breaking the long chain of illiterates, semi-literates, an obscure surname that would be charged with light for eternity. In a few years— three, five, ten, twenty—the book would end up on those shelves, in the library of the neighborhood where I was born, it would be catalogued, people would ask to borrow it to find out what the daughter of the porter had written. I heard the flush of the toilet, I waited for Maestro Ferraro to appear, just as when I was a diligent girl: the same fleshless face, perhaps more wrinkled, the crew-cut hair white but still thick over the low forehead. Here's someone who could appreciate what was hap-pening to me, who would more than justify my burning head, the fierce pounding in my temples. But from the bathroom a stranger emerged, a small rotund man of around forty.

"Do you want to take out books?" he asked. "Do it quickly because I'm about to close."

"I was looking for Maestro Ferraro."

"Ferraro is retired."

Do it quickly, he was about to close.

I left. Just now that I was becoming a writer, there was no one in the entire neighborhood capable of saying: What an extraordinary thing you've done.

121.

I didn't imagine that I would earn money. But I received the draft of the contract and discovered that, surely thanks to Adele's support, the publisher was giving me an advance of two hundred thousand lire, a hundred on signing and a hundred on delivery. My mother was speechless, she couldn't believe it. My father said, "It takes months for me to earn that much money." They both began to brag in the neighborhood and outside: our daughter has become rich, she's a writer, she's marrying a university professor. I flourished again, I stopped studying for the teachers' college exam. As soon as the money arrived I bought a dress, some makeup, went for the first time in my life to the hairdresser, and left for Milan, a city unknown to me.

At the station I had trouble orienting myself. Finally I found the right metro, and arrived nervously at the door of the publishing house. I gave a thousand explanations to the porter, who hadn't asked me anything, and who in fact, while I spoke, continued to read the newspaper. I went up in the elevator, I knocked, I went in. I was struck by how neat and tidy it was. My head was crowded with all that I had studied and I wanted to display it, to demonstrate that even if I was a woman, even if you could see my origins, I was a person who at twenty-three, had won the right to publish that book, and now, nothing nothing nothing about me could be called into question.

I was greeted politely, led from office to office. I talked with the editor who was working on my manuscript, an old man, bald, with a very pleasant face. We talked for a couple of hours, he praised me, he cited Adele Airota often, with great respect, he showed me some revisions that he suggested, he left me a copy of the text and his notes. As he was saying goodbye he added, in a serious voice, "The story is good, a contemporary story very well expressed, the writing is always surprising; but that's not the point. It's the third time I've read the book and on every page there is something powerful whose origin I can't figure out." I turned red, thanked him. Ah, how much I had been able to do, and how rapid it all was, how well liked I was and how likable I had become, I could speak about my studies, where I had done them, about my thesis on the fourth book of the Aeneid: I replied with courteous precision to courteous observations, mimicking perfectly the tones of Professor Galiani, of her children, of Mariarosa. A pretty, amiable woman named Gina asked if I needed a hotel and, at my nod of assent, found me one on Via Garibaldi. To my great amazement I discovered that everything was charged to the publisher, everything that I spent on food, the train tickets. Gina told me to present a record of expenses, I would be reimbursed, and she asked me to say hello to Adele for her. "She called me," she said. "She's very fond of you."

The next day I left for Pisa, I wanted to embrace Pietro. On the train I considered one by one the editor's notes and, satisfied, I saw my book with the eyes of one who praised it and was working to make it even better. I arrived very pleased with myself. My fiancé found me a place to sleep at the house of an old assistant professor of Greek literature whom I also knew. In the evening he took me to dinner and to my surprise showed me my manuscript. He, too, had a copy and had made some notes, we looked at them together one by one. They bore the imprint of his usual rigor and had to do mostly with the vocabulary.

"I'll take care of them," I said thanking him.

After dinner we walked to an isolated meadow. After we had held and touched each other for a long time in the cold, obstructed by coats and woolen sweaters, he asked me to revise and polish with care the pages where the protagonist loses her virginity on the beach. I said, bewildered, "It's an important moment."

"You yourself said that that part is a bit risqué."

"At the publisher no one objected."

"They'll talk to you about it later."

I became irritated, I told him that I would think about it and the next day I left for Naples in a bad mood. If that episode upset Pietro, who was a young man of wide reading, and had written a book on Bacchic rites, what would my mother and father say, my siblings, the neighborhood, if they read it? On the train I worked on the manuscript, keeping in mind the observations of the editor, and Pietro's, and what I could eliminate I did. I wanted the book to be good, I didn't want anyone to dislike it. I doubted that I would ever write another.

122.

As soon as I got home I had some bad news. My mother, convinced that it was her right to look at my mail when I was absent, had opened a package that came from Potenza. In the package she had found a number of my notebooks from elementary school and a note from Maestra Oliviero's sister. The teacher, the note said, had died peacefully, twenty days earlier. She had often remembered me, in recent times, and had asked that some notebooks from elementary school that she had saved be returned to me. I was distressed, even more than my sister Elisa, who wept inconsolably for hours. This bothered my mother, who first yelled at her younger daughter and then, so that I, her older daughter, could hear it clearly, commented aloud: "That imbecile always thought she was more of a mother than I am."

All day I thought of Maestra Oliviero and of how she would have been proud to know about my degree, about the book I was going to publish. When everyone went to bed I shut myself in the silent kitchen and leafed through the notebooks one after the other. How well she had taught me, the teacher, what beautiful handwriting she had instilled. Too bad that my adult writing had gotten smaller, that speed had simplified the letters. I smiled at the spelling mistakes, marked with furious strokes, at the *goods*, the *excellents*, which she wrote punctiliously in the margin when she found a good expression or the right solution to a difficult problem, at the high marks she always gave me. Had she really been more mother than my mother? For a time I hadn't been sure. But she had imagined for me a road that my mother wasn't able to imagine and had compelled me to take it. For this I was grateful to her.

I was putting aside the package to go to bed when I noticed in the middle of one of the notebooks a small, thin sheaf of paper, ten pages of graph paper fastened with a pin and refolded. I felt a sudden emptiness in my chest: I recognized *The Blue Fairy*, the story that Lila had written so many years before, how many? Thirteen, fourteen. How I had loved the cover colored with pastels, the beautifully drawn letters of the title: at the time I had considered it a real book and had been envious of it. I opened it to the center page. The pin had rusted, leaving brown marks on the paper. I saw, with amazement, that the teacher had written beside a sentence: *beautiful*. So she had read it? So she had liked it? I turned the pages one after the other, they were full of her *wonderfuls, goods, very goods*. I got angry. Old witch, I thought, why didn't you tell us that you liked it, why did you deny Lila that satisfaction? What drove you to fight for my education and not for hers? Is the refusal of the shoemaker to let his daughter take the admission examination enough to justify you? What unhappiness did you have in your head that you unloaded onto her? I began to read *The Blue Fairy* from the beginning, racing over the pale ink, the handwriting so similar to mine of that time. But already at the first page I began to feel sick to my stomach and soon I was covered with sweat. Only at the end, however, did I admit what I had understood after a few lines. Lila's childish pages were the secret heart of my book. Anyone who wanted to know what gave it warmth and what the origin was of the strong but invisible thread that joined the sentences would have had to go back to that child's packet, ten notebook pages, the rusty pin, the brightly colored cover, the title, and not even a signature.

123.

I didn't sleep all night, I waited until it was day. The long hostility toward Lila dissolved, suddenly what I had taken from her seemed to me much more than what she had ever been able to take from me. I decided to go right away to San Giovanni a Teduccio. I wanted to give her back *The Blue Fairy*, show her my notebooks, page through them together, enjoy the teacher's comments. But most of all I felt the need to have her sit beside me, to tell her, you see how connected we are, one in two, two in one, and prove to her with the rigor that it seemed to me I had learned in the Normale, with the philological persistence I had learned from Pietro, how her child's book had put down deep roots in my mind and had, in the course of the years, produced another book, different, adult, mine, and yet inseparable from hers, from the fantasies that we had elaborated together in the courtyard of our games, she and I con-

tinuously formed, deformed, reformed. I wanted to embrace
her, kiss her, and tell her, Lila, from now on, whatever happens
to me or you, we mustn't lose each other anymore.

But it was a hard morning, it seemed to me that the city did
everything possible to get between me and her. I took a
crowded bus that went toward the Marina, I was unbearably
squashed by miserable bodies. I got on another, even more
crowded bus, I went in the wrong direction. I got out, upset,
disheveled, I waited for a long time, angrily, to make up for the
mistake. That small journey through Naples exhausted me.
What was the use of years of middle school, high school, university, in that city? To arrive at San Giovanni I had forcibly to
regress, as if Lila had gone to live not in a street, or a square, but
in a ripple of time past, before we went to school, a black time
without rules and without respect. I resorted to the most violent dialect of the neighborhood, I insulted, I was insulted, I
threatened, I was mocked, I responded by mocking, a spiteful
art in which I was trained. Naples had been very useful in Pisa,
but Pisa was no use in Naples, it was an obstacle. Good manners, cultured voice and appearance, the crush in my head and
on my tongue of what I had learned in books were all immediate signs of weakness that made me a secure prey, one of those
who don't struggle. On the buses and the streets heading
toward San Giovanni I fused the old capacity to stop being
meek at the right moment with the pride of my new state: I had
a degree, I had had lunch with Professor Airota, I was engaged
to his son, I had deposited money in the Post Office, in Milan
I had been treated with respect by important people; how
could these shitty people dare? I felt a power that no longer
knew how to adjust to the *pretend not to notice* with which, in
general, it was possible to survive in the neighborhood and
outside it. Whenever, in the throng of passengers, I felt male
hands on my body, I gave myself the sacrosanct right to fury
and reacted with cries of contempt, I said unrepeatable words

like the ones my mother and, especially, Lila knew how to say. I was so excessive that when I got off the bus I was sure that someone would jump off behind me and murder me.

It didn't happen, but I walked away angry and scared. I had been much too neat when I left the house, now I felt mangled, outside and in.

I tried to compose myself, I said to myself: calm down, you're almost there. I asked the passersby for directions. I walked along Corso San Giovanni a Teduccio with the cold wind in my face, it seemed a yellowish channel with defaced walls, black doorways, dirt. I wandered, confused by friendly information so crowded with details that it turned out to be useless. Finally I found the street, the building. I went up the dirty stairs, following a strong odor of garlic, the voices of children. A very fat woman in a green sweater looking out of an open door saw me and cried, "Who do you want?" "Carracci," I said. But seeing that she was perplexed I corrected myself immediately: "Scanno." Enzo's surname. And then, afterward, "Cerullo." At that point the woman repeated *Cerullo* and said, raising a large arm, "Farther up." I thanked her, kept going, while she leaned over the banister and, looking up, shouted, "Titì, there's someone looking for Lina, she's coming up."

Lina. Here, in the mouths of strangers, in this place. I realized only then that I had in mind Lila as I had seen her the last time, in the apartment in the new neighborhood, in the orderliness that, however charged with anguish it had been, now seemed the backdrop of her life, the furniture, the refrigerator, the television, the well-cared-for child, she herself with a look certainly worn out but still that of a well-off young woman. I knew nothing, at that moment, of how she lived, what she did. The gossip had stopped at the abandonment of her husband, at the incredible fact that she had left a beautiful house and money and gone away with Enzo Scanno. I didn't know about the encounter with Soccavo. So I had left the neighborhood in the certainty that I would find her in a new house among open books and educational games for her son, or, at most, out momentarily, doing the shopping. And, out of laziness, in order not to feel uneasy, I had mechanically placed those images inside a toponymy, San Giovanni a Teduccio, beyond the Granili, at the end of the Marina. I went up with that expectation. I thought, I've made it, here I am at my destination. So I reached Titina. A young woman with a baby in her arms who was crying quietly, with slight sobs, rivulets of mucous dripping onto her upper lip from cold-reddened nostrils, and two more children attached to her skirts, one on each side.

Titina turned her gaze to the door opposite, closed.

"Lina's not here," she said, in a hostile tone.

"Nor Enzo?"

"No."

"Did she take the child for a walk?"

"Who are you?"

"My name is Elena Greco, I'm a friend."

"And you don't recognize Rinuccio? Rinù, have you ever seen this lady?"

She boxed the ear of one of the children beside her, and only then I recognized him. The child smiled at me, he said in Italian, "Hello, Aunt Lenù. Mamma will be back tonight at eight."

I picked him up, hugged him, praised how cute he was and how well he spoke.

"He's very clever," Titina admitted, "he's a born professor."

At that point, her hostility ceased, she invited me to come in. In the dark corridor I stumbled on something that surely belonged to the children. The kitchen was untidy, everything was sunk in a grayish light. There was a sewing machine with some material still under the needle, and around and on the floor other fabric of various colors. Suddenly ashamed, Titina tried to straighten the room, then she gave up and made coffee, but continuing to hold her daughter in her arms. I sat Rinuccio on my lap, asked him stupid questions that he answered with lively resignation. The woman meanwhile told me about Lila and Enzo.

"She makes salami at Soccavo," she said.

I was surprised, only then did I remember Bruno.

"Soccavo, the sausage people?"

"Soccavo, yes."

"I know him."

"They are not nice people."

"I know the son."

"Grandfather, father, and son, same shit. They made money and forgot they ever went around in rags."

I asked about Enzo. She said he worked at the locomotives, she used that expression, and I soon realized that she thought he and Lila were married, she called Enzo, with liking and respect, "Signor Cerullo."

"When will Lina be back?"

"Tonight."

"And the child?"

"He stays with me, eats, plays, does everything here."

So the journey wasn't over: I approached, Lila moved away. I asked, "How long does it take to walk to the factory?"

"Twenty minutes."

Titina gave me directions, which I wrote down on a piece of paper. Meanwhile Rinuccio asked politely, "May I go play, aunt?" He waited for me to say yes, he ran into the hall with the other child, and immediately I heard him yelling a nasty insult in dialect. The woman gave me an embarrassed look and shouted from the kitchen, in Italian, "Rino, bad words aren't nice, watch out or I'll come and give you a rap on the knuckles."

I smiled at her, remembering my trip on the bus. I also deserve a rap on the knuckles, I thought, I'm in the same condition as Rinuccio. When the quarrel in the hall didn't stop, we ran out. The two boys were hitting each other, throwing things and yelling fiercely.

124.

I arrived at the site of the Soccavo factory by a dirt path, amid trash of every type, a thread of black smoke in the frozen sky. Before I even saw the boundary wall I noticed a sickening odor of animal fat mixed with burned wood. The guard said, derisively, you don't go visiting your girlfriend during working hours. I asked to speak to Bruno Soccavo. He changed his tone, stammered that Bruno almost never came to the factory. Call him at home, I replied. He was embarrassed, he said that he couldn't bother him for no reason. "If you don't call," I said, "I'll go and find a telephone and do it myself." He gave me a nasty look, he didn't know what to do. A man came by on a bicycle, braked, said something obscene to him in dialect. The guard appeared relieved to see him. He began to talk to him as if I no longer existed.

At the center of the courtyard a bonfire was burning. The flame cut the cold air for a few seconds as I passed. I reached a low building of a yellow color, I pushed open a heavy door, I entered. The smell of fat, already strong outside, was unendurable. I met a girl who, obviously angry, was fixing her hair with agitated gestures. I said *Excuse me*, she passed by with her head down, took three or four steps, stopped.

"What is it?" she asked rudely.

"I'm looking for someone called Cerullo."

"Lina?"

"Yes."

"Look in sausage-stuffing."

I asked where it was, she didn't answer, she walked away. I

pushed open another door. I was assailed by a warmth that made the odor of fat even more nauseating. The place was big, there were tubs full of a milky, steaming water in which dark bodies floated, stirred by slow, bent silhouettes, workers immersed up to their hips. I didn't see Lila. I asked a man who, lying on the swampy tile floor, was fixing a pipe: "Do you know where I could find Lina?"

"Cerullo?"

"Cerullo."

"In the mixing department."

"They told me stuffing."

"Then why are you asking me, if you know?"

"Where is mixing?"

"Straight ahead."

"And stuffing?"

"To the right. If you don't find her there, look where they're stripping the meat off the carcasses. Or in the storerooms. They're always moving her."

"Why?"

He had a malicious smile.

"Is she a friend of yours?"

"Yes."

"Forget it."

"Tell me."

"You won't be offended?"

"No."

"She's a pain in the ass."

I followed the directions, no one stopped me. The workers, both men and women, seemed to be enveloped in a bitter indifference; even when they laughed or shouted insults they seemed remote from their very laughter, from their voices, from the swill they handled, from the bad smell. I emerged among women in blue smocks who worked with the meat, caps on their heads: the machines produced a clanking sound and a mush of soft, ground, mixed matter. But Lila wasn't there. And I didn't see her where they were stuffing skins with the rosy pink paste mixed with bits of fat, or where, with sharp knives, they skinned, gutted, cut, using the blades with a dangerous frenzy. I found her in the storerooms. She came out of a refrigerator along with a sort of white breath. With the help of a short man, she was carrying a reddish block of frozen meat on her back. She placed it on a cart, she started to go back into the cold. I immediately saw that one hand was bandaged.

"Lila."

She turned cautiously, stared at me uncertainly. "What are you doing here?" she said. Her eyes were feverish, her cheeks more hollow than usual, and yet she seemed large, tall. She, too, wore a blue smock, but over it a kind of long coat, and on her feet she wore army boots. I wanted to embrace her but I didn't dare: I was afraid, I don't know why, that she would crumble in my arms. It was she, instead, who hugged me for long minutes. I felt the damp material that gave off a smell even more offensive than the smell in the air. "Come," she said, "let's get out of here," and shouted at the man who was working with her: "Two minutes." She drew me into a corner.

"How did you find me?"

"I came in."

"And they let you pass?"

"I said I was looking for you and that I was a friend of Bruno's."

"Good, that way they'll be convinced that I give the son of the owner blow jobs and they'll leave me alone."

"What do you mean?"

"That's how it works."

"Here?"

"Everywhere. Did you get your degree?"

"Yes. But an even more wonderful thing happened, Lila. I wrote a novel and it's being published in April."

Her complexion was gray, she seemed bloodless, and yet she flared up. I saw the red move up along her throat, her cheeks, up to the edge of her eyes, so close that she squeezed them as if fearing that the flame would burn the pupils. Then she took my hand and kissed it, first on the back, then on the palm.

"I'm happy for you," she murmured.

But at the moment I scarcely noticed the affection of the gesture, I was struck by the swelling of her hands and the wounds, cuts old and new, a fresh one on the thumb of her left hand whose edges were inflamed, and I could imagine that under the bandage on her right hand she had an even worse injury.

"What have you done to yourself?"

She immediately withdrew, put her hands in her pockets.

"Nothing. Stripping meat off the bones ruins your fingers."

"You strip the meat?"

"They put me where they like."

"Talk to Bruno."

"Bruno is the worst shit of them all. He shows up only to see who of us he can fuck in the aging room."

"Lila."

"It's the truth."

"Are you ill?"

"I'm very well. Here in the storerooms they give me ten lire more an hour for cold damage."

The man called: "Cerù, the two minutes are up."

"Coming," she said.

I murmured, "Maestra Oliviero died."

She shrugged, said, "She was sick, it was bound to happen."

I added in a hurry, because I saw that the man next to the cart was getting anxious, "She let me have *The Blue Fairy*."

"What's *The Blue Fairy*?"

I looked at her to see if it was true that she didn't remember and she seemed sincere.

"The book you wrote when you were ten."

"Book?"

"That's what we called it."

Lila pressed her lips together, shook her head. She was alarmed, she was afraid of getting in trouble at work, but in my presence she acted the part of someone who does as she likes. I have to go, I thought.

She said, "A long time has passed since then," and shivered.

"Do you have a fever?"

"No."

I looked for the packet in my purse, gave it to her. She took it, recognized it, but showed no emotion.

"I was an arrogant child," she muttered.

I quickly contradicted her.

"The story is still beautiful today," I said. "I read it again and discovered that, without realizing it, I've always had it in my mind. That's where my book comes from."

"From this nonsense?" she laughed loudly, nervously. "Then whoever printed it is crazy."

The man shouted, "I'm waiting for you, Cerullo."

"You're a pain in the ass," she answered.

She put the packet in her pocket and took me under the arm. We went toward the exit. I thought of how I had dressed up for her and how hard it had been to get to that place. I had imagined tears, confidences, talk, a wonderful morning of confessions and reconciliation. Instead here we were, walking arm in arm, she bundled up, dirty, scarred, I disguised as a young lady of good family. I told her that Rinuccio was cute and very intelligent. I praised the neighbor, asked about Enzo. She was glad that I had found the child well, she in turn praised the neighbor. But it was the mention of Enzo that kindled her, she lighted up, became talkative.

"He's kind," she said, "he's good, he's not afraid of anything, he's extremely smart and he studies at night, he knows so many things."

I had never heard her talk about anyone in that way. I asked, "What does he study?"

"Mathematics."

"Enzo?"

"Yes. He read something about electronic calculators or saw an ad, I don't know, and he got excited. He says a calculator isn't like you see in the movies, all colored lights that light up and go out with a *bip*. He said it's a question of languages."

"Languages?"

She had that familiar narrow gaze.

"Not languages for writing novels," she said, and the dismissive tone in which she uttered the word "novels" disturbed me, the laugh that followed disturbed me. "Programming languages. At night, after the baby goes to sleep, Enzo starts studying."

Her lower lip was dry, cracked by the cold, her face marred by fatigue. And yet with what pride she had said: he starts studying. I saw that, in spite of the third person singular, it wasn't only Enzo who was excited about the subject.

"And what do you do?"

"I keep him company: he's tired and if he's by himself he feels like sleeping. But together it's great, one of us says one thing, one another. You know what a flow chart is?"

I shook my head. Her eyes then became very small, she let go of my arm, she began to talk, drawing me into that new passion. In the courtyard, with the odor of the bonfire and the stink of animal fats, flesh, nerves, this Lila, wrapped up in an overcoat but also wearing a blue smock, her hands cut, disheveled, very pale, without a trace of makeup, regained life and energy. She spoke of the reduction of everything to the alternative true-false, she quoted Boolean algebra and many other things I knew nothing about. And yet her words, as usual, fascinated me. As she spoke, I saw the wretched house at night, the child sleeping in the other room; I saw Enzo sitting on the bed, worn out from work on the locomotives in who knows what factory; I saw her, after the day at the cooking tubs or in the gutting room or in the storerooms at twenty below zero, sitting with him on the blanket. I saw them both in the terrible light of sacrificed sleep, I heard their voices: they did exercises with the flow charts, they practiced cleaning the world of the superfluous, they charted the actions of the day according to only two values of truth: zero and one. Obscure words in the miserable room, whispered so as not to wake Rinuccio. I understood that I had arrived there full of pride and realized that—in good faith, certainly, with affection—I had made that whole journey mainly to show her what she had lost and what I had won. But she had known from the moment I appeared, and now, risking tensions with her workmates, and fines, she was explaining to me that I had won nothing, that in the world there is nothing to win, that her life was full of varied and foolish adventures as much as mine, and that time simply slipped away without any meaning, and it was good just to see each other every so often to hear the mad sound of the brain of one echo in the mad sound of the brain of the other.

"Do you like living with him?" I asked.

"Yes."

"Will you have children?"

She had an expression of feigned amusement.

"We're not together."

"No?"

"No, I don't feel like it."

"And he?"

"He's waiting."

"Maybe he's like a brother."

"No, I like him."

"So?"

"I don't know."

We stopped beside the fire, she gestured toward the guard. "Look out for him," she said. "When you go out he's liable to accuse you of stealing a mortadella just so he can search you and put his hands all over you."

We embraced, we kissed each other. I said I would see her again, I didn't want to lose her, and I was sincere. She smiled, she said, "Yes, I don't want to lose you, either." I felt that she, too, was sincere.

I went away in great agitation. Inside was the struggle to leave her, the old conviction that without her nothing truly important would ever happen to me, and yet I felt the need to get away, to free my nostrils of that stink of fat. After a few quick steps I couldn't help it, I turned to wave again. I saw her standing beside the bonfire, without the shape of a woman in that outfit, as she leafed through the pages of the *Blue Fairy*. Suddenly she threw it on the fire.

125.

I hadn't told her what the story of my book was or when it would be in bookstores. I hadn't even told her about Pietro, of the plan to get married in a couple of years. Her life had overwhelmed me and it took days for me to restore clear outlines and depth to mine. What finally restored me to myself—but what myself?—was the proofs of the book: a hundred and thirty-nine pages, thick paper, the words of the notebook, fixed by my handwriting, which had become pleasantly alien thanks to the printed characters.

I spent happy hours reading, rereading, correcting. Outside it was cold, a frigid wind slipped in through the loose window frames. I sat at the kitchen table with Gianni and Elisa, who were studying. My mother was busily working around us, but with surprising care, in order not to disturb me.

Soon I went to Milan again. This time I allowed myself, for the first time in my life, to take a taxi. The bald editor, at the end of a day spent evaluating the final corrections, said to me, "I'll call you a taxi," and I didn't know how to say no. So it happened that when I went from Milan to Pisa, at the station I looked around and thought: why not, let's play the great lady again. And the temptation resurfaced when I returned to Naples, in the chaos of Piazza Garibaldi. I would have liked to arrive in the neighborhood in a taxi, sitting comfortably in the back seat, a driver at my service, who, when we reached the gate, would open the door for me. I took the bus instead, I didn't feel up to it. But something about me must have been different, because when I greeted Ada, who was taking her baby out for a walk, she looked at me distractedly, and walked by. Then she stopped, turned back, said, "How well you look, I didn't recognize you, you're different."

At the moment I was pleased, but soon I became unhappy. What advantage could I have gained from becoming different? I wanted to remain myself, chained to Lila, to the courtyard, to the lost dolls, to Don Achille, to everything. It was the only way to feel intensely what was happening to me. Yet change is hard to oppose: in that period, in spite of myself, I changed more than in the years in Pisa. In the spring the book came out, which, much more than my degree, gave me a new identity. When I showed a copy to my mother, to my father, to my sister and brothers, they passed it around in silence, but without looking through it. They stared at the cover with uncertain smiles, they were like police agents confronted with a fake document. My father said, "It's my surname," but he spoke without satisfaction, as if suddenly, instead of being proud of me, he had discovered that I had stolen money from his pocket.

Days passed, the first reviews came out. I scanned them

anxiously, wounded by even the slightest hint of criticism. I read the best ones aloud to the whole family, my father brightened. Elisa said teasingly, "You should have signed Lenuccia, Elena's disgusting."

In those frenzied days, my mother bought a photograph album and began to paste in it everything good that was written about me. One morning she asked, "What's the name of your fiancé?"

She knew, but she had something in mind and to communicate it she wished to start there.

"Pietro Airota."

"Then you'll be called Airota."

"Yes."

"And if you write another book, on the cover will it say Airota?"

"No."

"Why?"

"Because I like Elena Greco."

"So do I," she said.

But she never read it. My father didn't read it, Peppe, Gianni, Elisa didn't read it, and at first the neighborhood didn't read it. One morning a photographer came and kept me for two hours, first in the gardens, then along the *stradone*, then at the entrance to the tunnel, taking photographs. Later, one of the pictures appeared in *Il Mattino*; I expected passersby would stop me on the street, would read the book out of curiosity. Instead no one, not Alfonso, Ada, Carmen, Gigliola, Michele Solara, who, unlike his brother Marcello, wasn't a complete stranger to the alphabet, ever said to me, as soon as they could: your book is wonderful, or, who knows, your book is terrible. They only greeted me warmly and went on.

I encountered readers for the first time in a bookstore in Milan. The event, I soon discovered, had been urgently planned by Adele Airota, who was following the book's journey at a distance and traveled purposely from Genoa for the occasion. She came to the hotel, kept me company all afternoon, tried tactfully to calm me. I had a tremor in my hands that wouldn't go away, I struggled with words, I had a bitter taste in my mouth. I was angry with Pietro, who had stayed in Pisa, he was busy. Mariarosa, who lived in Milan, made a quick congratulatory visit before the reading, then she had to go.

I went to the bookstore terrified. The room was full, I went in with my eyes down. I thought I would faint with emotion. Adele greeted many of those present, they were friends and acquaintances of hers. She sat in the first row, gave me encouraging looks, turned occasionally to talk to a woman of her age who was sitting behind her. Until that moment I had spoken in public only twice, forced to by Franco, and the audience then was made up of six or seven of his friends who smiled with understanding. The situation was different now. I had before me some forty refined, cultivated strangers who stared at me in silence, with an unfriendly gaze; it was in large part the prestige of the Airotas that compelled them to be there. I wanted to get up and run away.

But the rite began. An old critic, a university professor much esteemed in his time, said as many good things about the book as possible. I couldn't understand his speech, I thought only of what I was to say. I fidgeted in my chair, I had a stomachache. The world had vanished into chaos, and I couldn't find within myself the authority to call it back and put it in order again. Yet I pretended self-assurance. When it was my turn, I spoke without really knowing what I was saying, I talked in order not to be silent, I gesticulated too much, I displayed too much literary knowledge, I made a show of my classical education. Then silence fell.

What were those people in front of me thinking? How was the critic and professor beside me evaluating my remarks? And was Adele, behind her air of cordiality, repenting her support of me? When I looked at her I realized immediately that my eyes were begging her for the comfort of a nod of approval and I was ashamed. Meanwhile the professor touched an arm as if to calm me, asked the audience for questions. Many stared in embarrassment at their knees, the floor. The first to speak was an older man with thick eyeglasses, well known to those present but not to me. At simply hearing his voice, Adele had an expression of annoyance. The man talked for a long time about the decline of publishing, which now looked more for money than for literary quality; then he moved on to the marketing collusion between critics and the cultural pages of the dailies; finally he focused on my book, first ironically, then, when he cited the slightly risqué pages, in an openly hostile tone. I turned red and rather than answer I mumbled some banal comments, off the subject. Until I broke off, exhausted, and stared at the table. The professor-critic encouraged me with a smile, with his gaze, thinking that I wanted to continue. When he realized that I didn't intend to, he asked curtly: "Anyone else?"

At the back a hand was raised.

"Please."

A tall young man, with long, unruly hair and a thick black beard, spoke in a contemptuously polemical way of the preceding speaker, and, a few times, even of the introduction of the nice man who was sitting next to me. He said we lived in a provincial country, where every occasion was an opportunity for complaining, but meanwhile no one rolled up his sleeves and reorganized things, trying to make them function. Then he went on to praise the modernizing force of my novel. I recognized him most of all by his voice, it was Nino Sarratore.

Elena Ferrante is the author of *The Days of Abandonment* (Europa, 2005), *Troubling Love* (Europa, 2006), and *The Lost Daughter* (Europa, 2008), soon to be a film directed by Maggie Gyllenhaal and starring Olivia Colman, Dakota Johnson, and Paul Mescal. She is also the author of *Incidental Inventions* (Europa, 2019), illustrated by Andrea Ucini, *Frantumaglia: A Writer's Journey* (Europa, 2016) and *The Beach at Night* (Europa, 2016), a children's picture book illustrated by Mara Cerri. The four volumes known as the "Neapolitan quartet" (*My Brilliant Friend, The Story of a New Name, Those Who Leave and Those Who Stay,* and *The Story of the Lost Child*) were published by Europa Editions in English between 2012 and 2015. *My Brilliant Friend,* the HBO series directed by Saverio Costanzo, premiered in 2018. Ferrante's most recent novel is *The Lying Life of Adults,* published in 2020 by Europa Editions.

THE NEAPOLITAN QUARTET
by Elena Ferrante

"Imagine if Jane Austen got angry and you'll have
some idea how explosive these works are."
—John Freeman

"Ferrante's novels are intensely, violently personal,
and because of this they seem to dangle bristling key
chains of confession before the unsuspecting reader."
—James Wood, *The New Yorker*

978-1-60945-078-6 • September 2012

"Stunning . . . cinematic in the density of its detail."
—The *Times Literary Supplement*

978-1-60945-134-9 • September 2013

"Everyone should read anything with Ferrante's
name on it."—Eugenia Williamson, *The Boston Globe*

978-1-60945-233-9 • September 2014

"One of modern fiction's richest portraits of a friendship."
—John Powers, *NPR's Fresh Air*

978-1-60945-286-5 • September 2015

Elena Ferrante's New Novel
The Lying Life of Adults

"Another spellbinding coming-of-age tale from a master."
—*People Magazine*

978-1-60945-715-0 • Available now

MY BRILLIANT
FRIEND

Elena Ferrante

MY BRILLIANT FRIEND

Book One: The Neapolitan Quartet
Childhood, Adolescence

Translated by Ann Goldstein

Europa

Elena Ferrante

MY BRILLIANT
FRIEND

Book One, The Neapolitan Quartet
Childhood, Adolescence

*Translated from the Italian
by Ann Goldstein*

Europa
editions

Europa Editions
1 Penn Plaza, Suite 6282
New York, N.Y. 10019
www.europaeditions.com
info@europaeditions.com

Translation by Ann Goldstein
Original title: *L'amica geniale*
Translation copyright © 2012 by Europa Editions

Library of Congress Cataloging in Publication Data is available
ISBN 978-1-60945-506-4

Ferrante, Elena
My Brilliant Friend

Book design by Emanuele Ragnisco
www.mekkanografici.com

Cover photo © Anthony Boccaccio/Getty Images

Prepress by Grafica Punto Print –Rome

Printed in Italy

THE LORD: Therein thou'rt free, according to thy merits;
The like of thee have never moved My hate.
Of all the bold, denying Spirits,
The waggish knave least trouble doth create.
Man's active nature, flagging, seeks too soon the level;
Unqualified repose he learns to crave;
Whence, willingly, the comrade him I gave,
Who works, excites, and must create, as Devil.

J. W. GOETHE, *Faust*,
translation by Bayard Taylor

CONTENTS

MY BRILLIANT
FRIEND

Index of Characters

The Cerullo family (the shoemaker's family):
Fernando Cerullo, shoemaker.
Nunzia Cerullo, wife of Fernando and Lila's mother.
Raffaella Cerullo, called *Lina*, and by Elena *Lila*.
Rino Cerullo, Lila's older brother, also a shoemaker.
Rino, also the name of one of Lila's children.
Other children.

The Greco family (the porter's family):
Elena Greco, called *Lenuccia* or *Lenù*. She is the oldest, and
  after her are *Peppe*, *Gianni*, and *Elisa*.
The *father* is a porter at the city hall.
The *mother* is a housewife.

The Carracci family (Don Achille's family):
Don Achille Carracci, the ogre of fairy tales.
Maria Carracci, wife of Don Achille.
Stefano Carracci, son of Don Achille, grocer in the family store.
Pinuccia and *Alfonso Carracci*, Don Achille's two other chil-
  dren.

The Peluso family (the carpenter's family):
Alfredo Peluso, carpenter.
Giuseppina Peluso, wife of Alfredo.
Pasquale Peluso, older son of Alfredo and Giuseppina, con-
  struction worker.

Carmela Peluso, who is also called *Carmen*, sister of Pasquale, salesclerk in a dry-goods store.
Other children.

The Cappuccio family (the mad widow's family):
Melina, a relative of Lila's mother, a mad widow.
Melina's *husband*, who unloaded crates at the fruit and vegetable market.
Ada Cappuccio, Melina's daughter.
Antonio Cappuccio, her brother, a mechanic.
Other children.

The Sarratore family (the railroad worker poet's family):
Donato Sarratore, conductor.
Lidia Sarratore, wife of Donato.
Nino Sarratore, the oldest of the five children of Donato and Lidia.
Marisa Sarratore, daughter of Donato and Lidia.
Pino, Clelia, and *Ciro Sarratore*, younger children of Donato and Lidia.

The Scanno family (the fruit and vegetable seller's family):
Nicola Scanno, fruit and vegetable seller.
Assunta Scanno, wife of Nicola.
Enzo Scanno, son of Nicola and Assunta, also a fruit and vegetable seller.
Other children.

The Solara family (the family of the owner of the Solara bar-pastry shop):
Silvio Solara, owner of the bar-pastry shop.
Manuela Solara, wife of Silvio.
Marcello and *Michele Solara*, sons of Silvio and Manuela.

The Spagnuolo family (the baker's family):
Signor Spagnuolo, pastry maker at the bar-pastry shop Solara.
Rosa Spagnuolo, wife of the pastry maker.
Gigliola Spagnuolo, daughter of the pastry maker.
Other children.

Gino, son of the pharmacist.

The teachers:
Maestro Ferraro, teacher and librarian.
Maestra Oliviero, teacher.
Professor Gerace, high school teacher.
Professor Galiani, high school teacher.

Nella Incardo, Maestra Oliviero's cousin, who lives on Ischia.

PROLOGUE

Eliminating All the Traces

1.

This morning Rino telephoned. I thought he wanted money again and I was ready to say no. But that was not the reason for the phone call: his mother was gone.

"Since when?"

"Since two weeks ago."

"And you're calling me now?"

My tone must have seemed hostile, even though I wasn't angry or offended; there was just a touch of sarcasm. He tried to respond but he did so in an awkward, muddled way, half in dialect, half in Italian. He said he was sure that his mother was wandering around Naples as usual.

"Even at night?"

"You know how she is."

"I do, but does two weeks of absence seem normal?"

"Yes. You haven't seen her for a while, Elena, she's gotten worse: she's never sleepy, she comes in, goes out, does what she likes."

Anyway, in the end he had started to get worried. He had asked everyone, made the rounds of the hospitals: he had even gone to the police. Nothing, his mother wasn't anywhere. What a good son: a large man, forty years old, who hadn't worked in his life, just a small-time crook and spendthrift. I could imagine how carefully he had done his searching. Not at all. He had no brain, and in his heart he had only himself.

"She's not with you?" he asked suddenly.

His mother? Here in Turin? He knew the situation perfectly

well, he was speaking only to speak. Yes, he liked to travel, he had come to my house at least a dozen times, without being invited. His mother, whom I would have welcomed with pleasure, had never left Naples in her life. I answered:

"No, she's not with me."

"You're sure?"

"Rino, please, I told you she's not here."

"Then where has she gone?"

He began to cry and I let him act out his desperation, sobs that began fake and became real. When he stopped I said:

"Please, for once behave as she would like: don't look for her."

"What do you mean?"

"Just what I said. It's pointless. Learn to stand on your own two feet and don't call me again, either."

I hung up.

2.

Rino's mother is named Raffaella Cerullo, but everyone has always called her Lina. Not me, I've never used either her first name or her last. To me, for more than sixty years, she's been Lila. If I were to call her Lina or Raffaella, suddenly, like that, she would think our friendship was over.

It's been at least three decades since she told me that she wanted to disappear without leaving a trace, and I'm the only one who knows what she means. She never had in mind any sort of flight, a change of identity, the dream of making a new life somewhere else. And she never thought of suicide, repulsed by the idea that Rino would have anything to do with her body, and be forced to attend to the details. She meant something different: she wanted to vanish; she wanted every one of her cells to disappear, nothing of her ever to be found. And since

I know her well, or at least I think I know her, I take it for granted that she has found a way to disappear, to leave not so much as a hair anywhere in this world.

3.

Days passed. I looked at my e-mail, at my regular mail, but not with any hope. I often wrote to her, and she almost never responded: this was her habit. She preferred the telephone or long nights of talk when I went to Naples.

I opened my drawers, the metal boxes where I keep all kinds of things. Not much there. I've thrown away a lot of stuff, especially anything that had to do with her, and she knows it. I discovered that I have nothing of hers, not a picture, not a note, not a little gift. I was surprised myself. Is it possible that in all those years she left me nothing of herself, or, worse, that I didn't want to keep anything of her? It is.

This time I telephoned Rino; I did it unwillingly. He didn't answer on the house phone or on his cell phone. He called me in the evening, when it was convenient. He spoke in the tone of voice he uses to arouse pity.

"I saw that you called. Do you have any news?"

"No. Do you?"

"Nothing."

He rambled incoherently. He wanted to go on TV, on the show that looks for missing persons, make an appeal, ask his mamma's forgiveness for everything, beg her to return.

I listened patiently, then asked him: "Did you look in her closet?"

"What for?"

Naturally the most obvious thing would never occur to him.

"Go and look."

He went, and he realized that there was nothing there, not

one of his mother's dresses, summer or winter, only old hangers. I sent him to search the whole house. Her shoes were gone. The few books: gone. All the photographs: gone. The movies: gone. Her computer had disappeared, including the old-fashioned diskettes and everything, everything to do with her experience as an electronics wizard who had begun to operate computers in the late sixties, in the days of punch cards. Rino was astonished. I said to him:

"Take as much time as you want, but then call and tell me if you've found even a single hairpin that belongs to her."

He called the next day, greatly agitated.

"There's nothing."

"Nothing at all?"

"No. She cut herself out of all the photographs of the two of us, even those from when I was little."

"You looked carefully?"

"Everywhere."

"Even in the cellar?"

"I told you, everywhere. And the box with her papers is gone: I don't know, old birth certificates, telephone bills, receipts. What does it mean? Did someone steal everything? What are they looking for? What do they want from my mother and me?"

I reassured him, I told him to calm down. It was unlikely that anyone wanted anything, especially from him.

"Can I come and stay with you for a while?"

"No."

"Please, I can't sleep."

"That's your problem, Rino, I don't know what to do about it."

I hung up and when he called back I didn't answer. I sat down at my desk.

Lila is overdoing it as usual, I thought.

She was expanding the concept of trace out of all proportion. She wanted not only to disappear herself, now, at the age of sixty-six, but also to eliminate the entire life that she had left behind.

I was really angry.

We'll see who wins this time, I said to myself. I turned on the computer and began to write—all the details of our story, everything that still remained in my memory.

CHILDHOOD

The Story of Don Achille

My friendship with Lila began the day we decided to go up the dark stairs that led, step after step, flight after flight, to the door of Don Achille's apartment.

I remember the violet light of the courtyard, the smells of a warm spring evening. The mothers were making dinner, it was time to go home, but we delayed, challenging each other, without ever saying a word, testing our courage. For some time, in school and outside of it, that was what we had been doing. Lila would thrust her hand and then her whole arm into the black mouth of a manhole, and I, in turn, immediately did the same, my heart pounding, hoping that the cockroaches wouldn't run over my skin, that the rats wouldn't bite me. Lila climbed up to Signora Spagnuolo's ground-floor window, and, hanging from the iron bar that the clothesline was attached to, swung back and forth, then lowered herself down to the sidewalk, and I immediately did the same, although I was afraid of falling and hurting myself. Lila stuck into her skin the rusted safety pin that she had found on the street somewhere but kept in her pocket like the gift of a fairy godmother; I watched the metal point as it dug a whitish tunnel into her palm, and then, when she pulled it out and handed it to me, I did the same.

At some point she gave me one of her firm looks, eyes narrowed, and headed toward the building where Don Achille lived. I was frozen with fear. Don Achille was the ogre of fairy tales, I was absolutely forbidden to go near him, speak to him, look at him, spy on him, I was to act as if neither he nor his family existed. Regarding him there was, in my house but not only mine, a fear and a hatred whose origin I didn't know. The way my father talked about him, I imagined a huge man, covered with purple boils, violent in spite of the "don," which to me suggested a calm authority. He was a being created out of some unidentifiable material, iron, glass, nettles, but alive, alive, the hot breath streaming from his nose and mouth. I thought that if I merely saw him from a distance he would drive something sharp and burning into my eyes. So if I was mad enough to approach the door of his house he would kill me.

I waited to see if Lila would have second thoughts and turn back. I knew what she wanted to do, I had hoped that she would forget about it, but in vain. The street lamps were not yet lighted, nor were the lights on the stairs. From the apartments came irritable voices. To follow Lila I had to leave the bluish light of the courtyard and enter the black of the doorway. When I finally made up my mind, I saw nothing at first, there was only an odor of old junk and DDT. Then I got used to the darkness and found Lila sitting on the first step of the first flight of stairs. She got up and we began to climb.

We kept to the side where the wall was, she two steps ahead, I two steps behind, torn between shortening the distance or letting it increase. I can still feel my shoulder inching along the flaking wall and the idea that the steps were very high, higher than those in the building where I lived. I was trembling. Every footfall, every voice was Don Achille creeping up behind us or coming down toward us with a long knife, the kind used for slicing open a chicken breast. There was an odor of sautéing garlic. Maria, Don Achille's wife, would put me in the pan of boiling oil, the children would eat me, he would suck my head the way my father did with mullets.

We stopped often, and each time I hoped that Lila would decide to turn back. I was all sweaty, I don't know about her. Every so often she looked up, but I couldn't tell at what, all that was visible was the gray areas of the big windows at every landing. Suddenly the lights came on, but they were faint, dusty, leaving broad zones of shadow, full of dangers. We waited to see if it was Don Achille who had turned the switch, but we heard nothing, neither footsteps nor the opening or closing of a door. Then Lila continued on, and I followed.

She thought that what we were doing was just and necessary; I had forgotten every good reason, and certainly was there only because she was. We climbed slowly toward the greatest of our terrors of that time, we went to expose ourselves to fear and interrogate it.

At the fourth flight Lila did something unexpected. She stopped to wait for me, and when I reached her she gave me her hand. This gesture changed everything between us forever.

2.

It was her fault. Not too long before—ten days, a month, who can say, we knew nothing about time, in those days—she had treacherously taken my doll and thrown her down into a cellar. Now we were climbing toward fear; then we had felt obliged to descend, quickly, into the unknown. Up or down, it seemed to us that we were always going toward something terrible that had existed before us yet had always been waiting for us, just for us. When you haven't been in the world long, it's hard to comprehend what disasters are at the origin of a sense of disaster: maybe you don't even feel the need to. Adults, waiting for tomorrow, move in a present behind which is yesterday or the day before yesterday or at most last week: they don't want to think about the rest. Children don't know the meaning of yesterday, of the day before yesterday, or even of tomorrow, everything is this, now: the street is this, the doorway is this, the stairs are this, this is Mamma, this is Papa, this is the day, this the night. I was small and really my doll knew more than I did. I talked to her, she talked to me. She had a plastic face and plastic hair and plastic eyes. She wore a blue dress that my mother had made for her in a rare moment of happiness, and she was beautiful. Lila's doll, on the other hand, had a cloth body of a yellowish color, filled with sawdust, and she seemed to me ugly and grimy. The two spied on each other, they sized each other up, they were ready to flee into our arms if a storm burst, if there was thunder, if someone bigger and stronger, with sharp teeth, wanted to snatch them away.

We played in the courtyard but as if we weren't playing together. Lila sat on the ground, on one side of a small barred basement window, I on the other. We liked that place, especially because behind the bars was a metal grating and, against the grating, on the cement ledge between the bars, we could arrange the things that belonged to Tina, my doll, and those of Nu, Lila's doll. There we put rocks, bottle tops, little flowers, nails, splinters of glass. I overheard what Lila said to Nu and repeated it in a low voice to Tina, slightly modified. If she took a bottle top and put it on her doll's head, like a hat, I said to mine, in dialect, Tina, put on your queen's crown or you'll catch cold. If Nu played hopscotch in Lila's arms, I soon afterward made Tina do the same. Still, it never happened that we decided on a game and began playing together. Even that place we chose without explicit agreement. Lila sat down there, and I strolled around, pretending to go somewhere else. Then, as if I'd given it no thought, I, too, settled next to the cellar window, but on the opposite side.

The thing that attracted us most was the cold air that came from the cellar, a breath that refreshed us in spring and summer. And then we liked the bars with their spiderwebs, the darkness, and the tight mesh of the grating that, reddish with rust, curled up both on my side and on Lila's, creating two parallel holes through which we could drop rocks into obscurity and hear the sound when they hit bottom. It was all beautiful and frightening then. Through those openings the darkness might suddenly seize the dolls, who sometimes were safe in our arms, but more often were placed deliberately next to the twisted grating and thus exposed to the cellar's cold breath, to its threatening noises, rustling, squeaking, scraping.

Nu and Tina weren't happy. The terrors that we tasted every day were theirs. We didn't trust the light on the stones, on the buildings, on the scrubland beyond the neighborhood, on the people inside and outside their houses. We imagined the dark corners, the feelings repressed but always close to exploding. And to those shadowy mouths, the caverns that opened beyond them under the buildings, we attributed everything that frightened us in the light of day. Don Achille, for example, was not only in his apartment on the top floor but also down below, a spider among spiders, a rat among rats, a shape that assumed all shapes. I imagined him with his mouth open because of his long animal fangs, his body of glazed stone and poisonous grasses, always ready to pick up in an enormous black bag anything we dropped through the torn corners of the grate. That bag was a fundamental feature of Don Achille, he always had it, even at home, and into it he put material both living and dead.

Lila knew that I had that fear, my doll talked about it out loud. And so, on the day we exchanged our dolls for the first time—with no discussion, only looks and gestures—as soon as she had Tina, she pushed her through the grate and let her fall into the darkness.

3.

Lila appeared in my life in first grade and immediately impressed me because she was very bad. In that class we were all a little bad, but only when the teacher, Maestra Oliviero, couldn't see us. Lila, on the other hand, was always bad. Once she tore up some blotting paper into little pieces, dipped the pieces one by one in the inkwell, and then fished them out with her pen and threw them at us. I was hit twice in the hair and once on my white collar. The teacher yelled, as she knew how to do, in a voice like a needle, long and pointed, which terrorized us, and ordered her to go and stand behind the blackboard in punishment. Lila didn't obey and didn't even seem frightened; she just kept throwing around pieces of inky paper. So Maestra Oliviero, a heavy woman who seemed very old to us, though she couldn't have been much over forty, came down from the desk, threatening her. The teacher stumbled, it wasn't clear on what, lost her balance, and fell, striking her face against the corner of a desk. She lay on the floor as if dead.

What happened right afterward I don't remember, I remember only the dark bundle of the teacher's motionless body, and Lila staring at her with a serious expression.

I have in my mind so many incidents of this type. We lived in a world in which children and adults were often wounded, blood flowed from the wounds, they festered, and sometimes people died. One of the daughters of Signora Assunta, the fruit and vegetable seller, had stepped on a nail and died of tetanus. Signora Spagnuolo's youngest child had died of croup. A cousin of mine, at the age of twenty, had gone one morning to move some rubble and that night was dead, crushed, the blood pouring out of his ears and mouth. My mother's father had been killed when he fell from a scaffolding at a building site. The father of Signor Peluso was missing an arm, the lathe had caught him unawares. The sister of Giuseppina, Signor Peluso's wife, had died of tuberculosis at twenty-two. The oldest son of Don Achille—I had never seen him, and yet I seemed to remember him—had gone to war and died twice: drowned in the Pacific Ocean, then eaten by sharks. The entire

Melchiorre family had died clinging to each other, screaming with fear, in a bombardment. Old Signorina Clorinda had died inhaling gas instead of air. Giannino, who was in fourth grade when we were in first, had died one day because he had come across a bomb and touched it. Luigina, with whom we had played in the courtyard, or maybe not, she was only a name, had died of typhus. Our world was like that, full of words that killed: croup, tetanus, typhus, gas, war, lathe, rubble, work, bombardment, bomb, tuberculosis, infection. With these words and those years I bring back the many fears that accompanied me all my life.

You could also die of things that seemed normal. You could die, for example, if you were sweating and then drank cold water from the tap without first bathing your wrists: you'd break out in red spots, you'd start coughing, and be unable to breathe. You could die if you ate black cherries and didn't spit out the pits. You could die if you chewed American gum and inadvertently swallowed it. You could die if you banged your temple. The temple, in particular, was a fragile place, we were all careful about it. Being hit with a stone could do it, and throwing stones was the norm. When we left school a gang of boys from the countryside, led by a kid called Enzo or Enzuccio, who was one of the children of Assunta the fruit and vegetable seller, began to throw rocks at us. They were angry because we were smarter than them. When the rocks came at us we ran away, except Lila, who kept walking at her regular pace and sometimes even stopped. She was very good at studying the trajectory of the stones and dodging them with an easy move that today I would call elegant. She had an older brother and maybe she had learned from him, I don't know, I also had brothers, but they were younger than me and from them I had learned nothing. Still, when I realized that she had stayed behind, I stopped to wait for her, even though I was scared.

Already then there was something that kept me from abandoning her. I didn't know her well; we had never spoken to each other, although we were constantly competing, in class and outside it. But in a confused way I felt that if I ran away with the others I would leave with her something of mine that she would never give back.

At first I stayed hidden, around a corner, and leaned out to see if Lila was coming. Then, since she wouldn't budge, I forced myself to rejoin her; I handed her stones, and even threw some myself. But I did it without conviction: I did many things in my life without conviction; I always felt slightly detached from my own actions. Lila, on the other hand, had, from a young age—I can't say now precisely if it was so at six or seven, or when we went together up the stairs that led to Don Achille's and were eight, almost nine—the characteristic of absolute determination. Whether she was gripping the tricolor shaft of the pen or a stone or the handrail on the dark stairs, she communicated the idea that whatever came next—thrust the pen with a precise motion into the wood of the desk, dispense inky bullets, strike the boys from the countryside, climb the stairs to Don Achille's door—she would do without hesitation.

The gang came from the railroad embankment, stocking up on rocks from the trackbed. Enzo, the leader, was a dangerous child, with very short blond hair and pale eyes; he was at least three years older than us, and had repeated a year. He threw small, sharp-edged rocks with great accuracy, and Lila waited for his throws to demonstrate how she evaded them, making him still angrier, and responded with throws that were just as dangerous. Once we hit him in the right calf, and I say we because I had handed Lila a flat stone with jagged edges. The stone slid over Enzo's skin like a razor, leaving a red stain that immediately gushed blood. The child looked at his wounded leg. I have him before my eyes: between thumb and index finger he held the rock that he was about to throw, his arm was raised to throw it, and yet he stopped, bewildered. The boys under his command also looked incredulously at the blood. Lila, however, manifested not the least satisfaction in the outcome of the throw and bent over to pick up another stone. I grabbed her by the arm; it was the first contact between us, an abrupt, frightened contact. I felt that the gang would get more ferocious and I wanted to retreat. But there wasn't time. Enzo, in spite of his bleeding calf, came out of his stupor and threw the rock in his hand. I was still holding on to Lila when the rock hit her in the head and knocked her away from me. A second later she was lying on the sidewalk with a gash in her forehead.

4.

Blood. In general it came from wounds only after horrible curses and disgusting obscenities had been exchanged. That was the standard procedure. My father, though he seemed to me a good man, hurled continuous insults and threats if someone didn't deserve, as he said, to be on the face of the earth. He especially had it in for Don Achille. He always had something to accuse him of, and sometimes I put my hands over my ears in order not to be too disturbed by his brutal words. When he spoke of him to my mother he called him "your cousin" but my mother denied that blood tie (there was a very distant relationship) and added to the insults. Their anger frightened me, I was frightened above all by the thought that Don Achille might have ears so sensitive that he could hear insults even from far away. I was afraid that he might come and murder them.

The sworn enemy of Don Achille, however, was not my father but Signor Peluso, a very good carpenter who was always broke, because he gambled away everything he earned in the back room of the Bar Solara. Peluso was the father of our classmate Carmela, of Pasquale, who was older, and of two others, children poorer than us, with whom Lila and I sometimes played, and who in school and outside always tried to steal our things, a pen, an eraser, the *cotognata*, so that they went home covered with bruises because we'd hit them.

The times we saw him, Signor Peluso seemed to us the image of despair. On the one hand he lost everything gambling and on the other he was criticized in public because he was no longer able to feed his family. For obscure reasons he attributed his ruin to Don Achille. He charged him with having taken by stealth, as if his shadowy body were a magnet, all the tools for his carpentry work, which made the shop useless. He accused him of having taken the shop itself, and transforming it into a grocery store. For years I imagined the pliers, the saw, the tongs, the hammer, the vise, and thousands and thousands of nails sucked up like a swarm of metal into the matter that made up Don Achille. For years I saw his body—a coarse body, heavy with a mixture of materials—emitting in a swarm salami, provolone, mortadella, lard, and prosciutto.

These things had happened in the dark ages. Don Achille had supposedly revealed himself in all his monstrous nature before we were born. *Before.* Lila often used that formulation. But she didn't seem to care as much about what had happened before us—events that were in general obscure, and about which the adults either were silent or spoke with great reticence—as about the fact that there really had been a before. It was this which at the time left her puzzled and occasionally even made her nervous. When we became friends she spoke so much of that absurd thing—*before us*—that she ended up passing on her nervousness to me. It was the long, very long, period when we didn't exist, that period when Don Achille had showed himself to everyone for what

he was: an evil being of uncertain animal-mineral physiog-
nomy, who—it seemed—sucked blood from others while
never losing any himself, maybe it wasn't even possible to
scratch him.

We were in second grade, perhaps, and still hadn't spoken
to each other, when the rumor spread that right in front of the
Church of the Holy Family, right after Mass, Signor Peluso had
started screaming furiously at Don Achille. Don Achille had
left his older son Stefano, his daughter Pinuccia, Alfonso, who
was our age, and his wife, and, appearing for a moment in his
most hair-raising form, had hurled himself at Peluso, picked
him up, thrown him against a tree in the public gardens, and
left him there, barely conscious, with blood coming out of
innumerable wounds in his head and everywhere, and the poor
man able to say merely: help.

5.

I feel no nostalgia for our childhood: it was full of violence.
Every sort of thing happened, at home and outside, every day,
but I don't recall having ever thought that the life we had there
was particularly bad. Life was like that, that's all, we grew up
with the duty to make it difficult for others before they made
it difficult for us. Of course, I would have liked the nice manners that the teacher and the priest preached, but I felt that
those ways were not suited to our neighborhood, even if you
were a girl. The women fought among themselves more than
the men, they pulled each other's hair, they hurt each other. To
cause pain was a disease. As a child I imagined tiny, almost
invisible animals that arrived in the neighborhood at night,
they came from the ponds, from the abandoned train cars
beyond the embankment, from the stinking grasses called *feti-
enti*, from the frogs, the salamanders, the flies, the rocks, the

dust, and entered the water and the food and the air, making
our mothers, our grandmothers as angry as starving dogs. They
were more severely infected than the men, because while men
were always getting furious, they calmed down in the end;
women, who appeared to be silent, acquiescent, when they
were angry flew into a rage that had no end.

Lila was deeply affected by what had happened to Melina
Cappuccio, a relative of her mother's. And I, too. Melina lived
in the same building as my family, we on the second floor, she
on the third. She was only a little over thirty and had six children, but to us she seemed an old woman. Her husband was
the same age; he unloaded crates at the fruit and vegetable
market. I recall him as short and broad, but handsome, with a
proud face. One night he came out of the house as usual and
died, perhaps murdered, perhaps of weariness. The funeral
was very bitter; the whole neighborhood went, including my
parents, and Lila's parents. Then time passed and something
happened to Melina. On the outside she remained the same, a
gaunt woman with a large nose, her hair already gray, a shrill
voice that at night called her children from the window, by
name, the syllables drawn out by an angry despair: Aaa-daaa,
Miii-chè. At first she was much helped by Donato Sarratore,
who lived in the apartment right above hers, on the fourth and
top floor. Donato was diligent in his attendance at the Church
of the Holy Family and as a good Christian he did a lot for her,
collecting money, used clothes, and shoes, settling Antonio, the
oldest son, in the auto-repair shop of Gorresio, an acquaintance of his. Melina was so grateful that her gratitude became,
in her desolate woman's heart, love, passion. It wasn't clear if
Sarratore was ever aware of it. He was a friendly man but very
serious—home, church, and job. He worked on a train crew
for the state railroad, and had a decent salary on which he supported his wife, Lidia, and five children; the oldest was called
Nino. When he wasn't traveling on the Naples-Paola route he

devoted himself to fixing this or that in the house, he did the shopping, took the youngest child out in the carriage. These things were very unusual in the neighborhood. It occurred to no one that Donato was generous in that way to lighten the burdens of his wife. No: all the neighborhood men, my father in the lead, considered him a womanish man, even more so because he wrote poems and read them willingly to anyone. It didn't occur even to Melina. The widow preferred to think that, because of his gentle spirit, he was put upon by his wife, and so she decided to do battle against Lidia Sarratore to free him and let him join her permanently. The war that followed at first seemed funny; it was discussed in my house and elsewhere with malicious laughter. Lidia would hang out the sheets fresh from the laundry and Melina climbed up on the windowsill and dirtied them with a reed whose tip she had charred in the fire; Lidia passed under her windows and she spit on her head or emptied buckets of dirty water on her; Lidia made noise during the day walking above her, with her unruly children, and she banged the floor mop against the ceiling all night. Sarratore tried by every means to make peace, but he was too sensitive, too polite. As their vindictiveness increased, the two women began to insult each other if they met on the street or the stairs: harsh, fierce sounds. It was then that they began to frighten me. One of the many terrible scenes of my childhood begins with the shouts of Melina and Lidia, with the insults they hurl from the windows and then on the stairs; it continues with my mother rushing to our door, opening it, and looking out, followed by us children; and ends with the image, for me still unbearable, of the two neighbors rolling down the stairs, entwined, and Melina's head hitting the floor of the landing, a few inches from my shoes, like a white melon that has slipped from your hand.

It's hard to say why at the time we children took the part of Lidia Sarratore. Maybe because she had regular features and

blond hair. Or because Donato was hers and we had understood that Melina wanted to take him away from her. Or
because Melina's children were ragged and dirty, while Lidia's
were washed, well groomed, and the oldest, Nino, who was a
few years older than us, was handsome, and we liked him. Lila
alone favored Melina, but she never explained why. She said
only, once, that if Lidia Sarratore ended up murdered she
deserved it, and I thought that it was partly because she was
mean in her heart and partly because she and Melina were distant relatives.

One day we were coming home from school, four or five
girls. With us was Marisa Sarratore, who usually joined us not
because we liked her but because we hoped that, through her,
we might meet her older brother, that is to say Nino. It was she
who first noticed Melina. The woman was walking slowly from
one side of the *stradone*, the wide avenue that ran through the
neighborhood, to the other, carrying a paper bag in one hand
from which, with the other, she was taking something and eating it. Marisa pointed to her, calling her "the whore," without
rancor, but because she was repeating the phrase that her
mother used at home. Lila, although she was shorter and very
thin, immediately slapped her so hard that she knocked her
down: ruthless, as she usually was on occasions of violence, no
yelling before or after, no word of warning, cold and determined, not even widening her eyes.

First I went to the aid of Marisa, who was crying, and
helped her get up, then I turned to see what Lila was doing.
She had left the sidewalk and was going toward Melina, crossing the street without paying attention to the passing trucks. I
saw in her, in her posture more than in her face, something that
disturbed me and is still hard to define, so for now I'll put it
like this: she was moving, cutting across the street, a small,
dark, nervous figure, she was acting with her usual determination, she was firm. Firm in what her mother's relative was

doing, firm in the pain, firm in silence as a statue is firm. A follower. One with Melina, who was holding in her palm the dark soft soap she had just bought in Don Carlo's cellar, and with her other hand was taking some and eating it.

6.

The day Maestra Oliviero fell from the desk and hit her cheekbone against it, I, as I said, thought she was dead, dead on the job like my grandfather or Melina's husband, and it seemed to me that as a result Lila, too, would die because of the terrible punishment she would get. Instead, for a period I can't define—short, long—nothing happened. They simply disappeared, both of them, teacher and pupil, from our days and from memory.

But then everything was surprising. Maestra Oliviero returned to school alive and began to concern herself with Lila, not to punish her, as would have seemed to us natural, but to praise her.

This new phase began when Lila's mother, Signora Cerullo, was called to school. One morning the janitor knocked and announced her. Right afterward Nunzia Cerullo came in, unrecognizable. She, who, like the majority of the neighborhood women, lived untidily in slippers and shabby old dresses, appeared in her formal black dress (wedding, communion, christening, funeral), with a shiny black purse and low-heeled shoes that tortured her swollen feet, and handed the teacher two paper bags, one containing sugar and the other coffee.

The teacher accepted the gifts with pleasure and, looking at Lila, who was staring at the desk, spoke to her, and to the whole class, words whose general sense disoriented me. We were just learning the alphabet and the numbers from one to ten. I was the smartest in the class, I could recognize all the letters, I knew how to say one two three four and so on, I was constantly praised for my handwriting, I won the tricolor cockades that the teacher sewed. Yet, surprisingly, Maestra Oliviero, although Lila had made her fall and sent her to the hospital, said that she was the best among us. True that she was the worst-behaved. True that she had done that terrible thing of shooting ink-soaked bits of blotting paper at us. True that if that girl had not acted in such a disruptive manner she, our teacher, would not have fallen and cut her cheek. True that she was compelled to punish her constantly with the wooden rod or by sending her to kneel on the hard floor behind the blackboard. But there was a fact that, as a teacher and also as a person, filled her with joy, a marvelous fact that she had discovered a few days earlier, by chance.

Here she stopped, as if words were not enough, or as if she wished to teach Lila's mother and us that deeds almost always count more than words. She took a piece of chalk and wrote on the blackboard (now I don't remember what, I didn't yet know how to read: so I'm inventing the word) "sun." Then she asked Lila:

"Cerullo, what is written there?"

In the classroom a fascinated silence fell. Lila half smiled, almost a grimace, and flung herself sideways, against her deskmate, who was visibly irritated. Then she read in a sullen tone:

"Sun."

Nunzia Cerullo looked at the teacher, and her look was hesitant, almost fearful. The teacher at first seemed not to understand why her own enthusiasm was not reflected in the mother's eyes. But then she must have guessed that Nunzia didn't know how to read, or, anyway, that she wasn't sure the word "sun" really was written on the blackboard, and she frowned. Then, partly to clarify the situation to Signora Cerullo, partly to praise our classmate, she said to Lila:

"Good, 'sun' is what it says there."

Then she ordered her:

"Come, Cerullo, come to the blackboard."

Lila went unwillingly to the blackboard, the teacher handed her the chalk.

"Write," she said to her, " 'chalk.' "

Lila, very concentrated, in shaky handwriting, placing the letters one a little higher, one a little lower, wrote: "chak."

Oliviero added the "l" and Signora Cerullo, seeing the correction, said in despair to her daughter:

"You made a mistake."

But the teacher immediately reassured her:

"No, no, no. Lila has to practice, yes, but she already knows how to read, she already knows how to write. Who taught her?"

Signora Cerullo, eyes lowered, said: "Not me."

"But at your house or in the building is there someone who might have taught her?"

Nunzia shook her head no emphatically.

Then the teacher turned to Lila and with sincere admiration asked her in front of all of us, "Who taught you to read and write, Cerullo?"

Cerullo, that small dark-haired, dark-eyed child, in a dark smock with a red ribbon at the neck, and only six years old, answered, "Me."

7.

According to Rino, Lila's older brother, she had learned to read at the age of around three by looking at the letters and pictures in his primer. She would sit next to him in the kitchen while he was doing his homework, and she learned more than he did.

Rino was almost six years older than Lila; he was a fearless boy who shone in all the courtyard and street games, especially spinning a top. But reading, writing, arithmetic, learning poems by heart were not for him. When he was scarcely ten his father, Fernando, had begun to take him every day to his tiny shoemaker's shop, in a narrow side street that ran off the *stradone*, to teach him the craft of resoling shoes. We girls, when we met him, smelled on him the odor of dirty feet, of old uppers, of glue, and we made fun of him, we called him shoe-soler. Maybe that's why he boasted that he was at the origin of his sister's virtuosity. But in reality he had never had a primer, and hadn't sat for even a minute, ever, to do homework. Impossible therefore that Lila had learned from his scholastic labors. It was more likely that she had precociously learned how the alphabet worked from the sheets of newspaper in which customers wrapped the old shoes and which her father sometimes brought home and read to the family the most inter-esting local news items.

Anyway, however it had happened, the fact was this: Lila knew how to read and write, and what I remember of that gray morning when the teacher revealed it to us was, above all, the sense of weakness the news left me with. Right away, from the first day, school had seemed to me a much nicer place than home. It was the place in the neighborhood where I felt safest, I went there with excitement. I paid attention to the lessons, I carried out with the greatest diligence everything that I was told to carry out, I learned. But most of all I liked pleasing the teacher, I liked pleasing everyone. At home I was my father's favorite, and my brothers and sister, too, loved me. The prob-lem was my mother; with her things never took the right course. It seemed to me that, though I was barely six, she did her best to make me understand that I was superfluous in her life. I wasn't agreeable to her nor was she to me. Her body repulsed me, something she probably intuited. She was a dark blonde, blue-eyed, voluptuous. But you never knew where her right eye was looking. Nor did her right leg work properly—she called it the damaged leg. She limped, and her step agitated me, especially at night, when she couldn't sleep and walked along the hall to the kitchen, returned, started again. Sometimes I heard her angrily crushing with her heel the cockroaches that came through the front door, and I imagined her with furious eyes, as when she got mad at me.

Certainly she wasn't happy; the household chores wore her down, and there was never enough money. She often got angry with my father, a porter at the city hall, she shouted that he had to come up with something, she couldn't go on like this. They quarreled. But since my father never raised his voice, even when he lost patience, I always took his part against her, even though he sometimes beat her and could be threatening to me. It was he, and not my mother, who said to me, the first day of school: "Lenuccia, do well with the teacher and we'll let you go to school. But if you're not good, if you're not the best, Papa needs help and you'll go to work." Those words had really scared me, and yet, although he said them, I felt it was my mother who had suggested them, imposed them. I had promised them both that I would be good. And things had immediately gone so well that the teacher often said to me:

"Greco, come and sit next to me."

It was a great privilege. Maestra Oliviero always had an empty chair next to her, and the best students were called on to sit there, as a reward. In the early days, I was always sitting beside her. She urged me on with encouraging words, she praised my blond curls, and thus reinforced in me the wish to do well: completely the opposite of my mother, who, at home, so often rebuked me, sometimes abusively, that I wanted to hide in a dark corner and hope that she wouldn't find me. Then it happened that Signora Cerullo came to class and Maestra Oliviero revealed that Lila was far ahead of us. Not only that: she called on her to sit next to her more often than on me. What that demotion caused inside me I don't know, I find it difficult to say, today, faithfully and clearly what I felt. Perhaps nothing at first, some jealousy, like everyone else. But surely it was then that a worry began to take shape. I thought that, although my legs functioned perfectly well, I ran the constant risk of becoming crippled. I woke with that idea in my head and I got out of bed right away to see if my legs still worked. Maybe that's why I became focused on Lila, who had slender, agile legs, and was always moving them, kicking even when she was sitting next to the teacher, so that the teacher became irritated and soon sent her back to her desk. Something convinced me, then, that if I kept up with her, at her pace, my mother's limp, which had entered into my brain and wouldn't come out, would stop threatening me. I decided that I had to model myself on that girl, never let her out of my sight, even if she got annoyed and chased me away.

8.

I suppose that that was my way of reacting to envy, and hatred, and of suffocating them. Or maybe I disguised in that manner the sense of subordination, the fascination I felt. Certainly I trained myself to accept readily Lila's superiority in everything, and even her oppressions.

Besides, the teacher acted very shrewdly. It was true that she often called on Lila to sit next to her, but she seemed to do it more to make her behave than to reward her. She continued, in fact, to praise Marisa Sarratore, Carmela Peluso, and, especially, me. She let me shine with a vivid light, she encouraged me to become more and more disciplined, more diligent, more serious. When Lila stopped misbehaving and effortlessly outdid me, the teacher praised me first, with moderation, and then went on to exalt her prowess. I felt the poison of defeat more acutely when it was Sarratore or Peluso who did better than me. If, however, I came in second after Lila, I wore a meek expression of acquiescence. In those years I think I feared only one thing: not being paired, in the hierarchy established by Maestra Oliviero, with Lila; not to hear the teacher say proudly, Cerullo and Greco are the best. If one day she had said, the best are Cerullo and Sarratore, or Cerullo and Peluso, I would have died on the spot. So I used all my childish energies not to become first in the class—it seemed to me impossible to succeed there—but not to slip into third, fourth, last place. I devoted myself to studying and to many things that were difficult, alien to me, just so I could keep pace with that terrible, dazzling girl.

Dazzling to me. To our classmates Lila was only terrible. From first grade to fifth, she was, because of the principal and partly also because of Maestra Oliviero, the most hated child in the school and the neighborhood.

At least twice a year the principal had the classes compete against one another, in order to distinguish the most brilliant students and consequently the most competent teachers. Oliviero liked this competition. Our teacher, in permanent conflict with her colleagues, with whom she sometimes seemed near coming to blows, used Lila and me as the blazing proof of how good she was, the best teacher in the neighborhood elementary school. So she would often bring us to other classes, apart from the occasions arranged by the principal, to compete with the other children, girls and boys. Usually, I was sent on reconnaissance, to test the enemy's level of skill. In general I won, but without overdoing it, without humiliating either teachers or students. I was a pretty little girl with blond curls, happy to show off but not aggressive, and I gave an impression of delicacy that was touching. If then I was the best at reciting poems, repeating the times tables, doing division and multiplication, at rattling off the Maritime, Cottian, Graia, and Pennine

Alps, the other teachers gave me a pat anyway, while the students felt how hard I had worked to memorize all those facts, and didn't hate me.

In Lila's case it was different. Even by first grade she was beyond any possible competition. In fact, the teacher said that with a little application she would be able to take the test for second grade and, not yet seven, go into third. Later the gap increased. Lila did really complicated calculations in her head, in her dictations there was not a single mistake, she spoke in dialect like the rest of us but, when necessary, came out with a bookish Italian, using words like "accustomed," "luxuriant," "willingly." So that, when the teacher sent her into the field to give the moods or tenses of verbs or solve math problems, hearts grew bitter. Lila was too much for anyone.

Besides, she offered no openings to kindness. To recognize her virtuosity was for us children to admit that we would never win and so there was no point in competing, and for the teachers to confess to themselves that they had been mediocre children. Her quickness of mind was like a hiss, a dart, a lethal bite. And there was nothing in her appearance that acted as a corrective. She was disheveled, dirty, on her knees and elbows she always had scabs from cuts and scrapes that never had time to heal. Her large, bright eyes could become cracks behind which, before every brilliant response, there was a gaze that appeared not very childlike and perhaps not even human. Every one of her movements said that to harm her would be pointless because, whatever happened, she would find a way of doing worse to you.

The hatred was therefore tangible; I was aware of it. Both girls and boys were irritated by her, but the boys more openly. For a hidden motive of her own, in fact, Maestra Oliviero especially enjoyed taking us to the classes where the girl students and women teachers could not be humiliated so much as the males. And the principal, too, for equally hidden motives, preferred competitions of this type. Later I thought that in the school they were betting money, maybe even a lot, on those meetings of ours. But I was exaggerating: maybe it was just a way of giving vent to old grudges or allowing the principal to keep the less good or less obedient teachers under his control. The fact is that one morning the two of us, who were then in second grade, were taken to a fourth-grade class, Maestro Ferraro's, in which were both Enzo Scanno, the fierce son of the fruit and vegetable seller, and Nino Sarratore, Marisa's brother, whom I loved.

Everyone knew Enzo. He was a repeater and at least a couple of times had been dragged through the classrooms with a card around his neck on which Maestro Ferraro, a tall, very thin man, with very short gray hair, a small, lined face, and worried eyes, had written "Dunce." Nino on the other hand was so good, so meek, so quiet that he was well known and liked, especially by me. Naturally Enzo hardly counted, scholastically speaking, we kept an eye on him only because he was aggressive. Our adversaries, in matters of intelligence, were Nino and—we discovered just then—Alfonso Carracci, the third child of Don Achille, a very neat boy, who was in second grade, like us, but looked younger than his seven years. It was clear that the teacher had brought him there to the fourth-grade class because he had more faith in him than in Nino, who was almost two years older.

There was some tension between Oliviero and Ferraro because of that unexpected summoning of Carracci, then the competition began, in front of the two classes, assembled in one classroom. They asked us verbs, they asked us times tables, they asked us addition, subtraction, multiplication, division (the four operations), first at the blackboard, then in our heads. Of that particular occasion I remember three things. The first is that little Alfonso Carracci defeated me immediately, he was calm and precise, but he had the quality of not gloating. The second is that Nino Sarratore, surprisingly, almost never answered the questions, but appeared dazed, as if he didn't understand what the teachers were asking him. The third is that Lila stood up to the son of Don Achille reluctantly, as if she didn't care if he beat her. The scene grew lively only when they began to do calculations in their heads, addition, subtraction, multiplication, and division. Alfonso, despite Lila's reluctance and, at times, silence, as if she hadn't heard the question, began to slip, making mistakes especially in multiplication and division. On the other hand, if the son of Don Achille failed, Lila wasn't up to it, either, and so they seemed more or less equal. But at a certain point something unexpected happened. At least twice, when Lila didn't answer or Alfonso made a mistake, the voice of Enzo Scanno, filled with contempt, was heard, from a desk at the back, giving the right answer.

This astonished the class, the teachers, the principal, me, and Lila. How was it possible that someone like Enzo, who was lazy, incapable, and delinquent, could do complicated calculations in his head better than me, than Alfonso Carracci, than Nino Sarratore? Suddenly Lila seemed to wake up. Alfonso was quickly out of the running and, with the proud consent of Ferraro, who quickly exchanged champions, a duel began between Lila and Enzo.

The two competed for a long time. The principal, going over Ferraro's head, called the son of the fruit and vegetable seller to the front of the room, next to Lila. Enzo left the back row amid uneasy laughter, his own and his friends', and positioned himself, sullen and uneasy, next to the blackboard, opposite Lila. The duel continued, as they did increasingly difficult calculations in their heads. The boy gave his answers in dialect, as if he were on the street and not in a classroom, and Ferraro corrected his diction, but the figure was always correct. Enzo seemed extremely proud of that moment of glory, amazed himself at how clever he was. Then he began to slip, because Lila had woken up conclusively, and now her eyes had narrowed in determination, and she answered correctly. In the end Enzo lost. He lost but was not resigned. He began to curse, to shout ugly obscenities. Ferraro sent him to kneel behind the blackboard, but he wouldn't go. He was rapped on the knuckles with the rod and then pulled by the ears to the punishment corner. The school day ended like that.

But from then on the gang of boys began to throw rocks at us.

9.

That morning of the duel between Enzo and Lila is important, in our long story. Many modes of behavior started off there that were difficult to decipher. For example it became very clear that Lila could, if she wanted, ration the use of her abilities. That was what she had done with Don Achille's son. She did not want to beat him, but she had also calibrated silences and answers in such a way as not to be beaten. We had not yet become friends and I couldn't ask her why she had behaved like that. But really there was no need to ask questions, I could guess the reason. Like me, she, too, had been forbidden to offend not only Don Achille but also his family.

It was like that. We didn't know the origin of that fear-rancor-hatred-meekness that our parents displayed toward the Carraccis and transmitted to us, but it was there, it was a fact, like the neighborhood, its dirty-white houses, the fetid odor of the landings, the dust of the streets. In all likelihood Nino Sarratore, too, had been silent in order to allow Alfonso to be at his best. Handsome, slender, and nervous, with long lashes, hair neatly combed, he had stammered only a few words and had finally been silent. To continue to love him, I wanted to think that was what it had been. But deep down I had some doubts. Had it been a choice, like Lila's? I wasn't sure. I had stepped aside because Alfonso really was better than me. Lila could have defeated him immediately, yet she had chosen to aim for a tie. And Nino? There was something that confused and perhaps saddened me: not an inability, not even surrender, but, I would say today, a collapse. That stammer, the pallor, the purple that had suddenly swallowed his eyes: how handsome he was, so languid, and yet how much I disliked his languor.

Lila, too, at a certain point had seemed very beautiful to me. In general I was the pretty one, while she was skinny, like a salted anchovy, she gave off an odor of wildness, she had a long face, narrow at the temples, framed by two bands of smooth black hair. But when she decided to vanquish both Alfonso and Enzo, she had lighted up like a holy warrior. Her cheeks flushed, the sign of a flame released by every corner of her body, and for the first time I thought: Lila is prettier than I am. So I was second in everything. I hoped that no one would ever realize it.

But the most important thing that morning was the discovery that a phrase we often used to avoid punishment contained something true, hence uncontrollable, hence dangerous. The formula was: *I didn't do it on purpose*. Enzo, in fact, had not entered the competition deliberately and had not deliberately defeated Alfonso. Lila had deliberately defeated Enzo but had not deliberately defeated Alfonso or deliberately humiliated him; it had been only a necessary step. The conclusion we drew from this convinced us that it was best to do everything on purpose, deliberately, so that you would know what to expect.

Because almost nothing had been done deliberately, many unforeseen things struck us, one after the other. Alfonso went home in tears as a result of his defeat. His brother Stefano, who was fourteen, an apprentice in the grocery store (the former workshop of the carpenter Peluso) owned by his father—who, however, never set foot in it—showed up outside school the next day and said very nasty things to Lila, to the point of threatening her. She yelled an obscenity at him, and he pushed her against a wall and tried to grab her tongue, shouting that he would prick it with a pin. Lila went home and told her brother Rino everything, and the more she talked, the redder he got, his eyes bright. In the meantime Enzo, going home one night without his country gang, was stopped by Stefano and punched and kicked. Rino, in the morning, went to look for Stefano and they had a fight, giving each other a more or less equal beating. A few days later the wife of Don Achille, Donna Maria, knocked on the Cerullos' door and made a scene with Nunzia, shouting and insulting her. A little time passed and one Sunday, after Mass, Fernando Cerullo the shoemaker, the father of Lila and Rino, a small, thin man, timidly accosted Don Achille and apologized, without ever saying what he was apologizing for. I didn't see it, or at least I don't remember it, but it was said that the apologies were made aloud, and in such a way that everyone could hear, even though Don Achille had walked by as if the shoemaker were not speaking to him. Sometime later Lila and I wounded Enzo in the calf with a stone and Enzo threw a stone that hit Lila in the head. While I was shrieking in fear and Lila got up with the blood dripping from under her hair, Enzo, who was also bleeding, climbed down the embankment, and, seeing Lila in that state, he, utterly unpredictably and to our eyes incomprehensibly, began to cry. Then Rino, Lila's adored brother, came to school and, outside, beat up Enzo, who barely defended himself. Rino was older, bigger, and more motivated. Not only that: Enzo didn't mention that beating to his gang or his mother or his father or his brothers or his cousins, who all worked in the countryside and sold fruit and vegetables from a cart. At that point, thanks to him, the feuds ended.

10.

Lila went around proudly for a while, with her head bandaged. Then she took off the bandage and showed anyone who asked the black scar, red at the edges, that stuck out on her forehead under the hairline. Finally people forgot what had happened and if someone stared at the whitish mark left on her skin, she made an aggressive gesture that meant: what are you looking at, mind your own business. To me she never said anything, not even a word of thanks for the rocks I had handed her, for how I had dried the blood with the edge of my smock. But from that moment she began to subject me to proofs of courage that had nothing to do with school.

We saw each other in the courtyard more and more frequently. We showed off our dolls to each other but without appearing to, one in the other's vicinity, as if each of us were alone. At some point we let the dolls meet, as a test, to see if they got along. And so came the day when we sat next to the cellar window with the curled grating and exchanged our dolls, she holding mine and I hers, and Lila abruptly pushed Tina through the opening in the grating and dropped her.

I felt an unbearable sorrow. I was attached to my plastic doll; it was the most precious possession I had. I knew that Lila was mean, but I had never expected her to do something so spiteful to me. For me the doll was alive, to know that she was on the floor of the cellar, amid the thousand beasts that lived there, threw me into despair. But that day I learned a skill at which I later excelled. I held back my despair, I held it back on the edge of my wet eyes, so that Lila said to me in dialect:

"You don't care about her?"

I didn't answer. I felt a violent pain, but I sensed that the pain of quarreling with her would be even stronger. I was as if strangled by two agonies, one already happening, the loss of the doll, and one possible, the loss of Lila. I said nothing, I only acted, without spite, as if it were natural, even if it wasn't natural and I knew I was taking a great risk. I merely threw into the cellar her Nu, the doll she had just given me.

Lila looked at me in disbelief.

"What you do, I do," I recited immediately, aloud, very frightened.

"Now go and get it for me."

"If you go and get mine."

We went together. At the entrance to the building, on the left, was the door that led to the cellars, we knew it well. Because it was broken—one of the panels was hanging on just one hinge—the entrance was blocked by a chain that crudely held the two panels together. Every child was tempted and at the same time terrified by the possibility of forcing the door that little bit that would make it possible to go through to the other side. We did it. We made a space wide enough for our slender, supple bodies to slip through into the cellar.

Once inside, we descended, Lila in the lead, five stone steps into a damp space, dimly lit by the narrow openings at street level. I was afraid, and tried to stay close behind Lila, but she seemed angry, and intent on finding her doll. I groped my way forward. I felt under the soles of my sandals objects that squeaked, glass, gravel, insects. All around were things not identifiable, dark masses, sharp or square or rounded. The faint light that pierced the darkness sometimes fell on something recognizable: the skeleton of a chair, the pole of a lamp, fruit boxes, the bottoms and sides of wardrobes, iron hinges. I got scared by what seemed to me a soft face, with large glass eyes, that lengthened into a chin shaped like a box. I saw it hanging, with its desolate expression, on a rickety wooden stand, and I cried out to Lila, pointing to it. She turned and slowly approached it, with her back to me, carefully extended one hand, and detached it from the stand. Then she turned around. She had put the face with the glass eyes over hers and now her face was enormous, with round, empty eye sockets and no mouth, only that protruding black chin swinging over her chest.

Those are moments which are stamped into memory. I'm not sure, but I must have let out a cry of real terror, because she hurried to say, in an echoing voice, that it was just a mask, an anti-gas mask: that's what her father called it, he had one like it in the storeroom at home. I continued to tremble and moan with fear, which evidently persuaded her to tear the thing off her face and throw it in a corner, causing a loud noise and a lot of dust that thickened amid the tongues of light from the windows.

I calmed down. Lila looked around, identified the opening from which we had dropped Tina and Nu. We went along the rough bumpy wall, we looked into the shadows. The dolls weren't there. Lila repeated in dialect, they're not there, they're not there, they're not there, and searched along the floor with her hands, something I didn't have the courage to do.

Long minutes passed. Once only I seemed to see Tina and with a tug at my heart I bent over to grab her, but it was only a crumpled page of old newspaper. They aren't here, Lila repeated, and headed toward the door. Then I felt lost, unable to stay there by myself and keep searching, unable to leave if I hadn't found my doll.

At the top of the steps she said:

"Don Achille took them, he put them in his black bag."

And at that very moment I heard him, Don Achille: he slithered, he shuffled among the indistinct shapes of things. Then I abandoned Tina to her fate, and ran away, in order not to lose Lila, who was already twisting nimbly between the panels of the broken door.

11.

I believed everything she told me. The shapeless mass of Don Achille running through the underground tunnels, arms dangling, large fingers grasping Nu's head in one hand, in the other Tina's. I suffered terribly. I got sick, had fevers, got better, got sick again. I was overcome by a kind of tactile dysfunction; sometimes I had the impression that, while every animated being around me was speeding up the rhythms of its life, solid surfaces turned soft under my fingers or swelled up, leaving empty spaces between their internal mass and the surface skin. It seemed to me that my own body, if you touched it, was distended, and this saddened me. I was sure that I had cheeks like balloons, hands stuffed with sawdust, earlobes like ripe berries, feet in the shape of loaves of bread. When I returned to the streets and to school, I felt that the space, too, had changed. It seemed to be chained between two dark poles: on one side was the underground air bubble that pressed on the roots of the houses, the threatening cavern the dolls had fallen into; on the other the upper sphere, on the fourth floor of the building where Don Achille, who had stolen them, lived. The two balls were as if screwed to the ends of an iron bar, which in my imagination obliquely crossed the apartments, the streets, the countryside, the tunnel, the railroad tracks, and compressed them. I felt squeezed in that vise along with the mass of everyday things and people, and I had a bad taste in my mouth, a permanent sense of nausea that exhausted me, as if everything, thus compacted, and always tighter, were grinding me up, reducing me to a repulsive cream.

It was an enduring malaise, lasting perhaps years, beyond early adolescence. But unexpectedly, just when it began, I received my first declaration of love.

It was before Lila and I had attempted to climb the stairs to Don Achille's, and my grief at the loss of Tina was still unbearable. I had gone reluctantly to buy bread. My mother had sent me and I was going home, the change clutched in my fist and the loaf still warm against my chest, when I realized that Nino Sarratore was trudging behind me, holding his little brother by the hand. On summer days his mother, Lidia, always sent him out with Pino, who at the time was no more than five, with the injunction never to leave him. Near a corner, a little past the Carraccis' grocery, Nino was about to pass me, but instead of passing he cut off my path, pushed me against the wall, placed his free hand against the wall as a bar, to keep me from running away, and with the other pulled up beside him his brother, a silent witness of his undertaking. Breathlessly he said something I couldn't understand. He was pale, and he smiled, then he became serious, then he smiled again. Finally he said, in school Italian:

"When we grow up I want to marry you."

Then he asked if in the meantime I would be engaged to him. He was a little taller than me, very thin, with a long neck, his ears sticking out a little from his head. He had rebellious hair, and intense eyes with long lashes. The effort he was making to restrain his timidity was touching. Although I also wanted to marry him, I felt like answering:

"No, I can't."

He was stunned, Pino gave him a tug. I ran away.

From that moment I began to sneak into a side street whenever I saw him. And yet he seemed to me so handsome. How many times had I hung around his sister Marisa just to be near him and walk part of the way home with them. But he had made the declaration at the wrong moment. He couldn't know how undone I felt, how much anguish Tina's disappearance had caused me, how exhausting the effort of keeping up with Lila was, how the compressed space of the courtyard, the buildings, the neighborhood cut off my breath. After giving me many long, frightened glances from a distance, he began to avoid me, too. For a while he must have been afraid that I would tell the other girls, and in particular his sister, about the proposal he had made. Everyone knew that Gigliola Spagnuolo, the daughter of the baker, had done that when Enzo had asked her to be his girlfriend. And Enzo had found out and got angry, he had shouted outside school that she was a liar, he had even threatened to kill her with a knife. I, too, was tempted to tell everything, but then I let it go, I didn't tell anyone, not even Lila when we became friends. Slowly I forgot about it myself.

It came to mind again when, some time later, the entire Sarratore family moved. One morning the cart and horse that belonged to Assunta's husband, Nicola, appeared in the courtyard: with that same cart and that same old horse he sold fruit and vegetables with his wife, going up and down the streets of the neighborhood. Nicola had a broad handsome face and the same blue eyes, the same blond hair as his son Enzo. Besides selling fruit and vegetables, he was the mover. And in fact he, Donato Sarratore, Nino himself, and Lidia, too, began to carry things downstairs, all sorts of odds and ends, mattresses, furniture, and piled it on the cart.

As soon as the women heard the sound of wheels in the courtyard, they looked out, including my mother, including me. There was a great curiosity. It seemed that Donato had got a new house directly from the state railroad, in the neighborhood of a square called Piazza Nazionale. Or—said my mother—his wife had obliged him to move to escape the persecutions of Melina, who wanted to take away her husband. Likely. My mother always saw evil where, to my great annoyance, it was sooner or later discovered that evil really was, and her crossed eye seemed made purposely to identify the secret motives of the neighborhood. How would Melina react? Was it true, as I had heard whispered, that she had had a child with Sarratore and then killed it? And was it possible that she would start shouting terrible things, including that? All the females, big and small, were at the windows, perhaps to wave goodbye to the family that was leaving, perhaps to witness the spectacle of rage of that ugly, lean, and widowed woman. I saw that Lila and her mother, Nunzia, were also watching.

I sought Nino's gaze, but he seemed to have other things to do. I was then seized, as usual for no precise reason, by a weariness that made everything around me faint. I thought that perhaps he had made that declaration because he already knew that he would be leaving and wanted to tell me first what he felt for me. I looked at him as he struggled to carry boxes filled to overflowing, and I felt the guilt, the sorrow of having said no. Now he was fleeing like a bird.

Finally the procession of furniture and household goods stopped. Nicola and Donato began to tie everything to the cart with ropes. Lidia Sarratore appeared dressed as if to go to a party, she had even put on a summer hat, of blue straw. She pushed the carriage with her youngest boy in it and beside her she had the two girls, Marisa, who was my age, eight or nine, and Clelia, six. Suddenly there was a noise of things breaking on the second floor. Almost at the same moment Melina began screaming. Her cries were so tortured that Lila, I saw, put her hands over her ears. The pained voice of Ada, Melina's second child, echoed as she cried, Mamma, no, Mamma. After a moment of uncertainty I, too, covered my ears. But meanwhile objects began to fly out the window and curiosity became so strong that I freed my eardrums, as if I needed clear sounds to understand. Melina, however, wasn't uttering words but only aaah, aaah, as if she were wounded. She couldn't be seen, not even an arm or a hand that was throwing things could be seen. Copper pots, glasses, bottles, plates appeared to fly out the window of their own volition, and in the street Lidia Sarratore walked with her head down, leaning over the baby carriage, her daughters behind, while Donato climbed up on the cart amid his property, and Don Nicola guided the horse by the bridle and meanwhile objects hit the asphalt, bounced, shattered, sending splinters between the nervous hooves of the beast.

I looked at Lila. Now I saw another face, a face of bewilderment. She must have realized that I was looking at her, and she immediately disappeared from the window. Meanwhile the cart started off. Keeping to the wall, without a goodbye to anyone, Lidia and the four youngest children slunk toward the gate, while Nino seemed unwilling to leave, as if hypnotized by the waste of fragile objects against the asphalt.

Last I saw flying out the window a sort of black spot. It was an iron, pure steel. When I still had Tina and played in the house, I used my mother's, which was identical, prow-shaped, pretending it was a ship in a storm. The object plummeted down and with a sharp thud made a hole in the ground, a few inches from Nino. It nearly—very nearly—killed him.

12.

No boy ever declared to Lila that he loved her, and she never told me if it grieved her. Gigliola Spagnuolo received proposals to be someone's girlfriend continuously and I, too, was much in demand. Lila, on the other hand, wasn't popular, mostly because she was skinny, dirty, and always had a cut or bruise of some sort, but also because she had a sharp tongue. She invented humiliating nicknames and although in front of the teacher she showed off Italian words that no one knew, with us she spoke a scathing dialect, full of swear words, which cut off at its origin any feeling of love. Only Enzo did a thing that, if it wasn't exactly a request to be her boyfriend, was nevertheless a sign of admiration and respect. Some time after he had cut her head with the rock and before, it seems to me, he was rejected by Gigliola Spagnuolo, he ran into us on the *stradone* and, before my incredulous eyes, held out to Lila a garland of sorb apples.

"What do I do with it?"

"You eat them."

"Bitter?"

"Let them ripen."

"I don't want them."

"Throw them away."

That was it. Enzo turned his back and hurried off to work. Lila and I started laughing. We didn't talk much, but we had a laugh at everything that happened to us. I said only, in a tone of amusement:

"I like sorb apples."

I was lying, it was a fruit I didn't like. I was attracted by their reddish-yellow color when they were unripe, their compactness that gleamed on sunny days. But when they ripened on the balconies and became brown and soft like small wrinkled pears, and the skin came off easily, displaying a grainy pulp not with a bad taste but spongy in a way that reminded me of the corpses of rats along the *stradone*, then I wouldn't even touch them. I made that statement almost as a test, hoping that Lila would offer them to me: here, take them, you have them. I felt that if she had given me the gift that Enzo had given her I would be happier than if she had given me something of hers. But she didn't, and I still recall the feeling of betrayal when she brought them home. She herself put a nail at the window. I saw her hang the garland on it.

13.

Enzo didn't give her any other gifts. After the fight with Gigliola, who had told everyone about the declaration he had made to her, we saw him less and less. Although he had proved to be extremely good at doing sums in his head, he was lazy, so the teacher didn't suggest that he take the admissions test for the middle school, and he wasn't sorry about it, in fact he was pleased. He enrolled in the trade school, but in fact he was already working with his parents. He got up very early to go with his father to the fruit-and-vegetable market or to drive the cart through the neighborhood, selling produce from the countryside, and so he soon quit school.

We, instead, toward the end of fifth grade, were told that it would be suitable for us to continue in school. The teacher summoned in turn my parents and those of Gigliola and Lila to tell them that we absolutely had to take not only the test for the elementary school diploma but also the one for admission to middle school. I did all I could so that my father would not send my mother, with her limp, her wandering eye, and her stubborn anger, but would go himself, since he was a porter and knew how to be polite. I didn't succeed. She went, she talked to the teacher, and returned home in a sullen mood.

"The teacher wants money. She says she has to give some extra lessons because the test is difficult."

"But what's the point of this test?" my father asked.

"To let her study Latin."

"Why?"

"Because they say she's clever."

"But if she's clever, why does the teacher have to give her lessons that cost money?"

"So she'll be better off and we'll be worse."

They discussed it at length. At first my mother was against it and my father uncertain; then my father became cautiously in favor and my mother resigned herself to being a little less against it; finally they decided to let me take the test, but always provided that if I did not do well they would immediately take me out of school.

Lila's parents on the other hand said no. Nunzia Cerullo made a few somewhat hesitant attempts, but her father wouldn't even talk about it, and in fact hit Rino when he told him that he was wrong. Her parents were inclined not to go and see the teacher, but Maestra Oliviero had the principal summon them, and then Nunzia had to go. Faced with the timid but flat refusal of that frightened woman, Maestra Oliviero, stern but calm, displayed Lila's marvelous compositions, the brilliant solutions to difficult problems, and even the beautifully colored drawings that in class, when she applied herself, enchanted us all, because, pilfering Giotto's pastels, she portrayed in a realistic style princesses with hairdos, jewels, clothes, shoes that had never been seen in any book or even at the parish cinema. When the refusal persisted, the teacher lost her composure and dragged Lila's mother to the principal as if she were a student to be disciplined. But Nunzia couldn't yield, she didn't have permission from her husband. As a result she kept saying no until she, the teacher, and the principal were overcome by exhaustion.

The next day, as we were going to school, Lila said to me in her usual tone: I'm going to take the test anyway. I believed her, to forbid her to do something was pointless, everyone knew it. She seemed the strongest of us girls, stronger than Enzo, than Alfonso, than Stefano, stronger than her brother Rino, stronger than our parents, stronger than all the adults including the teacher and the carabinieri, who could put you in jail. Although she was fragile in appearance, every prohibition lost substance in her presence. She knew how to go beyond the limit without ever truly suffering the consequences. In the end people gave in, and were even, however unwillingly, compelled to praise her.

14.

We were also forbidden to go to Don Achille's, but she decided to go anyway and I followed. In fact, that was when I became convinced that nothing could stop her, and that every disobedient act contained breathtaking opportunities.

We wanted Don Achille to give us back our dolls. So we climbed the stairs: at every step I was on the point of turning around and going back to the courtyard. I still feel Lila's hand grasping mine, and I like to think that she decided to take it not only because she intuited that I wouldn't have the courage to get to the top floor but also because with that gesture she herself sought the force to continue. So, one beside the other, I on the wall side and she on the banister side, sweaty palms clasped, we climbed the last flights. At Don Achille's door my heart was pounding, I could hear it in my ears, but I was consoled by thinking that it was also the sound of Lila's heart. From the apartment came voices, perhaps of Alfonso or Stefano or Pinuccia. After a very long, silent pause before the door, Lila rang the bell. There was silence, then a shuffling. Donna Maria opened the door, wearing a faded green housedress. When she spoke, I saw a brilliant gold tooth in her mouth. She thought we were looking for Alfonso, and was a bit bewildered. Lila said to her in dialect:

"No, we want Don Achille."

"Tell me."

"We have to speak to him."

The woman shouted, "Achì!"

More shuffling. A thickset figure emerged from the shadows. He had a long torso, short legs, arms that hung to his knees, and a cigarette in his mouth; you could see the embers. He asked hoarsely:

"Who is it?"

"The daughter of the shoemaker with Greco's oldest daughter."

Don Achille came into the light, and, for the first time, we saw him clearly. No minerals, no sparkle of glass. His long face was of flesh, and the hair bristled only around his ears; the top of his head was shiny. His eyes were bright, the white veined with small red streams, his mouth wide and thin, his chin heavy, with a crease in the middle. He seemed to me ugly but not the way I imagined.

"Well?"

"The dolls," said Lila.

"What dolls?"

"Ours."

"Your dolls are of no use here."

"You took them down in the cellar."

Don Achille turned and shouted into the apartment:

"Pinù, did you take the doll belonging to the shoemaker's daughter?"

"Me, no."

"Alfò, did you take it?"

Laughter.

Lila said firmly, I don't know where she got all that courage:

"You took them, we saw you."

There was a moment of silence.

" 'You' me?"

"Yes, and you put them in your black bag."

The man, hearing those words, wrinkled his forehead in annoyance.

I couldn't believe that we were there, in front of Don Achille, and Lila was speaking to him like that and he was staring at her in bewilderment, and in the background could be seen Alfonso and Stefano and Pinuccia and Donna Maria, who was setting the table for dinner. I couldn't believe that he was an ordinary person, a little short, a little bald, a little out of proportion, but ordinary. So I waited for him to be abruptly transformed.

Don Achille repeated, as if to understand clearly the meaning of the words:

"I took your dolls and put them in a black bag?"

I felt that he was not angry but unexpectedly pained, as if he were receiving confirmation of something he already knew. He said something in dialect that I didn't understand, Maria cried, "Achì, it's ready."

"I'm coming."

Don Achille stuck a large, broad hand in the back pocket of his pants. We clutched each other's hand tightly, waiting for him to bring out a knife. Instead he took out his wallet, opened it, looked inside, and handed Lila some money, I don't remember how much.

"Go buy yourselves dolls," he said.

Lila grabbed the money and dragged me down the stairs. He muttered, leaning over the banister:

"And remember that they were a gift from me."

I said, in Italian, careful not to trip on the stairs:

"Good evening and enjoy your meal."

15.

Right after Easter, Gigliola Spagnuolo and I started going to the teacher's house to prepare for the admissions test. The teacher lived right next to the parish church of the Holy Family, and her windows looked out on the public gardens; from there you could see, beyond the dense countryside, the pylons of the railroad. Gigliola passed by my window and called me. I was ready, I ran out. I liked those private lessons, two a week, I think. The teacher, at the end of the lesson, offered us little heart-shaped cookies and a soft drink.

Lila didn't come; her parents had not agreed to pay the teacher. But, since we were now good friends, she continued to tell me that she would take the test and would enter the first year of middle school in the same class as me.

"And the books?"

"You'll lend them to me."

Meanwhile, however, with the money from Don Achille, she bought a book: *Little Women*. She decided to buy it because she already knew it and liked it hugely. Maestra Oliviero, in fourth grade, had given the smarter girls books to read. Lila had received *Little Women*, along with the following comment: "This is for older girls, but it will be good for you," and I got the book *Heart*, by Edmondo De Amicis, with not a word of explanation. Lila read both *Little Women* and *Heart*, in a very short time, and said there was no comparison, in her opinion *Little Women* was wonderful. I hadn't managed to read it, I had had a hard time finishing *Heart* before the time set by the teacher for returning it. I was a slow reader, I still am. Lila, when she had to give the book back to Maestra Oliviero, regretted both not being able to reread *Little Women* continuously and not being able to talk about it with me. So one morning she made up her mind. She called me from the street, we went to the ponds, to the place where we had buried the money from Don Achille, in a metal box, took it out, and went to ask Iolanda the stationer, who had had displayed in her window forever a copy of *Little Women*, yellowed by the sun, if it was enough. It was. As soon as we became owners of the book we began to meet in the courtyard to read it, either silently, one next to the other, or aloud. We read it for months, so many times that the book became tattered and sweat-stained, it lost its spine, came unthreaded, sections fell apart. But it was our book, we loved it dearly. I was the guardian, I kept it at home among the schoolbooks, because Lila didn't feel she could keep it in her house. Her father, lately, would get angry if she merely took it out to read.

But Rino protected her. When the subject of the admissions test came up, quarrels exploded continuously between him and his father. Rino was about sixteen at the time, he was a very excitable boy and had started a battle to be paid for the work he did. His reasoning was: I get up at six; I come to the shop and work till eight at night; I want a salary. But those words outraged his father and his mother. Rino had a bed to sleep in, food to eat, why did he want money? His job was to help the family, not impoverish it. But he insisted, he found it unjust to work as hard as his father and not receive a cent. At that point Fernando Cerullo answered him with apparent patience: "I pay you already, Rino, I pay you generously by teaching you the whole trade: soon you'll be able to repair a heel or an edge or put on a new sole; your father is passing on to you everything he knows, and you'll be able to make an entire shoe, with the skill of a professional." But that payment by instruction was not enough for Rino, and so they argued, especially at dinner. They began by talking about money and ended up quarreling about Lila.

"If you pay me I'll take care of sending her to school," Rino said.

"School? Why, did I go to school?"

"No."

"Did you go to school?"

"No."

"Then why should your sister, who is a girl, go to school?"

The matter almost always ended with a slap in the face for Rino, who, one way or another, even if he didn't intend to, had displayed a lack of respect toward his father. The boy, without crying, apologized in a spiteful tone of voice.

Lila was silent during those discussions. She never said so, but I had the impression that while I hated my mother, really hated her, profoundly, she, in spite of everything, wasn't upset with her father. She said that he was full of kindnesses, she said that when there were accounts to do he let her do them, she said that she had heard him say to his friends that his daughter was the most intelligent person in the neighborhood, she said that on her name day he brought her warm chocolate in bed and four biscuits. But what could you do, it didn't enter into his view of the world that she should continue to go to school. Nor did it fall within his economic possibilities: the family was large, they all had to live off the shoe repair shop, including two unmarried sisters of Fernando and Nunzia's parents. So on the matter of school it was like talking to the wall, and her mother all in all had the same opinion. Only her brother had different ideas, and fought boldly against his father. And Lila, for reasons I didn't understand, seemed certain that Rino would win. He would get his salary and would send her to school with the money.

"If there's a fee to pay, he'll pay it for me," she explained.

She was sure that her brother would also give her money for the school books and even for pens, pen case, pastels, globe, the smock and the ribbon. She adored him. She said that, after she went to school, she wanted to earn a lot of money for the sole purpose of making her brother the wealthiest person in the neighborhood.

In that last year of elementary school, wealth became our obsession. We talked about it the way characters in novels talk about searching for treasure. We said, when we're rich we'll do this, we'll do that. To listen to us, you might think that the wealth was hidden somewhere in the neighborhood, in treasure chests that, when opened, would be gleaming with gold, and were waiting only for us to find them. Then, I don't know why, things changed and we began to link school to wealth. We thought that if we studied hard we would be able to write books and that the books would make us rich. Wealth was still the glitter of gold coins stored in countless chests, but to get there all you had to do was go to school and write a book.

"Let's write one together," Lila said once, and that filled me with joy.

Maybe the idea took root when she discovered that the author of *Little Women* had made so much money that she had given some of it to her family. But I wouldn't promise. We argued about it, I said we could start right after the admission test. She agreed, but then she couldn't wait. While I had a lot to study because of the afternoon lessons with Spagnuolo and the teacher, she was freer, she set to work and wrote a novel without me.

I was hurt when she brought it to me to read, but I didn't say anything, in fact I held in check my disappointment and was full of congratulations. There were ten sheets of graph paper, folded and held together with a dressmaker's pin. It had a cover drawn in pastels, and the title, I remember, was *The Blue Fairy*. How exciting it was, how many difficult words there were. I told her to let the teacher read it. She didn't want to. I begged her, I offered to give it to her. Although she wasn't sure, she agreed.

One day when I was at Maestra Oliviero's house for our lesson, I took advantage of Gigliola being in the bathroom to take out *The Blue Fairy*. I said it was a wonderful novel written by Lila and that Lila wanted her to read it. But the teacher, who for five years had been enthusiastic about everything Lila did, except when she was bad, replied coldly:

"Tell Cerullo that she would do well to study for the diploma, instead of wasting time." And although she kept Lila's novel, she left it on the table without even giving it a glance.

That attitude confused me. What had happened? Was she angry with Lila's mother? Had her rage extended to Lila herself? Was she upset about the money that the parents of my friend wouldn't give her? I didn't understand. A few days later I cautiously asked her if she had read *The Blue Fairy*. She answered in an unusual tone, obscurely, as if only she and I could truly understand.

"Do you know what the plebs are, Greco?"

"Yes, the people, the tribunes of the plebs are the Gracchi."

"The plebs are quite a nasty thing."

"Yes."

"And if one wishes to remain a plebeian, he, his children, the children of his children deserve nothing. Forget Cerullo and think of yourself."

Maestra Oliviero never said anything about *The Blue Fairy*. Lila asked about it a couple of times, then she let it go. She said grimly:

"As soon as I have time I'll write another, that one wasn't good."

"It was wonderful."

"It was terrible."

But she became less lively, especially in class, probably because she realized that the teacher had stopped praising her, and sometimes seemed irritated by her excesses of virtuosity. When it came time for the competition at the end of the year she was still the best, but without her old impudence. At the end of the day, the principal presented to those remaining in competition—Lila, Gigliola, and me—an extremely difficult problem that he had invented himself. Gigliola and I struggled in vain. Lila, narrowing her eyes to cracks, applied herself. She was the last to give up. She said, with a timidity unusual for her, that the problem couldn't be solved, because there was a mistake in the premise, but she didn't know what it was. Maestra Oliviero scolded her harshly. I saw Lila standing at the blackboard, chalk in hand, very small and pale, assaulted by volleys of cruel phrases. I felt her suffering, I couldn't bear the trembling of her lower lip and nearly burst into tears.

"When one cannot solve a problem," the teacher concluded coldly, "one does not say, There is a mistake in the problem, one says, I am not capable of solving it."

The principal was silent. As far as I remember, the day ended there.

16.

Shortly before the final test in elementary school Lila pushed me to do another of the many things that I would never have had the courage to do by myself. We decided to skip school, and cross the boundaries of the neighborhood.

It had never happened before. As far back as I could remember, I had never left the four-story white apartment buildings, the courtyard, the parish church, the public gardens, I had never felt the urge to. Trains passed continuously on the other side of the scrubland, trucks and cars passed up and down along the *stradone*, and yet I can't remember a single occasion when I asked myself, my father, my teacher: where are the cars going, the trucks, the trains, to what city, to what world?

Nor had Lila appeared particularly interested, but this time she organized everything. She told me to tell my mother that after school we were all going to the teacher's house for a party to mark the end of the school year, and although I tried to remind her that the teachers had never invited all us girls to their houses for a party, she said that that was the very reason we should say it. The event would seem so exceptional that none of our parents would be bold enough to go to school and ask if it was true or not. As usual, I trusted her, and things went just as she had said. At my house everyone believed it, not only my father and my sister and brothers but even my mother.

The night before, I couldn't sleep. What was beyond the neighborhood, beyond its well-known perimeter? Behind us rose a thickly wooded hill and a few structures in the shelter of the gleaming railroad tracks. In front of us, beyond the *stradone*, stretched a pitted road that skirted the ponds. To the right was a strip of treeless countryside, under an enormous sky. To the left was a tunnel with three entrances, but if you climbed up to the railroad tracks, on clear days you could see, beyond some low houses and walls of tufa and patches of thick vegetation, a blue mountain with one low peak and one a little higher, which was called Vesuvius and was a volcano.

But nothing that we had before our eyes every day, or that could be seen if we clambered up the hill, impressed us. Trained by our schoolbooks to speak with great skill about what we had never seen, we were excited by the invisible. Lila said that in the direction of Vesuvius was the sea. Rino, who had been there, had told her that the water was blue and sparkling, a marvelous sight. On Sundays, especially in summer, but often, too, in winter, he went with friends to swim, and he had promised to take her there. He wasn't the only one, naturally, who had seen the sea, others we knew had also seen it. Once Nino Sarratore and his sister Marisa had talked about it, in the tone of those who found it normal to go every so often to eat *taralli* and seafood. Gigliola Spagnuolo had also been there. She, Nino, and Marisa had, lucky for them, parents who took their children on outings far away, not just around the corner to the public gardens in front of the parish church. Ours weren't like that, they didn't have time, they didn't have money, they didn't have the desire. It was true that I seemed to have a vague bluish memory of the sea, my mother claimed she had taken me as a small child, when she had to have sand treatments for her injured leg. But I didn't much believe my mother, and to Lila, who didn't know anything about it, I admitted that I didn't know anything, either. So she planned to do as Rino had, to set off on the road and get there by herself. She persuaded me to go with her. Tomorrow.

I got up early, I did everything as if I were going to school— my bread and milk, my schoolbag, my smock. I waited for Lila as usual in front of the gate, only instead of going to the right we crossed the *stradone* and turned left, toward the tunnel.

It was early morning and already hot. There was a strong odor of earth and grass drying in the sun. We climbed among tall shrubs, on indistinct paths that led toward the tracks. When we reached an electrical pylon we took off our smocks and put them in the schoolbags, which we hid in the bushes. Then we raced through the scrubland, which we knew well, and flew excitedly down the slope that led to the tunnel. The entrance on the right was very dark: we had never been inside that obscurity. We held each other by the hand and entered. It was a long passage, and the luminous circle of the exit seemed far away. Once we got accustomed to the shadowy light, we saw lines of silvery water that slid along the walls, large puddles. Apprehensively, dazed by the echo of our steps, we kept going. Then Lila let out a shout and laughed at the violent explosion of sound. Immediately I shouted and laughed in turn. From that moment all we did was shout, together and separately: laughter and cries, cries and laughter, for the pleasure of hearing them amplified. The tension diminished, the journey began.

Ahead of us were many hours when no one in our families would look for us. When I think of the pleasure of being free, I think of the start of that day, of coming out of the tunnel and finding ourselves on a road that went straight as far as the eye could see, the road that, according to what Rino had told Lila, if you got to the end arrived at the sea. I felt joyfully open to the unknown. It was entirely different from going down into the cellar or up to Don Achille's house. There was a hazy sun, a strong smell of burning. We walked for a long time between crumbling walls invaded by weeds, low structures from which came voices in dialect, sometimes a clamor. We saw a horse make its way slowly down an embankment and cross the street, whinnying. We saw a young woman looking out from a balcony, combing her hair with a flea comb. We saw a lot of small snotty children who stopped playing and looked at us threateningly. We also saw a fat man in an undershirt who emerged from a tumbledown house, opened his pants, and showed us his penis. But we weren't scared of anything: Don Nicola, Enzo's father, sometimes let us pat his horse, the children were threatening in our courtyard, too, and there was old Don Mimì who showed us his disgusting thing when we were coming home from school. For at least three hours, the road we were walking on did not seem different from the segment that we looked out on every day. And I felt no responsibility for the right road. We held each other by the hand, we walked side by side, but for me, as usual, it was as if Lila were ten steps ahead and knew precisely what to do, where to go. I was used to feeling second in everything, and so I was sure that to her, who had always been first, everything was clear: the pace, the calculation of the time available for going and coming back, the route that would take us to the sea. I felt as if she had everything in her head ordered in such a way that the world around us would never be able to create disorder. I abandoned myself happily. I remember a soft light that seemed to come not from the sky but from the depths of the earth, even though, on the surface, it was poor, and ugly.

Then we began to get tired, to get thirsty and hungry. We hadn't thought of that. Lila slowed down, I slowed down, too. Two or three times I caught her looking at me, as if she had done something mean to me and was sorry. What was happening? I realized that she kept turning around and I started turning around, too. Her hand began to sweat. The tunnel, which was the boundary of the neighborhood, had been out of sight for a long time. By now the road we had just traveled was unfamiliar to us, like the one that stretched ahead. People appeared completely indifferent to our fate. Around us was a landscape of ruin: dented tanks, burned wood, wrecks of cars, cartwheels with broken spokes, damaged furniture, rusting scrap iron. Why was Lila looking back? Why had she stopped talking? What was wrong?

I looked more carefully. The sky, which at first had been

very high, was as if lowered. Behind us everything was becoming black, large heavy clouds lay over the trees, the light poles. In front of us, the light was still dazzling, but as if pressed on the sides by a purplish grayness that would suffocate it. In the distance thunder could be heard. I was afraid, but what frightened me more was Lila's expression, new to me. Her mouth was open, her eyes wide, she was looking nervously ahead, back, to the side, and she was squeezing my hand hard. Is it possible, I wondered, that she's afraid? What was happening to her?

The first fat drops arrived, leaving small brown stains as they hit the dusty road.

"Let's go back," Lila said.

"And the sea?"

"It's too far."

"And home?"

"Also."

"Then let's go to the sea."

"No."

"Why?"

I had never seen her so agitated. There was something—something she had on the tip of her tongue but couldn't make up her mind to tell me—that suddenly impelled her to drag me home in a hurry. I didn't understand: why didn't we keep going? There was time, the sea couldn't be too far, and whether we went back home or continued to go on, we'd get wet just the same, if it rained. It was a type of reasoning I had learned from her and I was bewildered when she didn't apply it.

A violet light cracked the black sky, the thunder was louder. Lila gave me a tug, I found myself running, unwillingly, back toward our own neighborhood. The wind rose, the drops fell more thickly, in a few seconds they were transformed into a cascade of water. It occurred to neither of us to seek shelter. We ran blinded by the rain, our clothes soaked, our bare feet in worn sandals that had no purchase on the now muddy ground. We ran until we were out of breath.

We couldn't keep it up, we slowed down. Lightning, thunder, a lava of rainwater ran along the sides of the road; noisy trucks sped by, raising waves of mud. We walked quickly, our hearts in a tumult, first in a heavy downpour, then in a fine rain, finally under a gray sky. We were soaked, our hair pasted to our heads, our lips livid, eyes frightened. We went back through the tunnel, we crossed the scrubland. The bushes dripping with rain grazed us, making us shiver. We found our schoolbags, we put over our wet clothes the dry smocks, we set out toward home. Tense, her eyes lowered, Lila had let go of my hand.

We quickly understood that things had not happened as we expected. The sky had turned black over the neighborhood just when school was over. My mother had gone to school with an umbrella to take me to the party at the teacher's. She had discovered that I wasn't there, that there was no party. For hours she had been looking for me. When I saw from a distance her painfully limping figure I immediately left Lila, so that she wouldn't get angry with her, and ran toward my mother. She slapped me and hit me with the umbrella, yelling that she would kill me if I did something like that again.

Lila took off. At her house no one had noticed anything.

At night my mother reported everything to my father and compelled him to beat me. He was irritated; he didn't want to, and they ended up fighting. First he hit her, then, angry at himself, he gave me a beating. All night I tried to understand what had really happened. We were supposed to go to the sea and we hadn't gone, I had been punished for nothing. A mysterious inversion of attitudes had occurred: I, despite the rain, would have continued on the road, I felt far from everything and everyone, and distance—I discovered for the first time—

extinguished in me every tie and every worry; Lila had abruptly repented of her own plan, she had given up the sea, she had wanted to return to the confines of the neighborhood. I couldn't figure it out.

The next day I didn't wait for her at the gate, I went alone to school. We met in the public gardens. She discovered the bruises on my arms and asked what had happened. I shrugged, that was how things had turned out.

"All they did was beat you?"

"What should they have done?"

"They're still sending you to study Latin?"

I looked at her in bewilderment.

Was it possible? She had taken me with her hoping that as a punishment my parents would not send me to middle school? Or had she brought me back in such a hurry so that I would avoid that punishment? Or—I wonder today—did she want at different moments both things?

17.

We took the final test in elementary school together. When she realized that I was also taking the admission test for middle school, she lost energy. Something happened that surprised everyone: I passed both tests with all tens, the highest marks; Lila got her diploma with nines and an eight in arithmetic.

She never said a word to me of anger or discontent. She began instead to go around with Carmela Peluso, the daughter of the carpenter-gambler, as if I were no longer enough. Within a few days we became a trio, in which, however, I, who had been first in school, was almost always the third. They talked and joked continuously with each other, or, rather, Lila talked and joked, Carmela listened and was amused. When we went for a walk between the church and the *stradone*, Lila was always in the middle and the two of us on the sides. If I noticed that she tended to be closer to Carmela I suffered and wanted to go home.

In this phase she seemed dazed, like the victim of sunstroke. It was very hot and we often bathed our heads in the fountain. I remember her with her hair and face dripping as she talked constantly about going to school the next year. It had become her favorite subject and she tackled it as if it were one of the stories she intended to write in order to become rich. Now when she talked she preferred to address Carmela Peluso, who had got her diploma with all sevens and had not taken the admission test for middle school, either.

Lila was very skillful at telling stories—they all seemed true—about the school where we were going, and the teachers, and she made me laugh, she made me worry. One morning, though, I interrupted her.

"Lila," I said, "you can't go to middle school, you didn't take the admission test. Not you and not Carmela."

She got angry. She said she would go just the same, test or no test.

"And Carmela?"

"Yes."

"It's impossible."

"You'll see."

But I must have rattled her. She stopped telling stories about our scholastic future and became silent. Then, with a sudden determination, she started tormenting her family, insisting that she wanted to study Latin, like Gigliola Spagnuolo and me. She was especially hard on Rino, who had promised to help her but hadn't. It was pointless to explain to her that there was now nothing to do about it; she became even more unreasonable and mean.

At the start of the summer I began to have a feeling difficult to put into words. I saw that she was agitated, aggressive as she had always been, and I was pleased, I recognized her. But I also felt, behind her old habits, a pain that bothered me. She was suffering, and I didn't like her sorrow. I preferred her when she was different from me, distant from my anxieties. And the uneasiness that the discovery of her fragility brought me was transformed by secret pathways into a need of my own to be superior. As soon as I could, cautiously, especially when Carmela Peluso wasn't there, I found a way to remind her that I had gotten a better report card. As soon as I could, cautiously, I pointed out to her that I would go to middle school and she would not. To not be second, to outdo her, for the first time seemed to me a success. She must have realized it and she became even harsher, but toward her family, not me.

Often, as I waited for her to come down to the courtyard, I heard her shouting from the windows. She hurled insults in the worst street dialect, so vulgar that listening to them made me think of order and respect; it didn't seem right to treat adults like that, or even her brother. Of course, her father, Fernando the shoemaker, when he lost his head turned ugly. But all fathers had fits of anger. And hers, when she didn't provoke him, was a kind, sympathetic man, a hard worker. He looked like an actor named Randolph Scott, but unrefined. He was rough, without pale colors, a black beard covered his cheeks, and he had broad, stubby hands streaked with dirt in every crease and under the nails. He joked easily. When I went to Lila's house he took my nose between index and middle fingers and pretended to pull it off. He wanted to make me believe that he had stolen it and that now, as his prisoner, the nose was struggling to escape and return to my face. I found this funny. But if Rino or Lila or the other children made him angry, even I, hearing him from the street, was afraid.

I don't know what happened, one afternoon. In the hot weather we stayed outside until dinnertime. That day Lila didn't show up, and I went to call her at the windows, which were on the ground floor. I cried, "Lì, Lì, Lì," and my voice joined Fernando's extremely loud voice, his wife's loud voice, my friend's insistent voice. I could hear that something was going on and it terrified me. From the windows came a vulgar Neapolitan and the crash of broken objects. In appearance it was no different from what happened at my house when my mother got angry because there wasn't enough money and my father got angry because she had already spent the part of his wages he had given her. In reality the difference was substantial. My father was restrained even when he was angry, he became violent quietly, keeping his voice from exploding even if the veins on his neck swelled and his eyes were inflamed. Fernando instead yelled, threw things; his rage fed on itself, and he couldn't stop. In fact his wife's attempts to stop him increased his fury, and even if he wasn't mad at her he ended up beating her. I insisted, then, in calling Lila, just to get her out of that tempest of cries, obscenities, sounds of destruction. I cried, "Lì, Lì, Lì," but she—I heard her—kept on insulting her father.

We were ten, soon we would be eleven. I was filling out, Lila remained small and thin, she was light and delicate. Suddenly the shouting stopped and a few seconds later my friend flew out the window, passed over my head, and landed on the asphalt behind me.

I was stunned. Fernando looked out, still screaming horrible threats at his daughter. He had thrown her like a thing.

I looked at her terrified while she tried to get up and said, with an almost amused grimace, "I haven't hurt myself."

But she was bleeding; she had broken her arm.

18.

Fathers could do that and other things to impudent girls. Afterward, Fernando became sullen, and worked more than usual. That summer, Carmela and Lila and I often passed the workshop, but while Rino always gave us a friendly nod of greeting, the shoemaker wouldn't even look at his daughter as long as her arm was in the cast. It was clear that he was sorry. His violent moments as a father were a small thing compared with the widespread violence of the neighborhood. At the Bar Solara, in the heat, between gambling losses and troublesome drunkenness, people often reached the point of *disperazione*—a word that in dialect meant having lost all hope but also being broke—and hence of fights. Silvio Solara, the owner, a large man, with an imposing belly, blue eyes, and a high forehead, had a dark stick behind the bar with which he didn't hesitate to strike anyone who didn't pay for his drinks, who had asked for a loan and didn't repay it within the time limit, who made any sort of agreement and didn't keep it, and often he was helped by his sons, Marcello and Michele, boys the age of Lila's brother, who hit harder than their father. Blows were given and received. Men returned home embittered by their losses, by alcohol, by debts, by deadlines, by beatings, and at the first inopportune word they beat their families, a chain of wrongs that generated wrongs.

Right in the middle of that long season an event took place that upset everyone, but on Lila had a very particular effect. Don Achille, the terrible Don Achille, was murdered in his house in the early afternoon of a surprisingly rainy August day.

He was in the kitchen, and had just opened the window to let in the rain-freshened air. He had got up from bed to do so, interrupting his nap. He had on worn blue pajamas, and on his feet only socks of a yellowish color, blackened at the heels. As soon as he opened the window a gust of rain struck his face and someone plunged a knife into the right side of his neck, halfway between the jaw and the clavicle.

The blood spurted from his neck and hit a copper pot hanging on the wall. The copper was so shiny that the blood looked like an ink stain from which—Lila told us—dripped a wavering black line. The murderer—though she inclined to a murderess—had entered without breaking in, at a time when the children were outside and the adults, if they weren't at work, were lying down. Surely he had entered with a skeleton key. Surely he had intended to strike him in the heart while he was sleeping, but had found him awake and thrust that knife into his throat. Don Achille had turned, with the blade stuck in his neck, eyes staring and the blood pouring out and dripping all over his pajamas. He had fallen to his knees and then, facedown, to the floor.

The murder had made such an impression on Lila that almost every day, with great seriousness, always adding some new details, she compelled us to hear the story as if she had been present. Both Carmela Peluso and I, listening to her, were frightened; Carmela couldn't sleep at night. At the worst moments, when the black line of blood dripped along the copper pot, Lila's eyes became two fierce cracks. Surely she imagined that the murderer was female only because it was easier for her to identify with her.

In that period we often went to the Pelusos' house to play checkers and three-of-a-kind, for which Lila had developed a passion. Carmela's mother let us sit in the dining room, where all the furniture had been made by her husband before Don Achille took away his carpenter's tools and his shop. We sat at the table, which was placed between two sideboards with mirrors, and played. I found Carmela increasingly disagreeable, but I pretended to be her friend at least as much as I was Lila's, in fact sometimes I even let her think that I liked her better. On the other hand I really did like Signora Peluso. She had worked at the tobacco factory, but had recently lost her job and was always at home. Anyway, she was, for better or for worse, a cheerful, fat woman, with a large bosom and bright red cheeks, and although money was scarce she always had something good to offer us. Also her husband seemed more tranquil. Now he was a waiter in a pizzeria, and he tried not to go to the Bar Solara to lose at cards the little he earned.

One morning we were in the dining room playing checkers, Carmela and I against Lila. We were sitting at the table, us two on one side, she on the other. Behind Lila and behind Carmela and me were the identical, dark wood sideboards with the mirrors in spiral frames. I looked at the three of us reflected to infinity and I couldn't concentrate, both because of those images, which disturbed me, and because of the shouts of Alfredo Peluso, who that day was upset and was quarreling with his wife, Giuseppina.

There was a knock at the door and Signora Peluso went to open it. Exclamations, cries. We looked out into the hall and saw the carabinieri, figures we feared greatly. The carabinieri seized Alfredo and dragged him away. He struggled, shouted, called his children by name, Pasquale, Carmela, Ciro, Immacolata, he grabbed the furniture made with his own hands, the chairs, Giuseppina, he swore that he hadn't murdered Don Achille, that he was innocent. Carmela wept desperately, they all wept, I, too, began to weep. But not Lila, Lila had that look she had had years earlier for Melina, but with some difference: now, although she remained still, she appeared to be moving with Alfredo Peluso, whose cries were hoarse, and frightening: *Aaaah*.

It was the most terrible thing we witnessed in the course of our childhood, and made a deep impression on me. Lila attended to Carmela, and consoled her. She said to her that, if it really was her father, he had done well to kill Don Achille, but that in her opinion it wasn't him: surely he was innocent and would soon get out of prison. They whispered together continuously and if I approached they moved a little farther off so that I wouldn't hear.

ADOLESCENCE

The Story of the Shoes

1.

O n December 31st of 1958 Lila had her first episode of dissolving margins. The term isn't mine, she always used it. She said that on those occasions the outlines of people and things suddenly dissolved, disappeared. That night, on the terrace where we were celebrating the arrival of 1959, when she was abruptly struck by that sensation, she was frightened and kept it to herself, still unable to name it. It was only years later, one night in November 1980—we were thirty-six, were married, had children—that she recounted in detail what had happened to her then, what still sometimes happened to her, and she used that term for the first time.

We were outside, on the roof terrace of one of the apartment buildings in the neighborhood. Although it was very cold we were wearing light, low-cut dresses, so that we would appear attractive. We looked at the boys, who were cheerful, aggressive, dark figures carried away by the party, the food, the sparkling wine. They were setting off fireworks to celebrate the new year, a ritual in which, as I will explain later, Lila had had a large role, so that now she felt content, watching the streaks of fire in the sky. But suddenly—she told me—in spite of the cold she had begun to sweat. It seemed to her that everyone was shouting too loudly and moving too quickly. This sensation was accompanied by nausea, and she had had the impression that something absolutely material, which had been present around her and around everyone and everything forever, but imperceptible, was breaking down the outlines of persons and things and revealing itself.

Her heart had started beating uncontrollably. She had begun to feel horror at the cries emerging from the throats of all those who were moving about on the terrace amid the smoke, amid the explosions, as if the sound obeyed new, unknown laws. Her nausea increased, the dialect had become unfamiliar, the way our wet throats bathed the words in the liquid of saliva was intolerable. A sense of repulsion had invested all the bodies in movement, their bone structure, the frenzy that shook them. How poorly made we are, she had thought, how insufficient. The broad shoulders, the arms, the legs, the ears, noses, eyes seemed to her attributes of monstrous beings who had fallen from some corner of the black sky. And the disgust, who knows why, was concentrated in particular on her brother Rino, the person who was closest to her, the person she loved most.

She seemed to see him for the first time as he really was: a squat animal form, thickset, the loudest, the fiercest, the greediest, the meanest. The tumult of her heart had overwhelmed her, she felt as if she were suffocating. Too smoky, too foul-smelling, too much flashing fire in the cold. Lila had tried to calm herself, she had said to herself: I have to seize the stream that's passing through me, I have to throw it out from me. But at that point she had heard, among the shouts of joy, a kind of final detonation and something like the breath of a wing beat had passed by her. Someone was shooting not rockets and firecrackers but a gun. Her brother Rino was shouting unbearable obscenities in the direction of the yellow flashes.

On the occasion when she told me that story, Lila also said that the sensation she called dissolving margins, although it had come on her distinctly only that once, wasn't completely new to her. For example, she had often had the sensation of moving for a few fractions of a second into a person or a thing or a number or a syllable, violating its edges. And the day her father threw her out the window she had felt absolutely certain, as she was flying toward the asphalt, that small, very friendly reddish animals were dissolving the composition of the street, transforming it into a smooth, soft material. But that New Year's Eve she had perceived for the first time unknown entities that broke down the outline of the world and demonstrated its terrifying nature. This had deeply shaken her.

2.

When Lila's cast was removed and her arm reappeared, pale but perfectly functioning, her father, Fernando, came to an agreement with himself and, without saying so directly, but through Rino and his wife, Nunzia, allowed her to go to a school to learn I don't know exactly what, stenography, bookkeeping, home economics, or all three.

She went unwillingly. Nunzia was summoned by the teachers because her daughter was often absent without an excuse, disrupted the class, if questioned refused to answer, if she had to do exercises did them in five minutes and then harassed her classmates. At some point she got a nasty flu, she who never got sick, and seemed to welcome it with a sort of abandon, so that the virus quickly sapped her energy. Days passed and she didn't get better. As soon as she tried to go out again, paler than usual, the fever returned. One day I saw her on the street and she looked like a spirit, the spirit of a child who had eaten poisonous berries, such as I had seen illustrated in a book belonging to Maestra Oliviero. Later a rumor spread that she would soon die, which caused me an unbearable anxiety. She recovered, almost in spite of herself. But, with the excuse that her health was poor, she went to school less and less often, and at the end of the year she failed.

Nor did I do well in my first year of middle school. At first I had great expectations, and even if I didn't say so clearly to myself I was glad to be there with Gigliola Spagnuolo rather than with Lila. In some very secret part of myself I looked forward to a school where she would never enter, where, in her absence, I would be the best student, and which I would sometimes tell her about, boasting. But immediately I began to falter, many of the others proved to be better than me. I ended up with Gigliola in a kind of swamp, we were little animals frightened of our own mediocrity, and we struggled all year not to end up at the bottom of the class. I was extremely disappointed. The idea began to quietly form that without Lila I would never feel the pleasure of belonging to that exclusive group of the best.

Every so often, at the entrance to school, I ran into Alfonso, the young son of Don Achille, but we pretended not to know each other. I didn't know what to say to him, I thought that Alfredo Peluso had done a good thing in murdering his father, and words of consolation did not come to me. I couldn't even feel moved by the fact that he had been orphaned, it was as if he bore some responsibility for the fear that for years Don Achille had inspired in me. He had a black band sewn on his jacket, he never laughed, he was always on his own. He was in a different class from mine, and the rumor was that he was really smart. At the end of the year we found out that he had been promoted with an average of eight, which depressed me hugely. Gigliola had to repeat Latin and mathematics, I managed to pass with sixes.

When the grades came out, the teacher summoned my mother, told her in my presence that I had passed Latin only thanks to her generosity, and that without private lessons the next year I certainly wouldn't make it. I felt a double humiliation: I was ashamed because I hadn't done as well as I had in elementary school, and I was ashamed of the difference between the harmonious, modestly dressed figure of the teacher, between her Italian that slightly resembled that of the Iliad, and the misshapen figure of my mother, her old shoes, her dull hair, the dialect bent into an ungrammatical Italian.

My mother, too, must have felt the weight of that humiliation. She went home in a surly mood, she told my father that the teachers weren't happy with me, she needed help in the house and I ought to leave school. They discussed it at length, they quarreled, and in the end my father decided that, since I at least had been promoted, while Gigliola had been held back in two subjects, I deserved to continue.

I spent the summer lethargically, in the courtyard, at the ponds, generally with Gigliola, who often talked about the young university student who came to her house to give her private lessons and who, according to her, was in love with her. I listened but I was bored. Every so often I saw Lila with Carmela Peluso; she, too, had gone to a school for something or other, and she, too, had failed. I felt that Lila no longer wanted to be my friend, and that idea brought on a weary exhaustion. Sometimes, hoping that my mother wouldn't see me, I lay down on the bed and dozed.

One afternoon I really fell asleep and when I woke I felt wet. I went to the bathroom to see what was wrong and discovered that my underpants were stained with blood. Terrified by I don't know what, maybe a scolding from my mother for having hurt myself between my legs, I washed the underpants carefully, wrung them out, and put them on again wet. Then I went out into the heat of the courtyard. My heart was pounding.

I met Lila and Carmela, and walked with them to the parish church. I felt that I was getting wet again, but I tried to calm down by telling myself it was the wet underpants. When the fear became unbearable I whispered to Lila, "I have to tell you something."

"What?"

"I want to tell just you."

I took her by the arm, trying to drag her away from Carmela, but Carmela followed us. I was so worried that in the end I confessed to them both, but addressing only Lila.

"What can it be?" I asked.

Carmela knew all about it. She had had that bleeding for a year already, every month.

"It's normal," she said. "Girls have it naturally: you bleed for a few days, your stomach and your back hurt, but then it goes away."

"Really?"

"Really."

Lila's silence pushed me toward Carmela. The naturalness with which she had said what she knew reassured me and made me like her. I spent all afternoon talking to her, until dinner time. You wouldn't die from that wound, I learned. Rather, "it means that you're grown-up and you can make babies, if a man sticks his thingy in your stomach."

Lila listened without saying anything, or almost anything. We asked if she had blood like us and saw her hesitate, then reluctantly answer no. Suddenly she seemed small, smaller than I had ever seen her. She was three or four inches shorter, all skin and bones, very pale in spite of the days spent outside. And she had failed. And she didn't know what the blood was. And no boy had ever made a declaration to her.

"You'll get it," we both said, in a falsely comforting tone.

"What do I care," she said. "I don't have it because I don't want to, it makes me sick. And anyone who has it makes me sick."

She started to leave but then stopped and asked me, "How's Latin?"

"Wonderful."

"Are you good at it?"

"Very."

She thought about it and muttered, "I failed on purpose. I don't want to go to any school anymore."

"What will you do?"

"Whatever I want."

She left us there in the middle of the courtyard.

For the rest of the summer she didn't appear. I became very friendly with Carmela Peluso, who, although she laughed too much and then complained too much, had absorbed Lila's influence so potently that she became at times a kind of surrogate. In speech Carmela imitated her tone of voice, used some of her recurring expressions, gesticulated in a similar way, and when she walked tried to move like her, even though physically she was more like me: pretty and plump, bursting with health. That sort of misappropriation partly repulsed and partly attracted me. I wavered between irritation at a remake that seemed a caricature and fascination because, even diluted, Lila's habits still enchanted me. It was with those that Carmela finally bound me to her. She told me how terrible the new school had been: everyone teased her and the teachers couldn't stand her. She told of going to the prison of Poggioreale with her mother and siblings to see her father, and how they all wept. She told me that her father was innocent, that it was a black creature who killed Don Achille, part male but mostly female, who lived with the rats and came out of the sewer grates, even in daytime, and did whatever terrible thing had to be done before escaping underground. She told me unexpectedly, with a fatuous little smile, that she was in love with Alfonso Carracci. Right afterward her smile turned to tears: it was a love that tortured her, and sapped her strength, the daughter of the murderer was in love with the son of the victim. It was enough for her to see him crossing the courtyard or passing by on the *stradone* to feel faint.

This was a confidence that made a great impression on me and consolidated our friendship. Carmela swore that she had never talked about it to anyone, not even Lila: if she had decided to open up to me it was because she couldn't bear to keep it inside anymore. I liked her dramatic tone. We examined all the possible consequences of that passion until school started again and I no longer had time to listen to her.

What a story! Not even Lila, perhaps, would have been able to make up such a tale.

3.

A period of unhappiness began. I got fat, and under the skin of my chest two hard shoots sprouted, hair flourished in my armpits and my pubis, I became sad and at the same time anxious. In school I worked harder than I ever had, yet the mathematics problems almost never gave the result expected by the textbook, the Latin sentences seemed to make no sense. As soon as I could I locked myself in the bathroom and looked at myself in the mirror, naked. I no longer knew who I was. I began to suspect that I would keep changing, until from me my mother would emerge, lame, with a crossed eye, and no one would love me anymore. I cried often, without warning. My chest, meanwhile, became large and soft. I felt at the mercy of obscure forces acting inside my body, I was always agitated.

One day as I came out of school, Gino, the pharmacist's son, followed me along the street and said that his classmates claimed that my breasts weren't real, I stuffed them with cotton batting. He laughed as he spoke. He said that he thought they were real, he had bet twenty lire on it. Finally he said that, if he won, he would keep ten lire for himself and would give me ten, but I had to prove that I didn't use padding.

That request frightened me. Since I didn't know how to act, I deliberately resorted to Lila's bold tone:

"Give me the ten lire."

"Why, am I right?"

"Yes."

He ran away, and I was disappointed. But soon he returned with a boy from his class, a skinny boy whose name I don't remember, with a dark down above his lip. Gino said to me, "He has to be there, otherwise the others won't believe I've won."

Again I resorted to Lila's tone.

"First the money."

"And if you have padding?"

"I don't."

He gave me ten lire and we all went, silently, to the top floor of a building near the public gardens. There, next to the iron door that led to the terrace, where I was clearly outlined by slender segments of light, I lifted up my shirt and showed them my breasts. The two stood staring as if they couldn't believe their eyes. Then they turned and ran down the stairs.

I heaved a sigh of relief and went to the Bar Solara to buy myself an ice cream.

That episode remained stamped in my memory: I felt for the first time the magnetic force that my body exercised over men, but above all I realized that Lila acted not only on Carmela but also on me like a demanding ghost. If I had had to make a decision in the pure disorder of emotions in a situation like that, what would I have done? I would have run away. And if I had been with Lila? I would have pulled her by the arm, I would have whispered, Let's go, and then, as usual, I would have stayed, because she, as usual, would have decided to stay. Instead, in her absence, after a slight hesitation I put myself in her place. Or, rather, I had made a place for her in me. If I thought again of the moment when Gino made his request, I felt precisely how I had driven myself away, how I had mimicked Lila's look and tone and behavior in situations of brazen conflict, and I was pleased. But sometimes I wondered, somewhat anxiously: Am I being like Carmela? I didn't think so, it seemed to me that I was different, but I couldn't explain in what sense and my pleasure was spoiled. When I passed Fernando's shop with my ice cream and saw Lila intently arranging shoes on a long table, I was tempted to stop and tell her everything, hear what she thought. But she didn't see me and I kept going.

4.

She was always busy. That year Rino compelled her to enroll in school again, but again she almost never went and again she failed. Her mother asked her to help in the house, her father asked her to be in the shop, and she, all of a sudden, instead of resisting, seemed in fact content to labor for both. The rare times we saw each other—on Sunday after Mass or walking between the public gardens and the *stradone*—she displayed no curiosity about my school, and immediately started talking intensely and with admiration about the work that her father and brother did.

She knew that her father as a boy had wanted to be free, had fled the shop of her grandfather, who was also a shoemaker, and had gone to work in a shoe factory in Casoria, where he had made shoes for everyone, even soldiers going to war. She had discovered that Fernando knew how to make a shoe from beginning to end by hand, but he was also completely at home with the machines and knew how to use them, the post machine, the trimmer, the sander. She talked to me about leather, uppers, leather-goods dealers, leather production, high heels and flat heels, about preparing the thread, about soles and how the sole was applied, colored, and buffed. She used all those words of the trade as if they were magic and her father had learned them in an enchanted world—Casoria, the factory—from which he had returned like a satisfied explorer, so satisfied that now he preferred the family shop, the quiet bench, the hammer, the iron foot, the good smell of glue mixed with that of old shoes. And she drew me inside that vocabulary with such an energetic enthusiasm that her father and Rino, thanks to their ability to enclose people's feet in solid, comfortable shoes, seemed to me the best people in the neighborhood. Above all, I came home with the impression that, not spending my days in a shoemaker's shop, having for a father a banal porter instead, I was excluded from a rare privilege.

I began to feel that my presence in class was pointless. For months and months it seemed to me that every promise had fled from the textbooks, all energy. Coming out of school, dazed by unhappiness, I passed Fernando's shop only to see Lila at her workplace, sitting at a little table in the back, her thin chest with no hint of a bosom, her scrawny neck, her small face. I don't know what she did, exactly, but she was there, active, beyond the glass door, set between the bent head of her father and the bent head of her brother, no books, no lessons, no homework. Sometimes I stopped to look at the boxes of polish in the window, the old shoes newly resoled, new ones put on a form that expanded the leather and widened them, making them more comfortable, as if I were a customer and had an interest in the merchandise. I went away only, and reluctantly, when she saw me and waved to me, and I answered her wave, and she returned to concentrate on her work. But often it was Rino who noticed me first and made funny faces to make me laugh. Embarrassed, I ran away without waiting for Lila to see me.

One Sunday I was surprised to find myself talking passionately about shoes with Carmela Peluso. She would buy the magazine *Sogno* and devour the photo novels. At first it seemed to me a waste of time, then I began to look, too, and we started to read them together, and comment on the stories and what the characters said, which was written in white letters on a black background. Carmela tended to pass without a break from comments on the fictional love stories to comments on the true story of her love for Alfonso. In order not to seem inferior, I once told her about the pharmacist's son, Gino, claiming that he loved me. She didn't believe it. The pharmacist's son was in her eyes a kind of unattainable prince, future heir of the pharmacy, a gentleman who would never marry the daughter of a porter, and I was on the point of telling her about the time he had asked to see my breasts and I had let him and earned ten lire. But we were holding *Sogno* spread out on our knees and my gaze fell on the beautiful high-heeled shoes of one of the actresses. This seemed to me a momentous subject, more than the story of my breasts, and I couldn't resist, I began to praise them and whoever had made such beautiful shoes, and to fantasize that if we wore shoes like that neither Gino nor Alfonso would be able to resist us. The more I talked, though, the more I realized, to my embarrassment, that I was trying to make Lila's new passion my own. Carmela listened to me distractedly, then said she had to go. In shoes and shoemakers she had little or no interest. Although she imitated Lila's habits, she, unlike me, held on to the only things that really absorbed her: the photo novels, love stories.

5.

This entire period had a similar character. I soon had to admit that what I did by myself couldn't excite me, only what Lila touched became important. If she withdrew, if her voice withdrew from things, the things got dirty, dusty. Middle school, Latin, the teachers, the books, the language of books seemed less evocative than the finish of a pair of shoes, and that depressed me.

But one Sunday everything changed again. We had gone, Carmela, Lila, and I, to catechism, we were preparing for our first communion. On the way out Lila said she had something to do and she left us. But I saw that she wasn't heading toward home: to my great surprise she went into the elementary school building.

I walked with Carmela, but when I got bored I said goodbye, walked around the building, and went back. The school was closed on Sunday, how could Lila go into the building? After much hesitation I ventured beyond the entranceway, into the hall. I had never gone into my old school and I felt a strong emotion, I recognized the smell, which brought with it a sensation of comfort, a sense of myself that I no longer had. I went into the only door open on the ground floor. There was a large neon-lit room, whose walls were lined with shelves of old books. I counted a dozen adults, a lot of children. They would take down volumes, page through them, put them back, and choose one. Then they got in line in front of a desk behind which sat an old enemy of Maestra Oliviero's, lean Maestro Ferraro, with his crew-cut gray hair. Ferraro examined the chosen text, marked something in the record book, and the person went out with one or more books.

I looked around: Lila wasn't there, maybe she had already left. What was she doing, she didn't go to school anymore, she loved shoes and old shoes, and yet, without saying anything to me, she came to this place to get books? Did she like this space? Why didn't she ask me to come with her? Why had she left me with Carmela? Why did she talk to me about how soles were ground and not about what she read?

I was angry, and ran away.

For a while school seemed to me more meaningless than ever. Then I was sucked back in by the press of homework and end-of-the-year tests, I was afraid of getting bad grades, I studied a lot but aimlessly. And other preoccupations weighed on me. My mother said that I was indecent with those big breasts I had developed, and she took me to buy a bra. She was more abrupt than usual. She seemed ashamed that I had a bosom, that I got my period. The crude instructions she gave me were rapid and insufficient, barely muttered. I didn't have time to ask her any questions before she turned her back and walked away with her lopsided gait.

The bra made my chest even more noticeable. In the last months of school I was besieged by boys and I quickly realized why. Gino and his friend had spread the rumor that I would show how I was made easily, and every so often someone would ask me to repeat the spectacle. I sneaked away, I compressed my bosom by holding my arms crossed over it, I felt mysteriously guilty and alone with my guilt. The boys persisted, even on the street, even in the courtyard. They laughed, they made fun of me. I tried to keep them off once or twice by acting like Lila, but it didn't work for me, and then I couldn't stand it and burst into tears. Out of fear that they would bother me I stayed in the house. I studied hard, I went out now only to go, very reluctantly, to school.

One morning in May Gino ran after me and asked me, not arrogantly but, rather, with some emotion, if I would be his girlfriend. I said no, out of resentment, revenge, embarrassment, yet proud that the son of the pharmacist wanted me. The next day he asked me again and he didn't stop asking until June, when, with some delay due to the complicated lives of our parents, we made our first communion, the girls in white dresses, like brides.

In those dresses, we lingered in the church square and immediately sinned by talking about love. Carmela couldn't believe that I had refused the son of the pharmacist, and she told Lila. She, surprisingly, instead of slipping away with the air of someone saying Who cares, was interested. We all talked about it.

"Why do you say no?" Lila asked me in dialect.

I answered unexpectedly in proper Italian, to make an impression, to let her understand that, even if I spent my time talking about boyfriends, I wasn't to be treated like Carmela.

"Because I'm not sure of my feelings."

It was a phrase I had learned from reading *Sogno* and Lila seemed struck by it. As if it were one of those contests in elementary school, we began to speak in the language of comics and books, which reduced Carmela to pure and simple listener. Those moments lighted my heart and my head: she and I and all those well-crafted words. In middle school nothing like that ever happened, not with classmates or with teachers; it was wonderful. Step by step Lila convinced me that one achieves security in love only by subjecting the wooer to hard tests. And so, returning suddenly to dialect, she advised me to become Gino's girlfriend but on the condition that all summer he agree to buy ice cream for me, her, and Carmela.

"If he doesn't agree it means it's not true love."

I did as she told me and Gino vanished. It wasn't true love, then, and so I didn't suffer from it. The exchange with Lila had given me a pleasure so intense that I planned to devote myself to her totally, especially in summer, when I would have more free time. Meanwhile I wanted that conversation to become the model for all our next encounters. I felt clever again, as if something had hit me in the head, bringing to the surface images and words.

But the sequel of that episode was not what I expected. Instead of consolidating and making exclusive the relationship between her and me, it attracted a lot of other girls. The conversation, the advice she had given me, its effect had so struck Carmela Peluso that she ended up telling everyone. The result was that the daughter of the shoemaker, who had no bosom and didn't get her period and didn't even have a boyfriend, became in a few days the most reliable dispenser of advice on affairs of the heart. And she, again surprising me, accepted that role. If she wasn't busy in the house or the shop, I saw her talking now with this girl, now with that. I passed by, I greeted her, but she was so absorbed that she didn't hear me. I always caught phrases that seemed to me beautiful, and they made me suffer.

6.

These were desolate days, at the height of which came a humiliation that I should have predicted and which instead I had pretended not to care about: Alfonso Carracci was promoted with an average of eight, Gigliola Spagnuolo was promoted with an average of seven, and I had all sixes and four in Latin. I would have to take the exam again in September in that one subject.

This time it was my father who said it was pointless for me to continue. The schoolbooks had already cost a lot. The Latin dictionary, the Campanini and Carboni, even though it was bought used, had been a big expense. There was no money to send me to private lessons during the summer. But above all it was now clear that I wasn't clever: the young son of Don Achille had passed and I hadn't, the daughter of Spagnuolo the pastry maker had passed and I hadn't: one had to be resigned.

I wept night and day, I made myself ugly on purpose to punish myself. I was the oldest, after me there were two boys and another girl, Elisa: Peppe and Gianni, the two boys, came in turn to console me, now bringing me some fruit, now asking me to play with them. But I felt alone just the same, with a cruel fate, and I couldn't calm down. Then one afternoon I heard my mother come up behind me. She said in dialect, in her usual harsh tone:

"We can't pay for the lessons, but you can try to study by yourself and see if you pass the exam." I looked at her uncertainly. She was the same: lusterless hair, wandering eye, large nose, heavy body. She added, "Nowhere is it written that you can't do it."

That was all she said, or at least it's what I remember. Starting the next day, I began to study, forcing myself never to go to the courtyard or the public gardens.

But one morning I heard someone calling me from the street. It was Lila, who since we finished elementary school had completely gotten out of the habit.

"Lenù," she called.

I looked out.

"I have to tell you something."

"What?"

"Come down."

I went down reluctantly, it irritated me to admit to her that I had to take the exam again. We wandered a bit in the courtyard, in the sun. I asked unwillingly what was new on the subject of boyfriends. I remember that I asked her explicitly if there had been developments between Carmela and Alfonso.

"What sort of developments?"

"She loves him."

She narrowed her eyes. When she did that, turning serious, without a smile, as if leaving the pupils only a crack allowed her to see in a more concentrated way, she reminded me of birds of prey I had seen in films at the parish cinema. But that day it seemed to me she had perceived something that made her angry and at the same time frightened her.

"She didn't tell you anything about her father?" she asked.

"That he's innocent."

"And who is the murderer?"

"A creature half male and half female who hides in the sewers and comes out of the grates like the rats."

"So it's true," she said, as if suddenly in pain, and she added that Carmela believed everything she said, that all the girls did.

"I don't want to talk anymore, I don't want to talk to anyone," she muttered, scowling, and I felt that she wasn't speaking with contempt, that the influence she had on us didn't please her, so that for a moment I didn't understand: in her place I would have been extremely proud. In her, though, there was no pride but a kind of impatience mixed with the fear of responsibility.

"But it's good to talk to other people," I murmured.

"Yes, but only if when you talk there's someone who answers."

I felt a burst of joy in my heart. What request was there in that fine sentence? Was she saying that she wanted to talk only to me because I didn't accept everything that came out of her mouth but responded to it? Was she saying that only I knew how to follow the things that went through her mind?

Yes. And she was saying it in a tone that I didn't recognize, that was feeble, although brusque as usual. She had suggested to Carmela, she told me, that in a novel or a film the daughter of the murderer would fall in love with the son of the victim. It was a possibility: to become a true fact a true love would have to arise. But Carmela hadn't understood and right away, the next day, had gone around telling everyone that she was in love with Alfonso: a lie just to show off, whose consequences were unknown. We discussed it. We were twelve years old, but we walked along the hot streets of the neighborhood, amid the dust and flies that the occasional old trucks stirred up as they passed, like two old ladies taking the measure of lives of disappointment, clinging tightly to each other. No one understood us, only we two—I thought—understood one another. We together, we alone, knew how the pall that had weighed on the neighborhood forever, that is, ever since we could remember, might lift at least a little if Peluso, the former carpenter, had not plunged the knife into Don Achille's neck, if it was an inhabitant of the sewers who had done it, if the daughter of the murderer married the son of the victim. There was something unbearable in the things, in the people, in the buildings, in the streets that, only if you reinvented it all, as in a game, became acceptable. The essential, however, was to know how to play, and she and I, only she and I, knew how to do it.

She asked me at one point, without an obvious connection but as if all our conversation could arrive only at that question:

"Are we still friends?"

"Yes."

"Then will you do me a favor?"

I would have done anything for her, on that morning of reconciliation: run away from home, leave the neighborhood, sleep in farmhouses, feed on roots, descend into the sewers through the grates, never turn back, not even if it was cold, not even if it rained. But what she asked seemed to me nothing and at the moment disappointed me. She wanted simply to meet once a day, in the public gardens, even just for an hour, before dinner, and I was to bring the Latin books.

"I won't bother you," she said.

She knew already that I had to take the exam again and wanted to study with me.

7.

In those middle school years many things changed right before our eyes, but day by day, so that they didn't seem to be real changes.

The Bar Solara expanded, became a well-stocked pastry shop—whose skilled pastry maker was Gigliola Spagnuolo's father—which on Sunday was crowded with men, young and old, buying pastries for their families. The two sons of Silvio Solara, Marcello, who was around twenty, and Michele, just a little younger, bought a blue-and-white Fiat 1100 and on Sundays paraded around the streets of the neighborhood.

Peluso's former carpenter shop, which, once in the hands of Don Achille, had become a grocery, was filled with good things that spilled out onto the sidewalk, too. Passing by you caught a whiff of spices, of olives, of salami, of fresh bread, of pork fat and cracklings that made you hungry. The death of Don Achille had slowly detached his threatening shadow from that place and from the whole family. The widow, Donna Maria, had grown very friendly and now managed the store herself, along with Pinuccia, the fifteen-year-old daughter, and Stefano, who was no longer the wild boy who had tried to pierce Lila's tongue but a self-possessed young man, his gaze charming, his smile gentle. The clientele had increased greatly. My mother sent me there to do the shopping, and my father wasn't opposed, partly because when there was no money Stefano wrote everything in a ledger book and we paid at the end of the month.

Assunta, who sold fruit and vegetables on the streets with her husband, Nicola, had had to retire because of bad back pain, and a few months later pneumonia almost killed her husband. Yet those two misfortunes had turned out to be a blessing. Now, going around the streets of the neighborhood every morning with the horse-drawn cart, summer and winter, rain and shine, was the oldest son, Enzo, who had almost nothing about him of the child who threw rocks at us: he had become a stocky youth, with a strong, healthy look, disheveled blond hair, blue eyes, a thick voice with which he praised his wares. He had excellent products and by his gestures alone conveyed an honest, reassuring willingness to serve his customers. He handled the scale adroitly. I liked the speed with which he pushed the weight along the arm to find the right balance, the sound of iron scraping rapidly against iron, then wrapped the potatoes or the fruit and hurried to put the package in Signora Spagnuolo's basket, or Melina's, or my mother's.

Initiatives flourished in the whole neighborhood. A young

dressmaker became a partner in the dry goods store, where Carmela Peluso had just started working as a clerk, and the store expanded, aspiring to become a ladies' clothing shop. The auto-repair shop where Melina's son, Antonio, worked was trying, thanks to the son of the old owner, Gentile Gorresio, to get into motorcycles. In other words everything was quivering, arching upward as if to change its characteristics, not to be known by the accumulated hatreds, tensions, ugliness but, rather, to show a new face. While Lila and I studied Latin in the public gardens, even the pure and simple space around us, the fountain, the shrubbery, a pothole on one side of the street, changed. There was a constant smell of pitch, the steamroller sputtered, advancing slowly over the steamy asphalt, as bare-chested or T-shirted workers paved the streets and the *stradone*. Even the colors changed. Pasquale, Carmela's older brother, was hired to cut down the brush near the railroad tracks. How much he cut—we heard the sound of annihilation for days: the trees groaned, they gave off a scent of fresh green wood, they cleaved the air, they struck the ground after a long rustling that seemed a sigh, and he and others sawed them, split them, pulled up roots that exhaled an odor of underground. The green brush vanished and in its place appeared an area of flat yellow ground. Pasquale had found that job through a stroke of luck. Sometime earlier a friend had told him that people had come to the Bar Solara looking for young men to do night work cutting down trees in a piazza in the center of Naples. He—even though he didn't like Silvio Solara and his sons, he was in that bar because his father was ruined—had to support the family and had gone. He had returned, exhausted, at dawn, his nostrils filled with the odor of living wood, of mangled leaves, and of the sea. Then one thing led to another, and he had been summoned again for that kind of work. And now he was on the construction site near the railroad and we sometimes saw him climbing up the scaffolding of the new buildings that were rising floor by floor, or in a hat made of newspaper, in the sun, eating bread with sausage and greens during his lunch break.

Lila got mad if I looked at Pasquale and was distracted. It was soon obvious, to my great amazement, that she already knew a lot of Latin. She knew the declensions, for example, and also the verbs. Hesitantly I asked her how, and she, with that spiteful expression of a girl who has no time to waste, admitted that during my first year of middle school she had taken a grammar out of the circulating library, the one managed by Maestro Ferraro, and had studied it out of curiosity. The library was a great resource for her. As we talked, she showed me proudly all the cards she had, four: one her own, one in Rino's name, one for her father, and one for her mother. With each she borrowed a book, so she could get four at once. She devoured them, and the following Sunday she brought them back and took four more.

I never asked her what books she had read and what books she was reading, there wasn't time, we had to study. She drilled me, and was furious if I didn't have the answers. Once she slapped me on the arm, hard, with her long, thin hands, and didn't apologize; rather, she said that if I kept making mistakes she would hit me again, and harder. She was enchanted by the Latin dictionary, so large, pages and pages, so heavy—she had never seen one. She constantly looked up words, not only the ones in the exercises but any that occurred to her.

She assigned homework in the tone she had learned from our teacher Maestra Oliviero. She obliged me to translate thirty sentences a day, twenty from Latin to Italian and ten from Italian to Latin. She translated them, too, much more quickly than I did. At the end of the summer, when the exam was approaching, she said warily, having observed skeptically how I looked up words I didn't know in the dictionary, in the

same order in which I found them in the sentence to be translated, fixed on the principal definitions, and only then made an
effort to understand the meaning:

"Did the teacher tell you to do it like that?"

The teacher never said anything, she simply assigned the
exercises. I came up with that method.

She was silent for a moment, then she said to me:

"Read the whole sentence in Latin first, then see where the
verb is. According to the person of the verb you can tell what
the subject is. Once you have the subject you look for the complements: the object if the verb is transitive, or if not other
complements. Try it like that."

I tried. Suddenly translating seemed easy. In September I
went to the exam, I did the written part without a mistake and
answered all the questions in the oral part.

"Who gave you lessons?" the teacher asked, frowning.

"A friend."

"A university student?"

I didn't know what that meant. I said yes.

Lila was waiting for me outside, in the shade. When I came
out I hugged her, I told her that I had done really well and
asked if we would study together the following year. Since it
was she who had first proposed that we meet just to study,
inviting her to continue seemed to me a good way of expressing my joy and gratitude. She detached herself with a gesture
almost of annoyance. She said she just wanted to understand
what that Latin was that those clever ones studied.

"And then?"

"I've understood, that's enough."

"You don't like it?"

"Yes. I'll get some books from the library."

"In Latin?"

"Yes."

"But there's still a lot to study."

"You study for me, and if I have trouble you'll help me. Now I have something to do with my brother."

"What?"

"I'll show you later."

8.

School began again and right away I did well in all the subjects. I couldn't wait for Lila to ask me to help her in Latin or anything else, and so, I think, I studied not so much for school as for her. I became first in the class; even in elementary school I hadn't done so well.

That year it seemed to me that I expanded like pizza dough. I became fuller in the chest, the thighs, the rear. One Sunday when I was going to the gardens, where I was planning to meet Gigliola Spagnuolo, the Solara brothers approached me in the 1100. Marcello, the older, was at the wheel, Michele, the younger, was sitting next to him. They were both handsome, with glossy black hair, white teeth. But of the two I liked Marcello better; he resembled Hector as he was depicted in the school copy of the Iliad. They followed me the whole way, I on the sidewalk and they next to me, in the 1100.

"Have you ever been in a car?"

"No."

"Get in, we'll take you for a ride."

"My father won't let me."

"And we won't tell him. When do you get the chance to ride in a car like this?"

Never, I thought. But meanwhile I said no and kept saying no all the way to the gardens, where the car accelerated and disappeared in a flash beyond the buildings that were under construction. I said no because if my father found out that I had gone in that car, even though he was a good and loving man, even though he loved me very much, he would have beat me to death, while at the same time my little brothers, Peppe and Gianni, young as they were, would feel obliged, now and in the future, to try to kill the Solara brothers. There were no written rules, everyone knew that was how it was. The Solaras knew it, too, since they had been polite, and had merely invited me to get in.

They were not, some time later, with Ada, the oldest daughter of Melina Cappuccio, that is the crazy widow who had caused the scandal when the Sarratores moved. Ada was fourteen. On Sunday, in secret from her mother, she put on lipstick and, with her long, straight legs, and breasts even larger than mine, she looked grown-up and pretty. The Solara brothers made some vulgar remarks to her, Michele grabbed her by the arm, opened the car door, pulled her inside. They brought her back an hour later to the same place, and Ada was a little angry, but also laughing.

But among those who saw her dragged into the car were some who reported it to Antonio, her older brother, who worked as a mechanic in Gorresio's shop. Antonio was a hard worker, disciplined, very shy, obviously wounded by both the untimely death of his father and the unbalanced behavior of his mother. Without saying a single word to friends and relatives he waited in front of the Bar Solara for Marcello and Michele, and when the brothers showed up he confronted them, punching and kicking without even a word of preamble. For a few minutes he managed pretty well, but then the father Solara and one of the barmen came out. They beat Antonio bloody and none of the passersby, none of the customers, intervened to help him.

We girls were divided on this episode. Gigliola Spagnuolo and Carmela Peluso took the part of the Solaras, but only because they were handsome and had an 1100. I wavered. In the presence of my two friends I favored the Solaras and we competed for who loved them most, since in fact they were very handsome and it was impossible not to imagine the impression we would make sitting next to one of them in the car. But I also felt that they had behaved badly with Ada, and that Antonio, even though he wasn't very good-looking, even though he wasn't muscular like the brothers, who went to the gym every day to lift weights, had been courageous in confronting them. So in the presence of Lila, who expressed without half measures that same position, I, too, expressed some reservations.

Once the discussion became so heated that Lila, maybe because she wasn't developed as we were and didn't know the pleasure-fear of having the Solaras' gaze on her, became paler than usual and said that, if what happened to Ada had happened to her, to avoid trouble for her father and her brother Rino she would take care of the two of them herself.

"Because Marcello and Michele don't even look at you," said Gigliola Spagnuolo, and we thought that Lila would get angry.

Instead she said seriously, "It's better that way."

She was as slender as ever, but tense in every fiber. I looked at her hands and marveled: in a short time they had become like Rino's, like her father's, with the skin at the tips yellowish and thick. Even if no one forced her—that wasn't her job, in the shop—she had started to do small tasks, she prepared the thread, took out stitches, glued, even stitched, and now she handled Fernando's tools almost like her brother. That was why that year she never asked me anything about Latin. Eventually, she told me the plan she had in mind, a thing that had nothing to do with books: she was trying to persuade her father to make new shoes. But Fernando didn't want to hear about it. "Making shoes by hand," he told her, "is an art without a future: today there are cars and cars cost money and the money is either in the bank or with the loan sharks, not in the pockets of the Cerullo family." Then she insisted, she filled him with sincere praise: "No one knows how to make shoes the way you do, Papa." Even if that was true, he responded, everything was made in factories now, and since he had worked in the factories he knew very well what lousy stuff came out of them; but there was little to do about it, when people needed new shoes they no longer went to the neighborhood shoemaker, they went to the stores in the center of town, on the Rettifilo, so even if you wanted to make the handcrafted product properly, you wouldn't sell it, you'd be throwing away money and labor, you'd ruin yourself.

Lila wouldn't be convinced and as usual she had drawn Rino to her side. Her brother had first agreed with his father, irritated by the fact that she interfered in things to do with work, where it wasn't a matter of books and he was the expert. Then gradually he had been captivated and now he quarreled with Fernando nearly every day, repeating what she had put into his head.

"Let's at least try it."

"No."

"Have you seen the car the Solaras have, have you seen how well the Carraccis' grocery is doing?"

"I've seen that the dry goods store that wanted to be a dressmaker's gave it up and I've seen that Gorresio, because of his son's stupidity, has bitten off more than he can chew with his motorcycles."

"But the Solaras keep expanding."

"Mind your own business and forget the Solaras."

"Near the train tracks a new neighborhood is being developed."

"Who gives a damn."

"Papa, people are earning and they want to spend."

"People spend on food because you have to eat every day. As for shoes, first of all you don't eat them, and, second, when they break you fix them and they can last twenty years. Our work, right now, is to repair shoes and that's it."

I liked how that boy, who was always nice to me but capable of a brutality that frightened even his father a little, always, in every circumstance, supported his sister. I envied Lila that brother who was so solid, and sometimes I thought that the real difference between her and me was that I had only little brothers, and so no one with the power to encourage me and support me against my mother, freeing my mind, while Lila could count on Rino, who could defend her against anyone, whatever came into her mind. But really, I thought that Fernando was right, and was on his side. And discussing it with Lila, I discovered that she thought so, too.

Once she showed me the designs for shoes that she wanted to make with her brother, both men's and women's. They were beautiful designs, drawn on graph paper, rich in precisely colored details, as if she had had a chance to examine shoes like that close up in some world parallel to ours and then had fixed them on paper. In reality she had invented them in their entirety and in every part, as she had done in elementary school when she drew princesses, so that, although they were normal shoes, they didn't resemble any that were seen in the neighborhood, or even those of the actresses in the photo novels.

"Do you like them?"

"They're really elegant."

"Rino says they're difficult."

"But he knows how to make them?"

"He swears he can."

"And your father?"

"He certainly could do it."

"Then make them."

"Papa doesn't want to."

"Why?"

"He said that as long as I'm playing, fine, but he and Rino can't waste time with me."

"What does that mean?"

"It means that to actually do things takes time and money."

She was on the point of showing me the figures she had put down, in secret from Rino, to understand how much it really would cost to make them. Then she stopped, folded up the pages she was holding, and told me it was pointless to waste time: her father was right.

"But then?"

"We ought to try anyway."

"Fernando will get mad."

"If you don't try, nothing ever changes."

What had to change, in her view, was always the same thing: poor, we had to become rich; having nothing, we had to reach a point where we had everything. I tried to remind her of the old plan of writing novels like the author of *Little Women*. I was stuck there, it was important to me. I was learning Latin just for that, and deep inside I was convinced that she took so many books from Maestro Ferraro's circulating library only because, even though she wasn't going to school anymore, even though she was now obsessed with shoes, she still wanted to write a novel with me and make a lot of money. Instead, she shrugged in her careless way, she had changed her idea of *Little Women*. "Now," she explained, "to become truly rich you need a business." So she thought of starting with a single pair of shoes, just to demonstrate to her father how beautiful and comfortable they were; then, once Fernando was convinced, production would start: two pairs of shoes today, four tomorrow, thirty in a month, four hundred in a year, so that, within a short time, they, she, her father, Rino, her mother, her other siblings, would set up a shoe factory, with machines and at least fifty workers: the Cerullo shoe factory.

"A shoe factory?"

"Yes."

She spoke with great conviction, as she knew how to do, with sentences, in Italian, that depicted before my eyes the factory sign, Cerullo; the brand name stamped on the uppers, Cerullo; and then the Cerullo shoes, all splendid, all elegant, as in her drawings, shoes that once you put them on, she said, are so beautiful and so comfortable that at night you go to sleep without taking them off.

We laughed, we were having fun.

Then Lila paused. She seemed to realize that we were playing, as we had with our dolls years earlier, with Tina and Nu in front of the cellar grating, and she said, with an urgency for concreteness, which emphasized the impression she gave off, of being part child, part old woman, which was, it seemed to me, becoming her characteristic trait:

"You know why the Solara brothers think they're the masters of the neighborhood?"

"Because they're aggressive."

"No, because they have money."

"You think so?"

"Of course. Have you noticed that they've never bothered Pinuccia Carracci?"

"Yes."

"And you know why they acted the way they did with Ada?"

"No."

"Because Ada doesn't have a father, her brother Antonio counts for nothing, and she helps Melina clean the stairs of the buildings."

As a result, either we, too, had to make money, more than the Solaras, or, to protect ourselves against the brothers, we had to do them serious harm. She showed me a sharp shoemaker's knife that she had taken from her father's workshop.

"They won't touch me, because I'm ugly and I don't have

my period," she said, "but with you they might. If anything happens, tell me."

I looked at her in confusion. We were almost thirteen, we knew nothing about institutions, laws, justice. We repeated, and did so with conviction, what we had heard and seen around us since early childhood. Justice was not served by violence? Hadn't Signor Peluso killed Don Achille? I went home. I realized that with those last words she had admitted that I was important to her, and I was happy.

9.

I passed the exams at the end of middle school with eights, and a nine in Italian and nine in Latin. I was the best in the school: better than Alfonso, who had an average of eight, and much better than Gino. For days and days I enjoyed that absolute superiority. I was much praised by my father, who began to boast to everyone about his oldest daughter who had gotten nine in Italian and nine, no less, in Latin. My mother, to my surprise, while she was in the kitchen washing vegetables, said to me, without turning:

"You can wear my silver bracelet Sunday, but don't lose it."

I had less success in the courtyard. There only love and boyfriends counted. When I said to Carmela Peluso that I was the best in the school she immediately started talking to me about the way Alfonso looked at her when he went by. Gigliola Spagnuolo was bitter because she had to repeat the exams for Latin and mathematics and tried to regain prestige by saying that Gino was after her but she was keeping him at a distance because she was in love with Marcello Solara and maybe Marcello also loved her. Even Lila didn't show particular pleasure. When I listed my grades, subject by subject, she said laughing, in her malicious tone, "You didn't get ten?"

I was disappointed. You only got ten in behavior, the teachers never gave anyone a ten in important subjects. But that sentence was enough to make a latent thought become suddenly open: if she had come to school with me, in the same class, if they had let her, she would have had all tens, and this I had always known, and she also knew, and now she was making a point of it.

I went home with the pain of being first without really being first. Further, my parents began to talk about where they could find a place for me, now that I had a middle-school diploma. My mother wanted to ask the stationer to take me as an assistant: in her view, clever as I was, I was suited to selling pens, pencils, notebooks, and schoolbooks. My father imagined future dealings with his acquaintances at the city hall that would settle me in a prestigious post. I felt a sadness inside that, although it wasn't defined, grew and grew and grew, to the point where I didn't even feel like going out on Sunday.

I was no longer pleased with myself, everything seemed tarnished. I looked in the mirror and didn't see what I would have liked to see. My blond hair had turned brown. I had a broad, squashed nose. My whole body continued to expand but without increasing in height. And my skin, too, was spoiled: on my forehead, my chin, and around my jaws, archipelagos of reddish swellings multiplied, then turned purple, finally developed yellowish tips. I began, by my own choice, to help my mother clean the house, to cook, to keep up with the mess that my brothers made, to take care of Elisa, my little sister. In my spare time I didn't go out, I sat and read novels I got from the library: Grazia Deledda, Pirandello, Chekhov, Gogol, Tolstoy, Dostoyevsky. Sometimes I felt a strong need to go and see Lila at the shop and talk to her about the characters I liked best, sentences I had learned by heart, but then I let it go: she would say something mean; she would start talking about the plans she was making with Rino, shoes, shoe factory, money, and I would slowly feel that the novels I read were pointless and that my life was bleak, along with the future, and what I would become: a fat pimply salesclerk in the stationery store across from the parish church, an old maid employee of the local government, sooner or later cross-eyed and lame.

One Sunday, inspired by an invitation that had arrived in the mail in my name, in which Maestro Ferraro summoned me to the library that morning, I finally decided to react. I tried to make myself pretty, as it seemed to me I had been in childhood, as I wished to believe I still was. I spent some time squeezing the pimples, but my face was only more inflamed; I put on my mother's silver bracelet; I let down my hair. Still I was dissatisfied. Depressed I went out into the heat that lay on the neighborhood like a hand swollen with fever in that season, and made my way to the library.

I immediately realized, from the small crowd of parents and elementary- and middle-school children flowing toward the main entrance, that something wasn't normal. I went in. There were rows of chairs already occupied, colored festoons, the priest, Maestro Ferraro, even the principal of the elementary school and Maestra Oliviero. Ferraro, I discovered, had had the idea of awarding a book to the readers who, according to his records, had been most assiduous. Since the ceremony was about to begin and lending was suspended for the moment, I sat at the back of the room. I looked for Lila, but saw only Gigliola Spagnuolo with Gino and Alfonso. I moved restlessly in my chair, uneasy. After a while Carmela Peluso and her brother Pasquale sat down next to me. Hi, hi. I covered my blotchy cheeks better with my hair.

The small ceremony began. The winners were: first Raffaella Cerullo, second Fernando Cerullo, third Nunzia Cerullo, fourth Rino Cerullo, fifth Elena Greco, that is, me.

I wanted to laugh, and so did Pasquale. We looked at each

other, suffocating our laughter, while Carmela whispered insistently, "Why are you laughing?" We didn't answer: we looked at each other again and laughed with our hands over our mouths. Thus, still feeling that laughter in my eyes, and with an unexpected sense of well-being, after the teacher had asked repeatedly and in vain if anyone from the Cerullo family was in the room, he called me, fifth on the list, to receive my prize. Praising me generously, Ferraro gave me *Three Men in a Boat*, by Jerome K. Jerome. I thanked him and asked, in a whisper, "May I also take the prizes for the Cerullo family, so I can deliver them?"

The teacher gave me the prize books for all the Cerullos. As we went out, while Carmela resentfully joined Gigliola, who was happily chatting with Alfonso and Gino, Pasquale said to me, in dialect, things that made me laugh even more, about Rino losing his eyesight over his books, Fernando the shoemaker who didn't sleep at night because he was reading, Signora Nunzia who read standing up, next to the stove, while she was cooking pasta with potatoes, in one hand a novel and in the other the spoon. He had been in elementary school with Rino, in the same class, at the same desk—he said, tears of amusement in his eyes—and both of them, he and his friend, even though they took turns helping each other, after six or seven years of school, including repeats, managed to read at most: Tobacconist, Grocery, Post Office. Then he asked me what the prize for his former schoolmate was.

"*Bruges-la-Morte.*"

"Are there ghosts?"

"I don't know."

"May I come along when you give it to him? Rather, may I give it to him, with my own hands?"

We burst out laughing again.

"Yes."

"They've given Rinuccio a prize. Crazy. It's Lina who reads everything, good Lord, that girl is clever."

The attentions of Pasquale Peluso consoled me greatly, I liked that he made me laugh. Maybe I'm not so ugly, I thought, maybe I can't see myself.

At that moment I heard someone calling me. It was Maestra Oliviero.

I went over and she looked at me, as always evaluating, and said, as if confirming the legitimacy of a more generous judgment about my looks:

"How pretty you are, how big you've gotten."

"It's not true, Maestra."

"It's true, you're a star, healthy, nice, and plump. And also clever. I heard that you were the top student in the school."

"Yes."

"Now what will you do?"

"I'll go to work."

She darkened.

"Don't even mention it, you have to go on studying."

I looked at her in surprise. What was there left to study? I didn't know anything about the order of schools, I didn't have a clear idea what there was after the middle school diploma. Words like high school, university were for me without substance, like many of the words I came across in novels.

"I can't, my parents won't let me."

"What did the literature teacher give you in Latin?"

"Nine."

"Sure?"

"Yes."

"Then I'll talk to your parents."

I started to leave, a little scared, I have to admit. If Maestra Oliviero really went to my father and mother to tell them to let me continue in school, it would again unleash quarrels that I didn't want to face. I preferred things as they were: help my mother, work in the stationery store, accept the ugliness and the pimples, be healthy, nice, and plump, as Maestra Oliviero said, and toil in poverty. Hadn't Lila been doing it for at least three years already, apart from her crazy dreams as the sister and daughter of shoemakers?

"Thank you, Maestra," I said. "Goodbye."

But Oliviero held me by one arm.

"Don't waste time with him," she said, indicating Pasquale, who was waiting for me. "He's a construction worker, he'll never go farther than that. And then he comes from a bad family, his father is a Communist, and murdered Don Achille. I absolutely don't want to see you with him—he's surely a Communist like his father."

I nodded in assent and went off without saying goodbye to Pasquale, who seemed bewildered. Then, with pleasure, I heard him following me, a dozen steps behind. He wasn't good-looking, but I wasn't pretty anymore, either. He had curly black hair, he was dark-skinned, and sunburned, he had a wide mouth and was the son of a murderer, maybe even a Communist.

I turned the word over and over in my head, *Communist*, a word that was meaningless to me, but which the teacher had immediately branded with negativity. Communist, Communist, Communist. It captivated me. Communist and son of a murderer.

Meanwhile, around the corner, Pasquale caught up with me. We walked together until we were a few steps from my house and, laughing again, made a date for the next day, when we would go to the shoemaker's shop to give the books to Lila and Rino. Before we parted Pasquale also said that the following Sunday he, his sister, and anyone who wanted were going to Gigliola's house to learn to dance. He asked if I wanted to go, maybe with Lila. I was astonished, I already knew that my mother would never let me. But still I said, all right, I'll think about it. Then he held out his hand, and I, who was not used to such gestures, hesitated, just brushed his, which was hard and rough, and withdrew mine.

"Are you always going to be a construction worker?" I asked, even though I already knew that he was.

"Yes."

"And you're a Communist?"

He looked at me perplexed.

"Yes."

"And you go to see your father at Poggioreale?"

He turned serious: "When I can."

"Bye."

"Bye."

10.

Maestra Oliviero, that same afternoon, presented herself at my house without warning, throwing my father into utter despair and embittering my mother. She made them both swear that they would enroll me in the nearest classical high school. She offered to find me the books I would need herself. She reported to my father, but looking at me severely, that she had seen me alone with Pasquale Peluso, company that was completely unsuitable for me, who embodied such high hopes.

My parents didn't dare contradict her. They swore solemnly that they would send me to the first year of high school, and my father said, in a menacing tone, "Lenù, don't you dare ever speak to Pasquale Peluso again." Before she left, the teacher asked me about Lila, still in the presence of my parents. I answered that she was helping her father and her brother, she kept the accounts and the shop in order. She made a grimace of contempt, she asked me: "Does she know you got a nine in Latin?"

I nodded yes.

"Tell her that now you're going to study Greek, too. Tell her."

She took leave of my parents with an air of pride.

"This girl," she exclaimed, "will bring us great satisfaction."

That evening, while my mother, furious, was saying that now there was no choice but to send me to the school for rich people, otherwise Oliviero would wear her out by tormenting her and would even fail little Elisa in reprisal; while my father, as if this were the main problem, threatened to break both my legs if he heard that I had been alone with Pasquale Peluso, we heard a loud cry that silenced us. It was Ada, Melina's daughter, crying for help.

We ran to the window, there was a great commotion in the courtyard. It seemed that Melina, who after the Sarratores moved had generally behaved herself—a little melancholy, yes, a little absentminded, but in essence her eccentricities had become infrequent and harmless, like singing loudly while she washed the stairs of the buildings, or dumping buckets of dirty water into the street without paying attention to passersby—was having a new crisis of madness, a sort of crazy outburst of joy. She was laughing, jumping on the bed, and pulling up her skirt, displaying her fleshless thighs and her underpants to her frightened children. This my mother found out, by questioning from her window the other women looking out of their windows. I saw that Nunzia Cerullo and Lila were hurrying to see what was happening and I tried to slip out the door to join them, but my mother stopped me. She smoothed her hair and, with her limping gait, went herself to see what was going on.

When she returned she was indignant. Someone had delivered a book to Melina. A book, yes, a book. To her, who had at most two years of elementary school and had never read a book in her life. The book bore on the cover the name of Donato Sarratore. Inside, on the first page, it had an inscription in pen to Melina and also marked, with red ink, were the poems he had written for her.

My father, hearing that strange news, insulted the railway-worker poet obscenely. My mother said someone should undertake to bash the disgusting head of that disgusting man. All night we heard Melina singing with happiness, we heard the voices of her children, especially Antonio and Ada, trying to calm her but failing.

I, however, was overcome with amazement. On a single day I had attracted the attention of a young man like Pasquale, a new school had opened up before me, and I had discovered that a person who until some time earlier had lived in the neighborhood, in the building across from ours, had published a book. This last fact proved that Lila had been right to think that such a thing could even happen to us. Of course, she had given it up now, but perhaps I, by going to that difficult school called high school, fortified by the love of Pasquale, could write one myself, as Sarratore had done. Who knows, if everything worked out for the best I would become rich before Lila with her shoe designs and her shoe factory.

11.

The next day I went secretly to meet Pasquale Peluso. He arrived out of breath and sweaty in his work clothes, spotted all over with splotches of white plaster. On the way I told him the story of Donato and Melina. I told him that in these latest events was the proof that Melina wasn't mad, that Donato really had been in love with her and still loved her. But as I spoke, even as Pasquale agreed with me, revealing a sensitivity about things to do with love, I realized that, of these developments, what continued to excite me more than anything else was the fact that Donato Sarratore had published a book. That employee of the state railroad had become the author of a volume that Maestro Ferraro might very well put in the library and lend. Therefore, I said to Pasquale, we had all known not an ordinary man, put upon by the nagging of his wife, Lidia, but a poet. Therefore, right before our eyes a tragic love had been born, inspired by a person we knew very well, that is to say Melina. I was very excited, my heart was pounding. But I realized that here Pasquale couldn't follow me, he said yes only so as not to contradict me. And in fact after a while he became evasive, and began to ask me questions about Lila: how she had been at school, what I thought of her, if we were close friends. I answered willingly: it was the first time anyone had asked me about our friendship and I talked about it enthusiastically the whole way. Also for the first time, I felt how, having to search for words on a subject where I didn't have words ready, I tended to reduce the relationship between Lila and me to extreme declarations that were all exaggeratedly positive.

When we got to the shoemaker's shop we were still talking about it. Fernando had gone home for the afternoon rest, but Lila and Rino stood next to each other scowling, bent over something that they looked at with hostility, and as soon as they saw us outside the glass door they put it away. I handed Maestro Ferraro's gifts to Lila, while Pasquale teased Rino, opening the prize under his nose and saying, "After you've read the story of this Bruges-the-dead tell me if you liked it and maybe I'll read it, too." They laughed a lot, and every so often whispered to each other remarks about Bruges, which were surely obscene. But I noticed that Pasquale, although he was joking with Rino, looked furtively at Lila. Why was he looking at her like that, what was he looking for, what did he see there? They were long, intense looks that she didn't seem to be aware of, while—it seemed to me—Rino was even more aware of them than I was, and he soon drew Pasquale out into the street as if to keep us from hearing what was so funny about Bruges, but in reality irritated by the way his friend was looking at his sister.

I went with Lila to the back of the shop, trying to perceive in her what had attracted Pasquale's attention. She seemed to me the same slender girl, skin and bone, pale, except perhaps for the larger shape of her eyes and a slight curve in her chest. She arranged the books with other books she had, amid the old shoes and some notebooks with battered covers. I mentioned Melina's madness, but above all I tried to communicate my excitement at the fact that we could say we knew someone who had just published a book, Donato Sarratore. I murmured in Italian: "Think, his son Nino was in school with us; think, the whole Sarratore family might become rich." She gave a skeptical half smile.

"With this?" she said. She held out her hand and showed me Sarratore's book.

Antonio, Melina's oldest son, had given it to her to get it out of the sight and hands of his mother. I held it, I examined the slim volume. It was called *Attempts at Serenity*. The cover was red, with a drawing of the sun shining on a mountaintop. It was exciting to read, right above the title: "Donato Sarratore." I opened it, read aloud the dedication in pen: *To Melina who nurtured my poetry. Donato. Naples, 12 June 1958*. I was moved, I felt a shiver at the back of my neck, at the roots of my hair. I said, "Nino will have a better car than the Solaras."

But Lila had one of her intense looks and I saw that she was focused on the book I had in my hand. "If it happens we'll know about it," she muttered. "For now those poems have done only damage."

"Why?"

"Sarratore didn't have the courage to go in person to Melina and in his place he sent her the book."

"Isn't it a fine thing?"

"Who knows. Now Melina expects him, and if Sarratore doesn't come she'll suffer more than she's suffered till now."

What wonderful conversations. I looked at her white,

smooth skin, not a blemish. I looked at her lips, the delicate shape of her ears. Yes, I thought, maybe she's changing, and not only physically but in the way she expresses herself. It seemed to me—articulated in words of today—that not only did she know how to put things well but she was developing a gift that I was already familiar with: more effectively than she had as a child, she took the facts and in a natural way charged them with tension; she intensified reality as she reduced it to words, she injected it with energy. But I also realized, with pleasure, that, as soon as she began to do this, I felt able to do the same, and I tried and it came easily. This—I thought contentedly—distinguishes me from Carmela and all the others: I get excited with her, here, at the very moment when she's speaking to me. What beautiful strong hands she had, what graceful gestures came to her, what looks.

But while Lila talked about love, while I talked about it, the pleasure was spoiled by an ugly thought. I suddenly realized that I had been mistaken: Pasquale the construction worker, the Communist, the son of the murderer, had wanted to go there with me not for me but for her, to have the chance to see her.

12.

The thought took my breath away for a moment. When the two young men returned, interrupting our conversation, Pasquale confessed, laughing, that he had left the work site without saying anything to the boss, so he had to go back right away. I noticed that he looked at Lila again, for a long time, intensely, almost against his will, perhaps to signal to her: I'm running the risk of losing my job just for you. Addressing Rino, he said:

"Sunday we're all going dancing at Gigliola's, even Lenuccia's coming, will you two come?"

"Sunday is a long way off, we'll think about it later," Rino answered.

Pasquale gave a last look at Lila, who paid no attention to him, then he slipped away without asking if I wanted to go with him.

I felt an irritation that made me nervous. I began touching the most inflamed areas of my cheeks with my fingers, then I realized it and forced myself not to. While Rino took out from under the bench the things he had been working on before we arrived, and was studying them in bewilderment, I started talking again to Lila about books, about love affairs. We inflated excessively Sarratore, Melina's love madness, the role of the book. What would happen? What reactions would be unleashed not by the reading of the poems but by the object itself, the fact that its cover, the title, the name and surname had again stirred that woman's heart? We talked so fervently that Rino suddenly lost patience and shouted at us: "Will you stop it? Lila, let's get to work, otherwise Papa will return and we won't be able to do anything."

We stopped. I glanced at what they were doing: a wooden form besieged by a tangle of soles, strips of skin, pieces of thick leather, amid knives and awls and various other tools. Lila told me that she and Rino were trying to make a man's traveling shoe, and her brother, right afterward, made me swear on my sister Elisa that I would never say a word about it to anyone. They were working in secret from Fernando, Rino had got the skins and the leather from a friend who worked at a tannery at Ponte di Casanova. They would devote five minutes here, ten tomorrow, to making the shoe, because there was no way to persuade their father to help them; in fact when they had brought up the subject Fernando had sent Lila home, shouting that he didn't want to see her in the shop anymore, and meanwhile he had threatened to kill Rino, who at the age of nineteen was lacking in respect and had got it in his head to be better than his father.

I pretended to be interested in their secret undertaking, but in fact I was very sorry about it. Although the two siblings had involved me by choosing me as their confidant, it was still an experience that I could enter only as witness: on that path Lila would do great things by herself, I was excluded. But above all, how, after our intense conversations about love and poetry, could she walk me to the door, as she was doing, far more absorbed in the atmosphere of excitement around a shoe? We had talked with such pleasure about Sarratore and Melina. I couldn't believe that, though she pointed out to me that heap of leathers and skins and tools, she did not still feel, as I did, the anxiety about a woman who was suffering for love. What did I care about shoes. I still had, in my mind's eye, the most secret stages of that affair of violated trust, passion, poetry that became a book, and it was as if she and I had read a novel together, as if we had seen, there in the back of the shop and not in the parish hall on Sunday, a dramatic film. I felt grieved at the waste, because I was compelled to go away, because she preferred the adventure of the shoes to our conversation, because she knew how to be autonomous whereas I needed her, because she had her things that I couldn't be part of, because Pasquale, who was a grown-up, not a boy, certainly would seek other occasions to gaze at her and plead with her and try to persuade her to secretly be his girlfriend, and be kissed, touched, as it was said people did when they became boyfriend and girlfriend—because, in short, she would feel that I was less and less necessary.

Therefore, as if to chase away the feeling of revulsion these thoughts inspired, as if to emphasize my value and my indispensability, I told her in a rush that I was going to the high school. I told her at the doorway of the shop, when I was already in the street. I told her that Maestra Oliviero had insisted to my parents, promising to get me used books, for nothing, herself. I did it because I wanted her to realize that I was special, and that, even if she became rich making shoes with Rino, she couldn't do without me, as I couldn't do without her.

She looked at me perplexed.

"What is high school?" she asked.

"An important school that comes after middle school."

"And what are you going there to do?"

"Study."

"What?"

"Latin."

"That's all?"

"And Greek."

"Greek?"

"Yes."

She had the expression of someone at a loss, finding nothing to say. Finally she murmured, irrelevantly, "Last week I got my period."

And although Rino hadn't called her, she went back inside.

13.

So now she was bleeding, too. The secret movements of the body, which had reached me first, had arrived like the tremor of an earthquake in her as well and would change her, she was already changing. Pasquale—I thought—had realized it before me. He and probably other boys. The fact that I was going to high school quickly lost its aura. For days all I could think of was the unknowability of the changes that would hit Lila. Would she become pretty like Pinuccia Carracci or Gigliola or Carmela? Would she turn ugly like me? I went home and examined myself in the mirror. What was I like, really? What would she, sooner or later, be like?

I began to take more care with myself. One Sunday afternoon, on the occasion of the usual walk from the *stradone* to the gardens, I put on my best dress, which was blue, with a square neckline, and also my mother's silver bracelet. When I met Lila I felt a secret pleasure in seeing her as she was every day, in a worn, faded dress, her black hair untidy. There was nothing to differentiate her from the usual Lila, a restless, skinny girl. Only she seemed taller, she had grown, from a small girl, almost as tall as me, maybe half an inch less. But what was that change? I had a large bosom, a womanly figure.

We reached the gardens, we turned and went back, then walked along the street again to the gardens. It was early, there wasn't yet the Sunday commotion, the sellers of roasted hazelnuts and almonds and *lupini*. Lila was again asking me tentatively about the high school. I told her what I knew, exaggerating as much as possible. I wanted her to be curious, to want at least a little to share my adventure from the outside, to feel she was losing something of me as I always feared losing much of her. I was on the street side, she on the inside. I was talking, she was listening attentively.

The Solaras' 1100 pulled up beside us, Michele was driving, next to him was Marcello, who began to joke with us. With both of us, not just me. He would sing softly, in dialect, phrases like: what lovely young ladies, aren't you tired of going back and forth, look how big Naples is, the most beautiful city in the world, as beautiful as you, get in, half an hour and we'll bring you back here.

I shouldn't have but I did. Instead of going straight ahead as if neither he nor the car nor his brother existed; instead of continuing to talk to Lila and ignoring them, I turned and, out of a need to feel attractive and lucky and on the verge of going to the rich people's school, where I would likely find boys with cars much nicer than the Solaras', said, in Italian:

"Thank you, but we can't."

Marcello reached out a hand. I saw that it was broad and

short, although he was a tall, well-made young man. The five fingers passed through the window and grabbed me by the wrist, while his voice said: "Michè, slow down, you see that nice bracelet the porter's daughter is wearing?"

The car stopped. Marcello's fingers around my wrist made my skin turn cold, and I pulled my arm away in disgust. The bracelet broke, falling between the sidewalk and the car.

"Oh, my God, look what you've made me do," I exclaimed, thinking of my mother.

"Calm down," he said, and, opening the door, got out of the car. "I'll fix it for you."

He was smiling, friendly, he tried again to take my wrist as if to establish a familiarity that would soothe me. It was an instant. Lila, half the size of him, pushed him against the car and whipped the shoemaker's knife under his throat.

She said calmly, in dialect, "Touch her again and I'll show you what happens."

Marcello, incredulous, froze. Michele immediately got out of the car and said in a reassuring tone: "Don't worry, Marcè, this whore doesn't have the guts."

"Come here," Lila said, "come here, and you'll find out if I have the guts."

Michele came around the car, and I began to cry. From where I was I could see that the point of the knife had already cut Marcello's skin, a scratch from which came a tiny thread of blood. The scene is clear in my mind: it was still very hot, there were few passersby, Lila was on Marcello as if she had seen a nasty insect on his face and wanted to chase it away. In my mind there remains the absolute certainty I had then: she wouldn't have hesitated to cut his throat. Michele also realized it.

"O.K., good for you," he said, and with the same composure, as if he were amused, he got back in the car. "Get in, Marcè, apologize to the ladies, and let's go."

Lila slowly removed the point of the blade from Marcello's throat. He gave her a timid smile, his gaze was disoriented.

"Just a minute," he said.

He knelt on the sidewalk, in front of me, as if he wanted to apologize by subjecting himself to the highest form of humiliation. He felt around under the car, recovered the bracelet, examined it, and repaired it by squeezing with his nails the silver link that had come apart. He gave it to me, looking not at me but at Lila. It was to her that he said, "Sorry." Then he got in the car and they drove off.

"I was crying because of the bracelet, not because I was scared," I said.

14.

The boundaries of the neighborhood faded in the course of that summer. One morning my father took me with him. Since I was enrolling in high school, he wanted me to know what public transportation I would have to take and what route when I went in October to the new school.

It was a beautiful, very clear, windy day. I felt loved, coddled, to my affection for him was added a crescendo of admiration. He knew the enormous expanse of the city intimately, he knew where to get the metro or a tram or a bus. Outside he behaved with a sociability, a relaxed courtesy, that at home he almost never had. He was friendly toward everyone, on the metro and the buses, in the offices, and he always managed to let his interlocutor know that he worked for the city and that, if he liked, he could speed up practical matters, open doors.

We spent the entire day together, the only one in our lives, I don't remember any others. He dedicated himself to me, as if he wanted to communicate in a few hours everything useful he had learned in the course of his existence. He showed me

Piazza Garibaldi and the station that was being built: according to him it was so modern that the Japanese were coming from Japan to study it—in particular the columns—and build an identical one in their country. But he confessed that he liked the old station better, he was more attached to it. Ah well. Naples, he said, had always been like that: it's cut down, it's broken up, and then it's rebuilt, and the money flows and creates work.

He took me along Corso Garibaldi, to the building that would be my school. He dealt in the office with extreme good humor, he had the gift of congeniality, a gift that in the neighborhood and at home he kept hidden. He boasted of my extraordinary report card to a janitor whose wedding witness, he discovered on the spot, he knew well. I heard him repeating often: everything in order? Or: everything that can be done is being done. He showed me Piazza Carlo III, the Albergo dei Poveri, the botanical garden, Via Foria, the museum. He took me on Via Costantinopoli, to Port'Alba, to Piazza Dante, to Via Toledo. I was overwhelmed by the names, the noise of the traffic, the voices, the colors, the festive atmosphere, the effort of keeping everything in mind so that I could talk about it later with Lila, the ease with which he chatted with the pizza maker from whom he bought me a pizza melting with ricotta, the fruit seller from whom he bought me a yellow peach. Was it possible that only our neighborhood was filled with conflicts and violence, while the rest of the city was radiant, benevolent?

He took me to see the place where he worked, in Piazza Municipio. There, too, he said, everything had changed, the trees had been cut down, everything was broken up: now see all the space, the only old thing left is the Maschio Angioino, but it's beautiful, little one, there are two real males in Naples, your father and that fellow there. We went to the city hall, he greeted this person and that, everyone knew him. With some he was friendly, and introduced me, repeating yet again that in school I had gotten nine in Italian and nine in Latin; with others he was almost mute, only, indeed, yes, you command and I obey. Finally he said that he would show me Vesuvius from close up, and the sea.

It was an unforgettable moment. We went toward Via Caracciolo, as the wind grew stronger, the sun brighter. Vesuvius was a delicate pastel-colored shape, at whose base the whitish stones of the city were piled up, with the earth-colored slice of the Castel dell'Ovo, and the sea. But what a sea. It was very rough, and loud; the wind took your breath away, pasted your clothes to your body and blew the hair off your forehead. We stayed on the other side of the street in a small crowd, watching the spectacle. The waves rolled in like blue metal tubes carrying an egg white of foam on their peaks, then broke in a thousand glittering splinters and came up to the street with an oh of wonder and fear from those watching. What a pity that Lila wasn't there. I felt dazed by the powerful gusts, by the noise. I had the impression that, although I was absorbing much of that sight, many things, too many, were scattering around me without letting me grasp them.

My father held tight to my hand as if he were afraid that I would slip away. In fact I had the wish to leave him, run, move, cross the street, be struck by the brilliant scales of the sea. At that tremendous moment, full of light and sound, I pretended I was alone in the newness of the city, new myself with all life ahead, exposed to the mutable fury of things but surely triumphant: I, I and Lila, we two with that capacity that together—only together—we had to seize the mass of colors, sounds, things, and people, and express it and give it power.

I returned to the neighborhood as if I had gone to a distant land. Here again the known streets, here again the grocery of Stefano and his sister Pinuccia, Enzo who sold fruit, the Solaras' 1100 parked in front of the bar—now I would have paid any amount for it to be eliminated from the face of the earth. Luckily my mother had never found out about the episode of the bracelet. Luckily no one had reported to Rino what had happened.

I told Lila about the streets, their names, the noise, the extraordinary light. But immediately I felt uncomfortable. If she had been telling the story of that day, I would have joined in with an indispensable counter-melody and, even if I hadn't been present, I would have felt alive and active, I would have asked questions, raised issues, I would have tried to show her that we had to take that same journey together, necessarily, because I would be enriched by it, I would have been a much better companion than her father. She instead listened to me without curiosity, and at first I thought it was malicious, to diminish the force of my enthusiasm. But I had to persuade myself it wasn't so, she simply had her own train of thought that was fed on concrete things, a book, a fountain. With her ears certainly she listened to me, but with her eyes, with her mind, she was solidly anchored to the street, to the few plants in the gardens, to Gigliola, who was walking with Alfonso and Carmela, to Pasquale, who waved at her from the scaffolding of the building site, to Melina, who spoke out loud of Donato Sarratore while Ada tried to drag her into the house, to Stefano, the son of Don Achille, who had just bought a Giardinetta, and had his mother beside him and in the backseat his sister Pinuccia, to Marcello and Michele Solara, who passed in their 1100, with Michele pretending not to see us while Marcello gave us a friendly glance, and, above all, to the secret work, kept hidden from her father, that she applied herself to, advancing the project of the shoes. My story, for her, was at that moment only a collection of useless signals from useless spaces. She would be concerned with those spaces only if she had the opportunity to go there. And in fact, after all my talk, she said only:

"I have to tell Rino that Sunday we should accept Pasquale Peluso's invitation."

There I was, telling her about the center of Naples, and she placed at the center Gigliola's house, in one of the apartment buildings of the neighborhood, where Pasquale wanted to take her dancing. I was sorry. To Peluso's invitations we had always said yes and yet we had never gone, I to avoid arguments with my parents, she because Rino was against it. We often saw him, on holidays, all cleaned up, waiting for his friends, old and young. He was a generous soul, he didn't make distinctions of age, he brought along anyone. He would wait in front of the gas station and, one or two at a time, Enzo and Gigliola, and Carmela who now called herself Carmen, and sometimes Rino himself if he had nothing else to do, and Antonio, who had the weight of his mother, Melina, and, if Melina was calm, also his sister Ada, whom the Solaras had dragged into their car and driven who knows where for an hour. When the day was fine they went to the sea, returning red-faced from the sun. Or, more often, they all met at Gigliola's, whose parents were more tolerant than ours, and there those who knew how to dance danced and those who didn't learned.

Lila began to go to these little parties, and to take me; she had developed, I don't know how, an interest in dancing. Both Pasquale and Rino turned out to be surprisingly good dancers, and we learned from them the tango, the waltz, the polka, and the mazurka. Rino, it should be said, as a teacher got annoyed immediately, especially with his sister, while Pasquale was very patient. At first he would have us dance standing on his feet, so that we learned the steps, then, when we became more skilled, we went whirling through the house.

I discovered that I liked to dance, I would have danced for-ever. Lila instead wore the expression of someone who wants to understand how it's done, and whose pleasure seems to con-sist entirely in learning, since often she stayed seated, watching us, studying us, and applauding the couples who were most in synch. Once, at her house, she showed me a book that she had taken from the library: it was all about the dances, and every movement was explained with black-and-white drawings of a man and woman dancing. She was very cheerful in that period, with an exuberance surprising in her. Abruptly she grabbed me around the waist and, playing the man, made me dance the tango as she sang the music. Rino looked in and saw us, and burst into laughter. He wanted to dance, too, first with me, then with his sister, though without music. While we danced he told me that Lila had such a mania for perfection that she was obliged to practice continuously, even if they didn't have a gramophone. But as soon as he said the word—gramophone, gramophone, gramophone—Lila shouted at me from a corner of the room, narrowing her eyes.

"You know what kind of word it is?"

"No."

"Greek."

I looked at her uncertainly. Rino meanwhile let me go and went to dance with his sister, who gave a soft cry, handed me the dance manual, and flew around the room with him. I placed the manual among her books. What had she said? Gramophone was Italian, not Greek. But meanwhile I saw that under *War and Peace*, and bearing the label of Maestro Ferraro's library, a tattered volume was sticking out, entitled *Greek Grammar*. Grammar. Greek. I heard her promising me, out of breath:

"Afterward I'll write gramophone for you in Greek letters."

I said I had things to do and left.

15.

She had begun to study Greek even before I went to high school? She had done it on her own, while I hadn't even thought about it, and during the summer, the vacation? Would she always do the things I was supposed to do, before and better than me? She eluded me when I followed her and meanwhile stayed close on my heels in order to pass me by?

I tried not to see her for a while, I was angry. I went to the library to get a Greek grammar, but there was only one, and the whole Cerullo family had borrowed it in turn. Maybe I should erase Lila from myself like a drawing from the blackboard, I thought, for, I think, the first time. I felt fragile, exposed, I couldn't spend my time following her or discovering that she was following me, either way feeling diminished. I immediately went to find her. I let her teach me how to do the quadrille. I let her show me how many Italian words she could write in the Greek alphabet. She wanted me to learn the alphabet before I went to school, and she forced me to write and read it. I got even more pimples. I went to the dances at Gigliola's with a permanent sense of inadequacy and shame.

I hoped that it would pass, but inadequacy and shame intensified. Once Lila danced a waltz with her brother. They danced so well together that we left them the whole space. I was spellbound. They were beautiful, they were perfect together. As I watched, I understood conclusively that soon she would lose completely her air of a child-old woman, the way a well-known musical theme is lost when it's adapted too fancifully. She had become shapely. Her high forehead, her large eyes that could suddenly narrow, her small nose, her cheekbones, her lips, her ears were looking for a new orchestration and seemed close to finding it. When she combed her hair in a ponytail, her long neck was revealed with a touching clarity. Her chest had small graceful breasts that were more and more visible. Her back made a deep curve before landing at the increasingly taut arc of her behind. Her ankles were still too thin, the ankles of a child; but how long before they adapted to her now feminine figure? I realized that the males, watching as she danced with Rino, were seeing more than I was. Pasquale above all, but also Antonio, also Enzo. They kept their eyes on her as if we others had disappeared. And yet I had bigger breasts. And yet Gigliola was a dazzling blonde, with regular features and nice legs. And yet Carmela had beautiful eyes and, especially, provocative movements. But there was nothing to be done: something had begun to emanate from Lila's mobile body that the males sensed, an energy that dazed them, like the swelling sound of beauty arriving. The music had to stop before they returned to themselves, with uncertain smiles and extravagant applause.

16.

Lila was malicious: this, in some secret place in myself, I still thought. She had shown me not only that she knew how to wound with words but that she would kill without hesitation, and yet those capacities now seemed to me of little importance. I said to myself: she will release something more vicious, and I resorted to the word "evil", an exaggerated word that came to me from childhood tales. But if it was a childish self that unleashed these thoughts in me, they had a foundation of truth. And in fact, it slowly became clear not only to me, who had been observing her since elementary school, but to everyone, that an essence not only seductive but dangerous emanated from Lila.

Toward the end of the summer there was increasing pressure on Rino to take his sister on the group excursions outside the neighborhood for a pizza, for a walk. Rino, however, wanted his own space. He, too, seemed to me to be changing, Lila had kindled his imagination and his hopes. But, to see him, to hear him—the effect hadn't been the best. He had become more of a braggart, he never missed a chance to allude to how good he was at his work and how rich he was going to be, and he often repeated a remark he was fond of: It won't take much, just a little luck, and I'll piss in the Solaras' face. When he was boasting like this, however, it was crucial that his sister not be present. In her presence he was confused, he made a few allusions, then let it go. He realized that Lila was giving him a distrustful look, as if he were betraying a secret pact of behavior, of detachment, and so he preferred not to have her around; they were working together all day anyway in the shoemaker's shop. He escaped and swaggered like a peacock with his friends. But sometimes he had to give in.

One Sunday, after many discussions with our parents, we went out (Rino had generously come to my house and, before my parents, assumed responsibility for my person), in the evening no less. We saw the city lighted up by signs, the crowded streets, we smelled the stench of fish gone bad in the heat but also the fragrance of restaurants, of the fried food stalls, of bar-pastry shops much more lavish than the Solaras'. I don't remember if Lila had already had a chance to go to the center, with her brother or others. Certainly if she had she hadn't told me about it. I remember instead that that night she was absolutely mute. We crossed Piazza Garibaldi, but she stayed behind, lingering to watch a shoeshine, a large painted woman, the dark men, the boys. She stared at people attentively, she looked them right in the face, so that some laughed and others made a gesture meaning "What do you want?" Every so often I gave her a tug, dragging her with me out of fear that we would lose Rino, Pasquale, Antonio, Carmela, Ada.

That night we went to a pizzeria on the Rettifilo. We ate happily. To me it seemed that Antonio wooed me a little, making an effort to overcome his timidity, and I was pleased because at least Pasquale's attentions to Lila were counterbalanced. But at some point the pizza maker, a man in his thirties, began to spin the dough in the air, while he was working it, with extreme virtuosity, and he exchanged smiles with Lila, who looked at him in admiration.

"Stop it," Rino said to her.

"I'm not doing anything," she said and tried to look in another direction.

But things got worse. Pasquale, smiling, said that the man, the pizza maker—who to us girls seemed old, he was wearing a wedding ring, was surely the father of children—had secretly blown a kiss to Lila on the tips of his fingers. We turned suddenly to look at him: he was doing his job, that was all. But Pasquale, still smiling, asked Lila, "Is it true or am I wrong?"

Lila, with a nervous laugh in contrast to Pasquale's broad smile, said, "I didn't see anything."

"Forget it, Pascà," said Rino, giving his sister a cutting look.

But Peluso got up, went to the counter in front of the oven, walked around it, and, a candid smile on his lips, slapped the pizza maker in the face, so that he fell against the mouth of the oven.

The owner of the place, a small, pale man in his sixties, hurried over, and Pasquale explained to him calmly not to worry, he had just made clear to his employee a thing that wasn't clear to him, there would be no more problems. We ended up eating the pizza in silence, eyes lowered, in slow bites, as if it were poisoned. And when we left Rino gave Lila a good lecture that ended with a threat: Go on like that and I'm not taking you anywhere.

What had happened? On the street the men looked at all of us, pretty, less pretty, ugly, and not so much the youths as the grown men. It was like that in the neighborhood and outside of it, and Ada, Carmela, I myself—especially after the incident with the Solaras—had learned instinctively to lower our eyes, pretend not to hear the obscenities they directed at us, and keep going. Lila no. To go out with her on Sunday became a permanent point of tension. If someone looked at her she returned the look. If someone said something to her, she stopped, bewildered, as if she couldn't believe he was talking to her, and sometimes she responded, curious. Especially since—something very unusual—men almost never addressed to her the obscenities that they almost always had for us.

One afternoon at the end of August we went as far as the Villa Comunale park, and sat down in a café there, because Pasquale, acting the grandee, wanted to buy everyone a spumone. At a table across from us was a family eating ice cream, like us: father, mother, and three boys between twelve and seven. They seemed respectable people: the father, a large man, in his fifties, had a professorial look. And I can swear that Lila wasn't showing off in any way: she wasn't wearing lipstick, she had on the usual shabby dress that her mother had made—the rest of us were showing off more, Carmela especially. But that man—this time we all realized it—couldn't take his eyes off her, and Lila, although she tried to control herself, responded to his gaze as if she couldn't get over being so admired. Finally, while at our table the discomfort of Rino, of Pasquale, of Antonio increased, the man, evidently unaware of the risk he ran, rose, stood in front of Lila, and, addressing the boys politely, said:

"You are fortunate: you have here a girl who will become more beautiful than a Botticelli Venus. I beg your pardon, but I said it to my wife and sons, and I felt the need to tell you as well."

Lila burst out laughing because of the strain. The man smiled in turn, and, with a small bow, was about to return to his table when Rino grabbed him by the collar, forced him to retrace his steps quickly, sat him down hard, and, in front of his wife and children, unloaded a series of insults of the sort we said in the neighborhood. Then the man got angry, the wife, yelling, intervened, Antonio pulled Rino away. Another Sunday ruined.

But the worst was a time when Rino wasn't there. What struck me was not the fact in itself but the consolation around Lila of hostilities from different places. Gigliola's mother gave a party for her name day (her name was Rosa, if I remember right), and invited people of all ages. Since her husband was the baker at the Solara pastry shop, things were done on a grand scale: there was an abundance of cream puffs, pastries with cassata filling, *sfogliatelle*, almond pastries, liqueurs, soft drinks, and dance records, from the most ordinary to the latest fashion. People came who would never come to our kids' parties. For example the pharmacist and his wife and their oldest son, Gino, who was going to high school, like me. For example Maestro Ferraro and his whole large family. For example Maria, the widow of Don Achille, and her son Alfonso and daughter Pinuccia, in a bright-colored dress, and even Stefano.

That family at first caused some unease: Pasquale and Carmela Peluso, the children of the murderer of Don Achille, were also at the party. But then everything arranged itself for the best. Alfonso was a nice boy (he, too, was going to high school, the same one as me), and he even exchanged a few words with Carmela; Pinuccia was just pleased to be at a party, working, as she did, in the store every day; Stefano, having precociously understood that good business is based on the absence of exclusiveness, considered all the residents of the neighborhood potential clients who would spend their money in his store; he produced his lovely, gentle smile for everyone, and so was able to avoid, even for an instant, meeting Pasquale's gaze; and, finally, Maria, who usually turned the other way if she saw Signora Peluso, completely ignored the two children and talked for a long time to Gigliola's mother. And then, as some people started dancing, and the din increased, there was a release of tension, and no one paid attention to anything.

First came the traditional dances, and then we moved on to a new kind of dance, rock and roll, which everyone, old and young, was curious about. I was hot and had retreated to a corner. I knew how to dance rock and roll, of course, I had often done it at home with my brother Peppe, and at Lila's, on Sundays, with her, but I felt too awkward for those jerky, agile moves, and, I decided, though reluctantly, just to watch. Nor did Lila seem particularly good at it: her movements looked silly, and I had even said that to her, and she had taken the criticism as a challenge and persisted in practicing on her own, since even Rino refused to try. But, perfectionist as she was in all things, that night she, too, decided, to my satisfaction, to stand aside with me and watch how well Pasquale and Carmela Peluso danced.

At some point, however, Enzo approached. The child who had thrown stones at us, who had surprisingly competed with Lila in arithmetic, who had once given her a wreath of sorb apples, over the years had been as if sucked up into a short but powerful organism, used to hard work. He looked older even than Rino, who among us was the oldest. You could see in every feature that he rose before dawn, that he had to deal with the Camorra at the fruit-and-vegetable market, that he went in all seasons, in cold, in the rain, to sell fruit and vegetables from his cart, up and down the streets of the neighborhood. Yet in his fair-skinned face, with its blond eyebrows and lashes, in the blue eyes, there was still something of the rebellious child we had known. Enzo spoke rarely but confidently, always in dialect, and it would not have occurred to either of us to joke with him, or even to make conversation. It was he who took the initiative. He asked Lila why she wasn't dancing. She answered: because I don't really know how to do this dance. He was silent for a while, then he said, I don't, either. But when another rock-and-roll song was put on he took her by the arm in a natural way and pushed her into the middle of the room. Lila, who if one simply grazed her without her permission leaped up as if she had been stung by a wasp, didn't react, so great, evidently, was her desire to dance. Rather, she looked at him gratefully and abandoned herself to the music.

It was immediately clear that Enzo didn't know much about it. He moved very little, in a serious, composed way, but he was very attentive to Lila, he obviously wished to do her a favor, let her show off. And although she wasn't as good as Carmen, she managed as usual to win everyone's attention. Even Enzo likes her, I said to myself in desolation. And—I realized right away—Stefano, the grocer: he gazed at her the whole time the way one gazes at a movie star.

But while Lila was dancing the Solara brothers arrived.

The mere sight of them agitated me. They greeted the pastry maker and his wife, they gave Stefano a pat of sympathy, and then they, too, started watching the dancers. First, like masters of the neighborhood, as they felt they were, they looked in a vulgar fashion at Ada, who avoided their gaze; then they spoke to each other and, indicating Antonio, gave him an exaggerated nod of greeting, which he pretended not to see; finally they noticed Lila, stared at her for a long time, then whispered to each other, Michele giving an obvious sign of assent.

I didn't let them out of my sight, and I quickly realized that in particular Marcello—Marcello, whom all the girls liked—didn't seem in the least angered by the knife business. On the contrary. In a few seconds he was completely captivated by Lila's lithe and elegant body, by her face, which was unusual in the neighborhood and perhaps in the whole city of Naples. He gazed without ever taking his eyes off her, as if he had lost the little brain he had. He gazed at her even when the music stopped.

It was an instant. Enzo made as if to push Lila into the corner where I was, Stefano and Marcello moved together to ask her to dance; but Pasquale preceded them. Lila made a gracious skip of consent, clapped her hands happily. At the same moment, four males, of various ages, each convinced in a different way of his own absolute power, reached out toward the figure of a fourteen-year-old girl. The needle scratched on the record, the music started. Stefano, Marcello, Enzo retreated uncertainly. Pasquale began to dance with Lila, and, given his virtuosity, she immediately let go.

At that point Michele Solara, perhaps out of love for his brother, perhaps out of a pure taste for making trouble, decided to complicate the situation in his own way. He nudged Stefano with his elbow and said aloud, "Are you some kind of a sissy? That's the son of the man who killed your father, he's a lousy Communist, and you stand there watching him dance with the girl you wanted to dance with?"

Pasquale certainly didn't hear him, because the music was loud and he was busy performing acrobatics with Lila. But I heard, and Enzo next to me heard, and naturally Stefano heard. We waited for something to happen but nothing happened. Stefano was someone who knew his own business. The grocery was thriving, he was planning to buy a neighboring space to expand it, he felt, in short, fortunate, and in fact he was very sure that life would give him everything he wanted. He said to Michele with his enchanting smile, "Let him dance, he's a good dancer." And he continued to watch Lila as if the only thing that mattered to him at that moment were her. Michele made a grimace of disgust and went to look for the pastry maker and his wife.

What did he want to do now? I saw him talking with the hosts in an agitated manner, he pointed to Maria in one corner, he pointed to Stefano and Alfonso and Pinuccia, he pointed to Pasquale, who was dancing, he pointed to Carmela, who was showing off with Antonio. As soon as the music stopped Gigliola's mother took Pasquale under the arm in a friendly way, led him into a corner, said something in his ear.

"Go ahead," Michele said to his brother, "the way's clear." And Marcello Solara tried again with Lila.

I was sure she would say no, I knew how she detested him. But that wasn't what happened. The music started, and she, with the desire to dance in every muscle, first looked for Pasquale, then, not seeing him, grasped Marcello's hand as if it were merely a hand, as if beyond it there were not an arm, his whole body, and, all sweaty, began again to do what at that moment counted most for her: dance.

I looked at Stefano, I looked at Enzo. Everything was charged with tension. My heart was pounding as Pasquale, scowling, went over to Carmela and spoke sharply to her. Carmela protested in a low voice, in a low voice he silenced her. Antonio approached them, spoke to Pasquale. Together they glared at Michele Solara, who was again talking to Stefano, at Marcello, who was dancing with Lila, pulling her, lifting her, lowering her down. Then Antonio went to drag Ada out of the dancing. The music stopped, Lila returned to my side. I said to her, "Something's happening, we have to go."

She laughed, exclaimed, "Even if there's an earthquake coming I'm going to have another dance," and she looked at Enzo, who was leaning against a wall. But meanwhile Marcello asked and she let him draw her again into a dance.

Pasquale came over and said somberly that we had to go.

"Let's wait till Lila finishes her dance."

"No, right now," he said in a tone that would not admit a response, hard, rude. Then he went straight toward Michele Solara and bumped him hard with one shoulder. Michele laughed, said something obscene out of the corner of his mouth. Pasquale continued toward the door, followed by Carmela, reluctantly, and by Antonio, who had Ada with him.

I turned to see what Enzo was doing, but he was still leaning against the wall, watching Lila dance. The music ended. Lila moved toward me, followed by Marcello, whose eyes were shining with happiness.

"We have to go," I nearly shrieked.

I must have put such anguish into my voice that she finally looked around as if she had woken up. "All right, let's go," she said, puzzled.

I headed toward the door, without waiting any longer, the music started again. Marcello Solara grabbed Lila by the arm, said to her between a laugh and an entreaty: "Stay, I'll take you home."

Lila, as if only then recognizing him, looked at him incredulously: suddenly it seemed to her impossible that he was touching her with such assurance. She tried to free her arm but Marcello held it in a strong grip, saying, "Just one more dance." Enzo left the wall, grabbed Marcello's wrist without saying a word. I see him before my eyes: he was calm; although younger in years and smaller in size, he seemed to be making no effort. The strength of his grip could be seen only on the face of Marcello Solara, who let go of Lila with a grimace of pain and seized his wrist with his other hand. As we left I heard Lila saying indignantly to Enzo, in the thickest dialect, "He touched me, did you see: me, that shit. Luckily Rino wasn't there. If he does it again, he's dead."

Was it possible she didn't realize that she had danced with Marcello twice? Yes, possible, she was like that.

Outside we found Pasquale, Antonio, Carmela, and Ada. Pasquale was beside himself, we had never seen him like that. He was shouting insults, shouting at the top of his lungs, his eyes like a madman's, and there was no way to calm him. He was angry with Michele, of course, but above all with Marcello and Stefano. He said things that we weren't capable of understanding. He said that the Bar Solara had always been a place for loan sharks from the Camorra, that it was the base for smuggling and for collecting votes for the monarchists. He said that Don Achille had been a spy for the Nazi Fascists, he said that the money Stefano was using to expand the grocery store his father had made on the black market. He yelled, "Papa was

right to kill him." He yelled, "The Solaras, father and sons—
I'll cut their throats, and then I'll eliminate Stefano and his
whole family from the face of the earth." Finally, turning to
Lila, he yelled, as if it were the most serious thing, "And you,
you were even dancing with that piece of shit."

At that point, as if Pasquale's rage had pumped breath into
his chest, Antonio, too, began shouting, and it was almost as if
he were angry at Pasquale because he wished to deprive him of
a joy: the joy of killing the Solaras for what they had done to
Ada. And Ada immediately began to cry and Carmela couldn't
restrain herself and she, too, burst into tears. And Enzo tried
to persuade all of us to get off the street. "Let's go home," he
said. But Pasquale and Antonio silenced him, they wanted to
stay and confront the Solaras. Fiercely, but with pretended
calm, they kept repeating to Enzo, "Go, go, we'll see you
tomorrow." Enzo said softly, "If you stay, I'm going to stay,
too." At that point I, too, burst into tears and a moment afterward—the thing that moved me most—Lila, whom I had
never seen cry, ever, began weeping.

We were four girls in tears, desperate tears. But Pasquale
yielded only when he saw Lila crying. He said in a tone of resignation, "All right, not tonight, I'll settle things with the
Solaras some other time, let's go." Immediately, between sobs,
Lila and I took him under the arm, dragged him away. For a
moment we consoled him by saying mean things about the
Solaras, but also insisting that the best thing was to act as if
they didn't exist. Then Lila, drying her tears with the back of
her hand, asked "Who are the Nazi Fascists, Pascà? Who are
the monarchists? What's the black market?"

17.

It's hard to say what Pasquale's answers did to Lila. I'm in danger of getting it wrong, partly because on me, at the time, they had no concrete effect. But she, in her usual way, was moved and altered by them, so that for the entire summer she tormented me with a single concept that I found quite unbearable. I'll try to summarize it, using the language of today, like this: there are no gestures, words, or sighs that do not contain the sum of all the crimes that human beings have committed and commit.

Naturally she said it in another way. But what matters is that she was gripped by a frenzy of absolute disclosure. She pointed to people, things, streets, and said, "That man fought in the war and killed, that one bludgeoned and administered castor oil, that one turned in a lot of people, that one starved his own mother, in that house they tortured and killed, on these stones they marched and gave the Fascist salute, on this corner they inflicted beatings, these people's money comes from the hunger of others, this car was bought by selling bread adulterated with marble dust and rotten meat on the black market, that butcher shop had its origins in stolen copper and vandalized freight trains, behind that bar is the Camorra, smuggling, loan-sharking."

Soon she became dissatisfied with Pasquale. It was as if he had set in motion a mechanism in her head and now her job was to put order into a chaotic mass of impressions. Increasingly intent, increasingly obsessed, probably overcome herself by an urgent need to find a solid vision, without cracks, she complicated his meager information with some book she got from the library. So she gave concrete motives, ordinary faces to the air of abstract apprehension that as children we had breathed in the neighborhood. Fascism, Nazism, the war, the Allies, the monarchy, the republic—she turned them into streets, houses, faces, Don Achille and the black market, Alfredo Peluso the Communist, the Camorrist grandfather of the Solaras, the father, Silvio, a worse Fascist than Marcello and Michele, and her father, Fernando the shoemaker, and my father, all—all—in her eyes stained to the marrow by shadowy crimes, all hardened criminals or acquiescent accomplices, all bought for practically nothing. She and Pasquale enclosed me in a terrible world that left no escape.

Then Pasquale himself began to be silent, defeated by Lila's capacity to link one thing to another in a chain that tightened around you on all sides. I often looked at them walking together and, if at first it had been she who hung on his words, now it was he who hung on hers. He's in love, I thought. I also thought: Lila will fall in love, too, they'll be engaged, they'll marry, they'll always be talking about these political things, they'll have children who will talk about the same things. When school started again, on the one hand I suffered because I knew I wouldn't have time for Lila anymore, on the other I hoped to detach myself from that sum of the misdeeds and compliances and cowardly acts of the people we knew, whom we loved, whom we carried—she, Pasquale, Rino, I, all of us—in our blood.

18.

The first two years of high school were much more difficult than middle school. I was in a class of forty-two students, one of the very rare mixed classes in that school. There were few girls, and I didn't know any of them. Gigliola, after much boasting ("Yes, I'm going to high school, too, definitely, we'll sit at the same desk"), ended up going to help her father in the Solaras' pastry shop. Of the boys, instead, I knew Alfonso and Gino, who, however, sat together in one of the front desks, elbow to elbow, with frightened looks, and nearly pretended not to know me. The room stank, an acid odor of sweat, dirty feet, fear.

For the first months I lived my new scholastic life in silence, constantly picking at my acne-studded forehead and cheeks. Sitting in one of the rows at the back, from which I could barely see the teachers or what they wrote on the blackboard, I was unknown to my deskmate as she was unknown to me. Thanks to Maestra Oliviero I soon had the books I needed; they were grimy and well worn. I imposed on myself a discipline learned in middle school: I studied all afternoon until eleven and then from five in the morning until seven, when it was time to go. Leaving the house, weighed down with books, I often met Lila, who was hurrying to the shoe shop to open up, sweep, wash, get things in order before her father and brother arrived. She questioned me about the subjects I had for the day, what I had studied, and wanted precise answers. If I didn't give them she besieged me with questions that made me fear I hadn't studied enough, that I wouldn't be able to answer the teachers as I wasn't able to answer her. On some cold mornings, when I rose at dawn and in the kitchen went over the lessons, I had the impression that, as usual, I was sacrificing the warm deep sleep of the morning to make a good impression on the daughter of the shoemaker rather than on the teachers in the school for rich people. Breakfast was hurried, too, for her sake. I gulped down milk and coffee and ran out to the street so as not to miss even a step of the way we would go together.

I waited at the entrance. I saw her arriving from her building and noticed that she was continuing to change. She was now taller than I was. She walked not like the bony child she had been until a few months before but as if, as her body rounded, her pace had also become softer. Hi, hi, we immediately started talking. When we stopped at the intersection and said goodbye, she going to the shop, I to the metro station, I kept turning to give her a last glance. Once or twice I saw Pasquale arrive out of breath and walk beside her, keeping her company.

The metro was crowded with boys and girls stained with sleep, with the smoke of the first cigarettes. I didn't smoke, I didn't talk to anyone. During the few minutes of the journey I went over my lessons again, in panic, frantically pasting strange languages into my head, tones different from those used in the neighborhood. I was terrified of failing in school, of the crooked shadow of my displeased mother, of the glares of Maestra Oliviero. And yet I had now a single true thought: to find a boyfriend, immediately, before Lila announced to me that she was going with Pasquale.

Every day I felt more strongly the anguish of not being in time. I was afraid, coming home from school, of meeting her and learning from her melodious voice that now she was making love with Peluso. Or if it wasn't him, it was Enzo. Or if it wasn't Enzo, it was Antonio. Or, what do I know, Stefano Carracci, the grocer, or even Marcello Solara: Lila was unpredictable. The males who buzzed around her were almost men, full of demands. As a result, between the plan for the shoes, reading about the terrible world we had been born into, and boyfriends, she would no longer have time for me. Sometimes, on the way home from school, I made a wide circle in order not to pass the shoemaker's shop. If instead I saw her in person, from a distance, in distress I would change my route. But then I couldn't resist and went to meet her as if it were fated.

Entering and leaving the school, an enormous gloomy, run-down gray building, I looked at the boys. I looked at them insistently, so that they would feel my gaze on them and look at me. I looked at my classmates, some still in short pants, others in knickers or long pants. I looked at the older boys, in the upper classes, who mostly wore jacket and tie, though never an overcoat, they had to prove, especially to themselves, that they didn't suffer from the cold: hair in crew cuts, their necks white because of the high tapering. I preferred them, but I would have been content even with one from the class above mine, the main thing was that he should wear long pants.

One day I was struck by a student with a shambling gait, who was very thin, with disheveled brown hair and a face that seemed to me handsome and somehow familiar. How old could he be: sixteen? Seventeen? I observed him carefully, looked again, and my heart stopped: it was Nino Sarratore, the son of Donato Sarratore, the railroad worker poet. He returned my look, but distractedly, he didn't recognize me. His jacket was shapeless at the elbows, tight at the shoulders, his pants were threadbare, his shoes lumpy. He showed no sign of prosperity, such as Stefano and, especially, the Solaras displayed. Evidently his father, although he had written a book of poems, was not yet wealthy.

I was disturbed by that unexpected apparition. As I left I had a violent impulse to tell Lila right away, but then I changed my mind. If I told her, surely she would ask to go to school with me to see him. And I knew already what would happen. As Nino hadn't noticed me, as he hadn't recognized the slender blond child of elementary school in the fat and pimply fourteen-year-old I had become, so he would immediately recognize Lila and be vanquished. I decided to cultivate the image of Nino Sarratore in silence, as he left school with his head bent and his rocking gait and went off along Corso Garibaldi. Now I went to school as if to see him, even just a glimpse, were the only real reason to go.

The autumn flew by. One morning I was questioned on the Aeneid: it was the first time I had been called to the front of the room. The teacher, an indolent man in his sixties named Gerace, who was always yawning noisily, burst out laughing when I said "or-A-cle" instead of "OR-a-cle." It didn't occur to him that, although I knew the meaning of the word, I lived in a world where no one had ever had any reason to use it. The others laughed, too, especially Gino, sitting at the front desk with Alfonso. I felt humiliated. Days passed, and we had our first homework in Latin. When Gerace brought back the corrected homework he said, "Who is Greco?"

I raised my hand.

"Come here."

He asked me a series of questions on declensions, verbs, syntax. I answered fearfully, especially because he looked at me with an interest that until that moment he hadn't shown in any of us. Then he gave me the paper without any comment. I had got a nine.

It was the start of a crescendo. He gave me eight in the Italian homework, in history I didn't miss a date, in geography I knew perfectly land areas, populations, mineral wealth, agriculture. But in Greek in particular I amazed him. Thanks to what I had learned with Lila, I displayed a knowledge of the alphabet, a skill in reading, a confidence in pronouncing the sounds that finally wrung public praise from the teacher. My cleverness reached the other teachers like a dogma. Even the religion teacher took me aside one morning and asked if I wanted to enroll in a free correspondence course in theology. I said yes. By Christmas people were calling me Greco, some Elena. Gino began to linger on the way out, to wait for me so we could go back to the neighborhood together. One day suddenly he asked me again if I would be his girlfriend, and I, although he was an idiot, drew a sigh of relief: better than nothing. I agreed.

All that exhilarating intensity had a break during the Christmas vacation. I was reabsorbed by the neighborhood, I had more time, I saw Lila more often. She had discovered that I was learning English and naturally she had got a grammar book. Now she knew a lot of words, which she pronounced very approximately, and of course my pronunciation was just as bad. But she pestered me, she said: when you go back to school ask the teacher how to pronounce this, how to pronounce that.

One day she brought me into the shop, showed me a metal box full of pieces of paper: on one side of each she had written an Italian word, on the other the English equivalent: *matita*/pencil, *capire*/to understand, *scarpa*/shoe. It was Maestro Ferraro who had advised her to do this, as an useful way of learning vocabulary. She read me the Italian, she wanted me to say the corresponding word in English. But I knew little or nothing. She seemed ahead of me in everything, as if she were going to a secret school. I noticed also a tension in her, the desire to prove that she was equal to whatever I was studying. I would have preferred to talk about other things, instead she questioned me about the Greek declensions, and deduced that I had stopped at the first while she had already studied the third. She also asked me about the Aeneid, she was crazy about it. She had read it all in a few days, while I, in school, was in the middle of the second book. She talked in great detail about Dido, a figure I knew nothing about, I heard that name for the first time not at school but from her. And one afternoon she made an observation that impressed me deeply. She said, "When there is no love, not only the life of the people becomes sterile but the life of cities." I don't remember exactly how she expressed it, but that was the idea, and I associated it with our dirty streets, the dusty gardens, the countryside disfigured by new buildings, the violence in every house, every family. I was afraid that she would start talking again about Fascism, Nazism, Communism. And I couldn't help it, I wanted her to understand that good things were happening to me, first that I was the girlfriend of Gino, and second that Nino Sarratore came to my school, more handsome than he had been in elementary school.

She narrowed her eyes, I was afraid she was about to tell me: I also have a boyfriend. Instead, she began to tease me. "You go out with the son of the pharmacist," she said. "Good for you, you've given in, you're in love like Aeneas' lover."

Then she jumped abruptly from Dido to Melina and talked about her for a long time, since I knew little or nothing of what was happening in the buildings—I went to school in the morning and studied until late at night. She talked about her relative as if she never let her out of her sight. Poverty was consuming her and her children and so she continued to wash the stairs of the buildings, together with Ada (the money Antonio brought home wasn't enough). But one never heard her singing anymore, the euphoria had passed, now she slaved away mechanically. Lila described Melina in minute detail: bent double, she started from the top floor and, with the wet rag in her hands, wiped step after step, flight after flight, with an energy and an agitation that would have exhausted a more robust person. If someone went down or up, she began shouting insults, she hurled the rag at him. Ada had said that once she had seen her mother, in the midst of a crisis because someone had spoiled her work by walking on it, drink the dirty water from the bucket, and had had to tear it away from her. Did I understand? Step by step, starting with Gino she had ended in Dido, in Aeneas who abandoned her, in the mad widow. And only at that point did she bring in Nino Sarratore, proof that she had listened to me carefully. "Tell him about Melina," she urged me, "tell him he should tell his father." Then she added, maliciously, "Because it's all too easy to write poems." And finally she started laughing and promised with a certain solemnity, "I'm never going to fall in love with anyone and I will never ever ever write a poem."

"I don't believe it."

"It's true."

"But people will fall in love with you."

"Worse for them."

"They'll suffer like that Dido."

"No, they'll go and find someone else, just like Aeneas, who eventually settled down with the daughter of a king."

I wasn't convinced. I went away and came back, I liked those conversations about boyfriends, now that I had one. Once I asked her, cautiously, "What's Marcello Solara up to, is he still after you?"

"Yes."

"And you?"

She made a half smile of contempt that meant: Marcello Solara makes me sick.

"And Enzo?"

"We're friends."

"And Stefano?"

"According to you they're all thinking about me?"

"Yes."

"Stefano serves me first if there's a crowd."

"You see?"

"There's nothing to see."

"And Pasquale, has he said anything to you?"

"Are you mad?"

"I've seen him walking you to the shop in the morning."

"Because he's explaining the things that happened before us."

Thus she returned to the theme of "before," but in a different way than she had at first. She said that we didn't know anything, either as children or now, that we were therefore not in a position to understand anything, that everything in the neighborhood, every stone or piece of wood, everything, anything you could name, was already there before us, but we had grown up without realizing it, without ever even thinking about it. Not just us. Her father pretended that there had been nothing before. Her mother did the same, my mother, my father, even Rino. And yet Stefano's grocery store *before* had been the carpenter shop of Alfredo Peluso, Pasquale's father. And yet Don Achille's money had been made *before*. And the Solaras' money as well. She had tested this out on her father and mother. They didn't know anything, they wouldn't talk about anything. Not Fascism, not the king. No injustice, no oppression, no exploitation. They hated Don Achille and were afraid of the Solaras. But they overlooked it and went to spend their money both at Don Achille's son's and at the Solaras', and sent us, too. And they voted for the Fascists, for the monarchists, as the Solaras wanted them to. And they thought that what had happened before was past and, in order to live quietly, they placed a stone on top of it, and so, without knowing it, they continued it, they were immersed in the things of before, and we kept them inside us, too. That conversation about "before" made a stronger impression than the vague conversations she had drawn me into during the summer. The Christmas vacation passed in deep conversation—in the shoemaker's shop, on the street, in the courtyard. We told each other everything, even the little things, and were happy.

19.

During that period I felt strong. At school I acquitted myself perfectly, I told Maestra Oliviero about my successes and she praised me. I saw Gino, and every day we walked to the Bar Solara: he bought a pastry, we shared it, we went home. Sometimes I even had the impression that it was Lila who depended on me and not I on her. I had crossed the boundaries of the neighborhood, I went to the high school, I was with boys and girls who were studying Latin and Greek, and not, like her, with construction workers, mechanics, cobblers, fruit and vegetable sellers, grocers, shoemakers. When she talked to me about Dido or her method for learning English words or the third declension or what she pondered when she talked to Pasquale, I saw with increasing clarity that it made her somewhat uneasy, as if it were ultimately she who felt the need to continuously prove that she could talk to me as an equal. Even when, one afternoon, with some uncertainty, she decided to show me how far she and Rino were with the secret shoe they were making, I no longer felt that she inhabited a marvelous land without me. It seemed instead that both she and her brother hesitated to talk to me about things of such small value.

Or maybe it was only that I was beginning to feel superior. When they dug around in a storeroom and took out the box, I encouraged them artificially. But the pair of men's shoes they showed me seemed truly unusual; they were size 43, the size of Rino and Fernando, brown, and just as I remembered them in one of Lila's drawings: they seemed both light and strong. I had never seen anything like them on the feet of anyone. While Lila and Rino let me touch them and demonstrated their qualities, I praised them enthusiastically. "Touch here," Rino said, excited by my praise, "and tell me if you feel the stitches." "No," I said, "you can't feel them." Then he took the shoes out of my hands, bent them, widened them, showed me their durability. I approved, I said bravo the way Maestra Oliviero did when she wanted to encourage us. But Lila didn't seem satisfied. The more good qualities her brother listed, the more defects she showed me and said to Rino, "How long would it take Papa to see these mistakes?" At one point she said, seriously, "Let's test with water again." Her brother seemed opposed. She filled a basin anyway, put her hand in one of the shoes as if it were a foot, and walked it in the water a little. "She has to play," Rino said, like a big brother who is annoyed by the childish acts of his little sister.

But as soon as he saw Lila take out the shoe he became preoccupied and asked, "So?"

Lila took out her hand, rubbed her fingers, held it out to him. "Touch."

Rino put his hand in, said, "It's dry."

"It's wet."

"Only you feel the wetness. Touch it, Lenù."

I touched it.

"It's a little damp," I said.

Lila was displeased.

"See? You hold it in the water for a minute and it's already wet, it's no good. We have to unglue it and unstitch it all again."

"What the fuck if there's a little dampness?"

Rino got angry. Not only that: right before my eyes, he went through a kind of transformation. He became red in the face, he swelled up around the eyes and cheekbones, he couldn't contain himself and exploded in a series of curses and expletives against his sister. He complained that if they went on like that they would never finish. He reproached Lila because she first encouraged him and then discouraged him. He shouted that he wouldn't stay forever in that wretched place to be his father's servant and watch others get rich. He grabbed the iron foot, pretended to throw it at her, and if he really had he would have killed her.

I left, on the one hand confused by that rage in a youth who was usually kind and on the other proud of how authoritative, how definitive my opinion had been.

In the following days I found that my acne was drying up.

"You're really doing well, it's the satisfaction you get from school, it's love," Lila said to me, and I felt that she was a little sad.

20.

As the New Year's Eve celebration approached, Rino was seized by the desire to set off more fireworks than anyone else, especially the Solaras. Lila made fun of him, but sometimes she became harsh with him. She told me that her brother, who at first had been skeptical about the possibility of making money with the shoes, had now begun to count on it too heavily, already he saw himself as the owner of the Cerullo shoe factory and didn't want to go back to repairing shoes. This worried her, it was a side of Rino she didn't know. He had always seemed to her only generously impetuous, sometimes aggressive, but not a braggart. Now, though, he posed as what he was not. He felt he was close to wealth. A boss. Someone who could give the neighborhood the first sign of the good fortune the new year would bring by setting off a lot of fireworks, more than the Solara brothers, who had become in his eyes the model of the young man to emulate and indeed to surpass, people whom he envied and considered enemies to be beaten, so that he could assume their role.

Lila never said, as she had with Carmela and the other girls in the courtyard: maybe I planted a fantasy in his head that he doesn't know how to control. She herself believed in the fantasy, felt it could be realized, and her brother was an important element of that realization. And then she loved him, he was six years older, she didn't want to reduce him to a child who can't handle his dreams. But she often said that Rino lacked concreteness, he didn't know how to confront difficulties with his feet on the ground, he tended to get carried away. Like that competition with the Solaras, for example.

"Maybe he's jealous of Marcello," I said once.

"What?"

She smiled, pretending not to understand, but she had told me herself. Marcello Solara passed by and hung around in front of the shoemaker's shop every day, both on foot and in the 1100, and Rino must have been aware of it, since he had said many times to his sister, "Don't you dare get too familiar with that shit." Maybe, who knows, since he wasn't able to beat up the Solaras for chasing after his sister, he wished to demonstrate his strength by means of fireworks.

"If that's true, you'll agree that I'm right?"

"Right about what?"

"That he's acting like a big shot: where's he going to get the money for the fireworks?"

It was true. The last night of the year was a night of battle, in the neighborhood and throughout Naples. Dazzling lights, explosions. The dense smoke from the gunpowder made everything hazy, it entered the houses, burned your eyes, made you cough. But the pop of the poppers, the hiss of the rockets, the cannonades of the missiles had a cost and as usual those who set off the most were those with the most money. We Grecos had no money, at my house the contribution to the end-of-the-year fireworks was small. My father bought a box of sparklers, one of wheels, and one of slender rockets. At midnight he put in my hand, since I was the oldest, the stem of a sparkler or of a Catherine wheel, and lighted it, and I stood motionless, excited and terrified, staring at the whirling sparks, the brief swirls of fire a short distance from my fingers. He then stuck the shafts of the rockets in glass bottles on the marble windowsill, burned the fuses with the tip of his cigarette, and, excitedly, launched the luminous whistles into the sky. Then he threw the bottles, too, into the street.

Similarly at Lila's house they set off just a few or none, and Rino rebelled. From the age of twelve he had gotten into the habit of going out to celebrate midnight with people more daring than his father, and his exploits in recovering unexploded bottles were famous—as soon as the chaos of the celebration was over he would go in search of them. He would assemble them all near the ponds, light them, and delight in the high flare, *trac trac trac*, the final explosion. He still had a dark scar on one hand, a broad stain, from a time when he hadn't pulled back fast enough.

Among the many reasons, open and secret, for that challenge at the end of 1958, it should therefore be added that maybe Rino wanted to make up for his impoverished childhood. So he got busy collecting money here and there to buy fireworks. But we knew—he knew himself, despite the frenzy for grandeur that had seized him—that there was no way to compete with the Solaras. As they did every year, the two brothers went back and forth for days in their 1100, the trunk loaded with explosives that on New Year's Eve would kill birds, frighten dogs, cats, mice, make the buildings quake from the cellars up to the roofs. Rino observed them from the shop with resentment and meanwhile was dealing with Pasquale, with Antonio, and above all with Enzo, who had a little more money, to procure an arsenal that would at least make for a good show.

Things took a small, unexpected turn when Lila and I were sent to Stefano Carracci's grocery by our mothers to do the shopping for the dinner. The shop was full of people. Behind the counter, besides Stefano and Pinuccia, Alfonso was serving customers, and he gave us an embarrassed smile. We settled ourselves for a long wait. But Stefano addressed to me, unequivocally to me, a nod of greeting, and said something in his brother's ear. My classmate came out from behind the counter and asked if we had a list. We gave him our lists and he slipped away. In five minutes our groceries were ready.

We put everything in our bags, paid Signora Maria, and went out. But we hadn't gone far when not Alfonso but Stefano, Stefano himself, called to me with his lovely man's voice, "Lenù."

He joined us. He had a confident expression, a friendly smile. Only his white grease-stained apron spoiled him slightly. He spoke to both of us, in dialect, but looking at me: "Would you like to come and celebrate the new year at my house? Alfonso would really be pleased."

The wife and children of Don Achille, even after the murder of the father, led a very retiring life: church, grocery, home, at most some small celebration they couldn't skip. That invitation was something new. I answered, nodding at Lila: "We're already busy, we'll be with her brother and some friends."

"Tell Rino, too, tell your parents: the house is big and we'll go out on the terrace for the fireworks."

Lila interjected in a dismissive tone: "Pasquale and Carmen Peluso and their mother are coming to celebrate with us."

It was supposed to be a phrase that eliminated any further talk: Alfredo Peluso was at Poggioreale because he had murdered Don Achille, and the son of Don Achille could not invite the children of Alfredo to toast the new year at his house. Instead, Stefano looked at her, very intensely, as if until that moment he hadn't seen her, and said, in the tone one uses when something is obvious: "All right, all of you come: we'll drink spumante, dance—new year, new life."

The words moved me. I looked at Lila, she, too, was confused. She murmured, "We have to talk to my brother."

"Let me know."

"And the fireworks?"

"What do you mean?"

"We'll bring ours, and you?"

Stefano smiled. "How many fireworks do you want?"

"Lots."

The young man again addressed me: "Come to my house and I promise you that we'll still be setting them off at dawn."

21.

The whole way home we laughed till our sides ached, saying things like:

"He's doing it for you."

"No, for you."

"He's in love and to have you at his house he'll invite even the Communists, even the murderers of his father."

"What are you talking about? He didn't even look at me."

Rino listened to Stefano's proposal and immediately said no. But the wish to vanquish the Solaras kept him uncertain and he talked about it with Pasquale, who got very angry. Enzo on the other hand mumbled, "All right, I'll come if I can." As for our parents, they were very pleased with that invitation because for them Don Achille no longer existed and his children and his wife were good, well-to-do people whom it was an honor to have as friends.

Lila at first seemed in a daze, as if she had forgotten where she was, the streets, the neighborhood, the shoemaker's shop. Then she appeared at my house late one afternoon with a look as if she had understood everything and said to me: "We were wrong: Stefano doesn't want me or you."

We discussed it in our usual fashion, mixing facts with fantasies. If he didn't want us, what did he want? We thought that Stefano, too, intended to teach the Solaras a lesson. We recalled when Michele had expelled Pasquale from Gigliola's mother's party, thus interfering in the affairs of the Carraccis and giving Stefano the appearance of a man unable to defend the memory of his father. On that occasion, if you thought about it, the brothers had insulted not only Pasquale but also him. And so now he was raising the stakes, as if to spite them: he was making a conclusive peace with the Pelusos, even inviting them to his house for New Year's Eve.

"And who benefits?" I asked Lila.

"I don't know. He wants to make a gesture that no one would make here in the neighborhood."

"Forgive?"

Lila shook her head skeptically. She was trying to understand, we were both trying to understand, and understanding was something that we loved to do. Stefano didn't seem the type capable of forgiveness. According to Lila he had something else in mind. And slowly, proceeding from one of the ideas she hadn't been able to get out of her head since the moment she started talking to Pasquale, she seemed to find a solution.

"You remember when I said to Carmela that she could be Alfonso's girlfriend?"

"Yes."

"Stefano has in mind something like that."

"Marry Carmela?"

"More."

Stefano, according to Lila, wanted to clear away everything. He wanted to try to get out of the *before*. He didn't want to pretend it was nothing, as our parents did, but rather to set in motion a phrase like: I know, my father was what he was, but now I'm here, we are us, and so, enough. In other words, he wanted to make the whole neighborhood understand that he was not Don Achille and that the Pelusos were not the former carpenter who had killed him. That hypothesis pleased us, it immediately became a certainty, and we had an impulse of great fondness for the young Carracci. We decided to take his part.

We went to explain to Rino, to Pasquale, to Antonio that Stefano's invitation was more than an invitation, that behind it were important meanings, that it was as if he were saying: before us some ugly things happened; our fathers, some in one way, some in another, didn't behave well; from this moment, we take note of that and show that we children are better than they were.

"Better?" Rino asked, with interest.

"Better," I said. "The complete opposite of the Solaras, who are worse than their grandfather and their father."

I spoke with great excitement, in Italian, as if I were in school. Lila herself glanced at me in amazement, and Rino, Pasquale, and Antonio muttered, embarrassed. Pasquale even tried to answer in Italian but he gave up. He said somberly:

"His father made money on the black market, and now Stefano is using it to make more money. His shop is in the place where my father's carpenter shop was."

Lila narrowed her eyes, so you almost couldn't see them.

"It's true. But do you prefer to be on the side of someone who wants to change or on the side of the Solaras?"

Pasquale said proudly, partly out of conviction, partly because he was visibly jealous of Stefano's unexpected central role in Lila's words, "I'm on my own side and that's it."

But he was an honest soul, he thought it over again and again. He talked to his mother, he discussed it with the whole family. Giuseppina, who had been a tireless, good-natured worker, relaxed and exuberant, had become after her husband's imprisonment a slovenly woman, depressed by her bad luck, and she turned to the priest. The priest went to Stefano's shop, talked for a long time with Maria, then went back to talk to Giuseppina Peluso. In the end everyone was persuaded that life was already very difficult, and that if it was possible, on the occasion of the new year, to reduce its tensions, it would be better for everyone. So at 11:30 P.M. on December 31st, after the New Year's Eve dinner, various families—the family of the former carpenter, the family of the porter, that of the shoemaker, that of the fruit and vegetable seller, the family of Melina, who that night had made an effort with her appearance—climbed up to the fifth floor, to the old, hated home of Don Achille, to celebrate the new year together.

22.

Stefano welcomed us with great cordiality. I remember that he had dressed with care, his face was slightly flushed because of his agitation, he was wearing a white shirt and a tie, and a blue sleeveless vest. I found him very handsome, with the manners of a prince. I calculated that he was seven years older than me and Lila, and I thought then that to have Gino as a boyfriend, a boy of my own age, was a small thing: when I asked him to come to the Carraccis' with me, he had said that he couldn't, because his parents wouldn't let him go out after midnight, it was dangerous. I wanted an older boyfriend, one like those young men, Stefano, Pasquale, Rino, Antonio, Enzo. I looked at them, I hovered about them all evening. I nervously touched my earrings, my mother's silver bracelet. I had begun to feel pretty again and I wanted to read the proof in their eyes. But they all seemed taken up by the fireworks that would start at midnight. They were waiting for their war of men and didn't pay attention even to Lila.

Stefano was kind especially to Signora Peluso and to Melina, who didn't say a word, she had wild eyes and a long nose, but she had combed her hair, and, with her earrings, and her old black widow's dress, she looked like a lady. At midnight the master of the house filled first his mother's glass with spumante and right afterward that of Pasquale's mother. We toasted all the marvelous things that would happen in the new year, then we began to swarm toward the terrace, the old people and children in coats and scarves, because it was very cold. I realized that the only one who lingered indifferently downstairs was Alfonso. I called him, out of politeness, but he didn't hear me, or pretended not to. I ran up. Above me was a tremendous cold sky, full of stars and shadows.

The boys wore sweaters, except Pasquale and Enzo, who were in shirtsleeves. Lila and Ada and Carmela and I had on the thin dresses we wore for dancing parties and were trembling with cold and excitement. Already we could hear the first whizz of the rockets as they furrowed the sky and exploded in bright-colored flowers. Already the thud of old things flying out the windows could be heard, with shouts and laughter. The whole neighborhood was in an uproar, setting off firecrackers.

I lighted sparklers and pinwheels for the children, I liked to see in their eyes the fearful wonder that I had felt as a child. Lila persuaded Melina to light the fuse of a Bengal light with her: the jet of flame sprayed with a colorful crackle. They shouted with joy and hugged each other.

Rino, Stefano, Pasquale, Enzo, Antonio transported cases and boxes and cartons of explosives, proud of all those supplies they had managed to accumulate. Alfonso also helped, but he did it wearily, reacting to his brother's pressure with gestures of annoyance. He seemed intimidated by Rino, who was truly frenzied, pushing him rudely, grabbing things away from him, treating him like a child. So finally, rather than get angry, Alfonso withdrew, mingling less and less with the others. Meanwhile the matches flared as the adults lighted cigarettes for each other with cupped hands, speaking seriously and cordially. If there should be a civil war, I thought, like the one between Romulus and Remus, between Marius and Silla, between Caesar and Pompey, they will have these same faces, these same looks, these same poses.

Except for Alfonso, all the boys filled their shirts with firecrackers and missiles and arranged rows of rockets in ranks of empty bottles. Rino, increasingly agitated, shouting louder and louder, assigned to me, Lila, Ada, and Carmela the job of supplying everyone with ammunition. Then the very young, the young, the not so young—my brothers Peppe and Gianni, but also my father, also the shoemaker, who was the oldest of all—began moving around in the dark and the cold lighting fuses and throwing fireworks over the parapet or into the sky, in a celebratory atmosphere of growing excitement, of shouts like did you see those colors, wow what a bang, come on, come on—all scarcely disturbed by Melina's faint yet terrified wails, by Rino as he snatched the fireworks from my brothers and used them himself, yelling that it was a waste because the boys threw them without waiting for the fuse to really catch fire.

The glittering fury of the city slowly faded, died out, letting the sound of the cars, the horns emerge. Broad zones of dark sky reappeared. The Solaras' balcony became, even through the smoke, amid the flashes, more visible.

They weren't far, we could see them. The father, the sons, the relatives, the friends were, like us, in the grip of a desire for chaos. The whole neighborhood knew that what had happened so far was minor, the real show would begin when the penurious had finished with their little parties and petty explosions and fine rains of silver and gold, when only the masters of the revels remained.

And so it was. From the balcony the fire intensified abruptly, the sky and the street began to explode again. At every burst, especially if the firecracker made a sound of destruction, enthusiastic obscenities came from the balcony. But, unexpectedly, here were Stefano, Pasquale, Antonio, Rino ready to respond with more bursts and equivalent obscenities. At a rocket from the Solaras they launched a rocket, a string of firecrackers was answered by a string of firecrackers, and in the sky miraculous fountains erupted, and the street below flared, trembled. At one point Rino climbed up onto the parapet shouting insults and throwing powerful firecrackers while his mother shrieked with terror, yelling, "Get down or you'll fall."

At that point panic overwhelmed Melina, who began to wail. Ada was furious, it was up to her to get her home, but Alfonso indicated that he would take care of her, and he disappeared down the stairs with her. My mother immediately followed, limping, and the other women began to drag the children away. The Solaras' explosions were becoming more and more violent, one of their rockets instead of heading into the sky burst against the parapet of our terrace with a loud red flash and suffocating smoke.

"They did it on purpose," Rino yelled at Stefano, beside himself.

Stefano, a dark profile in the cold, motioned him to calm down. He hurried to a corner where he himself had placed a box that we girls had received orders not to touch, and he dipped into it, inviting the others to help themselves.

"Enzo," he cried, with not even a trace now of the polite shopkeeper's tones, "Pascà, Rino, Antò, here, come on, here, we'll show them what we've got."

They all ran laughing. They repeated: yeah, we'll let them have it, fuck those shits, fuck, take this, and they made obscene gestures in the direction of the Solaras' balcony. Shivering with cold, we looked at their frenetic black forms. We were alone, with no role. Even my father had gone downstairs, with the shoemaker. Lila, I don't know, she was silent, absorbed by the spectacle as if by a puzzle.

The thing was happening to her that I mentioned and that she later called dissolving margins. It was—she told me—as if, on the night of a full moon over the sea, the intense black mass of a storm advanced across the sky, swallowing every light, eroding the circumference of the moon's circle, and disfiguring the shining disk, reducing it to its true nature of rough insensate material. Lila imagined, she saw, she felt—as if it were true—her brother break. Rino, before her eyes, lost the features he had had as long as she could remember, the features of the generous, candid boy, the pleasing features of the reliable young man, the beloved outline of one who, as far back as she had memory, had amused, helped, protected her. There, amid the violent explosions, in the cold, in the smoke that burned the nostrils and the strong odor of sulfur, something violated the organic structure of her brother, exercising over him a pressure so strong that it broke down his outlines, and the matter expanded like a magma, showing her what he was truly made of. Every second of that night of celebration horrified her, she had the impression that, as Rino moved, as he expanded around himself, every margin collapsed and her own margins, too, became softer and more yielding. She struggled to maintain control, and succeeded: on the outside her anguish hardly showed. It's true that in the tumult of explosions and colors I didn't pay much attention to her. I was struck, I think, by her expression, which seemed increasingly fearful. I also realized that she was staring at the shadow of her brother—the most active, the most arrogant, shouting the loudest, bloodiest insults in the direction of the Solaras' terrace—with repulsion. It seemed that she, she who in general feared nothing, was afraid. But they were impressions I recalled only later. At the moment I didn't notice, I felt closer to Carmela, to Ada, than to her. She seemed as usual to have no need of male attention. We, instead, out in the cold, in the midst of that chaos, without that attention couldn't give ourselves meaning. We would have preferred that Stefano or Enzo or Rino stop the war, put an arm around our shoulders, press us to them, side to side, and speak soft words. Instead, we were holding on to each other to get warm, while they rushed to grab cylinders with fat fuses, astonished by Stefano's infinite reserves, admiring of his generosity, disturbed by how much money could be transformed into fiery trails, sparks, explosions, smoke for the pure satisfaction of winning.

They competed with the Solaras for I don't know how long, explosions from one side and the other as if terrace and balcony were trenches, and the whole neighborhood shook, vibrated. You couldn't understand anything—roars, shattered glass, splintered sky. Even when Enzo shouted, "They're finished, they've got nothing left," ours continued, Rino especially kept going, until there remained not a fuse to light. Then they raised a victorious chorus, jumping and embracing. Finally they calmed down, silence fell.

But it didn't last; it was broken by the rising cry of a child in the distance, shouts and insults, cars advancing through the streets littered with debris. And then we saw flashes on the Solaras' balcony, sharp sounds reached us, *pah, pah*. Rino shouted in disappointment, "They're starting again." But Enzo, who immediately understood what was happening, pushed us inside, and after him Pasquale, Stefano. Only Rino went on yelling vulgar insults, leaning over the parapet, so that Lila dodged Pasquale and ran to pull her brother inside, yelling insults at him in turn. We girls cried out as we went downstairs. The Solaras, in order to win, were shooting at us.

23.

As I said, many things about that night escaped me. But above all, overwhelmed by the atmosphere of celebration and danger, by the swirl of males whose bodies gave off a heat hotter than the fires in the sky, I neglected Lila. And yet it was then that her first inner change took place.

I didn't realize, as I said, what had happened to her, the action was difficult to perceive. But I was aware of the consequences almost immediately. She became lazier. Two days later, I got up early, even though I didn't have school, to go with her to open the shop and help her do the cleaning, but she didn't appear. She arrived late, sullen, and we walked through the neighborhood avoiding the shoemaker's shop.

"You're not going to work?"

"No."

"Why?"

"I don't like it anymore."

"And the new shoes?"

"They're nowhere."

"And so?"

It seemed to me that even she didn't know what she wanted. The only definite thing was that she seemed very worried about her brother, much more than I had seen recently. And it was precisely as a result of that worry that she began to

MY BRILLIANT FRIEND · 179

modify her speeches about wealth. There was always the pressure to become wealthy, there was no question about it, but the goal was no longer the same as in childhood: no treasure chests, no sparkle of coins and precious stones. Now it seemed that money, in her mind, had become a cement: it consolidated, reinforced, fixed this and that. Above all, it fixed Rino's head. The pair of shoes that they had made together he now considered ready, and wanted to show them to Fernando. But Lila knew well (and according to her so did Rino) that the work was full of flaws, that their father would examine the shoes and throw them away. So she told him that they had to try and try again, that the route to the shoe factory was a difficult one; but he was unwilling to wait longer, he felt an urgent need to become like the Solaras, like Stefano, and Lila couldn't make him see reason. Suddenly it seemed to me that wealth in itself no longer interested her. She no longer spoke of money with any excitement, it was just a means of keeping her brother out of trouble. But since it wasn't around the corner, she wondered, with cruel eyes, what she had to come up with to soothe him.

Rino was in a frenzy. Fernando, for example, never reproached Lila for having stopped coming to the shop, in fact he let her understand that he was happy for her to stay home and help her mother. Her brother instead got furious and in early January I witnessed another ugly quarrel. Rino approached us with his head down, he blocked our path, he said to her, "Come to work right now." Lila answered that she wouldn't think of it. He then dragged her by the arm, she defied him with a nasty insult, Rino slapped her, shouted at her, "Then go home, go and help Mamma." She obeyed, without even saying goodbye to me.

The climax came on the day of the Befana.[1] She, it seems, woke up and found next to her bed a sock full of coal. She knew

---

[1] In Italian folklore, the Befana is an old woman who delivers gifts to children, mostly in southern Italy, on the eve of the Epiphany (the night of January 5th), like St. Nicholas or Santa Claus.

it was from Rino and at breakfast she set the table for everyone but him. Her mother appeared: Rino had left a sock full of candies and chocolate hanging on a chair, which had moved her, she doted on that boy. So, when she realized that Rino's place wasn't set, she tried to set it but Lila prevented her. While mother and daughter argued, Rino appeared and Lila immediately threw a piece of coal at him. Rino laughed, thinking it was a game, that she had appreciated the joke, but when he realized that his sister was serious he tried to hit her. Then Fernando arrived, in underpants and undershirt, a cardboard box in his hand.

"Look what the Befana brought me," he said, and it was clear that he was furious.

He pulled out of the box the new shoes that his children had made in secret. Lila was openmouthed with surprise. She didn't know anything about it. Rino had decided on his own to show his father their work, as if it were a gift from the Befana.

When she saw on her brother's face a small smile that was amused and at the same time tormented, when she caught his worried gaze on his father's face, it seemed to her she had the confirmation of what had frightened her on the terrace, amid the smoke and fireworks: Rino had lost his usual outline, she now had a brother without boundaries, from whom something irreparable might emerge. In that smile, in that gaze she saw something unbearably wretched, the more unbearable the more she loved her brother, and felt the need to stay beside him to help him and be helped.

"How beautiful they are," said Nunzia, who was ignorant of the whole business.

Fernando, without saying a word, and now looking like an angry Randolph Scott, sat down and put on first the right shoe, then the left.

"The Befana," he said, "made them precisely for my feet."

He got up, tried them, walked back and forth in the kitchen as his family watched.

"Very comfortable," he commented.

"They're gentleman's shoes," his wife said, giving her son admiring looks.

Fernando sat down again. He took them off, he examined them above, below, inside and outside.

"Whoever made these shoes is a master," he said, but his face didn't brighten at all. "Brava, Befana."

In every word you heard how much he suffered and how that suffering was charging him with a desire to smash everything. But Rino didn't seem to realize it. At every sarcastic word of his father's he became prouder, he smiled, blushing, formulated half-phrases: I did like this, Papa, I added this, I thought that. Lila wanted to get out of the kitchen, out of the way of her father's imminent rage, but she couldn't make up her mind, she didn't want to leave her brother alone.

"They're light but also strong," Fernando continued, "there's no cutting corners. And I've never seen anything like them on anyone's feet, with this wide tip they're very original."

He sat down, he put them on again, he laced them. He said to his son: "Turn around Rinù, I have to thank the Befana."

Rino thought it was a joke that would conclusively end the whole long controversy and he appeared happy and embarrassed. But as soon as he started to turn his back his father kicked him violently in the rear, called him animal, idiot, and threw at him whatever came to hand, finally even the shoes.

Lila got involved only when she saw that her brother, at first intent only on protecting himself from punching and kicking, began shouting, too, overturning chairs, breaking plates, crying, swearing that he would kill himself rather than continue to work for his father for nothing, terrorizing his mother, the other children, and the neighbors. But in vain. Father and son first had to explode until they wore themselves out. Then they went back to working together, mute, shut up in the shop with their desperations.

There was no mention of the shoes for a while. Lila decided that her role was to help her mother, do the marketing, cook, wash the clothes and hang them in the sun, and she never went to the shoemaker's shop. Rino, saddened, sulky, felt the thing as an incomprehensible injustice and began to insist that he find socks and underpants and shirts in order in his drawer, that his sister serve him and show him respect when he came home from work. If something wasn't to his liking he protested, he said unpleasant things like you can't even iron a shirt, you shit. She shrugged, she didn't resist, she continued to carry out her duties with attention and care.

He himself, naturally, wasn't happy with the way he was behaving, he was tormented, he tried to calm down, he made not a few efforts to return to being what he had been. On good days, Sunday mornings for example, he wandered around joking, taking on a gentle tone of voice. "Are you mad at me because I took all the credit for the shoes? I did it," he said, lying, "to keep Papa from getting angry at you." And then he asked her, "Help me, what should we do now? We can't stop here, I have to get out of this situation." Lila was silent: she cooked, she ironed, at times she kissed him on the cheek to let him know that she wasn't mad anymore. But in the meantime he would get angry again, he always ended up smashing something. He shouted that she had betrayed him, and would betray him yet again, when, sooner or later, she would marry some imbecile and go away, leaving him to live in this wretchedness forever.

Sometimes, when no one was home, Lila went into the little room where she had hidden the shoes and touched them, looked at them, marveled to herself that for good or ill there they were and had come into being as the result of a design on a sheet of graph paper. How much wasted work.

24.

I returned to school, I was dragged inside the torturous rhythms that the teachers imposed on us. Many of my companions began to give up, the class thinned out. Gino got low marks and asked me to help him. I tried to but really all he wanted was for me to let him copy my homework. I did, but reluctantly: even when he copied he didn't pay attention, he didn't try to understand. Even Alfonso, although he was very disciplined, had difficulties. One day he burst into tears during the Greek interrogation, something that for a boy was considered very humiliating. It was clear that he would have preferred to die rather than shed a single tear in front of the class, but he couldn't control it. We were all silent, extremely disturbed, except Gino, who, perhaps for the satisfaction of seeing that even for his deskmate things could go badly, burst out laughing. As we left school I told him that because of that laughter he was no longer my boyfriend. He responded by asking me, worried, "You like Alfonso?" I explained that I simply didn't like him anymore. He stammered that we had scarcely started, it wasn't fair. Not much had happened between us as boyfriend and girlfriend: we'd kissed but without tongues, he had tried to touch my breasts and I had got angry and pushed him away. He begged me to continue just for a little, I was firm in my decision. I knew that it would cost me nothing to lose his company on the way to school and the way home.

A few days had passed since the break with Gino when Lila confided that she had had two declarations almost at the same time, the first in her life. Pasquale, one morning, had come up to her while she was doing the shopping. He was marked by fatigue, and extremely agitated. He had said that he was worried because he hadn't seen her in the shoemaker's shop and thought she was sick. Now that he found her in good health, he was happy. But there was no happiness in his face at all as he spoke. He broke off as if he were choking and, to free his voice, had almost shouted that he loved her. He loved her so much that, if she agreed, he would come and speak to her brother, her parents, whoever, immediately, so that they could be engaged. She was dumbstruck, for a few minutes she thought he was joking. I had said a thousand times that Pasquale had his eyes on her, but she had never believed me. Now there he was, on a beautiful spring day, almost with tears in his eyes, and was begging her, telling her his life was worth nothing if she said no. How difficult the sentiments of love were to untangle. Lila, very cautiously, but without ever saying no, had found words to refuse him. She had said that she loved him, but not as one should love a fiancé. She had also said that she would always be grateful to him for all the things he had explained to her: Fascism, the Resistance, the monarchy, the republic, the black market, Comandante Lauro, the neo-fascists, Christian Democracy, Communism. But to be his girlfriend, no, she would never be anyone's girlfriend. And she had concluded: "I love all of you, Antonio, you, Enzo, the way I love Rino." Pasquale had then murmured, "I, however, don't love you the way I do Carmela." He had escaped and gone back to work.

"And the other declaration?" I asked her, curious but also a little anxious.

"You'd never imagine."

The other declaration had come from Marcello Solara.

In hearing that name I felt a pang. If Pasquale's love was a sign of how much someone could like Lila, the love of Marcello—a young man who was handsome and wealthy, with a car, who was harsh and violent, a Camorrist, used, that is, to taking the women he wanted—was, in my eyes, in the eyes of all my contemporaries, and in spite of his bad reputation, in fact perhaps even because of it, a promotion, the transition

from skinny little girl to woman capable of making anyone
bend to her will.

"How did it happen?"

Marcello was driving the 1100, by himself, without his
brother, and had seen her as she was going home along the
stradone. He hadn't driven up alongside her, he hadn't called
to her from the window. He had left the car in the middle of
the street, with the door open, and approached her. Lila had
kept walking, and he followed. He had pleaded with her to forgive him for his behavior in the past, he admitted she would
have been absolutely right to kill him with the shoemaker's
knife. He had reminded her, with emotion, how they had
danced rock and roll so well together at Gigliola's mother's
party, a sign of how well matched they might be. Finally he had
started to pay her compliments: "How you've grown up, what
lovely eyes you have, how beautiful you are." And then he told
her a dream he had had that night: he asked her to become
engaged, she said yes, he gave her an engagement ring like his
grandmother's, which had three diamonds in the band of the
setting. At last Lila, continuing to walk, had spoken. She had
asked, "In that dream I said yes?" Marcello confirmed it and
she replied, "Then it really was a dream, because you're an
animal, you and your family, your grandfather, your brother,
and I would never be engaged to you even if you tell me you'll
kill me."

"You told him that?"

"I said more."

"What?"

When Marcello, insulted, had replied that his feelings were
delicate, that he thought of her only with love, night and day,
that therefore he wasn't an animal but one who loved her, she
had responded that if a person behaved as he had behaved
with Ada, if that same person on New Year's Eve started shooting people with a gun, to call him an animal was to insult ani-

mals. Marcello had finally understood that she wasn't joking, that she really considered him less than a frog, a salamander, and he was suddenly depressed. He had murmured weakly, "It was my brother who was shooting." But even as he spoke he had realized that that excuse would only increase her contempt. Very true. Lila had started walking faster and when he tried to follow had yelled, "Go away," and started running. Marcello then had stopped as if he didn't remember where he was and what he was supposed to be doing, and so he had gone back to the 1100.

"You did that to Marcello Solara?"

"Yes."

"You're crazy: don't tell anyone you treated him like that."

At the moment it seemed to me superfluous advice, I said it just to demonstrate that I was concerned. Lila by nature liked talking and fantasizing about facts, but she never gossiped, unlike the rest us, who were continuously talking about people. And in fact she spoke only to me of Pasquale's love, I never discovered that she had told anyone else. But she told everyone about Marcello Solara. So that when I saw Carmela she said, "Did you know that your friend said no to Marcello Solara?" I met Ada, who said to me, "Your friend said no to Marcello Solara, no less." Pinuccia Carracci, in the shop, whispered in my ear, "Is it true that your friend said no to Marcello Solara?" Even Alfonso said to me one day at school, astonished, "Your friend said no to Marcello Solara?"

When I saw Lila I said to her, "You shouldn't have told everyone, Marcello will get angry."

She shrugged. She had work to do, her siblings, the housework, her mother, her father, and she didn't stop to talk much. Now, as she had been since New Year's Eve, she was occupied only with domestic things.

25.

So it was. For the rest of the term Lila was totally uninterested in what I did in school. And when I asked her what books she was taking out of the library, what she was reading, she answered, spitefully, "I don't take them out anymore, books give me a headache."

Whereas I studied, reading now was like a pleasant habit. But I soon had to observe that, since Lila had stopped pushing me, anticipating me in my studies and my reading, school, and even Maestro Ferraro's library, had stopped being a kind of adventure and had become only a thing that I knew how to do well and was much praised for.

I realized this clearly on two occasions.

Once I went to get some books out of the library. My card was dense with borrowings and returns, and the teacher first congratulated me on my diligence, then asked me about Lila, showing regret that she and her whole family had stopped taking out books. It's hard to explain why, but that regret made me suffer. It seemed to be the sign of a true interest in Lila, something much stronger than the compliments for my discipline as a constant reader. It occurred to me that if Lila had taken out just a single book a year, on that book she would have left her imprint and the teacher would have felt it the moment she returned it, while I left no mark, I embodied only the persistence with which I added volume to volume in no particular order.

The other circumstance had to do with school exercises. The literature teacher, Gerace, gave back, corrected, our Italian papers (I still remember the subject: "The Various Phases of the Tragedy of Dido"), and while he generally confined himself to saying a word or two to justify the eight or nine I usually got, this time he praised me eloquently in front of the class and revealed only at the end that he had given me a ten. At the end of the class he called me into the corridor, truly impressed by how I had treated the subject, and when the religion teacher came by he stopped him and summarized my paper enthusiastically. A few days passed and I realized that Gerace had not limited himself to the priest but had circulated that paper of mine among the other teachers, and not only in my section. Some teachers in the upper grades now smiled at me in the corridors, or even made comments. For example, Professor Galiani, a woman who was highly regarded and yet avoided, because she was said to be a Communist, and because with one or two comments she could dismantle any argument that did not have a solid foundation, stopped me in the hall and spoke with particular admiration about the idea, central to my paper, that if love is exiled from cities, their good nature becomes an evil nature. She asked me:

"What does 'a city without love' mean to you?"

"A people deprived of happiness."

"Give me an example."

I thought of the discussions I'd had with Lila and Pasquale in September and I suddenly felt that they were a true school, truer than the one I went to every day.

"Italy under Fascism, Germany under Nazism, all of us human beings in the world today."

She scrutinized me with increased interest. She said that I wrote very well, she recommended some reading, she offered to lend me books. Finally, she asked me what my father did, I answered, "He's a porter at the city hall." She went off with her head down.

The interest shown by Professor Galiani naturally filled me with pride, but it had no great consequence; the school routine returned to normal. As a result, even the fact that, in my first year, I was a student with a small reputation for being clever soon seemed to me unimportant. In the end what did it prove? It proved how fruitful it had been to study with Lila and talk to her, to have her as a goad and support as I ventured into the world outside the neighborhood, among the things and persons and landscapes and ideas of books. Of course, I said to myself, the essay on Dido is mine, the capacity to formulate beautiful sentences comes from me; of course, what I wrote about Dido belongs to me; but didn't I work it out with her, didn't we excite each other in turn, didn't my passion grow in the warmth of hers? And that idea of the city without love, which the teachers had liked so much, hadn't it come to me from Lila, even if I had developed it, with my own ability? What should I deduce from this?

I began to expect new praise that would prove my autonomous virtuosity. But Gerace, when he gave another assignment on the Queen of Carthage ("Aeneas and Dido: An Encounter Between Two Refugees"), was not enthusiastic, he gave me only an eight. Still, from Professor Galiani I got cordial nods of greeting and the pleasant discovery that she was the Latin and Greek teacher of Nino Sarratore. I urgently needed some reinforcements of attention and admiration, and hoped that maybe they would come from him. I hoped that, if his professor of literature had praised me in public, let's say in his class, he would remember me and finally would speak to me. But nothing happened, I continued to glimpse him on the way out, on the way in, always with that absorbed expression, never a glance. Once I even followed him along Corso Garibaldi and Via Casanova, hoping he would notice me and say: Hello, I see we're taking the same route, I've heard a lot about you. But he walked quickly, eyes down, and never turned. I got tired, I despised myself. Depressed, I turned onto Corso Novara and went home.

I kept on day after day, committed to asserting, with increasing thoroughness, to the teachers, to my classmates, to myself my application and diligence. But inside I felt a growing sense of solitude, I felt I was learning without energy. I tried to report to Lila Maestro Ferraro's regret, I told her to go back to the library. I also mentioned to her how well the assignment on Dido had been received, without telling her what I had written but letting her know that it was also her success. She listened to me without interest, maybe she no longer even remembered what we had said about that character, she had other problems. As soon as I left her an opening she told me that Marcello Solara had not resigned himself like Pasquale but continued to pursue her. If she went out to do the shopping he followed her, without bothering her, to Stefano's store, to Enzo's cart, just to look at her. If she went to the window she found him at the corner, waiting for her to appear. This constancy made her anxious. She was afraid that her father might notice, and, especially, that Rino might notice. She was frightened by the possibility that one of those stories of men would begin, in which they end up fighting all the time—there were plenty of those in the neighborhood. "What do I have?" she said. She saw herself as scrawny, ugly: why had Marcello become obsessed with her? "Is there something wrong with me?" she said. "I make people do the wrong thing."

Now she often repeated that idea. The conviction of having done more harm than good for her brother had solidified. "All you have to do is look at him," she said. Even with the disappearance of the Cerullo shoe factory project, Rino was gripped by the mania of getting rich like the Solaras, like Stefano, and even more, and he couldn't resign himself to the dailiness of the work in the shop. He said, trying to rekindle her old enthusiasm, "We're intelligent, Lina, together no one can stop us, tell me what we should do." He also wanted to buy a car, a television, and he detested Fernando, who didn't understand the importance of these things. But when Lila showed that she wouldn't support him anymore, he treated her worse than a servant. Maybe he didn't even know that he had changed for the worse, but she, who saw him every day, was alarmed. She said to me once, "Have you seen that when people wake up they're ugly, all disfigured, can't see?"

Rino in her view had become like that.

26.

One Sunday, in the middle of April, I remember, five of us went out: Lila, Carmela, Pasquale, Rino, and I. We girls were dressed up as well as we could and as soon as we were out of the house we put on lipstick and a little eye makeup. We took the metro, which was very crowded, and Rino and Pasquale stood next to us, on the lookout, the whole way. They were afraid that someone might touch us, but no one did, the faces of our escorts were too dangerous.

We walked down Toledo. Lila insisted on going to Via Chiaia, Via Filangieri, and then Via dei Mille, to Piazza Amedeo, an area where she knew there would be wealthy, elegant people. Rino and Pasquale were opposed, but they couldn't or wouldn't explain, and responded only by muttering in dialect and insulting indeterminate people they called "dandies." We three ganged up and insisted. Just then we heard honking. We turned and saw the Solaras' 1100. We didn't even notice the two brothers, we were so struck by the girls who were waving from the windows: Gigliola and Ada. They looked pretty, with pretty dresses, pretty hairdos, sparkling earrings, they waved and shouted happy greetings to us. Rino and Pasquale turned their faces away, Carmela and I were too surprised to respond. Lila was the only one to shout enthusiastically and wave, with broad motions of her arms, as the car disappeared in the direction of Piazza Plebiscito.

For a while we were silent, then Rino said to Pasquale he had always known that Gigliola was a whore, and Pasquale gravely agreed. Neither of the two mentioned Ada, Antonio was their friend and they didn't want to offend him. Carmela, however, said a lot of mean things about Ada. More than anything, I felt bitterness. That image of power had passed in a flash, four young people in a car—that was the right way to leave the neighborhood and have fun. Ours was the wrong way: on foot, in shabby old clothes, penniless. I felt like going home. Lila reacted as if that encounter had never taken place, insisting again that she wanted to go for a walk where the fancy people were. She clung to Pasquale's arm, she yelled, she laughed, she performed what she thought of as a parody of the respectable person, with waggling hips, a broad smile, and simpering gestures. We hesitated a moment and then went along with her, resentful at the idea that Gigliola and Ada were having fun in the 1100 with the handsome Solaras while we were on foot, in the company of Rino who resoled shoes and Pasquale who was a construction worker.

This dissatisfaction of ours, naturally unspoken, must somehow have reached the two boys, who looked at each other, sighed, and gave in. All right, they said, and we turned onto Via Chiaia.

It was like crossing a border. I remember a dense crowd and a sort of humiliating difference. I looked not at the boys but at the girls, the women: they were absolutely different from us. They seemed to have breathed another air, to have eaten other food, to have dressed on some other planet, to have learned to walk on wisps of wind. I was astonished. All the more so that, while I would have paused to examine at leisure dresses, shoes, the style of glasses if they wore glasses, they passed by without seeming to see me. They didn't see any of the five of us. We were not perceptible. Or not interesting. And in fact if at times their gaze fell on us, they immediately turned in another direction, as if irritated. They looked only at each other.

Of this we were all aware. No one mentioned it, but we understood that Rino and Pasquale, who were older, found on those streets only confirmation of things they already knew, and this put them in a bad mood, made them sullen, resentful at the certainty of being out of place, while we girls discovered it only at that moment and with ambiguous sentiments. We felt uneasy and yet fascinated, ugly but also impelled to imagine what we would become if we had some way to re-educate ourselves and dress and put on makeup and adorn ourselves properly. Meanwhile, in order not to ruin the evening, we became mocking, sarcastic.

"Would you ever wear that dress?"

"Not if you paid me."

"I would."

"Good for you, you'd look like a cream puff, like that lady there."

"And did you see the shoes?"

"What, those are shoes?"

We went as far as Palazzo Cellammare laughing and joking. Pasquale, who did his best to avoid being next to Lila and when she took his arm immediately, politely, freed himself (he spoke to her often, of course, he felt an evident pleasure in hearing her voice, in looking at her, but it was clear that the slightest contact overwhelmed him, might even make him cry), staying close to me, asked derisively:

"At school do your classmates look like that?"

"No."

"That means it's not a good school."

"It's a classical high school," I said, offended.

"It's not a good one," he insisted, "you can be sure that if there are no people like that it's no good: right, Lila, it's no good?"

"Good?" Lila said, and pointed to a blond girl who was coming toward us with a tall, dark young man, in a white V-neck sweater. "If there's no one like that, your school stinks." And she burst out laughing.

The girl was all in green: green shoes, green skirt, green jacket, and on her head—this was above all what made Lila laugh—she wore a bowler, like Charlie Chaplin, also green.

The hilarity passed from her to the rest of us. When the couple went by Rino made a vulgar comment on what the young woman in green should do, with the bowler hat, and Pasquale stopped, he was laughing so hard, and leaned against the wall with one arm. The girl and her companion took a few steps, then stopped. The boy in the white pullover turned, was immediately restrained by the girl, who grabbed his arm. He wriggled free, came back, addressed directly to Rino a series of insulting phrases. It was an instant. Rino punched him in the face and knocked him down, shouting:

"What did you call me? I didn't get it, repeat, what did you call me? Did you hear, Pascà, what he called me?"

Our laughter abruptly turned to fear. Lila first of all hurled herself at her brother before he started kicking the young man on the ground and dragged him off, with an expression of disbelief, as if a thousand fragments of our life, from childhood to this, our fourteenth year, were composing an image that was finally clear, yet which at that moment seemed to her incredible.

We pushed Rino and Pasquale away, while the girl in the bowler helped her boyfriend get up. Lila's incredulity meanwhile was changing into fury. As she tried to get her brother off she assailed him with the coarsest insults, pulled him by the arm, threatened him. Rino kept her away with one hand, a nervous laugh on his face, and meanwhile he turned to Pasquale:

"My sister thinks this is a game, Pascà," he said in dialect, his eyes wild, "my sister thinks that even if I say it's better for us not to go somewhere, she can do it, because she always knows everything, she always understands everything, as usual, and she can go there like it or not." A short pause to regain his breath, then he added, "Did you hear that shit called me 'hick'? Me a hick? A hick?" And still, breathless, "My sister brought me here and now she sees if I'm called a hick, now she sees what I do if they call me a hick."

"Calm down, Rino," Pasquale said, looking behind him every so often, in alarm.

Rino remained agitated, but subdued. Lila, however, had calmed down. We stopped at Piazza dei Martiri. Pasquale said, almost coldly, addressing Carmela: "You girls go home now."

"Alone?"

"Yes."

"No."

"Carmè, I don't want to discuss it: go."

"We don't know how to get there."

"Don't lie."

"Go," Rino said to Lila, trying to contain himself. "Take some money, buy an ice cream on the way."

"We left together and we're going back together."

Rino lost patience again, gave her a shove: "Will you stop it? I'm older and you do what I tell you. Move, go, in a second I'll bash your face in."

I saw that he was ready to do it seriously, I dragged Lila by the arm. She also understood the risk: "I'll tell Papa."

"Who gives a fuck. Walk, come on, go, you don't even deserve the ice cream."

Hesitantly we went up past Santa Caterina. But after a while Lila had second thoughts, stopped, said that she was going back to her brother. We tried to persuade her to stay with us, but she wouldn't listen. Just then we saw a group of boys, five, maybe six, they looked like the rowers we had sometimes admired on Sunday walks near Castel dell'Ovo. They were all tall, sturdy, well dressed. Some had sticks, some didn't. They quickly passed by the church and headed toward the piazza. Among them was the young man whom Rino had

196 · ELENA FERRANTE

struck in the face; his V-necked sweater was stained with blood.

Lila freed herself from my grip and ran off, Carmela and I behind her. We arrived in time to see Rino and Pasquale backing up toward the monument at the center of the piazza, side by side, while those well-dressed youths chased them, hitting them with their sticks. We called for help, we began to cry, to stop people passing, but the sticks were frightening, no one helped. Lila grabbed the arm of one of the attackers but was thrown to the ground. I saw Pasquale on his knees, being kicked, I saw Rino protecting himself from the blows with his arm. Then a car stopped and it was the Solaras' 1100.

Marcello got out immediately. First he helped Lila up and then, incited by her, as she shrieked with rage and shouted at her brother, threw himself into the fight, hitting and getting hit. Only at that point Michele got out of the car, opened the trunk in a leisurely way, took out something that looked like a shiny iron bar, and joined in, hitting with a cold ferocity that I hope never to see again in my life. Rino and Pasquale got up furiously, hitting, choking, tearing—they seemed like strangers, they were so transformed by hatred. The well-dressed young men were routed. Michele went up to Pasquale, whose nose was bleeding, but Pasquale rudely pushed him away and wiped his face with the sleeve of his white shirt, then saw that it was soaked red. Marcello picked up a bunch of keys and handed it to Rino, who thanked him uneasily. The people who had kept their distance before now came over, curious. I was paralyzed with fear.

"Take the girls away," Rino said to the two Solaras, in the grateful tone of someone who makes a request that he knows is unavoidable.

Marcello made us get in the car, first Lila, who resisted. We were all jammed in the back seat, sitting on each other's knees. I turned to look at Pasquale and Rino, who were heading

toward the Riviera, Pasquale limping. I felt as if our neighborhood had expanded, swallowing all Naples, even the streets
where respectable people lived. In the car there were immediate tensions. Gigliola and Ada were annoyed, protesting that
the ride was uncomfortable. "It's impossible," they said. "Then
get out and walk," Lila shouted and they were about to start
hitting each other. Marcello braked, amused. Gigliola got out
and went to sit in front, on Michele's knees. We made the journey like that, with Gigliola and Michele kissing each other in
front of us. I looked at her and she, though kissing passionately, looked at me. I turned away.

Lila said nothing until we reached the neighborhood.
Marcello said a few words, his eyes looking for her in the rear-
view mirror, but she never responded. They let us out far from
our houses, so that we wouldn't be seen in the Solaras' car.
The rest of the way we walked, the five of us. Apart from Lila,
who seemed consumed by anger and worry, we all admired
the behavior of the two brothers. Good for them, we said,
they behaved well. Gigliola kept repeating, "Of course,"
"What did you think," "Naturally," with the air of one who,
working in the pastry shop, knew very well what first-rate
people the Solaras were. At one point she asked me, but in a
teasing tone:

"How's school?"

"Great."

"But you don't have fun the way I do."

"It's a different type of fun."

When she, Carmela, and Ada left us at the entrance of their
building, I said to Lila:

"The rich people certainly are worse than we are."

She didn't answer. I added, cautiously, "The Solaras may be
shit, but it's lucky they were there: those people on Via dei
Mille might have killed Rino and Pasquale."

She shook her head energetically. She was paler than usual

and under her eyes were deep purple hollows. She didn't agree but she didn't tell me why.

27.

I was promoted with nines in all my subjects, I would even receive something called a scholarship. Of the forty we had been, thirty-two remained. Gino failed, Alfonso had to retake the exams in three subjects in September. Urged by my father, I went to see Maestra Oliviero—my mother was against it, she didn't like the teacher to interfere in her family and claim the right to make decisions about her children in her place—with the usual two packets, one of sugar and one of coffee, bought at the Bar Solara, to thank her for her interest in me.

She wasn't feeling well, she had something in her throat that hurt her, but she was full of praise, congratulated me on how hard I had worked, said that I looked a little too pale and that she intended to telephone a cousin who lived on Ischia to see if she would let me stay with her for a little while. I thanked her, but said nothing to my mother of that possibility. I already knew that she wouldn't let me go. Me on Ischia? Me alone on the ferry traveling over the sea? Not to mention me on the beach, swimming, in a bathing suit?

I didn't even mention it to Lila. Her life in a few months had lost even the adventurous aura associated with the shoe factory, and I didn't want to boast about the promotion, the scholarship, a possible vacation in Ischia. In appearance things had improved: Marcello Solara had stopped following her. But after the violence in Piazza dei Martiri something completely unexpected happened that puzzled her. He came to the shop to ask about Rino's condition, and the honor conferred by that visit perturbed Fernando. But Rino, who had been careful not to tell his father what had happened (to explain the bruises on his face and his body he made up a story that he had fallen off a friend's Lambretta), and worried that Marcello might say one word too many, had immediately steered him out into the street. They had taken a short walk. Rino had reluctantly thanked Solara both for his intervention and for the kindness of coming to see how he was. Two minutes and they had said goodbye. When he returned to the shop his father had said:

"Finally you're doing something good."

"What?"

"A friendship with Marcello Solara."

"There's no friendship, Papa."

"Then it means you were a fool and a fool you remain."

Fernando wanted to say that something was changing and that his son, whatever he wanted to call that thing with the Solaras, would do well to encourage it. He was right. Marcello returned a couple of days later with his grandfather's shoes to resole; then he invited Rino to go for a drive. Then he urged him to apply for a license, assuming the responsibility for getting him to practice in the 1100. Maybe it wasn't friendship, but the Solaras certainly had taken a liking to Rino.

When Lila, ignorant of these visits, which took place entirely at the shoemaker's shop, where she never went, heard about them, she, unlike her father, felt an increasing worry. First she remembered the battle of the fireworks and thought: Rino hates the Solaras too much, it can't be that he'll let himself be taken in. Then she had had to observe that Marcello's attentions were seducing her older brother even more than her parents. She now knew Rino's fragility, but still she was angry at the way the Solaras were getting into his head, making him a kind of happy little monkey.

"What's wrong with it?" I objected once.

"They're dangerous."

"Here everything is dangerous."

"Did you see what Michele took out of the car, in Piazza dei Martiri?"

"No."

"An iron bar."

"The others had sticks."

"You don't see it, Lenù, but the bar was sharpened into a point: if he wanted he could have thrust it into the chest, or the stomach, of one of those guys."

"Well, you threatened Marcello with the shoemaker's knife."

At that point she grew irritated and said I didn't understand. And probably it was true. It was her brother, not mine; I liked to be logical, while she had different needs, she wanted to get Rino away from that relationship. But as soon as she made some critical remark Rino shut her up, threatened her, sometimes beat her. And so things, willy-nilly, proceeded to the point where, one evening in late June—I was at Lila's house, I was helping her fold sheets, or something, I don't remember—the door opened and Rino entered, followed by Marcello.

He had invited Solara to dinner, and Fernando, who had just returned from the shop, very tired, at first was irritated, and then felt honored, and behaved cordially. Not to mention Nunzia: she became agitated, thanked Marcello for the three bottles of good wine that he had brought, pulled the other children into the kitchen so they wouldn't be disruptive.

I myself was involved with Lila in the preparations for dinner.

"I'll put roach poison in it," Lila said, furious, at the stove, and we laughed, while Nunzia shut us up.

"He's come to marry you," I said to provoke her, "he's going to ask your father."

"He is deceiving himself."

"Why," Nunzia asked anxiously, "if he likes you do you say no?"

"Ma, I already told him no."

"Really?"

"Yes."

"What are you saying?"

"It's true," I said in confirmation.

"Your father must never know, otherwise he'll kill you."

At dinner only Marcello spoke. It was clear that he had invited himself, and Rino, who didn't know how to say no to him, sat at the table nearly silent, or laughed for no reason. Solara addressed himself mainly to Fernando, but never neglected to pour water or wine for Nunzia, for Lila, for me. He said to him how much he was respected in the neighborhood because he was such a good cobbler. He said that his father had always spoken well of his skill. He said that Rino had an unlimited admiration for his abilities as a shoemaker.

Fernando, partly because of the wine, was moved. He muttered something in praise of Silvio Solara, and even went so far as to say that Rino was a good worker and was becoming a good shoemaker. Then Marcello started to praise the need for progress. He said that his grandfather had started with a cellar, then his father had enlarged it, and today the bar-pastry shop Solara was what it was, everybody knew it, people came from all over Naples to have coffee, eat a pastry.

"What an exaggeration," Lila exclaimed, and her father gave her a silencing look.

But Marcello smiled at her humbly and admitted, "Yes, maybe I'm exaggerating a little, but just to say that money has to circulate. You begin with a cellar and from generation to generation you can go far."

At this point, with Rino showing evident signs of uneasiness, he began to praise the idea of making new shoes. And from that moment he began to look at Lila as if in praising the energy of the generations he were praising her in particular. He said: if someone feels capable, if he's clever, if he can invent good things, which are pleasing, why not try? He spoke in a nice, charming dialect and as he spoke he never stopped staring at my friend. I felt, I saw that he was in love as in the songs, that he would have liked to kiss her, that he wanted to breathe her breath, that she would be able to make of him all she wanted, that in his eyes she embodied all possible feminine qualities.

"I know," Marcello concluded, "that your children made a very nice pair of shoes, size 43, just my size."

A long silence fell. Rino stared at his plate and didn't dare look up at his father. Only the sound of the goldfinch at the window could be heard. Fernando said slowly, "Yes, they're size 43."

"I would very much like to see them, if you don't mind?"

Fernando stammered, "I don't know where they are. Nunzia, do you know?"

"She has them," Rino said, indicating his sister.

"I did have them, yes, I had put them in the storeroom. But then Mamma told me to clean it out the other day and I threw them away. Since no one liked them."

Rino said angrily, "You're a liar, go and get the shoes right now."

Fernando said nervously, "Go get the shoes, go on."

Lila burst out, addressing her father, "How is it that now you want them? I threw them away because you said you didn't like them."

Fernando pounded the table with his open hand, the wine trembled in the glasses.

"Get up and go get the shoes, right now."

Lila pushed away her chair, stood up.

"I threw them away," she repeated weakly and left the room.

She didn't come back.

The time passed in silence. The first to become alarmed was

Marcello. He said, with real concern, "Maybe I was wrong, I didn't know that there were problems."

"There's no problem," Fernando said, and whispered to his wife, "Go see what your daughter is doing."

Nunzia left the room. When she came back she was embarrassed, she couldn't find Lila. We looked for her all over the house, she wasn't there. We called her from the window: nothing. Marcello, desolate, took his leave. As soon as he had gone Fernando shouted at his wife, "God's truth, this time I'm going to kill your daughter."

Rino joined his father in the threat, Nunzia began to cry. I left almost on tiptoe, frightened. But as soon as I closed the door and came out on the landing Lila called me. She was on the top floor, I went up on tiptoe. She was huddled next to the door to the terrace, in the shadows. She had the shoes in her lap, for the first time I saw them finished. They shone in the feeble light of a bulb hanging on an electrical cable. "What would it cost you to let him see them?" I asked, confused.

She shook her head energetically. "I don't even want him to touch them."

But she was as if overwhelmed by her own extreme reaction. Her lower lip trembled, something that never happened.

Gradually I persuaded her to go home, she couldn't stay hiding there forever. I went with her, counting on the fact that my presence would protect her. But there were shouts, insults, some blows just the same. Fernando screamed that on a whim she had made him look foolish in the eyes of an important guest. Rino tore the shoes out of her hand, saying that they were his, the work had been done by him. She began to cry, murmuring, "I worked on them, too, but it would have been better if I'd never done it, you've become a mad beast." It was Nunzia who put an end to that torture. She turned pale and in a voice that was not her usual voice she ordered her children, and even her husband—she who was always so submissive—to stop it immediately, to give the shoes to her, not to venture a single word if they didn't want her to jump out the window. Rino gave her the shoes and for the moment things ended there. I slipped away.

28.

But Rino wouldn't give in, and in the following days he continued to attack his sister with words and fists. Every time Lila and I met I saw a new bruise. After a while I felt that she was resigned. One morning he insisted that they go out together, that she come with him to the shoemaker's shop. On the way they both sought, with wavy moves, to end the war. Rino said that he loved her but that she didn't love anyone, neither her parents nor her siblings. Lila murmured, "What do you mean by love, what does love mean for our family? Let's hear." Step by step, he revealed to her what he had in mind.

"If Marcello likes the shoes, Papa will change his mind."

"I don't think so."

"Yes, he will. And if Marcello buys them, Papa will understand that your designs are good, that they're profitable, and he'll have us start work."

"The three of us?"

"He and I and maybe you, too. Papa is capable of making a pair of shoes, completely finished, in four days, at most five. And I, if I work hard, I'll show you that I can do the same. We make them, we sell them, and we finance ourselves."

"Who do we sell them to, always Marcello Solara?"

"The Solaras market them; they know people who count. They'll do the publicity for us."

"They'll do it free?"

"If they want a small percentage we'll give it to them."

"And why should they be content with a small percentage?"

"They've taken a liking to me."

"The Solaras?"

"Yes."

Lila sighed. "Just one thing: I'll tell Papa and see what he thinks."

"Don't you dare."

"This way or not at all."

Rino was silent, very nervous.

"All right. Anyway, you speak, you can speak better."

That evening, at dinner, in front of her brother, whose face was fiery red, Lila said to Fernando that Marcello not only had shown great curiosity about the shoe enterprise but might even be interested in buying the shoes for himself, and that in fact, if he was enthusiastic about the matter from a commercial point of view, he would advertise the product in the circles he frequented, in exchange, naturally, for a small percentage of the sales.

"This I said," Rino explained with lowered eyes, "not Marcello."

Fernando looked at his wife: Lila understood that they had talked about it and had already, secretly, reached a conclusion.

"Tomorrow," he said, "I'll put your shoes in the shop window. If someone wants to see them, wants to try them, wants to buy them, whatever fucking thing, he has to talk to me, I am the one who decides."

A few days later I passed by the shop. Rino was working, Fernando was working, both heads bent over the work. I saw in the window, among boxes of shoe polish and laces, the beautiful, elegant shoes made by the Cerullos. A sign pasted to the window, certainly written by Rino, said, pompously: "Shoes handmade by the Cerullos here." Father and son waited for good luck to arrive.

But Lila was skeptical, sulky. She had no faith in the ingen-uous hypothesis of her brother and was afraid of the indecipherable agreement between her father and mother. In other words she expected bad things. A week passed, and no one showed the least interest in the shoes in the window, not even Marcello. Only because he was cornered by Rino, in fact almost dragged to the shop, did Solara glance at them, but as if he had other things on his mind. He tried them, of course, but said they were a little tight, took them off immediately, and disappeared without even a word of compliment, as if he had a stomachache and had to hurry home. Disappointment of father and son. But two minutes later Marcello reappeared. Rino jumped up, beaming, and took his hand as if some agreement, by that pure and simple reappearance, had already been made. But Marcello ignored him and turned directly to Fernando. He said, all in one breath:

"I have very serious intentions, Don Fernà. I would like the hand of your daughter Lina."

29.

Rino reacted to that turn with a violent fever that kept him away from work for days. When, abruptly, the fever went down, he had disturbing symptoms: he got out of bed in the middle of the night, and, while still sleeping, silent, and extremely agitated, he went to the door and struggled to open it, with his eyes wide open. Nunzia and Lila, frightened, dragged him back to bed.

Fernando, however, who with his wife had immediately guessed Marcello's true intentions, spoke with his daughter calmly. He explained to her that Marcello Solara's proposal was important not only for her future but for that of the whole family. He told her that she was still a child and didn't have to say yes immediately, but added that he, as her father, advised her to consent. A long engagement at home would slowly get her used to the marriage.

Lila answered with equal tranquility that rather than be engaged to Marcello Solara and marry him she would go and drown herself in the pond. A great quarrel arose, but she didn't change her mind.

I was stunned by the news. I knew that Marcello wanted to be Lila's boyfriend at all costs, but it would never have entered my mind that at our age one could receive a proposal of marriage. And yet Lila had received one, and she wasn't yet fifteen, she hadn't yet had a secret boyfriend, had never kissed anyone. I sided with her immediately. Get married? To Marcello Solara? Maybe even have children? No, absolutely no. I encouraged her to fight that new war against her father and swore I would support her, even if he had already lost his composure and now was threatening her, saying that for her own good he would break every bone in her body if she didn't accept a proposal of that importance.

But I couldn't stay with her. In the middle of July something happened that I should have thought of but that instead caught me unawares and overwhelmed me. One late afternoon, after the usual walk through the neighborhood with Lila, discussing what was happening to her and how to get out of it, I came home and my sister Elisa opened the door. She said in a state of excitement that in the dining room was her teacher, that is, Maestra Oliviero. She was talking to our mother.

I looked timidly into the room, my mother stammered, in annoyance, "Maestra Oliviero says you need to rest, you're worn out."

I looked at the teacher without understanding. She seemed the one in need of rest, she was pale and her face was puffy. She said to me, "My cousin responded just yesterday: you can go to her in Ischia, and stay there until the end of August. She'll be happy to have you, you just have to help a little in the house."

She spoke to me as if she were my mother and as if my

mother, the real one, with the injured leg and the wandering eye, were only a disposable living being, and as such not to be taken into consideration. Nor did she go away after that communication, but stayed another hour showing me one by one the books that she had brought to lend to me. She explained to me which I should read first and which after, she made me swear that before reading them I would make covers for them, she ordered me to give them all back at the end of the summer without a single dog-ear. My mother endured all this patiently. She sat attentively, even though her wandering eye gave her a dazed expression. She exploded only when the teacher, finally, took her leave, with a disdainful farewell and not even a caress for my sister, who had counted on it and would have been proud. She turned to me, overwhelmed by bitterness for the humiliation that it seemed to her she had suffered on my account. She said, "The signorina must go and rest on Ischia, the signorina is too exhausted. Go and make dinner, go on, or I'll hit you."

Two days later, however, after taking my measurements and rapidly making me a bathing suit—I don't know where she copied it from—she herself took me to the ferry. Along the street to the port, while she bought me the ticket, and then while she waited for me to get on, she besieged me with warnings. What frightened her most was the crossing. "Let's hope the sea isn't rough," she said almost to herself, and swore that when I was a child she had taken me to Coroglio every day, so my catarrh would dry out, and that the sea was beautiful and I had learned to swim. But I didn't remember Coroglio or the sea or learning to swim, and I told her. And her tone became resentful, as if to say that if I drowned it would not be her fault—that what she was supposed to do to avoid it she had done—but because of my own forgetfulness. Then she ordered me not to go far from the shore even when the sea was calm, and to stay home if it was rough or there was a red flag. "Especially," she said, "if you have a full stomach or your period, you mustn't even get your feet wet." Before she left she asked an old sailor to keep an eye on me. When the ferry left the wharf I was terrified and at the same time happy. For the first time I was leaving home, I was going on a journey, a journey by sea. The large body of my mother—along with the neighborhood, and Lila's troubles—grew distant, and vanished.

30.

I blossomed. The teacher's cousin was called Nella Incardo and she lived in Barano. I arrived in the town by bus, and found the house easily. Nella was a big, kind woman, very lively, talkative, unmarried. She rented rooms to vacationers, keeping for herself one small room and the kitchen. I would sleep in the kitchen. I had to make up my bed in the evening and take it all apart (boards, legs, mattress) in the morning. I discovered that I had some mandatory obligations: to get up at six-thirty, make breakfast for her and her guests—when I arrived there was an English couple with two children—tidy up and wash cups and bowls, set the table for dinner, and wash the dishes before going to sleep. Otherwise I was free. I could sit on the terrace and read with the sea in front of me, or walk along a steep white road toward a long, wide, dark beach that was called Spiaggia dei Maronti.

In the beginning, after all the fears that my mother had inoculated me with and all the troubles I had with my body, I spent the time on the terrace, dressed, writing a letter to Lila every day, each one filled with questions, clever remarks, lively descriptions of the island. But one morning Nella made fun of me, saying, "What are you doing like this? Put on your bathing suit." When I put it on she burst out laughing, she thought it was old-fashioned. She sewed me one that she said was more modern, very low over the bosom, more fitted around the bottom, of a beautiful blue. I tried it on and she was enthusiastic, she said it was time I went to the sea, enough of the terrace.

The next day, amid a thousand fears and a thousand curiosities, I set out with a towel and a book toward the Maronti. The trip seemed very long, I met no one coming up or going down. The beach was endless and deserted, with a granular sand that rustled at every step. The sea gave off an intense odor and a sharp, monotonous sound.

I stood looking for a long time at that great mass of water. Then I sat on the towel, uncertain what to do. Finally I got up and stuck my feet in. How had it happened that I lived in a city like Naples and never thought, not once, of swimming in the sea? And yet it was so. I advanced cautiously, letting the water rise from my feet to my ankles, to my thighs. Then I missed a step and sank. Terrified, I gasped for air, swallowed water, returned to the surface, to the air. I realized that it came naturally to move my feet and arms in a certain way to keep myself afloat. So I knew how to swim. My mother really had taken me to the sea as a child and there, while she took the sand treatments, I had learned to swim. I saw her in a flash, younger, less ravaged, sitting on the black sand in the midday sun, in a flowered white dress, her good leg covered to the knee by her dress, the injured one completely buried in the burning sand.

The seawater and the sun rapidly erased the inflammation of the acne from my face. I burned, I darkened. I waited for letters from Lila, we had promised when we said goodbye, but none came. I practiced speaking English a little with the family at Nella's. They understood that I wanted to learn and spoke to me with increasing kindness, and I improved quite a lot. Nella, who was always cheerful, encouraged me, and I began to interpret for her. Meanwhile she didn't miss any opportunity to compliment me. She made me enormous meals, and she was a really good cook. She said that I had been a stick when I arrived and now, thanks to her treatment, I was beautiful.

In other words, the last ten days of July gave me a sense of well-being that I had never known before. I felt a sensation that later in my life was often repeated: the joy of the new. I liked everything: getting up early, making breakfast, tidying up, walking in Barano, taking the road to the Maronti, uphill and down, lying in the sun and reading, going for a swim, returning to my book. I did not feel homesick for my father, my brothers and sister, my mother, the streets of the neighborhood, the public gardens. I missed only Lila, Lila who didn't answer my letters. I was afraid of what was happening to her, good or bad, in my absence. It was an old fear, a fear that has never left me: the fear that, in losing pieces of her life, mine lost intensity and importance. And the fact that she didn't answer emphasized that preoccupation. However hard I tried in my letters to communicate the privilege of the days in Ischia, my river of words and her silence seemed to demonstrate that my life was splendid but uneventful, which left me time to write to her every day, while hers was dark but full.

At the end of July Nella told me that on the first of August, in place of the English, a Neapolitan family was to arrive. It was the second year they had come. Very respectable people, very polite, refined: especially the husband, a true gentleman who always said wonderful things to her. And then the older son, really a fine boy: tall, thin but strong, this year he was seventeen. "You won't be alone anymore," she said to me, and I was embarrassed, immediately filled with anxiety about this young man who was arriving, fearful that we wouldn't be able to speak two words to each other, that he wouldn't like me.

As soon as the English departed—they left me a couple of novels to practice my reading, and their address, so that if I ever decided to go to England I should go and see them— Nella had me help her clean the rooms, do the laundry, remake the beds. I was glad to do it, and as I was washing the floor she called to me from the kitchen: "How clever you are, you can even read in English. Are the books you brought not enough?"

And she went on praising me from a distance, in a loud voice, for how disciplined I was, how sensible, for how I read all day and also at night. When I joined her in the kitchen I found her with a book in her hand. She said that the man who was arriving the next day had written it himself. Nella kept it on her night table, every evening she read a poem, first to herself and then aloud. Now she knew them all by heart.

"Look what he wrote to me," she said, and handed me the book.

It was *Attempts at Serenity*, by Donato Sarratore. The dedication read: "*To darling Nella, and to her jams.*"

31.

I immediately wrote to Lila: pages and pages of apprehension, joy, the wish to flee, intense foreshadowing of the moment when I would see Nino Sarratore, I would walk to the Maronti with him, we would swim, we would look at the moon and the stars, we would sleep under the same roof. All I could think of was that intense moment when, holding his brother by the hand, a century ago—ah, how much time had passed—he had declared his love. We were children then: now I felt grown-up, almost old.

The next day I went to the bus stop to help the guests carry their bags. I was very agitated, I hadn't slept all night. The bus arrived, stopped, the travelers got out. I recognized Donato Sarratore, I recognized Lidia, his wife, I recognized Marisa, although she was very changed, I recognized Clelia, who was always by herself, I recognized little Pino, who was now a solemn kid, and I imagined that the capricious child who was annoying his mother must be the one who, the last time I had seen the entire Sarratore family, was still in a carriage, under the projectiles hurled by Melina. But I didn't see Nino.

Marisa threw her arms around my neck with an enthusiasm I would never have expected: in all those years I had never, absolutely never, thought of her, while she said she had often thought of me with great nostalgia. When she alluded to the days in the neighborhood and told her parents that I was the daughter of Greco, the porter, Lidia, her mother, made a grimace of distaste and hurried to grab her little child to scold him for something or other, while Donato Sarratore saw to the luggage without even a remark like: How is your father.

I felt depressed. The Sarratores settled in their rooms, and I went to the sea with Marisa, who knew the Maronti and all Ischia well, and was already impatient, she wanted to go to the Port, where there was more activity, and to Forio, and to Casamicciola, anywhere but Barano, which according to her was a morgue. She told me that she was studying to be a secretary and had a boyfriend whom I would meet soon because he was coming to see her, but secretly. Finally she told me something that tugged at my heart. She knew all about me, she knew that I went to the high school, that I was very clever, and that Gino, the pharmacist's son, was my boyfriend.

"Who told you?"

"My brother."

So Nino had recognized me, so he knew who I was, so it was not inattention but perhaps timidity, perhaps uneasiness, perhaps shame for the declaration he had made to me as a child.

"I stopped going with Gino ages ago," I said. "Your brother isn't very well informed."

"All he thinks about is studying, it's already a lot that he told me about you, usually he's got his head in the clouds."

"He's not coming?"

"He'll come when Papa leaves."

She spoke to me very critically about Nino. He had no feelings. He was never excited about anything, he didn't get angry but he wasn't nice, either. He was closed up in himself, all he cared about was studying. He didn't like anything, he was cold-blooded. The only person who managed to get to him a little was his father. Not that they quarreled, he was a respectful and obedient son. But Marisa knew very well that Nino couldn't stand his father. Whereas she adored him. He was the best and most intelligent man in the world.

"Is your father staying long? When is he leaving?" I asked her with perhaps excessive interest.

"Just three days. He has to work."

"And Nino arrives in three days?"

"Yes. He pretended that he had to help the family of a friend of his move."

"And it's not true?"

"He doesn't have any friends. And anyway he wouldn't carry that stone from here to there even for my mamma, the only person he loves even a little, imagine if he's going to help a friend."

We went swimming, we dried off walking along the shore. Laughing, she pointed out to me something I had never noticed. At the end of the black beach were some motionless white forms. She dragged me, still laughing, over the burning sand and at a certain point it became clear that they were people. Living people, covered with mud. It was some sort of treatment, we didn't know for what. We lay on the sand, rolling over, shoving each other, pretending to be mummies like the people down the beach. We had fun playing, then went swimming again.

In the evening the Sarratore family had dinner in the kitchen and invited Nella and me to join them. It was a wonderful evening. Lidia never mentioned the neighborhood, but, once her first impulse of hostility had passed, she asked about me. When Marisa told her that I was very studious and went to the same school as Nino she became particularly nice. The most congenial of all, however, was Donato Sarratore. He loaded Nella with compliments, praised my scholastic record, was extremely considerate toward Lidia, played with Ciro, the baby, wanted to clean up himself, kept me from washing the dishes.

I studied him carefully and he seemed different from the way I remembered him. He was thinner, certainly, and had grown a mustache, but apart from his looks there was something more that I couldn't understand and that had to do with his behavior. Maybe he seemed to me more paternal than my father and uncommonly courteous.

This sensation intensified in the next two days. Sarratore, when we went to the beach, wouldn't allow Lidia or us two girls to carry anything. He loaded himself up with the umbrella, the bags with towels and food for lunch, on the way and, equally, on the way back, when the road was all uphill. He gave the bundles to us only when Ciro whined and insisted on being carried. He had a lean body, without much hair. He wore a bathing suit of an indefinable color, not of fabric, it seemed a light wool. He swam a lot but didn't go far out, he wanted to show me and Marisa how to swim freestyle. His daughter swam like him, with the same very careful, slow arm strokes, and I immediately began to imitate them. He expressed himself more in Italian than in dialect and tended somewhat insistently, especially with me, to come out with convoluted sentences and unusual phrasings. He summoned us cheerfully, me, Lidia, Marisa, to run back and forth on the beach with him to tone our muscles, and meanwhile he made us laugh with funny faces, little cries, comical walks. When he swam with his wife they stayed together, floating, they talked in low voices, and often laughed. The day he left, I was sorry as Marisa was sorry, as Lidia was sorry, as Nella was sorry. The house, though it echoed with our voices, seemed silent, a tomb. The only consolation was that finally Nino would arrive.

32.

I tried to suggest to Marisa that we should go and wait for him at the Port, but she refused, she said her brother didn't deserve that attention. Nino arrived in the evening. Tall, thin, in a blue shirt, dark pants, and sandals, with a bag over his shoulder, he showed not the least emotion at finding me in Ischia, in that house, so I thought that in Naples they must have a telephone, that Marisa had found a way of warning him. At dinner he spoke in monosyllables, and he didn't appear at breakfast. He woke up late, we went late to the beach, and he carried little or nothing. He dove in immediately, decisively, and swam out to sea effortlessly, without the ostentatious virtuosity of his father. He disappeared: I was afraid he had drowned, but neither Marisa nor Lidia was worried. He reappeared almost two hours later and began reading, smoking one cigarette after another. He read for the entire day, without saying a word to us, arranging the cigarette butts in the sand in a row, two by two. I also started reading, refusing the invitation of Marisa to walk along the shore. At dinner he ate in a hurry and went out. I cleared, I washed the dishes thinking of him. I made my bed in the kitchen and started reading again, waiting for him to come back. I read until one, then fell asleep with the light on and the book open on my chest. In the morning I woke up with the light off and the book closed. I thought it must have been him and felt a flare of love in my veins that I had never experienced before.

In a few days things improved. I realized that every so often he would look at me and then turn away. I asked him what he was reading, I told him what I was reading. We talked about our reading, annoying Marisa. At first he seemed to listen attentively, then, just like Lila, he started talking and went on, increasingly under the spell of his own arguments. Since I wanted him to be aware of my intelligence I endeavored to interrupt him, to say what I thought, but it was difficult, he seemed content with my presence only if I was silently listening, which I quickly resigned myself to doing. Besides, he said things that I could never have thought, or at least said, with the same assurance, and he said them in a strong, engaging Italian.

Marisa sometimes threw balls of sand at us, and sometimes burst in, shouting "Stop it, who cares about this Dostoyevsky, who gives a damn about the Karamazovs." Then Nino abruptly broke off and walked along the shore, head lowered, until he became a tiny speck. I spent some time with Marisa talking about her boyfriend, who couldn't come to see her, which made her cry. Meanwhile I felt better and better, I couldn't believe that life could be like this. Maybe, I thought, the girls of Via dei Mille—the one dressed all in green, for example—had a life like this.

Every three or four days Donato Sarratore returned, but stayed at most for twenty-four hours, then left. He said that all he could think of was the thirteenth of August, when he would settle in Barano for two full weeks. As soon as his father appeared, Nino became a shadow. He ate, disappeared, reappeared late at night, and didn't say a single word. He listened to him with a compliant sort of half smile, and whatever his father uttered he gave no sign of agreement but neither did he oppose it. The only time he said something definite and explicit was when Donato mentioned the longed-for thirteenth of August. Then, a moment later, he reminded his mother—his mother, not Donato—that right after the mid-August holiday he had to return to Naples because he had arranged with some school friends to meet—they planned to get together in a country house in the Avellinese—and begin their summer homework. "It's a lie," Marisa whispered to me, "he has no homework." But his mother praised him, and even his father. In fact, Donato started off right away on one of his favorite topics: Nino was fortunate to be able to study; he himself had barely finished the second year of vocational school when he had had to go to work, but if he had been able to study as his son was doing, who knows where he might have gone. And he concluded, "Study, Ninù, go on, make Papa proud, and do what I was unable to do."

That tone bothered Nino more than anything else. Sometimes, just to get away, he went so far as to invite Marisa and me to go out with him. He would say gloomily to his parents, as if we had been tormenting him, "They want to get an ice cream, they want to go for a little walk, I'll take them."

Marisa hurried eagerly to get ready and I regretted that I always had the same shabby old dress. But it seemed to me that he didn't much care if I was pretty or ugly. As soon as we left the house he started talking, which made Marisa uncomfortable, she said it would have been better for her to stay home. I, however, hung on Nino's every word. It greatly astonished me that, in the tumult of the Port, among the young and not so young men who looked at Marisa and me purposefully, he showed not a trace of that disposition to violence that Pasquale, Rino, Antonio, Enzo showed when they went out with us and someone gave us one glance too many. As an intimidating guardian of our bodies he had little value. Maybe because he was engrossed in the things that were going on in his head, by an eagerness to talk to me about them, he would let anything happen to us.

That was how Marisa made friends with some boys from Forio, they came to see her at Barano, and she brought them with us to the beach at the Maronti. And so the three of us began to go out every evening. We all went to the Port, but once we arrived she went off with her new friends (when in the world would Pasquale have been so free with Carmela, Antonio with Ada?) and we walked along the sea. Then we met her around ten and returned home.

One evening, as soon as we were alone, Nino said suddenly that as a boy he had greatly envied the relationship between Lila and me. He saw us from a distance, always together, always talking, and he would have liked to be friends with us, but never had the courage. Then he smiled and said, "You remember the declaration I made to you?"

"Yes."

"I liked you a lot."

I blushed, I whispered stupidly, "Thank you."

"I thought we would become engaged and we would all three be together forever, you, me, and your friend."

"Together?"

He smiled at himself as a child.

"I didn't understand anything about engagements."

Then he asked me about Lila.

"Did she go on studying?"

"No."

"What does she do?"

"She helps her parents."

"She was so smart, you couldn't keep up with her, she made my head a blur."

He said it just that way—*she made my head a blur*—and if at first I had been a little disappointed because he had said that his declaration of love had been only an attempt to introduce himself into my and Lila's relationship, this time I suffered in an obvious way, I felt a real pain in my chest.

"She's not like that anymore," I said. "She's changed."

And I felt an urge to add, "Have you heard how the teachers at school talk about me?" Luckily I managed to restrain myself. But, after that conversation, I stopped writing to Lila:

I had trouble telling her what was happening to me, and anyway she wouldn't answer. I devoted myself instead to taking care of Nino. I knew that he woke up late and I invented excuses of every sort not to have breakfast with the others. I waited for him, I went to the beach with him, I got his things ready, I carried them, we went swimming together. But when he went out to sea I didn't feel able to follow, I returned to the shoreline to watch apprehensively the wake he left, the dark speck of his head. I became anxious if I lost him, I was happy when I saw him return. In other words I loved him and knew it and was content to love him.

But meanwhile the mid-August holiday approached. One evening I told him that I didn't want to go to the Port, I would rather walk to the Maronti, there was a full moon. I hoped that he would come with me, rather than take his sister, who was eager to go to the Port, where by now she had a sort of boyfriend with whom, she told me, she exchanged kisses and embraces, betraying the boyfriend in Naples. Instead he went with Marisa. As a matter of principle, I set out on the rocky road that led to the beach. The sand was cold, gray-black in the moonlight, the sea scarcely breathed. There was not a living soul and I began to weep with loneliness. What was I, who was I? I felt pretty again, my pimples were gone, the sun and the sea had made me slimmer, and yet the person I liked and whom I wished to be liked by showed no interest in me. What signs did I carry, what fate? I thought of the neighborhood as of a whirlpool from which any attempt at escape was an illusion. Then I heard the rustle of sand, I turned, I saw the shadow of Nino. He sat down beside me. He had to go back and get his sister in an hour. I felt he was nervous, he was hitting the sand with the heel of his left foot. He didn't talk about books, he began suddenly speaking of his father.

"I will devote my life," he said, as if he were speaking of a mission, "to trying not to resemble him."

"He's a nice man."

"Everyone says that."

"And so?"

He had a sarcastic expression that for a few seconds made him ugly.

"How is Melina?"

I looked at him in astonishment. I had been very careful never to mention Melina in those days of intense conversation, and here he was talking about her.

"All right."

"He was her lover. He knew perfectly well that she was a fragile woman, but he took her just the same, out of pure vanity. Out of vanity he would hurt anyone and never feel responsible. Since he is convinced that he makes everyone happy, he thinks that everything is forgiven him. He goes to Mass every Sunday. He treats us children with respect. He is always considerate of my mother. But he betrays her continually. He's a hypocrite, he makes me sick."

I didn't know what to say. In the neighborhood terrible things could happen, fathers and sons often came to blows, like Rino and Fernando, for example. But the violence of those few carefully constructed sentences hurt me. Nino hated his father with all his strength, that was why he talked so much about the Karamazovs. But that wasn't the point. What disturbed me profoundly was that Donato Sarratore, as far as I had seen with my own eyes, heard with my own ears, was not repellent, he was the father that every girl, every boy should want, and Marisa in fact adored him. Besides, if his sin was the capacity to love, I didn't see anything particularly evil, even of my father my mother would say angrily, Who knows what he had been up to. As a result those lashing phrases, that cutting tone seemed to me terrible. I murmured, "He and Melina were overcome by passion, like Dido and Aeneas. These are things that are hurtful, but also very moving."

"He swore faithfulness to my mother before God," he exclaimed suddenly. "He doesn't respect her or God." And he jumped up in agitation, his eyes were beautiful, shining. "Not even you understand me," he said, walking off with long strides.

I caught up to him, my heart pounding.

"I understand you," I murmured, and cautiously took his arm.

We had scarcely touched, the contact burned my fingers, I immediately let go. He bent over and kissed me on the lips, a very light kiss.

"I'm leaving tomorrow," he said.

"But the thirteenth is the day after tomorrow."

He didn't answer. We went back to Barano speaking of books, then we went to get Marisa at the Port. I felt his mouth on mine.

33.

I cried all night, in the silent kitchen. I fell asleep at dawn. Nella came to wake me and reproached me, she said that Nino had wanted to have breakfast on the terrace in order not to disturb me. He had left.

I dressed in a hurry, and she saw that I was suffering. "Go on," she yielded, finally, "maybe you'll be in time." I ran to the Port hoping to get there before the ferry left, but the boat was already out at sea.

Some difficult days passed. Cleaning the rooms I found a blue paper bookmark that belonged to Nino and I hid it among my things. At night, in my bed in the kitchen, I sniffed it, kissed it, licked it with the tip of my tongue and cried. My own desperate passion moved me and my weeping fed on itself.

Then Donato Sarratore arrived for his two-week holiday. He was sorry that his son had left, but pleased that he had joined his schoolmates in the Avellinese to study. "He's a truly serious boy," he said to me, "like you. I'm proud of him, as I imagine your father must be proud of you."

The presence of that reassuring man calmed me. He wanted to meet Marisa's new friends, he invited them one evening to have a big bonfire on the beach. He himself gathered all the wood he could find and piled it up, and he stayed with us until late. The boy with whom Marisa was carrying on a half-steady relationship strummed a guitar and Donato sang, he had a beautiful voice. Then, late at night, he himself began to play and he played well, he improvised dance tunes. Some began to dance, Marisa first.

I looked at that man and thought: he and his son have not even a feature in common. Nino is tall, he has a delicate face, the forehead buried under black hair, the mouth always half-closed, with inviting lips; Donato instead is of average height, his features are pronounced, he has a receding hairline, his mouth is compact, almost without lips. Nino has brooding eyes that see beyond things and persons and seem to be frightened; Donato has a gaze that is always receptive, that adores the appearance of every thing or person and is always smiling on them. Nino has something that's eating him inside, like Lila, and it's a gift and a suffering; they aren't content, they never give in, they fear what is happening around them; this man, no, he appears to love every manifestation of life, as if every lived second had an absolute clarity.

From that evening on, Nino's father seemed to me a solid remedy not only against the darkness into which his son had driven me, departing after an almost imperceptible kiss, but also—I realized with amazement—against the darkness into which Lila had driven me by never responding to my letters. She and Nino scarcely know each other, I thought, they have never been friends, and yet now they seem to me very similar: they have no need of anything or anyone, and they always know what's right and what isn't. But if they're wrong? What is especially terrible about Marcello Solara, what is especially terrible about Donato Sarratore? I didn't understand. I loved both Lila and Nino, and now in a different way I missed them, but I was grateful to that hated father, who made me, and all us children, important, who gave us joy and peace that night at the Maronti. Suddenly I was glad that neither of the two was present on the island.

I began reading again, I wrote a last letter to Lila, in which I said that, since she hadn't ever answered me, I wouldn't write anymore. I bound myself instead to the Sarratore family, I felt I was the sister of Marisa, Pinuccio, and little Ciro, who now loved me tremendously and with me, only with me, wasn't naughty but played happily; we went looking for shells together. Lidia, whose hostility had conclusively turned into sympathy and fondness, often praised me for the precision that I put into everything: setting the table, cleaning the rooms, washing the dishes, entertaining the baby, reading and studying. One morning she made me try on a sundress that was too tight for her, and, since Nella and even Sarratore, called urgently to give an opinion, thought it very becoming, she gave it to me. At certain moments she even seemed to prefer me to Marisa. She said, "She's lazy and vain, I brought her up badly, she doesn't study; whereas you are so sensible about everything." "Just like Nino," she added once, "except that you're sunny and he is always irritable." But Donato, hearing those criticisms, responded sharply, and began to praise his oldest son. "He's as good as gold," he said, and with a look asked me for confirmation and I nodded yes with great conviction.

After his long swims Donato lay beside me to dry in the sun and read his newspaper, *Roma*, the only thing he read. I was struck by the fact that someone who wrote poems, who had even collected them in a volume, never opened a book. He hadn't brought any with him and was never curious about mine. At times he read aloud to me some passage from an article, words and sentiments that would have made Pasquale extremely angry and certainly Professor Galiani, too. But I was silent, I didn't feel like arguing with such a kind and courteous person, and spoiling the great esteem he had for me. Once he read me an entire article, from beginning to end, and every two lines he turned to Lidia smiling, and Lidia responded with a complicit smile. At the end he asked me, "Did you like it?"

It was an article on the speed of train travel as opposed to the speed of travel in the past, by horse carriage or on foot, along country lanes. It was written in high-flown sentences that he read with great feeling.

"Yes, very much," I said.

"See who wrote it: what do you read here?"

He held it out toward me, put the paper under my eyes. With emotion, I read: "Donato Sarratore."

Lidia burst out laughing and so did he. They left me on the beach to keep an eye on Ciro while they swam in their usual way, staying close to each other and whispering. I looked at them, I thought, Poor Melina, but without bitterness toward Sarratore. Assuming that Nino was right and that there really had been something between the two of them; assuming, in other words, that Sarratore really had betrayed Lidia, now, even more than before—now that I knew him somewhat—I couldn't feel that he was guilty, especially since it seemed to me that not even his wife felt he was guilty, although at the time she had compelled him to leave the neighborhood. As for Melina, I understood her, too. She had felt the joy of love for that so far from ordinary man—a conductor on the railroad but also a poet, a journalist—and her fragile mind had been unable to readjust to the rough normality of life without him. I was satisfied with these thoughts. I was pleased with everything, in those days, with my love for Nino, with my sadness, with the affection that I felt surrounded by, with my own capacity to read, think, reflect in solitude.

34.

Then, at the end of August, when that extraordinary period was about to come to an end, two important things happened, suddenly, on the same day. It was the twenty-fifth, I remember with precision because my birthday fell on that day. I got up, I prepared breakfast for everyone, at the table I said, "Today I'm fifteen," and as I said it I remembered that Lila had turned fifteen on the eleventh, but, in the grip of so many emotions, I hadn't remembered. Although customarily it was the saint's day that was celebrated—birthdays were considered irrelevant at the time—the Sarratores and Nella insisted on having a party, in the evening. I was pleased. They went to get ready for the beach, I began to clear the table, when the postman arrived.

I stuck my head out the window, the postman said there was a letter for Greco. I ran down with my heart pounding. I ruled out the possibility that my parents had written to me. Was it a letter from Lila, from Nino? It was from Lila. I tore open the envelope. There were five closely written pages, and I devoured them, but I understood almost nothing of what I read. It may seem strange today, and yet it really was so: even before I was overwhelmed by the contents, what struck me was that the writing contained Lila's voice. Not only that. From the first lines I thought of *The Blue Fairy*, the only text of hers that I had read, apart from our elementary-school homework, and I understood what, at the time, I had liked so much. There was, in *The Blue Fairy*, the same quality that struck me now: Lila was able to speak through writing; unlike me when I wrote, unlike Sarratore in his articles and poems, unlike even many writers I had read and was reading, she expressed herself in sentences that were well constructed, and without error, even though she had stopped going to school, but—further—she left no trace of effort, you weren't aware of the artifice of the written word. I read and I saw her, I heard her. The voice set in the writing overwhelmed me, enthralled me even more than when we talked face to face: it was completely cleansed of the dross of speech, of the confusion of the oral; it had the vivid orderliness that I imagined would belong to conversation if one were so fortunate as to be born from the head of Zeus and not from the Grecos, the Cerullos. I was ashamed of the childish pages I had written to her, the overwrought tone, the frivolity, the false cheer, the false grief. Who knows what Lila had thought of me. I felt contempt and bitterness toward Professor Gerace, who had deluded me by giving me a nine in Italian. The first effect of that letter was to make me feel, at the age of fifteen, on the day of my birthday, a fraud. School, with me, had made a mistake and proof was there, in Lila's letter.

Then, slowly, the contents reached me as well. Lila sent me good wishes for my birthday. She hadn't written because she was pleased that I was having fun in the sun, that I was comfortable with the Sarratores, that I loved Nino, that I liked Ischia so much, the beach of the Maronti, and she didn't want to spoil my vacation with her terrible stories. But now she had felt an urge to break the silence. Immediately after my departure Marcello Solara, with the consent of Fernando, had begun to appear at dinner every night. He came at eight-thirty and left exactly at ten-thirty. He always brought something: pastries, chocolates, sugar, coffee. She didn't touch anything, she kept him at a distance, he looked at her in silence. After the first week of that torture, since Lila acted as if he weren't there, he had decided to surprise her. He showed up in the morning with a big fellow, all sweaty, who deposited in the dining room an enormous cardboard box. Out of the box emerged an object that we all knew

228 · ELENA FERRANTE

about but that very few in the neighborhood had in their house: a television, an apparatus, that is, with a screen on which one saw images, just as at the cinema, but the images came not from a projector but rather from the air, and inside the apparatus was a mysterious tube that was called a cathode. Because of that tube, mentioned continuously by the large sweaty man, the machine hadn't worked for days. Then, after various attempts, it had started, and now half the neighborhood, including my mother, my father, and my sister and brothers, came to the Cerullo house to see the miracle. Not Rino. He was better, the fever had definitely gone, but he no longer spoke to Marcello. When Marcello showed up, he began to disparage the television and after a while he either went to bed without eating or went out and wandered around with Pasquale and Antonio until late at night. Lila said that she herself loved the television. She especially liked to watch it with Melina, who came every night and sat silently for a long time, completely absorbed. It was the only moment of peace. Otherwise, everyone's anger was unloaded on her: her brother's anger because she had abandoned him to his fate as the slave of their father while she set off on a marriage that would make her a lady; the anger of Fernando and Nunzia because she was not nice to Solara but, rather, treated him like dirt; finally the anger of Marcello, who, although she hadn't accepted him, felt increasingly that he was her fiancé, in fact her master, and tended to pass from silent devotion to attempts to kiss her, to suspicious questions about where she went during the day, whom she saw, if she had had other boyfriends, if she had even just touched anyone. Since she wouldn't answer, or, worse still, teased him by telling him of kisses and embraces with nonexistent boyfriends, he one evening had whispered to her seriously, "You tease me, but remember when you threatened me with the knife? Well, if I find out that you like someone else, remember, I won't merely threaten you, I'll kill you." So she didn't know how to get out of this situation and she still carried her weapon, just in case. But she was terrified. She wrote, in the last pages, of feeling all the evil of the neighborhood around her. Rather, she wrote obscurely, good and evil are mixed together and reinforce each other in turn. Marcello, if you thought about it, was really a good arrangement, but the good tasted of the bad and the bad tasted of the good, it was a mixture that took your breath away. A few evenings earlier, something had happened that had really scared her. Marcello had left, the television was off, the house was empty, Rino was out, her parents were going to bed. She was alone in the kitchen washing the dishes and was tired, really without energy, when there was an explosion. She had turned suddenly and realized that the big copper pot had exploded. Like that, by itself. It was hanging on the nail where it normally hung, but in the middle there was a large hole and the rim was lifted and twisted and the pot itself was all deformed, as if it could no longer maintain its appearance as a pot. Her mother had hurried in in her nightgown and had blamed her for dropping it and ruining it. But a copper pot, even if you drop it, doesn't break and doesn't become mis-shapen like that. "It's this sort of thing," Lila concluded, "that frightens me. More than Marcello, more than anyone. And I feel that I have to find a solution, otherwise, everything, one thing after another, will break, everything, everything." She sent me many more good wishes, and, even if she wished the opposite, even if she couldn't wait to see me, even if she urgently needed my help, she hoped I would stay in Ischia with kind Signora Nella and never return to the neighborhood again.

35.

This letter disturbed me greatly. Lila's world, as usual, rapidly superimposed itself on mine. Everything that I had written in July and August seemed to me trivial, I was seized by a frenzy to redeem myself. I didn't go to the beach, I tried immediately to answer her with a serious letter, one that had the essential, pure yet colloquial tone of hers. But if the other letters had come easily to me—I dashed off pages and pages in a few minutes, without ever correcting—this I wrote, rewrote, rewrote again, and yet Nino's hatred of his father, the role that the affair of Melina had had in the origin of that ugly sentiment, my entire relationship with the Sarratore family, even my anxiety about what was happening to her, came out badly. Donato, who in reality was a remarkable man, on the page became a banal family man; and, as far as Marcello was concerned, I was capable only of superficial advice. In the end all that seemed true was my disappointment that she had a television at home and I didn't.

In other words I couldn't answer her, even though I deprived myself of the sea, the sun, the pleasure of being with Ciro, with Pino, with Clelia, with Lidia, with Marisa, with Sarratore. Thankfully Nella, at some point, came to keep me company on the terrace, bringing me an *orzata*. And when the Sarratores came back from the beach, they were sorry that I had stayed home and began celebrating me again. Lidia herself wanted to make a cake filled with pastry cream, Nella opened a bottle of vermouth, Donato Sarratore began singing Neapolitan songs, Marisa gave me an oakum seahorse she had bought at the Port the night before.

I grew calmer, yet I couldn't get out of my mind Lila in trouble while I was so well, so celebrated. I said, in a slightly dramatic way, that I had received a letter from a friend, that my friend needed me, and so I was thinking of leaving before the appointed time. "The day after tomorrow at the latest," I announced, but without really believing it. In fact I said it only to hear Nella say how sorry she was, Lidia how Ciro would suffer, Marisa how desperate she would be, and Sarratore exclaim sadly, "How will we manage without you?" All this moved me, making my birthday even happier.

Then Pino and Ciro began to nod and Lidia and Donato took them to bed. Marisa helped me wash the dishes, Nella said that if I wanted to sleep a little later in the morning she would get up to make breakfast. I protested, that was my job. One by one, they withdrew, and I was alone. I made my bed in the usual corner, I looked around to see if there were cockroaches, if there were mosquitoes. My gaze fell on the copper pots.

How evocative Lila's writing was; I looked at the pots with increasing distress. I remembered that she had always liked their brilliance, when she washed them she took great care in polishing them. On them, not coincidentally, four years earlier, she had placed the blood that spurted from the neck of Don Achille when he was stabbed. On them now she had deposited that sensation of threat, the anguish over the difficult choice she had, making one of them explode like a sign, as if its shape had decided abruptly to cede. Would I know how to imagine those things without her? Would I know how to give life to every object, let it bend in unison with mine? I turned off the light. I got undressed and got in bed with Lila's letter and Nino's blue bookmark, which seemed to me at that moment the most precious things that I possessed.

From the window the white light of the moon rained down. I kissed the bookmark as I did every night, I tried to reread my friend's letter in the weak glow. The pots shone, the table creaked, the ceiling weighed oppressively, the night air and the sea pressed on the walls. Again I felt humbled by Lila's ability to write, by what she was able to give form to and I was not, my eyes misted. I was happy, yes, that she was so good even without school, without books from the library, but that happiness made me guiltily unhappy.

Then I heard footsteps. I saw the shadow of Sarratore enter the kitchen, barefoot, in blue pajamas. I pulled up the sheet. He went to the tap, he took a glass of water, drank. He remained standing for a few seconds in front of the sink, put down the glass, moved toward my bed. He squatted beside me, his elbows resting on the edge of the sheet.

"I know you're awake," he said.

"Yes."

"Don't think of your friend, stay."

"She's in trouble, she needs me."

"It's I who need you," he said, and he leaned over, kissed me on the mouth without the lightness of his son, half opening my lips with his tongue.

I was immobilized.

He pushed the sheet aside, continuing to kiss me with care, with passion, and he sought my breast with his hand, he caressed me under the nightgown. Then he let go, descended between my legs, pressed two fingers hard over my under-pants. I said, did nothing, I was terrified by that behavior, by the horror it created, by the pleasure that I nevertheless felt. His mustache pricked my upper lip, his tongue was rough. Slowly he left my mouth, took away his hand.

"Tomorrow night we'll take a nice walk, you and I, on the beach," he said, a little hoarsely. "I love you and I know that you love me very much. Isn't it true?"

I said nothing. He brushed my lips again with his, mur-mured good night, got up and left the kitchen. I didn't move, I don't know for how long. However I tried to distance the sensation of his tongue, his caresses, the pressure of his hand, I couldn't. Nino had wanted to warn me, did he know what would happen? I felt an uncontainable hatred for Donato Sarratore and disgust for myself, for the pleasure that lingered in my body. However unlikely it may seem today, as long as I could remember until that night I had never given myself pleasure, I didn't know about it, to feel it surprised me. I remained in the same position for many hours. Then, at first light, I shook myself, collected all my things, took apart the bed, wrote two lines of thanks to Nella, and left.

The island was almost noiseless, the sea still, only the smells were intense. Using the money that my mother had left me more than a month before, I took the first departing ferry. As soon as the boat moved and the island, with its tender early-morning colors, was distant enough, I thought that I finally had a story to tell that Lila could not match. But I knew immediately that the disgust I felt for Sarratore and the revulsion that I had toward myself would keep me from saying anything. In fact this is the first time I've sought words for that unexpected end to my vacation.

36.

I found Naples submerged in a stinking, devastating heat. My mother, without saying a word about how I had changed—the acne gone, my skin sun-darkened—reproached me because I had returned before the appointed time.

"What have you done," she said, "you've behaved rudely, did the teacher's friend throw you out?"

It was different with my father, whose eyes shone and who showered me with compliments, the most conspicuous of which, repeated a hundred times, was: "Christ, what a pretty daughter I have." As for my siblings, they said with a certain contempt, "You look like a negro."

I looked at myself in the mirror and I also marveled: the sun had made me a shining blonde, but my face, my arms, my legs were as if painted with dark gold. As long as I had been immersed in the colors of Ischia, amid sunburned faces, my transformation had seemed suitable; now, restored to the context of the neighborhood, where every face, every street had a sick pallor, it seemed to me excessive, anomalous. The people, the buildings, the dusty, busy *stradone* had the appearance of a poorly printed photograph, like the ones in the newspapers.

As soon as I could I hurried to find Lila. I called her from the courtyard, she looked out, emerged from the doorway. She hugged me, kissed me, gave me compliments, so that I was overwhelmed by all that explicit affection. She was the same and yet, in little more than a month, she had changed further. She seemed no longer a girl but a woman, a woman of at least eighteen, an age that then seemed to me advanced. Her old clothes were short and tight, as if she had grown inside them in the space of a few minutes, and they hugged her body more than they should. She was even taller, more developed, her back was straight. And the pale face above her slender neck seemed to me to have a delicate, unusual beauty.

She seemed nervous, she kept looking around on the street, behind her, but she didn't explain. She said only, "Come with me," and wanted me to go with her to Stefano's grocery. She added, taking my arm, "It's something I can only do with you, thank goodness you've come back. I thought I'd have to wait till September."

We had never walked those streets toward the public gardens so close to one another, so together, so happy to see each other. She told me that things were getting worse every day. Just the night before Marcello had arrived with sweets and spumante and had given her a ring studded with diamonds. She had accepted it, had put it on her finger to avoid trouble in the presence of her parents, but just before he left, at the door, she had given it back to him rudely. Marcello had protested, he had threatened her, as he now did more and more often, then had burst into tears. Fernando and Nunzia had immediately realized that something was wrong. Her mother had grown very fond of Marcello, she liked the good things he brought to the house every night, she was proud of being the owner of a television; and Fernando felt as if he had stopped suffering, because, thanks to a close relationship with the Solaras, he could look to the future without anxieties.

Thus, as soon as Marcello left, both had harassed her more than usual to find out what was happening. Result: for the first time in a long, long time, Rino had defended her, had insisted that if his sister didn't want a halfwit like Marcello, it was her sacrosanct right to refuse him and that, if they insisted on giving him to her, he, in person, would burn down everything, the house and the shoemaker's shop and himself and the entire family. Father and son had started fighting, Nunzia had got involved, all the neighbors had woken up. Not only: Rino had thrown himself on the bed in distress, had abruptly fallen asleep, and an hour later had had another episode of sleepwalking. They had found him in the kitchen lighting matches, and passing them in front of the gas valve as if to check for leaks. Nunzia, terrified, had wakened Lila, saying, "Rino really does want to burn us all alive," and Lila had hurried in and reassured her mother: Rino was sleeping, and in sleep, unlike when he was awake, he wanted to make sure that there was no gas escaping. She had taken him back to bed.

"I can't bear it anymore," she concluded, "you don't know what torture this is, I have to get out of this situation."

She clung to me as if I could give her the energy.

"You're well," she said, "everything's going well for you: you have to help me."

I answered that she could count on me for everything and she seemed relieved, she squeezed my arm, whispered, "Look."

I saw in the distance a sort of red spot that radiated light.

"What is it?"

"Don't you see?"

I couldn't see clearly.

"It's Stefano's new car."

We walked to where the car was parked, in front of the grocery store, which had been enlarged, had two entrances now, and was extremely crowded. The customers, waiting to be served, threw admiring glances at that symbol of well-being and prestige: a car like that had never been seen in the neighborhood, all glass and metal, with a roof that opened. A car for wealthy people, nothing like the Solaras' 1100.

I wandered around it while Lila stood in the shadows and surveyed the street as if she expected violence to erupt at any moment. Stefano looked out from the doorway of the grocery, in his greasy apron, his large head and his high forehead giving a not unpleasant sense of disproportion. He crossed the street, greeted me cordially, said, "How well you look, like an actress."

He, too, looked well: he had been in the sun as I had, maybe we were the only ones in the whole neighborhood who appeared so healthy. I said to him:

"You're very dark."

"I took a week's vacation."

"Where?"

"In Ischia."

"I was in Ischia, too."

"I know, Lina told me: I looked for you but didn't see you."

I pointed to the car. "It's beautiful."

Stefano's face wore an expression of moderate agreement. He said, indicating Lila, with laughing eyes: "I bought it for your friend, but she won't believe it." I looked at Lila, who was standing in the shadows, her expression serious, tense. Stefano said to her, vaguely ironic, "Now Lenuccia's back, what are you doing?"

Lila said, as if the thing annoyed her, "Let's go. But remember, you invited her, not me: I only came along with the two of you."

He smiled and went back into the shop.

"What's happening?" I asked her, confused.

"I don't know," she said, and meant that she didn't know exactly what she was getting into. She looked the way she did when she had to do a difficult calculation in her head, but without her usual impudent expression; she was visibly preoccupied, as if she were attempting an experiment with an uncertain result. "It all began," she said, "with the arrival of that car." Stefano, first as if joking, then with increasing seriousness, had sworn to her that he had bought the car for her, for the pleasure of opening the door and having her get in at least once. "It was made just for you," he had said. And since it had been delivered, at the end of July, he had been asking her constantly, not in an aggressive way, but politely, first to take a drive with him and Alfonso, then with him and Pinuccia, then even with him and his mother. But she had always said no. Finally she had promised him, "I'll go when Lenuccia comes back from Ischia." And now we were there, and what was to happen would happen.

"But he knows about Marcello?"

"Of course he knows."

"And so?"

"So he insists."

"I'm scared, Lila."

"Do you remember how many things we've done that scared you? I waited for you on purpose."

Stefano returned without his apron, dark eyes, dark face, shining black eyes, white shirt and dark pants. He opened the car door, sat behind the wheel, put the top down. I was about to get into the narrow back space but Lila stopped me, she settled herself in the back. I sat uneasily next to Stefano, he started off immediately, heading toward the new buildings.

The heat dissipated in the wind. I felt good, intoxicated by the speed and by the tranquil certainties released by Carracci's body. It seemed to me that Lila had explained everything without explaining anything. There was, yes, this brand-new sports car that had been bought solely to take her for a ride that had just begun. There was, yes, that young man who, though he

knew about Marcello Solara, was violating men's rules of masculinity without any visible anxiety. There was me, yes,
dragged furiously into that business to hide by my presence
secret words between them, maybe even a friendship. But what
type of friendship? Certainly, with that drive, something significant was happening, and yet Lila had been unable or
unwilling to provide me with the elements necessary for understanding. What did she have in mind? She had to know that
she was setting in motion an earthquake worse than when she
threw the ink-soaked bits of paper. And yet it might be that she
wasn't aiming at anything precise. She was like that, she threw
things off balance just to see if she could put them back in
some other way. So here we were racing along, hair blowing in
the wind, Stefano driving with satisfied skill, I sitting beside
him as if I were his girlfriend. I thought of how he had looked
at me, when he said I looked like an actress. I thought of the
possibility of him liking me more than he now liked my friend.
I thought with horror of the idea that Marcello Solara might
shoot him. His beautiful person with its confident gestures
would lose substance like the copper of the pot that Lila had
written about.

We were driving among the new buildings in order to avoid
passing the Bar Solara.

"I don't care if Marcello sees us," Stefano said without
emphasis, "but if it matters to you it's fine like this."'

We went through the tunnel, we turned toward the Marina.
It was the road that Lila and I had taken many years earlier,
when we had gotten caught in the rain. I mentioned that
episode, she smiled, Stefano wanted us to tell him about it. We
told him everything, it was fun, and meanwhile we arrived at
the Granili.

"What do you think, fast, isn't it?"

"Incredibly fast," I said, enthusiastically.

Lila made no comment. She looked around, at times she

touched my shoulder to point out the houses, the ragged poverty along the street, as if she saw a confirmation of something and I was supposed to understand it right away. Then she asked Stefano, seriously, without preamble, "Are you really different?"

He looked at her in the rearview mirror. "From whom?"

"You know."

He didn't answer immediately. Then he said in dialect, "Do you want me to tell you the truth?"

"Yes."

"The intention is there, but I don't know how it will end up."

At that point I was sure that Lila must not have told me quite a few things. That allusive tone was evidence that they were close, that they had talked other times and not in jest but seriously. What had I missed in the period of Ischia? I turned to look at her, she delayed replying, I thought that Stefano's answer had made her nervous because of its vagueness. I saw her flooded by sunlight, eyes half closed, her shirt swelled by her breast and by the wind.

"The poverty here is worse than among us," she said. And then, without connection, laughing, "Don't think I've forgotten about when you wanted to prick my tongue."

Stefano nodded.

"That was another era," he said.

"Once a coward, always a coward—you were twice as big as me."

He gave a small, embarrassed smile and, without answering, accelerated in the direction of the port. The drive lasted less than half an hour, we went back on the Rettifilo and Piazza Garibaldi.

"Your brother isn't well," Stefano said when we had returned to the outskirts of the neighborhood. He looked at her again in the mirror and asked, "Are those shoes displayed in the window the ones you made?"

"What do you know about the shoes?"

"It's all Rino talks about."

"And so?"

"They're very beautiful."

She narrowed her eyes, squeezed them almost until they were closed.

"Buy them," she said in her provocative tone.

"How much will you sell them for?"

"Talk to my father."

Stefano made a decisive U turn that threw me against the door, we turned onto the street where the shoe repair shop was.

"What are you doing?" Lila asked, alarmed now.

"You said to buy them and I'm going to buy them."

37.

He stopped the car in front of the shoemaker's shop, came around and opened the door for me, gave me his hand to help me out. He didn't concern himself with Lila, who got out herself and stayed behind. He and I stopped in front of the window, under the eyes of Fernando and Rino, who looked at us from inside the shop with sullen curiosity.

When Lila joined us Stefano opened the door of the shop, let me go first, went in without making way for her. He was very courteous with father and son, and asked if he could see the shoes. Rino rushed to get them, and Stefano examined them, praised them: "They're light and yet strong, they really have a nice line." He asked me, "What do you think, Lenù?"

I said, with great embarrassment, "They're very handsome."

He turned to Fernando: "Your daughter said that all three of you worked on them and that you have a plan to make others, for women as well."

"Yes," said Rino, looking in wonder at his sister.

"Yes," said Fernando, puzzled, "but not right away."

Rino said to his sister, a little worked up, because he was afraid she would refuse, "Show him the designs."

Lila, continuing to surprise him, didn't resist. She went to the back of the shop and returned, handing the sheets of paper to her brother, who gave them to Stefano. They were the models that she had designed almost two years earlier.

Stefano showed me a drawing of a pair of women's shoes with a very high heel.

"Would you buy them?"

"Yes."

He went back to examining the designs. Then he sat down on a stool, took off his right shoe.

"What size is it?"

"43, but it could be a 44," Rino lied.

Lila, surprising us again, knelt in front of Stefano and using the shoehorn helped him slip his foot into the new shoe. Then she took off the other shoe and did the same.

Stefano, who until that moment had been playing the part of the practical, businesslike man, was obviously disturbed. He waited for Lila to get up, and remained seated for some seconds as if to catch his breath. Then he stood, took a few steps.

"They're tight," he said.

Rino turned gray, disappointed.

"We can put them on the machine and widen them," Fernando interrupted, but uncertainly.

Stefano turned to me and asked, "How do they look?"

"Nice," I said.

"Then I'll take them."

Fernando remained impassive, Rino brightened.

"You know, Ste', these are an exclusive Cerullo design, they'll be expensive."

Stefano smiled, took an affectionate tone: "And if they

weren't an exclusive Cerullo design, do you think I would buy them? When will they be ready?"

Rino looked at his father, radiant.

"We'll keep them in the machine for at least three days," Fernando said, but it was clear that he could have said ten days, twenty, a month, he was so eager to take his time in the face of this unexpected novelty.

"Good: you think of a friendly price and I'll come in three days to pick them up."

He folded the pieces of paper with the designs and put them in his pocket before our puzzled eyes. Then he shook hands with Fernando, with Rino, and headed toward the door.

"The drawings," Lila said coldly.

"Can I bring them back in three days?" Stefano asked in a cordial tone, and without waiting for an answer opened the door. He made way for me to pass and went out after me.

I was already settled in the car next to him when Lila joined us. She was angry.

"You think my father is a fool, that my brother is a fool?"

"What do you mean?"

"If you think you'll make fools of my family and me, you are mistaken."

"You are insulting me: I'm not Marcello Solara."

"And who are you?"

"A businessman: the shoes you've designed are unusual. And I don't mean just the ones I bought, I mean all of them."

"So?"

"So let me think and we'll see each other in three days."

Lila stared at him as if she wanted to read his mind, she didn't move away from the car. Finally she said something that I would never have had the courage to utter:

"Look, Marcello tried in every possible way to buy me but no one is going to buy me."

Stefano looked her straight in the eyes for a long moment.

"I don't spend a lira if I don't think it can produce a hundred."

He started the engine and we left. Now I was sure: the drive had been a sort of agreement reached at the end of many encounters, much talk. I said weakly, in Italian, "Please, Stefano, leave me at the corner? If my mother sees me in a car with you she'll bash my face in."

38.

Lila's life changed decisively during that month of September. It wasn't easy, but it changed. As for me, I had returned from Ischia in love with Nino, branded by the lips and hands of his father, sure that I would weep night and day because of the mixture of happiness and horror I felt inside. Instead I made no attempt to find a form for my emotions, in a few hours everything was reduced. I put aside Nino's voice, the irritation of his father's mustache. The island faded, lost itself in some secret corner of my head. I made room for what was happening to Lila.

In the three days that followed the astonishing ride in the convertible, she, with the excuse of doing the shopping, went often to Stefano's grocery, but always asked me to go with her. I did it with my heart pounding, frightened by the possible appearance of Marcello, but also pleased with my role as confidante generous with advice, as accomplice in weaving plots, as apparent object of Stefano's attentions. We were girls, even if we imagined ourselves wickedly daring. We embroidered on the facts—Marcello, Stefano, the shoes—with our usual eagerness and it seemed to us that we always knew how to make things come out right. "I'll say this to him," she hypothesized, and I would suggest a small variation: "No, say this." Then she and Stefano would be deep in conversation in a corner behind

244 · ELENA FERRANTE

the counter, while Alfonso exchanged a few words with me, Pinuccia, annoyed, waited on the customers, and Maria, at the cash register, observed her older son apprehensively, because he had been neglecting the job lately, and was feeding the gossip of the neighbors.

Naturally we were improvising. In the course of that back and forth I tried to understand what was really going through Lila's head, so as to be in tune with her goals. At first I had the impression that she intended simply to enable her father and brother to earn some money by selling Stefano, for a good price, the only pair of shoes produced by the Cerullos, but soon it seemed to me that her principal aim was to get rid of Marcello by making use of the young grocer. In this sense, she was decisive when I asked her:

"Which of the two do you like more?"

She shrugged.

"I've never liked Marcello, he makes me sick."

"You would become engaged to Stefano just to get Marcello out of your house?"

She thought for a moment and said yes.

From then on the ultimate goal of all our plotting seemed to us that—to fight by every means possible Marcello's intrusion in her life. The rest came crowding around almost by chance and we merely gave it a rhythm and, at times, a true orchestration. Or so at least we believed. In fact, the person who was acting was only and was always Stefano.

Punctually, three days later, he went to the store and bought the shoes, even though they were tight. The two Cerullos with much hesitation asked for twenty-five thousand lire, but were ready to go down to ten thousand. He didn't bat an eye and put down another twenty thousand in exchange for Lila's drawings, which—he said—he liked, he wanted to frame them.

"Frame?" Rino asked.

"Yes."

"Like a picture by a painter?"

"Yes."

"And you told my sister that you're buying her drawings?"

"Yes."

Stefano didn't stop there. In the following days he again poked his head in at the shop and announced to father and son that he had rented the space adjacent to theirs. "For now it's there," he said, "but if you one day decide to expand, remember that I am at your disposal."

At the Cerullos' they discussed for a long time what that statement meant. "Expand?" Finally Lila, since they couldn't get there on their own, said:

"He's proposing to transform the shoe shop into a workshop for making Cerullo shoes."

"And the money?" Rino asked cautiously.

"He'll invest it."

"He told you?" Fernando, incredulous, was alarmed, immediately followed by Nunzia.

"He told the two of you," Lila said, indicating her father and brother.

"But he knows that handmade shoes are expensive?"

"You showed him."

"And if they don't sell?"

"You've wasted the work and he's wasted the money."

"And that's it?"

"That's it."

The entire family was upset for days. Marcello moved to the background. He arrived at night at eight-thirty and dinner wasn't ready. Often he found himself alone in front of the television with Melina and Ada, while the Cerullos talked in another room.

Naturally the most enthusiastic was Rino, who regained energy, color, good humor, and, as he had been the close friend of the Solaras, so he began to be Stefano's close friend, Alfonso's,

Pinuccia's, even Signora Maria's. When, finally, Fernando's last reservation dissolved, Stefano went to the shop and, after a small discussion, came to a verbal agreement on the basis of which he would put up the expenses and the two Cerullos would start production of the model that Lila and Rino had already made and all the other models, it being understood that they would split the possible profits half and half. He took the documents out of a pocket and showed them to them one after another.

"You'll do this, this, this," he said, "but let's hope that it won't take two years, as I know happened with the other."

"My daughter is a girl," Fernando explained, embarrassed, "and Rino hasn't yet learned the job well."

Stefano shook his head in a friendly way.

"Leave Lina out of it. You'll have to take on some workers."

"And who will pay them?" Fernando asked.

"Me again. You choose two or three, freely, according to your judgment."

Fernando, at the idea of having, no less, employees, turned red and his tongue was loosened, to the evident annoyance of his son. He spoke of how he had learned the trade from his late father. He told of how hard the work was on the machines, in Casoria. He said that his mistake had been to marry Nunzia, who had weak hands and no wish to work, but if he had married Ines, a flame of his youth who had been a great worker, he would in time have had a business all his own, better than Campanile, with a line to display perhaps at the regional trade show. He told us, finally, that he had in his head beautiful shoes, perfect, that if Stefano weren't set on those silly things of Lina's, they could start production now and you know how many they would sell. Stefano listened patiently, but repeated that he, for now, was interested only in having Lila's exact designs made. Rino then took his sister's sheets of paper, examined them carefully, and asked him in a lightly teasing tone:

"When you get them framed where will you hang them?"

"In here."

Rino looked at his father, but he had turned sullen again and said nothing.

"My sister agrees about everything?" he asked.

Stefano smiled: "Who can do anything if your sister doesn't agree?"

He got up, shook Fernando's hand vigorously, and headed toward the door. Rino went with him and, with sudden concern, called to him from the doorway, as Stefano was going to the red convertible:

"The brand of the shoes is Cerullo."

Stefano waved to him, without turning: "A Cerullo invented them and Cerullo they will be called."

39.

That same night Rino, before he went out with Pasquale and Antonio, said, "Marcè, have you seen that car Stefano's got?"

Marcello, stupefied by the television and by sadness, didn't even answer.

Then Rino drew his comb out of his pocket, pulled it through his hair, and said cheerfully: "You know that he bought our shoes for twenty-five thousand lire?"

"You see he's got money to throw away," Marcello answered, and Melina burst out laughing, it wasn't clear if she was reacting to that remark or to what was showing on the television.

From that moment Rino found a way, night after night, to annoy Marcello, and the atmosphere became increasingly tense. Besides, as soon as Solara, who was always greeted kindly by Nunzia, arrived, Lila disappeared, saying she was tired, and went to bed. One night Marcello, very depressed, talked to Nunzia.

"If your daughter goes to bed as soon as I arrive, what am I coming here for?"

Evidently he hoped that she would comfort him, saying something that would encourage him to persevere. But Nunzia didn't know what to say and so he stammered, "Does she like someone else?"

"But no."

"I know she goes to do the shopping at Stefano's."

"And where should she go, my boy, to do the shopping?"

Marcello was silent, eyes lowered.

"She was seen in the car with the grocer."

"Lenuccia was there, too: Stefano is interested in the porter's daughter."

"Lenuccia doesn't seem to me a good companion for your daughter. Tell her not to see her anymore."

I was not a good companion? Lila was not supposed to see me anymore? When my friend reported that request of Marcello's I went over conclusively to Stefano's side and began to praise his tactful ways, his calm determination. "He's rich," I said to her finally. But even as I said that I realized how the idea of the riches girls dreamed of was changing further. The treasure chests full of gold pieces that a procession of servants in livery would deposit in our castle when we published a book like *Little Women*—riches and fame—had truly faded. Perhaps the idea of money as a cement to solidify our existence and prevent it from dissolving, together with the people who were dear to us, endured. But the fundamental feature that now prevailed was concreteness, the daily gesture, the negotiation. This wealth of adolescence proceeded from a fantastic, still childish illumination—the designs for extraordinary shoes—but it was embodied in the petulant dissatisfaction of Rino, who wanted to spend like a big shot, in the television, in the meals, and in the ring with which Marcello wanted to buy a feeling, and, finally, from step to step, in that courteous youth

Stefano, who sold groceries, had a red convertible, spent forty-five thousand lire like nothing, framed drawings, wished to do business in shoes as well as in cheese, invested in leather and a workforce, and seemed convinced that he could inaugurate a new era of peace and well-being for the neighborhood: it was, in short, wealth that existed in the facts of every day, and so was without splendor and without glory.

"He's rich," I heard Lila repeat, and we started laughing. But then she added, "Also nice, also good," and I agreed, these last were qualities that Marcello didn't have, a further reason for being on Stefano's side. Yet those two adjectives confused me, I felt that they gave the final blow to the shine of childish fantasies. No castle, no treasure chest—I seemed to understand—would concern Lila and me alone, intent on writing our *Little Women*. Wealth, incarnated in Stefano, was taking the form of a young man in a greasy apron, was gaining features, smell, voice, was expressing kindness and goodness, was a male we had known forever, the oldest son of Don Achille.

I was disturbed.

"But he wanted to prick your tongue," I said.

"He was a child," she answered, with emotion, sweet as I had never heard her before, so that only at that moment did I realize that she was much farther along than what she had said to me in words.

In the following days everything became clearer. I saw how she talked to Stefano and how he seemed shaped by her voice. I adapted to the pact they were making, I didn't want to be cut out. And we plotted for hours—the two of us, the three of us—to act in a way that would quickly silence people, feelings, the arrangement of things. A worker arrived in the space next to the shoe shop and took down the dividing wall. The shoemaker's shop was reorganized. Three nearly silent apprentices appeared, country boys, from Melito. In one corner they continued to do resoling, in the rest of the space Fernando arranged benches, shelves, his tools, his wooden forms according to the various sizes, and began, with sudden energy, unsuspected in a man so thin, consumed by a bitter discontent, to talk about a course of action.

Just that day, when the new work was about to begin, Stefano showed up. He carried a package done up in brown paper. They all jumped to their feet, even Fernando, as if he had come for an inspection. He opened the package, and inside were a number of small pictures, all the same size, in narrow brown frames. They were Lila's notebook pages, under glass, like precious relics. He asked permission from Fernando to hang them on the walls, Fernando grumbled something, and Stefano had Rino and the apprentices help him put in the nails. When the pictures were hung, Stefano asked the three helpers to go get a coffee and handed them some lire. As soon as he was alone with the shoemaker and his son, he announced quietly that he wanted to marry Lila.

An unbearable silence fell. Rino confined himself to a knowing little smile and Fernando said finally, weakly, "Stefano, Lina is engaged to Marcello Solara."

"Your daughter doesn't know it."

"What do you mean?"

Rino interrupted, cheerfully: "He's telling the truth: you and Mamma let that shit come to our house, but Lina never wanted him and doesn't want him."

Fernando gave his son a stern look. The grocer said gently, looking around: "We've started out on a job now, let's not get worked up. I ask of you a single thing, Don Fernà: let your daughter decide. If she wants Marcello Solara, I will resign myself. I love her so much that if she's happy with someone else I will withdraw and between us everything will remain as it is now. But if she wants me—if she wants me—there's no help for it, you must give her to me."

"You're threatening me," Fernando said, but halfheartedly, in a tone of resigned observation.

"No, I'm asking you to do what's best for your daughter."

"I know what's best for her."

"Yes, but she knows better than you."

And here Stefano got up, opened the door, called me, I was waiting outside with Lila.

"Lenù."

We went in. How we liked feeling that we were at the center of those events, the two of us together, directing them toward their outcome. I remember the extreme tension of that moment. Stefano said to Lila, "I'm saying to you in front of your father: I love you, more than my life. Will you marry me?"

Lila answered seriously, "Yes."

Fernando gasped slightly, then murmured, with the same subservience that in times gone by he had manifested toward Don Achille: "We're offending not only Marcello but all the Solaras. Who's going to tell that poor boy?"

Lila said, "I will."

40.

In fact two nights later, in front of the whole family except Rino, who was out, before they sat down at the table, before the television was turned on, Lila asked Marcello, "Will you take me to get some ice cream?"

Marcello couldn't believe his ears.

"Ice cream? Without eating first? You and me?" And he suddenly asked Nunzia, "Signora, would you come, too?"

Nunzia turned on the television and said, "No, thank you, Marcè. But don't be too long. Ten minutes, you'll go and be back."

"Yes," he promised, happily, "thank you."

He repeated thank you at least four times. It seemed to him that the longed-for moment had arrived, Lila was about to say yes.

But as soon as they were outside the building she confronted him and said, with the cold cruelty that had come easily to her since her first years of life, "I never told you that I loved you."

"I know. But now you do?"

"No."

Marcello, who was heavily built, a healthy, ruddy youth of twenty-three, leaned against a lamppost, brokenhearted.

"Really no?"

"No. I love someone else."

"Who is it?"

"Stefano."

"I knew it, but I couldn't believe it."

"You have to believe it, it's true."

"I'll kill you both."

"With me you can try right now."

Marcello left the lamppost in a rush, but, with a kind of death rattle, he bit his clenched right fist until it bled.

"I love you too much, I can't do it."

"Then get your brother, your father to do it, some friend, maybe they're capable. But make it clear to all of them that you had better kill me first. Because if you touch anyone else while I'm alive, I will kill you, and you know I will, starting with you."

Marcello continued to bite his finger stubbornly. Then he repressed a sort of sob that shook his breast, turned, and went off.

She shouted after him: "Send someone to get the television, we don't need it."

41.

Everything happened in little more than a month and Lila

in the end seemed to me happy. She had found an outlet for the shoe project, she had given an opportunity to her brother and the whole family, she had gotten rid of Marcello Solara and had become the fiancée of the most respectable wealthy young man in the neighborhood. What more could she want? Nothing. She had everything. When school began again I felt the dreariness of it more than usual. I was reabsorbed by the work and, so that the teachers would not find me unprepared, I went back to studying until eleven and setting my alarm for five-thirty. I saw Lila less and less.

On the other hand, my relationship with Stefano's brother, Alfonso, solidified. Although he had worked in the grocery all summer, he had passed the makeup exams successfully, with seven in each of the subjects: Latin, Greek, and English. Gino, who had hoped that he would fail so that they could repeat the first year of high school together, was disappointed. When he realized that the two of us, now in our second year, went to school and came home together every day, he grew even more bitter and became mean. He no longer spoke to me, his former girlfriend, or to Alfonso, his former deskmate, even though he was in the classroom next to ours and we often met in the hallways, as well as in the streets of the neighborhood. But he did worse: soon I heard that he was telling nasty stories about us. He said that I was in love with Alfonso and touched him during class even though Alfonso didn't respond, because, as he knew very well, he who had sat next to him for a year, he didn't like girls, he preferred boys. I reported this to Alfonso, expecting him to beat up Gino, as was the rule in such cases, but he confined himself to saying, contemptuously, in dialect, "Everyone knows that he's the fag."

Alfonso was a pleasant, fortunate discovery. He gave an impression of cleanliness and good manners. Although his features were very similar to Stefano's, the same eyes, same nose, same mouth; although his body, as he grew, was taking the same form, the large head, legs slightly short in relation to the torso; although in his gaze and in his gestures he manifested the same mildness, I felt in him a total absence of the determination that was concealed in every cell of Stefano's body, and that in the end, I thought, reduced his courtesy to a sort of hiding place from which to jump out unexpectedly. Alfonso was soothing, that type of human being, rare in the neighborhood, from whom you know you needn't expect any cruelty. We didn't talk a lot, but we didn't feel uncomfortable. He always had what I needed and if he didn't he hurried to get it. He loved me without any tension and I felt quietly affectionate toward him. The first day of school we ended up sitting at the same desk, a thing that was audacious at the time, and even if the other boys made fun of him because he was always near me and the girls asked me continuously if he was my boyfriend, neither of us decided to change places. He was a trusted person. If he saw that I needed my own time, he either waited for me at a distance or said goodbye and went off. If he realized that I wanted him to stay with me, he stayed even if he had other things to do.

I used him to escape Nino Sarratore. When, for the first time after Ischia, we saw each other from a distance, Nino came toward me in a friendly way, but I dismissed him with a few cold remarks. And yet I liked him so much, if his tall slender figure merely appeared I blushed and my heart beat madly. And yet now that Lila was really engaged, officially engaged— and to such a fiancé, a man of twenty-two, not a boy: kind, decisive, courageous—it was more urgent than ever that I, too, should have an enviable fiancé and so rebalance our relationship. It would be lovely to go out as four, Lila with her betrothed, I with mine. Of course, Nino didn't have a red convertible. Of course, he was a student in the fourth year of high school, and thus didn't have a lira. But he was a lot taller than I, while Stefano was an inch or so shorter than Lila. And he spoke a literary Italian, when he wanted to. And he read and discussed everything and was aware of the great questions of the human condition, while Stefano lived shut off in his grocery, spoke almost exclusively in dialect, had not gone past the vocational school, at the cash register had his mamma, who did the accounts better than he, and, though he had a good character, was sensitive above all to the profitable turnover of money. Yet, although passion consumed me, although I saw clearly the prestige I would acquire in Lila's eyes if I were bound to him, for the second time since seeing him and falling in love I felt incapable of establishing a relationship. The motive seemed to me much stronger than that of childhood. Seeing him brought immediately to mind Donato Sarratore, even if they didn't resemble each other at all. And the disgust, the rage aroused by the memory of what his father had done without my being able to repulse him extended to Nino. Of course, I loved him. I longed to talk to him, walk with him, and at times I thought, racking my brains: Why do you behave like that, the father isn't the son, the son isn't the father, behave as Stefano did with the Pelusos. But I couldn't. As soon as I imagined kissing him, I felt the mouth of Donato, and a wave of pleasure and revulsion mixed father and son into a single person.

An alarming episode occurred, which made the situation more complicated. Alfonso and I had got into the habit of walking home. We went to Piazza Nazionale and then reached Corso Meridionale. It was a long walk, but we talked about homework, teachers, classmates, and it was pleasant. Then one day, just beyond the ponds, at the start of the *stradone*, I turned and seemed to see on the railway embankment, in his conductor's uniform, Donato Sarratore. I started with rage and horror, and immediately turned away. When I looked again, he was gone.

Whether that apparition was true or false, the sound my heart made in my chest, like a gunshot, stayed with me, and, I don't know why, I thought of the passage in Lila's letter about the sound that the copper pot had made when it burst. That same sound returned the next day, at the mere sight of Nino. Then, frightened, I took cover in affection for Alfonso, and at both the start and the end of school I kept near him. As soon as the lanky figure of the boy I loved appeared, I turned to the younger son of Don Achille as if I had the most urgent things to tell him, and we walked away chattering.

It was, in other words, a confusing time, I would have liked to be attached to Nino and yet I was careful to stay glued to Alfonso. In fact, out of fear that he would get bored and leave me for other company, I behaved more and more kindly toward him, sometimes I even spoke sweetly. But as soon as I realized that I risked encouraging his liking me I changed my tone. What if he misunderstands and says he loves me? I worried. It would have been embarrassing, I would have had to reject him: Lila, my contemporary, was engaged to a man, Stefano, and it would be humiliating to be with a boy, the little brother of her fiancé. Yet my mind swirled without restraint, I daydreamed. Once, as I walked home along Corso Meridionale, with Alfonso beside me like a squire escorting me through the thousand dangers of the city, it seemed to me right that the duty had fallen to two Carraccis, Stefano and him, to protect, if in different forms, Lila and me from the blackest evil in the world, from that very evil that we had experienced for the first time going up the stairs that led to their house, when we went to retrieve the dolls that their father had stolen.

42.

I liked to discover connections like that, especially if they concerned Lila. I traced lines between moments and events distant from one another, I established convergences and divergences. In that period it became a daily exercise: the better off I had been in Ischia, the worse off Lila had been in the desolation of the neighborhood; the more I had suffered upon leaving the island, the happier she had become. It was as if, because of an evil spell, the joy or sorrow of one required the sorrow or joy of the other; even our physical aspect, it seemed to me, shared in that swing. In Ischia I had felt beautiful, and the impression had lingered on my return to Naples—during the constant plotting with Lila to help her get rid of Marcello, there had even been moments when I thought again that I was prettier, and in some of Stefano's glances I had caught the possibility of his liking me. But Lila now had retaken the upper hand, satisfaction had magnified her beauty, while I, overwhelmed by schoolwork, exhausted by my frustrated love for Nino, was growing ugly again. My healthy color faded, the acne returned. And suddenly one morning the specter of glasses appeared.

Professor Gerace questioned me about something he had written on the blackboard, and realized that I could see almost nothing. He told me that I must go immediately to an oculist, he would write it down in my notebook, he expected the signature of one of my parents the next day. I went home and showed them the notebook, full of guilt for the expense that glasses would involve. My father darkened, my mother shouted, "You're always with your books, and now you've ruined your eyesight." I was extremely hurt. Had I been punished for pride in wishing to study? What about Lila? Hadn't she read much more than I had? So then why did she have perfect vision while mine deteriorated? Why should I have to wear glasses my whole life and she not?

The need for glasses intensified my mania for finding a pattern that, in good as in evil, would bind my fate and hers: I was blind, she a falcon; I had an opaque pupil, she narrowed her eyes, with darting glances that saw more; I clung to her arm, among the shadows, she guided me with a stern gaze. In the end my father, thanks to his dealings at the city hall, found the money. The fantasies diminished. I went to the oculist, he diagnosed a severe myopia, the glasses materialized. When I looked at myself in the mirror, the clear image was a hard blow: blemished skin, broad face, wide mouth, big nose, eyes imprisoned in frames that seemed to have been drawn insistently by an angry designer under eyebrows already too thick. I felt disfigured, and decided to wear the glasses only at home or, at most, if I had to copy something from the blackboard. But one day, leaving school, I forgot them on the desk. I hurried back to the classroom, the worst had happened. In the haste that seized us all at the sound of the last bell, they had ended up on the floor: one sidepiece was broken, a lens cracked. I began to cry.

I didn't have the courage to go home, I took refuge with Lila. I told her what had happened, and gave her the glasses. She examined them and said to leave them with her. She spoke with a different sort of determination, calmer, as if it were no longer necessary to fight to the death for every little thing. I imagined some miraculous intervention by Rino with his shoemaker's tools and I went home hoping that my parents wouldn't notice that I was without my glasses.

A few days afterward, in the late afternoon, I heard someone calling from the courtyard. Below was Lila, she had my glasses on her nose and at first I was struck not by the fact that they were as if new but by how well they suited her. I ran down thinking, why is it that they look nice on her when she doesn't need them and they make me, who can't do without them, look ugly? As soon as I appeared she took off the glasses with amusement and put them on my nose herself, exclaiming, "How nice you look, you should wear them all the time." She had given the glasses to Stefano, who had had them fixed by an optician in the city. I murmured in embarrassment that I could never repay her, she replied ironically, perhaps with a trace of malice:

"Repay in what sense?"

"Give you money."

She smiled, then said proudly, "There's no need, I do what I like now with money."

43.

Money gave even more force to the impression that what I lacked she had, and vice versa, in a continuous game of exchanges and reversals that, now happily, now painfully, made us indispensable to each other.

She has Stefano, I said to myself after the episode of the glasses. She snaps her fingers and immediately has my glasses repaired. What do I have?

I answered that I had school, a privilege she had lost forever. That is my wealth, I tried to convince myself. And in fact that year all the teachers began to praise me again. My report cards were increasingly brilliant, and even the correspondence course in theology went well, I got a Bible with a black cover as a prize.

I displayed my successes as if they were my mother's silver bracelet, and yet I didn't know what to do with that virtuosity. In my class there was no one to talk to about what I read, the ideas that came into my mind. Alfonso was a diligent student; after the failure of the preceding year he had got back on track and was doing well in all the subjects. But when I tried to talk to him about *The Betrothed*, or the marvelous books I still borrowed from Maestro Ferraro's library, or about the Holy Spirit, he merely listened, and, out of timidity or ignorance, never said anything that would inspire me to further thoughts. Besides, while in school he used a good Italian; when it was just the two of us he never abandoned dialect, and in dialect it was hard to discuss the corruption of earthly justice, as it could be seen during the lunch at the house of Don Rodrigo, or the relations between God, the Holy Spirit, and Jesus, who, although they were a single person, when they were divided in three, I thought, necessarily had to have a hierarchy, and then who came first, who last?

I remembered what Pasquale had once said: that my high school, even if it was a classical high school, was surely not one of the best. I concluded that he was right. Rarely did I see my schoolmates dressed as well as the girls of Via dei Mille. And, when school was out, you never saw elegantly dressed young men, in cars more luxurious than those of Marcello and Stefano, waiting to pick them up. Intellectually, too, they were deficient. The only student who had a reputation like mine was Nino, but now, because of the coldness with which I had treated him, he went off with his head down, he didn't even look at me. What to do, then?

I needed to express myself, my head was bursting. I turned to Lila, especially when school was on vacation. We met, we talked. I told her in detail about the classes, the teachers. She listened intently, and I hoped that she would become curious and go back to the phase when in secret or openly she would eagerly get the books that would allow her to keep up with me. But it never happened, it was as if one part of her kept a tight rein on the other part. Instead she developed a tendency to interrupt right away, in general in an ironic manner. Once, just to give an example, I told her about my theology course and said, to impress her with the questions that tormented me, that I didn't know what to think about the Holy Spirit, its function wasn't clear to me. "Is it," I argued aloud, "a subordinate entity, in the service of both God and Jesus, like a messenger? Or an emanation of the first two, their miraculous essence? But in the first case how can an entity who acts as a messenger possibly be one with God and his son? Wouldn't it be like saying that my father who is a porter at the city hall is the same as the mayor, as Comandante Lauro? And, if you look at the second case, well, essence, sweat, voice are part of the person from whom they emanate: how can it make sense, then, to consider the Holy Spirit separate from God and Jesus? Or is the Holy Spirit the most important person and the other two his mode of being, or I don't understand what his function is."

Lila, I remember, was preparing to go out with Stefano: they were going to a cinema in the center with Pinuccia, Rino, and Alfonso. I watched while she put on a new skirt, a new jacket, and she was truly another person now, even her ankles were no longer like sticks. Yet I saw that her eyes narrowed, as when she tried to grasp something fleeting. She said, in dialect, "You still waste time with those things, Lenù? We are flying over a ball of fire. The part that has cooled floats on the lava. On that part we construct the buildings, the bridges, and the streets, and every so often the lava comes out of Vesuvius or causes an earthquake that destroys everything. There are microbes everywhere that make us sick and die. There are wars. There is a poverty that makes us all cruel. Every second something might happen that will cause you such suffering that you'll never have enough tears. And what are you doing? A theology course in which you struggle to understand what the Holy Spirit is? Forget it, it was the Devil who invented the world, not the Father, the Son, and the Holy Spirit. Do you want to see the string of pearls that Stefano gave me?" That was how she talked, more or less, confusing me. And not only in a situation like that but more and more often, until that tone became established, became her way of standing up to me. If I said something about the Very Holy Trinity, she with a few hurried but good-humored remarks cut off any possible conversation and went on to show me Stefano's presents, the engagement ring, the necklace, a new dress, a hat, while the things that I loved, that made me shine in front of the teachers, so that they considered me clever, slumped in a corner, deprived of their

meaning. I let go of ideas, books. I went on to admire all those
gifts that contrasted with the humble house of Fernando the
shoemaker; I tried on the dresses and the jewelry; I almost
immediately noticed that they would never suit me as they did
her; and I was depressed.

44.

In the role of fiancée, Lila was much envied and caused
quite a lot of resentment. After all, her behavior had been irritating when she was a skinny little child, imagine now that she
was a very fortunate young girl. She herself told me of an
increasing hostility on the part of Stefano's mother and, especially, Pinuccia. Their spiteful thoughts were stamped clearly
on their faces. Who did the shoemaker's daughter think she
was? What evil potion had she made Stefano drink? How was
it that as soon as she opened her mouth he opened his wallet?
She wants to come and be mistress in our house?

If Maria confined herself to a surly silence, Pinuccia couldn't
contain herself, she exploded, speaking to her brother like this:
"Why do you buy all those things for her, while for me you've
never bought anything, and as soon as I buy something nice
you criticize me, you say I'm wasting money?"

Stefano displayed his tranquil half smile and didn't answer.
But soon, in accord with his habit of accommodation, he
began to give his sister presents, too. Thus a contest began
between the two girls, they went to the hairdresser together,
they bought the same dresses. This, however, only embittered
Pinuccia the more. She wasn't ugly, she was a few years older
than us, maybe her figure was more developed, but there was
no comparison between the effect made by any dress or object
when Lila had it on and when Pinuccia wore it. It was her
mother who realized this first. Maria, when she saw Lila and

Pinuccia ready to go out, with the same hairstyle, in similar dresses, always found a way to digress and, by devious means, end up criticizing her future daughter-in-law, with false good humor, for something she had done days earlier—leaving the light on in the kitchen or the tap open after getting a glass of water. Then she turned the other way, as if she had a lot to do, and muttered, "Be home soon."

We girls of the neighborhood soon had similar problems. On holidays Carmela, who still wanted to be called Carmen, and Ada and Gigliola started dressing up, without admitting it, without admitting it to themselves, in competition with Lila. Gigliola in particular, who worked in the pastry shop, and who, although she wasn't officially with Michele Solara, bought and had him buy pretty things, just to show off on walks or in the car. But there was no contest, Lila seemed inaccessible, a dazzling figurine against the light.

At first we tried to keep her, to impose on her the old habits. We drew Stefano into our group, embraced him, coddled him, and he seemed pleased, and so one Saturday, perhaps impelled by his sympathy for Antonio and Ada, he said to Lila, "See if Lenuccia and Melina's children will come and eat with us tomorrow evening." By "us" he meant the two of them plus Pinuccia and Rino, who now liked to spend his free time with his future brother-in-law. We accepted, but it was a difficult evening. Ada, afraid of making a bad impression, borrowed a dress from Gigliola. Stefano and Rino chose not a pizzeria but a restaurant in Santa Lucia. Neither I nor Antonio nor Ada had ever been in a restaurant, it was something for rich people, and we were overcome by anxiety: how should we dress, what would it cost? While the four of them went in the Giardinetta, we took the bus to Piazza Plebiscito and walked the rest of the way. At the restaurant, they casually ordered many dishes, and we almost nothing, out of fear that the bill would be more than we could afford. We were almost silent the whole time, because

Rino and Stefano talked, mainly about money, and never thought of involving even Antonio in their conversations. Ada, not resigned to marginality, tried all evening to attract Stefano's attention by flirting outrageously, which upset her brother. Then, when it was time to pay, we discovered that Stefano had already taken care of the bill, and, while it didn't bother Rino at all, Antonio went home in a rage, because although he was the same age as Stefano and Lila's brother, although he worked as they did, he felt he had been treated like a pauper. But the most significant thing was that Ada and I, with different feelings, realized that in a public place, outside of our intimate, neighborhood relationship, we didn't know what to say to Lila, how to treat her. She was so well dressed, so carefully made up, that she seemed right for the Giardinetta, the convertible, the restaurant in Santa Lucia, but physically unsuited now to go on the metro with us, to travel on the bus, to walk around the neighborhood, to get a pizza in Corso Garibaldi, to go to the parish cinema, to dance at Gigliola's house.

That evening it became evident that Lila was changing her circumstances. In the days, the months, she became a young woman who imitated the models in the fashion magazines, the girls on television, the ladies she had seen walking on Via Chiaia. When you saw her, she gave off a glow that seemed a violent slap in the face of the poverty of the neighborhood. The girl's body, of which there were still traces when we had woven the plot that led to her engagement to Stefano, was soon banished to dark lands. In the light of the sun she was instead a young woman who, when on Sundays she went out on the arm of her fiancé, seemed to apply the terms of their agreement as a couple, and Stefano, with his gifts, seemed to wish to demonstrate to the neighborhood that, if Lila was beautiful, she could always be more so; and she seemed to have discovered the joy of dipping into the inexhaustible well of her beauty, and to feel and show that no shape, however beautifully drawn, could contain her conclusively, since a new hairstyle, a new dress, a new way of making up her eyes or her mouth were only more expansive outlines that dissolved the preceding ones. Stefano seemed to seek in her the most palpable symbol of the future of wealth and power that he intended; and she seemed to use the seal that he was placing on her to make herself, her brother, her parents, her other relatives safe from all that she had confusedly confronted and challenged since she was a child.

I still didn't know anything about what she secretly called, in herself, after the bad experience of New Year's, dissolving margins. But I knew the story of the exploded pot, it was always lying in ambush in some corner of my mind; I thought about it over and over again. And I remember that, one night at home, I reread the letter she had sent me on Ischia. How seductive was her way of talking about herself and how distant it seemed now. I had to acknowledge that the Lila who had written those words had disappeared. In the letter there was still the girl who had written *The Blue Fairy*, who had learned Latin and Greek on her own, who had consumed half of Maestro Ferraro's library, even the girl who had drawn the shoes framed and hanging in the shoe store. But in the life of every day I no longer saw her, no longer heard her. The tense, aggressive Cerullo was as if immolated. Although we both continued to live in the same neighborhood, although we had had the same childhood, although we were both living our fifteenth year, we had suddenly ended up in two different worlds. I was becoming, as the months ran by, a sloppy, disheveled, spectacled girl bent over tattered books that gave off a moldy odor, volumes bought at great sacrifice at the secondhand store or obtained from Maestra Oliviero. She went around on Stefano's arm in the clothes of an actress or a princess, her hair styled like a diva's.

I looked at her from the window, and felt that her earlier shape had broken, and I thought again of that wonderful passage of the letter, of the cracked and crumpled copper. It was an image that I used all the time, whenever I noticed a fracture in her or in me. I knew—perhaps I hoped—that no form could ever contain Lila, and that sooner or later she would break everything again.

45.

After the terrible evening in the restaurant in Santa Lucia there were no more occasions like that, and not because the boyfriends didn't ask us again but because we now got out of it with one excuse or another. Instead, when I wasn't exhausted by my homework, I let myself be drawn out to a dance at someone's house, to have a pizza with the old group. I preferred to go, however, only when I was sure that Antonio would come; for a while he had been courting me, discreetly, attentively. True, his face was shiny and full of blackheads, his teeth here and there were bluish; he had broad hands and strong fingers—he had once effortlessly unscrewed the screws on the punctured tire of an old car that Pasquale had acquired. But he had black wavy hair that made you want to caress it, and although he was very shy the rare times he opened his mouth he said something witty. Besides, he was the only one who noticed me. Enzo seldom appeared; he had a life of which we knew little or nothing, and when he was there he devoted himself, in his detached, slow way, and never excessively, to Carmela. As for Pasquale, he seemed to have lost interest in girls after Lila's rejection. He took very little notice even of Ada, who flirted with him tirelessly, even if she kept saying that she couldn't stand always seeing our mean faces.

Naturally on those evenings we sooner or later ended up talking about Lila, even if it seemed that no one wanted to name her: the boys were all a little disappointed, each one would have liked to be in Stefano's place. But the most unhappy was Pasquale: if his hatred for the Solaras hadn't been of such long standing, he would probably have sided publicly with Marcello against the Cerullo family. His sufferings in love had dug deep inside him and a mere glimpse of Lila and Stefano together dimmed his joy in life. Yet he was by nature honest and good-hearted, so he was careful to keep his reactions under control and to take sides according to what was just. When he found out that Marcello and Michele had confronted Rino one evening, and though they hadn't laid a finger on him had grossly insulted him, Pasquale had entirely taken Rino's part. When he found out that Silvio Solara, the father of Michele and Marcello, had gone in person to Fernando's renovated shoe store and calmly reproached him for not having brought up his daughter properly, and then, looking around, had observed that the shoemaker could make all the shoes he wanted, but then where would he sell them, he would never find a store that would take them, not to mention that with all that glue around, with all that thread and pitch and wooden forms and soles and heels, it wouldn't take much to start a fire, Pasquale had promised that, if there was a fire at the Cerullo shoe shop, he would go with a few trusted companions and burn down the Solara bar and pastry shop. But he was critical of Lila. He said that she should have run away from home rather than allow Marcello to go there and court her all those evenings. He said she should have smashed the television with a hammer and not watched it with anyone who knew that he had bought it only to have her. He said, finally, that she was a girl too intelligent to be truly in love with a hypocritical idiot like Stefano Carracci.

On those occasions I was the only one who did not remain silent but explicitly disagreed with Pasquale's criticisms. I refuted him, saying things like: It's not easy to leave home; it's not easy to go against the wishes of the people you love; nothing is easy, especially when you criticize her rather than being angry at your friend Rino—he's the one who got her in that trouble with Marcello, and if Lila hadn't found a way of getting out of it, she would have had to marry Marcello. I concluded by praising Stefano, who of all the boys who had known Lila since she was a child and loved her was the only one with the courage to support her and help her. A terrible silence fell and I was very proud of having countered every criticism of my friend in a tone and language that, among other things, had subdued him.

But one night we ended up quarreling unpleasantly. We were all, including Enzo, having a pizza on the Rettifilo, in a place where a margherita and a beer cost fifty lire. This time it was the girls who started: Ada, I think, said she thought Lila was ridiculous going around always fresh from the hairdresser and in clothes like Princess Soraya, even though she was sprinkling roach poison in front of the house door. We all, some more, some less, laughed. Then, one thing leading to another, Carmela ended up saying outright that Lila had gone with Stefano for the money, to settle her brother and the rest of the family. I was starting my usual official defense when Pasquale interrupted me and said, "That's not the point. The point is that Lina knows where that money comes from."

"Now you want to drag in Don Achille and the black market and the trafficking and loan sharking and all the nonsense of before and after the war?" I said.

"Yes, and if your friend were here now she would say I was right."

"Stefano is just a shopkeeper who's a good salesman."

"And the money he put into the Cerullos' shoe store he got from the grocery?"

"Why, what do you think?"

"It comes from the gold objects taken from mothers and

hidden by Don Achille in the mattress. Lina acts the lady with the blood of all the poor people of this neighborhood. And she is kept, she and her whole family, even before she's married."

I was about to answer when Enzo interrupted with his usual detachment: "Excuse me, Pascà, what do you mean by 'is kept'?"

As soon as I heard that question I knew that things would turn ugly. Pasquale turned red, embarrassed. "Keep means keep. Who pays, please, when Lina goes to the hairdresser, when she buys dresses and purses? Who put money into the shoe shop so that the shoe-repair man can play at making shoes?"

"Are you saying that Lina isn't in love, isn't engaged, won't soon marry Stefano, but has sold herself?"

We were all quiet. Antonio murmured, "No, Enzo, Pasquale doesn't mean that; you know that he loves Lina as we all of us love her."

Enzo nodded at him to be quiet.

"Be quiet, Anto', let Pasquale answer."

Pasquale said grimly, "Yes, she sold herself. And she doesn't give a damn about the stink of the money she spends every day."

I tried again to have my say, at that point, but Enzo touched my arm.

"Excuse me, Lenù, I want to know what Pasquale calls a girl who sells herself."

Here Pasquale had an outburst of violence that we all read in his eyes and he said what for months he had wanted to say, to shout out to the whole neighborhood: "Whore, I call her a whore. Lina has behaved and is behaving like a whore."

Enzo got up and said, almost in a whisper: "Come outside."

Antonio jumped up, restrained Pasquale, who was getting up, and said, "Now, let's not overdo it, Enzo. Pasquale is only saying something that's not an accusation, it's a criticism that we'd all like to make."

Enzo answered, this time aloud, "Not me." And he headed

toward the door, announcing, "I'll wait outside for both of you."

We kept Pasquale and Antonio from following him, and nothing happened. They didn't speak for several days, then everything was as before.

46.

I've recounted that quarrel to say how that year passed and what the atmosphere was around Lila's choices, especially among the young men who had secretly or explicitly loved her, desired her, and in all probability loved and desired her still. As for me, it's hard to say in what tangle of feelings I found myself. I always defended Lila, and I liked doing so, I liked to hear myself speak with the authority of one who is studying difficult subjects. But I also knew that I could have just as well recounted, and willingly, if with some exaggeration, how Lila had really been behind each of Stefano's moves, and I with her, linking step to step as if it were a mathematics problem, to achieve that result: to settle herself, settle her brother, attempt to realize the plan of the shoe factory, and even get money to repair my glasses if they broke.

I passed Fernando's old workshop and felt a vicarious sense of triumph. Lila, clearly, had made it. The shoemaker's shop, which had never had a sign, now displayed over the door a kind of plaque that said "Cerullo." Fernando, Rino, the three apprentices worked at joining, stitching, hammering, polishing, bent over their benches from morning till late at night. It was known that father and son often quarreled. It was known that Fernando maintained that the shoes, especially the women's, couldn't be made as Lila had invented them, that they were only a child's fantasy. It was known that Rino maintained the opposite and that he went to Lila to ask her to intervene. It was known that Lila said she didn't want to know about it, and so Rino went to Stefano and dragged him to the shop to give his father specific orders. It was known that Stefano went in and looked for a long time at Lila's designs framed on the walls, smiled to himself and said tranquilly that he wanted the shoes to be exactly as they were in those pictures, he had hung them there for that purpose. It was known, in short, that things were proceeding slowly, that the workers first received instructions from Fernando and then Rino changed them and everything stopped and started over, and Fernando noticed the changes and changed them back, and Stefano arrived and so back to square one: they ended up yelling, breaking things.

I glanced in and immediately fled. But the pictures hanging on the walls made an impression. Those drawings, for Lila, were fantasies, I thought. Money has nothing to do with it, selling has nothing to do with it. All that activity is the result of a whim of hers, celebrated by Stefano merely out of love. She's lucky to be so loved, to love. Lucky to be adored for what she is and for what she invents. Now that she's given her brother what he wanted, now that she's taken him out of danger, surely she'll invent something else. So I don't want to lose sight of her. Something will happen.

But nothing happened. Lila established herself in the role of Stefano's fiancée. And even in our conversations, when she had time to talk, she seemed satisfied with what she had become, as if she no longer saw anything beyond it, didn't *want* to see anything beyond it, except marriage, a house, children.

I was disappointed. She seemed sweeter, without the hardness she had always had. I realized this later, when through Gigliola Spagnuolo I heard disgraceful rumors about her. Gigliola said to me rancorously, in dialect, "Now your friend is acting like a princess. But does Stefano know that when Marcello went to her house she gave him a blow job every night?"

I didn't know what a blow job was. The term had been

familiar to me since I was a child but the sound of it recalled only a kind of disfigurement, something very humiliating.

"It's not true."

"Marcello says so."

"He's a liar."

"Yes? And would he lie even to his brother?"

"Did Michele tell you?"

"Yes."

I hoped that those rumors wouldn't reach Stefano. Every day when I came home from school I said to myself: maybe I should warn Lila, before something bad happens. But I was afraid she would be furious and that, because of how she had grown up, because of how she was made, she would go directly to Marcello Solara with the shoemaker's knife. But in the end I decided: it was better to report to her what I had learned, so she would be prepared to confront the situation. But I discovered that she already knew about it. Not only that: she was better informed than me about what a blow job was. I realized it from the fact that she used a clearer formulation to tell me it was so disgusting to her that she would never do it to any man, let alone Marcello Solara. Then she told me that Stefano had heard the rumor and he had asked her what type of relations she had had with Marcello during the period when he went to the Cerullo house. She had said angrily, "None, are you crazy?" And Stefano had said immediately that he believed her, that he had never had doubts, that he had asked the question only to let her know that Marcello was saying obscene things about her. Yet he seemed distracted, like someone who, even against his will, is following scenes of disaster that are forming in his mind. Lila had realized it and they had discussed it for a long time, she had confessed that she, too, felt a need for revenge. But what was the use? After talk and more talk, they had decided by mutual consent to rise a step above the Solaras, above the logic of the neighborhood.

"A step above?" I asked, marveling.

"Yes, to ignore them: Marcello, his brother, the father, the grandfather, all of them. Act as if they didn't exist."

So Stefano had continued to go to work, without defending the honor of his fiancée, Lila had continued her life as a fiancée without resorting to the knife or anything else, the Solaras had continued to spread obscenities. I was astonished. What was happening? I didn't understand. The Solaras' behavior seemed more comprehensible, it seemed to me consistent with the world that we had known since we were children. What, instead, did she and Stefano have in mind, where did they think they were living? They were behaving in a way that wasn't familiar even in the poems that I studied in school, in the novels I read. I was puzzled. They weren't reacting to the insults, even to that truly intolerable insult that the Solaras were making. They displayed kindness and politeness toward everyone, as if they were John and Jacqueline Kennedy visiting a neighborhood of indigents. When they went out walking together, and he put an arm around her shoulders, it seemed that none of the old rules were valid for them: they laughed, they joked, they embraced, they kissed each other on the lips. I saw them speeding around in the convertible, alone even in the evening, always dressed like movie stars, and I thought, They go wherever they want, without a chaperone, and not secretly but with the consent of their parents, with the consent of Rino, and do whatever they like, without caring what people say. Was it Lila who had persuaded Stefano to behave in a way that was making them the most admired and most talked about couple in the neighborhood? Was this her latest invention? Did she want to leave the neighborhood by staying in the neighborhood? Did she want to drag us out of ourselves, tear off the old skin and put on a new one, suitable for what she was inventing?

47.

Everything returned abruptly to the usual track when the rumors about Lila reached Pasquale. It happened one Sunday, when Carmela, Enzo, Pasquale, Antonio, and I were walking along the *stradone*. Antonio said, "I hear that Marcello Solara is telling everyone that Lina was with him."

Enzo didn't blink. Pasquale immediately flared up: "Was how?"

Antonio was embarrassed by my and Carmela's presence and said, "You understand."

They moved away, to talk among themselves. I saw and heard that Pasquale was increasingly enraged, that Enzo was becoming physically more compact, as if he no longer had arms, legs, neck, as if he were a block of hard material. Why is it, I wondered, that they are so angry? Lila isn't a sister of theirs or even a cousin. And yet they feel it's their duty to be indignant, all three of them, more than Stefano, much more than Stefano, as if they were the true fiancés. Pasquale especially seemed ridiculous. He who only a short time before had said what he had said shouted, at one point, and we heard him clearly, with our own ears: "I'll smash the face of that shit, calling her a whore. Even if Stefano allows it, I'm not going to allow it." Then silence, they rejoined us, and we wandered aimlessly, I talking to Antonio, Carmela between her brother and Enzo. After a while they took us home. I saw them going off, Enzo, who was the shortest, in the middle, flanked by Antonio and Pasquale.

The next day and on those which followed there was a big uproar about the Solaras' 1100. It had been demolished. Not only that: the two brothers had been savagely beaten, but they couldn't say by whom. They swore they had been attacked on a dark street by at least ten people, men from outside the neighborhood. But Carmela and I knew very well that there were only three attackers, and we were worried. We waited for the inevitable reprisal, one day, two, three. But evidently things had been done right. Pasquale continued as a construction worker, Antonio as a mechanic, Enzo made his rounds with the cart. The Solaras, instead, for some time went around only on foot, battered, a little dazed, always with four or five of their friends. I admit that seeing them in that condition pleased me. I was proud of my friends. Along with Carmen and Ada I criticized Stefano and also Rino because they had acted as if nothing had happened. Then time passed, Marcello and Michele bought a green Giulietta and began to act like masters of the neighborhood again. Alive and well, bigger bullies than before. A sign that perhaps Lila was right: with people like that, you had to fight them by living a superior life, such as they couldn't even imagine. While I was taking my exams in the second year of high school, she told me that in the spring, when she was barely sixteen and a half, she would be married.

48.

This news upset me. When Lila told me about her wedding it was June, just before my oral exams. It was predictable, of course, but now that a date had been fixed, March 12th, it was as if I had been strolling absentmindedly and banged into a door. I had petty thoughts. I counted the months: nine. Maybe nine months was long enough so that Pinuccia's treacherous resentment, Maria's hostility, Marcello Solara's gossip—which continued to fly from mouth to mouth throughout the neighborhood, like Fama in the Aeneid—would wear Stefano down, leading him to break the engagement. I was ashamed of myself, but I was no longer able to trace a coherent design in the division of our fates. The concreteness of that date made concrete the crossroads that would separate our lives. And, what was worse, I took it for granted that her fate would be better than mine. I felt more strongly than ever the meaninglessness of school, I knew clearly that I had embarked on that path years earlier only to seem enviable to Lila. And now instead books had no importance for her. I stopped preparing for my exams, I didn't sleep that night. I thought of my meager experience of love: I had kissed Gino once, I had scarcely grazed Nino's lips, I had endured the fleeting and ugly contact of his father: that was it. Whereas Lila, starting in March, at sixteen, would have a husband and within a year, at seventeen, a child, and then another, and another, and another. I felt I was a shadow, I wept in despair.

The next day I went unwillingly to take the exams. But something happened that made me feel better. Professor Gerace and Professor Galiani, who were part of the committee, praised my Italian paper to the skies. Gerace in particular said that my exposition was further improved. He wanted to read a passage to the rest of the committee. And only as I listened did I realize what I had tried to do in those months whenever I had to write: to free myself from my artificial tones, from sentences that were too rigid; to try for a fluid and engaging style like Lila's in the Ischia letter. When I heard my words in the teacher's voice, with Professor Galiani listening and silently nodding agreement, I realized that I had succeeded. Naturally it wasn't Lila's way of writing, it was mine. And it seemed to my teachers something truly out of the ordinary.

I was promoted to the third year with all tens, but at home no one was surprised or celebrated me. I saw that they were satisfied, yes, and I was pleased, but they gave the event no weight. My mother, in fact, found my scholastic success completely natural, my father told me to go right away to Maestra Oliviero to ask her to get ahead of time the books for next year. As I went out my mother cried, "And if she wants to send you to Ischia again, tell her that I'm not well and you have to help me in the house."

The teacher praised me, but carelessly, partly because by now she took my ability for granted, partly because she wasn't well, the illness she had in her mouth was very troublesome. She never mentioned my need to rest, her cousin Nella, Ischia. Instead, surprisingly, she began to talk about Lila. She had seen her on the street, from a distance. She was with her fiancé, she said, the grocer. Then she added a sentence that I will always remember: "The beauty of mind that Cerullo had from childhood didn't find an outlet, Greco, and it has all ended up in her face, in her breasts, in her thighs, in her ass, places where it soon fades and it will be as if she had never had it."

I had never heard her say a rude word since I had known her. That day she said "ass," and then muttered, "Excuse me." But that wasn't what struck me. It was the regret, as if the teacher were realizing that something of Lila had been ruined because she, as a teacher, hadn't protected and nurtured it well. I felt that I was her most successful student and went away relieved.

The only one who congratulated me without reserve was Alfonso, who had also been promoted, with all sevens. I felt that his admiration was genuine, and this gave me pleasure. In front of the posted grades, in the presence of our schoolmates and their parents, he, in his excitement, did something inappropriate, as if he had forgotten that I was a girl and he wasn't supposed to touch me: he hugged me tight, and kissed me on the cheek, a noisy kiss. Then he became confused, apologized, and yet he couldn't contain himself, he cried, "All tens, impossible, all tens." On the way home we talked a lot about the wedding of his brother, of Lila. Since I felt especially at ease, I asked him for the first time what he thought of his future sister-in-law. He took some time before he answered. Then he said:

"You remember the competitions they made us do at school?"

"Who could forget them?"

"I was sure I would win, you were all afraid of my father."

"Lina, too: in fact for a while she tried not to beat you."

"Yes, but then she decided to win and she humiliated me. I went home crying."

"It's not nice to lose."

"Not because of that: it seemed to me intolerable that everyone was terrified of my father, me first of all, and that girl wasn't."

"Were you in love with her?"

"Are you kidding? She always made me uncomfortable."

"In what sense?"

"In the sense that my brother really shows some courage in marrying her."

"What do you mean?"

"I mean that you are better, and that if it were me choosing I would marry you."

This, too, pleased me. We burst out laughing, we said goodbye, still laughing. He was condemned to spend the summer in the grocery store, I, thanks to a decision of my mother more than my father, had to find a job for the summer. We promised to meet, to go at least once to the beach together. We didn't.

In the following days I reluctantly made the rounds of the neighborhood. I asked Don Paolo, the pharmacist on the *stradone*, if he needed a clerk. No. I asked the newspaper seller: I wasn't useful to him, either. I went by the stationer's, she started laughing: she needed someone, yes, but not now. I should come back in the fall when school began. I was about to go and she called me back. She said, "You're a serious girl, Lenù, I trust you: would you be able to take my girls swimming?"

I was really happy when I left the shop. The stationer would pay me—and pay well—if I took her three little girls to the beach for the month of July and the first ten days of August.

Sea, sun, and money. I was to go every day to a place between Mergellina and Posillipo that I knew nothing about, it had a foreign name: Sea Garden. I went home in great excitement, as if my life had taken a decisive turn. I would earn money for my parents, I would go swimming, I would become smooth and golden in the sun as I had during the summer in Ischia. How sweet everything is, I thought, when the day is fine and every good thing seems to be waiting for you alone.

I had gone a short distance when that impression of privileged hours was solidified. Antonio joined me, in his grease-stained overalls. I was pleased, whoever I had met at that moment of happiness would have been greeted warmly. He had seen me passing and had run after me. I told him about the stationer, he must have read in my face that it was a happy moment. For months I had been grinding away, feeling alone, ugly. Although I was sure I loved Nino Sarratore, I had always avoided him and hadn't even gone to see if he had been promoted, and with what grades. Lila was about to complete a definitive leap beyond my life, I would no longer be able to follow her. But now I felt good and I wanted to feel even better. When Antonio, guessing that I was in the right mood, asked if I wanted to be his girlfriend, I said yes right away, even though I loved someone else, even if I felt for him nothing but some friendliness. To have him as a boyfriend, he who was an adult, the same age as Stefano, a worker, seemed to me a thing not different from being promoted with all tens, from the job of taking, with pay, the daughters of the stationer to the Sea Garden.

49.

My job began, and life with a boyfriend. The stationer gave me a sort of bus pass, and every morning I crossed the city with the three little girls, on the crowded buses, and took them to

that bright-colored place of beach umbrellas, blue sea, concrete platforms, students, well-off women with a lot of free
time, showy women, with greedy faces. I was polite to the
attendants who tried to start conversations. I looked after the
children, taking them for long swims, and showing off the
bathing suit that Nella had made for me the year before. I fed
them, played with them, let them drink endlessly at the jet of a
stone fountain, taking care that they didn't slip and break their
teeth on the basin.

We got back to the neighborhood in the late afternoon. I
returned the children to the stationer, and hurried to my secret
date with Antonio, burned by the sun, salty from the sea water.
We went to the ponds by back streets, I was afraid of being
seen by my mother and, perhaps still more, by Maestra
Oliviero. With him I exchanged my first real kisses. I soon let
him touch my breasts and between my legs. One evening I
touched his penis, straining, large, inside his pants, and when
he took it out I held it willingly in one hand while we kissed. I
accepted those practices with two very clear questions in my
mind. The first was: does Lila do these things with Stefano?
The second was: is the pleasure I feel with Antonio the same
that I felt the night Donato Sarratore touched me? In both
cases Antonio was ultimately only a useful phantom to evoke
on the one hand the love between Lila and Stefano, on the
other the strong emotion, difficult to categorize, that Nino's
father had inspired in me. But I never felt guilty. Antonio was
so grateful to me, he showed such an absolute dependence on
me for those few moments of contact at the ponds, that I soon
convinced myself that it was he who was indebted to me, that
the pleasure I gave him was by far superior to that which he
gave me.

Sometimes, on Sunday, he went with me and the children to
the Sea Garden. He spent money with pretended casualness,
though he earned very little, and he also hated getting sun-

burned. But he did it for me, just to be near me, without any immediate reward, since there was no way to kiss or touch each other. And he entertained the children, with clowning and ath-letic diving. While he played with them I lay in the sun read-ing, dissolving into the pages like a jellyfish.

One of those times I looked up for a second and saw a tall, slender, graceful girl in a stunning red bikini. It was Lila. By now she was used to having men's gaze on her, she moved as if there were no one in that crowded place, not even the young attendant who went ahead of her, leading her to her umbrella. She didn't see me and I didn't know whether to call her. She was wearing sunglasses, she carried a purse of bright-colored fabric. I hadn't yet told her about my job or even about Antonio: probably I was afraid of her judgment of both. Let's wait for her to notice me, I thought, and turned back to my book, but I was unable to read. Soon I looked in her direction again. The attendant had opened the chaise, she was sitting in the sun. Meanwhile Stefano was arriving, very white, in a blue bathing suit, in his hand his wallet, lighter, cigarettes. He kissed Lila on the lips the way princes kiss sleeping beauties, and also sat down on a chaise.

Again I tried to read. I had long been used to self-discipline and this time for a few minutes I really did manage to grasp the meaning of the words, I remember that the novel was *Oblomov*. When I looked up again Stefano was still sitting, staring at the sea, Lila had disappeared. I searched for her and saw that she was talking to Antonio, and Antonio was pointing to me. I gave her a warm wave to which she responded as warmly, and she turned to call Stefano.

We went swimming, the three of us, while Antonio watched the stationer's daughters. It was a day of seeming cheerfulness. At one point Stefano took us to the bar, ordered all kinds of things: sandwiches, drinks, ice cream, and the children imme-diately abandoned Antonio and turned their attention to him.

When the two young men began to talk about some problems with the convertible, a conversation in which Antonio had a lot to say, I took the little girls away so that they wouldn't bother them. Lila joined me.

"How much does the stationer pay you?" she asked.

I told her.

"Not much."

"My mother thinks she pays me too much."

"You should assert yourself, Lenù."

"I'll assert myself when I take your children to the beach."

"I'll give you treasure chests full of gold pieces, I know the value of spending time with you."

I looked at her to see if she was joking. She wasn't joking, but she joked right afterward when she mentioned Antonio:

"Does he know your value?"

"We've been together for three weeks."

"Do you love him?"

"No."

"So?"

I challenged her with a look.

"Do you love Stefano?"

She said seriously, "Very much."

"More than your parents, more than Rino?"

"More than everyone, but not more than you."

"You're making fun of me."

But meanwhile I thought: even if she's kidding, it's nice to talk like this, in the sun, sitting on the warm concrete, with our feet in the water; never mind if she didn't ask what book I'm reading; never mind if she didn't find out how the exams went. Maybe it's not all over: even after she's married, something between us will endure. I said to her:

"I come here every day. Why don't you come, too?"

She was enthusiastic about the idea, she spoke to Stefano about it and he agreed. It was a beautiful day on which all of us, miraculously, felt at our ease. Then the sun began to go down, it was time to take the children home. Stefano went to pay and discovered that Antonio had taken care of everything. He was really sorry, he thanked him wholeheartedly. On the street, as soon as Stefano and Lila went off in the convertible, I reproached him. Melina and Ada washed the stairs of the buildings, he earned practically nothing in the garage.

"Why did you pay?" I almost yelled at him, in dialect, angrily.

"Because you and I are better-looking and more refined," he answered.

50.

I grew fond of Antonio almost without realizing it. Our sexual games became a little bolder, a little more pleasurable. I thought that if Lila came again to the Sea Garden I would ask her what happened between her and Stefano when they went off in the car alone. Did they do the same things that Antonio and I did or more, for example the things that the rumors started by the two Solaras said she did? I had no one to compare myself with except her. But there was no chance to ask her those questions, she didn't come back to the Sea Garden.

In mid-August my job was over and, with it, the joy of sun and sea. The stationer was extremely satisfied with the way I had taken care of the children and although they, in spite of my instructions, had told their mother that sometimes a young man who was my friend came to the beach, with whom they did some lovely dives, instead of reproaching me embraced me, saying, "Thank goodness, let go a little, please, you're too sensible for your age. And she added maliciously, "Think of Lina Cerullo, all she gets up to."

At the ponds that evening I said to Antonio, "It's always

been like that, since we were little: everyone thinks she's bad and I'm good."

He kissed me, murmuring ironically, "Why, isn't that true?"

That response touched me and kept me from telling him that we had to part. It was a decision that seemed to me urgent, the affection wasn't love, I loved Nino, I knew I would love him forever. I had a gentle speech prepared for Antonio, I wanted to say to him: It's been wonderful, you helped me a lot at a time when I was sad, but now school is starting and this year is going to be difficult, I have new subjects, I'll have to study a lot; I'm sorry but we have to stop. I felt it was necessary and every afternoon I went to our meeting at the ponds with my little speech ready. But he was so affectionate, so passionate, that my courage failed and I put it off. In the middle of August. By the end of the month. I said: you can't kiss, touch a person and be touched, and be only a little fond of him; Lila loves Stefano very much, I did not love Antonio.

The time passed and I could never find the right moment to speak to him. He was worried. In the heat Melina generally got worse, but in the second half of August the deterioration became very noticeable. Sarratore returned to her mind, whom she called Donato. She said she had seen him, she said he had come to get her; her children didn't know how to soothe her. I became anxious that Sarratore really had appeared on the streets of the neighborhood and that he was looking not for Melina but for me. At night I woke with a start, under the impression that he had come in through the window and was in the room. Then I calmed down, I thought: he must be on vacation in Barano, at the Maronti, not here, in this heat, with the flies, the dust.

But one morning when I was going to do the shopping I heard my name called. I turned and at first I didn't recognize him. Then I brought into focus the black mustache, the pleasing features gilded by the sun, the thin-lipped mouth. I kept going, he followed me. He said that he had been pained not to find me at Nella's house, in Barano, that summer. He said that he thought only of me, that he couldn't live without me. He said that to give a form to our love he had written many poems and would like to read them to me. He said that he wanted to see me, talk to me at leisure, that if I refused he would kill himself. Then I stopped and whispered that he had to leave me alone, I had a boyfriend, I never wanted to see him again. He despaired. He murmured that he would wait for me forever, that every day at noon he would be at the entrance to the tunnel on the *stradone*. I shook my head forcefully: I would never go there. He leaned forward to kiss me, I jumped back with a gesture of disgust, he gave a disappointed smile. He murmured, "You're clever, you're sensitive, I'll bring you the poems I like best," and he went off.

I was very frightened, I didn't know what to do. I decided to turn to Antonio. That evening, at the ponds, I told him that his mother was right, Donato Sarratore was wandering around the neighborhood. He had stopped me in the street. He had asked me to tell Melina that he would wait for her always, every day, at the entrance to the tunnel, at midday. Antonio turned somber, he said, "What should I do?" I told him that I would go with him to the appointment and that together we would give Sarratore a candid speech about the state of his mother's health.

I was too worried to sleep that night. The next day we went to the tunnel. Antonio was silent, he seemed in no hurry, I felt he had a weight on him that was slowing him down. One part of him was furious and the other subdued. I thought angrily, He was capable of confronting the Solaras for his sister Ada, for Lila, but now he's intimidated, in his eyes Donato Sarratore is an important person, of a certain standing. To feel him like that made me more determined, I would have liked to shake him, shout at him: You haven't written a book but you are much better than that man. I merely took his arm.

When Sarratore saw us from a distance he tried to disappear quickly into the darkness of the tunnel. I called him: "Signor Sarratore."

He turned reluctantly.

Using the formal *lei*, something that at the time was unusual in our world, I said, "I don't know if you remember Antonio, he is the oldest son of Signora Melina."

Sarratore pulled out a bright, very affectionate voice: "Of course I remember him, hello, Antonio."

"He and I are together."

"Ah, good."

"And we've talked a lot—now he'll explain to you."

Antonio understood that his moment had arrived and, extremely pale and tense, he said, struggling to speak in Italian, "I am very pleased to see you, Signor Sarratore, I haven't forgotten. I will always be grateful for what you did for us after the death of my father. I thank you in particular for having found me a job in Signor Gorresio's shop. I owe it to you if I have learned a trade."

"Tell him about your mother," I pressed him, nervously.

He was annoyed, and gestured at me to be quiet. He continued, "However, you no longer live in the neighborhood and you don't understand the situation. My mother, if she merely hears your name, loses her head. And if she sees you, if she sees you even one single time, she'll end up in the insane asylum."

Sarratore gasped. "Antonio, my boy, I never had any intention of doing harm to your mother. You justly recall how much I did for you. And in fact I have always and only wanted to help her and all of you."

"Then if you wish to continue to help her don't look for her, don't send her books, don't show up in the neighborhood."

"This you cannot ask of me, you cannot keep me from seeing again the places that are dear to me," Sarratore said, in a warm, falsely emotional voice.

That tone made me indignant. I knew it, he had used it often at Barano, on the beach at the Maronti. It was rich, caressing, the tone that he imagined a man of depth who wrote poems and articles in *Roma* should have. I was on the point of intervening, but Antonio, to my surprise, was ahead of me. He curved his shoulders, drew in his head, and extended one hand toward the chest of Donato Sarratore, pressing it with his powerful fingers. He said in dialect, "I won't hinder you. But I promise you that if you take away from my mother the little reason that she still has, you will lose forever the desire to see these shitty places again."

Sarratore turned very pale.

"Yes," he said quickly. "I understand, thank you."

He turned on his heels and hurried off toward the station.

I slipped in under Antonio's arm, proud of that burst of anger, but I realized that he was trembling. I thought, perhaps for the first time, of what the death of his father must have been for him, as a boy, and then the job, the responsibility that had fallen on him, the collapse of his mother. I drew him away, full of affection, and gave myself another deadline: I'll leave him after Lila's wedding.

51.

The neighborhood remembered that wedding for a long time. Its preparations were tangled up with the slow, elaborate, rancorous birth of Cerullo shoes: two undertakings that, for one reason or another, it seemed, would never come to fruition.

The wedding put a strain on the shoemaker's shop. Fernando and Rino labored not only on the new shoes, which for the moment brought in nothing, but also on the thousand other little jobs that provided immediate income, which they needed urgently. They had to put together enough money to provide Lila with a small dowry and to meet the expenses of the refreshments, which they intended to take on, no matter what, in order not to seem like poor relations. As a result, the Cerullo household was extremely tense for months: Nunzia embroidered sheets night and day, and Fernando made constant scenes, pining for the happy days when, in the tiny shop where he was king, he glued, sewed, and hammered in peace, with the tacks between his lips.

The only ones who seemed unruffled were the engaged couple. There were just two small moments of friction between them. The first had to do with their future home. Stefano wanted to buy a small apartment in the new neighborhood, Lila would have preferred to live in the old buildings. They argued. The apartment in the old neighborhood was larger but dark and had no view, like all the apartments there. The apartment in the new neighborhood was smaller but had an enormous bathtub, like the ones in the Palmolive ad, a bidet, and a view of Vesuvius. It was useless to point out that, while Vesuvius was a shifting and distant outline that faded into the cloudy sky, less than two hundred yards away ran the gleaming tracks of the railroad. Stefano was seduced by the new, by the shiny floors, by the white walls, and Lila soon gave in. What counted more than anything else was that, not yet seventeen, she would be the mistress of a house of her own, with hot water that came from the taps, and a house not rented but owned.

The second cause of friction was the honeymoon. Stefano proposed Venice, and Lila, revealing a tendency that would mark her whole life, insisted on not going far from Naples. She suggested a stay on Ischia, Capri, and maybe the Amalfi coast, all places she had never been. Her future husband almost immediately agreed.

Otherwise, there were small tensions, more than anything echoes of problems within their families. For example, if

Stefano went into the Cerullo shoe shop, he always let slip a few rude words about Fernando and Rino when he saw Lila later, and she was upset, she leaped to their defense. He shook his head, unpersuaded, he was beginning to see in the business of the shoes an excessive investment, and at the end of the summer, when the strain between him and the two Cerullos increased, he imposed a precise limit on the making and unmaking by father, son, helpers. He said that by November he wanted the first results: at least the winter styles, men's and women's, ready to be displayed in the window for Christmas. Then, rather nervously, he admitted to Lila that Rino was quicker to ask for money than to work. She defended her brother, he replied, she bristled, he immediately retreated. He went to get the pair of shoes that had given birth to the whole project, shoes bought and never worn, kept as a valuable witness to their story, and he fingered them, smelled them, became emotional talking of how he felt about them, saw them, had always seen in them her small, almost childish hands working alongside her brother's large ones. They were on the terrace of the old house, the one where we had set off the fireworks in competition with the Solaras. He took her fingers and kissed them, one by one, saying that he would never again allow them to be spoiled.

Lila herself told me, happily, about that act of love. She told me the day she took me to see the new house. What splendor: floors of polished majolica tile, the tub in which you could have a bubble bath, the inlaid furniture in the dining room and the bedroom, a refrigerator and even a telephone. I wrote down the number, with great excitement. We had been born and lived in small houses, without our own rooms, without a place to study. I still lived like that, soon she would not. We went out on the balcony that overlooked the railroad and Vesuvius, and I asked her warily:

"Do you and Stefano come here by yourselves?"

"Yes, sometimes."

"And what happens?"

She looked at me as if she didn't understand.

"In what sense?"

I was embarrassed.

"Do you kiss?"

"Sometimes."

"And then?"

"That's all, we're not married yet."

I was confused. Was it possible? So much freedom and nothing? So much gossip in the neighborhood, the Solaras' obscenities, and there had been only a few kisses?

"But he doesn't ask you?"

"Why, does Antonio ask you?"

"Yes."

"No, he doesn't. He agrees that we should be married first."

But she seemed struck by my questions, much as I was struck by her answers. So she yielded nothing to Stefano, even if they went out in the car by themselves, even if they were about to get married, even if they already had a furnished house, a bed with a mattress, still in its packing. And I, who certainly would not get married, had long ago gone beyond kissing. When she asked me, genuinely curious, if I gave Antonio the things he asked for, I was ashamed to tell her the truth. I said no and she seemed content.

52.

I made the dates at the ponds less frequent, partly because school was about to start again. I was sure that Lila, because of my classes, my homework, would keep me out of the wedding preparations, she had got used to my disappearance during the school year. But it wasn't to be. The conflicts with Pinuccia had intensified over the summer. It was no longer a matter of dresses or hats or scarves or jewelry. One day Pinuccia said to her brother, in Lila's presence and unambiguously, that either his betrothed came to work in the grocery, if not immediately then at least after the honeymoon—to work as the whole family always had, as even Alfonso did whenever school allowed him to—or she would stop working. And this time her mother supported her outright.

Lila didn't blink, she said she would start immediately, even tomorrow, in whatever role the Carracci family wanted. That answer, as Lila's answers always were, always had been, though intended to be conciliatory, had something arrogant, scornful, about it, which made Pinuccia even angrier. It became clear that the two women saw the shoemaker's daughter as a witch who had come to be the mistress, to throw money out the window without lifting a finger to earn it, to subdue the master by her arts, making him act unjustly against his own flesh and blood, that is to say against his sister and even his mother.

Stefano, as usual, did not respond immediately. He waited until his sister's outburst was over, then, as if the problem of Lila and her placement in the small family business had never been raised, said calmly that it would be better if Pinuccia, rather than work in the grocery, would help his fiancée with the preparations for the wedding.

"You don't need me anymore?" she snapped.

"No: starting tomorrow I have Ada, Melina's daughter, coming to replace you."

"Did she suggest it?" cried his sister, pointing to Lila.

"It's none of your business."

"Did you hear that, Ma? Did you hear what he said? He thinks he's the absolute boss in here."

There was an unbearable silence, then Maria got up from the seat behind the cash register and said to her son, "Find

someone for this place, too, because I'm tired and I don't want
to work anymore."

Stefano at that point yielded a little. "Calm down, I'm not
the boss of anything, the business of the grocery doesn't have
to do with me alone but all of us. We have to make a decision.
Pinù, do you need to work? No. Mammà, do you need to sit
back there all day? No. Then let's give work to those who need
it. I'll put Ada behind the counter and I'll think about the cash
register. Otherwise, who will take care of the wedding?"

I don't know for sure if Lila was behind the expulsion of
Pinuccia and her mother from the daily running of the grocery,
behind the hiring of Ada (certainly Ada was convinced of it
and so, especially, was Antonio, who began referring to our
friend as a good fairy). Of course, she wasn't pleased that her
sister-in-law and mother-in-law had a lot of free time to devote
to her wedding. The two women complicated life, there were
conflicts about every little thing: the guests, the decoration of
the church, the photographer, the cake, the wedding favors,
the rings, even the honeymoon, since Pinuccia and Maria considered it a poor thing to go to Sorrento, Positano, Ischia, and
Capri. So all of a sudden I was drawn in, apparently to give
Lila an opinion on this or that, in reality to support her in a difficult battle.

I was starting my third year of high school, I had a lot of
new, hard subjects. My usual stubborn diligence was already
killing me, I studied relentlessly. But once, coming home from
school, I ran into Lila and she said to me, point-blank, "Please,
Lenù, tomorrow will you come and give me some advice?"

I didn't even know what she meant. I had been tested in
chemistry and hadn't done well, and was suffering.

"Advice about what?"

"Advice about my wedding dress. Please, don't say no,
because if you don't come I'll murder my sister-in-law and
mother-in-law."

I went. I joined her, Pinuccia, and Maria uneasily. The shop was on the Rettifilo and I remember I had stuck some books in a bag, hoping to find some way of studying. It was impossible. From four in the afternoon to seven in the evening we looked at styles, we fingered fabrics, Lila tried on the wedding dresses displayed on the shop mannequins. Whatever she put on, her beauty enhanced the dress, the dress enhanced her beauty. Stiff organza, soft satin, airy tulle became her. A lace bodice, puff sleeves became her. A full skirt and a narrow skirt became her, a long train and a short one, a flowing veil and a short one, a crown of rhinestones, of pearls, of orange blossoms. And she, obediently, examined styles or tried on the models that were flattering on the mannequins. But occasionally, when she could no longer bear the fussiness of her future relatives, the old Lila rose up and, looking me straight in the eye, said, alarming mother-in-law, sister-in-law, "What if we chose a beautiful green satin, or a red organza, or a nice black tulle, or, better still, yellow?" It took my laughter to indicate that the bride was joking, to return to serious, rancorous consideration of fabrics and styles. The dressmaker merely kept repeating enthusiastically, "Please, whatever you choose, bring me the wedding pictures so that I can display them in the shop window, and say: I dressed that girl."

The problem, however, was choosing. Every time Lila preferred a style, a fabric, Pinuccia and Maria lined up in favor of another style, another fabric. I said nothing, stunned by all those discussions and by the smell of new fabric. Finally Lila asked me in vexation:

"What do you think, Lenù?"

There was silence. I suddenly perceived, with a certain astonishment, that the two women had been expecting that moment and feared it. I set in motion a technique I had learned at school, which consisted of this: whenever I didn't know how to answer a question, I was lavish in setting out premises in the confident voice of someone who knows clearly where he wishes to end up. I said first—in Italian—that I liked very much the styles favored by Pinuccia and her mother. I launched not into praise but into arguments that demonstrated how suitable they were to Lila's figure. At the moment when, as in class with the teachers, I felt I had the admiration, the sympathy of mother and daughter, I chose one of the styles at random, truly at random, careful not to pick one of those that Lila favored, and went on to demonstrate that it incorporated the qualities of the styles favored by the two women, and the qualities of the ones favored by my friend. The dressmaker, Pinuccia, the mother were immediately in agreement with me. Lila merely looked at me with narrowed eyes. Then her gaze returned to normal and she said that she agreed, too.

On the way out both Pinuccia and Maria were in a very good mood. They addressed Lila almost with affection and, commenting on the purchase, kept dragging me in with phrases like: as Lenuccia said, or, Lenuccia rightly said. Lila maneuvered so that we were a little behind them, in the evening crowd of the Rettifilo. She asked me:

"You learn this in school?"

"What?"

"To use words to con people."

I felt wounded. I murmured, "You don't like the style we chose?"

"I like it immensely."

"So?"

"So do me the favor of coming with us whenever I ask you."

I was angry. I said, "You want to use me to con them?"

She understood that she had offended me, she squeezed my hand hard. "I didn't intend to say something unkind. I meant only that you are good at making yourself liked. The difference between you and me, always, has been that people are afraid of me and not of you."

"Maybe because you're mean," I said, even angrier.

"Maybe," she said, and I saw that I had hurt her as she had hurt me. Then, repenting, I added immediately, to make up: "Antonio would get himself killed for you: he said to thank you for giving his sister a job."

"It's Stefano who gave the job to Ada," she replied. "I'm mean."

53.

From then on, I was constantly called on to take part in the most disputed decisions, and sometimes—I discovered—not at Lila's request but Pinuccia and her mother's. I chose the favors. I chose the restaurant, in Via Orazio. I chose the photographer, persuading them to include a film in super 8. In every circumstance I realized that, while I was deeply interested in everything, as if each of those questions were practice for when my turn came to get married, Lila, at the stations of her wedding, paid little attention. I was surprised, but that was certainly the case. What truly engaged her was to make sure, once and for all, that in her future life as wife and mother, in her house, her sister-in-law and her mother-in-law would have no say. But it wasn't the ordinary conflict between mother-in-law, daughter-in-law, sister-in-law. I had the impression, from the way she used me, from the way she handled Stefano, that she was struggling to find, from inside the cage in which she was enclosed, a way of being, all her own, that was still obscure to her.

Naturally I wasted entire afternoons settling their affairs, I didn't study much, and a couple of times ended up not even going to school. The result was that my report card for the first trimester was not especially brilliant. My new teacher of Latin and Greek, the greatly respected Galiani, had a high opinion of me, but in philosophy, chemistry, and mathematics I barely passed. Then one morning I got into serious trouble. Since the religion teacher was constantly delivering tirades against the Communists, against their atheism, I felt impelled to react, I don't really know if by my affection for Pasquale, who had always said he was a Communist, or simply because I felt that all the bad things the priest said about Communists concerned me directly as the pet of the most prominent Communist, Professor Galiani. The fact remains that I, who had successfully completed a theological correspondence course, raised my hand and said that the human condition was so obviously exposed to the blind fury of chance that to trust in a God, a Jesus, the Holy Spirit—this last a completely superfluous entity, it was there only to make up a trinity, notoriously nobler than the mere binomial father-son—was the same thing as collecting trading cards while the city burns in the fires of hell. Alfonso had immediately realized that I was overdoing it and timidly tugged on my smock, but I paid no attention and went all the way, to that concluding comparison. For the first time I was sent out of the classroom and had a demerit on my class record.

Once I was in the hall, I was disoriented at first—what had happened, why had I behaved so recklessly, where had I gotten the absolute conviction that the things I was saying were right and should be said?—and then I remembered that I had had those conversations with Lila, and saw that I had landed myself in trouble because, in spite of everything, I continued to assign her an authority that made me bold enough to challenge the religion teacher. Lila no longer opened a book, no longer went to school, was about to become the wife of a grocer, would probably end up at the cash register in place of Stefano's mother, and I? I had drawn from her the energy to invent an image that defined religion as the collecting of trading cards while the city burns in the fires of hell? Was it not true, then, that school was my personal wealth, now far from her influence? I wept silently outside the classroom door.

But things changed unexpectedly. Nino Sarratore appeared at the end of the hall. After the new encounter with his father, I had all the more reason to behave as if he didn't exist, but seeing him in that situation revived me, I quickly dried my tears. He must have realized that something was wrong, and he came toward me. He was more grown-up: he had a prominent Adam's apple, features hollowed out by a bluish beard, a firmer gaze. It was impossible to avoid him. I couldn't go back into the class, I couldn't go to the bathroom, either of which would have made my situation more complicated if the religion teacher looked out. So when he joined me and asked why I was outside, what had happened, I told him. He frowned and said, "I'll be right back." He disappeared and reappeared a few minutes later with Professor Galiani.

Galiani was full of praise. "But now," she said, as if she were giving me and Nino a lesson, "after the full attack, it's time to mediate." She knocked on the door of the classroom, closed it behind her, and five minutes later looked out happily. I could go back provided I apologized to the professor for the aggressive tone I had used. I apologized, wavering between anxiety about probable reprisals and pride in the support I had received from Nino and from Professor Galiani.

I was careful not to say anything to my parents, but I told Antonio everything, and he proudly reported the incident to Pasquale, who ran into Lila one morning and, so overcome by his love for her that he could barely speak, seized on my adventure like a life vest, and told her about it. Thus I became, in the blink of an eye, the heroine both of my old friends and of the small but seasoned group of teachers and students who challenged the lectures of the teacher of religion. Meanwhile, aware that my apologies to the priest were not enough, I made an effort to regain credit with him and with his like-minded colleagues. I easily separated my words from myself: toward all the teachers who had become hostile to me I was respectful, helpful, cooperative, so that they went back to thinking of me as a person who came out with odd, but forgivable, assertions. I thus discovered that I was able to behave like Professor Galiani: present my opinions firmly and, at the same time, soften them, and regain respect, through my irreproachable behavior. Within a few days it seemed to me that I had returned, along with Nino Sarratore, who was in his fifth year and would graduate, to the top of the list of the most promising students in our shabby high school.

It didn't end there. A few weeks later, unexpectedly, Nino, with his shadowy look, asked me if I could quickly write half a page recounting the conflict with the priest.

"To do what with?"

He told me that he wrote for a little journal called *Naples, Home of the Poor*. He had described the incident to the editors and they had said that if I could write an account in time they would try to put it in the next issue. He showed me the journal. It was a pamphlet of fifty pages, of a dirty gray. In the contents he appeared, first name and last name, with an article entitled "The Numbers of Poverty." I thought of his father, and the satisfaction, the vanity with which he had read to me at the Maronti the article he'd published in *Roma*.

"Do you also write poetry?" I asked.

He denied it with such disgusted energy that I immediately promised: "All right, I'll try."

I went home in great agitation. My head was already churning with the sentences I would write, and on the way I talked about it in great detail to Alfonso. He became anxious for me, he begged me not to write anything.

"Will they sign it with your name?"

"Yes."

"Lenù, the priest will get angry again and fail you: he'll get chemistry and mathematics on his side."

He transmitted his anxiety to me and I lost confidence. But, as soon as we separated, the idea of being able to show the journal, with my little article, my name in print, to Lila, to my parents, to Maestra Oliviero, to Maestro Ferraro, got the upper hand. I would mend things later. It had been very energizing to win praise from those who seemed to me better (Professor Galiani, Nino) taking sides against those who seemed to me worse (the priest, the chemistry teacher, the mathematics teacher), and yet to behave toward the adversaries in such a way as not to lose their friendship and respect. I would make an effort to repeat this when the article was published.

I spent the afternoon writing and rewriting. I found concise, dense sentences. I tried to give my position the maximum theoretical weight by finding difficult words. I wrote, "If God is present everywhere, what need does he have to disseminate himself by way of the Holy Spirit?" But the half page was soon used up, merely in the premise. And the rest? I started again. And since I had been trained since elementary school to try and stubbornly keep trying, in the end I got a creditable result and turned to my lessons for the next day.

But half an hour later my doubts returned, I felt the need for confirmation. Who could I ask to read my text and give an opinion? My mother? My brothers? Antonio? Naturally not, the only one was Lila. But to turn to her meant to continue to recognize in her an authority, when in fact I, by now, knew more than she did. So I resisted. I was afraid that she would dismiss my half page with a disparaging remark. I was even more afraid that that remark would nevertheless work in my mind, pushing me to extreme thoughts that I would end up transcribing onto my half page, throwing off its equilibrium. And yet finally I gave in and went to look for her. She was at her parents' house. I told her about Nino's proposal and gave her the notebook.

She looked at the page unwillingly, as if the writing

wounded her eyes. Exactly like Alfonso, she asked, "Will they put your name on it?"

I nodded yes.

"Elena Greco?"

"Yes."

She held out the notebook: "I'm not capable of telling you if it's good or not."

"Please."

"No, I'm not capable."

I had to insist. I said, though I knew it wasn't true, that if she didn't like it, if in fact she refused to read it, I wouldn't give it to Nino to print.

In the end she read it. It seemed to me that she shrank, as if I had unloaded a weight on her. And I had the impression that she was making a painful effort to free from some corner of herself the old Lila, the one who read, wrote, drew, made plans spontaneously—the naturalness of an instinctive reaction. When she succeeded, everything seemed pleasantly light.

"Can I erase?"

"Yes."

She erased quite a few words and an entire sentence.

"Can I move something?"

"Yes."

She circled a sentence and moved it with a wavy line to the top of the page.

"Can I recopy it for you onto another page?"

"I'll do it."

"No, let me do it."

It took a while to recopy. When she gave me back the notebook, she said, "You're very clever, of course they always give you ten."

I felt that there was no irony, it was a real compliment. Then she added with sudden harshness:

"I don't want to read anything else that you write."

"Why?"

She thought about it.

"Because it hurts me," and she struck her forehead with her hand and burst out laughing.

54.

I went home happy. I shut myself in the toilet so that I wouldn't disturb the rest of the family and studied until three in the morning, when finally I went to sleep. I dragged myself up at six-thirty to recopy the text. But first I read it over in Lila's beautiful round handwriting, a handwriting that had remained the same as in elementary school, very different now from mine, which had become smaller and plainer. On the page was exactly what I had written, but it was clearer, more immediate. The erasures, the transpositions, the small additions, and, in some way, her handwriting itself gave me the impression that I had escaped from myself and now was running a hundred paces ahead with an energy and also a harmony that the person left behind didn't know she had.

I decided to leave the text in Lila's handwriting. I brought it to Nino like that in order to keep the visible trace of her presence in my words. He read it, blinking his long eyelashes. At the end he said, with sudden, unexpected sadness, "Professor Galiani is right."

"About what?"

"You write better than I do."

And although I protested, embarrassed, he repeated that phrase again, then turned his back and went off without saying goodbye. He didn't even say when the journal would come out or how I could get a copy, nor did I have the courage to ask him. That behavior bothered me. And even more because, as he walked away, I recognized for a few moments his father's gait.

This was how our new encounter ended. We got everything wrong again. For days Nino continued to behave as if writing better than him was a sin that had to be expiated. I became irritated. When suddenly he reassigned me body, life, presence, and asked me to walk a little way with him, I answered coldly that I was busy, my boyfriend was supposed to pick me up.

For a while he must have thought that the boyfriend was Alfonso, but any doubt was resolved when, one day, after school, his sister Marisa appeared, to tell him something or other. We hadn't seen each other since the days on Ischia. She ran over to me, she greeted me warmly, she said how sorry she was that I hadn't returned to Barano that summer. Since I was with Alfonso I introduced him. She insisted, as her brother had already left, on going part of the way with us. First she told us all her sufferings in love. Then, when she realized that Alfonso and I were not boyfriend and girlfriend, she stopped talking to me and began to chat with him in her charming way. She must have told her brother that between Alfonso and me there was nothing, because right away, the next day, he began hovering around me again. But now the mere sight of him made me nervous. Was he vain like his father, even if he detested him? Did he think that others couldn't help liking him, loving him? Was he so full of himself that he couldn't tolerate good qualities other than his own?

I asked Antonio to come and pick me up at school. He obeyed immediately, confused and at the same time pleased by that request. What surely surprised him most was that there in public, in front of everyone, I took his hand and entwined my fingers with his. I had always refused to walk like that, either in the neighborhood or outside it, because it made me feel that I was still a child, going for a walk with my father. That day I did it. I knew that Nino was watching us and I wanted him to understand who I was. I wrote better than he did, I would publish in the magazine where he published, I was as good at school and better than he was, I had a man, look at him: and so I would not run after him like a faithful beast.

55.

I also asked Antonio to go with me to Lila's wedding, not to leave me alone, and maybe always to dance with me. I dreaded that day, I felt it as a definitive break, and I wanted someone there who would support me.

This request was to complicate life further. Lila had sent invitations to everyone. In the houses of the neighborhood the mothers, the grandmothers had been working for months to make dresses, to get hats and purses, to shop for a wedding present, I don't know, a set of glasses, of plates, of silverware. It wasn't so much for Lila that they made that effort; it was for Stefano, who was very decent, and allowed you to pay at the end of the month. But a wedding was, above all, an occasion where no one should make a bad showing, especially girls without fiancés, who there would have a chance of finding one and getting settled, marrying, in their turn, within a few years.

It was really for that last reason that I wanted Antonio to go with me. I had no intention of making the thing official—we were careful to keep our relationship absolutely hidden—but I wished to keep under control my anxiety about being attractive. I wanted, that day, to feel calm, tranquil, despite my glasses, the modest dress made by my mother, my old shoes, and at the same time think: I have everything a sixteen-year-old girl should have, I don't need anything or anyone.

But Antonio didn't take it like that. He loved me, he considered me the luckiest thing that had ever happened to him. He often asked aloud, with a hint of anguish straining under an appearance of amusement, how in the world I had chosen him, who was stupid and couldn't put two words together. In fact, he couldn't wait to appear at my parents' house and make our relationship official. And so at that request of mine he must have thought that I had finally decided to let him come out of hiding, and he went into debt to buy a suit, in addition to what he was spending for the wedding gift, clothes for Ada and the other children, a presentable appearance for Melina.

I didn't notice anything. I struggled on, between school, the urgent consultations whenever things got tangled up between Lila and her sister-in-law and mother-in-law, the pleasant nervousness about the article that I might see published at any time. I was secretly convinced that I would truly exist only at the moment when my signature, Elena Greco, appeared in print, and as I waited for that day I didn't pay much attention to Antonio, who had got the idea of completing his wedding outfit with a pair of Cerullo shoes. Every so often he asked me, "Do you know what point they've reached?" I answered, "Ask Rino, Lila doesn't know anything."

It was true. In November the Cerullos summoned Stefano without bothering to show the shoes to Lila first, even though she was still living at home with them. Instead, Stefano showed up for the occasion with his fiancée and Pinuccia, all three looking as if they had emerged from the television screen. Lila told me that, on seeing the shoes she had designed years earlier made real, she had felt a very violent emotion, as if a fairy had appeared and fulfilled a wish. The shoes really were as she had imagined them at the time. Even Pinuccia was amazed. She wanted to try on a pair she liked and she complimented Rino effusively, letting him understand that she considered him the true craftsman of those masterpieces of sturdy lightness, of dissonant harmony. The only one who seemed displeased was Stefano. He interrupted the warm greetings Lila was giving her father and brother and the workers, silenced the sugary voice of Pinuccia, who was congratulating Rino, raising an ankle to show him her extraordinarily shod foot, and, style after style, he criticized the modifications made to the original designs. He was especially persistent in the comparison between the man's shoe as it had been made by Rino and Lila in secret from Fernando, and the same shoe as the father and son had refined it. "What's this fringe, what are these stitches, what is this gilded pin?" he asked in annoyance. And no matter how Fernando explained all the modifications, for reasons of durability or to disguise some defect in the idea, Stefano was adamant. He said he had invested too much money to obtain ordinary shoes and not—precisely identical—Lila's shoes.

The tension was extreme. Lila gently defended her father, she told her fiancé to let it go: her designs were the fantasies of a child, and surely the modifications were necessary, and, besides, were not so great. But Rino supported Stefano and the discussion went on for a long time. It broke off only when Fernando, utterly worn out, sat down in a corner and, looking at the pictures on the wall, said, "If you want the shoes for Christmas take them like that. If you want them exactly the way my daughter designed them, have someone else make them."

Stefano gave in, Rino, too, gave in.

At Christmas the shoes appeared in the window, a window with the comet star made of cotton wool. I went by to see them: they were elegant objects, carefully finished: just to look at them gave an impression of wealth that did not accord with the humble shop window, with the desolate landscape outside, with the shop's interior, all pieces of hide and leather and benches and awls and wooden forms and boxes of shoes piled up to the ceiling, waiting for customers. Even with Fernando's modifications, they were the shoes of our childish dreams, not invented for the reality of the neighborhood.

In fact at Christmas not a single pair sold. Only Antonio appeared, asked Rino for a 44, tried it. Later he told me the pleasure he had had in feeling so well shod, imagining himself with me at the wedding, in his new suit, with those shoes on his feet. But when he asked the price and Rino told him, he was dumbstruck: "Are you crazy?" and when Rino said, "I'll sell them to you on a monthly installment," he responded, laughing, "Then I'll buy a Lambretta."

56.

At the moment Lila, taken up by the wedding, didn't realize that her brother, until then cheerful, playful, even though he was exhausted by work, was becoming depressed again, sleeping badly, flying into a rage for no reason. "He's like a child," she said to Pinuccia, as if to apologize for some of his outbursts, "his mood changes according to whether his whims are satisfied immediately or not, he doesn't know how to wait." She, like Fernando, did not feel in the least that the failure of the shoes to sell at Christmas was a fiasco. After all, the production of the shoes had not followed any plan: they had originated in Stefano's wish to see Lila's purest caprice made concrete, there were heavy ones, light ones, spanning most of the seasons. And this was an advantage. In the white boxes piled up in the Cerullos' shop was a considerable assortment. They had only to wait, and in winter, in spring, in autumn the shoes would sell.

But Rino was increasingly agitated. After Christmas, on his own initiative, he went to the owner of the dusty shoe store at the end of the *stradone* and, although he knew the man was bound hand and foot to the Solaras, proposed that he display some of the Cerullo shoes, without obligation, just to see how they went. The man said no politely, that product was not suitable for his customers. Rino took offense and an exchange of vulgarities followed, which became known in the whole neighborhood. Fernando was furious with his son, Rino insulted him, and Lila again experienced her brother as an element of disorder, a manifestation of the destructive forces that had frightened her. When the four of them went out, she noticed with apprehension that her brother maneuvered to let her and Pinuccia go on ahead while he stayed behind to talk to Stefano. In general the grocer listened to him without showing signs of irritation. Only once Lila heard him say:

"Excuse me, Rino, do you think I put so much money in the shoe store like that, without any security, just for love of your sister? We have the shoes, they're beautiful, we have to sell them. The problem is to find the right place."

That "just for love of your sister" didn't please her. But she let it go, because the words had a good effect on Rino, who calmed down and began to talk, in particular to Pinuccia, about strategies for selling the shoes. He said they had to think on a grand scale. Why did so many good initiatives fail? Why had the Gorresio auto repair shop given up motorbikes? Why had the dressmaker in the dry goods store lasted only six months? Because they were undertakings that lacked breadth. The Cerullo shoes, instead, would as soon as possible leave the local market and become popular in the wealthier neighborhoods.

Meanwhile the date of the wedding approached. Lila hurried to fittings for her wedding dress, gave the final touches to her future home, fought with Pinuccia and Maria, who, among many things, were intolerant of Nunzia's intrusions. The situation was increasingly tense. But the damaging attacks came from elsewhere. There were two events in particular, one after the other, that wounded Lila deeply.

One cold afternoon in February she asked me out of the blue if I could come with her to see Maestra Oliviero. She had never displayed any interest in her, no affection, no gratitude. Now, though, she felt the need to bring her the invitation in person. Since in the past I had never reported to her the hostile tones that the teacher had often used about her, it didn't seem to me right to tell her then, especially since the teacher had recently seemed less aggressive, more melancholy: maybe she would welcome her kindly.

Lila dressed with extreme care. We walked to the building where the teacher lived, near the parish church. As we climbed the stairs, I realized that she was nervous. I was used to that journey, to those stairs; she wasn't, and didn't say a word. I rang the bell, I heard the teacher's dragging steps.

"Who is it?"

"Greco."

She opened the door. Over her shoulders she wore a purple shawl and half her face was wrapped in a scarf. Lila smiled and said, "Maestra, do you remember me?"

The teacher stared at her as she used to do in school when Lila was annoying, then she turned to me, speaking with difficulty, as if she had something in her mouth.

"Who is it? I don't know her."

Lila was confused and said quickly, in Italian, "I'm Cerullo. I've brought you an invitation, I'm getting married. And I would be so happy if you would come to my wedding."

The teacher turned to me, said: "I know Cerullo, I don't know who this girl is."

She closed the door in our faces.

We stood without moving on the landing for some moments, then I touched her hand to comfort her. She withdrew it, stuck the invitation under the door, and started down the stairs. On the street she began talking about all the bureaucratic problems at the city hall and the parish, and how helpful my father had been.

The other sorrow, perhaps more profound, came, surprisingly, from Stefano and the business of the shoes. He had long since decided that the role of speech master would be entrusted to a relative of Maria's who had emigrated to Florence after the war and had set up a small trade in old things of varied provenance, especially metal objects. This relative had married a Florentine woman and had taken on the local accent. Because of his cadences he enjoyed in the family a certain prestige, and also for that reason had been Stefano's confirmation sponsor. But, abruptly, the bridegroom changed his mind.

At first, Lila spoke as if it were a sign of last-minute nervousness. For her, it was completely indifferent who the speech master was, the important thing was to decide. But for several days Stefano gave her only vague, confused answers, and she couldn't understand who was to replace the Florentine couple. Then, less than a week before the wedding, the truth came out. Stefano told her, as a thing done, without any explanation, that the speech master would be Silvio Solara, the father of Marcello and Michele.

Lila, who until that moment hadn't considered the possibility that even a distant relative of Marcello Solara might be present at *her* wedding, became again the girl I knew very well. She insulted Stefano grossly, she said she didn't want to ever see him again. She shut herself up in her parents' house, stopped concerning herself with anything, didn't go to the last fitting of the dress, did absolutely nothing that had to do with the imminent wedding.

The procession of relatives began. First came her mother, Nunzia, who spoke to her desperately about the good of the family. Then Fernando arrived, gruff, and told her not to be a child: for anyone who wanted to have a future in the neighborhood, to have Silvio Solara as speech master was obligatory. Finally Rino came, and, in an aggressive tone of voice, and with the air of a businessman who is interested only in profit, explained to her how things stood: Solara the father was like a bank and, above all, was the channel by which the Cerullo shoe styles could be placed in shops. "What are you doing?" he shouted at her with puffy, bloodshot eyes. "You want to ruin me and the whole family and all the work we've done up to now?" Right afterward even

Pinuccia appeared, and said to her, in a somewhat artificial tone of voice, how pleased she, too, would have been to have the metal merchant from Florence as the speech master, but you had to be reasonable, you couldn't cancel a wedding and eradicate a love for a matter of such little importance.

A day and a night passed. Nunzia sat mutely in a corner without moving, without caring for the house, without sleeping. Then she slipped out in secret from her daughter and came to summon me, to speak to Lila, to put in a word. I was flattered, I thought for a long time which side to take. There was at stake a wedding, a practical, highly complex thing, crammed with affections and interests. I was frightened. I knew that, although I could argue publicly with the Holy Spirit, challenging the authority of the professor of religion, if I were in Lila's place I would never have the courage to throw it all away. But she, yes, she would be capable of it, even though the wedding was about to be celebrated. What to do? I felt that it would take very little for me to urge her along that path, and that to work for that conclusion would give me great pleasure. Inside, it was what I truly wanted: to bring her back to pale, ponytailed Lila, with the narrowed eyes of a bird of prey, in her tattered dress. No more of those airs, that acting like the Jacqueline Kennedy of the neighborhood.

But, unfortunately for her and for me, it seemed a small-minded act. Thinking it would be for her good, I would not restore her to the bleakness of the Cerullo house, and so a single idea became fixed in my mind and all I could do was tell her over and over again, with gentle persuasion: Silvio Solara, Lila, isn't Marcello, or even Michele; it's wrong to confuse them, you know better than I do, you've said it yourself on other occasions. He's not the one who pulled Ada into the car, he's not the one who shot at us the night of New Year's, he's not the one who forced his way into your house, he's not the one who said vulgar things about you; Silvio will be the speech master and will help Rino and Stefano sell the shoes, that's all—he'll have no importance in your future life. I reshuffled the cards that by now we knew well enough. I spoke of the before and the after, of the old generation and of ours, of how we were different, of how she and Stefano were different. And this last argument made a breach, seduced her, I returned to it passionately. She listened to me in silence, evidently she wanted to be helped to compose herself, and slowly she did. But I read in her eyes that that move of Stefano's had shown her something about him that she still couldn't see clearly and that just for that reason frightened her even more than the ravings of Rino. She said to me:

"Maybe it's not true that he loves me."

"What do you mean he doesn't love you? He does everything you tell him to."

"Only when I don't put real money at risk," she said in a tone of contempt that I had never heard her use for Stefano Carracci.

In any case she returned to the world. She didn't appear in the grocery, she didn't go to the new house, in other words she was not the one who would seek to reconcile. She waited for Stefano to say to her: "Thank you, I love you dearly, you know there are things one is obliged to do." Only then did she let him come up behind her and kiss her on the neck. But then she turned suddenly and looking him straight in the eyes said to him, "Marcello Solara must absolutely not set foot in my wedding."

"How can I prevent it?"

"I don't know, but you must swear to me."

He snorted and said smiling, "All right, Lina, I swear."

57.

March 12th arrived, a mild day that was almost like spring.

Lila wanted me to come early to her old house, so that I could help her wash, do her hair, dress. She sent her mother away, we were alone. She sat on the edge of the bed in underpants and bra. Next to her was the wedding dress, which looked like the body of a dead woman; in front of us, on the hexagonal-tiled floor, was the copper tub full of boiling water. She asked me abruptly: "Do you think I'm making a mistake?"

"How?"

"By getting married."

"Are you still thinking about the speech master?"

"No, I'm thinking of the teacher. Why didn't she want me to come in?"

"Because she's a mean old lady."

She was silent for a while, staring at the water that sparkled in the tub, then she said, "Whatever happens, you'll go on studying."

"Two more years: then I'll get my diploma and I'm done."

"No, don't ever stop: I'll give you the money, you should keep studying."

I gave a nervous laugh, then said, "Thanks, but at a certain point school is over."

"Not for you: you're my brilliant friend, you have to be the best of all, boys and girls."

She got up, took off her underpants and bra, said, "Come on, help me, otherwise I'll be late."

I had never seen her naked, I was embarrassed. Today I can say that it was the embarrassment of gazing with pleasure at her body, of being the not impartial witness of her sixteen-year-old's beauty a few hours before Stefano touched her, penetrated her, disfigured her, perhaps, by making her pregnant. At the time it was just a tumultuous sensation of necessary awkwardness, a state in which you cannot avert the gaze or take away the hand without recognizing your own turmoil, without, by that retreat, declaring it, hence without coming into conflict with the undisturbed innocence of the one who is the cause of the turmoil, without expressing by that rejection the violent emotion that overwhelms you, so that it forces you to stay, to rest your gaze on the childish shoulders, on the breasts and stiffly cold nipples, on the narrow hips and the tense buttocks, on the black sex, on the long legs, on the tender knees, on the curved ankles, on the elegant feet; and to act as if it's nothing, when instead everything is there, present, in the poor dim room, amid the worn furniture, on the uneven, water-stained floor, and your heart is agitated, your veins inflamed.

I washed her with slow, careful gestures, first letting her squat in the tub, then asking her to stand up: I still have in my ears the sound of the dripping water, and the impression that the copper of the tub had a consistency not different from Lila's flesh, which was smooth, solid, calm. I had a confusion of feelings and thoughts: embrace her, weep with her, kiss her, pull her hair, laugh, pretend to sexual experience and instruct her in a learned voice, distancing her with words just at the moment of greatest closeness. But in the end there was only the hostile thought that I was washing her, from her hair to the soles of her feet, early in the morning, just so that Stefano could sully her in the course of the night. I imagined her naked as she was at that moment, entwined with her husband, in the bed in the new house, while the train clattered under their windows and his violent flesh entered her with a sharp blow, like the cork pushed by the palm into the neck of a wine bottle. And it suddenly seemed to me that the only remedy against the pain I was feeling, that I would feel, was to find a corner secluded enough so that Antonio could do to me, at the same time, the exact same thing.

I helped her dry off, dress, put on the wedding dress that I—I, I thought with a mixture of pride and suffering—had chosen for her. The fabric became living, over its whiteness ran Lila's heat, the red of her mouth, her hard black eyes. Finally

314 · ELENA FERRANTE

she put on the shoes that she herself had designed. Pressed by Rino, who if she hadn't worn them would have felt a kind of betrayal, she had chosen a pair with low heels, to avoid seeming too much taller than Stefano. She looked at herself in the mirror, lifting the dress slightly.

"They're ugly," she said.

"It's not true."

She laughed nervously.

"But yes, look: the mind's dreams have ended up under the feet."

She turned with a sudden expression of fear.

"What's going to happen to me, Lenù?"

58.

In the kitchen, waiting impatiently for us, were Fernando and Nunzia. I had never seen them so well dressed and groomed. At that time Lila's parents, mine—all parents—seemed to me old. I didn't make much of a distinction between them and my grandparents, maternal and paternal, creatures who in my eyes all led a sort of cold life, an existence that had nothing in common with mine, with Lila's, Stefano's, Antonio's, Pasquale's. It was we who were truly consumed by the heat of feelings, by the outburst of thoughts. Only now, as I write, do I realize that Fernando at that time couldn't have been more than forty-five, Nunzia was certainly a few years younger, and together, that morning, he, in a white shirt and dark suit, with his Randolph Scott face, and she, all in blue, with a blue hat and blue veil, made an impressive sight. The same goes for my parents, about whose age I can be more precise, my father was thirty-nine, my mother thirty-five. I looked at them for a long time in the church. I felt with vexation that, that day, my success in school consoled them not at all, that in fact they felt, especially my mother, that it was pointless, a waste of time. When Lila, splendid in the dazzling white cloud of her dress and the gauzy veil, processed through the Church of the Holy Family on the arm of the shoemaker and joined Stefano, who looked extremely handsome, at the flower-decked altar—lucky the florist who had provided such abundance—my mother, even if her wandering eye seemed to gaze elsewhere, looked at me to make me regret that I was there, in my glasses, far from the center of the scene, while my bad friend had acquired a wealthy husband, economic security for her family, a house of her own, not rented but bought, with a bathtub, a refrigerator, a television, and a telephone.

The ceremony was long, the priest drew it out for an eternity. Coming into the church the relatives and friends of the bridegroom had all sat together on one side, the relatives and friends of the bride on the other. Throughout the ceremony the photographer kept shooting—flash, spotlights—while his young assistant filmed the important moments.

Antonio sat devotedly next to me, in his new tailor-made suit, leaving to Ada—who was really annoyed because, as the clerk in the bridegroom's grocery store, she might have aspired to a better place—the job of sitting at the back next to Melina and keeping an eye on her, along with the younger children. Once or twice he whispered something in my ear, but I didn't answer. He was supposed simply to sit next to me, without showing a particular intimacy, to avoid gossip. I let my eyes wander through the crowded church, people were bored and, like me, kept looking around. There was an intense fragrance of flowers, a smell of new clothes. Gigliola looked pretty, and so did Carmela Peluso. And the boys were their equal. Enzo and especially Pasquale seemed to want to demonstrate that there, at the altar, next to Lila, they would have made a better showing than Stefano. As for Rino, while the construction worker and the fruit and vegetable seller stood at the back of the church, like sentinels for the success of the ceremony, he, the brother of the bride, breaking the order of family ranks, had gone to sit next to Pinuccia, on the side of the bridegroom's relatives, and he, too, was perfect in his new suit, Cerullo shoes on his feet, as shiny as his brilliantined hair. What a display! It was clear that no one who had received an invitation wanted to miss it, and they came dressed like grand ladies and gentlemen, something that, as far as I knew, as far as everyone knew, meant that not a few—perhaps first of all Antonio, who was sitting next to me—had had to borrow money. Then I looked at Silvio Solara, a large man in a dark suit, standing next to the bridegroom, with a lot of gold glittering on his wrists. I looked at his wife, Manuela, dressed in pink, and loaded down with jewels, who stood beside the bride. The money for the display came from them. With Don Achille dead, it was that man with his purple complexion and blue eyes, bald at the temples, and that lean woman, with a long nose and thin lips, who lent money to the whole neighborhood (or, to be precise, Manuela managed the practical side: famous and feared was the ledger book with the red cover in which she put down figures, due dates). Lila's wedding was an affair not only for the florist, not only for the photographer, but, above all, for that couple, who had also provided the cake, and the favors.

Lila, I realized, never looked at them. She didn't even turn toward Stefano, she stared only at the priest. I thought that, seen like that, from behind, they were not a handsome couple. Lila was taller, he shorter. Lila gave off an energy that couldn't be ignored, he seemed a faded little man. Lila seemed extremely absorbed, as if she were obliged to understand fully what that ritual truly signified, he instead turned every so often toward his mother or exchanged a smile with Silvio Solara or scratched his head. At one point I was seized by anxiety. I thought: and if Stefano really isn't what he seems? But I didn't follow that thought to the end for two reasons. First of all, the bride and groom said yes clearly, decisively, amid the general commotion: they exchanged rings, they kissed, I had to understand that Lila was really married. And then suddenly I stopped paying attention to the bride and groom. I realized that I had seen everyone except Alfonso, I looked for him among the relatives of the bridegroom, among those of the bride, and found him at the back of the church, almost hidden by a pillar. But behind him appeared in full splendor Marisa Sarratore. And right behind her, lanky, disheveled, hands in his pockets, in the rumpled jacket and pants he wore to school, was Nino.

59.

There was a confused crowding around the newlyweds, who came out of the church accompanied by the vibrant sounds of the organ, the flashes of the photographer. Lila and Stefano stood in the church square amid kisses, embraces, the chaos of the cars and the nervousness of the relatives who were left waiting, while others, not even blood relations—but perhaps more important, more loved, more richly dressed, ladies with especially elegant hats?—were loaded immediately into cars and driven to Via Orazio, to the restaurant.

Alfonso was all dressed up. I had never seen him in a dark suit, white shirt, tie. Outside of his modest school clothes, outside of the grocery apron, he seemed to me not only older than his sixteen years but suddenly—I thought—physically different from his brother Stefano. He was taller now, slender, and was handsome, like a Spanish dancer I had seen on television, with large eyes, full lips, still no trace of a beard. Marisa had evidently stuck with him, their relationship had developed, they must have been seeing each other without my realizing it.

Had Alfonso, however devoted to me, been won over by Marisa's curls and her unstoppable chatter, which exempted him, who was so shy, from filling the gaps in conversation? Were they together officially? I doubted it, he would have told me. But things were clearly going well, since he had invited her to his brother's wedding. And she, surely in order to get her parents' permission, had dragged Nino along.

So there he was, in the church square, the young Sarratore, completely out of place in his shabby old clothes, too tall, too thin, hair too long and uncombed, hands sunk too deep in the pockets of his trousers, wearing the expression of one who doesn't know what to do with himself, his eyes on the newlyweds like everyone else's, but without interest, only to rest them somewhere. That unexpected presence added greatly to the emotional disorder of the day. We greeted each other in the church, a whisper and that was it, hello, hello. Nino had followed his sister and Alfonso, I had been grabbed firmly by the arm by Antonio and, although I immediately freed myself, had still ended up in the company of Ada, Melina, Pasquale, Carmela, Enzo. Now, in the uproar, while the newlyweds got into a big white car with the photographer and his assistant, to go and have pictures taken at the Parco della Rimembranza, I became anxious that Antonio's mother would recognize Nino, that she would read in his face some feature of Donato's. It was a needless worry. Lila's mother, Nunzia, led that addled woman, along with Ada and the smaller children, to a car and they drove away.

In fact no one recognized Nino, not even Gigliola, not even Carmela, not even Enzo. Nor did they notice Marisa, although her features still resembled those of the girl she had been. The two Sarratores, for the moment, passed completely unobserved. And meanwhile Antonio was pushing me toward Pasquale's old car, and Carmela and Enzo got in with us, and we were about to leave, and all I could say was, "Where are my parents? I hope someone is taking care of them." Enzo said that he had seen them in some car, and so there was nothing to do, we left, and I barely had time to glance at Nino, standing in the church square, in a daze, while Alfonso and Marisa were talking to each other. Then I lost him.

I became nervous. Antonio, sensitive to my every change of mood, whispered, "What is it?"

"Nothing."

"Did something upset you?"

"No."

Carmela laughed. "She's annoyed that Lina is married and she'd like to get married, too."

"Why, wouldn't you like to?" Enzo asked.

"If it were up to me, I'd get married tomorrow."

"Who to?"

"I know who."

"Shut up," Pasquale said, "no one would have you."

We went down toward the Marina, Pasquale was a ferocious driver. Antonio had fixed up the car for him so that it drove like a race car. He sped along, making a racket and ignoring the jolts caused by the bumpy streets. He would speed toward the cars ahead of him as if he wanted to go through them, stop a few inches before hitting them, turn the wheel abruptly, pass. We girls cried out in terror or uttered indignant instructions that made him laugh and inspired him to do still worse. Antonio and Enzo didn't blink, at most they made vulgar comments about the slow drivers, lowered the windows, and, as Pasquale sped past, shouted insults.

It was during that journey to Via Orazio that I began to be made unhappy by my own alienness. I had grown up with those boys, I considered their behavior normal, their violent language was mine. But for six years now I had also been following daily a path that they were completely ignorant of and in the end I had confronted it brilliantly. With them I couldn't use any of what I learned every day, I had to suppress myself, in some way diminish myself. What I was in school I was there obliged to put aside or use treacherously, to intimidate them. I asked myself what I was doing in that car. They were my friends, of course, my boyfriend was there, we were going to Lila's wedding celebration. But that very celebration confirmed that Lila, the only person I still felt was essential even though our lives had diverged, no longer belonged to us and, without her, every intermediary between me and those youths, that car racing through the streets, was gone. Why then wasn't I with Alfonso, with whom I shared both origin and flight? Why, above all, hadn't I stopped to say to Nino, Stay, come to the reception, tell me when the magazine with my article's coming out, let's talk, let's dig ourselves a cave that can protect us from Pasquale's driving, from his vulgarity, from the violent tones of Carmela and Enzo, and also—yes, also—of Antonio?

60.

We were the first young people to enter the reception room. My bad mood got worse. Silvio and Manuela Solara were already at their table, along with the metal merchant, his Florentine wife, Stefano's mother. Lila's parents were also at a long table with other relatives, my parents, Melina, Ada, who was furious and greeted Antonio angrily. The band was taking its place, the musicians tuning their instruments, the singer at the microphone. We wandered around embarrassed. We didn't know where to sit, none of us dared ask the waiters, Antonio clung to me, trying to divert me.

My mother called me, I pretended not to hear. She called me again and I didn't answer. Then she got up, came over to me with her limping gait. She wanted me to sit next to her. I refused. She whispered, "Why is Melina's son always around you?"

"No one is around me, Ma."

"Do you think I'm an idiot?"

"No."

"Come and sit next to me."

"No."

"I told you come. We're not sending you to school to let you ruin yourself with an auto mechanic who has a crazy mother."

I did what she said; she was furious. Other young people began arriving, all friends of Stefano. Among them I saw Gigliola, who nodded to me to join them. My mother restrained me. Pasquale, Carmela, Enzo, Antonio finally sat down with Gigliola's group. Ada, who had succeeded in getting rid of her mother by entrusting her to Nunzia, stopped to whisper in my ear, saying, "Come." I tried to get up but my mother grabbed my arm angrily. Ada made a face and went to sit next to her brother, who every so often looked at me, while I signaled to him, raising my eyes to the ceiling, that I was a prisoner.

The band began to play. The singer, who was around forty, and nearly bald, with very delicate features, hummed something as a test. Other guests arrived, the room grew crowded. None of the guests disguised their hunger, but naturally we had to wait for the newlyweds. I tried again to get up and my mother whispered, "You are going to stay near me."

Near her. I thought how contradictory she was, without realizing it, with her rages, with those imperious gestures. She hadn't wanted me to go to school, but now that I was going to school she considered me better than the boys I had grown up with, and she understood, as I myself now did, that my place was not among them. Yet here she was insisting that I stay with her, to keep me from who knows what stormy sea, from who knows what abyss or precipice, all dangers that at that moment were represented in her eyes by Antonio. But staying near her meant staying in her world, becoming completely like her. And if I became like her, who would be right for me if not Antonio?

Meanwhile the newlyweds entered, to enthusiastic applause. The band started immediately, with the marriage processional. I was indissolubly welded to my mother, to her body, the alienness that was expanding inside me. Here was Lila celebrated by the neighborhood, she seemed happy. She smiled, elegant, courteous, her hand in her husband's. She was very beautiful. As a child I had looked to her, to her progress, to learn how to escape my mother. I had been mistaken. Lila had remained there, chained in a glaring way to that world, from which she imagined she had taken the best. And the best was that young man, that marriage, that celebration, the game of shoes for Rino and her father. Nothing that had to do with my path as a student. I felt completely alone.

The newlyweds were obliged to dance amid the flashes of the photographer. They spun through the room, precise in their movements. I should take note, I thought: not even Lila, in spite of everything, has managed to escape from my mother's world. I have to, I can't be acquiescent any longer. I have to eliminate her, as Maestra Oliviero had been able to do when she arrived at our house to impose on her what was good for me. She was restraining me by one arm but I had to ignore her, remember that I was the best in Italian, Latin, and Greek, remember that I had confronted the religion teacher, remember that an article would appear with my signature in the same journal in which a handsome, clever boy in his last year of high school wrote.

At that moment Nino Sarratore entered. I saw him before I saw Alfonso and Marisa, I saw him and jumped up. My mother tried to hold me by the hem of my dress and I pulled the dress away. Antonio, who hadn't let me out of his sight, brightened, threw me a glance of invitation. But I, moving away from Lila and Stefano, who were now going to take their place in the middle of the table, between the Solaras and the couple from Florence, headed straight toward the entrance, toward Alfonso, Marisa, Nino.

61.

We found a seat. I made general conversation with Alfonso and Marisa, and I hoped that Nino would say something to me. Meanwhile Antonio came up behind me, leaned over, and whispered in my ear.

"I've kept a place for you."

I whispered, "Go away, my mother has understood every-thing."

He looked around uncertainly, very intimidated. He returned to his table.

There was a noise of discontent in the room. The more ran-corous guests had immediately begun to notice the things that weren't right. The wine wasn't the same quality for all the tables. Some were already on the first course when others still hadn't been served their antipasto. Some were saying aloud that the service was better where the relatives and friends of the bridegroom were sitting than where the relatives and friends of the bride were. I hated those conflicts, their mounting clamor. Boldly I drew Nino into the conversation, asking him to tell me about his article on poverty in Naples, thinking I would ask him afterward, naturally, for news of the next issue of the journal and my half page. He started off with really interesting and informed talk on the state of the city. His assurance struck me. In Ischia he had still had the features of the tormented boy, now he seemed to me almost too grown-up. How was it possible that a boy of eighteen could speak not generically, in sorrowful accents, about poverty, the way Pasquale did, but concretely, impersonally, citing precise facts.

"Where did you learn those things?"

"You just have to read."

"What?"

"Newspapers, journals, the books that deal with these problems."

I had never even leafed through a newspaper or a magazine, I read only novels. Lila herself, in the time when she read, had never read anything but the dog-eared old novels of the circulating library. I was behind in everything, Nino could help me make up ground.

I began to ask more and more questions, he answered. He answered, yes, but he didn't give instant answers, the way Lila did, he didn't have her capacity to make everything fascinating. He constructed speeches with the attitude of a scholar, full of concrete examples, and every one of my questions was a small push that set off a landslide: he spoke without stopping, without embellishment, without any irony, harsh, cutting. Alfonso and Marisa soon felt isolated. Marisa said, "Goodness, what a bore my brother is." And they began to talk to each other. Nino and I also were isolated. We no longer heard what was happening around us: we didn't know what was served on the plates, what we ate or drank. I struggled to find questions, I listened closely to his endless answers. I quickly grasped, however, that a single fixed idea constituted the thread of his conversation and animated every sentence: the rejection of vague words, the necessity of distinguishing problems clearly, hypothesizing practical solutions, intervention. I kept nodding yes, I declared myself in agreement on everything. I assumed a puzzled expression only when he spoke ill of literature. "If they want to be windbags," he repeated two or three times, very angry at his enemies, that is to say anyone who was a windbag, "let them write novels, I'll read them willingly; but if you really want to change things, then it's a different matter." In reality—I seemed to understand—he used the word "literature" to be critical of anyone who ruined people's minds by means of what he called idle chatter. When I protested weakly, for example, he answered like this: "Too many bad gallant novels, Lenù, make a Don Quixote; but here in Naples we, with all due respect to Don Quixote, have no need to tilt against windmills, it's only wasted courage: we need people who know how the mills work and will make them work."

In a short while I wished I could talk every day to a boy on that level: how many mistakes I had made with him; what foolishness it had been to want him, love him, and yet always avoid him. His father's fault. But also my fault: I—I who was so upset by my mother—I had let the father throw his ugly shadow over the son? I repented, I reveled in my repentance, in the novel I felt myself immersed in. Meanwhile I often raised my voice to be heard over the clamor of the room, the music, and so did he. From time to time I looked at Lila's table: she laughed, she ate, she talked, she didn't realize where I was, the person I was talking to. Rarely, however, did I look toward Antonio's table, I was afraid he would make me a sign to join him. But I felt that he kept his eyes on me, that he was nervous, getting angry. Never mind, I thought, I've already decided, I'll break up tomorrow: I can't go on with him, we're too different. Of course, he adored me, he was entirely devoted to me, but like a dog. I was dazzled instead by the way Nino talked to me: without any subservience. He set out his future, the ideas on the basis of which he would build it. To listen to him lighted up my mind almost the way Lila once had. His devotion to me made me grow. He, yes, he would take me away from my mother, he who wanted only to leave his father.

I felt someone touch my shoulder, it was Antonio again. He said, "Let's dance."

"My mother doesn't want me to," I whispered.

He replied, tensely, "Everyone's dancing, what's the problem?"

I half-smiled at Nino, embarrassed, he knew that Antonio was my boyfriend. He looked at me seriously, he turned to Alfonso. I left.

"Don't hold me close."

"I'm not holding you close."

There was a loud din, a drunken gaiety. Young people, adults, children were dancing. But I could feel the reality behind the appearance of festivity. The distorted faces of the bride's relatives signaled a quarrelsome discontent. Especially the women. They had spent their last cent for the gift, for what they were wearing, had gone into debt, and now they were treated like poor relations, with bad wine, intolerable delays in service? Why didn't Lila intervene, why didn't she protest to Stefano? I knew them. They would restrain their rage for love of Lila but at the end of the reception, when she went to change, when she came back, dressed in her beautiful traveling clothes, when she handed out the wedding favors, when she had left, with her husband, then a huge fight would erupt, and it would be the start of hatreds lasting months, years, and offenses and insults that would involve husbands, sons, all with an obligation to prove to mothers and sisters and grandmothers that they knew how to be men. I knew all the women, the men. I saw the gazes of the young men turned fiercely to the singer, to the musicians who looked insultingly at their girlfriends or made allusive remarks to one another. I saw how Enzo and Carmela talked while they danced, I saw also Pasquale and Ada sitting at the table: it was clear that before the end of the party they would be together and then they would be engaged and in all probability in a year, in ten, they would marry. I saw Rino and Pinuccia. In their case everything would happen more quickly: if the Cerullo shoe factory seriously got going, in a year at most they would have a wedding celebration no less ostentatious than this. They danced, they looked into each other's eyes, they held each other closely.

Love and interest. Grocery plus shoes. Old houses plus new houses. Was I like them? Was I still?

"Who's that?" Antonio asked.

"Who do you think? You don't recognize him?"

"No."

"It's Nino, Sarratore's oldest son. And that's Marisa, you remember her?"

He didn't care at all about Marisa, about Nino he did. He said nervously, "So first you bring me to Sarratore to threaten him, and then you sit talking to his son for hours? I have a new suit made so I can sit watching you amuse yourself with that kid, who doesn't even get a haircut, doesn't even wear a tie?"

He left me in the middle of the room and headed quickly toward the glass door that opened onto the terrace.

For a few seconds I was uncertain what to do. Join Antonio. Return to Nino. I had on me my mother's gaze, even if her wandering eye seemed to be looking elsewhere. I had on me my father's gaze, and it was an ugly gaze. I thought: if I go back to Nino, if I don't join Antonio on the terrace, it will be he who leaves me and for me it will be better like that. I crossed the room while the band kept playing, couples continued to dance. I sat down.

Nino seemed not to have taken the least notice of what had happened. Now he was speaking in his torrential way about Professor Galiani. He was defending her to Alfonso, who I knew detested her. He was saying that he, too, often ended up disagreeing with her—too rigid—but as a teacher she was extraordinary, she had always encouraged him, had transmitted the capacity to study. I tried to enter the conversation. I felt an urgent need to be caught up again by Nino, I didn't want him to start talking to my classmate exactly the way, until a moment earlier, he had been talking to me. I needed—in order not to rush to make up with Antonio, to tell him, in tears: yes, you're right, I don't know what I am and what I really want, I use you and then I throw you away, but it's not my fault, I feel half and half, forgive me—Nino to draw me exclusively into the things he knew, into his powers, to recognize me as like him. So I almost cut him off and, while he tried to resume the interrupted conversation, I enumerated the books that the teacher had lent me since the beginning of the year, the advice she had given me. He nodded yes, somewhat sulkily, he remembered that the teacher, some time earlier, had lent one of those texts to him and he began to talk about it. But I had an increasing urgency for gratifications that would distract me from Antonio, and I asked him, without any connection:

"When will the magazine come out?"

He stared at me uncertainly, slightly apprehensive.

"It came out a couple of weeks ago."

I had a start of joy, I asked, "Where can I find it?"

"They sell it at the Guida bookstore. Anyway I can get it for you."

"Thank you."

He hesitated, then he said, "But they didn't put your piece in, it turned out there wasn't room."

Alfonso suddenly smiled with relief and murmured, "Thank goodness."

62.

We were sixteen. I was sitting with Nino Sarratore, Alfonso, Marisa, and I made an effort to smile, I said with pretended indifference, "All right, another time." Lila was at the other end of the room—she was the bride, the queen of the celebration—and Stefano was whispering in her ear and she was smiling.

The long, exhausting wedding lunch was ending. The band was playing, the singer was singing. Antonio, with his back to me, was suppressing in his chest the pain I had caused him, and looking at the sea. Enzo was perhaps murmuring to Carmela that he loved her. Rino certainly had already done so with Pinuccia, who, as she talked, was staring into his eyes. Pasquale in all likelihood was wandering around frightened, but Ada would manage so that, before the party was over, she would tear out of his mouth the necessary words. For a while toasts with obscene allusions had been tumbling out; the metal merchant shone in that art. The floor was splattered with sauces from a plate dropped by a child, wine spilled by Stefano's grandfather. I swallowed my tears. I thought: maybe they'll publish my piece in the next issue, maybe Nino didn't insist enough, maybe I should have taken care of it myself. But I said nothing, I kept smiling, I even found the energy to say, "Anyway, I already argued once with the priest, to argue a second time would have been pointless."

"Right," said Alfonso.

But nothing diminished the disappointment. I struggled to detach myself from a sort of fog in my mind, a painful drop of tension, and I couldn't. I discovered that I had considered the publication of those few lines, my name in print, as a sign that I really had a destiny, that the hard work of school would surely lead upward, somewhere, that Maestra Oliviero had been right to push me forward and to abandon Lila. "Do you know what the plebs are?" "Yes, Maestra." At that moment I knew what the plebs were, much more clearly than when, years earlier, she had asked me. The plebs were us. The plebs were that fight for food and wine, that quarrel over who should be served first and better, that dirty floor on which the waiters clattered back and forth, those increasingly vulgar toasts. The plebs were my mother, who had drunk wine and now was leaning against my father's shoulder, while he, serious, laughed, his mouth gaping, at the sexual allusions of the metal dealer. They were all laughing, even Lila, with the expression of one who has a role and will play it to the utmost.

Probably disgusted by the spectacle in progress, Nino got up, said he was going. He made an arrangement with Marisa for returning home together, and Alfonso promised to take her at the agreed-on time to the agreed-on place. She seemed very proud of having such a dutiful knight. I said uncertainly to Nino:

"Don't you want to greet the bride?"

He gestured broadly, he muttered something about his outfit, and, without even a handshake, or a nod to me or Alfonso, he headed toward the door with his usual swinging gait. He could enter and leave the neighborhood as he wished, without being contaminated by it. He could do it, he was capable of doing it, maybe he had learned years before, at the time of the stormy move that had almost cost him his life.

I doubted that I could make it. Studying was useless: I could get the highest possible marks on my work, but that was only school: instead, those who worked at the journal had sniffed my report, my and Lila's report, and hadn't printed it. Nino could do anything: he had the face, the gestures, the gait of one who would always do better. When he left it seemed that the only person in the whole room who had the energy to take me away had vanished.

Later I had the impression that a gust of wind had shut the door of the restaurant. In reality there was no wind or even a banging of doors. There happened only what could have been predicted to happen. Just in time for the cake, for the favors, the very handsome, very well-dressed Solara brothers appeared. They moved through the room greeting this one and that in their lordly way. Gigliola threw her arms around Michele's neck and drew him down next to her. Lila, with a sudden flush on her throat and around her eyes, pulled her husband energetically by the arm and said something in his ear. Silvio nodded slightly to his children, Manuela looked at them with a mother's pride. The singer started *Lazzarella*, modestly imitating Aurelio Fierro. Rino with a friendly smile invited Marcello to sit down. Marcello sat down, loosened his tie, crossed his legs.

The unpredictable revealed itself only at that point. I saw Lila lose her color, become as pale as when she was a child, whiter than her wedding dress, and her eyes had that sudden contraction that turned them into cracks. She had in front of her a bottle of wine and I was afraid that her gaze would go through it with a violence that would shatter it, with the wine spraying everywhere. But she wasn't looking at the bottle. She was looking farther away, she was looking at the shoes of Marcello Solara.

They were Cerullo shoes for men. Not the model for sale, not the ones with the gilded pin. Marcello had on his feet the shoes bought earlier by Stefano, her husband. It was the pair she had made with Rino, making and unmaking them for months, ruining her hands.

ABOUT THE AUTHOR

Elena Ferrante is the author of *The Days of Abandonment* (Europa, 2005), *Troubling Love* (Europa, 2006), and *The Lost Daughter* (Europa, 2008), soon to be a film directed by Maggie Gyllenhaal and starring Olivia Colman, Dakota Johnson, and Paul Mescal. She is also the author of *Incidental Inventions* (Europa, 2019), illustrated by Andrea Ucini, *Frantumaglia: A Writer's Journey* (Europa, 2016) and *The Beach at Night* (Europa, 2016), a children's picture book illustrated by Mara Cerri. The four volumes known as the "Neapolitan quartet" (*My Brilliant Friend*, *The Story of a New Name*, *Those Who Leave and Those Who Stay*, and *The Story of the Lost Child*) were published by Europa Editions in English between 2012 and 2015. *My Brilliant Friend*, the HBO series directed by Saverio Costanzo, premiered in 2018. Ferrante's most recent novel is *The Lying Life of Adults*, published in 2020 by Europa Editions.

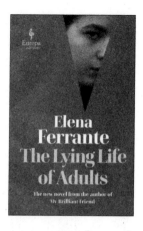

The Lying Life of Adults

Translated by Ann Goldstein

The new novel from the author of
The Neapolitan Quartet

"*The Lying Life of Adults* affirms that Ferrante is an oracle among authors, writing literary epics as illuminating as origin myths, explaining us to ourselves."—Claire Luchette, *O, The Oprah Magazine*

"*The Lying Life of Adults* lives up to its author's reputation, and then some . . . [Giovanna] is one of this year's most memorable heroines."—Bethanne Patrick, *The Boston Globe*

"Ferrante captures the interior states of young people with an unflinching psychological honesty that is striking in its vividness and depth."
—Dayna Tortorici, *The New York Times Book Review*

"Ferrante's women go so spectacularly to pieces that it is easy to forget that the vast majority of her novels have, if not happy endings, then notes of reconciliation."—Parul Sehgal, *New York Times*

Available everywhere books are sold

hardcover 978-1-60945-591-0
paperback 978-1-60945-715-0
ebook 978-1-60945-592-7